W9-DAD-332
YA

THE CASTINGS TRILOGY

PAMELA FREEMAN

By Pamela Freeman

The Castings Trilogy

Blood Ties

Deep Water

Full Circle

Ember and Ash

THE CASTINGS TRILOGY

PAMELA FREEMAN

The characters and events in this book are fictitious. Any similarity to real persons, living or dead, is coincidental and not intended by the author.

Orbit
Hachette Book Group
237 Park Avenue, New York, NY 10017

Orbit is an imprint of Hachette Book Group, Inc.
The Orbit name and logo are trademarks of Little, Brown Book Group Limited.

ISBN 978-1-61129-306-7

Printed in the United States of America

Contents

Book One
Blood Ties
Page 1

Book Two
Deep Water
Page 379

Book Three
Full Circle
Page 875

ICE KING'S
COUNTRY
Cliffhaven
Hidden
Valley
Spritford
Sharp River
Death Pass
WESTERN
MOUNTAINS
DOMAIN
Whitehaven
SOUTH
DOMAIN
FAR SOUTH
DOMAIN
Turvite
WIND CITIES

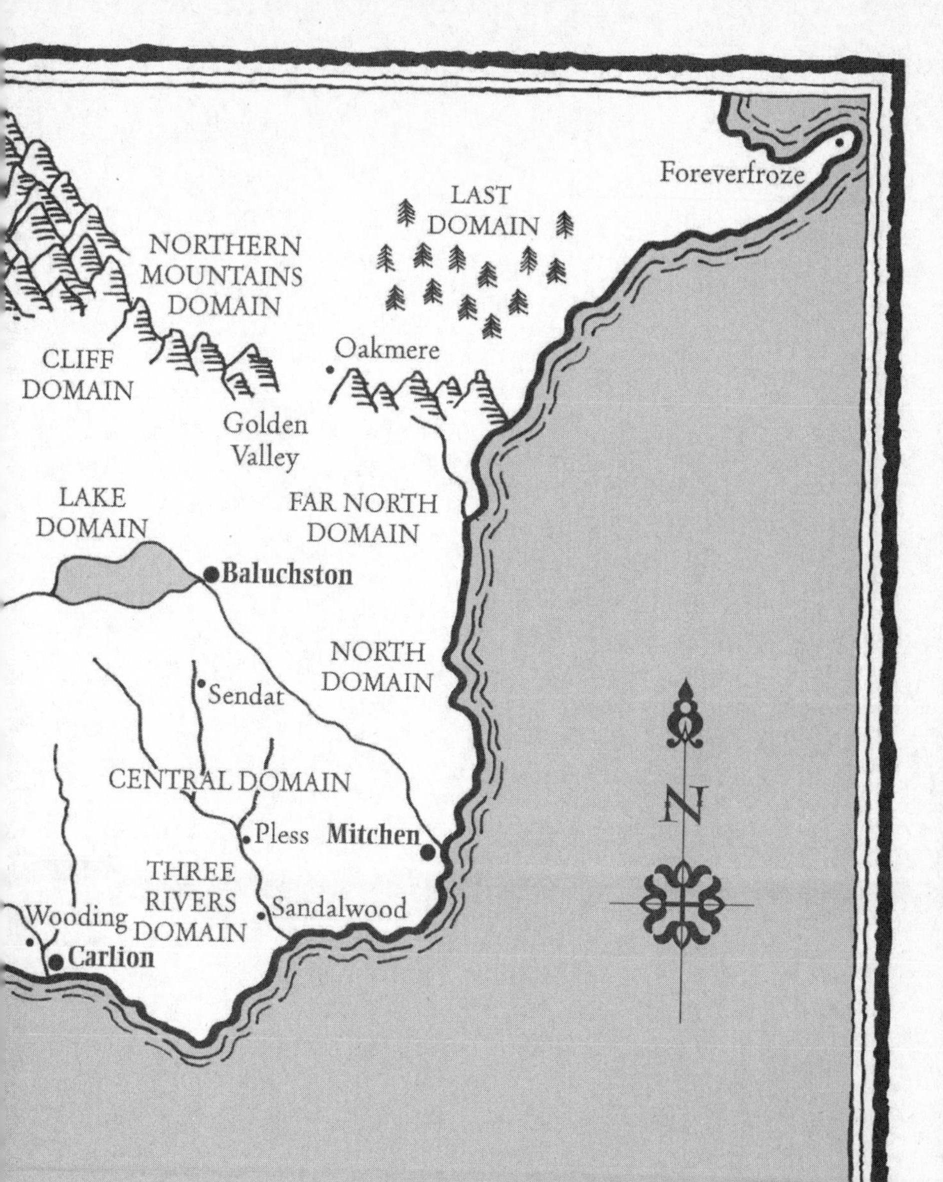
Foreverfroze
LAST DOMAIN
NORTHERN MOUNTAINS DOMAIN
CLIFF DOMAIN
Oakmere
Golden Valley
LAKE DOMAIN
FAR NORTH DOMAIN
Baluchston
NORTH DOMAIN
Sendat
CENTRAL DOMAIN
Pless
Mitchen
THREE RIVERS DOMAIN
Wooding
Sandalwood
Carlion
N
THE ELEVEN DOMAINS

BOOK ONE

BLOOD TIES

To Stephen

THE STONECASTER'S STORY

THE DESIRE TO KNOW the future gnaws at our bones. That is where it started, and might have ended, years ago.

I had cast the stones, seeing their faces flick over and fall: Death, Love, Murder, Treachery, Hope. We are a treacherous people—half of our stones show betrayal and violence and death from those close, death from those far away. It is not so with other peoples. I have seen other sets of stones that show only natural disasters: death from sickness, from age, the pain of a broken heart, loss in childbirth. And those stones are more than half full with pleasure and joy and plain, solid warnings like "You reap what you sow" and "Victory is not the same as satisfaction."

Of course, we live in a land taken by force, by battle and murder and invasion. It is not so surprising, perhaps, that our stones reflect our history.

So. I cast the stones again, wondering. How much of our future do we call to ourselves through this scrying? How much of it do we make happen because the stones give us a pattern to fulfill?

I have seen the stones cast too many times to doubt them. When I see Murder in the stones, I know someone will die. But would they have died without my foretelling? Perhaps merely saying the word, even in a whisper, brings the thought to the surface of a mind, allows the mind to shape it, give it substance, when otherwise it might have remained nothing more than vague murmurings, easily ignored.

Death recurred again and again in my castings that night. I did not ask whose. Perhaps it was mine, perhaps not. I had no one left to lose, and therefore did not fear to lose myself.

There was someone at the door, breathing heavily outside, afraid to come in. But he did, as they always do, driven by love or fear or greed or pain, or simple curiosity, a desire to giggle with friends.

This one came in shyly: young, eighteen or nineteen, brown hair, green trousers and blue boots. He squatted across the cloth from me with the ease of near-childhood. I held out my left hand, searching his face. He had hazel eyes, but the shape of his face showed he had old blood, from the people who lived in this land before the landtaken, the invasion. There was old pain, too, old anger stoked up high.

He knew what to do. He spat in his own palm, a palm crisscrossed by scars, as though it had been cut many times, and clapped it to mine. I held him tightly and reached for the pouch with my right hand. He was strong enough to stay silent as I dug in the pouch for five stones and threw them across the cloth between us. He was even strong enough not to follow their fall with his eyes, to hold my gaze until I nodded at him and looked down.

He saw it in my face.

"Bad?"

I nodded. One by one I touched the stones lying faceup. "Death. Bereavement. Chaos. This is the surface. This is what all will see." Delicately I turned the other two stones over. "Revenge and Rejoicing. This is what is hidden." An odd mixture, one I had never before seen.

He brooded over them, not asking anything more. The stones did not speak to me as they often do; all I could tell him were their names. It seemed to be enough for him.

"You know what this refers to?" I asked.

He nodded, absently, staring at Rejoicing. He let go of my hand and slid smoothly to his feet, then tugged some coins out of a pocket and let them fall on the rug.

"My thanks, stonecaster." Then he was gone.

Who was I to set Death on the march? I know my stones by their feel, even in the darkness of the pouch. I could have fumbled and selected him a happy dream: Love Requited, Troubles Over, Patience. I could have soothed the anger in his eyes, the pain in his heart.

But who am I to cheat the stones?

After he left, I cast them again. This time, Death did not appear. She had gone out the door with the young one and his scars.

SAKER

SAKER REMEMBERED the first time he had tried to raise the dead. It was the night after Freite, the enchanter, had finally died. By then he had been her apprentice for thirteen long years, but only in the last two had she shared any real secrets with him, and only then because he had threatened to leave her if she withheld.

Freite had wept for her great age and his refusal to any longer give his power for her extended life. She had no more to offer him. He had learned everything she had to teach of her Wind City magic, and it had not included pity, or generosity. So he refused to touch her in her extremity, knowing she would drain the power out of him to give herself another day, another week, a month if she was lucky... She had died cursing him, but he was cursed already, so he disregarded it.

After she was buried, the Voice of Whitehaven had pronounced Freite's bequests and he had found that her house had passed into his hands, along with her savings, which were much greater than he had imagined. So there he was, rich but without a plan. He had gone to the stonecaster to find out what the gods wanted him to do next. And the stonecaster had sent him out the door with Revenge and Rejoicing awaiting him.

That first time, he hadn't even known he needed the actual bones for the spell to work. The enchanter had told him half-truths, half-spells, trying to hoard her knowledge as though it could ward off death. Saker knew, certain sure, nothing kept Death away for good. That Lady tapped everyone on the shoulder, sooner or later. But sometimes, just sometimes, she could be tricked.

He raised the black stone knife level with his palm, forcing his hand not to shake. *This must work*. Now, finally, he had the means, seven years since the stonecaster had set him on his path...

"I am Saker, son of Alder and Linnet of the village of Cliffhaven. I seek justice."

He began to shake with memory, with yearning, sorrow, righteous rage. There lay the strength of his spell. He touched the never-closing wound in his mind, drew on the pain and set it to work. The rest of the spell wasn't in words, but in memories, complex and distressing: colors, phrases of music, a particular scent, the sound of a scream…

When he had gathered them all he looked down at his father's bones on the table, his father's skull staring emptily. He pressed the knife to his palm then drew it down hard. The blood surged out in time with his heart and splashed in gouts on the chalk-white bones.

"Alder," he said. "Arise."

BRAMBLE

THE BLOOD TRAIL was plain. Every few steps a splotch showed brilliantly red. There were tracks, too. In summer it would have been harder, but in this earliest part of spring the grasses and ferns were thin on the ground, and the ground was soft enough to show the wolf's spoor.

Even the warlord's man would have been able to track this much blood; for Bramble it was like following a clearly marked highway, through new fern fronds and old leaf mold, down past the granite rocks, through the stand of mountain ash, blood marking the trail at every step, so fresh she could smell it. The prints on the right were lighter; it was favoring the wounded side.

It wasn't sensible to go after a hurt wolf with just a boot knife in her hand. She'd be lucky to get home without serious injury. She'd be lucky to get home at all. But she couldn't leave a wounded animal to die in pain, even if she hadn't shot it.

The brown wolf had limped across the far end of the clearing where she had been collecting early spring sorrel at the edge of a small stream, too intent on its own pain to even notice Bramble.

The forest had seemed to hush the moment she saw the arrow, the wolf, the blood dripping from its side. The glade glowed in the afternoon sunlight. Rich and heady, the smell of awakening earth, that special smell that came after the snowmelt was over, rose in drifts around her. She heard chats quarreling far overhead. The trickle of the stream. A squirrel leaping from branch to branch of an elm, rattling the still-bare twigs. It paused. The wolf stopped and looked back over his shoulder, seeing her for the first time. She waited, barely breathing, feeling as if the whole forest waited with her.

"There he is! See him? Don't lose him!"

"Quiet, idiot!"

The voices broke the moment. The wolf slipped into the shadow of some pine trees. The squirrel, scolding, skipped from elm to willow to alder and was gone. Bramble looked around quickly. The warlord's men were close. Nowhere to hide except up a tree. She dropped the sorrel and sprang for the lowest branch of a yew. Its dark branches would hide her, unlike the easier-to-climb willow next to it whose branches were still showing catkins, but no leaves.

She climbed fast, without worrying about scratches, so she was bleeding in a dozen places by the time she had reached a safe perch. She grabbed some of the yew leaves and crushed them in her hands, wringing them to release the bitter-smelling sap, then rubbed it on the trunk as far down as she could reach, to confuse the scent in case they had hounds, who would sniff out the blood for sure and certain.

She wondered who they were chasing. An actual criminal? Or just someone who'd looked at them the wrong way? Someone old Ceouf, the warlord, had taken against, maybe, or someone who had complained? Bramble smiled wryly. At least it wasn't a woman. Everyone knew what happened to a woman found alone by the warlord's men.

It angered her, as it always did. More than that, it enraged her. The warlords claimed that they protected the people in their Domain, from other warlords, of course, and in earlier days from invaders. Perhaps they had, once. But a couple of generations ago the warlords of the Eleven Domains had made peace, and there hadn't been more than a border skirmish since. The warlord's men weren't soldiers anymore, just thugs and bullies. You stayed out of their way, didn't draw their attention, and spat in the dust of their footprints after they'd gone.

It's not meant to be like this, she thought. *No one should have to hide in fear of the people who are supposed to protect them.*

Today she had been happy, happier than she had been for months, since her sister had married and moved away to Carlion, the nearest free town. She had been out in her forest again, rejoicing in the returning spring, giving thanks for new life. And they had brought death and fear with them, as they did everywhere. Her chest burned with resentment. Some part of her had always refused to be sensible about it, as her parents demanded. "The world's not going to change just because you don't like it," they'd said, time after time. She knew they were right. Of course she knew it, she wasn't a child or a fool. And yet, some part of her insisted, *It's not meant to be like this.*

"This way!"

The voice came again. Bramble parted the needles in front of her until she could see the clearing below. There were two men, one blond, one red-haired, in warlord's gear, with a blue crest on their shoulders to show their allegiance to this, the South Domain. They were young, about her age. Their horses were tethered near the trail that led into the clearing. One was a thin dark bay, the other a well-muscled roan. The trail ended there, she knew, and the forest, even in early spring, was too dense from here in for mounted men to ride.

"I know I got it," the blond said. "I winged it, at least."

"If you want to finish it off, you'll have to go on foot," the redhead said. They looked at the undergrowth consideringly, and then the blond looked down at his shiny riding boots.

"I just bought these," he complained. He had a sharp voice, as though it were the other man's fault that his boots were new.

"Leave it," the redhead said, clearly bored now.

"I wanted the skin. I've always wanted a wolf skin." The blond frowned, then shrugged. "Another day."

They turned and went back to their horses, mounted, and rode away without a backward glance.

Bramble sat appalled and even angrier. He had left a wounded animal to die in agony so he wouldn't get scratches on his boots! *Oh, isn't that typical!* she thought. *They're the animals, the greedy, heedless, bloody shagging bastards!*

She waited until she was sure they weren't coming back, then swung down from the tree, pulled her knife from her boot, and went to look for the wolf.

She followed the blood trail until it disappeared into the big holly thicket. She skirted the sharp leaves and picked up the trail on the other side. It finally came to an end near the stream in the center of the forest.

The wolf had staggered down to drink and stood, legs shaking, near the water's edge. Then it saw Bramble, and froze with fear. But it was foaming at the mouth, desperate for water, and she stayed very still, as still as a wild creature in the presence of humans, until it took the last few steps to the water and drank. The black-fletched arrow, a warlord's man's arrow, stuck out from its side.

After drinking, it collapsed on the muddy edge of the stream and panted in pain, looking up at her with great brown eyes, pleading wordlessly.

Bramble came to it gently, making no sudden move that might startle it. "There now, there now, everything's all right now…" she crooned, as she did to the orphan kids she raised, or the nannies she helped give birth. She lowered her hand slowly, softly onto its forehead and the wolf whined like a pup. "Not long now, not long," she said softly, stroking back to grip its ears. She gazed into its eyes steadily until it looked away, as all wild animals will look away from the gaze of anything they do not wish to fight, and then she cut its throat, as quickly and painlessly as she could.

Bramble sat waiting, her hand still on its head, ignoring the tears on her cheeks, while the blood pulsed out into the stream, swirling red. There wasn't much blood. It had bled a lot already. Her fingers gentled its ears as though it could still feel, then she stood up.

She hesitated, looking at the caked blood on its side, then stripped off her jacket, shirt, skirt and leggings, so she wouldn't stain them. She had to hope that the warlord's men wouldn't change their minds and come back. She could just imagine *that* scene.

Her knife was only sharp enough to slit through the hide. She had to heave the carcass over to peel the skin off and it was much heavier than she thought. There was blood all over her. She wrinkled her nose, but kept going. It was a good, winter-thick pelt and besides, taking it gave the death of the wolf some purpose, instead of it being a complete waste of life. She cut the pelt off at the base of the skull. It was worth more with head attached, but Bramble had always felt that tanning the head of the animal was a kind of insult.

She would have left the carcass for the crows and the foxes, but she didn't want the warlord's men to find it, if they came looking for the hide later. Let him think that he had missed. She dragged it up the hill to a rock outcropping, and piled stones on it. At least it would make a meal for the ants and the worms.

She washed the blood off both her and the hide, put her clothes back on, tied up the hide and hoisted it over her shoulder. It weighed her down heavily, but she could manage it easily enough. She set off home.

The way was through the black elm and pine forest, and normally she would have lingered to admire the spring-green leaves that were beginning to bud, and listen to the white-backed woodpeckers frantically drilling for food after their long migration. She had been observing a red-breasted flycatcher pair build their nest, but today she passed it by without noticing, although she stopped to collect some wild thyme and sallet greens, and to empty one of her snares. She found a rabbit, thin after winter but good enough for a stew, and the pelt still winter-lush. Her hands did the work of resetting the snare but her mind was elsewhere.

The forest was ostensibly the warlord's domain, but was traditionally the hunting or grazing ground for a range of people, from foragers like Bramble to charcoal burners, coppicers, chair makers, withiers, pig farmers and woodcutters. It was a rare day that Bramble didn't meet someone in the forest; depending on the season, sometimes she saw as many people there as in the village street. It was just her bad luck that today she had seen the warlord's men.

She came out of the forest near the crossroads just outside Wooding and realized that it hadn't been just bad luck. There had been an execution today.

Her village of Wooding saw a lot of executions, because it was on the direct road from Carlion to the warlord's fort at Thornhill. For centuries the South Domain warlords had used the crossroads just outside Wooding as the site for their punishments. There was a scaffold set up for when the warlord felt merciful. And for when he wasn't there was the rock press, a sturdy wooden box the size of a coffin, but deeper, where the condemned were piled with heavy stones until their bones broke and they suffocated, slowly.

Today they had used the rock press. There was blood seeping out of the box at the corners. The condemned often bled from the nose and mouth in the final stages of pressing. Bramble slowed as she walked past the punishment site. Did she want to know who they had killed this time? What was the point?

She went over to the box and looked in. No one she knew, thank the gods. Some stranger—the Domain was large, and criminals were brought to the warlord from miles away. Then she looked closer. A stranger, but just a boy. Fourteen, perhaps. A baby. Probably accused of something like "disrespect to the warlord." Her heart burned again, as it had in the woods. Anger, indignation, pity. She would have to make sure she was nowhere near the village the next morning, when the warlord's men rounded up the villagers to see the boy's corpse removed from the box and placed in the gibbet. She doubted she could applaud and cheer for the warlord over this execution, as the villagers were expected to do.

Some did so gladly. There were always a few who enjoyed a killing, like the crows that nested in the tree next to the scaffold and descended on the corpses with real enthusiasm. But the rest of the villagers had seen too many people die who looked just like them. Ordinary people. People who couldn't pay their taxes, or hadn't bowed low enough to the warlord. Or who had objected to their daughter being dragged away to the fort by the warlord's men. It was important to attend the executions, and to cheer loudly. The warlord's men were always watching. Bramble had cheered as loudly as anyone, in the past, and had been sick later, every time.

So the warlord's men would have done their job today and gone home as soon as the boy stopped breathing. The blond had probably taken the shortcut through the woods and had seen the wolf by accident. He couldn't resist tracking it a little way. Couldn't resist killing again.

A hunter who didn't care if the animal he shot suffered deserved nothing but contempt. He certainly didn't deserve the hide of the animal he had abandoned to pain and slow death.

But the *sensible* thing to do would be to take the skin to the warlord's fort, say it had one of the warlord's arrows in it when she found it, and let the blond claim it. Let him have his prize for killing.

Bramble looked at the boy in the box, whose face was still contorted in pain. "Well, no one ever said I was sensible," she said.

She skirted the village and came to the back of her parents' house, through the alders that fringed the stream. She dumped the wolf skin behind the privy, then went the whole way back so she would be seen to come home through the main street with nothing in her hands but rabbit and greens.

Bramble passed the inn and ignored the stares of the old men who sat on the bench outside the door, tankards in hand, until one of them called out, "Got your nose stuck in the air, I see! Too high and mighty to tell us how that sister of yours is doing off in Carlion!"

It was Swith, the leatherworker's father, both hands cramped around his mug. He was a terrible gossip, but that wasn't why he had called Bramble over. He wanted her to notice his hands. The arthritis that kept him sitting here in the mild sun had swelled his knuckles up like a goat's full udder.

"She's well, she says," Bramble replied. "They're building a new house, on the lot next to his parents'."

"Ah, she's done well for herself, that Maryrose!" cackled Swith's crony, old Aden, the most lecherous man in the village in his day, and still not to be trusted within arm's reach. "She wasn't an eye-catcher like you, lass. But he got a good hot bed to go to, I'll say that, her town clerk's son!"

The other men frowned. Maryrose had been liked by everyone in the village, and she was certainly no light-skirt.

"That's enough of that, Aden," Swith said reprovingly. "Your mam and da will be missing her," he said with a cunning sideways look. "She was their favorite, wasn't she?"

It was an old match of his, trying to get Bramble to give him back a short answer. It kept him amused, and it didn't do her any harm. Everyone knew that Maryrose was the favorite.

"They are missing her, of course, Swith," Bramble said. Then, feeling she had given Aden and the others enough entertainment, she said, "I notice your hands are bothering you. Could I be helping? Give them a rub, maybe?"

"If you want to help a man by rubbing something—"

"Close that dirty mouth, Aden!" Swith bellowed then glanced a bit shamefacedly at Bramble. "Well, lass, now you mention it..."

She smiled at him. "I'll come by after supper."

It was a more or less regular thing she did, massaging goose grease and comfrey into the old people's hands and feet. Not all of them, of course. Just the cross-grained ones who couldn't find anyone else to help them. She was glad Aden didn't have arthritis; she wasn't about to get within groping distance of him.

She hefted the rabbit and greens in one hand. "I have to get these to Mam." None of them had mentioned the rabbit, though they had eyed it and no doubt would have liked to hear all the details on where she had trapped it and what kind of snare she had used, the kind of talk that kept them occupied for hours. To ask would have been against custom, since they all knew Swith had called her over to ask her a favor, which she was granting. If she wanted to tell them about her hunting, she would, in her own good time.

If she hadn't offered to help Swith, it would have been a different story, she thought with amusement as she walked up the street, exchanging greetings with Mill the charcoal burner, home at his grandparents' until after the snowmelt and spring rains, and ignoring the tribe of dogs that swirled around her heels as they always did. But she had made the offer, so the old men couldn't cross-question her without being unforgivably rude.

"I have a doe ready to drop twins, Bramble," called Sigi, the new young brewster who had doubled the inn's clientele after she had married its owner, Eril. Sigi's three toddlers, who ran around her feet as she brought in her washing, were screaming with excitement about a maggot one of them had plucked from the rubbish pile. "If she doesn't have enough milk for both, can I bring one to you?"

"Of course, and welcome," Bramble called back. "I've no orphans this season so far."

When Sigi had first met Bramble, she had reacted as many people did, with suspicion at Bramble's dark hair and eyes. In this land of blonds and redheads, a dark-haired person was assumed to be a Traveler, a descendant of the original inhabitants of the Domains, who had been invaded and dispossessed a thousand years ago. Old history. But no one trusted Travelers. They were thieves, liars, perverts, bad luck bringers. Bramble had heard all the insults over the years, mostly (though not always) by people who didn't know her, like ordinary travelers on the road through Wooding to Carlion.

Sigi had finally overcome her suspicion, and Bramble was trying hard to forget the insult. It would be nice to have a friend in the village, now Maryrose was gone, and Sigi was the best candidate. The other girls had long ago shut her out after she had made it clear that she didn't have any interest in the things that obsessed them, like boys and hair ribbons and sewing for their glory boxes. Not that boys weren't a pleasure, now and then.

Sigi's oldest child grabbed the maggot and dropped it down her brother's back and the resultant wailing distracted Sigi completely. Bramble laughed and went on to her own home, following Gred, the goose girl, as she shepherded her waddling, squabbling, hissing flock back to their night pasture outside the mill.

Bramble's family lived in an old cottage, a house really, bigger than it looked from the street, as it ran far back toward the stream. It was built of the local bluestone, all except for the chimney, which was rounded river stones in every shade of gray and brown and dark blue. It was thatched with the herringbone pattern you found on every roof around here, although in Carlion they thatched a fish-scale pattern, when they didn't tile in slate. The front garden caught the morning light, so it was full of early herbs just pushing through the soil. The vine over one corner was still a bare skeleton, but the house had a cheerful, open look with its shutters wide and its door ajar.

The door was ajar because her mother was in the road sweeping up the droppings the geese had left behind. The Widow Farli was doing the same thing outside her cottage a little farther down. Goose droppings were good fertilizer, and for someone like Widow Farli, who only kept a couple of scraggly hens, they were important. Bramble's mother, Summer, kept pigs, as well as goats and hens, and really didn't need them.

"No use wasting them," her mam said as Bramble came up. She swept the droppings onto an old piece of bag. "Here, go and give them to Widow Farli." She held the bag out.

Bramble took the droppings and handed the wild thyme and the sallet greens and the rabbit carcass to her mother.

Farli had a face you could cut cheese with, and the tip of her nose was always white, as if with anger, but at what, Bramble had never figured out. She stared past Bramble and said snidely, "Nice of your *mother* to take the trouble. *She*'s not one to go off gallivanting and leave all her work to others."

"Just as well," Bramble said, smiling sweetly, "or what would become of you?"

Farli's face flushed dark red. "Your tongue'll get you into mischief one day, young lady, you mark my words! Mischief or worse!"

She turned on her heel and flounced toward her back garden, keeping a tight hold of the bag of droppings.

Bramble grinned and went home. She had a pelt to cure. She fetched it from behind the privy and went to the kitchen door to ask her mother for a loan of the good knife to scrape the skin down.

"A *wolf?*" her mam said, that note in her voice that meant "what will the girl do next?" She had her frown on, too, the "what have I done to deserve this?" frown.

Bramble had grown up knowing she'd never be the daughter her parents wanted—never be like her sister, Maryrose, who was a crafter born, responsible, hard-working, loving in the way they understood. Maryrose looked like her mother, tawny-haired and blue-eyed, clearly one of Acton's people, while Bramble looked like her granda, who had started life a Traveler. He looked like the people who'd lived here before Acton's people had come over the mountains. Along with her coloring—or perhaps due to the way people looked askance at her because of it—Bramble had inherited the Traveler restlessness, the hatred of being enclosed. Where Maryrose was positively happy to stay seated all day at the loom with her mother, or stand in the workshop shaping and smoothing a beech table with her father, Bramble yearned to be in the forest, for the green luxuriance of summer growth, the sharp tracery of bare branches in winter, the damp mold and mushroom smell of autumn.

She had spent all her free time there as a child, and a lot of time when she should have been learning a trade. While she never did learn to weave or carpenter, by the time she was old enough to marry, a good proportion of the family food came to the table from her hands, and a few luxuries as well. Their flock of goats came from Bramble's nursing of orphan kids or the runty twin of a dropping. If she raised a kid successfully, she got either half the meat if it was a billy, or the first kid if it was a nanny. She had a knack with sick animals, and sick people, too. In the forest, she set snares, gathered greens, fruits and nuts, herbs and bulbs. In early spring, the hard time, it was her sallets and snowberries that kept the family from the scurvy, her rabbit and squirrel that fed them when the bacon ran out and the cornmeal ran low. They could have bought extra supplies, of course, but the money they saved, then and all through the year, from Bramble's gathering, made the difference between survival and prosperity, between living from day to day and having a nest egg behind them. And her furs brought in silver, too, although they weren't the thick, expensive kind you got from the colder areas up north near Foreverfroze. And old Ceouf, the warlord, took a full half of what she made on them, for a "luxury" tax.

There was always someone in the village ready to spy for the warlord. At Wooding's yearly Tax Day in autumn, it was amazing how the warlord's steward seemed to know everything that had been grown or raised or sold or bought in the last year. Bramble suspected Widow Farli of being an informer, but she couldn't blame her. A woman alone needed some way of buying the warlord's protection.

Bramble had never brought home a wolf skin before, but her mam thought poorly of it for one of those "it isn't respectable" reasons that she could never quite follow.

"The gods alone know what'll become of you, my girl," Mam said. That wasn't so bad; it was said with a kind of exasperated affection. But then she sighed and couldn't resist adding, "If only you were more like your sister!"

When Bramble was six, and seven, and eight, that sigh and that sentence had made her stomach clench with anguish and bewilderment. At nineteen, she just raised an eyebrow at her mother and smiled. It did no good to let it hurt; neither she nor her parents were going to change. *Could* change. And if there was still a cold stone, an empty hollow, under her ribs left over from when she was little, it was so familiar she didn't even feel it anymore.

"I'll make you a gorgeous coat out of it, Mam," she said, and winked. "Just think how impressed they'll be at the Winterfest dance."

Her mother smiled reluctantly. "Oh, yes, of course you will. I can just see myself in a wolf-skin coat. A lovely sight I'd be. No, thank you." She looked down at the rabbit and greens. "Well, these'll make a good meal."

Bramble nodded at the implied thanks, took the good knife her mother held out and went down to the stream to scrape the hide down thoroughly.

Every so often she couldn't help looking up to where flocks of pigeons and rooks, coming home for summer, circled the sky. High above them in the uplands of the air, a blue heron glided, like the old song said, free from care. It came from beyond the Great Forest, from up near Foreverfroze. She longed to see what it had seen. One day, but not yet, because the gods forbade it.

"Time and past to milk the goats, Bramble!" her mother called from the back door.

Bramble groaned and trudged off toward the goat shed. She lingered for a moment at the gate, watching the sky turn that pale, pale blue that wasn't quite gray, as it did on these spring evenings, just before it darkened. She wondered, for the hundredth time, or maybe the thousandth, where the birds had been. She had wanted to take the Road all her life. When she was a child, listening to her grandfather's Traveling stories, she had promised herself that one day she would. Just go. But as she grew older she watched the Travelers who came to Wooding and realized that they all had trades. Skills. Tinkering, music, singing, tumbling, mural and sign painting, horse breaking... Bramble had no skills worth anything to anyone else. She could hunt and forage, but on the Road, far from the forest, what good would that be to her?

So she laid her plan: she would save her coppers and head north, to the Great Forest in the Last Domain, where the mink and the weasel and the fox furs were so thick that the city folk would pay good silver for them. She would not Travel, but travel, to where her skills were useful and could earn her bread. She would see the oldest forest in the world and learn its secrets and there, in its green darkness, she would be rid of this yearning.

When she came back to the house with a pail of frothy milk, her mam had warmed water for her to wash in, and had laid out cheese and bread and some dried apple, "to keep the wolf from the door until the stew is ready." Bramble smiled—it was her mother's way of making a joke, and making amends for maybe speaking too sharply. She never said sorry, but the dried apple was running low this side of winter, and to bring some out just for a snack was the only apology Bramble needed.

A while later, her da and granda came in from the workshop smelling of cedar and sat down eagerly to the rabbit stew.

"What are you working on?" Bramble asked.

"A blanket chest for the innkeeper. I told him that camphor laurel would do as well as cedar to keep away the moths, but he thinks that town-bred Sigi of his deserves the very best," Da said, smiling.

"She's the reason he can afford a new chest," Granda said. "She's a better brewer than he ever was."

"Wouldn't be hard," Mam said, sniffing. Mam, rather surprisingly, liked a good strong brown ale, though, less surprisingly, she never had more than one.

The meal went on as normal; they discussed the day's events and the village gossip, and wondered, as always, how Maryrose and Merrick were doing and when there'd be news of a grandchild on the way. Mam said nothing of the wolf skin and Bramble kept silent, too, not sure how much of the story to share. None, maybe. If there was trouble, she knew her family would be safer if they knew nothing.

Again she felt impatient, itching with annoyance. It was wrong that they had to go in fear of the warlord's men all their lives. Sitting at the table as she'd done every night of her life, she was overcome by a familiar rush of feeling: the desire to get away, somewhere, *anywhere*, anywhere but here. It was so familiar that she knew what to do about it. Nothing. The next thing that would happen would be the voice of the local gods in her ear saying *Not yet*. They'd said it every time she'd felt like this, from the time she could understand the words. And every time she thought back to them: *When?* But they never answered.

But this time, when she was filled with impatience and the desire to fly away like the wild geese in autumn, there was no message from the gods. Nothing but silence. It sent a chill through her, to have one of the deep patterns of her life broken without warning, but it sped up her heart as well. She breathed more deeply, thinking about it.

After supper she went out into the windy, cold dark and made her way unerringly to the black rock altar in the wood near the village. Not the deep forest, this, but a beech wood of skeleton branches, floor clear of everything but last year's leaves and a frail flush of new ferns. The altar was close to the burial caves, as it should be, in a clearing surrounded by other trees: oak, ash, hawthorn bushes, rowan, and willows near the stream that provided the gods with music. Bramble came to the rock at moonrise. It was a thin sliver of moon, on the wane, with the evening star underneath the crescent: a bad-luck moon, but beautiful.

She knelt at the rock and felt the presence of the gods lift the hair on her neck, as it always did. She didn't pray, or offer sacrifice. She had just come to ask a question.

"When?"

The wind stilled. The glade filled with the presence of the gods, like pressure, like swimming deep down into the quarry pool until she could feel the weight of the water begin to push against her chest and eyes, like being smothered in strength.

Soon.

They spoke into her head, as they always did, and then left. The glade was now empty, the pressure was gone.

Soon.

What, she wondered, had changed?

She went home via Swith's and massaged his hands, but she was so quiet he actually apologized for Aden's crudity that afternoon. She laughed it off, but that night in her dreams she was a wild goose, flying forever across a gold-leafed forest.

The next morning she asked Gerda, the tanner, for advice about how to treat the hide, in case there was anything different about wolf skin from weasel and fox. There wasn't, but she paid for the advice with a basket of tiny sweet strawberries that she'd collected from the deep glade where an old oak had fallen.

It was a lovely pelt, thick and glossy. Bramble slung it over the chair in her room and ran her hand over it every time she passed. The fur sprang back against her hand as though the living body had leaped and a small fillip of pleasure went through her each time she felt it.

She didn't want to flaunt it, but risked wearing it out anyway. Looking back, she was sorry she hadn't hidden it in the forest and brought it back home after dark, sorry that she'd asked Gerda for advice.

The warlord's man tracked her down in the clearing near the Springtree. She wasn't gathering hawthorn, like the other girls were doing this day before the Springtree dance, but checking that the beehive she'd found last autumn had survived the winter. The hive was in the fork of a linden tree just breaking into leaf. The tree was one she'd climbed often as a child, playing a game with Maryrose where they had to get from village to home without touching the ground. It had been tricky but possible to jump from tree to tree to fence to tree all the way.

The hive was in good order, buzzing companionably. She sat on the limb a safe distance away, and talked to the bees awhile. She resolved to come back often enough through the summer so they'd get used to the sound of her voice, and not attack her when she came to smoke them and steal their honey.

A rider appeared from behind the big willow. It was the blond. Seen closer, he was a stocky, broad-shouldered man with the pale hair and blue eyes of Acton's people, mounted on a powerful-looking roan gelding. She grew wary, but he was far enough off that she could be out of the tree before he could get to her. The linden boughs intermeshed with a big willow; she could be away and into the forest before he could get off his horse. She stood up on the bough, one hand on the trunk.

"Greetings, mistress," he said, smiling the smile men so often used, the one that was meant to charm but never did. She nodded, not minded to give him any more than that until she knew what he wanted. Even smiling, he had a mean mouth and narrow eyes, for all that he was no older than her.

He was annoyed that she hadn't given him greetings. He frowned, then she saw his frown soften as he looked at her breasts. She knew that look, too. It wasn't desire, but lust, and took no account of what she thought or felt. Men who looked at you like that never met your eyes.

"Why not come down and talk?" He held out his hand invitingly.

"No, thank you."

He looked at her face then and she saw him register her black hair and eyes, saw the contempt in his face. She could see it made him angrier that a Traveler was resisting him. He drew himself up in the saddle, puffed out his chest like a ten-year-old boy trying to impress. She nearly laughed, but he was no less dangerous for that.

"Stop playing games, missy. You know why I'm here. Give me the wolf skin and I'll forget about your stealing it from me."

"If you've got a claim on something of mine you can take it to the village voice and he'll settle the dispute," Bramble said.

A voice was elected by each village and made decisions in disputes between villagers, as well as representing them in dealings with the warlord. The warlord's men never showed much respect to them. She didn't think the man would like to submit to the voice's ruling, but it was worth a try. The roan was fidgeting, ears back; Bramble could see it getting nervous as the man grew impatient. She refused to let her own nerves take over. It was better to be annoyed than afraid.

"We don't ask favors of villagers," he said with derision. "Where did you get it?"

"From a wolf."

"From *my* wolf." He swept a black-fletched arrow out of the quiver at his back and shook it at her. "It had a black arrow in it, didn't it, when you found it?" He shot the arrow back into the quiver with a thump that made the roan flinch. Bramble felt a quick surge of fellow feeling for it. "You found the carcass and skinned it...well, there's no harm in that. But it's my skin and I want it."

"Did you kill the wolf?" she asked quietly.

He hesitated. "I shot it."

"But *I* killed it. If you won't go to the village voice, perhaps the warlord should decide it?"

He didn't like that idea, having to admit to his overlord that he'd failed to finish off the wolf. The roan jumped as he put in the spurs. It took a step forward, only to be reined in hard.

"Just give it here or you'll be sorry." He loosened his sword in his scabbard deliberately.

Her toes gripped the bark firmly. She was suddenly angry past common sense or reason at his arrogance. It was typical of the warlord's men, of all the men who carried sword and shield. Typical that he hadn't followed the wolf and finished him off, as any compassionate hunter would do. That wolf had looked at her with pleading in its eyes, and she knew enough of animals to know when it was for help, and when it was for a quick end to pain. She had done this man's job for him, and she would keep the results.

"I think I'd rather go to the warlord."

It had been a mistake to stand up. She saw him looking up at her legs, bare under her skirt. Her stomach turned over with revulsion at the thought of him touching her and there was a flutter of panic beneath her breastbone. She pushed it down. Men like him lived for the fear in others.

The intention to hurt was in his eyes and in the hands hard on the reins, but he hesitated. The warlord allowed his men great license, but there were limits. He couldn't just beat her and take the skin. She might go to the warlord and say that she had been happy to accept his judgment on the matter. If the blond just took things into his own hands, he knew he'd be in trouble. The roan snorted and backed away a little. He curbed it savagely but otherwise ignored it. She could see the thoughts move behind his eyes, saw him looking for a way to discredit her before the warlord. It chilled her.

"Black hair and black eyes," he sneered. "You're a Traveler wench, aren't you? Is it true what they say, that you'll go with anyone?"

"No." Her voice was as cold and firm as she could make it.

She saw some flicker of reaction on his face and the spark of warning inside her grew stronger. Old Ceouf was famed for allowing his men to get away with rape. If she complained to him later about the way his man had dealt with the wolf, the blond would deny it, and accuse her of trying to revenge her rape. And he'd be believed. She would have to give him the wolf skin and then go straight to the warlord and lay it all before him. It was her only chance. Her hand moved slowly to the skin, but he misinterpreted, thought she was taking hold of it in ownership.

"You'd better do as you're told, girl. You don't want anything to happen to your family, do you?" His hand moved again to his sword hilt.

Of course he would threaten like that, the coward. She felt the contempt take over her face and saw his reaction to it. But she wasn't prepared for the speed with which he moved.

He kicked the horse forward and reached to pull her down. She drew back one foot, tough as an old boot from seasons of barefoot running, and kicked him in the head. Her heel connected with his face and he fell backward off the horse. She turned to run, but from the corner of her eye she saw that he lay very still. As still as death.

She looked back slowly. As the roan shifted uneasily sideways, she saw that he lay on his back, eyes wide, his face with a curious crumpled look. His long nose was shortened like a pig's. She realized that she had kicked him flat on the nose, that the bone had gone back and entered his brain like a spear. She had killed him.

She'd meant to run, she'd *planned* to run. But in the moment when he reached for her, an instinct stronger than reason had taken over. Her leg had seemed to move of its own accord, but it had, she realized, been guided by some dark, bone-deep refusal to run: a rejection of fear, of the surrender that comes with fear, an inability to accept that he was worth her fear.

She hoped that when the warlord's men found the body it would look as though he had ridden thoughtlessly fast under the low linden bough and been hit in the face, and the horse had ridden to the forest. Would it look like an accident? She didn't know enough to predict their reaction, so she shrugged the worry away.

She'd killed a lot of things—the wolf, rabbits, weasels and stoats, fish and fawns. It was a job that had to be done. But she'd always meant to do it. To kill without meaning seemed... well, it seemed a waste. A waste of what, she wasn't sure. Life? Purpose? Or something harder to name, though she could feel it. Her own soul? She couldn't look away from his face. He seemed improved by death; his face had lost its scowl. It felt odd to have interrupted the life of someone she knew nothing about, to kill someone she had only just met, as though killing needed intimacy, deep knowledge of the other, to make it all right. She forced herself to look away from him, and immediately realized that she had better get away, and fast.

Her heart was racing, her stomach clenched, her skin was clammy.

Fear or the exaltation of escape? She didn't know. But although fear was as good a name as any, the same impulse that had sent her foot against his face now prevented her from naming her racing heart as fearful. Excitement, the need to get moving, were better reasons.

She slid onto the broad back of the roan and gathered up the reins with clumsy hands. She couldn't reach the stirrups and it seemed somehow impolite to just kick the horse, so she clicked with her tongue, as plowmen did to draft horses, and the roan willingly moved off toward the trees. Even then, in the first moment of riding him, she wanted to keep him, felt that they had already become attached by fellow feeling against the man.

It was the first time Bramble had been on a horse since old Cuthbert, a Traveling tinker, had given her rides on his cart horse when she was six. It was a long way to the ground. She swallowed as the horse's swaying walk seemed to poise her over a long drop twice at each stride. The stirrups thumped against his side as he moved and he quickened his pace to a bumpy trot, and then to a canter.

She grasped the pommel and held her breath, feeling for the first time the intoxicating sense of power under her, the sense of being extended, that the horse's speed and strength and agility were all hers, even if only temporarily. It was an uncomfortable, unsteady passage, but by the end of it she was in love with riding.

She took him to a narrow gully in the depths of the wood, to her cave. It was less a cave than a cleft between two huge rocks that formed the end of the gully. She had come here since she was a child, whenever she wanted somewhere cool and quiet, somewhere to think or to pray. The rocks were covered with moss at the base and their cracked faces were shaded even in the middle of summer, since the trees around them were mostly evergreen, cedar and yew. It was a strange place, always quiet. Birds calling in the trees above sounded far away; water from a tiny spring where the two rock faces met trickled down gently, constantly, even when all the streams were frozen. It felt holy, but there were no gods here, just silence.

With a long tether made of strips of her underskirt, Bramble staked out the horse at the end of the cleft. It wouldn't stop him if he wanted to run, but nothing she had could. The cleft was just big enough to hold him. If wolves came the horse could retreat into it and protect himself with his front hooves. He was safe enough. She unsaddled and unbridled him, wiped off his sweat with a bunch of grass then leaned her back against the cool rock and watched him graze all afternoon. She went home with the memory of the warlord's man buried under thoughts of the roan.

The memory came back that night, though, in her dreams, where she endlessly kicked at his face, but he kept reaching for her anyway, over and over. She woke awash with sweat in the bed that she and Maryrose had shared, and wished that Maryrose was still here. If the warlord's men came to arrest her, she would go with them quietly and they'd have no excuse to bully her mother or father. But no one came except Eril, the innkeeper, to pick up the blanket chest in his handcart. He was full of the news that one of the warlord's men had been found dead.

"A riding accident," he said, shaking his head. "One of these harum-scarum young lads, it was, rode right into a linden bough and—phut!—dead! The warlord's not too pleased, they say, and the horse is missing, too, though that's not a loss to him up yonder, for it was the lad's own horse, they say. Keep an eye out for it, lassie," he said. "You might get a reward."

She didn't even consider turning the roan in for a reward.

That morning, before dawn, she had gone to the black rock altar in the forest. She approached silently, hiding in the thick growth of alders along the stream. She didn't want any of the villagers to see her and start asking questions about what she might be praying for.

There was no one there; she had come early enough. She stepped toward the rock, quietly, as she had always felt the local gods preferred. The villagers often laughed and joked as soon as they'd backed away from their prayers here, but she'd never understood that. Couldn't they feel the presence of the gods, that hair-raising, spine-chilling stroke along the skin, *beneath* the skin? Perhaps they couldn't. Perhaps that was part of the Traveler blood she'd inherited from her granda, just as she'd inherited his black eyes and black hair.

She sat down carefully, cross-legged in front of the rock, and bowed her head. Today she had a favor to ask, and there were time-honored ways of doing that.

"Gods of field and stream, hear your daughter. Gods of sky and wind, hear your daughter. Gods of earth and stone, hear your daughter."

Perhaps she should have brought a sacrifice; one of her goats had dropped a kid the night before. They liked young sacrifices, it was said. But the blood would have been noticed. The village snoops wouldn't have stopped until they'd found out who had made the sacrifice, and why. She forced her thoughts back to her petition.

"Gods of fire and storm, hear your daughter. Of your kindness, keep my family safe. Keep the warlord's men from them, keep them whole and happy."

She took out her knife and cut off a lock of her hair at the roots near her nape and laid it on the rock.

"Take this offering as a symbol of my reverence. Use it to bind safety around my family. Use it to bind me more surely to your service."

The hair stirred in a breath of air that Bramble couldn't feel. The gods were testing her sacrifice. The eddy of air turned and ruffled the hair on her head. In her mind she felt the tickle that meant the touch of the gods and, as always, the world spun around her as they tasted her thoughts. She rocked between joy and a holy terror that was completely different—cleaner—than the fear she had refused to the warlord's man. When her sight was clear again she saw that the hair on the rock had disappeared. The gods had accepted her sacrifice.

She let out a long breath of relief. There was nothing more she could do. Slowly, she got up and backed away. It was probably just superstition that said it was bad luck to turn your back on the gods, but she wasn't willing to risk bad luck just now.

She realized the gods had listened when at home she found her mam and da reading a letter from Maryrose and her husband, Merrick, inviting them all to come and live in Carlion. Mam had learned to read from her mother, who had been a waiting woman to the old warlord's wife, and she had taught her husband and both the girls.

They had talked about moving before, in a casual way, during the preparations for Maryrose's wedding, but now it was time to decide.

"They say they're building the new house big enough to fit all of us," her da said. "Merrick must be doing well."

"You should go," Bramble said. The memory of the warlord's man came up to confront her—his threats and the menace she'd read in his eyes—and it had made her voice harsh. She thumped some rabbit carcasses down on the table. "Get yourselves into a free town, where you're safe from the warlord's men."

They were startled.

"They've never bothered us," her father said.

"But they could. Anytime they want to. In Carlion you only have to worry about the town council." She tried to smile, to turn it into a joke. "Who knows, maybe you'll end up a councillor yourself!"

"It's a big shift, to leave everyone we know. All our friends," her father said, but he sounded excited by the idea of change. Mam sniffed.

"There's a few I'll not miss," she said, then paused. "And a few I will. But Maryrose is there...and any grandchildren we're likely to have will be Carlion born and bred."

From that moment, Bramble knew it was decided, although her mother wondered aloud how Bramble would cope with town life.

"For you're always in the forest," her mam said.

Bramble felt herself start to shrug, always her answer to that old complaint, but stopped. It was probably the last time she would ever hear it. "Don't worry about me," she said, eyes passing from her mam to her da.

But of course they did. They kept discussing it endlessly over breakfast. Bramble wished her grandmother was still alive. She would have forced them to admit they all wanted to go. No patience for dithering, her grandam. Bramble sighed. It was clear to her that the only thing holding them back was the thought that she would be unhappy in Carlion. She knew that as soon as she left they'd be packing up to make the move. She didn't try to explain that she probably wouldn't be with them. That would just lead to more questions, which she knew she couldn't answer.

After breakfast she went to her room and rolled her bag of silver, the wolf skin and some clothes in a blanket, to make a bedroll. It seemed to her that the gods' "soon" might mean very soon, and she had better be ready. She kissed her parents goodbye before she went to the forest. They were surprised; kisses were for bedtime.

She grinned at them reassuringly. "Just felt like it."

They were so surprised they didn't think to ask where she was going with her blanket. She crossed the stream at the bottom of their garden and headed for the forest. The roan was waiting for her, or at least waiting at the end of his tether, with his head high and his ears pricked. She stashed the bedroll and silver inside the cave then greeted him gently, stroking her hand down his neck, feeling very fragile next to his warm strength.

"Gods," she said, looking at his broad back and powerful rump. "Let's hope you're a good-natured fellow, because you'll have to be patient with me."

She contemplated the saddle. Not only did it look complicated, but it was branded with the warlord's mark. If she was found on the roan, she could claim that she had found it wandering in the forest, but if it had the warlord's saddle on it, she would be branded herself, as a thief. Or worse. Horse stealing was a garoting crime. So she left it aside with a feeling of relief. She didn't like the idea of having straps and buckles and harness on the roan. It felt wrong to tie up a fellow creature that way, like putting him in prison.

The blanket from under his saddle wasn't marked, so she slid that over him and then looked at the bit and bridle. It had a nasty look, all steel and sharp edges. The roan's mouth had calluses at the edges, marks of old wounds. She remembered the arrow in the wolf's side and threw the bridle away. The horse startled back a little when it hit the ground with a jingle.

"Shh, shh, now," she said, using the same tone she used with the sick lambs and kids she nursed back to health. "It's all right, everything's all right... "

She ran her hands over him, noting the marks beneath the hair and hating the warlord's man even more when she realized they were scars from whip and spur.

"Nothing to fear here, sweetheart," she crooned. She undid the tether and gathered it up. It was tied loosely around his neck and she used it to pull him over to a large rock.

"Now I know you could get rid of me with just a shake of your rump," she said, climbing on top of the rock, "but how about you don't? Let's see what we can do together, you and I."

She mounted carefully and adjusted herself on the blanket, pulling up the skirt she had worn over her breeches so that she sat comfortably. Then she leaned forward and undid the tether, stuffed it in a pocket and took a deep breath. How high she was! How far it seemed to the ground. The roan's hide was warm, even through the blanket. He seemed as solid as the rock she had climbed from.

And here I sit, she thought, smiling, *looking like a frog on a stone, with no idea what I'm supposed to do.*

"Up to you, horse," she said. "Let's go."

She clicked her tongue as she had before. The roan's ears flicked back in response. She did it again and squeezed his sides, very gently, with her legs. It felt like trying to squeeze a tree trunk, but the roan walked forward, then stopped. She squeezed again, a little harder, and he began to walk with more confidence, down the hill.

Excitement spiraled up from her stomach. She squeezed again. The roan broke into a trot. Bramble could feel her balance going and windmilled her arms, but she slid off sideways, anyway, right into a patch of nettles. She wanted to shout and curse, but she bit it back in case she frightened the horse, the completely untethered horse, into running.

She dragged herself up, thanking the gods for her breeches. The roan was standing, looking at her with amused, knowing eyes. He whickered to her softly.

"Yes, very funny," she said. "Perhaps we'll just stick to walking today, eh?"

He waited calmly while Bramble walked up to him. She took him by the forelock and led him uphill to the mounting rock. He nuzzled her shoulder. Up until that moment, she had seen him as a creature from the warlord's world that she could use, a living thing, yes, but like the goats and the chickens that she cared for at home. A domestic animal.

But the way he looked at her with amusement, she was sure, the way he greeted her with affection, the realization that he was here because he had chosen to wait for her, made her feel that he was more than that, that he was something she had never really had before. A companion.

It felt just as wrong to give him a name as to use a bit and bridle.

Owners gave names. She wasn't the owner, not in any sense. It wasn't like she had any real control over him: they were just fellow creatures, spending time together. If he thought of her at all, it was probably as "the human," and so she would think of him as "the horse," or maybe, "the roan."

She practiced walking him around all day and by the time she went home, she could hardly walk, her thighs were rubbed raw and her hips ached. But nothing could have kept her away the next day.

When she groomed him—she had watched ostlers at the inn attend to horses—she found more scars from the spurs and whip, and thought with satisfaction of the warlord's man going down under her foot. The next moment she made a sign of warding, because of the nightmares. She had forced herself to shake them off as soon as she woke. She wondered if she'd have the nightmares as long as she kept the horse, the spoils of her murder, but even if that were true, the roan was worth it.

She had laughed at the other girls when they breathlessly waited for one of the lads to glance their way, or dreamed over him through their chores, planning what to say when they next met. But she was just as bad with riding. That night, in between the nightmares, she dreamed about riding, about the surge as the horse set off, the muscles sliding beneath her. All the next morning she daydreamed about the wind in her hair, forgot to water the beans because she was planning their next excursion, and was abstracted when her parents spoke to her. They lifted eyebrows at each other and nodded wisely when she blushed. She thought they were relieved to have her acting like an ordinary girl for once, but couldn't tell them the truth. If the warlord's men ever found out what had happened, everyone who knew the truth would be killed.

She distracted them with talk about the move to Carlion, pretending enthusiasm so well that they actually started planning the move. Her father went out, then and there, to book the carrier's cart, and they even started packing. The house was dismantled slowly around them and every blanket and piece of cloth was commandeered to wrap around breakables.

"We'll have to leave the loom until last," her mother said, and started to make lists of all the things they would have to do before they left.

Bramble took the chance to escape and went to the roan. His breath snuffled in her face in greeting as he came to meet her at the end of his tether. She watered him and then rode him again, despite the pain in her thighs. She guided him with touches on the neck or a tug on his mane, but didn't take him far for fear the warlord's men would recognize him. So she rode as much as she dared around the confines of the deep forest. They rode that day as far as the chasm.

Wooding was in a valley around a small river that fed the much larger Fallen River, which flowed all the way to Carlion and the sea. Just outside Wooding, the Fallen curved around and dropped suddenly into a deep chasm, an abyss so far down it took a day to climb down and another to climb back up. There was one wooden bridge slung precariously across the drop, on the main road that a little farther on led through the village. The bridge was one of the reasons Wooding was more prosperous than most villages: there was no other way to get to Carlion. Unlike the bridge site, here in the forest the chasm was much narrower and the rock on both edges was soft and crumbling.

Bramble didn't take the roan too close to the edge, but they stood there for a while in the mist and moisture that rose from the wild turbulence of the river below, where the water leaped and spouted over huge boulders which had fallen from the cliffs. The noise of the falls, just out of sight around the bend upstream, shook the ground and made the roan uneasy. Bramble slid down from his back to soothe him.

"Nothing to frighten you here, sweetheart," she said.

She loved this place. She loved the sudden drop that seemed to entice her to fly out and fall, loved the raging of the river below, the clouds of foam that boiled over the edge of the falls and along the rocks. In the clouds and mists of the chasm, there were swarms of swifts that lived their whole lives on the wing, landing only to build nests and lay their eggs in the crevices of the cliff face. Peering over, it was as if the birds were emerging from the water, their curves and turns in the air like the splashes of white foam. Stunted trees clung to the ledges and crevices and there were ferns in every tiny niche: the cliff wall was itself a waterfall of green and golden stone.

Unexpected and dangerous and beautiful, the chasm was the wildest thing she knew, and she had come here all her life when she felt too enclosed in the village. The roan quieted under her hands and voice, and even put his head forward to inspect the chasm with interest.

Bramble took him back to the cave and groomed him thoroughly, reluctant to leave him. She finally tethered him for the night and ran home.

After dinner, the third evening after she'd killed the man, she leaned on the gate next to her granda and looked down the road that led out of the village.

"Don't you miss it?" she asked him, meaning what Travelers called the Road, the wandering life. She meant all the things she yearned for but couldn't describe.

"Why would I, with all that I love right here?" Granda replied.

It was the same answer to that question that she'd heard all her life. She'd been ten or eleven before she realized that he never answered her straight, but always with another question. And was thirteen, maybe, before she could read the look in his eyes when he stood at that gate and looked down the road to the horizon.

Tonight she wasn't minded to accept his answer.

"If you had things to do over again," she said, "would you have settled?"

He turned to look at her. Though his pate was bald, he still had a rim of dark hair around his scalp. He still walked strongly upright. Bramble could see the man he had been at eighteen, when he'd broken his hip and couldn't walk for a season. His parents, who were drystone fencers, had paid for Bramble's great-granny to board him until he could travel to meet them. But long before that, he and Bramble's gran had snuck off to the haystack and made her da, so he ended up staying and learning to be a carpenter from her great-granda.

He searched her eyes. "You're thinking of taking the Road," he said with certainty.

"Been thinking of that all my life," she said cheerfully, surprised by how well she could hide it. "No change there."

He looked relieved. "It's a hard life for a young girl, all alone. Travelers aren't liked anywhere. Well, you know that."

"I know it, but I've never understood why."

"Some Travelers say the sight of us reminds them that they don't really belong here, that what they have they stole. And that makes them angry. But I reckon it's just that everyone likes to have someone to look down on. When the warlord rides roughshod over you, it's good to be able to curse or hit or kick someone else, someone weaker. Makes you feel strong."

"And the strong hate the weak," Bramble said.

Her grandfather looked sideways at her, his brows lifted.

"That may be. No matter what the way of it, Traveling alone is dangerous. No warlord will give justice to a Traveler. Theft, beatings, even murder, it seems it doesn't count if it's a Traveler who's hurt. That's the worst of it. Even at the best, we're treated like foreigners. Like we don't belong anywhere. That can be hard, to be told you don't belong in your own land. Especially if you love it." His voice grew reminiscent. "You can't help but love it. From the cold north to the southern deserts, it's all beautiful. Travelers love the whole of it, not just the part they were born in."

"You do miss it."

"Sometimes." He paused. "But in the end, it's the people you love that matter. Traveling—it doesn't keep your heart warm. Remember that, sweetheart. It may make your heart beat faster, but it doesn't keep it warm. So, yes, I reckon I would settle, if I had to do it over again. Your gran was worth it, and I pray the gods give her rest until I join her, so we can be reborn together."

It wasn't, in a way, what she had wanted to hear, but it was reassuring nonetheless.

In the morning, Bramble washed and dressed carefully. She fed the goats and the chickens, carried water from the stream to the kitchen, swept out the cottage, laid her room straight and tidy, even weeded the front herb bed. At last it was time to go.

She walked down to the stream and turned east to follow it to the linden tree where his ghost would rise. Udall, the old thatcher, was gathering reeds in the stream and he nodded politely to her, though he didn't speak. He only spoke when he needed to: a silent, gray man, who lived alone and liked it. No need to worry about him gossiping with the neighbors about where she was off to at lunchtime. He looked at her with no curiosity at all, just recognition, and she wondered what he could see in her face.

It wasn't merriment, that was for sure and certain. She had a job to do, and the least she could do was show some respect. Just before noon, it would be three full days since she had kicked the warlord's man. Killed the warlord's man. And as his killer, it was up to her to lay his ghost when it quickened.

UDALL'S STORY

IT BEGAN on Sylvie's roof. My hands were cold. I blew on them to warm them, then gripped the ladder with my right hand, hoisted the third yelm of reeds onto my left shoulder and began to climb. My back was aching, low down, as it did those autumn mornings.

"Past my prime," I said to the reeds, and the reeds whispered back, as they always did.

Balanced carefully, I walked along the ridge pole of the roof to the southern end of the gable, the high end where the ladder didn't reach, and laid down the bundles of reed. My lashing awl was in my pocket. I sat astride the ridge pole and began to place the yelms so the reed lay snug and watertight, yelm over yelm. Then I lashed them with the crisscross herringbone pattern of the thatchers of Laagway.

"Getting too old for this," I said to the reeds. "They'll be cutting you and drying you and lashing you, too, for a long time yet, but I'm not sure I'll be doing it."

"Do they talk back?" A voice came from below me.

The stonecaster was standing in the room under me, looking up. She grinned. "It's an odd thing, to have your home open to the sky. I think I like it," she said.

"You always were an odd magpie, Sylvie. You wouldn't like it open when the winter rains set in."

"That's why I'm paying you, old man."

She stepped up onto a chest by the wall and stuck her head through the empty rafters to face me. "If you're feeling old, Udall," she said, "you should take an apprentice."

"Pot calling the kettle black."

"Ahah! But I'm taking a youngling on, soon."

This was news. Sylvie had refused to take an apprentice for all the time I had known her. "Who is it?" I asked.

She shrugged. "I don't know. Someone's due to turn up any day now. That's why I thought I'd get the thatch done. So it'll be over and done with by the time he comes."

"So...it's a he. What else do the stones say?"

"You don't want to know." Sylvie shook her gray hair over her eyes and peered up at me, like a storyteller pretending to be a stonecaster, and spoke in a long, wavering voice. "Oh, good sir, you don't want to know the future! It's too terrible."

I smiled. It was a very good impersonation of Piselea, a story-teller who'd drunk his way through the inn's beer all summer. "Tell me anyway."

"They say it's time you got married," she said briskly, shaking back her hair. "I did a casting for you this morning. I had a feeling in my bones."

"Married. Me—married." I smiled wider. "Very funny."

But she was serious.

"The stones say it, and they mean it, my friend. Married before Midwinter's Eve."

Well, it was a shock. I'd lived alone for four years, since Niwe, my sister, had died. Married. Who? There was no one in the village, and though I traveled for my work throughout the district, still, I'd not met anyone who'd taken my fancy for...well, not since Merris married Foegen the butcher, over at Connay. And that was six years since. No, seven.

Married. Who?

I lashed and hooked the reed all day, and if Sylvie had a watertight roof come winter, it was because my hands knew their job better than I did, at times, and I could tie my herringbone lashing blind drunk and three parts asleep, if I had to. For certain, my mind was elsewhere.

All day on the ladder I went over the roll of women I knew, talking each one over with the reed and dismissing each. For Mathe was as ill-tempered as a vixen, and Sel was too young, and Aedwina much too old, besides having that young bull of a son living with her. I puzzled over it mightily, I can tell you, and as the short autumn dusk closed in, I climbed down the ladder and knocked at Sylvie's door to ask for a casting. She sat me down on the rug.

"Who is it?" I asked, and spat in my palm.

She spat in hers and joined hands with me. As our hands locked I looked at Sylvie with new eyes, feeling the strength in her grip and the softness of her palm. Not her, surely?

She drew the five stones from her bag and cast them out. They were all faceup, plain as day.

"The Familiar," she said, and raised her eyebrows. "Woman. Well, no surprise there. Child. Love. Death." She brooded over them, touching them lightly. "So. A woman you know, with one or more children, someone you love or will love, brought to you by death. Accidental death, I think." Her eyes grew compassionate. "It may not be who you think, Udall."

"No?" I broke the handhold, and sat back on my heels. "Someone I love, or will love, with a child. It has to be Merris. Who else? So Foegen dies?"

"It may be. It may be not so. Don't try to look further than the stones show you. Don't try to change your future."

"Are you saying the future's fixed? That I don't have any say in what happens to me at all?"

"Udall, I sit on this rug and cast the future. And I see folk try to avert what's to happen to them. I see them frantic, trying to change what's been foretold. And every time, the very thing they do to try to change things is what brings their fate to them. This is the way of it. Act selfishly, to change your fate, and it brings that fate rushing to your door."

So I got up and walked out. I packed up the thatch and left all tidy, and next morning I was back to finish the job, though I'd had little sleep the night before. The lashing straw went over and under, around and between, and so did my thoughts. If I went to warn Foegen, would I merely arrive in time to comfort Merris in her grief, to have her turn to me at last? Or worse, would me being there actually cause the accident to happen? Would I have to bear the guilt of Foegen's death and Merris's love the rest of my life?

I had a job starting two days later in Pank, thatching a mill house. It was three months to midwinter. I could think about it later.

I spent the next day bundling reed into yelms and tying them firmly, ready for the mill. Each knot I tied made me think of Merris, whom I had taken for apprentice ten years before. I had taught her to tie each of these knots, her brown fingers fumbling at first and then surer, her soft hazel eyes intent on the reed so I could watch her unawares.

My sister had liked her, too. Niwe was always telling me to make a move, to say something to Merris. "Court the girl properly," she'd said, and every time she said it something curled up tighter inside me, for the truth was that Merris was a girl, and I was too old for her. Too old, too set in my ways, too boring. I went to Sylvie for advice, and she had refused to cast for me.

"You know perfectly well what you should do, Udall," she had scolded. "You're just afraid."

So I had been, and very afraid, too. I'd been afraid to shatter the growing pleasure of working with Merris, the rhythmic, side-by-side movements of bundling, laying, lashing, hooking, netting. Afraid of seeing pity or disgust in her eyes.

That hadn't changed.

But—I thought secretly, and did not even say it to the reeds—she'd be a woman with two children to keep. She might be glad of a husband with a good craft, someone who would love her and be good to her and the children.

I stopped bundling in disgust at myself. To think that I'd take advantage of a woman's grief, just to have her sitting at my table. Lying in my bed. I twisted the lashing straw so hard it cut my hand, but the thought remained, all the long night, and left me sleepless again.

I set out for Connay at daybreak. If Merris was going to be a widow and in need of comfort, it wouldn't be because I hadn't tried to warn Foegen.

The road to Connay ran along the side of a brown stream, bordered with rushes and reeds, so that their familiar whispering soothed me as I walked. I even whistled through the brisk autumn morning, and lopped the heads off milk thistles with my ash stick as I went.

It was dinnertime when I came into Connay, and the street was quiet. Foegen and Merris lived at the other edge of town, where the steers could be pastured until killing time, away from the shop in the main street and its charnel stink.

"I'll just stop in the shop and have a quick word with Foegen,"

I told the reeds growing by the stream. "Then I'll turn back again. I don't think I'll see Merris this visit." I stopped whistling at the thought of Merris's smile.

The shop was closed. So I walked reluctantly to the house, past ten or more houses thatched with my own pattern of herringbone and Merris's special under-and-over netting, and knocked on the door.

It was Merris's oldest, Beals, who opened the door, but the others crowded around fast enough: Merris, her face alight, Broc, the toddler, grabbing my boot and trying to eat the ash stick, and Foegen, saying, "Udall, welcome, well come! We're just sitting to dinner, come and eat!"

I didn't want to worry Merris, so I said nothing, just sat at the table with Broc in my lap and ate as little as I could without it causing comment. My gut was clenched tight and I felt a kind of terror at what I was about to do. But in the babble of talk and questions from Beals—"Uncle, why is it always an ash stick? Why not some other wood? Uncle, how far is it to Pank? Why is it called Pank? What does Connay mean?"—my silence went unnoticed.

After dinner I grabbed the chance when Foegen said, "Come and I'll show you the new draft of steers arrived yesterday. I've got them settling in the barn until I can get that stream fence mended. I wanted to take a look at them anyway."

We went out alone, Merris calling Beals back softly, "Come help your mam."

The animal barn, behind the vegetable garden, was a lofty wooden building with, of all things, a slate roof. It had been built by the last butcher, whose brother was a roof tiler. On the lookout for accidents, I foresaw a slate sliding off that roof and crushing Foegen's head. Or one of the steers goring him, or . . . I decided I would warn him as soon as we got inside.

Foegen stumbled. I put out my hand without thought, steadying him upright.

"Swith the strong!" Foegen said, his voice shaking. "Look what you saved me from."

On the path in front of him, half hidden by the seed-heavy autumn grass, a scythe lay, blade up and glinting.

"If I'd fallen I'd have cut my throat open on that. I was working here yesterday when the steers arrived. I meant to come back for it but..." Foegen was shaking, knowing too well what blade did to flesh. "Gods, if you hadn't been here, Udall..."

We went back to the house, steers forgotten, and Merris made much of us both, but more of Foegen.

She kissed my cheek goodbye as I left, and thanked me. On the way home, I told the reeds, "Ah, it wouldn't have worked, anyway. I'm too old for her." But when the reeds whispered back, they didn't sound convinced.

At the next casting, there was no sign of the Marriage stone. I tried to be glad, for Merris's sake. And Foegen's, too. He made her happy, after all.

"Try to avoid your fate and it rushes to you," Sylvie said to me. "Selfishness draws disaster, they say. Me, I've never known a case where a man tried to avert another's fate, for no better reason than love. But then, love breaks all fates."

ASH

There was blood on the wall. Ash could smell it. Steam rose from the body at his feet. He thought briefly of warming his hands at the open wound, but realized that the thought was the thin edge of hysteria, part of the shocked giggles he could feel working their way up his throat. He didn't have time for hysteria.

Ash wiped his dagger on the corpse's sleeve, and ran. He ran like a fit, sober young man, not the drunken sot he'd pretended to be as he had entered the alley, reeling from wall to wall, and talking to himself loudly about how it was definitely time to go home now that he'd won so much at three-card draw. He'd made himself bait and the bait had been taken. The girl had come at him with a cosh and a hidden knife, and she'd intended to kill him right from the start. She'd been skilled, too. He barely escaped the knife after he'd hit the cosh from her hand.

As he ran, he listened. His footsteps pounded like the muffled drums at a funeral, but they were the only footfalls. The others who had been following him had gone. They had thought he was an easy mark and when he proved differently they had melted away.

He ran out of the dark alleys and into a street he knew was respectable, safe, rich, because the householders had paid to have torches set at each street corner. Around the fifth corner he found himself back in Acton Square, with late-night strollers coming in bunches toward him, from behind him, and a slew of restaurant tables in front of him. He pretended to cough and turned aside, then slid his dagger back into his belt unobtrusively. He wasn't even breathing hard, and that seemed impossible. He felt as though he should be panting, sweating—showing *something*.

When Ash had first come to Turvite, Acton Square had astounded him. A large cobbled space between two-storied brick houses, it was always full of people. During the day, it was the market square, and the ground was covered by stalls and barrows and blankets spread with wares from every corner of the world. And unlike every other market he had ever seen, it didn't smell, because the fish market was down by the docks, where the fishing fleet came in. In the evening, when the market was packed away, the eating houses and restaurants that surrounded the square put out chairs and trestle tables—some even with tablecloths!—and the rich of Turvite came to eat and stroll and be seen.

On this fine early summer night the square was full of people dining on freshly caught fish and salted beef, eels in aspic, grilled squab and fried finches wrapped in spinach leaves, with the waiters sliding like snakes between the tables. The smell of food turned Ash's stomach.

Doronit had followed Ash unnoticed all the way through the "exercise." She watched him for a moment before she made herself known. He was flushed and a little walleyed, like a spooked horse, as she had expected, but he was not out of control. His dark hair was even darker with sweat, but it was a warm night so no one would think anything amiss. She saw him take a deep breath and turn pale with the smell of food. It was time to bring him back to earth. She slid around the alley corner and approached him from behind so that she would seem to have come from nowhere.

"Good," she said softly. "Almost perfect, sweetheart."

He had done better than she had hoped. It was always hard to predict how the softhearted ones would react afterward, even when she had trained them twice as hard as this one. His hand started a fine tremor, which was always the first sign of panic. Time to take control. There was nothing like sex to distract a young man from moral scruples.

She smiled at him and patted his cheek lingeringly. "You should have slowed a little before the square and put your dagger away. But that's a small fault."

Ash stared at her. She was dressed like a well-to-do city woman, with wide navy trousers tucked into soft yellow boots, dark brown hair neatly braided, and a shawl pinned at the shoulder by a brooch set with sapphires. To match her eyes, he thought. Even dressed demurely, she was so beautiful that men stared as they went by, and women glanced sideways with a mixture of envy and rueful acceptance. Doronit was all curves, smoothly rounded; there wasn't a hard line anywhere on her, from crown to toe. The girl in the alley had been curved, too, although skinny. He felt himself begin to shake.

Doronit tucked her hand into his elbow. "A nice hot cha, that's what you need. Come."

Ash tried not to react to the touch. Doronit thought his shakes were a reaction to the killing, and maybe they were, but he had never wanted her so badly. He couldn't believe that he could feel so aroused, so alive, just after killing someone. Did that mean he was mind-sick—a killer at heart, who enjoyed it? He took his cloak off as though he were hot, and held it in front of him. Doronit smiled as though she knew why, and he flushed more. She always made him feel like an unschooled virgin, which he hadn't been since he was fourteen. With Doronit any confidence he had disappeared and he was left, like now, holding his cloak in front of him and feeling like a fool. He clung to that feeling as a bulwark against the memory of the girl sliding down the wall, against the smell of her blood still in his nostrils.

They went to an eating house at the side of the square, sat on the bench in the farthest corner ("Never expose your back" had been one of his first lessons) and Doronit ordered cha and honey cakes. There was a piper outside the eating house playing "The Long Way Home." Badly. It grated on his nerves, but the words rolled out inside his head, automatically. *It's a long, long way, and I'll be dead before I get there…*

Ash forced the words from his mind and sat still, as Doronit had taught him, drew his breath down, down farther, let it out slowly, allowing the shakes to go with it until he was calm again.

"Well done," she said. "You are ready to talk it over now?"

Her voice, as always, was soft, with a slight lisp, that faint hint of accent.

He shivered and nodded, losing some of his calm. "I killed her."

"Yes," Doronit mused. "A shame you had to use two strikes. That one to the shoulder left blood on the wall where she fell back against it. In this situation it doesn't matter, but if you wished to dispose of the body without anyone knowing whether death had occurred, you would have found that awkward."

Her words were a cold wind and steadied him faster than anything else could.

She sipped her cha and stroked his hand. "But I'm sure you won't do it again."

Silently, he shook his head. He hadn't expected this—that she would analyze this exercise as she had every other lesson she had taught him. Surely killing was different from weapons practice or scribing?

"Good." She held his hand lightly for a moment. He could feel the softness of her skin.

Trying to seem oblivious to her, he looked around at the activity in the square.

It was as busy as it always was in midevening. The swirl and chatter of people made no impression on Ash—but he was sharply aware of the safeguarders standing at the open doors of moneylenders, singlestaves in one hand and the other not far from their daggers. Ash looked at them with envy. Soon he'd be fully trained and one of them. Then he wondered if *they* had had to kill someone as part of their training. From where he stood he could see a good twenty safeguarders outside private offices and the Moot Hall. That was a lot of dead people.

Doronit tapped his arm to regain his attention. "Tonight you acted in self-defense. So. Killing is easy that way. Perhaps the time will come when you will have to kill someone who is not trying to kill you. What will you do then?"

He sipped his cha, playing for time. "If they were trying to kill—hurt someone else...I'd protect them..."

She smiled, for once, truly pleased. "Well, and that is what a safeguarder does, after all," she said reassuringly. "They protect."

The first step was killing to protect oneself. The second would be killing to protect someone else, an innocent. The third, to protect someone who'd paid for protection precisely because they weren't innocent. In a year he'd be slitting the throat of anyone she told him to, and sleeping twice as well as normal afterward.

She woke him before dawn, when he was in the middle of a dream about her. He blushed, thinking she might have realized (what had he said or done while she was watching?). But she merely nodded to the door.

"Sometimes," Doronit said, "you will have to go without sleep for days. This is a talent that can be developed. So. Run."

Ash ran. He would have done anything for her. He knew how much he owed her. He had known from the first day, when his parents had brought him to Doronit, not really believing that she would take him on as an apprentice, not when the baker and the butcher and even the slaughterhouse had refused, because he was a Traveler and therefore not to be trusted. Why would a safeguarder house take on someone who was traitorous by blood, he had wondered, when its very business was being trustworthy?

But they had tried Doronit because she had the dark hair of the old blood, and, Ash realized now, because his parents had probably known that she placed little importance on the opinions of others, being so sure of her own. He found that surety comforting, particularly because she seemed certain he could be valuable to her. Once he was trained. At the moment, he knew that all he was doing was eating her food and using up her time with no return for her. And at nineteen, he was old for an apprentice, although Doronit had said that she had no use for the usual fourteen- and fifteen-year-olds.

"Not strong enough," she had said, moving her hand admiringly down his arm. "Not mature enough to deal with the work we do."

So he ran through the thickening heat of the morning, trying as hard as he could. The skills he did have amounted to nothing off the Road: being a mediocre drummer and knowing hundreds of songs by heart (but not being able to sing them) weren't much use to anyone. If Doronit was prepared to take him on with nothing, no skills, no silver, no family with business contacts, he would burst his heart trying to please her.

Mountain girls are mighty kind
And river girls are pretty

Round the yard first, then down to the docks. His feet hit the hard stones of the street and slipped on the morning dew.

But Turvite girls are kinder still
To a smart boy from the city…

As always, he ran to the rhythm of "Turvite Girls," a rousing drinking song. The song, he had discovered, was most popular with the Turvite women themselves. Singing it in his head kept his feet moving fast enough to make him sweat, but not so fast he became breathless.

He turned the corner onto the drumming wooden planks of the docks. The fishing boats weren't home yet. The merchanters raised their single masts brown against the gray clouds, and the shrouds rattled down from the mastheads like dice in a cup, tantalizingly just out of rhythm. Behind him the hills stretched up, blocking out half the sky.

Turvite rose from its harbor in tier upon tier of houses, ascending in a semicircle of hills between two sheer cliff headlands. Down here near the harbor—immersed in the smells of old fish heads, rotten mud and bilges—the houses were wooden or wattled, with the occasional brown-brick inn.

Ash looked up and back, toward Doronit's house, wondering what she was doing, who she was seeing. Her house was amid the whitewashed brick buildings, halfway up the hills, with balconies out over the street. Farther up, on the highest tiers, the houses were golden stone mansions set in gardens full of small shrubs.

He stopped for a moment at the lowest part of the harbor to get his breath before he began the long climb. This was the best part of the day in Turvite, the only quiet time. The gulls were off chasing the fishing boats and the only sound was the wind moaning through the rigging.

For Carlion girls like salted flesh
And Pisay girls like bulls
But the Turvite girls love a city boy
Who'll fill their cup to full.
Bodgers and todgers and sailors all know
Yes, the fellows all agree

There's no finer girls in the wide, wide world
It's a Turvite girl for me.

He remembered asking his mother why everyone laughed at the chorus—he must have been five, or six. She'd said that the words were just clever, and that was why people laughed. He was twelve or so before he found out what the "sailors knew." He'd known there was another meaning, even at five, and he'd tucked it away in his mind, determined to find out the truth. He'd felt great satisfaction when he'd finally understood. Doronit said that only the truly determined survived, but he didn't know the difference between "determined" and "truly determined." He guessed he'd find out.

The first time he came to Turvite he had been a child. They had gone to the harbor to find lodgings, of course; it was in the old part of the city where Travelers, if not welcome, were tolerated. Coming down the hill on the main road that cuts the town in two, moving from the rich to the poorer quarters, Ash had been overwhelmed by the noise and bustle: pedlars shouting their wares, spruikers calling for shops and breweries, delivery wagons and handcarts trundling over the cobbles and, above him, the neighbors gossiping over their washing, strung between the balconies that almost met over the street. And down by the harbor, there had been more to marvel at: shouts and whistles from the stevedores, the slap of the tide against the wooden docks, and above everything, like a clean descant to a muddy melody, the calls of the gulls. His ears had rung for days after they arrived.

That first day, down at the harbor and almost onto the wharves, his father had turned him around to show him the city they had just walked through. It rose in layers of brown and white and gold.

"There's no green," Ash had said, feeling stupid. How could there be no green? The whole world was green, except in the snow country.

His mother sniffed. "Turviters think trees suck up the goodness from the air."

"It looks like a layer cake," Ash said, awestruck, and was thinking, Sweet. Rich. Delicious.

"Like old stale cake," his mother said. "And full of maggots and weevils."

A group of women in bright shawls and dresses without trousers underneath had walked past, laughing loudly.

"A few butterflies and ladybirds around, too," his father said drily.

"Where you get sailors you get butterflies," his mother retorted, then her face softened and they both laughed.

For years afterward Ash had looked for butterflies near any harbor they went to, but he had discovered they were few and far between.

Ash put the memory away from him and kept running. He rounded the Customshouse near the docks and began to climb the hill, past the swaying ghost of the drunk bosun's mate loitering on the steps where he'd broken his neck, and past darkened taverns and brothels where only a single torch hung outside. The whores were asleep. Even the Sailor's Rest, which never closed, had its door shut against the early morning chill.

He wanted to slacken off, to slow down as he breasted the hill, but he forced himself on, muttering the chorus once again. His feet slapped the cobbles a little faster. There was a drunk asleep in front of the Watering Hole. Probably asleep. Perhaps dead.

The girl's face leaped to his mind: young, she had been, fourteen maybe, with pale hair and quick hands. She'd have had him, if he'd been the sozzled young merchant she'd taken him for. She'd have slit him from balls to throat and smiled while she was doing it.

But after she died—*after he'd killed her*—her face had been washed clean of all the greed and hatred. She had lain like a child fallen asleep, waiting for her parents to come home.

Ash threw up in the road. Bile burned his throat. He stayed for a moment, bent over with his hands on his knees, panting. He forced down the memories of the girl, of the smell of her blood, the heat of her body against his hand as he slammed her against the wall, the soft sigh as her last breath escaped her. He pushed them all back down and his gorge with them. Then he straightened up and began to run again. Doronit was waiting.

His memory flashed back three months to the first time he had seen her. It was early in the morning. The day before had been very long, very dispiriting. No matter where they went, no one had been interested in employing a Traveler boy with no skills and no references. Most tradesmen and merchants had refused to even see him, and those who had were scathing. "Wouldn't sleep safe in my bed with one of you lot in the house!" said the butcher, who had been their last hope. Ash hadn't been sure whether to be disappointed or relieved. He had dreaded the charnel house and the dismembering, the constant stench of blood. But at least, he had thought, butchers ate well.

They had gone back to their lodgings and sat slumped at the table. Even his mother had been diminished by a full day of hatred and distrust.

"Perhaps we could find a Traveler to take you on. A tinker or farrier, or someone like that," his father had said.

"No," his mother said. "There's one more person left to try. Tomorrow."

"Who?" Ash asked.

"Her name is Doronit. She's settled. She hires out safe-guarders."

"Swallow!" his father protested.

"I know it can be dangerous. But it's a trade that will never go short of work. And it is . . . respectable."

His father fell silent, passing his hand over his head in tiredness or uncertainty.

"I don't mind," Ash said. "There've been times I would have liked to know how to fight."

His mother nodded. "That's true. There's always times for a Traveler when it would be good to know how to fight."

His father stared at him. "If you fight, they kill you."

"Worse things than death," his mother replied.

His father smiled at that, the wide, wondering smile he kept for her. "They should have named you Hawk instead of Swallow," he said, and kissed her.

The next morning, early, they'd gone to Doronit's house, halfway up the thoroughfare leading to the most exclusive street in the city, a brick building painted pale yellow to mimic the golden stones of the rich. They had been impressed. But Ash knew now that she hungered to live at the very top, in one of the solid stone mansions.

She'd come to the door to answer their knock herself, dressed as most women in the city dressed: wide trousers tucked into boots, with a soft three-quarter skirt over the top, a wool shawl around her shoulders over a simple shirt. Her clothes had combined different hues of the same green. It was a modest, sensible, reassuring outfit. It should have made him feel that he was applying to work in a respectable, comforting, solid enterprise.

But he had been nineteen so he'd looked straight through the clothes to the body beneath, which was curved and full and promising; he'd looked at the face, with red mouth, even teeth, long, dark lashes and something about the sapphire eyes that was neither respectable nor comforting. Their eyes met and he saw hers widen, but he'd been overtaken by breathlessness and he still wasn't sure if it had been simple desire or something else, something like the pressure he felt when he knelt at the gods' altars. He had coughed with embarrassment and turned aside a little, shuffling his feet, and he'd seen out of the corner of his eye that she was smiling at him in amusement. That he had made a fool of himself. He'd flushed. Had thought that she'd never take him on. He'd suddenly burned to work for her, to prove himself to her, to wipe out this first impression of gaucheness and adolescent stupidity. He had been following his parents around for days trying to find a job because he needed to eat; because he had to leave them; because there was no place for him on the Road. He hadn't cared where he ended up if he couldn't make music. But he'd desperately wanted a place with Doronit.

His father had explained that they'd been looking to apprentice Ash. Ash had again been aware of her assessing stare and then a smile. But this time the smile had been fixed with pleasure, not amusement.

"Come in," Doronit had said, her voice as beguiling as a tenor flute. "I would be happy to take this young man."

From that moment he had dedicated himself to pleasing her.

Doronit owned a complicated business, the simplest part of which was the hire of safeguarders to other merchants. From protecting people who had been threatened, to guarding valuable shipments going from one town to another, to just standing around menacingly when large sums of money were being exchanged, safeguarders were as central to the merchants' business as their own staff. But unlike their own staff, merchants didn't need them every day, yet didn't like hiring them off the streets or out of the taverns. So Doronit had seen an opportunity, a service that supplied safeguarders only when they were needed. She had a core staff of six and could call on another twenty or so at need. Of them all, only Ash was boarded in her house. That was part of the articles of apprenticeship, of course, and nothing to be proud of, but it still gave him a small satisfaction every time the others went home and he turned indoors with her.

By the time Ash reached the yard again, panting and sweating, the other six had arrived. Aylmer was sandy-haired and blue-eyed with broad shoulders and slightly long arms. He had taught Ash to stand absolutely still: he was the stillest person Ash had ever met. He was quick when he needed to move, but when he came to a stop—he just stopped. There was Hildie, tiny and fast, who was teaching him to spot pickpockets—mostly by teaching him how to pick pockets himself. Elfrida, who usually posed as a waitress, with long blond braids and rosy cheeks, had once knocked him backward clear through a window with one swipe of her singlestick.

And then there were the three others: large, alike, fair-haired, and with faces scarred and scowling. Their last job had been as night-soil carters and they were known, collectively, as the Dung Brothers. Ash could never tell them apart and no one ever used their real names. They didn't seem to mind and, since they preferred to work together, an order to one was an order to all three. They were slower than the others at singlestave, but were so strong that one blow was all they needed to knock an opponent unconscious.

They practiced singlestave all morning, until Ash's head was swimming with hunger and fatigue and the Dung Brothers hit him across the room once each, three in a row. They grinned, identical grins, and turned their backs on him dismissively. He was too tired even to feel angry. Then Doronit let him eat.

She led the way to the front room. Her room. The pale cream walls, unlike the bright colors most Turviters painted their houses, were just a backdrop for the other colors in the room. Margolin rugs on the floor, traded across the desert and then over the mountains, sang indigo and russet in the cool darkness. Blue silk curtains embroidered with dark green butterflies dressed the window. A line of matching glasses sat on the high shelf to the left—clear glass, worth a warlord's ransom—with a bronze lamp kept alight underneath them to call up their multicolored fire.

The table, with a centerpiece of indigo linen, had been laid for a formal dinner: two knives, two spoons, a long spoonlike thing with a narrow cup on the end, like a tiny ladle. There were glazed ceramic plates instead of wooden trenchers and a piece of sea sponge floating in a pottery bowl.

"So. We begin the next phase," Doronit said. "In order to be most useful, you will need to blend in with your customers. Sit down." She picked up the tiny ladle. "This is for eating marrow bone."

A month later, Ash carefully wiped his fingers and mouth with a sponge, and dropped it back into the bowl.

The town clerk was about to speak. Ash angled on his bench so that he could see down the room, as well as to the center table. He gave half an ear to the speech, and all of his sight to scanning the room for trouble. It was the main chamber of the Moot Hall, with a gilded ceiling and huge wrought-iron candle-rings on the walls. The tables were set with Caranese pottery and glass goblets. He'd seen rooms like these many times before, when his parents performed at feasts, but he'd never imagined himself being a guest in one of them. Well, perhaps not a guest. He was here to work. But he sat at the same table as the guests, and ate the same food; the serving staff spoke to him with the same respect. He felt warmth spread in his chest. His parents, for all their skill, had never sat at a waxed wood table and been offered food and drink by servants in livery. And thanks to Doronit, his table manners were as good as any merchant's.

He brought his attention back to the present with a frown for his woolgathering, although he didn't expect any trouble. The Annual Gifting Dinners were hardly dangerous. Everyone already knew what they were getting from the city profits for the year. The infighting was over. The grudges were being nursed. But there wasn't likely to be any...

At the back of the room a door curtain waved in a draft. The councillor's ghost standing beside it turned her head to look through the gap. Ash stood up and made his way quietly toward the door. That door led deeper into the Moot Hall, not out. There should be no draft. The Dung Brothers, on the other side of the room, watched him impassively.

He flicked the curtain aside, his hand on his dagger. Doronit was behind it, smiling.

"Good," she said. "Very good."

She patted his cheek, then looked through the doorway to where the merchants sat. Doronit was dressed in blond lace and dark rose silk, cut low across her breasts. Her dark hair with its touch of red was dressed high with sapphire pins. More beautiful than any woman there. More desirable. But not exactly an honored guest; only the most important merchant families were given grants at the Gifting Dinners. She was there to work, like him. He could read in the tension in her arms and the set of her cheek her desire to be in the select company at the high table.

"You deserve to be at the high table more than any of them," he said. "Whatever I can do... You should have everything. You know I want to help... I could... I mean..."

What did he mean? That he was a prattling fool was what he meant. She would despise him, turn away from him. But although she had stiffened, displeased by his perceptiveness when he first spoke, by the end of the muddled speech she was smiling.

"I know I can trust you. It is good to know I have someone who cares for my interests," she said warmly. But she gave him a little push, like one you would give a child. "Go back to your place, sweetheart."

He went, the feeling of Doronit's hand on his back, on his cheek, still warm, not knowing if she laughed at him or valued him, turning her words from this way to that in his mind. But because he wanted her to value him more than he wanted anything else, on the way back to his seat, he watched for signs of trouble. The councillor's ghost watched Doronit out of the corner of her eye.

Ash knew Doronit was training others. She disappeared, sometimes for days. She had other houses in the city, other businesses apart from hiring out safeguarders. He didn't even know how many. It disturbed him, if he let himself think about it.

Were her other employees better than he was? Quicker, smarter? Better at killing? He needed to be indispensable to her.

And when she was gone, maybe she was meeting a lover...someone more her own age, more sophisticated, more intelligent, more charming...She was twice his age, he knew; he couldn't think of any reason why she would be interested in him. Yet she had taken him to live in her house; she was kind to him, buying him clothes, teaching him herself rather than leaving it to one of the others. She touched him...He remembered every touch, every glance, every smile. Surely she wouldn't act like that if she didn't like him? If he worked hard, learned quickly, became polished and strong, maybe then...?

At the town clerk's dinners and the Merchant House settling days, when merchants and creditors came together in the house's settling room, to pay their debts and strike new bargains, he kept a lookout for others she favored. But he couldn't, even using her training on how to read people's eyes and faces, find anyone she smiled at with more warmth than him. She employed many other safeguarders, but no young ones, like him. No one who lived in her house, ate at her table. He let that comfort him. And finally her lessons turned to areas where he was not entirely ignorant.

Doronit had timed it carefully. She needed, she thought, to bring him closer to her before Midwinter's Eve, so she called him into her office one morning in early autumn. The office was a plain room at the front of the house where she organized contracts with her customers. No glass or silk curtains here, she thought with satisfaction. The workmanlike wood and leather and painted shutters were a kind of disguise to reassure the merchants, who were about to entrust their treasures to her staff, that she was efficient, businesslike, although in an unusual trade for a woman. Her office looked organized, which she was, and simple, which she was not. There was a big slate on the desk, with chalk laid ready.

She gestured him to it. "Geography. I suppose you know the main trade routes, but can you draw a map?"

He grabbed the chalk and began to draw confidently, marking the outlines of the Domains, all eleven of them, and then the main rivers and towns, barely hesitating, whispering under his breath as he marked each one.

"What's that?" Doronit asked.

"It's a teaching song from Foreverfroze," he said, "about Domain rivers."

He was clearly embarrassed, using a child's song to aid his memory, but Doronit nodded. "Useful."

It didn't take him long to finish the map. "Those are the main routes," he said, dusting the chalk from his fingers. "I could put in the secondary roads if you wanted..."

She smiled. "So. In this I think the student knows more than the teacher. I will come to you when I want information about secondary roads."

Doronit was more than pleased, and not just at his skill, but at the strength and surety with which he'd completed the task. For a while, while he concentrated, he had been a man instead of a boy. She sighed a little inside, imagining what it would be like to have someone she could trust, a strong man, at her back. She'd never found anyone she could rely on, but perhaps this boy would become what she needed.

"I suppose you know your history, too?" she said, and gave him a flirting smile.

He reddened a little, but sat up straight, looking her in the eyes. "Yes."

"Are you sure?" A strong man sometime in the future was all very well, she thought, but she couldn't afford to have him become cocky right now. "Tell me about the war between the Western Mountains and the Central Domains."

"Which one?" She paused, unsure for once, and he smiled at her, but it was a happy smile, not a cocky one. "There have been three, in the last thousand years."

Her first impulse was to slap him down, but she restrained herself. This could be another moment to bind him to her, to make him love her as well as want her. She laughed, making it clear she was laughing at herself, not at him.

"And I thought I knew my history!" she said. "How do you know all this?"

He shrugged, clearly pleased but trying not to show it. "There are songs. Just about every important moment in time has its own song. At least one."

"But you can't know them all!" This time she really was astonished.

"Maybe not *all,*" he said, being modest. "But most."

He was close to cockiness now, buoyed up by his first sense of superiority over her. She couldn't allow that.

"But you never sing," she said, and watched the knife go home.

He paled, picked up the chalk and fiddled with it, marking an unimportant tributary of the Knife River.

"No," he said quietly. "I can't sing. But I know the songs."

There it was, the sense of uselessness that his parents had drummed into him, the fools! But it was helpful to her. He'd soon be at the point where only her opinion mattered.

"How wonderful," she said warmly, and he looked at her in surprise, taking self-respect from her and drawing himself up. She patted his hand and then waved dismissively at the map. "None of my other safeguarders care about the past. They probably don't even know that there used to be only six Domains instead of eleven."

He smiled tentatively. "North and South, Far North and Far South, Western Mountains and Central."

She patted him on the shoulder. "Acton may have been a great war leader, but he didn't have much imagination when it came to naming things, did he?"

They laughed together and then she sent him out to deliver a message. It was to Hildie, who had been hired out for the day to a jeweler expecting a big shipment of rubies.

The jeweler's workshop was a simple shopfront in the middle tier of the city, two streets above Acton Square: close enough to the houses of the rich that they wouldn't think it a trouble to walk there, but low enough down to have a reasonable rent. When Ash arrived, the counter had been drawn up and locked, so he knew that the rubies had arrived. He went in cautiously, whistling his identity code so that Hildie wouldn't jump him as he came through the door. He didn't see her as he entered, then felt her breath on his neck and spun around.

"Gotcha!" she said, and laughed at him. "Ya shoulda waited till I whistled back, young'un."

He blushed. He'd never get the feel for this constant suspicion and caution. "At least I remembered to whistle."

"Aye," she nodded, and showed him the knife in her hand. "Otherwise you'da been whistling through a new hole in your windpipe."

She smiled as she said it, and he wasn't sure how true it was. She was probably just trying to make him feel even younger and stupider.

The jeweler was examining the rubies before signing the receipt. She was a big woman, tall and solid, beginning to run to fat, with gray eyes and light brown hair plaited down her back. She wore blue trousers and black boots with a gray work smock—simple, inexpensive, misleading clothes—and showed a placid face to the world, although Ash knew she was considered one of the sharpest traders in the city. The ruby seller, a thin, sharp-nosed man with an enormous mustache, was fidgeting from one foot to the other, anxious to have the gems off his hands. If they were stolen before he got a receipt, it would be his loss, Ash knew.

"Well, you're a welcome sight," Hildie said to him. "Better two sets of eyes and hands right now—we's at the sharp moment now." She grinned. "Even your eyes might be useful."

He rolled his eyes in acknowledgment of her right to tease him, but he kept his face to the door and his eyes on the street.

"You're to report to the town clerk at eight tomorrow," he said, "for a meeting with some merchants from the Wind Cities."

"Why does the old fart need safeguarding from foreign merchants?"

Ash shrugged, but the jeweler chipped in, looking up from the lens she had suspended over the tray of rubies. "Because last time they threatened to cut his balls off if he substituted second-grade iron ore for the top grade they'd paid for."

"Ah . . . " Hildie nodded wisely, "and he's afeared they'll really try it this time and find out he don't have any, right?"

They all laughed, even the nervous ruby seller.

"All correct and accounted for," the jeweler said.

She packed the gems away into her strongbox and put it aside, then handed up a pouch of money.

The mustachioed vendor accepted the pouch and pulled something from his pocket with a flourish, all his nervous energy released once the jewels were safely paid for. "Something special," he said. "Unique."

He laid it out on the jeweler's tray—a big cloak brooch that mimicked a shield in intricate metal- and enamelwork. Bronze wire turned like hearts, or maybe faces, around a central circle with three curving enamel—*What?* Ash wondered. *Claws, birds' heads, scythes?*—coming out from the center. There was something about it that caught the eye. On one glance it looked calm, balanced, pretty; on another look it was packed with threatening shapes in a whirling dance. Unsettling.

"It's old," Ash said, and moved to see it better.

"Ancient," the man said, smoothing one end of his mustache into a curling tip. "As old as the Domains."

"I deal in gemstones," the jeweler said dismissively. "This isn't even gold, it's just bronze."

"They say—" The man paused dramatically. "That it belonged to Acton."

"And my grandmother's still alive and dancing the hornpipe every night at the Drunken Sailor."

"No, really! I got it in the west, near where Acton's people first came over the mountains. He gave it to some woman's ancestor."

"Why?"

The man shrugged. "Because she was a good shag, I guess. It was usually something like that with Acton, wasn't it?"

"And this woman gave it to you?" the jeweler said. "Because *you* were a good shag?"

He sniffed, which made the mustache bounce. "Because the warlord there's a right bastard and she needed to pay her taxes. But if you're not interested, I'll take it elsewhere."

"It may be old, but it's not in my line—Acton's or not. I'll just keep the rubies, thanks."

The man turned to Ash and Hildie. Hildie hadn't taken her eyes from the street the entire time.

"What about you two?"

"Not interested in anything of Acton's," Hildie said, her voice flat. Ash saw the man register Hildie's Traveler accent and sneer a little.

"What about you, lad?"

"He's an apprentice," Hildie cut in. "He couldn't afford a *fake* bronze brooch."

"Too bad," the man said.

"Yes," Ash said, his eyes still on the curving bronze. "Too bad." He was drawn to it; he wanted to pick it up and run his fingers across the intricate scrolling. What if this *had* belonged to Acton? The man who'd invaded this country and disinherited Ash's people, turned them off their land and made them into Travelers—the man who'd changed everything. The first warlord.

Half the old songs were about Acton—about his courage and leadership and humor and, of course, his love life, which by all accounts had been prodigious. He loomed larger than life in the minds of everyone in the Domains, perhaps all the more because no one knew what had happened to him. He had ridden out one day from a camp up near the Western Mountains and disappeared. The legend said that his last words had been, "I'll be back before you need me"; and in the countryside a surprising number of people believed he *would* come back one day, from wherever he had ridden away to, if the country was in deadly peril.

The brooch seemed to shimmer in front of Ash's eyes, speaking of choices long made and chances long forfeited. Perhaps there had been a moment when his ancestors could have united and fought Acton off; but they hadn't. Their settlements had been too widely scattered, the people living in the central lands had depended on the mountain people to repel any raids, so when Acton broke through that defense there was no one to stop him. There was no one who really knew how to fight and no one to rally the far-flung villages and make a stand.

So Ash stood here in a jeweler's shop in Turvite, which had been founded by those ancestors but was a city of Acton's people now, and he didn't even know what the birthright was that had been stolen from him. It was so far in the past—a thousand years!—that no Traveler alive today knew the history of their people before Acton came. Not for sure and certain, although Ash's father had taught him what was known of the old language. All they had were a few scraps of songs and stories, some of the traditions and habits and superstitions . . . and the casting stones, which predated not only Acton but Ash's ancestors as well, and had come, they said, straight from the gods.

The man wrapped the brooch up again, tucked his purse securely inside his shirt and did up his coat over it. Ash blinked; it seemed the shop was darker than before.

"Any more business for me?" the man asked the jeweler.

She shook her head. "I'll let you know if I have another order."

The trader still had his hand over his pocket. It seemed to occur to him for the first time that a money pouch could be stolen as easily as a pouch of rubies. "Walk me back to my lodgings, young'un?" he asked. "Standard rate?"

"Danger rate," Ash said. "They could be waiting for you to make the trade—most thieves prefer money to gems."

The man sniffed, then nodded and waited for Ash to go out the door before him.

"'Acton, lucky under the sword, lucky under the sheets, favored by gods and by all the unseen . . .'" Ash murmured.

"Huh?" Hildie said.

"An old song," Ash shrugged. "I'll see you later."

He went quietly, carefully, out the door and escorted the trader to his inn with no trouble. But on the way back to Doronit's he had the rest of that song singing in his head: *Acton, brother of horses, Acton, brother of wolves, Acton, father of hundreds, Acton, father of us!*

It made him feel a bit sick. Acton, the killer. Ash had always despised him. But he was a killer himself, now. The girl's face rose in his mind, as it sometimes did before he went to sleep or, worse, in his dreams. Such a young face. So concentrated on him, on his death. The knife in her hand, held low. Her pale hair, her pale face, relaxed after she fell, her thin chest still, her hand letting go of its clutch on the knife. What he felt wasn't exactly guilt, more sharp regret; he regretted whatever it was—circumstance, fate, bad luck—that had brought them both to that alleyway.

MARVEL'S STORY

THE WORLD's full of easy marks, but I never took myself for one of them, not me, not little Marvel. That's what they called me in the back alleyways of Turvite, a marvel 'cause I was so fast with my hands and light with my fingers. It's not a bad life, pickpocket and thief. Gods, why should I lie? It's shagging horrible—scary and dirty and hand-to-mouth and always scrounging. Better off dead, they say in other towns, but in Turvite we've too many ghosts to believe that. Not many neck themselves around here. No use complaining, that's what I say, not when you might get an easy mark around the next corner, with a fat purse and a yellow heart.

And I was lucky enough, though I'd had to kill a few times to get that purse. Life's not worth much in the alleyways. "Gutter" they called me, as well as Marvel. I'm not tall, see, and I can't reach a grown man's throat at the right angle to slit it neatly and quietly. Putting a shiv into the heart's tricky business, no matter what you've heard, specially if they're fat, so my best bet was to put the blade in just over their pubes and slit them from fork to gullet. The other thing is, if they're wearing a winter coat, most of the time it doesn't get much blood on it, so you can fence that, too.

It's good, when you're little and young, to have a reputation as a gutter. Keeps the thugs off you. Keeps the pimps away and the girlers who heave a woman or two aboard ships bound for the Wind Cities, to keep the sailors happy and sell to the brothels at the other end. One girler who tried that on me ended up with his balls in his throat, and they didn't get there through his mouth.

Never had to shag for my supper. Not once. My brother used to earn his bread that way before the poppy juice got to him and I swore I'd never let anyone do that to me. Better kill fifty men than have one of them on top of me like that.

Life got easier after my brother died and I didn't have to find enough silver to buy his juice. I started saving up for...something, I didn't know what. To learn a trade? Start a business of my own? I thought I could maybe sell fish down at the harbor market, or make candles. It wasn't so far-fetched. Look at Doronit. She arrived in Turvite as poor as me and now she gets invited to the Merchants' Banquets! I wanted to be like her. Makes you laugh, doesn't it?

Sometimes, when I was washing my hands afterward, I thought about going to the Valuers' Plantation. I liked Valuer thinking: that there shouldn't be any warlords or high families, that no one's life is worth more than another's—all valued alike—and that the rich should share with the poor so no one goes hungry. They say anyone is welcomed at the plantation, anyone at all. But I wondered what they'd say to me—I lived as though no one's life had any value at all.

I thought, sometimes, in the early morning before I went to sleep, *I'll save up and go to the Well of Secrets, and confess.* She can magic the blood off your hands, they reckon. *Then I'll go to the Valuers and maybe, if I have clean hands, they'll take me in.* It got so I was thinking about that night as well as morning, thinking through the journey up through Carlion and then inland to Pless and farther up, imagining the welcome at the end of it. I went out more than I should have, maybe, to find fat purses and yellow hearts. Took risks, like going after young men as well as old. Should have known better.

I should have smelled a rat when I saw that drunk young cully reel down the alley where I kept watch, his fat purse clinking against his side. Looking back, I realize he was a bit too young, he moved a bit too well to be a stumbling sot of a merchant's son, no matter how he was dressed. But Shiv and Dimple had seen him, too, and started to follow him, and I thought, *Got to get to him first, got to get that juicy purse.*

So I ran and I leaped, and when he turned suddenly, sharp as the knife he cocked at me, it was too late. I almost had him—I was quick, I was bloody quick. But he was quicker. I recognized him as he took me in the shoulder—Doronit's new boy, the Traveler. His eyes were wide with fear and horror. *He doesn't have a taste for killing*, I thought, as though it mattered to me. Not yet he didn't. Then his knife went in again and it was over.

Surprising, there's not so much pain when the knife goes in; it's when it comes out again that it hurts. Wasn't a bad death, all things considered. Quick. Clean. Over. And that was a relief. Seemed to me—at the moment when I stopped seeing anything and felt myself, my *self,* still go on—that maybe I owed Doronit's boy for setting me free.

I'd like to get to the Valuers' one day, though. If not in this life, maybe the next.

SAKER

HE NEEDED bones. The right bones, restless in the earth. He went to his workroom, to the big map spread out on the table, the most complete map of the Domains that he had been able to buy. There were a few massacre sites marked in red—Death Pass, Turvite, Carlion. But too few. So many more had been slaughtered. Carefully stored scrolls filled the shelves around him, but so little of their information was useful. What did he care about the names of the killers, or who their fathers had been? Why should he want to know how they had held their weapons, how they had swung them against his people—his peaceful, gentle people? The poems and histories had been written by the invaders, and gave no details about those killed, least of all where to find their bones.

Saker slumped at the table, head in hands, another night's study ending in frustration. There must be other scrolls, other histories . . . He felt the bag of stones at his waist. At least Friete, the enchanter, had taught him how to cast, had given him a way of supporting himself. It was useless to cast for oneself, every stonecaster knew that. Either useless or dangerous—one or the other. But sometimes the temptation was irresistible. He dug his hand in the pouch and drew out the necessary five stones, cast them with a practiced flick of the wrist. But they landed, not spread out across the table in an arc, but in a huddle on one spot, facedown. Right on top of Connay, north of Whitehaven. Two days' walk away.

He didn't bother to turn the stones over. Their position was enough. *Connay*. The gods had spoken. He would find what he needed in Connay. He packed, and then picked the stones up almost reluctantly: Revenge and Rejoicing, Death and Bereavement, and the Chaos stone lying on top of them all. His spirits rose. They were exactly the same stones as that first stonecasting after Friete's death. Saker wondered why Death, Bereavement and Chaos were now facedown. *Secrecy,* he thought. *I must work secretly. That is the message of the stones.* He went out whistling, headed for Connay.

BRAMBLE

BRAMBLE WANTED to arrive at the linden tree early, just in case. Ghosts rise, if they rise, three days after death, but not to the minute. It might be an hour earlier or two hours later. Some ghosts never came—those who had died slowly, and knew they were dying and had said all their farewells. "May you have no quickening" was a blessing, a wish that the gods would give you a good death, where you had no need to come back to say goodbye or ask for forgiveness or confront your killer, where you went straight on to new life. "May you quicken and never be reborn" was a curse.

It was hard to see ghosts in daylight. Most ghosts were just a pale waver in the air, like heat shimmer above paving, but some were more substantial, blobs of white in the shape of the dead person. Travelers, it was said, could see ghosts better than other people, but Bramble had never found it so. Maybe she didn't have enough Traveler blood in her. But she had attended a few quickenings in her time, as most people had, and she knew she would recognize the chill of the flesh as the ghost arrived.

As she approached the linden tree, she heard men's voices. She stopped behind a yew and watched. *So he had some friends,* she thought. There were three men in warlord's uniform, sitting at the base of the tree, on the other side from where the blond had fallen. They were talking idly. One was throwing pebbles at the nearby willow; another, an older man with brown hair and a beard, had his head tipped back to look at the leaves above him; the third—the redhead who had been with the blond in the forest when the wolf had been shot—was sharpening his dagger with a small whetstone. He spat on the stone as she watched and honed the blade with deep concentration, as though preparing it for someone's flesh.

Bramble couldn't decide whether to leave immediately, or wait. If the blond quickened—and he would, she knew it in her bones—she should know what happened. His friends were here because he had died suddenly, but they thought it was by accident. If the ghost was strong enough to be seen clearly, it could let them know the truth. On the other hand, if they found her here, at this place, at this time, death was the best she could hope for.

The ghost decided for her. It took form, shimmering and pale gray, lying on the ground just as the warlord's man had lain three days ago. Bramble felt her skin chill and grow goose bumps, even from so far away. The three men jumped to their feet, and the ghost did too. They confronted each other. The dead man was just a blur, but it was clear enough for his friends.

"You're dead," the redhead said, gently enough. "You rode into the tree limb." He pointed to the branch above their heads. "Three days ago. This is your quickening."

The ghost put out his pale arms and waved negatingly.

"Yes, yes," the redhead said soothingly. "I know it's a shock. But you really are dead."

The ghost pointed to the tree limb and waved both arms again.

"Yes, that's the branch," the older man said. His voice was very deep, and hard. He sounded bored. "Just accept it, Swith. You're dead. No use going on about it."

Swith. Somehow it troubled Bramble that the blond should have the same name as her crotchety old friend. She didn't want to think of him as a real person, with a name and friends who cared about him.

The ghost waved an arm, shook a fist in the direction of the tree branch.

"He's not acting like it was an accident," the redhead said uneasily. "He's not being reasonable."

"You expect him to be different now from when he was alive?" the older man said scathingly. "Come on, we've done what we came for. Let's get back to Thornhill. I've got work to do even if you haven't."

The redhead looked troubled. "What if it wasn't an accident?"

The ghost pointed his arms at his friend and seemed to nod, although it was hard for Bramble to see.

"It wasn't an accident?" the redhead said. The ghost made a victory gesture above his head.

"Oh, shagging gods!" the older man said. "Of course it was an accident. Swith just doesn't want to be remembered as the idiot he was."

The youngest of the three, a man with big ears, sniggered.

The ghost fell down upon his knees. It sobered even the sniggerer.

"They never found his horse, Beck," the redhead said quietly.

Beck, Bramble thought, *that's the warlord's second in command.*

"That was a good horse," Beck said thoughtfully. "I trained him myself. Worth killing for, if you had somewhere safe to take him."

"I think we'd better talk to the warlord. Try to find the horse. If it's still out in the forest, well, then it's an accident. If not..."

The older man sniffed, then nodded. "All right. I'll talk to him. Let's go."

She waited until the three men had mounted and left. The redhead clearly felt awkward about riding away from the ghost, just leaving it standing there by the tree. He tried to wave goodbye to it, but halfway through caught the eye of the older man and he turned the movement into a fumble on the reins.

They went west up the slope, toward Thornhill, without looking back. When they were out of sight, Bramble slowly came forward, her knife tight in her hand. When the ghost caught sight of her, he pointed one long pale arm at her head, turned as though to call back the men, then realized he couldn't. Bramble swallowed. Up close, the chill was much worse. She took a deep breath. Words had been laid down for this, words that had to be said.

"I am your killer," she said to him, trying to look him in the eye. "Lo, I proclaim it, it was I who took your life from you. I am here to offer reparation, blood for blood."

She cut her wrist with a sure flick of the knife and offered it to him, her whole body tensed against what was to come. But the ghost backed away and waved his arms: *No*. She could almost see his mouth, a slightly darker shape, form the word.

"If you do not forgive me, you will be caught here in this place, with no chance of rebirth," Bramble said.

He lunged forward, his hands out for her throat, forgetting for a moment that he no longer had a body to do damage with. His pale form passed right through her; she felt a horrible chilly wave. The burial cave smell enveloped her and she fought to stop herself vomiting.

The ghost turned, furious, unappeased, and raised its fists to the sky in anger.

It was enough. Bramble turned and ran back toward the stream. *Now,* the gods said in her mind. *Now.* She ran home, straight to her mother's workshop.

She fetched up at the side of the loom, panting. "I'm leaving. I—I'll go to Maryrose. I'm going now. Don't worry. And if you're asked, you know nothing of where I am or why I've gone. You all come soon."

Her mother sat with her mouth open, astonished. Bramble moved around the corner of the loom, hugged her briefly, kissed her cheek, and ran out headed for her father's workshop before her mother could recover her breath.

Her da and granda were standing at the workbench, looking at some plans. As she ran to them they turned to face her. She reached up to kiss each of them on the cheek—*NOW,* the gods insisted—then ran out without speaking. She ran for the forest as though she were a wild goose flying.

She found the roan waiting for her. He nuzzled her shoulder while she tried to calm herself. His warm breath steadied her nerves, brought her back down to earth. She found that she had cut her forearm on the wild dash through the trees; it had ripped against a branch. Without thinking, she took her skirt off in haste and staunched the blood flow, then realized the stains she was making on the fabric. *Rot it,* she thought, *I could have used this skirt.* She tore enough off to make a bandage then tossed it aside. Her breeches would be enough. It would probably be better if she looked like a boy anyway. She pinned up her braid and put on a tight-fitting leather hood that she usually wore against the winter snow, and retrieved the carefully packed bundle from the rear of the cave and tied it to her back. Then she led the roan to the mounting block and climbed on his back.

"Come on, then," she said. "Go."

She found that her mind had been working on its own these past three days. There was a plan all ready in her head, though she hadn't been conscious of working it out. She would head for Carlion immediately, but through the forest, not on the road where the warlord's men would be sure to find her. It would take longer, because she would have to go up beyond the waterfall, beyond the chasm, to find a ford where she could cross the river, so she could circle down to the road through the forest on the other side. Longer but safer. The warlord's men would start their search from the linden tree, so she had time.

She knew the forest better than anyone, but the roan couldn't move through the undergrowth as she could, so they kept to the track, as they had the day before. The roan recognized the way and went happily enough. It was a warm day, with sun filtering down to her where the trees were less dense. They moved from shade to sun and back again, warmth and coolness, like the rhythm of the roan's soft hoofbeats. It had lulled her, so the sound of men's voices at a distance, the jingling of harness, caught her by surprise.

They had started their search from Thornhill, not from the linden tree. And they were coming steadily from the west. She turned to head more directly for the chasm. There were rocks near the waterfall, with caves...Perhaps she and the roan could hide there. These men didn't know the forest the way she did. She was confident that she could outsmart them in her own territory. Then she heard the baying of the hounds.

The roan's head went up, too, and he took a breath to whinny. She leaned forward quickly and held his nostrils closed. He looked at her reproachfully and she stared back at his enormous eyes.

"No noise, my friend," she whispered.

He let his breath out slowly, and she let go, then urged him to a quick walk.

The hounds' note changed. Bramble had watched the hunt go by too many times not to recognize it: "We are on the scent!" The roan quickened his pace when he heard men's voices urging on the hounds. He jumped at one voice in particular. A deep, hard voice. *Beck's,* Bramble thought. *The older man. The clever one.* The roan almost stumbled, then began to move faster, taking the rough ground in his stride, ignoring Bramble completely. She lay down low and clung to his neck with both hands as they moved rapidly through the undergrowth.

Behind them the hounds were belling furiously. Bramble tried desperately to think what to do. There was no time to hide. No way to get up above the chasm in time to cross the river and confuse the scent. She tried to think of other streams nearby, but there weren't any. She could probably climb a tree and let the roan go—the hounds would follow the horse scent. That would be the sensible thing to do. But she couldn't. She couldn't abandon him to the chase. What if the hounds' master didn't whip them back in time? What if the bloodlust got too much for them? What if they brought him down? These hounds were used to hunting people and horses as well as deer: they would leap for the throat. If she was still on the roan, at least she could help fight them off until Beck controlled them. He had admired the roan; he would save him. She decided that they would stand at bay at the chasm—a bad place but it was all they had.

She clung on as the roan raced faster through the trees. She craned for one look over her shoulder. Beck was in the lead, his face pale beneath the beard, his eyes intense.

"There!" he shouted. "It's just a boy! Get him!"

The roan broke into a panicked gallop. Bramble suddenly knew who had been responsible for those welts and scars on his hide. But they were going too fast... They were too close to the chasm: they'd never be able to stop in time.

The roan didn't falter as they broke from the trees and headed wildly toward the abyss. Bramble considered tumbling from his back before he reached the edge. Then she heard Beck's voice calling.

There were worse things than death.

There would be a leap and a moment suspended, and then a long hopeless curve to the rocks and the river below. They would fall like leaves between the clouds of swifts and then be washed away by the thundering rapids. Bramble clung to that thought. If their bodies were washed away then there could be no identification, no danger of reprisals on her family.

She hung on tighter.

The roan's hindquarters bunched under her and they were in the air.

It was like she had imagined: the leap, and then the moment suspended in the air that seemed to last forever.

Below her the swifts boiled up through the river mist, swerving and swooping while she and the roan seemed to stay frozen above them. Bramble felt, like a rush of air, the presence of the gods surround her. The shock made her lose her balance and begin to slide sideways.

She felt herself falling.

With an impossible flick of both legs, the roan shrugged her back onto his shoulders. Then the long curve down started and she braced herself to see the cliffs rushing past as they fell.

Time to die.

Instead, she felt a thumping jolt that flung her from the roan's back and tossed her among the rocks at the cliff's edge on the other side.

On the other side.

The roan slowed down and turned to head back for her. She stood slowly, muddled and shaken. She couldn't see properly, everything was in shadow, as though it were night. She reached out to touch the roan's shoulder. She knew she was touching him, but she could barely feel the warmth of his hide. She could barely hear; everything seemed distant, dull. She was breathing, but the breaths gave her no life. She felt like a dead woman breathing out of habit, as ghosts do when they first quicken, before they realize they are dead.

Her sight cleared, although the light still seemed dim. Her hearing came back a little. On the other side of the abyss a jumble of men and horses and hounds were milling, shouting, astonished, and very angry.

"You can't *do* that!" one yelled. "It's impossible!"

"Well, he shagging did it!" another said. "Can't be impossible!"

"Head for the bridge!" Beck shouted. "We can still get him. I want that horse!"

That got her moving, got her onto the roan's back and riding. The world still felt distant, but the roan, once she was on his back, was as sharp and clear to her as ever, each hair in his coat distinct, each movement warm and vital beneath her. Around her the forest was like a dream, but he was real. The need to keep him safe drove her on.

She didn't know this part of the forest quite as well, but well enough. She made her way as fast as they could go, cantering where the trees thinned out, walking quickly when they closed in. The roan was pleased with himself, she could tell; he cantered with his ears pricked up and almost pranced through the clearings. She showered lavish praises on him and he took it all in and pranced some more, until she almost laughed aloud.

She thought back to the leap. That moment in the air had been...magnificent. But once was enough. She wasn't sure, now, if the gods had merely surrounded her to taste the moment, as they sometimes did, or if they had actually held her and the roan up in the air for one crucial heartbeat.

Whether they had or not, she felt an obscure certainty that she had been meant to die in that chasm—that her time had been up. She should be tumbling in the white water of the river right now, being swept to sea, the roan beside her. It was only because the roan had made that extraordinary midair shrug that she hadn't fallen.

The fact that she was still alive felt wrong, out of balance. She didn't feel special, or protected, or gods-bound. She thought that the gods had acted to protect the roan, and she had just been along for the ride. It was the roan who was special, not she.

I should be dead, she thought. If she was dead, then it would all be settled. The warlord's men would have been satisfied to see her body swept away, the roan would have been safe from Beck's whip, the ghost of the man she had killed could have gone to his rest. There was a rounding off—a justice—in her death. But alive, no one was satisfied and no one was safe.

She looked ahead in her life and saw emptiness. If she should be dead, then there was no hole in the world she was destined to fill, no home, no place for her to find and claim. It was only now that she realized, when she had thought of the Road, her underlying assumption had been that she would travel until she found where she belonged. But if she belonged in the burial caves, then...

It seemed as though she was looking at the world through clouded glass. Noises were still muted in her ears. Was it shock? Maybe it meant something else. She didn't know. The only thing she was sure of was that the roan had saved her life, and she was in his debt. She murmured thanks to him as they rode, gave thanks and endearments and pats and encouragement, and he took it all as his due.

She would think about this again once they were past the Second River and farther away from the South Domain. Beck and his men *might* make it to the bridge and cut across to intercept her, but they were well behind.

She came to the Second at sunset, hearing the hounds far behind them. It took her a little while to find a place to ford, but the noise of the hounds grew no louder. They were on a false scent. She sighed with relief as they crossed the river. Once she had forded the Second she was in Three Rivers Domain, and they couldn't touch her or the roan without formal application to the Three Rivers warlord. Now it was an easy ride to Carlion, and Maryrose.

She knew that once she reached Carlion, she would be completely safe. There were arrangements for criminals to be sent back to the Domain they had come from but the free towns demanded a very high degree of proof before they would surrender anyone to a warlord's punishment, and Beck just didn't have any proof against her. In their own Domain, that wouldn't matter: he could act with the warlord's authority and no one could object. But the free towns were truly free, and because they were the centers of trade across the Eleven Domains, their councils were rich and powerful.

She rode through the night despite the lack of moon, trusting to the gods who had seen them safe thus far. The road was good, anyway, being the main road between the warlord's fort near Wooding, and Carlion, the second biggest free town in the world. The city was set on a natural harbor, almost as big as Turvite's, but the space between the harbor and the encircling hills was small and steep, so the buildings were crammed in tightly and the town huddled on the rim of the sea.

Bramble could smell the brine as she came down the hill to the first houses, and hear the rhythmic shushing of the waves against the rocks. But both smell and sound were muted by the fog in her head. The sharp salt smell only reached her nose, and didn't lift her spirits as it had on her last visit. The sound of the waves was dull instead of soothing.

She rode between the high, narrow brick houses, and the stones of the street were dark and slippery with sea spray. She clopped her way down Maryrose's street and into her yard before even the starlings were stirring.

She had first come to Carlion when Maryrose had married Merrick, who was a carpenter, like their da and Maryrose. Merrick's mother was the town clerk and he was well established, so Maryrose's new house was substantial, with a yard and stable, although they kept no horses yet. Quietly, Bramble let herself and the roan into the stable. She rubbed him down, fetched him water, then rolled herself in her blanket and slept until the town noises became too loud to be ignored.

Outside the kitchen door she hesitated. What if Maryrose looked at her and saw a walking corpse instead of a living sister? What if she really was dead and just didn't know it? It occurred to her for the first time that perhaps her body *was* lying in the bottom of the chasm, and the men had been chasing the roan, not her. What if she was a ghost who had quickened too soon? There was only one way to find out.

She popped her head around Maryrose's back door. "Any breakfast for a starving sister?"

Maryrose dropped the ladle into the porridge pot with a splash. She swept across the kitchen and enfolded Bramble in a hug. She smelled of woodsmoke and wool and wood, with a hint of lavender underneath, as she always did. Bramble was glad marriage hadn't changed that, at least. But even Maryrose's familiar scent seemed lost to her, somehow distant. A smell remembered rather than lived. But she definitely had a solid body that Maryrose could see and touch. Bramble returned the hug, her heart lifting and settling all at once, so that she was calmer than she had been since she killed the warlord's man. It was foolish, because it had been years since Maryrose could do anything for her that she couldn't do for herself. Come to think of it, she thought, there were a score of things Maryrose could do that she couldn't—weave, carpenter and cook in a hearth among them.

"How did you get here? Where are Mam and Da and Granda? What are you doing here?"

"Can I eat first and talk later?" Bramble said. "I'm starving."

It was true that she hadn't eaten since the day before, but the sensation of emptiness that filled her was stronger than hunger. She sat at the table and took the bowl of porridge that Maryrose handed her. It smelled nutty and sweet, but very faintly, as though she were smelling it from another room. She sprinkled on a bit of salt from the salt pig on the table and took a good mouthful. The taste was also muted. Like a damped-down fire, she thought, or sun behind clouds. She ate anyway. Maybe if she kept acting as though she were alive, the fog would burn off and she would be normal again. She didn't really believe that, but what else could she do? Lie down and die for real and true? Who would look after the roan then? She took another mouthful of porridge.

"Mam and Da and Granda are at home. I came on a horse overnight—he's in your stable. I'm —" Bramble hesitated.

She had come to Maryrose instinctively, but now she was here, she knew she couldn't stay. Already, after less than an hour, the solid walls of the town seemed to lean in on her, with a much more unpleasant pressure than when the local gods were present. She couldn't live in this comfortable, secure house. She'd go mad. It was time to put her original plan into action, and head for the Great Forest.

"I'm Traveling," she said at last.

Maryrose quieted immediately, served herself a bowl and sat opposite Bramble, gazing at her as though she could search her mind, or at least her emotions. Bramble endured it patiently. Maryrose had looked at her like that often enough before.

Maryrose was opening her mouth to speak when Merrick came in. He was as surprised as Maryrose had been, but a lot quieter about it.

"*Hullo.* Come to visit?"

She'd always liked Merrick, and this quiet welcome, complete with smile and pat on her shoulder, confirmed that regard.

She nodded. "Just a couple of days."

Maryrose was eating her porridge thoughtfully. She went, as she always did, to the heart of things.

"Where did you get a horse?" she asked.

So Bramble told them the whole story, nothing left out, although she found it difficult to explain the way she felt about the roan, about riding. It was a relief to tell Maryrose what had happened. If her sister had been at home Bramble would have shared it with her long ago.

The only thing she kept back from them was her conviction that she had been meant to die. They listened with growing concern and astonishment.

"You jumped the *chasm?*" Maryrose kept saying.

"The roan jumped the chasm," Bramble corrected her drily. "I just hung on."

"They thought you were a boy...?"

"Yes, but they might start asking questions... So it's a good thing Mam and Dad and Granda are coming here to live with you. Just in case."

"They're coming? Good." Maryrose spoke absently, turning the story over in her mind. "Yes, it's reassuring to live in a free town. One good thing Acton did, anyway."

"What do you mean?" Merrick asked.

Maryrose lifted an eyebrow at him. "Acton established the free towns so that people would have a place to go where no warlord could follow them or have power over them. I love the fact that within the walls of Carlion we're out of their control! It was Acton's idea to make the main towns of the Domains subject only to their town councils."

"Well, I know *that,*" Merrick said. "It was a stroke of genius—trade between the free towns keeps the Domains linked as they would never be if the warlords controlled everything. But why was that 'one good thing'? You talk as though Acton didn't do anything else good."

They both stared at him. Bramble saw, as if for the first time, his brown hair and hazel eyes, a legacy of the second wave of Acton's people who had come over the mountains after Acton's death. They had hoped to take land while the first tribe of invaders were leaderless, but Acton's son had dealt with them—done deals, traded, apportioned out land to the west and south. But even though a thousand years ago Acton would have been an enemy of his ancestors, Merrick still hero-worshipped him. That was plain in his indignation. Bramble looked at Merrick and Maryrose, sitting side by side but now with an indefinable distance between them. She hoped it wouldn't last.

"Our granda was a Traveler," Maryrose said slowly, as if thinking it through for the first time. "I suppose we were raised to... to think of

Acton differently. As the man who had headed an invasion force that killed off almost all of this land's people."

"And forced the rest onto the roads as Travelers," Bramble added. "Except for the Lake People, of course, and he tried with them, but the Lake stopped him. A stone-cold, bullying murderer, that was Acton."

"No..." Merrick paused and looked from one to the other, from dark Bramble to red-haired Maryrose.

People often looked from one of them to the other, wondering how they could be sisters. But Merrick's eyes weren't suspicious or harsh when he looked at her. Merrick was a logical man, as well as kindly—*almost* good enough for Maryrose.

"Well...of course a lot of people were killed," he continued. "But he established our civilization, our whole way of life. And you—you're both three-quarters Acton's blood."

Bramble laughed. "Not me—not according to anyone who's ever met me. They take one look and think 'Traveler' and that's how they treat me."

"You can't reject your heritage because of a bit of prejudice."

"Be sure I can," Bramble said. "I'm taking to the Road, where I belong."

Merrick turned to Maryrose. "What about you, love?"

She smiled tenderly at him, kissed his cheek and twined her hand in his. "I'm no Traveler, Ric. I'm a crafter, through and through. But I can't just sing Acton's praises when I know how much pain he caused—and all for greed."

"Greed?" Merrick protested again. "His people were being attacked from the north, squeezed back into uninhabitable lands. They would have starved."

"So they attacked other innocent people in turn. And they'd been raiding over the mountains for years," Maryrose said, a little exhausted.

Bramble waved her hand dismissively. "Oh, it doesn't matter, Maryrose. We have to live in the present. It's ridiculous, anyway—what happened a thousand years ago can't touch us now."

She was glad to see both Merrick's and Maryrose's faces lighten and their shoulders lean together to touch again. But she had shivered as she said those last words, the same kind of shiver that she felt when she sat by the black rock and opened her mind to the local gods. It was the first strong feeling she had experienced since she landed on the other side of the abyss, and she welcomed it even while it frightened her.

"Will you stay?" Maryrose asked, hesitantly.

Bramble shook her head. She could see her parents being happy enough here, but she knew she couldn't stay. She needed open air—field or forest or mountain. And underneath her breastbone, in that hollow place, there still lurked a fear that she was dead, was in some way just a ghost moving a body around, and that she should avoid all the people she loved, for their sakes. Even talking to Maryrose, a cloudy glass was between them, an insuperable barrier between life and death, and she was lucky to have been granted this chance to say her goodbyes before death caught up with her.

"No," she said to them. "I'm no city girl. I'm heading north."

She stayed another day, pretending everything was fine, chatting and currying the roan—while her sister looked on, astonished—and sitting in the big front room where Maryrose had her loom and Merrick his carpenter's bench.

They didn't mention Acton again, or Travelers, or warlords. Instead, Bramble told funny stories about the lambs she had hand-reared, the squirrels who scolded her in the forest as she watched at their nut store, about her first fumbling efforts to ride the roan, and the pain she'd been in afterward.

"I swear," she said, "I was walking like a woman who's just given birth, with my legs as far apart as they could go so the chafing didn't kill me. And Widow Farli comes out of the potter's and takes one look at me—reeling from side to side—and shouts 'the falling sickness, the falling sickness!' and runs to get the village voice. So I straightened up—and believe me, it hurt, every step—and when she dragged the voice out to see me, there I was, walking quietly along like a little lady, smiling kindly at the poor, deluded thing. So he turns to look at her as though *she's* got the sickness and she gets all in a snit and says, 'Don't you look at *me* in that tone of voice!'"

Maryrose giggled helplessly, her shuttle faltering halfway across the warp, and Ric shook his head, smiling as he planed a piece of sweet-smelling cedar. Bramble was happy, simply happy, but it was the happiness you feel when you remember a good memory, or as a ghost might smile, recalling the life that was over.

As she was packing to leave, Merrick brought her a present, a pair of horse bags that didn't need a saddle to hang off.

She was touched, and kissed his cheek. "Thanks, Ric."

She packed them evenly—one side for her gear, the other for the roan's feed and hobbles and curry combs that she had bought at Carlion market—then slung them across his withers. He was eager to be off, too; she could feel it.

She kissed them both goodbye, hugged Maryrose a couple of times, then used the mounting block in the yard to climb onto the roan. She grinned determinedly, nudged the roan through the gates, and took the Road. It was a beautiful morning, with gulls wheeling in the sky and a fresh salt breeze blowing. Bramble moved through it without truly feeling anything, as though only her body were present, not her soul.

Three-quarters of the way up the hill on which Carlion was built, she passed a house with a red leather pouch hung outside the door to show it was a stonecaster's. She rode past, but then stopped the roan and turned back. It was better to know than to wonder, she thought.

She put a loose strap around the roan's neck so that any passersby would think he was tethered to the bootscraper by the door, and knocked.

"Come, come," a brusque voice told her.

She found herself in a square green room with a white ceiling and furnished only with a dark blue rug. A middle-aged man sat slouched on the rug, running his fingers through a leather pouch the exact red of the one hung outside. She couldn't tell if he was a Traveler or one of Acton's people, because he was completely bald and kept his eyes on the pouch.

"Sit, sit, girl," he said.

She sat down cross-legged and spat in her left palm. The stonecaster did the same and they clasped hands.

"Do you want to say your question out loud?" he asked, as if he didn't care one way or the other. Bramble knew that the more specific the question, the better the results, so she thought carefully.

"What happened to me during the jump over the chasm?"

The stonecaster looked up at that, but his eyes told her nothing. They were nothing eyes—not blue, not brown, not green—that seemed to change color depending on what he was looking at. He brought out the stones, cast them across the rug and looked down.

"Death," he said. "Destiny. Rescue. All facing up. Spirit, facing down. And Confusion."

"What do they mean?"

He cocked his head, as though listening, as she had known other stonecasters to do. They said the stones talked to them, but she had never felt the presence of the gods at a casting.

The stonecaster sat upright, startled, and let go of her hand. "They say you died," he said. "That it was your time to die and you died. Your spirit should have moved on to rebirth. But your body—was saved?"

"Yes," Bramble said. "My horse saved me."

This time the stonecaster looked at her with compassion. "I have never heard of something like this, where someone's destiny has been broken."

"Love breaks all fates," Bramble said.

"Love from a horse?" the stonecaster said. "Well, maybe, it may be... However it happened, body and mind are alive, spirit is—not yet gone, but not really here. Ready to be reborn but unable to because it's still tied loosely to the body."

"Like a ghost who has quickened but not been laid to rest?"

"Perhaps. Perhaps, yes. It may be so."

"I have another question."

"Of course," he said. "What should you do, yes?"

She nodded.

They clasped hands again and with his right hand he gathered the stones from the rug and cast again. Bramble found herself concentrating on the stones as they fell, as though she could change their message. Casting stones were all natural, not shaped, and they came in every color of rock imaginable. These five were a pattern of ocher, gray, brown and black on the dark rug.

Destiny again, she recognized. And she knew the Rebirth stone. The others were strange to her.

"Love," the stonecaster said, touching the ocher one lightly. "Endurance through trials. And the blank stone, which means anything is possible."

"What do they mean?

He cocked his head again, then shrugged. "What you see is all I can tell you. Destiny, Rebirth, Endurance... There is a way through for you, but it's not one the stones can easily describe."

"And in the meantime I'm dead?"

"Not dead, exactly. Detached from your spirit, which is your connection to the living world."

Detached, Bramble thought. Yes, that was how she felt. Detached and unfeeling. Even this casting, horrific though it was, left her with only a mild sensation of shock and despair, like an echo.

"Endurance," she said.

"Yes," said the stonecaster. "You must endure." He would accept no payment. "Not for news such as that," he said, his changeable eyes reflecting the green walls and reminding her of the forest she was heading toward. "Remember, there was love in the reading."

Riding out of Carlion east along the coast, Bramble almost felt calm. She knew the worst. She merely had to endure. At some point her body would die, as every body did in time, and her spirit would be free to be reborn. She might have to endure a very long time. If that were so, the forest was even more the place she should be. It would be easier to endure death surrounded by the myriad life of the woods. She turned the roan's nose and urged him to a canter.

MARYROSE'S STORY

BEFORE YOU were born and after the sun first shone, there was a girl. She was a young girl, a wild girl: there has been a girl like her in every village and town since the world was born. The girl whose first word is "No!," the girl who runs away from parents and sisters and rolls in the dust with dogs, who throws stones at boys and breaks the pots she is set to wash. The girl who can soothe a colicky baby or a frightened doe rabbit, the girl whose grandfather shakes his head over her but slips her honey cake under the table, the girl wreathed in flowers with bare feet and big eyes, the girl called Bramble, the interesting one.

Well, this is a story about me, her sister Maryrose, who had to stay home and milk the goats while Bramble roamed over the hillsides. Who held the timber still for our father, the carpenter, to saw, while Bramble hunted wild honey. Who threaded the loom for our mother, the weaver, while Bramble waded in the cool green creek. Who learned both to weave and carpenter, because there were only the two of us, and our parents had to teach someone—and Bramble was never there. Except at mealtimes.

Oh, believe me, I didn't dislike Bramble, not at all. Because, truth be told, I liked having my parents all to myself. And I liked weaving and carpentering and the cool green of the creek didn't tempt me at all, with the good wood whispering under my plane, with the bright wool whispering between my fingers and the sharp *clack, clack* of the shuttle flicking across the warp like a dragonfly.

But I worried about Bramble. For how was she to care for herself when she grew up, who knew nothing and could do nothing useful except gather wild food from the forest? I could see a time, after our parents' deaths, when Bramble would be forced into the cold, cold world unless I myself wove enough cloth and shaped enough wood to support both of us. And that, for I was only human after all, I was determined not to do.

So I looked at Bramble and I considered her, and I came to a conclusion that the one thing that she had in abundance, and which I lacked, was looks. She was a true briar flower: curly black hair, black sloe eyes and smooth skin, a pink flush in her cheeks, and the grace of a fawn. It occurred to me that some good man might not mind that Bramble could not even bake bread, if he was bewitched enough by her beauty and her charm (for Bramble, when she cared to, could charm the birds down out of the trees and onto her fingers). Then the man could take care of Bramble, and I wouldn't need to worry about her, ever again.

So I decided to look for a man for Bramble. A man who was hardworking, where Bramble was shiftless. A man who was prosperous, where Bramble had nothing. A man who was young and good-looking, or else Bramble would never look twice, let alone marry. A man who was merry and good-tempered, who wouldn't be irritated by the many things Bramble didn't know, but would value the wild spirit in her. A man who was strong—for somewhere, sometime, Bramble must be tamed. Maybe love could do it where everything else had failed.

I started looking in our own village. But there was no man there to fit the bill. For Wilf was sweet but ugly. Carl was hard-working, but timid as a mouse, and quailed whenever Bramble cast him a scornful look. Neither Aelred nor Eric, Ralf nor Martin were even-tempered enough, for Bramble could try the patience of a stone, when she came home singing late in the long summer evenings, when the dinner was cold and dried out, when the chores had all been done.

The other boys had parents who glared hard-eyed at Bramble when she danced (the lightest, the merriest of all) round the Springtree, and held back their sons from her light feet and shining hair. And none of the boys had strength enough to gainsay them.

So I looked elsewhere. When I was nineteen and Bramble a year younger, I took the cloth to market for the first time on my own, to the Winterfair in the city. It was good cloth—my mother and I wove so alike that no one could tell where one left off and the other began. We had dyed it a serviceable dark brown, a good yeoman color for jerkin or capuchin or cloak. As well I took a piece I'd woven all myself, on the lap loom, from scraps and scourings of wool, with a pattern of autumn leaves, bright as fire and gold as sun against the color of evergreens.

I set out my wares in the great trade hall, on a trestle table I had rented from the organizer of the fair, the town clerk. I spread out the good solid brown lengths and then, across the front of the table, I laid the bright piece. I watched the craftsmen and the craftswomen set up their tables around me; but mostly I watched the craftsmen, thinking, "No, he's too old for Bramble, that one's too young, that one's too short, he's too skinny, too mean a mouth, too flighty . . . " I turned them over in my mind as my customers turned over the lengths of wool on my table. I would have bought none of them for Bramble.

Many people approached, drawn by the swathe of autumn fabric, but I liked that piece and had no real wish to sell it, so I put a high price on it, and many who came to finger the red and gold and green I sent away with sensible brown. Then the town clerk came, with her husband the silversmith, her daughter the jeweler, and her son the woodcarver. The town clerk wanted the bright piece as a Winterfest present for her husband, to make a fine waistcoat and scarf. What could I do? For all traders know that the town clerk can make or mar your Winterfair, this one or next, by where she put your table and how much rent she charges for it.

So I named my price and gave the town clerk a good discount. I reluctantly handed the piece to the husband, and the family moved away. But the son, the woodcarver, lingered behind.

"It's hard," he said, "giving up something you've made, something you love, to a stranger."

I looked at him properly for the first time, and I liked what I saw. For he was comely, with autumn hair the color of turning oak leaves, and warm brown eyes, and good hands with calluses from chisel and saw. They were the same calluses as I had on my hands, the same as my father's. So I knew that he was hardworking at his trade, and I knew by his smile that he was merry. I set myself to find out more about him, for here at last was someone who might do for Bramble.

"It is hard," I acknowledged.

"My name is Merrick," he said. "What's yours?"

The more I knew him, the more I was sure. He was hard-working and prosperous, young and good-looking, merry and even-tempered, and strong—all the things I had wanted for Bramble. For the length of that Winterfair we were together, even after I'd sold all my cloth, for there was a heavy snowfall and the roads were blocked. So we walked together and talked together, and mostly what we talked about was Bramble. I told him about my sister: her beauty, her wildness, how she had never cared for a man, nor deigned to even smile at a suitor. For my grandmother had once told me that men love to hunt what they cannot have, so I made Bramble seem aloof and uncatchable—like a pure white hind in the forest—and that was the truth, after all.

Perhaps Grandam was right, for when the snow stopped and the roads were cleared, Merrick asked my permission to journey back to the village with me, to meet my family. The town clerk beamed and Merrick's sister kissed me on the cheek, and filled my knapsack with freshly baked bread and russet apples.

It was a happy journey. Merrick kept me laughing all the way, and when we were not laughing, we talked, comfortably, about timber: oak and ash and beech, pale, smooth lime, and rare, fragrant cedar. Then we laughed again.

But oddly, the closer I came to the village, the heavier my heart became. When finally we stood outside our front gate, and the door opened and Bramble came flying down the path to meet us with bare feet and black eyes and red cheeks, I couldn't bear to look at Merrick in case my plan had worked after all, and he was bewitched by her beauty and charm.

And maybe he would have been if he'd met Bramble first, black hair bright against the snow and red lips smiling. For Bramble, there was no doubt, was intrigued by him. She sat at his feet in front of the fire and made him laugh, and pelted him with questions about the city, and being the town clerk's son, and traveling as a journeyman, and seeing the wide world, and about life and death and even, once, about love. It seemed to me that we all stopped, breathless, to hear his answer.

He shook his head, laughing. "My mother always said I had a heart of oak," he said. "No softness in it for any maid." He reached out and brushed a flake of ash, casually, from my shoulder.

That was the moment when I realized that, Bramble or no Bramble, I was going to marry Merrick, and if I had to support her for the rest of my life to pay for it, then I would.

So we married and I moved to town, but underneath my joy was always the nagging worry—what would happen to Bramble? And then she went on the Road and my worry grew, for who knew what might happen to her out there? But there was no use trying to stop her, for nothing and no one ever has, nor ever will.

ASH

A WEEK AFTER their visit to the jeweler's, Doronit called Hildie and Ash into her office from the training floor.

Hildie slipped through the door without knocking and Ash, looming over her, followed, carrying his knives and staves. He was coming along well, Doronit thought. Improving rapidly at singlestave and knifework, and learning to read and write surprisingly quickly. He'd actually be making her real money soon. And then there were his *special* gifts...though it wasn't time for those yet. He had to be bound even more firmly to her. And this assignment might be another knot in that rope.

She smiled at them impartially, the boss's smile. "You know Martine, the stonecaster?"

Hildie nodded, Ash shook his head.

"Lives down near the shambles," Hildie said to him. "Got a good name. Accurate, like."

"She has the Sight, apparently," Doronit said, "and has Seen a...an attempt on her life. Soon."

"Ranny?" Hildie said sharply.

Doronit shrugged. "It doesn't matter who's behind it. Martine wants us to provide protection. You two can take the first watch. And no staves. We don't carry staves through the city without good cause. Knives will do. Off you go."

She let them turn to the door, then she called Ash back. "There will be death tonight, Ash. The stonecaster saw it. Make sure it isn't yours."

He nodded, grave-faced, and followed Hildie.

Doronit was only a little worried. She'd made the caster check that he'd be safe and, though no casting could be relied upon entirely, Martine had said that Ash should come through the encounter intact. She was less sure about Hildie. Doronit wasn't so concerned; risk was the nature of her business, and anyway, Hildie didn't have the same gifts as Ash. Those were . . . well, not irreplaceable, but rare. Very rare.

She went to the corner of the room where a concealed panel in the floor hid her cashbox, and deposited Martine's payment. She smiled, as always, at the sight of her treasures. She had hiding places all through the house and outbuildings, and in other places too, and she felt safe every time she looked at them. They reassured her that she'd never go without a meal or decent clothes, even if she lived to be a hundred. She'd been dressed in castoffs and rags for too long when she first came to Turvite. She smoothed the fine wool of her trousers under her hands and smiled again, then closed the panel and went to inspect the Dung brothers' attempts at archery.

Hildie led the way to Martine's through part of the city Ash had rarely visited, the oldest part, which predated Acton's invasion. They went through a small open space not far from the docks, which Ash had never seen before, but it set his nerves strumming. He had heard of this place: Doronit had mentioned it, laughing. His father had once taught him a song about it, a song of melancholy chords and dying cadences. In a past so long ago that even the stone-dwellers who live under the cliffs had forgotten, the place was once a ford over an open stream, the song said, and next to the stream was a black rock, a sky-born rock, where the local gods came to meet their worshippers.

The tip of the black rock still jutted through the cobbles and gravel of modern Turvite, no more than two hands' width showing above the ground. Next to it, encircled by roots, stood the only full-grown tree in the city, throwing around it in summer an umbrella of green. It looked both incongruous and right, that oak tree, Ash thought. It towered over the cottages around it, out of place, out of scale. Yet if he looked only at the tree, he could see its shapeliness. The sweep of its branches had grace, and the yellowing leaves were pale flames against the sky.

Even in the heat of summer, though, Turviters did not sit under that tree. As Ash and Hildie went through, he noticed that others passed by almost as though they hadn't seen it. The song had said that Turviters never spoke of the place to each other nor mentioned it to visitors. The open space had no name, although every other crumb of the busy cake had a label, every crooked alley and dead-end street in the city had a name.

Ash could feel the tree at his back as they went into a small side street, could sense the black rock sitting there, its power seething. How could the Turviters ignore it? It called him back with a whisper of many voices saying his name. The voices were cajoling, inviting, familiar, like the voice he had heard in the cradle, the voice he heard in his own head. He had to force himself to go on with Hildie, feeling a cold sweat crawl down his back.

As they disappeared into the winding streets, the voices died, disappointed, like a wind dropping. He found himself walking more briskly, as though while he had heard the voices they had drained him, but now his energy returned. What would have happened if he'd gone back? *I won't go back,* he thought, *not ever*. But a part of him, a small trickle of desire, sent his thoughts back to the tree and the rock. He knew he would be able to point in its direction no matter where he was in the city, as though it were a lodestone and he a compass needle.

"Were you talking about Ranny of Highmark?" he asked Hildie, to take his mind off the altar stone.

"Mmmm."

Ash had never met Ranny. He'd heard stories: she was wild, profligate, ruthless, intelligent enough to know when others were more intelligent and to hire the best minds she could find. She was the head of a large merchant family that spread over half the world.

"She wants Martine dead. Tried to hire Dufe to kill her."

Dufe was a safeguarder Ash met occasionally in the taverns. He had worked for Doronit briefly before Ash had come to Turvite.

"Why?"

Hildie shrugged. "Goes back to a reading Martine did for her, they say. Told her she knew the day and the time of her death, and the cause of it, but wouldn't tell her anything more. Said it were against her code."

"It is," Ash nodded. "There's no stonecaster born will tell you the time you're to die. They say it takes all the joy out of living."

"Ranny reckoned she'd avoid her death altogether. Be somewhere else. She offered Martine... well, she offered her a lot, just to tell her *where* she was going to die. So she could avoid the place. But Martine wouldn't do it."

Ash grinned. "Traveler's proverb: 'He who runs away from Death has Her as a traveling companion.'"

"Tell Ranny that."

"I still don't understand why Ranny wants Martine dead."

"Because if Ranny can't know the time of her death, no one's going to know. That's what she said."

"How do you know?"

"Dufe told me."

Ash laughed to himself. Ranny had picked the wrong man there. Dufe was as far from a killer for hire as a safeguarder could be, which made him wonder if he'd ever gone through one of Doronit's tests in the back alleys of Turvite. Would he have killed the girl thief? Somehow Ash didn't think he would have walked down the alley in the first place. Maybe that was why Doronit had fired him.

They reached the stonecaster's house at dusk. It was a small house in the middle of the old part of town, with the caster's sign outside: an outsize canvas pouch hanging from the balcony, which jutted out over the street. He would have known anyway—there was a ragged circle of ghosts standing back from the door, waiting to be let in. Most of them were standing in the middle of the road, but they didn't care—ghosts in Turvite were used to being walked through without so much as a by-your-leave.

Martine was on the balcony looking down at them, so the first sight he had of her was her face upside down, with long dark hair falling either side so that it was like looking up a tunnel, with her pale face the light at the end. She seemed very tall.

"Push it," she said. "It's always open." Her voice was strong, but with an undertone of sweetness, like fresh mead.

The ghosts eddied and moved forward, but only one came to the door with them. The stonecaster must have spelled the door. It was often done. A ghost could only enter if it had some connection with the human visitor.

Hildie held the door open for Ash but he waited for the ghost to go ahead of him. Ash swallowed hard, to stop his gorge rising. It was the girl he had killed, clear as day, with the strong paleness of the newly dead, as though someone had drawn her with white wax on a black slate. He could see through her, of course, but it was like seeing through mist, or through a cobweb. He hung back, but she gestured him forward and he realized that the spell meant that he had to go in first, with the ghost following behind him in a wave of cold and burial cave stench.

He went past her with that chill that he always felt passing a spirit, and stepped through the door with all the prickles raised on his spine. They didn't seem to affect the Turviters. He supposed that if you were surrounded by ghosts from the time you were born, you got used to them. He'd been pleased, when he first came to Turvite, to find that everyone could see the ghosts. In most places he'd been the only one, he and his mother, although she always acted as if she couldn't see them. In Turvite the ghosts were so strong that everyone knew they were there—they were proud of them.

He turned in time to see the ghost slide in behind him. Hildie kept the door open for a moment more before following, as though she wasn't quite sure if the ghost were entering or not, then closed it with the snap of a good latch.

The room was bright with lamplight and firelight shining on pale yellow walls and bright blue painted woodwork. There was a frieze of leaping fish against the yellow around the ceiling. It was like coming into daylight after the dim dusk of the street. Ash blinked and looked away from the ghost.

The stonecaster had come down to meet them. She *was* tall, with very white skin and long green eyes. A strange, foreign face in this city of yellow hair and blue eyes, but beautiful in its own way. She held her head very high. Ash was reminded of the stories of the Lake People, the only people of the old blood who had withstood Acton's invasion. They were said to hold their heads like that, proud and undefeated. Most Travelers looked down, not up, in case their glance was seen as insolence and invited a curse or a blow. Ash had been taught by his parents to look, not down, but sideways, to keep his chin pointed ahead rather than up. "No need to invite trouble," his father had said, and his mother had been in a dark mood all that day.

The stonecaster looked at the ghost and sighed. "Well? What is this?" she asked Hildie.

"I killed her," Ash answered.

The stonecaster turned to look at him, and as her green eyes met his, he felt the same churning in his stomach that he felt with Doronit, and the same confusion, and a kind of recognition. These, like Doronit's, were eyes that he knew, and more, she had a pattern of speech and lilting voice almost completely obscured by Turviter inflection, but still there—a palimpsest of an earlier tale. That voice brought back nights on the Road around the fire circle, and stories and songs in a language the Turviters would not have understood.

"She was trying to kill me," he added, carefully suppressing everything but the business at hand. He turned to the ghost. "Weren't you?"

The ghost looked at him blankly.

He wasn't going to let her get away with that. His voice sharpened. "*Weren't you?*"

Reluctantly, the ghost opened her mouth. "Aye."

As always, it was a deep, scraping voice like rock on steel, a sound that sent shivers down to the fingertips. The three humans shuddered as one, and Hildie looked shocked and a little worried. She looked at Ash as if she'd never seen him before.

"Didn't know they could talk," she said.

The stonecaster raised an eyebrow, not at the ghost, but at Ash. She didn't seem surprised. "Well. Sit, then."

The ghost, Martine and Ash sat on the rug. He could faintly see the yellow and blue of the wool through the ghost's body.

Hildie took a breath, recovering her normal calm. "Naught to do with me," she shrugged. "I'm here to keep watch." She dropped the bar across the door and produced a wooden wedge from her pouch to fix it firmly in place, then moved to the window that gave onto the street. She settled into the window seat, turning her head from left to right and back again in a slow, steady scan.

Martine spat in her left palm and held it out to the ghost, who laid her own hand into it. Ash could see the shudder go through Martine at the touch; he knew that feeling, that sudden scent of earth and touch of cold stone.

The caster produced her pouch of stones and with her right hand threw five of them on the rug. The stones fell across the pattern, and every one of them landed on the yellow. And every one of them was facedown.

Ash stared at them as she turned them over.

"Death. Hidden Death. That's yours," she said to the ghost.

The ghost nodded.

"Then Flight. Danger. Liberation." She turned the last stone over and hesitated.

"What is it?" he asked.

"Death of the soul," Martine said softly. She looked up into the empty eyes of the ghost. "This is him, not you."

"I don't understand," Ash said.

Martine became brisk. "These stones tell the story of her death: Death, Flight—that's you running away—and Liberation. I would say that this young woman is finding death more pleasant than life."

The ghost nodded. Ash felt a stab of pity go through him.

"I'm...sorry," he ventured, and looked for a moment too deeply into the ghost's eyes and grew dizzy.

"So," Martine said. "She has come to pay her debt to you by warning you. You are in danger—danger of losing your soul, losing who the gods want you to be. Do you understand?"

"But...from what?"

The ghost shook her head at him, smiling in derision.

He got angry. Even the ghosts were laughing at him now. "*From what?*" he shouted at her.

The dead voice came again, reluctantly. "From who, cully," it said. And that was all. The pale, young face faded away, still smiling.

Martine let her left hand fall back into her lap. "That one is gone for good," she said. "She's paid her debt and left. It was well done." She looked at him curiously. "It seems you lead an interesting life, young man."

Hildie, standing beside the window, whistled sharply. Ash was on his feet with his dagger out, his back flat to the wall behind the door, before his mind even registered the danger signal.

"Three of 'em," Hildie said. "They was keeping watch behind the baker's. Man and a boy, at the door. One's gone round the back, quick as bedamned. He's the one to ware of."

Hildie had never tried to sound like a Turviter, Ash thought, then shook his head. "*Irrelevant,*" he could hear Doronit say. "Concentrate or die."

There was a knock at the door. Martine moved toward it, looking questioningly at Hildie. Hildie signaled for her to stay still. Ash heard the faint shuffle of feet behind the door. He nodded to Hildie and she slipped out to the back room.

Martine collected the cast stones and put them back into her pouch. She hesitated, then sat back cross-legged on the rug and cast the stones again. All were facedown. She didn't bother to turn them over, simply collected them, dropped them into the pouch and reached in for five more. She seemed too calm.

Ash pulled his attention away from her. The knock came again, harder.

"Stonecaster, ho!" a deep voice called. A hand tried the door latch then jiggled it impatiently.

Poor training, he thought, one ear cocked for sounds from the back room. Then he heard the muffled scratch of boots on the roof. On the balcony. He whistled low to Hildie, *watch out,* and went to the stairs, flattening himself against the wall so he would be invisible from above.

The rattling of the latch grew louder. The bar began to lift a little with each jerk. The wedge that Hildie had jammed in would soon bounce out of its socket. He wanted to call to Martine, but it was too late. There were feet on the stairs. Almost silent. And fast.

Ash moved as the man hesitated at the bottom of the stairs, looking through the doorway to where Martine sat, casting the stones, her dark head bent. The men in the street were swinging the door latch as hard as they could. He knew what the man on the stairs was considering: do it now or wait until the others break in?

Ash moved. He slammed against the man shoulder to shoulder and sent him sprawling across the floor. But the man was quick, and rolled and came back to his feet in an instant, dagger ready. Martine retreated to the hearth, holding a white-handled dagger behind her skirt, and the pouch in her other hand ready, it seemed, to throw in the fire.

Ash felt his concentration narrowing, as it always did in a knife fight, blocking out everything except the other's blade, the muscles of his chest where movement would first be seen, the play of his feet. In this circle of tension it was curiously silent. "Don't look at the face," he heard Doronit say in his head. "Don't engage until you're ready to kill. If you're not ready to kill, don't fight with a knife."

The other man was cautious, too, but all he had to do was delay until the others broke the latch. Ash had to move fast. He feinted right, dropped to one knee and struck up as the man moved to block him. The dagger went up under the ribs. Doronit had shown him the spot, had traced it on his bare skin with one finger.

The door latch broke as he pulled the dagger out and blood splashed over the blue and yellow rug. The man fell.

The two from the street charged in. The boy headed toward Martine but halted when she raised her knife. The man centered on Ash, his dagger poised. There was no sound but hard breathing. The man was bigger than him, huskier, and with a much longer reach. That was bad.

They faced each other across the corpse. Ash crouched, dagger edge out and ready. The other gazed at his face. *Mistake,* Ash thought, as he reversed the knife and threw it. *Bad mistake, cully.* "When you throw to kill," Doronit had said, "aim for the throat. It's the only spot you can be sure the knife will go in." She was always right.

The dagger went in through the voice box and the man was choking to death, clawing at his throat and turning blue, taking final gasping breaths. Ash knelt on the man's chest and drew out the knife, cutting the big artery as he went. His hand was quite steady. He had time to wonder at that.

Behind him he heard scuffling as Hildie sprang from the stairs to deal with the boy.

"No!" Martine said. "Just hold him."

Ash turned. Hildie was about to cut the boy's throat. Martine's knife was already in his shoulder, the hilt sticking out stark white against the blood. The boy was in his twenties, pale-haired, like most Turviters, but with large dark eyes that spoke of other blood, and a face all smooth skin and fine bones. Ash swallowed against the sudden block in his throat. The boy's eyes were searching everywhere for an escape and flinched away from the bodies of his two colleagues.

"Now," Martine said, and pulled the dagger out from his shoulder. The blood flowed after it, sluggishly, and the boy turned as white as the hilt. "Who sent you?"

There were two corpses on her floor, but her voice was calm. Too calm, her breath too even. It was the voice of someone who had seen events so terrible that nothing would ever be able to shock her again. He was reminded of Doronit, and the thought surprised him. What had Doronit seen that was so terrible?

The boy was silent.

"The mootstaff will not care if I have three corpses instead of two," Martine said. "Who sent you?"

Hildie pricked his throat with the knife.

"Ranny," the boy whispered.

Martine relaxed. "Thank you," she said.

Hildie tightened her grip on the knife and looked to Martine for instructions. Martine jerked her head toward the door. Hildie loosened her grip. The boy bolted for the street, rushing through the crowd of mingled ghosts and neighbors who were staring at them through the doorway.

There was nothing left but the cleaning up. The bright yellow and blue rug was ruined. Ash helped roll it up with shaking hands. ("A reaction, and perfectly normal," came Doronit's voice in his memory, "but try not to let the customer see—it undermines their confidence in us.") He thought he managed to hide them from Martine, though Hildie cocked an eye at him. Once he was used to scenes like this, as she was, the shaking wouldn't happen. He hoped. He was almost sure he hoped it.

Hildie fetched the mootstaff leader, Boc, who came with a handcart to take the bodies out to the graveyard (no burial caves for these ones). Boc was relieved to know there was no problem with the deaths. "Housebreakers coming by their just deserts," he said, nodding, as Martine explained, and asked Hildie to give his regards to Doronit. Doronit kept in well with Boc.

The mootstaff were supposed to keep the peace, but there was far too much crime on the streets of Turvite for a handful of men to control. That was why safeguarders were needed. And Turvite lived by the old laws, as did all of the free towns: you could—you *should*—defend your home to the death against all comers, even if all they had in mind was a little pilfering. Ash had sometimes wondered if it dated back to the invasion, when, if you didn't defend your home, you were dead.

Boc left with a helper trundling the handcart along the cobbles. And that was all. Hildie nodded to Martine and made for the door, but Martine put her hand out to stop Ash from following her.

"Three days' time," she said. "Be here."

He nodded and followed Hildie.

Doronit was pleased with them, he knew by the way she smiled gently at him. She was less pleased when she heard he would need to go back in three nights.

"That's the festival. We're booked at the Town Moot." She shrugged. "Well, get it over with early and join us there. We can't get a reputation for failing to clean up after ourselves."

The next day, Doronit sent Ash back to Martine to escort her on a visit to Ranny of Highmark.

"Ranny makes a bad enemy and we don't want to antagonize her," Doronit said to Ash before he left. "Just be businesslike toward Martine, not friendly, you understand?"

The Highmarks were a smallish, tight clan, Doronit had explained. Ranny had two brothers, younger than she and not as bright. Her father was dead, and her mother remarried to a Reacher from the mansion next door, a good marriage with fine trade concessions attached. Ranny ruled Highmark under the eyes of her grandparents, both physically hale and still sharp-minded but disinclined to continue running the business day-to-day.

Highmark ancestors included four mayors and eighteen town clerks—the family knew where power resided and preferred it to pomp and ceremony. They took their name from the golden mansion at the very top of the hill overlooking Turvite, the first to be built at that height and still the second biggest.

It seemed to Ash, as they stood outside Highmark, that Martine was unimpressed. "This won't take long, I just need to talk to her," she said. "What is your name, anyway?"

"Ash," he said, startled to realize that after all that had happened, they were still virtually strangers. He felt as though they had known each other much longer than a single day.

"Well, Ash, maybe we can sort this out without more killing."

Ash stood to one side as Martine knocked at the door and asked to see Ranny. They were let in straightaway by a young woman with chestnut hair and hard eyes who kept her hand near her belt knife and made them walk down the corridor ahead of her to the office.

Ranny was a slight, fair-haired woman with the pale blue eyes you only got when there was no Traveler blood at all in the family. She looked the opposite to Martine in every way.

Ash took up the standard safeguarder position just inside the room. The chestnut-haired girl stood on the other side of the door in the same position. They nodded to each other, the careful, deliberate nod that said, "Neither of us wants any trouble here but we're both ready for it." Her hand kept going to her knife and Ash realized that she was nervous of him. Then he remembered that he had killed two of her... what, colleagues? Either way, to her he was dangerous. A part of him was pleased to be thought dangerous by a pretty girl, but he brought his attention back to Martine and Ranny.

They were facing each other. Martine seemed to radiate calm over the desk to the other woman. It didn't work.

Ranny glared at her, her hands fidgeting with a stick of sealing wax. "What's the point of you coming here?" she demanded.

"I hoped to negotiate a truce."

Ranny snorted. "Fine. Tell me what I want to know and we'll have a truce."

Martine had considered it, she had told Ash on the walk there. But to tell someone the date of their death was to blight their life. And surely Ranny deserved it now, Ash thought, had invited it, even, by trying to kill her? Still, a swift death and rebirth was one thing; a living death, tormented, was another...

Martine shook her head and made her voice gentle. "You won't believe me, but I keep that secret out of a wish to not hurt you more than I have done so far."

"You should never have told me that you knew!"

Martine bowed her head so that the curtain of black hair hid her face. "That is true. I should have concealed it from you. But I was surprised it was there, so clear in the stones."

Ranny scowled at her. "Hypocrite!" she hissed. "No decent stonecaster would ever let someone know that they had discovered the date of a death."

"That is true," Martine said.

"Well then!" Ranny exclaimed. She got up from the desk and paced around the room. "Just tell me *when*. If I knew when, I could plan."

Ash could see Ranny's dilemma: should she have children if she wouldn't live long enough to bring them up? Should she have them immediately so that her bloodline would continue? Should she train one of her brothers to take over so the family wouldn't suffer when she died? Or, if she outlived them, would training one to rule, when he would never get a chance, sour and embitter him?

"I need to *know,*" she said. "You owe it to me."

"You tried to kill me," Martine replied.

"You ruined my life. I can't sleep, I can't work... With you dead, I could at least be back where everyone else is, with no way of finding out."

"Ah..." Martine was startled at that explanation, but it was one Ash understood. Yes, there was a logic and even a justice in it. Martine nodded, also understanding.

"You think you can choose for me, but I should be able to choose for myself," Ranny said. "You are treating me like a child because you have the Gift and I don't."

There was enough truth in that, too, to give Martine pause. Stonecasters did tend to look on their clients like children to be guided, but not by them—by the stones. Had Martine allowed herself to become arrogant, to make choices that rightfully belonged to Ranny?

Ash looked into the pretty blue eyes and saw ambition, anger, ruthlessness, but not much wisdom. Perhaps Martine was treating Ranny like a child, but it might be that it was safer to do so.

"I need to know *when*," Ranny said.

Martine shook her head.

"Then you're going to die."

Ranny walked out of the room and the girl escorted them silently to the front door.

Ash was on full alert the whole way back to Martine's, wishing that Doronit had sent Hildie or Aelred as well, to guard their backs. It was a relief to shut the door of Martine's house behind them.

"Do you think I did the right thing?" Martine asked, handing Ash his payment.

Ash paused. "I don't know," he said eventually. "I would probably have told her, but—she doesn't look like a woman who would accept any fate. If you told her, you'd be setting her off on a path to avoid her death, and then…"

"'She who runs away from Death has Her as a traveling companion,'" Martine said.

Ash nodded. "You know that's true."

"Yes," Martine said, relaxing a little. "I know less every day, but that I do know." She smiled. "Thank you, Ash. I'll see you in two days."

After Ash had killed the men at Martine's, he found his mind returning to one point of the night: the moment when Hildie had pressed the point of the knife against the boy's throat, and looked at Martine for instructions. If Martine had said, "Kill him," what would Hildie have done? He shied away from the thought, not wanting to imagine himself in Hildie's place, but it drew him back, time and again, during singlestave practice, on his runs along the sea cliffs, at night. Was that expected of safeguarders? To kill if the client said so?

It was autumn. The days were bright and crisp, the sea was glowing ultramarine, as it did near festival time, and crashing higher against the cliffs at the full of each tide. It seemed a time of clarity and light. But his mind kept returning to that yellow and blue room.

Other thoughts of the boy kept coming back—of his dark eyes and smooth skin. They were eyes like his own. Ash slept badly and, when he did sleep, he dreamed of Doronit standing by smiling while he killed the boy. By festival night he was twitchy and couldn't concentrate. Doronit dismissed him to the stonecaster's with a frown that made his stomach drop into his boots.

"Go on, then, get yourself quit of these spirits. Come to the Town Moot as soon as you can."

She was dressed for the festival, her face painted with expensive silver tint, her clothes ghost-pale and flowing. She looked very beautiful, he thought, staring helplessly at her. She ran her hand down his arm, making his skin tickle and his eyes burn.

"Come soon," she said.

He walked through the streets to Martine's, resenting that he couldn't go with Doronit. He walked with desire running through him and no end to it in sight. *Very well,* he thought. After he finished at Martine's, he'd find himself a brothel and do something about it. If he couldn't have Doronit tonight, he'd have someone else. She didn't have to know. Then he thought of all the things Doronit knew that you didn't expect. All the people who sold her information, or owed her favors. She *would* find out. And then what? Either she'd laugh at him or be angry—he didn't know which was worse.

The streets were full of people enjoying themselves, painted like ghosts, wearing white, or silver if they could afford it. It was a city of happy ghosts. He hadn't wanted to dress up. It wouldn't have been very respectful to the ghosts he was going to meet. Of course, that was the point of the festival, held on the anniversary of Acton's victory over the city, to show the ghosts that no one was afraid of them.

He had been to the festival once before, when he was seven and his parents came to Turvite to perform for the merchants. He remembered that night vividly. The whole city was full of ghosts, it had seemed to him. He hadn't realized that some silver shapes were actually people in costume. He hadn't understood why he could see through some and not others, why some made so much noise, laughing and singing the "Fly Away Spirit" song, while others drifted silently, shrinking into corners as the revelers careered by.

He remembered his parents practicing in the courtyard of Merchant

House earlier in the day. His mother had sung "The Taking of Turvite," while his father played the flute.

Acton killed them all, she chanted.
All on the streets of Turvite
Their spirits rose up with a soundless cry
Their spirits rose up to cry to their gods
The faces of death stalked the streets of Turvite
The faces of death haunted the killers

Then she swung into the chorus, with Alured, their drummer, picking up the beat so that Ash hopped from foot to foot in time.

And the killers laughed!
Yes, they laughed!
And Acton laughed loudest of all.

He had tried to sing along, but, as always, his mother had laid a finger across her lips, not before he had seen a spasm of pain pass over his father's face. Looking back, he realized that that was the last time he had tried to sing for his parents. It was the day he had understood that he would never be a singer, as he yearned to be. If he was going to be a musician, he would have to play the flute like his father.

The sun was setting when he reached the stonecaster's house. There was only one ghost left there, a thin, old wraith who looked as if he had seen a thousand festivals. Ash nodded to him and the ghost nodded back. Behind the ghost, the sky was a mixture of orange and gold, a real autumn sunset. It cheered him and he knocked at the door with more energy than he'd felt for days.

Martine let him in. The bloodstained rug had been replaced by a mat of lambskins, gleaming white in the lamplight. Martine sat cross-legged on the edge of the mat, and gestured for him to sit beside her. He sat aware of her long hands and hooded eyes. There was a darkness in the way her blood moved in her veins, as though she carried a secret.

"It's not always three days to the minute," she said. "Sometimes it takes a few hours. But then, this isn't the first quickening you've been to, is it?"

Ash shook his head and was aware, by the lift of Martine's eyebrow, that the answer had made him seem more of a killer than he really was, but didn't want to explain his past any further. He didn't want to talk about his parents. Musicians were often asked to quickenings in the far west of the country. There, the people believed that soft music helped the spirit on its way, especially the spirits of those killed by accident or violence or sudden illness. These were the ones who quickened back into the waking world. His mother had taught him that the other spirits, who had nothing left unsaid, went on to be reborn straightaway. Although the ghost was said to quicken three days after its death, his parents had often played through the night or through the day before the ghost had appeared. Outside Turvite, a quickening was the only time that most people could see a ghost, not that those spirits had been as . . . vivid as they were in Turvite. Turvite had the strongest ghosts in the world.

"You have old blood in your face," Martine said, studying him. For a moment he thought she meant real blood, branding him a killer. She saw his confusion. "I mean, you have the look of the ones who were in this land before—the original inhabitants."

He felt forced into an explanation. "I'm a Trav—my parents was, were, Travelers. Musicians. They say that when Acton and his men came, a lot of the old people took the road, having no land of their own left to them."

"Yes," Martine said, brooding. "That is so. Did you know that that is why you can see the ghosts?"

"Everyone can see them here!" he protested. He had no mind to be any more set apart than he already was by his dark hair and eyes.

Martine smiled at him and shook her head. "No. In Turvite, where the ghosts are strong, everyone can detect . . . something. A shimmer in the air, a scent on the wind, a paleness where there should be darkness. Sometimes they catch a glimpse of eyes, hair, a hand. They feel cold as they pass. That's all."

"But the Turviters talk about the ghosts all the time. They're so clear here! It's like looking at . . . at white people."

"That is so for me, for you. I think for Doronit. For one in a thousand, perhaps. And only one in a thousand thousand can make them speak, as you did three nights ago. I cannot."

Ash believed her and was saddened. One of the things he loved about Turvite was that everyone else could see ghosts; he'd spent his whole life seeing things that others couldn't. But he had never understood how the people of Turvite could just walk straight through ghosts as if they weren't there. They seemed proud of their ghosts and proud of their indifference to them. The children of Acton, they called themselves. Acton, who had been faced by the ghosts—thousands upon thousands of the slaughtered Turviters whom he and his men had killed—and had laughed them down. "If we could vanquish you alive," he had said, "why should we be frightened of you dead?" And his people had moved into Turvite and taken it over from cellars to attics, had lived ham by haunch with the spirits of the dispossessed and had grown proud of it.

Ever since then, those who died in Turvite, even Acton's people, had strong ghosts. Ash's father had told him that it was a relic of the spell used to call up the Turviters' ghosts after the battle with Acton and his men. An enchanter who lived in Turvite had tried to give the ghosts physical strength, so that they could continue to fight. "She failed," his father had said, "but the ghosts became strong in other ways—they persisted, they could be seen or sensed by everyone." Acton's men cornered her on the cliffs north of the harbor, but Acton forbade anyone to kill her, in case that made the ghosts fade. He wanted his people to live with a reminder of their victory. He laughed as he said it, and she cursed him—he would never have what he most wanted—but he shrugged and said that he already had it, and gestured to the city. Then she shook her head and smiled a smile of sweet revenge and jumped off the cliffs.

No one knew her name now, and Ash supposed it didn't matter anyhow, because she was wrong. Acton lived for years afterward and by all accounts was a happy man. It was he who started the Ghost Begone Festival at the autumn equinox, when they found that the enchanter's death hadn't made the ghosts go away after all, and there were more every day as Acton's own people died, until there was no corner of Turvite inhabited by more people than ghosts.

Outside Martine's, the sound of the festival was growing louder. A party of young women went by singing "Fly Away Spirit" in high, sweet voices. Ash thought of his mother, who could see spirits just as he could, and sang higher and sweeter than any other voice on the Road. His throat tightened. He wondered where she was singing tonight, what accompaniment his father was providing. He wondered if they felt freer, happier, without him . . . and thought they probably did.

Then the ghosts quickened.

The big man roused first, solidifying on the floor as he had lain in the first moment after death. Ash saw the pale shape grow before him: white, transparent, but recognizably the same burly, hairy figure who had crashed through Martine's door. He sat up and struggled to his feet as though he still had a body. New ghosts were always like that. They acted as though they still had muscles and bones attached to their will. The older ones just floated, drifted wherever they chose, from floor to ceiling.

The ghost looked around, searching for his friend. The new rug confused him. He tried to touch it, saw his hand pass through the white tufts, and screamed. His mouth opened, the muscles of his face in a rictus of horror. But no sound came out.

Ash was crying hard, hot tears. There was too much pain in this face. He forgot, for a moment, that this man had been a killer for hire and had tried to kill him.

The ghost saw them. He stilled then moved for his dagger. It was gone. He held up his hands to show them he was unarmed. It seemed he thought they were still in the middle of the fight.

"It is three days later," Martine said quietly to him. "You are dead. This is your quickening."

"*No,*" he mouthed, and shook his head.

"Yes," Martine answered. "This is your killer."

Remembrance flooded over his face as he looked at Ash —remembrance and hate and grief. He looked again, frantically, for his colleague, then turned to Martine with pleading hands.

"He will come. Wait."

So they waited, Martine and Ash sitting still, the ghost rubbing his face against his hands, shaking his head, crying without sound, mouthing *no,* and what looked like *Dukka,* over and over.

Dukka came. He formed and solidified just like the first, but then rolled and jumped to his feet, his dagger ready in his hand. They had not been able to pry it from his grasp before the mootstaff took him away.

"Wait," Martine said. She rose and confronted him, pointed to his friend. "Look. He is dead. You are dead."

Dukka turned slowly to his friend.

"Speak to him, oh gods, *speak,*" Ash whispered to himself. He couldn't bear any more silent screaming.

"Hwit," Dukka said, the harsh ghost voice grating on the nerves as it always did. "Oh, my boy."

The two spirits moved toward each other and attempted to touch. But even a ghost cannot touch another ghost. Their hands passed through each other's faces. They cried aloud.

They turned to him.

"You," Dukka spat. "You killed him."

Martine intervened. "You were, if you remember, trying to kill him."

Astonishingly, Hwit let out a laugh. "True for you," he said, and his voice was the same, exactly the same, as the dead voice of the smaller man. Even though Ash was expecting it, it was always hard to hear that the voices of the dead were all alike, as though identity could not survive past the door of death.

Hwit grinned at Dukka. "Fair's fair," he said. "At least we're together."

For a moment Hwit held his friend's gaze, and the anger seemed to drain out of him. "Fair's fair. Knife cuts knife," he said.

They both turned to Ash. He had been to enough quickenings, so he knew what to do.

"I am your killer," he said to them. "Lo, I proclaim it, it were I who took your lives from you. I am here to offer reparation—blood for blood."

He pushed up his left sleeve and held out his arm, then took his dagger and cut the skin just above his wrist. His hands were steady, but his body was shaking as though with cold. The blood welled out slowly, dark red. It caught the lamplight.

Dukka moved forward and bent his head to the cut. Hwit laughed and joined him so that the two pale tongues reached his flesh and touched, granting their bodies only enough solidity at this moment to taste the blood of their killer, and enough to touch each other, once more.

The burial cave smell arose around Ash and he almost choked. The touch of the ghosts' tongues was ice, hot ice, cold fire. He trembled.

The ghosts raised their heads. As soon as they left contact with his blood they were wraiths again and the final drops of blood fell from their lips straight through their bodies to the rug.

"I release you," Dukka said.

"And I." Hwit leaned forward. "One day you'll follow us, lad."

The dead voice made it sound like a threat, but was it? Martine bared her arm and raised her dagger, but Dukka shook his head.

"It was because of me Ash was here. I am responsible," she said.

Dukka shrugged.

She snapped at Ash, "Get him to s*peak* to me."

"Speak," Ash whispered.

"We release you," Hwit said. "We don't need any more. Blood must be spilled, but one killer's blood is enough."

And they faded.

"Just like that?" Ash squeaked, and then coughed to clear his voice. "That's it?"

"That's all," she said. "They were generous, those two. I suppose they recognized a fellow professional. Knife cuts knife, as he said."

That made him feel worse than anything else he had done. "Those *voices,*" he said, shuddering. "I hate those voices worst of all."

Martine looked at him and repeated the Traveler proverb, "From the grave, all speak alike."

"Well, they shouldn't," Ash said.

Ash stood at the bottom of the Moot Hall steps looking up. The Moot glowed orange at every window with lamp- and firelight. The music was loudest here, drums thumped out a jig-and-spin, an old one that he recognized, the "Drunken Tailor." There were very few songs or dances that he didn't know, though he couldn't play any of them himself. He'd been no better a flautist than a singer. He could feel the music in him, but he couldn't bring it out. He couldn't even dance in time.

His parents had tried to make the best of it by getting him to drum for them. He'd been able to do it, barely, but not by feeling it. He had to watch his father's hands on the strings or the note holes and match his own hands to their stroke. It had been good enough for taverns and country towns, but not for places like Turvite and Carlion, not for warlords' courts, where they made a good deal of their money.

Then one night, not far from Turvite, the three of them had met up with another Traveler, a drummer, who was camped at the site they had planned to use, a common with a stream and a copse nearby for firewood.

His parents had hesitated as they caught sight of the stranger already encamped, but he had looked up and smiled and said, "Fire and water"—the Travelers' greeting. "Fire and water and a roof in the rain," Ash's mother had said. So they moved down to the campfire and shared their food and some stories as well. Inevitably, after dinner his father had drawn out the flute, and the other drummer, after waiting politely for Ash to find his drum, had pulled out a small tambour.

They had started with songs everyone knew: ballads and drinking songs, cradle and teaching songs. The drummer had played with his blood and his soul, and Ash had known by the end of the second song that his parents needed someone who could play like this, who could lay down the dark heart of the song behind the melody, could call out the dancing feet. By the third song he had known that he would never play the drum again, never pretend that he might be good enough someday, with enough practice. By the fourth song they had forgotten him altogether, and after the fifth they had started talking excitedly of where they could go next, to play together.

Ash had gone off, away from the fire, and fallen asleep wrapped in his blanket, as he had almost every night of his life, but this time knowing that the next day would be the end of the only life he had known.

Over breakfast, his mother had noted his quietness and hesitated, clearly weighing what to say. He hadn't wanted to hear it.

"I'd better find something else to do with my life, right?" he said.

Though he had tried to keep the bitterness out of his voice, he hadn't quite succeeded. It had banished any softness from his mother's face.

"You heard. You have ears, even if you can't play," she said. "He's what we need."

"It will free you to do something else," his father said. "After all, lad, how can you be happy doing something you don't love?"

Ash had stared at him, astonished that he hadn't understood, that he mustn't have understood Ash at all to be able to say that.

"I do love it," he said. "I just can't do it as well as you."

It had taken both mother and father aback—they were musicians born, not made, and although they practiced daily, obsessively, it had never occurred to them that someone could love the actual making of music and yet not be good at it. To love music was the basis of being human, of course, but to love the making, the crafting—they had thought the love and the skill went together.

Typically, his mother had been the first ro recover. "We'll find you another trade that you can love," she said.

But they hadn't, of course, because no one except Doronit had wanted a gangly nineteen-year-old whose only skills were a poor hand on a drum and a memory crammed with every song known on the Road. So Ash had learned to be a killer, and wondered, now, if this was a craft that those who practiced it loved.

He stopped on the first step of the Moot as a rush of warm air and perfume and food smells swept over him. It was packed; latecomers spilled down the steps and out onto the street, all dancing and singing along. Silver and red and blue painted faces grinned and kissed and warbled, "*He was drunker than a wine vat, drunker than a rotten fart, ooooh, he was the drunken tailor of Pii-ii-say*..."

"An' I loved her, Arvid, I really did," a man wept on his friend's shoulder at the bottom of the steps. "But she was a lying vixen, just like her mother."

The silver paint was rubbing off on Arvid's jacket. He stroked the man's hair, hand curiously tender, then looked up and met Ash's eyes, and blushed. He stuck his hand back into his pocket.

"Don't worry about her, Braden," he said. "Come inside and get drunk."

"You're my best friend, Arv, my very best friend in the world..."

They turned back up the steps, arms around each other, and blundered into a couple who were kissing as they came down. For a moment Ash thought it was Doronit; she had the same dark hair, the same kind of silver floating dress. He felt as though he'd been kicked in the stomach. Then he realized it wasn't her, but was still awash with his reaction: pounding heart, churning gut, sweating and cold at the same time.

He ran. He kept to the back streets, where there were fewer people, and he ran as hard as he did in training sessions when Doronit was waiting for him. He ran through the markets, alive with food vendors' and winesellers' calls, away from the shouts of those he brushed past, unheeding, and through the curling streets of private houses, with light and ghost pennants streaming from each window. He kept running until he reached the long hill that led to the cliffs outside town.

Everywhere he ran, he saw ghosts.

On the cliff tops they huddled in groups near the edge, waiting for morning. They watched the city lights. Some of them were fading already, although it was nowhere near dawn. That was the purpose of the festival, to cull out the city ghosts, to scare away the weak and insult the strong so they left forever. Without the festival, his father had told him, there would be many more ghosts than people in Turvite. He wondered now what his father saw when he looked at a ghost.

Old and young, big and small, they clung together. There seemed to be nowhere he could go to get away from them, no place he could be alone to think things through. It wasn't fair. It never had been.

He had come to Doronit as though to a safe harbor, a place in the world he could finally make his own. But if it meant he had to be a stone-cold killer, like Dukka and his friend, he wasn't sure he wanted it. Not even for Doronit. He didn't want to be the knife that cuts the knife. But if he didn't become that, what else could he become? There were no doors open to him except this one. He wanted to shout, or protest, but what good would it do? He was a Traveler who had lost the Road, and there was nowhere and nothing else in Acton's land for him.

His mother had taught him never to compel a spirit to speak unless it was really necessary, but that night he didn't care. He faced the multitude of pale forms and threw up his arms. He could feel the power to make them speak flood through him. He had never opened himself to it like this before; it was like a thousand drums beating together, like the crash of the waves on the rocks below, thunderous, overwhelming.

"Speak!" he conjured them. *"Speak."*

Instantly a great moan went up from them. It was the strangest sound he had ever heard, for though it came from a thousand mouths, each made the same sound: dead, grating, harsh as stone on stone, it was a cry of pain. Silence followed as each ghost realized that it had made a true sound, that its screams were no longer silent.

"Speak," he conjured them again, at that moment hating everything, everyone, himself, wanting to hit back, wanting the ghosts to scream his own protests. "Speak all the night through!"

The ghosts cried out again, then turned to the city and began to move toward it. Slowly, then faster. They rushed past him in a wind of cold air, and as they gained speed they made a deep, screeching moan, repeated and modulated. It was the sound of desperation.

He sank down and clasped his hands around his knees. He giggled so that he wouldn't cry. He felt drunk, crazy, lost.

"Hah!" he said. "It may be I shouldn't have done that." And stubbornly, though he knew his voice was harsh, he began to sing "Fly Away Spirit."

BRAMBLE

So in my next life I'm going to get the gods to make me a big blond man, Bramble thought. *Really big. Really blond. Maybe really stupid, too. Big, blond, stupid men seem to have a good time around here.*

The four big, blond and, quite possibly, stupid men were certainly having a good time standing in the middle of the road and not letting her pass. They were having a good time yelling things, too.

"Show us your teats!" was the favorite of the youngest and stupidest. His big brothers—or his inbred cousins—had other ideas.

"Gods, I love taking it from Traveler bitches!" the oldest said with a smirk.

The other two sniggered.

"Come on down, slut, and we'll show you what real men are like."

"Wait till you try a taste of my sausage, girlie!"

"Nah, not him, try me!"

"She'll have us all, and like it," the oldest said.

The others had just been having fun, but he meant it. His eyes never left her face; he was waiting for fear to show. There was a part of her that wondered what it mattered. She was dead anyway. But another, deeper part answered: *He can wait until hell melts*. The thought and the feeling cut through the fog she had been riding in and sharpened her attention.

"Get her down, Than. Grab her bridle first." He pushed the youngest forward.

The boy, no more than fifteen, hesitated. "She's not got a bridle, Cal."

They blinked, uncertain for a moment. Bramble drove her heels into the roan's sides and thundered forward. Cal made a grab for her, but she kicked him on the side of the head and was almost unseated when the roan kicked his back legs at the same time to knock over two more of them. *He's battle trained,* she thought with a chill. Then they were through and galloping. The men were left swearing and cursing her as they picked themselves up.

She let the roan slow, but kept him to a canter until they had passed two more villages. At the next stream she let him drink, and then walked him to cool down while her own trembling subsided.

She hadn't expected this sort of thing. Oh, from warlords' men, yes, of course. But not from ordinary men. Those big yokels were just like boys from her own village. She shuddered to think of Carl or Wilf or Eric treating some chance-met Traveler girl like that. Would they? Not Wilf, surely? She remembered lying with Wilf in the shade of a big willow tree last summer, his hands gentle on her, his body a pleasure. They had not been in love, but it had been lovely. Surely Wilf couldn't act like that?

But another voice, just as strong, reminded her: *To them, you're just a Traveler. They can do anything they like to Travelers.*

In the many full moons since she had left Carlion moving slowly along the coast toward Central Domain, she'd learned a bit about how Acton's people treated Travelers. She looked the part, of course, except for the horse. On close inspection her clothes were crafter clothes, even if she was wearing breeches. But at first glance she was just another Traveler girl. And that was the way she was treated.

When she'd asked for a room at the inn on the first night, they'd shouted her out of doors. "The kitchen door next time for you, girlie, and the stable's the best your kind'll get anywhere in this Domain!" the innkeeper had yelled, then set the boys in the village to throw stones at her as she left.

She had slept in the woods after that; she couldn't bring herself to go to the kitchen door, not while the spring and summer nights were warm.

She had food. Shops would serve her, she'd found, if she waited at the back until everyone else had been served first. They charged her more though, and if she protested they took back the food.

"Go hungry, then," the baker had said.

She was tired of being tensed, ready for a harsh word or a thrown stone, tired of being hated for no reason at all. Quite a few people in

Wooding hadn't liked her, partly because she looked like a Traveler, but more, she realized now with a wry smile, because she had been wild to a fault. But even Aelred's mother hadn't looked at her with the blank eyes of hate, the eyes that don't see what's really there, don't see a person but only a Traveler. The warlord's man had looked at her like that before she killed him, but she hadn't recognized it then. She had thought it was more personal than it really was.

At night she dreamed of the blank eyes and sometimes she kicked out as she had kicked the warlord's man, and woke sweating and swearing and exhausted. She would turn to the roan for comfort, leaning her face against his warm side while he snuffled curiously at her hair. She dreamed, too, of the dark after death, from where she would be reborn. Those dreams were comforting, reassuring her that even if she were meant to be dead, even if she *felt* dead, there would be a new life someday.

The haze only lifted when the sun was on her back, the track seemed endless in front of her, or when she smelled the hedgerows at dawn as the wildflowers released their fragrance to the new warmth. She loved the sense that no one was waiting for her, that there was nowhere she *had* to be: no goats to be milked, no garden to be weeded, no orphan kid to be fed, nothing needed her except the roan. The idea of freedom was the only thing that seemed real to her. She was still looking through a cloudy glass, and was trying to accept that she might stay like this forever. But thoughts of the Great Forest kept her going.

She came toward Sandalwood halfway through the early autumn afternoon, with the wild geese practicing their flights overhead, calling as they went. In the past, Bramble had listened to those calls with a longing to be off, on the Road, going who knew where. Now the call did nothing to her heart except remind her that the year was turning.

There was a party of pilgrims waiting for the ferry by the river. Sandalwood was a big town, but there were no houses near the dock, just flat green fields. Their leader was carrying the traditional staff with its bunch of green leaves tied to the top, and saw her looking.

"Floodplain this side," he said. He smiled expansively. "I'm Marp.

Used to be a trader, selling rugs and suchlike up from the Wind Cities. Know all of this Domain and a good few others."

"Not many people as well traveled who aren't Travelers," Bramble remarked.

"True, that is, true enough." He glanced quickly at her black hair and away again. "I take people as I find them, no matter what they are. The Wind Cities is full of people who look like Travelers, and they're just the same as anybody else, I reckon."

"What do you do now?"

"Why, guiding pilgrims, guiding pilgrims is my life's work now, lass." He beamed beatifically. "Well of Secrets, she told me that's my life's work. What she says, you know is true."

How do you know? Bramble asked herself. She'd heard the same thing said by people who'd never met the Well of Secrets, and doubted it as she doubted most things. But Marp seemed an intelligent, sensible man who'd thrown up his old life on the say-so of a stranger. Why? They said she could forgive, too, for sins and worse, but sometimes she demanded more changes than people were willing to make.

Bramble wondered if the Well of Secrets could lead her to rebirth or at least tell her how long she had to endure this half life.

The Well of Secrets was living in the far north at that time, in Oakmere, Marp told her, a small village on the road to Endholme, in the Last Domain. It had been a small village, but what it was after a couple of years of pilgrimages was anyone's guess. Bramble could imagine what would have happened if the Well of Secrets had moved to her village, Wooding. She could see the hastily built inns, the brothels, the shops with expensive food, the eating houses, the souvenir sellers... There was greed enough to go around, even among their handful of families.

The ferry was a flat barge, good for horses and carts as well as people. It wasn't rowed, but pulled along by a rope between two huge pulleys on either bank. The ferryman and his helper simply heaved on the rope and the ferry moved across as the rope moved around in an endless circle. The ferryman took Bramble over last, even though it was clear that she had been first to the dock. Marp tried to protest on her behalf, but she waved him to not bother. There was no point complaining. The pilgrims walked on through the town, but by the time Bramble and the roan arrived, she was tired and thirsty and headed for the nearest inn.

She wondered if the innkeeper would throw her out, but no one paid any attention to her as she sat down at a small table in the corner. She saw, looking around, that there were other Travelers drinking there. Two, at least, were unmistakable: young men with jet hair and sloe eyes, good-looking and all the more striking because they were twins.

The afternoon had turned a little cool, so she had the wolf skin around her shoulders. It, or maybe something else about her, attracted the twins' attention and they came over with their drinks.

"Mind if we sit here?" one of them asked. He had a nice smile. She could see that he was the cheeky one of the two, the one who liked excitement and a bit of risk. No wonder he was interested in a girl in a wolf's skin. A Traveler girl, too. He was someone she might have had a yen for in the days before the abyss. But the part of her that felt desire seemed dead too.

She shrugged and moved down to make room for them.

"I'm Ber," the young man said, "and that's Eldwin." He was nodding his head toward his twin.

"Bramble," she said.

"So, tell me all about yourself," he said softly, sliding his hand near hers so the backs of their fingers touched.

She had to laugh, it was so transparent, and he laughed with her, confident in his charm.

Then she shivered as the air suddenly turned cold. All around them it grew quiet and dark, like something was absorbing all the light. Ber grew pale and sweat popped out on his forehead. The others at the table edged away from him. Bramble wondered if a fever had taken him suddenly. His eyes were blank and he started to shake. A fit, maybe. She took hold of his arm to steady him, and saw his brother do the same on the other side. Her hair lifted on her neck, but it wasn't the presence of the gods. The gods had nothing to do with this. Then he spoke.

"Born wild," he said, and it was like his voice, and yet not quite the same. "Born wild and died wild, and not fit for this young man," he continued. "No one will ever tame thee, woman, and thou wilt love no man never. Give over. Begone."

Bramble snatched her hand away. Ber's eyes closed and he toppled over sideways. Without thinking, because she didn't want to think about what he had said, she helped his brother lay him out on the bench. She patted his cheek and, when he roused, his eyes focused but bemused, she gave him water to sip.

Then she slipped away. Still not allowing herself to think, she rode straight through the town, and only when she was on the open road, between fields of ripening oats, did she let herself remember. It had not been the gods who spoke. She knew that, knew their presence as she knew her own voice. But it was something else unearthly. Something more than human, other than human. A demon, maybe, and demons were supposed to know the future and the past. Its words rolled around her mind: *Born wild and died wild. Not fit for this young man...thou wilt love no man never...begone...begone...never...never.*

She didn't want to think about them, but the words kept coming back. She was not only dead, but without love. The dead could not love, or be loved, except in memory. They could not find new love, except through rebirth. When she found tears on her cheeks, she urged the roan into a canter, trying to escape the sensation that a knife was carving a hole in her chest, below her breastbone, a hole that would never be filled. She knew that feeling. It was like when her mother said, "If only you were more like your sister," but somehow much worse. There was no hope in it, no room for change. *Never,* the demon said in her mind, and she pushed the roan into a gallop. But she couldn't outrun that voice. She had just enough sense to steer the roan onto the soft grass verge so he wouldn't be hurt by the jarring pace. He slowed on his own eventually, having enjoyed the chance to stretch out after four days of slow walking.

She forced herself to be calm, to take control.

"Enough," she said out loud. "I won't think about it again. It might be right, it might be wrong. All I can do is live and find out." Her breathing steadied. "Forget it," she told herself. "Forget it. Endure."

ELDWIN'S STORY

THE FIRST TIME the demon spoke to us, I was just two months out from my seventeenth birthday, from our birthday, my twin's and mine. We were sitting around a table at an inn, the Wide-Mouthed Jug, in Sandalwood, and it'd been a good day for both of us, Ber and me.

We were feeling like men: there was silver in our pockets and a good day's work behind us. And there was no one at home to worry over us, for Mam took our comings and goings with never a hair turned, and our da, what used to worry himself over us, he was dead two months gone.

We just wanted a drink, and maybe a few light words with a pretty girl. Ber found one, pretty enough but a bit wild-looking, with a wolf skin around her shoulder. He took her hand. Then he started foaming at the mouth and spouting demon words, and fainted away afterward. I thought he was dead. My heart stopped its beating for one long space and then I saw his breath bubble the foam on his lips, and it started again with a heavy thump.

When he opened his eyes, they were cloudy, and he remembered nothing. "I was holding your hand," he said to the girl, "and then I was lying on the bench. What happened?"

But I had to take him out of the inn and back to our caravan before I could tell him, for the innkeeper wanted us and the girl out, and she weren't a woman to argue with.

We never saw the girl again. Sometimes, when Ber talks about it all, sometimes I think she's what he thinks on most, even now, like it was her who called up the demon in him.

But I don't think so.

The hardest part, I think, was the way it changed Mam.

She used to be free and easy, never caring where we were or what we were up to, and we'd come home and tell her all about it, whatever it was, and she'd scold us and laugh at us and there'd be no trouble at all. It was Da who worried about us. How that man could worry! From the time we was just walking, he'd take us with him on his tinker rounds, and he'd have us walk ahead of him, "Where I can keep an eye on you." He kept lookout for strange dogs and strange men, for sharp rocks at our feet and snakes in the grass.

He didn't even teach us tinkering till we were nearly thirteen. Then he'd make us do everything twice and three times, and over again under his eye, before he'd let us do it on our own. And Mam would shake her head and laugh at him. He wouldn't hear of us going off on the Road by ourselves, though he had broken from his family when he was fifteen, and married only two years later.

On our seventeenth birthday, around the fire after dinner, we pushed him on it, pushed him for our share of the profits for the summer, for we'd worked long hours and made as much as he.

"Just give us that, Da," I said. "Give us our silver for the summer and we'll be off together."

"I will not!" Da said. "I wouldn't if I could and I can't, anyway—I've spent it already on a nice caravan. It'll sleep all of us, snug and sound. I'm picking it up tomorrow from Oswald the Bodger."

Ber and I looked at each other.

"You had no right to do that," Ber said.

"No right at all," I agreed.

"'Twere our silver, just as much as yours."

"You should have asked us both, and Mam, too, before you did a thing like that."

"It won't stop us," said Ber. "We'll go anyway, with no silver behind us, and trust to luck we'll get work before winter."

"Aye," I said. "We'll go tomorrow."

"No!" Da shouted, jumping to his feet. "You're too young, you're too flighty—the first stranger you meet you'll be fleeced by, I can just see it happening. You're no more fit to be on the Road than when you were babies. I've taken care of you all your lives and I tell you I'm not going to stop now —"

But stop he did, with a look of wild surprise on his face, and he fell down at our feet, the breath gone from his body, tears in his eyes, just like that, dead.

At first, it wasn't so bad. Once the first shock of the grief and the guilt were done, Mam was strong enough. For there was a load of guilt, for all of us, no doubt of that. But after the first time the demon spoke through Ber, she changed. And maybe I did, too.

It was the not knowing when it would happen. Anytime of the day or night—no telling. But it was always in company, so we got out of the habit of going to inns, Ber and I, and we didn't linger with our customers to chat no more.

We knew what they said—"Not like their father, those boys. Why, Griff'd have you there all day, talking about those two, and now they don't give you the time of day..."

But we were good tinkers, Ber and I, so we didn't lose much custom by it, and we explained the demon away as fits, to them that asked. Maybe we even got more custom—people coming to take a look at the possessed man.

Mam kept a close eye on us, now, and wanted us home in the fire circle by dark; though the demon came in the daytime, too, so what difference that made I don't know. She fussed over Ber, though she used to treat us two so alike, sometimes we joked she couldn't tell us apart. Now it was like I was older, more responsible. And I did it myself, too, like he had a mortal illness and I had to tend to him.

Yet he was no different in himself, nervier, maybe, but sometimes I think it was Mam and I made him so. He had no memory of it, see, no memory of the fire growing dark and the air growing cold, of the hair standing up on your neck, and the flesh crawling on your bones...as that thing used him, used his mouth and his tongue and his eyes...

It never did us any harm direct. When it spoke, it spoke only warnings. Sometimes we didn't even understand what it said, but whoever we were with understood all right. I've seen grown men go white and run from the room at a single word. It might be a name, or a place, and once in Fiton, it were just, "twelve silver pieces," and an old man, white-haired and rheumy-eyed, shuffled out of the inn like Death herself were after him. She caught him later that night, we heard, when he hanged himself in his own barn. We don't go back to Fiton now.

It went on like that for two years. I was thinking about leaving, about just plain running somewhere, anywhere I didn't have to watch Ber every second. But how could I leave him? Or Mam? He was half of my heart's blood, and she was the other. So I thought, *Next time it comes, I'm going to talk to it, ask it to leave us alone. Beg with it. Bargain with it, need be.*

For we'd never had the courage to speak to it directly. It was too hard, it using Ber's voice, and always so calm and reasonable, even when it was accusing some poor soul of murder, or worse. I couldn't bear to look at him when he was foaming at the mouth and blank-eyed. But I had to. Mam was withering away, not eating, not smiling. She'd be sick, come winter, I knew.

So I was waiting, on edge, all that summer. We worked our way through Pless and Carlion, down the Long Valley to Margarie, then made north to Freewater as the leaves started turning. All that time the demon was quiet, and we kept ourselves to ourselves. It was a beautiful summer—hot days and cooler nights—and autumn came in on a whisper of cold in the early mornings, such that one day we woke to find Ros, our mare, had her winter coat and we hadn't even noticed.

Now we had the caravan, we didn't need to winter over in a town, but this year I wanted to because Mam was looking so thin and frail.

"Back me up," I said to Ber. "She'll get sick otherwise for sure."

He was uneasy with the idea. "Freewater's a big place. Lot of people." He was worried about the demon coming. And I saw he was more pained by it all than I'd known, feeling set apart, like, and not safe for others to be around.

"It'll be all right, twin," I said. "You do no harm, and never could."

"Not I, but it."

I hugged him, feeling suddenly that I knew what Da felt when he worried after us. "What will happen, will happen. And might be there's a stonecaster in Freewater can tell us what it is."

That cheered him, and me too, for it was a good idea and I should have had it before.

So we found a barn on the outskirts of Freewater, and the farmer let us use it and draw water from his well. Ber and I set Mam up good, and that first night we chopped her wood and fetched her water and sat down for dinner with her, and it was like it always had been, she was bright and laughing for once. It was like a gift, and it decided me to act then and there.

"We're going into Freewater," I told her straight after dinner, while she was putting the plates away. "We're going to a stonecaster to see what they say about this thing."

She went pale, standing there, and Ber had to take the plate out of her hand lest she drop it, but she nodded and sat down. "Aye. It's time and past time to face it." But her eyes filled with tears. And the room grew cold. "Oh, gods, preserve us," Mam whispered.

Ber stood up, blank-eyed, shivering, and the light faded. My gorge were rising, like it always did, but this time I stood and faced the demon, eye to eye.

"Do not go to the stonecaster," it said.

"What do you want with us? Why do you come? Why are you tormenting us like this?" I had a hundred questions, but I could barely force myself to speak.

It tilted Ber's head, and on his face was puzzlement; it was the first feeling it had ever shown. It seemed to search for words, where words had always come easily before.

"I help," it said finally.

"You steal my brother's body and call that helping?"

"I . . . warn. Danger comes, I tell you."

Anger was taking me over; I could feel it, and I knew I had to hold it back or any damage I did would be to Ber. "Why us? Why follow us? Leave us alone! Let us go our own road."

"No!" it howled, foam coming out Ber's mouth. "I've taken care of you all your lives and I tell you I'm not going to stop now—not now, not yet —"

"Griff," Mam said, so quiet, so gentle it would break your heart. "Griff, you're dead, love. Time to let go. Time to say goodbye."

It shook Ber's head, shook his whole body. "No, no, no, no . . . "

"They're grown men, love." Mam touched Ber's face, looked into his blank eyes. "They can look after themselves."

I was shaking, too, finally hearing Da's voice underneath Ber's. But he wasn't listening to Mam. "Can't you see what you're doing to us,

Da?" I said. "You think you're protecting us, but you're sucking the life out of us all, not just Ber."

"I'd never hurt —"

"Every time it hurts! You've got no right. You never had no right to hold on to us. It killed you trying. Let go—for pity's sake!"

"Let go, love," said Mam.

"Love —" it whispered.

"Aye," she said, "aye, I know you do."

He turned Ber's head to look at her, and for a moment he was truly there, looking out of Ber's eyes—my old da, stubborn as ever.

"Love —" he said again, then Ber's eyes closed and he fell over.

Seems to me I watched my da die twice, and both times I killed him. I went to the stonecaster after, and she picked Guilt out, and Death and Love—all lying facedown. But faceup were New Beginnings and the blank stone, which means the future's open-ended, and anything could happen from here on in.

SAKER

THE GODS *had* led him to Connay, Saker decided as he listened to the high, perfect voice of the woman singing. The inn crowd didn't care about her perfection; they banged their tankards on the table in time to the insistent drum and tapped their feet to the flute. After a couple of verses they were shouting out the chorus with smoke-roughened voices.

And Acton laughed!
Yes, he laughed!
He laughed and killed them all!

Verse after verse, the song went through Acton's exploits on the battlefield; a litany of murder, thought Saker, a canticle of death. Then he realized what he was hearing: a map.

When they took a break he fought his way to the small stage. "How many of the old songs do you know?" he asked the flautist.

The flautist was a man of middle years, with intense black eyes. "I know all of them," he said matter-of-factly, using a kerchief to clean the spit out of the flute.

The gods *were* leading him!

"My name is Penda," Saker said. It was a name he used whenever he pretended to be one of Acton's people, the name of one of Acton's companions in Death Pass. Penda was the last one through the pass, just as Saker was the last of the old blood, undiluted. It was a little irony he carried around with him. "I am a student of the old times. I would like to learn the songs, to write them down."

The man shook his head decidedly. "No. The songs must be passed from mouth to ear—never written. If you don't promise this, I cannot help you."

Saker recognized the tone in his voice: absolute certainty. Gold wouldn't change his mind. Nothing would. "Could I write down some of the things the songs talk about? Names, places, what was done there? A history?" he asked.

The man looked uncertain. The singer came and placed a hand on his arm and his hand went up automatically to cover it gently. They smiled at one another, the unbidden smile of long-time lovers, more a softening around the eyes than anything else. Husband and wife, Saker thought.

"The songs *are* the history," the man said finally, and made to turn away.

"But how many people know the songs?" Saker asked, desperation flaring. "How many people have you taught?"

The flautist paused, some pain flickering on his face. "My son. But..."

"But he has left the Road," the woman said, "as he needed to. We are teaching Cypress, here." She gestured to the drummer. Even concentrating on the flautist as Saker was, he noticed the gracefulness of her hand movement, her beauty. Her features matched the beauty of her voice. "It will do no harm for him to write down the names and places, Rowan," she said.

The man hesitated. "It's not the tradition."

"But he's one of us," the woman said. "One of the old blood."

Saker felt himself pale. How could she know? He had dyed his hair red-brown, his eyes were hazel: he looked exactly like any other descendant from the second wave of Acton's invasion.

She smiled at him with pity. "The old blood recognizes itself," she said. "You are driven to find out what happened in the time past."

He nodded.

"I see it. It gives you no peace. Perhaps when you know the total, you will find a way to peace. Help him, Rowan."

She moved away and bent over to talk to the drummer, Cypress.

"If Swallow wants to help you, you'll be helped—one way or another," the man said. "I will tell you the songs and you may write your history. But, Penda, there are many songs and we must travel. You will have to come with us."

Saker nodded. "Of course, of course. And I can pay you —"

"Good," the drummer broke in. "You can start by buying a round of drinks!"

BRAMBLE

BRAMBLE LET THE ROAN travel along for the whole autumn evening, hearing over and over again the... the what? Curse? Prediction? That demon voice could not be contradicted. *Born wild and died wild. Thou wilt love no man never. No one will ever tame thee.*

The words had hit her like wood because they rang true, because they chimed not only with her feeling of having escaped death, her fate, by a mistake, but with an empty place that she had always known was inside her. She thought that place had finally been filled, by the love of riding and by loving the roan, but she'd been wrong. It was still there, just better hidden, buried deeper. She felt it ache.

She was more disturbed than she wanted to admit to herself by the prophecy that she would never love. Of course, she had wondered, time and again, when the other girls her age had giggled during the Springtree dance as the boys twirled them and smiled at them, when they had gossiped about this one's eyes or that one's hands, why she had felt nothing beyond desire for any of them, and only liking for Wilf, the sweet but ugly boy the other girls ignored.

She had wondered and then let it go, until Maryrose brought Merrick home to meet the family. She could see why Maryrose loved him, but couldn't imagine doing so herself, although she tried and tried hard.

Did she have so hard a heart? She could be kind—her ability to raise orphaned lambs and kids, to gentle them and give them the will to live was well known. She was known, too, as a good nurse for children and old people. "A wild heart but soft hands" was how one granfer had described her. She could be compassionate to young things and old, to the sick and the dying, the unhappy and the mad.

But love... Love for a man was something she'd never been able to come to. Perhaps she never would, now that she was a being of flesh and blood but without feeling. Perhaps she would never love, never marry.

"Is that so terrible a thing, horse?" she asked, and the roan whickered back at her and rubbed his soft nose against her bare leg. She was a little comforted, and hoped to be comforted more by the quiet of the Great Forest.

The road was longer than she had expected and she only came toward Pless as the autumn began to bite down and her money was almost exhausted.

In the late afternoon on a cloudy day, with the threat of a storm in the air, she rode down the main road to Pless, through a valley of pastureland flanked on both sides by deep forest. Halfway down the valley the roan stopped dead in the road.

Bramble sat, surprised, not knowing why he had paused. She clicked her tongue encouragingly, but instead of continuing, he executed a smart quarter turn and trotted through an open gate beside the road. He had never acted like this before, but it was as though he knew exactly where he was going. So Bramble let him go and just tried not to fall off—trotting was the one pace she had not yet mastered. Sensing this, the roan slowed to a walk, and headed toward a fenced yard where a man was gentling a chestnut filly.

The man had dark brown hair and a tall, loose-limbed body that would have been gangly as a youth. He wasn't exactly comely, not like Merrick, although he had a charm about him in the way he talked to the horse, as though it were a person. But he was at least twice her age, no matter how charming he might be.

She watched for a while, smiling as he tricked the filly by walking away from her so that she followed out of curiosity. He moved quietly and gently, never intruding on her until she felt safe and secure in his hands. When he'd finally managed to slip the bridle on her head, he noticed Bramble at the fence, sitting, as she usually did, with one leg drawn up across the roan's shoulders, no saddle, no reins in her hands, no bit in the horse's mouth, but clearly comfortable.

He smiled at her, with a charm that shone through his gray eyes, with none of the automatic suspicion she'd encountered from most settled people since she had taken the Road. "Bring him in," he invited her. "It'll do the filly good to see another horse so friendly with a human."

She smiled back at him, a little surprised. The easy exchange made her feel more alive. So she touched the roan on the shoulder, clicked her tongue, and sat back as he made his own way to the gate which the man held open.

By the time she'd brought the roan in and turned him around, the man was grinning fit to burst.

"I'm Gorham."

"Bramble."

Gorham looked the roan up and down with a horseman's eye. "Nice conformation."

"Thanks." Bramble nodded at the filly. "Is she yours?"

He shook his head. "No. I'm training her up for a farmer over Sandalwood way."

Bramble was surprised. "That's a long way to bring a horse for training."

Gorham shrugged, as though it were usual. "He wants to run her in the chases."

If Gorham trained chasers from all over this Domain, he must be good at his job, Bramble thought. But then, she had seen that already in the way he handled the filly.

"I'm about to take a break," Gorham said. "Have a cup of cha?"

Bramble was tempted. It was a nice change to talk with someone pleasant. But she needed to keep moving. If she rode hard, they might get to the forest before winter set in. She knew how to survive in a forest, even in the cold months.

"Thanks, but no. I'd better be going," she said. "I want to make Pless by nightfall."

"You have a natural way with that roan," Gorham said. "I'll take you on if you're looking for work."

She shook her head. "No, thanks all the same." Gorham seemed so trusting, like another Traveler, that she felt she owed him an explanation. "I'm heading for the Great Forest. I want to get there before winter."

He nodded understanding. "Wind at your back," he said, the Traveler's farewell, confirming her suspicion that he was, or had been, on the Road.

"Gods be with you," Bramble said.

She touched the roan on the shoulder again and clicked her tongue, but he didn't move, except to shake his mane and stamp his foot in denial. The signs were clear, he wasn't going anywhere.

Bramble jumped off and walked around to look him in the eye. "What is it, lad?" she asked. "You like it here?"

His wise eyes regarded her but gave away no secrets. When she tried to lead him out of the yard he wouldn't budge. Well, she thought, they were partners in this journey and he had as much right as she did to decide where they should go and where they should stay—perhaps more. It was he the gods had kept alive.

She turned to Gorham and shrugged. "Looks like I want a job after all."

He looked surprised but he didn't comment. "I'll show you the lodgings."

The wattle-and-daub cottage, behind the yard and screened by a stand of maple, was more than adequate, with a bedroom and kitchen with a scullery attached. It needed cleaning badly, though, and there was no bed.

Gorham pulled at his lip. "Best you come home with me tonight," he said.

Bramble raised an eyebrow and he smiled, amused by her tacit suspicion. "My wife'll give you a bed for the night," he qualified.

Bramble nodded. "Fair enough."

Gorham mounted his rangy chestnut, which had been tied up on the other side of the yards. "I'm training him up for someone else," he said disparagingly, then looked the roan over. "Nice form, but he's got a bit of temperament, hasn't he?"

Bramble shook her head and smiled. "Not really." Then she went to talk to the roan. "We have to go to town tonight, but we'll come back in the morning."

Gorham hauled her up on the chestnut and they led off. The roan followed amiably, as though he'd never refused to move. Gorham glanced at Bramble with curiosity. "You've got to be boss of your animal," he said.

"Not this one."

As they rode back to town, they tried not to ask each other too many questions, out of respect, but some had to be asked.

"You were a Traveler?" Bramble asked.

Gorham was startled. "How'd you know?"

"The way you looked at me—I mean, the way you *didn't* look at me." She fumbled for what she meant. "No contempt... no suspicion."

Gorham nodded. "Aye, I know what you mean there, lass." He pulled at his lip again. "We *were* Travelers, my Osyth and I, but we came to Pless as crafters and there's no one here who knows what we were. You understand why?"

Bramble nodded. She understood perfectly.

"Osyth has a yen for me to be a town councillor." He chuckled. "I can't see any town voting in a Traveler as councillor, can you? So if you don't mind..."

"I won't mention it." She chuckled in turn. "I'm the opposite—raised crafter, just lately took to the Road."

"Well, it's a funny world," Gorham said comfortably. "We might not tell Osyth you're on the Road, then. What were your parents?"

"A carpenter and a weaver."

"Good, solid, respectable trades." He laughed as she made a face. "Aye, I know, you've had enough of respectability."

"I'd had enough of it in my cradle!"

He laughed again. "Well, then, we won't try to be too respectable out at the farm. We'll keep that for town."

They arrived at the townhouse—a fine, respectable house, she thought wryly—and went through the yard gate to the stables to settle the horses and wash their hands before entering the back door into the kitchen. Bramble hung back a little, suddenly unsure whether she wanted to spend the night inside bricks and mortar, but unable to think of an excuse.

Osyth was cutting carrots at the table. She rose briskly as Gorham came in, and gave him a brief kiss on the cheek. He looked at her for a moment, after she'd turned away, as though he was waiting for something more, then he sighed just a little and turned to Bramble.

"We have a guest," he said.

Bramble came forward. Gorham waited with some trepidation to see how Osyth took to her. The girl had a wilder version of Osyth's own beauty, he thought, that lithe, black-haired beauty, and she looked anything but ordinary. As they confronted each other, Gorham realized that he was also a little nervous about what Bramble thought of Osyth. It made him see his wife afresh, as Bramble might see her.

Osyth was still beautiful: a slight woman with black hair drawn back into a simple roll and small, graceful hands. Only her mouth, with the corners drawn in and the lips a little too firm, hinted at a lack of generosity. It was that and the way she stared at Bramble.

Gorham could see his wife assessing each item and read her reactions as easily as those of a horse to a new companion: narrowed eyes (her coloring, bad—a Traveler), a small nod (dressed like a man, but good quality), a disapproving sniff (no shoes), and arched eyebrows (her saddlebags—a guest for how long?). He remembered when his wife was more carefree, wilder herself. But that was before they'd had the children, before they'd settled. Something had changed long before.

There had been a time when Osyth, whenever they were together, would take his face between her hands and gaze lovingly at him. Over time, the gaze had become more searching, and eventually disappointed. It had leached away his love, that disappointment, as he felt diminished in her sight. But he still missed her looking at him, missed her paying attention to him, even if it brought disappointment. All she was interested in now was silver and becoming powerful in the town. But he wouldn't let her be dismissive of Bramble.

Osyth opened her mouth, but Gorham got in first. "Bramble's coming to work for us. Out at the farm. She'll go back there tomorrow and get the old cottage sorted out for herself. But tonight she needs a meal and a bed."

"I'm happy to sleep in the stable," Bramble said mildly. Gorham raised his hand to protest, but she shook her head at him. "*Really.*"

Osyth nodded, satisfied although not happy. "There's not much for supper," she said. "But I suppose I can find you something."

Gorham left it at that. He and Bramble sat by the hearth and talked about the horses out on the farm while Osyth served up supper, a stew with more lentils than meat, but sustaining and tasty.

As they ate, Gorham asked Bramble questions about her family.

Osyth listened to the answers, gradually relaxing as all the respectable details came out: carpenter, weaver, long established in their village, grandfather on her mother's side the village voice for twenty years before he died, sister married to the Carlion town clerk's son. She nodded in approval at the news of Bramble's parents moving to town to be with Maryrose.

Finally it seemed that there were no more details to share and Gorham sat brooding while Osyth picked at her food.

"Do you have any children?" Bramble asked.

His face lightened. "Two, then, we have—a girl and a boy, Zel and Flax. They're on the Road."

Osyth got up, her plate still half full, and walked to the hearth, shouting disapproval with her stiff back.

"It's like I told you," Gorham said quietly, "no one here knows we were Travelers. They don't know about the childer, either. They took the Road on their own before we settled here."

"Well, I won't tell anyone," Bramble said reassuringly, pitching her voice to reach Osyth.

"You won't have to tell anyone," Osyth said, turning around, "if Gorham keeps going around saying 'childer' instead of 'children'! That's a give away any crafter could pick."

Gorham flashed her a smile. "Go on, you know I never do it around town folk."

"*We're* town folk now—and don't you forget it." But she was smiling back at him for the first time, and Gorham saw her as lovely as when she was a girl, when she'd been less critical and more loving.

"I'll say goodnight then," Bramble said, picking up her saddlebags and heading for the door.

Osyth nodded at her; Gorham smiled and raised a hand. "Goodnight then, lass."

As Bramble shut the door behind her, Osyth looked at her husband. "Why take on someone who looks like a Traveler, for goodness sake, when we're trying so hard to start over?"

"But she's not a Traveler, love," Gorham said. "You can tell everyone that—drop in a few hints about her being the town clerk's niece-in-law and there'll be no trouble at all."

"Talking mills no corn—they'll still wonder. They'll wonder if you're shagging her, too."

He was still. "*You* don't think —"

She looked away. "Oh, no. I see how you treat her, just like Zel. Besides, your tastes don't run to young and dark, do they?"

He didn't know how to reply, there was so much bitterness in her voice. There was satisfaction in her eyes as she saw his discomfiture. She pushed her advantage.

"They'll all think she's a Traveler, with that hair and eyes."

"They don't think that about you."

"Of course they do! I've been asked who my folks were, where I come from. Not all of them believe what I tell them, either. Not by a long shot."

He hadn't realized that. They lived such separate lives now, he and Osyth. He was out on the farm, she was in town, absorbed in town doings, gossip and alliances, births and marriages, and getting fish for the best price, buying in bulk to save silver. He knew what they said about her: "Counts her change three times, she does," Maude had told him. But they'd not gone hungry since the day she took over the finances, and without her management he'd never have saved enough to buy the farm. He'd done it to please her, but now he realized that she'd known him better than he'd known himself; the farm was where he belonged. And he liked staying out there because he was away from the accusation in her eyes. Love, regret, shame and annoyance mixed equally in him, and hot. He needed to escape it.

"I might just go out for an ale..." he said.

She looked at him. He saw the anger rise in her, and saw her tamp it down with iron-hard control. "You can't go out with that girl staying here," she said. "You're her host. It wouldn't be fitting."

He was flummoxed.

"You wouldn't be back before breakfast," she said. "You never are. What would I tell Bramble?"

It was the first time she had ever alluded to his overnight absences. He thought resentfully that she'd use anything against him, but what could he say? They were skating on thin ice, here, neither mentioning where he'd really be going, neither prepared to acknowledge the truth.

If the truth were ever said aloud, they couldn't go on as they did, getting through their days with at least a little dignity and calm. Besides, he couldn't bear the fight that would erupt. He just wanted some comfort, some easygoing laughs and a cuddle or two. With Osyth, everything was so intense. Everything mattered, everything was life-or-death. She was too much for him, and that was the real truth. That was why she had always been disappointed when she looked into his eyes.

She was standing rigid, clutching a wiping cloth in both hands, with knuckles white. Waiting.

"Well, then, I suppose you're right," he said slowly, and he saw her relax, watched triumph curl at the corner of her mouth.

He let go of an image of Maude snuggling down with him on the rug in front of her fire, and managed to smile at Osyth. He wasn't strong enough to be what she wanted, but that wasn't her fault. And strangely, there was still love in that curdling mixture of shame and disappointment. So there he was, caught in her eyes and her grace and her fine-boned beauty, just as he'd been caught the first time he saw her juggling and tumbling with her sisters, out on the Road.

He walked over and touched her cheek. "Come on then, love, let's go to bed."

Her face flushed and she turned within his arm to walk up the stairs to the bedroom.

OSYTH'S STORY

THE SUMMER I was seventeen was a disaster. It rained three weeks before haying, and the hay rotted in the fields. More like lakes, they were, so the hay rotted from the bottom up, and stank like marsh gas. It rained for so long that the wheat lay flat and the grain sprouted on the stalk. The fruit swelled and turned rotten on the trees, and the few pieces that were harvested grew mildew overnight. Even the mushrooms washed away.

The grandams shook their heads and prophesied a desperate, hard winter, lean and hungry. Farmers decided which of their animals to kill, for they'd not have enough feed to last them through winter, and it was better to smoke some of the meat now and have enough left to keep the breeding stock going till spring.

The crafters in the town shook their heads and bought in as much as they could—barley and oats and lentils—till the price went up and the town councils argued bitterly over whether they had the right to set a price limit on staples. Some did, and some didn't, and where they didn't, the folk looked forward to a killing winter.

It frightened me. Life on the Road was hard enough in the good years, when the fields bloomed and farmers were hopeful enough to part with a few coins for the pleasure of seeing me juggle, or hearing my sisters sing. In a year like this there'd be no free food at farmhouse doors, no extra firewood for the price of a juggle and a tumbling run. And in the towns it'd be just as bad, with no prosperous farmers to commission work and no happy merchants with spare silver looking for ways to spend it; the crafters would be sitting idle. Even the innkeepers would have a bad year, for the barley was looking to be twice last year's price and hops worth their weight in coppers.

In high summer I looked forward to a cold, hungry winter, and it frightened me as naught had ever done before.

Me and Rawnie and Rumer had been on the Road for four years

on our own, since we'd cut loose of our mam and da in Foreverfroze, way up north. Da had taken a liking to the cold air and white sky of the north, and Mam had a mind to try fishing the way the Foreverfroze women did it. She was ever a good angler, was Mam, with a passion for whitefish and yellowback, which none of us could understand.

So my sisters and I took the Road and did pretty well, all told. We were Road children, after all, and all our life'd been spent following the drum on Da's back, along the high roads and the back roads, with Mam whistling behind to keep our spirits up on the long stretches.

I was the youngest and was used to being looked after. But it didn't take me more than two months to realize that neither Rumer nor Rawnie could handle silver without letting it slide through their fingers like water, just like our da. I was as hard-headed as Mam, and I took that purse out of their hands and doled them out copper like it was gold.

Soon enough it was I who was deciding where we should go and what we should sing, and it was I who made them keep ten silver bits in reserve, even when it meant shagging for our supper. 'Twas better to lie down for ten minutes, I said, and have food where we knew the innkeeper'd feed us for a shag, than find us one day stone broke in an inn with a woman keeper. "I'll not go hungry," I said, "and I'll not sleep in the rain. What's good enough for Mam and Da is good enough for us."

Don't mistake me, I spent time on my back, same as them, though I hated it worse, I think. I hated the blank look in the innkeepers' eyes and the scorn on their faces, the smell of them—the old-man smell more often than not, or else that dirty stale beer smell, and the leather smell from their jerkins—for it wasn't often they'd bother to undress, not for the price of a supper.

Rawnie and Rumer were even-tempered girls, light as thistledown in body and mind, as tumblers should be. They practiced as often as I wanted without begrudging it, but they were more interested in the young men than anything else. Once they earned their place for the night, if they had to, they washed and brushed their hair, put on their bright performing smiles, and sang and tumbled like nothing had happened. But they seldom had to, no more than once every two or three months, with us taking it in turn as we did. But I remembered every forced time like it was my right hand I'd lost, and I brooded on it, even though it was my idea.

Jugglers don't have to smile—it's better to pretend frowning concern to heighten the tension: will she drop a pin, will she catch on fire? In the town squares, sometimes I would send flaming batons up into the summer night sky, like distress beacons or warning fires, but to whom, I didn't know. On those nights the copper rained into our hands, and sometimes silver, too.

Rumer reckoned it hurt me worse than them because I'd never done it with a sweet young man, a douce young man with long fingers and soft lips. My first time'd been in Mickleton with a fifty-year-old innkeeper, who had two daughters older than me, and wanted me to call him "Da" all the way through it. Rawnie and Rumer hadn't known till it was over and they found me puking hard behind the horse barn, my fingers blue with cold and clutching onto the barn wall for balance. They'd have taken my place, wanting my first time to be soft and sweet, like theirs'd been, but I wouldn't let them. It wouldn't have been fair.

I remembered that time, and others, as the fruit rotted on the trees that summer, and the prices rose steadily in the towns. I could see a long winter ahead, and I couldn't face it.

We was in Carlion in the late days of summer and it was warm and dry and beautiful now, though it was too late to do any good. Among the townspeople worry bred a need for entertainment, and they walked the streets of an evening, and stopped in the green near the well to watch me juggling the shining silver-painted balls, and to hear Rumer and Rawnie sing sweet songs. "Keep it happy," I'd said. "They want to be taken out of their cares, and they depend on us to do it. They'll give us more that way." But even so, copper was scarce and silver was as rare as balls on a gelding.

There was one evening like that, no different from any other, when I saw a young man, a comely man, watching from the back of the crowd while the three of us tumbled and rolled, balanced and spun.

The crowd applauded. Panting, I saw the young man grin at us and clap heartily himself. Brown-haired, he was, with gray eyes like agate and a tall body that was only just free from the gangliness of youth. He had a pack on his back and he was clearly a Traveler, like us, but he was dressed as well as any merchant, and he had muscle, the kind you only get with regular food and work.

His name was Gorham. He came over to us at the end of the performance, after we'd finished collecting the few coins from the ground. That moment, his eyes rested on all three of us with equal pleasure, I think, but I moved forward to greet him. Rumer and Rawnie smiled at each other and slipped into the background, for, as one of them said to the other later, "It was the first time she ever did so much as look at a likely lad, and it's about time, too!" Of course they were thinking, the both of them, that me taking pleasure with a man would make their lives easier, and mine.

Gorham was a horsebreaker, so his pay didn't depend on how generous an audience felt: he set his prices and the owners paid. No one killed off a horse because of a bad winter; they just sold them to someone who could afford them. And young though he was, Gorham had a reputation already. He'd traveled all his life with his mam, who was a horsebreaker of great fame. Even Rumer had heard of Radagund the Horse Speller, who was said to use enchantments from the Western Mountains to bind the horses to her with chains of affection.

Gorham laughed at the stories. "Aye," he said, "it looked like that, with my mam. Come to that, it looks like that sometimes with me, though not so often. See, I reckon my mam was half a horse herself."

"That makes you a horse's grandson," I said, grinning.

"Aye," he said, "that's me."

He laughed, as he often did, then kissed me. That was his way, to laugh and then reach for what he wanted, as a man reaches who's rarely been refused anything. Radagund had reared her son the way she'd reared horses: with endless kindness and a firm hand on the reins. At nineteen, he was as honest and comforting as bread, and he smelled to me of safety and harborage and solace. I wanted him.

Not in the way Rawnie and Rumer wanted their young men, with a light lust, a giggle in the hay at the back of a barn, and a "wind at your back" the next day and off again—no one the worse and everyone better for it. No, I wanted Gorham the way the winter wind wants to get indoors, moaning at the cracks and crevices, rattling the panes of the window. I could see that after a week or so in Carlion he'd be off to his next yearling, and maybe he'd remember me with a smile in the long winter nights. Or maybe not.

"Oh, he's head over ears in love with you," Rumer said, pushing me on the shoulder as I stretched and warmed up for practice, so I fell over on my backside. "What's he like, eh?"

I shook my head and blushed, and that was enough to give Rawnie and Rumer the giggles. They got on with practice but, truth be told, I didn't know what he was like; I had been playing a teasing, waiting match with Gorham, knowing all too well that to keep him in Carlion a few days more was life and death to me, and knowing how often the young enjoyed and left.

So I went to the stonecaster, but not for a casting.

"A spell I want —" I said, my hard-won silver clutched in my hand.

The stonecaster laughed. "To make a young man fall in love with you," she said with certainty. She had a strange voice, strong and precise, not like a Traveler's lilt, nor a town dweller's burr.

"Aye," I said, without shame. "Love and need, I want, and certain sure and no wearing off."

"Don't we all?" Her voice was mocking and, underneath, pained. "But you won't find that here, girl. The tanner will help you—if it's help you call it. On Leather Street, where the juniper bush grows."

I nodded and made to rise, but the stonecaster stopped me.

"Wait. You interest me, girl. Let's see what the stones have to tell you. No charge." She laughed again, bitterly, drew five stones from the bag, and cast them across the blanket. I watched them fall with keen interest. "All facedown," the woman said. "Unusual." There was no trace of laughter in her, now, she was all serious eyes and pursed lips. She turned the stones over, one by one. "Magic—there's your spell, girl. And Pain. Silver. Children. Frost." She was silent a moment, then raised her dark eyes to mine. "A mixed blessing, you get with your spell, and all facedown, which means secret."

"Aye," I said. "Secret and sure. Silver and children."

"Pain and Frost."

"Nothing's without pain, dam, thou knowest that. Frost... well, with enough silver, you can protect yourself against frost. This'll suit me fine."

The stonecaster watched me out the door with a foreboding frown, but I shrugged it off. It was Gorham I wanted and Gorham I would have.

The tanner was more businesslike and much less pleasant. He stank like his tannery, and his spell powder stank even more.

"Give it to the young man in his cha, and sugar it well," he said. "He'll never notice if you're touching up his leg the while he drinks." He sniggered to himself and his hand brushed my breast as he handed it over. "Hope you treat him well," he said. "That stuff'll bind him to you for all his breathing days, and no mistake."

"It ought to," I snapped. "It cost enough."

Gorham drank it down like it was sweet cider, while I slid my hand up his leg and whispered in his ear. He was sleeping in the hayloft of a livery stable in return for grooming and cleaning tack, and later that night we snuggled in the hay and I opened myself to him body and soul, sure of him at last. For there was no doubt that his eyes were resting warmer on me than they'd ever done before, and his hands were more urgent and his words were all of love and staying together, forever. I had no doubt it was the spell. I drowned happily in the scent of him, the clean, rich smell of horses and hay, and if there came a moment or two when the memory of the old innkeeper slid between us, it was soon over and forgotten.

When he went on to Sandanie at the end of the week, I went with him. Rumer and Rawnie wailed like cormorants as we left, but it may be they were not so unhappy to see me go, when I'd given them two-thirds of our silver and left them free to go where they pleased and sing where they liked, without a baby sister scowling disapproval at them.

And with Gorham, Rawnie had said that I'd be safe and well looked after: "For he worships the ground you walk on, and has done since he laid eyes on you that first day!"

"He'll learn," Rumer grinned. "First time he tries to spend his silver for something she don't approve on. He'll learn."

I turned my nose up at her and we laughed.

But it seemed he never did. It seemed he liked the way I organized our lives, bargained with his customers, insisted on earning as much of my own keep as I could in the inns and on the town greens. I traveled with more pleasure than ever before, and I rounded out with good eating and warm living until I could only juggle, not tumble no more, for tumbling needs you thin and wiry.

The first babe was a girl, Hazel, that we called Zel, and the second, a boy. The years they were born, Gorham took on with a horse dealer for two whole seasons and we stayed planted in one place longer than either of us had ever done in our lives. Mitchen, that was, both times, where we lived in half a cottage that belonged to the horse dealer. The other half was rented by the dealer's farrier, Flax, who became the second child's namesake and taught Gorham all he knew of farriery in recompense, not having any young ones of his own.

I loved the long winter nights by the fire in a good sound cottage with food on the hob, and Gorham's big feet stretched to the blaze. Gorham teased me that I loved the cottage more than him, more than the babies, which wasn't so far from the truth, for I was never a motherly girl, not even when I was nursing. But I treasured those babes, for they were two more ties that kept Gorham bound to me, and not by no spell. For it seemed to me that the spell had worked too well, and had trapped me, too.

"Look at me, love," I'd say to him, and turn his eyes to me. I'd search his face over and over, holding him between my palms. I didn't even know what I was looking for, and was sure I never found it.

How could I? I was looking for real love, for love that wasn't called up by spells, for love that settled itself on me and not just on the girl who'd served him that cup of cha. Even if it had come, would I have seen it? Would it have been any different from the spell-wrought tenderness I'd seen on his face that first night? Surely it would be, I thought. Surely years of living together, loving together, would breed a truer kind of love than that.

But all I saw on his face was the same look he'd had that night in the stable loft.

We brought up the two young ones like true Travelers, to know the Road and love it, to walk uncomplainingly through cold winds and sweltering sun. Later, when times were good, we bought a cart and horse. It was a wild pony from the marshland, who'd been called unbreakable, but Gorham whispered him to sleep and gentled him awake until he was tame as a lovebird, and nibbled gently on Gorham's ear while he was being harnessed.

I taught my young ones singing and juggling, and as much tumbling as I could manage in those days. Zel was the spit of me, dark hair and dark eyes with a strong mouth, and no nonsense about her. Flax was sweet as honey, with a voice like a meadowlark that earned us good takings by the time he was waist-high.

"Look at me, love," I still said, from time to time, but I'd given up hope of ever finding what I was looking for.

Once, when we was back in Carlion, I tried to find the tanner again, to have the spell taken off. He was gone, the neighbors told me, murdered by a customer who hadn't liked the consequences of his spell. I felt a sweet shaft of satisfaction mingle with my disappointment; I knew how the customer had felt.

When Zel was fifteen and Flax twelve, they took to the Road by themselves, wild to try their wings.

Gorham didn't like it. "They're not old enough," he complained to me. "They'll get into all manner of harm."

"How old was you?"

"Fifteen —"

"And I was thirteen. They've traveled all their born days—they'll be fine."

He gave in, as he always did to me, but with a frown. I didn't care: he was mine again, it was just the two of us, and without the young ones to feed and clothe, we were riding high.

The night after they went I lay in his arms. "You don't look in my face no more," he said suddenly. "You've given it up, haven't you? Given up hoping you'll find whatever it was you were looking for."

My heart swelled and I kissed him and murmured, "No, don't be silly." But I had no real answer for him. He was right: I had given up hoping for real love.

That year we went to Pless for the horse fair. Our pony was getting old and we'd more than enough put away to buy a new one, perhaps, Gorham hoped, even a horse.

"No," I said definitely, "just a pony. We can't afford a horse."

"You've got enough silver to buy a whole string of horses, woman," Gorham shouted at me. It was a new thing, him shouting.

It stung me and I stung back. "We'd have no silver left at all if I let you spend what you liked when you liked! That silver's against our old age, man, against the year we'd freeze to death if we didn't have enough to pay our way."

He quietened and shook his head. "It may be that year'll come, and may be not, woman."

He went out of the horse barn where a friend of his was letting us stay, and I didn't see him again that night, though I stayed awake and waited all the night through, my heart knocking hard in me at every step, but it was never him. And that was new, too.

I went looking for him the next day, though I didn't tell anyone that I'd lost him, and that way I got to talking to a score of townsfolk. I came back to the horse barn bubbling with excitement, and found him sluicing himself down at the trough. He straightened hurriedly, with an apology on his lips, but I waved him silent.

"The farrier's dead and he's got no child!" I blurted out.

"What?"

"The horse dealer, old Tinsley. He died last week."

Gorham looked shocked. "I was planning to visit him this morning. He was only my da's age. What happened?"

"Stroke. Isn't it wonderful?"

"Wonderful? Woman!"

"Aye, I mean, of course, it's bad that he's dead. But he's got no child. And his widow's looking to sell the farm."

Gorham stared at me blankly. "Sell —"

"Aye! We've got enough, Gorham. Only just, we'd have nothing behind us, but we could do it. Sure and certain, we could settle here and be set for the rest of our lives."

I was ready with all the arguments but he didn't argue. He went thoughtful like, and quiet. "Let me think on it," he said. "A few days."

At the end of the week the bargain was made and we moved into the cottage out by the farm. It was just a few acres then, with a rickety stable and a couple of yards for training the horses. Tinsley's widow moved in with her sister, and the townsfolk nodded approval. Pless wasn't a town we'd been in much over the years, and it was clear that most folk didn't know that we'd been Travelers—with our good burghers' clothes and our solid cart. Crafters we was taken for, and I was pleased, having no wish to see contempt in anyone's eyes. For Travelers, there is no doubt, are scorned and mistrusted, and that's not good for business. We already knew how to talk like townsfolk; we'd done it for fun, pretended, but now it was real. I kept at Gorham until he agreed to leave our Traveler talk behind us.

I expected to be as happy as sky is blue in that sturdy cottage, with my trivet and my cupboards, and my pots and pans hanging from the hooks above the fire. So far as fire and clean water and a soft bed could make me happy, I was. But Gorham was away from that fire entirely too much. I didn't understand it at first; it'd seemed he wanted this move as much as me.

"Look at me, love," I said to him one night when we was in bed, when he was home for once at a reasonable hour, but he turned his face away as if I'd see something shameful there. I let it drop, but cold crept up my spine and my heart started thudding like it would shake the bed. I lay awake too long that night, and he was gone again when I woke up.

In the morning light I went to watch him in the yard with a new two-year-old, and found him humming at his work. He grinned at me but ducked his head out of sight. Too late. That grin was different from any he'd ever given me.

Of course, it was a woman in the marketplace who told me, the thin fishmonger with the buckteeth, "for your own good," she said, and "I think you ought to know." Gorham had a fancy woman.

Her name was Maude and she was a seamstress for the clothier, one of Acton's people, with fair hair and blue eyes, and not even younger than me—a year or two older. She'd been respectable up until this, the fishmonger said, but now it was all over Pless and no wonder, shameless as they both were about it, laughing in the inn together until after the late summer dark, walking back to her place bold as you please.

I believed it straightaway. Gorham would laugh and reach for what he wanted with no thought of consequences, just as he'd done with me.

But I searched his face when he ate at my table, while he slept. He had changed toward me, no doubt. Had the spell worn off? Or worse—had the spell never worked at all? Had Gorham's love been real all this time? Had I found a lie, even while he was showing me the truth? If I'd known, could I have kept his love, worked for it, instead of believing it was mine no matter what?

I was filled with rage…at the tanner, at the stonecaster who'd sent me there, at my own young self for being so foolish, so ready to believe, at Gorham, for not making me see—all these years—that I was really at the center of his heart, where Maude was now. I was murderous with rage, but I held it back. I was never no fool. Without Gorham, I had nothing: no house, no food, no fire. Without Gorham, it was back on the Road again, back into the desperate winters. I was too old for that.

Gorham never mentioned Maude's name. Nor did I. I accepted his absence from my bed without a word. I even turned toward him in the night, when he occasionally reached for me, hesitantly, thinking that maybe the day would come when he'd tire of his fancy woman and come back home to stay. I wanted him to, wanted another chance to make him love me real and true.

But it was too late, even when we did well enough to buy more acres next to ours, even when we prospered enough that we could move into a big house in town and give up the farm cottage altogether. It was bitter for me, that day. Everything I'd worked for, saved for, had come true, and all it meant was that he'd now find it even easier to slip along to Maude's and leave me alone.

When he was gone, in the dead of night, when he was sleeping warm and cozy with his fancy woman, I shook my bag of silver out onto my bed and counted the pieces, over and over, listening for his step. But all I heard was the clink and repeated clink of falling coins, and I wished the tanner was still alive so I could try his spell one more time.

ASH

ASH WATCHED Doronit carefully the few days after the Ghost Begone Festival, but she gave no sign that anything was amiss. She was quiet, but somehow pleased with herself. The whole city was quiet, recoiling from the shock of festival night.

Even the ghosts were quiet. They skulked in corners, and looked at passersby out of the corners of their white eyes, with half-smug, half-fearful smiles. Ash ignored them and they seemed happy to cooperate with him. No one suspected that he had set the ghosts loose to hag-ride the town.

Ash couldn't stop thinking about the girl he had killed. He wouldn't let himself think about the warning she had given, but he was ashamed that he hadn't gone back to the alleyway three days after he had killed her, to help her ghost move on, as he had with the two men who had tried to kill Martine.

That had been his responsibility, and he had failed. He had acted as though her ghost wasn't... wasn't *worthy* of being helped, as though she were not really human, just a doll in a game of Doronit's. He was black-burning ashamed of that, remembering her clear ghostly eyes and her wry mouth. He should have gone back to acknowledge his guilt in her death, paid the blood price and set her free. Instead, he was in her debt, no matter what Martine said. According to his mother, the debts he couldn't pay in this life must be paid in the next. He and the girl would meet again—somewhere, somehow—in another life.

He had avoided that alleyway since the night he had killed her, but now he found himself passing by on that side of Acton Square, glancing down the narrow, winding lane as if he might see her there. It was stupid. It was worse than stupid, it was now a habit, the kind of predictable behavior that safeguarders should never set up, in case anyone was looking for a place to waylay them. But he did it anyway.

A couple of weeks after Ghost Begone Night, Ash and Aelred were set to guard the gates of a select and seemingly endless party in one of the restaurants in Acton Square. After the party guests had gone home, Aelred slapped him on the shoulder with a quick "see you in the morning" and made off downhill toward the boardinghouse behind the Sailor's Rest, where he lived. Although the restaurant was on the other side of the square from the alleyway, Ash found himself drifting over there rather than setting out for Doronit's.

There was no one about at this time of night. His boots rang out in the cool air and he changed his footfall so that he walked silently. It had been a long time since he'd heard silence. He was used to it, out on the Road, but it was a rare thing in Turvite. He slowed his steps, enjoying it, but was still, compulsively, making his way to the alleyway. He knew she wouldn't be there. He knew there would be no clear-eyed ghost waiting for him near the wall where he'd killed her. But he was drawn there anyway; he would take one look, and go home.

He looked, and saw the girl's death reenacted. There she was, up against the wall. There he was, knife in hand, blade glinting as he drew it back for the second strike, the kill strike.

"NO!" he yelled, and leaped forward, reaching for that hand. He realized his stupidity as he leaped: he couldn't touch a ghost, couldn't touch a haunting, he would go straight through...

And he cannoned, instead, into a solid, muscular body, much larger than his. His mind stopped thinking altogether, but his body knew what to do. The months of training had taught him reflexes he hadn't known existed. *Keep the knife away, get rid of it.* In a single swift action, he grabbed the man's hand and slammed it down on the cobbles. The knife skittered away and they both rolled to their feet, and were now facing each other, wary.

He was a big man, stronger, no doubt. But Ash's first blow had done some damage: the man favored one leg, as though his ankle were twisted, and he winced as he put it to the ground. He saw Ash notice it and rushed forward, his big hands out for Ash's throat. *Under and up.* Ash ducked under the attack and used his opponent's momentum to throw him up into the air, across his back, so the big man landed heavily on the cobbles. Ash drew his boot knife. The knife in his hand, in this place, brought his mind back to life, put him in control of his reflexes. He didn't want to kill anyone else.

"I don't want to kill you," he said. He heard the sincerity in his own voice, and the complete belief that he would be able to kill this much larger man. The man heard it too, and scrambled up from the cobbles and then backed away with one hand raised in surrender. He pulled himself around the corner and Ash could hear his footsteps echoing fast across the square.

It was only then that Ash turned to the girl.

Of course, it wasn't the girl. Wasn't even *a* girl. It was the little jeweler with the big mustache. As soon as Ash helped him up from where he had fallen, he began babbling with gratitude and shock.

"Oh, gods, if you hadn't come, if you hadn't come, he was going to *kill* me, actually *kill* me... He had a knife, did you see, he had a knife, he was going to k-k-*kill* me..."

"It's a popular spot for that," Ash said, and then realized the man was shaking. "It's all right, it's all right, he's gone, he's not coming back... You're all right now." His words seemed to also calm himself down: he was a safeguarder with a client now, not a fool reacting to a ghost who wasn't even there.

After some time the jeweler finally swallowed hard, and seemed to pull himself back into something close to his normal cynical self-assurance. But his hands were still trembling. "I have to go back to my inn... It's down near the docks..." He peered fearfully out of the alleyway at the empty square. "I don't suppose you..."

"I'll come with you," Ash said resignedly. They walked together across the square, the jeweler looking over his shoulder at every second step. "What were you doing in that alleyway in the first place?" Ash asked. "It's not the safest place in the city."

"I wasn't in the alleyway!" the jeweler said indignantly. "I was just walking back to my inn, through the square, after dinner at a client's house and that... that *thug* grabbed me."

"You should hire a safeguarder if you're going to walk around the city at night," Ash scolded.

"I'm going home tomorrow," the jeweler said with obvious relief. "Back to Carlion. It's a lot safer there."

They walked in silence until they reached the Fifty Friends, a middlingly prosperous tavern with an extra house next door for guests.

The jeweler paused under the torch that helped guests climb the steps without falling over their drunk feet. "I'm in your debt," he said.

Ash shook his head. "No, really, you're not."

"Yes, yes, I know I am. I pay my debts." He scrabbled in his pouch and drew out a soft leather bag, about as big as his palm. "Here. You liked this the other day. Have it with my thanks." Then he darted up the steps and into the door, closing it firmly behind him.

Ash stared at the bag knowing, from the size and the weight, what he would find inside. He drew it out slowly. It glinted warmly in the torchlight, intricate and beautiful. It couldn't possibly be Acton's cloak brooch. Not truly. But something in its heaviness, its undoubted age, told him differently.

To get back to Doronit's house he had only to climb the hill. But his feet took him south from the docks, around the older part of the city, as he thumbed the pattern on the brooch. He walked past the black stone altar and heard, deep in his mind, the susurration of the local gods calling his name. They called whenever he came to this part of town, whenever he passed the altar. He tried hard to ignore them, but the brooch seemed to grow cold in his hands. He walked more quickly.

It was late. It didn't matter if it was Acton's brooch. But he had to know, beyond doubt. Martine would probably be asleep. It would do no harm to go and see. Stonecasters often worked late, their clients preferring the privacy of darkness.

There was a light on in the main room of Martine's house. He hesitated outside. Tonight there were no ghosts waiting for entrance, just the door, plain oiled wood. It was anything but portentous, that door, but it felt like the entrance to somewhere else. It was like the magic circle the Ice People believed in, which takes you to the world of the gods. The local gods whispered his name more loudly, and he raised his hand to knock on the door.

Martine opened it and greeted him without surprise. "Come in."

He sat down on the new fleece rug and she sat opposite him with her bag of stones in her lap. He spat on his palm and held it out. She spat on hers and they clapped and grasped hands. With his other hand he held out the brooch.

"Was this Acton's?" he asked.

She blinked in surprise, and looked at the brooch. Then she smiled, a strange, sideways smile, and reached into the bag.

Only one of the five stones she scattered was faceup. "Certainly," she said softly. "It was his." She turned the others over. "Betrayal. Blood. Murder. Guilt."

"Acton's all right," Ash tried to joke. His insides were churning; he was half nauseous, half excited. He dropped the brooch beside the stones. The fire flickered light over its intricate design.

"There is a story here," Martine said. Her eyes were unfocused while she listened to the stones. "But it is not our story to hear. Nor to tell." She shook her head and let his hand go. "That is all the stones have to say."

They both looked at the brooch. *Acton's.*

A visible shiver went through Martine. "This has seen its share of blood."

"He slaughtered thousands," Ash said slowly, "but I don't get any sense of evil from it. Do you?"

Martine shrugged. "It is just a thing that has passed through many hands since he last touched it. Maybe they have wiped it clean."

"Maybe."

They stared at it until Martine suddenly laughed. "Look at us! Entranced by a bauble! Come, sit up and I will make us some cha."

Ash smiled shamefacedly and sprang up to help her swing the kettle over the fire. They sat companionably in silence until the kettle boiled, and then drank the cha together.

"What am I supposed to do with it?" Ash said suddenly.

"You could sell it. I will give you a warranty that it's genuine. There are many among the old families who would pay well to have a thing of Acton's."

Deep in his mind the local gods whispered, *Keep it.* Martine's face changed, and he knew that she heard them too. It made him feel better.

"Or maybe I'd better not," he said drily.

She laughed. "There *is* some advice it is wiser to take."

"Will you keep it here for me?"

He was reluctant, very reluctant, to take it back to Doronit's, where he would have to conceal it. She would only see profit in it, and he knew she took no account of the local gods. He suspected she even took no account of the powers beyond them.

"That's a great trust," Martine said slowly.

He was surprised; he had taken it for granted that he could trust her, but he had no reason for that, after all, except that she had heard the gods speak to him. Or maybe there was something in her that was the opposite of Doronit—a lack of interest in profit beyond what was necessary to live—which he had recognized because he shared it.

"It's just a brooch," he said.

She smiled that sideways smile that told him she saw right through him. He couldn't help but smile back.

"All right," she said. She picked up the brooch and rose to place it on her mantelpiece. "It will be waiting here for you when you come back." Her words seemed to echo, as though they were part of a prophecy.

"When I come back," he confirmed.

In the silence that followed, the ease between them vanished and he became too aware of his feet and his hands. He reddened and got up.

"I...I'd better —"

"Yes," Martine said. "Go, but be careful of who you trust."

Ash blinked. "I'll try."

She closed the door behind him with a definite thud, as though she was glad to see the back of him, but when he looked at her window she was standing there, watching him, and she raised a hand in farewell as he turned the corner.

He felt lighter, walking home, and not just because he had left Acton's brooch behind him. Martine was the first friend he had found on his own, outside Doronit's control. Perhaps he could craft a life for himself in this city after all.

SAKER

EACH NIGHT, Rowan, Swallow and Cypress found a place to perform, usually in an inn. Where they were known from past visits they were welcomed, and got beds in the stables. "But no lights, understand," the innkeepers said. "We don't want any fires."

Most of the time, Rowan would make sure they performed at least one song from the distant past, usually about the invasion of the area or town they were in. The customers loved them, banged their tankards on the tables in time with the drumming, and slapped Rowan and Cypress on their backs afterward. While Swallow and Cypress sang, Saker would take notes.

In the vale of Wooding, in the forested valley,
six hundred were slain by the sword-wielding few.
Aelred, he led them, through clearing and coppice
Through river and rushes to victory sweet.

"Six hundred in Wooding," noted Saker. "Near the river."

By ford of the Sprit where water sprites lurk
great-hearted Garlok gathered his men,
led them to raven's nest, glade in the woods.
There were the enemy ranged up against them,
There were the enemy, mighty and strong:
Seven and forty the enemy fallen
By Garlok's strong blade and the blades of three friends.

"Spritford," wrote Saker. "Forty-seven. Raven's Nest Glade."

On nights when they were not performing, in between villages, Rowan and Swallow would perform some of the history songs that were not popular with Acton's people. Some had been written by Travelers.

Saker prized these the most as they often contained detailed information about the victims of an attack: ages, burial and battlegrounds. Rowan's flute cast a high lament into the night for those songs.

Sometimes Rowan would sing in a firm, mellow voice, and Swallow would drum quietly on her knee, showing Cypress the rhythm. Cypress listened as hard as Saker, but Saker could tell that all he really cared about were the rhythms and words, not what they meant.

Each night was precious to Saker because each song brought him closer to his goal, but other things were precious, too. Swallow's calm grace called up long-buried memories of his mother, who had been neither calm nor graceful, but who had shared Swallow's coloring and litheness.

Saker wept quietly into his pillow on the first night a memory returned to him. He saw his mother rushing around the house with a broom after his older sister, threatening retribution for some chore, he couldn't remember what, left undone. His sister shrieked with laughter as she scurried around the table, and his mother was trying not to laugh, too, but shouting, "You're lazy! What are you?" His sister answered breathlessly, hiccuping with laughter, "Lazy!" and finally his mother flung herself down on the settle by the fire, and giggled. He remembered laughing, too, laughing so much his eyes watered. But he couldn't remember when it had happened... how long before they were all dead. But it was a happy memory, and after the tears he went to sleep peacefully.

There was only a handful of memories, and each new one was priceless. To remember his father hale and strong and whole again just fed his resolution. He had only been able to remember his father after the attack, his head half crushed by a sword blow and the flesh ragged on his shoulder from the spur.

One night, after six long, sorrowful songs, Rowan stopped. "That's all," he said. "You have heard all of them now."

"*All* the old songs?" Saker asked, feeling strangely bereft.

"All the history songs. The others aren't of interest to you."

Saker sat quietly with his notebook on his lap. He looked at its fat pages, almost filled. He looked at Rowan and Swallow, then Cypress.

"Thank you. Then... I must be leaving you soon."

"We'll be in Carlion in a few days," Rowan said.

Saker nodded. The future looked curiously empty, despite all the work he had to do. He would need to go back to the enchanter's house, his house, and work on the map…There were to be no more companionable nights by the fire, no more buried memories surfacing like flowers in a cesspit. Over the last six months he had grown accustomed to being Penda, the student, one of a traveling group. It would take a little time to remember how to be alone again.

"It's been good, having you with us," Rowan said. "Like having our son back."

Swallow frowned. "Nothing like it!" she said sharply, but then smiled at Saker. "But good, nonetheless."

"So your work's over then, cully," Cypress said.

Saker looked at his notebook again, and slowly shook his head. "It's just beginning."

BRAMBLE

GORHAM TOOK HER out to the farm the next day early, after a breakfast of thin porridge, which wasn't half as good as Maryrose's. She turned out the roan in a small field next to the cottage, and set to work.

Cleaning out the cottage took most of the morning. They'd brought an old bed, which Osyth had produced from an attic somewhere, to save having to buy a new one. It was creaky with woodworm, but Gorham lashed it tight with greenhide strips, and with the new ticking (which he'd insisted on) stuffed with fresh straw, it was comfortable enough.

Bramble and Gorham had sat at the kitchen table the night before and made a list of the things she'd need at the cottage: cooking pans, bed linen, dishes, broom, scrubbing brush... Osyth sniffed as they wrote down each item but a few moments later she would appear with a tattered or half-broken or *almost* worn-out version. Bramble had to suppress a fit of the giggles. The shagging woman never threw anything out—not even a badly chipped chamber pot! It'd cut your bum to ribbons if you chanced to sit on it.

"Thanks," Bramble had said when she'd offered that, "but I think I'll buy one of my own."

So the cart had been packed with almost everything she'd need, even if most of it was in poor condition. Gorham fixed a broken leg on the table while Bramble cleaned, but she didn't want to waste too much time with the cottage. Maybe she would get around to prettying it up later.

Sitting on cords of wood at the newly mended table, she lunched on cheese and pickles with day-old bread ("No sense wasting it on the pig," Osyth had said). Gorham had fresh bread, and offered to share it, but Bramble shook her head; she didn't care much anymore. Her sense of taste was dull. She wondered, sometimes, if she would ever really enjoy anything again.

"No need. Besides, you want to be able to tell her that I ate it all up." She tilted her head sideways at him with no smile at all, careful to keep her face straight.

Gorham nodded.

That set the tone for all their exchanges about Osyth: tacit acknowledgment that she was, well, difficult, but never discussing it.

In the afternoon Gorham introduced Bramble to her new job.

She had never been employed before; she hated the idea of taking orders, of being subservient. She wondered if the fog that had surrounded her since the roan's jump would deaden her resentment of being bossed around. But Gorham didn't bark orders. Arriving in the morning, he might say, "I thought we'd see if the chestnut will eat from the hand today." Over those first two days he explained everything that had to be done to keep the farm operating, and what her part would be. And then he generally left her to it.

There was only one exception. She learned to wear boots because Gorham insisted on it. "If a sixteen-hand stallion trod on your bare foot, even accidentally, you'd be off work for weeks." With a stout boot it was merely temporary agony. The first time it happened, the pain cut through the fog all right, although only for a few moments.

She also learned to keep to a routine after she realized that animals thrived when their lives were predictable. She even learned to bite her tongue when clients tried to talk as though they knew one end of a horse from another, when clearly they had never really looked at their own animals.

It was a life they could bear, she and the roan. It made no demands on her that she couldn't fulfill, even with the cloudy glass of death between her and the world. Maybe the sense of detachment made her less restless. What did it matter where she was, after all?

She and the roan explored the countryside each morning before work, and in her time off—usually in the middle of the day—she roamed the forest that bordered Gorham's land. It was a remnant of the old forests that had covered the land before Acton's time: oak, mainly, and pockets of beech and elm, alder and willow along the streams, holly and rowan in thickets where old trees had fallen. She found much of her own food there, trapping rabbits and birds, searching out greens and berries in summer, nuts, acorns, mushrooms and truffles in autumn. She had always helped to fill her family's table and it had satisfied her deeply to sit down to a full meal of her own providing. She'd lost a certain sense of that satisfaction, but it was still good. She supposed that gardeners felt like this about fruit and vegetables they had grown, but why garden, she thought, when the forest did all the work for you?

Besides, what would she do if she didn't roam the forest? Sit in the cottage and knit? As she'd received her pay week by week, she'd replaced most of the broken-down things that Osyth had given her (giving them back punctiliously). Beyond utility, she had done almost nothing to the cottage: there were no curtains, no special plates or dishes, no rugs except one made from rabbit fur that she'd tanned herself. She had never cared about indoor things, and finally she didn't have her mam nagging, "Make your room look nice." Aside from housekeeping, she left the cottage alone and found a new kind of freedom in the unadorned walls and paucity of possessions. She felt light and almost free whenever she thought about how little she owned.

Gorham made her responsible for the physical care of the horses that were brought to them from all over the country for gentling, and mostly that meant becoming very well acquainted with manure and currycombs. But Gorham was a generous man and the day after she arrived, he began to teach her his craft. He was a renowned horse trainer, although by the end of the second year after Bramble joined him, he acknowledged that she was his equal. She might have taken the Road before that. She had certainly intended to. But that was before she saw the chases.

Pless was a famous center for chase races, and they were run at the Autumn and Spring Festivals—after harvest, and after sowing. That first autumn, Gorham took her to see a horse that he'd trained race in the biggest chase of all, the Pless Challenge.

She'd never seen a chase before, didn't even know the rules. The area around Wooding was too hilly and the gullies and chasms too frequent for chases. But she knew, of course, the superstitions.

The Autumn Chase was the oldest, the tradition going back since before Acton came over the mountains. The Kill, who led the chasers over the course, represented the death of the year, her grandam had told her once, and the chasers were the hunters who harried the year to its death. The red scarf the Kill carried was the symbol of its blood.

The Spring Chase was much younger, only a hundred years or so on horseback, although there had always been a footrace in spring to celebrate the new year. The Kill in spring represented new life and it was considered very good luck for one of the riders to actually catch the Kill before the finish line and grab the red scarf. If someone could do that, they became the Kill Reborn.

Although now it was more a sport than a ritual, many still believed that a rider who grabbed the red flag from the Kill in the Spring Chase was someone special, someone marked by the gods. But it was very unlucky for someone to catch the flag in the Autumn Chase. Then it was said that he or she was marked out for death within the year.

Bramble stood with Gorham on a hill a mile from Pless, along with the rest of the spectators, half the town at least, and watched as the riders gathered at the town gate. Among the swirling crowd of horses and riders, each with a brightly colored handkerchief around his neck, there was one, on a stocky gray, with a red scarf tied to a lance.

"That's the Kill," Gorham said. "He sets off before the others, then there's a count to fifty, and then the eight riders go. They have to follow his path exactly, over the obstacles he picks, and the first back to the finish line wins." He pointed to a fence a mile or so on the other side, where there was a small group of men waiting.

"That's it?"

"That's enough." Gorham smiled. "We're looking for Golden Shoes—his rider's wearing a blue kerchief."

She picked out Golden Shoes, a sprightly chestnut shying sideways, away from the Kill's red scarf. It had energy enough, she thought.

The Kill set out. The spectators on the hill spontaneously started counting in unison as the rider set his horse to the first fence, and at "...forty-eight, forty-nine, FIFTY!" the horses at the gate surged forward, fighting for position. They took the first jump over an easy post-and-rail fence, but as they scrambled up the hill toward the crowd Bramble caught her breath. She hadn't realized how fast they would go.

The Kill swept past in a gust of wind, red scarf fluttering, and after him the pack of horses came. She could hear the rumble of their hooves on the ground, then felt the ground start to shake.

The pack went over a stone wall and then a fallen tree. By now the best four riders were out in front, and Bramble was beginning to realize that it took more than a fast horse to win.

"They have to go over the same obstacles as the Kill," Gorham said in her ear, "but they can go over them at any point. The good riders take the straight line, even if it's more dangerous."

She could see that the leaders were not jumping their horses at exactly the same place as the Kill. They cut corners even if it meant setting their mounts at a higher section of a fence, or worse, a stone wall, where they couldn't see what lay on the other side.

The pack thundered up and flashed past them too fast for Bramble to take in more than a confusion of colors, shaking ground, flying dust and riders' shouts.

Bramble realized that she was shouting, too, that all of the spectators were urging on their favorites. She wasn't yelling for any horse in particular, she wanted them all to go fast—to go even faster. Her heart was pounding, her fists were clenched, and her body was leaning after the pack as though she could fly across the fields with them. For the first time since the jump across the chasm, she felt alive.

"Golden Shoes was second, did you see?" Gorham's hand gripped her shoulder. "There she goes!"

Bramble could just see the blue kerchief around the neck of the second rider. Coming downhill, the pack picked up speed. The next jump was over a stream. It looked deceptively easy, but it was muddy with autumn rain on both sides, and with the extra momentum the footing was treacherous. The first rider made it across safely. Golden Shoes slid a little on landing, but her rider gathered her nicely and she kept her feet. The third rider went down sprawlingly, and the horses behind were coming too fast to stop. Two riders managed to wrench their horses around to jump at a different angle, so they landed on either side of the fallen horse, but two others crashed straight over and were collected by the muddy bank.

The spectators on the hill froze with a collective gasp, except for one woman who cried out "Robbie!" and started running down to the stream. The others took breath and followed.

There were four horses down, three of them struggling back to their feet. The fourth, the bay, which had been the first to fall, was rocking backward and forward, trying to get his feet under him, but without success. His rider had been thrown off to one side, and was sitting with his head in his hands. The other riders were already standing by the time the group from the hill arrived.

The crying woman hurried through the stream careless of the wet and embraced the seated rider. "Gods, Robbie, gods," she said, again and again. "I thought you were dead." It was clear she was his mother.

Gorham had gone straight to the bay's head and helped him up, but it was now walking with a pronounced limp.

Using his mother's arm to stand, the rider came over, his face full of concern. "Is it broken?"

Everyone quieted for the answer. Gorham felt the fetlock carefully, his face grave, and then smiled. "Just a sprain," he said. He looked over toward the finishing fence and the others turned with him, curiosity rising now their worst fears had been allayed.

"Who got the Kill?" the rider asked, but no one knew.

Gorham cupped his mouth with his hands and shouted to the judges, "Who won?"

"Golden Shoes," came back the reply.

Gorham thumped Bramble on the shoulders. "I knew it," he said exultantly. "I knew that one had it in her."

Bramble looked at the four horses that had made it to the finish fence. They were circling, cooling down. Golden Shoes's rider raised the lance with the red scarf attached, clearly the symbol of victory.

She looked back at the riders leading their horses to and fro, checking their legs and their wind, seeming to have forgotten the fall already. One of them had blood coming from his nose, but he wiped it away with the back of his hand and examined his horse's off-hind hoof.

She looked up at the clear autumn sky, felt the thundering pulse in her blood begin to calm down, and smiled. The fog was gathering again, the glass clouding. But now she had a remedy.

"When's the next chase?" she asked Gorham.

"Not until next spring," he said with a knowing grin. "Got you hooked already, have we?"

She tried to seem unmoved, but found herself smiling in a way that was anything but calm, and said, "Next spring. Good. That will give me time to get the roan ready."

He was startled. "Ready for what?"

She gestured to the horses at the stream, to the finishing fence, to Golden Shoes and her rivals. "Ready for this. Next spring I ride."

Once he got over the surprise, Gorham was enthusiastic, although cautionary. "That roan's a good, strong horse, even though he's old enough that you'll only get a few years out of him," he said as they strolled back to the town gates. "He's got the bone for it, and he's got the hindquarters. But some horses aren't jumpers, and some horses aren't chasers, and you can't change that. It's in the blood."

"He can jump when he wants to," Bramble said drily, remembering the chasm beneath her and the jolt as they had landed. The gods may or may not have helped them over, but that first leap had been prodigious.

"Most horses can jump when they want to," Gorham said. "But will he jump when *you* want him to, and where, and at the right speed?"

He went on for some time like that, to prepare her for disappointment, but he could feel his own excitement rising. He'd trained others' horses to chase, but never one of his own. Well, the roan wasn't exactly his, but it would race from his stable, which was much the same thing. He had a brief vision of Bramble handing him the red scarf from the Kill's lance in front of the townsfolk, and smiled inside. Then he sobered, remembering the duties still awaiting him at home.

"I've got to go," he said at the gates. "Osyth's having a special postrace morning tea for the town council and the winning owner and rider." He paused. Osyth wouldn't thank him for inviting Bramble home, but it seemed rude to just leave her standing there.

"Better you than me," Bramble said, grimacing, releasing him from his predicament. She smiled, pleased that he had wanted to invite her, relieved that he hadn't, and knowing he had seen her relief. So they nodded and went their ways.

But later that afternoon Gorham arrived at the farm, rubbing his hands as he approached her, and comfortably back in his work clothes. "Well, no time like the present to find out if you've got a chance. He hasn't had any hard work today, we'll try him over a few small jumps," Gorham said, and Bramble realized that he was as excited as she was.

Yet when she had changed into her oldest clothes and was taking the roan out to the training paddock where Gorham was dismantling the big jumps, to leave small logs for her first training session, he stared disapprovingly at her.

"Where's his saddle?"

"I don't use a saddle. You know that."

"You have to when you jump—at least if you're jumping high fences at speed. You'll fall off if you don't." He watched as doubt crossed her face. "Trust me," he said. "You need to keep your own balance or you won't be able to balance the horse and he'll fall. Do you want him to break his leg because you have a fancy to ride bareback?"

It wasn't the words so much as the tone that convinced her. She realized that he used the same tone with uppity two-year-old colts who thought they could get the better of him, and laughed, but she went and got the saddle. The roan flipped his ears back at her as she put it on, but resignedly, as though he'd always known that the bareback days were too good to last.

That first day of training, the roan had lifted himself over the small logs as though they weren't there. Bramble, solid in her saddle, barely felt the motion. The fog didn't lift as she had hoped, but this was only the first step. She knew that when she was racing she would come alive again. She had to.

"Well, you might be lucky," Gorham said. "Seems he's done this before, and I'd say he knows how to set himself right."

He put up the next level of jumps. The horse dealt with these easily—it was Bramble who had to learn the skills, then, and on the days that followed, as the jumps grew higher.

"Keep your weight over his center of balance. No—*forward!*" Gorham yelled. "Keep your elbows in—one of the other riders is just as likely to grab one and hoist you off."

She stopped and stared at him, the roan snatching a mouthful of grass when he realized she was distracted.

"What, you thought this was a nice family outing?" Gorham laughed. "They're out to win and some of them don't care how. The winning rider gets a purse of silver, you know."

Bramble nodded, smiling tightly, and fleetingly thought of her foot snapping back that man's head. Anyone who meddled with her was going to get worse than he gave, she thought, then she put it out of her mind and concentrated on crouching in her stirrups to take her weight forward.

"It's not just jumping," Gorham said, over and over, as they cleaned tack or mucked out the stables. "It's strategy, and cunning, and knowing when to push your horse and when to let him take a rest."

Bramble shook her head. "Maybe. And maybe it's just a matter of going faster than anyone else."

Gorham shook his head back at her, but he chuckled as he did it. "If you can, lass, if you can."

Gorham had a long, unfenced stretch of land that bordered the forest: a smooth, rabbit-free length of grass, close-cropped by sheep that were folded each night by the farmer next door. She had tried the roan out there the morning after the chase, just on sunrise.

She had galloped the roan before, of course; how could she have resisted it? But racing speed was to everyday galloping as a full rose was to a bud. That morning as she steadied him, wanting to set off from a standing start, as though they were racing, she thought that she had forgotten what it was like to really look at the world. The fog was still with her, but there was a break in it now, and she could look through it, even feel through it.

The autumn air was rich with loam and mushroom scent, with moisture and the promise of a fine day. It was so early that not even the thrushes were singing. The horse moved like an extension of her, so that she was as strong as he, as fierce and agile and elemental. She sat, poised in a moment of perfect balance, perfect calm, and then pressed hard with her legs and said, "Go!" then, "Faster!" pressing harder, and "*Faster!*" leaning down on his neck, feeling the exhilaration sweep through the roan first and then up into her, the intoxication, the rushing splendor of speed.

When they were forced to draw up by the fence at the end of the paddock, she looked back on that moment of blissful calm before the run and wondered why she had thought she was so happy. It was nothing compared to a flat-out gallop!

She had been grateful for Gorham's training: the discipline of the training paddock, where each jump had to be attempted with calm and precision, was, she knew, necessary for both her and the roan. But on its own she knew it wouldn't help her win. She had to learn to jump at speed, across country, over streams and stone walls and brush fences and wooden rails. And this she had to do alone.

That training took up all her midday hours, the time she had liked to spend in the forest. Although she had loved those rambles, she let them go without a thought, and bought food from town instead. Chases were run in the midmorning, Gorham told her, or at noon, so she and the roan had to get used to racing in the full sun.

She started with the fences around the farm, learning to approach them at increasing speeds. When she could manage them easily at a half-speed gallop, she set out across country, jumping as many obstacles as she could, trying to improve their form in the time they had before the iron-hard ground of winter frost made riding dangerous for the roan.

By then she knew that a chase was to a gallop as a gallop was to a canter: the rush to the fence, the takeoff, the soaring speed through the air, the landing and swift, powerful thrust that got them to full speed again, were like drinking spirits on an empty stomach, like diving into the quarry, like love. And perhaps, she thought, this was what the Love stone had foretold in her casting.

She fell, of course. She fell into mud and onto gorse, pitched headfirst over stone walls and backward into cowpats. She fell, and learned to fall, and learned to keep hold of the reins as she fell. The horse, by some magic of his own, never hurt himself, although he, too, often fell. Always, she realized, it was her fault.

Because the roan was a natural jumper who loved speed as much as she did, it was usually imbalance, hesitation or stupidity on her part that set him wrong for a fence. She berated herself silently after each fall, and apologized to the horse, who snuffled in her hair and never held it against her. Even after the worst fall, standing wet with mud up to her armpits, her head splitting from contact with the ground, her shoulder almost dislocated from being wrenched by the reins, she was full of hope. But the rush of feeling died away when she was off his back and the training sessions were finally over.

She waited for the spring thaw with a little girl's impatience, and as soon as the ground was soft enough she and the roan went out in the early morning and at noon again, getting stronger, growing closer, and building on that wordless understanding that allowed them to act as one. The roan's jumping was flawless, joyful, exuberant; the only thing that concerned her was that he'd had no practice racing against other horses.

"Well, he'll either like it or hate it," Gorham said cheerfully, as they watched the first of the spring foals being born late one night. "Some horses just take to it, others never do. Try not to frighten him, that's all."

She snorted. "He doesn't know how to be frightened."

Gorham turned his head slowly to look at her, grinning. "That's because you haven't been frightened so far."

At that moment the foal began to slither down the birth canal onto the straw, and it took all their attention.

A little later Gorham continued as though there hadn't been an interruption. "What are you going to call him?"

It took Bramble a while to work out what he meant. "Call him? The Roan, I suppose."

"You can't call an entry in the chases 'The Roan.'" He shook his head decisively.

She smiled at him. "Well, you pick one."

He pulled at his lip. He'd always wanted to do this, to name a chaser. He had all sorts of names picked out: Gorham's Pride, Gorham's Mane, Silverfleet (chosen, he remembered with a chuckle, when he was very young and romantic). But naming a horse for someone else was a big responsibility. He looked at Bramble, her dark eyes and curling black hair, tanned skin and crooked smile.

He smiled back. "What about Thorn?" he said, and she laughed and laughed.

"Bramble on Thorn," she agreed, still chuckling as they walked back to the cottages. She paused at her door. "But that's not his name, you know."

Gorham nodded. "Not around here," he said, and she nodded back, a compact.

She'd never felt she had the right to name the roan. Maybe it was because he came to her through death, or that she owed him her life, but more likely it was because in her thoughts he didn't need a name. He was *the* horse: the others needed names because they were not. And it had to do with his own nature, with his sensitivity to her thoughts, and his courage. It had to do with all the reasons why she was sure they would win.

They arrived two days before the race, to give the roan time to rest. Gorham had registered the horse for the first available chase of the season; he wouldn't be eligible to enter any of the important races until he had won at least one. It was at Sendat, farther north, in Central Domain.

Maude, Gorham's fancy woman, came too. It was the only thing Bramble didn't like about Gorham, the fact that he kept a fancy woman. Not that he tried to hide it—the whole town knew. But having dealt with Osyth, Bramble was a little more forgiving of Gorham than she would have been otherwise.

Maude came up to Bramble at the beginning of the journey to Sendat and said that she had no mind to let Gorham go off on his own. "Not 'cause I'm suspicious-minded, like, lass," she said cheerily. "I just like the outing."

Bramble smiled at her; no one could help liking Maude, who carried her generous nature on her face as clearly as Osyth carried her miserliness. *Still*, Bramble thought, *I wouldn't put up with it. No man of mine would go off with a fancy woman and have me still there to come home to.*

They stayed in a comfortable inn in the center of town. The rooms were bright and smelled of lemon, but Bramble intended sleeping in the stable. In the afternoon she walked through the town to the chase fields. Sendat nestled under a tall hill, topped, as usual, by the local warlord's fort. At the base of the hill, where the smell wouldn't offend those in the fort, was the execution place. Instead of just one gibbet, this warlord had set up three, next to the scaffold and rock press. They were all full, and the bodies, only a few days old, showed the obvious marks of torture: burns, broken bones, scars that hadn't had time to heal. Bramble wondered if the warlord was using the spring chase to make a point; the gibbets were eloquent of power and control.

The warlord was called Thegan, the same name as Acton's son. No one was sure if it was his proper name or one he had assumed. Thegan was a new warlord, from the cold north, and he had married, a local told them, the old warlord's daughter, the Lady Sorn, and taken control. He still kept his old Domain in the north, which a son from an earlier marriage was overseeing for him. That was unusual. Bramble wondered whether the other warlords were happy about it, or if the long peace that had kept the Domains prosperous in recent years was at risk.

The waitress who told them about Thegan spoke with a mixture of admiration and circumspection, careful not to criticize him directly. That and the gibbets told Bramble all she wanted to know about him. She and Gorham had trained all the old warlord's horses, but she suspected they would look elsewhere for custom in the future. She felt vaguely sorry for the girl the warlord had married so conveniently, but her thoughts soon returned to the chase ahead.

Most Kills were experienced chase riders, and it was considered an honor if the warlord or town council asked you to set the course. The Kill could take any route he chose within set boundaries, any combination of fences, any direction, doubling back or straight ahead. Some Kills waited until the chase itself to decide their course, letting whim take over, while others planned obsessively, in secret, to make their course the most challenging.

Aside from the spectacle, the chase was now used mostly as a means of identifying good bloodlines for the warlords' messenger horses, and for gambling. The first Spring Kill was always the youngest person possible, for luck, to represent the new-born earth. And maybe, Bramble thought, always suspicious, to give the riders the best chance of catching the Kill and having a Kill Reborn, bringing luck to the town. But perhaps not. The Kill Reborn was the stuff of fire talk and bedtime tales; it hadn't happened for over thirty years.

The first Spring Chase was often dangerous, as a young, inexperienced Kill could choose the route badly, pick fences that were fine for one riding alone but death traps for three or four horses jumping at once.

She tried to plot all the potential courses, but it was impossible. She decided to follow her instinct: take the roan to the front immediately and stay there. She was certain in her bones that he would be faster than any of the others, and he was used to jumping alone. Staying in front would protect her from the underhanded tactics of the more experienced riders. She was not a cunning person, but she was determined to be very good at winning.

By the morning of the chase she was anxious past eating, almost past talking. The fog still surrounded her and she wanted the chase—the jumps, the speed, the danger—to bring her back to life again, at least for the duration of the race. Gorham counseled her on strategy over breakfast, while she saddled up, while they walked to the starting point. She nodded and didn't hear anything he said. The only thing she was aware of was the roan at her shoulder. She smiled at Maude and Gorham and then went to collect her neckerchief. It was bright blue: a good color, a lucky color.

She tied it on and swung herself up in the saddle as the other riders did the same, jostling and swearing at each other. They eyed her sideways. Women rode often enough in the chases, but none of them had seen this one before, looking like a Traveler with her black hair and eyes. Wasn't strong enough, most of them thought, not enough muscle, not enough guts, most likely, though her horse looked fit enough... too strong for a girl. Some noticed the set of her mouth and felt a momentary doubt, but pushed it aside to concentrate on their own mounts, fresh and restive, eager to race.

The Kill was a young man—very young, very fair—wearing the warlord's colors of brown and gold. He was pale with excitement and shifted his grip on the lance as his hands sweated. "Ride!" the counter shouted, and the Kill set off. "One, two, three... "

Bramble felt the fog lift, the glass clear. The riders counted with him, still jostling for position. Bramble found herself being edged to the back and shouldered the roan forward until she could see the Kill over another horse's head. She counted under her breath, tapping it out with one finger on the roan's neck. They had practiced this, too, the roan growing more and more eager to move as the taps continued. At "forty-nine" she flicked him hard and at "fifty" he was springing ahead, sliding through the gap in front to be among the first group away.

They headed downhill in a helter-skelter flurry of hooves and shouts. Bramble pressed the roan, fixed her eyes on the Kill ahead, and blocked out everything else. The horse was enjoying himself, his ears pricked and muscles springy, having a wonderful time. Bramble laughed under her breath and leaned forward into the first jump.

It was post and rails: easy for all the horses and reassuring to start with. One fell, all the same, at the back. There was a rise up to the second fence and some of the horses slipped back from the first group. Bramble found herself one of three: a chestnut mare on one side, and a dapple gray on the other.

They cleared the low stone fence with equal ease and curved to follow the Kill together. He was over a stream and heading for a high stone wall. They surged forward, increasing the pace on the flat. The chestnut misjudged the width of the stream and landed in the water. She splashed out but had lost time, so the gray and Bramble were now ahead.

There was a good distance to the wall, and the gray began to edge forward. Bramble didn't even have time to react: the roan surged ahead. She could feel his determination not to be beaten, and his pleasure at leaving the other horse behind.

They were a length ahead at the stone fence and two lengths ahead when they landed. The roan was a marvel, taking off at the perfect moment, and landing with a spring that got them straight back to racing speed. Bramble laughed again and set her eyes on the Kill.

There were two more fences. She and the roan took them alone, just as she had imagined. She was exultant, and so was he. They could both hear the hooves behind them, but nothing could catch them. The practice gallops had been nothing, a canter in comparison. *No one has ever been so fast,* she thought. She could feel the presence of the gods, but only faintly, as though not even they could keep up.

As the Kill labored up the last hill to the finish point, she and the roan flashed past him. The gods had finally caught up. She could feel their presence—the pressure of their attention—just as she had when they leaped the chasm. She reached out and plucked the lance from the Kill's hand, laughing aloud and ignoring the gasps from the crowd at the finish. She waved the lance with its red scarf above her head; she was fully alive again, the fog had gone completely, and she heard the crowd laugh and cheer with her, felt the gods themselves exult.

The roan reared in reaction to the crowd's cheers, the scarf swept out on the breeze, and Bramble was, for a moment, a heraldic figure, the crest for some great warlord: the Kill Reborn.

ASH

DORONIT KEPT Ash busy, training him in the use of poisons. He didn't like the catalog of symptoms, which was gruesome yet compelling.

"Why do I have to know all this?" he protested. "I don't want to poison people."

She smiled at him condescendingly so that again he felt like a child. He was so easy to read, so easy to manipulate; it exhilarated her like a sweet wine. Leading him, step by step, into intrigue and sophistication had become as much her favorite hobby as a way of crafting a useful tool.

"Of course you don't, sweetheart," she said, keeping her voice steady and warm, as to a child. "But others may want to poison you. You need to know what to look for, what to smell for; you need to recognize the effects. With the slower-acting venoms, it's possible to save yourself if you realize what's happened early enough. Come, don't be foolish."

Looking very foolish and rather adorable, he sat down next to her at the workbench in her cellar and examined the herbs she had spread out in front of him.

"Lily of the valley," she said, touching the leaves and red berries. "Yellow leaves are the strongest. They must be kept thoroughly dry, otherwise they grow moldy and lose their strength. This stops the heart, like foxglove. Some use it as a medicine."

And so she went on: meadow saffron, celandine, white hellebore, mistletoe, and rarer plants like yellow pheasant's eye and blackthorn.

"Now with rue," she said, "most use the leaves, but I've found that the stems are just as potent—" She pretended to catch herself up on that and looked at him to see if he had been paying attention. She had to ease him in with nothing too shocking, nothing he would think *unforgivable*. "Not for poison, of course, sweetheart. But... well, you're old enough to know the truth of it, yes? When a young woman wishes to be rid of a child in the womb, perhaps she might come to me, or to another herbalist, and we might give her an infusion of rue. You understand? It's dangerous for her, and certainly uncomfortable, but for some girls it's worth the risk."

It sounded plausible and, if he checked with a herbalist, he would find that rue was used in just such a way. She saw the momentary wariness in his eyes, shifted nearer to him, and laid her hand over his. "What, are you shocked after all, sweetheart? Didn't your roving parents teach you the truth about life? Or didn't they believe in forcing miscarriages?"

He stood up and pulled his hand away, stung. "If they had, I wouldn't be here," he said. "My mother told me that once. She tried to convince my father that it wouldn't be good for them to be burdened with a child, but he said they had to accept the consequences of their actions."

"So, they didn't want you. More fool them." Doronit's heart sped up with excitement. That was it, the cord that would bind him to her: being wanted. Being valued. Belonging. She'd suspected it before, but now she was sure. She stood next to him and slid her hand through his arm so he could feel her breast against his elbow. "I know how to value you," she said. "And you belong to me, now."

Ash swallowed down the lump in his throat. It was true. He did belong to her. Who else would want him? He was no good for anything, everyone knew it. Except Doronit. Doronit had taken him from his parents gladly.

"I won't let you down," he said, and for the first time dared to put his arm around her.

"I know you won't," she said. She stroked his cheek kindly then pulled away and sat back down at the bench. "Now, arnica," she said briskly, leaving him standing there feeling foolish, once again. "It's often used because there's no suspicion if someone finds it in your pack. It's used for so many other things . . ."

The training went on through the shortening autumn days and the chilling nights. Ash was earning money for her now, as a safeguarder at Merchant House functions, but some part of each day was still given over to training: concocting poisons, or their antidotes, singlestave and knife-throwing practice, hand-to-hand fighting, the system of whistles by which all of Doronit's people communicated (oddly enough, he could whistle those two-note signals easily, although he couldn't sing the same notes), and numbers and tallying.

"Never let a client cheat you," Doronit said as she showed him how to use a slate and chalk. "The only way to protect yourself is to be as fast with numbers as they are."

Ash put all thoughts of killing away from him. He was a safeguarder. It was a respectable profession, not important, perhaps, but respectable. He began to spend more time away from the house. Aylmer took him to taverns where the mead was strong and the music loud, and he met young men working for other guardhouses. One of them was Dufe, the safeguarder who had parted ways with Doronit the year before Ash had arrived in Turvite.

Dufe was a swarthy southerner with bright brown eyes and beautiful hands. Sitting next to him in the smoky din of the tavern, Ash noticed the same heart-thumping confusion he felt when Doronit touched him, especially when Dufe leaned across him to take a mug of mead from the waitress, and rested a hand on his thigh as he did so.

Dufe grinned at Ash's flushed face. "How old are you, young one?" he asked.

"Just turned twenty."

"You look younger. Doronit likes to get them young, doesn't she? The younger the better. She's got no morals at all, that woman."

Ash bridled instantly, his hand going to his dagger.

Dufe laughed at him and lifted his hands. "No, no, I won't fight you over that. She's the perfect woman, if you want to think so." He stood up and drained off his mug. His hand dropped on Ash's shoulder and he bent over. "A word of advice. Have a bit of fun away from the old woman. Find a nice young one like yourself. Doronit will eat your heart out bit by bit, and she'll do it so sly you won't even feel it going."

His grip on Ash's shoulder tightened, then he was gone. Aylmer turned back from the waitress he had been talking to and grinned at him. "Dufe gone? Oh, well, he's got a nice warm wife to go home to. Not that he does that often. He's one that likes to taste life."

"Mmmm." Ash wasn't sure whether to be angry or worried by Dufe's words. He shook them off and ordered another mead.

"Dufe's got a good heart," Aylmer said cheerfully. "That's why he and Doronit never got on. He was already fully trained when he came up from the south. She took him on, but he only lasted a month. He sets strict rules for himself...except when it comes to shagging." He chuckled. "The stories I could tell you about that man!"

Ash walked home alone. Aylmer had gone upstairs with the waitress. Ash didn't know if he envied him or not. In the quiet darkness the ghosts stood out more strongly than ever: pale forms clustering near doorways, or walking aimlessly through the night. They nodded to him as he passed, and he nodded back. They seemed as solid as he was. Perhaps they were. Perhaps he was as insubstantial. Perhaps nothing was as it seemed, Doronit included.

On Midwinter's Eve the Turviters shuttered the windows, set covers over the lamps and screens around the fires, so the bright colors of their walls were doused, and sat in pitch darkness, practicing for death. The youngest person in the house, and the oldest, recited together the Midwinter Prophecy, and then the door was set open to the ghosts. The ghosts entered where they pleased. And when they pleased, they set their hand on a man's head here, a woman's there, pointing out the people marked by illness who were to die before the next Midwinter's Eve. They did not always choose to enter.

"It's considered a blessing," Doronit explained to Ash. "It gives the person the chance to put their affairs in order, to say their goodbyes. The ghosts only do it for the people they like."

He looked around the empty room. "They don't come in here?"

She laughed shortly. "Not willingly. Come."

She led him out into the night. The streets were emptier than he had ever seen them.

"Why do the ghosts stay, Doronit?" He had wondered that for a long time.

"Because they're angry at being killed and their killers have not offered reparation. Because they don't want to leave the people they love. Because they owe a debt. Because they're afraid of the dark beyond the grave—as they should be."

"But beyond death is life again." That was what his parents had taught him.

"So *you* think. But who knows for truth? Perhaps there is nothing. Perhaps the spirit...shreds itself against death until there is nothing left."

"Is that what you believe?"

A person who believed that, he thought, would have no reason to live well. There would be no reason for honor or pity or generosity, which, his parents had taught him, were the qualities necessary for rebirth. "These are the things that work against the dark," his mother had said. "These are the only things that can pierce the dark beyond the grave and lead the spirit through to new life."

Doronit stopped. "I think not about it."

She had led the way to the open space where the black rock waited beneath its oak tree. It was the sacred place where, it was said, the gods of Turvite had once lived, before Acton came and drove them all away. Ash knew better. Although nothing called him by name, as it had last time he was there, he could feel the power in the stone beckoning.

They waited. The wind was biting. He felt his nose turning blue with cold. He rubbed it with gloved fingers. Doronit stood still. Gradually, the ghosts came, answering the call. One by one they left the houses and slid into the streets, all of them drawn to the same place.

"They come to greet the dawn at the old holy place," Doronit said quietly. "This will be the last night for those who have paid their debts."

"By giving warning of death?"

"What else can the dead do for the living?"

He thought of the girl he had killed. She had warned him, too, though not of simple death: "Death of the soul," Martine had said.

The ghosts swirled and eddied around the gods' stone. Doronit pointed to one, then another. "*Speak,*" she urged. "Tell me your secrets."

They spoke, reluctantly, one by one, some with sorrow, and some with hatred. They told her all they knew: the silly secrets, of first love and small vanities, and the deep secrets, their own and others'. They spoke of betrayal and murder and heartbreak, of violence, of fraud and lechery, greed and lies, domestic tyrannies and harsh cruelties.

Ash listened. Initially, as Doronit had commanded the first ghost to speak, he had felt elated: at last he knew someone like him, who could not only see ghosts, but compel them to talk. He wasn't a freak after all. But as he heard the stories that Doronit extracted from them, he started feeling ill. Stories flowed out of them of calumny, of rape behind closed doors, of small bribes and large corruption. The ordinary stories were the worst. They filled him so that he was close to tears; they were so full of love and grief, hatred and joy, the secrets of the heart. To listen made him ashamed. But still he listened. Doronit had brought him here for a reason and he needed to know what it was.

He thought of Dufe's scathing remark: "She's got no morals at all..." Was this moral? Was it wrong? Did the dead have the right to keep their secrets? They couldn't be hurt, could they? He tried to convince himself that they were hurting no one, but it was difficult to believe, looking at their faces and seeing how they hated giving up their secrets. Perhaps taking secrets to the grave was the only power the dead had, and Doronit was taking it away.

Doronit's voice was growing weaker. He realized that she was exerting her will as well as her voice, that it was her strength that was forcing the ghosts' revelations. She leaned against him for support as it continued. Finally, with still twenty or more of the spirits left to speak, she shook her head.

"That's it for me," she said. "Your turn, Ash."

He stared at her, incredulous. "Me?"

"Of course, sweetheart. That's why I brought you. Did you think I didn't know? After Ghost Begone Night? Half the ghosts in the city told me your name."

"I can't —"

"*Can't?*" she said. "What do you think I've trained you for?" She straightened. He could only see her face in the faint light reflected from the spirits, but he knew she was angry. "Why do you think I took you from your fools of parents, who couldn't see what they had in their hands? Why have I housed you and fed and—yes—*loved* you all this time? For *this,* stupid one. And now you say you can't?"

"I..." *She loves me, she says she loves me.* "But —"

She changed tone. "Sweetheart, sweetheart. This is why I'm successful, why I can charge the prices I do. Why the town clerk smiles at me in the street. I know *everything*. I could misuse this knowledge, but I don't. I don't blackmail anyone—I don't reveal any of these secrets. But for my own protection, and for yours, Aylmer's, Hildie's, and all the rest—I must know. I'm exhausted, I have no more strength. I need your help. Now."

He hesitated still.

She drew a breath. He wasn't as well trained as she had thought, but he could still be brought to heel.

"Of course," she said slowly, "if you don't do this, you're worthless to me. I have half a dozen who are better with the knife and singlestave. I'm fond of you, sweetheart, but I can't afford you if you don't earn your keep."

She saw the threat sweep through him, turning him cold. He pictured himself on the streets. He couldn't go back to his parents. He had thought he was doing well with the knife and the stave, but what did he know? Without her...

"*Speak,*" he said, and listened while his guts roiled with shame.

Ash sat on the side of his bed, his hands dangling over his knees. *My room,* he thought, *the first I've ever had. My bed.* He looked around. A cupboard, with several changes of clothing carefully folded, warm red blankets, a lantern on the table, an earthenware jug and mug, two pairs of boots and a pair of evening shoes... All his. The brick walls were painted sea green with a blue trim. The shutters were solid and fit tightly. Even on this midwinter night, it was not freezingly cold. The room glowed. It felt like home.

He thought about being outside, homeless, deserted, and began to shiver. After all, he reasoned, the ghosts were dead. She wasn't hurting them. And Doronit had said that she never used the information for ill. He clung to that even while he knew it was a lie and that she would use her knowledge any way she could, and all for her own good. But he didn't allow himself to think about it, any more than he let himself think about the Deep, or the demons there. He refused to think about how the demons would judge Doronit. This was his home, Doronit was all the family he had; he had to trust her.

He slept badly that night, but in the morning he got up and went to singlestave practice as usual, and smiled at Doronit afterward, while they shared breakfast.

Doronit was very loving to him for days afterward. More, she began to include him in business meetings with Merchant House, with sea captains who wanted protection for their goods heading for Mitchen and Carlion, with the owner of the Sailor's Rest who had been having trouble with some fishers from Foreverfroze, here to sell a cargo of seal fur and whitefish oil.

Aylmer clouted him on the shoulder and congratulated him the first time he negotiated a deal himself, with Doronit just smiling on.

"So you're the heir, then, eh?" Aylmer grinned over the singlestave, trying to distract him with talk. "She's grooming you to take over, youngling. You'll be worth a warlord's ransom."

Aylmer hit a glancing blow and then doubled it back fast to test his guard.

Ash parried it easily, grinned back and changed from shield to spear, trying to poke Aylmer in the stomach. "I'll be your boss!"

"Yes, sir, no, sir, whatever you say, sir." Aylmer backed out of stave reach and pretended to bow and scrape. "Well, I don't know why she's chosen you, lad, but I suppose you do?"

Ash blushed. It was true, he did know; the memory of Midwinter's Eve was still sharp in his mind, still brought a wave of nausea.

"No need to be embarrassed, lad." Aylmer chuckled. "She's not to my taste, but I can see you're sharper than I ever was—a bit of shagging here and there is a small price to pay for a good business."

Ash grinned halfheartedly. It would be easier to live with himself if Aylmer was right. But Doronit never touched him, except the occasional pat on the cheek or hand sliding down his arm. He had realized, after Midwinter's Eve, that she did it deliberately, to throw him off balance. But that didn't stop him stammering, or the hot wave of desire that swept over him.

He fed the memory of those moments into an attack on Aylmer: thrust, shield, sweep, spear, parry. He vented all his frustration and pushed his desire into the stave, and for the first time he beat Aylmer back. He rallied quickly but it wasn't enough. They ranged over the practice room, sweating and heaving, with no thought now for anything but the staves and each other's movement. Ash came forward with a step he'd only practiced alone, and took Aylmer by surprise on the back foot, swept his legs out from under him and had Aylmer with the stave at his throat.

"Hah!" Ash shouted, and his opponent threw his stave down in surrender. Ash was jubilant. It was the first time he had defeated any of the older safeguarders, and Aylmer was acknowledged as being very good with the stave.

Alymer grinned, but rubbed his back as he got up. "Trying to make me feel old, boy?" He looked at Ash with fresh interest. He'd always been fast at singlestave but he'd never shown the right mix of aggression and composure that made for a formidable opponent. That had changed; the diffident young man had vanished. Maybe becoming Doronit's chosen heir had given him confidence, Aylmer thought, or maybe he was just growing into himself, as boys often did around that age. It had made Aylmer feel the creeping touch of age. He was old enough to be Ash's father, and he winced as he bent over to pick up his stave.

"Come to the tavern," Ash said, bouncing on his toes, energy undiminished. "I'm buying."

As they walked out into the spring day, into the hawkers' cries and the rumble of carts, into the clamorous bargaining at the market, into the smells and sounds and life of Turvite, Ash felt his heart expanding. He did love this city, loved its energy and its venality, too, the way its citizens were sharp and generous at the same time, openhanded with food or drink, but otherwise kept track of every copper. He loved the sense of being part of something larger, of having his own role to play in the city's life, of sharing fellow feeling with every other inhabitant. He might not have had much to call his own, but he was a Turviter.

He bounded into the tavern and bought Aylmer a tankard of mead, not ale. "You want to get me drunk, boy?" Aylmer protested.

Ash just laughed. "Why not? It's the end of the working day, why shouldn't we get drunk?"

And later he went upstairs with one of the waitresses, the tall blond, buxom one (the one least like Doronit). He was too drunk to do much more than roll in the sheets with her laughing. But they slept, and when they woke up they laughed some more, and sighed, then shagged with satisfying energy until dawn.

He went home in the early morning light and let himself into the house quietly, but not quietly enough. As he walked down the hall, Doronit appeared at the door to her room and just stood there, looking at him. He forced himself to stand still, not to blush or stammer out excuses. She lifted an eyebrow at him and suddenly grinned; it was a real smile, unlike any he'd had from her before. He grinned back.

"I'll be calling you the same time as usual," she said. "You might be better off not going to sleep at all." She disappeared into her room.

He took her advice, his heart lighter, not just because of the night with the waitress, but because he had stood his ground with Doronit for the first time and her smile had acknowledged it. Perhaps he could work his way to some kind of equality with her.

SAKER

SAKER RETURNED to the house he had inherited from the enchanter, in Whitehaven, in the Far South Domain, and finally finished his map. Every massacre site was marked in red, not in blood—as Saker felt would have been appropriate—but at least in red. Every smaller battle site, where fewer than twenty had been killed, was marked in orange. The few individual murders he had managed to track down were marked in yellow. He had to use saffron for that, but it had been worth it. Every death, every desecration, would be remembered.

His walls were covered with scrolls: every account of the invasion still in existence, plus his own notes. It had taken Saker fifteen years to gather them all, once his reason for living had become clear to him. But they hadn't been enough. Only Rowan's songs had allowed him to complete his map. From their words—and from what they did not say—he had colored the Domains to show exactly where Acton's people had killed.

The colors followed the main rivers and the coastline, leaving empty spaces inland. He didn't know what to do about those empty spaces. They weren't empty any longer. In a thousand years Acton's people had spread right across the land, cutting down the forests that his people had left in peace, spreading anywhere there was a stream or a place to dig a well. There were no deaths to be avenged in those empty spaces, but the people living there had benefited from all the other deaths, all the red and orange and yellow. After an hour's brooding over the map, Saker delicately shaded those parts a pale green, for the death of trees. Perhaps the ghosts of the forests would come to join his army. Who could tell? These days he knew that anything was possible.

It was time to try the spell again. There had been something missing, but his Sight knew that it was only a small thing, a twist on what he was already doing... He went over to the cloth-shrouded box near his window and folded back the purple cover. The words of the spell weren't hard, but the concentration required was enormous. He shut out the sounds of the street below, the noise of pots being washed in the kitchen of the house next door, the intensity of his own heartbeat and breathing. Only the bones remained, with their faint earthy scent. He held the knife ready against his palm and made the cut without blinking.

His blood dripped onto the bones as he said the words of the spell, and he felt his heart swell with pain and love as his father's ghost rose before him, looking just as he had twenty-five years ago, in the moment before the warlord's axe had taken him. Saker had been five then. He took in the apparition: broad-shouldered but not tall, dark hair and eyes now pale; his strong, beloved face disfigured by the head wound that had killed him.

His father smiled at him, then raised an eyebrow questioningly.

Saker pointed to the map. "It's finished," he said.

His father moved slowly over to the table and looked down. He pointed to the green areas and looked at Saker.

"The death of trees," Saker explained.

His father nodded. He let his hand trace the contours of the Western Mountains, up to the foothills where their village, Cliffhaven, had been—and still was. He motioned as though to tap the table at that point.

Saker nodded. "I know," he said. "But not yet. We must try somewhere else first."

His father frowned and tapped the table impatiently, although the tip of his finger went straight through.

Saker felt the familiar lurch in his stomach, the desire to please his father tightening his guts. He hardened himself against it. "Soon," he promised. "I don't have enough blood for all the ghosts in Cliffhaven. We have to find a way to share the blood out without killing the spellcaster. We'll try somewhere else first."

His father still frowned.

"We're very close," Saker said. "I promise."

Then his father smiled and made as if to embrace him. Saker said the last few words of the spell, the words he had saved for this moment. His father's arms came around him and he moved happily into the firm hug, feeling his father's hands on his back, the shoulder under his cheek. He closed his eyes and surrendered to being a little boy again, when everything was all right.

The spell faded too soon. Saker covered the dry bones and wiped away his tears. He had to find a way to make it last, and not just for his father, but his sisters and cousins, and all his family. His mother's bones were beyond recovery, but he could call up everyone else...the entire village. And then they would take back what was theirs. Every bit of it.

ASH

AT THE vernal equinox, Doronit took Ash out to the cliffs beyond the harbor, where he had met and scattered the ghosts on festival night. It was a windy, damp night, with thin clouds covering a sickle moon, and the waves below thumping against the rocks.

She stood on the edge of the cliff and told him to stand behind her. Then she whistled.

The melody was a simple one: five notes repeated over and over in a minor key. Ash waited. Nothing happened.

Doronit kept whistling, on and on. He began to feel dizzy, as though he could lean against the wind and into the notes of the tune as he might lean against a breaking wave. He felt light-headed and heavy-hearted, sorrowful, almost, distant from his own body, yet sharply aware of the ground beneath his feet. Perhaps she had drugged him.

"Whistle," she said, and dug him in the ribs. He stumbled, almost sending them both over the cliff, but she pulled him back and shook him a little. Then she turned him to face outward over the water. "*Whistle!*"

He picked up the tune from her. Standing there, listening, the notes had wound themselves into his brain so tight he wondered if he'd never get them out. It was the first time in his life he'd ever managed to reproduce a tune. He was making music for the first time! He whistled enthusiastically, and she relaxed, satisfied.

Then he saw the wind wraiths coming, flying across the scudding clouds toward them.

He had seen water sprites once, dancing on a waterfall in the high mountains west of Circ. The wind wraiths were like them: sharp features, long fingers and claws, slitted eyes with no pupils, just all black, and hair that waved back from their smooth faces like seaweed under water. But where the water sprites were emerald and silver and blue, the wind wraiths were cloudy white and gray, half transparent, and as much sound as sight, rushing, wuthering, until the back of his head had a line down the middle where it felt like it was going to split open. There were only three wraiths, but they seemed to be everywhere.

"Greetings at the Turn of the Year, People of the Air," Doronit said.

Ash whistled. One of the wraiths slithered past him, beading his arm with moisture and bringing him up in goose bumps.

It faced Doronit, no more than a foot away. "Again, woman?" Its voice was like steam shrilling from a kettle. It pierced his ears.

"Again, honored ones. What news?"

"No news for our enemies." It smiled. Its teeth were square and blunt.

"I am thy friend," Doronit said. "I bring news. Two ships, but a day out from Turvite, bound for the islands. Two *old* ships."

The wraith moistened its lips and slid a finger down her cheek.

She flinched, but stood firm, looking straight into its eyes.

Ash's whistle slowed.

The wraith smiled and set one clawed finger at the corner of Doronit's mouth.

He whistled faster, back to the correct tempo, and the finger was withdrawn. His heart was pounding as though he were running. His mouth was drying out.

"What news for me, friend?" Doronit whispered.

"So sad, so sad..." The wraith smiled. "The *White Hind* gone in a late gale, the *Sunrise* lost its cargo, all jettisoned. The *Cloven Hoof* foundered, all hands dead. The sea is eating woven wool and fine timber, alum and indigo. It will be bluer than ever this summer."

"Ridiculous name for a ship, anyway," Doronit said. "My thanks, honored one."

The other wraiths gathered closer.

The wraith reached for Ash, to pull him over the cliff. Doronit hauled him back. He kept whistling.

"Our payment, friend," it said.

"Not this one. Not this year. I've given you two ships. That should be enough. North and southwest they're riding, with red sails."

The wraiths surrounded Ash, sliding against his skin, trying to disrupt the rhythm of the tune.

"Enough!" Doronit said. "Come, Ash." She pulled him away, walking backward to keep her face toward the cliffs and the wraiths.

"Fondness is foolishness," the wraith whispered to her, but she ignored it and began whistling.

It was a different tune, the same five notes, but in a different order. Ash couldn't stop whistling his own melody until she put a cold hand over his mouth. In an instant they shrieked away, like tattered cloaks streaming across the sky.

She waited for his questions as they walked back to town, but he said nothing. He was thinking about her words, "Not this year." So she had paid them in other years. But what coin had she paid in? Who had gone up with her to the cliffs last year?

That night in his dreams she turned into a wind wraith at the moment of climax, but even as a wraith she was beautiful, and he surrendered his throat to her claws in a kind of ecstasy. He woke, sweating, and lay in the dark, ashamed, but not knowing what he was most ashamed of—helping her with the wraiths, or being drawn to her even if she had a wraith's heart. Because if she had appeared at the doorway to his room at that moment he would have been filled with a fierce desire. He couldn't imagine being without her.

The next day Doronit paid a visit to the merchants who dealt in wool, and purchased a great deal of blue cloth: the blue that only merchants and their servants could wear. She bought up all the blue cloth in the city. A rumor spread that she intended to fit out all her safeguarders in blue tunics. Ash had started it, at her direction.

A week later news swept through port that Beasle's two ships, the *High Flag* and the *Winged Flag*, were lost with all hands and cargo in an unseasonable storm.

The following day Beasle visited Doronit, and that afternoon Doronit gave Ash silver for new spring clothes. When he went to show her what he'd bought, he saw there was a small coffer in her room, which had not been there the day before: a beautiful, painted coffer with very strong locks.

"How many people were on Beasle's ships?" he asked.

"I don't know. Twenty? Forty?"

"How much were they insured for?"

She smiled. "Quite a lot."

"And was there really as much cargo aboard as the insurers were told?"

She laughed. "Very good. Very good. You're doing fine. Now what have you bought for the Merchants' Banquet?"

The sailors were dead. There was no proof: the ships were old and there had been a storm. There was no doubt about the storm. Perhaps the ships would have sunk anyway. Perhaps the storm would have happened without Doronit. There was nothing he could do. Nowhere he wanted to go. Nowhere he *could* go.

The news of the *Cloven Hoof*'s sinking became known. Doronit "reconsidered" her decision to have tunics made for her staff, and resold half of her blue fabric to the wool merchants at double the price. The other half she kept: "On Ghost Begone Night the merchants give their servants their new livery for the year, so they look smart for the festival. The price will triple before then."

The year turned. The fishing boats at harbor began to stink in the sun. Ash ran and trained all through the summer heat as he had through the winter cold. "The weather won't abate itself because you're uncomfortable," Doronit had said. "What use is a safeguarder who has to sit down in the shade?"

On a gray, airless day in early autumn, before the first chill had come to break the summer stew, he loped into the courtyard with sweat running down his whole body, and found her waiting for him with a cool drink and a towel.

"What's happened?" he asked.

She smiled sideways at him. "Twelve months ago you wouldn't have asked anything. You would have blushed and smiled at me. Come."

She led the way into her room. He toweled off as he went and gulped down the juice.

Her room was cool and calm. Conscious of his sweat, he sat on the edge of the window seat, with his elbows on his knees. She sat next to him.

"We have a problem. I...have an enemy."

She pulled a twist of yellow paper from her pocket: a sweetmeat pouch, with balls of dried apricot and shredded nut meat. They were her favorites, from Perle, the confectioner.

"Smell them."

She held the paper under his nose, and he sniffed. Apricot, nut, honey...something else, faint and sharp, like almonds...

"Bitter almond," he said, shocked. "Not Perle?"

"No, no. I bought these yesterday, had some. I was fine, no? I left them here, on the little table. Today I saw three people here—Aylmer, Eral, from the Merchant Guild, and the stonecaster."

"Martine?"

"After she was gone I went to take a sweet. Something was...not right. I don't know. Perhaps the paper was twisted differently. I was careful. I smelled the poison."

"So Eral?"

"No, why would he? We do good trade together. Ten years, no problems. And Aylmer is loyal."

"Yes...yes, he is. But why would Martine—?"

"She came to warn me against Ranny, to tell me not to go into business with her. 'For your own good,' she said. She hates Ranny, everyone knows that."

"Aylmer said it was Ranny who hated Martine."

"Why not? It's natural to hate someone who hates you. But Martine has always hated Ranny and all her house. Why else would she tell her that she knew the date of her death and then tell her no more? That is something one would do only to an enemy. Place death in her mind, with no relief from wondering."

"I don't—"

"You like her. But she is dangerous."

He remembered Martine's knife in the boy's shoulder, her calm face as she stepped over two corpses bleeding on her own rug.

"Yes, but—"

"She tried to kill me." Doronit's voice was sharp.

Underneath his confusion and the shock of Doronit's near escape, he was skeptical about Martine being the culprit. It was hard to believe.

Doronit had a plan. She would ask to see Martine secretly, for a private reading. She would emphasize the need for confidentiality, say that she was coming alone. Ash would wait outside.

"If she wants me dead, she will try to take the opportunity. If she bears no ill will, I will have a reading and we will turn our eyes elsewhere."

There was a storm brewing, the first of the autumn storms. The Turviters were indoors, waiting for the deluge. Only ghosts roamed the darkened streets, glancing furtively at Doronit and Ash as they went past, melting backward into alleys and alcoves. He nodded at one or two, but they never took their eyes off Doronit. She ignored them.

There was a scurry of dead leaves and dust in circles at their feet. Lightning flashed in the distance.

"Hurry," Doronit said. "But stay back until she lets me in."

He hid in a doorway while Doronit approached Martine's door. The circle of ghosts around it drew back and Doronit went in.

Thunder clapped on the cliffs outside the city, and rumbled backward into the hills. Ash hesitated. Doronit wanted him to stay here, but if he went in the back way he'd be able to hear their conversation. Part of him, the remnant of the boy who had come to Turvite, resisted. Surely he could trust Doronit? But the part that remembered Midwinter's Eve and the ghosts' stolen secrets, the part that remembered the wind wraiths reaching for him on the cliffs, knew better.

He turned and ran for the back lane, jumped up over the bakery flour store, over the roof tiles, and across to Martine's roof. He slid his knife under the latch on the dormer window and dropped soundlessly to the floor. This was how the second assassin had got in. Martine should have nailed it shut.

He crept down the stairs. Murmuring came from the parlor. He froze in the dark as thunder crashed directly overhead. He heard a scuffle.

"Ash! To me! To me!"

He found them struggling with a knife, Doronit's skill almost matched by Martine's greater height and strength. He shouldered into both of them and sent them smashing to the floor. He picked up the knife.

"Kill her now!" Doronit said. "She tried to knife me. Slit her throat!"

The women stood up in a breath, glaring at each other. He was frozen, without words, almost without thought.

"Ash. Kill her now."

"She tried to kill you with this knife?" he asked, keeping a wary eye on Martine.

She stared back at him, her breath slowing. She said nothing, but stood a little straighter, less threateningly. She moved away from Doronit, toward the mantelpiece where Acton's brooch still lay.

"You saw!" Doronit said.

Ash was still watching Martine.

"Ash, sweetheart, I know you don't like killing, but sometimes it's necessary. Knowing when is what makes a good safeguarder. Someone I can trust. Someone I can keep with me. Forever."

It was more disguised than on Midwinter's Eve, but still a threat: do what I tell you or I will abandon you. Panic overtook him, just as it had then. He looked at the knife, at Martine, at the knife again.

"This," he said slowly, "is not her knife."

Doronit stared at him. "What?"

"This is not her knife. Her knife is white."

"Well, maybe she has two!"

"Maybe. Or maybe you set this up. How much is Ranny paying?"

For a moment she almost denied it. Then she laughed. "Ah, you have grown clever, no? Old enough now to be more than an apprentice. Ranny pays well—she pays *us* well, and more to come if we rid her of this thorn in her side."

Doronit was now standing close to him, her hand on his shoulder, her breath on his cheek: a moment of dizziness, of sweet closeness and belonging.

"She is nothing to us, Ash. Do it quickly and we will be gone."

For the first time he read desire for him in her eyes and realized that he would have to be a killer for her to want him.

Martine waited. He closed his eyes. Doronit's scent was around him: warmth, home...

He threw the knife to Martine, hilt first. "She says it's your knife. You'd better have it."

Doronit hissed. "You fool!" She swung at him, her ring scoring his cheek. "I would have made you my partner. My successor."

"Successor to fear and death," Martine said.

"Why not?" Doronit glanced at him. "Why should I care what happens to Acton's people? Why should you? The three of us are among the last of the old blood. Why should we care about the Turviters, who murdered our people and took our land and laughed at our ghosts? Why should I not make myself wealthy at their expense?"

After all the lies, he could still recognize the truth: she was driven by a long, twisted hatred. "So to revenge yourself on them, you try to kill Martine, one of the old blood?" He shook his head. "Your revenge has a mercenary tinge to it, I think."

For the first time, she was shaken. Her certainty quivered like wind on water. Then her mouth firmed. "I know enough to know that I can only look after myself. That is a lesson you will learn, boy, out on the Road with no skills and no guardian. You will remember. You will regret this."

She opened the door and walked into the slanting downpour. The wind blew in and rain drenched the rug.

Martine shut the door and put the knife down on the table, then took him by the arm and led him to the small fire. She built it up until the flame shadows danced on the ceiling.

He couldn't stop shaking. The sweat on his face was drying and it stretched his skin taut. There were raindrops hissing down the chimney and sputtering out. He noticed the smell of lavender, wood smoke, wet wool, cha, for the first time. Martine's long hair swung low as she stooped to the fire. She held a mug to his clenched teeth. Cha. The scent loosened his jaw and he sipped once, twice. She put the mug into his hands and he held it awkwardly.

Martine sat at his feet and cast the stones.

"Foresight. Liberation. Understanding. Pain," she said. "And the blank stone. That means anything may happen from now on."

DORONIT'S STORY

It's true my parents were Travelers by blood, but they were as settled as can be by nature. I was an only child, raised outside a small town way down past Turvite toward the Wind Cities. My father was a cowman for the biggest local farmer; my mother acted as evening dairymaid so the farmer's wife could get supper for her brood of children.

It was a happy childhood, I suppose, but a lonely one. None of the local children were allowed to play with me, the "Traveler brat." They threw stones but I learned to dodge them. I wasn't so skillful dodging the mud or the cow dung. If they'd come at me one by one I could have fought back, but they never did. I used to straggle home and just stand in the doorway until my mother saw me. She would get a look on her face. I thought, the first time it happened, that it was a look of exasperation with me, tempered with resignation at the work I made for her. I hung my head, but she chivvied me over to the fire and changed my clothes, speaking gently so I understood that it wasn't my fault, and cheered up.

Later my parents bought their own cow, and a few goats, and I had the keeping of them. I hated it, but what was the alternative?

The spring I was sixteen, I was walking down the lane toward our cottage, bringing watercress and some young nasturtium leaves from the stream nearby for supper. I was brooding over my life, the way you do when you're sixteen and think you're unhappy, and I didn't hear the horse come nosing up behind me until it was too late. I heard soft hoof noises on the gravel and then a snuffle and I turned, but the warlord's man was off the horse already and had hold of me a moment later. I knew him by sight and by reputation—violent, crazed almost, but one of the warlord's favorites. His name was Egbert, but they called him Fist. He was grinning at me.

What's the point of describing it? There aren't any words for the terror, the despair, the loneliness of it. He pushed me facedown into the spring mud until it was in my mouth and my nostrils, until I could hardly breathe, and took me from behind. Both passages. Grunting, "Traveler bitch, scum, whore, turd, filth..." And when he'd finished he got up, kicked me once in the ribs, got back on his horse, and rode off.

All I wanted to do was lie there and die. Then I started to vomit and I had to get up on my hands and knees to retch.

But you don't die, that's the worst of it: you have to stand up and stagger back home, walk in and see the look on your mother's face. I'll never forget her face that day. It was like the look she had given me each time I had come home covered in dung, but now I was old enough to read it. It wasn't just her immediate comprehension and the horror. There was a kind of humiliation, as well, and a giving in, a submission to our situation, to the position of Travelers in the Domains, an acceptance that nothing could be done, no justice could be expected. I knew in that instant that someone had once forced my mother facedown in the mud. Strangely, I was angrier about that long-ago violation than I was about my own, and that anger stayed with me and kept me from crying.

She stood for a moment, frozen, then came and cradled me and stripped me, and heated water and made it scalding hot, too, and made me sit in the bath, and drink the small amount of applejack my father kept behind the oats crock, and chew on some rue, while she washed my hair and my hands and crooned over me and urged me to cry, to let it out, let it go. I couldn't, though I wanted to, if only to make my mother feel better. I knew what she was trying to do, with the heat and the herbs and the liquor. But hot water and rue don't always work, and there wasn't enough applejack to make a squirrel sick, so three weeks later I knew I was pregnant.

"It's your own fault," my da said. "You shouldn't have been walking down that lane alone. You know that the warlord's men think Traveler girls are fair game."

"What's she supposed to do?" my mam said. "Never move out of doors?"

Her voice was gentle, though, and I couldn't be angry with him, either, for I'd seen him weep all the tears that I could not on the night it happened, standing, staring at the fire for hours, his hand clenching and unclenching, and that look on his face, too, the one that says: "I need to do something about this but there's nothing I can do that won't make it worse."

I hated the thought of the baby, of course, hated it with nausea and headaches and not eating, but it was a strong one and it clung onto life. Then one day I was out combing the goats for their fleece and I felt it move. I'd been dreading it, that moment, knowing it was coming, knowing I'd feel this product of rape inside me. I'd been waiting for it in horror. But when it came the touch was so soft. Tiny. Innocent. Completely innocent. How could I hate it?

My mam had said, "If you hate this child he will have ruined two lives." And I knelt in the straw of the goat shed and cried, remembering, accepting, coming to love. And I did love her, my darling, when she was born, loved her with all there was in me to love, my sweet-skinned, milk-scented, beautiful black-haired Larch, loved every bit of her from her fat wrists with the crease across them, to the incredible softness underneath her toes. Is there anything softer than feet that have never felt the hard ground? My parents loved her too; Da took a while, resenting her on my behalf, but when she held out her little hands to him and grinned, how could he resist?

So it went on for seventeen months, and the only change was that now the women in the market spat as I passed and said "Traveler whore" out of the sides of their mouths, even though my da had told the story abroad, and they all knew where the baby came from. I grew a shield on my heart, in that time. Inside were Mam and Da and Larch, outside were all of Acton's people, all the rest of the world. But it was only for protection, so I wouldn't care about the spitting and the curses. I didn't hate them, then.

In the early spring the warlord and his men raided the territory of the Wind Cities, in retaliation for raids they'd made on us the year before. It happened every year or so, and people had forgotten who had started it. I loved the spring raids—it meant all the warlord's men were away and I could go wherever I wanted to. It was the only time of year I was really free. But this year they brought back a fever with them, a plague they said was striking all the Wind Cities. Of course the warlord's men brought it back, but there was a Traveler family that had come to town from the north at the same time, a young tinker and his wife and twin baby boys, and the townsfolk blamed them for it. One of the babies had a fever, they said.

It went through the district faster than any other disease I've ever seen: whole families died in a couple of days. It was a swelling sickness, with great black boils under the arms and in the groin, and those who were stricken couldn't keep anything down. The district battened down and people huddled indoors, praying to the local gods (but when had they ever cared about humans?). We did the same, but it was too late. The farmer came down with it after an imprudent trip to market in the next town (he was hoping it hadn't reached there yet, but he was wrong). He came by on his way home to discuss the sale with my father. Da got sick two days later, and Mam that night. Then Larch.

I couldn't care for them all myself, but I tried. Larch didn't have it too badly, at first, and I hoped, gods, I hoped, that she would come through, as some had. Mam and Da needed more than I could do for them. They were bleeding at the gums, and the boils had started under their arms. It happened so fast. One hour I thought they'd be all right and the next they were screaming, begging for water, sweat pouring out of them as though they were water sprites hauled onto dry ground.

We got our water from the farmer's well, and I dared not leave them long enough to fetch it, but finally I had to. When I got to the farmyard, the gate was bolted shut against me. I put down the buckets and yoke to undo the bolts, and the farmer's wife appeared in the doorway, red-eyed, with a pitchfork in her hand.

"Get away from here, you Traveler bitch! It's 'cause of you and your kind that my man's dead and my children like to die! Get away from our well!"

I was aware of the fine summer morning, the sweet air, the chirp of starlings, a rustle in the grass...and the woman, staring at me with a hate that had always been in her, sleeping, until now. That was the moment I found out who I was and what I could do. I didn't care what she thought, or felt, or said, or did: I needed the water and I would take it across her dead body if I had to.

I climbed the gate, with her still screaming and waving the pitchfork, and opened it from the other side, picked up my buckets and moved to the well. She came at me with the fork. As if I'd practiced it all my life, as if I were one of the warlord's men, I stepped aside and hit her in the midriff with the bucket yoke. She folded up onto her knees and started to cry, but I ignored her. I filled the buckets, picked up the yoke and took the water back to my family.

By the time I got back Mam and Da were dead. I blamed the farmer's wife, and I still do, not for them dying, because they were bound for death, but for robbing me of their last moments, for making them die alone. If she hadn't bolted the gate it would have taken me only a few moments to fetch the water and maybe I'd have been back in time to ease their passing.

But my Larch was alive. She was hot, but she wasn't bleeding at the gums or pouring with sweat. It was the first stages. Sometimes, I'd heard, if the disease was caught early by the healer it could be eased—for those who didn't develop the pus-boils it was the fever that killed. I knew there were herbs that could lower fever. I didn't know what they were, except for feverfew, and we'd used all of that we had.

I decided to go to the healer in town. I carried her in, three miles and a bit, her body burning against mine, her little arms trying to hold on around my neck. Oh, that is the true feeling of motherhood, those little arms around your neck. I could feel her grip getting weaker and weaker and I hurried in response until I was running.

Every shop and house was barred and shuttered, even the healer's. I banged on the door and shouted for help until a window opened above me and the healer leaned out.

"What?" he said.

"My little one's just got the fever," I said. "No pus, no bleeding gums. Can't you help her? Bring the fever down so she's got a chance?"

"There's not enough herbs to go around for our own people," he said, and closed the shutter.

I thumped on the door again and again, but he ignored it. So I carried her back home, giving her as much water as I could along the way, and looking for feverfew beside the road, but there was none left anywhere. I took her out to the goat shed, away from the death inside the cottage, and I nursed her there. I bathed her body with cool water, spooned it into her mouth, and fanned her to keep her cool. But it was no use. She vomited the water up as soon as it went down, and the sweat started to stream off her as the sun went down.

If I'd had the herbs, help from a healer, she might have lived. Since then I've seen others live with fevers just as bad. She was dead before morning, in the still time when the tides of night change and the stars burn more brightly just before they begin to grow pale. She died with her little hand clutching at my shirt. When it loosened and fell away, it was like the world fell away too, or I fell from it, into darkness deeper than the sea.

I don't remember those first hours. My next memory is of standing next to the graves I had dug and filled in. The other dead of the town would lie in the burial caves, but I knew better than to ask that for Traveler scum.

It was getting on for sunset, three days after my parents had died. I hurried back to the cottage so I could be there when they quickened. I closed the shutters so I could see them better when they arrived. I'd always been able to see ghosts, like my da, but it didn't happen too often, apart from the ghost of the draper that haunted the well in the town square. I'd never been to a quickening, but my parents had described them to me. So I waited in the dark room, my heart beating fast, and they came. Their forms gathered on the beds where they had died, their faces still contorted with fever and thirst. Then they moved their heads, looking around, looking for me. I came forward and they saw me and smiled.

I'd thought my heart was numb, but it wasn't. It was full of heat and tears and acid. Yet I couldn't cry. "You are dead," I said.

Mam nodded, Da looked surprised, then saw Mam, misty and frail, and he sighed noiselessly. They reached hands toward each other and turned back to me. I couldn't cry. There was something I had to say.

"Look after Larch," I said.

Grief flowed into their faces and Mam reached out a hand to me. I felt for the first time the touch of a ghost on my cheek, that chill drift just under the skin. Then they faded.

A day later I sat in the goat shed and waited for my baby to come back to me. I made sure I was sitting in exactly the place I had been when she died. She came gently, her little body seeming to nestle into mine as it had so many times. She tried to clasp my shirt, but her hand passed right through. Then she sat up, surprised, and tried to touch my cheek, but her little hand slid through again. Then she got frightened and her face crumpled into silent tears.

"Oh no, little one, don't cry," I said, "please don't cry, talk to Mam instead."

"Mam," she said. "Want Mammy!" And she tried to grab hold of me and couldn't and cried out—"No!"—and her voice was the terrible voice of the dead, the stone-on-stone grating that the rock on the burial caves makes as it's rolled back. I'd just wanted to comfort her, to stop her soundless weeping. I didn't know then that it was possible to make ghosts speak. "Mam!" she cried, and reached for me again and then she faded.

I ran. I ran from the sound of that voice coming from my sweet girl's mouth, its emptiness and pain. I ran out of instinct to the forest, as though being hunted, until I was exhausted, until I could no longer hear the desolate voice, until I sank down and passed out.

I woke desperate for water and found a stream. I knelt and drank. A new beginning, that moment was. I had thought, waking, that the center of my heart was now empty, but kneeling, with the water cupped in my hands, I realized I was wrong. It was cold and numb and full of hate, but still dangerous. I would take payment for what Acton's people had done to me and mine. Revenge was all I had left.

SAKER

SAKER AWOKE from a dream of his mother calling his name and realized how stupid he'd been.

"Alder, arise," he had said. The one difference, the *only* difference, between the spell he had used on his father and those he had tried on other bones was his father's name. He needed names, not just bones.

But the names of the slain had been forgotten. The killers had not recorded the names of those they killed—they hadn't known them. How could he recover the names of those lost forever?

It was a cold night, but he was sweating with excitement. He got up and paced around his room, trying to work it out. Perhaps a spell? A divination spell? But the enchanter had never taught him those. He went down to his workroom and worried the problem all night, walking, talking it over with himself, consulting his scrolls in the hope that somewhere a name had been recorded. Nothing.

Then, as the sun edged over the low hills to the east of Whitehaven and lit the tops of the trees at the edge of town, he realized afresh how stupid he was. The people he wanted to raise were of the old blood. They would have followed the custom whereby the first living thing the mother sees outside the birthing room gives the child its name. It was considered good luck to see a bird; his own name, Saker, was a kind of falcon. In any large group of the massacred, there would be those named after birds, trees, flowers, animals...All he had to do was try some. Surely he would know when he had the right names—his Sight would tell him.

He stopped short as he realized what this meant. It was time to raise the dead.

BRAMBLE

As BRAMBLE grasped the red-scarfed lance, she felt the fog being ripped away by a wave of sensation: life was coming back, her spirit was returning. It hurt, as birth always hurts, but she welcomed it with astonished joy.

"Kill Reborn!" the crowd shouted, and she brandished the lance in triumph. She *was* reborn. The sights and sounds of the crowd, the other chasers, the vivid green of spring all around her were overwhelming. Gorham ran to the finish line and thumped her leg in congratulations, panting too hard to talk, grinning madly. She laughed back.

She followed him up to the counter and received the winner's bag of silver, still too dazed to speak. She just smiled, and smiled, and sometimes grinned, but everyone seemed to think that was quite normal.

The party that followed was long and loud and exuberant. Sendat was celebrating the good luck of being granted a Kill Reborn, and it was determined to celebrate thoroughly.

If she'd wanted to, Bramble could have got drunk ten times over without spending a copper. Everyone wanted to buy her a drink, clap her shoulder, smile into her eyes. Quite a few wanted more than that. She suspected that if she'd been clubfooted, squinty and with breath like a banshee she would have still had all the men after her. Good luck, they say, rubs off, and where better to rub it than onto a man's privates? She could see them reasoning that out.

After the fifth fumbling attempt to seduce her, she slipped out to the stable to talk to the roan, her blood bubbling with delight. She was alive again, aware of the pleasure of taking each breath: the glass was broken, the fog dispersed. From the moment she had grabbed the lance with the red scarf, death had retreated from her. She was truly reborn.

The waitress found her and hustled Bramble back into the common room. "The warlord's here! Come on, come on, don't keep him waiting, it's an honor," she said, picking bits of straw off her clothes and reproving her under her breath. She pushed Bramble forward to the hearth where the warlord stood with the inn's best tankard in his hand.

Thegan was a tall man, tawny-haired and blue-eyed, a bright cornflower blue, with a firm mouth and long, strong hands. He was dressed in dark brown, a good serviceable color, which was made luxurious by the cut and pile of the fabric and by the emblem stitched in gold on his shoulder: a spear and sword, crossed. Laughing at something one of his men had said, his face was alive with pleasure. Bramble could see why the waitress was blushing and fidgeting, hoping for him to notice her. He was comely enough to make any woman blush.

Then he turned his eyes on Bramble and she saw, without surprise, that they were cold as stone behind the cheerful facade. He had a mouth, in repose, that was joined to his nose by long lines that ran down to the corners, deeply etched: the mouth of a man with strong desires, who kept them under tight control. And hard eyes.

A woman moved forward beside him, a lady. There was only one person this could be. The warlord's lady, Sorn. She was like a picture of autumn in a tapestry, with rich auburn hair and green eyes, in a dark green dress with a border of embroidered claret and gold leaves around the hem, neck and cuffs. Her pale skin was fine-pored and delicate, showing the blue veins at temple and wrist. A lovely woman, Bramble thought, wrapped in femininity and assured grace. Only the nose was out of place, a man's straight nose, which gave her face strength but left it looking a little lopsided. But young—much younger than Thegan. Sold to the highest bidder, most like. She smiled at the woman companionably and Sorn smiled back.

"So this is our Kill Reborn," Thegan said. A cheer went up around the room and he smiled more widely. "It was well done."

No doubt she was expected to curtsy and blush and call him "lord." Bramble didn't know how to curtsy and she wasn't about to learn. "Thanks," she said.

His eyes narrowed. It was the same reaction she'd had from the warlord's man, but with a difference. The warlord's man didn't know how to control his anger; this one did, and that made him more dangerous.

"It was a good race," he said, testing her. Next to him, Sorn stayed perfectly still, watching Bramble intently.

Bramble nodded. "I enjoyed it."

They stared at each other for a moment, acknowledging enmity. Sorn bit her lip as though to hold back a smile. Then the innkeeper came up with a tray of drinks and food, and slipped between them, breaking the stare. And just as well, Bramble thought, making her way out to the stables again as the others clustered around the drinks. There was no way that could have ended well.

Gorham and Maude were happily ensconced in a corner talking horses with a bunch of chase enthusiasts. He raised a glass to her as she walked by and they smiled twin smiles of mutual congratulation. It helped her shake off any unease left from the encounter with Thegan. She slipped into the stable and laid her cheek against the roan's side. She was full to the brim with happiness and so was he, she could tell. He pricked his ears as though he heard again the cheers of the spectators and snorted as if he wanted to race again.

She patted him, fed him carrots and promised him they would race again soon.

They rode twice more that year, in different towns, and won each time, making them eligible for the Pless Challenge in autumn. She never overtook the Kill again—they had learned caution. Besides, she didn't want to take the risk: stealing the scarf and lance from the Kill in autumn was the worst of bad luck. She was reborn; it was best to leave well enough alone.

Thanks to being the Kill Reborn, Bramble was immediately as well known among chasers as the most experienced rider. She was offered more horses to ride than she could ever have taken, but she refused them all. She wasn't interested in chasing with another horse. She grew to enjoy the claps and calls as she mounted the roan before a chase, to relish the cheers afterward. But it was the ride itself that kept her at Gorham's, kept her from the Road—the chase, and the feeling of having escaped death. Perhaps she could escape the demon's prophecy as well. Perhaps, now she was alive again, she could love and be loved.

The Pless Challenge was the most prestigious and hotly contested chase in the Domains. No horse and rider combination could enter unless they had won at least three consecutive chases, so the competition was tough. Bramble studied the racecourse for days before the chase, although it was off limits to horses until race day. She saw other riders doing the same thing. Most she knew from the other chases, although one was new: a young man with long blond hair drawn back in the ponytail sported by most of the expert riders. He prowled the course with long, rangy strides as though he had to stop himself from breaking into a run. His ponytail bobbed along behind him and it made Bramble chuckle, although she couldn't have said why. His hearing was excellent. She was on the other side of a field, but his head went up (just like a horse, she thought) and he whirled around to see her.

He grinned and started to walk over to her. "The Kill Reborn!" he shouted halfway across the field. "I've heard about you!"

He sprang to a dead stop in front of her and examined her. "Ah, yes, a good native type, excellent conformation, not too much bone, though, may have trouble in heavy going."

Was that a joke? She couldn't quite tell, couldn't read him, but she decided to act as though it were. She examined him in turn. He was dressed as she was, in rider's leather trews and a loose linen shirt, nothing fancy, but good quality, with well-stitched boots. A red-fringed kerchief around his neck added a touch of flamboyance. He looked like a caricature of Acton's people: hair so blond it was almost white, pale blue eyes, fair skin, and a tall, loosely connected frame. He wore small gold earrings that drew attention to his long neck.

"Hmmm," she said. "Thoroughbred. Pure bloodlines, but a bit long in the back, and those pedigreed animals can be very nervous types. Waste a lot of energy. Expensive to feed, I'd say."

He laughed aloud, throwing his head back. She smiled involuntarily. "Gods, you're right there!" He grinned at her, showing crooked teeth. "I'm Leofric. Leof. Come and have a drink with me."

It was those teeth, she decided later, that threw her off balance and made her accept his invitation. They were so unexpected in such a beautiful man, and they got under her defenses. It was like Wilf back in her home village—sweet but plain—and imperfection somehow always made her gentler than she would be otherwise.

They walked back to Pless across the fields.

"So, the Kill Reborn in Sendat..." he said.

"That's me."

"How many chases had you ridden before that one?"

His intentions were obvious—size up the opposition. Fair enough.

"None." His eyebrows went up.

"But you've been riding a long time?"

"A few months." She saw with satisfaction the shock on his face.

"Gods...and you just decided to start chasing?"

"Yep."

"So, what, you've found some spell to make you win?" His face was suddenly intense, as though, if such a spell were possible, he would move heavens and earth to get it.

"That's me. An enchantress."

He dissolved into laughter, as though the intensity of the moment before had never happened. "Absolutely!" he said, batting his eyes at her. "I came under your spell as soon as I set eyes on you."

"What makes you think I'd bother putting a spell on you?"

He stopped and grasped her shoulder to turn her toward him, then tilted her face up toward his with a finger under her chin. She was torn between wanting to slap his hand away and wanting to rub her cheek against it. She kept still. He leaned closer to her until she could see the sapphire glint in his eyes.

"Wouldn't I be worth putting a spell on? They say that in the Wind Cities the women have a spell that turns men into love slaves. Wouldn't you like to use that one on me?"

His voice was low and intimate, practiced, assured. He was all too used to being irresistible, she decided. "Then I'd be responsible for feeding you—I can't afford it."

He chuckled again and let go of her chin. "Now that you mention it, I am famished!"

They went to the first inn they came to, the Shield, the most expensive inn in town, right next to the river.

"I'm staying here," Leof said. "It's not bad."

The taproom looked more like a restaurant than an inn, with the walls painted the green of spring beech leaves, and the frieze patterned with autumn leaves in russet and tan. There were long cushions on the benches and the tables shone with polish. It was a far cry from the inn nearest the farm, where she sometimes went with visiting grooms, or the alehouse in her home village.

They sat at a bench near the window and looked across the river to the chase grounds. Leof waved to the barman and he came over. Not quite a man, Bramble thought. He was no more than sixteen, a lithe boy who might have been good-looking without a disastrous case of pimples. He was trying hard to flirt with Leof, smiling, smoothing his brown hair back and standing as close to him as he could.

"Ale, maybe, and some new bread and cheese?" Leof suggested. She nodded. "Your best ale, now," he said to the boy, and winked.

The boy blushed and scurried off to the kitchen. Bramble raised an eyebrow at Leof. He laughed.

"No, no, I prefer women. But there's no need to be rude about it, is there? He seemed like a nice young lad."

She thought he just liked admiration, and didn't much care where it came from.

While they waited for the food and drink, Leof cross-examined her on the chases she had been in since the Kill Reborn in Sendat. Two could play at that game, she thought. He tried to shrug off her questions.

"Oh, I've ridden in a few chases, I suppose. It's not a bad inn, is it?"

"I asked how many," she said with a smile.

"Twelve," he said, smiling back.

The boy hurried back with a full tray and set everything out on the table. He lingered until Leof smiled at him again, then tucked the tray under his arm and strolled off, trying to be nonchalant.

"How many wins?"

He hesitated, pretending that he was deciding how much cheese to cut.

"If you don't tell me, someone else will."

He looked up and chuckled. "Well, that's true. Ten. Here, have a drink."

He passed her a tankard of ale and bit enthusiastically into the bread and cheese. Bramble watched, amused. He did everything enthusiastically. She was aware of her body and her immediate surroundings in the same way as when she was riding: the softness of the cushion under her buttocks and the hard edge of the bench against her calves, the smell of the beeswaxed table, aged cheese, and horse and hay from Leof and herself. All around them people were drinking, talking, eating, but those sounds seemed to disappear, leaving them in a quiet space, so quiet she could hear him swallow a gulp of ale. Everything seemed more alive, the colors were stronger, the sounds sweeter, the smells more evocative. He'd had that effect on the bar boy, too, as though Leof carried some music around with him that made life more intense.

"Why haven't I seen you before?" she asked.

"I'm from the north. I haven't raced in Pless before."

"And do you always take the opposition to an inn the day before a chase and try to get them drunk?"

"Only if they're as gorgeous as you."

Bramble felt the base of her spine tingle. She wanted to turn her arm over as it rested on the table, to expose the soft skin running from wrist to elbow . . . just to see if he'd notice, look . . . touch. It had been a very long time since she'd wanted to show anything of herself to anyone. She took her arm off the table and tucked her hand under her thigh.

Leof noticed and took her other hand from around the tankard. He stroked the ball of his thumb around her palm. She felt warm down to her toes, from the inside out, and her breath came faster. So did his.

"I tell you what," he said. "How about a wager? If I win, you make love to me. If you win, I make love to you."

She laughed. "What if neither of us wins?"

"Impossible! But if we don't, we make love to each other."

She pretended to consider it, nodding thoughtfully, bottom lip thrust out. "That sounds fair."

He clinked his tankard against hers, still keeping hold of her hand. "To victory!" he said.

"To victory!"

They finished the meal talking comfortably about chases and horses and riding, but his hand and hers were never out of touch for long, fingers entwined or brushed against each other. It was a match and Bramble played along, as familiar with the tactics as he clearly was, but a little off balance and uncertain underneath. She didn't quite like the feeling, but gods, he was gorgeous...

After lunch they walked back to the course.

"Come around with me?" Leof held out his hand, but Bramble shook her head.

"So you can watch my reactions and ask more questions about my strategy? Don't think so."

"Well, it was worth a try," he said, and winked.

She couldn't help but smile, but was glad enough to get away from him and feel normal again. She couldn't let a pretty face interfere with a chase. The familiar discipline of examining each potential jump and working out what her approach should be calmed her, and she ignored the occasional glimpses of Leof in the distance.

Bramble smiled as she walked toward Gorham's house, where she was staying that night. If he thought he'd distracted her from the chase, he was in for a surprise. But she was still smiling as she went to sleep that night. Win or lose tomorrow, her bed would be sweeter...

She dreamed all night about the demon that spoke from the boy's mouth in Sandalwood: *Thou wilt love no man never...Never...Never.* The words repeated themselves over and over, and when they stopped she saw her foot slamming into the face of the warlord's man. It was much clearer in her dream than in her memory, so that she could hear the ugly sound of the bone breaking and a kind of squelching noise as it shafted back into his brain. He raised his head from the ground, dead and deformed, and the demon's voice came from his mouth. *Not fit for this young man.* She woke, sweating and nauseous.

She sat for a few minutes on the side of the bed with her hands hanging between her thighs. "It's just guilt," she said out loud. "It doesn't mean anything." Her voice echoed in the dark room and she shivered.

She got dressed in the starlight from the window and went down the stairs, treading quietly so as not to wake Gorham and Osyth, to spend the rest of the night in the stable. The sight and smell of the roan calmed her. Until she laid her head on his warm side, she hadn't realized that she was still trembling. He nosed her hair and her pockets, looking for carrots, and she laughed a little. This was where she belonged. She found a carrot for him in one of the feed bins and lay down on his blanket in a corner of the stall. He lipped her shoulder and went back to standing with his head just out of the stall, and then slid back into horse sleep with his weight resting on his off hind. She slept more deeply than she had expected to, and didn't wake until the sun was fully up and Gorham appeared at the stable door, calling her to breakfast.

The weather had turned while she was asleep and it was a true autumn day: cold and windy with a lowering sky. It was a bad riding day, with poor visibility in hollows and streams filled with low-lying fog. The dull tan of the oak trees and the scarlet of the hawthorn berries were the only colors apart from the bright kerchiefs of the riders.

Bramble had brought out the roan early to warm up, along with the other riders, including Leof, who was riding a big bay mare. They all wore their lightest shirts and boots, because even the weight of a jacket could mean the difference between winning and losing. Leof smiled and waved at her, but they were both too focused for more.

The crowd soon assembled and the Kill was given his standard. As the riders jostled for position, Bramble found herself trying not to get near Leof, and she wasn't sure why. Perhaps she just didn't want to humiliate him by getting away from him at the start. *Too much overconfidence, my girl,* she thought sternly, *he's won ten—you've only won three*. But with the roan springing with energy at every step, it was hard not to be optimistic.

"Keep him steady, lass," Gorham called.

She raised a hand to him and concentrated on setting the roan straight for the start.

And then the Kill set off. The crowd counted out fifty—the number of men in Acton's first war band—and the riders were away in a thundering, determined mob of black and roan and bay.

The route was the hardest Bramble had faced yet, over high stone walls and water-filled ditches, through narrow paths between trees with low-hanging boughs. The second jump was a difficult stone wall with a small gap flanked by blackberry bushes. Bramble was well placed for the jump, but Leof, she saw out of the corner of her eye, was heading for the bushes. She heard him yell "Hah!" and his mare surged ahead to take the middle ground, forcing a chestnut straight into the blackberry thorns. The chestnut took the jump but its hind legs caught in the bushes and it tumbled over. Bramble and Leof took the jump together and he grinned at her as they landed.

By the third jump it was clear that the race was between Bramble and Leof. The bay was strong and a canny jumper, and Leof rode her with skill and sensitivity—there were no whips or spurs in sight. The mare had a tendency to jump a bit higher than she needed to, which lost her time. But she was a shade faster than the roan on the flat, so they were evenly matched.

They stayed neck and neck over the last jump and started together up the long hill that led to the finish. It was punishing at the end of a tough chase, and the horses started to show the strain. The mornings of practice paid off now, with the roan, at the peak of his fitness, just having the edge over the bay mare. She began to labor halfway up the hill, but Leof urged her on and she picked up the pace again. It was too late. She had lost too much ground to make it up, and the roan passed the finish half a length ahead of her.

Bramble took the red scarf from the Kill and flourished it, as expected, to the revelers, who were cheering madly to see a local horse win the biggest race of the year.

She escaped the crowd and walked over to Leof, wondering how he would take being beaten by a girl he was romancing. She held out her hand.

He was smiling in disbelief, but he returned the handshake. "Gods, girl, that's a horse and a half you've got."

She smiled widely, patting the roan on the neck. "That's the truth."

"You're a bloody fine rider, I'll give you that, but it was the horse that won that race."

She nodded. "I know."

"If I'd been riding him —"

"He wouldn't have tried that hard for you."

Leof stared at her, giving away nothing. "I don't doubt it." He smiled brilliantly. "We had a wager."

"So we did." She felt laughter bubbling up and let it out, throwing her head back. It was ridiculous to feel this happy.

"The party's at my house," Gorham shouted, and everyone started to move toward town.

Leof and Bramble rode together quietly, letting the horses cool down. She showed him to Gorham's stable and they tended their horses together, in a quiet intimacy shut away from the growing noise of the party in the house. They stood shoulder to shoulder for a few moments, watching the roan and the mare snort at each other and lip at their hay. Leof turned and slid his arms around Bramble's waist.

"Let's not go to the party," he said. He nuzzled the side of her neck. "I have to make good on my wager."

His mouth was soft and warm on her skin.

"Gorham will wonder where we are."

"Let him wonder."

His hands were traveling, then cupping her behind, drawing her against him. Their mouths met, and then loosened reluctantly.

"Let's go back to the inn," he said. "I'm not at my best on a pile of straw."

Bramble laughed, nervously, and went with him, leaving the prize bag of silver sitting on top of the feed bin.

His room at the inn was the most luxurious thing Bramble had ever seen: canopied bed, velvet bed throw, fine embroidered linen sheets. She smiled, thinking that she'd never actually shagged anyone in a bed. Riverside grass and haylofts, yes. Beds, no. She inspected the view from the window and found the river and hills beyond.

"Stop trying to distract yourself," Leof said. He pulled her into his arms. "If I can't make you yield in a chase, I bet I can here."

And he could. He paid the wager in full, with hands and lips and body. For the first time in her life, Bramble didn't try to stay in charge. She pressed into him, against him, around him; she let her mind go for once, and she trusted him.

They made love, slept, woke to evening light and moved again together, caressing and laughing, catching their breaths together like one creature instead of two. Afterward it was full night and the autumn air was chilly. Bramble smiled into the darkness, hoping that the warmth she felt meant that the demon's words had been all wrong. She was on the way to loving, surely?

Leof reached over her and fumbled for a tinderbox. She tickled him and it took three tries to light the candle.

"Stop it, woman! No more of that. I am *starving!*"

"Me too," she said.

He jumped out of bed and hurried into clean clothes from the press at the end of the bed, his pale flesh goose-bumped. Bramble smiled.

"Lots of food," she said.

He pulled on a brown jacket and saluted, his fist pressed to his chest. "Yes, ma'am!" As he took his hand down, a crest on his shoulder caught the light. It was a crossed sword and spear.

Bramble felt stupid, as though her thinking had slowed to a glacier pace. "You... you're a warlord's man."

He nodded, lacing up his boots. "One of Thegan's," he said. "I'm from Cliff Domain, but he's called me down to serve him in Sendat for a while."

"You're a *warlord's* man."

"Well, don't say it like that, love." He tied his boot off and stood up. "A big, big meal, eh? A bit of everything? And some wine?"

Bramble was shivering. She felt unbearably nauseous, wanting to be sick but unable to get past a huge lump in her throat. A warlord's man. She had wanted him. Let him... She wanted to get out of bed, drag her clothes on and run, but suddenly couldn't bear the thought of him seeing her naked.

"Why didn't you tell me?"

He stilled in his movement, searching her face. "What difference does it make?"

"A lot."

"What, you wouldn't have come back with me if you'd known I was one of Thegan's men?"

"I wouldn't have talked to you."

"Why not?" His astonishment was genuine.

"Warlord's men...aren't popular where I came from."

"Ah." He sat on the side of the bed. "It's true, some warlords use their power irresponsibly. And I suppose they attract the wrong kind of men. But we're not all bad, love."

He smiled tenderly at her and reached to brush a strand of hair from her face. She propelled herself backward until her head hit the wall. It was the same reaction that had made her kick the other warlord's man when he had reached for her leg. She couldn't bear for him to touch her.

He sat frozen. "That bad? You hate us that badly? All of us?"

"Warlord's men are thugs and bullies, living off the people like leeches."

"That's not how it is in Cliff Domain. I promise you."

"Really." She was unconvinced.

"Really!" He jumped up, angry now. "Without us, the people would be dead, or worse. We protect them."

"From other warlords! If we didn't have any warlords, they wouldn't need you, would they?"

"Yes they would! We protect them from the raiders, from the Ice King's people. Without us, the whole Domain would be laid waste, just like Cliffhaven was."

"What's Cliffhaven?"

"A pair of villages, up near the mountain pass. Twenty years ago the Ice King's men came down and killed everyone—everyone!—in both villages. I saw—my father took me to see, so I would know what we trained for, what we fought for. It was Thegan who forced them back across the ranges. He's a great man, a great leader. I'm proud to follow him!"

The nausea was dying, leaving emptiness behind. That hollow, dead place was still there, underneath everything. She'd thought that Leof...that the demon might have been wrong. But how could she love a warlord's man? Even one who believed he was doing good? And maybe up there in the mountains they did need protection, but he was still someone who dealt in blood and turned to fighting to find solutions. And he worked for Thegan, who had seemed so cold...She felt very tired.

"Go and get your dinner," she said. "Maybe I'll see you at another chase someday."

"That's it?"

"That's it."

"You can't see past the sword?" He gestured to the corner.

There was a sword in a leather scabbard leaning against the wall, an unobtrusive, unadorned weapon made for killing, not show. It seemed to grow larger as she stared at it, realized it had been there all along. She imagined the edge on it, the cutting blade, and shuddered.

"Well?" he said.

She stared back at him.

He turned and walked to the door.

"Leof." He spun around to look at her. "Don't trust Thegan. I've met him. He may be a great man, but he's not a good one."

His face hardened, as it hadn't done before. "Thegan is my sworn liege. You will not speak of him that way."

Their first recourse was always a threat. Even Leof. "Or what? What will you do to me?"

His face softened again and he suddenly looked like a boy of sixteen.

"Oh, Leof, just take care of yourself."

He went out the door silently.

She dressed and shuffled through the streets to Gorham's house where the party, incredibly, was still going. She went to the stable and sat between the roan and the bay mare, wanting to cry, but feeling that empty place expanding under her chest until there was no room for tears.

From then on she avoided socializing with the other riders, although sometimes, to her disgust, she dreamed of being in Leof's arms, dreamed of his lips and hands and warmth. Her own bed seemed colder when she woke, but she wouldn't let herself weep over it, nor consider running away. She was content, she told herself, to live out on the farm. She tried to ignore the memories of being on the Road, and pushed down the desire to move on, be free, feel the sun on her back as she headed north. There's enough sun here, she told herself. She tried to pretend that she wasn't afraid to take the Road, but she was.

If she stopped chasing, she finally admitted to herself one day, she might stop living, too, and go back to death in life. It was a spring morning and she looked up to watch the migrating birds pass over, snow geese and eider ducks and above, the tall cranes, heading north. She left the tack she was mending and took the roan for a ride in the forest. She couldn't still the sense that she wasn't quite where she was supposed to be. But in the end she stayed with Gorham, and relished the chases even more because of what she knew she was missing.

She took the midnight watches with the foaling mares while Gorham dined with the owners in town, and she was happy to take the yearlings and two-year-olds and gentle them, teach them, love them into willing cooperation with humans. The hard part was letting them go to who knew what kind of master; although, there was many a time when Gorham refused a sale because he didn't like the riding hands of the buyer, or the way they dug in their heels unnecessarily. He wouldn't even talk to one warlord's buyer who wore spurs.

Pless was a free town and a fair distance from that particular warlord's domain, so it was safe enough to refuse, but Bramble admired him nonetheless. Although he did begin to regularly sell horses to the warlord in Sendat, Thegan, despite Bramble's objections.

"No matter how he treats his people, he treats his horses well," Gorham said. "And he pays well, too."

In the late autumn two years after she had come to the farm, Gorham arrived one morning with a peculiar look on his face, half happy, half worried. He was distracted all day. Bramble stared when he couldn't find the mucking out fork for the third time in one hour, though it was standing there in full view.

"All right, what's happened?" she asked, placing the fork in his hand.

He stood looking at the fork and laughed shamefacedly. "Zel and Flax are here, my kids."

"Well, that's good. Isn't it?"

"Flax's sick. With the marsh fever. In the past they've stayed a few days and then taken the Road again. But with Flax sick, it looks like they'll be here all winter. And Osyth's worried the town will find out about them. They're singers and acrobats, you know, like Osyth used to be—the least respectable kind of Traveler." For a moment his face brightened. "You should hear Flax's voice—he sings like a meadowlark."

She shrugged, not too interested in Osyth's ambitions or Flax's voice. "You'll just have to keep them out of sight."

Over the winter Gorham became more silent and more haggard. He buried his worries in hard work, and there was plenty of that. The winter was too bitter and the ground too hard to let the horses go out to exercise in the fields, which meant snow had to be shoveled from the main yard every morning, pine bark and sawdust scattered. And the horses exercised there on a lunging rein for all the hours that daylight lasted.

Gorham was absent more often than he cared to be, because the town council elections were coming up. Osyth was taking every opportunity to consolidate Gorham's chances, giving parties, attending parties, "dropping in" on people to chat. She was probably bribing people, too, Bramble thought (if she could bring herself to hand over her silver). She shook her head at the idiocies most people were interested in, and concentrated on keeping the roan fit enough through winter so they could start training for the chases as soon as the weather broke.

Then one day Gorham came out to the farm gray-faced.

"Osyth's dead," he said. "Last night. I was with Maude. The catch broke on her window. She died of the cold in her sleep."

He said each sentence separately, as though they didn't follow on from each other. It seemed odd to Bramble: most people woke up when they got too cold.

Gorham noticed her reaction. "She took sleeping drafts sometimes," he said. "When I went to Maude's."

He felt guilty, she could see, but she thought that guilt was stronger in him than grief, and that maybe the guilt was so strong because there was some relief mixed in with the grief.

He went home after an hour; he'd cleaned the same bridle three times. Bramble tried to show sympathy, but she wasn't sure that sympathy was what he needed. Absolution, maybe.

She went to the funeral the next day, of course, and stood by

Gorham at the mouth of the burial cave and heard the town clerk speak the farewell words.

"May you not linger on the roads. May you not linger in the fields. Time is, and time is gone," he said.

"Time is, and time is gone," the mourners responded.

"May you find friends. May you find those you loved. Time is, and time is gone."

"Time is, and time is gone."

"Under your tongue is rosemary: remember us. In your hands are evergreens: may our memories of you be evergreen. Time is, and time is gone."

Then they placed her in the burial cave and rolled the stone back over the entrance.

Gorham's children weren't there.

"I told them they could come as far as I was concerned," Gorham said. "It was Osyth who cared about me getting on the town council, so people might as well know we were Travelers now. But Flax's still very sick and Zel won't leave him."

Maude was in the crowd but didn't go back to the house afterward for the mourners' honey and salt cakes. Flax and Zel didn't come downstairs, although Bramble saw Gorham go up to them a couple of times.

Two weeks later Gorham was elected to the town council.

"I forgot to take out my nomination," he said, a little dazed, at the election party in the town square.

Bramble smiled widely at him. "You got the sympathy vote, man," she said. "Wouldn't Osyth be pleased?" And that was somehow funny for both of them, that Osyth had got what she wanted, as though she was ordering his life even from the grave.

Bramble never did meet Gorham's children, for they left town as soon as the weather warmed up, by the northwest road. Three months later he married Maude, and became markedly more carefree, despite his new responsibilities as councillor.

At about the same time, Gorham bought himself a Golden Valley stallion with a prize-winning pedigree, a broad-chested palomino with a wicked eye.

The day he arrived, Gorham was beside himself, more excited than Bramble had ever seen him. "This is it," he said. "Now we stop training other people's horses and start breeding our own."

She smiled at him, for she was also pleased. They'd been gradually acquiring a brood-stock of mares, but they'd had to take them to other farms to be covered by a stallion. Bramble didn't like leaving her pregnant mares in someone else's hands, but since they had to be covered again within a month of dropping their foals, there was no alternative. Now the mares could stay home, and she'd have the fun of birthing the foals from the mares other people brought to their stallion.

Gorham had risked a lot on the purchase, but not as much as a Golden Valley stallion usually cost.

"They say he can't be tamed," Gorham said to Bramble as they watched the procession of horses make its way up the road, the blond mane waving in the middle of the pack and trying, again and again, to break to the front. There was energy there and to spare, Gorham noted with satisfaction, although the journey from Golden Valley through the mud and slush of early spring couldn't have been easy.

"They say he's never been ridden, that he'll take a leading rope but not a bit." Gorham snorted, confident, feeling excitement bubble up even more strongly inside him as the horses drew nearer. "As long as I can lead him within smelling distance of the mares, that's all we'll need. The foals we'll gentle ourselves from the day they're born—they'll take the bit all right." He danced from foot to foot. "He's by Gelt out of White Blaze!" he repeated for the fiftieth time. "Gelt!"

Gelt had won every chase in the country for four years straight, until there was no one left who'd take a bet against him. His owners had retired him to stud for two years, then brought him back to racing, but some rival fed him hemlock with his oats, so there were only two years' worth of his get. This three-year-old stallion was one of only four colts born, and his dam was herself a prizewinner.

"He looks well," Bramble said.

He did look well, prancing through the gate at the end of a long day's travel as though he'd just been for a stroll down to the river. He was a healthy, glossy, beautiful animal, with a mad sidestep and bared teeth for anyone who came near him, even his own groom.

Gorham nodded to Bramble and she moved in gently, silently, until she could breathe softly into his nostrils. He stood stock-still at the scent, then shook his head and moved backward, untrusting. Gorham and Bramble nodded to each other, satisfied. There was no malice in him, just mischief and a hatred of being confined and told what to do.

That Bramble understood. She felt his stubbornness—the will to never be mastered, never be compliant—as a kick in her own chest. If she hadn't liked Gorham, she might at that moment have leaped upon the stallion's back and let him race flat out until he was exhausted, using his desire to be free to release her from her own bondage...But she did like Gorham, and there was the roan to be considered, so she pushed down the urge to flight and showed the groom where the stallion should be stabled.

They passed a field where a mare and new foal were grazing, and the stallion broke free and jumped neatly across the fence as though it were only knee height.

"She's not due to come into season for another four days," Bramble said, surprised.

The groom shook his head. "Don't matter. He likes mares. Collects them, you might say, even when they're not in season."

And indeed, when they looked across, the stallion wasn't trying to mount the mare, just sidling around her, whickering, snuffling. He shook his head, the pale mane flying, and Bramble was abruptly reminded of Leof shaking the hair back out of his eyes as he smiled at her. She forced her attention back to the present. The mare was entranced, although she should have been warning this strange stallion away from her foal. They watched her sniffing in turn, smelling that unmistakable stallion musk, and as good as swooning. Bramble held on to the fence and laughed. Gorham stood there, legs apart, arms folded, beaming as though the stallion was his own son.

The stallion looked sideways at the mare, nickering softly, and she rubbed her head against his neck like a coquette. The onlookers shouted with laughter. The sound offended the stallion, who flung up his head to stare forbiddingly at them. That made them laugh more.

"The way he looked sideways at her!" Gorham chuckled, wiping his eyes.

"Like Acton, he is," the groom said, chuckling too.

The legend held that Acton had been irresistible to women. He'd had, they said, a way of looking sideways so that women just melted into his arms. In his own tribe, before the landtaken, they said all a woman had to do to excuse her infidelity with Acton was say, "But he looked sideways at me!" And husbands who followed Acton into battle were mostly hoping that over the mountains he'd find fresh girls to look at. His heir, Thegan, was born of a woman who had no time for men, but had said that if she were going to try it with anyone, it might as well be Acton.

"Like Acton," Gorham said thoughtfully. "So he is, and so we'll name him. Acton it is."

He and Bramble shared a grin, two Travelers making a joke about the old enemy of their people. Even the fair-haired groom smiled. "Aye," he said, "that's the name for him, rightabout."

Then the stallion came up to the fence where Bramble was leaning. He didn't get too close, but stood quietly next to her.

Gorham moved toward him but he flung up his head and moved back. Gorham paused, considering. "Talk him in, Bramble," he said.

So Bramble spoke quietly to the stallion, reeling him in on her voice like a fish on a line. "Here then, Acton, come on, Acton, here we are, come to Bramble, come on, boy."

The words were unimportant, it was all in the tone of voice. Gorham watched as Acton stepped carefully back to stand near Bramble's shoulder and snort at her, and reluctantly let his plans for schooling and gentling the horse himself slip away.

"Looks like he's taken to you, lass," he said. "Best for you to have the handling of him."

She was astonished and delighted, he could see. Never expected much for herself, Bramble, though she held her dignity so dear. Well, not dignity exactly, he thought. Freedom, maybe, or something like it. She'd never be beholden to anyone, not even for a scoop of oats for that roan gelding of hers. And how had a slip of a girl, as she had been then, got hold of a warhorse?

On the Road you didn't ask those sorts of questions, and even though he'd settled now, Gorham still knew better than to poke and pry where it didn't concern him. Bramble had been a gift from the local gods, as far as he was concerned. He considered himself to be the best horse trainer this side of the mountains, but Bramble, he knew, would outstrip him, or could, if only she could bring herself to truly master an animal instead of working out a compromise, where the beast was a partner rather than a servant.

Gorham loved horses, loved them with a rising of his blood whenever he was near them, loved training, grooming and, especially, riding them, as though their mere scent was his key to happiness. But they were only animals, after all, not people, and no matter how often you felt that wordless sense of accord, or found your horse responding as though it could think in tandem with you, they were still animals and bred to serve humans. Gorham knew Bramble didn't see it that way.

It didn't get in the way of day-to-day business, because a horse that has been bred right and trained right likes to be ridden, likes to have the partnership and even the hard work, so Bramble was happy to prepare them for their owners, or for eventual buyers, knowing Gorham didn't sell to the cruel or the stupid. But it worried him, sometimes, in case they ever came to a parting of the ways over it. And it worried him, briefly, as he put the stallion into her care, but he soon dismissed it. He told Bramble that Acton would have the life all stallions dreamed of: no work and an endless procession of mares to cover.

"Not endless," Bramble protested over an ale that night in the tack room in the stallion's stable block, sitting where they could both see Acton's head poked out over his stall. "Spring to midsummer. You won't get mares coming into season later than that."

"Well, all right," Gorham admitted. "He gets to rest in autumn and winter. But he'll need it by then! I've got twelve booked in for him already, not counting our own seven."

Gorham had built the stallion block big and beautiful, hoping that one day there'd be more than one stallion to house there. The spring wind was always from the east, so they'd put it easterly and well away from the foaling boxes and the mares' stalls, with the width of the breeding pens in between, and a stand of fragrant trees and plants for good measure. Gorham didn't want his carefully constructed stable kicked to bits by a stallion determined to get to a mare.

Acton's bright eyes watched them and his ears pricked forward to listen to them talk. His blond mane shone in the lantern light and his coat was as glossy as an hour's currying and combing could make it. Bramble had sung and whispered to him the whole time and could feel him settle in to the sound of her voice as she did, could sense his satisfaction in being groomed and later, the security of the routine. He might not like being bridled or ridden, but he enjoyed the benefits of human contact. He was too intelligent for his own good, the silly git, she thought, and was surprised to find how much affection she already felt for him.

In the months that followed, that affection grew. She never tried to ride him. Now and then, when Gorham saw how easily Acton came to her whistle, the whistle they used to call all their horses from the field, he hinted at her riding him in a chase. But she sidestepped the suggestion each time. She was happy to groom and lead him, bring him to the mating yard and calm him down afterward, and play games with him. But she felt, down deep in her bones, that if he were ever ridden, something would die in him, and something in herself, as well. Winning a chase, for Acton, would be a dishonor.

Gorham saw it, and sometimes, heading home to Maude, back to the four walls of his townhouse and the responsibilities of the town council, he was glad, too, to know one creature that had refused to be tamed. Acton, he thought, hadn't been gentled, or broken; he just liked Bramble, as all horses did, and went where she went and did as she suggested because he liked to please her. Anyone else, even Gorham, got a swift kick or a sharp bite if they tried to lay hands on him. You couldn't call that tame. So Gorham kissed Maude good evening and went off to his council meetings, but the wildness of Acton lay under his breastbone, sometimes a comfort, sometimes a source of restlessness, and he never tried too hard to get Bramble to ride the stallion.

Bramble developed a lucrative sideline: buying cross-grained, human-wary animals—biters, buckers and bitches, as she called them—and working them until they were safe with children on their backs. Sometimes it took a long time, but it was worth it. She sold them only for children, and only then if the child came to her to be taught to ride and look after it. She took half the profits of that and, as always, a quarter of the profits of the other training she did for Gorham.

She worked, she trained, and she chased. She won the first Spring Chase for three years straight. She'd been glad that the honor of hosting the race went to a different town each year, so she hadn't had to go back to Sendat and risk meeting Leof. She knew that he had taken part in other chases, but he had never raced against her again. Had never even come to watch. She told herself that she was glad of it, but wondered if it meant that he hated her. Her memories of him were so mixed: warm and funny and gentle, and then cold and sharp as his sword. She avoided thinking about him by concentrating on whatever work was at hand.

She trained the roan as usual through winter to be ready for the first Spring Chase, but the week before the entry money was due, she sought out Gorham in the tack room. She stood uncomfortably, fidgeting with a bridle, until he turned around and raised his eyebrows at her.

"What's the matter?"

"It's the roan..."

"Mmmm?" Gorham sat on a bale of straw and looked at her steadily. "What's the matter with him?"

"I'm not sure whether to ride him in the Spring Chase or not."

His eyebrows almost climbed off his face. "Why not?"

"He's lost speed," she said reluctantly. "He doesn't feel as fit as he should be."

"He won the last two chases all right."

"They were poor fields. They were mostly youngsters, entered for the experience. The good horses aren't put up against him anymore. He didn't have to try very hard."

Gorham pulled at his nose and then looked up at the roof, calculating. "He'd be, what, thirteen now?"

"I don't know exactly, but around thirteen, maybe fourteen, I think, by his teeth."

He nodded. "Well, you can't expect him to race forever. Your decision."

She reassured herself: the roan was fit enough, she was worrying unnecessarily, she should give him the chance. She was particularly nervous about missing the Spring Chase, the one where she had been reborn, and she wished that he'd lost fitness in the middle of the season. If she stopped chasing altogether, would she lose herself? It seemed more likely, somehow, if she missed the Spring Chase. She couldn't bear the thought of that fog descending on her again, of looking at the world through cloudy glass forever. So she paid the entry fee and prepared the roan for the race, trying to believe that he would be ready for it.

The Spring Chase was in Pless this year, and as the riders gathered for the start, Bramble felt nervous, sensing something was wrong. Then, as the caller signaled them forward to the start line, the roan stopped. He just stopped, as he had that day in the road outside Gorham's farm. She clicked her tongue and squeezed her legs against his sides, but he didn't move.

Bramble jumped off and moved to his head. He turned away from the start and faced toward home.

"What is it, lad?" she asked, as she had asked then. He looked her back in the eye and unlike that day, he was not calm, but restless, flicking his mane, flinging his head up. She put her hand on his neck and felt him quiet down. When the roan had decided to stop at Gorham's, she had accepted it and had now lived his choice for years. But this... She felt fear under her breastbone, the threat of emptiness and death. Without chasing, it might come back. At that moment, she was sure it would, sure that she would descend, once again, into the fog she had escaped from. She couldn't face it.

"Please," she said.

He let out a great breath through his nostrils, not really a neigh, but a sigh, then turned back to face the start.

It was a strong field and they got away to a quick start. The Kill was the young son of a nearby farmer, who spent every afternoon that he could sneak away from his work at Gorham's, begging to be taken on as an apprentice. He knew every inch of the terrain and had planned his route to get the most out of both horse and rider. It was the toughest course she had ever ridden, and by the approach to the third jump

Bramble knew the roan wasn't up to it. He was trying hard, but each jump was an effort, and he had lost the surge back to racing speed after the jump. He began to fall behind.

She had no experience riding in the middle of the pack: they had always led. Bramble found herself jostling for position, trying to see ahead over the other riders, making guesses about the best line to take through a jump. She and the roan were both unsettled. By the fourth jump they were lying fifth, and Bramble was figuring out a safe way to drop out of the race without being trampled by the pack.

The Kill led them at a knee-breaking pace down a half-wooded hillside and soared over a shallow stream that had cut deeply into its banks. There were rocks on the streambed, sharp and unforgiving. The horse in front fell as the bank collapsed beneath it, and the roan had to leap over it as well as the stream. It was a jump that in the past he could have taken with moderate effort.

He took off, but he didn't have the power to get all the way across the stream. For a moment he hung suspended over the gap, then fell heavily, turning as he hit the ground, to shake her off his back, kicking out behind and twisting so she didn't fall under him. She heard his head thwack into one of the rocks and reached for him, but the fall and the current in the stream threw her away. She crawled back against the flow, heedless of the pack jumping over her and thrashing up the farther bank. The noise was deafening, but she moved in a bubble of silence until she reached him and heard his rasping breath.

His head was covered in blood and his ribs were clearly broken, the bones piercing the skin. The stream was flowing red below them and his breath was coming harder and harder. She sat in the streambed and took his head in her lap. He stared up at her with resignation and nuzzled her in between bouts of coughing. "I'm sorry, I'm sorry," she said, over and over. The roan's breath became harsh, settling into the death rattle that meant the end was coming. Bramble put her head down on his to share every shake and shudder. When the shaking stopped, her whole body registered it. She raised her head slowly and looked at him, then gently closed his half-open eye.

She knew that it was her fault. She had known he wasn't fit enough to chase, but had forced him to, out of fear. She had given over to a fear of herself as she would never have to a threat from anyone else. She had sacrificed the roan. Betrayed him.

She was ready, she thought, to pay the price of betrayal. She felt numb, and welcomed the numbness. Then, all at once, her feeling came back. She saw the spring twilight ending with a haze of gold and lavender in the sky. She was aware of it, aware of every dust mote in the air, of the rough streambed beneath her, the texture of the roan's hair, roughened by sweat, under her fingers, the smell of horse, of blood, of leather. She saw the ripples in the stream glow and darken as the sunlight faded. She had passed beyond shock, she thought, to a state where everything seemed alive and full of clarity, full of meaning... If only she could understand it. But there was nothing to understand except the dead weight on her lap, and nothing to feel except shame and grief.

Gorham was standing on the bank with a few of the other riders. She eased her way from under the roan's head, but couldn't just put it down under the water. She knew that it was ridiculous—he was already dead. He wouldn't drown, wouldn't even feel the water closing over his head—but she still couldn't do it. Gorham came to her aid by removing the saddle and placing it under the roan's head.

Then he guided her to the bank and hugged her. She endured it, as she endured the other riders' pats of sympathy on her back. She didn't deserve sympathy.

Some of the riders brought shovels, and together they pulled the roan out of the water to a grave they had dug while Bramble had sat oblivious in the stream. She resented that, resented the blisters on their hands that should by rights have been hers, but she endured that loss, too, because a killer can claim no rights over her victim. She allowed herself to hold his head, though, as they dragged him out of the stream, and she filled in the grave herself, shaking her head when the others tried to help. "Come back with Maude and me tonight," Gorham said, but she shook her head and walked back to the cottage alone.

She sat without moving all night, remembering her betrayal. She intended to sit there forever. Looking back later, she realized that she had survived only because Gorham had pulled her out of the cottage the next morning and thrust a newly born foal into her arms. The warm, wriggling body dragged her attention back to the present. She started to cry, then let the foal go to raise her blistered hands to her face, and smelled the roan again. It was the last time she would know that scent.

Bramble worked through the spring foaling and the summer presentation of mares to the stallions. She worked silently, for the most part, and Gorham let her be. Maude tried a few times to "cheer her up a bit" but eventually realized that she couldn't, and left her alone. Through every day and most of every night, while her hands were busy, her mind went over every moment of her time with the roan, and every moment of his death. For three years she had clutched to the chase to protect her against the fog, against the knowledge that she should have died in the chasm, and for three years the roan had joyfully partnered her. Now it was over.

One day, in autumn, as the wild geese flew over, she suddenly remembered the demon's curse: *Born wild and died wild. Not fit for this young man. Thou wilt love no man never.* That had seemed a terrible curse to her then, and feasible after the chasm. But she had come back to life and, even with the roan's death, life showed no signs of deserting her. There was no fog, no clouded glass. She felt everything sharply, saw everything vividly. She wished she didn't.

Thinking of the light going out in the roan's eyes, she was reminded of the warlord's man's face as he fell, and was ashamed, suddenly, of killing him, and ashamed of not feeling worse about it when it happened. It was as though she hadn't really understood death before—had never felt its finality. Its eternity. Grief and guilt fought for space in her and both won.

She needed... something. Not just to take the Road again. Not just to face her fear of that hollow space within her. Something else. She needed forgiveness. But from where? The two she had injured were both dead. Then she remembered the pilgrims she had met at Sandalwood.

She would go to the Well of Secrets. A real pilgrimage, this time: a pilgrimage to seek forgiveness and absolution. As soon as she had made the decision, she felt better. Just as grief-stricken, just as guilty, but better. She wept again for the roan, gently, and fell asleep.

She left the next day, after a long hour with Acton in his stall.

He was getting older, too, had come into his full strength. His sons were adding to the stud's income, now. Gorham had three of his get, from different but equally well-bred mares, and another stallion from Golden Valley: the stallion stable block was finally full.

Gorham was in Pless at a council meeting. Bramble thought she would pack, then ride into town to say goodbye. She took her store of silver—mostly from winning chases—and the three horses she was working with at the time, Mud, Campanile and Trine.

Mud was a bay pony who had figured out early that he was much stronger than any human who tried to boss him around. He didn't bite or kick, just refused to cooperate with saddling and unsaddling by leaning his whole weight against you, or by sitting down on his haunches. His former owner had gelded him, but it hadn't made any difference to his temperament. After a month with Bramble he was grudgingly letting her do up the girths, and he would follow her if she was riding another horse. She used him as a packhorse.

Campanile (stupid name, thought Bramble, and called her Cam) was a flighty chestnut ex-chaser who'd been mistreated as a youngster and was terrified of the whip and even of the reins, if she saw them out of the corner of her eye. Bramble didn't even possess a whip and rode her without reins, as she had the roan. Six weeks after taking her on, Cam was tractable and even eager to be ridden, as long as the rider was Bramble. Given another six weeks she'd have been ready for the reins, and another rider, but Bramble figured she could train her on the road and sell her if she needed extra silver.

Trine was a bad-tempered, intelligent black who'd been sold to Bramble cheap because her rider had fallen to his death from her during a stag hunt. The horse had been labeled a killer. And it was possible she was—she certainly despised humans. She took every chance to nip and bite, and Bramble had clouted her on the nose each time, aware that, as Gorham had taught her, horses were herd animals and she had to establish that she was one of the older females who would have dished out punishment in the wild.

Gorham had found Trine for her only two weeks ago, in an attempt to spark her interest in riding again. Bramble's combination of discipline and loving care was just beginning to have an effect. Of all the horses she had trained, Trine was the most cross-grained and would take the longest to gentle. Bramble liked her.

Gorham arrived as she was settling the packs on Mud. He stood for a moment, taking it in, then silently helped her finish.

"Where are you going?" Gorham asked.

"Do you know where the Well of Secrets is these days?"

"Up north, I heard, in the Last Domain. You heading that way, then?"

Bramble stilled her hands against Mud's sides, spreading her fingers out to feel the warmth. It was a clear day, autumn just making itself felt.

"It's a bad time of year to be traveling north," Gorham said. "Winter comes early up there. I'd be heading for Mitchen, myself, or even Carlion, until after winter. Besides, you'd have to go through the Lake Domain."

"So?"

"The council's worried that war's coming between Central and Lake. Thegan's looking north, they say. Maybe you'd be best off taking the long way round, by the coast."

She smiled at him, warmed that he was not trying to persuade her to stay. The boy from the town who turned up every afternoon had been pestering Gorham for months to take him on as an apprentice, and he'd shown that he had a way with the young ones. She wouldn't be leaving Gorham all on his own. Still, he could easily have taken it amiss, she thought, that she was just up and leaving.

As though he read her mind, he smoothed down the pack and said a little regretfully, "It's been too long since I was on the Road myself."

"Maybe I will make for Carlion," she said. "That's good advice. Thanks."

They'd worked together long enough for him to hear all the other thanks in her voice, and the affectionate goodbye that neither of them was comfortable speaking.

"Wind at your back," he said as she jumped lightly onto Cam's back. The Travelers' goodbye.

"Fire in your hearth," she said in return, the Travelers' goodbye to those settled in towns, and he winced, but tried to smile at her in farewell.

She paused at the gate.

She could imagine walking into Maryrose's kitchen, into her welcome. She missed her more now than any time in the last few years and longed to be safe under Maryrose's loving, intelligent stare. Under that stare she felt herself to be just ordinary. Maybe the demon was right, and she would never love any man, but didn't the fact that she loved Maryrose count for something?

The road north led through Sendat, and in Sendat were Thegan, whom she had no wish to meet again, and Leof. Leof. She hadn't thought of him in a very long time, and there was no use thinking about him now. He lived by cold steel and blood, and she wanted nothing to do with him. She definitely didn't want to face the pain she had seen in his eyes. And Thegan, she was sure, even after that one brief meeting, was not to be trusted. It would be foolish to ride straight into his territory, especially with these rumors of war with the Lake People.

Half a mile down the road she stopped. Her stomach was churning. Taking this route, she was doing it again, ignoring her instincts. She needed more than Maryrose's hugs and scoldings. She needed more than anyone normal could give her. Forgiveness. She turned the horses north and immediately she felt better.

At last she was back on the Road. A wood pigeon lifted into the air nearby with that distinctive *slap slap slap* of wings, and her heart lifted with it. There was no sun on her back on this cloudy day, but she didn't care. *The Road is long and the end is death*, she said to herself, remembering one of her grandfather's sayings. *If we're lucky*.

ASH

HE WAS standing by the window keeping watch, knowing what he would have to do if Doronit sent Hildie or Aylmer back to kill Martine. Fight one friend to save another.

"I must leave," Martine said to Ash. "Doronit won't try to be subtle next time—it will be a quick knife as I walk past in the street."

She went to a cupboard and took out paper, brush and an ink block, then sat before the fire to write.

"I'm leaving instructions for my man of business to sell this house and keep the monies safe for me until I send for them," she said, concentrating on the paper.

Ash waited, silently. What could he do? He couldn't go back to Doronit's, not even to pick up his clothes. She would kill him as soon as look at him, he knew. All he had was what he stood up in and the few coins in his pouch. And Acton's brooch. He went over to the mantelpiece to look at it. It glowed in the firelight, larger than life. It seemed more important than he remembered. More alive than he was. It was warm to the touch, but he felt cold, his stomach like lead.

Martine finished writing and waved the letter in the air to dry it. "Call a messenger, Ash, and we'll send this off." The *we* was automatic, and it warmed him a little. He knew he could ask Martine for advice.

He opened the door and gave three sharp whistles to summon a messenger. The rain had stopped for a while, though the sky was green and threatened a storm. Even on a day like this, there were three children who appeared out of nowhere, jostling in the doorway to be the one who took the message. Martine chose the oldest of them, a thin blond girl.

"Here," she said, handing over the letter, "take this to the House of Surety for me. It's next to the Guildhouse. Get their stamp and I will pay you a penny."

"Yes, marm," the girl answered, and then ran up the street. She must have been hungry to run that fast.

Ash latched the door behind her. Martine looked at him carefully.

"I must pack what I can carry," she said. "Back on the Road, when I had thought I'd left it behind me forever. I should have cast my own future that day, not Ranny's." She laughed without humor. "So. I must take the Road, Ash." She paused. "I would welcome the company of a trained safeguarder."

His heart seemed to grow larger, enough to hurt his ribs. "I have no money," he said. "I'd be a burden to you. I'll probably never be able to repay you."

"Well, come to that, I think you just saved my life, so maybe the talk of repaying should be on my side."

He shook his head firmly.

"No..." she agreed, "maybe you and I should not talk of debts and repayment. But it is true I would welcome your company, and I have enough to pay for both of us—at least until we get where I think I need to go."

Ash was too relieved and grateful to even ask where that was. She smiled at him and disappeared upstairs. He sat down by the fire. He couldn't think; he just stared at the flames and let their warmth enter his cold bones. Later he would think about Doronit. Had he betrayed her or had she betrayed him? He wasn't quite sure. All he knew was that she had meant to use him as a tool, like she used the ghosts and the wind wraiths. He would not be a tool. He was sure of that, too. The storm outside began in earnest: lightning, thunder and then an avalanche of rain.

In the middle of it there was a bang on the door. He reacted as a safeguarder, springing up then putting his back to the wall behind the door as Martine came in from the kitchen to open it. She sighed at the knife in his hand. He hadn't even realized that he'd drawn it. But it could easily be Doronit or Hildie, or any of the others out there. He realized that he was ready to kill any of them instantly. It appalled him, but the determination was there, unflinching: he would kill them all before he let them kill Martine or him.

It was the messenger. She came in, drenched and crying, and held out her hand. "I had the stamp, honest, marm. He took the letter, honest. But the rain washed it off."

Martine looked at the hand and then at Ash. If there had been a stamp, it was gone now. "Never mind, child, I'll have to trust you."

The girl's face lightened.

"Come," Martine said. "I'm leaving today. I've packed what food we can carry. You and your friends can have the rest. Ash, would you bring the bag from the upper room, please?"

She took the girl into the kitchen and he went slowly up the stairs, thinking about what had just happened. He had broken from Doronit, but what she had expected from him—the cynicism and control and violence—were part of him now. They would, he suspected, be part of him forever. He *was* a safeguarder.

While a small part of him mourned the boy who had not known how to slit a man's throat or strangle someone with a scarf, most of him felt stronger. At least he had a real trade—the skills were valuable, if harnessed with his own conscience. Perhaps he could get work in another town, somewhere a long way away, where Doronit's influence could not reach him. As he brought down the large backpack from the bedroom, his step was surer and his heart beat more strongly. He smiled at Martine as she came out of the kitchen with another bag packed full. She was followed by the girl, carrying a box stuffed full of vegetables and bags of flour and other things he couldn't see.

"Thanks, marm, thanks, marm . . . " she kept saying.

"She lives across the street," Martine said to him. "Make sure she gets there with her booty?"

So he went across the street, the rain hitting his skin so hard it stung, and made sure the other children lurking in the doorways didn't rob the girl of her reward. It was a small door in an unpainted house that was much poorer-looking than its neighbors.

"Thanks to you, too, sirrah," she said, and beamed at him from the doorway. "Gods' blessings on you."

It was the first blessing he'd received since he left his parents, and his eyes softened. He lifted a hand to her and went back to Martine a little calmer.

She had the packs ready, together with a storm cape for him. The oiled canvas with hood would keep out the worst of the rain. He hoisted the big pack on his back and fastened the cloak around him, then headed for the door.

"You're forgetting something." Martine nodded toward the mantelpiece. The only thing on it was Acton's brooch.

Ash went over and picked it up. "Why do I feel all this has happened because of this?" he asked, and slipped it into his pouch.

"Perhaps it has. But Doronit wouldn't believe it." They grinned at each other. "Let's go."

They left under cover of the storm by the North Road and saw no one they knew.

Ash was happy, despite the storm and the colder weather ahead, despite his jaw clenching so tight, whenever he thought of Doronit, that his teeth were aching. He had no idea where they were going, and he didn't care. He was relieved to leave Doronit behind him, although he felt a pang for Turvite.

The brooch hung heavily over his left hipbone, but he refused just to be a tool, even of the gods. He was leaving because he'd been betrayed by a calculating, selfish woman—there were songs about that. It happened to men all the time. *Betrayed by a woman, cast out into the storm*... He recited "The Lying Sweetheart" in his head as they slogged through the mud, and he felt grown-up at last.

SAKER

THERE WAS a village on the way to the mountains, in the poor land west of the Lake. Saker had been there often before, as he had made his rounds of the country, drawing his maps and collecting old scrolls. There had been a massacre there, but a small one, just a village. Saker flinched as he realized what he'd thought: "just a village." *Every* death was important. *Every single one* had to be avenged.

The important thing about Spritford, this village, was that the invaders had buried the bodies. They'd learned by then about the stench and illness that came from rotting corpses. They'd gathered the dead and thrown them into a small dell, then shoveled enough dirt over them to keep out the scavenging animals. The dell was named in one of Rowan's songs: Ravensnest Glade.

Which meant that Saker could find the bones.

It wasn't hard for a stonecaster and a mule to make their way from Whitehaven to Spritford in the lengthening days of spring. Everywhere he went Saker mourned: the missing forests, the dead towns without trees where the pale-eyed townsfolk hurried about their greedy business. They had no beauty, no grace, none of the spirit-filled artistry of his own people. Without the Travelers, this land, these Domains would have no culture at all. It was people of the old blood who sang the songs and painted the walls and told the stories and danced the dances. *These invaders*, he thought, *just watch us because they can't do anything else. Maybe that's why they hate us so.*

He found Spritford easily enough, on the shore of the river Sprit, coming to it from the south toward the end of the day. Just as he came in sight of the Sprit, he saw a hawk stoop. It flashed down and struck, both feet extended forward, and then beat its wings twice powerfully to launch again, a ground squirrel dangling lifeless from its talons. As it rose slowly, he could see that it was a saker falcon, and he was immensely cheered by the omen.

"Fly well, brother," he said, and whistled as he rode toward the village.

The land rose beyond the cottages to a ridge that concealed the river Sharp. The Ravensnest Glade, the song said, was on the Sharp side of the village. He wanted to ride on, find the dell right away, but he made himself stop at the inn, take a room, and cast some stones for the innkeeper's sister in return for a meal, as he usually did. He didn't want to attract attention.

He found himself spending the evening casting stones for the villagers, trying not to show how irritated he was by their petty concerns: "Will my girl marry me?" "Does my husband know?" "Will the calf from the red cow live?" "Will I be lucky at dice this full moon?" They were obsessed with the trivial—all townsfolk were, and farmers no better. Never was there a question about truth, or justice, or even rebirth. They were pitiful, pale shadows of the men and women who had lived in this land before the invasion. The land would not miss them.

"I thought," he said carefully to the innkeeper's sister, a thin but red-cheeked woman, "that I would go to pay my respects to your gods tomorrow. Where is the altar?"

"Oh yes, sir," she said, "they'll like that, I'm sure. The rock is in Ravensnest Glade, on the Sharp side of the town. I'll point it out in the morning."

She left him to serve another customer. He sat, feeling his body grow cold. He'd only asked the woman where the gods were so he'd have an excuse to go off exploring in the morning. The gods were in the actual place of burial. He shivered, appalled. Had Acton's men been insane, to make the gods' place their dumping ground? And why had the gods allowed it?

The woman came sidling back, not sure if he would welcome more chat. She was smiling at him nervously, trying to ingratiate herself as though that would somehow ensure a better result at her next casting. She was one of those women who were excited by magic, by the lure of the stones. He despised them, all of them: they were eager to use the skills of the old blood but contemptuous of those in whose veins it ran.

"The gods used to be by the river, it's said," she offered. "After Acton's people came, they asked to be moved to the glade."

Very good, Saker thought, *the gods had decided it—to be near their dead*. That meant that the gods here, unlike most local gods, cared about what happened to the people in their charge. Most gods were not interested in temporal concerns, and seemed to care more about the beasts of the fields than about humans. Although they did like a sacrifice, so humans were useful to them in some ways.

These gods must be different. A shiver went through him at the thought, but he shook it away. Tomorrow he would raise the dead, feel their bones in his hands, replenish them with his own blood. And their gods would strengthen him when he cast the spell, so the dead could take back what was theirs.

ASH

ASH HAD grown up walking the Road, and he fell back immediately into that easy, unhurried pace that let you walk all day. He saw that Martine did, too, and remembered that she had said something about being on the Road before. They went on for an hour or so in the sharp rain, heading up over the hills surrounding Turvite. It was a steep climb, and for a long while he concentrated solely on putting one foot in front of the other. The rain lifted as they passed the top of the first line of hills and started down the other side. He hadn't realized how he had been hunched against the deluge, the sound as much as the cold, until it stopped.

"Where are we going?" he asked.

She turned her head and laughed at him. "Finally you ask!"

He grinned, too, and shrugged.

"We're going north, to Hidden Valley," she said. "To visit... well, let's call her an old friend." She looked at him again. "No, let's not call her that. I owe you more than a social lie."

"Elva is the daughter of two people I grew up with. There were the three of us the same age in our village, Lark and Cob and me—two girls and a boy. Lark and I were named on the same day, after the birds our mothers saw following the births—the lark and the house martin. We played together, got into trouble together, were punished together. When I was small it seemed it would always be the three of us. But, two girls and one boy... Of course we both fell in love with him. And when the time came to choose, he chose Lark."

She brooded over that for three paces, then went on.

"It was because I was... different. I already knew I could cast the stones—you know how children play at stonecasting?"

He nodded.

"Even before I could read the runes, I could tell what the stones meant. And there were other things... the ghosts, the local gods... When he was small, Cob just accepted it, but when it came time to choose who he'd lie with in the dark of night, he couldn't bring himself to choose someone who spoke to ghosts. He told me. So. Perhaps the gods were listening... because their daughter, Elva, was stranger far than me. The strangest child ever born to our blood."

Martine fell silent.

Ash gathered his courage. "What was strange about her?"

She blinked rapidly, forcing back memory.

"There's no color in her, nothing but white and pink—white skin, white hair, pink eyes. She cannot bear the rays of the sun. I've learned, since, that children are sometimes born that way, but we had never heard of it then. The village voice wanted her put out on the mountain to die, until the local gods spoke to him and said they wanted her to live. But Cob couldn't bear to have her near him, although Lark would have loved her, I think, if he'd let her. Then she started talking to the local gods—almost her first words were to them. Cob couldn't abide it. So I took her to live with me, with their blessing, as soon as she could walk properly."

"And you went on the Road?"

She paused, then clearly decided not to tell him another part of the story. He tried not to feel hurt. She had a right to her privacy.

"No. That came later."

"And then?"

"Then? We wandered. You know the life. I cast the stones, I bought our bread, I laid ghosts to rest, I tended Elva and fed her and loved her, too..."

Ash heard Doronit's echo—*Why have I housed you and fed and, yes, loved you all this time?*—and lost track of what Martine was saying for a moment.

"...and then we were in Carlion and Ranny of Highmark came for her reading. You know what happened. I was a fool, no? After that, it wasn't safe for Elva to be near me. Ranny would have loved to see me bereft and grieving. Elva was a woman by then, and beautiful... though few can see past her white skin. She left me to find her own place, five years ago, when she was sixteen. So. That is where we are going—to Elva."

"Just to visit?" he ventured.

She looked at him in the fading twilight, amused.

"Have you tried to cast the stones, boy? You see further than most. No, not just to visit. The stones have shown me...warnings, about Elva, though it's unchancy to cast for your own needs. A stonecaster rarely sees the truth about those she loves. Still, there are signs that Elva may be glad to see me, and not only because she loves me."

They walked the rest of the daylight in silence. Ash was lost in a daydream about this beautiful white-haired girl, only one year older than him...It stopped him thinking about Doronit, about what she was doing, whether she had replaced him already; it stopped him imagining what it would have been like, if he'd killed Martine and gone home to share Doronit's bed.

Martine said nothing until they reached a stream crossing the road, not far down from a camping place. "Time for fire," she said.

There was a tent in the bag Ash carried, so he set it up while Martine gathered firewood and some dry kindling from under a holly bush, disturbing a lizard, which skittered off into the growing dark. Every movement, every moment, reminded him of the long years of traveling with his parents. It was pleasure and pain, both.

They sat at the fire, ate, and then crawled into the tent, back to back, warmth to warmth. He waited until he could hear her breathing, slow and even, and then he let the tears creep out of his eyes and drip onto his sleeve, so there'd be no mark on the tent in the morning. He didn't think at all, just cried quietly and steadily until the moon set and he slept.

In the morning they packed up and Ash doused the fire while Martine brushed and braided her hair. It was a fine morning after the rain, though the bite of the autumn air in the highland was brisk. The sun caught the shine on Martine's hair. He stared out of the corner of his eyes, not just because she was beautiful, with her brush in her hand, standing and swaying with each stroke, but because the gleam of her hair, moving as the brush went through it, seemed to call his eye, seemed to weave shapes that he could almost make out. It was like sunlight on water, constantly changing, drawing him...The shapes were almost clear...He pulled his eyes away and went off to wait by the road. He'd heard of Travelers having the bright vision, the Sight that shows itself in light, but he didn't want any part of it. Even among Travelers, such folk were thought of as unchancy. He had enough that set him apart from everyone else. He wasn't minded to be any more different than he had to be.

Martine came to the road with her hair neatly braided, the plait hanging far down her back, and smiled at him. "So. Ready to go?"

They walked companionably, enjoying the still, crisp mountain air. "How about a song to pass the time?" Martine asked after a while.

Ash went red in the face and looked away. "I don't sing."

"Everybody sings," she said, surprised by his reaction.

He shook his head.

"Oh, come on. You know 'The Green Hills of Pless,' don't you?"

"I know lots of songs. My parents were musicians. But I don't—I *can't* sing."

She looked at him curiously. "Your voice can't be that bad, surely."

"Yes it is."

"Maybe to your parents, if they were professionals. But I'm just a stonecaster. What do I know about music? Give it a try. My own voice isn't that wonderful."

So, because he felt he owed her so much, he cleared his throat and began to sing "The Green Hills of Pless."

I have wandered the land from Domain to —

Before he finished the first line he saw the look on her face and stopped short. She came to a halt in the road, her face pale. He stopped a few steps farther on and looked back at her.

"It *is* that bad, isn't it?" he asked reluctantly.

She was frowning, as though he were a puzzle she was trying to solve. "It's the voice of the dead," she said.

"That bad, huh?" he said, trying to be casual about it.

"No, really the voice of the dead," she insisted. "Exactly the same."

Ash stared at her, memories cascading over him: the look of pain on his mother's face whenever he tried to sing as a young child; the way his father would turn away, abruptly, or walk out of the room; and, on the day he left them for Doronit, his mother saying "but music is dead to you, anyway," as though to remind him of something he knew already. He had not known. He had not sung since he was small. Not even when he was alone. His mother was right. Music was dead to him.

Strangely, it made him feel both shaken and comforted. To have the voice of the dead was a terrible thing, but it was clearly the work of the gods. It was not his fault that he could not sing; not his fault that music did not spring from him as it did from his parents. To be the son of singers and have a mediocre voice might be shameful, but what the gods visited upon you could not be a cause for shame. Now he could put it behind him and find a new place in the world.

Martine plopped right down in the middle of the road and took out her bag of stones. "Come on," she said, "give me your hand."

She spread out a piece of fabric with a flick of her wrist and held her left hand out to him imperatively. He sank down to the road slowly, but he spat in his hand and clasped hers. She took the five stones out of the bag and cast them across the fabric. They were all facedown.

"The meaning hidden," she said. She turned them over slowly. "Death. Pain. Bereavement. The blank stone, the random one. And here, look—Rebirth. But all hidden. All secret."

She stared at the stones intently.

"I can't make them speak," she whispered. "They know your secret, but they are dumb to me, as ghosts are." She paused, thinking. "Tell them to speak."

"What?"

"Tell the stones to speak."

He shook his head. "No . . . If they're dumb, maybe I'm not meant to know. Maybe it's better not to know."

"I spend my life seeking knowledge. I don't think it's ever better not to know."

He shook his head again, stubbornly. "You seek knowledge for those who want to know, who come to you to find things out. This was your idea, not mine."

She let his hand go with a sigh. "So. Maybe . . . maybe. For now, at least."

Then they'd had to dodge a cart full of cabbages, whose driver swore at them for feckless Travelers, sitting in the dirt and getting in the way of hardworking folk.

They grinned at each other, and kept walking.

They went on like that for days, stopping at villages where Martine exchanged castings for food and shelter. They slept in barns, shepherds' huts, on the floor of inn stables, in the tent. The hedges and trees were full of birds, and at evening and morning the sky was full of flocks making practice flights before their journey south for winter. Ash had forgotten the high, soaring skylark song and the way that, passing through a dell, the grasshopper shrill seems to deafen you.

They grew used to the smell of their own sweat until they didn't smell it anymore. But every Traveler knows that if you don't wash regularly, the townsfolk won't have anything to do with you—which is funny, his mother used to say, for most of them don't wash from one week to the next. But Traveler sweat smells strange to them, and unpleasant.

So they stopped at creeks and pools, thankful that it hadn't been a dry summer, and washed, each taking a turn as lookout for the other, and Ash trying not to think about what Martine looked like bathing when it was his turn to guard. He looked away when she brushed her hair each morning, too, determined not to be snared into the bright vision of the Sight. He filled his head with fantasies about the white-haired girl instead, and refused to think about Doronit.

There was no sign of Doronit's or Ranny's men on the road behind them, and in the end it felt almost like a holiday, except that Martine was worried about Elva. She didn't say it, but he could tell. She would walk for a while in silence, her face gradually becoming more severe, a frown appearing. Then she would shake her head and turn to him almost desperately, saying, "How about a song, then?"

She'd discovered that even though he couldn't sing them, he could recite the verses of all the ballads, histories, and love songs, though love songs didn't work so well as walking songs. And some of the histories were very old.

"What's the oldest one you know?" Martine asked him one day.

"Oh, that's the invasion song, 'The Landtaken Ballad.'"

"I haven't heard that one."

So he began, although it was a song that always left him both excited—stirred up, as he often was by songs of battle and glory—and angry at how *happy* Acton's men had been as they had killed his ancestors.

Bright in the morning shone the spring sun
Bright in the sun shone the spears of our host
Bright the fierce eyes of Acton the bold
As they took the cold road that led to Death Pass.

Death Pass was where Acton and his men had come over the mountains in the first invasion. They had come at the first sign of spring thaw in the lowlands, plowing their way through chest-high snow, moving as silently as possible so they would not trigger the terrible avalanches that gave Death Pass its name. It was an insane thing to do, which was why they were able to massacre the people living on the other side of the pass. In previous years those people had armed themselves well against the annual summer raids of Acton's tribe, but they had been taken by surprise when their enemy appeared out of the snow and mist, swords and spears in hand.

Bright flowed the blood of the dark-haired foe
Red flowed the swords of the conquering ones
Mighty the battles, mighty the deeds
Of Acton's companions, the valiant men.

No one had been left alive, not even the babies. In the past, the tribe from beyond the mountains had raided, killed some men, raped some women, loaded themselves up with booty and gone home again. This time they stayed. The *landtaken,* Acton called it, the theft of land; it was the biggest theft there had ever been. And when Death Pass cleared in spring, across the mountains came the women and children of the tribe, and they moved into the empty cottages, while the men swept down into the lowlands, killing and keeping what they overran. That first village was renamed Actonston, of course.

Remember their names, and praise them daily:
Acton and Aelred, the boon companions,

Beorn and Baluch, Merrick and Mabry,
Aelric and Asgarn, Garlok and Gabra…

They walked silently for some time after he had finished reciting the song. Ash kept his eyes on the road, not wanting her to see the turmoil the song raised in him.

"So. The world changed in a day," Martine said eventually.

He nodded. "In a day, and a few hundred years. The landtaken took a long time to finish. More tribes followed Acton's people over the mountains, and the Domains are large. It took them a long time to wipe out every settlement."

"Yes," she said. "Longer than you might think."

They made their way gradually north, toward the mountains. Elva lived in a village at the foothills, Martine had said. At first they traveled through farmland, land that had been settled even before Acton came. But as they moved farther from Turvite they came upon more and more patches of wild land—forest, or marsh, or heath.

After two weeks on the Road they were having to walk a whole day to get to the next village by nightfall, and in the evenings their breath clouded on the chilling air. Even though Ash had been on the Road for most of his life, some parts of the country seemed strange to him: moors where the wind wuthered through the gorse; or stretches where granite cropped out from grass that looked as close mown as if sheep had grazed there for a thousand years, but there were no sheep anywhere to be seen, and the granite never took warmth from the sun, no matter how hot the day; or stands of pines where the sun never reached the path, even at midday.

On the fifteenth day, they came late in the twilight to a village set in foothills, and as they came down over a ridge they saw the lights just being kindled in cottages. There was no inn, but a bush hanging above the door of one cottage showed them where the ale was brewed, so they went on down and knocked.

"Come along in," came a man's voice.

"Blessings on this place," said Martine as they entered.

It was a drinking place like you'd find in any village. There were a few tables with benches, a few chairs near the fire for the old men, a couple of kegs against the wall, a shelf of tankards gleaming cheerily in the firelight. Ash felt his spirits rise, and they rose further when the brewer came toward them and smiled, the first smile they'd had from an innkeeper since they'd left Turvite. He was a broad, strong-looking man, though not tall, with wide-set blue eyes and laugh lines at the corners of his eyes and mouth.

"Travelers, then?" he asked. "Singers, storytellers?" His tone was hopeful, the voice of a lover of tales and one starved of entertainment. It was easy to see why he had become a brewer; he relished the company and the talk around the fire.

Martine held up her pouch, and his face fell.

"Stonecaster," he said. "Ah, well, no less welcome for that. I'm Fiske. Come, sit by the fire."

Fiske fed them pea soup, grilled trout, greens, carrots and baked parsnips. The food was good, and they ate hungrily. Fiske sat down and ate with them, asking for the news of the Road. There was a good deal they could tell him about the nearby villages, but he didn't care about news from Turvite, dismissing it with a wave of his hand.

"Foreigners," he said, and asked instead about the horse race in the town they had just passed through. He had a bet on, and he was very pleased when they told him that his horse had won. "Hah! I knew it. With Bramble not riding Thorn last spring, the chases have opened right up again. I knew Silver Shoes could win! Golden Shoes was his dam, you know." He looked at their blank faces and smiled. "You don't follow the chases, then?"

They shook their heads.

"Shame, shame..." Fiske said. "It's a great sport." He realized that he had distracted them from their meals. "Eat, eat."

They returned with pleasure to the sweet crispy-skinned trout and when they were finished, Martine asked where they might find somewhere to sleep for the night.

Conversation around the room seemed to hush.

Fiske pulled at his lip. "Well..." he said, considering.

The crowd of men at the tables and round the fire looked on, but kept out of it. Ash realized that Fiske must be the village voice, the one who acted as mediator and arbiter in village disputes: not quite a mayor, not quite a judge, not quite a peacemaker, but something of all three.

"I reckon you'd be happiest at Halley's place," he said, finally. "I'll take you."

"I'd better pay you first," Martine said, laughing at him.

He laughed, too, throwing his head back. "Aye, aye, so you'd better!"

So she paid and they followed Fiske out into the dark. He led them to a cottage on the other side of the village, near the southern road.

There was a ghost waiting outside the door. It was pale and wraith-like after the clarity of the Turvite ghosts, but Ash could see it plain enough, though it was clear that Fiske couldn't. It was an elderly man with a big mustache, dressed as a villager. They nodded to it and it nodded and grinned back, gesturing excitedly as if it had something to say. Martine gave it a short nod and tilted her head to Fiske, to show that it should wait until he went away. The ghost nodded.

Fiske, oblivious, knocked at the door. "Ho, Halley, open up! I've got guests for you."

A young man opened the door. He was in his late twenties, maybe, with the fair hair of Acton's people but with dark eyes. The knock had caught him in the middle of getting ready for bed, it was clear—his shirttails were out and he had one boot off.

"Fiske?" he said, in a light tenor voice. "What's the matter?"

"No problem, lad, just some guests for the night—a stonecaster and her boy. Thought you'd welcome them, for your da's sake."

Halley nodded at once and opened the door wide. The ghost slipped in and they followed, into a space that doubled as sitting room and cobbler's workshop.

Fiske raised his hand in farewell.

"Thank you, Fiske," Martine said.

"Welcome, welcome always," he said, and smiled at her, maybe a little more warmly than a brewer would smile at a customer.

She did look very beautiful in the light from the lantern, tall and slender and graceful. She smiled back at him, maybe a little more warmly than a customer would smile at a brewer. Ash raised an eyebrow. He suspected that Martine would not have smiled so warmly if they weren't due to leave tomorrow. In her own way, she was as self-contained as Doronit.

Halley shut the door and gestured to them to sit down on the settle by the fireplace. The fire had been banked for the night and he stirred it up again, and added more wood. Apple wood, Ash thought, by the smell of it. The ghost stood by the fire, waiting, its eyes on Martine and Ash.

"You've had a death in the family recently," Martine said to Halley as he turned from the fire.

He was surprised. "Yes, yes, my father... Fiske told you?"

Martine shook her head. "No. A man with a mustache?" she asked. "Balding on top but with curly hair around his ears?"

Halley went pale. "Yes, that's him. How—"

"He is here," Martine said gently. "He wishes to speak to you."

The ghost nodded urgently.

"H-here?" Halley said, looking around nervously.

"Trust us," she said, and turned to Ash, a question in her eyes. Ash nodded. "My friend here will ask him to speak, but you must be prepared. It will not sound like your father. It will sound... harsh." She held Halley's eyes until he nodded, then she nodded in turn to Ash.

Ash looked at the ghost. "Speak," he said.

"Burn them, burn them!" the ghost said quickly, as though he were afraid the charm would be too brief.

Halley flinched at the grating graveyard voice and looked around the room wildly. He made the sign against evil and backed into a corner near the fire. "That's not my f-father! It's a d-demon! It wants to kill us all!"

"No," Ash said, pitying his fear. "All the dead speak in that voice. Don't be afraid. Nothing will harm you."

Halley calmed a little but wouldn't come out of the corner.

"Burn what?" Martine asked the ghost patiently.

"The stones, the stones, purify them, burn the bag..." the ghost said.

Halley flinched again, and looked for the source of the voice.

"Ah." Martine turned to Halley. "Your father was a stonecaster?" Halley and the ghost both nodded. "He died suddenly?"

"His h-heart."

"And you inherited his pouch and stones. You have been using them."

Again they nodded, the identical gesture marking them as father and son, although in features they were very different.

"Give me the pouch, Halley." Martine's voice was very gentle.

Wordlessly he went to a cupboard opposite the door and took out a stonecaster's pouch, dark blue leather with a red drawstring. He handed it to Martine, who had wrapped a fold of her tabard around her hand.

She walked to the fire and threw the pouch in. "Fire free thee, fire speed thee, fire light thy way," she said, and smiled at the ghost.

Halley protested and moved to the fire as though to pluck it out. Ash didn't understand what was going on, but he trusted Martine and held Halley back until the leather pouch had flared and seared, the smell of burned leather forcing them all to breathe shallowly. The stones fell out of the pouch as it disintegrated and lay amid the wood, their runes glowing white against the dark granite fireplace. The shapes seemed to call his eyes as the light in Martine's hair had done. He looked away.

"Stonecasters," said Martine, "put a little of their soul into their stones and pouch. There's no spell to it—it's just that over the years, with handling, and concentration, and constantly wearing the pouch, the two grow together. The stronger the caster, the more this is so. When a caster dies, the pouch and stones must be purified with fire to cut the tie so that the spirit can travel on. Unknowingly, you have been keeping your father from his journey."

Halley relaxed against Ash's arm, and Ash realized that he had again automatically reacted as a safeguarder, keeping him in a wrestling hold.

When the leather pouch had finally fallen apart, the ghost began to fade and he gestured urgently to Ash.

"Speak," Ash said again.

The voice of death sounded harsher than ever, but this time Halley listened carefully.

"I am in your debt, so I repay the only way I can... The road you are traveling will take you to the dead."

Ash shivered, full of sudden alarm, but Martine just raised her eyebrows. Then the ghost crossed the room and made as though to caress the head of his son, a curving gesture full of love and regret that faded before it was completed. Ash felt his eyes fill and looked at Martine. Her eyes were dark, but not full of tears. He wondered what it would take to make her cry, or show fear.

"He loved you," he said to Halley. It was important that Halley should know it, all the more because he couldn't see his father's ghost. "He wanted to embrace you."

Halley stood, confused, shaking his head in mingled grief and shock.

Martine looked at him with interest. "You are not completely of the old blood," she said slowly. "Nor was your father."

"No...It was his grandmam was a Traveler."

Martine studied the stones glowing in the fireplace. "I'm thinking," she said, "that I might take these stones with me when we go."

"But they—"

"The thing of it is," she cut across him, "you don't have enough of the Sight to make it safe for you to use them. You'll be seeing the wrong things, five times out of ten, or not be able to hear them when they speak."

"Speak?" he said.

That seemed to decide her. "You cannot see your father's ghost, you cannot hear the stones speak—you should not be using them." She softened a little. "It's no disgrace. You have another trade."

Halley sat down in a chair by the table, his working chair. "I used to watch him, and wonder how he knew. The stones...I always wanted to play with them, but he would never let me. When he died, handling them made me feel like he was close to me..."

"He was," she said softly. "But he's gone now."

Halley put his hands in his hair and began to cry, the hard, coughing sobs of deep grief. Martine just stood there, so Ash went to him and laid an arm across his shoulders.

"Out of the dark, new life is born," he said, quoting an old Traveler saying. "The spark flies upward and becomes a star."

He didn't think Halley heard him.

"'The road you are traveling will take you to the dead,'" he quoted to Martine as they spread their blankets on the floor in front of the fire.

"The Road is long and the end is death," she said.

"I don't think that's what he meant."

"What can we do? 'The dead' is not the same as 'death,' of course. But this is a road I must travel." She turned her head and looked sideways at him from under the dark fall of hair she had loosened, as she always did before sleep. "But it's not your road, Ash. You can take another turning anytime you want."

Alone on the roads... A shudder ran through him. "No," he said. "Our road lies together. For as long as you want." He had tried to sound adult and sure of himself, but his voice trembled a little.

She smiled. "You may change your mind about that one day, youngling." She yawned suddenly and stretched. "All right then. We take the Road tomorrow together, and see what comes."

"And if it's the dead?"

She chuckled. "Of all the people in the world, we have least to fear from the dead. They need us too much."

They left in the early morning, with hot porridge warming their insides and Halley's father's stones tucked safely into Martine's pack. The air smelled of hay and ripe apples and they set off with surprisingly light hearts, considering the solemn warning.

They were heading for the ford across the Sharp River, the river that eventually curved around and flowed into Mitchen Harbor. The Sharp divided the Domains into two unequal parts, north and south, with all the fertile flatlands between Turvite and the river. Past it, to the north, was pastureland, heath, swamp and rock. Here there were fewer birds, fewer animals, and fewer insects, except in the swamps. Even the earth was different: much poorer and coarser. The southern curve, as they called it in those parts, was where the people of the old blood had retreated to when Acton's men invaded. They were left alone there for quite a while—the land deemed not worth the trouble—until the invaders ran out of room in the lowlands. Then the push north started, and gradually the people of the old blood were either killed off or forced out and scattered to go where they could. Many became Travelers.

Ash remembered his father teaching him the history of these lands as they walked through. "I say 'people of the old blood,'" his father had said, "because we never had a name for ourselves, not one that suited everyone. We were not a nation, just a collection of villages and towns, each independent but dealing with the others in peace—mostly. *My* father told me that we thought of ourselves as 'Turviters' or 'Plessans' first, and only secondly, loosely, did we see any connection between us and those from other towns. That was one of the reasons Acton succeeded so well—there was no way of bringing the men of the towns together to fight. The towns fell, one by one, to the fair-haired warriors."

That last phrase, Ash remembered, was from one of the long Traveler ballads in the old tongue. He had learned that ballad, and countless others, as his father had learned them, by word of mouth. The people of the old blood had no tradition of writing, just the runes, which were too powerful to be used for anything other than stonecasting.

"Tell me another history ballad," Martine said as they walked.

Ash grimaced. "They're all depressing," he said. "All about death and beheadings and villages put to the sword."

"There must be some lighthearted songs! Something not death. Traveler songs. I know there are..."

"Oh, there's plenty about how wonderful it all was before Acton came. If you can believe the songs, our culture was complex and exquisite—our artisans produced the most beautiful of objects, all that was good was shared, no one went hungry, our poets sang songs of such beauty that no one could listen dry-eyed..."

Martine's mouth made a quirk. "You don't believe them?"

"Well...There are a few songs from that time that survived. They're good songs—that's why they survived, and a couple are beautiful." He paused, remembering his mother's voice soaring into the descant of "Falling Water." "Yes, very beautiful. But they are human songs, after all, not songs from water sprites, whose songs are so beautiful they can steal your soul away.

"It seems to me..." he said with a sudden release of a long-held belief, one he hadn't even known was there, "it seems to *me* that old people always say everything was better in the past. Maybe it was, but what difference does it make now?"

Martine thought for a moment. "Maybe it gives us something to aspire to?"

"Maybe. And maybe it gives us an excuse not to aspire."

She nodded. "Likely. Very likely."

They spent a night camping in a copse of pine trees near the track, and made it to the ford toward the end of the next day.

SAKER

THE GLADE was ringed with scraggly pine trees, untidy, like the raven nests that crowned them. It was not like most of the gods' places, which tended to be beautiful, peaceful, lush. This was just a scrubby glade in the middle of a large pine copse, with brown winter grass waiting for the first snowfall, and a few rabbit burrows at the edges, well away from the black rock at its center.

They were all the same, those rocks, cold even in the summer sun and differing only in size. The gods, it was said, had sent them all to Earth at the same time, at the birth of life. Some said the stones had brought the first life, or they were what remained of the gods' sweat from laboring to create the living world. No matter how they had come, they belonged, everywhere, to the gods.

Saker knelt before the rock and bowed, waiting for the itch under the skin that meant the gods were with him. He felt nothing. Astonished, and a little alarmed, he prayed.

"Gods of field and stream, hear your son. Gods of sky and wind, hear your son. Gods of earth and stone, hear your son. Gods of fire and storm, hear your son."

Nothing.

He sat back on his heels, thinking hard. Did the gods disapprove of his plan? Surely not. Perhaps they had removed themselves so their presence would not interfere with his spell. Yes! *Of course.* His human magic might not work in their holy sphere, so they had left to allow him free rein.

"Thy son thanks you, gods of all."

He began to dig at the far north side of the glade, where Rowan's song had said the bones of the Spritford victims had been casually buried.

He found them easily, for bedrock was only a few feet down. The brittle bones of human skeletons, brown with age and dirt, mingled together; the skulls, with gaping holes, missing jaws, and empty eyes, willed him to work faster. The song had said forty-seven, men and women and children. He found twenty-nine skulls in three hours, and was satisfied. He placed the children's skulls to one side, cradling a baby's tiny head in his palm. He had to stop for a moment, to acknowledge the waste, the crushed bone, the toothless mouth. He laid it down, gently, and returned to the adult bones strengthened in purpose. They would pay. They would pay in blood every part of their debt.

He stood over the skulls, took out his knife, and began the spell.

I am Saker, son of Alder and Linnet of the village of Cliffhaven.
I seek justice. Justice for Wren, for Jay, for Lark, for Sparrow—

There was a little *flick* in his mind at the name Sparrow, and he said it again, but the sensation didn't come again, so he continued.

I seek justice for Falcon, for Owl—

There it was, a strong response this time: his Sight was coming alive and showing him, in his mind's eye, a small man with beautiful hands and angry eyes. He continued with new zeal.

I seek justice for Owl and all of his comrades, unjustly slain and buried in this place.

He could feel that the one name was enough. The bones were singing to him now, not all of them, but many. The spirits of the dead were listening, finally. The rest of the spell wasn't in words, but images in his mind, complex and distressing: colors, phrases of music, the memory of a particular scent, the sound of a scream...

He paused and looked down at the skulls. They seemed to shout silently for him to hurry. He pressed the knife to his palm and drew it down hard. The blood surged out in time with his heart and splashed in gouts on the lifeless bones.

"Arise, Owl and all his comrades," he commanded. "Take your revenge."

ASH

ASH HAD ALWAYS wondered why the river was called Sharp. When the road reached the ford, it was easy to see why.

They came down a ridge into a strange world. It was as though the land had been picked up and turned upside down, so that layers of rocks stuck up straight into the air, instead of lying flat under the ground. The wind had worn them into a maze of razor edges all the way to the water. The road picked its way between them, zigzagging wildly to find the safest way. It was hard on foot, Ash thought; taking a cart through would have been close to impossible.

Ash was nervous. It was an unchancy place, and the ghost's warning still troubled him. He made Martine follow him, and he kept his hand on his dagger as they made their way through the labyrinth. At every turn he expected Death herself to jump out at them, but other than startling some ravens picking over a rabbit's corpse, nothing happened. It darkened as they moved into the valley, and when the sun finally disappeared between one step and the next, his unease grew.

Only the wind's moan through the rocks followed them; only the river's rush awaited. The ford was at a wide, hence calm, stretch of the river, but it was still dangerous: just a series of stepping-stones joined the banks across the turbulent stream. Ash went first, testing each rock to make sure it would bear his weight, careful on the slick, worn granite. He was almost to the other side when he saw the water sprite, lying between the last rock and the bank, staring up at him with malice and a smile.

"Ware, Ash," Martine called at the same moment.

"I see it," he said, hesitating.

The water sprite couldn't hurt him if he stayed on land. In air, their flesh melted away into smoke. But if he stumbled and fell into the water, or even lost balance for a moment and dipped his foot in, she could pull him under. No one knew what happened to those who were taken by the sprites: no trace was ever found.

But he had a pretty good idea, looking at those long clawed hands and the sharp teeth that smiled at him. Suddenly Doronit's voice came back to him vividly: "Whistle." And it was as though he stood again on the cliffs outside Turvite with the wind wraiths trying to tug him over to his death.

He thrust the thought away from him. He knew if he moved while he was remembering that moment, he would fall. He swallowed hard and strode onto the last rock, then jumped as assuredly as he could to the shore. He stumbled, from fear or clumsiness, but fell face forward and grabbed hard at good, safe land. The sprite laughed at him.

Martine was safe beside him before he had picked himself up. She landed lightly and bent down to him, but he brushed off her hand, embarrassed and angry with himself.

"No harm done," she said, amused.

He grunted and then turned to watch the sprite swim away. It moved like a dolphin, smoothly and powerfully. But it could never leap into the air for joy, he thought, and felt a brief spasm of pity; then he shivered with relief.

The road ahead rose steeply through more of the sharp rock maze, but going up toward the sky, even a twilight sky, felt to Ash like waking up on a fine holiday morning. At the top of the ridge they both paused and looked back. The river spurted and foamed around the ford rocks. It looked perilous, and he shivered again.

The other side of the ridge was different country; they had passed into the sparser, harsher land of the north. Still, it was a kind of country they both knew well. From the ridge they could see the road wind down for miles into a long, broad, shallow valley until it came to a stream, a tributary of the Sharp. Specks of light appeared on the other side of the stream, and Ash realized that the dark shapes he had taken for rocks were really cottages. It was much farther away than it had looked, and he remembered that distances were often deceptive in these wider lands.

"That's Spritford. We'll reach there sometime tomorrow," Martine said. "Let's find somewhere for tonight."

Neither of them felt like going back to the river for water, so they cast about until they found a little pool in the rocks that had enough rainwater to make cha.

"It'll be safe enough if we boil it," Ash said.

There was enough shelter in the rocks to make an autumn night there not too unpleasant, although the ground was bruising to their hips. They drank, ate cheese sandwiches and some plums that Halley had given them, and settled back to sleep.

The next day was unseasonably hot and airless. The land was dusty, with flocks of goats grazing here and there, watched by young boys squatting on rocks who stared hard at them and sometimes deigned to nod when the pair waved. The scent of wild thyme and sage was strong and after a few hours Ash had a headache.

They rounded a low hill and found themselves on the final stretch of track down to the stream, with the village they had seen the night before on the other side.

BRAMBLE

RIDING NORTH, she was riding into autumn. In these parts, the season came in with a biting wind that crisped the leaves on the trees and bent the heavy grass heads flat by the side of the road. The horses didn't like it. It was cold enough for their breath to form plumes in the air. They were fidgety, reluctant to do anything she asked. Bramble wasn't any happier than the horses, and by late afternoon she was more than glad to see roofs above a rise in the ground up ahead.

The village was only a huddle of houses beside a stream. Like most of the country houses in this district, they were two stories: the lower one for the animals to winter in, the upper for the family. She stopped at the largest house and banged on the door with her fist.

"I need lodgings," she shouted. "I can pay."

The door edged open just enough to let her and the horses in, and was slammed shut behind them. The relief of being out of the wind was immediate. The stable felt stuffy, even warm, although she could still see her breath on the air. There were livestock in the stable, a cow and a nanny goat. A couple of dogs, which clearly had been curled up in the straw, bounced around them, sniffing avidly at Bramble's crotch. She pushed them away.

"Gods! It's cold enough to freeze the nuts off a gelding out there!" a voice boomed.

Bramble turned, unwound the scarf from her head and smiled. "It is that."

The voice belonged to a tall blond woman, with strong arms and big hands that she was using to unsaddle Cam. Bramble left her to it and saw to the other horses. Even the relief of being out of the cold hadn't sweetened Trine's temper. She tried to kick one of the dogs and was clouted firmly on the nose.

"That's it," the blond said. "You've got to show them who's boss."

She turned and shouted up the wooden stairs. "Lace, put a bran mash on. She's got three poor beasts here near dead with cold."

Side by side they rubbed the horses down in silence until Lace, who turned out to be a skinny adolescent girl in thick orange socks, brought down a wide pan of warm mash and emptied it into the feed trough. The three horses jostled to nose into it. The blond woman watched with satisfaction.

"That'll do 'em. Come on." She led the way to the living area above.

The room was untidy and sparsely furnished with wooden settles and a table and chairs, but softened by thick fleeces on the floor. Bramble, noting belatedly that her hostess had her boots off, took hers off too and sank cold toes into the fleece gratefully. Her feet tingled as the blood flowed more warmly in them.

"I'm Butterfly," the blond said, and jerked a thumb toward the girl. "Lacewing." Bramble didn't show her amusement, but Butterfly grimaced anyway. "They call me Fly and her Lacy," she said. "Our mother must have been crazy, but all the girls in her family were named for things that fly."

Bramble smiled. "I'm Bramble," she said. "With us, it was plants."

Fly guffawed and relaxed.

Bramble sat at the table as she and the girl made cha and cooked bacon and eggs.

"Bad time to start a journey, winter coming on," Fly said, glancing sideways as she turned the bacon.

"I'm on my way to the Well of Secrets," Bramble replied. "Didn't expect the cold to come on so soon."

"Keep going the road you're on, you'll have more to worry about than the cold."

Bramble raised her eyebrows.

"It's shaping up for war, girl, and those horses of yours are like gold around here. Why do you think my stable's empty?"

"The warlord?"

Fly snorted. "Shagging right. He's commandeered every horse within thirty miles. Took both my broodmares—though thank the gods he's breeding them, not using them as troopers. Wants to breed and train a cavalry, for the gods' sake! If it weren't for me being female, he'd have me up at the fort training the horses!"

"I don't quite understand what this war's supposed to be about."

Fly scooped the bacon and eggs onto rounds of bread on wooden plates and slammed them down on the table. "Lace! Eat!" she shouted. "Thegan *says* it's because the Lake People are bleeding us dry with the tolls they charge to ferry our goods across the Lake to the roads beyond, and because they won't let us build a bridge instead, and besides, our Lady Sorn, his wife, has a right to the Domain through her grandfather."

"And what's the real story?"

"Well, look at the map, girl! He's got the Cliff Domain already, now he's married Central, if he takes the Lake he's got the whole middle of the Domains under him, all the way to the coast. He'll have cut us in two."

Bramble considered it. "He won't have a port, though. It's all cliffs along the Central Domain coast."

"If I were Carlion, I'd be feeling nervous."

"He wouldn't invade one of the free towns!"

The free towns had been set up by Acton, and they had *always* been free to govern themselves. No warlord had entered a free town by force in a thousand years. It was unthinkable.

"Who's to stop him?" Fly answered.

The three of them ate thoughtfully for a moment.

The Domain nearest Carlion was South, where Bramble came from. The warlord there was better at encouraging his men to bully and steal than at training them for war. Three Rivers Domain was the next closest, but it was small.

Fly was right. Bramble grew cold from her toes to the tips of her ears. There was no one to stop him. Maryrose lived in Carlion. Perhaps she should turn around right now, go back to Carlion and warn them.

"Someone should warn Carlion," Lace said.

"They wouldn't believe us, honey. If I didn't know Thegan, it wouldn't even have occurred to me. But that one will stop at nothing."

Bramble thought it over. The news of war with the Lake People would get to Carlion soon enough. There were people of intelligence there, not least Maryrose's mother-in-law, the town clerk. They would see the need and recruit help. Few Domains would refuse. It was in everyone's best interests to keep the free towns *free*.

Bramble relaxed a little. "He has to win the war with the Lake People first."

"Easier said than done," Fly said, nodding. "But he's claiming the gods are behind him, because everything has gone so well in Sendat since the Kill was Reborn."

"The shagging bastard! The pox-ridden, slimy little thief!"

Fly's jaw dropped and then she shouted with laughter. "Bramble! Gods, it was you! The Kill Reborn!" She got up and made a mocking bow. "Well, well, well. So the Kill Reborn doesn't support Thegan. He's not going to like that, girl. Better not go to Sendat."

For once, Bramble was inclined to listen to advice. Following her instinct was what she'd decided to do, and her instinct was to stay well away from anything to do with Thegan. It made her skin crawl just to think of him. He was everything she'd always hated about the warlord system: selfish, brutal, power hungry. He had tainted her by claiming her luck as his own, implicating her in his evils. She had never been so angry. Her blood seethed, hissed in her ears. Like the warlord's man, she wanted Thegan's face under her foot.

But not badly enough to seek him out.

She stayed the night with Lace and Fly, asking no more questions and having to answer none.

She packed early the next morning and was off just after dawn, paying Fly more than the woman wanted to take.

"Saved my life," Bramble said.

"Good," Fly retorted, putting the coppers back into Bramble's pocket. "It's good luck to help the Kill Reborn. I might need me some good luck soon—don't take it away by paying me."

Bramble wasn't comfortable with the gesture, but thanked her and raised a hand goodbye. She had exulted in becoming the Kill Reborn, but carrying the name made her uneasy. It was as though the gods walked with her even when she couldn't feel them, as though some other force used her feet to walk and her mouth to speak. All the more reason to be angry with Thegan, she thought, for using what belonged to the gods.

She turned back on her tracks. Fly had said that there was a minor road—"nearly a track, girl"—two miles back on the right, which would take her in a wide curve around Sendat and up to the top of the Lake, where she could take a ferry across and have an easy ride to the main north road.

It had rained overnight and she rode into a landscape of moving water: drops falling from leaves, streams rushing between hedges of reeds, trickles along the rutted road, and dew-laden sere grasses lifting to the weak morning sun. It was beautiful, musical, magical. Bramble felt the horses detect her stir of blood and lift of heart, and quickened their pace as much as she dared.

Thegan's men saw her just before the turnoff. It was sheer bad luck. As she looked up into the morning glare, she saw six of them, picking their way down the road on sturdy mountain horses that were just bigger than ponies and starting to get shaggy with winter coats. Something about their silhouettes raised a shiver up her spine. She didn't even consider running, the feeling of inevitability was so strong. Besides, she had two packhorses. They'd catch her in seconds.

Bramble was thankful that the sergeant didn't look like either Thegan or the warlord's man she had killed. He was in his fifties, an ordinary looking gray-haired man with the beginnings of a cold. He kept sniffing and turning his head politely to spit out phlegm. It gave a strange rhythm to their conversation.

"Where are you off to, girl?" he asked civilly, and spat.

"Carlion." Eventually, she hoped.

He sniffed, but not in disapproval. "Well, sorry, lass, but you're coming to Sendat today. Warlord's orders."

"I'm on a free road, going to a free town!"

"Warlord's orders. All horses to be collected and their riders brought in for questioning, unless they're on warlord's business. What's your name?"

"Bramble."

He nodded and gestured for her to turn around.

She fell in with them and noted their professionalism: their way of surrounding her without jostling her, the sheen on their weapons, and the good condition of their tack. They all carried the short bows which work best on horseback, and they were slack but ready to be strung at a moment's notice, the quivers full and protected by leather hoods. Thegan kept a disciplined guard, trained and well equipped. It didn't make her like him any more. Trained to kill. Equipped to capture the innocent and steal from them. And what would happen to her once they reached Thegan's stronghold? Robbed and then turned out on the road to survive as best she could?

It took them most of the day to reach the fort above Sendat, on muddy, slippery roads that made the horses uncomfortable and twitchy, and unsure of their footing. They stopped whenever they found a patch of clear ground to rest the horses. When they stopped again to eat their lunch, the men offered to share their bread and bacon with Bramble, "to show there's no hard feelings, like," and she was glad she could show that her own bag was full of food, and refuse without giving offense. She didn't want to eat with them, or be beholden to them, but she wasn't stupid enough to antagonize them unnecessarily.

They talked at intervals about the coming war, which they all seemed to look forward to, especially one man, the sergeant's helper, the only one who kept his bow strung, "in case we see some rabbits for supper." He shot at two in one glade before Bramble had even seen them, the arrows finding sure marks. They all waited for him to gut them, while the horses nibbled lichen from the trunks of the birch trees. Bramble peeled a little of the bark and chewed on it.

The sergeant looked up at her. "Get used to the taste of it," he said sourly. "War in spring leaves the fields unsown and the granaries empty come winter. There'll be nothing *but* birch bark to eat this time next year."

The archer glared at him. "We don't talk about my lord Thegan's business to some Traveler slut."

The sergeant stared at him for a moment, reminding him of their different ranks, but the archer still glared, full of righteous indignation.

"He's not a god, Horst," the sergeant said, and spat tidily into the ditch.

Horst glowered at him but held his tongue.

They reached the fort an hour before sundown, filing up the narrow Sendat streets as the shopkeepers were folding in their counters. The sergeant exchanged greetings with a few of them. They looked at Bramble curiously. One, a middle-aged woman selling candles, let her mouth fall open and then called excitedly to someone inside her shop.

"Father! Father! It's the Kill Reborn! The Kill Reborn's come to join the warlord!"

Immediately others crowded out of the shop and people stared and pointed.

"That true?" the sergeant growled. "You *that* Bramble?"

"So what?"

He smiled. "Well, I don't think you need to worry about losing your horses, girl, ma'am, I mean. You're our luck! Everyone knows that." He paused. "I heard your Thorn passed on. I'm sorry."

He sounded genuine. She nodded.

"I'm Sig." He pulled off his glove and held out his hand.

For a moment she hesitated, not wanting to touch him, not wanting skin on skin with a warlord's man. The feel of Leof's hand leaped to her mind, warm, soft, strong. She reached out for Sig's hand to banish that memory and was astonished to hear the crowd break into cheering, interpreting the simple gesture as a symbol of something bigger, as though everything she did was a sign of the gods' will.

The fort was bigger than the one near Wooding. It covered the top of a plateau, maybe four or five hides of land, with a strong wooden palisade surrounded by a spiked ditch. As they rode through the gate Bramble saw that another wall, stone, was being built inside the wooden one. He's preparing for more than war with the Lake People, Bramble thought. He's making a palace like the kings of the Wind Cities.

The buildings were of stone below and wood above and rambled all over the southern side of the site, angled to the winter sun. The rest of the area was given over to stables and paddocks, with a huge gathering area in the center. That was where the sergeant led them.

"Wait here," he said, dismounting, and strode off into the main building.

Even so close to sundown, it was frantic with activity. The smithies, near the stables, were aglow and noisy; there were coopers hooping barrels in front of what looked like a warehouse; a wheelwright fitted an iron rim to a wheel near its wagon; and some fletchers were using the last of the sunlight to finish a batch of arrows—cloth-yard shafts, Bramble noticed, for the longbow that foot soldiers carried.

The yard to her right was full of horses. She edged Cam over to the railing, dismounted, and looked in. Over the past few years she and Gorham had trained quite a few horses for Thegan. They were all here. And more. He must have been buying up all the good mounts—or just taking them—from the local towns. Bramble recognized most of them in the yard. She whistled softly and they crowded to the rails, recognizing the whistle codes she and Gorham had taught them. She talked to them, deliberately taking a moment of calm before Thegan arrived. They snuffled into her hands, nuzzled her cheek, and shoved each other aside so they could get to her.

"And this," a warm, laughing voice said, "*this* is why the gods have led you to me."

She took a deep breath and turned. There Thegan was at last, slighter than in her memory, but still solid, with the big shoulders of a swordsman. He was welcoming, laughing with cold eyes, playing to the audience of crafters and soldiers who crowded, grinning, to see her.

"Our Kill Reborn!" he said loudly, inviting a cheer and getting one. "Welcome! You are thrice welcome to join us!"

"But I'm not joining you," she said quietly. "Your men arrested me and brought me here. So you could steal my horses, apparently."

His eyes went even colder, but he smiled.

"Following my orders, yes, but following the gods' commands, too, I think. They have led you here."

The crowd cheered and Thegan waved them backward a little so they could speak in private.

Bramble felt her whole body stiffen. She recognized, again, the itch under the skin that meant the gods were present, and she knew Thegan was right. The gods *had* led her here. But for what reason? Not to support Thegan. Of that, she was sure. The gods had their own secret purpose, which they weren't confiding to her. All she could do was act according to her nature—to the nature they had given her.

"But not to join you," she said, still keeping her voice quiet.

"Oh, yes," he said, just as quietly, moving closer until his breath ruffled her cheek. "You will join me, girl. You will train my horses and you will smile. And all men will say the Kill Reborn rides with Thegan and his luck warms his bed."

He didn't even bother to threaten her. There was so much menace in his voice that he didn't need to. She was trembling. At first she thought it was fear, compounded with the fear of humiliating herself in front of him by quivering in terror. Then she recognized it as anger so great that it threatened to rip her apart. It was anger greater than any she had ever felt, and she realized that she was filling with the gods' anger as well as her own. *Blasphemer,* she thought, and on the thought was calm again. She raised her head.

"No. I won't," she said.

For a long moment he looked at her. It was his true face for that moment, without the mask, and she saw the lines from nose to mouth, the deep-set curves at the corners of the mouth, the tracks at the eyes from squinting into snow glare, the pores growing coarser with age. He had a grown son, she remembered, who kept Cliff Domain in his name. He was feeling the sharp breath of the Lady of Death behind his shoulder, and he was reaching for glory to stave off her kiss. He was frightened and refused to know it. She knew that this was why the gods had brought her here.

Then his face was closed to her again, age and fear covered with assurance. "You will," he said.

"You are going to die," she said, "and nothing you do—no war, no conquest, no victory—can stop it. You will die and rot into dust, just like everyone else. That is the gods' message to you from me."

His face turned dark red with anger. "I will unite this brawling pack of warlords," he hissed. "I will create a united country, a great country, the country Acton intended, and I will leave such a legacy of prosperity and splendor that my name will live forever!"

She shook her head. "How many will you kill to ward off your fear of oblivion?" she asked.

He raised his hand as though to strike her, then turned it into a heavy-handed clap on the shoulder. "Let's get you in out of the cold!" he said loudly.

Another cheer went up, but stopped raggedly as the crowd parted to let a woman through. It was the Lady Sorn, shrouded in a cream cloak against the chill air. A young fair-headed maid held the hem of the cloak out of the mud. Sorn looked at her husband and then at Bramble.

The gods were still with her, Bramble realized, but they had turned all their attention to Sorn. They yearned for her, it felt like, but she stood quite still, as though she couldn't feel them at all. Perhaps she couldn't. It was often so, with Acton's people.

"A guest for us, my lord husband?"

"An honored guest, my lady. Bramble, the Kill Reborn."

Sorn smiled. "We are indeed honored. Come, then, my dear." She reached out and took Bramble's left hand in her right.

Bramble felt a stiffness, a piece of paper, pass to her hand before Sorn let go, moving as though to guide Bramble toward the buildings. She palmed it, shoving both hands in her pockets as though she were cold. She and Sorn moved through the crowd, followed by the maid, trying to keep up. There, near the huge open doorway to the main hall, stood Leof. Bramble stopped as she saw his face, saw his eyes go from her to Sorn in puzzlement, raise to Thegan, narrow in apprehension, and come back to her as if to a lodestone.

"Leof, look who has come to be our guest!" Thegan shouted jovially. "Your fellow chaser!"

Sorn, Thegan and Bramble stopped at the threshold beside Leof, who was searching for something to say. Bramble realized that at any other time she would have felt the kick in the stomach, the shock, at his nearness. But the gods filled her sight, darkening it, and there was thrumming in her ears. She felt the gods warning her not to step over the threshold. The maid dropped the edge of Sorn's cloak and held out a hand for Bramble's jacket. She hung back, looking for an excuse, and with gratitude felt Trine nip her on the shoulder. She turned automatically to clout her on the nose.

"Oh, my dear," Sorn said, "we've forgotten your horses, haven't we? Why don't you just turn them out in the yard with the others and one of the ostlers will see to them?"

"A good idea, my lady."

She took Trine's bridle and found Cam and Mud just behind her. She led them toward the yard and nodded to Sig as he swung the gate open for her. She paused and tied the two packhorses' leading reins securely to their packs, so they wouldn't trip over them. The other horses crowded forward, eager to get out, to be near her. She knew this would be her only chance.

At that moment the gods left her, emptied out of her into the sky. She had done whatever it was they wanted, and now they had no use for her. She was on her own. It left her relieved and desolate at once. But the fear rising in her stomach roused her into action: she would not give Thegan the victory of her fear.

She whistled, hard and loud, the code for "run to me," and swung up on Cam's back as the pack of horses turned itself into a herd and came rushing out. She urged Cam into a gallop from a standing start and swept out of the wooden gate in the middle of the herd, whistling "gallop" over and over again.

The men by the gate had no chance to close it, though they tried. For a moment she thought one of them was Beck, the warlord's man from her own domain who had pursued her to the chasm. Then one of the other men was pushed aside by the outside horses and she lost sight of him. She couldn't see if the man had been trampled, but said a prayer to the gods for him under her breath.

Then they were through, in a thundering avalanche of horseflesh, and heading down the steep streets of Sendat, the shadows closing over their heads as they left Thegan's stronghold behind.

FAINA'S STORY

DA CAME ROUND the back of the milking shed in the middle of the morning. I was distracted because the cheese was just setting and had to be watched. If you leave it in the hot water for too long it goes chewy. I hoisted the cauldron off the fire and began to scoop out the curds into the setting basket. He just stood there, fidgeting with his hands in his pockets.

"It's been a bad year, Faina," he began.

I made the sign against ill fortune and splashed some of the hot cheese on my hand, but I bit back my curse. Mam says for every curse the gods add a day to your stay in the darkness before you are reborn.

"Are you all right?" Da asked.

"Aye, I'm fine." I held my amulet for a moment and said a prayer against ill temper.

I kept scooping out the cheese, wondering what he wanted. He's a good man, my da, but women's work and men's work don't mix, he says; and he stays well away from the cheese making, knowing it's unchancy at best, getting the curds to turn, and a man there might set all awry.

"What's the matter, Da?" I asked finally.

"It's been a bad year."

Well, that was no news. What with late spring rains and early frost, and a stinging gale the week before the hay was ripe, it had been a bad year for the whole district. Mam said it was a sign from the gods, but she didn't know of what. That we weren't praying enough, likely.

"We can't pay the taxes, lass," Da said.

I put down the curd spoon and turned to him, drying my hands on my apron. This was serious news. The old warlord, Wyman, was dying of a wasting fever and with no firm hand on the reins, his men were getting out of control. They could take what they wanted in payment of taxes, and they would, too, and a bit over for themselves. We weren't poor, but we didn't have much to spare. If they took the cart, or the oxen, or the boar... it might make the difference between a bad year and a killing year.

"I thought... I wondered... It'd only be for a year. We're short only a bit."

"What do you mean, Da?"

"The Lady Sorn is getting married."

Well, we all knew that, too. She'd been married off to a man twenty years older, from Cliff Domain, where the men were as cold as their mountains. A shame, it was, we all thought, even those, like me, who lived in little villages and had never set eyes on the young lady.

"They need more maids at the fort. I've had a word to our village voice. The tax collector will take a year of service in exchange... Just a year, Faina..."

He was so apologetic, it took me a moment to realize that he was talking about me going into tax bondage. I was shocked, but then I was excited. To go to court! To help with the marriage celebrations! And tax bondage was honorable enough. Even the warlord's men didn't touch the bond servants. I didn't have to worry about rape, well, no more than living in my own village, where a girl who walked down a quiet lane always kept an ear out for the sound of horses' hooves.

"Of course I'll go, Da. It might even be fun," I said, and even if I hadn't wanted to go, it would have been worth saying so to see the relief on his face.

So I went to the court and I scrubbed out rooms that hadn't seen a brush for eighteen years, since the Lady Sorn's naming day. And I washed yellowing linen, carted water and emptied chamber pots, and I did all the work I always did at home, except cheese making and cooking. It *was* fun. There were lots of other girls like me, come specially for the year of the wedding, and our room at night was full of giggles and discussions about the best looking of the men at arms. We worked hard but we ate well, and some of us, I thought—looking at the scrawny ones—better than we'd ever eaten.

The only thing I didn't like was that most of the other girls were unbelievers. They cursed without thought; they had no respect for the gods. They laughed at me for getting up before dawn to go to the altar stone. What did they know?

To kneel by the altar stone in the gray half-light, to feel the winds of dawn and know that the gods woke, to say my prayers, to be in the presence of the gods, to know they listened: that was the center of my day, the center of my life, the calm point that let me work and laugh and eat and sleep with joy, because the gods went with me.

There was always the same handful of people at the altar stone: an old man from the stables, a woman from the kitchen called Aldie, a boy from the blacksmith's, a young woman from the court. We prayed in silence and waited for the dawn, and then moved away with a smile to each other.

It was the third day before I realized that the young woman was the Lady Sorn, and that was only because the old man said, "Tomorrow's the day, then, my lady," and she smiled at him and nodded.

"The Lord Thegan's son will be here at midmorning," she said.

"May all the gods bless you, my lady," he said.

"Thank you, Sip," she said. Then she looked at me curiously. "You're one of the new maids?"

I curtsied low. "Faina, my lady."

"You are very devout, Faina."

I blushed. Mam never thought so. "I like to come to the altar stone, my lady."

"So do I. But I've never had a maid who would accompany me." She smiled wryly, but those beautiful green eyes were warm. "You can't order someone to pray."

I smiled back. "No, my lady. The gods wouldn't like it."

"No, they would not. Come with me."

I followed her to her rooms and from that moment I was her own maid, her special maid. A blessing from the gods. No matter what else has happened, that was a blessing. I think, now, she might be one of those that the gods work through without them knowing it.

We talked often and long, she and I, though not so much that first day as there was so much to do getting ready for the wedding. But over the next weeks, and years, I learned about her life.

She had been cross to be married off without her father even asking, but she'd expected that long enough. The old lord, Wyman, treated his women like dogs and horses—breeding animals were only worth their keep if they bred true. Hah! Three wives he had and only the one ever caught a babe, and then he beat her for producing a girl until she died, lying in the straw still wet from the birth. The gods abhor a man such as he. He will scream at the edges of the dark, but it will be a warm night in hell before he gets reborn.

So he mistreated my lady all her life, for rage and disappointment that she wasn't a boy. And he pampered her, too, for show's sake, for his own pride's sake, so she was dressed in furs and silks and waited on with respect in the court, and then beaten behind doors. And all that time all everyone knew was that my Lady Sorn was beautiful and young and the best catch in the Eleven Domains, because her husband would rule the richest Domain of all when her father died, and he was dying fast from the wasting sickness.

They sent all manner of negotiators, the warlords from the other Domains. They wanted Central for their sons, or for themselves. Arvid, Lord of the Last Domain, was the only one who didn't court her. Central was too far, maybe, although of them all he was the closest in age. Thegan was old enough to be her father, almost. He has a son a couple of years younger, Gabra, who holds Cliff Domain for him, and at first the old warlord said that Sorn should be matched with him. All this happened through go-betweens, my lady told me.

Then Thegan arrived himself, with no warning, riding in large as life and twice as handsome, all gold hair and blue eyes and smiles, as irresistible as Acton himself. I wasn't there, but I can imagine it. I've seen him charm strangers a hundred times, seen that warmth flow out of him like honey, like sunlight. I don't think either my Lady Sorn or the old warlord even tried to resist him. They had the marriage two weeks later, an engagement just long enough to prepare the wedding and for my lord Thegan's son to arrive from Cliff Domain.

The first time I saw my lord Thegan was when he arrived in the hall in his wedding finery, all blue to match his eyes, smiling at my lady as though he had never seen anything so beautiful. And she was. Oh, yes, she was glowing. She believed in him, then. Loved him even.

We all believed in Thegan. After the old warlord died and my lord took the reins, he seemed sent by the gods to lead us. He used the lash and the gallows more than the old warlord, but then things had been let slide a while, and there were lawless men preying on merchants and farmers alike. They deserved the flayings and the hangings they got. At least I thought so—was sure so. After all, the Well of Secrets was Thegan's niece, as everyone knew. Surely that was a family led by the gods.

Just as I met my lady, I met my Alston at the altar stone in the dawn. He is a gods' man, my Alston, pure-hearted, and I loved him soon enough, as he loves me. He follows my lord like a child follows his father, and my lord Thegan trusts him.

About three years after my lady and my lord were married, Alston came to visit me one evening, excited and exalted. My lord had told him great news, news that filled him with hope for the future, our children's future. He explained everything to me, just as my lord had explained it to him: how the Domains were wasting away under lazy and evil warlords, and how they could be—should be—united to form a single great country, just as Acton had intended.

When Acton disappeared, a thousand years ago, he had been in the process of uniting the country. His death interrupted that, but now it was time to complete it—one country, strong and free and prosperous, under one law. Thegan's law. For he would be Overlord of the Eleven Domains. I could see it. It was a wonderful vision. For surely, the warlords cared too much for their own comfort and not much for the needs of their people. If there was an overlord, setting the law, making them abide by it, it could be a great thing for the common people.

My Alston said that Thegan's son in Cliff Domain, Gabra, wasn't strong enough to hold the country together after Thegan's death, but Thegan and Sorn's children would be raised from birth to know their destiny, and Thegan and Sorn's son would be overlord after Thegan. Then he swore me to secrecy, because there were spies from the other Domains who were our enemies, and no one should know for certain what the lord intended. I was so proud that Alston was one of my lord's trusted men. I gave a lock of my hair in thanksgiving to the gods that night, and when my lady asked me why, I told her, for of course Alston wouldn't have meant me to keep such a secret from my lady.

"All the Domains, Faina?" she asked quietly. "And how will he achieve this? He has sent out no letters for a council."

It had been twenty-two years since the last Council of Warlords, since the last attack on the Cliff Domain by the Ice King, where they had all agreed to send men to help drive back the ice warriors. Lord Thegan was one of the leaders of that campaign, along with his father and brother, and was the bravest of them all. That is why his men worship him so, Alston says. He is so driven in battle, but so careful about his men's lives. A true leader, my Alston says.

Looking back, it was after I told my Lady Sorn about the lord's plans that she changed. Stopped looking at him with that dazed, tremulous expression. I knew what that look meant. I'd heard her moaning in his bed, and crying out, and weeping, sometimes, too, but not weeping that needed comforting. For weeks after the wedding, he went around looking like a cat in a dairy and she was soft-eyed and languorous, as a new bride should be, but rarely is. It may be there was too much awakening too soon, for later she resented that her body had betrayed her, that when he called her to his bed she went despite herself, despite her suspicion and her distrust.

"I'm like a bitch in heat," she said bitterly to me one morning as we walked away from the altar stone a few weeks after I told her of the Lord Thegan's plans. "He snaps his fingers and I go running. And the things he does to me… " She buried her face in her hands, but I could see it was burning red with shame. "The things I do to him… " she whispered.

"But lady, he's your husband," I comforted her. "The gods enjoin us to cleave to our husbands and enjoy them."

"Not like this," she said quietly, then lifted her head and shook back her hair. "Well. He may have my body, but he won't have my mind. And maybe having the body will allay any suspicion of me. He will build his overlordship on the bodies of the innocent, Faina, and the gods cannot approve."

I admit, I was torn at that moment. If my lord Thegan was guided by the gods, then my lady should not be suspicious of him. Nor work against him. I thought, for a moment, that I should tell Alston that my lady mistrusted his master, but then something in me knew, and

I thought, no, she told me this for the gods alone to hear. Thank the gods I said nothing!

The preparations for war began, with the blacksmith working noon and night, although nothing was said openly. My lord began to buy all the horses he could, or take them in lieu of taxes if he couldn't buy them. And my lady started to walk all the courtyards and buildings of the fort each day, inspecting the preparations, listening to the sergeants at arms train their men.

Then the night came when the Kill Reborn was found and brought to the fort.

I followed my lady out into the night, intrigued to see the Kill Reborn join with my lord Thegan. Was it a true sign that he was doing the gods' will? Did they want the Domains united into one country, "a great nation" as my lord said, "renowned and strong and free..."?

I saw the Kill Reborn and it was a shock to realize she was a Traveler. But the gods often choose Travelers to carry their messages, I have noticed. So many stonecasters travel, it cannot be coincidence. Only a few can hear the gods. I've learned to pick them out of the crowd. I cannot feel the gods direct but, at secondhand, I am never wrong. The Kill Reborn travels with them on her shoulder. No doubt. I could feel them around her despite the dark, and the crowd, and the swords and shouts.

She was coming inside—*I might be able to serve her myself,* I thought, and was churned up with excitement—then she leaped upon her horse and whistled, and the whole pack of horses followed her. I felt my lady stiffen in surprise, then relax. My lord Thegan swore and stormed back toward the yard.

"Take her down," he ordered the archer, who was standing nearby, mesmerized by the spectacle.

The archer couldn't believe it at first, but he looked at my lord's face and then nocked his bow and swung it up to take aim. He pulled back the bowstring. My heart was huge in my throat. Blasphemy! Rank blasphemy to kill the chosen of the gods! I couldn't believe it.

"Leof!" my lady said urgently.

My lord Leof, one of the lord's lieutenants, sprang forward and knocked the bow out of the archer's hands.

Thegan rounded on him. "I gave an order!"

"My lord, think!" Leof said. "To shoot the Kill Reborn! The luck would leave you. I acted to save you, my lord."

My lady moved forward. "Not in front of everyone, Thegan."

Thegan stilled, control returning like water flowing into a jug. "Leof. You will find her and bring her back. You will send out men and recapture the horses. All of them. Do it now."

"Yes, my lord."

My lord Leof bowed and made his leave and my lady and I turned to go inside. I could hear the horses charging down the hill and I said a prayer for the Kill Reborn's safety on that slippery road. I stayed, for a moment, just inside the door, to touch the amulet at my breast and say the prayer.

And I heard Thegan beckon the archer.

"Horst."

"My lord."

"You're my man, I know."

"On my life, my lord."

"Follow Lord Leof. If he finds the girl, kill her. If he doesn't find her—she'll probably head north. I sent couriers north yesterday to Lord Arvid in the Last Domain. I will instruct Lord Leof to send you after them if he doesn't find the girl. You can catch up if you ride fast. Tell the Lord Arvid that I would take it as a mark of friendship to have the girl returned to me."

I stood for a moment, and then ran inside as though the Lady of Death herself was behind me. I knew that if he caught me there, having heard what I had heard, I was dead. And still, when I think of it, it was not the order to kill that shocked me the most. It was the way he talked about her. "The girl," he called her, as though she were nothing. No man with any belief in the gods could talk about the Kill Reborn like that. I realized he was without belief: the worst of all men, because there can be no redemption. Even the evil can be reborn if they repent to the gods in time. But to seek the gods' forgiveness you must first believe.

It was like the world had darkened to winter in the middle of spring: my days shortened, my skies clouded. It had been a golden time since they married, since the old warlord died and the reins came into Thegan's hands. He had brought so much joy and hope and energy to the Domain. He seemed to glow like the sun and we warmed ourselves from him. Now I felt cold. And older. Much, much older.

My lady was right. I prayed to the gods to give me the words to reveal the truth to Alston. I prayed to the gods for help, for comfort, for succor. Only they can guide us.

ASH

IN THE LATE afternoon light, the ghosts stood out surprisingly well, white against the rushing water of the stream, against the dull sage green of the bushes by the track.

"They're strong!" Martine exclaimed.

"As strong as in Turvite," Ash agreed. He felt light-headed, relieved. This was all the warning had meant. A group of ghosts! Then, as he and Martine neared the ford, he realized that these were not like any ghosts he had ever seen.

They were a mixture of men and women, but they all had the same look: an antique look, with strange clothes, dirty and disheveled. They were shorter than most people, with the tallest coming shoulder-high. The men were in knee-length skirts, bare chested, the women in long gowns that fell straight from shoulder to hip to ground without a break. Some of them had tears in their gowns; two of the men had the marks of wounds showing dark across their chests.

They had shawls over their shoulders, both men and women, and all wore long braids: the women, one down their backs, the men a series of shorter braids around their heads, tied down with a headband that crossed their foreheads. There were beads and feathers tied to the ends of the braids. Ash could tell that the braids were dark, and so were their eyes.

Each of them, men and women, clutched a tool, or maybe a weapon: sickles, knives, scythes, wooden rakes. Even ghost-pale, Ash could tell that the metal of the tools wasn't iron. Something about the way the light moved over the surface. Bronze, maybe? The ghosts held them in front of their chests as though unfamiliar with using them that way.

They were terrified—and angry. They stood absolutely still as Ash and Martine approached them, but poised, as though ready to run. Martine held out her hands in a gesture of peace. Their heads turned to follow the gesture, and the beads on the ends of their braids rattled.

Ash felt the blood drain from his head, it seemed from his whole body. That was not possible. Even on Ghost Begone Night—when he had set the ghosts of Turvite free to speak—they could make no other sound, not a clapping of hands, nor rustling of cloth as they ran, nothing. It *was not possible* for the beads on the head of a ghost to clink together.

"Ask them to speak, Ash," Martine said calmly.

He saw that there were drops of sweat starting out along her brow. She had heard it too. That was reassuring, in a way.

"Speak," Ash said gently, not wanting to startle them.

They looked at him, uncomprehending. The man in front, the tallest and brawniest, raised his scythe and made to move forward. There was a stain on the blade of the scythe, like blood. Ash swallowed against the stone in his throat. If the beads could rattle, could the scythe slice through flesh? He thought hard, and fast.

"Viven," he said, in the old tongue.

Relief flashed across all the ghosts' faces and they began to speak in a rush, gabbling the old language together. The man in the front waved them impatiently to silence, and spoke urgently, quickly, then waited for an answer to his question.

Ash could understand only one or two words in every six. The grating voice of the dead made it even harder to understand.

"Keiss," he said.

The man repeated his question.

Ash caught the words for invaders, yet where? He shook his head, dredging his memory for phrases from old songs. There was one, a lament...

"Sive keiss fardassane, loll parlan marl," Ash said. Go slowly from the battlefield, the invaders have gone.

"Loll?" the man said, eagerly.

Ash bit his lip. Shook his head. Swept his arm out in a circle that took in the whole country. *"Nurl loll,"* he said. *"Fessarna."* Gone everywhere. Conquered.

The group set up a wail, the same sound the ghosts from Turvite had made, a keening, echoing wail that set every nerve grating.

The sun touched the horizon and, as one, the ghosts turned to look at it, to raise their hands in gestures of homage and farewell.

"Wait!" Ash said, as they started to fade. "Who called you? Why? *Viven! Jli vivel? Se?*"

"*Carse,*" said the man, straining to stay a moment longer. He reached out and touched Ash's sleeve, gripped his arm with a strong and healthy hand. The edge of the scythe came nearer and Ash could smell the blood on its blade. Fresh blood. "*Carse. Sarat.*"

Then they faded.

"What did he say?" Martine demanded. "Who called them?"

"A carse is like an enchanter—but more than that. Someone who guides the tribe, a seer. Like the Well of Secrets."

"And *sarat?*"

"Revenge," Ash said blankly, with the smell of blood still in his nostrils, filling his head. "It means 'revenge.'"

They stood at the ford, reluctant to cross to the village.

"It would be more sensible to go around and find the road on the other side," Martine said.

"There was fresh blood on the scythe," Ash said. "We have to find out what happened."

"Why? Why us?"

"Because they spoke to us." Until he said it, he had not realized how strongly he felt about it. It was as though the ghost's words had put a yoke on him, a leash that pulled him to the village, to further knowledge, perhaps to greater responsibility. He didn't like the feeling. It was too much like walking past the black rock and oak tree in the center of Turvite and hearing the local gods call his name. Like watching the sheen and gleam of Martine's hair and knowing that if he just *concentrated,* he would see more... He shivered in the dusk, looking at the stream gurgling happily through the shallow rocks. But he could not turn away.

"I'm not sure I want to know," Martine said.

He stared at her. Her face had closed in, like the carvings of the dead the southern villagers sometimes did at the mouths of burial caves.

"I have seen enough blood," she said.

"What if this is the same thing that's threatening Elva?"

She shook her head, not in denial but as though to clear her thoughts. "You're right," she said. "It would be...that's the way the gods work."

So they crossed the ford and went up the slope to the village.

It was not a large place—a crossroads with some outlying streets that petered out into the woods on the far side. It had two inns, though, and a livery stable, and a couple of the houses on the ford side had notices on their front doors, drawings of a pillow and a plate, the standard sign for lodgings. Ash noticed that the drawings were done beautifully, elegantly sketched by brush rather than scrawled with charcoal, as they had been in other villages.

Every door was barred. There were some signs of disturbance: an overturned water barrel had made the dusty street mud halfway up, and there were broken windows with boards hastily nailed across them. From one cottage came the high, wailing sound of grief, rhythmically, as though whoever cried rocked to and fro in time to her keening. The shadows of evening seemed to lengthen in response.

Martine knocked on the door of the biggest inn. There was no answer, but a scuffling inside betrayed listeners behind the door.

"They've gone," Martine called. "They've gone."

"Who says so?" A voice came from behind the door.

"Flesh and blood."

"Stand by the window where we can see you."

They moved to the window. Between a crack in the shutters an eye stared out at them.

"Prove you're flesh and blood, then," a high voice said.

Martine shrugged, drew out her knife and pricked her thumb with the tip. A rich drop of blood welled up. The door opened cautiously.

"They're shagging Travelers!" Ash heard a voice say. "They probably brought the—the others... "

"Maybe not," the high voice said. "There's only two of them."

The woman in the inn door was bandaged across her cheek and around her head, and her arm was in a sling. She was thin, with lank blond hair, and had small hectic patches of red high on her pale cheeks.

"What do you want?" she asked, holding the door ready to close.

"To help," Martine said. "To find out what happened."

"We'll help our own," she said. "What do you think's happened?"

"We saw the ghosts, by the ford," Ash said. "What happened?"

"You *saw* them? They didn't attack you?" Her voice had sharpened into suspicion.

Behind her, a crowd of men and women shifted weapons more firmly into their grasp. Ash felt the hairs rise on his neck.

"They were going to," he assured her.

"But then they faded," Martine cut in, "as the sun set."

The crowd relaxed a little. Ash bit back his explanation of talking to the ghosts. Martine had more experience of people than he did; he would take her lead and ask questions later.

"Then they might be back in the morning," the woman said thoughtfully.

"Who knows. What did they do?" Martine asked.

The woman moved out of the doorway and indicated the room beyond. "Look for yourself."

Ash and Martine moved into the taproom. There were the normal long tables set up, but no one was sitting at them. Four shrouded bodies lay on them instead, the shrouds faintly marked with blood from the wounds underneath them. One of the bodies was a child. A woman sat by it, head on her arms in exhausted sleep, one hand still clutching a fold of the shroud.

Martine shuddered. The woman nodded, as though Martine had passed a test, and allowed them farther in. Ash found himself holding his breath. He didn't know what he was feeling.

"They came at noon," an old man said suddenly. "Right on noon, out of nowhere."

"Out of the forest," a woman said. "I was taking the vealer to butcher and they came out of the forest. I saw them in time and I hid in the stable."

"You couldn't stop them!" said a young man with deep cuts down his bare shoulders. "I had my hayfork and I got one right through the chest, but it didn't stop him!" He hesitated. "I—I ran," he admitted, and began to weep. "If I'd stayed . . . " He turned aside.

"They're dead already," the innkeeper said. "What could you have done? All that stops them is solid wood and stone. They couldn't get through the doors." She looked at the biggest of the shrouded bodies.

"My brother tried to stop them. *He* should have run." She moved toward the table slowly, until she stood by the corpse. "*Why didn't you run?*" She hit her brother's body with a closed fist, and began to sob.

Friends closed around her and a young man, patting shoulders, proffered hot drinks. Ash and Martine withdrew to a corner and sat down on a couple of stools.

"We need to know if there have been any strangers here," Martine said softly.

"The enchanter?"

She nodded. "It's a risk to ask, but we have to know. And then I think we leave these people to their sorrow. Before they turn on us."

She rose and moved to the innkeeper, who was calmer than the others.

"I think my friend and I will not trespass on your hospitality in these circumstances," she said gently. "You will not want strangers here now."

"Strangers, no..." The woman's face was suddenly stricken. "The stonecaster! Oh, gods, he was going to the forest yesterday and he hasn't come back! They must have found him..." She wept anew, although more quietly.

"A stranger?"

"No, no, he's been coming through here for years, now and then. Saker, his name is. He'd have no chance, he's only a thin little thing."

"We'll keep a lookout for him," Martine said, nodding to Ash.

They moved to the door and the young man with the wounded shoulder glared at them suspiciously. "You're going out into the night? With them out there?"

"We saw them fade as the sun went down. To tell the truth, my plan is to travel all night and be well away from here when the sun comes up. Just in case."

There was a murmur around the room.

"Good idea!" an old woman muttered. She turned to a younger woman by her side. "You go, too, Edi. Be away from here before daylight."

"Oh, no, Mam! I couldn't leave you. Besides, what if they're everywhere?"

Martine and Ash slipped through the door and it closed behind them as the argument went on.

"Why would they be everywhere?" the old woman said. "They were *our* ghosts!"

"Wait," Martine breathed. "Listen."

They stood in the full dark outside the door and listened.

"Other places have their own ghosts, Mam," the daughter replied. "They'll be just as bad as ours."

"How do you know they were Spritford ghosts, Mardie?" the innkeeper asked.

"Oh, lass, didn't you see the way they looked when they came into the town? The way they were dressed, the way they acted? Pointing at everything, looking up at the mountains to get their bearings and then looking at our buildings like they couldn't believe their eyes? They were ours, all right, from the old days. From Acton's time. Come back to take their revenge."

"But why have they come back *now?*" wailed the daughter.

"We'll go to the gods tomorrow," said the innkeeper, "and ask."

"Let's go," Martine said.

OWL'S STORY

I COULDN'T STOP them. I didn't even realize the village was being attacked, until they burst the latch like it wasn't there. There were three of them, tall like Acton's people always are, redheaded. And the biggest going straight for my Sparrow, ripping her gown right off her breasts. Oh, Sparrow, I tried, I tried, but they were so many, so strong. All I had was my hands. They had swords, axes, clubs. I tried to get to you, beloved, but they were... They held me, made me watch as they violated you and then slit your throat. Then they beat me to death with their hands and feet. Enjoying it. The blood and the pain. Monsters.

I died cursing them, promising revenge, and after death I brooded on it, locked in the cold dark with nothing to warm me but rage and a thirst for their blood. I yearned to be reborn, but the gods betrayed me and kept me there, waiting...

I don't know how long.

Then the enchanter came and set us free. So few of us, only nine: me, Marten, Squirrel, Hazel, Moth, Beech, Juniper, Cat and young Sage. Only nine of us had kept our anger strong enough to be called back from the dark. But not my Sparrow. Oh, that is the hardest thing, that Sparrow didn't wait for me, didn't cleave to me in the dark behind death. She has gone on and I have truly lost her. Forever. The killers took all the years we might have had together, and more, they took the rebirth together, which we had planned, had prayed for. They took our unborn children, and grandchildren, they took everything we could have had, should have had, but for them. I will never stop hungering for their deaths.

The enchanter was one of our blood, you could tell: dark and slight, though his eyes were lighter than ours. He spoke to us in the old tongue, but stiffly, as though he'd never spoken it before: "Take your revenge," he said. He pointed out of the glade toward the village, and we went, the weapons in our hands that we'd died holding.

We were ghosts. White and silent. I thought that I should feel cold, or shaken, but I was already cold, as cold as endless time.

Then the enchanter reached out and touched my arm. Touched it! My arm was as solid as his. He said again, "Take your revenge. Then go to the river."

As I realized what he was offering us, I was full of rage. And hope that my rage would be sated. I grabbed Sage's scythe—I knew I could make better use of it—and headed for the village. The others followed.

"Kill them all!" the enchanter shouted behind us.

I would.

The village made me understand how long I had been curled in the dark. First, there were no trees—not for a mile or more around. The land had had its bones laid bare, had been raped as my Sparrow had. There were brick and stone houses where our earthen cottages had been. Many more of them. They had prospered on our blood, and they would pay.

At the first house, I reached out my hand and opened the door. It moved. It was true, I could touch. I could act. At last.

Inside were a man and a woman, sitting at a table. Acton's people—pale-haired and blue-eyed. I swung the scythe before they realized what was happening. I made him watch her death as they had made me watch Sparrow's... The blood spurted all over him: hot blood, their blood, blood of the invaders, the rapists, the marauders. I was filled with holy exultation. I tried to shout my joy, but the dead cannot speak. So I swung the scythe again.

He was kneeling by his woman, cradling her head. Yes! Mourn as I mourned. I brought the staff of the scythe down on his neck and heard it snap.

How wonderful a sound.

SAKER

HE WAS still bleeding. Saker sat on the ground next to the bones and shook. Too much blood lost. He tried to bind the cut with a cloth he had laid ready, but his left hand trembled too much. In the end he put the cloth over his hand and clenched it between his knees until the bleeding stopped.

Part of him had never really believed it would work. His father, yes—that had worked—but that spell had been fueled by his deep grief, a need to hold his father again in his arms. Part of him had believed that his grief was the important ingredient in the spell. Part of him still believed it.

Then he remembered how he had lamented over the baby's skull just before he had cast the spell. Perhaps sorrow at the waste, at the shocking disregard for life, was enough. Compassion for those cut down without mercy by the invaders. Perhaps his heart was bigger than he had known.

When the shaking had stopped and he no longer felt faint, he got up, picked up his pack and followed the track the ghosts had left. It made him laugh. A track left by ghosts! Who would believe it? He was light-headed with blood loss and a growing euphoria. He was the master of the dead! No one had done it before—not even the enchanter of Turvite, who brought the ghosts back but could not give them strength.

The door of the first house was open, but there was no sound. He looked in cautiously. It smelt bad, of offal and dung.

Then he saw the woman, her guts oozing over the wooden floor. That was the smell. The man lay beside her, seemingly without a wound, but dead.

They were dead.

He groped his way outside and along the wall until he came to the corner of the house, where he turned his face into a breeze. He felt sweat cooling on his forehead, and tried to stop himself from vomiting. The bile rose in his throat and he fought it. And lost. The breeze blew some of the vomit over his boots, and he grabbed a handful of grass and frantically tried to rub it off…so his father wouldn't notice, wouldn't despise him for a weakling.

It was the smell, he told himself. He wasn't expecting that.

Enchanter training had taught him how to control errant thoughts and concentrate. He took the image of the dead couple and pushed it firmly to one side. Then he drew a deep breath.

"The first revenge," he said sonorously, as though his father were listening. "There will be more."

He skirted the village, in case someone had connected him with the ghosts' rising, and came out the other side, near the river, and waited in the shade of a small juniper tree. It was appropriate, he thought. The smell took him back to his early childhood, before the warlord's men had come…

There had been a juniper tree outside their house and his auntie used the berries for cooking. He had been forbidden to climb the tree because it was so old. "Older than Acton's people, that one," his father would say, patting the trunk fondly. "You stay away from it, boy."

Saker couldn't remember his father ever calling him by his real name. Saker was *boy,* or *you,* or, in a good mood, *young'un*. He hadn't minded. He had liked being called boy. His father had not much time for girls. He barely noticed Saker's three older sisters, or the baby.

He had tried hard to please his father. Everyone did, in the whole village. And not just because his father had been strong and liable to prove that strength on anyone who challenged him. He had been clever, too, known to be clever—known for his wit and guile. Saker had heard the other villagers say such things, usually when his father had got the better of one of Acton's people in a bargain.

That juniper tree…Its branches were so inviting, its trunk just right for holding as you climbed. From the top, he had thought, you would be able to see out of the valley and all the way to Cliffhold, where the warlord lived. He battled with himself for weeks, but one day, when he had thought his father was out in the fields with the new ewe, he climbed it.

He had been right, you could see right out of the valley, although not down as far as Cliffhold, which was a day's ride away. If he had looked the other way, if he had turned around to look at the sheer mountains behind, he might have seen them coming…

Over and over in the years since, he had played that scene in his mind, but this time he turned, this time he saw the warlord's men coming over the rise behind the village, swords out. This time he yelled and yelled and yelled so that the women had time to hide and the men had time to pick up weapons, and the children had time to scramble away into the underbrush…

Would it have made any difference? As an adult, he told himself that it wouldn't have. The warlord's men were soldiers who had known their job, and their job that day had been to kill. Everyone. From eldest to youngest. Old Auntie Maize to Saker's little sister, still at her mother's breast.

Everyone, except him. Because when the screaming had started and he *had* turned around, finally, too late, he froze where he was, had been too scared to move, too scared to help his father fight the men who were chopping down at his sisters with short, efficient strokes of their swords. He had been too frightened to jump on the back of the captain of the troop, although he had sat on his horse right below him, and maybe, maybe, he could have pulled him off into the dirt…

And what would he have done then? He scolded himself. He had only been five summers old. Five. The warlord would have batted him away like a fly. And he'd have been dead, like all the others.

Saker began to tremble with the effort of pushing aside *that* memory, the worst one, the one that came after the warlord's men had dragged the bodies away and the sun had gone down. He had stayed so long in the tree that he had wet himself, but he couldn't stay there any longer. His hands had started shaking with fatigue and he nearly fell. So he had made his way down slowly, cautiously, looking both ways at every step to make sure.

He had walked through the village that he knew, even at night, like his own home, but there was no one left. Just empty houses. And him.

The bodies had been piled up down the slope a little way. He avoided them, blocking his mind to the smell rising already, glad they had been hidden from him by the darkness. It had been strange, the way dreams can be strange, to be the only person there, it had reminded him of something. Then he had remembered. The songs and the stories about the first invasion told how Acton had ordered his men to kill the people but not burn the houses, so they could be used again.

The invasion had gone on almost a thousand years, Acton's people gradually pushing back farther and farther into the land, but that original order had always been followed. The last push from the fair-haired warriors had been less than two hundred years before. Saker's grandparents had talked about it as though it had been yesterday. In that last wave of the invasion, they had herded most of the people of the villages into the forest and killed them there. The remnants of those original people had come to live here, in Cliffhaven, on the poorest land in the Domains, the land that no one else had wanted.

Up until that day.

And, alone in his father's house, the young Saker had known they would come back. They would live in their houses and farm their land and milk their ewes and eat their food.

It had filled him with a vast, wavery anger that seemed larger than himself. It had gone beyond the shock of having seen his family killed. It had gone past the desolation of the empty village, to a mature, burning sense of injustice.

He would go to the gods.

He had seen his family dragged out and murdered in front of him. So he had found the house as it always was. There had been no corpses or blood awaiting him. The soldiers hadn't taken anything. As an adult, he had wondered about that. It wasn't usual. In every invasion song he'd heard, the villages had been preserved, by Acton's order, to give shelter to the old people and children who would follow the warriors across the mountains, but the warriors had stolen any loose items they could find, as battle spoil. But not here. Twenty years later, he still didn't understand why.

It had made it worse for the young Saker, to see every accustomed thing in its rightful place, without the people who used them. He had put his spare clothes and some food into his father's pack, feeling a twinge of guilt as he had taken it ("put that down, boy, it's not yours!"); but he had resolved to survive. He had taken his father's money from the brick under the hearth, his auntie's earrings and his biggest sister's bracelet, and a blanket and a kitchen knife, which he clenched in his hand. It was a black rock knife that his father had made, chipped from the black stone near the altar stone, with the gods' permission. His father had talked to the gods. He would talk to them, too.

He had slipped through the back window, just in case, and made his way by starlight to the gods' place. He had always been able to find it, no matter where he was. It had always called to him, but he had been considered too young to talk to the gods directly. That was for adults. Now *they* would have to talk to *him*.

The stone in its clearing had seemed to drink the light in. He had gone to it and had placed his hand on the cool surface. He had known the words.

"Gods of field and stream, hear your son. Gods of sky and wind, hear your son. Gods of earth and stone, hear your son. Gods of fire and storm, hear your son."

They had risen up in his mind, like pale shadows with dark eyes, whispering his name. He had ignored them, still angry.

"Why did you let this *happen?* How could you?"

The answer had come in a whisper through his mind, not his ears.

Human evil is outside our control. Accept. Live.

"NO!" he had screamed. "I will NOT! I WILL NOT!"

With relief he had erupted into a genuine tantrum, of the kind he hadn't had for over a year, since his father had beaten him for it. He had thrown himself full length and beat his fists on the stone and his feet on the ground. The unfairness of the world had swept over him and he had howled and cried and sobbed, pushed beyond the point where he could stop.

The gods had let him cry, soothing him with whispers.

Little child, little child, there is nothing you can do.

Having exhausted his passion, he had lain bereft on the grass.

Sleep, little child, the gods had whispered. *We will keep you safe tonight.*

He had no reason to trust them, but they were all he had left.

"I won't always be little," he had said, and fell asleep.

Under the juniper tree, Saker shook his head free of memories. It had been a long wait, but the ghosts were finally coming down the road toward the ford. He picked up his pack. Before he had a chance to move, he saw two strangers approaching on the other side of the ford.

Even at this distance, he could see that they were dark-haired and walked with the ease of long practice. Travelers.

He hesitated.

Would the ghosts harm them? Surely not. They were of the old blood, too. The ghosts would recognize that and welcome them. He could not be found with the ghosts. He had to remain hidden.

The ghosts seemed to talk with the Travelers, but he knew that was impossible. Then, the leading ghost, the strong-looking man, turned his head to watch the sun going down below the mountains.

The ghosts faded.

Saker stood, astonished and dismayed. This hadn't happened with his father. Although...he thought back. He had never raised his father's ghost close to sunset. The spell had always finished well before then. What difference did the sun make?

He would have to go to another village and wait for news of what had happened at Spritford. Find out how many had died, how thorough the revenge had been. And then work on the spell. Night was a good time for killing, he thought, turning away from the ford and threading his way back through the trees. He couldn't afford to lose the night...What if he started the spell at night...?

And next time, he thought, remembering his sister's scream as the sword came down, *I will use a bigger massacre site.*

BRAMBLE

THE HORSES surrounded Bramble in a great stampeding cloud. She kept her head as low as she could and urged them forward. They clattered through the cobbled streets of Sendat and were onto the road beyond in a matter of moments.

She felt the same exhilaration as when she chased: speed, horses, danger... She laughed aloud. The darkness made it more exciting. But more dangerous for the horses.

She slowed Cam after they left the town and whistled the other horses to slow, too. They did so reluctantly, and stopped when she stopped, milling around her in a loose herd. She called Trine and Mud and loosened their leading reins from where she had tied them, thanking the gods they hadn't come loose and tripped them up. She turned them to the north, then patted the necks of the horses she could reach and whistled the code for "stay."

They didn't want to let her move off without them, but she was firm. "Go on with you, you big softies, back to your yard and your stables and your dinner."

As they hesitated, she toyed for a moment with the idea of stealing the whole lot of them, depriving Thegan of the chance of going to war anytime soon. But there was no way she could hide such a thundering crowd anywhere in the settled farmlands around Sendat—and it was getting colder out here. She'd lose some of them for sure. So she whistled "stay" over and over until they stopped trailing her up the track, and turned to follow a big stallion called Sugar, which Bramble had trained herself. Sugar moved off, the others behind him, then turned his big head to look at her.

"Tell you what, Shoog," she said. "See if you can break his neck for me."

Sugar shook his mane and nickered at her.

Bramble nudged Cam. "Let's go, my friends," she said, "and let's go fast."

They were lucky. Half an hour after they left Sendat the clouds cleared and a half-moon shone enough light so that Bramble could see the road between its ditches. She pushed the horses hard, knowing that, while Thegan might assume she would head toward Carlion, he wasn't foolish enough to neglect other possibilities. There would be men after her, and soon. They would be mounted on their best horses, and they'd travel much faster than she could, with three.

She had to put as much space as she could between her and Thegan before sunup. Her only hope lay in reaching the Lake Domain before Thegan's men found her. Once she had crossed the border to another Domain, Thegan couldn't touch her. There was supposed to be a process where a warlord could request that a fleeing criminal be arrested and handed back to justice, but in practice it rarely happened. Besides, the Lake Domain didn't have a warlord, just the Lake and its people and Baluchston, its free town. In the Lake Domain, she knew she would be safe.

It was a wild ride. Clouds scudded across the moon and the wind was high. She was lucky it wasn't the freezing wind of winter; but it was chill enough to cut at her face and make her lips bleed. They rode past farmhouses, past mills with their locked mill wheels groaning against their rain-filled millraces. Through increasing patches of woodland, darkly threatening, she slowed the horses, although they wanted to speed through the gloom, fearing ancestral wolves. Each time they broke through to the moonlit road, the horses picked up their pace.

Bramble began to fret that they needed rest, but she didn't dare limit their pace. Once she stopped them for a few moments, and walked them around until they were cool enough to drink from the rainwater in the ditch by the road. She swapped Mud's burden to Cam so she could mount him, and give Cam a spell.

They started off refreshed, but not long after, all the horses began to tire and they had to slow to a walk.

The tidy farms around Sendat were long past, and the fields on either side of the road were given over to pasture or trees. The patches of woodland were wilder, not tamed by charcoal burners and coppicers. The undergrowth was heavy by the side of the road, though Bramble thought she could force the horses through it if Thegan's men caught up.

The wind dropped as she passed a lone farmhouse where a small light shone, the candle of a farmer getting ready to milk, and she knew it must be near dawn. She had no idea how far she had come. If she were a *real* Traveler, she would know the roads and the borders, but she didn't even know how far it was from Sendat to the border of the Lake Domain. More than a night's ride, that was certain.

At the next forest, she rode in a little way and then slowed the horses, looking for a track leading in deeper. The moon had set and the sky was not yet paling, so it was difficult to see. She tried three false trails before she found one the horses could manage in single file.

Beyond the heavy undergrowth near the road, she found the going easier. This wasn't the kindly wood of her childhood—it was a conifer forest, dark as pitch and smelling sharply of pine. The tall, scraggly trees creaked menacingly as the dawn wind picked up, and high above she could hear the ominous cawing and squabbling of rooks. Below, there was silence, the horses' steps muffled by the thick blanket of pine needles. Nothing else grew but the pines.

She dismounted to lead the horses, fearing they might walk into a branch in the gloom.

For the first time in her life, she was truly afraid. She feared nothing real—not Thegan's men coming after her, nor sharp branches or wolves. Yet it was deep in the marrow, like the terror brought by the gods. But if this was the gods' gift, they were darker and more terrible gods than any she had faced. She stood, trembling in the dark, and felt the urge to run, blindly, wildly, as fast as she could, to anywhere. Her legs twitched and her shoulders trembled with the strength of that desire. She fought it, but could feel herself losing... She felt a sharp pinch on her arm.

Trine had bitten her!

The pain brought her back to herself and she turned, from reflex, to clout the mare on the nose. Then she hugged her, tears on her cheeks, burrowing her face into the warm sweaty hide. Trine snorted astonishment and that made Bramble laugh.

"Yes, you're right, then, aren't you, I'm acting like a fool. Well, come on, then." She led the horses farther on and felt the panic recede, though it left her with a bad taste in her mouth, a distaste for the person she might have become without the horses. Fear diminished further as the dawn light swelled in the gaps between the trees, until she could see a good length in front of her. She hesitated as the trail petered out in the middle of nowhere, between two trees just like any other two they had passed.

"All right, it's up to you now," she told the horses. "Find us some water."

She mounted and relaxed the reins on Trine and sure enough, after snuffling the air for a moment, the mare headed off decisively, the other two following. They went straight, and soon Bramble could hear, under the sough of the wind, water chuckling.

It was only a small brown stream running over rocks, but it was life itself. Bramble didn't let the horses drink too much at once because the water was cold. She put on the horses' feed bags and then went through the packs to see what she had left for herself. Not much. Fly had packed her cheese and scones, but who knew how long they had to last her. She ate half of them, reasoning that she needed the energy. They would rest now, and then get going again in the late afternoon.

At last she had enough light to read the note Thegan's woman had given her. The parchment had been folded twice. Inside, the writing was formal and delicate, the writing of a court scribe—or a lady.

To the leader of the Lake Dwellers, greetings from Sorn, Lady of Central Domain.

Against my wishes, Thegan, warlord of Central Domain, will move against you on the first full moon night of spring.

Be prepared and beware. He comes with fire.

Sorn.

Bramble let out a long breath. *Oh, dung and pissmire. So much for staying out of things. So much for keeping my head down and disappearing. Thanks a lot, Sorn.*

She knew she had to deliver the message. The Lake. She had to cross it anyway, and at least there she'd be out of Thegan's Domain. Well, if she was lucky, she thought, this forest might stretch all the way there. Perhaps she could avoid the road altogether. Then she looked around. The pines grew so thickly, there was barely any sun on the forest floor. There were no living branches within reach; the lower branches had all died as the higher ones blocked out the sun. In this deep shade it was impossible to tell direction. She would have to climb tree after tree to find north. And as for that old tale about moss growing on the north side of trees—bah! Moss grew on *every* side of the trees. Who knew how lost she was already?

Well, better lost than dead, or a prisoner of Thegan's. She felt almost cheerful. She curled up in her bedroll on a soft patch of pine needles and went to sleep.

When she woke she peed behind a rock and laughed at herself for hiding from the horses as she did so. Then she climbed the nearest tree. It was a matter of nerve and hard hands rather than difficulty, as the branches were frequent but sometimes rotten and the harsh bark scraped her hands raw. Near the top, though, she could see the sun beginning to wester, and realized that her little stream ran west of north: the direction she needed to take to get to the Lake.

Hopefully it would take her the whole way.

They progressed easily enough at first, while the light lasted, following the stream down a gradual slope. Then it joined a larger stream, still heading roughly west by north. There was just enough space between the trees for the light to reach the banks and give life to the undergrowth; they were choked with the thorny stems of blackberry, the long canes of raspberry, and roots and remnants of other plants. In high summer, Bramble thought, she'd have been able to pick a nice salad along here: young dandelion greens, rocket, fennel, nasturtium, flat-lobed parsley, maybe even some tender young strawberries. As it got darker she dismounted and led the horses to keep warm.

The stream grew wider, fed by another stream of equal size, and the undergrowth grew bushier, with evergreen shrubs crowding the banks. Thickets of holly were interlaced with the long horizontal branches of firethorn, their crop of vivid red berries just beginning to ripen. Riding near them could scratch your eyes out. Bramble was forced to walk parallel to the stream about ten yards back.

Moving away from the stream meant moving away from the faint moonlight. Bramble waited until her eyes could adjust. Trine raised her head suddenly, reacting to something Bramble couldn't hear, and widened her nostrils, ready to whinny. Bramble reached up and nipped her nostrils closed just in time. Trine snorted softly, annoyed, and tried to bite her. Mud and Cam had ceded to Trine as herd leader, and waited for her to greet any strangers. As she stayed silent, so did they, their ears pricked forward. Bramble listened with them.

At the very edge of her hearing, she could make out *something*. Whispers? She tied the horses to a tree and went on. If Trine made too much noise and someone came to investigate, at least she wouldn't be there. It was a risk, but she had to know what had made the noise.

Moving silently through a forest at night is not a skill to be acquired in a hurry. Bramble had roamed the forests of her childhood, and those near Gorham's farm, night after night, watching badgers, finding the nests of owls, following bats to find the best fruit, high in the wild fig trees. This forest, with its needle-quiet floor, was child's play. But to follow the sound, she had to move closer to the stream for cover, and moving silently through holly and firethorn was difficult and painful.

She slipped through, never breaking a branch, going low under the firethorn branches and sliding around the dense pyramids of holly. The sounds grew louder, and then she could see the flicker of a small fire on the opposite bank of the stream. That would have been what Trine had smelled—that, and the other horses. There were two of them, dark in the shadows beyond the fire. There were two people sitting in front of it, their backs to her.

Bramble found a place where she could see their faces. They wore Thegan's uniform. She looked closely. Their horses' heads drooped from hard riding, and they themselves seemed very tired. Had they ridden after her from Sendat? She realized that they were camping at a ford; a road ran through the stream right here.

They seemed settled for the night. She could get back to the horses and lead them in a wide circle around the ford, and find somewhere else to cross the stream. Then she heard the sound of horses coming from the north, three or four of them, walking in the dark. The men at the fire stood up and took out their swords. One of them slipped back into the trees behind the fire, near the horses.

Four horsemen came into the clearing, splashing easily across the ford.

"Be at ease, Hodge," the leader called to the man at the fire. "Sully, come out of there."

It was Leof's voice. As he swung down from his mount she noted that he wasn't riding his mare; this was a bay gelding from Thegan's yard. So they'd got their horses back all right. The fire lit his pale hair and caught the metal around him—sword belt, hilt, dagger, boot buckles, earring—so that he walked, for a moment, in a constellation of stars.

Then he moved forward to the fire and she saw his face. He seemed tired, very tired, and something underneath that, something hard that hadn't been there before. *Thegan has tainted him,* Bramble thought with grief. *He has turned him into a killer.*

The other men were busy unsaddling the horses and letting them drink and eat. Sully came out of the trees to help them.

Hodge moved forward to take Leof's horse as he swung down. "Is it war, sir? Are we recalled?" he asked.

"Not yet, no. Your orders stand. You have the letter for Arvid?"

Hodge patted his breast. "Safe."

Leof nodded. "Well, you have extra duty now. You're to keep a lookout for a woman named Bramble. You may remember her—she was the Kill Reborn."

Hodge smacked a hand flat against his thigh. "Bramble on Thorn! I saw that race, saw her take the Kill's banner—as neat a thing as I've ever seen. What's the matter with her?"

Leof paused and weighed his words, then spoke slowly. "She's defied my lord Thegan. He wants her back to train his horses. If you find her on your way to the Last Domain . . . take her somewhere safe and send word to me. I'll be riding the border until she's found. If you find her on the way home, bring her back with you."

Hodge whistled. "Wouldn't like to be in her shoes, eh, if Thegan's got it in for her."

Leof frowned sharply. "Who?"

"My lord Thegan, I meant, of course, sir."

Hodge's back down was complete, but unconvincing, Bramble

thought. *He* seemed to have Thegan's measure, at least. By the horses, Bramble saw that Horst, the archer who had helped bring her to Thegan's fort, was whispering to the other men. He was probably telling the full story.

"She might be making for the border," Leof said.

The archer returned to the fire and eased a log farther onto the blaze with his toe. "She's cunning," he said dispassionately. "She's disappeared off the face of the world."

"That's a good trick," Leof said, smiling tightly. "There's times I wouldn't mind trying that myself."

Hodge grinned at him with easy familiarity. "Aye, we'd all like that now and then, sir."

"I've checked the other roads leading to the Lake," Leof said, "and no one's seen hide nor hair of her. We'll rest here tonight. The Lord Thegan wanted Horst to go after you and ask the Lord Arvid to return her if she makes it that far. But there's no need for three of you to go. Hodge, you can deliver that message."

Horst spoke up. "My lord Thegan told me to take that message, lord."

They stood in silence for a moment, each of them weighing his words.

"Yes," Leof said slowly. "All right, then. You and Sully can take the message to the Last Domain. Hodge and I will go on to the border tomorrow. She has to cross it somewhere."

Hodge scraped a thumb down his cheek, rasping stubble. "She's the Kill Reborn... maybe she has ways we don't."

"She's just a woman, sergeant," Leof said. "I've... raced against her, I know. But she's a woman with three horses, so if we can't find her, Thegan will have our thews for bowstrings."

"Aye, he will at that."

The men chuckled and settled down at the fire. Bramble waited until they were eating and slithered backward until she was completely screened by the undergrowth. Then she picked her way back to the horses. It was the firelight, she told herself fiercely, that had made her eyes ache as though she wanted to cry.

HORST'S STORY

This is how it happened. The old warlord, Wyman, was weak. I'd served him since I was ten, when my granda's wife sold me into tax bondage for five years, to pay off the debts my parents had left. The fever had got them, both at once, and me and my sisters were sent off to Granda's house. Might have been different, I reckon, if my grandam were still alive, but she weren't, and the new wife couldn't see any percentage in looking after young ones who were no blood of hers.

That's what she said, "There's no percentage in it, love," winding her arms around his neck, and my granda, old fool that he was marrying a chit half his age, just nodded and did what she wanted.

So I was sent to the old warlord's fort and my sisters, older than I was, were sent to be chambermaids and drudges at one of the inns in Sendat. One got pregnant by the ostler and married him; she did all right, seems happy enough. The other died of a cut that went bad. The shagging innkeeper didn't even get a healer in for her. Too tight with his money. I got him, though. I got my lord to fine him for losing me her wages, because by then I was a man, sixteen, and what she earned belonged to me, not to my granda. My lord backed me full and the innkeeper didn't argue it.

I gave some of the money to my other sister, though she had no claim to it under law. But then, our mam never liked that law. Said a woman's wages were her own in other Domains. That Central was the worst place for a woman to be. Da just laughed and said, "You do all right," and she'd look in the direction of the altar stone as if to ask the gods to witness his foolishness. But I reckon she did all right, too. Da never laid a hand on her unless she answered him back, and he never had a fancy woman. He kept a roof over her head and food on the table, most nights. But farming's a hard business when the rain is scarce and the taxes are high, and after they were dead there was nothing left.

So I went to the fort and was put to be the fletcher's boy. Making glue—gods, the headaches I got!—and plucking fowls. It wasn't just chickens, but the big birds, too—ravens, hawks when we could get them, grouse, pheasants. But never owls. Owls are unchancy birds and should be left alone. An arrow fletched with an owl's feather can't be trusted. That life wasn't too bad. I was fed and had somewhere to sleep, on the floor of the fletching shed. And old Fletcher didn't thump me unless I made a mistake.

After a couple of years Fletcher put me to making arrows, and that's where it all came apart. My eyes, now, they don't work so well up close. I can tell a hawk from a kite a mile off, but anything closer than my outstretched arm's a bit blurry. Arrow making, it needs good eyes for near work. So I got thumped a lot until they figured it out, and then, as I had my growth early, they put me to be boy to the warlord's men.

Looking back, I can see it was a bad time to be put there, but then I didn't know any better. The men were drunkards—rowdy, slovenly, no discipline, no pride. No purpose. I wasn't big enough to stand my ground, so I got what any young one got from them, and not just the shit work. The casual thumpings, the being pissed on, the insults. I didn't know then that the drunkards were the ones who should have been shamed by all that. I didn't know how real men should behave.

Then came the day my lady Sorn got married. I hadn't even seen her husband, just heard he was a lot older than her, and from the mountains. All it meant to me was that the men were drunk for days after the wedding, and I had a lot more vomit to clean up than usual.

But a week after the wedding, he came into the guardhouse. My lord Thegan. He stood at the door, with the sun behind him. One of the men had just emptied a chamber pot over my head and I stood there with the piss running down my face. Just piss, thank the gods. They were all laughing. He stood at the door, all clean and neat and... perfect, like, and looked around at the men. Half of them tried to straighten up but the other half were laughing so much they didn't even notice he was there.

He looked at me. I was cherry red, expecting him to laugh, too, and feeling like I couldn't bear it if he did.

He smiled at me. A real smile. "What's your name, boy?"

"Horst," I said.

He nodded. "Is this the way they normally are, Horst?"

I shrugged. But he kept looking at me and smiling as though we were friends, as though he understood everything that had ever been done to me. And I think he did. So I nodded. "Mostly. A bit worse than usual, because of the wedding drink."

"The wedding was a week ago," he said softly.

And just from the note in his voice, suddenly all around the guardhouse men were standing up, trying not to fall over, trying to look sober.

"The wedding was a week ago," he said again, and the scorn in his voice was like acid. "I am ashamed of you." He spaced the words out slowly, and looked each man in the eyes as he said them. By the end of it, we were all looking at the floor, ashamed of ourselves, too.

Then he came over to me. *To me.* And he clapped his hand on my shoulder and he said, "But not of you, lad. None of this is your fault. Go and get cleaned up."

I turned to leave, lifted up by his words. My heart was flying.

"And Horst," he added, remembering my name as though I were someone who mattered. "Tell the sergeant at arms to get down here now."

That was the first order he ever gave me. I ran to do it.

Now I'm his man, and part of the best disciplined, most skilled, most dedicated force in the Domains. He made us. Like he made me. He was the one who saw that my long-sightedness made me a good archer. But he had the real long sight. He's the only man I ever met who sees past the next meal and the next woman. He's the one with the vision to see how the Domains could be united, made one country the equal of any—*better* than any in the world.

He's a great man, my lord, a great man. He'll take us all to greatness. And I'll be one of his men helping to bring his vision to life. Following him, no matter what. Because on my life, I am Lord Thegan's man.

BRAMBLE

SHE FOUND the horses again half by chance and half by smell: as she got closer she could trace the faint scent of fresh horse dung. The relief almost brought her to tears. This place, so different from the forests she had known, sapped her strength. She had never felt so alone, as though she had been traveling among the creaking pines for weeks instead of days. The earlier panic had left her, but a deeper sadness grew in its place. The elements closed in around her: dark forest, heavy pine scent, the soughing of the branches above her as a wind picked up, the still, foreboding air hanging quiet below, surrounded by enemies, nowhere that was home. Again she thanked the gods for the horses. Without them she might have handed herself over to Leof and his men, just to have someone to talk to.

She shook her head briskly and gathered up the leading reins, murmuring softly to the horses, "come on then, come on then," to reassure both them and herself.

They headed west, as far as she could reckon it. She planned to move back on Leof's tracks and cross the border halfway between his resting place and the next border post.

She fondled Trine's nose and pulled her hand away before it could be bitten. "With luck, we'll be across before morning."

Four hours later, with dawn filtering down through the dark branches, she cursed herself for having said it out loud, positively inviting the forest spirits to lead her astray.

Well, maybe it wasn't that. Closer to the Lake, the forest was crisscrossed with streams, small and large, some of them sluicing noisily through deep defiles. She had been forced to detour around two of them for some way before she found a ford, and she had lost her direction. Dawn would allow her to climb a tree and find out which way she was heading.

She tethered the horses, put their nose bags on, and went looking for a tree to climb. It took longer than she had thought. These trees were real giants, so big around the trunk that three men holding hands couldn't have circled them, and their first branches were far out of Bramble's reach. She kept looking, getting more anxious, until she spotted light ahead. One of the giants had fallen and created a clearing. The branches of the trees on the edge of the clearing swept the ground, luxuriating in the light.

She climbed up one of the low-hanging branches wearily. It had been a long night. Her hands still hurt from the last time she had done this, and her thighs were shaking with fatigue. Worse, when she got to a branch from where she could look out, she realized they had been heading northwest instead of west, and were probably far too close for comfort to the border post Leof had spoken of.

But she could see the Lake—or at least the huge beds of reed that covered it at her end. It lay only a couple of miles away, which meant that the border had to be almost at her feet.

The scrape of her boots down the trunk was too loud.

"What's that?" she heard below her.

She froze against the trunk. The voice had come from the clearing. Two men stood up, coming out of the shelter they had formed under the dead tree's roots. Wonderful. She had chosen a tree right next to the border post. As the men moved forward, she realized it was worse. One was Leof. He must have left the campsite last night and come back here to rejoin his men.

Even in the dull early light, Leof seemed to glow, golden and energetic. He *was* gorgeous. She found it hard to hate him, even if he was a warlord's man. But his face was more serious than she had known it. He was concentrating, working, looking for her so he could take her back to Thegan to be enslaved. This was his work, to hunt people down, to obey the orders of a killer...She thought of the full gibbets outside the fort at Sendat and her heart hardened inside her. She could feel it tighten, feel its stone under her breastbone. She clung to the trunk and prayed that the horses, thankfully out of their sight, wouldn't whinny or move.

There were four of them. Leof signaled to two to take the other side of the clearing. They slipped into the trees, swords in hand. Leof and the other man came toward her. It was an archer, she saw, the one who carried a bow instead of a sword. The same man who had been with Leof the night before. Leof sent him farther down, toward the Lake, away from her horses. Then he came, slowly, through the trees toward her. He leaned against the trunk of her tree, casually, and brought his boot up as though to get a stone out of it.

Her heart was thumping so hard she thought he would feel it, like a drum, through the trunk.

"Bramble?" he said quietly. "Don't answer me. Just in case Horst comes back. Are you all right?"

He glanced up at her, like a man judging the time by the sun. Their eyes met. She nodded.

"He—Thegan . . . tried to kill you as you rode away." The words came out with difficulty, as though torn from him. "Why?"

"I defied him," she whispered.

"That can't have been all!" He pushed away from the trunk and began to pace back and forth, pretending to examine the ground. "There must have been another reason."

"He threatened me," she whispered. "He said I would train his horses and warm his bed whether I wanted to or not. I said no."

He stopped, staring at the ground, his shoulders hunched, his hands dangling. He looked like a young boy.

"Found anything, Captain?" Horst called from the clearing.

Leof turned, instantly strong, full of purpose and certainty. "Nothing here. Go and call the others back, Horst. I think we're chasing a forest sprite."

"Aye, maybe so." Horst turned and disappeared into the trees on the other side of the clearing.

"Stay where you are. I'll move them out straightaway. Which way are you heading?"

"To the Lake."

"And then?"

She hesitated. Right now his sympathies were with her. But back under Thegan's eye, who knew where his loyalties would take him?

"Who knows?" she said, reluctant to actually lie to him.

He stood for a moment, then tilted his head back to stare at her. "I could have loved you."

She nodded. "I know."

It was all she could give him. What could she say? That maybe, if he hadn't been who he was, she could have loved him, too? That if he hadn't pulled on that uniform, they could still be curled up together, making love? The uniform *was* him.

"Take care," she said. "Don't trust him."

He made a gesture as though warding off her words, and moved quickly into the clearing.

"Right, let's get going. I want to make all the border posts today, starting with the west."

They went through the business of packing up and loading their horses, which, it turned out, were tethered down by a stream north of the clearing.

Leof was the last to leave. He didn't look back, but raised a hand as if in salute as he rode out of sight. She could deal with that. It was the sight of his ponytail bobbing up and down in time to the horse's movement that filled her eyes with tears.

ASH

DAWN BROKE in a prodigal outpouring of rose and gold across the pale blue sky and the tops of the far mountains lit like beacons. The mountain air coaxed the first faint tendrils of scent from the scrubby herbs and flowers: thyme, sage, gorse. Underneath the scent was the smell of dry earth, and the dawn wind brought a thread of cold air from the west. Skeins of snow geese took off from a long, narrow lake as the sun rose, wing after wing of white birds with black wing-tips lifting into the wind and turning south, away from the autumn chill. Their calling deafened Ash, and the wind from their wing beats buffeted his face. He and Martine stood still to watch them go out of sight, although their calls drifted back for some time after they had disappeared.

Back to the south on the back of the wind
At home in the uplands of the air
Wild as the seal that springs from the ice
Are autumn birds free from care.

"I don't know that one," Martine said.

"It's from Foreverfroze. A song from the Seal Mother's people," Ash said. "That's a loose translation."

"Nothing is truly free from care," Martine said. "Not on this side of death."

"Or on the other. Those ghosts. They wanted *revenge*. A thousand years later! How can the need for revenge last that long?"

"'Old revenge tastes sweeter,'" Martine quoted.

"That's an Ice People saying. Not one of ours. How was it that *none* of those from the landtaken were reborn?" He prayed that she would have an answer. Because if none of the ghosts of the landtaken had been reborn, that would mean—surely—that rebirth was only a story, a hope for the hopeless in the dark times.

"Perhaps some were. Do you know any songs about the taking of Spritford? About how many were killed?"

Ash thought for a few moments. Fragments of songs played in his head, about the taking of the Sharp River settlements, and working west toward the mountains. But these songs were only a few hundred years old, he realized by their phrasing, as this part of the land had been taken late in the invasion.

"Well, it wasn't a thousand years ago," he said, almost reluctantly. "There is a song." He paused, remembering, saying the words under his breath. "Seven and forty, the enemy fallen," he said at last.

"Forty-seven?"

Ash nodded.

"But there were only nine ghosts. Only nine had enough hate in them to resist rebirth, to turn away from it in search of revenge. The others were reborn—count on it," Martine said.

He felt cheered by that, but underneath the lift in his spirits was terror: the oldest terror, the fear of the dead, of the dark beyond the grave, of something out there.

Something was out there.

"Is there anyone we can warn?" Ash asked.

"Spritford will send messages out."

"We know more."

"We're Travelers."

Ash nodded. Travelers were automatically suspect, automatically disregarded. Even stonecasters. Try to tell the local warlord about talking ghosts and evil enchanters and they'd be lucky to escape a beating. Or the warlord would decide *they* were causing all the trouble and a quick solution would be a couple of garrotings.

They rested for a few hours. Ash slept fitfully. The voices of the dead echoed through his dreams and brought him awake, time after time, repeating invitations in the old tongue: "Revenge! Join us and revenge yourself! Take back what was yours!" He couldn't remember anything else, just the sound of the dead speaking to him, only to him, and the cold and dry feeling as though ghost after ghost had passed through him.

Then he fell into a deeper sleep and was caught in a dream that seemed infinitely worse, for the ghosts here were his parents. They looked like they had when he had last seen them, but pale, dead pale, and they came to him in his room at Doronit's, the only real home he had known, and laid solid, dead hands against his chest and on his cheek and whispered, "Join us." And although he knew, in the dream, that they were dead, still he reached out for them as if still a little child, and laid his head on his mother's cold breast and sobbed.

He woke with wet cheeks and stared at the ground for a long time before he rolled over to face Martine, knowing she would have heard him crying. She was sitting with her back to a rock, casting the stones on their cloth.

"I dreamed my parents were dead," he said. "Maybe they are. Maybe the ghosts have risen everywhere at once. Will you cast for me?"

She nodded and held out her hand. He spat into his palm and took it. "Are my parents dead?" he asked, then waited while she cast.

All the stones were faceup, except one.

"Life," Martine said immediately, finger on one stone. "They live. Work, or a task to be done. Travel. Music. So, all as usual, no? And the hidden stone..." She turned it over. "Responsibility. Hidden responsibility. That may be you. I'm sorry, Ash, this is a true reading, but the stones are not speaking to me. Perhaps I care too much what the answer is, for your sake. The stones do not like the caster to care too much."

He smiled, so relieved by the first stone that he had hardly heard the others. "It doesn't matter—they're alive. We should go."

They started off again through the thyme-scented scrub and the goat-browsed heather. They turned from the main road around noon and headed north by east, climbing with aching legs toward a high ridge, which stood back from the cliffs that now began to rim the horizon. The cliffs looked closer than they were, taller than seemed possible, and got taller slowly, very slowly, as they climbed.

It took them two full days of walking to reach the top of the ridge. Below was a valley the likes of which Ash, for all his wandering, had never seen before. The Hidden Valley lay in a deep, wide cleft in the hills, protected from the mountain cold by the steep-sided ridges on either side.

They stood still on the chill ridge, Martine smiling at Ash's astonishment, and saw, far below them, deer in still green glades, squirrels bounding from branch to branch, and even, farther off, an elk dipping antlers to drink at a stream. As the valley moved into shadow, birds settled, quarreling, into their roosts. Farther down, where the hillsides were terraced, cows and goats threaded their way along to be milked; and a group of women, seeming tiny at this distance, balanced jars of water on their hips as they climbed up steps set into the bank of the river, which ran through the center of the valley.

It was the most beautiful place Ash had ever seen. The dying light, gold and purple, seemed heartbreaking, as though the precious valley were slipping away from them, sliding beyond reach into the dark.

"Let's get down before nightfall," was all he said, but his voice wavered.

They climbed down into shadow and sunset. Darkness fell before they were halfway to the village, but it was a night of clear skies and blazing stars, so they could see just enough to follow the road.

Martine stopped at a field by the side of the road, with a small hut next to a black rock. Mist was rising from the stone and Ash felt the itch under his skin that meant this was the place of the local gods. But unlike the altar stone in Turvite, no one here was calling his name. These gods were satisfied by their worshippers.

A girl was sitting by the rock. She rose as they came nearer and ran across the field to them, despite being heavily pregnant.

"Careful, love!" Martine scolded, running to meet her. "Not so fast!"

"Mam!" the girl cried.

They embraced.

So this was Elva. Ash felt his stomach clench in disappointment, and then found grace to laugh at himself. So much for his fantasies! She *was* beautiful, her eyes darkened by the night and the starlight picking out the fine bones of her face. And she was *huge* with child. Martine wasn't surprised by it. She might have mentioned it, he thought, annoyed, then shook his head at his absurd expectations, and moved to greet Elva.

"This is Ash," Martine said, not looking away from Elva's face, one hand on the great curve of her belly, the other stroking Elva's cheek.

Ash found he had to look away from them. It was disturbing to see Martine's face naked with love.

"Welcome, Ash." Her voice was light and high, a soprano, but without much range, he judged.

"Blessings be," he answered.

"So. Come, come along in. I told Mabry you'd be here tonight, so they've got dinner going, and the girls are excited. They want you to cast the stones for them."

A prophet? Ash wondered. Or was she a stonecaster like Martine and the stones had told her? Or perhaps—a shiver ran across his skin and he knew this was the right answer—the gods had told her.

They followed her across the field and down a steep track to a homestead solidly planted on a terraced outcrop. There was light coming in stripes from behind the shutters, smoke rising straight from the chimney in the still air, a yap of dogs from a shed, which quieted as Elva shushed them, the soft sound of rustling wings as they walked past the dovecote. It was, as the valley had seemed from the ridge, a picture of peace and plenty. Ash thought of the blood on the ghost's scythe, and shuddered.

The door opened as they walked across the yard. A tall man stood there, as tall as Ash and more solid, curly brown hair haloed by the light inside.

"Elva? About time, love." He gathered her into the warm room with an arm around her waist, nodding to Martine as he did so. "Come away in and get warm. Gytha, shield the light."

Gytha—a tall woman some years older than Ash, with curly hair like Mabry's pulled back into a plait—had already moved to put small embroidered screens in front of the candles. Elva smiled at her and Gytha smiled back.

"Drema made the screens for me," Elva said to Martine. She turned to Ash. "To shield my eyes from the light." He nodded, astonished at how the strangeness of her pale skin, white hair and pink eyes shrouded the beauty he had seen so clearly by starlight.

Drema was sitting by the fire, embroidering a tiny felt coat clearly intended for the new baby. She was older and had a sterner face than her sister, Gytha. She got up and pushed Elva down into the chair.

"Sit you down, we'll manage, just you sit." She turned to Martine. "She does too much, outruns her strength. Maybe you'll be able to get her to slow down."

Martine smiled. "I doubt it. She always was a stubborn little lass."

Drema and Martine considered each other for a moment, and then both nodded slightly, confirming something, before they turned away, Drema to the fire where something was simmering, Martine to put her pack down by the stairs. Ash put his next to it. They smiled at each other, a mere softening of the eyes, acknowledging their success in making it here, then moved back to the fire and sat on a settle cushioned with a thick felt mat.

Sometimes, out on the Road with his parents, huddling in a tent while the wind howled outside, or picking leeches off his legs when they went through the swamps outside Pless, Ash had dreamed about a place like this. It was nothing fancy, just solid, strong walls and a rainproof roof, a warm fire, meat roasting on a spit, bread baking in an oven in the ashes, friends and family gathered around talking, laughing, sharing news. Of course, in his imagination there had been music, too; intricate but lively music from flute and pipe and drum, a melody he'd never heard except in this particular daydream.

Well, he could have the music in his head, at least. He stretched out his legs to the fire and listened to Martine and Elva talk, about the coming baby, mostly, about women's matters. The music ran underneath their words, filling in spaces and lifting his spirits even further.

Ash gathered from the conversation that Elva and Mabry had been married no more than a year, and before that she had lived in the little hut near the black stone altar. Mabry had been village voice then, and had been urged by the villagers to move her on, get her out of the gods' field.

"That was when we met," Mabry said. "I guess that was when I started to fall in love with her."

"You were just too soft to kick her out," Drema said. "But maybe that's why *she* started to fall in love with *you*."

"Has to be," Gytha teased him. "He hasn't got anything else to offer, now he's not village voice anymore."

"Now Mam's dead, I leave that to someone who really wants to do it," Mabry said comfortably.

Elva touched his hand, lightly. "Your mam is proud of you. They tell me so."

"They" were the gods, Ash realized. He wondered how it would be, to have the gods in and out of your head all day and night. Uncomfortable, he figured, but Elva seemed happy enough and Mabry was the most satisfied-looking man he had ever seen.

They ate at a big table in the corner. Ash was sorry to leave the fire, but glad for the food: roast kid and baked vegetables, gravy and spinach. He looked longingly at the new bread, fresh from the oven, but Gytha shook her head at him.

"You'd be awake with stomach pains all the night, if you ate it as fresh as that! Wait until breakfast."

It was like having older siblings suddenly, for that was how Mabry's two sisters treated him. And Mabry, after a few moments weighing him up, had done the same. He felt enveloped, welcomed, taken inside, where he had always been on the outside, and it overwhelmed him. He blinked back tears and concentrated on the fine, meaty texture of the goat. Travelers didn't develop many friendships with the settled; his parents had actively discouraged it. So this was his first experience of generous hospitality. But he was sure there was more to their welcome than hospitality. Martine was Elva's mam, more or less, so they were family.

He thought again of the blood on the ghost's scythe and grew cold, and then hot with determination. He would not let those ominous figures hurt this family. Never. No matter what it cost him.

"Hullo! Are you with us, Ash?"

Gytha waved her hand in front of his face and he started, recalled to the present suddenly. They all laughed at him.

"You were miles away," Mabry said.

"Yes, a long way away. But I'm glad to be back!"

They smiled at him, even Martine, although her eyes speculated on what thoughts had distracted him so thoroughly. Gytha and Drema were clearing the table so the others moved back to the fire.

"Give us a poem, lad," Martine said.

He nodded, seeing the women turn eagerly and Mabry sit forward on his chair.

"This is called 'The Homecoming,'" he said, smiling. "It's a song from the far north coast, about a sailor coming back from a fishing trip where he was nearly killed.

From the black eye of the storm
From the keen knife of the wind
From the long sharp fingers of the sprites of ice
From the pressure of the deep
From the terror of the waves
Seal Mother has delivered me…
And I am sailing home…
I am sailing home…

In his mind the music broke into the joyful swell of the song, and beneath it he could hear the creaking of the mast, the slap and thud of the waves breaking against the bow, the *crack* as an iceberg calved. Though he had never been that far north, and never been on a boat with sails. The song delivered the world of its maker sharp into his mind, clear as a memory of his own.

The songs had never come alive before, and he wondered why it was happening now. Because he had chosen the song to suit his own mood, and not to please someone else? He couldn't remember ever having done that before. But then, he'd only just started reciting the words of songs at all, with Martine.

"Oh, that was wonderful!" Gytha said, breathless. "It was like I was really there. Do another, go on!"

So he chose another, a song from the south, a ballad about a girl searching through the forest for her brother, because he felt he was searching for the truth to something, and this song fitted his mood, too. And, like the sailing song, as he said the words he heard the wind soughing in the pines, smelled the sharp scent of a fox as it flitted past, tasted the salt in the girl's tears as she cried in loneliness and despair. Then he felt the extraordinary surge of thankfulness and joy as she found him.

They applauded again and asked for more.

This time he chose songs he thought they would like; and nothing gave flight to the words but his own voice.

He tried to think it over later, alone in his blankets by the fire. Martine was in the only guest room, no more than a cubby-hole formed in the passage that used to lead to the back door. The door now led to a new room in the farmhouse that Mabry had built for Elva, the baby and himself. "So we won't be kept awake all night with the young one crying," Drema had said, in a stern voice, but with her hand gentling Elva's hair.

It was the first time since they had left Turvite that Ash had had time and solitude to think, and he knew that he should carefully go over everything that had happened. But his tiredness, the evening, the fellowship, the warmth, had left him swimming in a soft fog of comfort, and he decided not to spoil it. Instead, he curled up with his back to the solid warmth of the banked embers, laid his head on one of Gytha's felt cushions and slept dreamlessly all night.

Almost all the night. In the very early morning, in the gray light before dawn, Martine and Elva woke him and they went to see the gods.

Ash was familiar with the gods, of course. Every Traveler visited the sacred stones on their journeys, made sacrifices, prayed. His father had been very devout, but his mother less so.

"They don't really care much about people, you know," Swallow had said once, as Ash's father had prepared a gift for the local gods outside Carlion.

Rowan had shrugged. "But they are there, and deserve our worship."

"Maybe."

As a child, Ash had imagined that he heard the gods talking to him, but their voices were so faint that he could hardly hear them. That was until Turvite, and the black stone under the oak tree. He wondered, following Martine across the dew-soaked field, what he would hear now.

As they approached the stone he felt the hair on the back of his neck lift. They were here.

"They are always here," Elva said to him, as though replying directly to his thought.

Her eyes, colorless in the gray light, had lost their focus. She lowered herself awkwardly next to the stone and laid one hand on it, then her head dropped back and came up again.

Her voice, which had been high and a little thready, was now deep and sure. "We warn you," it said. The gods.

The gods were speaking through Elva.

Martine was pale, but it was obvious that she had seen it before and had expected it. "About what?" she asked.

"There is evil," said the gods. "Human evil. Great."

"The calling up of the dead?"

"The wall between living and dead may not be breached without harm to both. You must stop it."

"Us? Why *us?*" Ash cried.

Elva's sightless eyes turned toward him. "She will tell you."

"Elva?" Martine asked.

"The Well of Secrets."

"We must go to the Well of Secrets?" Ash asked.

"When the first thaw comes."

"Why not now?" he demanded.

But Elva's head had fallen back again and when she raised it her eyes were her own again.

"Oh, bugger," she said comfortably, as if just a little annoyed. "I wanted to find out if it's a boy or a girl."

"What?" Ash said.

"I thought they might stay a little bit longer so I could ask them about the baby."

He was speechless. The whole world was in danger and she wanted to ask the gods questions about a *baby*.

Martine was amused. "Elva can't change the future or the past, Ash," she said. "She's used to being the . . . the instrument through which the gods speak. And she really did want to know about the baby."

He shook his head. There was something here about the difference between men and women. He wanted to *act,* to *do* something immediately. The women seemed more interested in the coming birth than in the fate of the world.

When they went back to the farmhouse they told Mabry and his sisters the story of the ghosts and what the gods had said.

They heard the story quietly, then Mabry nodded. "We'd better tell the village voice," he said, "so she can warn everyone."

That was all.

Then Drema and Gytha simply went quietly about their business again.

Over the next few weeks, as winter settled into the valley, it began to really worry Ash that the others didn't want to discuss what was going to happen.

"They told us to wait," Martine said. "It's hard, but no good ever came of disobeying the gods."

Only Mabry, when Ash was helping him around the farm, would talk it over, and then just to ask Ash questions about the ghosts and what they could do. Half the work they were doing, Ash realized, was not ordinary farmwork, but Mabry's preparations in case the ghosts came.

"They couldn't get through the doors, you say?" he asked Ash, and went about repairing and putting up the heavy storm shutters. Others in the village were doing the same, but not all. Many villagers still thought Elva unchancy and wanted nothing to do with her or the family.

"They only had bronze weapons, you say?" Mabry asked, and he sharpened his steel knives and scythes and his axe, and kept at least one weapon to hand no matter where he was.

"You might not be able to kill them," he observed, "but if they're solid you ought to be able to cut off their arms."

Ash nodded. "If they can't hold a weapon there's a limit to the damage they can do."

Hesitantly, Ash offered to teach Mabry singlestave and fighting, and he was grateful for it. Soon there was a class in the small barn most afternoons, with a few friends of Mabry's joining in. Ash was surprised to find how much he knew; watching Mabry, a strong, able man, fumble with his stick and hit himself over the head with it made him realize that he was, in fact, quite accomplished. Although he still wouldn't have backed himself in a serious fight against someone like Dufe, or the Dung brothers.

The best of the village bunch was Mabry's tall dark-haired friend,

Barley, who wielded the singlestave with ferocious determination and had shoulders like an ox.

"I used to be a ferryman," he said briefly, when Ash commented on his strength. "But I'm a potter now."

Barley turned back to his practice, squaring up to his opponent, one of the boys from the farm next door, half his size but quick as an eel.

For the first time Ash felt part of something; it was the first time, he realized, that he'd ever *been* part of a group of just men, working together. It was a solid, comforting feeling and he relished it all the more because he knew he'd have to leave come spring.

BRAMBLE

BRAMBLE MOVED along the branch until she had a better foothold. She waited until Leof's party had had plenty of time to move off, and then scrambled as fast as cramped legs, tired arms and sore hands would let her. She went back for the horses. She had considered leaving them behind, just letting them loose to forage, but it would have felt like Thegan had beaten her in some way if she did, so she took them, despite the risk. Besides, later on she'd need them, she figured, to get over the pass into the Last Domain, the most northerly of the Eleven Domains, where the Well of Secrets was living.

She took their feed bags off and led them to water, which was not hard to find so close to the Lake, as all the streams converged. Every moment made her dance with impatience, but she knew that fed and watered horses were less likely to be noisy or troublesome. Finally they raised their dripping muzzles from the stream. She led them across, and made straight for the Lake, heading into a surprisingly thick mist.

It didn't take long. They came to the first reed bed, which emerged spikily out of the mist, after only half an hour. That meant they were safely across the border. She couldn't relax, though. The forest came right down to the shores of the Lake here, with pines perched on the few rocks, and a variety of trees growing where the sun could reach, with their roots in the water. The leaves of willows, alders, laurels were turning every color imaginable, flaming defiance to the cold wind. Bramble took it as a sign of hope.

She took stock, too. There were three ways across the Lake, if you didn't have a boat. There was a ferry at the neck of the Lake, where it emptied itself into the river that ran to Mitchen. The ferry was surrounded by Baluchston—founded by Baluch, one of Acton's fifty companions—and the second of the free towns, after Turvite. It was small, for a free town, existing mostly to provide the needs of travelers and traders operating on and around the Lake, and, of course, to charge a hefty toll to use the ferry. Baluchston could charge the toll because the river fell two trees' height into a narrow canyon, and was impassable.

It was a prosperous little town and Bramble wouldn't have given a copper for its chance of staying free once Thegan had taken the Lake Domain. But since it was still a free town, Thegan's men were as safe there as she was, and would be watching for her.

The second way to cross the Lake was to swim it. It had been done, once or twice, out of bravado or greed or sheer desperation. But for every man who had made it across, twenty had died in the attempt. The worst thing was, no one knew why. It *looked* safe, the Lake—once you were past the reed beds around the edges it was unruffled, shining water. The lake current was strong, of course, but men had also swum the river itself.

But Bramble had heard the stories of swimmers setting out in high hope and full fitness, simply stopping halfway across and disappearing. Sucked down, pulled down, who knew? The local gods would only say that there were no water sprites in the Lake, which in itself was worrying, when everyone knew they were everywhere in the Sharp River, which fed the Lake. So what kept them out? Something nastier than water sprites. Bramble shivered at the thought. Swimming was one risk she wouldn't take.

Which left the third way: the Lake Dwellers. And she had to head there anyway, to deliver Sorn's note.

Bramble had always been fascinated by the Lake Dwellers. When she was small she had pestered her grandfather to tell her all the Travelers' tales about them. They were the same people who had lived on the Lake in Acton's time: no invasion, no landtaken, had ever dislodged them. If they were threatened—and they had been threatened, time after time—they simply disappeared to the hidden islands in the vast reed beds that covered the northwestern end of the Lake. And anyone who went after them disappeared also.

Camps or towns set up around the edges of the Lake went up in flames. Farms were flooded as the Lake waters mysteriously rose over dry fields. Fishermen washed up on the shore, occasionally alive, and talked about monsters from the deep. And any attempt at building a bridge failed spectacularly, usually in flames and with a lot of screaming. The dwellers believed the Lake was alive, a being of some kind, and she didn't like being shackled by bridges.

Baluch had negotiated with them for the free town and the ferry. The ferrymen were all from two families. When the town was set up, their ancestors had been taken away into the reeds by the Lake Dwellers and brought back a couple of days later. They refused to talk about what they had seen, but they began to refer to the Lake as "She." At puberty, both boys and girls from those families were still taken into the reeds by the Lake Dwellers, and they still returned closemouthed about what they had seen.

She would have to go farther west and north to find the Lake Dwellers. Or, she could ask the Lake for help…

Horsetail, bulrush, nalgrass, birdgrass…Along the edges of the Lake there were a dozen different kinds of reeds. She looked through the hardening autumn stalks to the cold mud beneath. This was not going to be pleasant. She considered removing her boots, but once, in her forest near Wooding, she had tried to climb through a reed bed to get to a stream, and had cut her feet badly. So she put her booted sole firmly down in the squelching mud and forced her way through the reeds.

She was waist-deep and beginning to turn blue with cold by the time she reached a patch of open water. She took great gulping breaths and rubbed her arms, trying to jump up and down to keep the blood moving. She almost lost a boot.

"Oh, shag it!" she said. Then she laughed. Could she have looked more ridiculous, standing waist-high in freezing water, swearing blindly, waiting for—what?

She laughed again, feeling exhilarated, as though she were setting off on a chase, soaring over fences and streams. Her laughter bubbled up and spread out over the water. There were no solemn words, no invocations to the gods that would help her now. All she had to offer was the truth.

"Oh, Lake, Lake, here I am, come to ask for help. Come to give help if I can. Please send the Lake Dwellers to me before I freeze to death."

She laughed again. Was there ever a less elegant prayer? But around her the wind was rising, the mist was lifting, and she felt again the sense of freedom and joy rising in her, as it had when she rode the roan. It was not like the presence of the local gods, not steeped in holy terror, but it had the same *breadth,* as though her emotion were larger than she was—as her anger at Thegan had been not only hers, but also the gods'. Here, she shared her exhilaration with the Lake.

She was not surprised to hear the soft clucking of water beneath a boat, or to see the high black prow curving through the mist, or to feel hands under her shoulders pulling her up over the tightly bound bundles of reeds that formed the sides of the boat. She was, however, surprised to find that her three horses were already on board, huddled in a nervous group in the center of the boat's flat bottom. She turned to the men who had lifted her aboard.

"The Lake told us where to look," one of them said, and there was general laughing. "She likes you, that Lake." He added a comment in his own language, and at that the whole crew—eight of them—dissolved into backslapping mirth.

Bramble laughed too, sitting on the deck with her back to the strong, tar-smelling reeds, a pool of water gradually seeping out around her.

They were tall men, and lean, and they all wore odd hats woven out of split reeds. They weren't exactly hats, just rims that sat on their hair. Their hair and eyes were as black as Bramble's own. Their skin was darker, though, and she thought that all Travelers must once have had skin like this, before interbreeding with Acton's folk. It was like looking back through time, to before the landtaken. But these were real people, not noble relics from a distant past. One had acne scars all over his face, another had several teeth missing. One had the bowed legs that meant he'd had rickets as a child. That one looked at her the way most men looked: body first and face, a very late second.

The men went about their tasks single-mindedly, attending kindly to the horses, steering with the long pole that also moved them through the water, or busy with nets and craypots in the stern. Which left one, the oldest, to talk to her.

He was not that old—fifty, maybe. As he stood at the prow he looked stern and proud; her grandfather had talked about the Lake Dwellers' legendary pride. His eyes were so dark they seemed unfathomable, but he turned to grin at her and a web of laughter lines sprang up around his eyes and mouth.

"She told us to come and get you, but She didn't say why," he said conversationally, a faint accent softening the ends of his words. "I am Eel. I speak your language. The others, not."

"I'm Bramble," she said.

The Lake had led these people to her. Presumably, She trusted them. Bramble reached inside her jacket for Sorn's note and handed it to Eel. Maybe he wouldn't be able to read it, anyway.

But he did, his eyebrows moving up. "So," he said, and called out to the steersmen in a different language. The boat immediately began to swing around in a big curve, turning west.

"Um..." Bramble said. "I understand you want to take this to your council as soon as you can, but I need to get to the other side of the Lake."

Eel nodded. "We are going to the other side."

She settled back. They might end up a long way west, but at least Thegan's men wouldn't be looking for her there. *Let the Lake lead us,* she thought.

The journey lasted all day, with the steersmen taking turns at propelling the boat along. They had headed straight for the middle of the Lake, so far that the southern shore disappeared and the northern shore was only a line in the distance. Bramble had heard about how large the Lake was, but being out on it—in what seemed, in that expanse, a tiny boat—was sobering. Astonishing. And exhilarating. It seemed to her that the freedom she had been seeking all her life, had sought on the Road, might be here, on this wide stretch of water. When the wind picked up from the east, pushing them faster against the westerly current, she laughed, and the boatmen laughed with her.

The horses weren't amused. Bramble spent most of the trip soothing them. Trine alone was unconcerned.

The day was fine as the mist burned off. Autumn sun was warm on their faces and turned the Lake into slabs of polished steel. The boatmen shared their lunch with her: smoked fish, flat bread, dried fruit and sweet water drawn up from the Lake in a small bucket. Before they drank the water the men dipped their forefingers in their cups and drew a circle on the back of their hands. Bramble hesitated. Should she do likewise?

Eel saw her poise her finger uncertainly and shook his head, smiling. "Not yet," he said. "When you have been properly introduced."

She smiled back at him and drank. The water was clear and cold and tasted of snow, and something else, not quite a muddy taste, but a little bitter, like weak tea.

"The taste of the reeds," Eel said. He patted the side of the boat.

It was made of very long bundles of reeds lashed together and then covered with bitumen on the outside to make it waterproof. Inside, the floor and the crevices between floor and side were tarred as well. It made the whole boat smell, but she could see that the combination of lightweight, buoyant reeds and waterproofing made the boat practically unsinkable. It was, however, like tinder waiting for a match. Worse: it would flame up faster than tinder, faster than wood soaked with liquor, faster than straw. Bramble thought of Sorn's message: *Beware. He comes with fire.* She blanched, imagining it all too clearly. Thegan would smile as he set the boats alight. If he could find them.

Toward the end of the day they came to the northwestern reed flats. There was some talk between the men, with a couple of them gesticulating aggressively.

Finally, Eel came over to her reluctantly. "It is our custom not to let outsiders see the paths through the reeds. I know you are a friend of the Lake, but —"

She smiled and held up her hands soothingly. "It's all right. Frankly, I'd rather not know. Then I can't be a danger to you."

He nodded with satisfaction and spoke over his shoulder to the others. They, too, nodded approvingly at her. One brought over a scarf, which they tied over her eyes. It smelled of fish. She leaned back against the solid bulwark of reeds and listened to the soft sounds of the boat: the gurgles from the steering blade, the bare feet of the men on the floor, the horses whickering as they caught the scent of land and fodder. The sides of the boat scraped gently against reeds, and the sounds of wind rubbing stalk against stalk and the squawking and flapping from ducks or geese disturbed by the boat surrounded her. The music of the Lake continued for a long time, while the light seeping under the edges of the scarf faded away. When she could see only a deep golden glow under the scarf, frogs began to call, a few at first, and then more and more, until the boat vibrated with the noise. It filled the world.

Eventually, the prow of the boat scraped against earth and Eel removed the scarf.

Bramble stood up, blinking her eyes. It was almost dark, with just faint tracks of gold and rose far down on the flat horizon that seemed to curve away. Every distance here was filled with the reeds, rustling, swaying, singing with the almost deafening frog chorus. There were houses built out of reeds, half circles seeming to cling to the ground, some the length of a small field. All the buildings were on stilts at the edges of a thin island, like a lace hem on a petticoat. There were boats everywhere, being poled along, tied up, repaired, some as big as the one she was on, others tiny, just big enough for one person.

The island—precious, arable land—was the domain of cattle and crops. Goats were being folded in for the night by young boys. They called to one another in high, carrying voices, and shouted instructions and, if tone was anything to go by, insults at their charges. The smell was rich and complex: reeds, mud, manure, smoke from the fires the boys were lighting near the cattle pens, and something bready cooking somewhere. That smelled delicious.

Bramble turned to look back up the channel they had come down—nothing but reeds and the faint tip of another island. As she looked, a boy came down to the edge of that island and leaped into one of the small boats, crying aloud in a rhythmic shout. He pushed off from the land and began to pole toward them. He was followed, in single file, by huge big-horned gray cattle who stolidly walked into the water and began to swim, only their heads and horns showing. Astonished, Bramble watched as the boy arrived at the closer island, beached his boat and then led the phlegmatic file of cattle up into a yard.

"There is grazing over there," Eel said, laughing at her expression. "Come away from the mosquitoes. Come inside."

Underneath the drumming of the frogs was another, nastier thrumming: thousands of mosquitoes. She slapped a few away without being bitten and stepped up out of the boat onto a platform outside one of the long buildings.

"My horses?" she said.

Eel shouted back to one of the men in the boat and he waved in acknowledgment. "Pike will look after them," he said. "Come."

He led her into a dim, receding tunnel of reeds. At intervals, the huge bundles of reeds supported the roof, arching high overhead. Nearby, a lamp picked up the color of the reeds and gave it back again, so they were bathed in golden light, slightly hazy with reed dust, and smelling sweetly of the lamp's scented oil. Roses, she thought, and musk.

It was the most alien place she had ever encountered. The great curved ceiling made her feel small, which she wasn't sure she liked. And yet...how peaceful it seemed, how warm and welcoming, and alive. She saw more of Eel's people, all men, wearing little felt caps with side flaps to cover their ears, beautifully embroidered in patterns of flowers and plants. They were dressed in loose cream shirts, some over trews, some just over loincloths. They looked at her curiously, and she wondered what they saw. Someone of the old blood? Kin? Or just an outsider, and not to be trusted, like all outsiders?

A young man came in with only a loincloth on. He smiled brilliantly at her, then turned away to put on a long shirt.

Eel smiled with relief. "This is Salamander. He is better at your language than I. He lived with the ferry people for a while."

"I thought I was in love with the blacksmith's daughter," Salamander explained, with practiced charm.

One of the other men made a quick comment and the group chuckled.

Salamander threw up a hand in acknowledgment. "Yes, yes, I was very stupid and she wasn't that good-looking, I know." He leaned toward Bramble and lowered his voice conspiratorially. "She *was,* actually, but what a shrew! Complaining all day and all night—not about me," he added hastily, seeing the amusement in Bramble's face. "At least," he winked, "not at night."

He seemed so young and was so transparently trying to impress her that she laughed.

"Come, come," Eel said. "It is time to do what you came for."

The three of them walked down the long, dim room, between two lines of rugs that were set out against the wall. Eel carried a lamp, so that as they passed, the colors in the rugs leaped into life and then fell back into darkness again. Some of the dye they had used Bramble recognized: the orange of onion skins, deep pink of rose madder, tan of yarrow, yellow of clematis. But there were deep blues as well, and a pale green like the sky just before dawn, and a deep yellow like the sun. Beautiful. Each one of them was beautiful in its own way, alive with images of birds in flight, of vines and water lilies, and the patterns of reeds.

Salamander saw her looking at them. "The weaving gives work to the people who do not have cattle. They must do something to live."

"They're beautiful."

"Yes?" He looked surprised, then nodded. "They are very old, those designs. But weaving is for the worthless. And for women."

His tone indicated that the two were the same. Bramble wondered wryly if all the people of the old blood had felt like that about women. The people in the Wind Cities, who resembled Travelers, also thought poorly of women, it was said. Property. Cattle. So much for an ancient paradise.

They came to the end of the room, into another pool of lamplight. A woman and a man were sitting there, side by side, not looking at each other.

Eel indicated the man. "Our steersman," he said. "And this is the listener."

The steersman was a tall, craggy-faced man with hard dark eyes surrounded, incongruously, with laugh lines. He was dressed like the other men, in cream shirt, felt waistcoat, and cap. He had tucked the side flaps of the cap up behind his ears. He was impressive and impassive. But Bramble's attention was drawn to the woman. She was young, perhaps younger than Bramble, and as ugly as anyone Bramble had ever seen who was not actually maimed. It was not an ugliness of deformity; it just seemed that her features didn't belong together on the same face, that her big nose was stuck on, her eyes were not quite level, her mouth went a little awry, and her ears were far too large for her head. And yet, her eyes were merry, and she smiled at Bramble and Salamander and Eel as though life was always joyful.

Bramble smiled back involuntarily, a guileless, warm smile, the kind of smile she reserved for Maryrose.

Eel handed over the letter from Sorn to the steersman. He glanced at it, then gave it back to Salamander, who read it aloud in the Lake language.

The steersman's head went back at one point and he hissed through his teeth. The mention of fire, Bramble thought. The steersman turned and spoke to the listener.

Salamander translated quietly into Bramble's ear. "What does the Lake say?"

"The message, and the messenger, can be trusted." The listener spoke in Bramble's tongue.

The steersman looked hard at Bramble, and then nodded.

"It will be soon," Bramble said. "He's calling in all his resources."

They nodded.

"Our thanks," the steersman said. "You are our guest."

He gestured to Eel to take her away, but the listener held up a hand.

"Wait." She spoke directly to Bramble, the mismatched eyes steady and serious. "You are going to the Well of Secrets?"

Bramble nodded.

Part of her felt that she should have been surprised that the listener knew it, but she was slowly realizing that that part had come from Acton's people. Her Traveler blood understood that this woman was connected to the gods. And then she bit back a smile, because the thought reminded her so much of the old ballads her grandfather had liked to sing.

The listener smiled as if in response to Bramble's musing. "We are all in a story now, but what the ending may be, no one knows. Not even the Lake." The men looked worried. "You *must* go to the Well of Secrets, and you must go tomorrow."

Bramble nodded, but a little wearily. She had been looking forward to at least a couple of days' rest and the opportunity to explore this strange world of reeds. "Tomorrow," she said.

"Sleep well. The Lake rocks you in her bosom," the listener said.

The steersman nodded at her and Bramble, Eel and Salamander turned to walk back to the other end of the house, where there was food set out, and a kind of wine she'd never tasted before...and more men and more lamps.

"Only men?" she asked Salamander when they had settled down on a rug to begin their meal.

"Would you prefer to eat with the women?" he said anxiously. "Their food is not so good. But I will take you across to their house if you wish."

She shook her head, suddenly exhausted. "No. I just want to have something to eat and then go to sleep."

"We have a house for you alone to sleep in." He was proud of himself. "I told them that the town dwellers like to sleep alone."

It seemed like a great boon to Bramble, to lie down alone in safety and peace. "Thank you," she said sincerely. "Thank you very much."

Exhaustion swept over her as she sat on the rug with Eel and Salamander and ate from a common dish of braised kid and flat bread. It was good food, warm and fragrant, but it was strange, with spices she wasn't used to turning the familiar taste of goat into something alien. The golden glow, the voices of men all around, strange men at that, combined to make her uneasy.

She had never been in a room with *only* men before, except for cleaning tack with a couple of the grooms who brought mares to Gorham's. But that was different, on home turf. And there were only a couple of grooms at a time. As the meal went on, the house filled with more and more men, all looking, and even smelling, strange, and with the dark hair and eyes which were so rare elsewhere. Although she knew she was perfectly safe, she was also tense, unable to read the faces of the men, who talked and laughed and shouted as the wine went around, but whose eyes studied her, openly, with deep and serious interest.

She wished that she had gone to the women's house after all. She was too alone here. When Salamander touched her on the shoulder, she jumped, and was ashamed of herself.

He smiled at her. "Come on, now," he said soothingly, as to a child. She flushed. "I'll take you to your house."

That meant another trip in a smaller boat, with Salamander standing in the stern to pole it along. There were clouds, but the moon was up, half full, and wind raced the clouds across its face, sending flickers of silver across the waves, like fish leaping, over and over again. The Lake seemed alive with movement, even in the channels between the islands: a place that seethed with life.

She could hear the cattle and goats, smell the smudge fires they lit to keep the mosquitoes away from the herds, hear the whine of the mosquitoes themselves, the voices of women as they passed smaller houses, murmuring to children, singing lullabies, scolding. A child's cry of protest rose up into the night and sent goose bumps down her back. Then the mother's voice came, soothing, gentling, finally speaking firmly. The mother said the same thing several times, and then they were out of earshot.

"What did she say?" Bramble asked.

"'Listen to the Lake, she will hear you,'" Salamander said. "It is what mothers say here when their children are complaining and they've heard enough. Listen to the Lake. It means, if you are quiet, so that you can hear the Lake lapping under the house, then the Lake may grant your desires." He grinned. "But it really means 'No.'"

She smiled back. "Does the Lake never give a child what it wishes?"

He nodded. "Oh, yes, often. A lost toy floats back, the child catches a fine fish . . . many things. The Lake loves children and cares for them."

"And adults?"

This time, his smile was rueful. "The Lake will give an adult what he, or she, desires, but only once in a lifetime, so you have to be very sure of what you ask for. Some people go to their graves never having asked, for fear of getting it wrong and wasting it. Others ask too soon for things which are worthless and must live the rest of their lives with that mistake. Like me."

She looked at him questioningly.

He shrugged, his mouth wry. "I asked for the daughter of the blacksmith in the town. Well, I got her!" And then, irrepressibly, he threw back his head and laughed.

Bramble had to laugh too, although she wondered how much hurt hid behind his laughter, and how much the laughter of the other men had pushed him into making a mockery of himself. He needed to forget about it and find some way of proving himself to them so that they would stop laughing. She sobered. No doubt Thegan would give him plenty of opportunity.

"'She gives us all we need and requires obedience in return,'" Salamander said, clearly quoting.

Bramble raised her eyebrows. "What if She doesn't get obedience?"

"She takes what is her due, either in life or through death. Only a fool disobeys the Lake. They say the fish pick your bones very clean, but I'd rather have my body burned, as it should be. After a peaceful death from old age."

So much for the Lake's universal benevolence. Perhaps it was just as well. She would need to be ruthless to protect Her people from Thegan. Salamander brought the boat smoothly to moor against a small reed house, barely bigger than a room.

"Your sleeping house," he said. "Sleep well. Listen to the Lake and she will soothe you. Who knows? She may speak to you."

"I'll listen. Goodnight, and thank you."

Her packs were already inside, on reed mats, and there was a thick rug, which was clearly the sleeping place. Salamander had not left her a light, but the sliding shutters were pushed back from the windows and the fitful moonlight showed enough to let her find the chamber pot and use it, and then retrieve and curl up under her favorite blanket, with a bag as pillow. The autumn night was cool and she was glad of the blanket. She wondered where the horses were, but she had seen enough of the way Eel's men handled them to be sure they would be fine. She watched the moonlight and listened to the Lake, but all she heard was the low sound of water lapping at the stilts of the house until she slept.

She dreamed that Maryrose's voice called to her to get up. She stood up and went to the window where the voice had come from. Even as she walked, she knew it was a dream, because outside the window shone a full moon, where it had been only a half-moon when she went to bed. And the Lake water lapped at the sides of her hut, higher than before, as though it were spring and the Lake had risen with the melting snow. A warm, light breeze fanned her face.

Outside, she couldn't see any of the huts or the islands she and Salamander had poled through that night. Only the Lake, stretching endlessly in the moonlight, the waters shining silver so brightly it hurt her eyes.

Maryrose's voice came again.

"Will you help me?"

She didn't sound distressed, but calm, gentle, with even tones. But underneath the familiar, beloved voice was something else, another note that resonated with Maryrose's voice as the wind played across waves. Even in the dream, Bramble knew it was the Lake talking. But whether it was the real Lake or just her own dreaming of it, brought on by the strangeness of the place and Salamander's tales, she didn't know.

"Of course I will help, if you need it," Bramble said.

After all, wasn't that why she was here? She found that she was breathing hard, as she did when she rode in a chase. She had the same feeling of recklessnes, of exhilaration, that she got when she was a stumble away from death.

"Will you give me what I need?" the voice asked.

Bramble's heartbeat increased even more and she felt that one wrong word would shatter the dream, and perhaps shatter more than that. It was like talking to the local gods, she had that same feeling of being on a precipice, of pressure that threatened to take your breath if you said what was unwanted.

"You could take what you need," she said, finally, knowing it was true, that she had nothing the Lake could not take, including her life.

Maryrose's voice laughed, softly. "Never without asking. That is the compact. Will you give?"

"Yes."

"Ah." It was less Maryrose's voice now and more a shifting slide of sound—less human, more beautiful. "And will you become one of my children?"

She shook her head without thinking, knowing in her bones that she did not belong here and never would. The Lake was absolutely still, waiting for her answer. The waves against her hut were still, the breeze dead. The whole Lake waited. Bramble cleared her throat.

"Although it would be an honor, Lady, I think I belong elsewhere."

The waves began again, the breeze lifted her hair gently.

"So think I. Wise child, you have far to go before you reach your journey's end."

Then suddenly it was just before dawn, and Bramble was lying under her blanket in the clear gray light, with the air outside so cold that the tip of her nose ached. She lay for a moment, wondering, then heard Salamander call her name as his boat bumped at her doorstep.

"Time to go, beautiful rider," he said, poking his head through the door. "Your boat is waiting."

ASH

WINTER CAME, in a rush, in a matter of days. The last leaves fell, frosts hardened the ground, snow drifted down steadily and the animals were moved into the big barn, crowded by the fodder Mabry had stored there this year, instead of in the small barn. "We need to practice," he had said to Gytha, when she complained of having to squeeze through the hay to feed the chickens.

Three weeks after they arrived, at breakfast, Elva began to have birth pains. Ash was sent to get the midwife from the cluster of houses down near the river.

"Second on the left, no, right—the yellow house," Mabry gabbled, then raced back to the bedroom.

Ash ran, as fast as he could in the snow, slipping and sliding down the steep path in flurries of snow. But when the midwife heard why he'd come, she just nodded and went calmly about putting the things she needed into her bag. Ash hopped from one foot to the other impatiently. She shook her head at him tolerantly.

"First birth, just started the pains—she'll be hours yet, young'un."

So it proved. He followed the wiry legs of the midwife up the path and waited in the main room for hours. Gytha was the messenger, coming out to get fresh towels or a hot brick from the fire for Elva's back, and each time saying, "Don't fret, it's all going well."

It was dark before the midwife emerged. "Well, it didn't take as long as I thought, after all." She smiled at him. "Go on, then, go see the little lad."

Ash rushed into the bedroom and stopped at the door. It was like an image from an old song: the new parents, the mother holding the swaddled babe close, the proud father bending over them. He hardly saw the others. He was struck through with envy, with a desire for what Mabry had: a wife to love, a child to raise, a home to live in and work for, a place in a village where he was known and respected. They were things he would probably never have. For a moment, he hovered on the brink of hating Mabry for that, but he remembered Doronit, her face contorted by hate for Acton's people, and he turned the yearning into an even stronger determination not to let anything harm this family. Or, he thought for the first time, others like them.

Elva looked up from the child. "A boy. With dark hair!" she said. "I must look out the window. Draw back the shutters, Mabry."

They had discussed this, too, in the nights before the fire, and Mabry had agreed that Elva could name the baby the Traveler way, by the sight of the first living thing she saw outside after the birth. But Mabry was prepared to go with Traveler customs only so far, and he had laid plans with Ash. He nodded to Ash now, before he touched the shutters, and Ash ran outside to where they had potted up and hidden two small trees: a cherry for a girl and a tiny cedar sapling for a boy. He positioned himself by the window and called out to Mabry, who then opened the shutters.

"What are you doing, Ash?" Elva asked, and Mabry explained.

The two girls laughed, but Elva and Martine were silent. Ash peered in. They didn't look happy.

"Fine," Elva said. "I can see why you did it. But you have to take the consequences. The first living thing I saw was Ash. We'll call the baby Ash."

Mabry expostulated, but Elva held firm.

"The gods guide us in our choice of names," Martine said. "You think you're the first father who's tried to cast only the stones he wants? It never answers. It's bad luck."

So Mabry agreed, to Ash's delight. He wasn't interested in babies, but it was as though the gods had heard his yearning to be part of this family, and had given his wish to him backhandedly, as was their habit. An Ash, of Traveler blood, would grow up in this warm and loving spot, cherished and happy. *If they could stop the ghosts.*

The days shortened. This far north, so close to the mountains, the winters were long and very cold. The valley was protected from the worst of the winds, but even so, there were few days when they could walk out comfortably into crisp air. On those days the sky was deep blue and the air tasted sharp and bracing on the tongue, and the women came up from the village, to see the new baby and surreptitiously assess the strangers. A couple of men from the class in the barn came too, awkwardly, and Ash realized that they were courting Drema and Gytha. Gytha grinned and flirted with her beau, but Barley, courting Drema, had a harder task. Still, Ash thought, watching the way her eyes softened as he gingerly held the baby, he might have a chance.

The evenings were spent marveling over the baby and talking, with Ash reciting almost every song he knew. At Drema's request, he began to do it chronologically, working his way through the past, from the very earliest Traveler songs to the ballads of the landtaken and the love songs and nonsense songs of the present.

It sobered Mabry and his sisters a little. It was clear that, like most settled folk, they had never heard the full story of the landtaken: the full toll of the dead, the raped, the enslaved. The songs told of the ceaseless expansion north, which pushed back the old inhabitants to the poor, marginal land, and from there, pushed them onto the roads, to become Travelers.

The ballads were from an earlier, more robust age, where battle was a source of glory and the tally of those killed added to a warrior's renown. Acton's people had delighted in bloodshed. But Mabry's people were farmers, and it was too easy, with the ghosts perhaps gathering, for them to imagine the terror and despair of those attacked.

Holmstead fell! Giant Aelred, shield of iron
Mighty sword arm for his chief.
Down came Aelred, fierce with battle cry
Sweeping all before his blade
Sweeping all before to death.
The dark people leaped to battle
A hundred strong they leaped to battle
Wielded weapons in weak arms.
Mighty Aelred led his warriors
A score of warriors came behind him

Faced the hundred.
Killed them all.

"Do we have to listen to all this blood and death?" Gytha asked.

"I think we do," Drema said, and Mabry nodded.

"Yes. Better to know the truth. Better to understand why the enchanter the ghosts spoke of is seeking revenge."

"Keep to the history, Ash," Drema said. "We must start with the earliest and work our way up."

There were kinder songs, too, and they turned to those with relief. Ash dredged his memory for early songs that were not about battle. Several times he remembered songs, or fragments of songs, that he had heard his father sing at night near the fire, but never his mother. "Useless songs," she had said. They never performed them, because they were in the old Traveler language and would have been unpopular with audiences. But they were haunting, all in a minor key. Although it was difficult to figure out what they meant, even after Ash had translated them.

The gods' own prey is galloping, is riding up the hill
Her hands are wet with blood and tears and dread
She is rearing on the summit and her banner floats out still
Now the killer's hands must gather in the dead.

"It's not a very good translation," Ash said apologetically. "The original's better. It's a tricky rhythm."

"'The killer's hands must gather in the dead,'" Martine mused. "It sounds like a prophecy."

"Oh, gods, not a prophecy!" Elva exclaimed. "I hate those things. They never say what you think they mean and then they come up behind you when you least expect it and shove you into something horrible."

She scowled. Everyone but Martine looked surprised.

"Oh, it's not that bad, love," she said, and smiled. "It was only a little prophecy."

"Tell us," Mabry said.

Elva shook her head stubbornly, but Martine laughed. "One of the old women in our village foretold when Elva was born that she would live with the gods. She's never really known what it meant."

"But you've already done that, sweetheart," Mabry said. "When you first came here, you built a cabin next to the gods' stone and lived with them."

Elva's pale face went still for a moment and then broke into a wide smile. "I did, didn't I?" She laughed in relief. "All my life I've had that shagging prophecy following me around and it came true without me even noticing it! You see, that's what I mean, it's just typical of prophecies. You can't trust them."

"All right," Martine said soothingly, "we won't worry about some prey of the gods."

"After all," Ash said, "that song was written a thousand years ago. If it is a prophecy, it's not likely to come true right now."

"Enough songs for tonight," Drema said firmly. "Let's go to bed."

Rolled comfortably in his blankets by the fire, breathing in the warm scent of apples from the drying rack over the ashes, Ash drifted off to sleep immediately, but was woken in the middle of the night by little Ash's crying. He lay in the darkness and listened to Elva murmuring to him, and to the funny hiccup he always gave as he was put to the breast. Then there was silence, except for the slow creak of the roof under its burden of snow, the very faint hiss from the banked fire... and his own breathing, slow and steady.

Something about that rhythm brought back a memory from a long time before: he clung to his father's back as they walked a road, somewhere, sometime, when he was little enough for Da to carry him most of the day. His father was singing. His father's voice wasn't beautiful, like Mam's, but he liked its deep resonance, coming up through his back as Ash clung to his shoulders. Mam pushed their handcart behind them, and the rumbling of the wheels was even deeper. His father was singing old words, very odd words. Snatches of it came back to Ash, "knife cleansed, blood flows, memory calls, past shows, the bones beneath it all... "

"That's a song better forgotten." His mam's voice had come sharply.

"No song should be forgotten," his father had said.

Yes, Ash realized, this was why the incident had stayed in his memory, although he had been so tiny at the time. It was the first, one of the only times, he had ever heard his father disagree with his mother.

"No song should be forgotten," his father had repeated. "You remember that, Ash."

So he had. He remembered them all.

They had little Ash to thank that the winter did not seem endless. The few weeks before he was born had dragged out, but afterward the days flew, crammed from morning until night.

Ash would never have believed the difference one little baby made. None of them got enough sleep, except Gytha who could ignore his nighttime cries. They walked around during the day with dark circles under their eyes, and drank too many cups of cha to stay awake. Elva was the worst, of course, but she at least felt no shame in curling up with the baby for a nap. The others had chores to do, even in winter: animals to be fed and mucked out, thatch to be replaced on the barn roof, water to be carried, chamber pots to be emptied and cleaned, cooking, cleaning, felting, sewing, spinning, weaving, chopping wood.

Then there was the nappy changing, the clothes washing, the baby bathing before the fire, the walking and the soothing and the rocking to sleep. And just watching the changing expressions on that tiny face—it was a full-time job for all five of them, which was ridiculous. Perhaps not quite full-time, Ash conceded. They did have some time for other things.

Mabry was also a skilled woodcarver, and made delicate designs of flowers and plants on all sorts of items. He had made the baby's cradle before Martine and Ash arrived. The day after little Ash was born, he set to work to carve the traditional flower for Elva's child necklace, which all the women of Acton's people were given who had borne a child to their husband. Cornflower was for a boy, daisy for a girl, and carved and painted by the father—that was the tradition. A stillborn child's flower was left unpainted, to show the life unlived. When the woman died, she was buried with the necklace. The cornflower Mabry carved and painted for little Ash was a marvel, complex and delicate, almost alive. Through the long winter nights he worked at a pair of dinner plates, rectangles of wood on which he etched the spare outline of reeds.

As the days grew noticeably longer, Gytha spent nights out in the barn in case of early lambing.

Then came the first sign of spring thaw—a warm wind from the south. The five of them stood together outside, with little Ash in Martine's arms, looking south down the valley and watching chunks of ice break away from the riverbanks and be carried away.

"Time to go," said Martine.

Ash couldn't tell if there was sorrow or anticipation in her voice. Perhaps both.

So they packed up that day, saying little except to plan their route. "Down the valley's your best way," said Mabry. "Right to the end and then come up into Cliff Domain and strike east. The roads aren't good, but you'll get there in a few weeks. Then north through the Golden Valley and Quiet Pass into the Last Domain. They say the Well of Secrets is there now, in Oakmere." He paused. "It's a long trip."

Martine patted Mabry on the shoulder reassuringly. "We're Travelers, born and bred."

"The road is long and the end is death," Ash said cheerfully.

Mabry smiled. "If we're lucky." He had learned the Traveler's answer from Elva.

As they were packing, each of them came to give Ash and Martine a parting gift, things they'd worked on all winter that Ash never suspected could be for him. Gytha had woven a big goat's-wool blanket that would cover both of them. Drema had made them felt coats, beautifully embroidered, and far warmer than anything Ash owned. Elva had dried half an orchard's worth of fruit over the fire, "for the lean, hungry times," she said. And Mabry gave them the plates.

"A bit heavy to carry, but lighter than pottery," he said shyly.

Martine kissed him. Ash, embarrassed, pounded him on the shoulder.

The next morning, early, Ash, Mabry, Drema and Gytha waited outside while Martine and Elva said goodbye in the house.

"Take care of yourself," Mabry said to Ash.

"You too. All of you."

Mabry tried to smile. "Don't worry. We'll be ready."

Ash nodded. "Keep your guard up, then."

Then Martine came out, and Elva followed with tears streaking down her face. Martine's face was set, as he had seen it during the attack at her house, when she held the white knife to the young man's throat. He knew her better now, and it was a face that was holding back fear and sorrow.

There was kissing all round, and then they simply turned and walked away.

As they picked their way down the slushy path, Ash felt worse than when he had left his parents behind to go to Doronit's. This time he was leaving people who valued him, who had a place for him. *But only for the winter,* he reminded himself. *It was only ever just for the winter.* It wasn't where he really belonged.

But the winter's contentment had given him a new standard to measure life against. He wouldn't be satisfied, ever, until he could create a home as warm, and a life that meant as much.

"Oh, gods," he said aloud, thinking of what might lie ahead. "Why us?"

Martine glanced sideways at him. "Shagged if I know." She grinned at his surprise. "Look on the bright side, lad. We've full packs, a long road and a reason to walk it. What more do Travelers need?"

He smiled back, reluctantly, and settled his pack more comfortably on his back. She was right, they had a long way to go.

BRAMBLE

BRAMBLE'S HORSES were already loaded in Eel's big boat and were very glad to see her. They almost knocked her down, butting her side with their heads, nickering in her face, moving closer to her, even Trine. Eel waited patiently for them to settle down, smiling so hard his eyes almost disappeared into their laugh lines.

"They missed their *sisgara,*" he said. "Their herd leader. They were lost and lone without you."

"I was a bit lost and lone without them," Bramble confessed, absurdly uplifted by their greeting.

She rubbed their noses, clouted Trine on the shoulder when she tried to step on Eel's foot, felt herself surrounded by the familiar warmth and horse smells. She was no longer traveling alone in a strange land.

They came to bind her eyes again and she asked for just a moment to take in the dawn breaking over the Lake. The sky was streaked with clouds, which picked up every color imaginable: green and rose and gold, magenta and heliotrope and violet. All were reflected in the still water. It was a kaleidoscope of color, changing rapidly as the sun rose and the sky settled into duck egg blue, the pale clear blue of winter. Bramble took a great breath as though she could inhale the colors.

"All right," she said.

She closed her eyes and was blindfolded, then settled back against the side of the boat and listened again to the Lake.

They poled out slowly from the narrow channels, leaving the myriad noises of the village behind until there was nothing to be heard but the calls of birds and the rustle of the reeds and the lap of the Lake water. It chuckled against the prow, happy, but also urgent, as though it were pressing them to hurry. Whether Eel heard it like that she didn't know, but when they came to a larger channel, he picked up the pace and they were now moving much faster than they had the day before.

After some time, he came to unbind her eyes and give her water and cheese and bread. He shared the food with her, sitting cross-legged on the deck. They had drawn up in a small cove surrounded by willows and, standing farther back, elms. The willows had dropped almost all their thin yellow leaves, the elms were already winter bare. There was an autumn scent, of moss and drying earth, just perceptible over the pitch-tar smell of the boat. As they ate, Eel's men put out two gangplanks and led the horses, scrambling, onto the shore.

"We have taken you to the northern side, but a long way west of the town. There is a road, farther up, that you can join to take you to the Golden Valley, and from there over the Quiet Pass into the Last Domain, where you will find the Well of Secrets."

Bramble nodded. "Thank you." She wondered if she should tell him about the dream.

"Remember though," Eel went on, "the road is in the Cliff Domain—Thegan's son's Domain, the one Thegan ruled before he married the Lady Sorn. You must be wary."

Bramble went cold. She had hoped to cross the Lake as close as possible to Baluchston, which would have kept her out of Cliff Domain.

"He's going to come at you from both sides," she said.

"Yes. But do not worry. It has happened before, with men as greedy and blood hungry as he, and we are still here. We will always be here. We are the Lake's children and She cares for us, the way She cares for you."

She was surprised, and showed it.

"You think She does not care for you?" Eel asked, laughing. "Then ask yourself, how can you spend a night with open windows and come out the next morning without a single mosquito bite? She's never done that much for me!"

Bramble looked at her arms, and was astonished that it hadn't occurred to her before. Not *one* bite. Even though, as she and Salamander had poled toward her house, she had heard the insistent whine of the mosquitoes everywhere.

She opened her mouth, but didn't know what to say.

"I am honored," she managed finally.

Eel smiled at her again, and patted her shoulder. She suddenly felt very young and silly. It wasn't unpleasant.

"Then you will understand and forgive her," he said. "She takes only what she needs."

"What do you mean?" she asked, but he smiled and shook his head and gestured to her to follow the horses.

She looked at him for a moment, annoyed that he wouldn't explain, then followed the horses ashore. They came to nose into her shoulder, Trine shoving the others aside to get closer to her. She spent a few moments saddling up and securing their packs, trying not to think of the journeys she had taken with the roan. The hot ball of grief and guilt was never far away, but it could be lived with. She took a deep breath, pushing the memories aside, and decided to ride Trine again. This new affection should be nurtured.

As she was preparing to mount up, and wondering what to say to Eel, Salamander appeared from between the bare willow withes.

"Hallo!" he said cheerfully. "Are you ready?"

She looked at Eel.

"He will show you to the road." He looked at Salamander sternly. "Don't get yourself killed and don't fall in love with any drylander."

The men in the boat laughed.

Salamander sighed. "Uncle, I will try to avoid both."

"Good!" Eel smacked him between the shoulder blades in a gesture of affection and farewell, then turned to Bramble.

"Take care of him. My sister will use my guts as her fishing lines if he gets hurt."

"Oh, I think he can take care of himself," Bramble said drily. Salamander shot her a look of gratitude. "Goodbye. Thank you."

"No," Eel said. "Our thanks are to you for risking so much to bring us our warning." He bowed, formally, his hat in his hand. "The gods go with you."

"Blessings be on you and yours," Bramble replied.

She turned and led the horses off, Salamander by her side.

"I hate goodbyes," Salamander said happily. "This is the way."

He led her along a slender path she might easily have missed on her own, through an arch of bare elm branches. Dry leaves crunched under their feet and a cool breeze lifted off the Lake, as though to bid them farewell. As they walked through the arch, she felt a shiver, some kind of anticipation. Was it fear? she wondered. She ducked her head to avoid a low bough and when her head came up she almost bit her tongue off in surprise.

The elms around them were in leaf: bright yellow-green new spring leaves. The sun was higher in a sky patched with cloud, the air was rich with the heady, full smell of the earth after fresh spring rain. The breeze was warm, now, and looking back she could see that the level of the Lake was much higher, just as she had seen in her dream the night before.

Salamander turned to smile at her uneasily, half apologetic, half scared. “It’s only a little bit of time She has taken,” he said placatingly. “Just a few months.”

Her breath was coming as fast as though she had been running. *Then you will understand and forgive her,* Eel had said. This was what he had meant. *She takes only what she needs.* Bramble breathed in slowly, willing her heart to slow. She grinned suddenly. It answered her questions about whether the dream had been true. She felt again the rush of adrenaline and excitement from the dream. *Magic.* She’d never experienced real magic before, just the presence of the gods, which was part of her blood and bone. No, it couldn’t be magic—that was something humans did. To move two people and three horses through time was power of another kind.

Salamander regarded her anxiously.

“You’ve lost your time, too,” she said.

Salamander seemed pleased not to be shouted at. He smiled, immediately relaxed. “Oh, I volunteered,” he said. “Who minds missing winter? The road is this way.”

He led her up a winding path and she followed, the horses completely unperturbed by the sudden shift to spring, although their nostrils were wide, drinking in the full, living scent.

She looked over her shoulder at the Lake, expecting something, anything, a sign, an omen... But there was just the flickering of sun on the ripples and an empty cove that had last seen a boat in late autumn. Bramble turned in her saddle and stared resolutely ahead. Why had the Lake needed Bramble to be here, now? Right at this time. What was so special about *now?*

Nothing, it seemed, for the moment. Salamander led her down a winding path, through thickets of willow and alder. There were streams crisscrossing their track, bubbling with snowmelt and forcing them to turn aside several times before they found safe places to ford. All the streams looked alike, all the clumps of willow seemed the same. She would not have found the way by herself.

After a couple of hours they emerged onto pastureland where cows were grazing. These were a different breed from the Lake cattle, big bony black-and-white animals, and only a couple had calves. It must be very early spring. The land was dead flat and the sky was wide above them. It was as though they had been picked up and put down somewhere a world away.

"The road's over that way," Salamander said, pointing north. "Follow it east and take the first turning to the north. That'll lead you up to Golden Valley. It's a bit longer, but it'll keep you off the main track."

"Thanks. I hope you get back safely."

Salamander grinned. "Who'd want to hurt me?" He darted in and kissed her on the cheek before she realized what he was doing. "Had to do it," he said. "Couldn't resist."

Bramble's laugh made Trine toss her head at the end of her leading string, blowing loudly through her nose.

"Exactly," Bramble said. "Couldn't have put it better myself."

She unclipped the leading string and jumped up onto Trine's back. "Wind at your back," she said.

"Smooth water," Salamander replied, then turned and slipped into the cover of the willows.

Bramble rode away and had to resist the urge to turn around and wave at him like a child saying "bye-bye." But she rode away with a smile.

It was good to be on horseback again. She found the road easily, just a double cart track through the short grass, and followed it without meeting anything more alarming than cows. When it branched, she took the overgrown northern track, which led toward the foothills nearby.

She calculated that she had two days' riding to get to Golden Valley. She would be safe there. Golden Valley lay between Cliff Domain and

Far North Domain. It was terrible country for farming but it bred wonderful horses, with stamina and bone and heart. In the past, the two Domains had fought over the valley so often that trade from the far north, from the Last Domain and the Northern Mountains Domain, had almost stopped. About thirty years ago, just after he'd come into his inheritance, the previous warlord of the Last Domain had brokered a peace, and his son, Arvid, now safeguarded that peace. The Golden Valley was now a "free valley," as Carlion and Turvite were free towns. It belonged to no one and was governed by a council elected by its inhabitants. It was neutral territory and Thegan—and his son—could not touch her there.

The track wound higher into the foothills. Bramble felt lighthearted. The spring sun, the clear sky, the clarity of the hill air combined to buoy her spirits. She was across the Lake, had delivered her message, and was on her way again. The Well of Secrets would keep until she got to the Last Domain, and Oakmere. She whistled as she rode and talked to the horses, to Trine especially.

Her good mood lasted until dusk. They had climbed well into the foothills, and the mountains soared above them. She was looking for a place to camp for the night when she heard the howl of wolves.

Early spring, she realized immediately, as the horses whickered in fright and Cam reared up and tried to bolt, reverting in an instant to the flighty animal she'd been when Bramble first took her in. Bramble tussled with her and with the other two, talking to them, and regretting, for the first time, not putting a bit on Trine. They shuffled and twisted a good way down the path before she got them under control. *Early spring.* It would have been a long, hungry winter, and the baby calves and kids had not yet arrived. *No easy prey except us.*

She looked around frantically. There was no shelter here on the bare hillside. She would have to ride on, to a cave, a niche in the rocks, anything where the horses could have their backs protected while they used their front hooves to defend themselves. But it was getting dark, and the footing underneath was growing more and more treacherous. She clicked her tongue at the horses at the same moment the wolves' howl came again, and she had to hold them in hard to stop them galloping off down the uneven track.

"There now, just a little faster, that's it, you're all right, no need to worry, just pick up the pace a little, that's all," she crooned, calming them and herself at the same time.

She had the wolf skin around her shoulders and wondered if that was a good omen or a bad one. *Gods, aid your daughter,* she prayed, but there was no sense of the gods at all up here on the bare hillside.

They went on as fast as she dared through the darkening night until the track curved around a ridge of fissured granite. There were gaps in the rock as though someone had sliced a knife down a cake. She dismounted and led the horses up the hillside, slippery with loose rock, until she found a gap that was big enough for the three of them. It wasn't big enough for her as well, but if she had to, she resolved, she could lie across their backs... She tried not to think about sliding off the horses backward, in the dark, onto cold rock, to be trampled by thrashing, panicked hooves. The wolves might not come. *And spring will follow autumn next year,* she thought. *Of course they'll come.*

There was no wood up here to start a fire. She gave the horses a small drink of water, but not too much, then grabbed some of the oats from a saddlebag and fed them quickly. They'd need the energy if they had to run. She drank some water and ate the dried apricots and flat bread that Eel had given her. That seemed a long time ago. She laughed softly, and the horses shifted in response. It was a long time ago. Months. She settled down to wait, knife in hand. It was the same knife she had slit the wolf's throat with, back in Wooding. It didn't look very big.

They won't be long. Wolves liked to hunt at dusk, not at midnight. *They'll be here soon.*

They were.

They came from all directions at once, even from above the fissure, leaping down to swirl and growl and snap at the horses' hooves, trying to panic them into running. But the horses' instinct to run was overcome by another instinct—to stand and fight. They struck out with hooves flailing, the three standing together, with Trine a little to the front. As their hooves landed, sparks flew from the rocks. The night was full of noise: snarling, neighing, the thud and crack of hooves meeting flesh and rock, and her own shouting. She stayed just to one side of the cleft, out of reach of their hooves, but one of the wolves—the leader, she realized—circled around toward her.

She turned to face it. Here was the image from so many stories: the evil wolf, the northern wolf, sharp teeth bared, claws clicking on the rock, prowling, measuring up its prey. Childhood terror rose up in her. She saw the wolf's muscles tense, ready to spring.

She leaped forward and down a moment before it launched so that it passed just over her instead of reaching her throat. She thrust up with the knife at its belly and dragged the knife down. It felt like her shoulder was coming out of its socket, but she kept hold of the haft.

The wolf yowled in pain and twisted in midair, coming down heavily on its side. She jumped on it with both knees before it could rise. The sound of the air being forced out of its lungs was all she could hear.

And then the world went quiet.

The wolf writhed beneath her, impossibly strong. One claw ripped down her arm. She raised the knife in both hands and plunged it down as hard as she could. The wolf convulsed beneath her and then lay still.

For a moment, Bramble felt nothing but relief, as though it were all over. But noise crashed into the silence and she realized that the fight was still going on around her.

The big brown wolf leading the attack against the horses realized that its leader was down. It flung its head back and howled. Bramble stood up slowly, straddling the corpse, knife in hand, and snarled at the pack. She felt as rabid as she sounded. She would kill them all before she would let them hurt her horses.

There were only three of them left. It had seemed like dozens. One body was lying in front of Trine, smashed and bloody. The brown wolf—a female—stared at Bramble and snarled back. Bramble took a step forward, and the brown wolf broke. She yelped and turned and the other two followed her, only the whites on the undersides of their tails showing up in the almost dark as they ran.

Bramble checked the horses. They had got away with just a scratch or two, and none too deep. She cleaned out the wounds and then cleaned her own, a long ragged tear down her arm that would probably scar. She bound it up awkwardly with one of her shirts.

She dragged the two carcasses away from the fissure before she sat down. Once she sat she'd never be able to get up again, and there would be scavengers after the meat before dawn, and maybe other hunters, like bears. They would be satisfied with the wolf meat and not come looking for more.

Then she sat next to the fissure and let out her breath in a long *houf*. The horses were still fretting and were too frightened to wander off by themselves, and in a way she was relieved, because she didn't have the energy to get their tethers out and find rocks big enough to secure them to.

"Well, cullies, we're safe enough now," she told them. "Settle down, now, settle down."

They did settle down under the spell of her voice, and she even slept a little, sitting up against the hard rock, despite the pain in her arm. It seemed to throb and burn worse as the night went on, and she was afraid it was turning bad. She'd have to find a healer, but where?

In the morning the horses' scratches looked clean and on the mend, but her bandage was showing blood and her arm was hot and red. She fed and watered the horses but there was no water left for her. She had trouble lifting the saddlebags back onto Mud's back.

"Not good," she said to Trine. She was light-headed and not up to jumping on as she usually did, so she led Trine to a rock and climbed on from there. It seemed the wolves had knocked some of the arrogance out of Trine, because she stood still and let Bramble mount her without any objection. She even nosed Bramble's leg gently afterward.

They went as fast as they could on the rocky trail, with stones shifting under the horses' hooves. Mud proved to be most sure-footed, so they followed him and, like Trine, he was unusually cooperative with her. She wondered if killing the lead wolf had cemented her position as head of the herd. It was possible; and possible, too, that this far from their normal life, the horses just wanted the reassurance of someone telling them what to do.

She could understand that.

Just after midday she neared the top of the ridge they had been making toward all morning. She was pretty sure that Golden Valley lay over it. Maybe there she could find a healer. Her arm was getting worse. The trail led to a pass through even higher peaks, sharp and treacherous, with snow on their tops. She threaded her way through a recent rockfall of giant boulders that almost blocked the trail.

She reached the other side and was sure it was Golden Valley before her. It had been named in autumn, her da had told her once, because of the yellow leaves of the poplar trees that grew there. The poplar leaves were a brighter yellow-green now, in early spring, but the valley below seemed lit up with them, glowing in the sunlight. They followed the courses of innumerable streams and circled around ponds. She could see farmhouses and fenced paddocks far below...and horses. She smiled.

She followed the trail with her eye as it zigzagged down the hillside, making a steep way around clumps of bushes and pine trees. They started down carefully.

Two bends down, Trine neighed loudly and was answered by another horse hidden by the curve in the track. Bramble wasn't worried. Here in Golden Valley she was safe. She was just a...a horse trainer, looking for work on her way to the Well of Secrets. Plain and simple. The truth, in fact.

The riders below came around the bend. She was a moment slow in recognizing them. It was the two men Leof had talked to in the clearing—Horst and Sully, on their way back from the Last Domain. They stared at her in disbelief.

"Bramble!" Horst said. "It's bloody Bramble!"

"We're in Golden Valley," Bramble said quickly. "A free valley."

Horst looked up and down. There was no one in sight. "Aye," he said slowly. "But no one knows you're here, do they? I reckon we could have met you just the other side of the ridge."

"You'll be breaking the law."

Sully grinned. "You think my lord Thegan will *care*? Horst, my old mate, he's going to love us for this!"

"Don't take me back to him," Bramble said, her stomach turning over at asking a warlord's man for anything. "You know what he's like."

Sully glanced at Horst. "Aye. He's a coldhearted bastard who'd slit his own mother's throat if it was useful to him. And that's why we're taking you back, lass. Can you imagine what he'd do to us if we didn't?"

They were blocking the trail, but perhaps she had a chance of making it down the hillside to a lower part of the track. She had to try.

She made a feint to turn back up the trail, then, as they surged after her, she turned sideways and bolted across the hillside, dropping the leading reins and letting Cam and Mud follow as they could. She just hoped they wouldn't get entangled in the reins and fall. Trine picked up her pace and slipped across the loose scree on the hill and then turned to slide, dance, and finally leap down to the firmer footing between the trees that masked the lower bend of the trail.

Horst and Sully came after her as fast as they dared, but they kept to the trail so they were a little way behind her. And now it was just a chase. Bramble let everything go out of her head except getting farther ahead. The world narrowed to the track ahead of her, the ground, the way down. She was good at this, better than the men following. She knew how to find shortcuts, how to take risks. Trine wasn't the roan, but she was fast.

She was a fair way ahead of them at the bottom of the hill. The track branched and she swung left, farther into the valley, heading for houses and witnesses...and safety. But she felt increasingly lightheaded and hot. Her arm seemed to swell even more, and her heart was skipping its beats.

The track curved back and up the hill, heading for another pass. She had chosen the wrong track. She knew she had to turn back and go down the hillside, but not on the track, that would just head her into their arms. She faltered and turned Trine, her head swimming, but Trine balked at the steep descent and rocky surface, and Bramble felt herself falling, although it seemed to be happening a long way away.

She had just enough energy left to roll as she hit the ground. She wanted to just lie there for a moment. Just a moment. But she forced herself to clamber up. If she could get back on Trine...

Horst caught her as she grasped Trine's mane. He had leaped from his horse and grabbed her arms. She screamed with pain and he let her go in surprise. Trine swung around and bit him hard on the arm. He swore and drew his sword. Sully moved off to the side to stop her running back down the hill. He drew his sword as well.

"Give in, now, lass, give it over and come with us," Horst said gently. "You know you can't win."

Bramble knew he was right. But the same refusal to be frightened that had stopped her running from the blond, back in Wooding, stopped her from giving in now.

"I'd rather die than be used by Thegan," she said venomously. She drew her knife, and jumped toward Sully.

"Stupid Traveler bitch!" he yelled as he brought his sword down.

THE WELL OF SECRETS

THEY'LL BE meeting soon," Safred said casually to her uncle. "The other three. But there's no guarantee they'll make it through that moment."

"I'd spit for luck but my mouth's too dry," Cael said.

There was a distant commotion outside in the street. Cael raised an eyebrow. Safred's eyes hazed for a moment, then cleared.

"A healing," she said. "One of the pilgrims fell from the bridge."

"Can you help him?"

"Her. No. But I can save the baby."

And the family'll ask why I didn't foresee the accident and save them both, Safred thought. *I'd ask the same. But the only answer is "because the gods didn't will it" and what kind of answer is that?*

"There's one good thing," she said as she prepared to open the door. "The fifth will be along tomorrow."

"What fifth?" Cael looked at her. "What haven't you been telling me?"

Safred smiled sadly. "Too much. Life and death and destruction and rebirth. Everything, really."

She opened the door before they could knock on it. Three men rushed in carrying the injured woman and placed her on the bed where the Well of Secrets did her healing. She placed both hands on the woman's belly and looked at Cael, noting the increase in gray hairs, the slight blurring of muscle by a thin film of fat: the signs of age approaching, even if it was a long way off yet.

He glared at her as he often did, to remind her that though she was the healing miracle worker to everyone else, to him she was still the child he had raised. And to part of her he was still almost-father, the strong arms that had protected her. But he couldn't protect her from the gods.

She concentrated on the body beneath her hands and began to sing in horrible, grating tones that sounded like the voice of the dead, and the pain left the woman's face.

Cael pushed his way outside through the crowd gathered at the door, watching, worshipping as the gods showed their power.

CAEL'S STORY

There were fishers on the bank. When the boat came gliding down the stream toward them, a lantern at her prow and another at her stern, gleaming in the dusk, they thought it was a ghost ship, for surely no craft could navigate this high reach of the river, far above the falls.

There were rocks downstream and rocks upstream, white water churning endlessly, in and out of season. How could a ship come here?

So they ran, throwing down their rods and their gaffs, back to the village crying, "Death, disaster upon us!"

The ship rode the white water lightly, and survived the teeth of the rocks and the smiting of the stream. It smashed to pieces on the high falls—but by then it had served its purpose, and those on board were safe ashore.

I was one of those on board. So I, Cael, tell the tale as one who was there and who knows the truth.

When her time came upon the Lady and her pains drew close together, she called for me and entrusted the coming babe into my care.

"For," she said formally, "though you and I have contested more than once, and more than bitterly, still I know you are honest, and I know you are true. Take the child, and guard her from her father. For I would not travail thus to see her taken and raised at court, a pawn for alliances and treaty making. Teach her the new ways and let her not be seduced into bondage to her father, or to any other."

She did travail, indeed, and died therefrom. But the child survived.

I took her, and named her Safred, which means sorrow, for it was true her coming brought little joy. I found a wet nurse, and sent word to the warlord that the Lady and his daughter, both, were dead in the straw. He sent silver for their funeral, and an observer, and we sent two bodies to the burial caves, swathed tightly in the burial clothes, the Lady and a runt piglet.

We hid the child in a cave in the high woods, with the wet nurse and a guard. Later, when it was safe, we brought them back.

I raised the child with my own two. Perhaps I was not as kind to her. There are men who can love any child as though they were true sons or daughters; I am not one of them. When I looked at Safred, I saw her mother's eyes, and though her mother and I had disagreed many times, the lack of her was hard. Sometimes when I looked at her, I saw her father's very look and expression. Then I pushed her out of the house, because I did not like the fear that sprang in me at those times.

It might have been different if my Sage had not died of a fever when Safred was only two. She grieved for Sage a long time, as did my own girls. And I.

But overall she grew up happy enough, and never went in need. I myself taught her the contest, in words and in deeds, as I did my own girls. While March, my elder, took to the wordstriving as though born to argue, and while Nim was swift with hands or staff, Safred took no interest in either.

"Your mother was a great striver," I told her often, "you must have something of her in you."

She just looked at me sideways out of those green eyes. I am telling you, and I am telling you true. No matter what she became later, no matter what deeds of argument or arms she achieved, as a child she was slower than most.

Perhaps she practiced in secret; one cannot become a great striver without constant practice. She was secretive—well, all the world knows that. "The Well of Secrets" they called her in Parteg, and lined up halfway to Corpen to confess to her. But I am getting ahead of my story.

She learned quickly in other ways: learned to cipher and scribe, learned herbalry and leechcraft, husbandry and tillage, cooking and weaving. All the village taught her, as though they wished to make up for shunning her mother so when she first came home, big with child, and all knew the father's name. Safred was quick to learn, except when I was teaching her. Yet I swear I taught her as I taught my own, as I taught other village children.

Well, time passes and does not ask our consent. Soon enough my March and my Nim were in their own houses, and Safred and I were left alone. I had more time for her then. I discovered, then, about the gods' power.

At first it seemed no more than skill. When she tended an animal, say a milch cow with hard udders, the cow recovered quickly. So it might be with any skilled healer. The seeds she planted grew fast and strong; so it might be with any skilled tiller. The horses she gentled never kicked at her; so it might be with a beast handler of soft voice and quiet ways. Except that her voice was not quiet. Not usually.

Then Terin, the weaver's son, broke his leg falling from the walnut tree, broke it so the bone was sharp through the skin. And all wailed, for such a wound meant he was almost certain sure to lose his life through bleeding and, if not his life, his leg.

I was nearest the boy when he fell, so it was I who carried him to the leech's house, and Safred followed me. The healer, who must have known, I realized later, put water to boil and reached down the hanging herbs for a poultice, found wood for a splint, but left the tending of the boy to Safred.

That was the first time I heard her sing. Now singing is a bad word for it, as those who have heard it will tell you. For, and I tell you the truth, it sounded horrible. Like a bellows creaking with wind.

I would have stopped her, but the healer laid his hand on my arm and shook his head. Safred put her hands on the boy's shoulders. She looked into his eyes, deep in, with that wide green gaze I remembered from her mother, and breathed these strange sounds. Terin's eyes grew wide, wider, and his mouth dropped like one in sleep. Then she laid hands on his leg and brought the bone back into place as one might put back a hair comb that has fallen out of place—as simply as that. The boy made no noise, and no drop of blood left him.

In all my memory, that is the strangest time, despite all I saw later, and all I learned. The boy's leg was lying broken and white on the covers, his bone showing through his skin like a rock breaking through grass, but no blood, as though he were dead already, though he sat there breathing before me. Lo, that was the strangest sight of my life, and I did not know how to speak to her after—when the leech had bound the leg and poulticed it, and she had stopped singing.

She sat, staring up at me, waiting for my judgment, half resigned to my disapproval, half fearful of it.

"Your grandmother was a woman who walked with the gods," I said. "Your mother told me, once, that her mother was born an enchanter, but her father beat it out of her, for fear she should set a spell upon him or his beasts. For she did not love him, nor should she have."

Safred stirred then, and stood up. She was short, you know, and had to look up into my eyes.

"I set no spells for harm," she said.

"Nor did she," I said. "What's bred in the bone comes out in the flesh. Your mother would have been glad to see this, to see her own mother's gift brought to use. To good use."

She colored, for the first time I remember. After that, I think, we were better acquainted, and she kept fewer secrets from me. But secrets she had to have, no matter what. They were like meat and drink to her.

That was how she discovered the great power she carried with her. It started with a pedlar, a traveling man who had been in our village before: a dark man—not dark of countenance, but dark of spirit. He smiled, but under the smile was pain. Few could bear to talk with him for longer than it took to conclude their bargain, but still we bought from him because few others came our way, and perhaps out of pity.

When Safred was sixteen, the pedlar came to our house to show me new wool cloth from down valley. I was not home. I tell this part of the story as it was told to me by the pedlar. He came, he said, and called out, "Blessing on the house." Safred came out to him, and gazed at him with the green eyes of healing.

"Come in," she told him, and made him lay his pack aside and brewed him rosemary tea and talked with him. I think the man was starved for talk; perhaps that was all the healing he needed. But Safred said to him, "You carry a secret."

That was true. Now, I tell you, I do not know what the secret was, any more than you, for Safred was the deepest pit there ever was for secrets, and after a secret was told to her, the teller did not need ever to tell it again. But tell her he did, and went away a different man. Maybe she laid some blessing on him. Maybe the simple telling was enough. Maybe she forgave him, who could not forgive himself. I never told Safred a secret, so I don't know. I had no secret to tell her, for she had known me all her life. That, I regret—that I had no secrets then to give her.

After the pedlar, others came to her. At first they were just from our village, people who had known her all her life. Margery's neck pains went away; Dalis's breathing improved; but these were not the real miracles. It was the kindness that was true magic. Wherever a secret was washed by Safred's green eyes, that household rejoiced—and was kinder thereafter.

Some people said she laid a geas on them, to tell the secret to the person it most concerned, or to make reparation where reparation was due. Whatever she said, it was done.

Soon people began to come from elsewhere. And sometimes, when pilgrims were in the house with Safred, and I kept guard outside, I heard her singing that harsh song. But I heard no words, ever, though pilgrims sometimes swore they had shouted out their pain.

It was foreordained that her father should hear of it.

Now, I do not know what you have heard of Masil, her father, the warlord. That he was brave and handsome? True. That he was violent? Most true. That he was barbaric, insane, wicked? Perhaps true. But no one ever said that he was stupid.

When he heard of the wonders coming from our village, he sent a messenger to discover the truth, for even then he suspected that this green-eyed enchanter was the daughter of another green-eyed woman, who had bewitched him out of things he had wanted to keep: his heart and his manhood and his children. For they say that after the Lady, Masil could lie with no other woman, and I believe it.

When the messenger came, I knew it was time. For no one has ever called me stupid, either, and I had been preparing for this since the first pilgrim came. The village helped. We showed him Tamany, who was green-eyed enough, but could not have been the child of either Lady or warlord in a year of blue moons. He went away, but it was time to leave.

Safred wanted to stay until she had spoken to all the pilgrims who were waiting to see her. I knew that the train of pilgrims would not end. We argued bitterly. That was the first I knew of her skill at word-striving, and surprise silenced me. That was my great flaw. I should have overborne her. Everything then might have been different, and I might have children and grandchildren living still.

We stayed an extra week. On the last day, one of the goat-herds ran into the village, crying that the warlord was coming himself to see the witch. I called Safred out, but she would not leave her pilgrim, who was crying and wailing fit to die. So I dragged her out by her hair and shook sense back into her.

"Your mother died to give you freedom," I said, in no mind to be gentle. "Will you throw her gift back in her face, will you spit on her grave? Do you want to be a warlord's daughter, a pawn for alliances and treaty making?"

Perhaps part of her wanted to stay and set eyes on her father for the first time, but she came, half dazed, and I took her up the hill path, to the same cave where we had hidden her as a baby, where I had left our supplies. We were not quite fast enough. The scout from the warlord's party saw us, and they followed fast enough.

But I had prepared for this day, too, and for this danger. So I led her into the labyrinth of the caves, which I had spent months learning, months when I could no longer enter my house for fear of hearing another's secret, months when I imagined this day, over and over.

There were others in the village who knew the secrets of the caves. None would guide the warlord. So he put the village to the torch, and all the people in it, male and female, adult and child, and I lost my Nim and my March and their children, too, all three of them. I will never get them back. Nor cease to mourn them.

There is no darkness like the inner darkness of the earth. It lies solid on your eyelids. It is not cold there, nor ever hot, but it can be damp or dry, loud or silent, and all this depends on the waters that run through it. Our caves were formed by water, and water runs through them constantly, dripping, flowing, rushing, pounding. I navigated our way as much by sound as by sight or touch, following my ears as well as the marks I had laid down over many explorations.

There were wonders in that place I can never describe to you. It is one of the differences between Safred and me, that to her the caves were a place of horror and fear, while to me they were a miracle.

We made our way through the heavy dark with a small lantern, Safred whimpering all the way. And deep in the darkest cave, we met the delvers. I was there, and I tell you truth. They do exist, the dark people, the little people, the eaters of rock. Like boulders they seem at first, rounded and heavy. When they move it is slowly, far slower than you or I, yet nothing can stand in their way. They are blind, of course, though they smell their way, and their hearing is like a bat's. They surrounded us before we were aware. A deep grumbling filled the cavern. It was like the harsh sound Safred made when she spelled, but this was a song of anger and distrust. Until she answered them.

All this way, I had been the strong one, unafraid of the dark. But now, when I trembled with fear, Safred stood tall and sang her song of gentleness, of kindness and healing.

It didn't work very quickly. That was something I was to come to know—nothing worked quickly with the delvers. Oh, I spent a weary time there, listening to the two songs contest our safety. But she sang unwearied and finally, for a moment, they listened without singing back, and we were safe.

Or so we thought. In the village, Terin, afraid for his life and promised the lives of his mother and sister, agreed to guide the warlord through the caves. Even at that time, I could not blame him. If I had been faced with Nim and March, knife to throat, would I have had the loyalty to refuse Masil? I tell you the truth, and the truth is that I do not know.

The sound of the singing guided them as well as Terin, I would guess. Sound travels far underground. However that may be, they came upon us when the singing of the delvers had grown sweet and I was finally relaxing. I quenched the lantern, but it was too late. They had seen us. And we saw them. Lord Masil was flanked by two men with torches flaring.

"Greetings, my daughter," he said, and his voice was rich and warm. He did not realize that the singing he had heard came from the delvers. To his eyes they were boulders, dark and rounded. "I have waited long to see you."

It was the only time I have ever understood my sister Perian, when Masil stood there with his red hair shining in the flames and his shoulders broad. She had loved him, once. At that moment I was stricken with sorrow that I had hated her for her disloyalty, called her "the Lady" with scorn like the other villagers when she returned, strove to shame her.

When she died she was only eighteen, younger than my Nim.

At that moment I repented me of my hard thoughts.

"Time to come home, daughter," he said, and held out his hand.

But she said, "I have no home to go back to. You have destroyed it. How many people did you put to the torch before you found a guide?"

And so I learned of my girls' deaths, and learned hatred afresh.

The men behind him gasped at her Sight, but he was silent. Then, "As many as I had to," he said. "You are worth more to me than a thousand lives."

"I am worth," Safred said, "no more than any other. Nor are you."

Anger moved across his face. "I had this argument too many times with your mother. I will not listen to it from you. Take her."

His men moved forward, but Safred sang out a harsh note, quick and sharp. As they leaped toward her, it must have seemed to them that the very rocks had come alive beneath their feet, as the delvers rose and, as formidable as winter, pushed them back, slowly, solidly.

I took her and pulled her away, following a delver who sang softly to us to guide us. Her father shouted after us, "I will find you! I will search until I do, daughter!"

I knew it was the truth, for he was burning with the shame of being tricked out of her once, and he would not rest until that shame was erased. And I knew that they would find a way around the delvers, eventually, for the delvers have no weapons, only strength and surprise.

So I hurried her down the tunnel, through ways I had never been before, until we came, weary miles behind us, into the greatest cavern I have ever seen. And here we could see everything, for there was a glow coming up from a wide lake, a pearly light that showed us the cavern plain as day. There were wonders: shapes formed by the water into statues like people, and animals, and even trees. And there was one shape there I marveled over, for it was as like a ship as any I have seen riding at harbor in the city.

The delver took us to it, singing happiness and escape. For it was a ship, a ship beached high out of the lake, with no sign of damp or rot upon it, though by rights it should have been covered in the stone growth that had created the pillars and statues. Who placed it there? I do not know. There were people who in the past had buried their warlords in boats, but this ship was empty.

Safred laid her hand upon it. "There is a spell on this ship," she said. "A spell of forgetting. It has forgotten the ocean, the river, forgotten the very meaning of water."

Then she went to the lake and, gathering up water in her hands, she poured it over the prow of the ship as you might wash a baby's head gently. The ship shuddered. I would say it came back to life, except it was a made thing only, of wood and cloth and pitch. But it seemed to spring toward the lake as though set free from long bondage, and splashed gladly into the milky water.

Then it waited, quietly, while we said farewell to the delver and boarded, and Safred sang our thanks.

She laid her hand upon the ship and said, "My brother, take us to the light."

The ship turned silently into the current.

We slid down waterways of glowing white. Pale fish swam in the waters, blind as delvers. The whisper of the water against the ship's hull was soothing, and I slept, for the first time in a day and a night and a day, as far as I could reckon time. Perhaps Safred slept too. I did not need to guard her there.

We slid down a smooth current and gathered speed as we went, and we came to an area of sharp rocks and had to be ready to fend the ship off at every turn. We ate twice and slept once more, in turns, before we saw the light in the water growing less. I lit the lanterns at the prow and the stern of the ship. We carried on, an island of light in the darkness, until we realized that in the distance there was daylight.

So we emerged from the mountains into a strange country, onto a river we had never seen. Safred turned into my arms and we wept together as we came into the light again. There were fishers on the bank.

This is the first story of Safred, my sister's daughter. All her other stories can be told by other people, for her life was a public life, and her deeds known to all. But this story only I, Cael, can tell, for I was there, and I swear to you, what I have told you is truth.

ASH

THE TOP of that ridge, that's the border to Golden Valley," Martine said thankfully.

Ash nodded. He would be thankful, too, when they got out of Cliff Domain. The weeks of walking had been punctuated by bands of armed men riding or marching south, pushing everyone else off the roads and tracks. They weren't just warlord's men. The bands usually had two or three of those in charge, but they were made up of ordinary young men, farmers mostly, by the look of them, and the unpracticed way they held their pikes and shields. The warlord of Cliff Domain was either planning a war or expecting an attack from the south.

"They're taking all the protection away from the mountains," Martine had said a week earlier. "Let's hope the Ice King doesn't hear about it. He'd be over the mountains and raiding in a heartbeat."

"Does that still happen?" Ash asked. "I thought the Ice People had given up."

Martine was silent for a moment. "The last raid was twenty years ago," she said slowly. "It was . . . bad. Since then, the borders have been heavily guarded. Who knows what would happen if they weren't."

She seemed uneasy whenever they encountered the marching men, turning her eyes back to the high mountains behind them. Fortunately, none of the bands were interested in two Travelers who had enough sense to get out of the way as soon as they heard the tramp of marching feet. The men only whistled at Martine halfheartedly as they went past, not even bothering with ribald comments. They were tired, not used to walking so far, and not enthusiastic about where they were going.

In the villages, the gossip said the men were going to force the Lake People to stop charging such exorbitant tolls for ferrying goods across the Lake at Baluchston. But that sounded unlikely to Ash.

"Go to war because of tolls?" he said to Martine privately. "Seems a bit of an overreaction."

"Maybe the warlord here isn't planning to actually go to war. Just frighten them."

"Who's the warlord?"

"Gabra's in charge," Martine said, "but the actual warlord is his father, Thegan. Thegan's in the south, now. He married the daughter of the warlord of Central Domain, and left his son in charge of Cliff Domain." She snapped her fingers. "So. There you are. If he takes Lake Domain, he'll have all the middle of the country. From cliff to cove."

It was part of a Traveler saying—From cliff to cove, from sand to snow—that described the extent of the Domains, from the eastern sea to the western mountains and from the southern deserts to the northern ice.

They looked at each other. War. And in the middle would be the remnants of the old blood, the Lake People.

"The Lake protects her own," Ash said.

Martine nodded. "It might not be a bad thing," she said. "If more ghosts arise, it might not be a bad thing to have the middle of the country ready for a fight. With trained men in an organized army."

"You can't kill ghosts."

"No. But we might be able to cripple them. Stop them, as Mabry said. They have solid arms and legs. Without those... how much harm can they do? But that's real fighting and it needs trained soldiers to do it... Thegan might be doing us all a favor."

"The gods said that *we* have to stop them, not this Thegan."

"He might buy us time, though. I suspect we'll be short on time."

Without discussing it, they began to walk longer each day, into the early spring dusk and sometimes, when the moon was bright, into the night as well.

Now, finally, they were leaving Cliff Domain and going into Golden Valley. From there it was only a couple of days' walk to the pass over the northern mountains and into the Last Domain. They were only three or four days away from the Well of Secrets.

"Horses would have been nice." Ash sighed as his legs complained at the climb up to the ridge. "You'd think the gods could arrange a little thing like that."

They came over the ridge and immediately heard horses, several of them, going far too fast for the broken ground. The path below them was obscured by trees. Ash could just make out the shapes of horses coming up the trail—one in front and two following. It looked like a pursuit.

Then the horses broke cover. The first one, a black, was being ridden by a young woman with dark hair. Two men followed on the horses behind—warlord's men, here in Golden Valley, Ash realized, where no warlord had power.

The woman tried to turn the horse downhill, but the black propped and she fell. Ash found himself running down the trail, sliding and slipping on the loose rocks. She was up in a moment, to face her pursuers. They exchanged words. None of them saw Ash hurtling toward them.

The men drew their swords.

She pulled a knife and sprang as the shorter one raised his sword to strike her down.

Ash barreled into him as the sword was coming down, ducking his shoulder so that the blade went over him, and he and the man ended up sprawling, rolling, scrabbling for a foothold.

Ash had no time to think; the man was well trained and came back at him immediately with his sword, but he lost his footing and slithered back a little and his first blow missed. Ash went forward before the man could recover, drawing his knife without thinking, moved in and under the sword arm, stabbing upward.

The man fell, and from the way he fell Ash knew he was already dead. His sword clanged to the ground.

Ash snatched it up and turned to face the other man, who had moved toward him. The warlord's man was brought up short by the woman's knife at his throat from behind. But she wasn't going to be able to hold him long, Ash realized. She was flushed and shaking from fever, or a wound, or both. He noticed she had a wolf skin tied over one shoulder like a cape.

"Drop the sword, Horst," she said. Horst hesitated. "I don't want to kill you, but I will." She whispered the words, but she meant them.

Horst dropped the sword. Ash kicked it away, keeping his eyes steadily on the warlord's man.

The woman stepped back, shakily. "You'd better not take him home, Horst," she said. "Thegan doesn't like failure. If I were you I'd say he died of a fever on the road. I wouldn't mention me at all." Her face twisted a little. "He was going to kill me. It seems the gods protect the Kill Reborn."

Horst spat out of the side of his mouth. "Sully and me go back a long way. I'll not be lying about his death." He turned to look at Ash seriously. "Will you be here for his quickening?"

Ash flushed. They didn't have time... What was one ghost when so many might rise? "I'm sorry. We don't have time to wait three days."

Horst spat again, this time at Ash's feet. "A curse on you, then, and I'll be remembering you. And so will my lord Thegan. You've made yourself a bad enemy today, lad, and all for a Traveler bitch."

"All for a Traveler," Ash agreed.

Horst's eyes lifted, for the first time, to his hair, and Ash saw him realize that he too was a Traveler. It was as though the fact that Ash could fight had blinded Horst to his coloring. A look of horror came on Horst's face.

Ash smiled grimly at him. "It's a bad thought, isn't it, that we might learn to fight back?"

He was filled with fury, a long suppressed fury, born of all the nights sleeping in a stable instead of an inn room, all the times he'd been served last in a shop, all the times Acton's people had sworn at him or spat in the dust as he passed, or charged him twice the fair price, just because they could. For a moment he understood the enchanter, *knew* why he had raised the ghosts. His hand tightened around the sword hilt.

Then Martine's voice cut through. "Let him go, Ash."

The voice was a balm to him, banishing the rage and leaving him empty. He stepped back and gestured to Horst. "Take your friend and your horses, and get out of here."

Horst laid the body over Sully's horse, mounted his own, and led the horse downhill. When he was a fair way down the slope he turned and shouted.

"Don't think you'll find a welcome in Golden Valley. You've murdered here."

"You had no right to stop her here. It's a free valley," Ash called back.

"You attacked us unprovoked," Horst said, his face grim. "Who do you think they'll believe?"

Then he spurred his horse off down the track, Sully's horse following.

"He's right," Martine said. "They'll believe him."

"We have to get out of here," Ash said.

The woman was clinging to her horse. "Water?" she asked. Martine gave her the water bottle and she drank deeply, the color coming back a little to her face. "That's better. Thanks." She looked at Ash. "Thanks to you, too."

He nodded acknowledgment. He was saved from wondering what to say when her horse whickered loudly and was answered by two more horses that emerged from the clump of pines above them.

Ash looked at the sword and felt sick at the blood drying on it. But he knelt and wiped it on a tussock of grass, then slid it through his belt. He'd have to find a proper sheath for it later.

"Throw it away," Martine said.

"What?"

"You know the penalties for anyone other than a warlord's man carrying one of those. Throw it away."

It went against all his instincts.

"She's right," the woman whispered. "Cause you nothing but trouble."

Reluctantly, Ash slid it out of his belt and tossed it in the grass. Both women nodded, for a moment looking like sisters.

"I'm Ash," he said. "This is Martine."

"Bramble," the woman breathed. "Help me up."

"Your arm is hurt," Martine said. "We should see to that first."

Bramble shook her head. "We have to move now, before he gets a gang together to hunt us down." She whistled to the other horses and they came trotting forward, nosing her shoulder and cheek. She passed the reins of the bay to Martine and those of the chestnut to Ash. "Help me up?"

Ash hoisted her onto the black's back. She was unsteady on her feet, but rock solid on the animal's back.

"Can you ride?" she asked. They both shook their heads.

"Well, guess you're going to learn," she said, her eyes crinkling with amusement. "Use a rock to mount."

The bay tried to lean his full weight against Martine as she reached for his mane to pull herself up. Bramble scolded the horse and he stood upright. The chestnut skittered a little as Ash approached her and Bramble soothed her—"There, Cam, he's harmless"—and she stood calmly as he mounted.

"Are you a horse speller?" Martine asked.

Bramble smiled and shook her head. "Just a beginner at it," she said. "Let's go."

She led the way, walking first, then, as they reached the firm grass at the valley bottom, picked up the pace to a canter. They avoided the farmhouses and villages, skirting them as widely as possible. Ash and Martine's thighs were soon aching and chapped.

Bramble stopped at a stream to let the horses drink and Martine eased herself against Mud's saddlebags, and sighed. "You had to go and ask the gods for horses, didn't you?"

Ash snorted. "At least we'll get there faster."

"Where are you going?" Bramble asked.

Ash felt that she was pretending interest, trying to ignore the pain and swelling in her arm. She looked very pale. "The Well of Secrets," he answered. No reason she shouldn't know. Lots of people went to the Well of Secrets.

She looked sideways at him, eyebrows raised. Ash realized that she was really quite pretty, under the sweat and the pallor.

"Me too," she said.

They took each other for pilgrims, and no more was said. They started off again, a little slower this time as Bramble was beginning to look more drawn and wince every time her horse moved sharply.

Golden Valley wasn't large. A two-day walk was only a morning's ride at a good pace. They were braced for sounds of pursuit, but they heard no followers. They would hear them, Bramble knew, if their pace slackened any more.

Bramble gestured to Ash to take the lead. She was swaying, but managed to twist her hands tight in her horse's mane and she laid her head down on its neck. "Trine will look after me," she said. "You go ahead and she'll follow."

Martine stayed behind Bramble and came up next to her when the path was wide enough. They moved through green-gold poplar groves and sparsely grassed fields where granite boulders edged up through the thin dirt. They kept as close to the foothills as they could, away from the villages and main road.

When Martine found a clump of comfrey, she insisted that they stop to bathe Bramble's arm and put crushed leaves on it. It looked bad. Yellow pus was trapped under the skin and the whole arm was red and swollen.

"If we can't get to a healer here," Martine said, frowning, "the best thing we can do is make it to the Well of Secrets as fast as we can. She's supposed to be a healer."

Bramble chuckled painfully. "Well, if she's not I reckon there'll be a dozen who claim to be in Oakmere."

Martine smiled. "You may be right. Charlatans gather around crowds."

"Let's go," Ash said impatiently, watching behind them.

Bramble climbed painfully onto Trine.

It was late afternoon by the time they reached the end of the valley. They had to come back onto the main road to take the pass into the Last Domain, and Ash insisted that Martine take the lead so that he could guard their backs if necessary.

He was still jumpy from that morning: he didn't want to think about it, but he kept replaying the fight in his head. Could he have avoided killing that man, Sully? Could he have chosen some other way? Was there a moment when he'd decided to kill? He couldn't remember a moment. All he remembered was movement and action and instinct ruling him. But it was a trained instinct, and it had been trained, he realized, to kill. Not to safeguard, but to kill.

He pushed the thought away. He had been protecting Bramble and himself. Sully would have killed her—killed him. He'd had the right to... Did *anyone* have the *right* to kill? That was too hard a question.

He dismissed that thought, too, and concentrated on the increasingly difficult task of staying on a horse when his legs felt like jelly.

As they climbed the road to the pass they met a farmer with a bullock cart laden with apples coming the other way.

"Afternoon," he said affably, reacting to the horses rather than the riders. Then he looked again and scowled at them. "Got airs above your station, ain't you?" he said, and spat on the road behind them.

"Afternoon to you, too," Ash said.

He wanted to quicken their pace, but Cam had her own ideas about how fast you climbed a hill, and he didn't know how to persuade her otherwise.

By the time they had threaded their way into the pass, the sun was setting. The pass was a flattened part of a saddleback ridge, sharp as a knife everywhere but here. They stopped for a moment and looked down the long road before them. In the distance they could see a village by a river.

"Oakmere," Martine said, and smiled. "Not far."

"Let the horses take a rest," Bramble said. Her voice was thready.

Martine dismounted, groaning, and then stretched and went over to her. She didn't try to help Bramble down, just checked her arm and gave her water.

Ash climbed off Cam and discovered why Martine had groaned. Every muscle in his legs and most in his back wanted to lie down and die. As for the chafing... He'd wait until he was somewhere private before he found out how bad that was.

"Go faster," Martine said privately to Ash as they mounted. "She might lose that arm if it's not treated soon."

"Next stop, the Well of Secrets," Ash said cheerfully to Bramble.

She tried to smile at him. "And that's supposed to be reassuring, is it?"

The path was wide enough, so they set off down the long slope side by side.

THE WELL OF SECRETS

"THEY'RE ALMOST HERE, the other three," Safred said to her uncle Cael. "Get them to clear the street so the horses can get through easily. There's no time to be lost if we want to save that arm."

"Whose arm?" Cael asked, but she didn't answer.

She was listening to some other voice again. Then her eyes focused and she looked at him. "What comes after the healing, that's the hard part."

"Well, what comes after?"

"Nobody likes being destined to do something," she said, and he knew how little she relished her responsibilities from the gods.

"It's an affront to our sense of free will," he said mildly.

"Powerlessness without impotence. Purpose, but someone else's volition." She paused. "I must make it their own will if we are to succeed."

"Can you do that?"

She nodded slowly. Her mouth curved wryly. "I will have help. From Saker."

SAKER

HE RAISED the black stone knife level with his scarred palm. The bones of a thousand murdered innocents lay before him. He was at one of the largest massacre sites in the Eleven Domains.

"I am Saker, son of Alder and Linnet of the village of Cliffhaven. I seek justice for Owl, for Sparrow, for Lark, for Ash, for Oak, for Cedar..."

There were so many buried here that every name he spoke brought up an image in his mind: men and women, old and young, beautiful and ugly, strong and frail. But all angry. All thirsting for revenge.

The rest of the spell wasn't in words, but images in his mind, complex and distressing. Colors, phrases of music, the memory of a particular scent, and now, the memory of blood and broken bodies and exultation could be added...

He pressed the knife to his palm then drew it down hard. The blood surged out in time with his heart and splashed in gouts on the bones as he walked over the site, sharing his blood as widely as he could.

"Kinsmen," he said. "Arise."

Acknowledgments

An earlier draft of this book was my thesis for a Doctor of Creative Arts degree at the University of Technology, Sydney. Many thanks to my supervisor, Debra Adelaide, and to my examiners: Richard Harland, Van Ikin and Sophie Masson. Thanks also to my agent, Lyn Tranter, and to the people who read the manuscript in draft form: Stephen, Rose, Jeremy, Ron, Cathie, Leanne, Patricia, Judy and Jens.

Book Two
DEEP WATER

To Stephen and Robert

THE WELL OF SECRETS

"THE DESIRE TO know the future gnaws at our bones," said Safred, the Well of Secrets. "Or so a stonecaster told me."

Her uncle Cael grunted and kept cutting up the carrots. Carrots, beets, onion and garlic, lemon juice and oil. Delicious.

"Are you going to bake that?" Safred said hopefully. She wasn't fond of salad, but Cael loved it.

Cael grinned at her. "The desire to know the future gnaws at our bones."

She laughed, then sighed.

"They're coming. Send out the word. The girl is badly hurt." She paused. "They may not get here in time. It will be difficult."

"Don't tire yourself out."

"You'd rather I let her die? Besides, you'll like her, this Bramble. She's contrary."

He grimaced at her but went out to the street to spread the word, as she had instructed. The Well of Secrets sat for a few moments more, wondering if she had the strength to bring the Kill Reborn back from her second death. The gods were silent on the matter, although she had asked them, a thing she rarely did. Prophecy was all very well, but sometimes things came to a tipping point, where the future could go either way, or they came to a person who held the future in her hand, and this was such a time and Bramble such a person. If the Kill Reborn lived... if the girl Bramble survived... which was more important? Safred thought that not even the gods knew. What would happen in the next day would shape the future of the Domains, perhaps of the world, and Safred was as blind to it as—as Cael was.

"Gnaws like a rat," she said, and laughed so that she would not cry.

ASH

ASH! CATCH HER!" Martine shouted.

Ash moved by instinct, kicking his horse toward Bramble's as she swayed and slid sideways, her eyelids fluttering. He grabbed her awkwardly, her shoulder hitting his and almost pushing him out of his saddle. He gripped with his knees, but that was a mistake, because the horse—what was its name? Cam?—took that as a signal to go faster. They started to pull away from Bramble's horse, with Bramble still half out of the saddle and Ash's reins caught up underneath her back. She was not quite a dead weight, and she struggled weakly, as though she thought Ash was trying to pull her off the horse. Her skin was as hot as though he were holding a cup of fresh cha.

Bramble's horse blew out through her nose in disgust and stopped dead, and Ash's horse stopped with her. They were still badly aligned, but now he could hoist Bramble back onto her seat. He brushed her wounded arm as he steadied her, and she made a sound halfway between a moan and a scream, and fainted truly.

He managed to push her so that she fell forward, over her horse's neck. The arm that the wolves had savaged dropped and hung straight, and Ash could see for the first time just how swollen it was. The sleeve of her shirt, even pulled back as it was, cut deep into the puffy red flesh.

The wound, made by a wolf's claw, was starting to smell, the unmistakable sweet smell of decay.

Martine smelt it too. "The Well of Secrets is her only hope of keeping that arm," she said. "We'll have to ride faster."

They used a shift of Martine's to lash Bramble to the neck of her horse. Ash was nervous as he did it, because Trine had already tried to take a few bites out of him, but this time she waited patiently, occasionally turning her head to nose at Bramble's good shoulder.

Then they rode.

They had sighted Oakmere, where the Well of Secrets lived, from the top of the Golden Valley mountain pass just before sunset, and the town had seemed only an hour or so riding away. Ash had thought they would have plenty of time to reach it before the northern twilight ended. But as they went down into the valley, and then up the hill and down into the next valley, and the next, they realized that they had been deceived. They had stopped to rest the horses at a stream that flowed icy cold down from the mountains, but they didn't dare take Bramble off Trine in case they couldn't put her on again. They managed to get her to drink a little water, and Martine made a cold compress for the arm, but it was clearly useless.

"I don't know how fast we can go without risking the horses," Ash said with frustration.

"The horses can be sacrificed if necessary," Martine replied.

Ash's mouth twisted wryly. "As long as you tell her it was *your* decision!" he said. He had met Bramble only that morning, but he knew already that her horses were like gold to her—no, not gold, but something more precious. He didn't want to be the one to tell her one of them was dead.

Martine returned the half smile. "That's fair. Let's go."

Even tied on, Bramble swayed in the saddle. By sunset, she was delirious, muttering about guilt and death and someone called Leof who had let her go from somewhere, against orders. "Shagging pine trees!" she said suddenly, clearly, then moaned. Ash felt embarrassed and guilty, as he had when Doronit had made him listen to the secrets of the dead, back in Turvite. He tried not to listen, but his horse worked best with Trine, so he rode next to Bramble, supporting her, and he felt every word as well as hearing it.

Martine took their reins and led them both, to leave Ash's hands free. He trusted her to find the road and set the pace. All his attention spiraled down to Bramble. He was determined to save her. He had killed a warlord's man to protect her, back in the Golden Valley, and he didn't want that death to be for nothing. If Bramble lived, he would feel better about killing the man Sully. If she died—he didn't want to think about the waste of two lives, so he rode and rode and supported Bramble and prayed to the local gods.

The ride turned into a rhythm of canter and rest and canter. He was blind to the spring beauty of the mountains; deaf to the wind and the birds and the constant, rushing sound of the streams. All he knew was Bramble's back under his hands, his own back screaming in protest at the unnatural pose, his breath and the horses' drowning out hers. She was breathing in feeble gasps, as though each breath hurt.

Every hill forced her back in the saddle until she was supported only by the cloth under her armpits and by Ash's hands. Every downslope sent her sliding toward Trine's head, rubbing the inflamed arm and shoulder and making her cry out. She roused sometimes and blinked vaguely at Ash. He got her to drink whenever he could, but finally she didn't even react when her arm hit the saddlebow.

Ash raised his head and stared at Martine in despair. "She's dying," he said.

He became aware that it was growing dark. They had ridden through the long hours of twilight and into the night. The horses were laboring up another slope, a zigzag path that led to a high ridge. They were exhausted. Ash became abruptly conscious of the pain in his legs and back. His own tiredness almost overwhelmed him.

"It can't be far now," Martine said, but her tone was doubtful. She looked pale and her face showed more lines than usual. She eased her backside in the saddle and winced. "Let's hope she can cure saddle sores as well," she said.

It was a good try at a joke, but Ash was too tired to laugh. They plodded up the rise, sure that there would be nothing but another empty valley in front of them.

There were lights. Below them in the valley, there were lights beginning to shine. One by one they sparked up, flaring gold and white and yellow until the valley seemed carpeted with stars.

Ash tried to say something, but his mind refused to work.

Bramble breathed more harshly.

"That's the beginning of the death breathing. It will get louder, and then the rattle will start," Martine said, her voice tight. "Go! Go! There's still a chance!"

They set the horses at the downslope as fast as they dared. Then, Ash gritted his teeth, took the reins back from Martine, and urged

Cam and Trine even faster. If the horses broke a leg, so be it. Bramble's breathing was coming slower and louder. He put his head down and pushed the tired horses to their fastest pace. They couldn't do it for long, but he spoke to them, as he had heard Bramble doing back in Golden Valley.

"Come on, come on, you're her only hope! Come *on*!" he shouted.

Astonishingly, they responded, letting the momentum of the slope carry them, getting their legs under them by sheer luck and will, almost falling down the hillside. They left Martine behind.

Then the lights were around him, and people—people leading them to a house and saying things like, "The Well of Secrets wants you to take the sick lass straight to her!" and "Don't worry now, she'll fix her!" and "Someone get Mullet!"

It was disorienting, loud, deeply reassuring. All his senses had come abruptly alive, so that everything registered sharply: the golden lights and the night chill, the shining eyes of the people milling in a group behind the horses. His own tiredness washed away in a surge of relief and warmth.

Then there was a house, with wide double doors lit by oil lamps, and an old man waiting for them, so old his back was bent half over and his eyes were milky with rheum. He helped Ash dismount painfully, who then set to loosen the cloth under Bramble's armpits.

"I'm Mullet. She sent me to take care of the horses," the old man said, and reached for Cam's leading rein with the assurance of an ostler. Cam neighed in alarm and threw up her head. Ash couldn't believe it, but Bramble roused at that and looked at Mullet closely. He met her eyes and grinned, showing one tooth top and bottom on different sides of his mouth. "She'll be right with me, lass," he said. Bramble nodded and fell off the horse.

Before Ash could move to help, another man was there to catch her and cradle her. Ash assessed him. Tall, very strong, about fifty, with olive coloring and bright blue eyes, a neat beard that left his cheeks bare. Not a Traveler. He had come out silently, leaving the door wide open behind him, and now he simply turned and walked back inside with Bramble.

Martine arrived, scrambled off her horse and gave the reins to the grinning old man, who grinned even wider as he saw her limping. The man carrying Bramble didn't look back. Ash was annoyed that he and Martine were being ignored, but he reserved judgment. Saving Bramble's life was the important thing.

He stayed behind Martine as they went into the house. As they passed the threshold he shuddered, feeling suddenly edgy and dangerous with it.

"Remember, no killing the Well of Secrets," Martine said in a whisper, reading his mood as she so often did. "If she's really irritating, you can do it later."

He grinned involuntarily and relaxed a little as they went through the doorway into a room that took up the whole ground floor. The kitchen hearth was at the back, fire blazing, with a table and chairs before it, and a door near the hearth led to a yard he could see through a window. There were lamps alight everywhere, making the room as bright as day. At the front was a big open space with another table covered with a mattress and coverlet. An ordinary mattress, not a featherbed, and a coverlet of homespun wool dyed dark orange. He had had a coverlet of the same color in his room at Doronit's, when she first started training him to be a safeguarder. He was looking at the bed and thinking about coverlets because something in him did not want to look at the woman who stood on the other side of the table. To speak to her, to deal with her, would change life forever.

Every ounce of Sight in him had reared up and screamed the moment he had walked into the room. It was the first time he admitted how strong his Sight had become. If it were Sight. He didn't know if life would be changed for the better or worse. Just that it would be changed profoundly, irreversibly. The Well of Secrets caught the thought, Ash realized. He had *Seen* her catch it, seen the oddly bright green eyes smile a little, the head tilt up just a fraction, the short sandy eyelashes flicker.

"Nothing lasts forever, not even change," the Well of Secrets said directly to him, then she turned to the table where the man had already laid Bramble. She took a small knife from her belt and cut Bramble's shirt off, revealing the arm, so swollen and red that it looked like it didn't belong to her pale body. The original wound from the wolf claw had almost disappeared into the swelling. Bramble roused a little and whispered, "If I die, tell my sister. Maryrose. Carlion."

The Well of Secrets nodded matter-of-factly, and Bramble fainted.

She was deeply unconscious, alarmingly pale, and still beautiful, her upper body covered only by breastbands. Martine glanced at Ash, clearly wondering how susceptible he would be to this display of female flesh. That annoyed him. He was keeping watch on both doors and on the big man who had carried Bramble in. He glanced at the Well of Secrets, but turned away immediately. He couldn't spare any attention for Bramble. In a strange place, even one that had welcomed them, his safeguarder training took over. He had to mind their backs. He would think about Bramble being beautiful later—if she lived.

The Well of Secrets took hold of Bramble's arm and began to sing softly, in the harsh, grating voice of the dead, but modulated by a living body. *His* voice. Ash whipped around and took a step forward, but the big man put out an arm to bar his way. Ash didn't notice. All his attention was on the Well of Secrets, his guts churning with disbelief and a wild hope that, somehow, he was about to find the answer to his own strange voice. She sang a chant from the burial caves, a lament from beyond the grave, horrible, spine-chilling, nauseating. As she sang, the flesh on Bramble's arm cooled, paled. The red streaks, which had stretched threatening claws up to her shoulder, now shrank back and disappeared.

A part of him almost, *almost,* understood what she was chanting. Stray fragments whipped past him before he could fully grasp their meaning. Something about coolness, and wholeness... but he couldn't really understand. What he could feel was the ebb and flow of power. He closed his eyes, and it was plainer, like water flowing into a stream and being turned back by a strong current. The water flow increased, but it made no headway. The current was too strong. Ash could feel the sweat break out on his back and forehead. So much power being poured out. So much that the vessel itself might be emptied, and they would be left with two corpses. Because it wasn't working.

Bramble's breathing stopped.

The Well of Secrets turned sheet-white and staggered. She grabbed on to the edge of the table to stop herself falling. The man sprang forward to support her. While she stood, breathing fast and weak, the red marks began to creep up Bramble's arm again, but the girl lay still as stone.

The healer released herself from the man. She faced the table with determination and placed her hands again on Bramble's shoulder.

Ash moved forward and stood next to her, and put his own hand over hers. He didn't quite know why, but he was sure that he had to do it, sure with Sight and with something more familiar to him than Sight, a fighter's instinct, solidarity.

This time the Well of Secrets' song was stronger, like a call to arms. Sweat stood out on her forehead and her hands began to shake, but she kept singing. The song rose in pitch and loudness until it was painful to hear. Ash began to tremble and feel weak, but he didn't know if it were just the noise, or if power was being taken from him.

He closed his eyes and saw that both were true, that it was the song itself that siphoned strength from him. He could feel himself getting weaker, but he knew that it wasn't going to work. That Bramble was dead.

The Well of Secrets stopped singing.

Ash almost fainted as the power drained away, and he thought he might topple backward, but then he felt someone giving him a push in the back to steady him and he stood upright, firm on his feet. A surge of strength went through him and into the Well of Secrets. She began singing again, louder than before.

Bramble coughed and began to breathe again. Her eyes stayed closed, but she said, "Oh Maryro-ose!" in the voice of a young girl complaining about having to do something she didn't want to do—clean up her room, perhaps.

The Well of Secrets began to sing again, her voice dropping suddenly to a whisper, a plea. The wound disgorged a great gout of pus and then began to close, weeks of healing before their eyes. But it was greater than healing, because the wound itself disappeared. Then the chant died away and there was no mark on Bramble's arm, not even a scar to show where she had been wounded.

"She'll sleep the night through and wake hungry," the Well of Secrets said, her words blurred with exhaustion. She patted Ash's arm in acknowledgment and he almost fell. The big man guided her away, up the stairs. She only came up to his armpit. Not a tall woman, not beautiful, not commanding or elegant or motherly or any of the things that gave women power of various kinds in the world. Ordinary, except for those eyes. But there, thought Ash, lay Bramble whole and unmarked. And he himself was still trembling.

As they reached the bend in the stairs Martine found her voice. "Thank you," she said, her face showing that she knew the words were inadequate. The Well of Secrets smiled at her wryly, acknowledging the thought as well as the thanks, and continued up. The man stayed on the landing, watching until they heard a door close upstairs.

"Most people don't find their tongue so fast," he said. "She doesn't get many thanks." It was not clear whether he thought this was a good or bad thing. He came back down the stairs and turned to Ash. "She's not so good at giving them, either."

"It wasn't me," Ash said. "Something else helped."

The man looked at him skeptically and shrugged. "I'm Cael," he said. "You'd be Ash and Martine, yes?"

They nodded. Ash was uncomfortable and wondered instantly what else Cael knew about him. Martine's mouth was set. She didn't like it either. She sniffed, and then motioned to the pool of pus on the coverlet. "I'll clean that up, if you tell me where to find water."

He smiled with his eyes. "Most people don't think of that, either. Expect it to disappear by enchantment. Don't worry. There's someone paid to clean." He looked at Bramble. "Do you have another shirt for her?"

"Her pack is on her horse," Martine answered.

"I'll get it," Ash said, and he made for the open door, glad of the excuse to get out of the room, but still having trouble controlling his legs. Halfway to the door he had to sit down on a bench.

There was a crowd standing just outside. They had clearly been listening and watching. They looked at him with interest and his cheeks reddened.

"You, Little Vole, go and get the girl's pack from Mullet," Cael ordered a young blond boy. The boy ran off and Cael closed the doors. Ash let himself sit for a moment to recover. He didn't have to prove anything to anyone.

"They were expecting us to arrive," Martine remarked.

"She told them to keep the street clear so the horses could get through. She said there was no time to waste." Cael's voice held a slight disapproval.

"We came as fast as the horses could bear," Martine said. She shifted uncomfortably, aware abruptly of her own chafing and sore muscles. "And that was a good deal faster than I found comfortable, I can tell you!"

He laughed, a booming laugh as big as the rest of him, and Martine smiled, but she wasn't as easily distracted as that.

"Are we allowed to know who you are?" she asked.

"I'm uncle to the Well of Secrets." He used the honorific sarcastically. "Her real name's Safred. She told me to tell you."

"Why?"

He shrugged. "Fools need the mystery. Those who have mysteries of their own need the truth."

"Did she say that?"

He regarded her quizzically, head on one side and eyes bright.

"Nay. She's not one for turning phrases. She said other things, though. Like to find you lodgings somewhere cheap but clean, and look after the horses, and make sure the young lad eats well."

Martine laughed. "No fear there. He has the appetite of a wolverine."

The door banged open and the boy, Little Vole, ran in with Bramble's saddlebags. The men left it to Martine to dress Bramble in her clean shirt, and when she was ready, Cael picked her up and led the Travelers to their lodging house, around the corner in the marketplace.

Oakmere was not what Ash had expected. Although there were more inns and lodging houses than you would normally find in a town of middling size, there were no shanties on the edges, no crowds of beggars targeting new arrivals, no one selling souvenirs on the street, no one offering to guide them or cure them or sell them an underage daughter, guaranteed a virgin.

Ash walked behind, still guarding their backs. Oakmere had a thriving market, judging by the number of shuttered stalls and tents.

As in Turvite, in Sator Square, the marketplace was alive at night, with eating houses and a few stalls still open.

Two Travelers and a third being carried attracted some attention, but not the black looks he had been braced for, the type Travelers normally endured in small towns. Here, there was curiosity but no hatred. A couple of stallholders and diners even smiled at him. It unsettled him more than open hostility would have. He wasn't used to a world where Travelers were welcomed.

There was a large inn on the southern side of the marketplace, but Cael turned into a much smaller lodging house near it.

Despite Safred's advice Ash wasn't interested in finding dinner. They had settled into their room and Bramble was sleeping deeply on a bed in the corner.

"You heard. She sang with—with the voice of the dead." He sat on the edge of his bed, elbows on his knees, his hands hanging.

Martine looked at him with affection and some concern. "Well, she's a real healer, a prophet, a conduit for the gods."

"But the voice of the dead! That's *my* voice, the voice I sing in! Could—could I be a healer, too? She took my strength, she used it."

"I think you would know by now if you had that gift," she said gently. "Apart from anything else, I think Doronit would have found it out."

Ash flinched slightly at Doronit's name. She had trained him as a safeguarder, and he had planned to make his living that way since those were the only skills he had mastered, but now he had to ask, what was he? A healer? An enchanter? Or just someone with a bit of Sight that the Well of Secrets could use?

Martine reminded him, "The Well of Secrets said you had to eat."

"But why?" His voice rose like a young boy's and he flushed. Any message from Safred sounded portentous, threatening who knew what.

"I think just because she foresaw that you would be...overset a little, and wanted you to settle down."

"Does that mean she saw what I'd do?"

Martine shook her head. "No. I'm sure of that. She was surprised when you stepped forward. I don't think she's used to getting help, especially strong help."

He reddened and bent to fumble at his bootstrap to conceal it.

"Come downstairs and eat," Martine said as though she hadn't noticed.

The smell of fish frying was coming up from the kitchen. Saliva flooded into his mouth and he was suddenly hungry.

"I'm ravenous. Come and eat," she said again, and this time he came.

It was full dark as they sat down to the table in the kitchen below, and the other lodgers had eaten long ago. But the woman of the house served them, a young, squint-eyed red-head called Heron, wearing the brooch that widows in the Last Domain were given a year after their husband's death.

Heron sat down with them after she served their meals, with a cup of cha warming her hands. Ash ate without paying attention, food to mouth without looking and without tasting.

"Heron," Martine said. "That's an unusual name for a red-head. And we met a blond Vole earlier." Ash was curious about that, too, but he hoped the woman wouldn't take offense.

"A lot of us in the Last Domain have Traveler names now," Heron said easily. "I was named Freyt, but my parents learned Valuing a good twenty years ago and they renamed me."

Martine showed her surprise.

"You didn't know?" Heron said, surprised in turn. "We're most of us Valuers hereabouts. It's why she's safe here. She's one of us, you know. Raised as a Valuer, for all her father was a warlord."

They nodded. All the Domains knew that the father of the Well of Secrets had been a warlord, although rumor varied about who, exactly. More than one warlord had smiled when he was asked. None of them wanted to deny it, even those who were reputedly happily married at the requisite time.

Ash realized this explained the strange normality of Oakmere. Only in a Valuer town would the extraordinary powers of a Well of Secrets be housed in an ordinary house. Only in a Valuer town would a true prophet have to pay to have her cleaning done. Because in Valuer philosophy no one person was fundamentally more important than another. All lives Valued equally. Even Travelers. To show they believed it, Valuers took Traveler names. In a Valuer town, charlatans and treasure-seekers would find little to pick over, because Valuers were rarely rich. The rich had no time for a way of thinking that meant they were no better than the nightsoil collector. What was the point of being rich, if that were so?

Martine was smiling and gestured at her bag of stones to thank Heron for her explanation. “I could cast for you, if you like.”

Heron shook her head. “Safred will tell me if there’s anything I really need to know. But I give you thanks for the offer.” She collected the empty plates and went out to the scullery, leaving them to contemplate life in a town where their only valuable skill was considered worthless.

Martine shrugged and smiled at Ash. “Maybe I’ll have to learn to cook at last,” she said to him.

He looked at her blankly, realizing that he had heard the conversation, but had immediately forgotten it. His mind was still full of the ebb and flow of strange powers; he wondered if he would ever feel such strength again.

Martine sighed. “Come on, then. Time for bed.”

Ash lay in bed, looking up at the dark ceiling, and went over the healing again in his mind. He had done nothing, he realized. He had just stood there and let his strength be used. Just like he had let Doronit use him. It was why he had left her, because all she wanted to do was use his strength for death and destruction. But she had used him easily before that, because he had felt he had nowhere else to go, nothing to offer the world. She had used him again and again, and he had let her, out of fear and desire and a terror of being cast out into the world on his own. It wasn’t like his parents had wanted him. A singer who couldn’t sing, a musician who couldn’t play—what use was he to his parents, who were consummate performers? That was an old grief, and he forced it away by thinking of that moment when strength had flowed out of him to Safred.

Was that all he was good for? Giving his strength away to others—to women? The thought profoundly disturbed him, but he couldn't find an answer. He tried to feel again the power Safred had so easily drawn from him, but had no sense of it within him. Perhaps she had drawn it all away. Or perhaps she had emptied him temporarily and when he was recovered, he would be able to find it again.

He slept uneasily and dreamt of a tall red-headed woman standing in a doorway, nodding encouragingly at him.

SAKER

OH, IT WAS so easy! There were so many bones here, and not buried, just thrust into the cave like garbage, and the stone rolled across the cave mouth to keep down the smell. No laying out, no ceremony. There had been no sprigs of pine between these fingers, no rosemary under their tongues. Hundreds of bones, hundreds of skulls. So many names responding to his call.

He had an image, suddenly, of massacre sites like this one, scattered the length and breadth of the Domains. It had taken a thousand years, but Acton's people had killed, and killed, and killed again, until they owned the whole of the country, from cliff to cove, from sand to snow. His own village had been the last to live freely in the old way, and the last to be slaughtered. No doubt the invaders had thought themselves safe, then, thinking they had killed the last of the pure old blood. But they had overlooked him, and now he would bring about their ruin.

Saker looked greedily at the bones before him. Here was an army indeed, if even a fraction of those slaughtered by the invaders had stayed in the dark beyond the grave, yearning for revenge. He would give it to them, full measure and spilling over. They would take back their birthright and the land would flourish under its rightful owners. The people of the old blood—*his* blood—would live in freedom again, and he would be responsible.

To raise the ghosts of the dead, he needed to know their names. He had brought the skull of the man Owl from Spritford in case he could not See the names of the dead here, but that was not necessary. He could feel the presence of spirits already, and he was sure he would be able to sense them respond as he called a litany of Traveler names.

He placed Owl's skull at the entrance to the cave anyway. The man deserved to be recalled from death, and he was a good leader. Saker tolled the names with glee: "I seek justice for Owl, Juniper, Maize (he thought briefly of his Aunty Maize, cut down by the warlord's man),

Oak, Sand, Cliff, Tern, Eagle, Cormorant . . ." So close to the sea there were lots of seabird names, and even fish: Dolphin, Cod, Herring . . .

At almost every name there came the *flick* in his mind which meant that someone of that name was buried here, and in one out of ten a picture came to his head: men, women, grammers, granfers, all ages and conditions, with nothing in common but the fact that they were here, and angry. All of them, angry, and here in spirit, ready to take revenge for their deaths. It was the dark of the moon and he had used no light; they would be invisible to the inhabitants of the town below them. The brick houses of the harbor town looked more formidable than they really were. They would be upon the sleeping usurpers before they realized what was happening.

"I seek justice for Oak and Sand and Herring and all their comrades."

Saker paused. He could feel their anger, the desire for revenge, building beneath him, here on the hillside overlooking the harbor. It was dangerous, that anger, to him as well as to the invaders. He remembered when the ghosts of Spritford had met two Travelers at the river. For a moment, there, he had feared that they would strike down the Travelers, not recognizing their own. They had not. But because this was a night attack, when Traveler and invader would look alike, sound alike in the dark, he had made precautions. He entered the new part of the spell.

"I seek recompense for murder unjust, for theft of land, for theft of life; revenge against the invaders, against the evil which has come of Acton's hand . . . let no Traveler blood be spilled, let no brother or sister fall by our hands. Listen to me, Owl and Oak and Sand and Herring and all your comrades. Taste my blood and recognize it: leave unharmed those who share it with me and with you."

The spirits of the dead were listening. The rest of the spell wasn't in words, but images in his mind, complex and distressing. Colors, phrases of music, the memory of a particular scent, the sound of a scream . . . When he had gathered them all he looked down at the skulls. He pressed the knife to his palm then drew it down hard. The blood surged out in time with his heart and splashed in gouts on the bones. He flung his arm wide so that the blood touched as many bones as possible.

"Arise, Oak and Sand and Herring and all your comrades," he commanded. "Take your revenge."

This time, he had a sword ready to give Owl, symbolically making him the leader. The other ghosts accepted it. They looked to Owl immediately, and he pointed with his sword toward the sleeping town, his face alight with anticipation. Then he began to run toward the houses, and the others raced after him, each of them holding whatever weapon they had died with: scythe, hoe, knife, sickle. Not soldiers' weapons, but deadly enough.

Saker watched, smiling, as they streamed down the hill, toward Carlion, and then he went to follow.

LEOF

LEOF WAITED IN the cold before dawn for the signal to attack, hidden in the trees, calming his horse with a pat now and then. The still water of the Lake hid nothing, as Lord Thegan had said. Leof was sure that his lord must be right. The tales were nothing more than Lake people subterfuge.

"Perhaps there is a tricksy spirit," Thegan had told his men the night before. "Or perhaps the Lake People have some slight enchantment to call up illusions to frighten the cowardly. But remember, it is no more than illusion. It cannot be that the Lake has any real power."

He was reassured remembering those words, spoken with the confidence which inspired others. It was no wonder his men had followed Thegan here to the Lake so willingly. They believed everything Thegan said: that the people of Baluchston were strangling trade between the Domains by charging exorbitant prices for ferrying goods and people across. And there was no real reason a bridge couldn't be built, that Baluchston was just using old stories about the Lake so it could keep its monopoly. Old stories, and their mysterious alliance with the Lake People. An alliance which needed to be broken, so Baluchston could be taught a lesson.

The fact that, if Thegan took over Baluchston—a free town, for Swith's sake!—he would hold the entire center of the Domains, from Cliff to Carlion's borders, was never mentioned, but the men weren't fools. They knew and they approved. Their lord *should* be the most powerful in the Domains. They were sure he deserved it, and so did they. His power would be their power, and they would swagger and bask in it.

Leof checked the horizon again, but there were only whispering reeds and, far off, the sky starting to pale as dawn approached.

Thistle moved restlessly and Leof murmured softly to her. A good horse, Thistle, though not a chaser. He had left his chaser mare, Arrow, back at the fort.

Thoughts of Arrow inevitably made him think about Bramble; about their first race against each other, he and Arrow against her and her roan gelding; about the night that followed in his bed at the inn. That led him to memories of losing her, and losing her twice, when he had set her free to find her own way out of Thegan's territory, against the express orders of his lord. His unease over his disloyalty made Thistle shift beneath him, and he thought again of Arrow, burying memories of Bramble as deeply as he could.

When foot soldiers went against horsemen, they aimed to bring the horse down first, then deal with the rider. He had no mind to lose Arrow to a stray arrow or a spear thrust. His lord had scolded him about leaving her behind, but in that friendly, jovial way that meant he should not take it seriously. Leof had almost brought her, even so. Anything to show Thegan that he was loyal.

As though the thought had triggered it, the signal to advance rang out, a long horn call that echoed strangely through the pine trees. Leof urged Thistle forward, followed by the small squad of horsemen and the much larger group of archers and pikemen that Thegan had put under his command. Their task was simple: the horsemen were to secure the shore of the Lake so that the archers could shoot flaming arrows into the reeds. Then the whole troop would protect the area until the reeds had burned down to the waterline and the Lake was exposed. Thegan had placed bands all around the perimeter of the Lake, in both Central and Cliff Domains. His aim was to lay bare the secret lairs of the Lake People, the hidden islands where they were protected from attack. With the reed beds empty, Thegan would be able to see right across the Lake, into the heart of its mystery.

Leof gave his men hand signals, but they weren't really needed. These were experienced men, at least half of them from the Cliff Domain, most of whom had fought with him on past campaigns. Thegan had mixed the Cliff men up with the Centralites, putting battle-hardened men side-by-side with those who had never fought, "to make sure no one panics when the arrows start flying," he said, and Leof had nodded. That had been the moment when Thegan had forgiven him and started treating him again as a trusted officer. Thegan had smiled at him for the first time since he had stopped Thegan's archer from shooting Bramble in the back as she escaped from Sendat and said, "Just as well I have experienced officers, too," and clapped him on the back. The relief had been enormous.

Leof put the thought away from him and concentrated on getting this sortie right for his lord. The archers lined up a short distance back from the shoreline and set arrows to their bows. Broc, a boy barely old enough to fight, ran along the line with a blazing torch, setting each arrow alight, then stood well back from the horses so that none would be spooked by the flames.

Leof raised his hand and dropped it again, and the arrows flew, bright as shooting stars, into the air and onto the reed beds. It was a beautiful sight, the bright flame against the still-dark sky. They waited with all senses fully alert for response, waited for the reeds to catch, waited for the flames to rise, licking, into the sky.

At first it seemed that nothing was happening. The fire arrows burnt among the reeds, throwing writhing shadows over them. Then slowly, slowly, the reeds began to catch. Leof braced himself for the Lake's response. Lord Thegan had warned him that they had to stand firm against illusion. He had warned his men likewise and they were ready.

A deep vibration came from the Lake and the still water between the reeds began to whisper as though it were a quickly moving current. Leof felt the ground shake beneath him. His horse reared and only his long experience in chasing allowed him to anticipate the movement and jump off safely. Thistle tore the reins from his hand and bolted. Behind him, the other horsemen were falling as their mounts reared and then raced away to the forest. The archers, confused, stepped back, away from the Lake. Then, from beyond the reeds, there was a rushing sound, loud, sibilant, like wind through trees, like breath through giant lungs. It was moving closer, and it was nothing human. The archers broke and fled into the trees, followed by the horsemen, some limping, leaving only Leof standing firm; and Broc, behind him, clutching his torch.

"What is it, lord?" he asked.

The sound grew too loud to make a reply. *Illusion*, Leof thought, *to make us run away. I trust my lord. It's only illusion.* Before him, out of the darkness, roared a wave mounting higher than a house, higher than a tree, a hill of a wave that loomed above them. Broc screamed and ran, dropping the torch.

Illusion, Leof told himself, just before the wave hit.

BRAMBLE

THE CEILING WAS dark green, with wooden beams. Bramble had never seen a green ceiling before. She was more tired and more hungry than she had ever felt in her life, and she was disoriented by waking in a room with a green ceiling.

Then she remembered, and her body of its own accord curled into a tight ball of misery, head on knees, trying to shut out the world. Maryrose. Maryrose was dead.

She lay and shook for a while, remembering. She had died again, only this time it was her body that had died. She remembered lying on the Well of Secret's table, body in flames, arm hurting almost past her ability to bear it. Then she had—fainted? Died.

But instead of being in the Well of Secret's house she had been in Maryrose's front room, and Maryrose was lying dead, with Merrick next to her, dead, and she knew it wasn't a dream. She had been glad she herself was dead, and she called out, "Wait for me!" to Maryrose, so they could go on together to rebirth. She was glad to be out of it all, glad to be set free of whatever destiny the gods had planned for her.

She called out again, "Wait for *me*, Maryrose!" in exactly the same way she had called out to her big sister when she was tiny and Maryrose walked too fast on her longer legs.

And just like then, Maryrose heard her and came back for her. She—her spirit—appeared somehow, as though she had walked in from another room through a door that wasn't there, and stood looking at Bramble with the same loving annoyance as when they were children.

"What are you doing here?" she asked.

Bramble felt a moment of surprise. Ghosts weren't supposed to be able to talk. "I'm dead," Bramble said.

"Nonsense."

"I am so!"

"Well, you shouldn't be. Not yet. You've got work to do." She pointed to her own body, lying limp on the floor. "You're supposed to stop all this."

She put out her hands and turned Bramble so that she was facing the door, although ghosts were not supposed to be able to touch anything, not even each other. "Go on, then. Get back there."

Bramble hesitated, looking back to her. "Mam and Da? Granda?"

"They're fine. They went back to Wooding for Widow Farli's wedding to the smith. They missed all this."

"Mare —"

"Oh, don't worry," Maryrose said, the exasperated big sister. "I'll wait for you. We both will." Bramble smiled and she smiled back, exasperation melting into love. "You do what you're told and go back."

Then Maryrose pushed her between the shoulder blades and she took two steps and was through the doorway before she had finished saying, protestingly, "Oh, Maryro-ose." Then—nothing, until she had woken here, under this green ceiling.

She forced herself to uncurl. Maryrose was dead. Someone had killed her. It was Bramble's job to stop whoever it was. So. If that was the destiny the gods had in mind for her, she would embrace it. She would find the murderers, and disembowel them.

She lay for a moment, staring up at the ceiling, and then lifted her left hand, gingerly, to touch her shoulder. Her mind remembered the pressure, the pain, the burning and nausea and sheer *wrongness* of that swollen arm. But her body didn't. It was all gone. Cautiously, her head spinning, she sat up and examined her body. Not even a scar. She was starving, her body clamoring to replace the energy she had lost.

Suddenly, her hunger was gone, replaced by awe. What kind of person could do that, heal without leaving a scar? To heal was one thing, but to knit the flesh back to a state where it did not even remember being injured...that was tinkering with powers deeper even than the local gods.

The room had three beds, covered with green blankets matching the light color of the walls. It was like being inside a forest. She should find that comforting. She should be happy to be alive. Again. Twice she'd been pulled back from death by the power of the gods; and this time, by Maryrose.

The first time, when the roan had saved her in the wild jump across the chasm outside Wooding, she had entered a living death, her spirit split from her body, her senses dull, her heart empty except for love for the roan. It had only ended when she became the Kill Reborn, truly reborn by some power in the running of the Spring Chase.

Would she go back to that death in life again? It didn't feel like it. All her senses were sharp. She could hear footsteps outside, climbing the stairs. She felt the bed linen under her thighs, the warmth of the late afternoon sun that slanted through high windows to fall across her shoulders. Saw each individual dust mote as it danced in the sunbeam. Each beautiful detail of the day filled her with grief and anger that Maryrose had been cut off from the world so viciously.

She was so weak she couldn't even stand up. And she stank with old sweat. At that realization, her mouth twisted with amusement. At least the Well of Secrets couldn't bespell that away—she stank of the last few days and was glad of it.

Martine put her head around the door and smiled at her. "Hungry?"

Bramble nodded. If she was going to live, and find out what had happened to Maryrose, she had to eat. Martine came in with a laden tray, followed by Ash who carried a basin and ewer, the water steaming from the top.

Bramble sniffed. "It's true, I need that. One thing she couldn't take away was the stink."

Martine's eyes crinkled with laughter and understanding as though she, too, found the Well of Secrets daunting and was glad to make a little joke about her.

"Food first, though," she said, handing Bramble a warm roll dripping with butter. It disappeared in two bites.

"That was the best thing I ever tasted," Bramble said, wondering, feeling guilty that she could enjoy food knowing that Maryrose was...she couldn't think about that now. Her body was ravenous, demanding food, and she had to feed it. She had work to do.

"Near death lends spice to living," Martine replied.

"Not always."

The young man, Ash, was busying himself tidying the two other beds. Bramble realized he was trying not to look at her in her breast-bands. That was both endearing and a bit worrying. The last thing she needed was a youngling yearning after her. She pulled the sheet up to cover herself. He had, after all, saved her life. Both of them had.

"I have to thank you," Bramble said, pausing before devouring a mug of soup. It was hard to pause, she was so hungry. She took a tiny sip. Asparagus and cream. Wonderful. "I owe you my life."

Ash turned at that and Martine shrugged. "That's what happens when you travel with a safeguarder," she said, waving her hand at Ash. "People get safeguarded."

Bramble looked at Ash with new eyes and he flushed. Under his shaggy black hair, he was a bit older than she had thought, and strong with trained muscle. He smiled at her tentatively and she realized that he was unsure of himself despite his strength and agility. She smiled back.

"Thank the gods, then, that you came at the right time." And the Lake, she thought, that sent me there right then. She remembered leaving the Lake and being transported through time, late autumn becoming spring in a heartbeat. She shivered with remembered awe. That was true power.

"Mmm," Ash said. "It was their fault, all right."

Ah, Bramble thought, so it's not just me the gods have been ordering about. I'm not sure if that's good or bad.

"After you've washed," Martine suggested, "we should go to see Safred. The Well of Secrets."

"The Well of Secrets," Bramble echoed. "Yes. I suppose we must. After I've seen the horses."

Fed, washed, dressed in clean clothes and with her horses well cared for in the rooming-house stables, Bramble walked around the corner of an ordinary looking street to meet the Well of Secrets. She didn't pause, or knock. If this Safred was a prophet, she should be expecting them.

As she pushed open the big double doors, they were met by a tall, good-looking older man.

"Ah, you're on your feet!" he said. "Good, good."

It was odd to meet someone who clearly knew her but of whom she had no recollection. Bramble forced a smile. "Thank you for your help."

He waved that away and moved back from the door. "Come in, come in. I'm Cael, Safred's uncle. They're waiting for you."

Sitting at a table were two women and a boy of about fifteen. The younger of the women, a girl really, had the dark, lean looks of the Traveler and the flexible body of a tumbler or dancer. She sat with her legs drawn up on the chair, one arm around a raised knee. She reminded Bramble of Osyth, though Osyth would never have sat so casually. Pless, where she had worked for Osyth's husband Gorham the Horsespeller, seemed a very long time ago.

The boy had light brown hair and was taller, gangly with the swift growth of youth.

Then there was the other woman. Red-headed, older than her, around forty, stout but not fat. Bramble forced herself to look Safred in the eyes. Oddly, where she had expected to find something strange, something foreign, she found someone much like herself. Not an ordinary woman, but a woman nonetheless, beset by the gods and carrying a destiny unasked for. There was humor in the folds of her mouth and the lines around her intense eyes.

Bramble had no time for humor. "My sister's dead," she said. "Who killed her?"

Safred sat up straight, astonished. "How do you —" she began to ask.

Bramble cut across her. "Never mind how I know. Who killed her?"

Safred's face sharpened with interest; with a kind of hunger. "Tell me how you know," she asked again.

"Tell me who killed her."

The Well of Secrets wasn't used to being resisted. She swallowed and sat back in her chair, mouth tight. "His name is Saker."

"Saker?" Martine asked. Bramble had almost forgotten she and Ash were there.

"That is his name, the enchanter, the one who raises ghosts. Saker. A bird of prey. He has a flock of falcons at his command. Last night, he loosed them onto new victims. In Carlion."

Martine and Ash looked shocked.

"Ghosts?" Bramble asked. "Maryrose wasn't killed by ghosts. She was almost cut in two. Ghosts can't do that sort of thing."

"These can." Safred looked at Martine and Ash. "Tell her."

Martine described the attack on Spritford. The maimings, the deaths, ordinary people cut down in their homes and on the street by ghosts who could hold a weapon and use it against the living. An unstoppable force, because they could not be killed themselves.

The young man and woman listened with appalled interest, but it was clearly old news to the big man, Cael, although he asked several questions about the ghosts and the way they had looked and spoken. Bramble was astonished that anyone could make ghosts speak. Ash looked fixedly at the table at that point, as though he were not proud of the ability.

Bramble sat for a moment after Martine finished. "What does he want?" she asked finally.

"He wants the Domains," Safred said.

"Why?"

Safred picked up a jug of cha and began pouring out cups and handing them around. She gestured to Bramble and Martine and Ash to sit down, and they did.

"We don't know," she said reluctantly. "Yet. All we know is that the ghosts are those who have been dispossessed and are still angry. Perhaps they are taking back what was theirs before the invasion."

"Do we know where he is, so I can go and kill him?" Bramble asked. There was silence. She looked around the table at the mixture of surprise and shock in the others' faces. "What? It's the simplest solution."

Ash nodded agreement, and then looked unsure. He took the cup of cha and sipped, staring at the tabletop.

Safred shook her head. "The ghosts would still be there. Now they have been called up... the gods say that killing Saker will not end it. Others will learn how to call the ghosts. There are many who are angry. Now they have proof that an army can be conjured...even if Saker dies there will be others. Too many others, for too long. The Domains would be destroyed. Thousands would die."

"Deal with the others one by one, as they arise. Stop this one now."

"It seems to me," the dark-haired girl said unexpectedly, her voice deep and pleasant, "that the problem is the ghosts, not the enchanter. Without them, he's helpless."

Safred smiled at the girl. "That is true. It is the ghosts we must dispose of." She looked around the table and gestured to the girl and boy, introducing them. "Zel and Flax, Bramble, Martine, Ash."

The girl nodded and the boy smiled at them. Zel and Flax, Bramble thought. So she *did* look like Osyth—these were Gorham's children. Bramble had never met them, but Gorham had talked about them often enough. And Zel's careful speech, with no trace of Traveler in it—that was Osyth's training. Zel was trying hard to fit in here.

"When ghosts quicken, they must be laid to rest," Safred said.

They sat for a moment, thinking that through. Bramble remembered the last quickening she had seen, the warlord's man whom she had killed, rising three days later as ghosts did if they were not prepared for death. She had been ready to go through the ritual that would have laid him to rest, would have offered her own blood in recompense, but she had been prevented. She wondered, uneasily, if his ghost still haunted the linden tree near her home village.

Safred looked at Ash. "You have done it," she said.

He nodded. "They need blood."

"They need *specific* blood," Martine said quietly. "The blood of their killer."

"They need more than that," said Safred. "The blood is just a symbol."

"Acknowledgment," Ash replied. "The killer must acknowledge his guilt and offer reparation."

"These ghosts are hundreds of years old," Cael said slowly, his deep voice doubtful. "Their killers are long dead."

Safred nodded and placed her hands flat on the table. Ash noticed that they were not pretty hands, not the hands of a warlord's daughter. They were sun-speckled and the nails were cut short. Safred seemed to lean on the table for support, as though even she could not believe what the gods were asking.

"Yes. A thousand years dead. Like the one responsible. The one who can acknowledge what was done."

"One?" Cael asked. "Just one for all of them?"

Bramble went cold as she realized what Safred meant. "Acton."

Safred nodded. "Who else?"

Acton had led the invasion of the Domains, leading his men from beyond the western mountains through Death Pass in the last days of winter, falling upon the unprepared inhabitants like a wolf pack. He was a legend, a hero to most people in the Domains, a name out of history. Hard to think of him as an actual human being who might have a ghost, just like anyone else. Bramble's Traveler grandfather had raised her to consider him as an invading murderer, the leader of the dispossession, but even she was used to thinking of him as larger than life. More evil than anyone. Treacherous. Greedy. Filled with the lust for blood. They said he had laughed as he killed.

It was one thing to hear that an enchanter had conjured up ancient ghosts and given them bodily strength, but it was quite another to think about conjuring Acton's ghost. For surely that was what she meant. Which was ridiculous, wasn't it?

Bramble was abruptly aware that the sun was setting and the shadows in the corners of the room were reaching out. She shrugged off the feeling of unease and looked around the table. Each face had its own kind of uncertainty and reluctance. Except Ash's. His was carefully blank.

"According to the song about the enchanter from Turvite who raised the ghosts," Ash said quietly, "you need the bones of the person who was killed. Acton's body was never found. Even if we *could* learn how to raise a ghost, we wouldn't be able to find his bones."

"Why would he offer acknowledgment and reparation anyway?" Zel asked. "He weren't sorry for what he'd done while he were alive."

Bramble noted Zel's slip back into Traveler speech—it was a sign of how shaken she was by the idea of raising Acton. They all were. Ash's hand had gone to the little pouch on his belt.

"That is true," Safred said slowly, sitting back in her chair. "But the grave gives a different perspective."

"And the bones?" Martine asked.

"There is a way to find the bones, if Bramble and Ash are willing." She looked at Ash. "You have something of Acton's."

Ash already had it in his hand. He had been way ahead of the discussion, Bramble realized. He reached forward and placed a brooch in the center of the table. A man's cloak brooch, ornate and beautiful. It sat in a pool of sunlight, looking pretty but ordinary.

"This belonged to Acton?" Zel asked, fascinated. She reached out as though to touch it, then pulled her hand back and stuck it in her lap. Bramble raised an eyebrow at her.

"It's not going to bite. May I?" she asked Ash, and when he nodded she reached out to pick up the brooch.

Safred stopped her with a hand on her wrist. "No. To be used, the brooch must pass from its rightful owner to the Kill Reborn in the right time and place."

"Oh, shagging hells!" Bramble said. "Fight spells with spells, is that it?" She was very tired but sat in her chair with a straight back, determined not to show any weakness to Safred. The brooch seemed to draw her gaze. She felt a little dizzy, but that might have simply been from fighting the poisoning in her arm.

"Yes," Safred said quietly. "This is your task, Bramble. Not to kill, but to live."

Bramble dragged her eyes away from the brooch. "What do you mean?"

"Of all of us around this table, you are the only one with mixed blood. Cael and I are of Acton's people, the others are pure Traveler. You bring both together—the link to the gods through your Traveler blood, the link to Acton's people through your mother's line. You are the only one who can do it."

Bramble fell silent. Martine asked the question for her.

"Do what?"

"Find Acton's place of death."

"How, exactly?"

Safred looked uncomfortable. "I know the steps to take, but I don't know what will happen. Will you do it? Will you let the brooch guide you?"

The others held their breath, waiting for her to respond. Bramble wanted to say, "No. No, what I will do is ride to Carlion and make sure that Maryrose is dead and my parents are all right. Then I will find Saker and gut him." But she hunched her shoulders as she drew breath to say it and felt the smooth way the arm moved in its socket. She remembered that her arm had no scar. Remembered that yesterday she had been dying and now she was whole and healthy. Because of Safred. She let out her breath, suddenly feeling very weary.

"Can't the gods just tell us where the bones are?" she asked instead.

Safred seemed almost embarrassed. "They don't know."

"I thought they knew everything."

"They don't pay much attention to humans, you know. Only when something big happens, or when they take a liking to someone. Acton—I don't think they noticed much about the invasion in the early days. It was just humans fighting each other."

Bramble understood. Humans did fight each other. Look at Lord Thegan preparing for war with the Lake People. She saw, vividly, in her mind's eye, Maryrose's blood on the floor; Merrick's arm cut to the bone. A human enchanter had been responsible for that. Oh, yes, humans killed each other.

"What about the stones?"

Martine immediately pulled out her pouch and cast, then shook her head. "No. Nothing. They are not speaking to me." She looked at Bramble. "I'm sorry. It happens, sometimes, when the gods are involved."

Bramble stared at the tabletop. Her heart pulled her to Carlion; her instinct said to obey the gods. This kitchen was a long way from any altar, but... In her mind, as she used to do in her home village of Wooding, she asked them, Should I go to Carlion now? They replied, faintly, as they had done so often to keep her from Traveling, *Not yet.* Well, that was that. Safred studied her in shock, as though she had overheard the exchange. Maybe she had. Bramble returned her gaze blandly, enjoying her uncertainty.

"Will it take long?" she asked.

Safred hesitated. "I'm not sure... but we can't do it here. We must go to the Great Forest. There is a lake there, the gods say."

"So," Bramble said, "let me see if I understand you. I have to go to a lake somewhere, use the brooch in some way you don't understand to do something you don't understand to find out the death place of the biggest bastard who ever lived, who died a thousand years ago and whose bones may be irretrievably lost and who is unlikely to want to help us anyway."

The silence was heavy with antagonism. Bramble and Safred stared at each other.

"It's the only way," Safred said at last.

"Hmm," Bramble said.

Safred looked at her. "There is a risk... some who take such journeys do not come back."

Bramble bared her teeth in a semblance of a smile.

"Don't worry," she said. "I'm good at coming back." And *then* she would go to Carlion and find the enchanter and kill him.

ZEL'S STORY

MURDER'S AN UGLY word, don't never doubt that. But it's a solid one, like a stone in your hand. I went to a stonecaster, and she plucked that Murder right from the bag, and Necessity, too.

We was Travelers, my brer and I. We did the rounds, town to town, city to city. We scrounged off the land where we could, worked where we could, sang in the taverns every night for food, for a roof in winter, out in the stable. Sang till Flax's voice broke; ah, he had a voice could pierce right through your body and blood, sweet as first love. In the taverns, when Flax let out those high, quivering notes, even the rowdiest of them would calm on down and get sentimental; sometimes even throw coins. It weren't very often I had to shag for our supper.

Then his voice cracked and we knew he had to stop his singing or risk losing his voice for good and all.

We was in Sandalwood, then, on the outskirts near the tanneries. So we walked onto Pless, and we went on back to our parents' house.

They'd always been pleased to see us, before. They'd been Travelers, too, the both of them, roaming free all their youth, taking their knocks and their sweets, rambling all over the known world, my mam said once to me, even down to the sandy waste, and up to Foreverfroze, in the north. They'd met up on the road, my father a horsebreaker, my mam a juggler, like me.

They only settled down in Pless when my mam got the rheumatics and couldn't juggle no more, and my father found a fancy-woman there he'd a mind to keep. He set up as a horse trainer and it's true, it's a rare horse my da can't spell into manners.

We didn't want to Settle, so they laughed and let us go, but they'd taught us how to see trouble coming and my mam showed us a few sneaky moves with the knife. Since those days we'd come visiting every year, spend a week or so and back on the Road again, and there'd be smiling and hugging enough to last the year round.

This time it were different. It were a sharp, cold autumn already, with worse to come and the grandams saying it'd be a killing winter, graveyards fat by Winterfest. I thought we could rest out the winter there with Mam and Da, work on a new act, teach Flax some more juggling, maybe some tumbling or a mind-reading act. I could sing, but not like Flax, not with that clear, heart-aching sound that brought silver out of purses.

I didn't think they'd mind. I'd of worked for my keep, and for Flax's, if they'd wanted. I didn't realize they'd turned respectable. Da were setting his sights on the town council, and trying to forget his murky past; and Mam were pushing him hard as she could go. Me, I think it were the fancy-woman Mam had in mind; seems a town councilor got to be really respectable, and maybe the fancy-woman would of had to go.

It weren't the shagging that worried Mam; it were the silver that went to keep bread on that woman's table and clothes on her back. Mam'd stick to silver like it were her life's price to let it go; and maybe that were true, once, out on the Road.

So when me and Flax turned up, unexpected, at the door, with Flax half-grown out of his clothes and me none so clean, neither, with the track from Sandalwood coming through swamp as it do, well, they weren't exactly so pleased as we thought they'd be.

Maybe we shoulda turned and walked away right then and there, before that hurt got any deeper. Maybe we shoulda said the Traveler's goodbye, "Wind at your back," and scooted along to the tavern and juggled and sang till we got our eating silver and our traveling silver, and just kept on going. But we didn't. No, we was cold and hungry and hoping for some hugs, so we walked straight on in and sat by the fire, and listened to the news.

They told us about the town council straight off, and if I'd been paying attention I'da noticed that new look on her face, that wary, not-welcoming look; but Flax had a cough from the damp swamp air and I were bustling him close to the fire and getting him cha. I just took it like a joke and laughed; my da the town councilor!

The next few days, I were too busy nursing Flax to think much of it. There was people coming and going all the time, with Mam serving them hot wine and spice biscuits, the smell drifting up to us and making me hungry as a waking bear, but Flax were so sick he didn't even notice. It were a bad fever, and he were coughing up blood.

The herb woman said he'd be safe if he stayed mostly in bed all winter. That were bad news for Mam and Da. They'd not told anyone about us coming back; and then I remembered that the last couple of visits we spent a lot of time at home, not visiting or going out. I realized that not many people here knew Mam and Da even had young ones, let alone that we was Travelers—and that's how they wanted it.

So they told the herb woman Flax were their stableboy, and they made me promise not to come down the stairs when there was visits going on; and I shrugged and said, "If you want," for I didn't see much harm in it, then.

Mam wanted us out, though, that were certain. She got this worried look back of her eyes every time the door banged, for fear it were some neighbor dropping in. Da turned quiet, and went to the fancy-woman's for his evening meal more often than not. And that didn't help Mam's temper—not at all.

Now if Flax'd been hale, I woulda just packed us up and taken the Road again, winter or not, but the herb woman warned me, quiet in the corner, that it were his life's price to go on the road before spring, and I believed her, he were that quiet and pale after the fever left him, and still coughing like an old man.

They knew I wouldn't leave without him. They wouldn't let me sing in the taverns, or juggle, in case anyone found out I were their daughter, and though I put in what I could of our Traveling silver, I had to keep some back for spring, to set us on the road again. I did what I could around the house but it weren't much compared to what we was eating, especially Flax, now the fever were over and his real growing time began.

Da got broody over his ale next to the fire, when he were home, though mostly he were out at the farm, working the horses.

Then Mam started muttering and counting her silver in the dark of night. Night after night I'd wake up and hear her, clinking and counting, all alone in her bed in the clear frost silence, with Da off to the fancy-woman. Maybe it shouldna been so much of a surprise when I came through to Flax's room and found Mam with a pillow over his face.

I fought her off him and it shoulda been easy, an old rheumaticky woman and a young one like me, but it weren't easy at all. She fought like it were her life she were fighting for, and I had to fling her down on the floor before she give up. Flax slept through it all, and I knew she'd given him a sleeping draught in his cha.

"Eating us out of house and home," she said, staring up at me like a trapped rat. "You're sucking us dry, sucking us dry . . ."

"Let me go out to juggle, then," I said. "I'll pay for Flax and me, both."

"Nay, nay," she said, shaking her head so hard her hair came out of its braid. "You'll bring disgrace on us, and we're so close, so close."

"Keep away from him, then. If you hurt him, I won't sit quiet and say nothing. I'll brand you up and down the town a killer," I said. "Here we stay till spring, Mam, and Flax can take the road again. Make your mind up to it, that's the way it is. If your council's so important, then Flax's keep and mine is the price you have to pay for it."

She went away, but I knew that weren't the end. I'd have to keep an eye on her all winter, and I couldn't. I had to sleep sometime. To eat what she cooked and to drink what she brewed, like the others. It were too easy for her to slip something in.

I thought awhile on going to my father, but I knew him. He'd always gone along with her over everything except the fancy-woman, and now I thought on it, she'd never faced him down about that. If she had, I reckon he'da caved in, like he always did. If she'd managed to kill Flax, and me not knowing, he woulda asked no questions.

Now, I thought, she'd have to kill both of us.

That were when I went to the stonecaster, for, truth to tell, I couldn't see my way out of it. The caster pulled Murder from the bag, and Necessity. And I thought, her or me. Her or Flax.

Two lives for one, I thought. I did it that night, while Da were with the fancy-woman and Flax were sleeping deep, and Mam too, for I'd used her own sleeping powder in both their chas.

I broke the latch on her window, like a too-strong gust of wind had blown it open, then I closed her door behind me and left her to the killing frost.

It were a long winter, shut up in the house, me and Flax practicing the new act, him getting stronger every day. Da spent more time with us, less with the fancy-woman, but he didn't seem too upset, apart from that. Before we left he asked us how we'd feel if he married the fancy-woman. Maude, he called her. We shrugged and gave our blessing. It were no skin off our noses.

LEOF

LEOF WOKE WITH his mother's voice in his ears. "Go home, child," it said. "Leave this place in peace and go back to one who will love you."

He struggled up, murmuring, "Mam?," half-expecting to find himself in his bedroom at home, half-expecting to hear his brother's snoring and the well pulley clanking in the yard outside as the stableboys filled the horses' buckets.

He didn't expect to find himself in the top branches of a pine tree, precariously wedged between a limb and the trunk, his head aching so badly that it felt like it would blow apart. The dawn light was not golden, but gray, and it was a long, long way to the ground.

Shivering with cold, he took stock. He was wet but not sopping, as though his clothes had been dripping for some time; they were clammy against his skin. He smelt of lake weeds.

Struggling to a more comfortable position, he sat himself in the fork of the tree and looked out. The wave had carried him a long way inland; he could only just glimpse the Lake through the trees, and then only because so many of them were broken in half, or their branches had been ripped away. Below, the forest floor was a mess of broken limbs and fallen trees. And bodies. Oh, gods of wind and storm, the bodies of his men. He could see three, four, at least five. They lay with the abandonment of death, limbs crooked, some buried under trees, some splayed on top.

He had had six horses and fifteen archers under his command; perhaps the others had been lucky too. Leof paused at the thought, remembering the voice which had spoken to him as he had woken. Perhaps luck had nothing to do with it. Perhaps the Lake had preserved those she wished to preserve. In which case, why him? Why him and not, as he could see as he climbed down toward the nearest body, why not Broc?

Broc lay on top of a smashed tree trunk, his back as broken as the tree. He looked older than he had the night before, as though he had tasted pain and despair before he died. Leof remembered his father, taking him to see what the Ice King had done to the villages he pillaged. Twenty-two years ago, when he was eight. The bodies had lain everywhere, cut down mercilessly, and for what? A few trinkets and some goats. Barely anything had been stolen. His father made him look at each body—children, women, men, granfers and grammers—all slaughtered and left in their blood. The flies had swarmed over the face of a little girl about the same age as he was, and he had vomited. He had been ashamed, but his father had understood.

"You will lose men in battle," his father had said. "It will be hard. But it is not so hard as seeing the bodies of the innocent folk who you have failed to protect."

That had been the moment when Leof had sworn himself to be a soldier, to protect the people of his land from the raiders who had left not a single person alive in two whole villages. He had known then, and in the years since, when he had defended the Domain against the Ice King's raids, that he was doing the right work. No matter how hard killing was, it had to be done, to protect the innocent.

Now, he stared down at Broc, who was both a man he had lost in battle *and* an innocent he had failed to protect. Tears scalded Leof's eyes and he let them fall onto the boy's body. It was the only blessing he could give him, and a plea for forgiveness. He should have told Broc to run as soon as the ground began to shake. He should have run himself, as Thistle and the other horses, wiser than men, had done. He should have known the horses would not be affected by illusion. Lord Thegan had been wrong. This was his fault.

Leof banished the thought immediately. Commanders based their decisions on the information they had at the time. Thegan had not had the right information. The Lake was much more powerful than they had known. They would have to regroup and make new plans.

On that thought, his tears dried and he began to think again like an officer. He checked the other bodies, without trying to disentangle them from the branches and debris which lay over and under them like macabre winding sheets. Two archers, two horsemen. He would have to search further afield for the others. He sent out a halloo but heard no response, so he began the gruesome task of searching for more bodies, in case there was anyone left alive.

He found three more men dead and a horse he didn't recognize before the cold and dizziness made him stop. Although he didn't have any obvious injuries apart from bruising, his head was pounding and he was shivering in fits and starts. He needed to find help before nightfall, or he would become another of the Lake's victims.

Reluctantly, he turned toward the Lake shore. There would be searchers out, he was sure. Sooner or later, Lord Thegan would organize the remnants of his army. He would expect a report from his officers. There had been twenty of them, each with a troop stationed at intervals around the Lake, so they could attack it from all sides.

Leof approached the shoreline cautiously, wondering if he should call out to reassure the Lake that he meant no harm. Then he remembered the voice he had heard. It had not seemed violent or maddened, just sad. Somewhat reassured, he threaded through broken branches and climbed over fallen trees.

The Lake stretched before him, impossibly peaceful. The water was still and serene, reflecting a perfect blue sky—so still that even the reed beds were silent, their eternal whispering paused. This was how the Lake should be, not riven by war and death. Leof was overwhelmed by remorse. It came unexpectedly, so quickly that he was taken by surprise. We should not have come here, he thought. We have no right to invade these people. Then he wondered whose thought it was, his or the Lake's, and was frightened, truly frightened, for the first time since he was a boy, at the idea that the Lake could put a thought in his head.

To his relief, he heard a shout from his left and turned to find a search party of four men making their cautious way around the shoreline. Hodge led them, his grim face lightening as he saw Leof.

"My Lord Leof!" he called, raising his hand in greeting. "Thank the gods!"

Leof went to meet them and clasped forearms with Hodge, although that was a gesture used between equals, not between officers and sergeants.

"I'm glad to see you alive, sergeant," Leof said. Hodge nodded.

"Same with us, sir. You're the first we've found in this stretch."

"How far did it go?"

Hodge stared at him, surprised. "All the way around, sir. Wherever we had men, wherever the arrows caught the reeds. We've lost—I don't know how many, maybe a quarter of the men, a third of the horses."

"My Lord Thegan?"

"Thank the gods, he's safe. He was ordering the attack from a lookout point and it was almost higher than the wave. He just got a wetting."

Leof exhaled in relief. "He'll be angry."

"Cold angry, sir, and dangerous with it." Hodge cleared his throat, aware suddenly that sergeants don't make comments like that about their lords. At least, not to officers. "He wants all survivors to gather toward Baluchston."

"Baluchston?"

"Aye." Hodge spat to one side. "The wave didn't touch the town. So my lord reckons they've turned coat there, gone native, like. He's going to raze the town, he says, to teach them a lesson."

Leof went so still that he heard his heart thumping clearly, heard the blood thrum in his ears. He had to get to Thegan. Try to turn his anger away from the town. It was the Lake who had sent the wave, not the people of Baluchston. He knew that in his bones.

"Do you have horses, sergeant?"

"Aye," Hodge nodded. "We've been gathering up the strays. Most of the horses made it out. About ten minute's walk back that way, sir. We found your Thistle."

Thistle safe. Leof smiled and clapped Hodge on the back. "A silver piece to every man in your group, sergeant, when we get back to Sendat. That's the best news I could have had."

He started off toward the horses with a light step, but turned back somberly as he remembered. "You'll find eight men and a horse that way," he said, pointing back to the forest. "I couldn't find anyone alive."

"Aye, sir," Hodge said, nodding to his men to continue their search. "I think this section had the worst of it, by the numbers dead."

"The wind was at our backs," Leof said. "The Lake had only one chance to stop us."

"She only needed one chance, sir," Hodge said. Leof noticed that "she." He wondered if Hodge, too, had heard his mother's voice telling him to go home. He wished, with all his heart, that he could follow that advice. Instead, he kept walking around the shoreline, trying to think of arguments which would convince Thegan that no good would come of massacre.

SAKER

SAKER FLUSHED EVERY time he remembered throwing up after the battle at Spritford. If he was to take back this land for its rightful inhabitants, he had to get over his squeamishness. So he followed his ghosts, his little army, down into Carlion determined to be detached; to be strong.

What he saw tried his resolution. The people of Carlion were mostly asleep, although a few late drinkers were on the streets, making their way home. They died first, Owl and his followers smashing into them before they realized what was happening. They didn't even have time to raise the alarm.

Owl gave the first blow: a backhanded sweep with a sword which cut open a man's neck to the bone. There was no scream, just a gargling sound as the blood spurted on the street, covering Owl. He grinned and spun to strike at a woman. But he stopped in mid-stroke and pushed her aside, moving on swiftly to another target.

Ah, Saker thought, noting her dark hair as she ran, sobbing with fear, into an alleyway. The spell is working. It protects those of Traveler blood. He concentrated on the feeling of satisfaction that gave him, so he didn't feel sick at the terrible noises coming from the battle around him; so he didn't feel at all for the man who had just died. That man was an invader, he reminded himself. Living off the profits of murderers. Deserving of death.

Then the ghosts went to the houses. Carlion was a peaceful town. It had its share of robbers and tricksters, but they tended to concentrate on the country visitors and traders who passed through. The residents left their doors on the latch, except during the big Winterfair. That was why Saker had chosen it as the first city, instead of Turvite, where crime flourished and householders put good stout bars across their doors before they went to bed.

The ghosts simply walked in for their slaughter. They disappeared from the silent, moonlit street into houses all along the main street and a few moments later the screams started.

Saker began to tremble, but he breathed deeply and admonished himself, imagining what his father would say if he could see him. Just standing still wasn't enough. He had to be part of it, to see it.

So he followed Owl into the next house.

It was a brick house, well-to-do. The front room was used as a carpentry workshop but there was a big standing loom there, too. Stairs led up to the sleeping chambers. As the door crashed back and Owl rushed in, a voice was raised in question from upstairs. A young auburn-haired man ran down, staring blankly at Owl and Saker. He was tying his trousers as he came; he had no weapon. Behind him was a red-headed woman in a nightshirt: tall, with a strong, attractive face.

Owl raised his sword and the man, quicker than he looked, jumped the last few steps and caught up a long piece of wood which lay on the workbench. He brought it up in time to block Owl's stroke, but the wood shattered.

"Merrick!" the woman screamed. She grabbed Owl and pulled him back, giving the man time to recover and find another weapon. All he could find was a chisel with a long point. Sharp enough, but no use against a sword. As the woman grabbed him Owl turned and raised his sword to strike at her, then stopped as he had done with the woman in the street. He pushed the red-headed woman away. Saker couldn't believe it. This red-head was one of the old blood? No, surely not!

"Maryrose!" the man cried, and slid around Owl to her side, helping her up.

Owl grinned, satisfaction on his face as he prepared to strike the man. As the sword came down, knocking aside the chisel, the woman threw herself in front of the man. The sword almost cut her shoulder off and she dropped straight down, dead already. Merrick screamed in anguish and launched himself at Owl, but two more strokes stopped him. He fell beside her, but he wasn't quite dead. His blood flowed out across the woman's hair, turning it dark, like a Traveler's. He tried to turn himself toward her, but only managed to slide his hand along the floor to touch her face. Her eyes stared blindly, green as grass. The man's fingers slid, shaking, along her cheek and fell.

"Maryrose," he whispered. "Wait for me." Then he died.

Owl smiled and turned to the door. Saker was shaking, but he reminded himself that this was necessary. This was no more than the invaders had done to his people.

He followed Owl outside.

There were people on the street now, rushing out to see why their neighbors were screaming, some men already armed, as though they had been expecting trouble. There was confusion, shouting, men trying to form groups to fight, women collecting children who had wandered out in their nightclothes, yawning.

Many died. Mostly it was quick. But sometimes it wasn't. Even the men who had come ready for fighting were soon overcome. Those with swords didn't know how to use them. They did better with the tools of their trades: knives, hoes, scythes, axes. They fought with desperation but could not do well enough to save themselves. Not when a ghost could take a stab to the heart and still keep fighting.

Yet Saker was astonished to see how many the ghosts passed over. Traveler blood must account for it, because there was no visible difference—the ghosts slashed down at one man but merely shoved another aside; they ripped a scythe across a woman's throat and leapt over her almost identical neighbor.

No matter what the people of Carlion did, they could not defend themselves against his army.

The only house untouched was a stonecaster's house with a big red pouch hanging outside, which Saker's Sight could tell had a spell on the door against ghosts. So. Something to think about.

He had seen enough. He walked through the dying and the dead, past people cowering behind carts and children bleeding over the bricks of the street. Dawn would come soon and he suspected that the ghosts would fade, then. He had to be ready to leave as soon as they faded.

When he stood by the burial site and looked at the bones laid out before him, he had a revelation. He had raised Owl's ghost by simply using his skull. He didn't need to go from place to place, raising the local dead against the living. He could take them with him. A bone, just one bone from each, was enough. If he used fingerbones instead of skulls, he could carry an army in a sack!

Frantically he began to collect fingerbones, laying them on the sack he had wrapped Owl's skull in. He sent out his Sight so that he could feel the spirit of the person who had owned the bone—when he felt the tingle that said the ghost was walking, he put the bone on the pile. In the end, he had a pile of bones which would fit into his smallest coffer. He pulled out the scrolls he kept there and put them in the sack. They weren't as precious, now, as the bones.

By the time the sun edged above the blood-red horizon, Saker was ready, horse harnessed, reins in hand. As he felt the spell dissolve and the ghosts fade, he started off, leaving behind a carpet of bones cast across the disturbed earth.

ASH

Safred poured out another round of cha while Cael lit a lamp, making the shadows sharper and the dark outside the windows seem more threatening. She looked at Ash.

"There is more needed. Once we have the bones," Safred said, "we have to raise Acton's ghost. The gods say you must sing him up."

Ash felt as if someone had punched him in the stomach. He stared down at the table, his hands hidden but his shoulders hunched tight. Was *this* why he sang with the voice of the dead? To sing spells of resurrection? It had a nasty logic about it. But he couldn't sing up a ghost.

"I don't know how," he said.

"You'd better find someone to teach you," Bramble said. He looked at her sharply and then nodded, once, abruptly. Many things made sense to him, all of a sudden. If such songs existed, he knew where to find them. It was even the right time of year—and, of course, that was why the gods had told them to stay in Hidden Valley until the spring. So he would be able to go straight to the Deep and demand answers.

Unexpected anger swept over him. This was a matter of *singing*. Of *songs*. He was supposed to know all the songs. His father had said he had taught Ash all the songs there were. Then he paused, his anger faltering. That was not exactly what his father had said. He'd said, "That's the last song I can teach you, son." Ash had just assumed that meant his father didn't know any others. Because he had also said to Ash, "You must remember *all* the songs." He had remembered them all, but apparently he had not been trusted with every one. He felt sick, and angry enough to take on even the demons of the Deep.

"Yes," he said to Bramble. "I should. I should be able to...can I take a horse?"

Bramble nodded. "Yes, but you don't know how —" she started to say.

"Do you want me to come?" Martine asked.

Ash hesitated, and then shook his head reluctantly.

Safred chimed in at the same moment. "Martine comes with us."

"Really?" Martine's voice was dangerously calm. She clearly didn't like it. Her mouth was tight.

Safred put up her palms in the traditional mime of good faith. "Not *my* idea," she said hastily. They were all silent. It took some getting used to, this idea that the gods were organizing their lives. "Your destiny is here," Safred said in a small voice.

Then she sat up, regaining her confidence, turning to speak to Ash. "After Bramble finds Acton's death place, you and she can go to find the bones together."

"Did the gods say that, too?"

"No, but isn't it obvious?" Safred was becoming annoyed. She wasn't used to people questioning her.

Ash shook his head. "No. I have to go somewhere else first."

"Where?"

He just stared at her. "Set a meeting point," he said. "I'll join you later."

"You must be at the lake, to give the brooch to Bramble at the right time!" Safred insisted.

Ash wondered why Safred didn't simply take the brooch from the table.

Safred flushed. "To be used, the brooch must pass from its rightful owner to the Kill Reborn in the right time and place," she insisted.

Ash nodded, picked up the brooch and weighed it in his hand for a moment. Then he held it out to Martine. Her lips twitched, but she took it respectfully enough.

"I give you this brooch," Ash said. "You are now the rightful owner."

Martine nodded and slipped the brooch in her pocket. Safred frowned. She opened her mouth to speak, but Ash forestalled her, as though everything had been settled.

"If I'm Traveling alone...I don't really know how to look after a horse," he said to Bramble.

"Take Flax or Zel," she said. "They'll know more than I do. They're Gorham's children."

Ash had no idea who Gorham was, but the dark-haired girl's head came up.

"Flax stays with me," she said. "We'll both go."

There it was, a flat statement leaving no opening for discussion. Stone. But Ash was stone, too. He had to be.

"No. You can't come. I'll go alone."

Safred looked curiously at Ash, her eyes unfocused. Ash suspected she was listening to the gods. If so, they didn't tell her anything she wanted to hear. Her face tensed.

But she put her hand over Zel's.

"We have need of Flax. He should go with Ash."

"I look after him." Zel's voice was almost pleading.

"Yes," Safred said. "Perhaps it is time to share that privilege."

Zel's eyes were dark with internal struggle. Safred patted her hand gently.

"You have done enough." Again, there was a layer of meaning that Zel seemed to understand.

"I'm a safeguarder," Ash reminded them. "He can look after the horses, and I'll look after him."

Zel stared at him intently, trying to read his soul. "Do you promise to look after him? As though he were your own brer?"

Ash nodded. "I promise."

Zel let out a long breath. "All right then. He can go."

"Anybody planning to ask Flax what he thinks?" Ash asked.

Safred looked startled, which was satisfying. Ash was tired already of people who arranged other people's lives as though they were gods themselves.

But Zel laughed bitterly. "Oh, he wants to go," she said.

It was true. Flax's eyes were alight. No surprise, Ash thought. What boy wouldn't rather travel with another young man than with his sister?

"We must decide where to meet," Safred said. "But I think, not now. Tomorrow, at the altar for the dawn prayers. Let the gods guide us."

Ash felt a little uncomfortable at the thought, remembering two black rock altars—the one in Turvite, where the gods had called to him, and the one at Hidden Valley, where they had commanded him to come here, at this time. Or perhaps they had set the time so he could save Bramble's life by killing the warlord's man, Sully. The thought of Sully pierced him with regret. He hadn't meant to kill; his training had taken over. He hadn't been able to stay, as he should have, and attend the quickening of Sully's ghost. He should have been there, three days later, waiting, ready with his knife, to admit his guilt, cut his own flesh and offer blood to Sully's ghost as reparation for his death. He sat for a moment at the table as the others got up. To lay one ghost to rest, that he understood. That was personal, immediate, necessary. But to lay an army of ghosts, who had died perhaps a thousand years before...he shook his head and pushed back from the table, following the others toward the door. He couldn't imagine how that might work.

Flax was cock-a-hoop as Bramble led him and Ash to the stables so that she could check on the horses and introduce him to Cam and Mud. She wouldn't dare lend Ash Trine, she said. Besides, she liked the cross-grained animal the best.

Flax chattered happily about getting back on the Road. "I can't stand it in towns," he said. "They close in around me."

"Me too," Bramble said. "You've always Traveled?"

He nodded. "When our mam and da Settled, Zel and I took the Road together. Six years ago now."

Ash revised his estimate of Flax's age upward. He had to be at least seventeen, although he talked like a much younger boy.

Flax knew horses, all right, and he soothed them with his voice. Bramble relaxed about letting her precious horses go to someone else. After he had finished grooming them, Flax left with a cheerful "Wind at your back!"

After that, Bramble spent some time with Mud and Cam, teaching Ash about their grooming and feeding, telling the horses that she was sure they would meet again. Of course they would. They nuzzled her and whickered gently as though trying to comfort her against the coming separation—until Trine got jealous and nipped them away from her. She laughed, and dusted her hands off. She seemed revived by her contact with the animals, but she still looked very tired.

"Enough for one day," she said. She turned to Ash and raised her eyebrows. "Have you wondered, if we're going to lay all these ghosts to rest, who's going to give the blood the ritual needs?"

He had wondered. To set a murdered ghost to rest, the killer had to acknowledge guilt and then offer his own blood to the ghost. Ash shivered, remembering the touch of ghostly tongues on his own flesh, when he had offered his blood as reparation to two men he had killed—men, he reminded himself, who had been trying to kill Martine. No need to feel sorry for those two. But the ritual was specific. Each ghost needed blood. Although, he remembered, those ghosts had refused blood from Martine. "Blood's just a symbol," they had said. "Didn't you know?"

There was too much they didn't know, he thought, and that might be the death of them all.

After dinner at Heron's, he went out to the garden behind the house for a breath of air, then stayed, sitting on a bench, looking up at the clear sky. A big lilac bush shed its petals over him as the night breeze stirred its branches. The scent reminded him of another night, camping by an abandoned house whose garden was full of lilacs. His father had taught him the love counting song that night:

There are ten white flowers my lover gave to me
Here are the petals of those sweet sweet peas:
Honesty
That's one!
Verity
That's two!
Poetry
That's three!
And Lo-o-ove
Ch: Love can't be counted
Love can't be caught
Love must be given
Never sold or bought

It was a sugary, sentimental song and he'd never liked it, but his father, Rowan, had enjoyed playing it on the flute, giving it lots of trills and flourishes. Ash didn't want to think about his father, so he concentrated on identifying the northern stars he had heard about but never seen before. There was the white bear, there was the salmon...a noise behind him made him spin around, knife springing from his boot to his hand as if it had a life of its own.

Martine stood there, holding a cup of cha, her pale face showing clearly in the moonlight but her eyes unreadable. She raised an eyebrow at the knife.

"If I'd wanted to kill you, you'd have been dead long since," she said.

He flushed. He was so on edge that he'd almost welcome a good fight. "Sorry. But...I don't like it here much."

"Mmm. It's not a comfortable time, I'll give you that." She smiled suddenly. "Have a cup of cha, lad."

He took the cup with as good grace as he could and Martine sat down beside him, bringing her feet up to sit cross-legged.

"Do you want to tell me where you're going?" she asked.

He paused, not entirely sure what to say. "To find my father," he said finally.

"Do you know how to find him?"

He looked down at the cha and nodded. "I know where he'll be at this time of year."

"You're going to Gabriston?" Martine asked carefully.

His head whipped up in astonishment. She should not know. No woman should know.

"How . . .?"

Martine shrugged. "I'm a stonecaster. We get to know lots of things we shouldn't."

He relaxed a little, but he was worried, all the same. He didn't know how much she knew, and so couldn't risk talking about any of it. He thought, instead, of the fact that his father had not taught him all the songs. Not all.

After so long away from his parents, after so much doubt and betrayal with Doronit, after taking on responsibility from the gods, who would have thought two words could hurt so much? They knifed into Ash's stomach, into his heart. It had been the one certainty of his life, that his father had trusted him with all the songs, *all* the songs, so they could be preserved as they should be, voice to voice.

How could he go back and ask? If his father had wanted him to know—had *trusted* him—he would have taught him the songs already.

"How are you planning to pay your way?" Martine asked.

He'd been worried about that, too. He had nothing—and the only thing he owned of value, the brooch, had been commandeered.

"I thought, Cael might . . ."

"I'm not sure they have much to spare themselves," she said thoughtfully. "I think you might need these."

She pulled a pouch out of her pocket. For a wild moment, he thought she was giving him her own pouch of stones, but then he saw it was the stones she had taken from the stonecaster's son last autumn. It seemed like years ago that they had helped the stonecaster's ghost to find rest. He had made the new pouch for these stones himself last winter, sitting by the fire at Elva and Mabry's, the month before their baby was born. Just the thought of little Ash warmed him. Having a namesake who was being raised Settled, a loving family around him, strong walls to protect him, made Ash feel stronger himself. Older and more competent. Not enough to make him take the stones, though.

"You'll know them," Martine reassured him. "They speak loudly, at first. They want to be known. And remember, just answer whatever question you're asked. Don't make my mistake and tell people more than they ask for."

"I'm not a caster," he said hastily.

"You could be. You have the Sight. You know it."

He didn't *know.* Just suspected. He didn't *want* to know. He was strange enough already; able to see ghosts, to compel them to speak, speaking himself with the voice of the dead. Having the Sight would just make him even odder.

"Stonecasters aren't thought of as freaks, you know," Martine said, seeming to read his thoughts as she so often did. "We're just part of the furniture of the world, really."

He laughed unwillingly. It was true, stonecasters were accepted everywhere. When she offered him the pouch, his hand seemed to rise of its own accord to take it.

The heavy softness of the leather, the stones within it, fit into his palm as though he had held it a thousand times before.

"So," Martine said. "So." She sounded disappointed, and reached to take the pouch back.

"What?" Ash said, startled. His fingers tightened on the pouch. Martine paused.

"They are not in harmony," she said.

He had no idea what she was talking about. She was surprised in turn.

"You can't hear them?"

Ash shook his head. Martine's face was unreadable, as it had been the first time he met her. It was as though she had withdrawn from him. As though he had failed her.

"The stones sing. Well, not exactly. Not like humans. But when they do not have a caster, they sing constantly, out of tune, out of rhythm. It's unpleasant. That's why I rolled this pouch up in a blanket. So I wouldn't have to listen to them."

"And?"

Martine hesitated. "When they find their caster, and he or she takes them in their hand, they come into tune."

Ash stared down at the pouch, which seemed as silent as the grave to him. "I can't even hear them," he said. "So I suppose they didn't come into tune."

"No," she said gently, resting her hand on his shoulder. "I was sure you were a caster. I even cast the stones about it, and they said yes, definitely. I don't understand —"

"What's to understand?" he shot back, suddenly angry. He tossed the pouch into her lap. "I can't do it. Just like I can't sing. Or play the flute. Or *anything* to do with music."

"That may be," Martine said slowly. "But my casting was quite clear. I've never known the stones to be completely wrong. I'll cast again."

"Don't bother," he said. "I still won't be able to hear them."

He strode off and walked the streets of the silent town until the salmon star had swum its way below the horizon. Then he went back to the lodging house and lay in the green-ceilinged room, trying not to think of all the things he was useless at—all the people he had failed. Perhaps his father had been right not to trust him. The only thing he seemed to be good at was killing.

BRAMBLE

FIRST LIGHT WAS early so far north, even in spring, and they were all yawning and shivering as they met outside Safred's house and followed her through the alleys and streets of the town to a small wooded area on its outskirts. A score or so of townsfolk came with them, and they greeted one another with nods and yawning half-smiles so simply that Bramble knew they took the walk to the gods' wood every morning.

The wood was surrounded by fields and some houses, and it was clear that the town had expanded around the altar, but had left enough space to keep the gods happy. They didn't like being crowded, it was said.

Bramble could feel them, lightly, in her mind. It was not the uncomfortable pressure they used when they wanted her to do something. This was almost companionable. It was the first time she had felt this way, going to greet them. At home, in Wooding, she had hated the dawn prayers, surrounded by those afraid of the gods, or of life, by the pious and by those who wanted to be thought pious, like the Widow Farli. But here, she sensed nothing from these people but simple devotion. No doubt it was harder to pretend to be pious with the Well of Secret's eyes on you.

The rock was in a clearing, surrounded by old beech trees, huge and knotted and twisting overhead so that their branches met and the altar seemed to be at the center of a domed room. Moss and young grass covered the ground and Bramble could hear the trickle of a stream which the gods always liked to have nearby. Although they were close to the town, she felt as though she were deep in a forest, perhaps even the Great Forest that she had dreamed about so often. The hairs on the back of her neck raised, and she knew that the gods had turned their attention to all of their followers, not just her.

They came to the altar in the silver light just before dawn, and knelt together, in silence, as the winds of dawn began to blow. Safred bowed her head; Martine and Ash looked down at their hands, which was not quite the same thing. Zel was praying, her mouth moving silently, her hand clasping Flax's. His face was blank. Surprisingly, Cael was also praying fervently, hands clenched against his chest.

Bramble's mind was empty of prayers. All she could do was feel: grief for Maryrose and a dark scouring of blame and anger for the gods, because they hadn't protected her sister. They gave her no reply in words, but she had a strong sense of their regret. It wasn't enough to ease her grief, but her anger cooled a little, and turned toward Saker. I will kill him, she thought. The pressure on her mind increased with the thought, but for the first time ever, she had the sense that the gods were undecided. *Should I kill him?* she asked them, but she heard no answer except, *Not yet.*

As the first light touched the tops of the trees, throwing shadows down onto the altar, the other townsfolk stirred and got up, backing away respectfully until they were beyond the circle of trees. But Safred motioned to their group to come closer. She laid a hand on the altar.

"Today we part. But we'll meet again, to bring the parts of the answer together."

"Aye," Cael said. "But where, and when?"

They looked at Safred, who hesitated. Bramble could tell there was no answer from the gods.

It was Martine who answered. "Turvite," she said.

"The stones?" Safred asked. "The stones say so?"

"Common sense says so, which is worth more," Martine replied briskly. "It was Acton's last big battle. It's the biggest city in the Domains. Sooner or later this Saker will go there, and he will bring his army."

"Oh, yes," Bramble said, feeling Martine's words ring true. "He'll want Turvite. He'll want to succeed where the old enchanter failed."

"Yes. He will want to surpass her," Safred said slowly.

"So," Cael said. "Turvite."

Ash flinched, just a little, as though Cael's voice had been a prod to his memory. "Um... Turvite might not be so healthy a place for Martine and me," he said.

Martine laughed. "True," she said. "Perhaps we should meet just *outside* Turvite. There's a village a few miles up the river, called Sanctuary. We could meet there."

"As soon as we can," Safred said reluctantly, and it was an irritant to her, they could all see, that she did not know the time and date.

"Where will you go to find the songs?" she asked Ash.

His face closed down. "South," he said.

"But I need to know —" Safred began, and at the same moment the gods roared into Bramble's head, forbiddingly. *No!* they ordered. Safred jerked as the command hit her. Ash shook a little, as though he had heard them too, but his face stayed stony.

"No," he echoed the gods.

Safred stared at him, her eyes burning and her face pale, but at last she nodded and the pressure in Bramble's mind eased off. Bramble could see the effort it took her not to ask more. She waited for Safred to say some final exhortation or blessing, but she just stepped back from the altar and walked away, her back to the altar. That unsettled Bramble, who always backed away, out of a mix of respect and caution. It seemed to her that Safred took the gods for granted, and that was not quite safe. She shrugged. None of her business. She had to see to the horses for the journey.

They walked back to the town and Bramble went straight to the stables instead of to Safred's house with the others. She led the horses around to the house, trying not to think about being separated from Cam and Mud. There was no choice, really, but she took a few moments as she led them to talk to them, telling them they would meet again, soon, soon. Trine got jealous and bumped her head against Bramble's side. Instinctively, she braced for a lance of pain from her arm, but of course there was none. She was healed. She wasn't sure she would ever get used to that.

Bramble had bought provisions for a few days' journey from Heron and had insisted on paying for the room as well, over Ash and Martine's protests. "Least I can do," she said. She never had liked being in someone's debt and only the knowledge that the gods had sent Ash and Martine to her at the right time allowed her to bear the gratitude she owed them. She grinned at Ash. He was still walking stiffly from the long ride. She remembered how much learning to ride hurt.

"Think you can manage another ride?"

He looked at Cam with some doubt. "If I have to," he said, then laughed with her. There was something false about the laughter, though, as if he was trying hard to seem light-hearted. Bramble felt a little protective of him, which was stupid, considering it was *he* who had saved *her* life. Zel brought a sack out from the house and dumped it next to the door frame.

"Another journey," Martine said. "Maybe Acton was right when he sent us on the Road. It seems like we can't get away from it no matter how we try."

"No rest for the Traveler," Ash said. "Not this side of the burial caves."

"I guess we must be Travelers, then," Martine said wryly. Zel went back in for another load, leaving the door open behind her. Martine said quietly to Ash, "I cast again, and the stones said the same thing."

He went very still for a moment, then shrugged. "Doesn't change anything."

"It may be that you need to find different —"

Ash cut her off. "Forget it. I can't do it, and that's all."

Bramble busied herself with checking the girths on the horses. No business of hers. They had the right to their own secrets. But she noticed distress in both their faces, although they tried to disguise it with the blank face so many Travelers seemed to develop. A protective face, that gave nothing away.

Safred's voice reached them, murmuring quietly. Then the sound of a man sobbing uncontrollably. One of the pilgrims, no doubt. Bramble was uncomfortable with this side of Safred's power. To heal flesh was extraordinary enough. To heal the spirit—something in her rebelled against that idea. To be so vulnerable to someone who was, after all, only another human... although at one time she had intended coming to the Well of Secrets for exactly that kind of healing, now it seemed inconceivable to her. There was no way she was baring her soul to Safred.

Safred's voice came again. Martine, Ash and Bramble exchanged glances. After a few moments the sobbing stopped and Safred appeared in the doorway, Cael behind her.

"Sorry to keep you waiting," she said cheerfully.

Bramble looked at Ash and smiled. "Parting of the ways. I guess we're not meant to travel together, lad," she said half-regretfully. He nodded, half-regretful himself.

Zel and Flax emerged from the house, Zel talking in a big-sisterly tone.

"You help as much as you can. Stay out of the inns. Wait until we're together again."

Flax bore her advice patiently; more patiently than most younger brothers would have. His mouth was crooked up a little at one corner, as though he found it amusing, but he listened and nodded and said, "Yes, Zel," in all the right places.

Mullet came around the corner leading four horses, three skittish chestnuts who looked like they had the same breeding and a much older, steadier bay. The old man nodded familiarly to Bramble. She nodded back and smiled. They had met already that morning to groom and saddle the horses. That had been the best time since she'd come to Oakmere, going quietly about the familiar tasks in the warm, lantern-lit stable, working companionably with Mullet as she had done so often with Gorham, the comforting smell of horses surrounding them.

She had been surprised to find the horses in such good condition after their frantic race to get her to Oakmere, but Mullet had grinned.

"Well of Secrets, she gave them a visit," he said.

"She *healed* them?" Bramble asked, astonished. It had not occurred to her that Safred would care about animals. Animals had no secrets.

"Said you'd need 'em," he confirmed. Yes, that made more sense. Safred might be a seer, but she was practical, too. She wouldn't let anything get in the way of the task at hand.

Now, as Safred swung up on the old bay, Bramble could tell that she had been right. Safred didn't care about the animal; it was just a way to get to where she was going. Bramble was trying hard not to dislike Safred, out of gratitude, but she suspected that it was a losing battle.

"Let's go," Safred said. "May the gods go with you."

"We might have less trouble if they didn't," Cael said softly to Bramble, and she chuckled.

Safred jammed a battered old leather hat on her head—all those freckles, thought Bramble, still amused, glad in some way to notice any weakness in her. They mounted their horses. They paused for a moment, exchanging glances: Zel and Flax, Ash and Martine. Then they rode away, Safred, Zel, Cael, Martine and Bramble to the north; Ash and Flax to the south.

Cael laughed openly at the look on Safred's face as she twisted in her saddle to watch the young men ride away.

"That boy has a secret," she said, her eyes hungry.

"And the right to keep it," Cael said.

Reluctantly, Safred nodded and started her horse off again. "For now," she said.

They rode out of the town toward the north, passing through streets which led to houses with large vegetable gardens and then a narrow strip of farmland, just showing the first greeny-purple tips of wheat above the soil. There were oats, too, in strips among the wheat, and cabbages, onions, beets—all the staples that would get a northern town through the long stretch of winter.

Not far from town they skirted a lake fringed with willows.

"Oakmere?" Bramble asked.

Cael grimaced. "They cut down the oaks to build the town, then someone brought a willow up from the south and they just took over."

Bramble pursed her lips. "Yes, incomers do that."

He gave her a look that showed he understood that she was talking about more than trees, but made no comment. She found herself liking him. He reminded her a bit of her own uncle, her father's brother, who was a chairmaker and woodcarver. She hadn't seen him often in her childhood because he lived in Whitehaven, where there was a bigger market for the intricate and expensive carving he loved, but she always enjoyed his visits. He was far more jovial and light-hearted than her parents, and took Bramble's daily explorations of the woods in his stride, unlike every other adult she knew. Cael had the same acceptance of life, the same good-natured easiness and enjoyment. But her uncle had been no fool, and neither was Cael.

Soon the farmland gave way to scrub and heath and then to sparse woodland, mostly birch and beech and spruce. It was clear that the trees were harvested by the townsfolk. There were stumps and coppiced trees, cleared areas where young saplings were springing up, the remnants of charcoal burners' fires.

The road was bordered by hedgerows—hawthorn, in flower, and wild white roses, which sent thorned canes onto the track and forced them to ride single file, Zel leading, ahead of Safred. Gorham must have thrown Zel up on a horse before she could walk; she rode as if she were a part of the animal. Safred was competent enough on a horse, Bramble had noted, but mounted clumsily, and she used reins and a saddle, which somehow surprised Bramble. She herself was riding Trine, not trusting her to anyone else, and as usual went without a bit. She had given Trine's saddle to Ash, for Mud, and rode Trine with just a blanket and saddlebags. The bags Merrick had given her. A torrent of grief broke over her at the memory and her chest felt painful, as though her heart was being squeezed. She forced herself to pay attention to where they were going. Ahead of them was a line of darker trees. Bramble couldn't see what they were—pine or larch or oak, maybe elms. There was no sense of a specific color green, just a wall of darkness which grew as they rode closer.

They reached a crossroads where a much larger road led off to the northwest. Safred dismounted and the others followed suit and stood by their horses. Martine and Cael thankfully stretched their legs.

"Ahead is the Great Forest," Safred said. She paused and took off her hat, pleating its crown without looking at it. "When we get to the altar we'll be safe, I think. Until then, be careful. Don't leave the path."

"They always say that in the stories," Bramble said involuntarily. "The old stories about children lost in the Forest always say, 'Don't leave the path,' and the child always does."

"Yes," Safred said. "Remember what they meet when they do."

They rode on.

The Forest began abruptly. There was a small slope covered with a dense thicket of wayfaring trees, not yet in flower. The grayish branches and rough leaves almost barred the path, but Cael pushed through, and they were suddenly among pine trees. Huge, straight, ugly. It was a little like the forest near the Lake, but *more.*

The enormous trees made Bramble feel as though she and the others had been shrunk to child size, or smaller; that they were toys pretending to be human, like the dolls Maryrose used to play with. She wondered if anyone or anything was playing with them, and what the game really was.

Under the high, intertwined branches, they rode in an artificial dusk that pressed heavily on them. The ground was covered by a carpet of browned pine needles so thick that the horses' hooves made no sound and Bramble was for the first time glad of the chink of bits and bridles from the others' horses. Far above them, patches of orange lichen spread like disease on the trunks. The smell of pine was so strong that after a while Bramble's nose blocked it out and she could smell nothing. See nothing except the gloomy brown and tan of the forest floor. Hear nothing except the faint sough of wind in the branches high above them. There were no stumps, no clearings. No one came here for wood or charcoal or pine, Bramble suspected. No one came here unless they had to.

Back at her home in Wooding, she had wanted so badly to come to the Great Forest, but this was not what she had hoped for. All her life, she had imagined herself running free here, but in her imagination it had been a wilder, more isolated version of her woods at home, filled with familiar, beautiful greens: oak and elm and alder and willow, holly and rowan and hazel, each a different shade, each taking its proper place in the burgeoning life of the wood.

This Forest's life was the opposite of that simple kitchen table they had sat around yesterday, of the daylight life of eating and drinking and talking and being. The opposite of the familiar stable where the horses' breath had showed misty in the chilly morning. Even the opposite of the gathering in the dawn around the black rock altar, where their own breaths had billowed out like steam. This was a place where breathing was foreign. Unwelcome. She felt the pressure of the Forest in her mind, like the pressure from the gods but with a different flavor. There was no voice here, as the gods had voices. There was nothing here but time, endless tree time, where a single heartbeat took a whole year and a thought might last the length of a human life.

Bramble remembered her panic in the forest by the Lake and how the presence of the horses had saved her from it. She saw that the others were starting to feel the same panic now. Picking up on their riders' anxiety, their horses were growing increasingly nervous, especially the two skittish chestnuts that Zel and Cael were riding. Bramble did not give into it so badly this time—perhaps because she had found a way through it before, and now kept her attention on Trine's warm hide and the way her muscles moved.

"Concentrate on your horses," she called to the others, her voice dropping flat and harsh into the silence. "Feel their warmth. Smell them. They'll comfort you."

Her companions turned back to look at her in surprise, then they nodded and moved with more confidence. Safred leaned down in her saddle to lay her face against the bay's neck. Zel dropped her hands so that they rested on the saddle bow, where she could feel the shift of her horse's muscles.

Bramble saw them relax a little and was pleased. Whatever they had to face in this forest, they weren't going to be in a panic when it found them.

Then they reached a stream, bubbling over flat, round stones, no more than a hand-span deep but too wide to jump across. At least, it was too wide for these horses. If the roan had been with her, they would have made it easily. She pushed aside a sharp pang of grief at the thought, but the memory of the roan lying in a stream much like this one, bleeding, his head in her lap, returned implacably. Guilt, as well as grief, welled up in her. It was her fault he had died. If she hadn't made him run in that last chase, he would never have fallen. He would still be alive. Concentrate! she told herself, and looked up and down the stream, searching for a crossing place.

The stream was wide enough that a shaft of sunlight made it down through the bordering trees, and bushes and grasses grew along its banks, their sharp green shocking in the gloom of the pine forest. It was the most cheerful place they had come to in the Forest, but the horses refused to cross. Bramble dismounted and walked to the front, leading Trine. There was a flat space on either side of the stream, but it was bare of any marks. Not even animals came here to drink. Trine snorted and backed away from the water.

"Water sprites?" Bramble asked Safred.

Safred shrugged, but Cael answered. "You can see water sprites, usually."

"What, then?" Bramble asked.

Martine bent to sniff the water. "It smells of something I've met before," she said thoughtfully, "but I can't quite place it."

In turn, they bent and sniffed the brown water. For all of them, it brought up an almost memory, a feeling that they knew the scent if only they could remember. It was neither pleasant nor unpleasant, but it was not pine or fruit or flower or bog or anything else that you would expect to find in a forest.

"If the horses don't want to cross it, I don't think we should," Cael said. The others nodded and Bramble was relieved. She trusted the horses' instincts more than the humans'.

The stream crossed the path at a right angle and there seemed no other way over it. The path clearly continued on the other side.

"Don't go off the path, children," she said wryly.

"Bramble's right," Zel said suddenly, not seeming to notice the wryness. "This might be a trick to get us off the path." She swung down from the chestnut and sat on the pine needles to take off her boots.

"Zel?" Martine said. "What are you doing?"

"I reckon I can make it across there," Zel muttered, pulling her boots off with a strange ferocity. "This is something *I* can do."

Bramble nodded. She'd feel like that, too, surrounded by people who can speak to ghosts and tell the future. Hells, she *did* feel like that, and she was the Kill Reborn. But although Gorham had told her that Zel was a tumbler, it was a very long way across that stream. She said nothing. The girl knew her own business best.

Cael wasn't so sure. He measured the stream by eye. "It's too far!" he said. "You'll fall halfway."

Zel jumped to her feet and began to do some limbering exercises, swinging her arms and legs. The horses edged away, the white of Trine's eyes showing. Bramble went to her head and soothed her.

"We'll see," Zel said. "If I get over we can string up a rope and you can slide across." She paused. "Do we have rope?"

"Aye," Cael said, his voice deep and comforting. "We've got rope. But that won't get the horses over."

"We'll have to leave the horses," Safred said, her voice tight. "We have to get to the lake by sunset."

Neither Bramble nor Zel liked that idea. Bramble didn't want to leave Trine in a strange place with who knew what hiding in the shadows. Zel, it was clear, had anticipated who would be left behind to look after the horses. She prepared for the jump with her mouth set.

Bramble found it hard to believe there was any danger. She remembered jumping the chasm near Wooding. *That* had been dangerous. This was just a shallow stream which, as the sun rose above the trees, began to sparkle in the sunbeams. But the horses wouldn't cross it. Bramble shrugged. Nothing was ever shagging easy.

Zel backed up the path and motioned them to move out of the way. Bramble and Cael took the horses off a little; Martine and Safred went to the other side of the track. Bramble expected Zel to run, instead, she took a couple of long paces and then started to do flip-flops, hands to feet to hands, building up speed. At the very edge of the water she jumped high and curled into a ball as she spun in the air, across the stream: once, twice, three times . . .

Her feet came down only a foot from the bank. She splashed heavily into the water, landing on hands and knees. The water flew up and doused her and the smell, whatever it was, immediately grew much stronger.

Zel knelt in the water, silent. She seemed frozen. Petrified.

"Zel?" Bramble called, but she didn't respond. Bramble edged down the stream, still holding the bridles, so she could see her face side on, but Zel's expression was fixed in a grimace of surprise.

"Turned to stone?" Cael wondered, voicing all their thoughts. He picked up a pinecone from the track and threw it at Zel's back. She twitched in response. He did it again and she scrambled up to her feet, her face changing gradually from surprise to fear, her eyes following something to her right, her head turning as she tracked something that wasn't there.

"Zel, keep going!" Safred called, but Zel remained still, breathing hard. Cael threw another cone, and another. Zel's back shrugged and involuntarily she took a half-step. Then she screamed, the scream of a child who has seen a monster. Bramble bent and grabbed a cone and threw it, too. Then they were all throwing cones, some landing near Zel, some hitting her legs and back, and one bouncing off her head.

"Aow!" she said, and took one more step. Enough to bring her out of the water. She stood looking down the track and shook her head as if to clear it. Then she turned, her flexible tumbler's body seeming heavy. Her feet fell solidly with a thwack into the mud.

"Are you all right?" Martine called.

Zel nodded and looked around again, clearing her throat as though she hadn't spoken for a long time.

"I'm fine."

"What happened?" Safred asked.

Zel shrugged. "I dunno. Everything…changed. Like I were somewhere different. There was elk. I think elk, but they was *huge*. A whole herd of 'em. And the trees was different—oak, I think, maybe some elm, and grasses and…and there were this *thing*, like a giant cat, shagging enormous, chasing the elk and they was running and running and the ground were shaking and then that thing, that big cat, it had these *teeth* down to here," she gestured to below her shoulders, "it stopped running and it turned to me and started to come. It were going to jump, like a wolf jumps—it were going to take out my throat, I could *smell* it. Then something hit me on the back of my head and I took a step and it—it was gone. All of it were just *gone*."

She sat down heavily, as though talking had exhausted her.

"You were right here," Cael reassured her. "You never left us."

Zel bit her lip. "If that thing had landed on me, I'd be dead," she said with certainty. "Here or not, there or not. I'd be dead."

"Mmm," Safred said. "Better not to take the horses through it, then."

"How do we get over?" Martine asked.

"We tie a rope high on one tree over this side," Cael said, "and then throw it to Zel. She can fix it lower to a tree on the other side and we slide down the rope. We can use one of the leading reins to hold onto."

Safred looked doubtful. "I'm not so good at climbing trees," she admitted. Bramble was amused to hear that the Well of Secrets had any flaws. "There's an easier way," she said. "It's simple. Just tie a rope around your middle, toss the other end to Zel and let her drag you across. Or if she's not strong enough, she passes it around a tree over there, throws it back and we all haul on it. Doesn't matter what you see or what you smell while you're going over, you'll be across in a moment and back to your senses."

"It's a risk," Cael said thoughtfully. "That cat thing might be waiting for the first one over."

"I'll go first," Bramble said.

"No," Safred said. "We need you. We can't risk you." She looked at Cael.

Silently, he took rope out of his saddlebags and prepared to throw it to Zel. Safred's eyes clouded for a moment and then she shook her head as if to clear it. Asking the gods? Bramble wondered. If so, she hadn't got an answer. Her face was hard to read. This was her uncle, after all, Bramble thought. She had to be worried, even if she didn't show it. Or was she so used to being controlled by the gods that she didn't fear anything they didn't tell her to fear?

Zel pushed herself to her feet and caught the rope Cael threw over easily, then passed it around a nearby pine at waist height and threw both ends back. He caught them and tied one end securely around his waist. They took hold of the other end and held the rope taut. Zel positioned herself at the tree to make sure the rope didn't catch on anything.

Cael walked back a few paces from the stream.

"I'm going to take a run-up so I'm moving fast when I hit the water," he said. "Ready? Pull!"

He ran at the water and they had to haul quickly on the rope to keep it tense. As his feet splashed into the stream his steps faltered. Unlike Zel, he kept going, but he slowed down and put his arms out in front of him as though warding something off. Bramble was closest to the stream and she hauled hard on the rope, jerking Cael forward.

"Pull!" she commanded and they pulled together, leaning into the rope and walking backward up the path. Cael was drawn forward across the stream but he went in staggering paces, arms frantically trying to clear something from in front of him as he went. He grunted with effort as he swept his arms from side to side. A couple of times he jerked as though he had hit something. He stepped sideways and the rope went slack. He was only a few steps from the bank. Zel was shouting at him, waving her arms near his face, balancing precariously on a rock at the water's edge, all her tumbler's agility called into play. He didn't react to her at all.

"Pull!" Safred shouted and they pulled more desperately, tightening the rope and dragging him facedown into the water. The smell of the stream became much stronger, making them gag. Then he was flung up in the air, his arms flailing, by a force none of them could see, although they felt the strength of it as the rope was jerked through their hands, burning as it pulled. Cael was thrown up and forward, as dogs who are gored by a boar fly through the air from the boar's tusks. He landed heavily on the side of the stream. His shoulders were above the stream and Zel grabbed them and hauled him as they pulled the rope. As though aware of her for the first time, he rolled to his hands and knees and shuffled himself out of the water, then collapsed on the ground, his hands shaking as he tried to undo the rope.

There were scratches all over his face and his clothes were ripped across the chest. A long, shallow gash cut across the width of his body. It looked much like a tusk wound, Bramble thought, widening as it went from a narrow point. He had been very lucky.

"Are you all right?" Safred called. He nodded and touched his face. Blood was welling in a dozen scratches.

"Uncle? Can you talk?"

"I always told you to get outside and play more when you were little. You should have listened to me and climbed a few trees while you could because, niece, I think you should climb one now." Cael was trying hard to speak light-heartedly, but long tremors wracked him, the aftermath of terror.

"What was it?" Martine asked, but he shook his head, shuddering at the memory.

"Tell me," Safred said urgently, her eyes intent.

He smiled shakily at her. "At last, I have a secret that you want! But this is not the time, niece."

"Tell me," she said again, pleadingly.

He shook his head. "Never mind about it now. Just rig up that rope and hold on tight."

Safred's face was a mixture of exasperation and thwarted desire. Bramble realized that knowing things, being *told* things, was as necessary to Safred as breathing. She was called the Well of Secrets because once told, the secrets were never spoken of again, disappearing as if into a deep well; but she drew those secrets to her more like a whirlpool than a well. She sucked them in as though they were air to breathe. Martine was staring at Safred, too, as though comprehending the same thing. She saw Bramble looking at her and raised an eyebrow, as if to say, "Interesting, isn't it?"

Cael tied off the rope around the pine tree they had used as a pulley and Martine pulled the rest of it back to their side. She looked doubtfully at the nearest tree. Bramble took the rope from her, exasperated, then took a rein from Zel's chestnut and tucked it into her belt.

"Don't tell me *you* didn't climb trees when you were a youngling either?" she said as she swung up onto the lowest branch. Fortunately, near the stream the pine branches grew close to the ground and were relatively easy to climb.

Martine didn't respond, but Zel answered for her.

"Travelers don't, mostly," she said. "You get yelled at if anyone sees you. Sometimes they throw rocks."

Bramble sniffed. She had been yelled at more times than she could count, climbing other people's trees, but no one had ever thrown rocks at her. Because she wasn't really a Traveler, just Maryrose's wild little sister. Gods she hated that whole way of thinking about Travelers! It stank like rotten fish. She put her anger into her climb and ignored the scratches from the pine twigs and bark. At a point where a branch had broken away, leaving a gap they could swing through, she attached the rope firmly to the trunk, making sure it was lodged securely on the stub of the branch. The line stretched tight right across the stream. She would have to bring her legs up at the end, though, to stop them splashing in the water as she landed.

She balanced on the branch below and doubled the rein, then flipped the doubled length over the rope and caught it with her other hand. She understood the theory. You were supposed to hold on to the rein and your body weight would slide you down the rope to the other side. From here, the rope looked frayed and the rein too thin. Break your neck, or simply fall into the stream and be ripped apart by whatever had attacked Cael. She grinned, feeling her blood fizz with the familiar excitement of danger, and launched herself from the tree.

The rush through the air was dizzyingly fast. Bramble tried to bring her legs up in time so that they did not hit the water on the far side of the stream, but just as she began to lift them, something invisible grabbed her ankle and yanked. She fell into the water with a flurry and splash that blinded her.

Scrambling to her feet, she blinked the water from her eyes and found that the something was not invisible after all. It was a man—no, a woman—no, a *something* almost human which stood, lounging, on the bank, laughing at her dishevelment and her astonishment.

Everything around her had changed, and she was caught in a surprise so profound that it left no room for other emotions.

Movement caught her gaze, and the being on the bank looked with her, still laughing. Fleeing through the trees was a herd of brown deer, but of a kind she had never seen before, with a broad white stripe down their back and black legs. They bounded over bushes and fallen trees, through undergrowth which masked the rest of the Forest. What had been pine trees were now elms. There were birds singing. Thrushes. The stream was narrower, and clearer, the water less brown, the stones rougher under her feet.

Her companion had a long knife in its hand. A stone knife, the kind that never dulls. It looked sacrificial. As she thought it, the laughter stopped. The person on the bank looked at her and smiled a kind, terrifying smile. It was thin, and no taller than she, and beautiful the way a hunting cat is beautiful, the way a hawk is beautiful as it hovers, waiting for the kill. There were hawk's feathers woven into its hair, so that she could not tell where the feathers stopped and the hair began, and its eyes were gold and slitted like a hawk's. Behind her, the undergrowth rustled and she wondered how many of them there were, and why she was still alive. Astonishment gave way to acceptance. If it was her time to die, so be it.

"Will you not run, as the deer run?" it asked. Its voice was warm and oddly husky, as though it spoke little.

Bramble shook her head. "I have done running," she said. "If you want to kill me, go ahead." She knew the edge of the stream would get her back to her own people, her own—what, time? place? world? She also knew she couldn't get to the edge of the stream before that wicked blade took her throat. She wasn't inclined to run for its amusement.

Concern filled its eyes but it came a step closer. Its bones moved oddly under its skin, more like a cat than a person. Another step. It raised the knife to her throat but did not touch her.

"There must be fear to cleanse the death," it whispered.

Bramble knew that she should be shaking in terror, but the feeling refused to come. She wasn't good at fear, never had been. With the roan and Maryrose both gone, there was nothing in this life she would mind leaving. It would take more than the threat of death to make her afraid. As though it recognized the thought, the hunter frowned.

"There must be fear," it repeated. It increased the pressure on Bramble's throat until she felt a runnel of blood make its way down her skin.

"I've been dead," Bramble said. "There are lots of things worse than a clean death."

It began to shake, its face crumpling with uncertainty. "Without fear, the death is tainted. The hunter becomes unclean."

"Then don't kill me."

"But the Forest requires it. All who see us must die." Then it cocked its head as though listening. "If I do not kill, I betray . . ."

Bramble listened too. Around them, everything became quiet. The thrushes stopped their trilling, the wind died, the stream itself seemed to pause. Then a shiver came through the trees, not from the wind but from the earth, a shiver that passed *up* the trees and lost itself in the gray sky above. Bramble felt that a message had been sent, but in a language she could not hear. The golden eyes filled with tears which trickled slowly down its face, as though the message had been one of great grief. It lowered the knife and slowly slid it into a belt sheath.

"I may not kill you now. The Forest knows you, Kill Reborn. You may travel safely here."

"And my friends, too," Bramble demanded. "And our horses."

It nodded. "If you will it. But the Forest says, move swiftly. The time is almost ripe."

It drifted back toward the undergrowth, and as it went, the scent from the stream intensified.

"Wait," Bramble said. "What *is* that smell?"

It laughed bitterly. "Memory," it said. "Memory and blood."

She took a step forward to follow it, to ask it more about the Forest, but the step took her from the elms back to the pines, to a blue sky above and Cael grabbing her hands, hauling her out of the water.

"How long was I there?" Bramble said. Safred and Martine, on the other side of the stream, opened their mouths to ask questions but Cael waved them silent.

"Only a moment. How long was it for you?" he answered.

Bramble considered. "A few minutes, maybe. Hard to tell. Long enough to almost be killed."

"What did you see?" Safred called. Her face was intent.

"Later," Bramble said. "There was a message from the Forest. Travel swiftly, it said. The time is almost ripe."

"Aye," Cael said grimly. He called to Martine. "Keep your legs well up, lass, when you come over."

Bramble shook her head. "No, it should be all right now. The Forest has given us leave to travel."

Immediately, Safred plunged into the stream, crossing in a few strides without incident. She reached the other side and Cael took her hand to haul her up. He grinned at her.

"Should have gone first if you wanted to know what was out there, girl," he said. She looked sideways at him, annoyed.

The smell had gone from the stream. Martine led the horses to the water and this time they ambled across willingly, snatching mouthfuls as they went.

Safred laid her hand on Cael, her eyes closing. Martine said quietly to Bramble, "Healing him," and Bramble nodded. Safred opened her mouth to sing and Bramble felt a shock go through her when the song came: grating, horrible, somehow familiar. She turned to Martine.

"Is that how she healed me?"

Martine nodded. "With a little help from Ash."

Knowing how horrendous her own injury had been, Bramble expected Safred to deal with Cael's scratches easily. But the song continued, louder, and Safred was frowning. Cael looked down at his chest, where the long gore mark stood out livid against his skin. It began to bleed. Sluggishly, then faster and stronger. His face paled and he reached up to grip Safred's wrist. She stopped singing and her own face was so white each freckle showed up clearly.

"They are not there," she said. "The gods are not there."

There was such desolation in her voice that Bramble went to her instinctively and put a hand on her shoulder.

Safred looked at Bramble's hand. It was scratched and bleeding from climbing the pine tree. Safred touched it lightly and closed her eyes. The scratches disappeared, fading away completely, just as her shoulder wound had. Safred didn't even need to sing.

Her eyes opened full of relief, but as she looked at Cael, she was at a loss. "I don't understand. They were there, easily, then. For Bramble."

"But not for me," Cael said. His face was unreadable.

"You said," Bramble reminded Safred, "that whatever guides you is weak in the Forest. Perhaps a wound that the Forest has inflicted is beyond their power here."

"You got that scratch from the Forest."

Bramble shook her head. "Not from the Forest. Just from a tree. There's a difference."

Cael shook his head as though it were too hard for him. He went to his horse, pulled a kerchief out of his saddlebag and mopped the blood from his chest.

"Enough," he said. "If the Forest wants me to bleed, then I'll bleed. Let's get going."

Safred studied him with a worried face, but eventually she nodded.

In silence, they mounted up and followed the trail before them.

"Me first this time, I think," Bramble said and Safred nodded agreement.

"Quickly, then. The lake is not far now."

THE HUNTER'S STORY

I WAS THE FIRST the fair-haired invaders killed here, but of course I did not die. I think the blue-eyed people did not understand what I was; where I was; when I was. I have heard that there was no Forest where they came from; only trees, here and there, lonely and longing for the Wood.

So perhaps they did not understand about me; us; all of us who are the Forest. They were surprised when I did not fall as they hacked at me; they became afraid and ran. Their running became part of me, as the running of the aurochs is part, and the running of the deer. All the hunted are part of me, because how else can I be a hunter?

Only the hunter who knows the fear of the chase can feel the true, pure victory; only the hunter who pays for his prey with terror is washed clean of guilt. To feel what they feel; to run as they run; to die as they die is the only way. If you hunt without it, you too will die in turn, as the humans do.

It is not hard to kill. The hard part is to do so while feeling all that the prey feels, and yet keep the clarity of purpose that allows the killing stroke, the slash of the knife to the perfect spot which will cause the least pain.

I remember my first kill. Who does not? It was so long ago that the Forest itself was different. I remember the cycads and the ferns. I remember the big lizards, which were never hunted, because they did not fear as we did. Their feelings were so far from us that it was never clear if we were clean after, so the flock leader ordered us to leave them alone. To prey only on the warm-blooded ones, who were enough like us, social and grouping together and fearing sharply the rustle in the bushes which said the killer was hiding, waiting, watching . . .

Blood is good when it is warm. Just one sip is all we need. Blood is life and more than life—the knowledge of life, which is what the animals lack and we provide for the Forest. Only those who kill understand life completely; only those who witness the eyes as they dull know the value of what leaves the body with the last breath.

Predators are the cull: we keep the bloodlines clean, the herds healthy, the memories alive. All the memories. None we have killed is forgotten. None we have killed truly dies. Each of our hunts lives forever in the Forest, in the special places of remembrance. We live there, also, alive at once in a dozen times, alive only at the times of the hunt, feeling again each kill: the aurochs, the deer, the boar, the humans. The humans feel fear the most vividly and are hardest to encompass in the moment of death, but we can do it. We must. The Forest requires us to kill all those who see us, so we have learnt how to kill men.

I know how to kill humans, but not the Kill Reborn. She had no fear. In all the untold years I had never met prey that had no fear of me. It changed me, that moment. To look into a human's eyes and see only calm, acceptance, interest—that is not what a hunter sees. But I had seen it. So what was I now? If I were not a hunter, did that mean I was a mortal, like her, subject to death as she was? I feared so. I knew I had to follow this Kill Reborn until I could taste her fear, until the Forest allowed her death. For all humans die. Then I would be a hunter again, and cleansed, and the memory of her death would join the other memories of my hunts.

Memories of death are eternal, kept in the Forest until the sun becomes ripe and is eaten by the gods. The Forest itself is smaller than it was; the places of remembrance fewer and busier than they were, with memories circling through them faster than in the past. This is due to the fair-haired men. But the Forest has withstood much in the past: fire and flood and ice. What is a thousand years? Nothing. Always it has recovered, and it will recover from this. Because we know, we hunters, that if necessary, we could take back the Forest land from the newcomers. I alone culled those first fair-haired men, and we could kill the others. We have had practice.

Although holding their fear and their pain would stretch us, we could do it, if we had to. If we were asked to. If the Forest woke.

LEOF

WITH THISTLE UNDER him and seeming to have taken no hurt, Leof felt steadier, more competent. His clothes were mostly dry by now, which also helped. He followed the directions the horse detail had given him and found the road to Baluchston only ten minutes' ride south. He swung onto it, joining the remnants of Thegan's army, all of them looking bedraggled and quite a few still dazed.

Wherever he could as he passed, he identified sergeants and told them to organize the men into squads so that by sunset, as they approached the outskirts of the town and could see the Lake again on their left, he was at the head of a reasonably well-ordered force, although the men were marching slowly and showed the tell-tale signs of exhaustion, shuffling feet and hanging heads.

"Fire and food in camp," he encouraged them and was as glad as they were to see the tents and campfires which marked their goal.

He coaxed a canter from Thistle and went ahead to alert the sergeants-at-arms who would be responsible for billeting the men. Several men hailed him boisterously as he entered camp, comrades from both Sendat and Cliffhold. He greeted them with a similar relief. Not all gone. Not all dead.

In fact, looking around he realized that the Lake had been remarkably merciful. There were far more men gathered here than he had expected. He had been stationed almost at the far end of the Lake, and his ragtag assortment of men were the last in. Although their numbers were much diminished, Leof reasoned that at least half the survivors were still on the other side of the Lake, the Cliff Domain side. If what he saw around him represented the other half, then they had not been as badly hurt as Hodge had suggested. Perhaps he and his men had, indeed, taken the worst beating.

He dismounted and handed Thistle's reins to a young ostler with a nod of thanks.

"Where's my lord?"

"In his tent," the boy said. Leof was reminded for a moment of Broc, but put the thought aside. There were always casualties in battle.

He found Thegan's tent easily enough. It was placed in the center of camp. It looked just as it always did on campaign, the brown canvas with gold ties at the corners both workmanlike and impressive, just like my lord Thegan. Leof hesitated at the door flap, then went through.

Thegan was seated at his map table, three of his officers behind him. Leof recognized them and was relieved to see them. They were older than he was, and sensible. He was sure they would see the folly of razing the town.

Thegan looked up as he entered and jumped to his feet.

"Leof!" He strode around the table and clasped Leof's upper arms. "Gods be blessed!" He smiled with real pleasure and Leof smiled back, warmed and thankful in turn. This was the Thegan who had earned his loyalty.

Since that disastrous night when he had stopped Horst from shooting Bramble in the back, Thegan had been distant with him, particularly when he returned empty-handed after searching for her. He thrust down his guilt that he had in fact found her but let her go. That had been true disloyalty to his lord, and there was no arguing it away. He had wondered, uncomfortably, for weeks afterward, if he had acted merely to show her that he was not the killer for hire she thought. That her distrust of warlord's men was unfounded. But he thought, bleakly, that it was more likely that he was just too soft to take a woman prisoner. Particularly Bramble, so wild and reckless. It would have wounded his heart to bind her hands and force her back to serve the warlord.

Well, if he couldn't serve his lord by giving him Bramble, he would have to serve him some other way.

"My lord."

"How many did you lose?"

"I think about half my squad," Leof answered, sobered.

Thegan clicked his tongue and let go of his arms, moving back to the table and looking down at the map of the Lake that lay there.

"That's the worst we've heard so far," he said quietly.

"The wind was at our back, my lord," Leof explained. "The Lake needed to make sure we were knocked out."

Thegan looked at the other men, as though Leof's words were significant.

"You think it was the Lake, then?"

"Well, of course... what else could it be?"

"The town wasn't touched." Thegan's tone was grim.

"But, my lord, isn't it known that the Baluchston people have an agreement with the Lake? That it leaves them alone?"

"We know that they, unlike everyone else who settled this Lake, live in safety. The Lake is dangerous, I grant you that. So is the sea, and the storm. But to plan and execute an attack like last night took intelligence, and I do not believe that the Lake has that. Anymore than the storm does."

"Perhaps that is so," Leof said slowly, wondering for the first time why he had assumed that the Lake was acting on its own behalf, without guidance. Was it just the voice he had heard, or was it all the stories that were told about the Lake, stretching back centuries? Stories about attacking forces befuddled, turned around in the middle of battle so that they were fighting their own side, or gone missing altogether only to turn up weeks later, swearing they had no memory of the time in between. Those stories were part of every child's upbringing in the Domains, and so were stories about the mysterious Lake People, the only original inhabitants who had successfully resisted Acton's forces. And still did.

"Why should it be the Baluchston people who planned it?" Leof said. "Why not the Lake People?"

"The Lake People are nothing but Travelers who do not travel," Thegan said impatiently. "Do you think if they had power like that they would skulk in the reeds like water rats? Do you think they would let Baluchston stand and the ferries run across their precious Lake?" He shook his head. "No, if the Lake People controlled the Lake they would have taken it back from Baluchston long since. As they haven't, the control must reside in Baluchston."

"But what would they gain from attacking us?" Leof asked. He wasn't convinced, but he knew Thegan in this mood. No argument would change his mind.

"They hope to maintain their freedom."

"They have freedom. They're a free town."

Thegan looked at him, an amused twist at the end of his mouth. "They *had* freedom. They are clever enough to realize that if I hold both Central and Cliff Domains, and cleared the Lake, their freedom would mean very little."

Leof paused. The other men were carefully not reacting to that statement. Now was not the time to argue for the continued liberty of the free towns. Towns outside the warlords' control had always been a sore point with Thegan, despite the fact that Acton had established them himself to encourage trade between the Domains. Better to cut to the core of the debate.

"My lord, what if no one controls the Lake? What if it *is* intelligent?"

There was silence in the tent for a long moment. Thegan seemed to think about it, but Leof realized with a shock that he was only pretending.

"If it *is* intelligent," he said eventually, "then it will be pleased that we are ridding it of Baluchston. If it is not, then we will destroy those who control it. Each and every one of them."

Leof felt forced to protest. "What if it was only a few, or just one enchanter working on his own?"

Thegan did pause at that, then shrugged. "We'll give them a chance to surrender the enchanter and swear their loyalty. If they don't, we fire the town."

But if there is no enchanter, if the Lake is intelligent, then you have just invented the perfect reason to destroy a free town, Leof thought. He felt colder than he had when he woke that morning. Because he didn't know if Thegan really believed what he was saying, or if he had just seized the chance to take control of a free town without protest from the other warlords.

"Come, you look like you need some food and a sleep," Thegan said to him, once again the commander concerned for his men. "The men need a rest, too. Tomorrow will be soon enough to march on Baluchston."

SAKER

FOR THE FIRST few miles out of Carlion, Saker was surrounded by other carts, riders and people on foot. The roads, caught between dry-stone walls, were so clogged that the walkers were faster than the carts.

His disguise was perfect, except that he was traveling alone. So he stopped and offered a lift to an old couple carrying a baby. They accepted with relief. The old man climbed into the back of the cart with some help from Saker; the woman clambered up next to Saker with more agility. She carried the baby in a shawl tied around her chest. It was not a newborn. Its curly yellow hair waved in the breeze as it popped its head up out of the shawl and looked around. Saker hated it. It was the inheritor of Acton's brutality. With hair like that, it would never be treated like an animal. Never be spat at, or cursed, or refused service. He set his heart against it.

Then he wondered, why were they alive? Had they run away so fast that the ghosts hadn't got to them? He asked his passengers.

"Ghosts? No bloody ghosts, sir, they were demons from the cold hells! Ghosts can't do what they did!" the man shouted over the noise of the wheels on the rough road.

"They killed our daughter's husband, they did, right in front of us," the woman confirmed.

"And your daughter?"

"Oh, she's been dead these ten months, birthing this one," she said, smoothing down the baby's curls.

"They didn't attack you?"

"It was strange, it was," she said, thinking hard. "It was like we weren't even there. Like they only saw him. As though Lady Death had sent them specially to get him."

She sounded as though she didn't mind that idea. Saker gathered that the baby's father had been disliked. It worried him, though, that three blond people had been overlooked by the ghosts. Surely they couldn't be Travelers in disguise, too? He thought of the red-headed woman. He would have sworn she was one of Acton's people, but Owl had thrust her aside; protected her, until she threw her life away to protect the man. Useless sacrifice. But if she had old blood, if the blonds beside him had old blood, if so many of the inhabitants had that blood running in their veins...where did that leave his crusade?

Perhaps he could refine the spell. Set the barrier higher, so that only those with *enough* old blood would be protected. But how much was enough?

All day, he pretended to be a kind young stonecaster who had been caught in Carlion unawares. He delivered the old couple and the baby to the woman's brother's cottage in a village on the boundary of Three Rivers Domain, left amidst their effusive thanks, and found a room for the night at the local inn.

He sat in a corner of the common room and listened to the talk around him. It ranged from disbelieving to hysterical, from terrified to belligerent. No one spoke of anything but the stories from Carlion. They didn't realize where he had come from and he kept silent rather than be deluged with questions. Halfway through the evening the door opened to let in a family: parents and two young girls, just out of childhood, both with light brown hair like their father. They were carrying bundles of cloths, with oddments sticking out of them: a candlestick, a tinderbox, an empty waterskin. He knew instantly that they were from Carlion, and as soon as the innkeeper realized it, too, she bustled them off into the corner next to him and interrogated the parents.

"We don't know what happened," the man said. "We were sleeping, and then the door banged back and these...these *things*, like ghosts but real, burst in on us. They had swords, just like warlords' men!"

"I screamed," one girl said.

"It was like they didn't see us," the mother added. "They looked us over but they didn't see us. Thank the gods!" She began to cry, taking off her headscarf to mop up her tears and revealing, not the black hair Saker had expected, but pure gold. "They killed our neighbors. Both sides. Just slaughtered them in their beds. Half the town's dead!"

The older girl started to cry, too, but the younger set her mouth and sat closer to her father.

"We're not going back there!" the mother said wildly, and the younger girl nodded decisive agreement.

"It's shagging cursed," the girl said. The mother immediately scolded her for swearing. Saker saw the satisfaction on the girl's face and realized she had planned it that way, to stop her mother crying. She was of Traveler blood through her father, he was sure, even if her mother wasn't. But then why did the ghosts ignore the mother? He would have to smooth out any inconsistencies in the spell next time.

He wondered where to go next. He wasn't ready for Turvite. He would be, soon, but not yet. For Turvite, his army needed better weapons. Mostly they had scythes and sickles. They needed swords. He wouldn't find those in a free town. Inevitably, he thought about a warlord's fort. Fighting a warlord's force would garner many weapons. His army wasn't big enough to do that yet. But if he moved through Central Domain, gathering bones, he could take his force against Sendat, and get all the weapons he wanted.

Saker nodded, forgetting for the moment the red-headed woman who had betrayed her blood. Central Domain. He would stay here and aim for Sendat before autumn.

Then Turvite. He would succeed where the old enchanter had failed. He laughed to himself in the inn chamber. No one had ever been as powerful. His head swam. Loss of blood, he thought. Yes, a time quietly collecting bones would be good for him as well as for his plan. When they attacked Sendat, he would need lots of blood to raise his army.

BRAMBLE

ONCE THEY CROSSED the stream, the horses splashing through the shallow water, the Forest changed to a mix of trees, elm and oak and beech. Now, Bramble felt, she was moving in the Great Forest of her imaginings, the complex, vivid forest alive with bird calls and insect humming and the rustle of small animals and lizards. The trees were giants, particularly the beeches, a kind she had never seen before reaching huge arms to the sky. It could take minutes to move from one side of their canopy to the other. Here, the leaf fall from last winter was soft under the horses' hooves, and the heady, fragrant scent of damp spring earth was enough to make her light-headed.

As they went further along the track, there were more oaks and fewer other trees. Eventually they were riding through a forest entirely made up of oaks—vast, ancient trees that shaded the forest floor almost as thoroughly as the pine trees had. But this part of the Forest wasn't gloomy. The green of the oak leaves and the way they shifted in the breeze let little pockets of light dance across the ground between the trees, which meant there was grass and small plants covering the ground. There were snowdrops, primroses and daffodils.

Her surroundings should have filled Bramble with happiness. But underneath the surface, she could still sense—something. The sense of being *listened* to was very strong. Not exactly watched, the Forest had no eyes. But it was paying attention to them, and the sensation was not pleasant. Somewhat like the pressure of the gods in her mind, but far more alien. The sense of time—endless, unchanging time—was very strong, and made her feel like a mayfly, so short-lived that her life was worth nothing. She and her companions were there on sufferance, and only because she was the Kill Reborn.

The Forest respected killing and its aftermath. The flutter of birds above, the buzzing of insects, the rustle of animals in the undergrowth, these were all sounds of death as well as life. Each of those animals was hunting and being hunted. Bramble had always accepted that she was part of a great intricate web of life and death, of prey and predator, but she realized now that she had accepted it so easily because she had always been the predator.

She would stay that way, she decided. The prey fears, and she had learnt already from the hunter that, in the Forest, fear was dangerous.

Before them the track ended, in a wide circle obviously cleared so wagons could turn, although shrubs and saplings were springing up across the clearing. Beyond, there was only forest.

"Why would anyone bring a wagon all the way out here and then just turn around and go back?" Zel wondered.

"Not a wagon," Cael answered. "A sleigh. In winter, the trappers organize for supplies to be brought out. They meet the sleigh, and then it goes back." He spoke with a little effort, his chest wound still paining him. Safred looked concerned, but said nothing.

"So," Bramble said. "Where to now?"

"The lake is east of north from Oakmere," Safred said uncertainly, her eyes unfocusing as they did when she listened to the gods. Then she shook her head in disappointment. "That's all I know."

Bramble pointed ahead and to their right. "That's that way."

"That's not east of north," Cael objected.

"No. We've swung around a bit, following the trail. But it's east of north from Oakmere."

"How do you know?" Zel asked. The question surprised Bramble. She had thought that a good sense of direction was a gift all Travelers had. She had certainly inherited hers from her Traveler grandfather. It had only ever let her down once, in the pine forest near the Lake, and even there she had been mostly on the right heading. Explaining her certainty was curiously hard.

"I just know," she said.

Cael shrugged. "All right, then," he said. "Let's go that way."

Threading through the forest was much slower than riding on the track. There was more time to imagine eyes watching them. Ears listening. Noses smelling. The sense of being listened to, being observed, was getting stronger.

But at least the trees here were centuries old, and beneath them only ferns grew, and mushrooms, so the going was easy. They walked the horses under trees so tall that they were unclimbable, so densely leaved that the sun was invisible. The air grew close and hot, smothering. Bramble found herself becoming more and more tense, ready for an attack that never came.

They reached a stream where she thought they should water the horses, so she dismounted and turned to face the others as they came up. Then she saw that the attack had been going on all the time. Cael, who had been immediately behind her, was shaking with pain and weakness, his face clammy white. His shirt was stained with blood. She went to help him down, and he came heavily into her arms, leaning on her shoulder.

"Why didn't you *say* anything?" Safred said, helping Bramble to sit him down on the grass. Martine grabbed a cup from her saddlebag. She went to the stream to get water while Bramble eased the shirt away from the wound. It didn't look good: red and puffy and still bleeding sluggishly from the tip.

"The Forest is keeping the wound fresh," he said. "I can feel it. Nothing to be done."

Martine came back with the water. "I think it's safe," she said. "It doesn't smell of anything." Cael drank it gladly and held out the cup for more.

"If Safred can't heal him, we'd better get the Forest to do it," Bramble said. "Wait here."

She knew what she needed, and the edges of a stream were a good place to find them: feverfew, comfrey, heal-all, greenwort. It took her only a few minutes to find them all.

When she came back, Martine was tearing up a shirt for bandages and Safred was washing Cael's wound, but in an unpracticed way that made Bramble's mouth twist awry. Never had to learn simple healing, she thought. Just a moment with the gods and it all went away. Live and learn, cully.

"Make a compress of the heal-all and comfrey," she said to Safred, handing her the leaves. Bramble picked up the cup and crushed some of the feverfew leaves into it, then filled it from the stream and set it to steep on the ground beside Cael. "It won't be as good as a tisane, but I think we'd better not light a fire here."

He nodded with an effort.

"It's an odd wound," she said. "What made it?"

Safred paused as she wrapped some linen around the plants. Listening hard.

"I cannot name them," he said slowly. "They were big. Flying. But not birds. Not bats, either. No fur. Huge. Clawed. One almost took me as a hawk takes a chicken, but I twisted and —" He gestured to his chest. "Then *I* flew, for a moment!" He tried to smile, turning to Zel. "Then this little one dragged me out of there." She reddened a little and mumbled something inaudible.

They managed to get Cael back on his horse and he seemed a little better for the feverfew. Bramble gave the rest of the herbs to Safred and told her to make him a tisane tonight from the feverfew and greenwort.

"I have willow bark," Martine offered.

"Good. That, too, then. It will help him sleep."

"How do you know so much about healing?" Safred asked.

Bramble laughed at her. "Safred, almost every woman in the Domains knows what I know. When you have a sick baby or an accident happens, not everyone can run to the Well of Secrets to be cured!"

Safred flushed and let her horse drop back until she rode next to Cael. Bramble thought she should have felt worse about teasing her—Safred was genuinely worried about Cael. But she didn't. She was too caught up in wondering what would happen when they got to the lake. Surely there would be an altar?

She yearned toward it. She imagined a clearing. The black rock, the familiar presence of the gods. They would be safe there, and Cael could rest—perhaps Safred would find the strength there to heal him.

The light shifted to gold, even through the oak leaves, and the few shadows there were began to lengthen. The sun was setting. The land tilted sharply upward. They climbed a ridge and they were at the edge of the trees, as though the Forest had been cut off abruptly.

Beyond them there was water, surrounded by a ring of oak trees and then grass that sloped steeply up to the edge. After the darkness of the trees, the water shone brilliantly. Still as ice, it reflected better than any mirror, doubling the rose and pink and gold of the light, the small reddened clouds, the darkening sky. Not quite a lake but more than a pool, it was perfectly circular, and it was the strangest thing Bramble had ever seen.

At the margin, instead of mud or reeds or pebbles, a sheer edge rose up out of the ground, so that the whole lake looked like a big dish which had been almost buried and then filled with water. The edge caught the dying sun and glinted sharply.

In the very center of the water was a small island, with a black rock altar at its heart. Much larger than most altars, Bramble thought it would be at least chest high on her; perhaps higher. Colored the normal flat matte black, the rock it stood on gleamed darkly green.

Bramble swung down from Trine and patted her absently, then walked forward over close-cropped grass, down to the water. The rim around the lake was rock. Or glass. A mixture of both? She had never seen anything like it. A green so dark it was almost black, on the western side, facing her, it reflected every bit of light from the dying sun. She went closer, carefully, and squatted down to study it.

The rim came up above her knees, and the level of water within it was higher than the grass outside, as if the lake truly was a dish. She reached out, waiting to see if the gods would warn her not to touch, but although she could just feel their familiar presence in her mind, they exerted no pressure on her. The rock was mostly smooth—smoother than river stones, as smooth as glass—but cut across with rougher streaks like the darker stripes in marble. It narrowed to a thin edge at the top. She leaned over the edge to look at the inside of the bowl, and found herself staring into water so clear that she could see her own reflection and the bottom of the bowl at the same time, so that it looked as though she were lying on the floor of the lake, looking up. Like a water sprite.

That unsettled her. She pulled back and her wrist grazed across the top of the rim. The edge was so sharp that she didn't realize she had been cut until the blood started to drip; some on the grass, some on the rock rim, some into the water.

As the first drop hit the lake, a wind seemed to shiver across the surface, ruffling the perfect reflection. Bramble shivered, too. Whatever this place was, it was not the home of her familiar gods.

"How are we going to get out there?" Martine asked from behind her.

Bramble stood up, wiping the blood on her breeches.

"Look," she said.

As the sun dropped lower and the reflection paled, they could see that there were rings of rock leading to the island, like the edge around the lake, just under the surface. They weren't very thick, but they were each no more than a pace apart.

"Stepping stones?" Martine said doubtfully. "What if we fall?"

Bramble shrugged. "We get wet. And worse, maybe."

Safred, Zel and Cael joined them. Cael was pale but looked a little better now he was out of the trees. He bent down to peer at the rock rim.

"Obsidian," he said.

"Obsidian?" Martine repeated. "This is *Obsidian Lake*?"

"What's Obsidian Lake?" Bramble asked.

"It's where the first black rock altar fell from the sky," she replied, her voice faltering a little. "It's a place from Traveler legend. Not a place for people, they say. Only for the gods."

Martine was hesitant, and that was so unlike her that Bramble frowned.

"But the gods have brought us here, right?" she asked Safred, who nodded.

"Yes. We are where we are meant to be. We must do the work set out for us." Her certainty reassured them all, but Bramble made a face.

"You sound like my grandam."

"I'm sure she was a very wise woman."

"Wise enough," Bramble said, "to know the signs of the Spring Equinox."

"You have a good sense of time," Safred said thoughtfully. "That may be useful. Perhaps it's just as well you became the Kill Reborn instead of the one who was meant to."

"The one who was meant to?" Bramble felt something tighten in her, but not unpleasantly. It was as though she were about to have a question answered that she had wondered about for a long time. She didn't know what the question was; but the answer was important.

"The gods didn't tell you?" Safred seemed surprised. "You were supposed to die, you know."

"At the chasm?" She knew the answer. Of course at the chasm. She relived that moment: the men chasing her, the roan making that extraordinary, impossible jump, and halfway over, her own fall and the roan's shift in midair to save her. Then, afterward, the death-in-life existence she had led. The stonecaster in Carlion had told her—she had died, truly, and her spirit had left her, but the roan had saved her body. She would still be dead inside, if he had not run so fast in her first Spring Chase that she overtook the Kill, snatched his banner, and became the Kill Reborn, symbol of new life. Unlike the other Kill Reborns of history, who just won a race by a big margin, she had been truly reborn.

"Yes," Safred said. "The gods helped the roan make the jump, not you. The roan should have gone to Beck, so he could become the Kill Reborn."

"*Beck*?" The face flashed before Bramble's eyes—a thin, older man with brown hair and a small beard, the face that had led the pack which hunted her to the chasm. She remembered, too, the scars and marks on the roan's hide that Beck had laid there. "They were going to give him to *Beck*?"

"He was a good rider. Good enough to be a Kill Reborn. He had mixed blood, too, and was certainly a killer. He was suitable for this task."

Bramble was furious. "And too bad for the roan, given to a cruel master!"

"Yes," Safred said quietly. "Too bad for the roan. But the roan loved you and saved you, to have you instead. So we are here."

" 'Love breaks all fates,' " Cael quoted, a slight rebuke in his voice. Bramble knew he was trying to turn her anger away from Safred, and knew that he was right. This wasn't the Well of Secrets' fault. Nor, really, was it the gods'. They were doing the best they could to restore balance to chaos. It was Saker's fault, and he would pay.

She scowled, but looked out at the lake, watching as the ripple of wind died away and the surface returned to pure reflection.

"What did you mean," Martine asked, " 'he was certainly a killer'?"

Safred looked at her wryly. “Haven’t you wondered why you were chosen by the gods? It is because you are all killers, and have deaths to expiate.”

Zel hung her head, but Martine met Safred’s gaze coolly.

“I have killed only where I had no choice, to protect my life or the life of another,” she said. “I have no regret and no guilt.”

Safred nodded. “That is the attitude of our enchanter,” she said. “It is good that you share it.” Martine went still for a moment. Safred looked at Zel, then covered Zel’s hand with her own. Zel’s head came up.

“I did what I had to do,” she said. “I must pay for it.” Her mouth was firm and Bramble was reminded even more of Osyth. Zel was like stone, as Osyth had been, a person who could not be turned from her course by anything.

Then Safred looked at her.

“I didn’t mean to kill him,” she said. “I don’t think I have reparation to make.”

Safred kept looking at her, drawing her somehow so that all she could see was the bright eyes.

“I was not talking about the warlord’s man,” she said softly. “He was not the only one who died because of you.”

Abruptly Bramble was back in the field outside Pless, the roan’s head in her lap, the stream flowing past them, guilt and grief and pain pounding her in waves. It had been her fault, and she would live with that forever. She dragged in a deep breath and pulled herself back to the present. “I have made my apologies for that,” she said angrily. “It has *nothing* to do with you.” She was furious that this—this *woman* would use her love and grief for the roan to manipulate her. Let her rot in the cold hells, she thought. She doesn’t own me.

“ ‘No one wilt ever tame thee,’ ” Safred whispered.

Bramble breathed in sharply in shock, then was strengthened by her anger. “Shagging right,” she said. “Get another lackey.” Then she thought about Safred’s claim that they were there because of being killers. It made some deep sense that she couldn’t quite puzzle out. If the gods needed a killer, she would be a killer indeed; and Saker would be her victim. “After I do this thing with Acton,” she said, “can I kill Saker?”

"Who knows?" Safred said wryly. "No one's told me."

The black rock stood glinting sharply with light, bright where before it had been dark. It beckoned to Bramble, and to the others, too, she could tell. Martine shivered whenever she looked at it, and Safred completely avoided looking at it. But it won't go away, cully, Bramble thought. Not on your life, or on mine. Or on Maryrose's.

They had only minutes before it was time to walk out to the altar, but setting up camp seemed too mundane a thing to do when the lake shimmered in front of them, reflecting the darkening sky, the first evening star.

Bramble looked after Trine, glad to have something to do to keep her mind off those sharp ridges of rock and the clear water that seemed, somehow, so threatening. Trine was perfectly happy under the trees, but she would not move out onto the short grass that ringed the lake, and Bramble did not try to persuade her. Cael had already tethered the other horses to a tree.

"I'll set up camp while you do whatever it is you have to do," he said.

"When I come back, I'll try again," Safred said to him and he nodded before gently shooing her away to join the others.

Safred, Martine and Bramble walked slowly down to the rim almost an hour after sunset, moving toward darkness, with a sky of red and gold and purple clouds behind them. The evening breeze had picked up and whipped the water into small waves. It was chilly but not cold, breezy but not windy, dim but not dark, although the pale spring moon was hidden behind the clouds.

Bramble felt her spirits rising as the night grew wilder, felt a lifting of the heart that was as familiar to her as the beginning of a chase. She went first. She thanked Gorham for making her wear tough boots as her feet would have been cut to the bone at the first step up onto the rim. She found her balance and then stepped toward the next rim of rock. If she fell, she would die. She was quite certain of that, sure beyond words or reason. The gods confirmed it: *Walk carefully,* they said. *Come to us.*

Each step was precarious, and each grew harder as the light faded away. After a handful of steps, she looked back. Safred and Martine were poised on the ridges behind her, reminding her of the Wind City legend, the Sea Woman who walked on water. Bramble shivered a little. The Sea Woman was a nasty spirit, no friend to humans. She shook off the thought and started to enjoy herself, enjoy each moment her foot found the next stepping place and the quick excitement of shifting her balance with a hop so that she moved firmly onto the ridge and still kept her balance. The water was cold in her boots, and her feet began to go numb.

Halfway across, the moon emerged from the clouds and the lake became a bowl of silver, cupping them, the Forest beyond a dark wall. She had the sense that the water itself was curved upward, that the island truly lay in the bottom of a bowl. It felt dangerous, and Bramble was glad of it. The promise of danger gave her relief from mourning.

She was only three paces from the island, then two, and one—she stepped onto the darker surface of the island expecting to find dirt and grass. Instead, she slipped and fell as her feet slid out from under her. The island was made of the same smooth, dark green glass as the lake bowl. She looked up at the altar; it was fused into a spire of the rock so that she couldn't tell where the lake rock ended and the altar began. That felt unchancy. Wrong. She struggled up and planted her feet firmly on the rock, then helped Safred and Martine across safely.

She began to move toward the altar, but Safred stopped her with a hand on her arm.

"I don't know what will happen," she said, her voice low. "You will see the past, the gods say, but they don't say how."

Bramble shrugged. "Guess I'll find out soon enough."

Safred smiled tightly, and motioned her toward the altar. Breast-high, it was larger than any Bramble had seen. She came toward it with another familiar sensation. The gods were waiting. The pressure on her mind was there, as it always was at an altar; the hair-raising, spine-chilling stroke along the skin, *beneath* the skin. She took a breath with difficulty, like breathing under water, but before she could lay her hand on the rock, mist began to rise from the altar's surface.

Gentle wisps at first. Then deepening to fog, swirling upward in a column which flattened out to spread in a dome over them, coming down onto the water and moving outward, until the sky was blocked, and the land was invisible, and they were encased in a brilliant, moonlit cloud. Bramble shivered with a simple chill as the mist droplets settled on her skin.

The mist was unchancy, no doubt, but the gods were there, solid in her mind, and she knew the fog was to protect her. She just didn't know from what. They could hear the wind in the Forest, and the waves on the lake, but inside the mist everything was still. Gradually, the stream of mist died away and the altar was left bare, not even damp. She reached out and placed her hand on it.

"Martine," Safred said quietly. Safred had her listening look on, and Martine's face mirrored hers. She placed the brooch on the altar next to Bramble's hand. It clinked, softly, as she set it down and immediately the wind died in the Forest, the waves subsided, the trees ceased to whisper. There was complete silence as she spoke.

"This is mine by right, by gift. I cede it to you, to the gods of field and stream, of fire and storm, of earth and stone, of sky and wind." She paused then, and as though prompted further, added, "I cede it to the gods of water and memory, that good may come of evil, that life may come from death."

She took Bramble's hand and placed it over the brooch.

For a moment Bramble's hand was caught between the warmth of Martine's hand and the cold of the brooch, then Martine lifted her hand and Bramble's fingers curled around the heavy circle.

"Gods of water and memory, aid your daughter," Safred said, her voice very gentle. Then she began to speak in the guttural, screeching voice of the dead.

The world grew darker and the land rocked beneath Bramble's feet. The waves were rising. The mere was turning against them. In her head the pressure of the gods intensified. She didn't feel fear, because the pressure didn't leave any room for fear, but it did leave room for action. She turned from the altar and tried to warn the others but as she opened her mouth to tell them to run the waters rushed over them and she was drowning.

LEOF

IN THE VERY early morning, Leof woke in the officers' tent with his mother's voice whispering in his ear: "Go home, little one, go home . . ." His face felt surprisingly cold; when he raised a hand to his cheek he found that he had been crying, but he didn't know for what. His drowned men? His mother? He scrubbed all traces of the tears away, as embarrassed as a child might be, and rolled out of bed. The men around him were still asleep.

Even so early in the morning the latrine pits were busy. He made his visit and went to stand by the edge of the camp, looking toward the Lake, where the houses of Baluchston showed their roofs as black triangles against the paling sky. It was going to be a beautiful spring day. A good day for attacking a town, he thought wryly. A good day for destroying a thousand years of tradition. A thousand years of freedom.

He knew he had to talk to Thegan, and knew also that it would make no difference.

As a rider in the chases, he had loved it when the chases were held at the free towns, because they brought competitors from all over the Domains, all keen to see if their horses were the fastest. That was how he had met Bramble, at a chase in Pless. One of the most prestigious chases, because Pless was a horse-breeding area and had a strong local field as well as the riders like him who brought their horses from far and wide.

He liked the free towns. He liked the sense of purpose in them, even if the purpose was mostly about making silver. He liked the casual warmth of their people, the way they walked with heads high, unafraid. Since he had come to Central Domain he had noticed how few people looked up, in case they met the eyes of a warlord's man and were—what? Beaten for insolence, perhaps? It was not like that in Cliff Domain, where the warlord's men were a disciplined fighting force, respected for protecting their people against raids by the Ice King's men.

Perhaps my lord Thegan is right, he thought with a kind of despair. Perhaps what this country needs is to be brought together under the rule of one overlord, someone who knows how to keep discipline among his men, someone who could protect the rights of the ordinary people. But whether Thegan was the right person to do that, he did not let himself consider.

Leof knew that no matter what he said to Thegan, Baluchston's freedom was over. The best he could do was prevent the sacking of the town. There were lots of stories about the sacking of towns from earlier wars between Domains—Leof didn't want to be part of one.

He left the gradually lightening sky and went to Thegan's command tent. Dawn was usually a good time to catch Thegan alone.

Thegan looked up from a pile of papers as Leof entered, and smiled at him.

"Just the man I need," he said. "I want a thorough tally of who we have lost so that the families can be informed. You know most of the men, don't you, even the Centralites?"

"Yes, my lord," Leof answered by rote. Then he took a breath and plunged in. "But there is another duty I would prefer."

Thegan leaned back a little from his table and pushed the papers away, his eyebrows rising. He looked mocking and suddenly older, as if Leof were an importunate child.

"Prefer? I don't remember asking your preference, officer."

There was a lump in Leof's throat, which he had to swallow down.

"My lord, I would ask that you let me parley with Baluchston. Let me convince them to surrender."

"To surrender the enchanter?"

Leof paused. He had to say this just right, or Thegan would take offense. "My lord, if I were that enchanter, I would have left the town long ago. The town may not be able to produce him."

"Then —"

"Then they must surrender to us, to prove their good faith," Leof said hurriedly. "It seems to me that no matter what they do, only the surrender of the town will prove their good intent."

Thegan smiled slowly. "That is very well thought out, Leof. Yes. Good. You may put that argument to the Baluchston Voice. I think they have kept the custom of a Voice, rather than a Mayor." He paused for a moment, considering that. "In fact, it could be argued that Baluchston is not, and never has been, a free town. It was not founded by Acton or his son. It keeps the customs of a village. It has no charter with any warlord." He smiled with genuine pleasure, seeing potential problems with other warlords disappear with that argument. "It has no claim on anyone's protection. Go and tell them so, and tell them that they have until noon to make up their minds."

Leof nodded and turned to go, his stomach churning. But he should have known Thegan would not let him go so easily.

"Leof?"

He made sure his face showed nothing as he turned back. Thegan was smiling, but it was the dangerous smile, the one that tightened the corners of his mouth but didn't reach his eyes.

"After you have parleyed, I want that list of the dead by noon."

Leof nodded. "Of course, my lord."

He left the tent with a sense of overwhelming relief, and realized that for a few moments he had been in as much danger as Baluchston.

"Hodge," he called as the sergeant went past. "My lord wants a tally of the dead. Get three of the men who can write to make a list. Then come to my tent with an honor guard. We're going to Baluchston."

He rode in on Thistle, with Hodge and three others on matching bay geldings, Thegan's honor guard horses which had somehow escaped the wave. Men and horses were as polished as a quick brushup could make them and the Baluchston people stopped in the street to look at them. Their expressions were odd: a mixture of fear and surety, as though they believed that, though the soldiers could try, nothing could hurt them. But the trying would be painful.

Leof had been an officer of one kind or another since he was eighteen, carrying the burden of ensuring his men's safety, but he had never felt responsibility weigh so heavily before. Not soldiers but townsfolk at risk... Riding through the town with everyone looking was like the beginning of a chase, when the competitors lined up in front of the crowd. He tried to feel some of the same exhilaration chasing brought, but the stakes were much too high.

Leof knew, theoretically, how to handle this. He could not stop and ask for directions to the Voice's house. Thegan would say that would show weakness. So they rode to the market square, which led directly onto the Lake shore and the ferry wharves. It was disconcerting, to have an open side to a town square, a side which moved and glinted as the current sent the Lake water downstream toward the high, impassable falls that plummeted to the Hidden River. The open side made him uneasy, as though the Lake were watching, as though the ground were shifting under his feet.

He stopped the small troop in the middle of the square and simply waited until, some minutes later, a fat old lady tramped out of one of the shops and came to stand in front of him.

"I'm the Voice," she said simply. "My name's Vi. What can we do for you?"

Her voice was dark and somehow comforting, the voice of the wise old women of the fireside stories. Wise old women are sometimes enchanters, Leof reminded himself. He gave the signal to dismount, swung down from Thistle and handed her reins to one of the men, patting her absently on the flank.

"I speak for the Lord Thegan," Leof said formally, bowing. "I would have speech with you on his behalf."

She nodded and led him toward the draper's shop from which she had emerged. A number of other townsfolk watched. Vi looked at them as though to invite them to join the discussion, but they shook their heads.

"Best you handle it, Vi," one called. She nodded and ducked into the dark interior of the shop.

Hodge began to follow them, but Leof signaled him to wait with the horses. Hodge didn't look happy but he obeyed. Leof relaxed a little. Better to have no witnesses to this.

"We don't bother with a Moot Hall," she said as she threaded her way past bolts of fabric, skeins of wool and a pile of cured sheepskins. "We generally have our meetings in here."

The room beyond was a light-filled kitchen, smelling of fried fish, centered around a large pine table, scrubbed white. Leof stood, unsure. The protocol of a warlord's fort he understood, but not that of a kitchen!

"Sit you down, lad." Vi smiled with real humor, as though enjoying his uncertainty.

Suddenly Leof laughed. Solemnity wasn't natural to him, and Vi's casual welcome suited him much better than it would have suited any of the other officers. Better to parley with humor and wisdom than with protocol and hostility. He sat down, not at the head of the table, but in the middle, and Vi, as though appreciating his tact, sat opposite him and poured them both some cha from a jug standing ready. Equals. His mouth twitched, imagining Thegan's reaction to that. That sobered him.

On the way into town, Leof had practiced a dozen different ways of beginning this conversation, but he discarded them all. It was clear to him that Vi knew why he was here.

"Well, now, my chickling," she said in her deep, comforting voice. "Here's a pretty pickle."

"He wants the town," he said simply. "And he'll take it, however he needs to. If you resist, he'll kill every one of you. Not one warlord will object. He'll make it sound so *inevitable* that they won't be able to."

Vi nodded. "So?" she prompted.

"So you should surrender. Save the lives of your people."

Vi's eyes were hooded as she looked down at her mug of cha, nodding. Then she looked up challengingly. "Might be that the Lake will have something to say about that."

Leof paused, not sure how to reply. Truth, perhaps, was all the weaponry he had.

"He doesn't believe in the Lake. He...he *can't* believe in it, I think."

She nodded. "Doesn't mean the Lake will ignore *him.*"

"He says it was an enchanter who called the waters up."

Vi sniffed with contempt, reminding Leof vividly of his aunty Gret. He paused, then said delicately, "The question is, *when* would the Lake act, and what would she do? She can't just inundate the town—that would cause more deaths than Thegan. What can she do to protect you?"

"You don't know?" Vi seemed surprised. "Hmm. Well, best not to tell you, then, I think." She thought it over. "I'll go talk to her. This is a decision best left to her."

"You only have until noon. After that, he attacks."

Vi drank her cha slowly, deliberately. "Better if he doesn't," she said just as deliberately. "Best if you stop him, lad. Or the Lake might do more harm than she has already."

The cha was good, and brought him a clearer head than he'd had since the Lake had risen.

"You're Acton's people," he said. "Are you sure she'll protect you?"

Vi laughed. "Oh, lad, we stopped being Acton's people a long time ago. We're Baluch's children. Baluch's and the Lake's. She'll look after us, don't you worry." She reached across the table with some effort, and patted his arm. "Looks to me like you might have stopped being one of Acton's people yourself."

He pushed back from the table and stood up, appalled. "I am my lord Thegan's man," he said furiously. "My loyalty is to him and to my comrades. I came to warn you, to convince you to surrender so that lives would not be lost needlessly. Do not impugn my honor!"

"Oh, lad," Vi said sympathetically. "You've got more honor in your little finger than Thegan has in his whole body."

"Until noon. You have until noon by the grace of your lord Thegan."

She shook her head. "He's no lord of mine, lad, nor ever will be. But I'll talk to the Lake and see what she says. Won't be back by noon, though. I'll have to go out to the deep water and that takes time. Sunset, say. I'll be back by sunset. Do what you can to stay his hand until then."

Leof turned on his heel and walked out without replying. Stay his hand? Might as well try to stop a storm. Baluchston was doomed.

ASH

Riding south out of Oakmere felt wrong to Ash. For one thing, he wasn't comfortable on a horse, and the chafing from his last ride was already making itself felt. For another, it felt disloyal to send Martine off with the others, even though he couldn't take her where he was going.

He had woken and gone through the process of leaving Oakmere with a fragile shell of normality carefully built around him. He pretended that nothing was wrong, but he knew that Martine wasn't fooled. Maybe not Bramble, either. But what could he do about it? He couldn't change who he was, no matter how many people he disappointed. Now, as he rode, it felt like there was an empty place on his belt, where the stones should have hung.

They had reached the beginning of the ascent to the Quiet Pass by the time he came back to himself.

"Um, south?" Flax asked hesitantly. "Just 'south'?"

Flax had apparently been waiting for his attention to return. The lad, it was clear, was good at reading moods.

"I couldn't tell her more. We're going to the place that is not talked about," Ash said, reluctant to say even that much. He shot Flax a glance and then looked more closely as he realized the words meant nothing to him.

"Where'd that be, then?" Flax asked.

"Your father must have taken you there?" Ash was astonished. Unless he had misunderstood, Flax had been on the Road all his life, and so had his parents until recently. But Flax shook his head.

Ash didn't know what to say. It wasn't his job to tell Flax about the Deep. It was his father's. In fact, it was forbidden to speak of it.

"Your father was a Traveler?" He had to make sure, before he said anything.

Flax nodded. "Aye, he were."

Flax was certainly talking like a Traveler, although back at Oakmere, he had chattered to Bramble as though he'd been born a blond. Ash shrugged that away. He spoke mostly like one of Acton's people himself, after intensive training by Doronit. Lots of Travelers spoke with two voices. But he had to make sure Flax had the right to go to the Deep.

"And your grandfather? Your father's father?"

"He died when Da were a baby. Da were brought up by his mam, Radagund the Horse Speller."

Even Ash had heard of Radagund. Flax was very proud of his famous grandmother. But it explained why he didn't know about the Deep. His grandfather had never taken his father there. But surely other Traveling men could have?

Delicately, he asked, "Was your grandam friendly with other Travelers?"

Flax shrugged. "I suppose. She worked mostly for Acton's people, though. Travelers don't have horses, much."

So, here he had a young Traveling lad who hadn't heard of the Deep. Well, there was no doubt he had a right to know, even if Ash wasn't the perfect person to tell him. But there was the prohibition against speaking of the Deep outside. He had to respect that.

"Before I tell you where we're going, you have to promise not to repeat anything I say. To anyone. Especially women. But not even to other male Travelers. If you do . . . you will die."

"What, you'd kill me?"

Ash looked down at the ground, then straight into Flax's eyes, mouth firm. "If I had to."

Flax's eyes widened, and then he grinned, as though it was an adventure.

"I promise."

Ash wasn't sure he trusted any promise from Flax, but he *was* sure that after the demons at the Deep had him, he would keep the secret.

"We are going to a place . . . a place where men go. Men of the old blood. Only men."

Strongly interested, Flax leaned forward in his saddle to stare more directly at Ash. Cam increased her pace in response, but Flax pulled her back to a walk.

"What for?"

Ash hesitated. "That depends. It's a craft thing. What they do depends on who they are...how they make a living. What do you do?"

"Me? Oh, I sing," Flax said.

Ash felt like he'd been thumped simultaneously in the stomach and the head. Why hadn't anyone *said*? Because Martine didn't know and the others didn't know it mattered.

"A singer?" he forced himself to ask, thinking, Please, gods, make him bad at it.

"Mmm," Flax said. He launched into a cheery song about a summer's day.

Up jumps the sun in the early, early morning
The early, early morning
The early dawn of day
Up wings the lark in the early light of dawning
The early light of dawning
When gold replaces gray.

Ash remembered his mother singing that song. He remembered learning it. Flax's voice rose as clear and full as a nightingale's. His tenor could have been designed to match with Ash's mother's soprano. Ash could hear his mother singing the words in his head, and they blended so perfectly with the beauty of Flax's voice that it brought tears to his eyes.

Ash knew, sickeningly, what would happen at the Deep. His father, finally finding the son who would complete their music, who would enable them to perform all those songs that needed two strong, perfect voices as well as the flute and drum. All the descants, all the harmonies, all the counterpoints. They could even sing the sentimental duets that the inn crowds so loved, because Flax wasn't their real son, so there was nothing unnatural about him and Swallow singing love songs together.

No doubt he would teach Flax *all* the songs.

"Come on, sing along," Flax said cheerfully, and started the second chorus.

For a long moment, Ash battled red rage: the desire to smash Flax's face, to leap upon him, drag him off the horse and slam his head against the road until there was no voice left to torment him. He shook with the desire, and the only thing that stopped him was the memory of promising Zel that he would look after Flax. Mud stopped in the middle of the road and shivered, too. Ash's hands clenched on the reins. It wasn't Flax's fault, he told himself. But he had to find someone to be angry with. The shagging gods! he thought finally, seizing on the idea with relief. They don't care who they hurt, what they do. *They're* the ones who brought us here. It's *their* fault.

With an effort, Ash took a breath and let it out, hearing Doronit's voice in his head saying, "Control. A safeguarder must have control." He took a second breath, a third, a fourth, and then felt calm enough to say, "I don't sing."

"Everybody sings!" Flax said, but his voice was uncertain as he looked at Ash's face.

Ash shook his head. "Not me."

Flax looked oddly at him, hesitating about whether to ask more questions. Ash felt both irritated and protective of him. The boy was his responsibility. He had promised Zel. Although she couldn't have known what it would require of him, he would keep his word.

"It's good that you're a singer," Ash said, with an enormous effort. "My father will be able to teach you what you need to know."

Flax nodded and stayed, blessedly, silent. As they continued up the long slope that led to the mountain ridge, passing the occasional cart or rider, Ash wondered over the fact that most people would think that fighting Sully and his friend when they were trying to capture Bramble was hard. That was easy, so easy, compared to *not* hitting Flax. Compared to handing Flax over, safe, to his father, and saying, "I have found a singer for you."

Which he must do. Because he had promised Zel. Then he wondered if Zel would thank him for that, if Flax found a way to Travel without her.

FLAX'S STORY

THAT NIGHT TWO years back it all changed, we were down the road apiece before I spoke up. "Sure you don't want to go on back?" I asked her.

Zel shook her head. "Never no more," she said, so quiet-like I could hardly hear. "Never no more in that place."

Well, we'd been Traveling together long enough for me to know when to keep my mouth tight closed, so I just hoisted the pack higher on my back and fell in step beside her.

It were a fine night, at least, and no suffering to be walking the roads under the new moon. I wished I could sing, but there were still three months to go then till my year was up. They say if a boy sings within a year of his voice breaking, it's gone for good. I wouldn't risk it, not for nothing. It's hard enough being without a voice for a whole twelvemonth—I couldn't keep me in my right mind if I lost my music for good and all. So we just walked.

After a few leagues, Zel stirred herself. "There's a good stopping place near the stream in the withy hollow," she said. "We'll lie there."

It were always Zel who decided where we stopped, where we went. When I were littler, I used to stravage her about it, but I know better now. 'Tisn't a thing in the world can push Zel from the path she's chosen. Earthquake wouldn't do it, nor death, neither, I reckon. Truth to tell, it were just being the little brer what made me tickle her about it anyway. I didn't know enough to make any choices. Now, I know more than she did then, and that's enough to know she chooses better'n me, most times.

Maybe not this time, though.

Maybe this time she were turning her back on a good thing, and maybe it were for me.

See, there were this man in the last town, in Gardea, and he were head over ears taken with Zel. Hanging around the tavern every night, digging in his purse for silver, clapping hard after we finished juggling and tumbling. Oh, he were smitten, hovering like a honey wasp over fallen fruit. Aegir, his name was. A cobbler.

Well, she's never one to turn a good-looking man away, not our Zel. So she went off with him one night, two, then three, but always came back before morning, grinning like a cat.

On the fourth night she came raging in, kicked the straw into a heap and threw herself down onto it loud enough that I knew she wanted to talk. We didn't have a lantern—not many tavern keepers let us have a lantern in the stable, for fear of fire—but my eyes were dark-ready, and I could see she was fuming.

"He wants to *marry* me!" she said, fierce and low, like it were an insult, like our own parents wasn't good and married before they had us.

"I said to him, 'You don't know me,' and he *laughs*. He laughs and says, 'Sure I know you, lass, inside and out.' Thinks he's so clever!"

"So what'd you say?"

"I didn't say. I just got on up and walked right out of there."

She settled down to sleep as though she'd finished even thinking about it, but I couldn't. I could see that cobbler, not understanding, lying bewildered in the dark somewhere.

Next night he were there, waiting for her after the act. But she pushed on past him like he were thin air, and we grabbed our packs and took the road, with him following like a duckling after its mam, shaking his head and trying to get her to speak with him. Zel kept her mouth tied up and her eyes down until he dropped back, still bewildered.

Myself, I think if he hadn't said he knew her, she mighta stayed. She don't like being known, our Zel. She don't like strangers knowing her business, she don't like family, even, knowing what she's thinking. Much less a cobbler from a tavern. She mighta stayed a bit, if he hadn't said that.

Not for long, 'cause she's a Traveler; or maybe she thinks she has to be one, because of me. There were no room in that cobbler's life for a brer who can't earn his keep 'cept by juggling in the taverns.

She knows I couldn't live in a town year round. It were hard enough the winter before, living with Mam and Da because I caught a killing fever, and couldn't take the road. I couldn't survive a spring indoors. But I think she were walking so hard away from that place 'cause some part of her wanted to stay, wanted that cobbler and that nice featherbed instead of straw in the stable with me. I thought, maybe some day that part'll be stronger than the part that wants to take the Road with me.

When we got to the stream near the withy hollow, there was Travelers already there. But it were near moonset, and we was tired, so Zel just went on down and said the Travelers' greeting, "Fire and water."

There was three of them, a mam and two brers, twin men fully grown. They had a fire going well, and they was roasting turnips and hedgehogs.

They nodded at Zel, and then at me. "Fire and water and a roof in the rain," the mam said, very polite. "Share our fire." Which were nice of her, for, say what you will, there are Travelers on the Road I wouldn't sleep easy near, let alone opening the fire circle to.

Zel looked sideways at her and at me, but we sat down and spread out our food: waybread and dried apples and ewe's cheese. We all shared and ate merrily enough, then Zel got out her little balls and juggled a time or two, for thanks.

They were tinkers, they told us. The mam was Aldith, and the twins were Ber and Eldwin. They were like as the two wings of the one bird, both dark-haired and dark-eyed, but the one, Eldwin, was a tad more heavyset and looked after Ber, passing him food like Zel did for me. The mam, too, fussed over him some, though he seemed hearty enough, and laughed a lot.

We sat, staring at the fire, like you do after a long day and a hard walk. It were peaceful, for a time. Then a cold shiver passed right through me and I looked up. It were quiet, suddenly. The mam and Eldwin was watching Ber, holding their breaths.

Ber shook his head, his eyes gone blank and wide in the firelight. I felt behind me for a heavy bit of wood, for I've seen men's eyes go like that in a baresark fury, but he didn't move. The fire dipped down to embers, like something was eating the light.

Eldwin said, "Oh, protect us from demons." The mam just moaned a little and rocked to and fro. Zel was tense beside me, ready to run or fight. Then Ber spoke.

"This fire circle," he said, "is closed to murderers." His voice were quiet and pleasant, like you'd say 'morning to a friend. Like he didn't know what he were saying. "There is a murderer here," he said. Next to me, Zel had her hand on her boot knife, easing it out of the sheath.

"A kin murderer," Ber said, or maybe it wasn't Ber, 'cause he were foaming a bit at the corners of his mouth, and the mam were rocking hard and stuffing her shawl in her mouth to stop herself from screaming.

"Why didst thou kill thy mam?" Ber asked Zel. She'd let go the knife and were staring at him like he were the entrance to the cold hells itself. I had no breath in my body, and my heart pounding were like a wind in my ears.

"Why didst thou kill thy mam?" the thing inside Ber asked again, its eyes fixed on Zel. She were sweating and shivering, both, as she resisted that voice.

"Why didst thou kill thy mam?" it asked, and no living being coulda denied it an answer.

"She was going to kill Flax!" Zel shouted suddenly. "She had the pillow over his face, smothering the life out of him. It was her or him." She quieted. "Her or me," she said. "Her or both of us."

"This fire circle," it whispered, "is closed to murderers."

Then it left Ber, as swift as it came, and the warmth came back to the night air and the fire sprang up high again. Ber closed his eyes and fell sideways. Eldwin leapt to catch him. They laid him down on the grass and poured water into his mouth and patted his cheeks until he stirred.

The mam looked at Zel and me, sitting frozen in our places.

"Wind at your back," she said. The Travelers' farewell. So we took our packs and we walked out of the hollow and onto the cold road without another word.

We walked along in silence.

"It were true, Flax," she said finally. "It were her or us."

"Because of me," I said. "Because you wouldn't leave me."

"She were mad on silver, you know that. Having us both to stay all winter, it were too much for her. Eating them out of house and home, she said we was."

"Because I were sick," I said. "If I'da been well we coulda taken the Road."

"That's so."

There's nothing on Earth or under it can sway Zel once she's made a choice. She made up her mind a long, long time ago that I were hers to look after, hers to guard. This were no different.

But I'm not the little brer I were. Already I'm taller than her.

Walking down that road, all I could think on was, sometime or other, my choice and Zel's choice would go different ways.

And what then?

BRAMBLE

BRAMBLE BECAME AWARE of a light. A candle floating in a small dish of water. Darkness around it, and everything blurred. She tried to look at the candle, but her eyes wouldn't obey her. They looked up, instead, to the horse that was standing quietly before her. Bramble assessed it automatically, the part of her mind that Gorham had trained noting its points: a short, stocky bay mare, a pony, really, but with heavy bones and a thick coat, bred for endurance in a cold climate. Her hands, of their own volition, rose to fasten the strap of the bag attached to the front of the saddle, but her eyes remained fixed on the saddle, as though she could do this job without thinking about it. As she could, normally.

It was a strange saddle, with a high pommel that formed two horns at the front and a matching pair of horns at the back. The stitching was large and it had a single girth plus a breastband and a breech strap which went around the rump. This saddle was clearly designed so the rider would find it hard to fall off. It was well-made and solid and would be reassuring to the rider. But Bramble knew there was no saddle like it anywhere in the Domains.

The saddlebag attached, her eyes dropped to her hands. A man's hands. Abruptly she was aware of her private parts. Oh, gods, that felt so...*wrong*.

She never allowed herself to be afraid, but now she was, even while she recognized that what she was seeing and feeling was the result of the spell. She was *inside* someone—maybe one of her ancestors? Seeing what he saw. The pony moved with a slight jingling of bridle. I'm hearing what he heard, she thought. She could smell, too, the familiar scents of a stable with another odor underlying it. The tallow candle, maybe, made from an unfamiliar animal.

Not only sight and smell and hearing, but everything else, too. Bramble realized that "her" heart was beating fast. The man was excited, or anxious, or happy. She didn't know which. Couldn't guess. Couldn't, thank the gods, hear his thoughts. All she could do was observe.

She tried hard to make him drop his gaze to the floor. But no matter how much she concentrated, her will had no effect.

Like a familiar embrace grown suddenly too tight, she felt the presence of the gods. Were they warning her to make no changes, to leave everything as it was? She stopped trying to control the man, and the pressure eased immediately.

Instead, she felt the gods' attention turn to the doorway, which opened to let a woman enter. She was bundled up, with a baby in a sling across her chest, and Bramble couldn't see her face within the hood made by her shawl.

The woman came forward into the small circle of light, skirting the horse casually, with a hand on its rump. It flicked its ears at her and whoofed a great breath out in a friendly fashion. She moved toward where the man stood.

"Gris," she said, putting back her shawl. She was very young and beautiful in that corn golden way of Acton's people, eyes like a summer sky and cheeks as pale as milk. Bramble had always disliked girls like that—they were often stupid and flighty, too obsessed with their own good looks to notice anyone else. But this girl was staring at the man with great concentration. Oddly, it felt like she was staring into Bramble's eyes, yet couldn't see her.

"Asa," he replied. Bramble felt sick to her stomach. It was a horrible thing, to feel one's lips move and words come out without any control. She remembered for a moment the Traveler boy in the inn in Sandalwood, who had been taken over by a demon. Had it been like this for him? She tried to pull back from the man's body, to reduce her awareness of him to what he saw, just what he saw. She was a little successful. The feel of rough cloth against his back receded. The sense of his genitals faded a little. At least he wasn't attracted to the woman. As soon as she had come in his heart had slowed, and her beauty made no impression on him at all. Asa, Bramble thought. That was the name of Acton's mother. She was reliving the past.

For the first time, she wondered if perhaps she could *change* history.

If Acton died now, the Domains would never be invaded. The original inhabitants would be safe. Perhaps Acton's people would die instead, she thought. They are both my people. At that thought, the pressure from the gods increased, as though they were agreeing with her. She relaxed. I will make no changes, she promised them. I will merely watch, and discover what we need to know. The pressure diminished immediately, but didn't disappear.

Bramble concentrated on what Gris and Asa were saying.

They were speaking a language she did not know. Some of the words were almost familiar, but pronounced oddly. The pressure of the gods increased in her mind, sending the voices fuzzy and warbling, then they steadied and she could understand what was being said. The gods had given her the ancient language as though it were her own.

"It's all ready," Gris said. "There's enough food to get you home. Do you have the things?"

From beneath her shawl, Asa produced some clothing and swaddling bands.

"Will they believe it?" she asked with intensity.

He nodded. "The cliff is an ancient sacrifice place. If they find your clothes and the baby's swaddling there, they'll assume you readied yourself for sacrifice and jumped."

"Naked?" she said doubtfully.

Gris smiled. Bramble could feel the face muscles moving, but she couldn't tell what kind of smile it was. It didn't feel happy.

"That is the way for sacrifices. They won't question it once I tell them about our conversation. How you couldn't bear to live with Hard-hand anymore. How the baby reminded you too much of him. And how I suggested you make a sacrifice to the gods in reparation for his murder."

She looked doubtful. "Make sure they don't blame you."

His mouth set firmly. The cheek muscles clenched. "I will," he said. Bramble could hear the determination in his voice. So could Asa. She nodded, then looked down at the covered baby. She drew the shawl away from his face and Bramble saw that he had inherited his mother's gold hair. He was not very old; no more than a month, maybe younger. Gris touched the baby's cheek softly with the back of one finger.

"Look after Acton," he said. "He is my heir."

She smiled then, a sweet smile, and nodded. Bramble tried to get a better glimpse of the baby's face, but Gris was looking at Asa.

"I will see you some other day," she said, and kissed his cheek. Bramble felt a flush creep up his face, but there was no response in his loins. He boosted Asa into the saddle and held the door open for her. She and the baby rode out into a windy, cloudless night and waters rose up around Bramble, as they had at the altar. This time she didn't fight them, but it was still unpleasantly gut-wrenching, the sensation of being overwhelmed, of actually dying, as strong as it had been the first time. She could easily be afraid, she thought, though she had given herself to the gods and had to trust in them. But it was hard to trust when the waves seemed intent on drowning her, on thrusting her down into darkness.

The sensation of goose bumps on her skin woke her. She was cold. She could tell she was thickly clothed, but she was still cold. She badly wanted to shiver, but her body wouldn't cooperate. Vision came slowly. She was in a big hall, with a fire in a circular fireplace in the middle of the room. There was no chimney. The smoke from the fire streamed upward to a hole in the roof. There were shuttered windows without any chinks of light. Either they were wadded against the cold or it was night.

Bramble noticed all this with difficulty, as though the person whose body she now observed from saw dimly. The body felt vaguely unwell and sluggish. But at least it was a woman. She was sitting at a table on a backless bench or stool.

The fire was too small to heat more than a tiny circle around it, but the people in the hall didn't seem to notice. There were twenty or so men sitting at long tables and eating from bowls. They were full-bearded and long-haired; their blond hair tied in plaits on either side of their face or loose down their back. They were dressed in leather and homespun and boots with the fleece left on the inside. Some women were sitting with them but more were serving. They wore long dresses, to the ground. That must make it hard to get around,

Bramble thought. Although she habitually wore breeches herself, most women in the Domains wore loose trousers under a full knee- or calf-length skirt. It was a good combination of modesty and practicality, she'd always thought, though she didn't bother much about modesty herself. Those long dresses were an invitation to trip.

The women carried bowls and spoons and bread on wooden plates from another room. The kitchen, Bramble supposed. There were children of all ages everywhere, the older ones sitting at the table, the younger ones running around and shrieking as they chased each other. Bramble had an impression of metal glinting above her head, but the woman she inhabited was too used to this room to look at the roof.

Then a woman with gold hair in two thick plaits came into view, carrying a bowl which she put down in front of the woman. It was soup and it smelled good, of lamb and barley.

"Here you are, Ragni," she said.

"Thanks, lass," Ragni replied. Out of the corner of her eye Bramble could just see the golden-haired woman. Yes, it was Asa. She looked much happier now. Then a toddler with her own bright gold hair ran up to her and grasped her by the legs. Ragni looked at him and her face creased in a smile.

"May the gods bless him, he's getting so tall!" she said. Her voice was quavery and when she reached out a hand to touch the child's cheek, it was wrinkled and spotted with age. Bramble was again conscious of how weak she felt. I should remember how this feels, she thought. I should have been more patient with Swith and his cronies when they complained about getting old.

"He's getting so cheeky!" Asa said, but she smiled as she swung the little boy up into her arms.

"Food!" he demanded. "More!"

"You've had your dinner, Acton, and there's no more until the men have finished eating," Asa said firmly.

"Acton man!"

Ragni, Asa and a couple of men sitting nearby laughed.

"Aye," one of them said, "you're a little man already, aren't you? Here, have some of ours."

Asa smiled at the man, the only red-head in the room. He held another toddler on his knee—an even paler blond than Acton—and was feeding him soup from his own bowl.

Asa put Acton down on the bench and the little boy on the man's lap wriggled down happily to sit next to him. Acton grabbed the piece of bread the young man held out. The other child held out his own hand for some.

"Share with Baluch, Acton," Asa said. Acton stuck his lip out and shook his head. Elric laughed and handed another piece of bread to Baluch.

"You're too soft on him, Elric Elricsson," Asa said with mock severity. Elric ducked his head and smiled and continued to share his soup with both boys. Acton swung his legs and grabbed for the spoon.

"No, Act'n," Elric's child said. "Da's spoon!"

"That's right, Baluch!" Asa said, and made Acton give it back to Elric.

"Let me know when you've had enough of him," she said to Elric, and went back to the kitchen.

"Wooing the babe so you can woo the mother, eh?" Ragni chuckled. "Well, your own wife's been in her grave long enough, I'll grant you. It's not a bad idea, lad, but you'll have to do more than share some soup. She's still the chieftain's daughter, and she's covered herself in glory these past years."

Elric was bright red with embarrassment. "Aye," he said. "I know. That's why I'm off in the spring."

"Trying to cover yourself in glory, too? Make sure you don't cover yourself in your own blood and guts instead. Glory costs too much, sometimes."

"I don't care what it costs," Elric said, looking toward the kitchen. "Whatever it costs will be worth it." Bramble felt the shiver that meant the gods were listening and grieved for the young man. Nothing good ever came of an oath like that.

Then the waters rose again and washed away the sight of the little gold-haired boy putting his face down into the soup bowl and slurping loudly. Somehow, although she was not conscious of having a body of her own, she felt herself smiling. It was hard to believe that this little scamp would grow up into the murderer and despoiler she knew him to be. The man who would slaughter thousands, and laugh while he did it, and then set up the whole system of warlordship which still tyrannized her country. Bramble felt her smile begin to fade, and then all sensation was swamped, as wave after wave broke over her until she felt nothing, saw nothing but the black of bottomless water.

Hearing came first. Panting, the thud of feet on the earth, and a swishing sound Bramble couldn't identify. She was moving, fast, shifting from side to side. The panting was her own breath, loud in her ears. She was holding something.

Her sight cleared as a sword came down toward her head, just like the sword that Thegan's man had aimed at her, but there was no Ash here now to save her. She had no time to feel anything, not even fear. Before she could react, her body swung its arms up and blocked the stroke with its own sword. Wooden, not steel. It was not a warlord's man attacking her, but a boy, aged eight or nine years old. A boy with shoulder-length golden hair caught in two plaits at the front.

"Hah!" he shouted, and lunged forward. The tip of his sword hit Bramble—hit the boy Bramble was inhabiting—just under the chest bone. He was wearing a padded jacket, but even so it hurt. She felt the pained exclamation making its way up his throat, and felt him bite it back. She understood that. Show no fear. Show no reaction to those trying to hurt you. Don't let Acton the bully scare you.

Then Acton grinned and clasped his opponent around the shoulders. Although he was not much taller, he seemed far sturdier.

"Baluch, that was a great match!"

The boy smiled, widely. Bramble became aware that they were surrounded by an audience of other boys and a few men, who were all stamping their feet and clapping with enthusiasm.

Baluch raised his hand in acknowledgment.

"How long did I last, Da?" he asked one of the men. Elric Elricsson, a few years older—and with only one arm. The right sleeve hung empty. So glory had had a high price, Bramble thought. I wonder if it got him what he wanted?

"A count of ninety," Elric said, smiling. "Well done, lad."

"That's better by fifteen than anyone else," another older man said approvingly. All the other men were graying or bald. Old men. Where were the young ones?

The old man turned to Acton. "You'd better watch yourself, little rooster, he might knock you off your perch."

Acton laughed heartily, but not in mockery. It was simple enthusiasm, Bramble saw. He was brightly, vividly alive and everyone there seemed to turn toward him, to angle themselves so they could see him. The other boys began a scuffle, looking out of the corner of their eyes to see if Acton was watching. Showing off for him. He didn't notice.

"Baluch could be better than me, *I* think," he said. "He thinks faster. He just needs to practice more."

Elric nodded. "That's what I keep telling him." He cuffed Baluch lightly on the back of the head. "Practice. That's the secret. But he's always off with his harp and his drum."

His voice was both faintly accusatory and proud. Bramble knew that tone. Her mother had used it whenever she talked about the food that Bramble brought home from the forest.

Acton let go of Baluch's shoulders and slapped him on the back.

"He makes the best songs," he said with admiration. Elric laughed.

"Maybe so, maybe so. But songs are for after battle, and you won't survive to get to the songs unless —"

"Unless I practice more. Yes, Da," Baluch said, with humor and resignation.

It still felt very odd to Bramble, to have someone else use her mouth and her tongue, to feel her body move and speak, it seemed, without her volition. But she was becoming accustomed to it, to distancing herself from the sensations so she could study Acton and her surroundings.

The group of boys was breaking up, allowing Bramble to see past them to the horse yard and the countryside beyond. Despite the summer-gold grass which covered its bones, it seemed barren to her, devoid of trees except for a few birches on the leeward side of hollows and small ridges. It was easy to tell which way the wind blew here—always from the snow-covered mountains, stunting and bending the trees until their top branches almost swept the ground. The mountains curved around, setting a barrier against the sky, the snow glowing orange and pink with the sunset. She had never seen mountains like these before—in comparison, the peaks near Golden Valley were mere foothills. She wanted Baluch to stand and stare at them, but he turned and followed Acton and the others toward a long building which she supposed was the hall she had been in earlier.

There were outbuildings beyond it—stables and byres, houses and animal enclosures. As she meshed her senses more fully with Baluch's, Bramble could smell the animals—horses, pigs, the wet-wool reek of sheep. She heard cows in the distance, saw hides stretching on drying frames. The frames were made from bones lashed together with leather strips. Timber was scarce, then. Valuable. As Baluch's eyes skimmed across the darkening grasslands, Bramble longed for the trees of home.

Baluch pulled a small wooden pipe from his belt and put it to his lips as he walked. He played a quick, flickering melody which made everyone increase their pace until they were striding along fast. Bramble wished that she could make music like this. She could feel his delight at the effect the tune was having. Then Acton halted, suddenly, and turned to look sideways at Baluch. It was a glance full of mischief and amusement and it made him seem older than he was.

"Stop it!" he ordered, half-laughing. "I'm not marching to anyone's tune!"

Baluch smiled. Bramble was beginning to get a sense of this boy's feelings. He was half sorry that his trick had been recognized, but also pleased that Acton was asserting his independence. He didn't really want to control people. Or at least, he didn't want to control Acton. Bramble knew that feeling, too. It was how she had felt about Acton the stallion, back in Pless. Famed for his wild strength and impossible to ride, the stallion had been a symbol to her of something she felt in herself. She had been glad every time she looked at him that something, some fellow creature, had refused to be tamed, as though that was a promise of equal wildness for herself.

Baluch stared at Acton, smiling, and Bramble stared too. He didn't look like a mad killer. He looked like a friendly, energetic boy who was used to being very, very good at things, better than anyone else, with a touch of the arrogance that that brought. He's a chieftain's grandson,

Bramble thought, remembering the old woman's words to Elric Elricsson. Her resentment at warlords rose up in her at the thought, but it was hard to sustain when Acton punched Baluch lightly in the arm and said, "Race you to the hall."

They sprinted off together, Acton in the lead, while the waters rose up and covered Bramble once again.

SAKER

THE NEXT DAY, Saker turned north from Three Rivers Domain and headed upriver toward Pless, into Central Domain. He had consulted his scrolls at length the night before, and had mapped out a wandering course that would let him visit all the massacre sites in the songs Rowan had shared with him. It would take him weeks, but that was all right. He had time.

He would not mention to anyone that he had come from Carlion. He was just a stonecaster, traveling the roads looking for customers, as he had been so many times before.

He considered raising the ghost of his father, Alder, to tell him the good news about Carlion, but he was so tired. Too much blood had been needed for Carlion. He would raise his father next time, so Alder could watch the invaders die, and be proud of him.

It was a fine day, and Central Domain was pretty country. Saker hummed as his horse ambled along the dusty roads, and did not admit to himself that he was glad there would be weeks before the next deaths.

MARTINE

"Do we move her?" Martine asked Safred.

Bramble lay sprawled across the rock at the base of the altar, her face scowling in concentration although her eyes were closed. She moved, twitched, frowned again.

The mist surrounded them still, spreading the moonlight into a blanket of silver around them. Martine didn't trust it, even if it did come from the gods.

Ever since Bramble had cried out in some kind of warning and collapsed at their feet, Martine had been fighting a sense of outrage, a feeling that no human should go through what Bramble was enduring. Her Sight told her that it violated more than time and space; it hacked at Bramble's identity and the center of who she was. Who knew what this experience would do to her?

"I think we must," Safred said, with the look on her face that meant she was listening to the gods. Martine listened, too, but although she could sense their presence they had never talked to her except through the stones. She was not like her daughter Elva, whose mind was taken over by the gods as casually as she might slip on a coat. She sent a prayer to whatever gods were listening for Elva's safety, and the safety of her husband Mabry and the baby Ash, back in Hidden Valley. Their home there had seemed a bastion of warmth and security, but nowhere was secure when ghosts carried weapons and used them for dark revenge.

As they stood, trying to decide what to do, the mist vanished as rapidly as it had come, leaving Martine feeling defenseless and exposed. It was growing dark rapidly, and the moon went behind the clouds. Martine dreaded the journey back across the sharp-edged rings of rock that were the only stepping-stones. She wasn't even sure it was possible.

"How can we?"

Safred gnawed at her lip. "The gods say, her spirit is in the water now, and the water knows her blood. We can float her back."

"Put her in the *lake*?" Martine shivered with a deep reluctance. "I think I'd rather wait with her here."

Safred looked puzzled, but shook her head. "The gods say that she is not safe here. That... that she might be *burnt*."

So. Martine let out a long breath. Yes. That was possible. On the night of the Spring Equinox, at a black rock altar, that was very possible. But she couldn't explain that to Safred.

"You know what they mean," Safred said accusingly.

"If she lies out here all day in the full sun, she *will* get burnt." Not a lie, but not the truth Safred wanted. Martine went on before Safred could ask another question. "Do the gods say whether *we* can float back, too?"

Immediately, Safred shivered. "No. No. They say on no account. We must walk. But she will float."

Martine untied her belt and strapped it around Bramble's chest. She held out her hand and Safred, after a moment of confusion, took off her own belt and gave it to her. Martine tied the two together and then took Bramble's shoulders while Safred took her legs. They slid her down the glassy rock to the edge of the water. Every bit of Sight Martine had told her that the water was dangerous, but they were here because of the gods, and it was a bit late to stop obeying them now.

"One, two, three," she said. They slid Bramble into the water. An expression of panic came over her face, but then it cleared and she floated easily, more easily than she should have, as though the water itself was supporting her, high enough to pass over the rock ridges which lay just under the surface. Her head floated easily, her mouth well clear of the water.

Martine gestured for Safred to go before her, and then she took hold of the two belt ends and stepped onto the first rock ring. As though the movement had caused it, the moon came out from behind the clouds and the lake burst into brilliant reflected light. Martine tugged at the belt and Bramble spun slowly, moving gently until her head bumped Martine's foot. It was as though she towed a corpse.

The journey back lived in Martine's memory as the strangest time of her life. Bramble lay as though dead, and it seemed to Martine that she towed death itself, life itself, memory and courage and grief, all in one package. The lake was calm, the small waves caused by Martine's steps soft against her boots. The moonlight cast long shadows so that she seemed to be a giant, striding across the face of the ocean, pacing not from rock to rock but upon some elemental power beyond her understanding. Although she had faltered and swayed on the journey out to the altar, now she walked with ease, each foot finding the perfect resting point on the next ring of rock. It seemed that the shore approached *her,* grew larger and wider until she lost all sense of size, until the trees seemed as big as mountains and the rim of the lake bowl was like a cliff, shivering with light under the moon.

Another sense, an older and more familiar sense, told her that it was wrong to walk away from the altar on the night of the Spring Equinox. That she still had work to do. *Later,* she told that voice, and on the thought everything returned to normal size, she took the final step over the knee-high rim, and brought Bramble safely to rest against the obsidian edge.

Cael was there, although she hadn't seen him waiting. She wondered if she had seen the real lake shore or some other country, some other time, but put the thought away. Cael went to lift Bramble out, but Martine stopped him. She gave him the belt, and he used it to drag Bramble half-upright, so he could grasp her without putting his hands in the water. Then he lifted her, with a grunt of effort that made Martine remember his wound, and carried her to the camp he had set up on the slope under the trees, where Safred was already warming herself by a fire. Through it all Bramble never opened her eyes, although her body was tense and her face set.

When it was approaching midnight, by the stars, Martine checked Bramble once again and gave her some water. She drank with a faint smile on her face, though there were dark circles under her eyes. Zel and Martine had stripped off her breeches and put a cloth under her, so they could give her water regularly without fearing that she would soil her clothes. They had laid a blanket over her for modesty, but now Martine tucked it in for warmth as well.

Martine gathered her flint, handstone and tinder. Spring Equinox.

She hadn't celebrated it since Elva left; it needed at least two Traveler women, one to hold the flint and the other to strike. Three was better, but tonight they had only two, her and Zel. And a black rock altar. Perhaps tomorrow night, or the next, Bramble would be with them. She hoped so. It was good to have three women for the third night, to represent the three sisters.

She really didn't want to walk out again on those precarious rock rings, but her Sight had been clear. The altar was waiting for the ritual, which was precise and demanding. No steel to strike fire from. Steel was too new a thing. The ritual went back far past the time humans first made steel. Fire must be made from stone and flint. The handstone must be old, the flint new, the tinder natural, not charred. That meant special tinder, because sparks from a handstone were not as hot as sparks from a firesteel. Birch tree fungus was the only tinder that caught readily. Martine, like all Traveler women, collected the fungus when she saw it, for any future need. She had gathered some in Hidden Valley, where the birch trees grew thickly on the upper slopes. She and Elva had gone out one clear winter day, saying only to Drema and Gytha that they were collecting firewood. Which they did, as well.

She went softly to where Zel was curled up in a nest of blankets, then paused. She didn't know how devout Zel's mother had been—perhaps Zel didn't know the rituals. But as she hesitated Zel's head came out of its nest, eyes bright in the starshine, and she slid to her feet without words, then reached down to pick up a small pile of kindling she had hidden under the blanket.

They walked toward the water.

"I have one new flint," Martine said quietly.

"I only have one, too," Zel said.

That was a problem. Each night of the ritual there must be a new flint, to call the wildfire. Three nights, two flints.

"We'll have to go looking for another," Martine said.

Zel nodded, but she looked anxious. "What if we don't find one? What happens if the ritual isn't completed?" Her voice rose with worry. It was odd to see her normally calm face twisted with concern. Zel didn't like not being in control of things, Martine knew. Something about Zel made her feel very old and not as wise as she should be. Like the fake grandmother she was. She wondered if she'd be wiser if Elva had been a true child of her body, not just her heart.

"What if he isn't pleased?" Zel insisted.

"Shh," Martine said. If Safred were to wake now, she'd sniff a secret and they'd never reach the end of her questioning. What could they tell her? She had no old blood at all—she'd said so. Martine handed Zel the birch fungus tinder.

Traveler women had tried to introduce women of Acton's blood to the fire once before, and Martine didn't want to be part of a disaster like that. Even the Well of Secrets wouldn't be safe from the fire. He didn't like strangers, they all knew that.

"I don't know," Martine said softly. "We'll worry about that if we need to."

Zel swallowed hard before she took the first step onto the seemingly blank face of the water, but she had a tumbler's balance and made the next step more easily than Martine. Martine was overwhelmed by the sense that the lake was watching. Not antagonistic, but ready to react to anything it deemed a threat.

They paced out, side-by-side as the ritual demanded, and stood at the altar. Martine stretched her senses, but the gods were not here. They were never here at the fire's time. She always wondered why—was it fear, or respect, or had some kind of deal been done? Then she reined in her thoughts. Cynicism had no place on this night.

Zel made a small nest of the tinder and kindling on the smooth face of the altar and stood back. Martine placed her striking stone and the new flint side-by-side on the altar next to the tinder, and stood next to Zel.

"We are daughters of fire," they said together, "daughters of Mim the firestealer, Mim the firelover, Mim the fire's love. The fire must never die."

Martine felt, as she always did in rituals, a mixture of self-consciousness and exaltation, of silliness and awe. There were tears in Zel's eyes. Together they took a pace forward.

Zel picked up the handstone and placed it close above the nest of fungus, bark and pine needles. Martine took the flint. She had to get the angle of the stroke precisely right, which was always harder when someone else was holding the stone, and harder still because of the height of this altar. But it wasn't the first time either of them had done this, which helped.

Zel braced herself, and nodded. Martine struck down cleanly into the shallow groove on the handstone and sparks flew down the groove straight onto the tinder. Immediately, it caught. They waited a moment for the spark to grow. It glowed in the darkness, a ring of light that gradually expanded. Zel folded the rest of the kindling over the top of it, and both of them crouched down so that their mouths were on a level with the kindling nest.

"Take our breath to speed your growth," Zel whispered. They blew softly, very softly, into the nest, and then there was flame as well as spark. They stood up and moved back a pace, waiting.

As the fire grew, licking at the kindling, Martine felt his presence. As always, it manifested within her body, not her mind, completely different from the presence of the local gods. Heat flooded her, spreading out from her solar plexus and her loins, making her nipples tight. Zel's head dropped back, her eyes closed and her breath quickened. It was worse—or better—when you were younger, Martine thought, but on the thought another wave of heat swept over her. Her body took control of her thoughts and filled her mind with images of fire, flames, burning gold. Each image brought a sense of touch, too, of stroke and probe, of caress and tease. She ached, deeply, for the fire's touch. For fulfillment.

Her body began trembling. She made the final step of the ritual, the one that was always hardest for her, and surrendered to him, although, always, always, there was a small part of herself she did not give; could not give. Her eyes closed and the fire filled her mind.

And died.

Martine opened her eyes slowly, gasping with disappointment and frustration. The kindling had burned away, cleanly, leaving nothing behind. No ash, no charcoal. Nothing to show there had been a fire at all. Of course. It always did, if the ritual had gone well.

It had been quick, but this was only the first night. Foreplay, nothing more. Heat drained away from her but left some things behind. Frustration. Readiness. A sharpening of her senses, so that everything made an impression: the cool breeze from the mere, the murmur of the trees, the dense blackness of the altar in the moonlight.

Zel wiped sweat from her face and shivered.

They looked at each other to make sure the other was ready to speak, and then said, together, "The fire will never die."

Then they turned and slowly, carefully, made their way over the water and back to camp. The campfire had flared up, as fires always did in the vicinity of the ritual. They banked it again and checked the area carefully. This close to the forest, every spark was a potential catastrophe.

Thank the gods—or the fire—that Safred was still asleep in her tent.

"After Bramble wakes up," Zel said quietly, as they paused before going to their blankets, "we is heading back to Oakmere, right?"

Martine nodded.

Zel grinned. "Good. Lots of likely lads in Oakmere! I love the week after Equinox!"

They stifled their laughter behind their hands. Martine knew she was acting like a silly girl, but she didn't care. That was part of the ritual, too. Zel was right. Traveler women who didn't have their own men came from the three-night vigil with the fire ready and eager for the first good-looking man who crossed their path. It was one of the reasons they had a reputation for being free with their bodies. But it was worth carrying that reputation for the rest of the year, to have the week after Equinox.

Martine took her blankets and stretched out next to Bramble, who was moving her legs restlessly. She straightened the blanket so Bramble's legs were covered, and checked the cloth they had laid under her. It was still dry, so she gave her more water. She had sweated a great deal already, and lack of water would kill her if they weren't careful.

Martine found it hard to sleep. Her body thrummed still with desire and arousal. She remembered past Spring Equinoxes, especially the ones after Elva was fully grown, when she had felt free to go out looking for pleasure. She smiled into the darkness. Shagging in the week after each Equinox, when all the senses had been brought to singing life, was like nothing else. It had been a long time since Martine had let herself enjoy it, though. Too long, she thought. Too long.

BRAMBLE

HER MOUTH WAS full of ashes. She was choking on them, smothering in them, coughing convulsively to clear her throat. She was coughing so hard that her eyes were streaming and she could see nothing, but she could hear a man shouting at her in a voice which showed he expected to be obeyed, a voice like a drum.

"The gods do not talk to children! They do not talk to half-grown boys too big for their boots! The gods talk only to the chieftain. So it is. So it will be."

Like an echo, other voices confirmed, murmuring, "So it is, so it will be."

The voice dropped lower, but became more menacing. "Do you understand, Baluch?"

Baluch could barely respond, his body was so wracked with coughs, but he nodded.

"A mouth full of ashes is the price for lying to your chieftain. It's a small price. If you were a man full-grown, I would have cut off your hand."

Baluch's eyes cleared at last. The speaker was a balding older man, fifty or so, with a bushy gray beard and bright blue, angry eyes. He was dressed as the men at the practice fight had been dressed, in baggy leggings and rough-spun tunic, but he had a great cloak of rabbit skins slung from his shoulders. With a shock, Bramble saw that the brooch which held the cloak was a larger version of the one she had laid her hand over on the black rock altar. For a moment she wondered how long she had been traveling, washed on wave after wave of ancestral memory. What were the others doing, there by the dark mere? The image of trees, water, the rising mist flashed across her mind and was swept away by the immediate sensation of Baluch spitting and spitting again, trying to get the ashes from his mouth.

"Enough, Father," Asa's voice came. "He understands."

She handed Baluch a horn of water and a basin. He grabbed at it and swilled his mouth over and over again.

"Hmmph," the chieftain grunted. "Very well. We will start the search for the child at first light."

He turned and walked away and only then was Bramble aware that they were in a corner of the large hall, where the shuttered windows showed a faint purple twilight. Outside, the wind whistled around the building and the walls radiated cold. The hall was packed with people, men, women and children, most of them moving uneasily, talking to each other, avoiding the central fire where a woman Asa's age sat rocking back and forth, her hands to her face, another woman patting her on the back.

Baluch had used up the water in the horn and his mouth felt almost normal, although puckered and sour. He stared into the grimy water in the basin. Bramble felt his despair and heard a faint dark music, deep notes sonorously played—a dirge. She knew it was from Baluch's mind, but he seemed unaware of it.

When a hand landed on his shoulder he didn't look up, as though he knew who it was. "I know where she is," he whispered.

The hand lifted and Acton came into view, looking about thirteen, perhaps less. "Where?"

Baluch gestured with the hand which held the drinking horn. "A cave, under a ridge. I can't describe it well enough, but I could find it."

"Mmm," Acton said.

Baluch raised his head. "I *could*. Your grandfather thinks I'm lying, but I'm not!"

"Shh," Acton cautioned him. "If he hears you say it again you *will* lose a hand. The gods talk only to the chieftain."

"But my mother had the Sight —"

"Athel was a woman, and under his control. No threat to him at all."

"But *I'm* not a threat. Everyone knows you'll be the next chieftain —"

"So," Acton said, ignoring him, suddenly cheerful, "maybe it isn't the gods. *Maybe* it's a friendly spirit."

"Uh, he won't believe that."

"No. But if we bring her back alive he'll pretend to believe it. Come on."

The music in Baluch's mind died away, changed to something warmer, deep notes still but with hope at the center of them. He followed Acton dumbly, out the back of the hall to a small chamber where Asa and a couple of women waited, holding candles.

"You'll get lost yourselves," one of them muttered, casting a dark look at Baluch.

Acton grinned at her, and kissed her cheek. "I know these hills like my own hands, Gret. Don't you trust me?"

She smiled despite herself. "I don't trust the weather. It smells like a blizzard to me."

Acton nodded, solemn, his gold hair glinting in the light of the candles.

"That's why we have to go now. A blizzard will be the death of her." As one, the women shivered and made a sign with their little fingers, clearly a ward against evil chance.

"Harald should —"

Acton cut her off firmly. "My grandfather is right. To go out now, not knowing where Friede is, would be foolhardy. More would be lost. But to go out knowing where she is, that is different."

"The gods —"

"Not the gods," Baluch said hastily. "A friendly spirit, that's all. Only the chieftain speaks with the gods."

Asa nodded approval. "Yes," she said. "A friendly spirit. Good. Go find her. But . . ." her voice faltered a little and she put out a hand to smooth Acton's hair. "Don't take stupid chances. One life is not worth two."

He smiled at her, but was clearly preparing to ignore her advice. His eyes sparkled with pleasure at the thought of the risks he was about to take. Bramble couldn't help but understand that. She had felt the same often enough herself, before a chase.

The women helped them into heavy winter clothing: shaggy sheepskin coats and leggings, felt hats with earflaps and long neck pieces to wrap around their throats, gloves. They took a pack with candles, tinderbox, dried apple, water, bread and another coat for the girl when they found her.

"She won't need boots," Baluch said dreamily. "We'll have to carry her back."

They went out into the sharp wind. It was almost full night, the sky a scudding mass of clouds flickering across a sickle moon. There was a thin layer of snow across the ground. Acton led until they were in the lee of the last outbuilding. Already Baluch's nose was red and sore. His ears were aching. The buffeting of the wind, which would merely have been uncomfortable to Bramble, was painful to him because of the insistent whuff and whine. It was as though his ears were more sensitive to the noise than to the cold. His inner music died under the clamor.

"Well?" Acton asked. "Which way?"

Baluch stilled, his head down. Bramble noted that the toes of his boots were scuffed like a little boy's, and was filled with a sudden maternal affection for him. This was, of course, the Baluch who had founded Baluchston. The one who had struck a deal with the Lake for a town and a ferry. The first ferryman. She had never quite understood why the Lake had made that agreement, but from inside Baluch's mind it made some sense. This boy would understand the Lake. So why was he best friends with Acton the warlord?

Bramble could feel the presence of the gods around Baluch, but the pressure on her own mind was light. All their attention was concentrated on him.

Then Baluch's head came up, and he pointed. "Up the northern flank," he said. "Over the sheep stream, beyond Barleyvale, and farther up."

Acton nodded. "You follow me," he said, "until we're there."

Baluch bit his lip as though not liking the instruction, but followed closely in Acton's footsteps. Bramble realized that Acton was taking the force of the wind, sheltering Baluch and making it easier for him. That made sense. Baluch was smaller, slighter—more likely to founder in the wind and cold. He was the one who could take them to the girl. It was a good tactical decision. Or perhaps it was simply a boy sheltering his best friend from a harsh wind. She didn't know which. The fact that she couldn't tell from Acton's manner annoyed her. What was to decide? He was Acton, warlord and murderer. So he had a friend. Even the worst of men may have friends.

But not, part of her mind suggested, friends like Baluch.

There was no room for further thought in the next two hours. The buffeting of the wind and cold took thought away, even though Bramble withdrew her senses as far as she could from Baluch's. She had wandered winter forests, been caught out in a snowstorm or two, but the temperate south had nothing like this, not even in the dead of winter. There was nothing in this harsh land to protect them except the occasional ridge or clump of rocks. They crossed thin, half-frozen streams, careful to keep their boots dry, and started on a steep upward slope.

The footing was treacherous: loose scree that shifted and tripped them time and again. Without the gloves, Baluch's hands would have been slashed and scored. Acton fell less often. From time to time he would put a hand back to help Baluch over a rough patch, or to pull him to his feet after a fall.

They had wrapped their scarves over their faces, leaving only their eyes visible, but even so Bramble could see that Acton was enjoying himself. At first it made her cross. She was *not* enjoying having to endure Baluch's struggle through wind and freezing cold, climbing a shagging mountain in the middle of the night. Then she thought, but I might, if I were really doing it. Not enjoy the physical discomfort, but the wildness of it, the sense of being on the edge of things, the knife's edge between joy and despair, success and failure. I might enjoy that.

They came to a sharp defile between two ridges, where they were protected from the wind. It felt almost warm by comparison and they pulled back their wraps so they could talk. Despite the shelter, they had to shout over the sound of the wind wuthering outside the defile.

"How far now?" Acton asked.

Baluch considered, again looking at his boots as the gods concentrated upon him.

"We have to climb the next ridge and then go around the rocks to the cave. Not far, but hard."

"How in the name of Swith the Strong did she get up here anyway?"

Baluch shrugged. "You know what Friede's like. It was a nice day this morning. She probably wanted to explore."

Acton shook his head, with some admiration. "More like a boy than a girl!"

Baluch grinned. "Asa's son should know how strong women can be."

Acton made a face but underneath it was pride for his mother. "Strong enough to tan our hides if we don't bring Friede back safe."

Baluch nodded, serious again. They wrapped themselves and started off, reluctantly leaving the shelter of the defile to climb the ridge before them.

"You go first, here," Acton said. Baluch looked quickly at him, as though surprised, but went willingly enough up the uneven slope.

The ridge was so steep that they had to go on all fours, grabbing at harsh rocks that cut through their gloves, and sending stones skittering down the slope beneath them. It was soon clear that Acton had the worst of it, as he had to avoid the rocks that slid from beneath Baluch's boots. The way broadened at one point so they could climb side-by-side and when it narrowed again, Baluch motioned for Acton to go first. Acton shook his head. Baluch pushed him, gesturing, Go on! Acton studied him for a moment, then shrugged and began to climb. They couldn't talk; the wind made speech impossible. It felt as though the wind wanted to pluck them off the ridge and cast them down onto the rocks below. Perhaps it did. Perhaps the howling was wind spirits, not just air streaming through gaps in the rocks.

Bramble forced her mind away from that disquieting thought and wasn't sure if it were hers or Baluch's. His breath was coming faster as they climbed and his legs ached and burned, but only from the knees up. Below that he was numb with cold. The clouds finally covered the moon when they were halfway up and the rest of the ascent was in the pitch dark, fumbling for handholds and footholds, grasping unseen outcrops, not knowing how securely they were anchored in what was now more cliff than ridge.

Baluch's attention narrowed to the feel of his hands, the rock beneath his feet. Occasionally he flinched as a rock dislodged by Acton's feet bounced past him. One stone the size of a fist thudded into his shoulder and made him lose his grip. His heart beat wildly as he lunged for another handhold, scrabbling until he was grasping the rock face securely. Bramble felt him begin to quiver deep inside, but he dragged in a great, gulping breath, the cold needling his lungs, and began to climb again, ignoring the quivering and the beating heart. Not long after, they reached a ledge and Acton squatted with his back to the cliff. Baluch joined him, both of them taking long breaths. Acton was tired, too.

Then Baluch stood and pointed, not up, but along the ledge. He edged toward a large whitish boulder which blocked it. Bramble was puzzled, at first, that she could see it. The night had been so dark before. Where was the light coming from? Then she realized that it was snowing and what she saw was the snow on the top of the rock, reflecting what little light there was. It had been snowing for a while, it seemed by the amount of snow on ledge and rock, but Baluch had been so concentrated on the next handhold, the next step, that he hadn't noticed, and so she hadn't noticed either.

There was a gap between the boulder and the rock face, and they edged between it, Acton having more trouble than Baluch. Beyond the rock face, the ledge curved around and ended in a cave mouth, darker by far than the surrounding rock. It was quieter in the lee of the boulder. Baluch went up to the cave mouth and unwrapped the neck piece from his mouth. It was stiff with snow and ice. He cleared his throat.

"Friede?" he called. "Friede?"

"Shhh!" a whisper came furiously from the dark cave. "Shhh! You'll wake her!"

Scrabbling noises were followed by a head appearing from the cave. Bramble could barely see, even though Baluch was standing close. It could have been any age child, boy or girl, from the voice and the hat, but Acton had that expression on his face that Bramble had seen so often from others when she herself had been young; the one that meant "this girl doesn't act as she should." Despite the fact that Friede was responsible for them having to make that horrible climb, she found herself liking her.

"Wake who?" Baluch said.

"Shh! The bear."

Both boys took an involuntary step backward and Friede made a reproving noise. "It's all right, she's in the winter sleep. But she'll wake up if you make too much noise."

"You're in trouble," Acton said. "What's worse, you got Baluch in trouble."

Friede emerged fully from the cave and stood awkwardly on the ledge. Astonished, Bramble saw that she was lame, with a crutch under her left arm. She was small; perhaps seven or eight.

"How did you get up here in the first place?" Baluch asked, exasperated.

"I fell from up there," Friede said, gesturing toward the top of the cliff. "It's not a bad walk if you take the long way around. And then I couldn't get down. Obviously." She seemed irritated rather than scared or upset, and Bramble adjusted her estimate of Friede's age upward, but she wasn't sure how far.

"So you just found a bear's cave?" Acton said. Bramble couldn't make out his face but his voice was amused.

"It was warm," Friede said dismissively.

"It may have to be warm," Acton said. "We'll have to stay in it tonight, all of us."

Immediately, Bramble felt the pressure of the gods grow greater around Baluch, and he shook his head.

"No, we have to go now, before the snow gets too deep. This blizzard is setting in for a long visit. Days, maybe weeks. We won't get home if we don't make a move right now."

Friede stared at him curiously.

Acton grinned. "The gods are leading him, girl. They must like you."

Friede took in a long breath. "The gods talk to you?" Her voice was full of wonderment and she looked at Baluch with a simple admiration which was clearly unusual in her.

"Sometimes," Baluch mumbled, head down.

"*So,*" Acton recalled them back to business, "we'd better go up rather than down."

"I can't climb up," Friede reminded him impatiently, back to her usual self.

"You can't climb down, either," Acton said. "If we have to carry you all the way home, I'd rather do it down a nice soft slope instead of the way we came, through the rocks."

"But to get to the slope . . ."

"Come on," Acton said, cheerful as though they were off for a picnic. "Climb aboard."

"Get her past the boulder first," Baluch advised. "The climb isn't as steep further down the ledge."

"Fine. Let's go."

They went back past the boulder, Acton leading, Friede edging along cautiously, Baluch behind ready to catch her if necessary. Once they were through, Baluch got the extra coat out of Acton's pack and helped Friede put it on. She sighed as she felt the warmth envelop her.

The ledge went back for another forty paces before it petered out, and the cliff was definitely at a less worrying slope at that end. Still, over the next half-hour Bramble wished that she could just withdraw from Baluch's mind altogether. She didn't understand why she had to live through this part of Acton's life.

Friede climbed on Acton's back without a word, as though she were used to this particular indignity. Baluch had to find their way up the ridge, and clear any loose rock or pebbles from their path. Acton stayed well back so that Friede wouldn't be hit by the debris, but followed Baluch's path faithfully. Baluch's hands were bleeding inside his gloves and only the warmth of the blood kept them from freezing, but Bramble knew that as soon as the blood stopped flowing it would freeze and cause frostbite. Baluch knew it too. He kept muttering, "Spare gloves, I should have known we'd need spare gloves," all the way up. Bramble could feel the burn and tremble of his legs and arms, the deep exhaustion which he kept back purely by will. She could only imagine how hard Acton was finding it with Friede on his back.

The climb didn't end suddenly, but slowly. The ridge folded back in a series of small summits, so that it seemed Baluch had reached the top several times before he actually did. Each time his heart leapt as the ground leveled out, and each time he set his mouth and kept going as he realized that the top was still above him. Finally he took three steps on level ground; four steps; five, and collapsed in gratitude. A moment later, Acton and Friede collapsed next to him.

They sat shoulder to shoulder, breathing hard.

"Well," Acton said. "At least that warmed me up."

Baluch choked with laughter and punched him on the arm. Friede stood, hoisting herself on her crutch.

"We'd better go," she said.

They were standing, Bramble saw, at the top of the ridge. On the other side, the ground sloped gently away, in a long hill that seemed endless in the darkness. She had no sense of direction without her own body to orient her, but Baluch seemed confident that they could find their way home.

"It's further, but at least we won't get lost," he said.

The snow was not so deep on the summit of the ridge, but as they moved down the long slope it lay thicker, and further down it had already shifted into drifts. On the upland, Friede had struggled with the crutch. Here, she had no chance. She fell three times before she would admit she couldn't cope.

"Told you we'd have to carry her," Baluch said. He presented his back to Friede and she climbed on with much less resignation than she had shown at the cliff face. She was slight, but any extra weight at all was a burden in these conditions. Baluch set his teeth and struggled on, with Acton going ahead to break the snow where it lay thickly, using Friede's crutch as a shovel where he could. The snow was falling more thickly now, the wind not as strong but still cutting.

Their exhaustion had moved past the point of physical pain. Bramble could feel that Baluch's arms and legs were protesting at each movement, but he seemed unaware of it, and unaware, too, of the music coursing through his mind, horns and fifes playing marching music, a steady, insistent beat. He and Acton both had settled into an unthinking, deliberate plodding that was like sleepwalking. Bramble worried that they would become lost through sheer inattention, but Acton seemed to be heading toward a particular goal. Often they had to skirt boulders or cracks in the rock, but always he would turn back to the same direction, like a sunflower turns toward sunlight.

The snow fell even more heavily, so they paused to tie themselves together with Friede's neck piece. She hid her face in Baluch's back and he could feel her breath, warm in the middle but cold on the edges, on the back of his neck. He couldn't feel his hands anymore, although Bramble knew they still supported Friede's legs.

After an interval that seemed to go on forever, they stopped to swap positions, with Acton taking Friede and Baluch going forward to tramp down the snow. Although Friede had been heavy, this was the more difficult task, requiring sheer dogged strength. Baluch couldn't sustain it as long as Acton, and they swapped twice more before, finally, they saw lights in the distance through the falling snow.

The snow was lying chest-deep and it needed both of them working together to force a way. But the sight of home filled them with energy and Baluch's steps were lighter even as he struggled through drifts.

They came back to exactly where they had started from, the back entrance to the hall. Acton banged on the door with a fist and Asa opened immediately, calling out loudly.

"Marte, she's here, she's here, they've brought her back!"

The woman who had been rocking by the fire, her face red and blotchy with crying, pulled Friede from Baluch's back, sinking down to the floor and stroking her hair, laughing and crying and shaking her. Baluch's legs shook. His face burned in the sudden warmth. His father, Elric, rushed over to support him. Baluch gladly grabbed on to his arm and tried to smile.

Acton unwrapped his face and shook himself free of snow, as energetic as if he had never left the room. He threw his hat and gloves onto a bench and hugged his mother with one arm.

"I need something warm to drink!" he declared. "It's as cold as the hells out there."

Asa laughed. Baluch was watching his father, whose eyes rested on Asa with appreciation, but without longing. He's given up trying to win her, then, Bramble thought, and wondered if his empty sleeve was to blame for Asa's lack of interest.

"I should beat you for this," Elric said, returning his attention to Baluch, but it was clear from his smile that he didn't intend to.

Other people crowded around them, exclaiming and shouting to others in the hall. Baluch felt overwhelmed by the noise. He tried to fumble his gloves off, but they were stuck to his hands by blood.

Acton noticed. He reached out and stopped Baluch. "You'll have to soak them off in warm water," he said gently. Elric took Baluch by the arm to lead him into the hall. As they turned toward the door, the chieftain appeared in it, rubbing his eyes.

"What in all the hells is going on?"

Silence fell, except for Friede's mother's quiet scolding. The chieftain looked at them for a long moment. Friede looked up and met his gaze.

"You are in trouble," he said. "I'll deal with you tomorrow." She nodded and yawned, which sent her mother and several of the other women into a scurry, saying, "Let's get her to bed, she's exhausted, tomorrow's soon enough to worry about tomorrow . . ." They took her out into the hall, leaving the chieftain staring at Acton and Baluch. Mostly, Bramble noted, at Acton. Elric tensed as though getting ready to resist any attempt to punish his son.

"It wasn't the gods, Grandfather," Acton said. "It was a friendly spirit."

"Hmph," his grandfather said. He turned to Baluch. "Is that so?" Baluch nodded silently. "No more to be said, then."

Elric relaxed, and so did Baluch. Moving back into the hall, Harald spoke over his shoulder, seemingly casual. "But you'd better have mulled wine to warm you. It's a man's drink, I know, but just this once . . ."

Acton smiled blindingly and slapped Baluch on the back. "Told you it'd be all right," he said. "Swith, I'm hungry! Mother, any meat left from dinner?"

Baluch followed him into the hall smiling, his internal music changing to triumphant horn blasts as the waters rose up and Bramble floated on their tide.

ASA'S STORY

THE WOMEN STAY in the women's quarters. Yes, of course. So the men think, if they think about it at all. But when the men venture away after the spring sowing, what do they think the women do? The ewes must be milked, the cows tended as they calve, the wheat weeded, the vegetables hoed, the barley malted and the ale brewed, and the women do it as they always do. But the sheep must be shepherded too, and the birds kept off the crops, and the horse yoked and the cart loaded for market. The wool is mostly spun in winter so the looms can be busy all through the long evenings of summer—but with the men away the wood must be chopped and the animals slaughtered and the meat butchered—yes, and the wolves chased away from the young lambs, too. The boys do some, of course, but without the women the men would find a cold hearth and an empty steading when they returned with their wounds and their tales and their glory.

So the women stay in the women's quarters, of course. But in the soft summer evenings after the light has faded too much to use the looms and the children are asleep, the women sit in the long hall and sing and laugh and drink small ale and make jokes about the men. As women always have.

So it was in our steading until the raiders came. For our men had sailed off, as they always did in summer, taking the pelts and the hides and the precious inkstone to the trading towns down south, sometimes all the way to the Wind Cities, and there was no one to protect us from the raiders.

The men came not from the sea, where we had a lookout placed, but over the mountains from the east. Not in the morning, when mostly they attack, but in the cool evening. So it was that the women were in the long hall, and that was the saving of us, because Eddi, Gudrun's son, called out loud enough from the stable before they killed him so that we had warning, and we could bar the doors and drag the tables across them. I thought they might burn us out, but it had been a long march and they wanted beer, and knew there would be barrels in the hall. So they battered the doors down. But we had time, Haena my mother, Gudrun and Ragni and I, to take down the ancestral shields that hung along the walls, and the spears that went with them.

My mother Haena was the oldest, white-haired and bent, but she straightened herself and faced them first, as she should, being our chieftain Harald's wife. The rest of us lined up behind her, hoping that by fighting we were dooming ourselves to die, and a quick death was what we prayed for, the best we could have, we thought.

They burst through the doors and came at us, but stopped in surprise when they realized it was only women facing them. Their leader was a tall strong man, sandy-haired and green-eyed, so green I saw it even in that moment of dread. I will not say his name in case his ghost seeks me out and takes revenge, but his use-name was Hard-hand, for indeed his hand was very hard on those he punished. He looked at us—and no doubt we looked ridiculous enough to his eyes—and laughed so hard he brought tears to his eyes. His men began to grin, then laugh, and lowered their weapons. Then Haena threw her spear and got one of them in the arm. He swore and pulled the spear out. The rest laughed even louder. Their leader had to prop himself up against the wall.

"Serve you right, Os!" he howled.

"Pierced by love's arrow!" said another, who looked to be the most intelligent of them. I found out later that he was their skald, their poet, and his name was Gris the Open-handed, for he was the most generous of men, even to strangers and women. He was Hard-hand's brother.

Then Gudrun heard her son Eddi's death cry come from the stable and grief took her and made her berserk. She ran screaming and struck at the leader. He swiped her aside with a casual blow with his sword, but such was his strength that the single blow near cut her in two and she fell, her scream turned to pain and then to silence before she lay full-length on the ground.

Hard-hand smiled, still, but his eyes were cold as he looked us over. He looked longest at me, and lingeringly. I knew that look and I hefted my spear higher. My mother Haena took a step back and rested her hand on my shoulder, giving me strength, because she knew that look too. Athel, my cousin, who was younger than I but had the Sight, dropped both spear and shield and put up a hand.

"Remember the strength of women," was what the men heard her say, but the women heard her voice, or perhaps the voice of the goddess, speaking under her words, saying, "Remember the strength of Haena's line."

We all remembered that the women of my mother's line had a power over men, only one kind of power, and only to be used once in a woman's life. My mother had used it to bind the man of her choice to her and so married my father Harald, and he was faithful to her lifelong. My grandmother had done the same with my grandfather, Sigur. So it went back for generations, and for the men concerned there was no shame, for to be chosen by a woman of our line was an honor-gift, and the power bound the woman as much as the man, to be faithful forever. We remembered that now, and I began to shake as I understood what was needed of me.

To bind this green-eyed man to me for life, for his life or mine, and to have no other man. I was very young and had not even exchanged courting glances at the Summer Gatherings. It seemed hard to me, too hard, to give away all that: all the possibilities of love and marriage and children and happiness. I felt I would rather die. But then I looked around the hall. There were nine of us, counting Gudrun, and I had the lives of seven other women in my hand. Women of our steading, for whom my family was responsible. My mother's hand on my shoulder tightened and then dropped as she left me to make the choice alone. I thought, I will make this choice, but my life will be short.

So I looked at that green-eyed man, and I looked with the eyes of power. They say the power came from the gods originally, and I believe it. At that moment I was more than a woman in her hall; more than a girl facing her enemy. I was greater, impossibly strong, impossibly desirable, impossibly desiring. I saw his face change, and I exulted.

"I will go with you," I said, in the trading language that my people and his shared. "If you and your men leave this steading and all its people in peace."

One of his men laughed. "You'll go with us if we choose and we'll all have you until you're —" Hard-hand smote him with the flat of his sword right across the mouth so that he fell to the floor, bloody, his teeth falling out into his palm, and he was called Bloody-mouth forever after. Hard-hand never took his eyes from mine.

"Willingly?" he asked. There was so much yearning in that question it made me both exultant and sick to my stomach with all it implied.

"If all are safe. Willingly," I said slowly.

"So be it," he said. "I will come in the morning and escort you to my home, where you will be my wife." At that his men almost fell over with astonishment, but they said nothing.

He turned slowly, reluctant to take his eyes from me, but once that contact was broken he whirled into action, ordering his men outside to retreat, to set up camp by the stream in the sheep meadow, to leave all their plunder behind them. They complained loudly, as such men do, but Gris quietened them. He looked strangely at me, Gris. Later, when I knew more of Hard-hand's life I understood why, for giving mercy to defenseless women was not something anyone who knew him would have expected.

I spent the night collecting my belongings and crying in my mother's arms. But in the morning I rose up and put on my traveling clothes. My mother pinned my cloak with her best brooch, that had been made by Elric the Foreigner in her youth at the behest of my father Harald, as a betrothal gift.

"You are a worthy daughter of a great line," she said formally. "May the gods protect you and bring you safe home."

"My mother, live long and die blessed by kith and kin, by wealth and weal, by fame and fortune."

"Fame I shall garner from your actions, fortune you have already been to me, kith and kin shall live here safe, remembering your name with praise."

She was proud and stately but her eyes were full of tears, as were mine. Tears of grief and fear, for who knew what waited for me over the mountains in the strangers' land?

Customs differ, but work is the same everywhere. What I found over the mountains was a strange life, yet in essence it was the same life I had left. There were no women's quarters or men's hall. Families had their own quarters and women lived with their own men and children, all in one small house. It is not a good system, for the children annoy the men and the men annoy the women and no one ever gets a moment to sit quietly alone. Women are kept apart from the other women who would give them comfort and advice and share the child-rearing and the cooking and the endless scouring of pots. That was different. The herbs they used for cooking and preserving were sometimes strange to me. But the work was the same: they had goats, not sheep, but though goats are cleverer than sheep they still need to be fed and milked and delivered of their young. The wool was softer but a little harder to spin; the blankets lighter but warmer. Small differences.

The great difference was Hard-hand. On that first morning, when I left my mother, he had given me a horse to ride, a pony that carried me sure-footedly over the mountain trails, even past a great chasm that reached so far down into the depths of the earth that the bottom could not be seen. Hard-hand had ridden beside me all the way, but there he got off his horse and led my pony. He remounted and I thanked him, and then he tried to talk to me, although he had trouble finding something to say. He was not a clever man. In the end he told me about his land, his manor as he called it, and the people who owed him fealty. He had been elected a chieftain, at least, and so I would not be shamed in lying with him.

The gods' power worked strangely on me. In my heart I hated him—not so much for his attack on our steading, for such things are to be expected—but for forcing me to make the choice I had made, for taking me from my family and friends, for stealing from me my right to choose my husband. For turning the great power of my mother's line, which should be used to create strong families living in joy, into a weapon. Yet his person was not distasteful to me. When he reached for my hand I did not feel the urge to snatch it away.

We came to his farmstead with its cluster of small buildings in the late evening after a long, long ride. I was swaying in the saddle and he looked at me with concern as he lifted me down.

"Siggi!" he yelled. A woman came out of his house and went to greet him, to kiss him, but he pushed her back roughly.

"This is —" It was then he realized that he did not know my name, that he had ridden beside me all day without asking. Gris laughed.

"Asa," he said. "Her name is Asa." I learned later that it was typical of him, to learn what others did not know, did not think worth knowing.

"Asa," Hard-hand said, his voice caressing. The woman Siggi heard it, and her face went hard. "She is to be my wife," he said. "Treat her well. Tonight I will sleep in my mother's house and in the morning we will be hand-fasted."

Siggi hated me from that moment, and I did not blame her. She had been his concubine for three years before I came, and had borne him two daughters. Now he looked at her as though she were no more than a servant. She wanted me dead, but she did not dare disobey him.

She took me inside and showed me a room to sleep in, for in this place they slept in separate rooms, alone or with their husbands and children, instead of all together as we did.

I slept well through exhaustion and rose to wash and ready myself. Hard-hand came at sunrise, as the custom was there, and we were hand-fasted over a holy fire struck from flint that had never been used before. Unlike us, where the chieftain is the go-between to the gods, these people had a seer to perform all the ceremonies, a man who could always hear the gods' voices, as Athel sometimes could. I discovered, after, that their gods are smaller than ours but much more approachable, and anyone could go to their black stone altar and speak to the gods, ask for favor, beg forgiveness. I never dared, being a child of different gods, but Siggi gained great comfort when the gods told her I would be gone within a year.

She told me that the morning after my wedding, when I rose from my marriage bed bruised and shaken. Hard-hand was bound to me, but that did not change his nature, and it was his nature to take what he wanted when he wanted it. And I was bound to be faithful to him until death.

Siggi taunted me, "The gods have promised me, you will be gone in under a year! He will tire of you and kill you and I will have him back."

"Is that what the gods say?" I asked, looking her straight in the eyes.

She shrugged, uncomfortable. "They say you will be gone in under a year, and *I* will be the chieftain's wife." Then she smiled maliciously. "You thought you had stolen him but he will come back to me when he tires of you."

I nodded. "Until then, I am his wife and the mistress of this steading. Fetch me water to wash in."

She glowered, but she obeyed. I washed slowly, thinking about her message from the gods. "Gone" they had said, not "dead." I would have been an honorable wife to him if he had treated me with honor. But he did not. I rinsed the blood from my thighs and decided, at that moment, to kill Hard-hand.

He was not an easy man to kill. He slept lightly, with his hand on his weapons. He ate no food that I had not eaten first. Although he wanted me nightly and the power of the gods meant that I did not resist, he never trusted me. Nor should he have. But when two months went by and we realized I was with child, he relaxed a little.

That was a hard moment for me. I had planned to kill Hard-hand and then myself, but a child changed everything. I could not take the life of an innocent. Which meant I had to live. To live with Hard-hand until the child was born and I was well enough to travel. The day I realized I ran down to the goatfold and sobbed into the side of a nanny as she suckled her twins. I raged against Hard-hand's gods, because I thought they had caused this as a punishment for not worshipping them. Now I think I was wrong, but then I felt caught in a trap from which there was no escape. Except one.

So I played the part of the willing wife. I worked hard. I joked with the other women and with his men. I pretended to have fallen in love with him at first sight and the only one who did not believe me was Gris, who had looked at my face in my father's long hall when all the other men were looking at my body. There was a reason for that. Gris did not lie with women. Nor with men, so far as I could discover, but then men lying with men was scorned in that place and he would have been dishonored by it.

As it was, his brother taunted him about his refusal to marry and advised him to get a woman from the far north, one of the Skraelings, who were so hairy they looked like men and might thus satisfy him. Hard-hand talked like this only in private, and I think did not understand that he was heaping dishonor on his brother. A joke, he thought it. But to Gris it was no joke, and his heart hardened against his brother day by day. The taunting became worse after my pregnancy started to show and the seer pronounced the child a boy. Hard-hand bragged that he was founding a dynasty and that his brother would never have descendants. That, I believe, truly hurt Gris, and I was sorry for him and tried to turn the talk away to other things. We became, in a sense, allies.

I began, through the winter, to squirrel food away against the time I had borne the child and recovered enough to travel. I would have to kill Hard-hand and try to escape over the mountains. Steal a horse. I did not ride well, but I could manage. Again, no one noticed except Gris. He came to me one afternoon in late winter. The rest of the men were out searching for missing cows. That day my back protested at every movement, I was so gravid. It would be only a matter of days before the child came. Gris handed me a travel pouch filled with dried meat.

"It is a hard journey even in summer," he said. "It will be early spring when you are fit to travel and you will need to keep your strength up on the road."

I nodded. I felt that more was needed, that this man and I were bound together in a great undertaking. "My son will be your son," I said. "When he is grown and you have need of an heir, send for him, and he will come."

He stood very still for a long moment. "He will unite our peoples," he said finally. "And rule with justice."

I nodded formally, accepting his words. I expected to have many sons, then; to marry again and have a family with a man of my choice. Later I found that the gods exact a price for every boon. Never again did I look on a man with desire, no matter how well favored he was, nor how kind. I would have married Elric Elricsson otherwise, because he was a good man and a kind father, but it would have been a poor bargain for him, getting a wife with no passion in her. I think the gods would have resented it.

The lying-in was hard, but then all are. The women did everything right and with gentleness, even though I was a stranger, even Siggi. She took the mattress from the bed-box and laid in the straw thick and deep, which was just as well for there was a deal of blood as well as the birth-waters. Well, no need to talk about it, maybe. Once it is over, birth is a private thing, a memory of darkness and pain and piercing joy.

Perhaps they were kinder to me than I expected because my pains started on the night before the first day of spring, as all were readying for the holiday, and spirits were light after the bleakness of winter. My son was born at sunrise the next morning, an omen among those people that he would achieve greatness. His father had been felling an oak sapling for the Springpole when he was called to see the baby, so he announced the child's name would be Acton, which means place of the oak tree. I was content with that name. The oak tree is strong and long-lived, and gives food and shelter generously to birds and beasts. Yet I have never understood why those people kill a tree to celebrate spring, the season of birth. Among my people, we use a living tree to wind the ribbons on and dance around.

I recovered quickly from the birth, but I pretended to be weaker than I was. I think Siggi suspected, but as it kept Hard-hand from my bed she said nothing. I put off the baby's naming ceremony as long as I could, until my strength returned, for I knew that Hard-hand would drink long that night and it was my best chance to escape. The baby was strong, too, and did everything lustily—yelled rather than cried, sucked eagerly at the breast, kicked and waved his little fists against the binding clothes. He would not go to sleep unless his hands were free. The other women scolded me for giving in to him.

"His arms will grow crooked if they're not strapped tight to his sides in the night," said one.

"He'll be untamable as a boy, if you don't bind him now," said another.

Well, she was right about that. But I was so tired that I left his hands free so he would sleep and I could sleep with him.

When it seemed we were due for a few days of good weather, I set the naming day for the next day. Just before dawn, I took off Acton's clothes and wrapped him in a shawl, as Siggi advised me. She was smiling, which concerned me, but she was often smiling now as the year passed and it came time for her gods' prophecy to come true. Hard-hand carried the child to the black altar stone and laid him on it, then took the shawl away so that my baby lay naked on the stone.

"Gods of field and stream, hear your son. Gods of sky and wind, hear your son. Gods of earth and stone, hear your son. Gods of fire and storm, hear your son. I bring you a new son: Acton, child of the spring. He is your sacrifice."

Then he drew his belt knife. I couldn't believe it. I started forward, but Siggi held me back, laughing nastily. Hard-hand lowered his knife to the altar. Then, at the last moment, as I dragged myself out of Siggi's grasp, the seer brought forward a young fawn and laid it over Acton so that the knife slit the fawn's throat and the blood spurted over both stone and child. My boy cried out, but not in fear, and tried, I swear, to grasp the knife. A great shout went up from everyone at that and Hard-hand swept the fawn aside and picked up the baby, holding him high above his head. The sun came over the mountain at that moment and lit him red, so that the blood showed black against his skin.

"My son is a man already!" Hard-hand shouted and everyone cheered.

Every one of them, men and women both, drank deep throughout the day and by dusk Hard-hand was almost snoring. When Acton was fed and asleep I went to Hard-hand, took him by the hand and led him to our room. His men made lewd jokes as we went and Hard-hand belched and laughed with them.

I lay with Hard-hand for the first time since Acton's birth. But this is the strange thing—for the first time, he was gentle with me. He had never come to me drunk before and I wondered, and have wondered many times since, was it his real nature coming through because he was disarmed by the drink and by happiness, or was it an aberration caused by the liquor? I killed him in his sleep with his own belt knife, driving the blade deep into his neck because I was not sure exactly where to strike to reach his heart, and he died never knowing I had betrayed him. Yet it would not have felt like a betrayal if he had not been gentle with me. Did I do wrong? Still I do not know if what I did was murder or something else which has no name, because the need of women to kill in silence has no name. But I left that room weeping, which I had not expected.

The men outside had fallen asleep where they sat, except for Gris. I picked my way through the snoring men with Acton in my arms and made it safely to the stable where Gris was waiting. He had a good pony already saddled for me, a map, and my saddlebag packed full of food and clothing. I gave him some of my clothes and Acton's swaddling bands. We had arranged that he would take them to a cliff which was used for sacrifices, and make it look as though I had killed myself and the baby.

"Go the long way I have marked on the map," he said.

I nodded and kissed his cheek before I left him. He flushed, and covered his embarrassment by boosting me into the saddle, baby and all. Then I left that place behind me without a backward glance and rode into the night. Going home.

ASH

FLAX LED THE way through Golden Valley.

"We've been this way a hand of times, back from Foreverfroze to see our grandam. It's always best to take the back roads, yes? We don't sing here, or tumble. It's too small a place, Zel says, and they don't like foreigners much. So. East or west?"

"East," Ash said.

They veered off the main road and went by smaller paths and back lanes, avoiding the towns and the big horse farms that filled the valley bottom, and by mid-afternoon Ash was sick and tired of hearing "Zel says."

Away from the rich river flats the valley was rocky and wooded with spruce and birch as well as the poplars which gave the valley its name. The eastern trail wound up and down foothills that were surprisingly wild for such a settled, prosperous valley.

"We should be all right," Flax reassured him. "In the daylight it's a nice ride, Da says. A chance to get off the roads and into the woods."

Rowan and Swallow, Ash's parents, stuck to the well-worn roads, the roads dotted with big inns where silver could be earned. The idea of taking a "nice ride" in the woods was alien to Ash. The only time he had been "off the roads" was when his father took him to the Deep.

Just thinking about the Deep felt wrong. That's what he had been taught, what all the boys had been taught: once you leave, wipe it from your thoughts like chalk from a slate. It doesn't exist. Don't talk about it to each other, don't even think about it. If Acton's people found out, heard even a whisper of Traveler men meeting in secret, there would be massacres. Ash knew that was right. He had passed enough crossroads with full gibbets and pressing boxes leaking blood from the executed. That was what warlords did to all wrong-doers, even to their own people. For Travelers suspected of plotting, there would be no mercy.

Boys, or men, who talked about the Deep were shunned their whole lives, cut out of Traveler society as though they had the plague. They didn't last long, Rowan had said seriously. "We of the old blood need each other, and without that contact...we sicken and die, or worse." Ash remembered one man, a dry-stone fencer, who wandered through the Domains like a ghost, talking to no one except the shopkeepers who served him reluctantly, as they served all Travelers, until he stopped even going into shops. He had jumped from a quarry cliff and broken his neck, or drowned in the deep green water, but before that he had thinned down to a wraith with haunted eyes. Ash had been sorry for him, but his father had said, "Leave him be, Ash," in that tone which could not be disobeyed, because it was used so rarely. "He spoke too much," his father explained quietly, and it was the year after Ash's first visit to the Deep, so that he understood, and his eyes grew round with astonishment, that anyone would—could—disobey the demons.

In the old days, those who talked, even to each other, were hunted down and killed by the demons. That death might have been kinder, Ash thought. At least it was quick.

Ash couldn't question the prohibition. It was what had kept the Deep safe for a thousand years, and the Deep was all they had left.

They met no one all morning, not even charcoal burners.

"Zel says the valley lot don't come up here much. Scared of bears and wolves, she says."

Ash kept a better lookout after that, and did see bear scat in a clearing. There were wolf tracks by the small pool where they stopped to water the horses. Cam and Mud didn't want to drink there, shifting nervously and showing the whites of their eyes. Flax gentled them and again quoted his father.

"Da says they'll never settle within scent of wolves." So they moved on quickly, eating in the saddle. Heron had made bacon rolls for them, and packed more food that would keep for a couple of days: hard cheese, dried apples, flat biscuits.

They had reached well into Golden Valley by sunset, and found a camp by a stream edged by birch trees. Ash had almost ridden past it, but realized in time that it was up to him to name the camping place. This was the first time he had been the oldest member of a Traveling party, and it was both unsettling and pleasant to take responsibility. Because Flax was certainly not going to.

Over the course of the day, Ash had passed through intense dislike to a simpler annoyance. Flax was so *young*. He rode along with a sunny smile, a song constantly on his lips. He didn't even realize he was singing, most of the time; it was as normal as breathing. His singing irritated Ash intensely.

At first he thought his irritation was because every pure note reminded him of his own inability to sing. But eventually he realized that it was because he carried his own songs with him, in his head, all the time, and Flax's singing cut across that internal music.

He had never thought about the music in his head before, except on odd occasions when he was particularly relaxed, as he had been the first night at Elva and Mabry's. But now, in competition with Flax's simple songs, he discovered complex layers of melody and harmony, the sounds of flute and drums and pipes and human voice, intertwining and shifting as the day lengthened and his mood changed.

The realization was disturbing. As though he had been living all this time with a stranger in his head; a stranger who could actually make music, even if it were music no one could hear. He wondered how he had remained unaware of it all this time. The question forced him back in memory to the days when he Traveled with his parents. He remembered days of intense concentration as his father taught him the songs; nights of intense listening as his parents performed. There had been no room in his head then, for any other music.

There had been one day, a lovely, calm summer day when they were in Carlion, staying down near the harbor. He and his father had sat side-by-side on the dock, watching the fishing boats go out at sunset. Ash couldn't remember how old he had been—ten, maybe, or eleven. The evening sky had started a phrase of flute music in his head. He remembered wanting to share it with his father, and not knowing how. He couldn't sing it, he couldn't even hum. He had tried to learn flute the year before and had done badly, and at that moment he had wished intensely that he had persevered, so that he could at least share this fragment of melody with his father, even if he would never be good enough to play for customers. Then he had had a wonderful idea.

"Is there any way to write down music?" he asked his father. If he could write it down, he could teach his father the melody and then his father could play it!

"No!" his father said sternly. "Never! Music must never be written down. From mouth to ear, from fingers to eye, from heart to heart, that is how music must be shared. Do you understand?"

Sternness was so rare for his gentle father that Ash had nodded, startled, the melody vanishing from his mind. He had known that *songs* mustn't be written down; but hadn't understood that the prohibition included all music. Looking back, Ash realized that that was the moment he had stopped paying attention to the music in his head—because what good was it, if it could never be shared with anyone?

As he and Flax put up their tents—separate, thank the gods and Cael—Ash wondered about that prohibition for the first time. He knew it was all of a piece with the philosophy of the Deep, but he did not really understand what purpose it served. He had followed his father's teachings with blind loyalty until now—but if his father had truly withheld songs from him, that loyalty had been...mistakenly given. The thought made him feel sick, but it stayed with him. And, ignoring a guilty sense of doing something shocking, he started once more thinking about writing down music.

They did without a fire—Ash felt that the less attention they called to themselves the better. So they sat beside the stream to eat their cold beef and bread and dried apples. Flax pitched a crust into the chuckling water and asked, "Where are we going?"

Ash's first thought was that he shouldn't say, but Flax would know, sooner or later. He remembered asking his father the same thing, the first time they had left his mother with her sister near the Lake and taken the Road by themselves. His father had stared at him, as though weighing his words, and said, "I am going where I must go, and you are going with me. That is all you need to know."

From father to son, that was reasonable. From man to man, it would be intolerably arrogant. But he couldn't tell Flax *what* they were going to. Or exactly where.

"The wilds near Gabriston," he said reluctantly. Gabriston was on a bluff downstream of the Lake. The Hidden River, which ran from where the Lake plunged into a gorge just below Baluchston, came out at Gabriston. The many streams which fed the Hidden River had carved the local sandstone into innumerable canyons and gullies. The place was as wild as still existed in the Domains, and it had a bad reputation.

Flax's eyes widened. Although it was just past sunset, Ash could see him clearly enough. He looked like a little boy being told a story.

"Zel says that place is haunted by demons and ghosts!"

"Well, *real* ghosts are nothing to worry about. And as for demons—I'll introduce you to a few when we get there." Ash grinned. He couldn't resist the temptation to scare the boy a bit. Just a bit. But while Flax was young, he wasn't stupid.

"So they aren't real?"

"Oh yes, they're real. But they're probably not what you expect."

Frowning, Flax took up the napkin his dinner had been wrapped in—probably by Zel. She had trained him well. He shook out the crumbs, folded it carefully, and tucked it back into his pack.

"What path will we take?"

"I'd rather not go into Thegan's territory," Ash said, reluctant to explain why. The man he had killed to protect Bramble had been one of Lord Thegan's men. He remembered the man's friend, Horst, saying, "You've made yourself a bad enemy today," and knew that he'd spoken the truth. Thegan was a very bad enemy to have made; but there was nothing he could do about that now, except avoid him. "So when we reach the mouth of the valley, we'll ride east into Far North Domain and swing around to come to the wilds below Baluchston."

Flax nodded. He glanced at Ash quickly, as if gauging his mood.

"What's wrong with Thegan?" he asked.

As they were Traveling together, Flax had the right to know. Slowly, Ash explained, "When Martine and I first came into Golden Valley on our way to the Well of Secrets, we found two of Thegan's men attacking Bramble. So I stopped them. One of them got killed."

"You *stopped* them? You killed a warlord's man?" Flax's voice was high with excitement and his eyes were round. "*How?* What happened?"

At first, Ash misread his reaction for that of a youngster wanting an exciting story, and it annoyed him. Then Flax continued, "I didn't know you could *fight* them!" and Ash realized that the wonder in his face was because a Traveler had stood up to a warlord's man and survived. Conquered. He looked at Ash with complete hero worship, which made Ash feel sick.

"Don't you try," he said. "I've been trained as a safeguarder. You haven't." He'd meant it as a dismissal of his own skill; to imply that that skill was nothing special, just an outcome of training, but Flax took it the other way. He nodded solemnly, even more impressed.

"Can you teach me?"

Could he teach Flax? Well, he *could*—but whether he *should* was another question.

"We have too far to ride and you have too many other things to learn when we get there," he said, not wanting to refuse outright. "Maybe later."

"Is it a long way?" Flax asked, disappointed but philosophical about it.

"A few days' ride."

"Zel told me not to sing for my supper," he said. "How will we eat?"

"Don't tell me you always do everything Zel tells you?" Ash said.

Flax grinned and got up. "Not always," he said. His smile was an invitation to share confidences, but Ash wasn't in the mood.

"Let's go to sleep," Ash said.

Flax nodded and moved to open his tent flap, but paused halfway inside. "You could sing with me," he said. "There are some good drinking songs that need two voices."

Gods, that boy was annoying. "I don't sing."

Flax shrugged and disappeared into his tent. Ash lay in his own tent and deliberately didn't let himself think about the stonecasting he could not do, which might have paid their way. Instead, he sent his thoughts out to Bramble. Tonight was the Spring Equinox; whatever journey she was going on would start tonight, he was sure.

"Gods of field and stream, shield your daughter," he whispered into the night, and felt better for it.

MARTINE

"SHE LOOKS UNCOMFORTABLE," Martine said.

"I daresay she is," Safred answered, smoothing back a strand of Bramble's hair.

Bramble lay curled up on her side, twitching slightly. Her black hair shone in the early morning sun, her skin pale, sweat beading her forehead and making stains on her back and under her armpits. Wherever she was, whatever she was doing, it was taking a lot of effort.

Every little while they would support her head and tilt water into her mouth. She swallowed reflexively but her eyes stayed closed. She made no sound, although sometimes she seemed to mouth words. Sometimes she smiled. She did not look like she was asleep, because there was no relaxation of her muscles. She stayed tensed against—something.

What was happening to her was horrible, worse somehow in daylight.

"She agreed to do it," Safred reminded Martine, reading her thought, as she so often did. "This was her task, and she knew it."

"That doesn't make it right," Martine responded.

Cael and Zel were off in the forest, hunting or foraging or perhaps just walking. No doubt Zel was searching for a new flint, too. They had struck up an odd friendship, speaking little but attending briskly to all the practical things that had to be done: setting up tents, seeing to the horses, cooking. Martine could see that there was a comfort in doing ordinary, necessary jobs, but she couldn't pull herself away from Bramble. She was in danger, Martine was sure. She felt that conviction deep in her bones, although she had no idea what threatened her. Obscurely, she felt that she owed it to Ash, who had risked his own life to save Bramble's, to make sure that the girl was all right.

"Is there danger?" she asked Safred abruptly. While it went against the grain to ask someone else instead of the stones, if you had a prophet handy, you might as well use her.

"There's always danger."

"From what?" she demanded and then, remembering the ghost of the girl Ash had killed in Turvite and her warning, she added, "From whom?"

Safred spread her hands. "I don't know." She was embarrassed. "But the Forest has said Bramble will be safe, and we must trust to that. The gods are guiding her, no doubt."

As so often with Safred, Martine felt that she meant more than she was saying, that she intended her to feel in need of guidance. She remembered Bramble's attitude to Safred, defiant and challenging, and smiled. Perhaps she needed some of Bramble's defiance in order to protect her. Perhaps she should trust her own annoyance, and let it guide her.

"It's the Forest that's hurting Cael," she said harshly.

Safred paled. "He's better this morning."

"When he comes out of the Forest, he'll be worse," Martine predicted. "You should keep him out of the trees."

She was right. When Cael and Zel emerged, he was leaning on her arm, shaky and pale, but he waved aside Safred's offer to try to heal him.

"I'll last until we're away from here," he said. "You can try again then."

"Stay out of the Forest," Martine said. "It will do you no good."

He nodded somberly and then smiled, as if he couldn't help it. "Caught between flint and striker," he said, gesturing from the trees to the lake. "If one doesn't get me, the other will. But we found a stream a little way back, where we can water the horses and fill our skins."

"Don't trust it," Martine said. "Check it every time, in case it has the smell of—whatever that was at the other stream."

Zel nodded. "Hell'll melt before I trust any stream in this place," she said. She looked at Bramble. "How's she?"

"Fighting something," Martine said. Bramble did, indeed, look as if she were fighting some internal battle, her face tight, her arms twitching, like a dreamer in a nightmare.

"Protect her, then, if you feel you must. She may be glad of it," Safred said.

Martine sat down next to Bramble. She doubted that the threat to Bramble would come from the outside, but she loosened the knife in her belt and the one in her boot and sat with her back to Bramble and the lake, scanning the Forest edge. But although she tried to put all her attention into her eyes, she was aware of Bramble, twitching slightly behind her, all her muscles taut as though she wanted to run, far away from here. Martine wanted to run, too. Her body was still keyed up from the ritual, and she was feeling unsettled and nervy.

She also didn't want to think about what "destiny" of hers required her to stay in the Last Domain instead of Traveling with Ash. She had seen many people meet their destiny, and it had mostly been very unpleasant, often deadly. She shrugged. Well, if it came, it came. Elva was safe, and that was all that mattered. Elva and the baby.

LEOF

HE HAD LET his anger at the Voice doom the town. He should have swallowed the insult and kept her talking, convinced her to surrender and *then* consult the Lake. Buy some time.

Leof rode back to the camp in a foul mood, angry with himself, Vi, Thegan, even the Lake itself, ignoring the glances Hodge and the men exchanged behind his back. What was the point of this? Fighting the Ice King's men when they had attacked the Domains, that had been *necessary.* This was just politics.

Thegan was overseeing the making of fire arrows, checking that the men didn't wind so much linen onto the arrowheads that they would go wildly off course when fired. Leof knew the drill. The arrows would be dipped in oil and lit just before they were shot into the air to rain down destruction on Baluchston, as they had tried to do to the reed beds. The Lake doesn't like fire, he thought. She won't be pleased about this. At noon, they won't even be spectacular. The thought gave him a thread to follow when he spoke to Thegan.

"It's a shame to fire these things in broad daylight, my lord," Leof said. "They're much more frightening at night. Sometimes you only need one or two before they surrender."

"So they're going to fight?" Thegan rested one brown boot on a barrel of oil and gazed sharply at him. The spring sun picked out the lines on his face, but it flattered him; he looked sharp as well, sharp and ready for action, ready for battle.

"The Voice has gone to 'consult with the Lake,' " Leof said deprecatingly, as though "consult with the Lake" was a euphemism for something else, something more political. "She says it will take until sunset. I don't think she—the Voice, I mean—will let her people be killed. She would surrender before that."

"So she will surrender as we approach the town."

"Mmm. If she's there. She said the consultation had to happen in deep water. That she—and perhaps others, do you think, my lord?—would be out on the water all day. If we attack when she's not there —"

"Then she will be spared the sight of her town being put to the flame," Thegan said briskly. "Order the men up for noon. Tell them to have their farings early, and to eat lightly. We don't want them weighed down and sleepy for the fighting."

Leof bowed. "My lord."

He knew Thegan well enough to accept that any attempt to sway him was useless. The only thing that could stop the sacking of the town was Thegan's death. Perhaps the Lake would accomplish that. Half of him was appalled at the thought, while the other—the part that had been well taught by Thegan, he recognized—knew that it was the simple truth. And although he winced at the thought of Thegan's men descending on the townsfolk, angry at the Lake's destruction of their comrades, and believing Thegan's claims about the enchanter from Baluchston, still he was Thegan's man, and would follow his orders. What else could he do? Set his own will up against that of the warlord? Claim some right to command, a right that didn't exist in any form? Nor would walking away, giving up his position, help. The town would still die. Perhaps he could keep the men under some control once the town was fired: keep the rapes and looting to a minimum. He wondered if Acton had ever faced a moment like this. But Acton had laughed as he killed, a thing Leof had never understood.

He called the sergeants together and gave them Thegan's orders. As they left, he called Hodge back, knowing that Thegan had been testing him all day, and would continue to test him.

"Get those lists of the dead ready for me. My lord wanted them before noon."

"Aye, my lord," Hodge said. He hesitated. "The old lady... she was the Voice?"

Leof nodded. "She's gone to consult the Lake. But my lord Thegan wants their surrender by noon, and if he doesn't get it . . ." Leof shrugged.

Hodge pulled at his lower lip, considering. "Seems like someone should have told her my lord doesn't like to be kept waiting. Saving your presence, my lord."

Leof chuckled without humor. "Perhaps someone did, sergeant. And perhaps she ignored it."

Hodge spat in the dust. "More fool her, then," he said dismissively, and went to follow his instructions.

The sun was climbing. Hodge brought back the list of the dead—too long, much too long, no wonder Thegan was angry, Leof thought. A waste of men, of time, of training—of sorrow and loss.

He presented it to Thegan in his tent.

"What a waste," Thegan said, frowning blackly. "When I think of all the training we put into getting the Central Domain men into shape!"

Leof said nothing. He was an experienced commander; he'd thought the same thing. It just sounded colder said aloud. He nodded and went back to readying his men, lecturing them about discipline and orderly occupation of the town, hoping to fend off the worst behavior.

"Kill only those who resist," he said. "Remember, we don't know how many were involved in the enchanter's plot. Most of the townsfolk are probably as innocent as you or I. No breaking into homes without orders. No rape. If a woman fights, kill her cleanly. No destruction. My lord Thegan wants this town intact for his own use, and I'd remember that if I were you." He said it with a smile and there were a few chuckles from the older men.

"Sergeants, you will be held responsible for the behavior of your men."

The sergeants turned as one to glare threateningly at their squads.

"We're like Acton's men," Leof concluded. "We don't want to destroy everything, because we'll have a use for it ourselves. Understood?"

The men nodded, but Leof doubted that, in the thick of it, amid the noise and the heat and the shouting, they would remember to control themselves. He'd done what he could.

The sun was climbing. Less than an hour to noon, and no word from Baluchston. Leof found himself checking the road to town every few moments, hoping to see a messenger bringing the surrender.

At noon, Thegan emerged from his tent and came to stand before his troops. The sun lit his fair head and reminded Leof of the old songs about Acton marching into battle with a head of shining gold.

"The town has defied us. The town has killed our comrades. The town will be taken. You have your orders. Kill any who resist." He paused deliberately. "There will be pleasures afterward, for those who fight well. But I want order and I want discipline." He smiled, that miraculous smile that no one could resist, and the men smiled back, even the crusty old sergeants. "Those who fight well today will be rewarded. Are you ready to avenge your comrades?" He raised his voice to a shout on the last words.

"*Yes! Aye!*" they shouted back.

Thegan nodded and turned to his officers.

"Tib, take the lead —" he began but a scuffle behind the men attracted his attention and a quick frown.

"What's toward?" Leof shouted at the rear.

"A messenger, sir," someone shouted back.

A stir went through the men, half of relief and half of disappointment. Leof sent a quick prayer of gratitude to the gods and shouted again, "Take his horse and let him through, fools!"

But the man who struggled through the troops was clearly not a messenger from Baluchston. He had ridden hard and long; ridden to the point of exhaustion. He was an older man, completely bald, wearing a dark robe and carrying a stonecaster's pouch at his belt.

He was staggering as he walked, and almost fell as he passed Leof. Leof supported him the last few steps to Thegan.

"My lord," the man said. His voice was hoarse with travel dust and he tried to clear it. Leof grabbed a waterskin from a nearby sergeant and gave it to him. He swallowed a mouthful and waved the rest away.

"Later. My lord, Carlion is attacked."

Thegan straightened, his attention like an arrow finding its mark.

"Who? Not old Ceouf?"

The man shook his head.

"Not by the living, lord. By the dead."

A stir ran through the men.

"To my tent," Thegan said, nodding to his officers to follow. Leof supported the man until he sank onto the bench before Thegan's work table.

"Now," Thegan said.

"I tried to warn the Council," the man said in a flat voice leached by exhaustion. "I'm a stonecaster, I saw disaster coming on us and I warned them. Every stonecaster in the city warned them, but there was no way we could read the truth in the stones and no way we could prepare for such an attack."

"The dead," Thegan said. "An attack by the dead?" His voice was carefully noncommittal.

The man smiled. An intelligent smile. "It sounds mad, I know. You remember the enchanter who tried to raise the ghosts against Acton? To give them strength and body?"

Thegan nodded. Everyone knew that story. After Acton's men had taken Turvite, a mad enchanter had tried to raise a ghost army against him, the ghosts of those he had killed. The story said she had wanted to make them solid so they could fight again, but when that failed, she tried to use the ghosts to frighten Acton away. Acton had laughed at her, asking why he should fear the dead when he had already defeated them alive? He wanted his people to live with a reminder of their victory. He laughed as he said it, and she cursed him with the loss of the only thing he held dear, that he should never have what he most wanted, but he shrugged and said he already had it, and gestured to the city. Then she jumped off the cliffs.

"Someone has found a way to do what she could not. Someone has given ghosts a strong arm." He paused, coughing, and Leof handed him the waterskin again. This time he drank deeply and sighed afterward.

"They came at night, maybe a hundred of them. Only a hundred, but nothing could stop them. We had been warning the town for a week and most men slept with their weapons by their bed, so the ghosts found resistance, but it was a slaughter anyway. How can you kill someone who is already dead? How can you stop someone who feels no pain, who does not bleed?"

Leof imagined such a battle and felt himself pale. The other officers clearly felt the same. Thegan's face was unreadable, but familiar to

Leof. It was the face of his general, a battle-hardened officer who had faced fierce enemies many times, and had found solutions where others had seen only disaster. The ability was one of the reasons his men followed him blindly—Thegan could always see a way clear even when they could not.

"Cut off their arms," he said. "Cut off their legs."

The man nodded. "Yes," he said. "That might work. But lord, it would take a trained fighting man to do that, and we were just merchants! They killed...they killed so many..."

"So you ran."

"I fought," the man said bitterly, and pulled his sleeve up to show a long wound, barely crusted over. "Then I realized that perhaps no one would survive, and what we needed was an army. So I came to you. I have been riding for...I don't know how long. Three horses have foundered under me. But it was the night after the full moon when we were attacked."

Thegan nodded. "You did the right thing. Go and rest now."

Tib went to the tent flap and called a solider to support the man and take him somewhere he could sleep.

"Wait," Thegan said. "Your name?"

"Otter," the stonecaster said. He hesitated. "Lord, when I rested a moment or two, I cast the stones. Carlion was just the beginning."

Thegan nodded, his face as grave as Leof had ever seen it.

"Rest," he said, his hand on Otter's shoulder comfortingly. "We will manage it from here."

Otter smiled, a startlingly sweet smile. His eyes were strange, not one color or another. Right now they reflected Thegan's brown uniform and shone dark with flecks of gold.

"I knew I was right to come to you. The stones told me so."

Thegan smiled at him and clapped him on the shoulder in farewell.

Thegan addressed his officers. "Strike camp. We march to Carlion. The nature of the attackers—that stays between us until the men need to know. We must avoid panic."

There was nothing else to be said. As Leof turned to go, Thegan stopped him with a hand on his arm.

"A wave from the Lake here, on the same night as the attack on

Carlion. No coincidence. Which means this was meant to weaken us so we could not aid the fight against this ghost army."

"So," Leof ventured, hoping to rescue something from this new development, "perhaps it was not a Baluchston enchanter at all? Someone who could raise the dead like this could certainly control the Lake . . .?"

Thegan looked sharply at him, but nodded. "Perhaps. Still, if one attack has been aimed at us, so may others be. I want you to ride immediately for Sendat and take control there. The reserves we left there must be trained up fast and hard; call in the oath men from the villages and begin training them too. We are going to need every spear, I think. As the stonecaster said, Carlion was just the beginning."

Leof nodded slowly. Every village owed the warlord men to fight in times of war—the men took an oath to come when called, and were given weapons and some training in return. But they weren't soldiers, and they would need much more training before they could fight effectively.

"I will send out messages from here to the other warlords," Thegan said. "We must all be prepared. Perhaps other things have happened elsewhere."

"Yes, my lord."

Thegan picked up a knife from the table and studied the way the light fell on its blade. "Protect the Lady Sorn," he said softly. "At all costs."

"With my life, my lord," Leof said immediately. Thegan shook his head and smiled—not the miraculous smile, but the real one, the one he kept for people he trusted. It was, as always, like being let into a secret room, a treasure house. Leof couldn't help but smile back.

"Not with your life, Leof. I need you to stay alive, too. Let others die for her."

The combination of intimacy and callousness left Leof not knowing what to say. Thegan threw the knife down onto the table so that the blade stuck in.

"Get my fort ready for war, Leof. You know what we'll need."

Leof nodded. "Train them how to cut off someone's arms while they're trying to kill you," he said dryly.

"Exactly," Thegan said and smiled the miraculous smile. He handed Leof a sheaf of papers. "Take the list of the dead with you and inform the families. Ride well."

Leof hesitated. "Do you have any word for me to take to the Lady Sorn?"

"No time. Just tell her the truth, and that I think of her."

Leof saluted and left; gathered Thistle, his two remounts, his groom and their gear and was on the road before the last of the tents had been struck.

Riding out of camp, he couldn't stop himself wondering why he had been chosen to guard Sendat. Thegan was on his way to give aid to a free town. To protect it. From inside its gates, no doubt. How long would it need that protection? Forever? Carlion's days as a free town were over, it seemed to Leof, and he wondered if he had been dispatched to Sendat in case he developed any inconvenient scruples about taking over a free town.

The only free town with a harbor near the Central Domain.

"From cliff to cove," he said aloud, and encouraged Thistle to a canter as they passed the last of Thegan's pickets. "He'll have it all."

Part of him was proud of his lord's success, his intelligence and strategy. That was the loyal part, the part that believed that Thegan's plan to unite the Domains would bring lawful prosperity to everyone. He concentrated on that part, on thinking those thoughts. Because that's who he was, even if he had let Bramble go against Thegan's orders. He was Lord Thegan's man, or he was no one.

BRAMBLE

THE SWORD IN her hand was heavy, but it was the smell that roused her: the acrid smell of fear-sweat on her own body. That smell was so unfamiliar to her that she reached out her other senses urgently, only to recoil when she found herself in a man's body, full grown. Full grown, but with only one arm. Elric? He was standing on a ledge a small way from the steading, looking out over the undulating landscape. She judged it was summer, and there was a band of men riding toward him, appearing and disappearing as they rode over the ridges and into the dales. They were moving fast. Elric was trying to still his quick breath, so he could shout. He turned half toward the steading.

"They're coming!"

An indistinct shout of acknowledgment came from the hall, and men with shields and spears ran out. They threw themselves flat on the ground, taking cover behind rocks and wedging shields in front of them. They held one spear in one hand and a couple more in the other, and waited, staring intently toward the riders.

A raiding party. A war party. Bramble didn't want to live through a raid. If Elric lived through it. She didn't want to die again. If Elric died while she was with him, what would happen to her? Don't think about it, she thought. There's nothing you can do, so forget it. Where is Acton?

Then she realized that Acton was one of the men—the very young, or old men—who were readying their spears. He was still only around thirteen or so, and he was smiling. There were other boys, who looked even younger. One of them was probably Baluch, but she had no idea which one. It was a strange thought, that she could know someone so deeply from the inside but have no idea what he looked like. The boys were all so young. Bramble supposed that most of the men were off raiding someone else's steading, and felt a stab of contempt for them.

Elric cleared his throat. "Wait," he ordered. "Make every shot count."

The band approaching them numbered about twenty men, all riding the short, stocky ponies Bramble had seen before. They wore leather fighting gear, with helmets of what looked like dark wood but which was probably leather. Oddly, they carried no shields. She was used to seeing the warlord's men riding, as Thegan's men had done, with shield on the left arm and right hand free for the sword. As though her thought had sparked the action, each rider reached for something slung across his back. A bow, short, curved, lethal-looking. They nocked arrows in unison and let fly. Elric dropped to the ground and Bramble heard the arrows whistle over, heard some thuds and swearing from his left. Someone had been hit. Elric lifted his face from the ground.

"Shields, ho!" he shouted, and jumped to his feet, letting go his sword and picking up a spear in one movement. Unlike the other men, he had no shield to cover him. He knew it; it was why he was sweating fear, she realized. He threw the spear, aiming not at the men, but at the horses. Of course, Bramble thought bitterly. They always suffer first.

Elric had no time to see if his spear had gone home. The raiders let loose another flight of arrows and one took him in the shoulder, a sudden thud followed by burning pain. She heard Acton shout, "Elric!" and then the waters came up and tumbled her away.

"There'll be more before they've finished," Asa's voice roused her. Bramble was back in a woman's body, thank the gods, looking down at Elric this time, swabbing blood away from his shoulder in the hall next to the fire. He looked very pale. With his shirt off, Bramble could see the scars of earlier fights, and the seared stump of his arm, the skin shiny with the burn marks of cauterization.

"You were lucky," the woman she looked through scolded him. It was old Ragni's voice. "You shouldn't have been out there at all, with no shield and jumping up just so they could get a good shot at you."

Elric bore it silently. "How many?"

Ragni quietened for a moment, spreading leaves—comfrey, from the smell—on the wound. "Two," she said softly. "Old Weoulf and that boy of Dati's. A few wounded."

"Baluch?"

"He's fine, he's fine," Ragni said, her voice back to normal. "He's off with Acton and Sebbi, burying the villains. No fire for them. They can rot in the cold hells."

A groan interrupted her. She looked over and spat on the floor next to a man lying flat, with no pillows or blankets under him as there were under Elric. He was bleeding slowly from a stomach wound. The enemy, Bramble presumed. He looked much like the people from the second wave of the invasion of the Domains, with Merrick's coloring, auburn hair and hazel eyes. Just another one of Acton's people, as far as Bramble was concerned. But not for Acton.

Acton then came in, followed by Asa and a stocky boy with wiry blond hair—Baluch? Bramble wondered—and stood staring at the man on the floor.

"Water," the man begged. Bramble understood him, but saw that neither Acton nor Asa did. The gods' gift worked for this man's language too, it seemed. But Ragni had seen a lot of men die in her time, and she knew what he needed.

"Wants water," she said, her voice cold.

"Give it to him," Acton commanded.

"Won't make any difference," Ragni said. "Gut wound like that, he's not got long."

"I want to talk to him," Acton said, his jaw set. "Give it to him."

She grumbled under her breath but she filled a drinking horn and handed it to Acton.

He squatted next to the man and lifted his head enough so that the man could drink. Half the water dribbled out the corners of his mouth. Bramble, too, had seen enough people die to know that Lady Death was standing close by.

"Why do you come?" Acton demanded. "Why do you attack us?"

The man understood. He smiled thinly and muttered three words, "The Ice King."

His speech was gibberish to everyone except Elric, who twitched on his blanket. "That was my father's tongue," he said. "It means the Ice King."

"Your king sends you?" Asa asked. "Why?"

The man smiled again, bitterly. He had to force the words out. "Ice King takes everything." That was all. His face paled and his eyes closed. Acton eased his head back onto the floor and turned away to talk to his mother. The stocky boy lingered a little longer, staring at the dying man.

"Don't waste your pity on him, Sebbi," Ragni said, venom in her voice. "Dati's boy is dead, and it might have been you."

Sebbi looked at her with shock but the waters came in a wave, a breaking wave, and threw Bramble backward into the dark, so she didn't hear his response.

The water trickled away and kept trickling, an intrusive and yet pleasant noise, a small stream over rocks. She was dabbling her fingers in it, sitting on grass beside the water and looking up. For a moment, that was all she knew: the sound and the feel; then her sight cleared and she found herself looking up at Acton. Not her, of course. Baluch. This time she recognized him immediately, the feel of his mind, with a faint pipe music interplaying with the sound of the water under his thoughts, the feel even of his body, was familiar.

Acton was standing by a small cliff where a spring issued from the rock and trickled down past Baluch. The contrast to the last time they were on the mountainside was striking. Now it was summer, warm and fragrant, the sky blue, the sun mid-morning high. The grass Baluch sat on was springy and bright green. Almost too green. Bramble smelled flowers—lilies of the valley, she thought, but she couldn't see them because Baluch was staring at Acton.

"Can you tell us *now*?" he said, his voice half-amused and half-exasperated. He glanced to his left where the stocky boy—Sebbi, Bramble remembered—was sitting. They exchanged looks of exasperation.

Acton grinned at them. He had grown a bit, was maybe a year older, fourteen or fifteen, as big as most men already, but she could see he hadn't come into his full growth.

"All right. We are going —" he paused for effect, but he looked a little hesitant as well "— to the Ice King."

"*What?* Are you insane?" Baluch jumped to his feet. Sebbi followed.

Acton grinned more widely, then sobered. "You remember that man who died? He said the Ice King had sent them."

"Of course I remember, but —" Sebbi said.

"We don't know enough! We don't know if they come willingly, what he wants, why he attacks us—we just don't know enough." Baluch regarded Acton. Bramble could tell that he was measuring him, weighing his words.

"So this doesn't have anything to do with Harald refusing to take you on the trading expedition?"

Acton scowled, for once looking like a typical boy. "I'm bigger than most of the men already!" he complained.

"Yes, yes, we all know that," Sebbi said, his tone mocking. "You're bigger and stronger and a better fighter, too."

"Well, aren't I?" Acton challenged him.

Sebbi paused and Baluch held his breath. Bramble realized that there seemed to be some tension between Acton and Sebbi which made Baluch uneasy. But neither of the others was tense, just concentrated. "In the practice yard, yes," Sebbi said. "You're good. But there is more to battle than skill. You've never killed."

"I have. I threw my spears. They fell."

Shrugging, Sebbi replied, "The horses fell. The men—some were killed by the fall, the hooves. Some by the second flight of spears. But who killed whom . . ." His tone was challenging.

Acton smiled, rejecting the challenge. "Only the gods know."

Sebbi laughed bitterly. "You're not the only one who missed out. They wouldn't let *me* go because it wouldn't have been fair to *you*. Even though I'm a year older. Even though *my* spear took one of them down cleanly."

"That's true. It was a fine cast," Baluch said quietly.

Acton nodded and the strain went out of Sebbi's face. Baluch sat again and plucked at the grass, avoiding Acton's eyes. Acton sat down beside him, hands hanging between his raised knees.

"We're ready, Bal. You know it."

"You're Harald's only heir. He doesn't want to risk you when things are so uncertain."

"I want to go to sea!" Acton said, yearning naked in his voice. "I've always wanted to."

"There may not be battle. It's just a trading journey."

Acton laughed. "Oh, yes, just trading. How many times have they come back from trading without having fought? Once, maybe, in our lifetimes? There are brigands on the dragon's road as well as on land. Besides, it's the sea itself I want, not just the fighting."

"The dragon's road itself is as dangerous as any battle," Sebbi remarked.

"Exactly!" Acton said, eyes shining.

"So if Harald won't let you risk your life there, you'll do it here?" Baluch's tone was dry.

Acton looked sideways at him, smiling, mischief in his eyes. "We do really need to know more, Bal. I'm not planning for us to fight. Just to scout. To see what we can see of this Ice King's country and his people. We've traded with them for generations and now suddenly they have nothing to trade and begin to attack us. This Ice King is driving them, but we don't know why. If we knew more, we might be able to make a truce. But right now, we're snowblind."

"Why now, when the men are away? Why not stay and help protect the steading?"

"This is more important." Acton had a stubborn look, but there was something underneath it. "The chieftains will meet at the autumn Moot."

"That's what you're planning! You're going to stand up in front of everyone and boast —" Sebbi accused.

"Not boast!" Acton protested. "Report back. To everyone, not just Harald. All of us." He avoided Baluch's eyes. "Decisions must be made by all the chieftains, not just my grandfather."

"What does your mother think of this?"

"Well, she said she'd leave our packs behind this rock . . ." Acton said, getting up and ferreting out three packs as he spoke. He dangled them from his hands, his eyes alight with mischief and excitement. "So I suppose she thinks it's a good idea!"

"Hmm," Baluch said, taking his own pack.

"Sebbi's mother helped. And if *your* mother objects," Acton added to Baluch, "she would have told the gods and they would tell you. But they haven't, have they?" There was a note of real anxiety in his voice.

Baluch shook his head.

"No. They haven't told me anything," he said reluctantly. Bramble could feel the gods listening, watching, but they exerted no pressure on either her or Baluch. For a moment, she seemed to catch one of Baluch's thoughts, a memory of his mother, dead in childbirth with him. The memory was sharp with long regret. She pulled away from it, not wanting to share his mind anymore deeply than she did already.

Acton whooped exuberantly, sounding much younger than he actually was. "So let's go!"

Despite themselves, the other boys smiled with excitement. "We're not in this for adventure," Baluch cautioned. "If we get caught . . ."

"No," Acton agreed immediately. "We mustn't be caught." His face became determined, and much older. "The chieftains need to know."

"So which way do we go?" Sebbi asked, settling his pack.

Acton shot Baluch a mischief-look. "I was hoping the gods might guide us."

"So that's why you brought me!"

Acton clouted him on the shoulder. "I wouldn't have gone without you, you know that!" They smiled at each other. "But it would be helpful if the gods —"

Baluch shook his head. Bramble could feel no pressure from the gods in either his mind or hers. "We'll have to make our own way." Almost in apology, he added, "They don't talk often, you know."

"Mmm. Well, I did bring a map, just in case you weren't feeling holy."

Baluch threw a pebble at him and they laughed. The trickle of the water became a flood and moved Bramble, tumbling, through the darkness.

She was singing, a kind of singing, a kind of calling out, calling something. Her throat tightened and relaxed rhythmically and the notes came out, not words but sounds, clear like bells, and underneath it a clicking sound, rhythmic too but uncoordinated with her calling. It was both musical and very irritating at the same time. Her sight cleared as the waters subsided, and she saw what she was calling. Goats. Goats with small blocks of wood tied around their neck, which clicked together as they moved. In Wooding, which seemed further than a thousand years away to Bramble, they had bells for their goats, at least for the lead wether and a couple of others. She wouldn't have thought the wooden blocks would make enough noise to keep track of the flock if they got lost in the forest.

Then she saw that they were on a steep hillside, with no trees, just low bushes and grasses covered with low-growing flowers. The girl stopped her singing–calling as the goats crowded around her, nuzzling at her hands and sides, one of them trying to eat her apron. She laughed and pushed the animal away. Bramble felt herself relaxing. This was known territory, at last. Animals, womanhood, the smell of goats and wild thyme, the bright blue of crane's-bill peeping from the rocks, all of it was familiar. Her mother used crane's-bill to make a blue dye. Bramble relaxed a little, but wondered why the gods had brought her here.

The girl clucked to the goats and sat down on the grass as they wandered nearby to graze. She pulled an apple and some cheese from her apron pocket and began to eat, her fingers teasing the blue crane's-bill flowers. From her hand and bare arm, she was quite young, and redheaded with freckles. Bramble was reminded of Safred jamming her old hat on her head. This girl apparently accepted her freckles.

The black nanny goat which had tried to eat her apron came over to see if she could cadge some of the girl's lunch, but the girl laughed and pushed the goat's inquisitive head away.

"Not enough for me, let alone you, too, Snowdrop," she said. "At least you can eat grass."

Bramble wondered at that. The season was high summer; there should have been enough crops ripe by now.

The girl plucked a flower and threaded it into her hair by her ear.

"You know, Snowdrop, they say if you sleep naked, wearing crane's-bill in your hair, on Mid-Summer's Eve, the Wise One will send you a dream of your future husband. Do you think it's worth a try?" Laughing, the girl lay back on the grass and closed her eyes. Taking advantage of her inattention, the goat came closer and stretched its neck to reach the cheese inside its cloth. The girl sat up, still laughing.

"I can't trust you for a second, wretched thing!" She pushed Snowdrop away firmly, the flesh warm and comforting under her hands.

The language the girl was speaking sounded different to Baluch's. Bramble could understand it, but the difference made her wonder just where she was. Over Snowdrop's back she saw three figures come into view around a curve of the mountain. Three young men. Acton and two others. One of them was Sebbi.

Bramble had seen Sebbi through Baluch's eyes; now she could see Baluch through the girl's. He was even fairer than Acton—a tow-headed, pale-eyed youth who next to Acton looked slight but who had a rangy strength of his own.

She watched his face as he looked at the girl and saw his hesitation, and then the pleasure and desire in his eyes. But the girl was looking mainly at Acton. Sebbi noticed that, too, and his mouth tightened. The girl didn't notice. She was smiling at Acton.

Oh no, Bramble thought. Not that. She could feel heat flowing through her, the quick heat of the young who want things immediately, right *now.* This girl was smitten with Acton at the first glance. He was worth looking at, Bramble admitted grudgingly, if you liked that tall blond muscly type. The girl obviously did. Bramble thought wryly that the gods were having a joke with her. The only person she'd felt comfortable being since this began was an empty-headed girl who wanted the man she hated most.

The boys hesitated as they saw her, but she had clearly seen them and there was nowhere to go on the bare hillside. Bramble could see Acton make the decision; let's pretend we're just harmless travelers, boys out for a lark. He'd noticed that she was pretty, just as Baluch had, but without Baluch's hesitation and reserve.

Acton smiled. Bramble wanted to think that it was a smile calculated to charm, like the way Thegan smiled, but even she had to admit that it wasn't. It was simply pleasure: a sunny day, a pretty girl, a chance to stop hiking and chat. And get information. Oh, yes, that was in his eyes, too: determination.

"Greetings," he said easily, in the girl's language. Bramble suspected that Acton had learned some of the foreigners' tongue from Elric.

The girl dimpled and played with one long red plait. "Greetings," she said. She flicked a glance at Baluch and Sebbi but returned immediately to Acton's face. "You're not from around here . . ." It was both question and invitation. Acton moved closer and sat down on a nearby rock.

"From a couple of valleys over," he said easily. Was that a lie or a simple understatement? Bramble glimpsed Baluch's face and realized he was undecided about the morality of lying to this far too trusting young woman. The girl wasn't interested in interpreting Baluch's expression, just Acton's, which was one of pure admiration.

"We thought we'd take a trip and, maybe...catch a glimpse of the Ice King."

His statement was daring, Bramble thought, said so straightforwardly, but perhaps it was safer than making up excuses.

The girl pouted. The movement was unfamiliar to Bramble, and she instantly hated the sensation. I am not like her! she thought defiantly to the gods. I just like goats. Her own emotions almost distracted her from what the girl was saying.

"Well, that's not hard. He's only one more ridge over. It's not like you can miss him."

Acton frowned, puzzled as Bramble was by the girl's tone, which was both resentful and dismissive, as though Acton had spoiled the afternoon by mentioning the king.

"Plenty of time for that later," Acton said, sliding down the rock so that he was sitting next to the girl. "There are more interesting things here."

She smiled and leaned back on her hands, tilting her head so that she looked at him from under her lashes. Her breasts were bigger than Bramble's and it was a strange sensation, to feel them move and shift under her dress. Acton smiled back and trailed one finger down her cheek. The girl's body came alight, on fire instantly. Acton's thumb rubbed against her lower lip and her tongue came out reflexively, licking both her lips and his skin. He leaned closer. The girl's eyes closed.

No, no, no! Bramble thought to the gods. Get me *out* of here! Now! But they didn't listen to her.

Baluch and Sebbi had disappeared from the girl's sight and thoughts, but just as Bramble felt the warmth of Acton's face next to the girl's and was bracing for his kiss, Baluch shouted loudly, "Acton! Get over here!"

Acton jumped to his feet immediately and ran, leaving the girl flustered and furious.

She jumped to her feet and turned on them. "What do you think you're *doing*?"

They were standing on the ridge, looking down into the next valley. Acton's hand had closed on Baluch's shoulder as if for support. The three stood silently, staring.

The girl advanced on them. "What's so important . . .?" Then she realized what they were staring at, although it was still out of her sight. Bramble impatiently willed her to go forward so that she could see.

"Oh, gods! Is that all?"

Acton turned to her. "*All?*"

She tossed her head, another action which Bramble immediately hated. "Oh, I know, he's destroying everything, he's wiping out all our farmland, we're all going to starve —" There was a sob in her voice and Bramble realized she was genuinely upset. "But there's nothing we can *do* about it and I thought we were going to have a nice day, just for once, just one day when I didn't have to think about disaster."

She moved a step forward, sank down and began to cry, but not before Bramble had seen what was in the next valley. Or rather, what was filling the next valley.

Ice.

The Ice King. Not a person, but a river of ice.

It filled the valley and covered the hills beyond. There were some peaks that stood out in the far distance, but each of the valleys between had been overrun. The ice stretched, white and blue and deep black where fissures broke the surface, as far as she could see. At its leading edge it showed as a striped cliff of blue and darker blue and white on top. It was too big to comprehend, too beautiful to be anything but terrifying.

As the girl's sobbing quietened, Bramble found that she could hear the crunch and screech of ice breaking, of rocks being slid along with force. The river was moving. Acton heard it too. He crouched down next to the girl.

"How fast does it move?" he asked gently.

She shrugged, still crying.

"How long has it been in that valley?" Baluch asked, not looking away from the ice.

"Since three days after the Springtree dance," the girl said, sniffing and wiping her nose on her sleeve.

"It's Mid-Summer tonight," Baluch said. "That means it's eaten the valley in less than two months."

"He eats everything," the girl said. "My gran says it's a punishment sent by the Wise One because we haven't been sacrificing enough."

"What do you think?"

She hauled herself to her feet as though she were as old as her gran.

"I think the world is coming to an end, that the ice giants are eating the world like the old stories say, and we'd better enjoy ourselves while we can." She looked at Acton and Bramble could feel, finally, the desperation under the coquetry. "What do you think?"

He came closer and framed her face with gentle hands. "I think you are beautiful, that you have eyes the color of the sea," he said, and Bramble could tell that there was no lying anywhere in him and perhaps never had been. So what changed him into Acton the invader?

He bent to kiss the girl.

Get me out of here *now*! Bramble screamed to the gods and at last they responded, sending the waters to tumble her away, to swirl her and shake her and land her somewhere, anywhere, but in Acton's arms.

ASH

THE NEXT DAY, a day of high white clouds and breezes, they rode through winding trails along the side of the mountain, heading south toward the pass into the North Domain. Ash considered all the different kinds of trouble they could get in, down in the populated parts of the valley. It was a truism among Travelers that two young men, Traveling together, were the most likely to attract unwanted attention.

"Bullies, bastards and bashers," his mother had warned him when he was only eleven or twelve. "They all go for the young men on their own."

He couldn't see any way around it, though. They had to head down to the river flats, to make their way around the eastern spur of the Northern Mountains that fenced in the valley. The bluff reared up in front of them, growing taller as they rode through the next day, a sheer cliff bespeckled by stunted trees clinging to ledges and crannies.

"Do you know any way *over* the bluff?" he asked Flax.

"I'm not going up there!" Flax retorted, alarmed. "That's wilderness!" Cam skittered a little, picking up on his fear.

Wilderness. Ash shivered. In wilderness, the old agreements with the wind and water spirits were void. Humans were prey, easy prey. The wilderness wasn't like the Great Forest, which had its own laws. There were no rules, and no help. Acton's people avoided the canyons near Gabriston because they believed them to be wilderness like that: fatal for humans. They were fatal, too, for anyone without Traveler blood in them. But the bluff ahead, that must be real wilderness, without demons, and no place for them. The valley was a haven in comparison. But they were likely to meet problems there.

Imagining all the problems, and planning how he'd deal with them if they arose, took enough of Ash's concentration—along with the riding, which still didn't come easily—so that he could mostly ignore Flax's incessant humming and singing.

He was so concentrated on the threats ahead that the shouts behind them took him by surprise.

"Oi! You! What do you think you're doing?"

They both turned in their saddles to see three men riding up behind them, on bay horses that even Ash realized were beautiful. The three men were all red-heads, brothers by the look of them, and they sat their horses in the same way that Bramble and Zel did, like they'd been born there.

"We'll never outrun them," Flax said quietly. "They're chasers."

Ash nodded. Better make sure they didn't have to run, then.

He raised a hand in greeting.

"Gods be with you," he said politely.

The greeting surprised them. But then they looked at his dark hair and dark eyes, and their own eyes narrowed. Flax moved forward a little and their expression lightened as they saw his fairer hair and hazel eyes. Ash dropped his gaze. Let them think he was a servant, if it made them feel better. "Pride gets you killed," his mother had taught him, and she was right.

"Greetings," Flax said, friendly and casual.

"What do you think you're doing, riding through our land?" The eldest of them spoke belligerently, but as though he always spoke like that, not with any especial malice.

"Sorry," Flax said. "I'm on my way to Mitchen, and I thought this was a public road."

"Why not take the main road, then?"

Flax waved his hand. "It's so pretty here, I just wanted to enjoy the ride."

They frowned. Ash thought it was probably a bad excuse. But the youngest man, a boy really, was looking at Flax with undisguised admiration. Flax smiled at him.

"It is beautiful," the boy agreed, pushing back his hair with one hand and smiling for all he was worth. His brothers shot him looks of annoyance, though clearly they knew all about his predilection for young men, because there was no puzzlement or disgust, just that look that brothers get when their younger siblings do something stupid. But the eldest wasn't minded to let it go that easily.

"What's *he* doing here?" he said, staring at Ash.

"He's my safeguarder," Flax said. It was an inspired idea. They looked taken aback, but not disbelieving.

Eyes still down, conveying no threat, Ash added, "Young master here likes to wander around. His father sends me to take care of him." He lifted his eyes and risked a conspiratorial smile. "Make sure he doesn't get into bad company."

The second man's mouth twitched, but big brother wasn't cozened so simply.

"A Traveler who can fight. Seems to me I've heard something about that recently . . ."

Ash shrugged, and Flax cut in.

"We've been up in Foreverfroze." He addressed the younger brother directly. "It's so beautiful up there. Have you been?"

"No, I always wanted to go but —"

His brother cut him off. "You're that one who killed the warlord's man."

Each man was suddenly still, staring at Ash. Except Flax.

"Oh, don't be silly. Why would he do that? And when, anyway? He's been with me." His manner was perfect, and the men relaxed. Ash was impressed by the quality of his lying. That had to come from practice. He wondered how much truth Flax told Zel.

"Off our land," the eldest brother said.

Flax and Ash both nodded, and turned their horses toward the river flats.

"Del, why don't you go with them and make sure they do leave?" the second brother said, amusement in his voice.

"Good idea!" the youngest said and didn't wait for endorsement from the eldest. He kicked his horse to move ahead and led them down a steep, stone-covered trail with the confidence of someone who'd done it all his life. Flax followed, just as flamboyantly. Ash came last with much more caution, finding another source of annoyance at Flax. It was all right for these boys who rode before they walked . . .

Del kept turning around in the saddle to flirt with Flax, who gave back smile for smile. Ash wasn't sure if it were acting or not. He suspected not, and wondered. Men shagging together was frowned upon among Travelers and it was one of the other differences between them and Acton's people. "We all have to do our duty to the blood," the boys had been told on his first visit to the Deep. "The blood must survive." And they were also told: no more than two children who needed to be carried. Children must be spaced so that, if necessary, parents could pick up one each and run. This was the man's responsibility, to refrain from sex so that there were never more than two young children at a time. Many Traveler families had grown-up children and then a new batch, young enough to be their siblings' children.

"Oh, there's no room at our house. My grands all live with us and my brother's brood and I've got four sisters, too, and none of them married yet," he heard Del say with mock outrage.

The prohibition against having more than two children at a time, combined with the Generation law, which for hundreds of years had forbidden Travelers to move in parties containing more than two generations—parents and children—meant that there were no large, happy, dark-haired families full of siblings who complained about each other and squabbled and borrowed each other's things and backed each other up in fights. Ash wondered what it would be like to live like that, in the middle of so many kin. But neither he nor any child of his was likely to find out.

They reached a ridge from which they could see the fertile valley, with wooden fences and houses looking like toys.

"This is the edge of our land," Del said with clear reluctance. He pointed south. "Follow the trail down that way and it brings you to the main road." He edged his horse closer to Flax and Cam. "Sure you can't stay?" he asked, resting a hand on Flax's shoulder. Flax looked a little downcast, too.

"I wish I could," he said. "But we have to get on."

They both sighed. Ash envied them for a moment: the quick solidarity, the easy friendship. Their ease together wasn't just being attracted to each other; they were the same kind of person, spoiled and cosseted and sunny-natured as a result, expecting the best from the world. But in Ash's experience, the best didn't happen often, if at all.

He coughed politely, as a servant might to remind his young master of the time.

"Yes, we have to get on," Flax repeated sadly. "Thanks for your help."

"If you're ever back this way . . ." Del touched Flax's cheek gently, and Flax nodded, then gave a cheeky grin.

"Oh, I'll pay a visit, don't you worry about that!" They both laughed and Del was still laughing and waving as they headed down the trail he had shown them and turned a corner, hiding him from sight.

"He was nice," Flax said.

Ash made a noncommittal noise of agreement, and Flax grinned at him.

"Not your type? You don't know what you're missing!"

For the first time they laughed together, so they were not on guard as they rounded another curve in the trail and found themselves on one of the roads that criss-crossed the valley floor. Ash hadn't realized how far down they'd come and it made him nervous. This road was used. He could see a cart in the distance to the south, coming closer, and to the north was a man on foot, with the heavy pack of a hawker. At least he was moving away from them.

"Look for a way to get off this road," Ash said. "We need to go the back ways."

Flax grinned. "*You* could always go over the bluff instead of around it. You're the one they suspect. I'll meet you on the other side."

Ash shuddered involuntarily, and Flax laughed.

"Very funny," Ash said sharply. He forced himself to look unconcerned, but the very thought of wind wraiths made him shake. Doronit had made him confront them—to tame them, even—but the memory of their long claws and sharp, hungry eyes still troubled his dreams.

He was so caught up in the memory of the night on the cliffs of Turvite when he had met the wraiths that he barely noticed the bullock cart coming toward him. His instincts kicked in at the last moment and he assessed the driver, a middle-aged man...someone he knew. Frantically, he tried to place the face, but it wasn't until the man spoke that he recognized him. This was the carter they had met, he and Bramble and Martine, on their journey out of Golden Valley to the Well of Secrets.

"You!" the man said accusingly, pointing at Ash. "You're that Traveler they're looking for! I saw you before, with the two whores."

Ash froze, caught between two equally strong impulses. The first, the oldest, was to run. The other was to kill. If they let the carter go, he would raise the valley against them. They would be tracked, captured, probably executed. Even the Golden Valley executed murderers. He thought fleetingly of the pressing box, and hoped it would be a quick hanging instead. But if he killed the carter now, it would buy them enough time to get out of the valley. Particularly if they hid the body and let the bullock loose... He found that his hand had moved to his boot knife without him willing it. He could hear Doronit's voice, teaching, "Assess the threats against you and then remove them."

It was good advice, and might save their lives. It might even save the Domains, because if they didn't complete their task and meet up with the others, there would be no one to stop the ghosts... One life against two. One against many... The time seemed to stretch out endlessly as he sat, poised between the two choices. The carter pointed his whip at them and almost snarled. Ash's fingers took a firmer hold, a throwing hold so he could draw and flip the knife right into the man's throat in one movement.

"You're scum, all of you!" the carter said. Ash's hand twitched, wanting to throw the knife.

"Death of the soul," he heard Martine's voice say quietly, and remembered another ghost, a girl he had killed, who had warned him against this path. His fingers loosened on the knife hilt.

"Say nothing. Just ride," he said to Flax quietly, and they swung around the man and pushed the horses to a canter. Once they were out of sight, they found the next path up into the hills and took it as fast as the horses could safely go on the steep ground.

They went fast and silently for an hour or two, cutting between tracks, heading back up the hillside, and then behind them they heard the belling note of hounds on the scent.

They looked at each other in alarm. The horses picked up on their nervousness and tossed their heads, Cam dancing a little sideways, which almost knocked Ash and Mud off the path. Ash recovered with difficulty and nodded his head to Flax to lead the way.

They came to a brook tumbling down the hillside in a mist of white spray, so they headed the horses upstream through the rocky flow and picked their way past two obvious trails until they came to a large stone jutting out into the water. Flax swung down from Cam and cajoled the horses into scrambling up onto the stone and stepping from there to a patch of thick grass, so that once the wet hoofprints had dried there would be no sign they had left the stream.

The sound of the dogs grew fainter behind them.

Ash felt as though he moved in a dream. After all, this was the stuff of Traveler nightmares: Acton's people on the hunt, dogs, a wilderness with no refuge, and he himself as guilty as he could be; no defense possible. He *was* a killer. Sully *was* dead. That thought made him wake up.

"They're after two of us," he said to Flax. "And you haven't done anything. If we split up, you should be all right."

Flax shrugged. "That carter saw me with you. He won't forget."

That wasn't quite true. The carter had stared at Ash the whole time.

"You know what the grannies say," Ash reminded Flax. "It's our duty to survive."

"Survive and breed?" Flax grinned. "Not likely to happen with me, anyways. Never saw a girl I'd give a tumble to. Come on."

He led the way up a narrow track, barely a deer trail, threading through the byways as quietly as they could. On the stony paths they had to move more slowly than Ash would have liked, but a lame horse would be the death of both of them.

Twice more during the day, in the distance, they caught the sound of baying hounds, and sweat broke out all over Ash. But the belling notes became no louder, and they found another path which took them further south.

"I just hope we don't go too far up," Flax said, giving the bluff ahead of them a worried look. They were much closer, but they wouldn't reach it that day.

Just before night they found a hollow in the cliff which trickled spring water down into a small pool. It was as good a stopping place as they could hope for on the hillside, screened from view from both sides. They couldn't risk putting up the tents, so they slept on the ground, rolled in a blanket, cold and uncomfortable, and they kept the horses tethered right next to them. Ash took the first watch. He was more used to going without sleep, and Flax was tired out. Waiting in the dark, danger lurking in every rustle of the bushes, he blessed Doronit for her relentless training. He and Flax might not get out of this alive, but at least he wasn't sitting here panicking and feeling helpless. If the hunters came, they'd get a fight.

BRAMBLE

THE DIRGE OF pipes being blown slowly filled her head. The sound was almost torture, but saved from that by the gradual change of tone in the music. There was melody there, if she could only concentrate enough to follow it. She strained through the darkness and found that, although her sight cleared, she was still in the dark.

All she could tell was that she was in a room, somewhere inside. The darkness pressed in on her as strongly as the sound of the pipes, droning outside. The dirge was a sound that remembered grief, or promised it. She, he—Baluch, she thought, from his reaction to the music—was sitting on the ground with his back to a wall, his knees drawn up in front of him. The air was hot. Too hot, but the only comfort in the place was the warmth of another body next to his, and he didn't move away. Acton, perhaps? Or Sebbi?

Without the sound of the pipes she would have believed them benighted in a cave. She was fairly sure that the pipes were real, not just in Baluch's head, but she couldn't be certain.

Then the pipes outside mounted in intensity and a door was flung open, letting in a blinding light.

"Come on, then," a voice boomed, echoing off the walls. Baluch turned his head. It had been Acton sitting next to him, with Sebbi on Acton's other side. They looked tired and Sebbi was trying not to look scared. Baluch's heart had started to beat wildly. Whatever was happening, Bramble thought, it's not good.

The voice belonged to a shortish, heavy-muscled man with red hair. His shoulders were huge and he wore only a length of undyed wool wrapped as a skirt. The rest of his body was warmed by a thick cover of hair. His beard obscured most of his face, and his head hair reached in many plaits down past his waist. There was so much hair on his face that it was easy to miss the sharp intelligence in his eyes.

"Out!" he ordered.

The three boys stood and walked slowly out the door, Acton first. They were all taller than the man, but Baluch, at least, didn't feel as if he were looking down on him. Bramble could feel the real fear that curled inside his stomach.

Outside, in pre-dawn light, there was a large circle of people, men and women and children, all with red hair. Bramble noted one girl with eyes red from crying, and thought, that's the one from the mountain, I reckon. Lost her lover. She couldn't feel much sympathy.

The hairy man took a knife from his belt—a black stone knife, the kind that never lost its edge. A knife from the gods.

"The Ice King has been sent as a punishment by the gods!" he declared, his deep voice booming over the silent gathering. "And why? Because we have been lax in our worship! We have foregone the ancient sacrifices! We have turned from the old, true ways and followed the ways of greed and easy living. So we are being punished!"

He pointed to the north. As one, the crowd turned to look and a moan broke from every lip. The Ice King towered over the village, less than an hour's walk away. Around the houses, Bramble could see carts laden with household goods. Ready to leave.

"It is time to return to the old ways!" the man announced. His eyes shone with fervor. "We do not even have to give up one of our own. The gods have sent us their sacrifice!"

He raised the knife and a roar went up from the crowd. He shook the knife in the air and they roared louder. Then he lowered the knife and they quietened.

"But the sacrifice must be chosen. I have inspected these gods' gifts and all are fit. So we will leave it to the gods."

He gestured to a woman standing nearby, a thin-faced woman with eager eyes who reminded Bramble of the Widow Farli in Wooding. She handed over three straws. One was short.

The hairy man turned away from the boys and put the straws in his fist, then turned back and offered it to them.

"What happens if we won't choose?" Acton asked.

The man looked hopeful. "Then you all die."

Acton looked at Baluch, and then at Sebbi. "If one of us is chosen, will you let the others go?"

The hairy man stilled for a moment, then nodded. "Aye."

"It doesn't matter who dies," Acton whispered. "What matters is that the others tell the chieftains about the Ice King."

Sebbi laughed shortly. "Hah! Easy to say."

The hairy man thrust his fist toward Baluch.

Bramble could feel the pressure of the gods suddenly descend. He hesitated. They were telling him which one to choose. He could perhaps save his comrades by choosing a different one, but then he would be disobeying the gods. She could feel him think it through. What if the hairy man was right, and the gods had chosen their sacrifice? Perhaps the one they wanted him to choose was the short straw. How could he know? He yielded to the pressure and closed his fingertips around the straw the gods insisted on, and drew it out slowly.

It was long.

Bramble found that she was almost as relieved as Baluch. Don't be ridiculous! she thought. You know he doesn't die here. He founds Baluchston. But somehow it didn't feel like that to her, as though they were living a history already laid down in stone. It felt as though Baluch had made a real choice, could have chosen differently, could have died here.

Acton nodded to Sebbi to choose. Giving him a better chance. Sebbi glared at him, but reached for a straw. Short.

"Hah!" the hairy man shouted. "The gods have chosen!"

The crowd roared again. Acton put his arm around Sebbi's shoulder. "I'll take your place."

Sebbi shrugged him aside. "The gods chose *me*, not you. It's my death will save these people."

Acton nodded respectfully. "Your choice."

He and Baluch both pretended not to see the sweat standing out on Sebbi's forehead.

In the crowd beyond, the men were assembling weapons. Spears, knives. No swords.

"I will be killed like an animal," Sebbi said, his face pale. "Without a warrior's death, how will I be reborn?"

Baluch moved to him and put a hand on his shoulder. "You will go straight to the gods, Seb. You are their chosen. Of course you will be reborn."

"Unless the sacrifice is not just this life, but all the lives I might have had," Sebbi said.

Neither of them knew what to say to that. They stood quietly, waiting. Baluch was fighting both grief and a kind of horror that life could go so quickly awry, so badly. Bramble could feel his longing for home. For once, there was no music in his mind. Then the pipes began again and he shuddered.

Sebbi noticed. "Thinking of music even now?" he mocked, his voice tight. "What's the matter, isn't it in tune?"

Baluch looked him straight in the eye. "I will write a praise-song for you and they will sing it until the end of time," he said.

Sebbi's eyes grew bright. "Yes," he said. "Give me life that way, Bal. If they take away all my rebirths, make sure I live in the memory of our people."

"I will," Baluch swore.

The hairy man approached them and took Sebbi by the arm, not unkindly. "It's time, lad," he said. "Come, you must be blessed."

He led Sebbi over to the space in front of where the men stood with their weapons.

"Can we do anything?" Baluch whispered to Acton.

Acton shook his head, his eyes fixed on Sebbi. "I'm not sure we should even try. Maybe this is what the Ice King needs. Besides, what's important here is that at least one of us gets back to the Moot."

His voice was implacable. There! Bramble thought with a strange relief. That's the invader. Ready to let others die for his own purposes.

The hairy man moved to strip Sebbi of his clothes, but Sebbi forestalled him and undressed himself quickly. Baluch mourned over him, but he was also noticing the details so he could work them into the song later: the way Sebbi stood tall in front of the crowd, the respect that had awoken in those watching as he had undressed, the way the light seemed to gather over his wiry golden head. The hairy man raised his knife and started to speak but Sebbi cut him off, shouting: "I come as a willing sacrifice, to help the peoples of this place. I take your message to the gods: Save us! Curb the Ice Giants and let us live in peace and plenty!"

The crowd erupted in acclamation. The men shook their spears in the air, the women cried out and called as the goat girl had called the goats, ululating.

The hairy man pointed to the horizon, where the sun was just about to appear. "Be ready!" he cried.

As the first gold edged over the mountain, he pushed Sebbi in the back. "Take our evils, take our lacks, take our contrition to the gods and beg them to hear our plea!" he said. "Run!"

Sebbi ran. As soon as he started, the men began to chant while the women sang a two-note hymn.

"Blood cleans, blood binds, blood scours, blood ties, blood washes, blood pulls . . ." they sang. The gods gathered, their pressure building, filling both Baluch and Bramble with holy terror. The gods' attention was stronger than she had ever known it.

Then Bramble realized the men were chanting numbers. They were counting. Counting as she had so often counted before a chase. But this was summer, not autumn. *After Mid-Summer*, the gods told her, absently, with only a part of their attention. *Any time after Mid-Summer, the sacrifice can be made.*

The Autumn Chase, Bramble thought, appalled. This is the real Autumn Chase. She was expecting them to count to fifty, but at forty-nine the men sprang away, led by the hairy man, and the gods went with them, leaving she and Baluch stunned.

The women followed the band of men, and the children ran beside them.

Acton turned to Baluch. "Let's go."

"We can't just leave!"

"We have to."

"But —"

Acton dragged him away. "He's going to die. Do you really want to watch?"

"Yes!" Baluch shouted. "I promised him a praise-song. I have to watch!"

He pulled his arm from Acton's grasp and ran after the crowd as fast as he could. He was much faster than the women with their long skirts and he passed them easily, although his legs were cramped from sitting so long in the dark.

The men were loping after Sebbi. Bramble could see him, going up a rise in the near distance. He was running smoothly, his bare legs flashing pure white in the early sun. The men increased their pace and Sebbi turned, curving his flight away from them toward the Ice King. Bramble could guess his reasoning: if he was to die to banish the Ice King, then the best place to shed his blood should be on the ice itself. The men agreed. They let out a howl of approval and quickened their pace. Baluch pushed himself to run faster. He angled across the grassland so that his path would intersect theirs close to the ice.

The ice had pushed boulders, soil and rubble before it. Collapsed houses. Precious spars of wood. Sebbi faltered as his foot landed on something sharp. Then he straightened and ran on, limping just a little. He left a clear trail of blood behind him. The chasers yelled in triumph. The blood heat was taking them over, the thrill of chasing. Bramble felt sick. This was what she had felt, chasing the Kill. This was her ritual, her greatest pleasure—her salvation. She realized that she had been truly reborn in the Spring Chase because somewhere, sometime, perhaps a thousand years before, a man had died in autumn. Life sacrificed, life returned, that was the bargain. It might even have been Sebbi's life that had given hers back to her.

He was at bay, now, standing bravely before the ice cliff. The men came within spearshot and howled triumph again. The spears flew. Baluch was counting them: ten, twelve, fifteen... Blood blossomed on Sebbi's chest and legs. He flung his arms wide, his jaw set, determined, then took the pain and used it to scream to the heavens: "Hear our plea! Save us!" Then he fell.

The men crowded around so that Baluch could not see, then broke apart as some of them picked up the body and hoisted it onto their shoulders, its arms and legs dangling. They were all smeared across their faces with Sebbi's blood. Bramble's gorge rose, but Baluch was calm now, all his grief transmuted into an arrow of concentration aimed at the party of men.

Acton appeared at Baluch's shoulder.

"Time to go," he said. The women came up, tearing at their faces and grieving for the young life cut down. But this, too, was part of the ritual and mostly their eyes were dry and bright with hope. Baluch put out a hand and stopped one of them, an older woman.

"What will happen to him?" He had spoken without thinking, in his own language, and she did not understand. Acton repeated it in her tongue. She hesitated.

"I do not know," she said finally. "In the old days, he would be torn apart and scattered on the fields to ensure good harvest. Now we have no fields... perhaps he will be scattered on the ice."

They could see, when they turned back to watch, that the chase party was following the line of the ice, stopping at intervals for prayer. Acton and Baluch watched long enough to see that the end of the prayer was followed by some part of Sebbi's body being cut off by the hairy man and thrown onto the ice.

"Will it work?" Acton asked Baluch in an undertone. "What do the gods say?"

Baluch shuddered. "The gods say nothing. But I think it will take more than one man's blood to satisfy the Ice King."

The men howled as Sebbi's hand was thrown high onto the ice cliff.

"Enough," Baluch said, turning away as the waters descended on Bramble like ice crashing down from the king.

LEOF

LEOF COULDN'T BITE back a smile when he saw the roofs of Sendat appear, and Thistle picked up her pace as she scented the stables of home.

"Good to be back, my lord," Bandy, his groom, said.

"Good and bad, man," Leof replied, waving to a few townsfolk as they made their way up the winding road to the fort.

He assessed it with new eyes as he came near. Although it was reasonably well fortified against normal attack, it would be helpless against an enemy which could not be killed. The walls needed to be much higher, giving defenders the chance to isolate and deal with individual attackers. The top of the walls needed to be sharp, rather than wide, and the defenders should be armed, not with spears, but with axes. Meat cleavers, even, lashed to poles, would do until they could get proper halberds made. The smithies would have to work overtime. Halberds were the best weapon, he was sure. The long blade fixed firmly to a long pole—it combined sword and spear, with the advantage that it kept your enemy at more than arm's length. A broadsword could hack off a limb, but it needed luck as well as strength and judgment. A good whack with a halberd, on the other hand, had so much leverage behind it that it frequently sent limbs flying. The weapon wasn't used much in close-quarter work because of the danger to your own troops, but a line of defenders, trained to work together...The plan was all Leof could think of, and he was miserably aware that it was full of flaws.

They rode into the muster area to shouts of welcome from the stables and the smithies. Leof dismounted thankfully and gave Thistle to Bandy, patting her and murmuring gratitude for her hard work as he did so. He ordered another groom to help Bandy before heading straight to the smithies, walking the kinks and aches from his legs and telling himself he was not at all tired.

The chief blacksmith, Affo, was a surprisingly small man, though with the massive arms of his trade. Leof didn't tell him the details of the attack on Carlion, just that the town had been attacked, and the warlord's men would be marching to give aid.

"We have perhaps a day before they march past us. And in that time . . ." he paused, unsure of how to phrase the order, then shrugged the problem aside. No good way to say it. "I want as many axes as you can produce."

"We're doing that already, lord," Affo said, surprised. "Battleaxes, halberds, even choppers."

"What?"

"The Lady Sorn ordered it, after that mad—after that messenger from Carlion came. She said," he added, clearly fishing for information, "that my lord Thegan needed them. She said not to worry about finishing them off, no decoration or such, just make them sharp?"

"If your warlord wanted you to know why, his lady would have told you, no?" Leof said severely.

"Aye, lord," Affo said. His expression plainly said, "All lords are mad." Leof hoped he'd keep thinking so, instead of wondering what kind of enemy needed to be attacked with axes. The thought hadn't occurred to Leof, but of course Otter would have come to Sendat first. Lady Sorn had reacted as befitted a warlord's lady. He breathed more easily. The men would not be going into battle badly armed, although they would only have enough axes for the forward guard.

He turned toward the hall and the Lady Sorn. He half-expected her to be waiting for him in the muster yard, but of course she would not do that. Not the Lady. She never intruded on the public spaces—the men's spaces. The hall, the residence and the gardens were her domain and she kept to them. Leof had approved of that when he first came to Sendat. She acted the way women should, modest and refined. Then he had met Bramble, and his ideas about what a woman should do had undergone considerable change.

Sorn was waiting by the fire in the hall, sitting in a pool of sunlight from one of the high windows. The light turned her auburn hair into fire and made her skin glow, enriched the deep green of her dress and sent flickers of light from her earrings into the corners of the room.

She seemed, for a moment, a creature of flame and leaf, like the embodiment of a forest, caught on a tapestry of the seasons between autumn and spring. Then he saw her face, calm as an iced-over pool, and thought, between autumn and spring is winter.

Normally, Sorn was surrounded by her maids and ladies, but now she was alone, except for the small hunting dog that was always at her side. She was waiting to hear her lord's message in private. Leof wished he had something better to tell her.

He bowed and saluted. Composed, Sorn rose and bowed back, protocol strictly observed, no trace of anxiety on her face. The little silvery whippet—what was its name, something odd, he couldn't remember—stood at her side, shivering as whippets do in the presence of strangers. She quieted it with a touch and it lay down again, head raised.

"My lady, I bring greetings from the Lord Thegan," Leof said.

"You are welcome, Lord Leof."

She gestured to him to sit beside her and he eased himself into a cushioned chair thankfully. Sorn poured him wine from a glass jug.

"You have heard the news, I gather, from Otter the Stonecaster?" He took a long swallow of the wine; it was a winter red from down south, full and comforting.

Sorn nodded. "I did what I could to prepare."

Leof smiled at her. "I've just come from the smithies. You did exactly right, my lady. My lord's men will be marching through here on the way to Carlion by tomorrow sunset, and it will... it may make a great deal of difference, having the axes ready for them to take."

She nodded, serious. "My lord?"

He hastened to reassure her. "He will be with them. He bids me to tell you that he thinks of you. He is well, although . . ." he took the sheaf of papers Thegan had given him from inside his jacket, "not all will be returning with him. The Lake—or, my lord thinks, some enchanter controlling the Lake—raised a great wave against us. Many were killed."

Sorn looked at the papers and went very still.

"How many?" she whispered. The whippet sprang to its feet and nosed her hand. She patted it absently. "Shh, Fortune."

"About a quarter of our forces," Leof said. "My lord has charged me with letting the families know."

Sorn reached for the papers. "This is my responsibility," she said, her voice low. "You will have enough to do." She hesitated. "And the Lake People?"

Leof sighed. "We never laid eyes on the Lake People," he said. "My lord blamed an enchanter from Baluchston for the wave and was about to punish the town when the messenger from Carlion arrived."

Sorn took a deep breath and let it out slowly, still looking at the list of names. "Baluchston is a thorn in his side," she said absently. "He will have it out one way or another." Then she looked up with anxiety in her eyes, as though he might hear that comment as disloyal. It was the first real emotion she had shown. The whippet stood alert, regarding him warily.

Leof smiled reassuringly at her. "One way or another," he agreed. She relaxed a little although, as always, she sat very straight. Fortune sat down again.

"Go to your quarters, my lord, and rest. Tomorrow will be soon enough to begin your work."

He smiled at her ruefully. "I doubt my lord would think so, I have a few hours' work yet before I can rest. But I would be glad of some food."

She smiled back, her face lighting with a hint of mischief. "I confess, I ordered a meal sent to the officers' workroom. It should be there by now."

He chuckled. "Too predictable, obviously. Thank you, my lady." He rose, bowed and went out, leaving her sitting quietly. The sun had moved past the window while they talked and she sat now in a pool of shadow, studying the lists of the dead, her dog at her side.

ASH

THERE WAS A trail, Flax said as they changed shifts at midnight, which skirted the upper bluff well above the road used by carts and riders. "Clings to the mountainside, like," he said, "about halfway up. It's *supposed* to be below the wilderness."

There was a silence as they both considered that, weighing dangers.

"Can we use it without being seen?" Ash asked.

Flax was only a patch of deeper darkness against the hillside, but somehow Ash knew he was pulling at his lip, considering.

"If we start early enough. Maybe."

So they started well before dawn, as soon as there was enough light for the horses to find their footing. The most dangerous part was where they had to descend a way into the valley, toward a larger road past a prosperous horse farm, from where the upper trail branched. Coming down the hillside was one of the hardest things Ash had ever done. He pulled up the hood on his jacket, just in case. He felt completely exposed in the dim light, as though a thousand eyes were watching him.

But they turned onto the trail without incident and continued quietly past the farm. It was so early that the dogs were still asleep, but as they passed the farm one woke and barked, waking the others until there was a chorus of barking. The door of the farmhouse crashed open to show the farmer, axe in hand, silhouetted in the opening. Ash stiffened, but Flax raised a hand.

" 'Morning," he shouted genially. "Sorry if we've woken you!"

Hesitantly, the farmer raised a hand in reply. Ash willed himself to keep Mud to a walk, matching Cam's gait. He didn't turn his head—with his hood up, the farmer couldn't see his hair or eyes, and wouldn't know he was a Traveler. Flax's light brown hair was clear in the growing light, and he hoped that would be good enough.

The farmer stood, scratching his head. He watched them until they were well past the boundary of the farm and the wild scrub started, but that was fair enough. Any farmer might do the same to strangers. Yet . . .

"Look back," Ash said. "Can you see him?"

Flax flicked a glimpse back over his shoulder. "Dung and pissmire!" he swore. "Someone's riding off the other way."

"They set a watch, in case we came this way," Ash said. His heart was beating faster and he felt fear coil in his gut.

They urged the horses to a canter and kept the pace up as long as they dared, until the trail became too steep and winding for it to be safe. There was no sense cutting across the trails they found. Now it was a race—they had to be around the bluff before they were caught. Had to be out of Golden Valley by nightfall, or they would not be leaving at all.

All morning they climbed up and southward into scrubby forest where rocks broke through the ground like warts on a toad. They stopped only to spell and water the horses. There was no food left and they filled their bellies with the cold stream, which only made Ash feel emptier. He allowed himself to hope, just a little. If they could just keep far enough ahead until nightfall . . .

"There they are!" a shout came from behind them. Immediately, Flax whistled, crouched low on Cam's neck and urging him on, pushing him to a canter and then a hard gallop along the narrow trail. Ash was taken by surprise when Mud responded enthusiastically to the whistle, following Cam along the trail. All he could do was cling on as the horses took the winding path as fast as they dared. His hood fell back in the rush.

"Get them!" the shout came behind them. "That black-haired bastard killed my friend!"

Ash recognized Horst's voice. Horst. Not some nameless pursuer, but a real enemy. But why was he still here? He realized with a shock that it had been only a couple of days since he had killed the warlord's man. Horst must have stayed for the quickening, which would come—oh, gods, was it tomorrow or today? Sully's ghost would rise, looking for acknowledgment and reparation from Ash, his killer. It was his duty to be there, to set his spirit at rest.

He couldn't. He had other duties, more important; he had to forget the image of Sully returning from beyond death to find his killer gone and his friend—his friend more intent on revenge than on freeing him for rebirth. Ash put his head down on Mud's neck and trusted to the horses and to Flax, because it was all he could do.

The shadows were closing in... if they could keep ahead until nightfall, and lose them in the dark... it was a forlorn hope. Ash could hear the sounds of pursuit getting closer. They were nearing the cliff face. There might be caves, but surely going into a cave would be stupid. There would be no way out.

The trail branched and Flax unhesitatingly took the left-hand fork. Around two bends, low branches whipping their faces, and then they had reached a clearing before the cliff, broken here by huge boulders. There *were* clefts in the rock, not caves so much as fissures, but they were narrow and no doubt had dead ends which would trap them. But if they could hide in one until the others passed . . .

The party behind had taken the wrong fork, but it wouldn't be long before they realized their mistake. Flax jumped off Cam and came to take Mud's reins so Ash could jump down, too.

"What now?" Flax asked. Off the horse, it seemed that authority had passed back to Ash.

"Hide," he said simply. They led the horses to one of the furthest fissures in the cliff face.

"They've got to be here somewhere," Horst's voice came. "I want them both, but don't kill the black-haired bastard. He's for me."

"You're not the law in Golden Valley." Ash recognized the voice of the second brother, the reasonable one. "We have no warlords here, and no warlords' men, remember?"

There were rumbles of assent from other men—at least six or seven, Ash estimated.

"Then I'll take him back to my lord Thegan and he can decide his punishment. Your laws allow for that, don't they?"

"Aye," the second brother said. "That's allowed."

Flax and Ash threaded their way through the fissure as fast as they could and found it led, not to a cave, but to another small clearing. Before them was a slope leading up to the top of the bluff. The going was rocky and perilous for the horses, full of sharp rocks and boulders, with no level ground at all. But they could manage it, if they had to.

At the top...wind spirits. Doronit had controlled them, with Ash's help, but he had only been helping. Just as with Safred, lending his strength to her will. He had never done anything like that by himself. He had a queasy suspicion that his own will wasn't strong enough, that the spirits would simply laugh at him if he tried to control them. Laugh and reach those long, clawed hands for his eyes...He shuddered. He couldn't do it. Better to face the trial and be hanged.

"They must be here somewhere!" Horst's voice came from beyond the fissure, startlingly loud. "I'll have both of them dragged before my lord and they'll pay."

Both. Ash looked at Flax, who was pinching the noses of both horses to prevent them from whickering. He had promised Zel he would look after him. Dung and pissmire.

"Here they are," the second brother said with a note of relief in his voice. Flax and Ash strained to hear and both they and the horses jumped when the hounds began to bay, the excited note of a fresh scent.

There was only one way to go. Up the slope, to wilderness. They scrambled as fast as they could on the rough surface, trying to find a way to go sideways, any way but straight up. Behind them, voices were arguing.

"I'm not losing my best pack for you!" the first brother's voice sounded. More shouting followed.

Any further and they would be beyond the screen of the trees, open to view—unless they threaded through the maze of rocks which led up to the bluff. The dogs were still sounding. Ash could hear them panting with eagerness—a sound from nightmares. He had once seen a man brought down by a warlord's dogs. Not even a Traveler—one of the lord's own farmers who had tried to cheat on his taxes. He had been begging for death by the time the warlord reached him.

Ash touched Flax on the shoulder and pointed upward. Flax paled and shook his head vigorously. Ash moved very close, until his lips were by Flax's ear. "I can control the spirits," he said.

Flax drew back in astonishment, staring at him. Ash shrugged, trying to look as though this was something he did every day. He saw the moment when hero-worship kicked in, when hope overcame fear in Flax's eyes, and it made him feel sick.

They started up the slope as quietly as they could in the fading light, Flax leading both horses as trustingly as a child, sure that if Ash said he could do it, he could.

But Ash wasn't sure at all.

BRAMBLE

THUMP. THUMP. REGULAR, deep, but not like a drum. More like... a fist on flesh. Yet not quite . . .

Bramble's sight cleared and she felt herself back in Baluch's body, then wished she weren't. The sound wasn't a fist on flesh, but a thick wooden rod. On Acton's bare back and sides. Harald was wielding it, his face red and furious. Acton held on to one of the posts in the big hall, his head hanging and his body shaking with each blow. Blood dripped onto the floor from where a roughness in the rod had caught him. Bruises were already appearing under the skin.

A circle of people watched—men and women, but no children. Bramble could hear them playing outside, pretending to be invaders and defenders. The contrast made her shiver, but Baluch was barely conscious of the noise. He flinched with every blow. Asa stood next to Acton, her face like stone.

"You disobeyed my orders," Harald said, finally standing back.

"He had good reason," Baluch said. "What we found —"

Harald wheeled on him. "Keep silence! The only reason I'm not belting you the same is that you were bound to follow his orders, as he was bound to follow mine."

Acton was breathing heavily. He used the post for support and pulled himself up to stand straight.

"We found —"

"I don't care what you found!" Harald shouted, breathing as heavily as Acton. He glared at his grandson. "I should have known you had treachery in your blood. Your father had to show himself in you sooner or later. You have lost a fine young man, a man who would have been valuable to our people. For a boy's prank! An adventure! It makes me sick to look at you."

He threw the rod on the floor and walked off. Asa picked it up and watched him walk out of the hall. Once he was through the door, she dropped the rod on a table and turned to Acton, putting an arm around him to support him. He pushed her gently away.

"I can walk."

He made it to a table in four faltering steps and sat down on a bench. Ragni was at his side immediately, with a warm bowl of water and soft rags for cleaning his blood away, but the deep injuries she could do nothing about. A woman passed Asa a drinking horn smelling of mead and she held it to Acton's lips. The mead brought a little color back to his cheeks.

He smiled ruefully. "I didn't expect him to be back so soon."

"That's why he's in a foul temper," Asa said. "The boats never sailed. First they had to fight their way through to the coast, past parties of raiders from the north, and then, when they got there, the bays were still iced over. In mid-summer. They couldn't get the boats out."

"It's the King," Baluch said. "He brings winter with him."

"Tell me," Asa said. The others crowded around to hear, but before he could speak a man ran into the hall. Tall, with wiry hair the same color as Sebbi's. Perhaps three or four years older. His face was pale, with tears running freely down his cheeks.

"You killed my brother!" he accused Acton.

Baluch intervened. "No, Asgarn. Sebbi was chosen by the gods to die a man's death. A great death, which shall be told in song and story for all the generations of our people."

Asgarn hesitated, and looked at Acton, who began to describe what they had found in the valley of the Ice King.

When Acton described Sebbi's death, Ragni said, "His mother should know of this, that he had a hero's death," and she hobbled out of the hall, looking as old as time itself.

After Acton had finished speaking, the hall was silent. Asgarn turned away, his shoulders hunched.

"He was only a boy," he whispered, but the hall was so silent that his words echoed.

"He died a man," Acton reassured him.

"For nothing! You say the ice will still keep coming." He walked out of the hall with his fists clenched. They watched him go silently.

"The Ice King takes everything," Baluch said. "Those from whom he takes must go elsewhere."

That brought a babble of talk, but one question kept recurring. Acton put it into words for them all.

"We can defend ourselves against the invaders, but if the sea lanes are blocked all year round, how can we trade? Without trade, we'll starve."

Asa considered. "There is a path over the mountains," she said finally. "People live there. Where there are people, there can be trade." She looked into Acton's face and smiled wryly. "I think it's time you met your uncle."

Bramble was beginning to get a sense of what the gods were showing her. Not just Acton's life, but its turning points. The moments of destiny. She wondered again if she should try to change the events she witnessed, but again the gods rose in her with immense pressure. *What has happened must happen*, they insisted, and she surrendered to their surety with something like relief, as the waters rose gently and floated her away. So, she thought, we go to meet the uncle.

"Cast!" someone yelled, and she felt her body draw back its right arm and throw something. Then again. This time, she could feel the smooth shaft of a spear in her hand, and her eyes took in the light just in time to follow its flight. The spear soared high, in a perfect arc, and came to earth in a man's neck. Blood spurted.

Suddenly she was aware of the noise: men were yelling, screaming defiance at the approaching war party. Those who had cast their spears rattled their swords on their shields. The band of men was below them on a slope, and although they threw their own spears they didn't have the same heft as the one thrown by—Baluch, was it? No, there was no music in this head. It was someone else who danced on the rock's edge and shook his sword in the air. The war party was made up of red-headed warriors who reminded her of the men who had cut Sebbi to pieces.

She saw Acton and Baluch out of the corner of the man's eye. Acton was shouting and thumping his sword. Baluch was quiet, but he hefted his sword more comfortably in his hand and set his feet to give him the surest footing. Acton gave a whoop of exhilaration and the man turned to grin at him, his cheeks drawn back wide in enjoyment.

"That's it, lad!" he bellowed to Acton. "Get your heart up!"

Acton grinned. "It's a good day for a fight, Eddil!" he shouted back.

There was no doubt that he was genuinely having fun. Wait until the fighting really starts, Bramble thought. This lot won't retreat because of a few spears.

Nor did they. The war party, thirty strong, forged up the hill and came to grips with the defenders. Eddil yowled and swung his sword; not, as Bramble had expected, at the man's head, but at his legs. The blow was blocked and the shock of that ran up Eddil's arm and made his fingers numb. He held on and swung his sword again. His blood was running light in his veins and his breath came easily. They had been training, then, Bramble thought, trying to hold on to her own mind in a deafening flurry of blows and counterblows, any one of which could have killed. She was not prepared for the clamor of battle. Or the smell of sweat.

Although she could not hear Eddil's thoughts, she could sense his feelings, as she had with the girl on the mountainside. He was exalted, feeling intensely alive, as she had felt during a chase. She concentrated on the man Eddil was fighting, trying not to think of him as her own enemy. He was around forty, she estimated, thin, and his eyes were deep-set, as though he had gone without sleep for some time. Every sword swing tired him more, and Eddil pressed forward harder, changing his grip so that as the man's sword drooped for a moment, he could use the sword like a dagger unexpectedly, piercing the man's side. The red-head gasped and sank as his knees buckled. Eddil pulled out the sword and ignored the fountain of blood that sprayed him. He leapt away to meet the next warrior, shouting, "Harald! Harald!" Then something—sword, spear, a block of wood was what it felt like—came down on his head and he stumbled. As his sight darkened and the waters rose up to carry Bramble away, she heard again Acton's whoop of delight and then his laughter. The old songs are true, she thought, he really did laugh as he killed.

A larger body, and older, was her first thought. She was squinting in bright light, looking west into the sunset, hand coming up to shade her eyes. She knew that hand. She searched her memory for the name. Yes, she was sure it was Gris. So, she thought, now comes the first meeting with the uncle.

Gris was watching a curve in a path that came from over the western hills into the valley. The hills were so close that when, sure enough, horses appeared, it took them only a few minutes to reach him.

Asa was in the lead, followed by Acton with a string of four laden ponies. Bramble realized with a shock that Acton was some years older—perhaps seventeen or eighteen. This was clearly not their first meeting. Gris shouted, "Welcome!" to them as soon as they appeared and called back to the steading, "They're here!"

As Asa and Acton dismounted from the stocky little horses, Gris embraced them both in turn while his people rushed to take the horses to the stable. Acton delayed long enough to lift his saddlebag from his pony and then allowed Gris to put an arm around his shoulders and usher him into the hall.

The hall was smaller than Harald's and had no shields or spears as decoration. Instead, antlers and animal skins were nailed to the wall: boar's tusks, a bear's jaw, even an eagle's talons. Bramble did not like to see trophies of death flaunted. On the other hand, these were people who valued hunting above fighting, as she did. That thought made her pause for a moment, remembering moments when she had hunted to live or to feed her family, and so she did not hear the first few words of conversation. When her attention returned, Acton, Asa and Gris were sitting by the fire pit in the middle of the hall, sipping beer and talking about the weather. Bramble almost laughed. The weather! The gods had brought her here to listen to weather talk!

"Yes, it's cold for this time of year," Gris said.

"Too cold," Asa replied. "The Ice King's talons reach further every year. We are hard pressed."

"The people unlanded by the King are seeking new lands, and they don't care who they take them from. Old friends are become enemies," Acton said. "Even the chiefs at the Moot look askance at each other."

"When your children are starving, you don't care who owns the bread, you just steal it," Asa said.

"Mmm." Gris drank, barely tasting the sharp beer. Bramble could not see into Gris's mind as she had Baluch's and it unsettled her. "Does it come so fast?" he asked.

"So fast and so far," Acton answered. "In a few more winters he will reach us."

Gris sat back in surprise. "Surely it will not come so far south!"

Acton shrugged. "Nothing has stopped him so far. Not summer, nor prayers nor...sacrifice." His voice roughened a little. "He comes, and we can't stop him."

"It's just ice," Gris said, determinedly practical.

"Perhaps. But what feeds the ice?" Acton asked. "If the old stories are true, and the Ice Giants will come to devour the earth...it may be that we are in the last days. Or," he paused, "it may be that he cannot cross these mountains. They are much higher than the northern hills."

His uncle was silent, turning the horn in his hands, avoiding their eyes.

"There was a day," Asa said gently, "when you named Acton your heir."

Gris's head came back up as though he heard a warning shout. His heart beat faster.

"I thought, as you know, that I would never have a son. But since then," he said, "I have married and I have two sons, Tal and Garlock. They are my true heirs."

Asa looked questioningly at him. "It was thought," she said carefully, "that you would never marry."

Gris smiled without humor. "It's astonishing what you can do when people expect it of you."

She raised her brows and nodded, then flicked her hand as though dismissing the subject. "This valley is large," she said. "Would you have room for others here?"

Gris got up and began pacing around the fire, breathing a little hard through strong emotion.

"I am not a man who fears," he said. "Any more than my brother was. But I tell you: I fear this. You are the only ones to know the way over the mountain. Thus we stay protected from the Ice King's people. But if I took your people in, many would know. Sooner or later, someone would tell, and our protection would be gone."

Asa nodded. "That is a fair statement, and I honor it. But my people are being pressed from all sides, and we have no escape but this!"

Acton, curiously, said nothing. He just looked at the fire. Had he expected to be his uncle's heir?

Gris stopped pacing. "I knew this was coming. From Acton's first visit, I knew this choice would be made. I have found another way."

Acton rose slowly to face him, but Asa stayed seated, looking up calmly. "Tell us."

Gris licked his lips. "There is another route through the mountains, through to the land beyond, which is as much larger than your country as your country is larger than this valley. We have raided there, from time to time. You remember, Asa, after you came here Hard-hand did not raid your people, and after you left I continued to respect your wishes."

"Why raid anywhere?" Acton asked.

Gris frowned, then smiled, his mouth twisted. "To keep our young men from killing each other, mostly. It's a small valley, and we needed thralls, goods. We have no access to the dragon's road, to trade with the Wind Cities. We had to have some way to build wealth."

Acton was frowning, as though familiar with these arguments and not convinced by them. "Thralls are slaves," he said.

"Your grandfather keeps slaves," Asa said impatiently.

"Yes," Acton said. "I know."

Asa gestured him quiet. "The way through . . ." she prompted.

"It's dangerous, even in summer," Gris said. "The pass is narrow. It's between two high peaks, Fang and Tooth, and they carry snow all year around. It's not unknown to have an avalanche there in midsummer. But it leads through, and the entrance is outside this valley. Our people could be left in peace."

"And once we were through?" Asa asked.

Gris shrugged. "That's up to you. There is a lot of land unsettled, beyond the mountains. The people there may let you pass."

Asa thought it over. "We will need to send emissaries. A treaty . . ."

"The chieftains will need to approve it," Acton cautioned. He seemed more unsure than Bramble had ever seen him. Was it the experience of battle that had sobered him? She doubted it. He was watching his mother closely. Perhaps it was something to do with Asa.

"Yes. Perhaps. But for our own people—we will do what we need to do to survive."

"My grandfather won't like it."

Asa laughed. "That is certain. We must leave tomorrow," she said with decision. "The All Moot will still be in session if we ride quickly. We will put the plan to the chieftains."

"You mean *I* will put the plan to the chieftain," Acton said. He didn't sound enthusiastic. "You are not allowed to speak."

Asa frowned. "There are laws which need to be re-examined," she said. "All should have the right to speak. Perhaps in the new land . . ."

"All?" Acton asked. "Even slaves?"

"Don't be ridiculous," Asa said. Gris laughed and she turned to him with mock severity.

"Don't you encourage him. He keeps making friends with the wrong people."

Gris smiled. Bramble could feel his body relaxing as the difficult part of the conversation ended. This was just family talk. "All boys do," he said.

"Acton is not a boy any longer. He is a man, and should act like one," Asa said, but she smiled as she said it and smoothed Acton's hair as though he were five summers old.

The waters this time were a river, sweeping her across country as well as time, moving her faster than she had gone before.

The smell was definitely male and definitely unwashed. It rose up around Bramble but didn't envelop her. As her sight cleared she seemed to see through a dozen pairs of eyes in turn; quick glimpses of the same scene from different positions, but without sound, as though she had gone deaf. Too many! she thought, fighting dizziness and nausea. Each pair of eyes saw the world differently. Color was brighter in one, perhaps a younger pair of eyes. For another person, color was less important but somehow the way people stood in particular groups had significance, and those eyes sorted the crowd that way. She paused there for a moment, as though the gods were testing whether this was the right observer, and in that moment saw a sea of men, filling a huge dip in the ground, one of the craters that the larger pieces of black rock had made when the gods sent it to earth. On one side of the crater a natural ledge held the men officiating. Acton was there, looking tall and strong.

The All Moot, Asa had said. They had Moot Halls where the ruling councils of the free towns met, like in Turvite and Carlion…her thoughts faltered at the memory that called up: Maryrose and Merrick showing her where his mother, the town clerk of Carlion, worked. In an office at the back of the Moot Hall. Maryrose had been so happy that day, two days before her wedding…The worst thing about living in someone else's body was that you could not weep when you needed to.

Bramble lost track of the switches from one pair of eyes to the next. Finally, she found herself looking out of the eyes of a man standing on the ledge. One of the chieftains, she presumed. An older man, then, but his body still felt strong and his eyes were sharp. He could see a feather stuck into the cap of a man in the very last group on the edge of the crater. A good archer, he would make, Bramble thought.

All this time, her hearing had been clouded, but now it sharpened and she could understand what was being said. The oldest man on the ledge, whose long beard was white streaked with gray, was speaking. He held a stick with eagle feathers bound to its top.

"Does the youngling Acton speak with the voice of his chieftain, Harald?" Though he was old, his voice rang out clearly across the Moot.

Harald was standing behind Acton. As the question was asked he stepped forward, shouldering Acton aside. The old man handed him the stick.

"He does not!" Harald declared. A murmur ran through the Moot. Harald handed the stick back to the old man.

"Then Acton, son of Asa, cannot be heard."

Bramble saw Acton's face harden. He wasn't surprised, and he had prepared for this.

"So, Oddi, you will let your people die rather than break a rule of precedence?" he said loudly.

The crowd and the men on the ledge burst into shouting, some saying, "Let him speak!" and others calling shame on him for speaking without the Mootstaff. Bramble felt the heart of her chieftain speed up, but he kept silent.

The old man held up his hands for quiet and her chieftain looked up, tensing.

"It is true these are desperate times," he said. "But should we thus forsake the ways of our ancestors, we risk becoming men without honor, without ties, without land, as our enemies are."

Bramble felt the chieftain clear his throat.

"Swef?" the old man inquired.

Swef stepped forward in boots of a distinctive red leather. She knew that leather—it was traded up from the Wind Cities and even in her time it was expensive. He took the staff. "Acton. I know what you would say here, and I say this: the youngling Acton speaks with my voice, if he wishes."

Silence fell over the Moot. Bramble realized that this was more than just a way around the rules. If she understood correctly, Swef was asking Acton to transfer his allegiance from his grandfather to him, in return for being allowed to speak.

Acton turned to Harald. "Grandfather . . ." he said pleadingly. Harald stared away from him in silence, his arms folded. Acton swallowed hard, and then took a deep breath and reached for the Mootstaff. Swef handed it to him, and patted him on the arm as he did so. Acton nodded acknowledgment. He was paler than Bramble had seen him before.

"Because the future of my people—my grandfather's people—is at stake, I speak here with the voice of Swef."

Bramble expected the crowd to react noisily, but they were completely silent, although some moved uneasily, putting their hands to their swords, or stroking their beards as if for comfort. Some of them had wounds bandaged; a few had an arm or an eye or an ear missing, the wounds still red and proud. Recent fighting, then. A lot of it.

"Brothers," Acton said, "we all know the dangers facing us. If danger was all that confronted us, we would laugh at it." The men below nodded. "If fighting were all that was required of us, we would fight. If dying were required of us, we would die. If killing were required of us, we would kill the enemy in their thousands!" They were nodding harder. "We are warriors and we do not flee any man!"

They shouted agreement.

"But it is not men who confront us. It is the Ice King."

He let that sink in. The crowd subsided, murmuring.

"I have seen the Ice King," Acton said quietly, so that they had to be silent to hear him. "I have seen the Ice King," he said a little louder. "I have seen the Ice King," he shouted. "And we cannot survive him!"

They were silent. Swef watched their faces—singling out some for special attention, Bramble realized. Key men. The ones whose opinions would sway others. Some were unconvinced, but most looked suitably grave. Bramble wondered how Acton knew what to say. She was reminded of the way Thegan had put on an act for his people at the Sendat fort, but that had been pure play-acting. No matter how rehearsed his words, Acton meant them. She wasn't even sure they were rehearsed. Perhaps he was speaking from the heart, remembering Sebbi and the cliffs of ice.

"He will come, and he will grind our halls into splinters and our fields he will crush and cover until there is no place to lay our heads nor even any place to burn our dead!" That was heartfelt, all right. Acton licked his lips, shifted his grip on the Mootstaff a little, and continued. "To flee the Ice King is not cowardice, but courage. Courage to admit that he is greater than any of us. Courage to save our women and our children and our beasts from hunger and misery and want. Courage . . ." he paused, gauging the mood of the crowd. Swef seemed amused at the tone of the speech; Bramble felt him suppress a chuckle. "Courage to leave the land of our fathers and find new lands to make our own."

The crowd stirred at that and one man shouted out, "The sea lanes are closed!"

"But the mountains are not," Acton replied. "There is a way through the mountains. A way of danger, a way for heroes. On the other side, with the good will of the people already there, we shall find a wide, empty land for us to settle. A good land, away from the fear of the Ice King. A land for adventure and trade and prosperity. If my brothers wish it so."

The crowd clamored, most in favor, it seemed to Bramble, but some objecting strongly.

Acton handed the stick back to the old man and, after hesitating, came to stand next to Swef. They exchanged glances. Swef murmured, " 'With the good will of the people there'? That's a big if."

Acton grinned at him, restored to his usual cheerfulness. "First things first," he whispered back. "Let's get the Moot's permission and then go negotiate."

Swef clapped him on the back. "You're your mother's son," he said, laughing as the waters rose up like a clear spring and floated Bramble away.

Not again! Bramble thought. The noise of battle was unmistakable. This time she was in Baluch's head, no doubt about it—each sword stroke was accompanied by martial music, horns and drums. His eyes were clouded by blood—he reached up to wipe it away and winced as the back of his hand caught on a tear in his scalp. From his right, an auburn-haired giant with plaits down to his waist screamed and brought down an axe—not a battleaxe, but the kind you used to chop wood. Baluch raised his shield, but it was clear the blow would shatter it and break the arm underneath, leaving him wide open for a killing blow.

Acton appeared out of nowhere and tripped the man neatly, so that he landed at Baluch's feet, face in the churned dirt. Baluch swallowed and brought his sword down on the man's neck. It was a huge blow. He was reluctant and spurred by his own reluctance and the shame it brought to greater strength. Blood spurted wildly and the legs and arms twitched while the head rolled away from the neck, showing the man's wild, dim eyes. Baluch spun away to block a spear thrust from another huge attacker. He and Acton stood back to back and fought together.

Around them, the melee swirled, blond heads and auburn heads intermingled, swords and shields swinging, spears flashing down and dripping as they came up again. The noise was tremendous, but Baluch didn't seem to hear. He was concentrated on the rhythm of sword stroke and shield parry. Acton pointed to the side. Harald was nearby, standing on a small rise, laying about him with vigor. Acton broke from their back-to-back position and moved toward Harald, Baluch guarding their progress from behind. But before they could reach the chieftain, a grinning berserker rose up behind him with spear in hand and thrust down hard into his back. Harald's arms went up in the air and he fell forward.

Acton shouted and surged ahead, heaving aside ally and enemy alike until he reached his grandfather's side. He sank to his knees beside Harald's dead body. Baluch stood over them, fending off two attempts to spear Acton. The berserker returned and Baluch dropped his shield to make a huge two-handed blow straight down on his head. It split the auburn head, the left ear coming away with part of the skull, soft brain oozing out. Astonishingly, the man stood, swaying but still alive. Baluch put a foot on his chest and kicked him away, then swooped to pick up his own shield in time to take the next blow from a raider on his flank. Baluch's chest was tight and tears were running down his cheeks as he swung his sword. Bramble realized belatedly that they were not for Harald. Elric, Baluch's father, was lying beside his chieftain, a great wound in his chest, the blood already drying. Acton rolled both men into seemly positions, then rose and lifted his sword.

"To me!" he shouted. "To me!"

The blond heads, one by one, turned and began to fight their way back toward the rise. Some fell on the way. When they were gathered, surrounded by a ring of swords and spears, Acton moved forward. He pointed with his sword to an older man to the far right of the attackers.

"That is their chieftain," he yelled to Baluch. "We will feed him to the ravens!" Then he began to fight his way toward the man. His men fell in behind him, Baluch at one shoulder, Asgarn coming up to shield the other side.

"Kill them all!" Acton shouted, and his men howled back: "Acton! Acton! Acton! Kill them all!"

Energy ran back into Baluch's limbs as the shout went up and he followed Acton with enthusiasm.

"Kill them all!" he shouted with the rest, the music in his head rising and rising until he could not think at all, just react: stab, swing, parry, block, swing again and rejoice as one of the attackers fell. No more reluctance, no more tears, just action and the satisfaction of killing those who deserved to die. Despite herself, Bramble was caught up in the storm of feeling and movement, in the music and the blood and the shouting. She felt Baluch's blood rise in a kind of exaltation.

Part of her, the part that had kicked the warlord's man out of instinct, out of a refusal to be conquered, understood that exaltation. Shared it. Kill them all, she thought. That's how it works. You have to try to kill them all, or die.

She was glad when the waters came like a thumping ocean wave, lifting her and tumbling her and scouring her mind clean of killing. So glad she wanted to cry, but she wasn't sure whether the tears were hers or from somewhere deep inside Baluch.

MARTINE

ON THE SECOND night of the vigil, Cael and Safred stayed up talking around the fire until late. Zel was sitting with Bramble for a while. She and Martine had fallen into shifts. Cael was ruled out from that duty because they had been successful at getting Bramble to drink, which meant that occasionally she pissed and had to be cleaned up, and they all knew she wouldn't want Cael involved with that. Or Safred, though it was trickier to justify her exclusion. They let her sit with Bramble every so often, in broad daylight, when one or the other of them was near, so it wasn't so obvious, but they both knew Safred realized what they were doing, and she didn't like it.

She retaliated by questioning them about their involvement with the gods. She wanted to know everything about Martine's journey from Turvite, every detail she could remember about the ghosts, what the gods had said through Elva, and then everything about Elva and her relationship with the gods. To Martine it seemed that Safred was both reassured and piqued to learn that another woman had so close a tie to them. She questioned Martine closely about how the gods possessed Elva, how they spoke through her, what their voice was like when they did.

Martine called a halt. If they didn't go to bed now, the others wouldn't be asleep by midnight. "When you meet her, you can ask her yourself—or see for yourself. But I'm going to bed."

"I just want to know —"

Martine lost patience. "Safred, I know it bothers you that other people have dealings with your gods, but they were our gods first. Lots of us have special dealings with them. It's part of our lives. Every stonecaster in the Domains hears the gods talk at some point. If you try to know everything about every person who deals with the gods, you'll be dead of old age before you get halfway through."

Safred went very still, a look in her eyes that balanced between hurt and revelation. She opened her mouth to ask another question, but Cael shook his head at her. He nodded to her tent. "Bed, niece."

She did what she was told.

Martine liked Cael, and right now she was thankful for his presence, but every now and then she looked at him and saw one of Acton's men: the big, fair-haired invaders who had dispossessed her people. She could imagine him laughing as he killed. The image made her voice sharper than she intended. "Good night, Cael."

He looked at her with surprise, but silently went to his bedroll, while she turned her back and walked over to Zel and Bramble. Bramble was crying, silently, tears rolling down her cheeks, her face set. It was a terrible sight, and Zel had hunched over so she didn't have to look at her, fighting her own tears.

Martine was struck again with the sense that what Bramble was undergoing was profoundly unnatural; that only grief would come of it. Saker, she thought, falcon, predator—you have hurt more people than you realize.

She stayed with Bramble while Zel went to the privy and then went herself, gathering dead pine needles for tinder as she walked back. Midnight wasn't far off, by the stars. Telling midnight by the stars at Spring Equinox was a trick every Traveler woman was taught by her mam. Martine wondered, not for the first time, what happened at the Autumn Equinox. The ritual then was reserved for older women, women who had gone through the change, the climacteric, and were past child-bearing age.

I'll find out soon enough, she thought wryly. Another ten, maybe fifteen years, and I'll be there. Excluded from the spring rituals, included in the autumn. Part of her found that depressing; part comforting. Somewhere to go to, somewhere where age had a purpose. Old women returned from the Autumn Equinox chuckling and grinning, but they didn't seek out men afterward.

Martine and Zel walked out to the altar as they had done the night before, becoming a little more confident in finding their footing. Martine had no sense that the lake resented the ritual, but she did, again, have the feeling that it was watching. Tonight, it was Zel's turn to provide the flint and Martine's to hold the striking stone.

The small pile of birch fungus caught alight immediately, and the ritual went on as it had done the previous night, except that, as always on the second night, the kindling burned more slowly and Martine's arousal was greater, her need more intense. She surrendered to the fire more easily, closing her eyes and releasing her body, if not her whole mind, to feel whatever he wanted it to feel. Desired, that was what she felt. His great gift. No matter what she looked like, every Traveler woman knew, deep inside, that she was desirable, because he desired her. Often, the plainest women were the fire's most ardent followers.

As the fire died and she returned to herself, shivering, Martine wondered, as she often had, what it was they were doing. The ritual wasn't worship. The contact between fire and woman was too intimate for that. They didn't ever talk of the fire as a god, just as "him" or "he." But—he gave and they took; they gave and he took. Was it simply a bargain, made and kept? Or was it something deeper? The old women said that it kept the Domains in balance. Woman to fire, man to water, they said in whispers. Sometimes they had whispered it to their stone-caster so that Martine had learned things young women did not normally know, and the stones had said the same thing, in whispers to her, many times over the years.

There was healing in the ritual, too. Women who had been raped were placed closest to the fire, and he healed them, burned away any disgust or hatred of men or self-recrimination. Set them free to feel and love again. That was a great gift. The one time that Traveler women had tried to introduce a woman of Acton's blood to the fire, it had been out of compassion for her, because she had been raped by a raiding party from the next Domain, in the time when all the warlords raided each other.

The fire had burnt cleanly away and the altar was untouched. That was always a good sign—a sign that he was pleased with them. Martine flushed with gratification at the thought, then smiled at herself. Like a young girl with her first love. Well, the fire was everyone's first love. Some women's only love. Some never got over their first Spring Equinox. Never found satisfaction with a human male. Would rather have the intensity without the fulfillment than the flesh and blood encounter, which never quite matched up for them. Others went the opposite way; clung to flesh and blood and rejected the fire; stayed away from the ritual, especially those who secretly preferred women to men. Zel had said her mother had been like that—so obsessed with her husband that she had no interest in the ritual and only took Zel the one time, because it was her duty to introduce her to the fire. Martine's mother had steered the middle course that Martine tried for: to perform the ritual but not be consumed by it.

"The fire will never die," they said in unison, and sighed.

Martine took Zel's hand and they went back to the camp, banked down the fire which was now leaping high, gave Bramble some water and lay down either side of her.

Zel sighed in the darkness. "It's a shame he don't like us pleasuring our own selves after," she said wistfully.

Martine laughed softly. "He won't come tomorrow night if you do," she warned, as her own mother had warned her.

"I know," Zel sighed. "Dung and pissmire. By the day after tomorrow, even Cael's going to start looking good to me!"

Bramble was shivering as though she, too, were feeling the effects of the Equinox, arousal without release. Martine reached out and patted her hand soothingly.

"Shh," she said. "It's all right. Shhh."

Bramble quieted a little, and Martine let her hand fall away. She looked up into the star-blazing sky and wondered what they would do if they couldn't find a flint tomorrow. There was only one solution she could see, and it terrified her.

BRAMBLE

HER NOSE WAS twitching, like a rabbit's. The cold air hit as though a door had opened into hell. The body she was in was a man's. Don't think about it, she told herself, trying to ignore the sensation of testicles contracting as the cold surrounded them. She strained to see and suddenly was blinded by whiteness: snow lit by high sun, dazzling, painful. On one side cliffs sheered up to the bright blue sky, on the other, a high slope covered with snow threatened them. Snow thin on the ground, gray stone, a thin, rocky trail between high boulders. Any noise here would echo off the cliffs and grow as it echoed. Bramble wanted to shiver—fortunately, the man she was with was shivering anyway.

The man was riding a chestnut horse, last in a line of four of the stocky little horses she had seen before. Asa was in the lead, followed by Acton, with another man behind them. That man wore bright red boots. Bramble felt herself smile at the sight of them, as if she had glimpsed something homely and reassuring. Swef, she thought. All she could see was his back, which was broad. Younger than Harald, but with gray hair showing beneath his cap, red to match his boots. He sat his horse well enough, but without the ease that familiarity brought. The bridle and bit were muffled with rags, and the hooves of the horses in front were in rag boots. Swef looked apprehensively up at the snow-covered slopes.

Death Pass, Bramble thought. They were in Death Pass. She realized she was looking through Gris's eyes.

There was an end to the defile in sight just ahead. She had only a glimpse of the mountain falling away sharply, of green land below, of trees far beneath and then the waters swept in and seemed to knock her sideways.

A fire. Warmth. Flickering shadows. A deep, accusing voice.

"You ask for privileges in words you learned from those of our people whom you stole to be your slaves!"

Gris raised his head to stare straight into the speaker's eyes. A younger man than Bramble expected, only about forty, and at last, at last, someone with dark hair! She hadn't realized how much the eternal blondness and redness was irritating her. The man stared back at Gris with something like hatred.

"True," Gris said. "We have stolen. We have enslaved. We have killed. That is true. Have you never raided, Hawk?"

The man looked aside, and then brushed the question away. His hand movements were odd: larger than Bramble was used to, and with the second finger touching the thumb. They were sitting by a proper hearth, not a fire pit, in a house which only seemed small because she had become accustomed to the large halls of Acton's home. The walls of the house were wattle and daub, but the chimney was made of flat field stones, intricately pieced together without mortar.

"We have had no time for raiding for some years. We must defend ourselves instead," the man—she must not think of him as a Traveler—said.

"But what if that were to change?" Asa leaned forward to speak persuasively. "What if your people were returned to you? If you no longer had to worry about raids? If you had strong friends at your back?"

Hawk ignored her as though she were not there.

"We could make you strong," she said, trying again. She exchanged a puzzled glance with Acton and gave a little shrug.

Acton raised his eyebrows and repeated, "We could make you strong."

"At what cost?" he countered immediately. In the pause that followed, he turned to Asa as though seeing her for the first time.

"The women are in the scullery," he said, and pointed to an open door on the far side of the fireplace.

For a moment, the three other men froze. Swef bit his lip. Asa's face went blank but Bramble could almost hear the thoughts racing through her mind: her dignity was not important enough to risk this negotiation.

"My mother is a wise counselor," Acton began, but she hushed him.

"I will speak to the women," she said. She rose and went in stately silence to the door. The dark-haired man smiled thinly in triumph.

Bramble was shocked. She had always assumed that women were less esteemed than men in the Domains because of the invasion, because Acton's people were flawed. She had never wondered how they had been treated in the old days.

"How strong can men be who take counsel from women?" Hawk asked scornfully.

Gris smiled. "Easy enough to control weak women, cowed from birth. It takes a real man to control a woman who knows her own mind."

"And you do?"

"My wife has a sharp mind and a sharp tongue, but she follows my lead."

"As you would have me do. You wish me to follow your instructions like a woman."

Bramble lost interest in the maneuvering for position and dominance, in the promises of alliance and mutual support. What was the point of listening, she thought, when they didn't keep any of those promises? When they slaughtered everyone instead? She wondered what Asa was doing and saying in the kitchen. Probably promising the women that their stolen children, siblings and husbands would be returned to them. Bramble suspected that even in this culture, men listened to their women behind closed doors. Unlike the sleeping halls of Acton's people, there were lots of closed doors in houses like these.

Her attention was reclaimed when Swef sat up straight and said, "So it is agreed?"

The man put up a delaying hand. "It is agreed that I will discuss it with my advisers, and ask their counsel. If they agree, we may try next summer—a small settlement, to the north where the forest ends. If that is successful, more may be possible." He spoke as though he were a chief and they were slaves, but Gris nodded in thanks.

Acton looked impatient, and annoyed by the man's pretensions. "Hawk, who will decide if it is successful?" he asked.

Well done, lad, Bramble thought. That's the real question. Who's got the power?

"I will," Hawk said, standing and looking down his nose at the three of them, even though he was shorter than they were. Swef let out a breath that was almost a snort. Gris simply nodded.

A girl came from the scullery with a platter of cheese and bread and apricots and put it down on a small stool next to Acton. She was pretty: black-haired and dark-eyed, honey skin and red lips, slim and very slight compared to the blond girls over the mountains. He smiled at her, that sideways smile that all the old stories mentioned, and she blushed and smiled back. Bramble could see why. That smile *was* attractive, the invitation to shared mischief, if you didn't know that this man would soon butcher all your relatives—perhaps even the girl herself.

This is dispiriting, Bramble thought, and if the water which came up then had been real she would not have had the energy to save herself.

Still in Gris's body—she was coming to recognize his scent, if not his mind—she surfaced to find him in a cave with Hawk and Acton and a woman. Bramble wondered where Swef was, whether this was another visit altogether. Jumping about in time was wearying. She longed for it to be over.

The woman was old, the oldest person Bramble had seen so far on this journey, and she wore animal skins roughly stitched together. Her white hair was felted together like a mess of snakes and her skin was dirty. She sat on a bear skin in front of a small fire, toying with a set of stones. The air should have been smokier here than it was.

Acton seemed to share the thought, because he looked up to the shadows above, and Gris followed his glance. The smoke wound its way out of a vent at the top of the cave. The woman caught Acton looking and gave a toothless grin.

"Clever one, aren't you?" she asked, casting stones casually across the skin. Without looking at them, she gathered them in.

"I don't understand you," Acton said slowly, still finding his way in a foreign tongue. "What do you want?"

"Sit down," the woman said, but it wasn't a reply. She was looking at Gris hard and leaned forward, as he sat on the other side of the bear skin, peering into his eyes. Her breath was rank, like dog breath.

"And you, kinslayer, you've got a passenger. Hello, girl."

If she'd been in her body, Bramble would have jumped at the words. The woman was clearly looking straight at her, *seeing* her in Gris's eyes. Gris had tensed at her words, but more at the word "kinslayer" than the greeting.

"Dotta!" Hawk reproved her. "This is important."

"You think this is not?" Dotta replied, but she leaned back and spat into her left hand. Hawk copied her and they clasped, palm to palm. Hawk prepared himself, as though he had thought the question out carefully.

"What will be the results of allowing the strangers to settle in our territory?"

Dotta drew out the five stones—so little of this ritual has changed, Bramble thought, I wonder why? The stones were mountain stones, gray and black and silverfish. They fell face up.

"Death. Betrayal. Chaos. Ruin. Destiny." Dotta poked at each stone in turn like a baker testing if dough has risen enough, then gathered them in. She didn't look at the men.

"Hah!" Hawk broke his hand free and glared at Gris. "So."

"Wait!" Acton said. "I have a question."

Dotta didn't speak; she simply spat in her hand again and held it out to Acton. Reluctantly, he spat in his own palm and clasped hers. They don't have stonecasting, Bramble realized. I never thought before, but no one consulted the casters about the Ice King. The stonecasting is part of the Domains, not the Ice King's land... she wasn't sure what that meant, but it seemed important, somehow.

Acton's gold hair shone in the firelight. He bowed his head for a moment as though praying, then asked carefully, in a halting accent, "What will be the results of *not* allowing us to settle in your territory?"

Dotta laughed and cast the stones.

"Death. Betrayal. Chaos. Ruin. Destiny," she chanted as they fell. They stared at her in astonishment, but she was right. The same stones, in the same order. Dotta hawked and spat in the fire and laughed at their expressions. "Did you think the Destiny stone meant nothing?"

"If we don't let them come . . ."

"They will come anyway," she said. "If not these men, then others. I have advice for you, Hawk, which you will not take. Run! Take your women and your children and your animals and your chattels and run a long, long way from here. The world is wide, but the Ice King's country is small and getting smaller. Run, little one! Or you will not see two more summers."

Hawk sat very still. "Is that prophecy?"

"It's common sense, which is worth more!" she retorted, reminding Bramble of Martine in Oakmere.

He relaxed a little. "Then there is still room to prevent the worst." He turned to Gris. "If we let your people in, you can support us against the others. The stones say Death and Ruin, but not *whose* death. Let us make it the deaths of others!"

Dotta made a disgusted noise and rose with audibly creaking bones. "You," she said to Gris. "Come."

She picked up a piece of bone with a plug on one end. It hung by a cord from her fingers. With the hem of her skirt guarding her other hand, she plucked an ember from the fire and dropped it in the bone, and put in tinder which she had had lying ready. Then she took a step back and began to swing the bone around and around her head, like a slingshot. Gris, Acton and Hawk scrambled up and out of the way. Dotta chuckled.

"The old ways still work," she said. The tinder burst into flame like a torch. "My sisters are dead," she added, "but I still keep the flame. My sister's daughters have taken it now, far away, where it will be safe. For a time, a long time."

The men were silent.

"Come," she said again to Gris, swinging the bone lightly from side to side, so that the tinder burnt just enough to give off light.

He followed her deeper into the cave, to a passageway. She turned and put her hand on his sleeve, looking into his eyes intently. Her smell was overwhelming, so close.

"Girl," she said. "Remember this. You will have need of it later."

Bramble shivered and wondered if it were her own body or Gris's that trembled. There was no doubt that Dotta was seeing her, talking to her as though Gris weren't there.

She led him through a labyrinth of passageways, telling Bramble each turning. "Three down and then left. Two down and right. Four down, past this outcrop and sharp right. Down on your knees, now, for a while . . ."

The path went on for some time, Bramble trying frantically to memorize all the turnings and twistings. At last they came to a larger space and Dotta stopped. She whirled the bone on its cord in a wide circle above her head, illuminating the walls and ceiling of a large cave. There, floating on the walls above them, vivid with ochre—red and brown and charcoal black—were paintings. Animals. Aurochs, the wild cows that still could be found in these mountains, even in Bramble's day. Hares, their long ears absurdly pricked. Elk raising noble antlers to the sky. Deer running and leaping in a herd. Running from a pack of men with spears. Tiny black figures, but unmistakable. Other figures, too, smaller, rounder, darker altogether. Bramble had no idea what they were.

"Why have you brought me here?" Gris asked with a croaking voice. He cleared his throat. "What do you want?"

Dotta moved closer to Gris and looked into his eyes. "You'll need this place, girl, when you make your search. This is a place where calling is done. When you need the earth spirits, come here and call them."

"What are you talking about, woman?" Gris said, his mind feeling deeply unsettled. But Bramble was tense with frustration. *How?* She wanted to shout.

Dotta smiled, the toothless mouth gleaming wet in the flickering light. "How?" she echoed. "The way the hunters drew the prey to them. How else?"

She touched the wall lightly where the dark, rounded shapes were. Shadows flowed across them as the bone swung back and forward, making them seem to move, seem to writhe and deform. "The prey must be called with love, though, or it does not come. Remember that."

Bramble stared at the drawings, trying to remember the sequence of passages and turns that had brought them here.

"You can go now," Dotta said casually, and as if at her command the waters rose and carried Bramble away.

DOTTA'S STORY

My aunty Lig was one of three sisters, as her mother had been, and her mother before her. She was the middle child. Brond was the eldest and Gledda the youngest, and they lived together. The way I was told it, Brond was Mim's mother, both of them black-haired charmers, and she was carrying a second girl. Gledda was sure that the father was the traveling skald who'd been around the season before.

"Well, we'll never know," Lig said philosophically, "for sure as ash follows flame, Brond'll never tell us, and there'll be no telling from looking at the baby."

She knew the new baby would have red hair, like Lig. And the third girl, which was me, whom Brond would bear in a couple more years, would be chestnut-haired, like Gledda, flame there, but buried deep. It was always so in our family: three girls, the first black-haired, like charcoal, the second with hair as red as flame, the third with hair like banked embers. But only one of them would bear children, and then there would be three daughters, and three daughters only.

Our lives had been so for as long as memory, since the first Mim had made her bargain with the Fire God and brought down a piece of the fire mountain to warm the hearth of her people. The Byman girls, our family were called, which means burning, and alone of all the women of our people, we didn't attend the ritual at Spring Equinox, because the wildfire was with us all year round.

The Byman girls didn't have much need for men, except to get their daughters. We did for ourselves, as crafters of one kind or another, but mostly potters. Over the generations our old stone house had filled with the results of our work and it was like walking into a treasure chamber, with old wall-hangings and shining platters on the wall, with glazeware in every color gleaming: pale green and midnight blue, and the special deep red glaze that people from as far away as Turvite came to buy. That red glaze made looking into a bowl like looking into the depths of the earth, and there were some who said that the recipe for it had been given to the first Mim, from the Fire God himself. But when I asked one of my aunts, all she would do was smile and say, "I learned it from my mother, and where she learned it, only she knows." Which was no help at all because their mother and their aunts were dead, since the winter after young Mim was born.

That was the way it always happened, too.

Lig told me she had always hoped that she would be the one to have the children. When she was little, she planned what she would call them. Bryne, perhaps, or Ban, for the bone the first Mim had carried down the mountainside, full of fire. Or even, daring thought, Rosa, the name of her friend from the village. She played with dolls, while Brond and Gledda were only interested in messing around with clay. Even her mother thought she would be the one to carry on the line.

"Look at her," she would say to her sisters, watching Lig croon a dolly to sleep, "she's made for it."

"Well, I hope so," the girls' Aunt Bryne had answered once, thinking Lig couldn't hear, "for she's not half the potter the others are."

Lig knew it was true. Brond and Gledda were potters born, crafting reasonable bowls before they could sew. So as she grew up she took on most of the cooking and the cleaning, and left them free to perfect their craft, sure that she would have the most important role of all, to mother the next batch of daughters.

But by the time she was old enough to dance the Springtree and run off to the woods afterward with a sweet young man, Brond was already pregnant with Mim. That first Springtree morning had put a sharp taste in her mouth, the taste of uselessness. For if Brond was bearing, then she and Gledda were barren. That was the way of it. Poor Ham the farrier hadn't known what to do when she'd rolled away from him, after, and cried into the new grass. She'd tried to reassure him, but to the day of her death when he looked at her a cloud went over his face, as it will over the face of a man who remembers failure. He married Rosa and had six children who followed him around like puppies. Lig had always known he'd make a good father. She didn't go to their house much, though, and her old friendship with Rosa withered away.

Brond had been glad enough to let her look after Mim, especially during the bad time, when they were dealing with the shock of their mother's death, and then their aunts'. Even though they knew it was coming, it was still a shock. No one had told them what to expect until after Mim was born.

"You mustn't tell her or the other girls, when they come," Aunt Bryne had said sternly, coughing her life away with fever. "For then they'd never try for a child until you were all dead, and it might be too late. Just let them choose their own time, and be thankful."

"Aye," their mam said. "We've made a good bargain with the Fire God. He gives us health and prosperity, he protects us from ill, and he gives us a quick death when the time comes. But he likes his servants to be young, and vigorous, like him. Small blame to him."

"Our line will never die," Aunt Aesca breathed. "Remember that. Never so long as the fire burns."

That was small comfort to Lig or to the others, as they watched the three of them, their three beloveds, waste away and die. Afterward, though, they clung to it as a solace. At least there was a reason for the deaths. Most people, Brond pointed out, die for no reason at all. Surely that would be harder to cope with.

Lig wondered.

Watching Brond feed Mim had been like a pain, like an ache in her own breast, but it was bound up with the general pain of grief and misery they all lived in at the time. Since then she had grown to love Mim as her own.

But she didn't think she could bear to see Brond have another daughter, and this one a girl with flame hair, like hers.

"She should be mine," Lig muttered to her pillow. "We should have one each. That would be fair."

As Brond rounded out and slowed down, sitting more by the fire in the kitchen than by the potter's wheel in the workshop, Lig found it hard to be in the same room with her. She spent more time in the garden. She raised most of their food anyway: vegetables and herbs, fruits, chickens and ducks and eggs. There were two gardens: a walled garden next to the kitchen, and an orchard which ran from the other side of the house down to the river.

In the walled garden she grew vegetables and herbs and kept two espaliered fruit trees, apricot and cherry. Her aunt Aesca had tended the garden while she was alive, and she had believed that it was no use growing anything you couldn't eat or use for medicine. There were no flowers, except the few plants she let grow to seed for next years' planting. Nothing there just for the beauty of it.

"A rose," Lig thought one day, on her knees by the carrots. "A white rose. That's what I'd like. A white rose."

It was only a small tradition she was breaking, but it felt satisfying all the same. She traded a blue bowl for a cutting of a white rose from Vine the thatcher's garden, and planted it and some cornflower seeds, for good measure.

She tended that baby rose all through spring and all through summer, mulching and watering it, soaping off the aphids and using dark brown ale on the thrips. She left the kitchen to Brond, before and after the baby's birth. They called her Blaise and she was as red-headed as Lig.

Lig couldn't help but love her, but this time she left the tending of her to Brond, along with tending the fire.

The fire didn't like it.

That was what they told me, when I was old enough to hear the story, when my chestnut hair was down past my shoulders and I could climb Aunty Gledda's legs like climbing up a tree, her strong hands helping me. They said that Lig had made a mistake, thinking that the Fire God only cared about the ones he'd blessed with children, when he cared more, maybe, about the other two, the ones he had all to himself.

Lig decided, they said, that if she couldn't leave a child in the world, she'd leave a rose. A perfect white rose, more beautiful than any anyone had ever seen. So she begged cuttings from anyone who had a rosebush, and she went out searching the hillsides for wild roses, and she moved the carrots and the spinach and the onions out to the edge of the orchard, and took over the walled garden for her roses.

Some had small, tender buds. Others were wide, blowsy things with few petals but a rich, heady scent. I can just remember the smell, dizzying in the walled summer garden. Years it took her, to match and cross the blooms.

With each year of neglect for the vegetable garden, the fire grew angrier.

Not that it wasn't tended. No, all of them tended it. Brond and Gledda, both, and Mim, too, when she was old enough. And then Blaise. Even me. And Lig, when she felt like it, when she was passing.

But she didn't sit staring into the flames anymore, and she didn't sing softly to it as she went about the cooking and the cleaning, for she was thinking about her roses. She smelt of rose, now, not of charcoal and warm wool. Even in winter. She made rose-petal jam, rose-leaf pillows and rosehip tea. After much trial and error, she learnt to make an unguent of roses, and the merchants who came to buy glazeware began to buy her vials of perfume and unguent as well.

It soothed an old hurt, I suspect, to be able to bring silver into the house as well as food from her garden.

The fire smouldered.

Then came the year when Lig achieved her goal. The perfect white rose. She ran into the house one spring morning and dragged us all out to the garden. My feet were cold in the dew, I remember, and I couldn't understand why Aunty Lig was so excited about a tiny rosebush, no bigger than I was, with only one rose on it.

We went into breakfast, Lig floating.

"If I never do anything else in my life," she said. "I've done this. The perfect rose."

The fire blazed up in a roar.

I remember it. The terror of it, the sound, the fierce heat. I remember Mam Brond grabbing me and running, calling for Blaise and Mim, screaming to Lig to run, run, *run*!

For Lig was standing there, staring at the fire as if bespelled. As if in love.

"For me?" she said. "You've come just for me?"

I looked back from the door and I saw him. I saw him reach out for her, and I saw her smile and walk straight into his arms.

He consumed the house and everything in it. Only the stone walls were left. But he left the orchard and the pottery alone.

We huddled in the street, watching, and Mam Brond and Aunt Gledda stopped anyone going too close or trying to put it out. The heat drove us back fifty paces. The thatch flamed so bright we couldn't look at it. Then it was gone. Just gone in a moment, as if it had never been.

We spent the night at Vine's, sitting close together, not talking. Blaise cried, they say, and I just sucked my thumb and clung to Mam. In the morning we went back.

The main room was still uncomfortably warm. There was nothing left, not even the shapes of things. Everything was consumed except the glazeware, which was all cracked and broken, crazed and dull, but there. The floor was slate, and it had cracked as well, but it was so well packed down on the earth below it that we could walk on it safely. The ashes crunched beneath our feet. Gledda cried as she walked.

The crock where the silver was kept had cracked open and the silver had melted into a sharp-edged puddle.

The kitchen was just a shell. Here, even the glazeware hadn't survived. All that remained was the chimney and the hearth. There were no bones, no sign of Lig at all. In the hearth, burning cheerfully as though this were any ordinary morning, was the fire.

Gledda went out straightaway to get it some kindling. Mam went into the garden.

He had swept through the garden so fast that he just sucked the moisture out of everything and left it charcoal. Each rosebush was a ghostly black image of itself. On Lig's special bush, her perfect bud was still there, every petal intact, black and crisp and dead as Lig itself.

"It was a warning," said Mam Brond.

"It was a punishment," said Gledda, tending the fire frantically.

"It was a bloody temper tantrum," Mim said, years later, but only outside, in the market, away from the fire.

Blaise, whose daughters grew up to tend the Fire God in their turn, said, "It was love abandoned."

But I saw it, over Mam's shoulder, and it was murder and love fulfilled, both at once. I saw it, and I wondered, all through the years of my girlhood: Does he love all of us, or only Lig? Was it simple jealousy of her time and care, or a deeper jealousy of living things?

After Blaise had her first daughter, and I knew there would be no children for me, I wondered: Would he come for me if *I* planted a rose?

I knew the answer, knew it certain in my bones, and that was how I found I had the Sight, and I had to combine his service with service to newer gods, and they extended my life after my sister's daughter bore her first girl. But still, even as I cast the stones and listened to them whisper the black rock gods' answers, still and always I tended the fire.

ASH

HARD COUNTRY BY daylight was a nightmare in the dark, and soon they were leading the horses as much by feel as by their sight, the strengthening starlight interrupted by cloud and trees and towering rocks. Irrationally, Ash felt safer on the ground, although he would be far safer on Mud if the dogs ever caught up to them. He had to hope that the first brother wouldn't risk his hounds in the wilderness, but if he did, they could be caught between two sets of claws and teeth. He distracted himself from that thought by trying to remember the sequence of notes Doronit had whistled to send the wind wraiths away. He had stood on the cliffs above Turvite with her and she had whistled two tunes: one to control them, so they could parley, and one to send them away. He had tried to forget that night . . .

As they made their way upward, the slope grew steeper, the trees fewer, and the rocks slid beneath them. The horses didn't like it when the trail shifted under their hooves, especially Cam. She shied and slid again, pulling on the reins so often that Flax had to swap over with Ash to give his arms a rest.

The last stretch was the steepest, the horses scrabbling for purchase, Flax and Ash on hands and knees. At the top they paused for a moment, and Ash was sure he could hear the scrabbling sounds continue. An echo? Or . . . Surely the men wouldn't follow them up here? They'd be insane to do so.

The top of the bluff was a plateau, dangerous even in daylight, and crowned with whirling winds which ripped between boulders and down crevices moaning unendingly. The horses didn't like it at all. A little way forward, Mud stuck his hooves in the thin soil and refused to go any further.

"We have to find shelter until daylight," Ash shouted above the wind. There was a sudden silence. The wind just stopped, as though it had heard him.

"That's not good," Flax said.

Wind wraiths, Ash thought in terror, just before they came. He and Flax were outside the old compact between the wind wraiths and humans: they could not take humans unless the humans were delivered to them by an act of treachery. The agreement was so old that some believed it had been arranged by the gods themselves, long, long before Acton's forces had come over the mountains. But it had force only in settled lands. He and Flax were in the wilderness, and they were fair game.

The thin, pale wraiths swerved in from all directions, around large boulders and small, screaming and moaning, sounding like all the storms, all the evil, in the world. Close enough, Ash thought, as he tried frantically to remember the sequence of notes that Doronit had used to send them away.

Like all the air spirits, wind wraiths liked to play with their prey. They streamed past, thin claws flicking out at the last moment to scratch a cheek, a hand, to cut through a shirt. Although they ignored the horses, Cam and Mud had their hooves firmly planted, shaking with frozen terror. The wind wraiths licked their claws and rounded back again, six of them, swirling like a cloud with needles hidden in its center. Ash couldn't remember the notes that would send them away. In desperation, he worked his dry mouth to make saliva and began to whistle. Five notes, notes that had been burned into his brain in the dark wind above Turvite. Five notes which controlled them.

They shrieked with displeasure, but their wild flight slowed and they came to hover in front of Ash. Flax looked from side to side, as though he couldn't quite see them, just hear them.

"Who calls us?"

Flax, getting the idea, was picking up the tune and whistling too. Ash waited until he was perfect in rhythm, perfectly in pitch, and then stopped, and spoke.

"We do."

The leading wraith spat on the ground and snarled at Ash, arms stretched toward his face, claws curling. He forced himself to remain still. "*Name*, ignorance."

"Ash." Flax flicked him a look, as though to say "What about me?" but Ash didn't know what the consequences would be of giving your name to a wind wraith, and he didn't want Flax to suffer if the results were bad.

"What would you have us do, *Ash*, little tree? Remember, trees can be uprooted if the wind is strong enough." It laughed.

"Leave us alone."

Flax gestured strongly to the horses.

"Leave us and our horses alone," Ash amended. "Let us pass safely through this place."

"What do you offer in exchange?" the wraith hissed. It looked consideringly at Flax.

Ash thought fast. He was certainly not going to make the kind of bargain that Doronit had. She had traded lives for information, had told them where to find whole ships for killing so she could collect the insurance silver. He would not trade Flax's life for his. But he had to give them something . . .

Behind them, stones shifted and scraped each other. The wind wraiths whirled up and shrieked and Ash risked a glance behind them. He began to whistle again, in case this was a trick to distract them. No trick. Behind them was a man, wrapping one arm around his head to protect his face from the wind wraiths' claws and swiping the air with his sword uselessly. The man was hard to see in the starlight, but Ash had no doubt about who it was. He made sure Flax was still keeping time, keeping pitch, and then he stopped whistling.

"Horst!" he called. "Come this way."

Horst stumbled toward them, the wind wraiths following and slicing at him viciously. They plucked away the sword in his hand and let it drop.

"You have brought us a sacrifice, friend!" the leading wraith said with satisfaction. "It is a good bargain!"

The wraith reached long claws toward Horst's face. He stepped back, screaming, "No!"

"No!" Ash shouted at the same moment, and batted the wraith's hands away.

The wraiths shrieked and spurted upward again, coming down a little further away. Ash had a moment to think. *Should* he sacrifice Horst?

He glanced at Flax and saw that he was just plain terrified—that he'd accept any bargain to get them out safely. Ash saw himself on the cliffs above Turvite, whistling frantically to keep himself and Doronit safe. If someone had said to him then, "Sacrifice someone who wants you dead and you'll be safe," what would he have answered?

Tactically, he knew what he should do. Probably no one, not even Martine, would blame him. But he had made this decision when he hadn't killed the carter, and besides that, he couldn't, he just *couldn't*, hand another person over to the wraiths.

"No," he said. "This is not a sacrifice. The bargain includes his safety."

Horst looked at him in astonishment.

"What do you offer, then," the wraith hissed, "that is worth three lives?"

Ash cast around frantically for something, anything, he could offer them. "Information," he said at last.

"What?"

Ash swallowed. He just hoped this news would be astonishing enough. "The barrier between life and death has been breached. Ghosts walk the land, killing the living."

"Sooooo." The wraith shot up into the sky like a fountain of white and returned to hover again in front of him. "Broken by a *human*?"

Ash nodded.

"Where?"

"South," Ash said. "In Carlion."

"Come, then, brothers," it shrieked. "Come to feast."

Laughing, cackling, screaming, the wraiths sped into the sky and headed south, a cloud traveling as no cloud could or ever should, against the wind.

Horst sank to the ground, shivering, blood running down his face and arms from hundreds of tiny wounds. The wraiths had done much more damage to him, thinking he was theirs.

Ash and Flax remained stock still for a long moment, until they were sure the wraiths weren't coming back, and then checked the horses, patting their sweating flanks and murmuring comfort, taking reassurance from their warmth and solid flesh, trying to keep an eye on Horst at the same time.

"What have you done?" Flax asked.

Ash wondered that himself. It hadn't occurred to him that the wraiths would react like that—he had just hoped that the information would be enough to make a bargain. He licked his lips nervously. He knew he was going to get into trouble over this, but he didn't know from whom.

"I . . . I don't know. But at least we're alive. Let's get going before they come back."

That got through to Horst. He clambered to his feet and faced Ash. "You could have fed me to them. You'd have been safe, then."

Ash shrugged. What could he say? In the darkness Horst's face was hard to see, but his voice was full of emotion: confusion, gratitude, anger. Ash would feel like that, too, if an enemy had saved him.

"I can't let you go," Horst said reluctantly. "It's my duty to my lord to take you back. Or kill you."

Ash felt very tired. "Kill me if you want, but you're still in Golden Valley and that makes it murder, not warlord's justice."

Horst hestitated. Ash wished he could see better, but the starlight was faint and interrupted by high clouds.

"I have to take you back," Horst said eventually.

"You can't," Ash said. "There are two of us, and we're both armed. We have horses, you don't. You're wounded. There's no chance you could take us both and drag us down the side of this shagging mountain without one of us clouting you on the head with a rock. And your lord should know the news we gave to the wraiths. There is an enchanter raising ghosts and giving them body. Your lord should be told."

The next pause seemed very long as Horst considered. Flax moved quietly around the side of the horses, trying, Ash could see, to get behind Horst in case it came to a fight. But then the wind wuthered through a gap in the rocks, sounding just like a wind wraith, and they all flinched. Horst let out a long sigh.

"You'll still be a wanted man," he said. "I can't let you off Sully's murder."

Ash nodded. "Fair enough," he said.

Horst turned back the way he had come, then paused. Speaking with difficulty, he said, "Thanks." Then he started walking, head down.

Flax came up beside Ash and clapped him on the shoulder. "Let's get out of here," he said.

It was easier said than done. The moon was on its downward slide and its light was interrupted by clouds building from the south. Ash and Flax took it in turns to go in front of the one leading the horses, poking at the ground with a stick to make sure it was solid, to make sure they wouldn't tumble headlong into a crevasse or have one of the horses break a leg in a pothole. All the time the wind was building, sounding more and more like the wind wraiths returning, until they were soaked with sweat from the tension and the concentration. When the moon was about to set, Ash decided they had to find somewhere to spend the rest of the night.

They found a nest of large boulders which had a sheltered spot in the center and a small overhang where they could sit, glad to have their backs against something solid, glad to be out of the wind, but not willing to sleep. Just in case. The horses, however, settled down as soon as they came within the circle of rocks, and Ash decided to take that as a sign they were safe. As they unsaddled and groomed the horses, the dusty scent of their hides and the routine way Mud shifted to let Ash move from one side to the other created a sense of normalcy that settled him, too.

They drank in silence while the horses found rainwater in hollows and lipped at the coarse grass. Ash wondered where the wind wraiths were, what they were doing. But there was nothing he could do about it. He remembered Doronit saying, "Concentrate on things you can do something about." She had been right. He had to concentrate on getting Flax and himself safely to the Deep. At least this trail should cut their travel time down considerably. Once they were off the plateau, they should be only a couple of days' ride to Gabriston. And then, the Deep.

"What made you think of the lie, back there?" he asked, after a long silence.

"What lie?"

"You being a rich kid of the new blood."

Flax laughed. "It *was* a good notion, wasn't it? I can go as one of them, just like my da. Comes in handy, sometimes."

Ash could imagine his mother's reaction to that. She despised Travelers who impersonated Acton's people. She could always pick them, and Ash had heard her snap her knowledge out of the side of her mouth as they passed someone pretending. She wouldn't approve of this charade. His mouth firmed. Well, it wasn't her life at risk, was it? She had given up all right to tell him what to do when she had handed him over to Doronit. Time for him to make his own decisions.

"I think we should keep up the act," he said.

"Sure and certain," Flax said comfortably. "I might even get you to shine my boots!"

Ash laughed unwillingly. He had never been closer to liking Flax. "Safeguarders are skilled professionals, I'll have you know," he said with mock sternness. "We don't shine boots."

"Shame." Grinning, Flax settled down with his head on Cam's saddle. "You can take first watch."

Liking him didn't last long, Ash thought. Spoiled brat. But there was something comforting about Flax's insouciance, about his resilience after the terrors of the night. Ash loosened his knife, just in case, and watched as the moon set and the dark crowded in.

In daylight the plateau was still remarkable, windshaped rocks taking on the appearance of hunched figures, of curving waves, of flames reaching to the sky. There was rainwater in rock hollows to drink, but nothing to eat, and Ash's stomach growled constantly once the sun was high.

Then they reached the edge of the bluff, and could see Far North Domain spread out below them. Wheat fields shining golden in the sun. As they took their first steps off the plateau, Ash felt sharp relief flood him. They were out of the wilderness now, and safe from the wraiths. Flax grinned at him, mirroring his relief.

The way down was treacherous, the ground covered with scree that shifted under their feet and the horses' hooves. They slithered down as much as walked, leading Cam and Mud, who picked their way delicately, lifting their hooves high and looking hard done by.

Reaching the valley floor was almost an anticlimax. They found a small waterfall trickling over the rocks and flung themselves down to rest while the horses drank. Ash's legs were so rubbery, he almost looked forward to getting back on Mud.

They had descended into a wide valley, with the first shoots showing in the ploughed fields. This was grain country, the Far North Domain; not an area Ash had been in much, but he knew it well enough to know that the valley held the Snake River—called so because of its curving, curling path that snaked around the flat valley bottom so much that there were places where it almost met itself. Villages were found in the center of the curves, protected on three sides by water, but vulnerable to flooding, so their houses were built high on stone pilings, with chicken roosts and rabbit hutches underneath, and stone-built silos were connected with the houses by causeways an arm's length off the ground.

As Ash and Flax rode along the rutted track that passed for the main road, they passed farm after farm where wild-eyed cats spat at them from barn doorways, and terriers yapped at their heels, while freckle-faced children peered at them from around corners.

"They're not called cats and dogs around here," Ash said to Flax as Cam kicked out at a snapping brindled mutt. "They're called mousers and ratters. Their job is to keep the pests from the grain."

"Do *I* look like a rat?" Flax demanded. Then he laughed. "Don't answer that!"

The farmers and their wives were out in the fields planting the second spring sowing, hoeing vegetable rows, tending the few new calves and lambs. There was not much pasture, here, where most land was given over to wheat and oats and maize.

The black stone altars were few and far between, but they found one in a grove of trees in a river bend and each sacrificed a lock of hair for their salvation on the plateau. Ash prayed for Sully, the man he had killed, who would have quickened yesterday. He hoped that Sully's ghost would find rest even though his killer had not offered reparation.

Sully's quickening set him wondering, as he had often wondered, about the dark after death, and the gate to rebirth. His father had told him that those who earned it were reborn. Rebirth was bought with courage and compassion and perseverance, tolerance and joy and generosity. There was a song... Ash stopped himself thinking about the song because any thought of his father teaching him—and *not* teaching him—made his gut clench. Rebirth—think about rebirth. The gods said it was true, but they refused to tell how, or when, any person would be reborn, or anything about someone's last life. Live the body in the body, Elva had told him they said, one morning when they'd been washing dishes together in the kitchen in Hidden Valley. No one knew for sure if the rebirths were endless, or if somehow, sometime, you stopped. Some people said that if you were good enough, wise enough, kind enough, you eventually became a local god. Elva had asked about that, she had said, and the gods just laughed, which could have meant anything.

They stopped in a village to buy supplies, and Ash stood scowling while Flax bargained amiably with the market stall owner. No doubt, he got a better price than Ash would have, and the man threw in a joke for good measure, about staying clear of the black dog, the spirit that led you astray.

Flax laughed and lifted a hand in farewell. Ash realized that the resentment he felt was not just because fairer-haired people were treated so differently. He also resented Flax's ease with people, his self-assurance, his conviction that everyone would like him, because everyone always had.

He pushed the emotion down. Why should he envy Flax? After all, from what he could gather, Flax's parents had sent him out on the Road when he was only twelve. At least *his* parents had waited until he was old enough to look after himself. Of course, Flax had Zel... Yes, he thought, he was definitely better off than Flax, and smiled to himself. Poor Zel, worrying about her little chick, gone off exploring the world.

The people of Far North had mined their fields for stones and built their houses, their silos, and weirs across their slow-flowing rivers to make races for the water mills which ground their grain. There was no need for ferries, or bridges, or fords. The horses crossed with no more than wet ankles, and Ash and Flax didn't have to pay tolls.

"I like this country!" Flax said, popping a strawberry into his mouth. The horses liked it too, and cantered happily on the grass by the side of the track, so that they made good time.

Ash's purse was empty.

They had to get some silver. Copper even, would do. "Guess it's up to me, then," Flax said cheerfully.

"I thought Zel told you to stay out of taverns?" Ash said. He raised his eyebrows to imply that Flax couldn't do anything that Zel forbade.

Flax made a face back at him, looking very young. "I don't have to go to a tavern to make silver," he said.

They had a choice of ways not long after. Either would lead them eventually to Gabriston, although the road that went by Cold Hill, the next town, was longer. At the crossroads, Ash knew they ought to take the shorter way, but the other road called to him strongly, with something like Sight but not exactly the same. The sensation worried him, but in the end he decided on the longer way, reasoning that they were being led by the gods, and shouldn't ignore Sight or anything like it if they hoped to get through the journey unscathed.

In Cold Hill, which was barely larger than a village, they tied their horses next to a horse trough on the green, unsaddled them and gave them nosebags. Flax made his way to the side of the green closest to the inn. They had ridden all day, and it was evening, the night approaching in the slow, incremental way it did in the north, the sky lavender and lilac, the evening air scented with a stand of lilies growing in the inn's front garden. There were tables set out there, and most of the inn's patrons had chosen to bring their tankards out to sit in the mild air.

Flax stopped opposite the inn, put down a large square of umber cloth, and began to sing. He just stood there, unself-conscious, relaxed, and let the warm notes rise gently over the drinkers' heads.

He sang a popular, sentimental song, to get their attention. Ash had seen it done often enough. Get them listening, without realizing it, and then bring out some louder or more startling song. He sighed. I should do my bit, he thought. There was a bench not far away, set no doubt for the use of older people when the green was busy as a market square. He knelt down beside it and began a gentle drumming on it with the flat of his hands, underscoring the rhythm of the song. Flax cast him a startled glance and then grinned.

In the cool wilds of twilight, my lover comes to me,
Gold in the sunset, her hair like summer corn
Deep in the Forest, snug beneath a tree
My love and I lie warm until the morn . . .

They were listening. How could they not? Ash thought. He had half-wished that Flax would be bad, would have no strength to his voice to buttress the sweetness Ash had already heard while they were riding. But no, his voice rose strong and clear and wholly beautiful, and he sang without strain, without effort, letting the notes go fully, opening himself to the song so that it was like the song sang him instead of the other way around. He had been well taught, somewhere, somehow. Ash felt the labor with which he was drumming and flushed. It was a simple rhythm and in his head it was clear and easy, but once he tried to reproduce it his hands faltered.

He concentrated. He could do this; he *had* done it, night after night, well enough so that the drinkers never noticed that he wasn't a real musician. But what did they know? If he made a mistake, Flax would certainly notice, and he couldn't stand that.

He made it to the end of the song without an error and relaxed a little, rubbing his reddening hands and wishing he had a drum. A few of the drinkers nodded to him and kept drinking, without so much as looking like throwing a coin. Ash didn't worry. This was the way it worked.

Flax looked at him and mouthed: "Death Pass?" Ash nodded. The ballad about Acton was a well-known and much-loved one and it had a strong beat. You couldn't do it without a drummer; there were sections where only the rhythm moved forward. He flexed his fingers and used his full palm to make the starting drumbeats as loud as he could. The drinkers stopped and looked, and Flax launched into the chorus straightaway. A good decision. They grinned and listened, and a couple, who'd clearly had the most to drink, even sang along.

Bright flowed the blood of the dark-haired foe
Red flowed the swords of the conquering ones
Mighty the battles, mighty the deeds
Of Acton's companions, the valiant men.

Ash wondered about Bramble. He kept his mind on the drumming, but the lower level of thought had to be busy with something, and he didn't want to think about Flax, about how perfectly he sang, about how he was exactly the son Ash's parents had hoped for. So he thought about Bramble instead, and wondered what was happening to her. They came to the first section where he had to drum alone and he cast everything out of his thoughts except the rhythm, determined not to disgrace himself in front of Flax. Flax came back in exactly on the beat, as precise as Swallow, and Ash increased the pace, as he was supposed to. It felt as bad as drumming for his parents. Worse, because he had been in constant practice then. He hadn't played this song for more than three years. But the music was clear in his head. If nothing else, he knew the songs. Except the ones his father hadn't taught him.

That thought made his hands falter, although he corrected himself immediately. Flax didn't appear to notice, but Ash was sure he would have. His face burned red. But the drinkers hadn't noticed. They were banging their tankards in time with his drumming, so that he could ease off a little to protect his hands. When Flax sang the first words of the chorus again, the drinkers joined in enthusiastically. They sang the last chorus three times and this time, when the song ended, coins came flying through the air to them.

Then the innkeeper came out with a small beer each and invited them to move to the inn garden.

"I guess that's not exactly *in* a tavern, is it?" Flax said, grinning.

Ash moved to a table, which was better for his back and gave more resonance, but still hurt his hands. Flax stood beside him, and they performed another half-dozen songs; war songs and love songs and, at the end, when the innkeeper nodded to them to finish up, a cradle song that everyone present had always known.

Close your eyes, close your eyes,
My own little sweetheart
You are tired, little boy
So sleep now, my joy . . .

Grown men wept the easy tears of the drunk as they remembered dead mothers, and young women grew sentimental, thinking of the children they would have someday. The soft notes rose clear and gentle into the dark sky, floating away to join the stars. This song needed no drumming. Flax sang alone, using the high part of his register so that it might well have been a woman singing. Ash felt almost as if he could hear an accompaniment, some impossible instrument which could play high and low at the same time, resonating behind and before each note. He wasn't sure if the music was in his own mind or some quality of echo from the inn walls. While it was beautiful, the last, soft song hardly ever produced coins. Still, it sometimes produced other things, like a girl to spend the night with or a place in the inn stable.

As he finished, Flax remained standing there, waiting. Ash realized, with a flash of humor, that he was waiting for Zel to come over and organize him. Instead, it was the innkeeper, bringing them ale.

"Bring your animals round to the stable," she said, kindly enough, as she handed the mugs to Ash. "But no light in there."

"Thank you, keeper," Ash said. He resisted the temptation to tell Flax what to do. He wasn't Flax's big brother, and the boy was old enough to work out for himself what should be done next.

But with the singing finished, Flax seemed a little dazed, so in the end Ash chivvied him over to the horses and got them, their gear and Flax around to the stable and settled in. They sat with their backs to the stable wall and slowly drank their ale. There was enough light coming from the inn's windows for them to see each other and the horses. Cam and Mud shifted from hoof to hoof and whoofed their breath out a couple of times, half-talking to each other and half-reassuring themselves that this strange stable was *their* stable, at least for tonight.

It had to be said, although he'd rather have cut out his tongue. "You sing well."

"Thanks," Flax said.

Ash wanted to hit him. It was all so *easy* for him. He just stood there and sang, and everyone around him managed life so that he could. "Who taught you?"

"Mam, to start with, while I were a youngling. Then Zel organized it. Anytime we met up with other singers on the Road, she'd bargain for me to have some lessons. Mostly people was free with their time. Travelers, that is. We never asked blondies."

"Have you ever Traveled with anyone else?"

Flax laughed shortly. "Not Zel. Keeps herself to herself. I don't mind. We do all right."

Ash imagined Zel and his mother coming up against each other, and shivered. There'd either be coldness like the chill of hell, or they'd take one look at each other, recognize a like spirit, and be unbreakable allies. Either way, the men in their families would fall in with their wishes, as they always had. Except, of course, for the matter of the Deep. Swallow had never quite approved. She didn't like having to stay alone with the wives of the other musicians, camping out or taking over a cottage for the days the men were away. Ash never asked what went on during those days, and she had not volunteered the information, but he had gathered from some of the other women that a lot of praying went on, and a lot of partying, and his mother was not fond of either. But she always met them with a heavy purse, because the parties included dice, and she had Death's own luck with the bones.

Ash thought of Swallow's face: thin, intense, beautiful. Bramble was beautiful, too, but although her coloring was Traveler, her bone structure and build were more like Acton's people. Her face was broader across the high cheekbones and her chin was less pointed. She looked more robust. His mother looked like a wind would blow her away, which was so misleading as to be funny. No one was tougher or healthier. He had inherited that from her, at least. He was never sick. The longer he sat in the dark, the harder it was to keep his thoughts from the sharp realization that he would have to take Flax to meet Swallow, afterward. That he would have to hand him over to her and watch her listen to him sing. The meeting with his father would be bad enough. With Swallow, who lived singing so much that the rest of the world was a shadow to her, it would be a knife in his guts.

Well, he had learned about knives, and how to avoid them, and how to take them if he had to, for the benefit of others. That was what a safeguarder did.

Obscurely comforted by the thought, he got up to lay out his blankets, but was interrupted by a sound from outside. He drew his knife and put his back to the door, motioning to Flax to stay back. Flax just stared, his eyes wide.

The door creaked open slowly. Ash tensed, ready for anything. There was a noise outside that he had never heard before. Like someone—a whole group of people—humming. Singing. Very high, very deep, some sweet and some harsh. Not quite on the same note. The noise set his teeth on edge and yet he wanted to hear more of it. Was this how the people of Cold Hill came to kill Travelers? Singing?

"Hello? Is anyone there?"

It was a man's voice, unsure of itself. He was standing in the light from the doorway. Ash peered through the gap between door and hinge and examined him carefully. A Traveler. Ash relaxed and slipped the knife back into his boot.

"We're here."

The man pushed the door fully open and peered into the dark. "I can't see you."

Ash stepped forward, making sure that he was balanced and ready to fight in case this was a trick.

"Oh, there you are," the man said, sounding relieved. "I have something for you." He held out a pouch. A stonecaster's pouch.

"They've been calling for a week now," he said.

Ash swallowed. He could hear the same descant that he had heard while Flax was singing the lullaby, and it was coming from the pouch. He could *hear* the stones. Just as Martine had said.

"For me?" he said.

The man nodded. "I thought it mighta been for the singer, but no, it were you, drummer." He gestured with the pouch. "Go on. Take them."

There was something in his voice, a deep desire to be rid of the pouch, that made Flax reach out and put a hand on Ash's arm.

"Don't take them. It's a trick," he said.

"No trick!" the man said. "I'm not out to cause anyone harm. My name's Auroch—I'm a chimney-maker, well known in these parts. And I'm a stonemaker, which aren't so well known, if you take my meaning."

They did. Stonemakers were few and far between and only stone-casters really knew who they were. Flax relaxed a little, but he still held Ash back. Ash wanted to throw him off and grab the stones, but he knew Flax was being sensible, so he stayed still. But his eyes never left the pouch of stones.

"Why are you so keen to give my friend the pouch?" Flax asked suspiciously.

"To get rid of it," Auroch said honestly. "It's an unchancy set, this one." His voice dropped to a whisper. "It's got a new stone in it."

They stood in silence. Ash breathed heavily, remembering a song his mother had only sung once, about the stones.

Cast a new stone, cast a new stone
And change the woven power of the world

So. This was why the other stones were wrong for him, yet Martine's casting insisted he was a stonecaster. These had been waiting for him. A new set. A new stone.

He reached out his hand for the pouch, and Auroch dropped it into his palm, and then turned and hurried off into the darkness.

A crescendo of song enveloped Ash, the stones singing high and low, sweet and harsh, loud and soft, each with its own note, all of them blending into something extraordinary. There was a central note, he could hear it, could hear how all the others twined around it.

Something no stonecaster had ever heard before.

AUROCH'S STORY

I NEVER WANTED IT. When I were a nipper and my mam told me the stories about stonemakers who were chosen to find a new stone, I thought, I hope that don't happen to me. A new stone coming into the pouch means the world's going to change, because the stones and the world reflect each other, although which is the reflection I've never figured. I wondered, sometimes, how stonecasters could walk around so easy with the world hanging at their waist.

Changing the world seemed too big a thing for me. Too scary. So. I were right there. Maybe it picked me because I didn't want it. That's likely. That's how the gods work. Or maybe I was just the only one nearby. There's only three of us stonemakers living, after all. It runs in families, like with my mam and me, and somehow it only goes to one or two in a generation.

Stonemaking's not all I do. Stones can't be bought or sold, only given. Just as well. A good stonemaker might make twenty sets, their whole life, and Travelers aren't the richest customers, so you'd never make a living.

I'm a chimney-maker by trade. You might think that any builder can make a chimney, but once you get more than one fireplace on the flue it's an expert job, and the best builders know it, and bring me in for that part of the job.

Turvite's got so big we are half Settled now, me and Cricket and Grass, our daughter. Winters here, summers on the Road. It's in the summer that I find the stones. Up north, mostly, because the northerners like chimneys made of river stones, and I go collecting. River stones are good for about half the casting stones. They carry the changing elements: Birth, Death, Chaos, Travel, Growth. They whistle and sing and hum to me as I handle the larger chimney stones, and I slip them into my pocket as gently as a bird lays moss in her nest.

The rest I find as I go. The harsh stones call strongly: Murder, Betrayal, Anger. A good Jealousy stone is the loudest of all. The last one I found fairly shouted at me from the side of a track way up near Mitchen, a flint in a field of chalk.

I don't like finding the harsh stones. The cry they make in my mind is as nasty as their meaning, and I get a headache for days afterward.

Now the puzzling thing about stones is that they don't all like each other. Each new stone has to pick its set, and some of them are very choosy. I had three sets building at the time this happened. Two almost done, waiting for a couple of stones. One of those needed only the blank stone. Another one just started, with only three in it; the ones that always come first when a set starts: Birth, Death, Rebirth. The blank stone is always last, and that tells you the set is complete, even if it doesn't have every single stone you know exists. That's because some stonecasters can also hear their own stones before they are in the pouch. They pick them up as children and use them for luck, although they don't understand why at that age. If you make a set with a stone missing, sure enough you'll find the person the pouch goes to has the missing stone in their pocket. Then all you have to do is mark one side of it for them and tell them which stone it is, though once it gets with the others in the pouch it usually starts to talk to the caster.

It might take ten years to make a set, normally. As it happened, one set that were nearly complete had taken me almost all my life. I'd found the first stone when I were only a babe, my mam said, playing by the side of a stream where she was searching for lily roots. I grubbed in the river sand with my fat baby hands, she said, laughing, and then tried to eat what I found. I would have choked on Birth, she said, if she hadn't heard the stone call out and grabbed it out of my hands.

So that were my first stone ever, and it is beautiful: flat and oval, smooth white quartz without a seam in it. Rare, and singing of beginnings whenever I went near it. I loved that stone, and thought I'd have it always.

Then, when I were eight or so, and my first set was starting to weigh heavy in the pouch, I were with my mam when she went to see a stonecaster who'd taken on a new apprentice. Mam was checking to see if the set she'd completed the winter before would suit this young one.

Someone from the outside wouldn't have seen much. We sat down, the old stonecaster served us some tea, he chatted with Mam about nothing much: the weather, the warlord's latest execution, the price of barley. The apprentice, a plain young woman who seemed grown up to me then but who was surely only sixteen or so, sat and looked hard at Mam's pouch on the table. I could hear the stones talking in their darkness, as they always did, out of tune and jangling, each of them trying their best to be heard, although some, like Justice, speak in a whisper, and some shout.

The apprentice heard them too, I were sure from the look on her face. Her hand crept closer and closer to the bag. Then the strange thing happened, which changed my life. As her hand approached, the stones began to change their noise. The closer she came, the more they seemed to sing together, the harsh stones providing the rhythm of the song, the gentle ones the melody. When she actually touched the pouch, they came into full harmony, all singing the same song, although the harsh was still harsh and the soft was still soft. Mam nodded at her kindly.

"I reckon they're yours, right enough," she said with satisfaction. The apprentice beamed at her, looking suddenly beautiful. That moment, I realized that all my work'd be for other people. That my lovely Birth stone would go to someone else; that no matter how many sets I made, none of them would sing for me the way that pouch had sung for her. That I could not bring the stones into tune.

On the way home, Mam were cock-a-hoop.

"No doubt about that," she said. "It's nice when it's so clear cut. Sometimes the stones stay a little out of tune, and it's hard to know whether that means they need another caster, or just that the young one hasn't grown into themselves yet."

I said nothing, and she looked at me.

"What's the matter?"

"Nothing," I said, but she knew me too well to take that. She cuffed me lightly on the back of the head.

"What?" she demanded.

"We never get to keep them," I said. "They never sing like that for us."

"They change their song when we make a set complete," she said.

"Not like that. Not *singing together.*"

She were quiet for a bit, then sighed. "No. That's so," she admitted. "But think of it like this: a builder builds a house for a new couple. Does he expect to live in it? A brewer makes a cask of ale for the warlord. Does she expect to drink it? Or even closer, a flute-maker makes a flute: does he expect to perform with it?" She shook her head. "We're makers, Auroch, and that's the fate of makers: to give what we make to others."

I hung my head. "Flutes aren't alive. They don't sing differently for maker and flautist."

"No?" Mam laughed. "That's not what my friend Rowan says. He reckons his flute don't sound the same for anyone else."

I hunched my shoulders at her and she tousled my hair. "It's the way of things, lad," she said sympathetically. "No stonemaker has ever been a stonecaster. They are different talents. Remember, without us, there'd be no stonecasting. Think of that."

I did think about it, on and off, about a world where the future were blank and dark, where fears could not be examined and lessened, where hopes could grow unchecked by reality. I imagined a world with no sense of what were to come, and I shivered and thought my mother were right. We was important. But I didn't realize then that the future can change; I didn't know that I would change it.

So that day, that fine spring day, I were working on a chimney in a village called Cold Hill. I were building with bricks, not stone, but that was the owner's problem; bricks are easier to lay, but not so good at holding heat. It were going to be a big, two-story house with four fireplaces and two chimneys, and the owner were trying to talk me into putting another little fireplace up in the attic, which woulda ruined the draw of the flue and made the lower hearths smoky in bad weather. But would she listen? No. She were arguing without taking breath so I stopped attending to her, and then I heard it calling.

A song, a call, a cry I'd never heard before from any stone, out of the pouch or in it. I'm not a word-maker, I can't describe it. It was like the hum of a distant beehive, or the constant sound of the surf from a long way off. Not loud, but soothing, somehow. I must have looked strange, because the owner said, "Well, if that's your attitude, I can always get another builder!"

"Go ahead," I said. I walked away from the chimney and the house, down to the stream at the end of the garden, where the call were coming from. As I got closer it became more like a song: all on a single note, like a singer trying to impress the audience with the size of his lungs. But that note had tones in it that I couldn't quite hear. They buzzed at the back of my head, they made lights dance in front of my eyes. The stone were easy to find, although it were buried a foot deep. I just reached down and pushed through the soft, cool mud and took it up in my hand. It weren't big, half the size of most stones, but it felt good in my hand, and as I touched it the note changed, deepened, quickened somehow, as though the stone itself were excited.

I washed it off. Jet black, it were, black as pitch. Blacker. That's rarer than you think, a completely black stone. It were perfectly round, and perfectly flat on both sides, like a coin. But the strange thing was that it weren't any of the stones I knew. That song, that feel, didn't belong to any of the stones in any pouch anywhere in the Domains. As I realized that, I felt cold all over, and began to shake. But it might be a stone that were common in other countries. The Wind Cities had stones we did not, and I knew the names of them all.

"What are you?" I whispered, and the stone sang back. Evenness, it said. Balance on the scales.

I'd never heard of that stone, and I felt sick. To bring a new stone into the world was to change the world itself... it were still too big for me. I didn't know what to do. I wished that my mam were still alive.

I left the stream and the complaining house owner and walked back to the cottage where we was staying, renting a room from a Settled Traveler. As I went through the cottage gate I heard a song from a little further down the road. A song I knew. The blank stone. It were just lying there in the middle of the track, plain and simple, as though it had been waiting for me to notice it. Gray, with silver streaks. Nothing special. I'd seen blank stones like this one a dozen times. It meant the set was complete.

I sat at my work table and looked at the stone, then took out the flint I used to make a mark on one side of each stone in the pouch, except the blank stone. Some stones tell you which side to make the mark on. Others don't care. But as I brought the flint closer to the black stone, it shrilled a warning. No mark, it sang. We are the same, both sides. That is the point.

My stomach churned. I went to my chest and got out the pouch, the set that just needed a blank stone—the set that I had been making my whole life. I put the blank stone in the pouch but kept the other tight in my fist. When a set is made complete, the cries of the stones change. Just a little. But not this time. The blank stone made no difference. I loosed my hold on the other stone and put it in the pouch.

The stones began to sing. Just like they had for the apprentice, just like they had for other stonecasters I had given pouches to.

They sang for me.

I shoulda been happy. At last, they was singing. But I were afraid, and a moment later I knew that though the set were singing, it weren't singing for me. They was calling their stonecaster. Calling like the goatherds in the Western Mountains yodel the flock home. The calls became notes, deep and high. Under them all I could hear the new note, the call of the black stone. The sound of the world changing.

LEOF

THE MEN CAME marching through the next afternoon, after what had clearly been a short night's rest. They looked ragged with exhaustion, even the officers on their mounts. Thegan kept them marching, allowing family and friends to walk alongside and hand over extra food or comforts, snatch a kiss or two, as long as they didn't slow the pace.

"Who knows what difference an hour may make?" he said to Leof, who came to ride alongside him through the town.

"We have thirty-seven axes of various kinds ready, my lord," Leof reported. "I have loaded them into a cart so that the men will not tire from carrying them. Also, a quantity of boar spear." That thought had come to him late the night before and he had rousted out every huntsman in Sendat to find the spears. Boar spears had a crosspiece about halfway up, intended to stop a boar simply running up the length of the spear to gore the spearsman, which they were prone to do. Too stubborn to know when they were dead, boars. Like the ghosts.

Thegan nodded approval. "You have done a great deal in a very short time."

"Otter came through here trying to find you, my lord. The Lady Sorn ordered the axes made ready."

Thegan raised an eyebrow, amused. "She is very martial of a sudden!"

"She acts to protect you and your men," Leof said.

Thegan nodded. "She's a warlord's daughter, after all. I suppose she's learned something of warfare, living in a fort all her life." He dismissed the thought and turned to other matters. "The fort —"

"Aye." Leof nodded. "The fortifications won't stop the ghosts. They'll need to be rebuilt, and more axes, more boar spears made. The call has gone out to the oath men this morning."

"Good. I'll leave you Alston for their training; he's reliable. Tell him the truth. And the men will need reprovisioning. We don't know what we will find in Carlion."

"At least ghosts don't eat much," Leof said dryly. "They won't strip the land bare as a living enemy might."

"Who knows what these ghosts will do. If they have flesh, perhaps they eat." Thegan paused, choosing his words carefully. "I know you would rather be with me in battle, but I need someone I can trust here. Supply lines, provisioning, they are the heart of warfare, no matter what the songs say. Men will not fight for glory on an empty stomach, with empty hands." They had reached the end of town, and Thegan gestured to the townsfolk to fall back and let the men proceed.

"I will do the best I can, my lord," Leof said formally, and saluted. Thegan returned the salute gravely, hand over heart, and then smiled.

"Keep my fort safe, boy," he said, spurring the chestnut gelding he rode to a canter, taking the lead, his banner rider following close behind so that the gold and brown banner floated out behind him—sword and spear crossed, glittering in the sunlight. The Lady Sorn had sewn that banner, Leof remembered, all of last winter.

He returned to the fort and only on the way up the hill realized that Thegan had left no word for his lady, hadn't even thought about visiting her, however briefly. When he came into the hall, hesitantly, she was waiting for him again in the shaft of sunlight. She saw his face, and smiled reassuringly.

"My lord does *not* send to say that he thinks of me?" she said, laughter in her voice. "I did not expect that he would, my lord. When a warlord goes to war, he thinks of nothing else."

He smiled back, relieved to find her so reasonable. Other women, he reflected, might well have taken offense. His mother, for one, would have had his father's ears pinned to the black rock altar if he'd slighted her so. Thank the gods Sorn was different. Later, though, he wondered why a great lady expected so little attention to be paid to her.

The oath men—farmers, laborers, tax bondsmen—came straggling in reluctantly the next day. Alston, the sergeant Thegan had detached for training duty, was younger than most sergeants and less annoyed than most would have been to miss the fighting, due to him being body and soul in love with the Lady Sorn's maid, Faina. Being around her made him cheerful and energetic, both qualities that were needed in turning the raggle-taggle mass of men into a fighting force. A force that could hew off arms and legs.

Alston was one of those sensible, stalwart men that every officer dreamed of having as a sergeant. He was tall and had light brown hair, a physique big enough to impress young recruits and a hand hard enough to impress the old campaigners. He brooked no nonsense, but he wasn't cruel and he didn't seek out power. He just did his job.

Fortunately, none of the oath men had given service before, so they didn't question the training methods Leof and Alston had devised, which were certainly not standard. They taught the men to work in pairs—one to engage the enemy and keep him at a distance, the other to come in from the side and hack off the arm. It occurred to Leof that outnumbering the enemy wasn't a bad approach to normal opponents, either. That cheered him somewhat, although he worried a lot about what would happen if the ghosts outnumbered them.

More and more, Leof blessed his experience in fortification and long defensive campaigns in the Cliff Domain. The Centralites had no real idea what war could be like. Moreover, since the rumors about why the men had marched to Carlion were even more unlikely than the truth, no one took the preparations all that seriously, no matter how hard Leof drove them. They were the strongest Domain of the Eleven; they had Lord Thegan leading them; why should they worry about attack? Only a fool would attack Sendat.

That was the general belief, and it made getting masons and carpenters to work all the hours of daylight difficult. They grumbled, they moaned, and they frequently slipped away to do some "little job" in the town. The blacksmiths were even worse. In the end, Leof decided that he had to confide something—not everything—to Affo and the head mason, Gris.

He took them and Alston into the tack room of the stables, where he had some strong brown ale ready, and served them himself. That alone put them on the alert. He chuckled as he saw their faces.

"No, no, lads, I'm not going to ask you to work through the night, don't worry." They smiled back and relaxed a little, but remained wary. "But I do need your help," he continued, growing serious. "I can't tell you everything... my lord has given strict instructions. But I can tell you that we were attacked by the Lake."

They nodded. Old news. The list of the dead had gone around; the families had been personally informed by the Lady Sorn, who had been generous—astonishingly generous—for those left without support.

"What you do not know," Leof paused, milking the moment for all the suspense he could. They leaned forward. "What you do not know, is that my lord believes it was *not* the Lake who attacked us."

They sat up at that, the two of them. He had their full attention now.

"My lord has found out that there is an enchanter working against the people of the Domains. That is what we prepare against."

"Swith the Strong!" Gris exclaimed. "He's good enough to control the Lake?"

"So it seems," Leof said, hoping the gods would forgive the lie, not sure if it were a lie. "This information is secret," he cautioned. "Only those in this room know it. If it comes to be talked about abroad, I will know who to blame, and I will dispense my lord's justice swiftly."

Affo and Gris nodded in unison, like twins, and he fought down a smile. One day his sense of humor would get him into trouble. His mother had always said so.

"You see why I need you to push your men. We don't know when this enchanter may strike again."

"He's attacked Carlion?" Affo asked. "That's where the troops have gone, isn't it?"

Leof assumed an air of great solemnity. "I can tell you no more," he said, "without betraying my lord." That was the simple truth. "Will you help us?"

They nodded again, and this time he let himself smile, a friendly smile that had them smiling back.

"Good. Drink up, then, and back to work."

He and Alston watched them go, talking animatedly to each other.

"They'll tell their wives," Alston said gloomily, "and then it'll be all over town."

"Have you told Faina?" Leof asked.

Alston blushed and shook his head. "She'd never ask," he said simply. "She belongs to the gods, that one, and can't do a dishonorable thing."

Leof clapped him on the back and sent him back to the muster yard, where the last batch of oath men were laboring to swing the weighted poles they practiced with. Affo's men were working to make spears and axes for them in time. But in time for what? Leof wondered. They were expecting word from Carlion any moment; the messenger horses were fast and surely there had been time by now to get a message back?

He went into supper as the sun dipped below the western hills, and found Lady Sorn and the two junior officers Thegan had left at the fort already eating at the glass table. It was called that because those who sat there had their wine served to them in clear glass goblets instead of pottery ones, and it was a pretty sight, the flames of the candles reflecting in the curved glass. He had always enjoyed it at Cliff Domain, watching Thegan and his father and the other lords draining their glasses so that the fire winked from the bases like stars. Now he was nominal lord here. He felt a poor substitute for his father, and wondered what Cliff Domain was doing to prepare. Thegan would have sent word there and to the other warlords.

Sorn and the officers rose and bowed as he approached. He bowed back, apologizing as he did so. "I seem to be always tardy these days, my lady," he said. Sorn smiled and sat again, gesturing for her maid, Faina, to serve him. He watched Faina curiously. Not all that pretty, but with big blue eyes that looked on the world as cleanly as a child, yet with a woman's intelligence. He could see why Alston, a man of clear thoughts and absolute loyalty, would be attracted. But then, he thought ruefully, I can always see why a woman is attractive. He wondered how long it had been since he had lain with anyone. It felt like months since that waitress in Connay, when he went there for the chases, but surely it couldn't be that long? After Bramble, he had pursued women obsessively for almost a year, trying to prove that she had been nothing special, and when that hadn't worked he'd let the women pursue him, when they chose, which was often enough to keep him satisfied. But it had been a while.

He smiled his thanks at Faina for the roast kid and vegetables she served, then poured more wine for the Lady Sorn.

"How goes it, Lord Leof?" she asked, the question she asked every evening.

He outlined the day's work and she listened and nodded and gave compliments, as she always did. He was never sure how much she understood of the technical aspects of what he told her, but he suspected it was more than she showed. He suspected that Sorn always knew and felt much more than she showed.

He was deep in an outline of the need to requisition more stone from the blue stone quarry in Springhill, a nearby town, when there was a disturbance at the door and Hodge entered the hall. Sorn and Leof both rose and moved to meet him.

He was dusty from the road and tired, but he bowed formally to them both and then looked from one to the other, not sure to whom he should report.

"If your news is private, sergeant, the Lord Leof can take you to my setting room."

Leof nodded, but motioned her to join them. "My lord said to keep you informed," he told her, and saw her flush, delicately, as though she had not expected that. Fortune came prancing up to Sorn as they went into the setting room, but Sorn shushed him and he went back to his accustomed place by the fire, head up, watching the flames and Sorn alternately.

As soon as the door closed, Hodge came to the point. "The ghosts were gone when we arrived, but the town was a shambles. They'd killed, we think, about half of the townsfolk. We're not sure, because some of them jumped off the cliffs to get away and we couldn't get all the bodies back, and others simply ran and haven't returned. I don't blame them."

"My lord is occupying the town?" Sorn asked.

Hodge nodded. "The town clerk and most of the council are dead. The townsfolk are terrified that the ghosts will come back. They welcomed us with open arms. The lads are living high—there's plenty of room for them." He spoke grimly, and Leof caught a sense of what the town had been like when he had arrived.

"Lord Thegan is organizing what's left of the townsfolk to fortify the town; taking stone from the empty buildings to make walls and so forth."

Leof nodded. "What does he need from us?"

Hodge handed over a list. "Supplies; armor; weapons, mostly. And to recruit some stonemasons from other towns to go to Carlion to help fortify it. But he says on no account deplete the workers from Sendat."

"Anything else?" Leof asked, studying the list. Hodge hesitated. "For your ears only, my lord." He looked at Sorn. "And I suppose yours, too, my lady…we found, out beyond the town, a great burial uncovered. Bones everywhere. Old bones. Very, very old."

Sorn went quiet, and then began pacing around the room, as though she could not contain her anger. "He is using the bones to raise the ghosts," she said. "The bones of the slain. Angry bones. Oh, this is a great blasphemy against the gods!"

Leof had never seen her show such emotion.

"Then let us hope they will aid us," he said seriously.

Sorn nodded. "I will pray for it," she said simply, then turned to Hodge.

"Sergeant, come and I will arrange food and rest for you."

Hodge smiled. "Thank you, my lady, but I have a home of my own to go to in the town. With my lord's permission?"

Leof motioned for him to go. "But be back here early. Does my lord want you back?"

Hodge shook his head. "I'm to help Alston train the oath men. We know more about how these ghosts fight, now." He paused, as though wondering if he should launch into a description now.

"In the morning," Sorn said, with mock severity. "Go to your home now."

"Thank you, my lady," Hodge said and left with more energy than he had when he arrived.

Sorn and Leof looked at each other. He wondered if Sorn had understood the implications of what Hodge had said.

"So," she said carefully, "my lord is now the warlord of a free town, with a nice, deep harbor."

He drew in a deep breath. She understood, that was certain. "Aye," he said. "Without a single protest."

Their eyes met and they nodded, very slightly, aware of Thegan's ambitions and, surprising to learn of each other, uncomfortable with them.

"I wonder," Sorn said, "if anyone has asked the local gods of Carlion what they think should be done?"

"Thegan doesn't consult the gods," Leof said without thinking. But it was true. Thegan never prayed at the altar except on festival days, in front of everyone.

"I know," Sorn said. That was all. But Leof suddenly saw a deep fissure between Sorn and Thegan, this matter of belief. She was devout, as everyone in Sendat knew, and he... Leof wasn't sure Thegan even believed in the gods, although how someone could not was beyond Leof's understanding. But it was obvious in Thegan's attitude to the Lake—as though he could not bear *anything* to be more powerful than he was.

Pity this enchanter, Leof thought, if Thegan gets hold of him. If he can't bear the gods to be powerful, he will do more than destroy a man who had such power.

Sorn stood, her earlier energy contained again. "Your meal is unfinished, and you should announce that all our people are safe and have come to the aid of Carlion after an attack by an unknown aggressor."

"Yes," he said, nodding. "That is exactly what I should do."

She flushed, as though caught out in something dishonorable. "My lord, I did not mean to instruct you —"

He laughed. His reaction startled her, but she smiled tentatively back. Fortune sprang gladly up from the hearthrug, ready for a game. He sidled up to Leof and Leof pulled gently on his ears, grinning at Sorn.

"My lady, I find myself in unknown country without a map, and I am grateful for any instruction."

She smiled more widely at that, a true smile with a hint of humor in it. "We are all walking unknown paths, my lord, and some of them are very rough."

"Well, we'll just have to help each other not to fall smack on our behinds," he said cheerfully, offering her his arm to go back into the hall.

She began to laugh. It was the first time he had heard her laugh, and it was a very pleasant sound. He had missed the sound of women's laughter. They walked back into the hall together still laughing, Fortune dancing behind them, and he saw that it was the best thing they could have done, because the tension in the room reduced immediately and was banished altogether by Leof's announcement. Banished by gossip and speculation about the "unknown aggressor."

Speculate all you like, Leof thought. None of us can tell you who he is. He handed Sorn into her chair and sat back down to a fresh plate of kid, conjured from somewhere at Sorn's signal. He ate it gratefully, and smiled at her as he swallowed. A woman who fed you was worth just as much as a woman who bed you, he thought. Sorn smiled calmly at him, the lady in her hall back in full force. What a warlord she'd make! Leof thought idly, then laughed at himself. Calm, serene ladylike Sorn! He was more tired than he'd realized. At least tonight he could sleep without wondering what was happening in Carlion.

BRAMBLE

"YOU CAN GO now," Dotta had said, as though she were a warlord's wife dismissing a servant. Bramble found it amusing rather than annoying, but knew she was using the laughter as a distraction to hide her uncertainty. What did it mean, that Dotta had seen her? Was she *really* present, then, truly experiencing these times and events? Half of her had thought it was like a story being played out in front of her, a message from the gods put into her mind. Part of her had thought she was, in truth, back at Oakmere, and these were just illusions—true illusions, perhaps, faithful to history, but still just a glamour the gods had cast.

If she was really here... Could she change things?

She'd thought it before, but not seriously. The gods had showed their disapproval even of the thought. But as the waters floated her away, the thought came back stronger than ever. If it were possible to change things, to communicate with Baluch, say, or Gris... If she could shift events so that the peoples of the Domains didn't die... The best way would be to make an avalanche in Death Pass as Acton and his men were coming through that first spring morning.

Change history. Kill Acton and Baluch and the rest, the invaders.

She remembered Dotta saying, "Did you think the Destiny stone meant nothing?"

She remembered Acton saying, "I have seen the Ice King and we cannot survive him!"

She remembered Sebbi's blood, sprayed across the ice.

If she changed history, Acton's people would die.

Her people. Her ancestors.

She understood, bitterly, why Safred had needed someone of mixed blood for this task. Someone with divided loyalties, who could not, in the end, be on anyone's side.

If she did not change history, her people would die. If she did, her people would die. There was no good outcome. She was under no illusion that she could change things enough so that the invasion would be peacefully negotiated. Even if she could take over Acton's mind, that wouldn't happen. There were too many men too used to fighting to let it happen. Men who *liked* fighting, who enjoyed the intensity, the vividness of life on the edge of death, as she had liked the intensity of chasing.

If she let the invasion go ahead, she was as guilty as Acton.

She let that thought settle into her as the waters buoyed her up and landed her on another shore.

At least it was warmer, but the yoke she carried on her back was so heavy that when her sight cleared all she could see was the earth in front of her. Stony earth, the kind you got near mountains, full of sharp stones and hidden rocks. She was pulling. Gods, she was pulling a plough! No wonder it was shagging hard work. Hadn't these people learned how to use oxen for this? Or horses, even? They had horses!

"Get moving, thrall!" a voice shouted. "We need to get the seed in before the rains come!"

A thrall. Not quite a slave, not in the way the Wind Cities kept slaves. They weren't locked up at night or sold off. They were perhaps more like bond-servants. At least, some of the old stories Bramble had heard said so. But there were no thralls in the Domains. She wasn't sure why. The stories said Acton had forbidden it...that only free men could cross the mountains. No doubt she'd find out the truth of it, sooner or later . . .

The thrall paused and wiped sweat from his face—definitely *his*; a woman couldn't have pulled this plough through the stony ground. Not far away, Acton and a group of young men were building a house from wood and stone. An older man, the stone-layer, probably, was directing them, choosing the stones for each course, making sure they fitted together and sloped gradually inward from the wide base. There was no mortar. At intervals, strong posts were held up by younger boys until the stones reached high enough to support them. The posts, Bramble thought, would form the basis for the wattle sections that were being woven by a group of women sitting under a tree. Asa was there, and the mother of the girl Friede who had been lost in the storm.

There the girl herself was, a woman now, limping along with her crutch, carrying a bundle of wattle withies on the other shoulder. She was laughing at something her mother had said, and her face was alight. Not beautiful, but strong and happy, despite the ever-present crutch. She dumped her bundle of withies at Asa's feet and rolled her shoulders as if they had been heavy. Her mother said something, with a face full of concern, but Friede brushed it off and swung around to collect another bundle from a group of young girls who were stripping the willow branches of their leaves. It was typical of Friede, Bramble thought, that she didn't simply sit down and strip leaves with the others. Typical of her to take the harder task; the more active. She wished for a moment that she could see this world through Friede's eyes instead of the thrall's. She suspected she would feel right at home in that mind.

The sun was at mid-morning and Bramble realized that it was coming not from the mountains but from the plains beyond. They were in the Domains, building a new settlement. She was puzzled. Had the battle of Death Pass already happened? Was the invasion over? She thought it would be just like the gods, to let her agonize over whether to stop the invasion and then to move her straight past it. A weight of responsibility lifted from her shoulders.

Now all she had to do was watch Acton until he died, and see where his bones lay. No decisions, no need to understand. The invasion was over and a thousand years past and no business of hers. She felt light, and free, even under the heavy yoke. It was not her burden, after all.

The thrall reached the end of the furrow and stopped to rest, looking down the valley to where a rough track emerged from a stand of larch and spruce. The grass either side of the track was spring green, but there was snow on the hillsides not far up and the air nipped cold at the thrall's lungs. He had a quick, lively mind, if the rhythm and speed of his glance could be read right. He took the opportunity to observe all he could: the house-building, the women (lingering on one girl in particular, a young blond who giggled to Friede about something), the track again. There were riders coming out of the trees and the thrall raised a shout. Warning or welcome? Bramble wondered.

The men stopped working on the building and dusted off their hands, moving to greet the newcomers. Hawk was in the lead on a chestnut, a longer-legged version of the shaggy hill ponies from the other side of the mountain. One of the Wind Cities' desert horses cross-bred with the mountain horses?

As he dismounted and threw his reins to one of his followers, Hawk pointed at the thrall and laughed. "Have you tamed no working beasts, then, in your Ice King's country?"

Although she had thought exactly the same thing, Hawk's mocking tone annoyed Bramble. Who was he to criticize?

Acton came forward, smiling. "Our ox broke his leg on the mountain path, and fell," he said. "The wolves will eat well for a while. We make do."

"Hmm." Hawk pretended to consider, sending quick glances toward the women who had stopped work to listen. Asa had apparently accepted Hawk's contempt toward women, for she made no move to join the men. Hawk's glance lingered on the blond girl and Friede. The thrall saw it, and his heart sped up, his hands clenched.

"So," Hawk said. "Perhaps we can lend you one of our beasts until you can bring another over the mountains."

Cooperating? Hawk letting Acton build a settlement near his land? No! This wasn't what had happened! Could she have changed history without even knowing it? Could the past have shifted so much just because she had observed it? Or had Dotta changed things somehow?

"That would be most kind." Swef's voice came from behind the thrall and he and the others turned around in surprise. Swef moved easily down the hillside, carrying a huge pile of withies across his shoulders. For this gathering chore, he had swapped his good red leather boots for the plain sheepskin ones everyone else wore. "If we do not get the seeds in, it will be a hard winter and a harder spring."

Hawk nodded. Swef dumped the withies at the feet of the blond girl. She giggled. Gods give me patience! Bramble thought. What *is* it about pretty girls and giggles? But she knew very well what it was. Every man there was aware of the blond. Except Acton, who was ignoring her, inspecting the next set of stones for the wall. Now that was strange. She didn't want her opinion of him to improve, but she had to admire his lack of interest in the giggler.

Asa rose and took several of the girls behind the building to where a line of carts with blankets stretched between them served as storage as well as sleeping tents. She came back with drinking horns and sent the girls around with them. Even Friede took a horn to a young man working a little way away, using a hatchet to lop branches and bark from more of the thick supporting posts. It was Baluch. He had grown and filled out, like Acton, so that he looked more like a young man than a boy. Acton was handsome in a lithe, muscular way, and he moved like a hunting animal, but Baluch had a grace of movement which said to Bramble that he was working in time to some internal music. Friede lingered as he drank and took back the horn with a few words. Baluch laughed. Friede was attractive in a way completely different from the giggling blond, and Baluch clearly knew it. Their eyes were warm on each other.

The thrall's gaze returned to Hawk and Swef, who were looking over the new building. Acton was a little way off, staring back toward Baluch. Or toward Friede? Bramble wondered, but doubted it. Unlikely that a warrior like Acton would want a girl on a crutch.

"Acton!" Swef called. "Show our guest your work!"

Acton went over to them readily enough to point out the elements of the building. The thrall lost interest and began to settle the yoke back onto his shoulders. He still watched the chieftains. Delaying the moment of hard work a little longer, Bramble guessed.

"Only one building?" Hawk asked, that superior tone in his voice.

"The hall comes first. After that, the women's quarters and the outbuildings."

"You don't have separate houses?" Again the barely suppressed scorn. Acton smiled, a smile the thrall recognized as dangerous, because he gripped the yoke harder as though he held a weapon, ready to defend if necessary.

"We do best when we live and work together," Swef said smoothly. "You can see," he pointed to the carts lined up behind the building, "we need a good large storage area before anything else."

"Yes," Hawk said. "I can see that."

Swef laid a hand familiarly on his shoulder, guiding him away from the building toward where the thrall was working. He smiled a companionable smile, but the thrall still kept hold of his yoke. "We're planning to put our sheepfold over here."

The waters came as a surprise. But what happened? Bramble thought as they tumbled her helplessly, as though she were a leaf in a mountain stream. What had happened to change history? Cooperation. Peace. A gradual settlement, not sudden invasion. Bramble swelled with gratitude and happiness. No matter how it had happened, there it was. There was only one thing which worried her now. If the past had changed so that the invasion was peaceful, why was she still here? Perhaps, in the Domains created by this new past, she didn't exist? Or was she condemned to live out Acton's life no matter what happened in it? The thought puzzled her, but it could not cut deeply into the great sense of relief and joy she felt.

Her bones ached. Every bone, each of them with its own special pain.

"I'm too old," her voice was saying, creaking a little. "I'm too old to go stravaging across mountains like a goat."

"Never too old, Ragni," Acton's voice came back, warm and teasing. "You're just a lass! Never fear, I'll carry you across myself and give you a good cuddling on the way!"

Ragni laughed and coughed as she laughed. She was sick, clearly. Every cough hurt her chest like it was being torn open. Phlegm filled her throat and she turned to spit politely in the fire. It was the fire in Harald's hall. They were back over the mountains at Harald's steading and it was cold, cold, colder than hell. Much colder than it had been the night Acton and Baluch had gone looking for Friede. Was that the Ice King's doing?

"You save your cuddles for them as wants them!" Ragni scolded Acton tenderly. "There's plenty as does, I hear!"

Acton shrugged. He was sitting with his back to the fire, resting against the raised stones of the hearth. His hair was lit up and his face was in shadow, but Ragni saw something, Bramble couldn't tell what, and leaned forward.

"What is it, lad?"

"Oh, the only girl I want doesn't want me, of course," he said, brushing off her concern as a joke. "Isn't that always the way of it?"

Ragni clucked her tongue. "She's a fool, then," she said roundly. "Her loss, lad, her loss."

"Mmm . . ." he said.

"It's not that silly chit Edwa, is it?" Ragni said sharply. "She's got all the boys after her but she's not worth a piece of rag, not in her bones. She'd make a bad wife, boy, a bad, willful wife."

Acton chuckled. "No, no, I'm not such a fool as that. I can't stand the giggles!"

Ragni nodded with satisfaction. "Well, then. Who?"

Acton shook his head, his face unreadable. "Fewer words, less regret," he said. It was a very old saying. Bramble had always thought it was a Traveler proverb.

"Huh . . ." Ragni said, unconvinced. "Well, it's good to have you back from Swef's new steading, lad. It was the worst day's work Harald ever did, when he let you go. Asgarn has done as he should, letting you come back, even if it's only for a visit."

"Asgarn's a good chieftain," Acton said. "He's looking after things well, and he'll lead you well when the time comes to make the trip across to the new settlement."

Ragni sniffed and spat again, looking across the fire to where a table of men sat, talking. Asgarn was one of them, Bramble saw, and the others were some of the chieftains who had stood on the ledge at the All Moot.

"You should be over there," Ragni said stubbornly.

"Oh, I'm no good at figuring how many barrels can fit into so many carts, Ragni," Acton said comfortably. "They can have their planning, and welcome to it. We'll need good plans, to get everyone who wants to come over the mountains and into good, solid halls by next winter."

"It's not going to work."

"Not in one year," Acton agreed. "It'll have to happen in stages, as the steadings closest to the mountains move over first, and let the ones further out, the ones who are being hard-pressed by the Ice King's men, shift in as they leave."

"Thought you were no good at planning?" Ragni said. He laughed.

The fire spat and hissed as a cow pat broke apart and burnt, smouldering. "That's the scent of home," Acton said. "Over the mountains they burn wood all the time, can you believe it?"

Ragni sniffed. "I miss your mother," she said.

Acton patted her on the knee—a comforting touch, warm and gentle.

"So do I," he agreed.

He looked up as the door opened to show a winter evening, light snow falling steadily, transformed for a moment into small flames by the light of the fire.

"Here's Baluch," Ragni said with pleasure. "Give us a tune, boy."

Baluch came in unwinding a hat-scarf from around his face. He pulled off his gloves and coat and sat down gladly by the fire, fishing a pipe out of his pocket. "It's building up to be a wild night," he said cheerfully. "I wonder how they're doing, over the other side of the mountain? I'll wager it's not as cold as here."

Acton grinned at him. "And there's no Asgarn to make you go out in the cold to tend the sheep," he teased.

"You'd be just as bad, over the mountains," Baluch retorted.

"Oh, I'm not chieftain there, Bal, any more than I am here. I'm just another pair of hands."

"You're Swef's heir," Ragni interjected with energy. "Don't you let him forget it!"

Acton laughed. "Wili is Swef's heir, Ragni."

"A girl! Well, there's a way to solve that. It'd be a good marriage for you both, and your place as chieftain would be safe."

Acton waved that idea away. "Tell you the truth, Ragni, I don't care if I'm never chieftain, there or anywhere."

The old woman made the sign averting evil. "Don't let the gods hear you say that, lad!"

Both the young men laughed, as Ragni shook her head at them, clucking her tongue.

"Tch! You should be ashamed, laughing at an old woman!" But her tone was indulgent.

Bramble wondered again if she were just going to live through Acton's life now, day by day, bit by bit, until he died and the spell came undone. Then where would she find herself? Back at Obsidian Lake, or in the darkness beyond death, waiting to be reborn? Part of her didn't really care. Then, as if in response to her thought, Baluch stopped laughing and stood up.

His face was white, his eyes stretched wide as if trying to see beyond the walls of the hall. He dropped the pipe and it fell into the fire, but he didn't notice. Acton tried to flick it out with a stick, but the pipe flared up in a sudden brightness. The flame lit Baluch's face from below, turning it into a death's head, a skull mask over the man beneath.

No, Bramble thought, recognizing the gods' touch even at a distance, feeling them pour into Baluch and open his mind. *No. It was going so well . . .*

Baluch screamed. His mouth opened wider than seemed possible and the scream came out wild and tortured, without thought or control. It was the kind of scream a woman makes in childbirth, when the pain has pushed her beyond being human, back into the animal life. But worse, because underneath was grief and horror.

Everyone in the hall came to their feet. Acton stood close to Baluch, a hand reaching out but pausing, waiting. Asgarn and the chieftains ran from the other side of the fire and stopped as he screamed again, and then gulped air and started to speak, his eyes wide but his own again, Baluch's eyes.

"Stop! Stop!"

"Is it a fit?" one of the chieftains asked.

Acton shook his head. "No. No. Sometimes, the gods speak to him."

"He's not a chieftain," Asgarn said.

"Even so, Ragni knows."

The old woman nodded. "Harald would never accept it, but we all knew. The gods speak to him."

Acton laid his hand delicately on Baluch's shoulder. Baluch was trembling.

"What has happened?" Acton asked gently.

Baluch's shaking increased until only Acton's support kept him from falling.

"They are killing them."

"Who?" Asgarn said. He moved closer, taking command, and Acton fell silent but put his arm around Baluch, physically holding him up.

"Hawk. Hawk and his men . . ." Baluch's eyes snapped shut as though he couldn't bear to look at something. "*No!*" he howled. "Friede!" He struggled against Acton's hold as if he could walk through the fire to save her. Acton's face paled but he hung on tighter.

"Hawk has attacked?" Asgarn asked.

"Attacked," Baluch moaned. "Killed. Friede. All the men. Taken. Edwa! Asa . . ." He drew out Asa's name on a long breath and then fell silent.

The hall was deathly quiet. Baluch's head dropped and Bramble could feel the gods leave him. If she had been in her own body she would have been shaking and crying with anger. How could she have thought it would happen easily? Why had she let herself hope? Cooperation! Hah! You couldn't expect cooperation from warriors, she didn't care what color hair they had. All they wanted to do was kill. Her heart had shriveled inside her and sat in her chest like a sharp rock. Or was that Ragni's pain?

Baluch raised his head and turned it with an effort, looking into Acton's eyes. "Asa. Your mother fought. She killed one as he, as he tried to . . ." Baluch shook his head. "Another struck her down."

"She has killed a rapist before," Acton said, his voice flat. "My father will no doubt welcome him to the coldest pit of hell."

"Friede . . ." Baluch sighed.

"Tell us of Friede," Acton said, suddenly urgent.

Baluch hid his face in his hands and wept. "She fought also. Swef tried to protect her. It took three of them to kill him. Then they killed her. It was —" His voice hiccupped. "It was quick, at least."

Acton turned away. Ragni watched him, her heart twisting in her. The one girl, Bramble thought, who wasn't interested in him . . . She didn't want to feel sympathy for any of them, but how could she help it?

"Edwa?" Asgarn said. "You said her name . . . ?"

Baluch wiped his tears away and looked around the group of chieftains. "They have taken the younger girls. To use later. To be slaves. Killed the men, stole everything, burnt the hall. They . . ." he faltered, "they killed the older women, too, after they... used them. Who kills women who don't fight? More than a raid. It was more than a raid. They wanted to wipe us out."

"She's still alive?" Asgarn was intent.

"Edwa. Wili. A few others. The prettiest ones." His voice was thick with scorn and hatred.

As if Baluch's words were a signal, talk broke out in the hall. Shouts, cries, sobs. Acton turned back to the group of chieftains. Baluch sank down and laid his head in Ragni's lap. She stroked his hair unsteadily.

"I claim revenge," Acton said. "My mother. My chieftain. My friends." He turned to Asgarn. "I know you are chieftain here now, and that I do not dispute. But we must return death for death to these animals, these lying, scheming traitors, and I will do it."

His voice was without emotion. His anger, his grief, had pushed him past feeling. All that was left was the desire to kill, and it shone clearly in his eyes and showed in the set of his shoulders and the tightness of his fists. At last, Bramble thought, with a kind of relief. Here he is: Acton the killer. He's so young. What, eighteen? Nineteen? Young.

She wanted to fall backward into hate for him, back into the scorn and anger she had always felt toward Acton the invader. There he was, wanting to kill, wanting to wipe out. But she remembered how she had felt, after she'd learned of Maryrose's death. Just like this. Exactly. Her face had been set in the same dead calm. Wanting to kill, wanting to wipe out. If Saker had been there, she would have done it. If Saker appeared before her when she awoke at Obsidian Lake, she would do it then. Gladly. Fiercely. Without regret. Just like Acton. She pushed the thought away from her. Killing one man, the murderer of your loved ones, that she could understand. But Acton had killed a whole nation.

The chieftains exchanged glances, nodding to each other. There was something there, Bramble thought, something they're not saying, not out loud. But there was an element of calculation in their assessment of Acton. Something... political.

"Kill them all," Asgarn said softly. "We will kill them all and take everything they have and laugh while we do it. Yes. You have the right, Acton. You will be the hand of the gods on these butchers."

The other chieftains murmured agreement. Acton nodded and stood straighter. Ragni put a hand to her heart and then to her mouth, as though she wanted to stop her own words. She began to sob quietly, and Baluch raised his head in her lap to comfort her, patting her shoulder, rising to put an arm around her, rocking her.

The old man from the Moot, the one who had controlled the staff, laid a hand on Acton's shoulder. "For this battle, you shall be the lord of war, Acton. We so appoint you and bind ourselves to support you."

Silence fell. Through Ragni's tears, Bramble could read the faces of the chieftains. The old man had gone further than they had intended. That was a mistake, old man, she thought bitterly. A bad, bad mistake.

MARTINE

After lunch, Zel and Martine buried the food scraps under a tree not too far into the Forest, in case they attracted bear or wolverine.

"We don't have a new flint," Zel said as she filled in the hole. "I looked all morning, but there are none around here at all."

"I know. I looked too, yesterday."

"What are we going to do?"

Zel looked worried, as she should be. Martine thought about the warnings she had received so many times as a youngster: the ritual was three nights, and all three must be completed, or disaster would occur during the following year. There were always lots of instances cited, too: forest fires, houses burnt down, even people themselves suddenly bursting into flame. At a time like now, with the future in balance, they couldn't afford to anger him.

Martine had thought about the problem, but she was still unsure of her answer. "One of my casting stones is a flint," she said.

Zel stopped shoveling and stared at her. "Use a casting stone?" she queried. "Can you do that?"

Martine shrugged. "I don't know. I've never heard of anyone doing it, but it was a flint before it was a casting stone."

Zel thought about it. "Which stone is it?"

"The blank stone."

"Dung and pissmire, Martine, are you crazy?" Her voice rose in panic. "That's the Chaos stone! Anything could happen!"

"The blank stone represents possibilities."

"Bad ones as well as good ones," Zel said.

"It's all we've got—unless you want to chip off a piece of the lake obsidian and use that."

A shudder went through them both.

"No," Zel said, breathless with horror at the thought. "No."

"Well, then. We can't leave the ritual unfinished. It would set him loose on us and those with us."

Zel was silent for a moment, her face unreadable, then said, "Ask 'em. Ask the stones if you should use it."

Martine crouched on the grass, spat on her hand and held it out to Zel. She couldn't ask herself. A fool's pursuit, when a caster threw for herself, but if Zel asked it might work.

Zel clasped her hand and whispered, "Should we use the blank stone as our new flint?"

Martine's fingers in the pouch drew five stones without hesitation. That alone told her it was a real casting, strong and true. She cast the stones. The blank stone, first. Then Mystery, Night, Rejoicing and Sorrow.

"Shagging hells!" Zel said.

Martine smiled grimly. "Well? Will you risk it?"

"Are they talking to you?"

She shook her head. "But it's a true casting. As true as you'll get. We'll have both rejoicing and sorrow, and anything could happen."

Zel straightened up in a smooth movement that made Martine envy her youth. She stood for a moment, staring out at the altar.

"If it gets bad, we can jump in the mere," Zel said.

"It'd have to be pretty bad before I'd jump in there."

They stood in silence. The breeze had died. The mere reflected the sky perfectly, so that it seemed to hold all the heavens. Only the altar was dull, a black stain on the blue.

"The altar should not be dark on this night," Martine said, suddenly sure. "We will use the tools we have."

Zel nodded. "If you say so."

Zel held the casting stone and Martine hit it cleanly with the striking stone, hard and fast as it should be done, so that bright sparks leapt out onto the tinder. Zel blew softly to make the sparks catch, and Martine said, "Take our breath to speed your growth."

As the tinder caught and small flames started to lick upward, she felt him come. But there was no gradually building arousal, no heat in her loins, no sense of being desired. There was just fire, shooting upward.

She hurriedly moved back, dragging Zel with her.

A lifetime of living with the gods hadn't prepared her for this. The fire roared up, higher and higher, far beyond the capacity of the fuel they had given it. The heat was intense; they fell back further, to the edge of the island. Martine hesitated: should they turn and run, or would that make it worse?

Then the choice was taken from them.

Obsidian Lake responded. Around them, in a perfect circle, the waters of the mere rose like a rampart, shielding the Forest from the fire, cutting off their escape. The waters began to move, to spin skyward, becoming a whirlpool with standing sides, rising higher and higher until they were stranded between fire and water, both roaring, both rearing, enemies confronting each other, implacable.

Zel stood immovable, eyes wide and fixed on the fire.

Martine looked where Zel looked, and saw him.

She had thought she was old enough to be invulnerable to the lure of the wild boys, the bad boys with full mouths and piercing eyes. She had thought she was too old for the promise of unbridled sex, unconstrained, unashamed—that she would never give anyone complete surrender, not even him.

But if he had looked at her as he was looking at Zel, she would have thrown herself into the fire without a second's thought.

Zel took a step forward. He reached out a hand. He was everything puberty promised but never delivered: intensity, ecstasy, freedom.

Zel took another step, her gaze never leaving his.

Martine was torn. Should she stop Zel? Did she have the right? Was it her choice, or Zel's? Or his? In desperation, she found her voice.

"We are daughters of the fire," she said to him. "Will you destroy your daughter?"

He turned his head and stared at her. Then he smiled and she saw death through his eyes, as a glorious transfiguration into flame.

She was transfixed, longing herself for that exaltation. The heat from the past two nights had come back as soon as he looked at her, wilder, stronger, more insistent. The aching need for him felt as though it would split her in two. She took a step toward him. But he didn't want her. He looked back to Zel. The young one.

Too late. When he looked back Zel was no longer staring at him, but at the ground.

"Hazel?" the fire said, in a voice of rushing wind and crackling power and deep, deep longing. Martine was filled with envy, wanting him, oh, wanting him to look at her like that, to say her name.

But Zel's mouth was set like stone. "I have to look after Flax," she said.

It was enough. He would never plead, never beg. He invited. Or he took. Martine grabbed Zel and began to pull her back, away, toward the wall of water. Better drowned than burnt, as he would burn them now. The heat escalated suddenly, harsh on their skin where it had been loving. He reached for them and the flames began to spread outward from the altar.

As though Zel's rejection of him had given the waters strength, they began to grow higher, curving over at the top so that the altar was almost enclosed in a dome of waves, an impossible inverted whirlpool. The air was sucked upward through the small opening at the top, and Martine staggered as the wind whipped around them, blinded them, caught their breath away, dragged them toward him. Waves from above crashed onto the island, plumes of water splashing down on the base of the altar, drenching them. Every drop stung like acid but the fire was so strong that their clothes dried again almost instantly.

Martine forced herself to turn around, fighting the pull of the wind toward the center, the heat scorching on her back. She and Zel clung to each other, crouching at the very edge of the water, Zel's head in Martine's arm, hiding her eyes against him as though she didn't trust her own resolution. She was trembling violently.

The flames were struggling, now. He could live without fuel, but not without air. Surely he would not let himself be extinguished? Martine looked back at him.

As if in response to her thought, he stared straight at Martine and then the fire rose in a single great column, pure flame, no sign of him left, and pierced through the narrow opening between the waves.

Steam hissed. The water faltered and the spin slowed, droplets falling and spitting on the altar. The column of fire left the altar, shooting straight up through the waves, rising impossibly fast toward the night sky until it became another star, and was gone from sight.

For a moment the waves loomed over them and Martine wondered if the mere needed some acknowledgment, some recompense for the trouble they had caused. But she was not minded to apologize to water.

"We are daughters of the fire," she said clearly. "What was done was done with respect and reverence."

The water slowed its spin, sinking gradually back toward the surface of the mere. Zel and Martine stayed where they were, not too near the altar which still gave off a startling heat, as the waters became calm again.

Before she moved, Martine forced herself to wait for one moment more, though every instinct was shouting at her to run. She took Zel's hand and squeezed it.

"The fire . . ." she prompted, waiting for Zel to catch up with her. Zel's eyes went wide but she cleared her throat with some difficulty.

"The fire," she said, and they completed it together, as it had to be said, "will never die."

Martine felt a slight easing in the tightness around her heart, as though the fire had heard them and acknowledged their fealty. The water paused in its movement, as though stopped in time. Martine went cold. Had they offended the mere? But the ritual had to be safely ended, or the fire could return whenever he wanted. That was part of the bargain. Perhaps the mere knew that, because after a heart-shattering pause it allowed the waters to continue settling.

When the water was once again clear and flat, reflecting the sky, they went back, holding hands, shaking, expecting Safred and Cael to meet them full of questions and exclamations.

But the camp was quiet, Cael and Safred still asleep. Martine and Zel sat well away from the campfire, shoulder to shoulder, still shaking.

"The ground was dry," Zel said finally, as though grabbing onto something real.

"What?" Martine said. Her mind felt overloaded, like a mill race with too much water going through it. She couldn't concentrate on anything except her memory of him.

"On the island, the ground was dry. As though the waves hadn't been there at all. *We're* dry. My skin—the water felt like it burned...but there are no marks." She paused, indicating Cael in his blanket and Safred's tent. "They didn't hear anything. Did it—was it real?"

Her tone was wistful. That jolted Martine into paying attention.

"If you mean, would you have burnt to a crisp if you'd walked into the fire, yes, you would have," she said tartly.

Zel bit her lip, tears rising in her eyes. "He'll never forgive me," she said.

"No. He never forgives."

"I'll never be able to do the ritual again."

Martine nodded, thinking it through. "You'd be too much of a risk to the others with you."

Zel looked down at the ground, her head hanging. "But we saw him," she whispered.

Martine felt the triumph, the astonishment, and finally the exaltation he had promised them. She smiled slowly. "Yes. We saw him. Remember," she touched Zel's shoulder, "it was you he wanted."

Zel turned curious eyes to her. "You didn't mind?"

How to answer that honestly? Martine felt again the agony of realizing it was Zel he was staring at. The envy. The despair. The longing.

"I minded," she said. "But now that he's gone, I know he was right. Of the two of us, it should have been you. I have not enough passion left for him."

She believed the words as she spoke them, but as soon as they had left her mouth she knew them to be a lie. Every breath taken in the memory of him told her that she was as made of passion as he was. She had forgotten it, but now her body remembered, and she and Zel wept in each other's arms because they were alive, and without him.

ASH

ASH SAT IN the dark stable for more than an hour, sliding the stones through his fingers, listening as they whispered their names: Love, Chaos, Murder, Revenge, Child, Woman, Death, Evenness . . .

Each stone was different, and each fitted his fingers and his mind as if crafted especially for him. He knew that a stonecaster's stones and his soul became entwined, and he could feel it happening, slowly, feeling the stones become *his*; only his. The process was both terrifying and exhilarating; scary and deeply comforting. There was nothing else that was *his*. He began to understand why stonecasters all seemed to have an unshakeable air of calm around them. The center of their lives was not touched by time or circumstance; their souls were as safe as stone.

Unlike Flax's singing, the stones didn't cut across his own mental music; rather, they seemed to harmonize with it, giving it more depth and color. He longed to use them. Flax was sitting beside him, nursing the last of his ale. He had the gift of happily doing nothing, which Ash had never mastered.

"I think I should practice before I try a paying customer," Ash said, as nonchalantly as he could. "Do you want me to read for you?"

Flax smiled with pleasure. "Oh, yes." He wriggled around until he was facing Ash and then spat in his left hand and held it out expectantly.

Ash put the pouch on the ground in front of him, spread out his own napkin, and spat in his own palm. They clasped hands.

"Ask your question," he said.

"Um . . . will Zel ever get married?"

Ash didn't let his surprise show, because that was also part of being a stonecaster, keeping your face blank. But he was suddenly curious about Flax; about whether he wanted the answer to be yes, or no. Was he so dependent on Zel that he couldn't bear the thought of her leaving? Or was he chafing under his big sister's competent management?

The stones in the bag were both strange and familiar to his fingers. It was a different feeling from just touching them, as he had earlier. Some seemed to slide past his fingertips as though waxed, others clung to his hand. It was easy, the work of only a moment, to gather the five that wanted to be drawn out. Ash breathed deeply to control his astonishment. He had always thought it was just chance—well, chance controlled by the gods—which stones were chosen. He'd had no idea that the stones chose themselves. The choice was so *clear.* It was so easy to tell which ones to grasp and which to let go. He felt euphoria building in him. This was something he could do, after all, something respected far more than safeguarding, something that—something that could take him back on the Road. With his parents, if they wanted.

A whole bright future rolled out in his mind in the moments that his hand drew the five stones out of the bag and cast them on the napkin of undyed linen. The stones stood out clearly against the pale fabric, but Ash didn't need the fading light to know which stones lay there. It was easy.

Then, as the stones spoke to him, it stopped being easy. He touched them, one by one, as he had seen Martine do, and they reached up into his mind and spoke, in sounds and music and images and smells. The smell of blood. The flight of an arrow. The sound of the sea.

"Time," he said with difficulty, and was appalled at the sound. The words came out harsh, grating, the unmistakable voice of the dead.

Flax recoiled, paling, and let go of Ash's hand. Then, slowly, he took it again, ignoring the fact that Ash was shaking.

"That's the voice of the Well of Secrets," he said slowly. "That's how she heals. With that voice."

Ash looked down at their hands, not sure what to say. Not wanting to admit to speaking with the voice of the dead. He shrugged, trying to imply that it was a surprise to him, too. But Flax had seen that already.

"You weren't trying to use that voice?" he asked warily.

Ash shook his head, afraid to speak. Afraid, oh gods, that his normal voice had gone completely.

"Has it happened before?"

"Only when I sing." The admission burst out before he could stop it, and it was his own voice, although a little higher than normal because he was frightened. But it was his voice. Turning back to the stones lying on the napkin was one of the hardest things he had ever done. He took a very deep breath, and touched one.

"Parting," he said, in the voice of the dead, and as he spoke the images, like memories, washed over him, full of treachery and blood. "Woman. Change. The blank stone."

He sat breathing heavily, glad it was over, not meeting Flax's eyes. But Flax was a Traveler born and bred, and the Sight, whatever form it took, was a part of his world. He accepted Ash's voice without further comment and looked at the blank stone consideringly.

"So. That means anything can happen, yes?"

Ash paused. The blank stone *did* mean that, but the stones were telling him something else; death, they said, murder. Yet those stones were not on the napkin. So what should he say to Flax? How much should he say? It might not be Zel's death, he told himself, although he was sure it was. But if the death stone wasn't there...perhaps Flax wasn't meant to know...Ash could have screamed from frustration. This was supposed to be a practice run, not an impossible choice! Then he remembered Martine's voice, "Answer the question. Don't make my mistake...don't give them more than they ask for."

"I don't . . ." Thank the gods, it was his own voice again. Perhaps the other voice only came when he was touching the stones, or naming them. "I don't see a wedding," he said and tried not to laugh hysterically at the understatement. "But there is a parting of the ways." A big parting, but perhaps not the final one. Perhaps that was what the blank stone meant.

Flax scratched his chin, a curiously old movement. "Time," he said.

"Yes," Ash replied, sure of that. "Months, at least."

Flax let go of his hand. "Months," he said, in a tone which meant that months might as well have been years. "I thought...there was a cobbler who wanted to marry her a while back. I just wondered...but I guess not, huh?"

Ash shrugged and swept the stones up into the pouch. They were once again just pieces of rock with carvings on them. That was all. The surge of feeling, of sight and smell and what had seemed like memory, was gone. He felt empty and tired.

"You know, I don't think your average stonecaster talks like that," Flax said. "Might cause a bit of a stir."

He was right. No one would want to consult a stonecaster who grated an answer like stone on stone. Like Death herself. They certainly didn't want to attract attention while they were on their way to the Deep.

"Dung and pissmire!" Ash cursed. All his bright plans crashed around him. Even this talent was useless to him. "Go to sleep!" he snarled at Flax, as though it were all his fault. Flax grinned and rolled himself into his blanket as though nothing were wrong.

The next day, they were more circumspect on the Road, because they were closer to Gabriston. Although Flax complained, they camped that night instead of going to one of the village inns.

"We don't need more silver. Best not to draw attention," Ash said. "That's the way of it, going to the Deep. Don't draw attention."

Or someone, sometime, would notice the trickle of Traveler men heading through Gabriston into the wilds, and ask questions. That would mean death, for someone—the questioner or the questioned. So the demons said.

They bought small amounts of food in each village they passed the day after, until their saddlebags were swollen, so they could skirt Gabriston and go onto the wilds without being noticed.

They were out of grain country now and into North Domain's vineyards, famous from cliff to cove for their fine vintages. Flax eyed the inns with some wistfulness, but Ash was firm.

"On the way out, maybe. Maybe, if all goes well. But no sane man goes to the Deep with drink in him."

The vines were planted on hillsides, so steep that in some places they were terraced to make more flat ground. The hills grew rougher, and the vines less abundant as they approached the wilds. Finally, they found their way to a bluff which overlooked the wilds: a network of canyons and chasms, stream-cut gorges and dead ends, all formed of the red sandstone that was quarried further downstream and sent all over the Domains. In Turvite, in rich merchants' houses, Ash had seen intricately carved mantelpieces and balustrades in the fine stone, streaked golden and blood red in intertwining layers. The sandstone was very beautiful, but the sight of it had always made him nervous—it reminded him of the Deep, and the Spring Equinox.

The canyons of the wilds had been worn away by water over thousands of years, many more thousands than Acton's people had been in the Domains. Every spring, his father had said, the singers and the poets had made their way here. Spring was the time for music and stories, he said, when things began to flow again. Summer was the time for those in the living trades: horse trainers and animal healers and drovers. Autumn for the dead trades: tinkers and painters and drystone wallers. Winter for the wood trades: carvers and carpenters and turners, chair-makers and basketweavers. Every craft had its time, its gods-chosen time, for the Deep. Except, Ash thought now, looking down at the stream below the bluff as it leapt and danced over the red rocks, except safeguarders. Perhaps he belonged with the shepherds. He laughed, shortly, and nudged Mud with his heels. The sun was setting. It was time for the Deep.

SAKER

SAKER HAD DECIDED to get well away from Carlion before he searched for more bones. Yet no matter where he went, people were afraid. They gathered in inns, talking agitatedly, calling each other over to confirm some part of the story, worrying, fretting. Or else they shut themselves up in their houses.

Whenever he passed a black rock altar there were people making sacrifices to the gods, praying hard. Useless, he wanted to tell them. The gods have sent me. Once, there was a Traveler family at the altar, and he wanted to stop and say, "You don't need to worry. If you stay out of the way, you won't be hurt." But of course he couldn't, without revealing himself.

In each village he passed, men and women were out nailing shutters firmly to the windows, or installing bars for the doors. Carpenters had notices pinned to their workshop doors: Too busy!

Smiths were making weapons instead of horseshoes. The local officers, who held large sections of the land in the warlord's name, had sent their sergeants out to collect their oath men, and hauled them away, complaining, from barricading their cottages.

All the activity should have made him feel triumphant. He had done this. *He*, Saker, had scared all these people. Part of him wished his father could be here to witness it. But... he didn't want it to be like this. The anxiety—oddly, he'd never imagined his actions leading to worry. Terror, yes. Terror in the night, death cleanly delivered a moment afterward, he had been expecting that. The killing was necessary, to retrieve the land from its usurpers. But worry, even this extraordinary worry, he hadn't expected that, and it felt wrong.

He knew what his father would say: you just didn't think it through, boy! He'd said it often to Saker in his childhood, when Saker rushed impetuously into some scheme. Like the time he'd wanted to raise snails to eat, as he'd heard the Wind Cities people did, and the box overturned. The snails got into the vegetable garden and ate all his father's plants. He winced at the memory of that beating, and of his father's voice saying, "You just didn't think it through, did you, boy? Well, think this through!" Down came the cane.

When he stopped for the night at an inn where he had been once before in his wanderings, he was besieged for castings. But he shook his head.

"Even the gods do not know the outcome," he said portentously. The innkeeper's wife burst into tears and his son paled, but the man himself sniffed.

"Good. You remember that, boy. Our fate is in our own hands."

Saker disliked him intensely in that moment, and it was only later that he realized the man reminded him of his father. But he didn't think about that. By that time he was occupied in finding bones.

LEOF

THE NEXT FEW days were a whirl of messages and reports. Leof sent recruiting parties to towns in the Domain furthest from Carlion. There was no use trying to get masons in closer towns to go to Carlion; refugees from the slaughter had already spread the story of the ghosts and the nearest towns were busy fortifying themselves.

The stories reached Sendat. Hodge came to Leof in the officers' workroom, where he was sorting through reports from two recruiting parties who had managed to scrape up some apprentice masons eager for adventure and a couple of older men who didn't work much these days but were prepared to take a trip to the coast at the warlord's expense. There was no door to the officers' workroom—it was an annex between the room where Thegan held his meetings and Thegan's workroom. Hodge stood a little uncomfortably in the doorway and cleared his throat.

"Yes?" Leof said, looking up. "Oh, it's you, Hodge. What's the problem?"

"We've got some people from Carlion come to town, my lord. Paying for their drinks at the inn with stories."

Leof put down the papers he had been reading. "Well, it had to come sometime. Call a muster and send to the town to say I'll address everyone in the square an hour before sunset."

Hodge nodded and left. A moment later Leof heard the bell that called the men to muster. He went out of the barracks building and stood in front of the hall. Should he tell Sorn? Hodge was waiting by the muster point.

"Sergeant, go and tell the Lady Sorn that she and her ladies and the rest of the household are invited to this muster. And get me a halberd."

Sorn had been waiting for this moment, it was clear. The maids had probably brought back the news from the town as well—maybe that was how Hodge had found out. She swept out of the hall with her ladies and maids in tow, Fortune hiding in her skirts, and behind them came the cooks and the kitchen boys and the fire tender; and from around the side of the hall came the gardeners and the dairymaid and the woodman and the lads who looked after the chickens and the ducks and the pigs. The brewer came out from her oast-house, the cheese-maker from her loft, the carpenter from his workshop. Leof hadn't reflected before on how big and complex the staff was that Sorn managed.

They waited to the side of the assembled troops. Knowing that it was bound to come, Leof had worried over what to say in this moment. But it was a lovely day, spring edging into summer, and all their own people were safe for the moment. His natural optimism asserted itself so that he smiled at the assembly with real reassurance.

"You've all heard the stories," he said simply. "Evil bloodsucking ghosts rising from the dead to slaughter us, yes?" Men in the ranks nodded, a little shamefacedly, expecting to be told none of it was true, that they were fools for listening to fireside tales. They shuffled their feet, a soft susurration in the dust.

"As far as we know, they don't suck blood." As they realized what he meant, they stood still and silence fell. "There are ghosts, raised by an enchanter. They do have bodily strength. They cannot be killed again."

Murmurs rose from both the men and from Sorn's household. One girl was giggling wildly, another gasping with fright and looking around as though expecting the ghosts to jump on them immediately.

"*But* . . ." Leof shouted, and they quieted. "But, the spell is of limited time. In Carlion, they faded as the sun came up. They have no more strength than they had when they were alive. Although they cannot be killed, they can be stopped. They cannot enter a barred door or a shuttered window, anymore than a man can." He held out his hand and Hodge put the halberd into it. He brought it round in a wide, hissing swipe and smacked the pole into his other hand. All eyes followed its sweep. "If you cut off their arms, they will do no more damage."

A few men in the ranks began to smile. Leof nodded to them.

"Yes. That is why we have been practicing with battleaxes and halberds these last days. That is why you will all learn to use boar spear, because if you impale one of these ghosts on one, he will be easy prey for the man with the battleaxe. Do you understand?"

"Aye, my lord," a few enthusiastic ones shouted.

"Do *all* of you understand?" Leof called.

"*Aye,* my lord," they shouted back.

He nodded to them and smiled again. "They are an unusual enemy, my friends. But they are *not* unstoppable. So far they have taken on unarmed townsfolk, who have never before even *seen* an enemy. I think they will get a surprise when they come up against *us.*"

He tossed the halberd in the air so that it gleamed in the sun and caught it again with a flourish and they cheered. Then he turned to the household and bowed to Sorn. "My lady, you and your people should be in no fear. Sendat is well protected and well armed against this enemy. You are in no danger."

She smiled at the halberd in his hand with real humor. "So I see, my lord."

The cook laughed at that and, when Sorn smiled in response, the others laughed, too. Sorn and Leof bowed to each other and she went back in to the hall, calm as ever. Leof watched her go with a half-smile on his face. She made everything so easy.

Hodge dismissed the men and Leof went down to the town to make the same speech, with a few small variations, to the townsfolk. To them he emphasized the fact that barred doors and good shutters would keep out the ghosts, and that the fort was being rebuilt so that, in an emergency, it would safely hold all the people from the town.

"Not that we'll need that," he said cheerily. "My men are training now to make sure that, *if* these ghosts turn up anywhere near here, they'll have their arms and legs cut off and be squirming on the grass like fat white worms before they know what's hit them!"

They laughed a little, but were not so easily reassured as the soldiers had been. Leof sobered.

"Remember, my friends, these ghosts have not been seen again since Carlion. It may be that this was a spell which could only be used there."

"What about Spritford?" someone at the back yelled.

"You, come forward," Leof said. He thought quickly as the older woman struggled toward the bench on which he stood. If there had been another incident, it would be best if news didn't get out about it now. He leapt down from the bench and waited for her to reach him.

The woman was middle-aged and truculent, in no mind to take orders from a young man, even a warlord's officer.

"Spritford?" Leof said quietly. "When was that?"

"Last autumn," she said. "My sister's man was killed there, and she came to live with me."

"So," he said, raising his voice, "nothing has happened since Carlion?"

She shook her head, and the people around her relaxed.

"Wait here for a moment," he said to the woman and climbed back on the bench. "My friends, you know the truth now. Go home and prepare, as we have been preparing for you. Remember that your warlord ordered you to secure your homes many months ago, so that no matter what enemy faced us, you would be safe. Remember that he lent you his own carpenters and smiths to help fortify your homes."

"That's true," he heard someone mutter. "We're in good shape."

"Go home and give thanks to the gods for our safety and pray to them for the warlord's well-being."

They drifted away, some to their houses but more to the road that led outside town to the black rock altar near the stream. The woman waited stolidly.

"Can you bring your sister to the fort?" Leof asked. She nodded and turned away.

Leof wondered if he should go with her and see the woman straightaway; but he wanted Sorn to be part of this meeting. She will be better at talking to women, he told himself. Particularly a grieving widow.

He went back to the fort and found Sorn in the kitchens, discussing the evening meal with the cook. She looked up and smiled as he came in.

"Roast kid for supper, my lord?" she asked.

"Always good," Leof said half-heartedly, his mind on Spritford and ghosts.

She mistook his lack of enthusiasm. "Something different tomorrow perhaps, then, Ael. An ash-baked dish, perhaps. Lamb with onions and wild greens and parsnips in some stock with lemon and rosemary, I think."

The cook shrugged, resigned. "Too late to start that tonight, my lady."

"Which is why I said 'tomorrow,' " Sorn said gently. The cook flushed and shifted his feet. "Tonight you will take the roast kid and fry it with brown ale and onions and thyme and some of the olives from the Wind Cities. You will cook the carrots with honey and serve a bitter salad of dandelion greens and wilted spinach in lemon juice, to aid digestion. There will also be dessert."

"Yes, my lady. What kind of dessert?"

It amused Leof to see how thoroughly Sorn had cowed the cook, who was a big man and known to be free with his fists after he'd had a few drinks. Sorn smiled graciously at him and turned to Leof.

"My lord? Do you have a favorite dessert?"

"Strawberries?" Leof suggested.

"Griddle cakes served with strawberries and the first skimming of cream," Sorn instructed.

"Yes, my lady," the cook said, looking at his feet.

Leof's lips twitched and a dimple showed briefly in Sorn's cheek but was banished immediately. She patted the cook on the arm.

"The bacon and barley soup was excellent this noon, Ael," she said.

The cook looked up, met her smile and smiled back. "Thank you, my lady," he said.

Fortune was waiting resignedly outside the kitchen door, and jumped up, barking softly, as Sorn appeared. Leof clicked his fingers and the dog danced up to him and licked his thumb. Sorn smiled. They strolled back to the hall together.

"You have a big household," he commented.

"It was enlarged considerably when I was married," she said. "My father did not care for home comforts in the same way that my lord Thegan does."

Leof had never thought of Thegan as caring about comfort in any way.

Sorn caught his expression and smiled, a little grimly. "My lord appreciates good food and good service," she said. "Such things do not happen by chance."

Leof nodded. "Anything of excellence is the product of hard work," he agreed. He led Sorn over to her customary chair and seated her with the appropriate bow. Fortune gave a sigh as he realized they were not going for a walk, and sat down. "Your household is exemplary and I am interested in how you organize it. Unfortunately, there is another matter to deal with at this time. A woman in the town reported an earlier uprising of ghosts in a town called Spritford."

"That is in the Western Mountains Domain, near the Sharp River," Sorn said.

Leof was surprised that she knew the Domains so well, and it showed in his face. She smiled wryly.

"I was courted by quite a few warlords and their sons and for a while studied the other Domains with a great deal of interest."

He laughed. "No doubt you did!"

She smiled back and laughed a little herself, her green eyes shining, then sobered quickly. "Spritford," she said. He sobered, too, indicating the door where the woman from the town had appeared, arm-in-arm with a slighter, shorter woman with strikingly similar features.

Sorn rose immediately and went to greet them. They bowed low, but she raised them up by the arms and led them to seats. Fortune hid behind Sorn's chair from the strangers.

"Come," she invited them. "Tell us about these ghosts."

The shorter woman, Ulma, was as stern-faced as her sister, and stoic. Not the wailing widow Leof had expected, but the grief was real enough. She told the story: ghosts appearing out of nowhere, solid, armed, angry. Seven dead in Spritford, she said, including her husband, struck down by a small man wielding a scythe, in the full light of the sun. That was unwelcome news; more welcome was the fact that they had faded at sunset.

"So I came here," she said finally, "thinking to find safety, but it seems maybe there's no safety anywhere."

Sorn nodded sympathetically, asked a few tactful questions about finances and ways she could help, and eased the women out the door having charmed them thoroughly. No, Leof corrected himself, watching as Sorn bid them farewell at the door, they're not charmed. That's respect in their faces, and not simply because she's the Lady. They are strong women and they recognize strength when they see it in others.

That was a striking thought, because strength was not a quality he had associated with Sorn. His own mother was strong, but in a very different way—decisive, outspoken, like many of the women in Cliff Domain, where the men were away fighting so often that the women had had to learn how to do without them. Sorn was another vintage entirely.

"That news is not good," she said seriously, coming back to where he stood, resting her hands on the back of her tall chair. "Fighting in broad sun. They are not restricted to the night, it seems."

"But they faded at sunset," he replied. "Perhaps they may have a night or a day, but not both?"

"It has been months since Spritford. Perhaps there have been other quickenings that we have not heard of?"

Leof shrugged. They just didn't know enough. "I'll send news of this to my lord," he said. "Do you have any message for him? I would be happy to include a letter in the package . . ."

Sorn considered, then shook her head. "My lord is involved in men's business. The only news I have is about women's work, and would not interest him." She said it simply, without resentment, but her reply sent a pang through Leof. It spoke of loneliness. She had no real friends among her ladies, he realized. Her maid, Faina, was devoted, but hardly a friend. There was no nearby officer's estate with its complement of wives and daughters who might provide companionship—only Fortune.

Difficult for her, he thought. Well, perhaps he could provide some friendly company while her lord was away. Impulsively, he reached out and touched the back of her hand.

"Anything about you must interest him," he said. Too late, he heard the note of sincerity in his voice. In that moment Leof felt the softness of her skin. Warmth and silk moving swiftly under his fingers. He felt a flood tide of desire sweep through him, overwhelm him as surely as the Lake had done. He was just as helpless as he had been then, tossed on a wave too big for him.

Sorn flushed and pulled her hand away. She half-turned, as though to leave, then stopped herself.

Leof spoke quickly. He couldn't bear to see her force herself to look at him. "I will send your regards in my letter, my lady."

Then he turned and left the hall, breaking etiquette by not waiting for her dismissal; not daring to wait for it.

ASH

COMING TO THE Deep set Ash's hair prickling on the back of his neck.

From the bluff outside Gabriston, they could see the wilds that lay to the north of the Hidden River. On the other side of the water was a simple cliff, but on this side the soft sandstone had been eroded by countless streams into a nightmare maze of canyons and crevasses, impossible to map. In the middle of the maze was the Deep, a series of caves and canyons which led to the heart of the demons' mysteries. Each man who came to the deep found something different there, but each man also found the same thing: the truth about himself. Which was why Ash's heart was pounding.

They paused at the beginning, at the bottom of the bluff, where the canyons started and the sound of the river swelled into a chorus that filled his head. He must make Flax swear the oath. He remembered the words easily enough. He spat in his hand and offered it to Flax, who copied him and grasped firmly.

"This is the oath we ask of you: will you give it? To be silent to death of what you see, of what you hear, of what you do?"

Flax had picked up on his mood and was uncharacteristically solemn. "I swear," he said.

"Do you swear upon pain of shunning, never to speak of this place outside of this place?"

"I swear."

"Do you swear upon pain of death never to guide another to this place who has not the blood right?"

Flax swallowed. "I swear."

"Do you swear upon pain beyond death, the pain of never being reborn, to keep the secrets of this place with your honor, with your strength, with your life?"

This time, Flax had to work his mouth for enough spit to form the words. "I swear."

There was sweat on Flax's forehead. Ash was glad to see it.

He let go of the boy's hand.

Ash led Flax down one narrow defile after another, the fern-covered walls of red sandstone rising higher as they went, until they moved in a green gloom. Water seeping through the stone made it glisten in the shadows, as though the hills were bleeding. Ash always felt that he should have smelt blood here, and death, instead of the clear scent of water, the must of leaf mold, and the occasional waft of early jasmine. His nose told him it was safe, but his ears strained past the endless trickle of water and the wind moaning through the rocks, waiting to hear the demons.

He checked on Flax regularly, knowing the lad was nervous and knowing he should be. The Deep was dangerous, and not just because of the demons. Vipers, spiders, scorpions lurked beneath every rock, every leaf. Poison tainted the beauty; he was reminded of Doronit.

The outsiders, Acton's people, thought the stones were a maze, difficult to find the way through because of their complexity. But that was just the wilds, the outside skin of the Deep, where the River allowed the fair-haired ones to penetrate. Further in, the truth was stranger. Ash had been here six years running with his father, the years between his voice breaking and his apprenticeship to Doronit, and it had never been the same twice. No one could penetrate the Deep unless the River willed it. Rock walls shifted; streams bubbled up where there had been solid rock the day before; bogs appeared that could suck a man down in three heartbeats, too quick even for a scream. Ash had seen that, once, when he was fourteen.

"Turn away," his father had said. "He came here with treachery; the River claimed him."

Ash found a clearing, a place with good water and grass, where they could leave the horses. They watered and groomed them and hung nosebags from the cliff wall as temporary mangers. By that time it was dark.

"Do we light a fire?" Flax asked hopefully.

Ash shook his head. "Follow me. Your eyes will adjust."

This was his favorite time in the Deep, just after sunset when the enchantment started. At least it had seemed enchantment, the first time, and every time afterward, too, even when he understood how it happened. As they walked further into the difficult passageways of stone, the walls began to acquire stars. Small, green, they glowed so faintly that it seemed like a trick of the eyes. Then, as the darkness gathered and his eyes adjusted, they became brighter, casual constellations scattered across the rock walls, clumped together in shining clusters, lighting their way.

Ash looked back at Flax, and was satisfied by the wonder on his face.

"What are they?" Flax asked.

Ash contemplated telling him the truth: little glowing insects. Glowworms. But he'd always hated that name. It diminished the beauty.

"The stars of the Deep," he said. "Come on."

They turned a corner and found themselves in a larger defile, with a stream pelting down the middle, splashing and leaping, throwing small pebbles and grit into the air. The edges of the defile were covered with fallen rocks and the way out was blocked by them, except for the stream, which launched itself from a small gap between the rock walls into the darkness. If they tried to wade through the stream and edge through the gap, they would be thrown helpless as dolls against the sharp rocks, or over the edge, to where they could hear the water plummet down to smash on rocks far below.

"Careful," Ash said. "From here, the demons watch."

He stood up straight and said clearly, "I am Ash, son of Rowan. I am known to this place. My blood is known. I give it again, that this place may know me afresh."

He took his belt knife and moved to the stream, then pricked his finger and let three drops of blood fall into the water. The stream quietened immediately. The water still flowed fast, but it no longer leaped and challenged.

Ash beckoned Flax toward him. As he approached, the stream again became wild, leaping high in menace. Ash took Flax's hand and held it over the stream.

"This is Flax, son of Gorham, come to meet his blood in the Deep." He pricked Flax's finger and let the blood drop into the water. It calmed immediately.

"Come on," Ash said. "Now."

Quickly he led Flax into the stream, stumbling a little on the rocky bottom, but striding as fast as he dared through the gap in the rocks. The stream pushed against his boots, but it didn't thrust him hard enough to make him fall; it didn't suddenly spring up when they were halfway through. He had seen that happen, too, to a scrawny friend of his father's, a storyteller. The man's body was never found.

"The River protects itself, and us," his father had said, as though trying to convince himself. But no one had said what the River was protecting itself from that day.

They had to turn at the very edge of the waterfall and sidle along a ledge. The ledge was narrow and there were rocks underfoot. It led along a sheer cliff wall to another gap in the rocks, and another canyon beyond. They stepped carefully through the gap and made their way down the canyon, and from there onto another high ledge. Ash could hear Flax breathing hard. He remembered the first time he had done this, or something like it, because it was never the same twice. The physical danger hadn't been as bad as the threat of the unknown, the demons waiting out in the darkness.

As though the thought had called them—and maybe it had—they heard the demons howling. The sound wasn't exactly like the howling of wolves, but it wasn't human. Flax stumbled as the first long wail reached them and Ash put out a hand to push him safely against the cliff face. They stopped for a moment, listening to the grief and hunger in the demon howl. Both of them were shivering.

Beyond this canyon was another one, and then another one after that. They twisted and turned and Ash knew it was useless to try to remember them, but he tried anyway. His safeguarder training was no use here, but he had been trained so long that he couldn't just abandon it.

Finally, they came into a large space ringed with cliff walls that were broken by caves and cracks. Inside one of the caves, a fire blazed just out of sight. Shadows flickered on the cave walls and out onto the beaten earth floor of the clearing. The sudden gold and orange of its light was almost too much for their dark-adjusted eyes.

Flax gasped. From behind rocks, from fissures and caves, figures emerged from the darkness. Naked, male, thin and solid, and tall and short, all with dark hair across their arms and bodies. The bodies seemed to be striped with blood. But it was their faces which had scared him, Ash knew. He remembered the first time he had been confronted by those snarling snouts, the sharp teeth, the animal eyes. Each man had the head of an animal: badger or otter or fox or deer, varied but all wild animals. There were no cows or pigs or sheep. A wildcat, but no cats; a wolf, but no dogs.

He knew what Flax was thinking: masks, surely they were masks? But they were not. Of course not. What would be the point of pretending? Dressing up in silly clothes, painting their bodies—that would not be work for men.

The demons closed toward them, slowly, and in their hands were stones; flint, sharp as knives. Flax's breathing was faster and shallower. He was getting ready to run. Ash put a hand on his arm, to calm him.

"We are members of the blood," he called to the demons. "I am Ash, son of Rowan, whose blood has calmed the waters." He nudged Flax. Flax had to clear his throat before he could talk.

"I am Flax, son of Gorham... whose blood has calmed the waters."

The hands holding the stones lowered to the men's sides. One of them, a badger, came forward to place his hands on Ash's shoulders. Ash looked deep into the dark eyes which glinted orange in the firelight and breathed in the sharp badger scent. He felt a swirl of emotions: anger, happiness, resentment, love.

"Fire and water, Father," he said.

BRAMBLE

THERE WAS A marching song playing at a dirge pace in her head—in Baluch's head. Bramble felt relief at being back with Baluch, despite the severe cold. Vision came back with a rush of white, dazzling. Snow, everywhere. Rough ground underfoot, invisible under the snow. Cliffs on one side, a high, rocky white slope on the other. Oh gods, Bramble thought. We're in Death Pass again! On the slope lay tons of snow which would crash down to bury them all at the slightest sound. Even though Bramble knew that the raiders—the invaders—had made it through unscathed, the sight of that burden of snow made her nervous, threatening with the same kind of impartial animosity as the Ice King. The silence was intense; the men pushed through the snow so slowly that even Baluch's sharp ears could only just catch a faint susurration at each step.

Acton was in front of Baluch, his gold head shrouded in hat and scarf, his shield slung over his shoulder, but his back unmistakable as he waded slowly through the breast-high snow. For a moment, hysteria flickered in Bramble. How had she become so shagging familiar with Acton's back? But she was, or Baluch was, or both. Baluch could see the profile of the man next to Acton—it was Asgarn, which vaguely surprised Bramble. Asgarn hadn't seemed the type to volunteer for something as chancy as this. Perhaps, she thought, the lord of war picked his men. Part of Bramble found that amusing; that Asgarn might have been caught in his own snare, and then she wondered why she assumed Asgarn had been laying traps, why she just plain didn't like him.

Acton and Asgarn led, just as in all the ballads, the two thickset men ploughing gradually, silently, toward the gap between cliff and slope, toward the triangle of ridiculously blue sky. Bramble had always imagined this day as being cloudy and gray, but it was a beautiful day, crisp and sunny.

The man next to Baluch stumbled and flung out a hand. Baluch grabbed it and hauled him back up. The man's gasp sounded overly loud and the entire band paused, terrified, in mid-step. A thin trickle of snow slid off a rock on the lower slope. They froze in place, waiting. Baluch was praying, Bramble realized, opening himself to the gods, but the gods refused to come. There was only a long moment of fear before the trickle of snow stopped.

They began moving again, slower than before despite the cold. Baluch's hands and feet were numb but his cheeks burnt and his mouth ached every time he drew a breath. For a while it seemed that the end of the pass was as far away as ever, that they would trudge through burning cold forever. But gradually, inevitably, the triangle of blue grew larger. Then the snow was not breast-high, but waist-high. Then thigh-high. Knee-high. Then the triangle of blue stretched to cover the whole sky, and they were out of the pass, standing on a lip of ground looking down into the valley, slapping each other on the back in congratulation, but silent still.

Silent, because below them in the morning light lay Hawk's steading. Smoke rose from its chimneys, but no one was about yet. There were no guards. The steading was undefended in early spring, because Death Pass was its defense. Silently, Acton drew his sword and settled his shield onto his left arm. The others did the same. Acton nodded to them, all fifty of them, and slapped Baluch on the arm. For a moment his face was serious, then he grinned at them, the joy of battle alight on his face. Baluch smiled involuntarily and hefted his sword. Bramble could feel the tension in him but also the excitement and, with it this time, a sense of grim purpose. Acton saw it in his face and nodded, a darker expression in his eyes.

"Let us take our revenge," he said so quietly that the others had to strain to hear. "Make them regret their treachery."

"Yes," Asgarn said. "Kill them all."

Baluch raised his sword high in acknowledgment, and the others copied him. The sun shimmered off their blades and blinded Baluch; and for a moment it became morning sunlight on water and the water rose to blind Bramble in its turn.

Blood in her mouth. Blood trickling down from her lip onto her chin. Her back was against a wall, and her legs were unsteady. The woman—yes, this was definitely a woman, a young woman clutching a blanket to her naked chest—lifted a hand to wipe away the blood. The movement brought back sight, and Bramble wished it hadn't. They were inside, in a small wooden room with a shuttered window and a bed. It smelled of woodsmoke and sex and fear.

The girl who had giggled, Edwa, lay on the bed, trying to pull her shift down around her buttocks. She was bleeding, too, the blood oozing down her inner thighs. There were bruises on her legs and arms. Her long hair was loose and snarled.

"Please . . ." Edwa said, raising her face in supplication to the man who stood in front of her, his left arm raised high as though about to strike her. Hawk. Edwa's face was dark with bruises all down one side. Hawk lowered his arm and began to undo his trouser drawstring.

"Come to your senses, have you?" he snarled.

Bramble could feel the woman whose eyes she saw through move her lips, her tongue, wanting to say something, to protest. But she had clearly learned that protesting brought nothing but blows. She dug her fingers into her own palms in an effort to keep quiet.

Bramble desperately wanted to be somewhere else, to *not see*. She was shocked to the core. Hawk was black-haired. Black-eyed. Like her. She had *known* that he and his men were using the girls, but to *see* it. To see a Traveler, as he looked to her, abuse a gold-haired girl . . . It went against all her prejudices, all that she wanted to be true.

Come on, Acton, she thought, where are you? Get in here and save them. Then she realized that she was urging on the invasion. She didn't know which made her sicker, the impending rape or her own thoughts.

The noise started outside: yells, the crash of swords and shields, screams. Hawk spun around at the sounds, his back to both women. He fumbled to pull up his trousers.

The woman dropped the blanket to the floor and jumped on his back as he bent over. She grabbed his belt knife at the same time. He straightened explosively, trying to throw her off. She locked her arms around his neck and strained to pull his head back, but he was too strong.

"Edwa!" she yelled, "take the knife."

Hawk was trying to drag the woman off his back, but she was

holding on with all her strength. Edwa put out both hands for the knife. The man whirled and the knife slashed across the back of her hand, drawing blood. She ignored the wound and his clubbing hands and grabbed the knife, holding it confidently, as though she had been longing for this moment. With both hands now free, the woman dragged back his head. As soon as his throat was bared, Edwa raised the knife and plunged it deeply into his neck. Blood spurted out, *poured* out all over her. Hawk fell to the floor with a wet gasp, dead already. Bramble was ashamed of how satisfied she felt as he collapsed.

The other woman ran to the door and shut it, then began looking around for something to barricade it with. Her red-gold braid lay over her wrist, matted and untidy. Bramble was abruptly aware of her smell. It had been a long time since anyone had let these girls wash.

"Help me move the bed against the door, Edwa," the woman ordered, but Edwa just stood, looking at the knife and the body.

The woman took her by the shoulder and shook her. "Don't you understand? They've come for us! I knew Acton wouldn't leave us here! All we have to do is keep Hawk's men out until after it's over and we'll be safe."

Edwa focused on her face, her blue eyes becoming less clouded. "They're here?" she whispered. The woman nodded. She began to dress herself hurriedly, dragging on shift and dress and snatching up a man's leather belt to girdle herself. She shook Edwa again, and this time Edwa moved, but not to help. She went down on one knee and got Hawk's other knife out of his boot. It was much longer, a dagger for fighting rather than the eating knife they had used to kill him.

The woman nodded. "Good. We might need that." She went to the other side of the bed and began to push it toward the door. "Come and *help*, Edwa! We can't let Hawk's men use us as hostages!"

Edwa was staring at the two knives, one in each hand. She put the smaller one against her wrist and drew it down slowly. Blood welled.

Bramble expected the woman by the bed to jump up and grab the knife, but she stayed very still. "Edwa?" she said gently.

"They mustn't see, Wili. They mustn't see me," Edwa whispered, finding a new place to cut and pushing the knife in.

Wili straightened up from the bed and turned to look fully at Edwa. The blond girl was painted in blood. Her hair was as dark as a Traveler's now, and her face was smeared and purple with bruises. Bramble could feel Wili's heart beating in deep, heavy thumps. Her sight blurred as the girl's eyes filled with tears.

"That won't kill you, Edwa," she said with a break in her voice. "It'll just make you more bloody."

Edwa looked up at Wili. Her eyes were dry and bleak. She nodded slowly, as though Wili had told her something hard to understand, but important. She dropped the belt knife and, bringing her other hand up in the same movement, thrust the long dagger in under her breastbone. Then she crumpled to the floor.

Wili sat down on the bed, as though it didn't matter anymore if Hawk's men found her. She stared at her hands. The nails were bitten down to the quick. Bramble could feel the knot of grief between her breastbone and her throat, and feel something else as well, a kind of heaviness that made movement impossible, even the movement that would be needed to cry.

The door slammed back and Acton sprang into the room, his sword and shield ready, blood and sweat running down his cheeks. He saw Wili first, and shuddered to a halt, visibly changing from berserker to concerned friend.

"Wili! Are you all right?" He closed the door behind him.

Wili's eyes overflowed and she started to cry. Not the choking sobs of grief, Bramble thought. That would come later. These were the tears of relief. She brushed them away almost angrily and stood up.

"*I'll* survive," she said, and looked at Edwa.

Acton knelt beside Edwa's body. He put down his shield but not his sword and reached his shield hand to touch the knife hilt that stood out from her shift. It had an antler handle, Bramble saw, left rough for a better grip. Edwa's hold had loosened and her hands had fallen away to lie empty and soft on the wooden floor. Acton closed the dull blue eyes and looked up at Wili.

"She didn't want you to see her—anyone to see her, after what had happened." Wili's voice was astonishingly calm, the tears gone.

"You didn't stop her." His tone wasn't accusing, not even wondering. He just said it.

"Her choice," Wili said. "I understood why."

Acton nodded slowly and stood up. He picked up his shield and gripped his sword more firmly. Bramble saw the fury build in him again and, like Wili, she understood it.

"Close the door behind me," he said. "I'll be back for you."

Wili nodded. He faced the doorway and then hesitated, turned back, as if he were impelled to ask.

"Friede?"

Wili shook her head. "She died in the attack. Took three of them with her, too, because they weren't expecting a cripple to fight." Her voice was bitter. "I should have fought harder. Maybe they would have killed me as well."

Acton raised his hand in denial, the sword pointing up. His eyes were dark with fury and determination. "You are the treasure we have saved from this wreck," he said. Bramble felt the warmth spread out from Wili's gut at his words, as though she had been waiting for a judgment, a death sentence, and had instead received a reprieve.

Acton went out the door in a rush, back into the shouting and screaming and hard, thudding noise. "Kill them all!" he shouted as he went, sword ready.

Wili began to cry again, sinking down to the floor and letting her head droop. The tears washed Bramble away gently, like a soft slide into sleep.

All she could feel was her heart, beating too fast, as though it was going to spasm. She couldn't catch her breath. It took all her strength, but she pulled back from the mind she was in, from the body's distress. She could see little except some cracks of light. A small room. Maybe a storeroom. Her hands were bound with cloth. The air was cold; her breath was the warmest thing here. *His* breath; it was a man, again, but she couldn't tell whom. His mind had a faintly familiar taste to it, but he was so frightened that all personality had been stamped out.

A door in the wall opposite crashed back and a red-headed man appeared. He was followed by a stocky blond with big shoulders. Together, they hoisted the man under the armpits and dragged him out the door, then threw him down onto the cold ground of a yard behind a big building. Hawk's house? Bramble wondered.

Acton and Baluch were standing there, their clothes smirched with blood, their eyes red with exhaustion. Acton was cleaning his sword with a snatch of cloth, paying great attention to the detail around the hilt. Baluch looked at him in concern, and then cast a quick glance at a corner of the yard. The man she inhabited looked too, and shuddered. A woman's body lay sprawled against the wall of an animal shed. Bramble could hear pigs inside squealing for food, that terrible squeal that sounded like they were having their throats cut.

Acton was very definitely not looking at the body of the woman. The red-head and the blond came back to the yard and dragged the corpse away, and only then did Acton look up, in time to see Asgarn pass the two and come on without a glance. Acton sheathed his sword as though he were glad to put it away.

Asgarn was in high spirits. He was just as bloody as the others, and just as tired, but he was smiling in satisfaction.

"That's a good day's work," he said. He clapped a hand on Baluch's shoulder. "Maybe you'll make a song of it, eh? The Saga of Hawk's Hall."

Baluch shook his head. "The Saga of Death Pass, maybe." Bramble wanted to smile. He'd clearly been thinking about it already, probably while they were making the trek through the pass.

"There's no one left?" Acton said.

"Except this one." Asgarn casually kicked the man on the ground. "When you say, 'Kill them all' that's what we do." Acton winced. "You did *want* them all dead, didn't you?"

"The men," Acton said. "I wanted the warriors killed."

"Ah . . ." Asgarn shrugged. "Well, next time you'd better tell us that first, lord of war." He turned away and kicked the man again, hard, on the shoulder. "So, what do we do with him, then? You want me to finish him off?"

"No!" Acton said. He looked at the man more closely, and was surprised. "You're one of ours, aren't you? One of Swef's thralls? Uen, isn't that your name?"

Baluch looked at Uen in surprise. Uen was looking up in hope. Bramble could feel the welling up of pleading; he was trying not to beg. She recognized his mind now. The thrall who had been ploughing the day Hawk came to visit Swef's steading.

"One of *ours*?" Baluch said. His voice was dark. Shaking. With compassion, or something else?

Acton reached down to help Uen up, but Baluch put out a hand and stopped him.

"If he's one of ours," he said, his voice flat, his hand on his sword hilt, "why was he the one who killed Friede?"

Acton froze and pulled his hand back. Put it on his sword hilt. Uen's heart had started to thump and leap wildly with panic, and memories flooded his mind. Bramble caught at them with determination. She had liked Friede. She wanted to know the truth.

Uen's memory was one of noise and shouting and rushing; rushing through Swef's big, new-smelling hall, its walls barely smoothed. The rushes on the floor made him stumble, he was running so fast and, unlike the men around him, who were just hacking at anyone they met, he was searching for someone. Friede. He was frantic, looking for her, running and dodging because he had no time to fight, he had to find her first, before any of Hawk's men. But he was too late.

She was in the kitchen. She had wedged herself in a corner and was using a stool as a shield and her crutch as a weapon. So many years of hobbling had made her arms strong. There was a man on the ground in front of her, his skull stove in. She was keeping the other two off, but only barely. One man's sword cut into the stool and as he wrenched it back the stool came with it, dragged out of her hand.

"Stop!" Uen said, and leapt toward them, pulling on the men's shoulders with wild hands. "Stop! This one is mine."

They turned in exasperation. "What?"

"My lord Hawk gave her to me. She's mine!"

They sneered at him, dark eyes scornful. "Oh, it's the traitor. Hah! Take her, then, oath breaker." Their backs were toward Friede and she took the opportunity to hit twice more, hard, with full control. They dropped like felled bullocks and Friede and Uen were left staring at each other.

"Traitor?" she said with venom.

"They were going to attack anyway," Uen said, desperate. "This way I got to save you."

She raised her crutch and hit at him, but he pushed it sideways.

"Oath breaker!" she shouted.

"I never took an oath! I'm a thrall, remember!"

She paused, considering, her green eyes cold. "That's true. Good. You'll go to the cold hells, then, not to Swith's Hall." She raised her crutch again deliberately.

"I love you," he said.

"I spit on you," she said, and brought the crutch down.

A scream rose in Uen's throat and he brought his sword around in a great flat circle. He had no skill, but he was very strong from years of physical work. The stroke almost cut her in half. Then he fell on his knees and gathered her into his arms and wept.

Now, in the courtyard, he wept again, the tears a mingling of grief and fear. He held out supplicating hands to Acton. His bladder loosened and urine gushed down his legs, but he barely felt it.

Acton drew his sword in one movement and swung it, much as Uen had swung. As the sword bit into Uen's neck the water rose, but it was blood this time and it was warm, sickeningly warm, so that Bramble wanted to vomit at the touch and at the memory of the cold fury on Acton's face and the thwarted desire on Baluch's. He had wanted to kill Uen himself, but he had waited too long to act. As the blood swamped her she heard Asgarn laughing.

"That's it! Kill 'em all," he said.

UEN'S STORY

I'D DO IT again. Even having to kill her, I'd do it again.

It was sweet to see them go down under the dark-hairs' swords. They weren't expecting anything, and they died like flies. Hah!

By all the gods that are, I am not an oath breaker. What were Swef's people to me? Gaolers. I am, I *was,* a thrall. If the only freedom I could have was death, then I took it with both hands.

Better than thralling. Better than carrying muck and being used as an *ox,* as though I was no better. Better than being yelled at and struck at when I was too slow and never thanked, no matter how hard I tried.

Except by Friede. Oh, and that friend of hers, Wili. But it was Friede who set the example. She was so kind, always.

I didn't expect her to hate me.

But I'd still do it again.

Because Swef was very loud, talking about the new land, the fresh land, the big land that had room for all. But it was too late for my people, wasn't it? Too late for the ones the Ice King had already conquered, who had to go cap in hand to the southerners to beg for living room. My father went. We were a small valley. There weren't enough of us to fight for new land. We kept to ourselves, we did, and that had worked well enough in the bountiful days, but when the King clawed our land away from us we had no allies to turn to.

So my father, who was chieftain, and his brother, who would have been lord of war if we'd fought, went to the Moot and asked for land. But none would give it. And then they asked for honorable service, as oath men to a chieftain. But none would give it. So rather than have their families starve, they agreed to thraldom, until they had worked back their price, which was the price of feeding them and housing them and clothing them, and so would *never* be worked back, not in a thousand generations, but they didn't realize it then because they were not *clever*, like Swef. Not *cunning*, like Swef. Not *evil*.

I was fifteen. I had been the chieftain's son and they made me do women's work. I would have accepted a man's job. I could have been a shepherd, or worked at a trade like smithing. Even being a tanner would have been honorable. But no, I had to feed the pigs their swill and carry chamber pots and scour cooking pans. It was shameful, and I hated them all. Except Friede, because she was kind to me and because her red hair reminded me of home.

My father and my uncle could not stand the shame. They raised their voices and then their hands to their captors and they were punished: the first time a beating, the second time the left hand cut off, the third time death from spearing. "I will keep no insolent servants," Swef said in his pride. My mother killed herself that night and took my two baby sisters with her. Because she was a thrall they would not give them a proper funeral pyre. The wood was too precious, Swef said. They *buried* them, like the carcass of an animal gone off in the summer heat.

That was the moment I decided to kill Swef, if I could, when I could; as the clods of dirt covered my sisters' shrouds and took my mother from my sight.

I said nothing. I did nothing. I worked hard and made him trust me. When the time came to select the staff for the new steading, there was no question but that I would go, too. He thought I was loyal, but I took no oath except the oath to make his death. That oath I kept.

When Hawk sought me out and asked me to lift the bars on the hall door, I was glad. But I made sure Friede would be safe. She would have been safe, too, if only she'd *listened* to me . . .

I only have one regret. I wish that I had let her kill me, because then I would have had a warrior's death. At a woman's hands, I know, but Friede had a heart as strong as any warrior's, and I am sure the men she killed are feasting with Swith in his Hall.

But mostly I wish that the Ice King had been satisfied before he ever ate my home; before our beautiful valley was crushed and ground in his grasp. While I waited for them to drag me out to Acton, I set myself to remember all of it I could, because I am the only one who remembers. All the others are dead, and when I cease to remember, that valley, green and shining and lovely, will vanish altogether. Hawk's people say there is no such thing as Swith's Hall; that we will go onto rebirth if we have lived well. But I would rather not be reborn. I would rather go on remembering; go on keeping my valley alive, until the Ice Giants eat the sun.

LEOF

LEOF WALKED OUT of the hall feeling like he was going into battle. The feeling was the same: the absolute necessity of not showing others how he felt, in order to save lives. In battle, it was the lives of others he held in his hands; the men under his command, who needed him to be calm and disciplined and rational, or they would die. Now, if he showed how he felt, *he* would die. Any officer who desired a warlord's wife knew the penalty was death.

He had to fill his head with warnings because he could still feel Sorn's pulse leap under his fingers and see the flush sweep up her cheeks as he touched her hand. As he had, all unwittingly, looked into her eyes and wanted her.

He had let it happen because he had thought he was in love with Bramble. Without the memories of her—on the roan, at the inn, in bed, absurdly, terrifyingly, high in that pine tree—occupying his mind and making him guilty, he would have considered whether it was wise to spend so much time with his warlord's young wife. He would have noticed her with his mind, instead of with his heart. Would have appreciated the gentle grace of her walk, the firm curve of her smile. And, appreciating, kept his distance, aware of the danger. Gods knew he would have relished the sight of her in any other circumstances; would have smiled and cozened her into bed in a heartbeat if she'd been just another girl.

As it was, he had been blind, and walked into a snare of his own devising. Worse than blind, because he had snared not only himself but her in the net. At least, he thought he had.

She had been brought up as the lady of the fort, which meant that she was trained to hide her feelings; trained to be calm, serene, unflappable. The flush on her cheeks when he had unthinkingly touched her hand could have meant any number of things. Anger at his impudence. Surprise. Warmth at simple human contact. Swith knew she got little of that, especially with her lord away. His touch could have meant nothing to her, or been a petty annoyance. She might not even have realized how he felt. It was over in a moment, after all; how much could she have read in his eyes?

The thought should have been a relief, but instead it wracked him with doubt and the desire to know. To be sure.

He went about the rest of the day doing all his duty plus some extra, like inspecting the smithies, and made sure his work was exemplary. He might betray his lord in his thoughts, but he would never betray him in reality. It was a fine, noble thought, but every time he assured himself, he remembered disobeying Thegan's orders to capture Bramble. He had betrayed his lord for a woman once before . . .

He debated whether to have his supper in his room or in the hall with Sorn. If she had not guessed, if she thought his touch a momentary inattention to etiquette, he could still present an unruffled front and they could continue as they had been, with their dignity unimpaired and loyalty intact.

He walked into the hall and up to the high table and saw immediately, from the paleness of her cheeks and the determined way she tilted her head up to face him, that she had wrestled all day with the same snares as he had, and come to the same conclusion. Underneath the tension and the concern, he realized that he felt a kind of triumph—not as pure as joy, not as simple as happiness. They couldn't possibly have joy or happiness, but still, she felt it too, and something in him exulted.

So he sat down beside her, as always, and greeted her formally, as always, and as always she asked him how the preparations for war were progressing. He told her about the smithies and their output of helmets and swords; she inquired if the fletchers needed more feathers; they discussed killing several of the swans for the feast on Thegan's return and harvesting the feathers.

"I have heard that fletchers like swan feathers," Sorn said, clearly inviting comment not just from him but from the other officers, making the conversation general. She steered the talk between Leof, Gard and Wil on to a discussion of arms and armament and then fell silent, as was fitting for a woman during such talk. Leof carefully did not look at her except when he offered her bread, or salt to season the kid with olives. Carefully, she smiled her thanks and gazed on him and the others impartially. It was a pretense so well devised that he realized she must have been aware for much longer than he had; he wondered how many meals he had shared with her, not knowing that she played this difficult role. How many times had he made it harder for her, unthinkingly blind?

Well, now they would pretend together, and together construct a bulwark against betrayal.

"My lady, would you have more kid?"

"Thank you, my lord, but no. I am satisfied."

A small ironic curve showed in the corner of her mouth and then disappeared so quickly that he wondered if he had truly seen it. Satisfied was the one thing she must not be, and she knew it. He must resist the temptation to increase their intimacy, even by talking together in public.

"The sweetmeats, perhaps, my lady?"

"Just one, I thank you."

So, he thought, no great play of denial. She was alert, too, to the desire for secret signals and to the danger they represented. There must be *no* layers to their talk; no secrets shared; no hidden understanding. What is hidden may be uncovered. What is fed, grows. Sorn was far more in control of this situation than he was. Far more practiced. She had sat through many such meals, he thought, and not just since I arrived. Meals where what she felt and what she showed were completely at odds.

Leof wondered about her childhood. He had heard that her father had been a hard man and for the first time felt that sudden empathy, the quick wrench of the heart which can herald love, not just desire. *No!* he thought, appalled. Not that. But helplessly, although his face showed nothing, as it showed nothing when he led his men into battle, he conned the way the fire slid shadows across her face, the way her eyelids curved when she smiled, the sudden flash of green when her gaze sharpened on a serving maid who flirted too openly with one of the sergeants in the lower hall. He moved away a little so that he could not smell her scent, rising softly from her warmed skin.

"We will need more heavy drays," he said instead to Wil. "But we cannot leave the farmers without a way to harvest, or there will be dearth and death before spring."

They launched into a discussion of the best way of balancing the needs of the warlord and the needs of the land, and Leof was successful, for a time, at ignoring her. Until she rose to bow good night, and the men rose with her and bowed back, and their eyes met—as she met all their eyes, for that was the etiquette, and there must be *nothing*, not even a lack of courtesy, to show that they treated each other differently. But at that moment he saw, behind the calm, behind the courtesy, behind even the hidden desire, fear.

He worried over that glimpse all night. What was she afraid of? Betrayal? Love? Or the thing he did not want to acknowledge . . . was she afraid of Thegan?

Inwardly, he knew she was right to be afraid. Thegan would be unforgiving. No warlord would countenance any hint of infidelity in his wife, the producer of his heirs, even if the woman was innocent. There must be no whisper to taint the rightful inheritance of the Domain. It was only twenty years since the warlord in the Far South Domain, old Elbert, had had his wife garrotted because she danced with another man at the Springtree celebrations. He'd had no trouble getting a second, younger wife, because all the observers had agreed she'd brought it on herself. Though there'd been no children from the second marriage, so maybe the gods thought otherwise.

It came down to inheritance. If Leof cuckolded Thegan—the thought popped into his head unbidden, full of danger and excitement—Leof's sons could inherit the Domain. Which made him wonder why Sorn had not borne children. Thegan had a son—only one, true—and he was an attractive man who had not been celibate since his wife died. Before his marriage to Sorn, he'd had a dozen women that Leof knew of for certain, and no doubt many more. But there were no bastards, none in Cliff Domain, at least, and none that he knew of here. Warlords commonly flaunted their bastards. Not Thegan.

His thoughts turned to Gabra, the son in Cliff Domain who had never had much of his father's love, that Leof had seen. He wondered whose son Gabra might be, and whether Thegan had accepted him unknowingly, cuckolded, or had arranged for his birth. Pimped his wife? No, no, that was not possible. Bramble's warning echoed in his head: Don't trust him. Feverishly, Leof plunged back into memories of Bramble, using her as a preventative against treason. But his memories of her had been leached clean of desire, and they were no use as a defense against desire for Sorn.

Perversely, his lack of desire for Bramble made him readier to believe her warnings. Or was it just easier to think that betrayal was excusable if committed against someone unworthy of his loyalty? He punched his pillow and forced himself to go over the inventory of spears and slingshots in the armory until his thoughts grew quiet and he slept a long time later, then rose in the early light, determined to continue pretending until the pretense was made real.

That morning he supervised the construction of a drying house, on the edge of the fort plateau, just inside the walls. By autumn they would have half a herd slaughtered and the meat drying for winter stews and campaign food. He skipped lunch to oversee the laying of the foundation stones for the new gate in the southern wall. That had to be done right. Any gate was a potential breach in a time of siege and if the foundations weren't strong the fort would be lost.

He approved of all the fortifications Thegan was introducing at Sendat. In Cliff Domain, not only was the warlord's dwelling fortified, but most of the towns. There had been years past, when the Ice King's people had raided, that those towns had been glad indeed that some warlord, sometime, had put time and silver into building proper defenses. So it might be at Sendat. Soon.

BRAMBLE

HEARING CAME BACK first, but it was dulled. Bramble strained to make out the sound of voices. Then sight returned, but the light was dim. She could see candle flames flickering, or was it oil lamps? There were a dozen of them in a small room, but still her eyes saw vaguely. Everything seemed fogged. But she was seeing through a man's eyes, that was certain.

The man blinked several times and made an effort to see and suddenly everything came clear, although she could feel the strength he was using to pay attention. Only the body lay open to her: she could barely feel this mind. It was opaque, shut off. Not from her, she didn't think. This was a mind which habitually guarded its thoughts. She tried to get a sense of what he was thinking, or feeling, and was disoriented. He thought in intricate layers, convoluted and intertwined, like the threads in a complex weaving. Thoughts linked to other thoughts in endless speculation. She could make no sense of it, catch not even one clear emotion. This mind was alien to her in a way none of the others had been, not even the goat girl on the mountain. This mind was old, and it schemed.

"Oddi," a voice said respectfully. His gaze sharpened on the speaker—Asgarn, his wiry hair catching the light from the candles and seeming fairer than ever. "Are you ready, Oddi?"

Oddi, Bramble thought. That was the name of the old man at the Moot, the one who held the Mootstaff, the one who had made Acton into the lord of war. He had been much stronger then. Age had caught up with him.

Oddi nodded, and Bramble could hear the bones of his neck creaking. Very old. But he still held the power in the room.

She wondered about him. He had let Acton make his speech at the Moot. He had made Acton lord of war. But now, as Acton stepped forward to bend one knee in front of him, she sensed no affection in him;

no softness. Whatever he had done for Acton, he had done for reasons of policy.

"Acton," Oddi said, his voice clear but not loud. "You have served this council well as our lord of war. You have avenged the deaths of our people and secured this territory for our people."

Agreement rose in chorus. "Well done," "Aye, that's so," "A great lord of war!" Bramble realized that the shadows held a big group of men. Chieftains? she wondered. The same men who were meeting in Asgarn's hall when Baluch saw Hawk's attack?

"We are in your debt," Oddi went on. "To pay this debt, we are minded to grant you this steading for your own, to hold as chieftain in your own right."

Astonishingly, Acton was shaking his head. He sprang to his feet and moved back a space so he could look down at Oddi. "I thank the council, but this is not my desire."

A murmur of surprise went around the room.

Oddi frowned, but didn't seem entirely surprised. "You reject this gift?"

"I mean no disrespect, but the steading cannot be mine. There is someone who has a better right."

Oddi spread his hands. "Swef is dead, and you were his heir. Surely his steading falls to you, by both right of inheritance and right of conquest?"

Acton shook his head. "There is still one alive who should have precedence. Wili."

A buzz rose from the men, half-angry, half-astonished. "A *woman*?"

"Swef's niece. If he had not adopted me, she would have inherited his steading. Has she not the right to keep it? And if we speak of the rights of conquest, the lord of this steading died by her hand, not mine. Has she not earned it?"

There was silence, as Oddi calculated. He exchanged glances with Asgarn, who looked thoughtful. They nodded at each other, pleased in some obscure way Bramble couldn't fathom.

"Is there dissent?" Oddi asked. Although the men shifted uncomfortably, no one spoke.

"Very well," he concluded. "If Wili was Swef's heir, he would have found her a husband to run the steading for her. This council will do as much. We will consider who best might be chosen." Again he exchanged glances with Asgarn. Hah! Bramble thought. They'd better ask Wili first. She's been through too much to put up with being parceled off like a prize heifer.

As though catching the thought, Acton spoke. "I think, honored counselors, that you had best consult Wili about that. She is no untried girl, to do as she is told just because a man tells her to."

A stir went through the room as the men realized what he meant. What Wili had suffered.

"True," Asgarn said. "She has earned the right to choose her husband."

You're sure she'll pick you, aren't you, you arrogant bastard? Bramble thought. But only if she doesn't have Acton around to compare you to.

Oddi looked at the two of them, now standing side-by-side, both tall, both blond, both strong. He pursed his lips, as though wondering which of them Wili might choose.

"There is still the matter of our debt to you," he said to Acton. "Is there something you desire?"

Acton nodded, for once intense and serious. "There is."

"Tell us."

"The river outside this steading leads to the sea. To the only port in this land. T'vit, they call it. Along the coast there are only cliffs. T'vit is the one harbor."

"And so?"

"In the bright days, before the Ice King came, we were a prosperous people. Our prosperity came from the sea. From trading." There were noises of agreement from the men listening. "If we are to be prosperous again, we need a port. If you wish to reward me, give me T'vit."

Oddi sat back in his chair, astonished—and surprised at being astonished. That emotion Bramble could read clearly. Oddi was rarely surprised; he was used to being several steps ahead of anyone else. "T'vit . . ." he said softly.

"Two boats of men," Acton said eagerly. "Give me boat builders and two crews and next summer I will take them down the river and secure us the port. Then our boats can take the dragon's road as they used to. To the Wind Cities and further."

The audience of chieftains liked that idea. "Bold thinking!" one said approvingly. "Trust Acton to see the way clear!"

Oddi looked at Asgarn. Asgarn was smiling, and so was Oddi. What were they scheming? Try as Bramble might, she could not read Oddi's thoughts. Acton, the big idiot, didn't even notice. She could have hit him.

"It is a good request, and a fitting reward. But if you are to take this port for our people, Acton, you must take it as our lord of war."

Acton nodded, although Asgarn shot Oddi a look of astonishment and chagrin. Oddi smiled sourly at him. So, Bramble thought, Asgarn isn't entirely in his confidence.

"Thus you will act with our authority, and what you annex will be ours to administer," Oddi added.

Light dawned on Asgarn's face, and he began to smile. He turned it into a smile of congratulations for Acton, but Bramble was not fooled. Nor was Acton.

"But I will be given T'vit, if I take it? That will be my reward?" he insisted.

Oddi looked around the room, checking with the other chieftains. The dark figures nodded, one by one. "T'vit itself will be yours. This is our oath."

Acton smiled widely. "I will take it for you. That is mine."

This time the sea came to reclaim Bramble; she even smelt its saltiness and heard the slap of waves on a beach, before the waves rolled her away into deeper water.

Her hands were busy, cutting up onions. She could smell the sharp tang and her eyes were stinging. The hands belonged to a woman, and they were familiar. Wili. Bramble relaxed a little. Wili's was a good mind to be in.

"They want to marry me off to Asgarn," Wili said, and glanced over her shoulder to where Acton was perched on a stool, honing his dagger on a small whetstone.

"Oddi?" he asked. Wili nodded. "What have you said to him?"

"That I am not ready for marriage."

He grinned, his blue eyes shining. "How did he take that?"

"He grumbled. But he can't actually *force* me." She paused, looking at the knife. "Can he?" Bramble could feel the fear rise up in her, scalding.

Acton shook his head. "Not while I'm around," he said comfortably.

She relaxed immediately, as though his word was solid rock to lean on. "How are the boats coming along?" she asked.

Acton's face lit up. "They'll be finished by spring, I think. We're having some trouble getting pitch, but Baluch has heard there's a natural source by a lake somewhere to the east. He's leaving tomorrow to see if we can trade for it with the lake people. Once we have that, we will be ready."

"More people will die," she said, not looking at him as she said it, then glancing over.

"Those who die in battle go to feast with Swith the Strong," he said. "I feel no sorrow for them. We all die. To give a good death to another warrior is a boon."

He looked up and met her eyes and Bramble could see that he meant it.

"What about the ones who aren't warriors? What about the women? The children?"

"I will try, Wili," he said softly. "I will try to protect them."

"Hmph. Try hard," she said.

Bramble wanted to hear his response, but the waters were a solid slap in the face, knocking her backward into darkness.

The waters were rushing over her, around her—no, under her filling her with the sound. Water splashed in her face and she shook it out of her eyes and held on tight to . . . to what?

"Yeayyyy!" the man whooped as the floor fell out from under him and he crashed down, then pulled himself upright again by the prow of a boat. They were in a boat, and she was with Baluch, unmistakable from the blare of horns in his head, the beating of drums that rose every time the boat shifted. He clung to the high, carved prow and peered ahead, one arm above his head. He moved his arm as he saw rocks approaching and the boat turned to avoid them. Bramble realized he must be signaling to the steersman.

It was a frantic race through white water, boulders rising up out of the fast-flowing river like demons, ready to rip out the bottom of the wooden boat. Bramble couldn't help thinking that the reed boats of the Lake People would be much better suited to this river, riding high on the water as they did. This boat dragged too much; had too much of its keel under the surface, where rocks could, and did, grab at it.

On either side of the river, forest crowded the banks, a lush summer green, with ferns and wild roses and blackberries spilling over the banks to dip leaves in the stream. They poured down the river as fast as the current itself. Plummeting down small cascades, swinging the boat wildly around to avoid being smashed to pieces, scraping along ambushing rocks, wind in Baluch's face, water splashing in his eyes, bouncing and rocking and jumping over the lip of the rapids like a runaway horse. It was wonderful—the best thing that had happened so far.

Baluch laughed and whooped as they went, and behind him she could hear Acton doing the same. Baluch cast one quick look back and they exchanged glances, eyes bright with shared laughter and a kind of joy. Risk, Bramble thought. They love it; and so do I.

It was over too soon. The boat tilted over the lip of the last of the rocks and swung wide into a shingled pool formed by a beaver dam. The stumps of the narrow birches they had felled to make the dam surrounded the pool, and further back there was real forest; birch and beech and oak and alder, rowan and one large, dark holly tree on the very edge.

Acton called out, "Beach her here, boys," and the men, about twenty of them, four to a bench, dipped their oars in the water and rowed the boat to shore, driving it up onto the shingle with one last huge thrust. They scrambled out with some relief. One man, a tall redhead with a slight squint in one eye, grumbled all the way.

"No life for a warrior," he said to a shorter blond man with very broad shoulders. "I want to die with a sword in my hand, not an oar."

The man clapped him on the back and the red-head smiled at him involuntarily, as one smiles at a very old and beloved friend.

"There'll be swords enough even for you soon, Red," Acton called across to him and grinned. "They won't give up the port without a fight."

Red smiled sourly and pointedly took off his jerkin and squeezed a stream of water out of it into the pool. The men laughed.

A moment later a second boat arrived, a little more slowly. Asgarn stood at the prow. He raised a hand in greeting and the boat came to land next to Acton's.

His men dragged the boat up the shingle and Asgarn leapt off. He didn't look like he'd enjoyed the trip much. "We can rest here, then. Good," he said.

Baluch left them to unpack food and wandered upstream, to a point above the beaver dam where the forest met the stream. He stayed, looking into the shadowed green, his mind making music with flute and pipe, a wistful, calling music that brought an ache up under his breastbone.

Acton joined him and sat on a rock at the edge of the stream, jutting out over the rushing water. "I still can't get used to it," he said, looking at the dense forest. "So many trees!"

Baluch nodded. "It's a rich land. The forest stretches all the way to the Lake."

"You'll have to take me there, one day," Acton said comfortably.

Baluch bit his lip. "Once you have T'vit, I'll be going again," he said.

"Going where?"

"Back to the Lake."

Acton stood up and faced him. "Something happened there, didn't it?" His face lit with a teasing smile. "Did you fall in love with one of the Lake girls?"

Baluch ducked his head. Bramble thought he was embarrassed, but his heart was beating in its normal pattern. There were memories moving in his mind, just under thought, but she couldn't catch them.

"Not with one of the girls." He paused, as though searching for the right words. "Something . . . calls me. Even now, I can hear it. Like music, or a whisper in the night. The Lake calls me. I have to go back."

Acton frowned. "Not by yourself," he said. "Come on the first trip to the Wind Cities with me, and when I get back I'll go with you." Baluch made a face, and Acton punched him lightly on the shoulder. "You can't trust strange women who whisper to you in the night, lad. You need your uncle Acton to look after you and protect you from hussies and enchantresses."

Baluch smiled at that. "You just want some for yourself!" he said. They laughed.

"Come with me to the Wind Cities, Bal," Acton said, almost wheedling. "Then I'll go with you to your lake."

Baluch sighed. Bramble could hear the music in his head grow fainter, as though he had turned his thoughts away from it, but it didn't entirely fade. "All right," he said. "I suppose someone has to look after you, too."

They went back to the others and ate smoked trout and pickled onions and brown bread. Two of the men had a belching contest. The red-head's friend, whose named turned out to be Geb, won.

"Should have bet on me, Red," he said, laughing, as the red-head handed coins over to one of the others.

Red grinned and nodded. "Should have known you were full of hot air, you mean," he retorted.

The men laughed and joked as they packed their supplies away and launched the boats again. Acton and Baluch watched them from the bank, chuckling, as Red tried to duck Geb in the river. Geb pushed him away, mock-scowling. Red hoisted himself into the boat and held a hand out to Geb.

"Oh, no!" Geb said, standing alone in the stream, thigh-deep, half-laughing. "You'll let me get halfway up, then you'll let go."

Red shook his head. "No, I won't. Truly."

"Get moving," Asgarn called impatiently from the other boat.

Geb took Red's hand and began to pull himself up. Sure enough, halfway up he fell back into the water. The others laughed, but Red shouted, "Geb!" and grabbed for him, pulling on his shoulders. Then

Geb started screaming—a high, disbelieving scream like a child in a nightmare.

There was blood in the water. Water sprite, Bramble thought, they're probably in every major stream in this time.

"Pull him up, pull him up!" Red shouted, and the other men rushed to grab Geb's shoulders and haul.

Acton stood to jump into the water, but Baluch held him back. The music in his head was warning, now, harsh and clamorous, full of fear. "No," he said. "There's something down there."

The men pulled, and pulled again, and suddenly Geb came free of the water. Something was clinging to his legs, but as they watched the water sprite dissolved into air, like mist, like fog dissipated by wind. It cried as it went, a thin, mournful cry that set the hairs up on the back of Baluch's neck.

Geb was bleeding hard, the big veins in his legs pumping the life out of him. Red cradled him, trying to put pressure on the worst wound, but there was no hope. Geb gripped Red's jacket and said, "Meli . . ."

"I'll look after her," Red promised. Geb nodded feebly, once, and died.

Acton and Baluch climbed into the boat from the shingle, careful not to let their feet get in the water. Red looked up at Acton with accusing eyes. Wild eyes, full of grief.

"You didn't even try to help," he said. Then he bent his head over Geb's body and began to weep. Acton stared at him, his mouth grim. Bramble thought he looked older, that the lines in his cheeks showed more clearly than they had a few moments ago.

"Come with me, Baluch, Den, Odda. We'll gather wood in the forest for his pyre," he said. He leaped from the boat as though glad to leave it behind. The others followed him. One splashed in the shallows as he landed and stumbled, terrified, up the shingle, almost crawling in his haste to get away from the water.

"This land is cursed!" Red said.

Baluch made the sign to avert evil and moved closer to Red. "Acton tried to help. I stopped him."

Red glared at him. "No one stops him doing what he really wants to do."

Bramble thought that was a fair comment. No one stopped Acton. Baluch turned away to follow Acton.

Red raised his voice. "When we go on, I'm thinking I'll be in Asgarn's boat."

Baluch paused. He didn't turn around, but he nodded, then jumped for the shore. In the middle of the jump, in midair, the waters came sideways and swept Bramble away in a flurry of foam and bubbles.

She was playing a drum in a simple, repetitive rhythm. In her head, another rhythm echoed and flicked in counterpoint. It has to be Baluch, Bramble thought. Coming back to Baluch at least had the virtue of familiarity; she could relax a little, read his thoughts a little. He clung to the prow with one hand and beat the drum with the other.

He began to whistle, and with the sound her vision cleared and she saw that they were on the river and his drumbeat was keeping the oarsmen in time. The river was calmer here than in the rapids, but its surface was deceptive—the boat was traveling very fast. They were rowing because the river was about to join another big stream and they would need to make their way against the crosscurrents and eddies that the confluence created.

Between the two rivers was a sheer clay bluff that came to a ragged point with a tiny beach where several small round boats were tied down. Baluch looked up and Bramble could see a village on top of the bluff; smoke came from drying racks with rows of fish tied to them; some laundry was spread out on bushes to dry.

The bluff was lined with women watching, children crowded between their mothers' legs to peer over at the strangers. Baluch waved to them and a couple of the children waved back. Then the men appeared. Some had slingshots; others carried head-sized rocks.

"Row!" Acton called. "Head for the bank!"

They bent their backs to the oar as Baluch increased the speed of the drumbeat, marking the time strongly. The boat seemed to pause and then leap away from the village toward the near bank. But stones were raining down on them already. One from a slingshot, about the size of a fist, hit Baluch in the shoulder and spun him around onto the deck. It knocked the wind out of him and for a moment all Bramble could see was the rough-finished boards of the hull, all she could think about was the aching desire to breathe... then he gasped and dragged a breath in and hoisted himself up.

The large rocks were mostly falling short but one had caved a hole in the side of the boat, just above the waterline. Several men were bleeding from the ears or nose. One nursed a broken hand. It was clear that the slingshotters could send their stones right to the bank—there was no safety there.

"Back!" Acton called. "Backwater!"

The unharmed men reversed themselves on the bench and spun their oars around. Baluch sprang down to a bench to replace an injured man and they rowed strongly until they were out of range. The men on the bluff shook their fists in the air and cheered. Their women hugged and kissed them. Bramble wanted to cheer with them. No one ever told this story, did they? About the ones who fought back. Oh, no, the stories were all about massacres, not about brave villagers who repulsed the invaders.

Asgarn's boat, following theirs, was keeping still in the water, rowing against the current just enough to let Acton come level.

"We need to find a place upriver to come ashore," Acton called to him. Asgarn nodded and ordered his men to reverse oars, then they rowed hard until they came to a sand beach on the far bank of the river.

Careful not to put their feet in the water, they lifted the wounded off the boat and tended them. One man had been hit in the head. There was no split in his skin and he said he was fine, but a few minutes after he sat down on a rock he began to bleed from the nose, and a moment after that he was dead.

Acton looked at his body with tight lips. Baluch's mind was full of mourning music, low and solemn.

"Elric," he said. "He was named for my father."

Looking down at the man, Bramble recognized in his features one of the boys who had played with Baluch and Acton the first time she had come into Baluch's mind. She remembered him, too, as one of the boys who had showed off, trying to attract Acton's attention.

"We would have done them no harm," Acton said angrily.

"They didn't know that," Baluch said. "We're strangers. Maybe they've heard some story about what happened to Hawk and his people."

Acton was stone-faced. Asgarn put his hand on Acton's shoulder.

"We have to take the village," he said, "or we can forget about getting to T'vit."

"Yes," Acton said. "Tonight."

"Night?"

"Oh, yes. They won't expect it. We land upstream of them and go in, hidden by darkness. We make noise. We threaten. We let them leave, if they want to."

"What if they don't?" Asgarn said, loud enough for the others to hear.

"Then we kill them all!" Red exclaimed, and the men cheered.

Acton took a breath, and then let it out. Baluch, even Baluch, was nodding.

"They challenged us," he said. "They killed first. There are consequences to murder."

"The women and children will not be harmed —" Acton began.

"Unless they fight," Asgarn concluded. The men nodded.

"Unless they fight," Acton conceded.

Bramble really didn't want to be present for the raid on the village. But the gods decided otherwise. She waited with Baluch, feeling his heart beating faster, in the darkness outside the village, until everyone was in bed except the single lookout. She watched Asgarn slit the lookout's throat. She crept with Baluch and the other men until they had surrounded the quiet houses and, as Acton nodded, she felt Baluch's throat contract and release in an unearthly, high-pitched scream. In an instant, all the men were screaming, a terrifying ululation that sounded completely inhuman.

In the houses, there were shouts and cries and clangs as people tumbled from beds and peered out of windows and doors. Acton raised a hand and the men stopped screaming.

"People of this village," Acton said, in the language he had learned from Gris. "You have killed one of my men, and for that your punishment is death."

The cries rose again but now they were human voices, Acton's men cheering, villagers protesting.

"But I am merciful," Acton shouted over the top of them, and they fell silent. "If you choose to leave this place forever, taking with you whatever you can carry, I will let you live."

"Never! We'll never leave!" an old woman's voice shouted back. "This is our place, you thieving bastards!"

There were shouts of agreement from men and women both.

"I will even let your women and children go before this battle, if you refuse to leave."

"We'll stay!" a younger woman's voice came. "We'll fight by our men and we'll see your souls to hell!"

Baluch stood close by Acton, as if worried about him.

"Well, Wili, I tried," Acton muttered. He turned to Baluch. "You'll tell her I tried, Bal?"

Baluch nodded. "They've chosen death. It's their right."

That seemed to comfort Acton, which annoyed Bramble. He was about to kill a whole village, and he wanted to feel good about it, to feel good that he had given them a choice between losing everything they had, everything they'd worked for, and dying. He had no idea what he was asking! She was angry again, and she welcomed the anger, because it strengthened her against what she knew was coming.

"For Elric!" Acton cried aloud, and his men echoed the cry as they rushed forward.

There had been men with torches hidden in the undergrowth. Now they threw the torches onto the thatch of the roofs and the houses came alight with a whoosh of air, the sudden heat on their faces, sudden light almost blinding them. The village men came out of the houses waving slingshots, with hatchets, with spears, with staves, but without a sword between them. The women came behind them with anything they could find, from a cooking pot to a kitchen knife. Some of them had babies tied to them with shawls. The children followed them, with little knives, with small slingshots, with bits of wood snatched from the kindling. "For the River Bluff!" they cried as they attacked.

They fought fiercely, children included, but they had no hope. There was a lot of blood, and Baluch spilled his fair share of it, including a young boy who came at him with a knife. He swiped him away with the flat of his sword, but Bramble heard the boy's neck crack. Baluch paused for a second, but the rapture of battle overtook both him and Acton and he charged villager after villager with real enjoyment, part of him relishing the image of fire against the dark sky, of sparks flying upward, of flames glinting on raised swords, of the rushing river encircling them with constant music.

Bramble fought against being caught up in the surge of emotion, but it was hard, so hard, to stay separate when Baluch's mind was so close to hers. She pulled herself as far back as she could and made herself think of other things; and then she thought that someone should stand as witness to the slaughter, for the children if for no one else, so she made herself watch it all, and feel it all, the exhilaration and the horror mingling in her until she couldn't split them apart, until it felt that she was drowning in fire and blood.

Was this what it had been like in Carlion, when Maryrose and Merrick had been slaughtered? Had the ghosts felt the same combination of excitement and repulsion? Or were they simply glad to kill?

She wished she could weep.

When the villagers were all dead and the fires had begun to burn down into the stone foundations of the houses, Acton called them together to count their losses. There were none. They whooped and slapped each other's backs and cheered for Acton a few times.

A couple of them went off to look for drink in the sheds which they claimed they had carefully *not* set fire to, because sheds were usually where the beer was brewed. This raised a laugh and a cheer. Baluch was exhausted. He slumped on a bench under an elm tree, incongruously untouched, as though ready for a picnic.

"Women and children," Acton growled to him. "Such great warriors we are."

"Their choice," Baluch said, his voice flat, his mind suddenly replaying the moment when he had killed the boy. All music emptied out of him and he hung his head between his knees, fighting nausea. Bramble felt a sour satisfaction, all the more so because there had been moments when she had been too involved with Baluch, had shared too closely with his pleasure as his sword had swung cleanly, had killed efficiently.

Baluch sat up, leaned his head back against the elm and closed his eyes.

"We're not going to do it this way when we get to T'vit," Acton said.

Bramble deeply wanted to hear him say it, wanted him to reject the warrior creed that he had lived his life by. She was surprised by the depth of her desire, the strength with which she silently urged him to put an end to the killing. Perhaps, just perhaps, he was changing . . .

"I don't want any of the houses lost," he said. "No fires. We're going to need the houses and boatsheds, and the boats, too. Tell the others. Kill the men, leave the houses alone."

She should have known. She hated him more in that moment than she had ever hated any warlord or warlord's man. He was as bad as she had always known. She felt as though her chest was being sawn open with a blunt knife. Why should it hurt her so much? She had always known what he was.

Baluch kept his eyes closed as though he didn't want to look at Acton's face. "And the women and children?"

Acton paused. "We'll give them the choice. Then it's up to them."

Bramble could have cried with thankfulness when the waters rose, gently, to carry her away in a deep and silent current.

The current washed her up, again in Baluch's mind, looking at another village by daylight, a whole, undamaged village of about twelve houses lying in a flat bend of the river, untouched, calm, perfect. Except that there were no people.

Acton and Baluch and Asgarn waited while the men went into the houses and searched. One by one, they came out and spread their hands.

"No one. Nothing," Red said. "They're all gone."

Asgarn laughed heartily. "They must have heard about River Bluff," he said.

The men began to smile, and then to laugh, too. "They've heard about our lord of war!" one said. "Acton the invincible!"

Acton smiled reluctantly and Baluch grinned.

"Let's hope they take the news to T'vit," Acton said. "I wouldn't mind taking the port this way!"

His men decided that was the funniest thing they had ever heard. Maybe it was relief at not having to fight. Maybe it was disappointment. But they collapsed in laughter while Acton and Baluch watched, smiling.

Except Asgarn. He smiled, but his eyes were cold.

As cold as the water that came down upon Bramble in a deluge.

ASH

Animal throats could not talk, but ears could listen, and human minds could understand. Ash kept his counsel about the songs he needed until he could talk with his father in daylight, man to man, but he could at least start Flax on the road he needed to walk. He moved back from his father and pulled Flax forward.

"This is Flax, whose father Gorham was raised by his mother and never brought to the Deep. Will you teach him what he needs to know?" He hesitated, but it had to be said, or Flax would not be accepted. "He is a singer."

The men nodded. Two of them, a deer with wide antlers and a squirrel, whose head looked odd on his large body, came forward and started to strip Flax's clothes off. He exclaimed and looked for help to Ash. Ash grinned at him. He had already started to undress.

"In the Deep, we show our true shapes." That was true in a way that Flax wasn't ready for yet. But he would be, one day soon.

The badger, his father Rowan in his true guise, put a hand on Ash's arm and led him forward to the cave—or rather, to the caves. The fire cave was only the first in a long series. It was open to all whose blood calmed the waters. Year after year, the boys were taken further in, further down, into the Deep. Ash had been told that before Acton came, each year would add a new scar to the boy's body until he was marked formally as a man. But not now.

"Travelers must travel unnoticed. Scars show, sooner or later, and lead to questions. There must be no questions about the Deep," he had been told.

In the old days, men wore the masks of their animal in the ceremonies, once it had been revealed to them by the water. But since Acton came, the River had granted them their true shapes, to be and then wear inside, afterward.

"This is the River's gift. This is how Traveler men stay men," his grandfather had told him, in the first year. "The fair-haired ones look at us with scornful eyes, and a man might come, in time, to believe that he is worthy of scorn. But *we* know that what they see is not what we truly are. The man who knows what he truly is, and accepts it, cannot be diminished by another's gaze. This is the River's gift: when they look at you with hate and disdain, you will think, 'You do not know me; you know nothing.' Then, though you look at the ground, pretending humility to prevent a beating, you will not feel humbled in your heart, because you know who you are."

Ash had always felt that it was a great gift, even though, when he went to Turvite, he had forced himself to banish even a stray thought about the Deep. It had been pure superstition; he was afraid then, that he would never return, that he had been cast out of the society of Travelers, forced to Settle, because there was no place for him on the Road. He was afraid that the River would reject him if he had tried to come here without his father.

He was still afraid of that, but there were more important things than his fear. He watched his father who had joined in the testing of the new boy. The demon forms prowled around Flax, growling softly, reaching out hands curled like claws to touch his face, to poke his side, to scratch.

"If you hold still and show no fear, you won't be harmed," Ash said quietly. It was what he had been told by his grandfather, who had met him and his father here the year before the old man died—the first year that Ash came and had been tested as Flax was being tested now. He believed it was true, but the demons chuckled to themselves disquietingly. Ash wondered what happened to the boys who broke and tried to run.

This was only the first test, but it lasted until dawn, until Flax was swaying with tiredness and fear had passed out of him because he was too exhausted to feel it. As the dawn broke somewhere outside the canyon, the sky lit with rose and orange glory and the demons lifted their heads and howled, a long ululation, then turned as one and jogged inside the big cave.

Ash came over to Flax and supported him to a seat on a flat rock. He brought water in a curved shell from a tiny stream flowing between two boulders, and held it so Flax could drink.

"W-why . . . ?" Flax stuttered.

"That was the first test," Ash said. "There'll be others."

"Demons. One of them was your father?"

Ash nodded. "You'll meet him soon."

"That's why he'll know the right songs? Because he's a demon?"

"Ah, no, not exactly."

"You could have warned me!" With his legs no longer wobbling and his thirst slaked, Flax had found enough energy to be angry.

"No, I couldn't," Ash said. "I'd sworn secrecy. I *did* warn you it was dangerous."

"Yes, but . . . *real* demons."

Ash laughed. "Oh, they're not so bad when you get to know them!" It hadn't occurred to him that Flax would think he was demon-spawned, that he wouldn't immediately understand who the badger-headed figure really was. He couldn't resist letting him continue to think it. The misunderstanding wouldn't be for long, anyway. He collected his and Flax's clothes and they dressed, glad to escape the chill.

Flax rummaged in their bags for something to eat, but Ash moved away, waiting for the sun to come up over the lip of the canyon wall. He knelt by the stream, trailing one hand in the cold water, and wondered what was happening up north, with Bramble and the others. He missed Martine. Oakmere was a long way north of where his ancestors had lived—there were no Traveler songs about it, and right now he was glad. He was sick of songs. Heartsick.

He had held them inside all his life, although again and again they had almost burst his chest with the pressure to sing. But he had never sung, because of the look on his parents' faces whenever he tried. Now he knew that he had sung with the voice of the dead, and his parents' reaction was understandable. But then, when he had been three and four and five years old, all he had known was that his voice was so horrible that even his father could not bear to listen. Yet his father had taught him the songs. Taught the music, on the flute and drum. Taught the lyrics, and heard Ash recite them all until he was word perfect.

All. That was the point—that had *been* the point—that he had learned all that his father had to teach. That his father had entrusted the songs to him, so that someday he could teach someone else . . . his own son, his own daughter...and the songs would continue, as they had continued for more than a thousand years. All of them. If his father had not given him all the songs, then none of them was worth anything.

None.

He wished he could wipe his memory clean of every song he had ever known.

The breeze carried the sounds of the Deep with it; birds, beetles, small animals in the carpet of leaves, and the Hidden River rushing through its banks. He found the Deep disturbing, always, but the sounds of life lifted his spirits. Perhaps—perhaps his father did not *know* the songs Safred was talking about. A small sound came from behind him, a foot on pebble, and he swung around, drawing his knife as he turned.

The men were coming out of the cave, still naked but with their own faces returned to them. Ash stowed his knife hurriedly. His father came first, smiling broadly, and embraced him.

"Ash! You made it!"

Ash knew he should have left his clothes where they were, but embracing his father while they were both naked always felt bizarre, and he'd rather have to strip off again later than experience that oddity.

Flax was looking from one face to another, one body to another, and coming to a conclusion.

"They're *not* demons?" he asked Ash, outraged.

"Only at night." Rowan laughed. "When the River gives us our true faces."

Flax opened his mouth to complain, but Ash forestalled him. "We have more important things to talk about." He looked around the circle of faces he knew so well. Friends, an uncle of his mother's, his father...They looked at him with welcoming eyes, but would they still look like that after he had demanded to be taught the secret songs? Or would he be cast out, never to return? Would he lose his place in the world all over again? His heart beat faster, but he had to speak.

"There are things happening in the world outside which you must know about," he said. "And there is a thing I must ask from you."

MARTINE

CAEL'S WOUND WASN'T healing. It wasn't getting any worse, and his fever was low, but it was constant. He was losing weight. Zel and Martine had to search further in the Forest to find feverfew and comfrey.

"You have to come out to the island," Safred said at breakfast. "I'm sure I could heal you at the altar."

Cael looked at the lake with loathing. "I'm all right. I'll last until we get out of the Forest."

"You look tired," Zel ventured.

"I'm sleeping fine. Slept like the dead last night. Every night since we've been here." He sounded faintly surprised.

Safred looked thoughtful. "So have I," she said. "What about you two?"

Martine didn't look at Zel. "I had trouble getting to sleep last night," she said truthfully, "but then I slept soundly."

"Me, too," Zel said.

"Maybe there's something in the air," Safred said.

Something from the gods, Martine thought. Or the fire, safeguarding us. She was warmed by the thought that even in his rage he hadn't lifted that protection. Bramble began to move, twisting from side to side as though in pain. Martine bent over her and smoothed her hair. She tried to give Bramble water, but her mouth stayed firmly closed.

"It doesn't matter if you're sleeping," Safred said sternly to Cael. "You have to be healed. Come to the altar."

He looked resigned. "All right."

"Safred," Martine said, "I don't think the gods want you to."

From the center of the black altar, mist was rising. There had been fog on the water when they woke at dawn, but it had disappeared when the sun hit it. Now, at noon, in full warm sun, mist was pouring off the altar and spreading outward, across the lake, toward them, as it had the first night, when they had taken Bramble to the altar.

"Dung and pissmire!" Zel said.

"I don't think now is a good time to go out there, niece," Cael said. But the mist didn't react to this retreat.

"Sit down around Bramble and hold hands!" Martine ordered. Zel grabbed her hand and Safred's and they formed a circle, Cael between Safred and Martine, Bramble in the middle, lying silently, frowning a little. Cael's hand *was* too hot, Martine thought. Then the mist rolled over them and they could see nothing.

BRAMBLE

For once, sight came back first. Bright light, sun shining, reflecting off water—water moving, shifting, breaking in brilliance. The sea, Bramble realized. The eyes she looked through were straining to see out past the breaking waves to where a boat with a square sail was making for the narrow harbor entrance. Cliffs reared up on either side, sheer and menacing, making a hazardous corridor to the open ocean. On the left-hand cliff, the northern side, were men, pushing large rocks toward the edge. If the rocks fell as the boat was making its way through the corridor, it would be smashed.

She saw through a woman's eyes. Her hand was at her throat and her heart beat fast, as though she were mortally afraid. She jiggled a baby on her left hip without looking at it. The baby chortled and patted her face with a soft hand, but although Bramble could clearly feel the touch, the woman seemed unaware of it. Out of the corner of her eyes, Bramble could see other people watching the boat's progress. Dark-haired people. After so long spent among the tall, burly men of Acton's world, they seemed small to her.

The men on the cliffs had hair that shone bright gold in the sunlight. They were big, too, and strong. Although the rocks had clearly been piled up ready for any attempted invasion from the sea, they were still a fair way away from the edge, and these men trundled them across the uneven ground with ease. Bramble could see that their hair was in plaits. Acton's men.

This must be Turvite. The battle for Turvite had been fought outside the town, up on the hills that surrounded the city, the stories said, because the men of Turvite wanted to have the advantage of the high ground. The elevation hadn't helped them: they'd all been killed.

Bramble could just imagine Acton laughing as he swung his sword, shouting "Kill them all!" There he was, himself, unmistakable, standing tall on the cliff edge, shouting down to someone in the boat. There was a woman on the boat who was shouting up. Bramble couldn't be sure why, but there was something about the way she stood and her long white hair that made her think of Dotta. Then Acton motioned his men back from the cliff's edge and gestured to the boat—you can leave, the gesture said. Take the open sea. The old woman waved her thanks.

The woman with the baby gasped and began to cry. There was a mixture of joy and sorrow swirling inside her that Bramble found difficult to experience. This was a woman who felt intensely, far more so than Ragni, or the girl in the meadow. Baluch turned all his feelings into music, and somehow that contained them; Gris had kept control of his through long practice. But this woman had almost no control at all, and it was dizzying.

Next to her, another woman, older, turned and put an arm across her shoulders. "Now, now, Piper," she scolded gently. "He's safe now. They've let the boat go."

"I'll never see him again, Snapper!" Piper wept.

"Better that than seeing him as a corpse," Snapper replied. "At least you know he's safe. Him and the other young ones. You've still got this little lady, Searose, to look after, remember. That tall one with the golden hair said we had until sunset to bury our dead and get out of the town. Lucky to get that much time, I reckon." She put her hands out to the baby and the baby launched herself happily into her arms.

"Your son is safe on the boat," Snapper said. "Time to deal with the dead."

That quietened Piper, which Bramble was glad of—and then realized that preferring to deal with dead bodies rather than living emotions showed how many dead bodies she'd seen lately. She was getting used to it. She wondered how much more used to it Acton's men were. After all, she merely dipped into their lives, while they kept fighting when she was not observing. Perhaps they were so used to it that death didn't even mark them anymore. Perhaps they just didn't notice it. Was that true of Acton?

That was a disquieting thought, and she pushed it away and made herself concentrate on Piper as she and the crowd of women who had watched the boat leave walked slowly away from the harbor, up the hill which cupped Turvite. This wasn't the place of Bramble's imaginings.

Where was the great and glorious city of Acton's triumph? The songs all talked about Turvite's magnificence—except that really old one, that just talked about the ghosts. There was no magnificence here. Turvite was barely more than a village. Bigger than her home village of Wooding, admittedly, but not by much, and different from it mainly in the number of trees that grew among the houses.

Down by the harbor there were no docks. The boats—small fishing smacks with a single mast—had been drawn up on the narrow shingle beach. There were some timber houses, some huts, a few shanties close to the beach, but no large buildings and seemingly no center to the town.

Piper and Snapper and the other women walked through an open space surrounded by oak trees. Trees that must have been carefully tended to grow here, in the path of the salt sea breezes. Bramble felt the call of the gods in her mind. The women dipped their heads to an altar in casual familiarity, although one at the back of the group spat on the ground as she passed.

"What shagging good are they?" she asked angrily, when the other women looked askance. "Didn't keep our men alive, did they?"

"Not their job, Crab," Snapper said. Bramble felt the attention of the gods center on Snapper approvingly. "People die," she continued. "Everyone dies. What do they care then? Months and years don't make any difference to them. Their job is to make sure that rebirth happens. That life continues."

"Easy enough to say," Crab snarled, and then pushed past them and strode up the hill. The women watched her go.

"She's carrying," a thin, older woman said. "And she's lost husband and brother and father this day."

"So have we all." Snapper sighed.

They kept walking, passing through the screen of oak trees back into the main street of the town. Some of the women were weeping quietly, others had set faces. Some had the blank look of shock, and were shepherded along by others. Halfway up the hill, a door opened and a woman came out. Dark-haired, of course, and a bit stout, maybe fifty or more. A woman who moved as if surety of her own competence was so deep that she couldn't imagine failing at anything. She had a knife in one hand; a black stone knife that she gripped as if she would never let it go.

"Tern!" Snapper said gladly.

Piper's heart gave an odd kick as she looked at Tern, as though frightened. But she came forward with the other women, murmuring greetings. Bramble noted that they kept a clear space between themselves and Tern. There were no embraces, no shared consolation with this woman.

Tern raked them all with a glance and moved up the hill, walking briskly. "Come!" she said. "It's time to take back what is ours."

Ah, Bramble thought, the enchanter who raised the dead. Good. I've been hoping for this.

The hill was steeper than it looked and Snapper had to hand the baby back to Piper. Piper began puffing as they climbed higher and the baby thought it was a game. Every time Piper forced out a breath, the baby laughed. Instead of making Piper happier, each laugh brought her closer to tears.

"Searose doesn't know what trouble we're in," Piper gasped to Snapper as they reached the top of the hill and started down the other side.

Snapper smiled grimly. "As it should be. Pray to the gods that she keeps unknowing."

Just over the ridge there was a haphazard pile of bodies. There had been no attempt to lay them out. They sprawled, with limbs askew. Blood was turning brown on their clothes and skin. A couple of severed arms had been tossed on top of the pile, like an afterthought. The smell, of pierced gut and vomit and blood and old urine, was horrible. Crab stood there, staring. Piper gagged, and then ran forward, pushing past Tern to reach one of the bodies, whose face could barely be seen under another man.

She pushed the body on top away and wailed, "Salmon," as she took the corpse's head in one hand. The other still gripped Searose fiercely. Grief rose up in her like vomit, unstoppable, and Bramble was shaken by the strength of it—true grief, untainted by fear for her own future or by anger or confusion. Pure as snowmelt, hot as fire. It seared Piper into scalding tears and Bramble found it almost unbearable. The strength of it brought back all her own grief, every grief she had ever felt, but particularly the newest one, for Maryrose. She almost envied Piper's ability to let it loose; to surrender to it as to a huge wave.

Around her, other women were discovering the bodies of their husbands, fathers, brothers, sons. Sobbing, wailing, choking tears, swearing, praying…Bramble felt breathless under the onslaught.

Then Tern touched Piper on the shoulder. "Sister," she said, "hold your tears. Wait, and watch, and listen."

She drew Piper up and passed her back to Snapper, who held her while Piper blinked at Tern in confusion. The other women moved away also, as though afraid of Tern.

As she passed, Tern looked closely at each woman. Bramble hurriedly drew her attention back from Piper's mind, trying to make herself invisible to the enchantress. Another encounter like the one with Dotta would be too unsettling. Something in her didn't want to be seen by Tern, whom she was rapidly coming to dislike, perhaps because, although she looked again and again into the eyes of women distraught with grief and fear, she showed no sign of compassion.

Tern stopped at last when she reached the woman who had spat at the altar. "You," she said. "Crab, isn't it? I need you. I need your anger. Will you give it?"

"What do I get for it?" Crab asked.

"Revenge."

Crab nodded decisively, and Tern smiled. Bramble thought, that's what we're fighting. That look. That's the look the enchanter Saker must have, just before he kills. The look that thirsts for blood. Yet, when I was a child and Granda told me the story of the enchantress of Turvite, I thought she was a hero. She felt a great sadness that was separate from her share of Piper's grief; the same kind of sadness that she had felt the first time she had realized that her father was not the strongest, wisest man in the world; that her mother was not the best woman in the village. The sadness of reality intruding on a dream. Of certainties melting.

Tern stood by the bodies, the women in a semi-circle watching her. She held the knife high, and began to speak.

"Gods of field and stream, hear your daughter. Gods of fire and storm, hear your daughter. Gods of earth and stone, hear your daughter." Bramble knew this incantation. For the first time since she had understood that the gods were translating for her, she was sharply aware of the doubling of meaning, because these were words that she knew. She heard them in both languages, her own and Tern's.

"Gods of sky and wind, hear your daughter," Tern said. She took Crab's hand in her free one and held tightly. Crab became pale, but she kept her expression of anger and determination. Tern continued to ask the gods for something, but for the first time, the gods failed to translate. It was as though they didn't want Bramble to hear these words, to understand them. Bramble tried frantically to remember, but the words were too alien to her—and to everyone else, she realized, because Snapper was staring in puzzlement. Bramble caught a sound here and there, but understood nothing and was as surprised as Piper when Tern raised the black rock knife and cut her hand open, swinging her arm wide so that the drops of blood fell on all the corpses.

The ghosts rose, stepping up from their bodies to stand unsteadily, confused, next to them. They had died clutching their weapons, so they had them in death: a few swords, some cleavers, mostly hunting spears. They were far clearer to see than any ghost Bramble had ever witnessed quicken. She couldn't see through them. They were solid. Real.

Bramble felt Piper's throat clench, her whole body tense, as Salmon rose and looked around, and saw her. The upsurge of love that poured through her was overwhelming. It shook Bramble. Salmon was an ordinary man, medium height, plain face, pockmarks. He held a sword, and his throat was cut through, the dark gash showing horribly. His eyes were kind, though, and it was in his eyes that Piper searched for something; whatever it was, she found it, because she relaxed and sighed a long, tremulous sigh.

Salmon started to move toward Piper, but Tern waved him back. "You are dead," she said. "I have raised your ghosts to take your city back from the invaders. You cannot die again, but they can. Follow me. Destroy them, and your wives and children can still be safe."

Salmon reached out a white hand and tried to touch her, but his hand went right through. Tern didn't even shiver, and that was when Bramble knew she was mad. She remembered that feeling, and only someone living completely inside the world in their head could stay unaffected by it.

Salmon looked at his hand in puzzlement, looking questioningly at Tern. "I will give you strength," she reassured him. "My death will give you bodies to fight with."

The other ghosts were raising clenched fists in the air, shouting words of defiance that no one could hear. Their wounds showed up clearly; some were missing arms, others had guts hanging out of their bellies.

Salmon nodded, then looked across at Piper and smiled, or tried to. His face was full of difficult and deep emotion, and Bramble understood that the same torrent of love was pouring through him. For the first time, she envied another woman. To feel so strongly, and be matched in that feeling... Well, she could let that dream go, too. A demon who had stolen a human body had told her that, at an inn in Sandalwood. Thee wilt love no human never, he had said, and she thought she had accepted it. Must accept it. But it was hard, even though she knew that love had brought the great grief she felt still pulsing through Piper. The baby shifted in Piper's arms and Salmon's eyes went to it and grew soft. Their love had brought Piper the baby and that, too, was no small thing.

Motherhood was not something Bramble had yearned for, but she was no stranger to the appeal of looking after something small and soft and vulnerable—she had nursed too many poddy calves and kids not to understand. Piper looked at Searose and truly saw her for the first time since the vigil on the beach. Bramble felt her fill immediately with a complex intertwining of emotions: a softer, warmer kind of love, pity, grief for the father Searose would never know, and a great, bone-shaking fear that the baby would die, too. Which wasn't unreasonable, Bramble thought, remembering River Bluff and the children who died there.

Around them, women were going up to the men they had loved, saying things to them in low voices, the things they hadn't had a chance to say before they died. At least Tern had given them that. All the women seemed to care so much that Bramble wondered for a moment whether there were no unhappy marriages in Turvite. But as Tern led the ghosts up over the hill and down through the town, followed proudly by Crab and then the other women and children, she realized that the women who did not care were busy packing their belongings, getting ready to leave. Handcarts stood outside many houses, bags were ready in doorways, women were ordering children to gather what they could. Only the truly grieving had gone to bury the dead.

As the ghosts went by, the women came out of their houses, snatched their children back from the procession, made the sign against evil and then, as though enchanted themselves, fell in behind the other women and followed. They marched silently up the hill that led to the cliff. Some women walked beside their men, others behind.

Acton saw them coming. Although his men had taken barrels of beer and were drinking freely, he had still set lookouts. He was standing a little way off, talking to—arguing with—Asgarn. Baluch stood nearby, listening. Seeing Baluch gave Bramble a strange feeling—as though he should be aware of her. She knew him well enough by now to tell that he wasn't happy with whatever Asgarn was saying. She had felt that particular frown often enough. When the lookout called, the three men turned as one and suddenly had swords in their hands, glinting in the midday sun.

At first there were shouts and alarms as Acton called his men to order. They sprang up a little unsteadily from where they had been sprawled, but Bramble saw that they were not really drunk, just a bit merry. They were certainly sober enough to kill. They clutched their swords and presented their shields, although they clearly weren't sure what was happening.

Then the first rank of soldiers realized what was facing them. "Ghosts!" they screamed. "The dead are come back!" They backed away, their faces white, until they stood at the edge of the cliff, and had to stop. They were terrified. Some crouched to pray, some cast around wildly for a way out.

The women held back, but Tern and the ghosts moved forward.

One of Acton's men screamed, "I killed you, I killed you, you're dead!" and jumped from the cliff. His fellows barely noticed.

As they neared Acton, Bramble was struck by how small the ghosts seemed. Much shorter and slighter. They looked almost childlike compared to the tall, strongly muscled fighting men.

"Who is the leader here?" Tern demanded.

Acton stepped forward. In contrast to the ghosts, he seemed full of color. His blue eyes were bright, his hair shone deep gold, his skin glowed with health. Even the simple dun and cream of his clothes seemed rich in comparison to the whiteness of the Turvite men. He was vividly alive; more alive, it seemed to Bramble, than anyone else there, even Tern. She felt relieved to see him, which was ridiculous, because she knew the gods always brought her to him, in every time she visited. He wore the brooch on his cloak. Baluch stood at his shoulder; paler hair, paler eyes, but fully there, listening as he always did.

"I am Acton, son of Asa. I am the lord of war," he said.

"Go from here," Tern declaimed, "and you will be spared, as you spared the women of Turvite. Stay and be slaughtered."

Behind Acton, his men shifted uncomfortably, muttering among themselves. Some were praying. Acton tilted his head, listening to them, and turned to face them, smiling.

"Lord," one said, "let us go from here." It was the man Red, whose friend had been killed by the water sprite. He looked shaken and tired. The other men murmured agreement, watching the ghosts with terror and fascination.

"We faced these men when they were alive, and killed them all," Acton reassured them. "Why should we fear them dead?"

Then, without warning, he laughed, spun, and swung his sword straight at the nearest ghost. Salmon. Salmon raised his own sword, but of course it was futile—Acton's blow went right through his sword and then through him as though he were not there, leaving Salmon unharmed, untouched—and no threat at all. All the women made some kind of sound: gasp, cry, moan. Acton's men whooped and cheered. They yelled, "Ac-ton! Ac-*ton*!" and beat their swords on their shields.

"You'll never scare our lord of war, bitch!" a man yelled. "Our lord fears nothing!"

Tern moved aside, toward the cliff. At first Acton let her go, assuming that she was retreating. Then she turned to face him again, and he saw her face. His laughter died, and his eyes narrowed. Bramble, through Baluch, had seen him look at enemies like that. Tern raised her hand and pointed at him.

"I curse you, Acton son of Asa. You shall never have what you truly want."

Bramble had known what she was going to say, and yet the words cut through her. It was her reaction, not Piper's. Piper was watching, but her attention was mostly on Salmon, who was staring bleakly at his useless sword. She didn't care what Tern said to the blond man. But the curse seemed to drain strength and warmth from Bramble. She felt shaky, as though her own body were close to fainting. She had felt like that a couple of times before, when she had been thrown from the roan and had the breath knocked out of her; panicky and shaky with shock. She didn't understand it. Why would she react like that to something she had heard in stories a dozen times before?

But Acton clearly felt none of her disquiet. His face lightened and he laughed again, eyes creasing up in genuine merriment. His hand went out, gesturing toward Turvite.

"I already have it," he said gaily. Bramble felt the shakiness begin to leave her. Acton's strength seemed to steady her as well as his men. His laughter was comforting. She felt vaguely ashamed of that.

Tern shook her head. Bramble felt the gods flow around Tern, but she couldn't tell if they were arriving or leaving.

"Never," Tern said. "Brothers of mine, I give you my strength."

The gods were leaving Tern. Something was missing. Bramble felt that Tern should have given something else—other words, some other action. No—feeling. That was what was missing. Feeling. Tern didn't really care about the dead men, and her words were only words.

Baluch had moved forward at the first moment that the gods had begun to move, instinctively reaching out for Tern, but he was too late. She stepped over the cliff and dropped out of sight. It was so sudden that even Bramble was startled. Piper and the other women cried out. Acton's men shouted, half of them jubilant, half appalled.

They all crowded to the cliff edge to peer over, but there was no sign of her in the churning surf below.

Piper turned back to watch, eagerly looking for Salmon. The ghosts had been startled by Tern's disappearance, but now they hefted their weapons. One of them, the one Crab had walked beside up the hill, looked at her. She nodded. He nodded back, then threw his spear with all his might at Acton.

Acton raised his shield but the spear never reached it. It vanished in thin air once it left the ghost's hand, melting as the water sprite had melted. Some of Acton's men jeered, but other Turviters gripped their spears and rushed. Acton's men scrambled to meet them, training and experience pushing them to present shields as a solid fence. Acton and Asgarn were in the center. Baluch took the rear, organizing another line of men behind them in case any attackers broke through. Bramble almost expected the clang of spear on shield, all the unholy noise of battle that she had come to know so well.

But the ghosts silently slid into and through the fence of shields, through the line of swordsmen, and out the other side, stumbling to a stop before they got to Baluch's line. Acton's men shivered and made faces of disgust as the ghost chill hit them, but then they realized what had happened and broke ranks, laughing and jeering and whooping with relief.

The women watching cried out in despair. Piper's heart was beating too fast for comfort; too fast for safety. It seemed to swell in her chest as though it were going to burst. Bramble realized that Piper felt like she was going to die—wanted to die, to join with Salmon. No! Remember the baby, Bramble thought toward her. Willed her to look at Searose, to remember that her baby needed her. Astonishingly, Piper did. She turned her face away from Salmon and looked at Searose, clutched her tighter and cried over her wispy black hair. Bramble wasn't sure if Piper had really responded to her thought, or if it were just mother love working. It didn't matter. The dangerous moment had passed.

At least, one dangerous moment.

The ghosts had backed away toward the cliff behind Acton's men, leaving nothing between them and the women. Acton's men, now the first jubilation had worn off, were glowering at the women. They were tossing down their swords and shields. Some of them were smiling, and it wasn't a smile Bramble liked. Then Acton stepped forward.

"I gave you until sunset to bury your dead and leave your houses. I think you have just forfeited the right to bury your dead. Clearly, you don't care if they sleep in peace or not. So I say now: take your things and go."

"They've forfeited more than their right to bury their dead," Asgarn objected. He came to stand next to Acton, glaring at the women. "They've forfeited everything."

Acton shook his head, and smiled irrepressibly. "Come now, Asgarn. It was a good try, but it failed. You would have done the same, if you thought it might work. I would have."

Asgarn looked exasperated and wiped one hand over his chin as though buying time to decide what to say. "The men deserve —"

Acton cut him off, his face for once serious. "The men deserve to be treated as though they are men of honor and not rutting drunken hogs."

"Honor operates between equals," Asgarn said. He gestured to the women in disdain. Piper's heart leapt in fear as his glance passed over her and the baby yelped as she gripped her too hard. "These are not equals. Look at them. They're barely human. Runts." The last word was spoken with scorn, a contempt that Bramble had heard many, many times on the Road. "Shagging Travelers," were the words usually spoken in her time, but the tone was the same. The men rumbled their agreement, but Acton wasn't moved.

"I gave my word," he said. "Go," he said to the crowd of women.

Some of them turned to head down the hill, but Snapper folded her arms. "Where do we go?" she asked. "A bunch of women and childer, with no way of making a living. We know how to fish, but this is the only harbor from here to forever. Easy to save our lives and feel good about yourself, but we're still dead by the end of winter, with no shelter and no food."

Asgarn turned away with a shrug of distaste, but Acton listened, his face growing serious. Baluch said something quietly in his ear, and he nodded.

"There's a village," he said. "It's abandoned. You can have it on two conditions. One is that our boats are left undisturbed as they go up and down river. The other is that you accept any other . . ." he searched for a word, but failed to find it, by the look on his face, "any other people who need shelter. I don't know what the place is named, but it's a few miles upstream of here. Call it Sanctuary."

"Go on, then," he added to the women, as though shooing a flock of chickens from his door, "go on, get going." Laughter threaded underneath his words and Bramble felt a mixture of annoyance and admiration. He was such a—an *idiot*! He could be as generous as a rich man on his deathbed, but he couldn't see that Asgarn was dangerous. He was too straightforward himself to recognize the point where shrewdness turned to deviousness. That was a point that Asgarn had reached long ago.

The women gazed at their men, gathered on the cliff edge. Acton's men didn't like it. They glared at the women and then one of them started to bang his sword on his shield and shout, "Ac-*ton*! Ac-*ton*!" Others joined in. Where before it had been a noise of celebration, now it was a threat.

The women hastily gathered their children and turned to go, talking about the new village as if to pretend that they weren't frightened. Some of them knew it. They carefully didn't mention why a village would be abandoned, but after the threats from the soldiers, they were filled with relief to turn toward their houses. Except Piper. She looked helplessly toward Salmon. He pointed to the north, toward a group of large boulders down the hillside about fifty paces away. She nodded and gave the baby to Snapper, kissing her on the head first. Then she walked down with a group of other women, slipping between a gap in the boulders as they passed so that Acton's men wouldn't realize she was there.

Salmon was waiting for her. They came close together, but couldn't touch. He curved his hand as though touching Piper's face, and the tears flowed hot down her cheeks. Bramble was tired of grief. She felt exhausted by it. There had been so many deaths: Sebbi and Elric and Asa and Friede and Edwa, so much grief and so much mourning and so much revenge. She wondered why the gods were keeping her here, now the important part of the story had happened. What use was it, forcing her to see, to feel this, too?

"Herring got away on the boat," Piper said to Salmon, talking around the lump in her throat, sobbing a little. His face lit with relief. His son then, too, was safe. Bramble wondered how old Herring was. Where the boat had gone, if this was the only port "from here to forever." The Wind Cities, maybe. Surely these people had heard of them?

Then Acton appeared through the gap in the rocks, fumbling with his trousers. He had clearly slipped away for a quiet piss, and he stopped in surprise and a little embarrassment as he saw Piper and Salmon.

"You'd better get going," he said to Piper. "My men are drinking again. I can hold them a while longer, but after that, I make no promises."

"I don't understand why you are stopping them," Piper said. "I always heard the blond barbarians raped and tortured women."

Acton's face filled with incongruous enjoyment, as though she had made a joke. "My mother had strong views about rapists," he said, his eyes dancing, and even Piper, standing by her dead husband, was warmed by that smile. Bramble felt a stab of irritation with her. He's your enemy, she wanted to say. But he was also Piper's protector, which had not been part of the story. Bramble had never heard of Sanctuary.

Acton looked at Salmon, who was glaring at him, and back at Piper. "Your man will be fine, you know," he reassured her. "He died fighting, his sword in his hand. Swith the Strong will welcome him into the hall of heroes, and he will feast in the company of the brave forever." His tone was earnest. There was no doubt that he believed it.

Piper looked at him, bewildered. "What are you talking about?" she said. "Death is just a door. Afterward, we go on to rebirth, if we have lived well and justly and pleased the gods."

Acton's face twisted in surprise.

Astonishingly, this was what the gods had wanted her to see, to hear, because the waters rose up like a breaking wave and smashed her away into darkness.

LEOF

KEEPING ARROW, HIS chaser, in condition was the perfect excuse to get away from the fort. Leof felt ashamed that he needed to, but it had been two days since Arrow had been exercised, and she was getting restive. His groom was quite capable of riding her usually, but in this mood Leof wouldn't trust her to anyone but himself. That was his excuse, anyway. He rode down the valley, inspecting the ditches and stake-traps which were being built in rings around the hill. Every man from the town who could be spared was working there, for all the daylight hours, but even so, it was progressing slower than Leof would have liked. That was another good reason for a ride, to encourage the workers and speed up the work.

At the bottom of the hill he turned aside and went down his favorite path, which led through the valley to a spring-fed pool which flowed out to become the best water source for miles. He told himself he was looking for a way to defend that water, which was crucial for the farmers in the valley. The pool itself was on common ground, and no one's direct responsibility. Which made it his.

The pool was overshadowed by a huge old cedar tree, the fruit of some long-ago warlord's trade with the Wind Cities. The story went that he had swapped his daughter for the seedling, but Leof doubted that. No warlord would give away so great a prize without getting a lot more than a tree back.

Under the sweeping branches the cedar scent was so strong that Leof felt slightly drunk. He dismounted and led Arrow to the pool and waited while she dipped her head to drink, glad of a moment's quiet. It was cool and beautiful here, and it seemed a long way away from the noise and movement at the fort. The pool was ringed with moss-covered rocks and the water spread out between them serenely, with only the faint ripple from the underground spring disturbing its reflection of the tree.

Leof was watching a branch reflected in the water, thinking about Sorn and the way her hair caught the light with sudden fire, when he saw a face appear in the pool.

He jumped back, startled, and Arrow's head came up with a whicker.

There was a man standing on the other side of the pool, smiling at him, his hands raised to show that he meant no harm. Leof relaxed a little, although he was silently berating himself. No one should have been able to sneak up on him like that! He was a warrior, not a lovestruck mooncalf.

The man was old, very old, with long white hair braided into plaits around his face and with the back left free. He had a full beard, too, which was unusual. So were his clothes—leggings and gaiters and a long, full tunic, almost like a woman's. He wore a gold arm-ring in the shape of a dragon high on his left arm. His eyes were very blue and he had surprisingly good teeth for such an old man. Leof wished his own teeth were that straight.

He nodded. "Greetings, sir."

"Greetings to you also, young man." The old man looked at him consideringly.

Then a voice seemed to come from inside Leof's head, or from the water, or from the air itself; it surrounded him, it filled him.

"Listen," it said. It was his mother's voice.

He and Arrow had ridden to this pool a hundred times before, but Leof felt suddenly that he had ventured into an unknown wilderness, where anything might happen. His heart sped up, his hands were clammy, and he felt for his sword.

"The Lake sent you," Leof said with certainty.

The man smiled. "Well done! I was expecting you to ask, 'Who are you?' Indeed, I am her ambassador. Her mouthpiece, if you will." He had a beautiful voice, warm and deep and flexible, but there was a hint of an accent, a slight brogue. A voice it would be easy to trust.

Leof set his heart against being persuaded by that voice. "And?"

"Child, there is great danger approaching, and you will need the powers of the Lake to survive it."

"*I* will need?"

"Your people. All our peoples. The Lake is not your enemy, but she will not be conquered. There is no living power in this world which could conquer her."

Leof latched on to that hint. "What about the power of the dead?"

"If the dead acquire such power as that, your people will be in a sorry state. Convince your lord."

Leof smiled ruefully. "My lord goes his own way."

The man laughed, companionably. "So did mine, once. But if you are loyal to him, you will convince him. The Lake will resist."

Leof hesitated, but his inborn impulse to honesty won out. "He doesn't believe in the Lake," he admitted.

The man went very still and his eyes widened a little. He whistled in disbelief. Leof was surprised by the purity of the sound—it was like the whistle of a young boy.

"That—explains." He lifted a hand. Oddly, given the roughness of his clothes, his fingernails were long and well cared for. "Be resolute," he said.

Leof blinked. The man was just—gone. Just *not there.* He hadn't stepped away, he hadn't moved. Just disappeared. Leof began to shake. True enchantment. *True* enchantment, not necromancy or trick or potion. He had never heard of such power—and Leof knew that it was the power of the Lake, not of the man. The man had been an ordinary human. Leof forced himself to cross the stream on the stones that ringed the pool and look at the ground where the man had stood.

He felt a great relief when he saw footprints, even though they only led from the pool *to* the tree, and not away from it. At least his sense that the man was alive and real had been right. An ambassador from the Lake. He jumped back across the stream with more energy, and collected Arrow.

The question was, should he tell Sorn about this? He should tell Thegan, no doubt, although Thegan would jump to the conclusion that this man was the enchanter he had declared was his enemy. His shocking ability to disappear would be the proof. Leof paused, reining Arrow in at the end of the river path, looking across the field to the fort on its hill. *Should* he tell Thegan? If he didn't, was that treason? Consorting with the enemy?

He longed to discuss it with Sorn, to lay it all out for consideration by those wise green eyes. But private conversation had to be avoided at all costs. So, what if he said nothing? If Thegan ever found out, it would be the pressing box for sure, and then the gibbet. The sun was going down. He would miss evening muster and inspection of the horses. He clicked his tongue to Arrow and she started off gladly, happy to be heading home. He put aside the decision for now. Or perhaps . . . This would be a good excuse to go to Carlion. He could put Wil in charge for a few days and ride down to tell Thegan personally. It was too . . . odd . . . to put in a message. How could he describe it properly?

Then he could leave Sorn for a while. Let them both recover. Perhaps even persuade Thegan to keep him in Carlion and send Eddil back to command in Sendat. He had at least as much experience as Leof.

He *had* to tell Thegan. The man had even *asked* him to. He ignored a suspicion that it would make the situation in Baluchston worse. But Thegan wasn't going to listen to him about the Lake anyway. He cantered Arrow up the hill more cheerfully. Secrecy wasn't in his nature and he felt much better having decided to take action.

As he went, he saw a local farmer pacing out the course of the next chase. He sighed. As temporary lord in Sendat, he couldn't compete in any of the chases. He had to hand out the prizes if asked. Since Bramble's roan, Thorn, had died he'd gone back to racing in every chase he could, instead of just the ones Bramble wasn't in, and he missed the regular dose of excitement. Missed winning, too. He patted Arrow on the neck and said, "One day soon, girl," and she tossed her head in response as he headed her for home.

Leof left the next morning, with no more than a public explanation to Sorn that he needed to discuss some elements of the fort's defense directly with Thegan. She was puzzled, he could see, and so was Wil, but they both accepted his statement. Sorn organized food for him to take and Bandy, his groom, prepared for the trip with enthusiasm. He had a ghoulish curiosity and couldn't wait to take a look at the wreckage the ghosts had caused.

The trip to Carlion was uneventful, although everywhere they stopped he was besieged with people wanting to be reassured that they weren't going to be murdered in their beds. He did the best he could, thinking wryly that they'd never have dared accost Thegan in the same way.

Carlion itself was... odd. Leof realized that he'd expected to see the kinds of things he had seen in other towns in Cliff Domain which had been attacked by the Ice King: houses burnt down, or stripped bare of all they had. But ghosts had no reason to loot. It appeared they didn't use fire, either. They just killed.

So the streets of Carlion were the same as ever, aside from a few shattered and hastily repaired shutters and doors. But there were far fewer people on the streets than the last time he was there. He saw fearful eyes peering out at him from behind windows and doors as he rode down the steep streets toward the Moot Hall. But the fearful people staying indoors weren't enough to account for the emptiness of the streets. Carlion was a town stripped bare, but of people, not things. Arrow's hoofsteps echoed forlornly from the brick walls, too easy to hear now the normal bustle of cart and handbarrows and vendors was gone. Leof could even hear the seagulls down at the harbor, and the wash of the waves against the docks.

The Moot Hall, he found with some relief, was bustling as usual, although most of the bustle was provided by men in Thegan's uniform. He was hailed immediately by one of the sergeants.

"My lord's in his office. Top of the stairs. Is there news from Sendat?"

There was anxiety in his voice and Leof remembered that he was a local man, with family in the town below the fort. Leof shook his head and smiled reassuringly. "Would I be here if there was?"

He handed Arrow over to Bandy and left him to organize their quarters. No doubt there would be plenty of choice.

Thegan's office—once the Town Clerk's, Leof had no doubt—was opulent in a way that sat oddly with Thegan's disciplined style. It was furnished in walnut and rosewood, and every piece of seating was cushioned in yellow velvet. There were golden curtains at the windows and the frieze that ran around the room was of sunflowers and green leaves. Leof remembered that the last Town Clerk of Carlion had been a woman. Dead, now, he presumed. Thegan looked slightly out of place in the office, but it was clear that he was unaware of his surroundings.

"Leof!" he exclaimed, waving away a Carlionite, a small man with a merchant's potbelly and huge mustaches. "Trouble?"

The small man raised worried eyes to Leof and visibly braced himself for bad news.

"No, no, no problems," Leof said, smiling at the man. He was so tired of smiling reassuringly. "But I needed to speak to you privately, my lord."

The man immediately packed up his papers and bowed himself out. "Tomorrow, Sirin," Thegan said. "In the morning."

Leof waited until the door was closed and then bowed.

"Well?" Thegan demanded. "I hope you have a good reason for this."

"I think so, my lord, or I would not have come."

Thegan nodded and gestured to Leof to sit down. He lowered himself onto the velvet cushion with some relief. The ride had been a long one. He couldn't resist a quick glance around the room and a smile at Thegan. Thegan smiled back, the real smile.

"I feel like I'm in a bordello," he admitted, leaning back in his chair. "But it reassures the Carlionites if I keep changes to a minimum."

Leof nodded, and hesitated. He wasn't quite sure how to proceed, although he had practiced this scene in his head on the way. "The Lake sent an ambassador," he said finally. He described what had happened by the pool.

Thegan sat upright. "So . . ." he said. "Our enchanter shows himself."

"Or the Lake —"

An impatient wave cut him off. "The Lake! It's just water, for Swith's sake! It can't *think*! This man, this old man, yes, he's the one we have to search for. Did you send out search parties?"

Leof gaped. It had not even occurred to him to look. The old man's disappearance had been so . . . final.

"I . . . I searched myself, around the site, my lord," he said carefully, "but there was no sign. Not even a footprint of him leaving."

"Where did he arrive from, then?"

Reluctantly, Leof said, "The pool."

"So he came from the Lake by boat —"

"No, my lord," Leof said firmly. "That pool does not connect with the Lake. It flows to the Simple River and thence to the sea."

Thegan paused. "So he is very powerful, then. Well, you did right to come to tell me. I will consider it. Go and have your meal."

He turned away to look out the window, but Leof lingered. "My lord, I hoped... I hoped I might be able to stay here and help you. Perhaps Eddil could take over at Sendat . . ."

Thegan stared at him, frowning. "Bored already? Defending my fort is not unimportant, Leof."

"My lord, I know that. But the defenses are proceeding, the smiths know their tasks... I could be of more use to you here. Eddil has more experience than I do at fortifications."

Thegan's mouth relaxed. "True. But I wouldn't leave my wife alone with that tomcat for more than an hour."

"He would never betray you!"

Thegan grinned. "Some men can't help themselves. At the least, he'd make a play for that holy little thing who waits on Sorn, and then there'd be a real problem! Officers are one thing, but a good sergeant like Alston is hard to find."

He came around the desk and laid his hand on Leof's shoulders. "I know it doesn't seem too exciting, Leof, but you are where I need you."

Leof nodded. What could he say? "You shouldn't trust me around your wife, either?" A death warrant for both of them.

"Do you have a report of your progress?" Thegan asked, all business again.

Leof handed over the detailed report which he had spent his last night in Sendat compiling. Unless the ghosts attacked again, he thought, I'm doomed to go back. He had a dreadful double impulse, to run as far as he could from Sendat—to take ship for the Wind Cities, perhaps, and leave everything he knew behind—and to ride immediately for Sendat and throw himself at Sorn's feet, declaring his love.

What shocked him most about the thought was that he really didn't know which he wanted more.

BRAMBLE

THERE WAS WATER moving nearby. Bramble could hear the slap and hiss of small waves on shingle, a sound that took her back to a day spent with Maryrose in Carlion before the wedding, when they had wandered over the town and the harbor, down to the small beach, and looked out over the waves. They had talked about their parents moving in to Carlion to live with Maryrose and Merrick in the new house after it was built.

"They'll be safer here than in Wooding, so near the fort," Maryrose had said, and Bramble had nodded agreement. Yes, Carlion was much safer. So they had thought. But now there were no safe places anywhere, and the dead could rise with axes in their hands and kill, and nothing could stop them. Except Acton, maybe. She forced down the choke of grief and concentrated as her sight cleared. If she had to live every second of Acton's life, she would.

They were down at the beach, sure enough, in Turvite, on a cold still day. Late autumn, maybe. But where before fishing boats had been drawn up on the shingle, now there were boat cradles reaching high ribs that seemed to mimic the cliffs around the harbor. Three of them. They were holding the skeletons of larger versions of the boats Acton had rowed down the river. But these, it was clear, would have masts as well as oars. They were long, flat-bottomed boats with high prows and sterns, a shape much like the reed boats of the Lake People, but bigger. Ships.

She was inhabiting a man, and she was so inured to it by now that when he hitched his trousers to get a more comfortable position for his privates, she didn't even wince. She thought at first that it was a stranger, but then the man reached out a hand past the cradle rib to touch the side of the ship and she recognized the hand. Baluch, but a Baluch so enraptured by the ships that he had not a single part of his mind to give to music.

"You've done well while I've been away," a voice said. Baluch turned and there was Asgarn, wiry hair bristling with energy, blue eyes bright with admiration. He, too, was entranced by the ships.

Acton's voice replied from behind Baluch. "We'll be ready by summer." Baluch turned as Acton slapped the side of the ship as Bramble would give a friendly slap to a horse. "We're collecting cargo now. I'm sending trappers out during winter for pelts and I've got a lumber crew in the forest picking out fine hardwood. That's scarce in the Wind Cities, the old men say."

Asgarn nodded. "Next year we might have grain as well. Bone carvings, too, when our men have more time."

Baluch added, "Metalwork, once the forges are set up. I'm sending out a message inviting charcoal burners to come to T'vit."

Asgarn looked skeptical. "Why would they leave their steadings to join you?"

Baluch traded glances with Acton, and abruptly the music was back, a low horn note. Bramble was good enough at deciphering his thoughts now to know that the note—and the look—meant warning. But Acton grinned at him. Not reassuring, just shagging cheeky. Acton knew that whatever he was about to say would cause a stir.

"Because here they'll be living in a free town."

Asgarn frowned. "What does that mean?"

"It means that T'vit is governed by a town council. Like the Moot, but permanent. It decides how the town is run. The council is elected by the people who live here." With an air of getting it all out, even the worst, he added, "Including women."

Bramble thought Asgarn might have an apoplexy, he turned so red. "Are you insane? And what do you mean, 'is'? Have you set this up already?"

Acton nodded. "It's going well. I'm the head of the council at the moment, of course, but in time I may be able to hand it over altogether."

"Did you consult the Moot about this?"

For a moment, Acton looked very much like his grandfather. The same stubbornness. "They gave me T'vit. I can do what I like with it."

"Give away your power? What kind of fool does that?"

"One who doesn't want it," Baluch said.

"Then hand it over to someone who'll use it properly! Not a bunch of traders and...and *charcoal burners*!" Asgarn took a step closer to Acton and reached out a hand in supplication. Bramble thought that he really did want Acton's understanding. That he respected him enough to want his support. "Can't you see the opportunity we have here? This country is *empty*. We needed the Moot before because we were all crowded up ham by haunch and we had to have a way of resolving disputes. But there's so much land here that each chief could rule a vast territory, rule without concerns about how his decisions would be greeted by others. There could be *real* power, not negotiations and bargains and paying compensation because a cow cropped another man's pasture! Can't you *see* what we could have?"

Acton was staring at him with a frown. Bramble tensed. This was the moment, then. This was the time when Acton helped establish the warlords. No wonder she'd never liked Asgarn. Baluch, however, didn't seem to pay much attention. He looked back at the ship instead of at Acton, smoothing his hand over the planks of the keel. Bramble could have hit him. Look at them! she thought. Look!

"The Moot has served us very well," Acton said. Baluch looked up and nodded agreement.

Asgarn set his mouth. "One man ruling a large territory would be better. A clear line of command, a clear area of responsibility, each chieftain able to work for his own good and secure his own power."

So there it was, spelled out. The warlord's creed. Bramble was sickened by it, and yet felt curiously exalted, because Acton was shaking his head. "Have you discussed this with the Moot council?"

Asgarn hesitated, and Bramble knew what that meant. He'd been sounding out the members of the council, doing deals, finding out what each man most wanted. Acton waited.

"Not in full council, no," Asgarn said. "But I am sure they will see the truth of what I say."

"That may be. But I think I will have a few words to say as well."

In Baluch's head, the warning music rose sharply at the look on Asgarn's face.

"Perhaps we should go together," Asgarn said slowly. Baluch put a cautioning hand on Acton's arm. Acton grinned at him.

"Baluch reminds me that we have much more to do here if we want to take the dragon's road in Spring. I will follow you to Wili's steading for the Mid-Winter Moot."

Asgarn nodded sharply, turned on his heel and headed up the shore toward the houses of T'vit. Acton and Baluch watched him go.

"Don't trust him," Baluch said.

"I don't," Acton replied. "But I didn't think he was mad enough to destroy the Moot."

"He's never forgiven you for Sebbi's death."

Acton's eyes clouded. "I've never forgiven myself."

"What will you do at the Moot?"

Acton grinned, his eyes gleaming with anticipation. "It's a different kind of battle. I've watched Harald fight that fight enough times to know how it's done. Don't worry. The Moot will survive."

Bramble was astonished and elated that Acton had refused Asgarn's arguments, but she was also confused. What had happened to change things? To make Acton a warlord, to have him help set up the warlord system? What had they offered him that had won him over?

She didn't have time to speculate further, because the waves on the beach rose suddenly and crashed over her, tumbling her into darkness.

There was warmth on her shoulder: warm lips, moving, kissing, a tongue touching. Her side was pressed up against something warm, all down her naked flank there was warmth. For one long moment, Bramble simply felt it; heat, comfort, teasing pleasure. Something loosened inside her and relaxed. Then a hand stroked down from her shoulder to her breast and she realized: Acton! That's Acton's hand!

At the same moment sight came back and she saw him, gold head bent to kiss the soft flesh above her breast, hand cradling the breast itself. Get me out of here! she shouted in her mind to the gods, but they did nothing.

Then the woman pushed him away. Bramble felt a combination of emotions from her—affection, unease, a lingering pleasure mixed with revulsion. It was so much like her own emotions that she couldn't quite tell where the woman's feelings stopped and her own began. Acton sat up and looked at her ruefully, as though he were aware how she felt. He had shaved off his beard. She wondered why. It made him look younger.

"Oh, Wili," he said regretfully, "was it that bad?"

Wili smiled carefully. Her eyes pricked with tears, but she didn't let them fall. Bramble could sense that she didn't want to hurt his feelings; but that she wanted to be out of that bed and dressed, securely, with trousers and belt and a good strong knife at her waist.

"Not *bad,*" she said. "Well, I had to do it, but I don't think I'll be doing it again."

A light broke on Bramble and she thought, they just made his son. The son of the woman who would have nothing to do with men, except that she tried it once with Acton . . .

He grimaced. "I'm sorry. I did the best I could."

She reached out and tousled his hair, making him look like a five-year-old. "It was a good try. But —"

"It'd be different if you loved me."

"Or if you loved me? I don't think so."

His face clouded. Wili drew her knees up to her chest and hugged them. She felt safer that way. Calmer. The feeling of wanting to cry faded from Bramble's mind.

Wili risked letting go with one hand and touched the back of his arm.

"If I loved you the way I loved Friede," he said, "it would have to make a difference."

Wili made a noise of disbelief. "I doubt it."

He was offended, but she smiled grimly. "You didn't love her," she said simply. "She knew it."

He sat up straight in indignation, the blanket falling away to show his muscled chest. "I did!"

"Ha!" Wili seemed to take some satisfaction in cutting him down to size. "You liked her. Maybe you were fond of her. Maybe you wanted her. But you didn't love her."

He looked worried, perhaps sad. "Did she tell you that?"

"She did. Not that she had to. I could tell. If she'd gone to your bed like the rest of them you'd never have given her another thought!"

"That's not true! Friede was... different."

"Because you thought she needed to be protected. She hated that, you know. She didn't want to be protected. That's why she loved Baluch. He never protected her. Didn't think she needed protection."

Acton looked down at the bed and stayed silent for a while. "I don't understand love," he admitted finally. "All women are beautiful, even the ugly ones. All of you are delicious."

"We're not honeycakes," Wili said quietly, but not to interrupt him.

"Friede was my friend, and that felt different from all the others."

"So maybe you just called it love, when it was friendship all the time." Wili patted his hand. "Friendship's nothing to be ashamed of."

He looked up and smiled, mischief gleaming. "Do you think I'll ever love?"

"Not while you go around bedding every woman you meet!"

He grinned, mischief growing, and was clearly ready to tease Wili about being one of those women. Time to change the subject, girl, Bramble thought, and Wili did think a lot like her, because immediately she said, "What is the Moot saying?"

His face became serious. "I have ratification for the free towns, to be set up like Turvite, with town councils elected by the people. I have agreement that there will be no thralls."

"How did you get that?" she asked, astonished.

"Fear. I used that traitor Uen as an example. We are too vulnerable, here in a new land, to have men with us who are not oath-sworn, who do not have a stake in our future here." He smiled slowly. "It took some time, but they agreed. Now we just have to re-establish the All Moot and I can go back to actually getting some work done!"

So, Bramble thought, it *was* his idea to get rid of thralls. That was well done. But was fear his real reason, or was it something else? Free towns, no thralls—how could that come from the man who established warlords? Did he simply get voted down? She was tired of being confused about him. She wanted some solid sense of what he was really like. Something beyond fighting and politicking and taking revenge. Or was that all there was to him? She didn't believe that.

Mainly because of Baluch and Wili. They didn't think that, and they were not fools.

Wili laughed at him and asked, as she had asked once before, "How are the boats coming along?"

The gods were not interested in his answer because the waters rolled over her and dumped her down a cascade. Bramble was falling, and falling, with nothing solid to hold on to.

As soon as she came to herself, she knew that she was not with Baluch. This was a much taller man who moved heavily, shifting from foot to foot with a perceptible thump. For the first time she became aware of how lightly Baluch moved, how easily his body obeyed him. She hadn't noticed before because it was how her own body moved, and so she had just accepted it. But this body was clumsy, lumbering. A big man, with big muscles, she thought, and weighed down somehow, not just by the heavy winter clothes he wore against the biting cold.

He was standing in a wood on a hill, a spur of pines on the edge of a much greater forest. He looked down to a steading, a snow-covered collection of houses and barns surrounded by pasture and some fenced fields, although pasture and ploughed ground looked alike under the thick snow. Bramble realized that it was Hawk's—that is, Wili's—steading. She had not seen it from exactly this angle before, but she was sure. There were some figures, well wrapped up, moving between house and animal barns. A woman emerged and shook out a blanket. Bramble recognized her: Wili. Her pregnancy wasn't showing yet, so not much time had passed. Wili had named the child Thegan, she remembered. He had finished what Acton started, the invasion of the Domains, right up to the Sharp River. Wili stood upright and looked up the slope, shading her eyes. Two children raced out the door past her and she called them back.

The sky was gray, but there was no wind. The man Bramble inhabited put up a hand to shake the snow from his collar, and she saw that he had copper hair springing thickly on hand and wrist. Maybe the one who had been in the boat with Acton, whose friend had died? Red. The more she thought about it, the more she was sure, because the only emotions she could sense were grief and fear, combined. It was a familiar grief, constantly refreshed, and it was threaded with guilt, because he was still alive.

Bramble knew that feeling. She felt sorry for him, but she was worried. What was he doing up here in the woodland, waiting, skulking? Where was Acton? Surely it was too soon for him to die? He couldn't be much older than the last time she had seen him, not if Wili were pregnant. The stories all talked about him ruling Turvite, setting up the warlord system, pushing the invasion further and further—surely that would take years more?

Then Red saw Acton, down at the steading, coming out of the main house, talking briefly with Wili, and then going to a barn. A few moments later he emerged, riding one of the stocky little ponies Bramble had come to admire.

He rode up the slope and passed Red, whose breathing came faster as Acton went by. Red reached down and brought a knife out of his boot. Not an eating knife. This was a fighting dagger, meant for killing.

Acton rode further up the slope, his breath and his horse's blowing clouds of steam. He was growing another beard, but it was still short and outlined his face. His expression was hard to read; the set look might just be due to the cold, but she didn't think so. He looked like someone going to do a job he disliked.

Halfway up, though, his face changed. He looked into the woodland and smiled, as though he had seen someone he knew. Bramble knew that smile, the sideways smile that he cozened women with. Bramble could have hit him. He was courting someone again. Now, of all times! But instead of riding toward whatever girl was smiling back at him, he raised a hand in farewell and continued on.

Further up the hill the forest curved around and continued in a thick ribbon of larch and spruce trees along the lower slopes of the mountains. As Acton disappeared into those, Red followed him, skirting the open spaces until his path crossed Acton's tracks just inside the belt of trees. Then he followed the tracks through the trees. Where they ended, he waited. Acton was higher up the steep hillside, near the cliff which showed the entrances to some caves. Dotta's caves? Bramble wondered, and then was sure. It had to be, so close to Wili's settlement.

Acton tethered his horse to a low bush and disappeared inside the cave. Immediately Red started to run forward, treading as much in the horse's tracks as he could. He fetched up, breathing hard, against the cliff face next to the cave entrance, and peered cautiously around into the cave. The passageway, winding between rough walls, was empty, but Acton's tracks were clear in the dirt, overlaying another set of footprints.

So someone was waiting for you, Bramble thought. What a surprise. I wonder if Asgarn is man enough to do his own killing.

That was the moment that Bramble understood. Acton never had set up the warlord system. They had killed him first and used his name afterward to gather support.

She was filled with rage. Asgarn and shagging Oddi. This was their doing.

Red crept along down the passageway as stealthily as he could, and paused at a turn, where the rock screened the cave beyond. There were voices, hard to decipher. Red didn't have Baluch's sharp ears. He edged closer to the opening.

Then Bramble heard Acton laugh in response to some comment. "Is this what you and Oddi have been scheming about? The Moot has ruled us for a thousand years, would you give all that history away? The Moot *works*. It has proved itself. That's why I copied it in T'vit. It's a curb on the headstrong and the foolish. The weak are protected."

"The weak are *favored*, you mean." That was Asgarn's voice, of course, bitter and harsh.

Red slid to the very edge of the opening and peered around. Beyond was Dotta's cave, but it smelt stale, of old ashes and grease from the small oil lamp that sat on a rock, giving a wavering and fitful light. Dotta was long gone, and her sacred fire with her. Bramble hoped she was safe.

Acton and Asgarn were facing each other, looking like two versions of the same man. Both tall, both fair, both strong and wide across the shoulders. Only the hair was different, and the way they stood: Asgarn with shoulders hunched and fists clenched; Acton upright and at ease, Asa's brooch on his cloak catching the lamplight like a star. Oh, be careful! Bramble thought. Don't be so sure of yourself.

"The strong are forced to carry the weak," Asgarn said.

Acton looked at him with curiosity. "Because we are all one people, of one blood. Should we not help each other?"

"The strong don't need help and the weak should pay for the help they need."

"Pay how?"

"In obedience. And other ways, if necessary. Labor. Gold. Goods."

"No," Acton said. "The chieftain has a duty to his people. Generosity pleases the gods."

"A ruler should look to his own interests first, and then give what he can, in return for loyalty."

Acton paused, as though he could see that this argument could go on forever without either of them shifting position. "I cannot support you," he said. "I think you will find that most of the Moot council is of my view. I have already received endorsement for my free towns."

"Aye, they're short-sighted, like you. They don't see where that will take us. But uninterested in power? I don't think so. I think enough of them like the idea of being fully in control of their own territory. But it would be just like you to convince them. Just like you to lead us all into disaster, like you always do. Come over the mountains! you said, and so all of them went and died, just so you could feel good. If we'd taken this territory in the first place, Swef and Asa—yes, and Friede, too—they'd all still be alive."

"That's true," Acton said quietly.

"Oh, yes, admitting it makes you sound so noble, doesn't it? You're good at that, aren't you? At having grand schemes. You're good at convincing people to die for some stupid noble idea. Like you convinced my *brother*!"

Asgarn sprang, drawing the knife from his belt. Like Red's, this was a killing dagger, not a belt knife. Acton was ready for him, his own knife out and his arm up to deflect the first blow. They began to wrestle for supremacy, kicking and hitting, shouldering each other around the cave.

Bramble could feel Red tensing, getting ready. If only Acton had lived! If only he had swung the Moot his way, there would have been no warlords, ever. How different the future might have been. The future came down to now, to this moment in a cave. To Red.

Because it was clear that Asgarn was tiring. Acton's immense strength was slowly winning out, forcing Asgarn back, step by step. Once he was pressed against the wall of the cave he would have no chance. If Red chose not to help Asgarn . . .

Bramble felt his muscles tense in preparation and screamed into his head: *No! Noooo!* He faltered and she was exultant. She *could* stop him. She *would*, and take whatever consequences that came.

She gathered her strength to shout again into his mind, but the gods flooded into her, overwhelmed her, pressed her back, silenced her, and Red leapt from the shadows and raised his knife high.

He swung the knife down into the middle of Acton's back, and then reversed his grip so he could strike up, under the ribcage, up into the heart. Bramble was straining to break free of the gods, straining to touch his mind again, so as the knife went up, and in, it was as though her own hand guided it, her own arm gave it strength.

Acton slumped down, the knife still in him. Asgarn kicked him as he fell and bent over him to say harshly, "Before you go to the cold hells, tell my brother from me that I have avenged him." He glanced at Red, who stood frozen, staring at Acton, his heart thumping and his eyes burning dry. Asgarn's face drained of fury. "And tell Geb the same, for Red."

At the name, Red's eyes filled with tears and he took a deep, sobbing breath. He nodded slowly, in a kind of desolate satisfaction.

Acton's eyes had rolled up and his labored breathing changed to the death rattle. Bramble was almost angry with him. It seemed impossible that he should be lying there. He was so strong! He was too full of life to let a nothing like Red overcome him. Each labored breath dragged the air from her own lungs, so that it felt like she was dying, too. She needed him to get up. Get up! she pleaded silently. But his breaths were weaker, the rattle more pronounced. Her eyes were full of tears, but they were Red's tears, and his heart, beating fast, and his lungs at last dragging breath into them. She wanted to reach out and touch Acton, to at least ease his passing, but of course Red did not respond to the thought. She had never felt so helpless, not even when the roan was dying in her arms. At least she had been able to comfort the roan in his last moments.

Asgarn reached out and ripped the brooch from Acton's cloak. He gave it to Red, and put a hand on his shoulder. "That was well done. Keep this in memory of a great deed that must remain secret."

Red nodded. His heart was slowing, his eyes clearing as he wiped tears away. There was a sense of freedom from pain and pressure, as though Acton's death had lanced a boil.

"You know where to put the body?"

"Aye."

Asgarn clapped him on the shoulder again. Playing the part of the warlord, Bramble thought bitterly.

"Loyalty will be rewarded," he said. He shrugged his cloak back into place and strode out of the cave without a backward glance. Red looked down at Acton. Blood was seeping out of his back and spreading across the cave floor, but he was still breathing, just.

Red bent and took him under the arms. Bramble had so wanted to touch him, but not like this... not to take him to his grave. Red began dragging him to a passageway in the back of the cave, the same passageway that Dotta had led Gris down, the one she had told Bramble to remember.

Bramble braced herself for the long, winding path down to the painted cave, but the waters came: as slow and inexorable as funeral music, as strong as winter. The water covered her, smothered her, stopped her breathing as Acton's breathing was stopping. She had killed him, and now she was dying, and that was as it should be. She was content with that; so when the waters receded and left her high and dry under the trees of the Forest, it seemed like a betrayal.

MARTINE

THE MIST WAS so thick that they could barely see each other's faces, but there was movement out there, beyond their circle. From the corner of their eyes, by the prickling on the back of their necks, they knew something, or some things, were out there, circling them, watching, listening. Searching.

Martine opened her mouth to speak, but Safred put her finger to her lips, signaling for silence. They leaned close together over Bramble so that their heads were almost touching.

"This isn't about you going to the island," Martine whispered. She was sure of that, somehow. "What are they looking for?"

Safred looked down at Bramble. "We should have left her out there," she breathed, worried. "Rigged up a sun shelter or something. She would have been safe there."

"What do you mean?"

"What she's doing leaves her soul unprotected. Going, she was protected by the gods at the altar. If she is coming back... perhaps the mist is their protection against—against whatever threatens."

"The Forest?"

Safred shrugged helplessly. "I don't think so. Something beyond life."

Zel interrupted. "You don't want to say it, but it's the demons that eat souls, isn't it?"

Safred's face confirmed it. Martine had never quite believed in that story—the demons were supposed to eat the souls of those who had lived badly, without generosity or courage or kindness. The souls of the evil, the petty, the mean-spirited. She wondered if they had eaten Acton's soul. It would be ironic, if all this effort had been for nothing, because his soul was long since dead.

"They're real?" she asked.

"I don't know," Safred whispered. "The gods won't answer when I ask. But, there's something out there."

"Is there anything we can do?" Cael's face was pale. It was the first time he had shown any fear, and that made Martine's gut turn over.

Safred hunched her shoulders, uncertain.

"There is a . . . a spell," Martine said.

Zel looked at her, shocked. When the old women were at the Autumn Equinox, the young women sang the dark song, the song of protection against evil, to guard their families against the coming winter. Against all demons. But it was secret, passed from mother to daughter of the old blood.

Oh, Mam, forgive me, Martine thought, but I can't leave Bramble unprotected. She began to sing.

There were five notes only, repeated over and over again. The words didn't matter, Martine had been told, but the melody must be precise. Usually, women sang the names of their loved ones, or words like "safe" and "protected" and "life." Martine sang "Bramble," spreading the word out over all five notes, repeating and repeating.

After a moment's silence, Zel joined in, her hand sweaty in Martine's.

The moving shadows in the mist seemed to pause as they sang. Then, as though they had been waiting for some sound, something to center upon, they gathered closer. Gods protect us, Martine thought, I hope I haven't doomed us all.

Then Safred joined in, singing not in the terrible, dead voice she used to heal, but in her own light alto. Cael opened his mouth to begin, too, but Martine warned him with a shake of the head, no. She didn't know what would happen if a man sang those notes.

The mist began to draw back, leaving them in a small circle of clear air. But as it did, screaming began around them. It was the sound of a rabbit screaming as the fox bites down, the sound of the lamb under the eagle's claws, of a child falling over a cliff. Small, defenseless, and totally false, it tried to lure them into breaking the circle, shock them to their feet. Cael jerked as the first cry tore the air, but Martine had him by one hand and Safred by the other, and they held fast, singing louder.

The noises changed into howls, threatening, louder than Martine thought her ears could stand; the sound crept into the back of her brain and urged her to run. Flee! Take cover! It was hard, very hard, to stay still when every instinct said to move, and move fast. Zel was sweating, staring at Safred as though her life depended on it. Cael sat with hunched shoulders, gripping their hands so hard that Martine's fingers were losing all feeling. Safred's legs twitched as if she had started to move and then stopped herself. If only they could *see* what was out there. But perhaps the mist was to protect them from seeing. Perhaps seeing would send them mad.

Bramble jerked and groaned as though she had been wounded. The movement was enough to distract their attention from the howling and bring it back to her. Their song became stronger, and immediately the mist circle moved further outward, pushing back. They were safe within that circle, Martine was sure, but the howling and shrieking were growing louder and the shadows in the mist darker, clearer.

Larger than humans, moving with cumbersome, swinging movements, the shadows changed as they watched: grew arms and legs, flexed claws, divided one head into three. It was profoundly unsettling—not just fearsome, but striking at Martine's understanding of how the world worked. This was not the world she knew; this lake, this Forest, were connected to the world beyond this one, where humans did not belong. Perhaps rebirth was simply the way humans escaped from the terrible darkness beyond death, if that darkness held these beings.

Bramble shivered, and shuddered, and began to thrash her arms and legs. Her knee struck Safred's and Zel's hands and almost broke their hold. The howling intensified, the shapes throwing themselves at the circle and being stopped by the edge of the mist, their bodies too visible as they flattened themselves against the circle. Much too visible, because they were not animals, nor wraiths like the water sprites or wind wraiths, nor even demons as some storytellers described them. They were human, and yet not. Some elongated, some compressed, some twisted around on themselves like snakes, some wizened away like dried leaves.

Martine sang although her throat was raw, sang with a dry mouth and cracked lips, sang and sang and sang again, the five notes that her mam had taught her, and did not look at the faces of the demons in case she saw her mam's face there, or her da's, or Cob's or any of her loved ones who had gone with Lady Death, because she did not want to know if they had not been reborn, if they had swollen with pride or shrunken with envy or turned awry with greed and become one of these shrieking, hungry monstrosities.

Bramble gasped, gasped as though she were drowning, and woke.

LEOF

THEGAN TURNED TO look down at the map spread out over a side table. It showed the Domains in detail, and an outline of other lands as well. It was the largest map Leof knew. He had seen it before, many times, and every time there was more information marked on it—more details about the Wind Cities, about the Ice King's land, about the Wild Shore on the other side of the Eastern Sea, and the Long Coast beyond the Wind Cities. He saw now that the area above Foreverfroze had been filled in—although there was not much to mark in the freezing lands. Leof wondered which of Thegan's agents had ventured so far north.

"We could make this a great country, Leof," Thegan said somberly. "We talk about the Wind Cities with awe because they are so rich, yet the Domains are ten times their size *and* more fertile. But when they trade, they speak with one voice. They play us off against each other and we let them. *We* must speak with one voice."

"And that voice will be yours," Leof said. The words came out without thought, and he tensed against Thegan's reaction. But Thegan took it as a compliment, or maybe a vote of confidence, because he laid his hand on Leof's shoulder and shook it gently.

"One day. Soon, perhaps." Then a sudden gaiety overtook him, as it did sometimes when they talked about the future. "We're going to need a new name," he declared, smiling. "A fitting name for our united country. What about Actonsland?"

"What about Thegansland?" Leof countered, smiling back.

Thegan laughed, but shook his head. "No, we need something to unite us, not set us quarreling. 'Thegansland' would be seen as a boast, a spit in the face."

"Sornsland, then," Leof said, only half-joking. "She will be a most beloved Overlady, and they would see it as a romantic gesture. Particularly since she will be bearing your heirs."

Thegan had laughed at the idea of Sornsland, but at the last sentence his brows came together and his mouth hardened. Part of Leof watched him with satisfaction. Yes, there was some problem there that bothered him. But Thegan recovered himself quickly.

"Still too divisive, lad," he said. "Actonsland will bring us all together."

"Except the Travelers," Leof said.

Thegan shrugged. "They ceased to matter a thousand years ago. They're nothing."

"Except this raiser of the dead. He's likely Traveler blood," Leof reminded him.

Thegan looked at him with puzzlement. "You've changed. You're more serious than you were. Older."

Flushing, Leof looked away. "You shouldn't have put me in charge," he tried to joke. "That's enough to give gray hairs to anyone."

Thegan smiled and nodded. "But is anything better than being in command?" he asked, not needing an answer, and dismissed Leof to his meal with a gesture as he sat at his desk and began reading Leof's report.

Leof left the office with the last comment echoing in his head. It was true for Thegan—to be in command, to be in charge, was the best thing possible. Power—Leof couldn't quite understand it. Of course, it was a good feeling when your men obeyed you, trusted you to give them the right orders, followed you into battle and committed themselves, body and soul, to supporting you. There *was* nothing like that wave of loyalty and trust, buoying you up so that you were greater than you could ever be on your own. But after battle? Command was the boring part of being an officer, Leof had always thought. Making inspections, reading and writing reports, having to take responsibility... Well, his mother had always said he was irresponsible, except with his men. She claimed that he would have been married long since and given her grandchildren if he'd had any sense of family responsibility. Perhaps she was right. He'd worked hard as Thegan's officer, but he'd played hard, too. He smiled at the memory of the chases, the girls, the hunting. Just as well I'm not ambitious, he thought wryly. The last thing Thegan wants is an officer who really yearns to command.

ASH

DAYLIGHT, IN THE Deep, was for sleeping and singing. The other men, with their own faces returned to them, wandered away to curl up on blankets. One older man had even brought a mattress. Ash's father shook his head and laughed.

"Plum says he's getting too old for sleeping on the hard ground. I know how he feels." He looked at Ash with undisguised pleasure and put both hands on his shoulders. "It's very good to see you. You're looking well? You've certainly filled out!"

It was a question. Ash smiled. He certainly had filled out over the past two years. He had been little taller than his father for quite a few years, but now he was bigger, too. Stronger.

"Yes, I'm well."

"What happened with Doronit?"

Ash's face closed in. He could feel it, feel the muscles tense and the jaw set, and he forced himself to relax. "I've left Doronit. It was necessary."

His father looked at him shrewdly and, to Ash's surprise, decided to change the subject. He turned to Flax.

"Welcome to the Deep, lad. Flex, your name is?"

Ash smothered a laugh. "Flax," he corrected.

Rowan chuckled gently. "Badger ears are sharp but they don't hear human speech all that well," he explained. Flax goggled at him, clearly astonished that he would refer so casually to his transformation.

"Oh. Um . . ."

Rowan took pity on him. "You're a singer?"

Flax nodded.

"Well then, let's hear something."

This was the moment Ash had been dreading. He took a step back, to have a clear view of both Flax and his father's face. Flax coughed nervously, no doubt wondering what would happen to him if he sang poorly. Then he took a deep breath and let out a single, clear note; the beginning of the most famous love song ever written, *The Distant Hills.*

From the high hills of Hawksted, my lover calls to me
The breeze is her voice, the wind becomes her breath
From the high hills of Hawksted, above the settled plain
My lover sings so sweetly, sings the song of death

The song told of a pair of separated lovers. From the words it wasn't clear whether the beloved was far away or actually dead, and singers differed in their interpretation. The song could have been sentimental, but the music was spare and dignified and it was one of the treasures of Domain culture. The men puzzled over it in the Deep, as they talked over many songs—who might have written it? No one knew where Hawksted was. None of their extensive traditions mentioned the song, but the scale used and the melody line showed that it was very old and probably written by someone of the old blood.

Flax's voice, always beautiful, was taken and magnified by the high walls of the Deep. It took on resonance and depth that sent chills down Ash's spine, but it kept its haunting clarity on the high notes. Rowan's face was unreadable, but the other men came back, slowly and quietly, not wanting to disturb the singer. Halfway through the song there was traditionally a flute solo. Rowan fished his smallest flute, a wooden willow pipe, from his pocket and was ready; he picked up the melody from Flax without a break and when Flax came back in for the last verse he kept on playing softly, so that the flute and the voice wound around each other like the lover's voice and the wind.

Afterward, every man there had tears in his eyes. Even Ash, although he didn't know if he were crying for the song or for the look on his father's face.

Rowan carefully shook the spit out of his flute and put it back in his pocket. "Well," he said. "Well." He turned to Ash. "You did right to bring him."

Ash nodded. Their meeting had happened just as he had imagined. Rowan would welcome Flax and train him and take him to meet Swallow and they would Travel together and be a family. So, although he felt as though a hole had been scoured out of his gut, he had to remember that this was not important.

"Yes. But I didn't come here because of Flax. I came because I need something from you." His father turned, surprised, and Ash motioned him away from the others.

"Of course, son. What is it?"

"I need the secret songs," Ash said.

Rowan went very still. "I can't teach you those." His voice was flat.

"Because you don't trust me," Ash said. "You told me you taught me all the songs, but you didn't. Because I'm not a singer. Or a musician."

He couldn't stop the pain from appearing in his voice. Rowan heard it, and bit his lip. But he still shook his head.

"Not for those reasons. I trust you. Truly. But the songs are not for young men. Not for *any* young men, no matter how trustworthy."

Ash stared at him, wanting to believe him. Rowan took him by the arm and dragged him back to the group seated around the fire.

"Ask them, if you don't believe me."

"Ask us what, lad?" one of the men said.

"I need to know the secret songs," Ash said baldly.

The men, just like Rowan, went very still and the atmosphere chilled. One of them got up and stepped forward; a stocky, balding man whom Ash had met here before. Skink, that was his name. He glared at Ash, and then around the circle of men.

"What do you know about the secret songs? Who's been talking?" he asked.

"The Well of Secrets," Ash said.

That astonished them, he was glad to see. Before they could collect their thoughts, he explained everything: the enchanter, the ghosts, the need to find Acton's bones and raise his ghost. At that, they looked at each other and shook their heads. They were going to refuse him.

"I *need* the songs," he said in desperation. "Or we all might be wiped out."

A thin-faced man named Vine pursed his lips. "But this enchanter wants to take the land back for us, doesn't he? For Travelers? Why not just let him?"

The other men seemed to be considering this. Ash couldn't believe it.

"Let hundreds, maybe thousands of people die? People you all know! Children. Babies. They're killing *everyone.*"

"But not us," Vine said.

Ash was astounded that the other men were looking thoughtful, some of them even nodding.

"Really? I know they've killed at least one person with some of the old blood in her. How are they going to know who is a Traveler and who not?" He turned to an older man with a bald pate and a fringe of white hair and hazel eyes. "How will they know who *you* are, Snake? You've pretended to be one of Acton's people often enough. How will ghosts know the difference?"

"Lad's got a point," Snake said, embarrassed.

"But he can't have the songs," Vine said firmly.

"Why *not*?" Ash was exasperated.

"Let's sit down and discuss it," Rowan said, smoothing things down.

Ash sat down in the fire circle. The fire was low, cooking some parsnips in the embers, but it gave a kind of formality to the gathering, as though they were assembling a council.

Ash sat next to Rowan. Flax hovered behind until Rowan pointed to the place on his other side.

"Sit here, lad." Yes, Ash thought, momentarily distracted. Of course you have to sit next to him. He was surprised that he felt no real hatred of Flax for usurping his place. It felt so inevitable, as though it had been planned by the gods, that he could no longer feel anything but pain and resignation.

When everyone was seated, Rowan cleared his throat. "So. We have two things to decide, it seems to me. Firstly, will we resist this enchanter? Secondly, will we give the… the songs to Ash so that he can resist him by following the Well of Secrets' plan?"

The other men nodded.

Skink leaned forward and took over. Ash remembered that in other years, it was Skink who ran discussions and gave orders when orders were needed.

"I can tell you one thing. If Acton's people work out *why* this enchanter is loosing the ghosts on them, every Traveler in the Domains will be slaughtered overnight."

They sat, recognizing the truth when they heard it. There had been massacres before, for no more reason than a Traveler man seducing a blond woman; or a child sickening after a Traveler family had passed by. For a reason, a *real* reason such as this, the massacre would spread like fire through a pine forest.

"We should not only resist him, we should be *seen* to resist him," Skink concluded.

The other men nodded, even Vine.

"So," Rowan said.

"So," Skink echoed. "The second question. I say, Ash is not ready for the songs. Someone else should sing them."

"How do you know I'm not ready?" Ash challenged him.

Skink laughed shortly. "Are you married? Do you have a family? You are not ready."

Ash was intent on arguing, but Rowan intervened. "There are seasons in a man's life, son. Babyhood, childhood. Then youth, when a boy first comes here. Then the wild time, when he Travels and lives and is irresponsible. And then maturity, which comes with marriage and children."

"And then age," Snake said dryly, "which comes to us all, whether we like it or not."

"If we're lucky," Ash said out of habit. The others nodded and said, "Aye, if we're lucky," and spat on the ground for luck.

"I don't understand . . ."

"The songs you're talking about . . ." Skink stopped and looked at Rowan for help.

"Songs of power," Rowan said. "They are songs of power."

"Exactly!" Ash said. "That's why we need them."

"Power like that—young men want to change the world, Ash. Just like this enchanter does. So we protect the power from the impetuousness of youth. No man may learn those songs until he has a stake in the future. Until there is a risk to him in changing things."

Ash was confused. "I don't understand."

"Until you have children," Flax hissed at him. "Until you're a father."

The men nodded. Oh, Ash thought. It wasn't me. Father didn't refuse *me*. He would have taught me later. He would have trusted me. But although he was flooded with relief that his father hadn't deliberately withheld the songs, a small doubt remained. He had left the Road, after all, and gone to Turvite. Would his father have ever sought him out again? Visited, no doubt, when they were in Turvite, but that only happened every decade or so. Would his father have come to teach him the songs when the time came?

He couldn't brood over it; there was too much at stake to let his attention wander.

"You have no stake in the future yet," Skink said. "One of us will sing the songs."

"It won't work," Ash said.

"Oh, only you can sing?" Vine mocked him. "Hah! I've never heard you sing a single note ever."

There it was, the moment he had dreaded. He opened his mouth to try to forestall it, but Flax got in ahead of him.

"You don't understand!" he said. "He has the prophet's voice, like the Well of Secrets when she heals!"

Ash was surprised by this championship. Flax's voice was full of awe, and it impressed some of the men, but Vine was still skeptical.

"A prophet's voice? What does that sound like?"

Flax opened his mouth to explain, but Ash put up a hand.

"It's not a prophet's voice. Is it, Father?"

Rowan shook his head. The other men looked at him. "It is the voice of the dead," he said.

There was silence. Then Flax spoke, his brow furrowed. "The dead don't speak. *Can't* speak."

Rowan explained reluctantly, not looking at Ash. "Some people have the power to compel the dead to speak. When they do . . . 'from the grave, all speak alike, and it is not easy to hear.' "

"But that saying means that the dead are silent!" Snake objected.

Rowan and Ash both shook their heads. The movement was identical, and as Ash realized that his heart contracted inside him.

"No, it doesn't mean that," Ash said. "It means that the voice of the dead is terrible."

"You didn't think to share this with us, all these years, Rowan?" Skink asked quietly.

Rowan flushed. "It's not one of the secrets of the Deep," he said. Ash knew that it would have been his mother's decision to keep the information within the family. He was almost certain that he had inherited the ability from her.

"I was told," Ash said, to distract the men from his father's discomfort, "that only one in a thousand thousand can compel the dead to speak."

"And that's you, is it?" Vine asked.

"Yes."

Skink was still gazing at Rowan as though he had betrayed them all. Rowan cleared his throat.

"It is a great blasphemy to compel the dead to speak. It is a power best left unused." His voice was urgent, utterly convinced. "That is why we did not teach Ash about his...ability. Blasphemy must be avoided."

Ash remembered the shame and excitement of standing next to Doronit at Mid-Winter, compelling the ghosts of Turvite to speak. He remembered the ghost of the girl he had killed, and the stonecaster's ghost, anxious to help his son and go onto rebirth.

"To compel a ghost to speak is blasphemy," he said. "But if a ghost wishes to speak, the power can be a blessing."

It was the first time in his life he had disagreed with his father. Rowan looked at him in surprise.

"I still don't believe he can sing the songs," Vine said.

Ash stood up, trying to relax his throat muscles. He knew how he was *supposed* to sing; knew about breath control and pitch and phrasing. But he had not sung aloud since he was a small child, and the ring of faces was hostile, except for Flax and his father. He felt his gorge rise, and forced it down. Then, deliberately making it as bad for himself as he could, so there could be nothing worse waiting for him, he chose to sing *The Distant Hills*.

As the first note left Ash's throat, he saw them all flinch. His father kept his head bowed; Flax and the others stared straight at him, mouths agape. Except for Vine, who looked away and then back again, over and over.

He sang the first two lines, which was more than enough. The grating, stone-ripping-stone sound was magnified by the rock walls, just as Flax's voice had been, but with Ash the sound became unbearable, unthinkable, the howling of demons. He watched their faces. They were horrified. Repelled. Just as he had known they would be.

At the end of the second line Ash fell silent and stood there, waiting.

"So?" Flax said eventually, running out of patience.

"Mmm," Skink said. "He was on pitch."

Ash gaped at him. The last thing he had expected was a critique. "I —"

"That's a voice to make a man's balls climb up into his gut. But the phrasing wasn't bad. He was in tune, though it's not an easy melody line." Skink spoke as if Ash were any young singer, come to the Deep to learn the old songs. He had seen the older men do this, time and again—take a young singer and groom him. He had never expected it to happen to him. He felt a warm ball of gratitude to Skink grow in his belly.

Vine looked sour. "I don't care if he can hit the highest note in the scale. He's a child. He has no stake in the future and he shouldn't be taught the songs. That's the real issue."

"He doesn't even know his true self yet!" Snake added.

Ash could see what was happening. Better to keep things the way they always had been. Better to be in control; especially when the alternative was to give away power to someone strange, like him. Someone incalculable. What he had to do was to make himself unthreatening: to meet their demands in a way they could accept.

"I have a stake in the future," he said softly.

They looked at him, puzzled.

"Got some girl pregnant in Turvite, did you?" Vine snapped. "Might have known."

"No," Ash said, controlling his impulse to slap Vine backward onto the hard rock. "No, not that. But friends of mine had a baby last winter. He's being raised in Hidden Valley, and I have sworn to protect him and his family. He is my stake in the future." He paused for a moment, trying to look them all in the eye, one by one, to convince them. "His name is Ash."

Skink considered, pulling at his lip while he thought. "I will ask you some questions. If the answers are sufficient, then we will think about the next step."

"What's that?" Flax jumped in.

"No man may learn the songs unless he knows his true nature. If we accept that Ash has a stake in the future, he must find his true shape. Only if the River accepts him can he learn the songs."

Ash breathed out, hard. Another step, and another step. Fighting was a lot easier.

"When the child was born, what did you feel?" Skink said. Ash knew by his tone that the question was more complicated than it appeared.

"Well . . ." he said, trying to give himself enough time to think it through, then realizing that all he could do was tell the truth. "Firstly, just thankfulness that everything was all right; that his mother was safe and he was well."

The men nodded.

"Then, when I saw him, I felt . . ." Ash paused. What had he felt? "I was surprised, because he was so little and so . . . red and scrunched up."

Some of the men laughed, but it was the laughter of recognition.

"Then he was named for me, and I held him for the first time and I felt . . . joy. But later, when I thought about it, I felt afraid. Afraid for him. Afraid of all the things that could happen to him. Like the ghosts. That was when I swore to protect him."

His answer poured out of him, each emotion vividly alive again. He was still afraid for little Ash, and it showed, he knew from the looks on their faces. Rowan had tears in his eyes. But it wasn't enough.

"Have you sung to him?" Skink asked, putting him in his place.

Ash felt his face harden. "No," he said.

"And you have left him." There was condemnation in Skink's tone. Traveler children were few, and cherished. Rowan placed his hand on Ash's shoulder in support and warning. Be calm, he meant. Ash could almost hear the words. He took a breath and let it out slowly, then answered.

"The gods willed it. Go to the Well of Secrets, they said, and she sent me to find the secret songs."

"There is one last question. Is the child of the old blood?"

"His mother was a Traveler."

"Was?"

"She has Settled."

Skink, Vine and Snake exchanged glances. Vine shrugged, and the other two nodded.

"It is enough," Skink said. "We declare that Ash, son of Rowan, has a stake in the future in the form of the boychild Ash."

"When the time comes," Vine added, "Ash, son of Ash, son of Rowan, will be admitted to the Deep and meet the River."

"As you will do, tonight," Skink said, "when you make your climb."

BRAMBLE

FOR A MOMENT, Bramble wondered whose body she was in. Whosever it was, it was achy and cold, with sleep-encrusted eyes. She wanted to open those eyes and see, and astonishingly, they opened as soon as she thought it. There were faces staring down at her that she knew, looking scared and relieved at the same time.

She was back.

Her eyes closed again for a heartbeat, in a mixture of thankfulness and loss, then opened again.

They weren't on the island anymore, but under the trees. They were holding hands around her, which seemed strange. She was half-naked under a blanket. As she struggled to sit up, they sprang into life, supporting her, getting her water to drink, pulling up the blanket which threatened to slip down.

"Are you all right?" Martine asked.

Bramble nodded and swallowed more water. Her mouth was as dry as a Wind Cities' river in the hot season. "I have to go to the Western Mountains near Actonston," Bramble said. No sense wasting time. "That's where he...where the bones are." She turned her thoughts firmly away from Acton's death to consider how she was going to get there. Forget him, she told herself. Think about it later.

"I need Zel," Bramble continued. Her mind was crystal clear, as though she had thought through this plan for days. Perhaps she had. She had no idea how long it had been since she left Acton.

"I'd rather stay with Safred," Zel said quietly.

"Maybe. But we're going to the Western Mountains, and I am not going through Thegan's territory to get there."

Safred frowned, pleating the crown of her hat in her hands. "So? How will you go?"

"The sea ice will be breaking up about now. By the time we ride to Foreverfroze it should be free and we can take a ship for

Turvite, then ride up the southern bank of the White River to Actonston."

They were all silent, surprised.

"So I need Zel," Bramble repeated. "She's the only one of you who knows enough about horses to help me on board ship."

Zel nodded slowly. "You'll need help, sure enough, if we take those chestnuts. But why will you need more than your own horse?"

"Because I need Cael, too," Bramble said.

Safred started to argue, but Cael held up one hand. "Why?" he asked.

Bramble hesitated. "The bones are in a cave; maybe thrown down a shaft, I'm not sure. We might need some muscle."

"We'll all go," Safred said.

"How are we going to afford a trip like that?" Cael asked. "We don't have enough for even Bramble and Zel, let alone all of us."

"If we wait a day," Safred said, her eyes unfocused, "we will meet someone on the Road who will help with that."

Bramble thought it odd, that she could never feel the gods coming and going from Safred, the way she could with Baluch. Maybe they didn't come and go. Maybe they were there all the time.

Then Cael moved away so she could put her breeches back on in privacy, and she became consumed with thoughts of food. She was starving.

In the middle of the night, after the moon had gone down, Bramble woke with a sudden jerk. Had she heard something? She drew her knife and rolled out of her blankets, glad to be disturbed from a sleep choked with dreams of Acton's blood. It was a cloudy, flickering night, with a wind high in the sky sending the clouds streaming in tatters across the stars, so that the light varied from faint to none unpredictably. An unchancy night to meet something vicious in the dark.

The others had told her about the mist, although she had a feeling they were leaving out the details. Since then, they had set a watch. She had thought it was Martine's turn, but she could not see her anywhere on the perimeter of the camp, where she was supposed to be. She didn't wake the others. Not yet. Just in case the noise she had heard was Martine making her rounds.

She prowled the border of the camp closest to the Forest, but heard nothing but the sough of the branches. Then she realized that something was moving down at the water. She paused, her heartbeat increasing. That mere... They could probably cope with wolf or bear, but a creature from the depths of the lake... She forced her imagination away from the thought.

She walked down toward the water, which was lying still even in the increasing wind. There was a figure at the water's edge, pacing backward and forward—Zel. It must be later than she had thought, if it was Zel's watch. She felt adrift in time, where before she had always been securely anchored.

"Sorry if I woke you," Zel said. They moved closer together so they would not disturb the others.

Bramble shrugged. "No matter." In the past, she would have just turned and gone back to bed, but in the moonlight she could clearly see the little telltale signs that Zel was worried, or upset, and somehow she didn't want to just leave her to her troubles.

"Are you all right?" she asked, although it went against all her habits and felt like prying.

Zel fiddled with her belt and half-shook her head. "Just thinking about Flax."

"Mmm." Well, Bramble could understand that. When Maryrose had left for Carlion, Bramble had worried about her every day, too. I was right to worry, she thought, grief clutching her throat. She should say something comforting, like, "He'll be all right," but with Maryrose's death so fresh she couldn't bring herself to say a well-meaning lie. He was abroad in a world where ghosts killed the living. Who knew if he would be all right or not?

Zel looked down at the ground, and then out at the mere, then back, as if it were hard for her to talk. "Um... I wanted to ask... what was he like?" she said finally.

"Acton?"

Zel nodded.

Bramble shook her head, not to refuse the question, but to clear her thoughts. "He was very alive. It's hard to believe he's dead."

"Are the songs true? Did he really laugh during battle? While he was killing people?"

Bramble hesitated, then shrugged. "Yes," she said. "He laughed."

"Did he really say, 'Kill them all'?"

"Yes," she said. "He said that."

"And that they should keep the houses intact so his people could use them?"

"Yes."

Bramble could see that Zel was somehow eased by the knowledge that Acton was as bad as she had imagined—that the songs didn't lie. Bramble stared out at the lake. Her eyes filled with tears. Why did it feel like betrayal to tell the truth? Acton *had* done all those things. He had killed and massacred and taken this land for his own people, he had *enjoyed* battle. He had. But he was not what people thought he was. She thought that even now she didn't really know what he was. No—what he *had been*. She mustn't forget that he was dead, even though it seemed to her that she could take the brooch in her hand again and swim through the waters to find him; to watch him; to perhaps finally understand him.

"He was a man of his time," she said, and blinked away the tears before they fell. She sat on a rock at the edge of the mere and stared at the still water, trying to find calmness in its serenity.

"Do you want company?" Zel said.

Bramble stiffened. "No. No, with thanks. I've slept too long, I think, and now my body doesn't know when to rest. Go back to sleep. I'll keep watch."

"Good night, then," Zel said.

Bramble watched all night by the mere, trying not to remember. The silent water should have been soothing, but it wasn't. It reminded her too much of the waves that had risen up, over and over again, to take her away from Acton's life. She knew she couldn't sleep. She kept seeing Red's arm—her arm, it had felt like—strike at Acton. Kept feeling the knife go in.

If she had been told, before she grasped the brooch, that she would have the chance to kill Acton, she would have rejoiced. But all she felt was horror. How could she be lamenting his death—the death of the invader?

It was because of the future that had been killed, she decided. The future where all towns would have been free towns, where every person, Travelers included, would have had a say in how things were done. The gods had stopped her from creating that future, and no doubt they had their reasons, but she mourned for that world, for the nation the Domains could have become, for the freedom lost.

She still had a chance to save *this* world. Maybe, afterward, there would be a way to create the future she had seen, if only briefly, in Acton's eyes. She put that thought aside. There was no use thinking about it now. Now they had to stop Saker.

But walking by the lakeside, she kept wondering what she could have replied to Zel's questions. "Yes, but he wasn't that bad?" He *was* what Zel believed: a killer, an invader, a destroyer of too much. He *had* laughed as he killed, in the battle light-heartedness that all his people seemed to share. He *had* said, "Kill them all." The provocation didn't matter, did it? Had Hawk and his men deserved to die? Maybe. But their women and children? No. And yet, he had been upset about that... Oh, it was too much to think about, Bramble told herself. It was over, and she had to get on with things.

She went to the privy before she woke the others, and was returning to the camp when the trees shimmered in front of her eyes and her hunter appeared next to a huge oak, its gold eyes gleaming in the shadow as though reflecting light from some other place or time. She controlled her shock instinctively. Show no fear, she thought.

"Kill Reborn," it said, "you are in haste."

She didn't care how it knew, only what it might be able to do.

"I need to get to the Western Mountains quickly," she said. "Can you help me?"

It tilted its head as though listening to the Forest. Then it nodded.

"It will not be easy."

"What do I have to do?"

"Trust me."

Bramble laughed. This was better. No more discussions or plans or arguing. Just a leap of faith.

“I have to tell them, get my saddlebags.”

“Just come,” the hunter said. “Or not.”

She paused. Just walk away? Oh, that was tempting. She would have done it, too, except for Trine.

“I have to make sure my horse is looked after,” she said. “That’s my duty.”

The hunter understood duty, and the husbanding of animals, even if its way of husbanding was to cull. It nodded.

“Be quick,” it said. The hawks’ feathers in its hair caught the light as it shifted backward into the undergrowth and disappeared.

Bramble ran back to the camp. Her saddlebags were by her bedroll. She grabbed them. Her last memory of Maryrose was wound up with these bags, and she wasn’t going to leave them behind.

Zel woke immediately when she touched her shoulder.

“Look after Trine for me,” Bramble said softly. “I’ve found a quicker way. I’ll meet you in Sanctuary.”

Zel barely had time to nod and no time for questions, before Bramble was racing for the Forest.

She found her way back to the oak and stood on the same spot as before. “I’m ready,” she said.

The air shimmered and the hunter appeared.

“Then walk with me,” it said.

MARTINE

SAFRED WASN'T HAPPY, with Bramble or with Zel, and Martine felt increasingly annoyed with her as they rode single file back through the Forest and she maintained the sulk. Trine was sulking, too, lagging as much as she could on the leading rein Zel had secured to her own saddle. Zel already had bites on both hands from bridling her. Martine thought that Safred and Trine had the same expression, and the horse had more cause.

Nothing happened to disturb them. They crossed the stream without incident; they weren't even bothered by the strange panic that they had felt earlier. It was all easy—too easy, Martine felt, as though the Forest wanted to see the back of them and was urging them on.

At the point where the trail into the Forest crossed the northwest road, they dismounted so that Safred could heal Cael.

"Out of the Forest," she said, smiling. She placed her hand on his chest confidently, and sang a high chant in her terrible voice. When she took her hand away the wound was as bad as ever. She tried twice more, with the same result, until her face was white with effort and she swayed on her feet.

"Enough," Cael said. "Let it heal on its own." His face was solemn and wary. "Don't kill yourself for something impossible," he added gently.

Safred's eyes filled with tears. "I can heal everyone else, why not you?"

He shrugged and helped her to mount. They all settled back into their saddles, while Safred recovered a little. Martine could see that she was getting set for a long, involved discussion of why and why not and what could be done about it, and she was thankful, at first, when they were interrupted by a party of riders cantering down the northwest road. Then she saw they were a warlord's men and she felt the familiar tightening in the gut that armed men always brought, anywhere in the

Domains. But Safred smiled for the first time since she had woken to find Bramble gone.

"Arvid!" Her voice rang with pleasure. "It's you!"

She was calling to a man with light brown hair, dressed as the others were in simple green uniforms without emblems. No crossed sword and spear here, as there was on Thegan's uniforms. Arvid. The warlord himself. He was about forty, maybe a bit older, with a smiling, open countenance that invited trust. With very shrewd blue eyes. Martine felt another jolt in her gut, but this one brought heat with it, fire licking along her nerves and into her bones. She wanted to melt into her saddle, but she stiffened her back and kept her face impassive. The week after Equinox, she thought with resignation. All the body wants is to be satisfied, and it doesn't care who does it.

"They didn't tell you who to expect?" he asked, smiling.

Safred laughed too, ruefully. "No. Just that we would meet someone." She looked quizzically at him. "Someone who would give us silver."

He laughed. "Oh, yes, that's all I'm good for, I know," he said with mock humility. "Just the treasury, that's me."

He was easy to like, but he was still a warlord, Martine reminded herself.

Safred introduced her companions by name, but with no other information. Martine nodded at him, and received a nod and an assessing glance in return, which warmed into admiration.

"You travel with beautiful companions, Saf," Arvid said, nodding politely to include Zel, but looking at Martine. She felt the color rise in her cheeks. The fire was getting entirely too strong for comfort.

"I am riding to the Plantation, and then to Foreverfroze," Arvid said. "There is a question of markets, of sending food to Mitchen for sale. The Valuers and I are combining to hire a ship, to trade down the coast."

"As far as Turvite?" Cael asked, edging his chestnut forward.

Arvid looked surprised. "We hadn't *intended* so," he said with a question in his voice.

Safred answered. "We need to get to Turvite. We were headed for Foreverfroze, to find a ship to take us there. The gods said we would find someone here today to help. I *thought* they meant with silver, but a ship would be even better!"

Cael laughed at her enthusiasm and at Arvid's long-suffering expression.

"It seems to me that the gods use me like a banker!"

"At least you have some use," Martine said quietly.

His gaze lifted quickly to meet her eyes, and this time he was the one who flushed. "Not all warlords are useless," he said.

"So they say," Martine replied. She wasn't going to give in to the fire, no matter how hard her heart beat when Arvid looked at her. This was just backwash from the ritual, and nothing personal.

One of his men moved his horse closer, as though Martine might be a threat, and scowled at her with ferocious loyalty. "My lord is the best warlord in the Domains!" he declared. Martine saw with surprise that it wasn't a man but a brown-haired woman of about thirty, strong and tall and flat-chested. The woman continued, "My lord shares his wealth and his power. He's even set up a council of all the Voices in the Domain to guide his laws!"

"Does he abide by their advice?" Martine asked, looking at Arvid.

He smiled and answered her directly. "He does, when he can. When he can't, he explains why and gets their agreement."

"Always?"

Arvid nodded. "So far. The Voices are usually reasonable people. And an increasing number are Valuers, which makes coming to an agreement easier."

"A warlord who values Valuers?" Martine's tone was skeptical, but her eyes never left his. That would be more than unusual—it would be extraordinary. Could he be that extraordinary?

"My mother was a Valuer," was all he said.

Martine nodded, once, and looked away. If she maintained that gaze any longer she would drown in it. Valuer mother or not, he was a warlord and no concern of hers. The thump her own heart gave at the thought surprised her.

"Let's get going," she said.

Arvid nudged his horse into a walk and somehow managed to get it next to Martine's chestnut. "The Plantation for the night, and then

Foreverfroze," he said companionably. Martine turned to look at him, making her eyes as unreadable as she could. He smiled, nonetheless. "I'm not a despot," he said quietly. "Don't condemn me without evidence."

She sniffed in exaggerated disbelief, but her hand went to the pouch of stones at her belt for comfort. She wished that she could cast the stones for herself, to see what he would mean to her. The last time her heart had beaten this fast for a human man was when she was a girl, with Cob. That had led to heartbreak, and he had been one of her own kind. No good could come of encouraging Arvid. But she let him ride beside her, with Safred, Cael and Zel behind, and she was aware of every movement of his thigh against the horse, every shift of his hands on the reins. She was glad when Trine took a dislike to Arvid's horse and surged forward to kick it, because it made Arvid give a rueful shrug and move up the column to get away from her.

Martine had heard about the Valuers' Plantation all her life and had, as most Travelers had, imagined living here in comfort and beauty. But it was just a farm. A very big farm, admittedly, with quite a number of houses and sheds and barns, and dairies and forges and one big meeting hall.

A tall, solid woman named Apple, with graying yellow hair, met them with a smile and arranged for them to have lunch in the meeting hall with the Plantation council, but there was no special banquet organized. The councilors came from the fields in their work clothes, and Arvid was treated the same as the other guests. Children ran in and out of the hall constantly, cajoling food from their parents and from other people, including Arvid, who sat up one end of the table with the councilors, engaged in serious discussions.

Martine noticed that the children looked up into the adults' eyes, instead of down at the ground in respect as they did in other places. She mentioned it to Apple as she passed a plate of ham and pickles to go with her bread.

"They're taught that they are the equal of all. To look up, not proud, or cheeky, because that means you are more important than the other person. But of equal value." The words came easily to her, and it was clear this was a lesson she had recited many times to her own children.

"*Thinking* you're equal won't stop the warlords' men from beating you if they think you're disrespectful," Martine said.

Holly, Arvid's guard, laughed, unoffended.

"Aye, in other places, that's so, and we've all had cause to know it," Apple answered around a mouthful of ham. "But Arvid is a Valuer himself, or as good as one."

"His mam was raised Valuer, just like mine," Safred said unexpectedly. "But she stayed with her lord. She's still alive. Almond, her name is, but they named the baby Arvid after his grandfather, instead of Cedar, like she wanted."

There was a brief, uncomfortable silence. Safred grinned.

"The gods didn't tell me that. Almond did."

Cael laughed and had to cover his mouth to stop crumbs flying out. Then he winced, and his hand went surreptiously to his chest, as though to ease the pain of the wound there. Safred noticed and her face tightened, but she said nothing.

Martine turned to look thoughtfully at Arvid, who was smiling courteously at an older man as he laid down the law about something, poking Arvid in the chest with one bony finger as he spoke. She couldn't imagine a warlord like Thegan even sitting at the same table as a farmer in dirty boots. Anyone who poked him in the chest would be poked back with a sword through the heart.

They were parceled out among the cottagers for the night, and Martine was placed with Apple. She was grateful when Martine offered to cast the stones for her, but refused.

"There're questions which shouldn't be asked, and there're questions which aren't worth asking, and those are the only two kinds I've got," she said, smiling, but with a tightness behind the smile that told Martine she'd seen some pain in the past.

Apple sent her son, Snow, over to stay at a friend's place, and Martine slept in his bed, in clean sheets scented with the rosemary bushes they had dried on. The Plantation wasn't paradise, and no doubt they had a long, cold winter of it so far north, but Martine thought as she drifted off to sleep that it was the best life she had seen so far in a warlord's territory.

She dreamt of Arvid. They were naked, encased in flames that did not burn, but sent impossible heat through every nerve. Her hair floated about her as though they were in water, and he tangled it in his hands and brought her head toward him, seeking her mouth as though frantic for her, as she was for him. She woke the moment before their lips touched and lay, aching, staring at the window, wanting him to climb through like a lover from a story.

I must be mad, she thought. This is more than the normal backwash from the Equinox. Perhaps it's punishment from the fire. Lord of Flames, she prayed, forgive me and set me free from this. But her skin was tender as though exposed to too much heat, and every movement of her breath rasped the sheet across tight nipples. She had to curl up in a ball, like a child, for hours before she fell asleep again.

She dreamt of Arvid.

APPLE'S STORY

WHAT GOOD WAS it? Where was the use? I had served, worked, been loyal—for what? An empty alleyway. Yet now they expected me to go on. To serve, as if nothing had happened. As though the alleyway still led home.

I stood with the tray in my hands, looking over at the glass table.

"You're lucky to still have a job," the cook said gently, "Go on. The lord is waiting."

Let him wait, I thought. Let him wait until the giants eat the sun.

I put down the tray and walked out of the hall, straight out of the fort enclosure and down the hill to the gibbet and the pressing box. The guard on the gate called out as I went, "I'll be closing up in a few minutes, girl," but I ignored him. I was not coming back.

I went to the gibbet. The crows had had three days at Lidi already, and I didn't want to look. I watched the gallows instead, and I was ready when his ghost quickened.

Lidi came back not in midair, where I'd been expecting him, but on the platform, which meant that he hadn't had the quick death I'd thought. He rose, slowly, knowing where he was, knowing what had happened, and I went forward so that he could see me.

He reached out to me, and I to him, but what good was that? His hands and mine passed through each other with a chill that went to my bones. It's a cruelty of the gods, that they let us see our dead, but not touch them.

"They will not offer reparation," I said, and only as I said it did I realize that I was crying, hiccuping with a tearing grief. "They never do. But don't let them condemn you in the next life as well. Cheat them. Go onto rebirth."

He reached for me again, his face bereft. I put my hand up near the side of his face. He pointed at me and spread his hands as though asking a question.

"I'm leaving," I said. "I'm going to the Plantation."

He stilled and nodded, and then tried to smile. He raised his hand and blew me a kiss, and that was the hardest moment of all, I remember, because it was a thing he never did. I used to do it to him as I left for work every morning, but it was a joke between us, that he would never copy me. "It's a girl's thing to do," he'd say. So he blew me a kiss and smiled and faded, gone before I could return the kiss, and I sank down at the foot of the gibbet, my legs unsteady. His body hung above me, laced in chains, three days' dead.

I couldn't touch his ghost, but I could touch his body, for the last time. So I reached out and put my hand on his foot, still in the shoes he had made himself. I didn't mean to, but I set him swinging and his chains rattled. It was like he was sending me a message, and the message was: *Run!* So I ran. I ran back through the alleyway to the rooms we had called home and I packed everything I could carry into his old backpack and I left, right then, no thinking about it, no planning, I just left and headed north. I spat on the road that led to the fort as I passed. They said he had withheld taxes, but the truth was that he had not bowed low enough. That he was disrespectful.

So he was, and so he should have been. What was there on the hill to respect? I'd always said, "No, love, don't anger them, just look at the ground as they pass by," but now I was filled with the anger that had filled him, the anger that had pushed him too far, pushed him right to the gallows.

So I went to the Valuers. We'd talked about it, Lidi and I, in the winter nights, snuggled under our thin blankets. We'd talked about making the trip north, to the Plantation. But I was still in tax bondage, from the bad summer when Da's crop failed, and they would have chased me and brought me back and branded me too, like as not, if not condemned me to the pressing box. So we stayed, and worked, and saved until I had worked out my tax bondage. We were planning to go that summer. It was Lidi's dream, not mine, but I would have gone anywhere with him.

Now there was just me, and I was going for him.

Well, it's a long trip and it took me a good long while to do, and made no easier by the fact that a month out of Whitehaven I found I was carrying. I sat by the side of a stream, my road-sorry feet in the water, and took a moment to count the days. Then I realized—understood that my tiredness wasn't just from walking so far. Lidi's baby. Oh, gods rest him, he'd wanted a child so much. I didn't know whether to laugh or cry, so I did both. I was more determined to get to the Plantation, so that Lidi's baby would grow up without any overlord, free in mind as well as body.

But it took a long time, and I had to winter over in Pless. I got work as a maid in the clothier's on the market square. One of the women spoke up for me, said that I was just traveling, not a Traveler, that they should let me stay long enough to have the baby and recover. I don't know why she did it, but it was life itself to me. Maude, her name was, she was kindness itself. Had no children, she told me, and always wanted one to fuss over, so she helped as though she'd been the aunty. She was a seamstress for the clothier and she made a whole set of baby clothes for me. So beautiful. Fit for a—I was going to say a warlord's child, but sackcloth would suit one of those better. Fit for a prince from the Wind Cities.

My own little prince was born in the middle of a winter storm, when the wind howled against the shutters and the snow blew sideways down the city streets. So I called him Snow, and it was a good name for he was as fair as Lidi had been. I was glad of that. I'm red-blond myself, but my great-grandmother had been a Traveler, and they say the dark hair can skip generations and appear at any time. I knew it would go harder for a child with black hair, and it had been worrying me—one of those silly worries a pregnant woman gets, yet real for all that. Life is harder for a dark-haired child, there's no doubt. But my Snow was a tiny blond scrap with long fingers that clung to mine and a cry that went right through your head and out the other side. Oh, he was a cryer, that one! Just as well I was living at the back of the workshop and not in someone's house, for he would have woken the dead with his bawling. But it was just colic, and he got over it after a month or so, though for that month I walked around like one dazed and the seamstresses were lucky if they got anything to eat or drink, let alone what they'd asked for. But they paid me, and I saved every skerrick.

When spring came, I decided to head north again. Maude tried to get me to stay. “It’s a free town,” she said. “He’ll be as free here as on the Plantation.”

Maybe she was right, but I’d promised Lidi’s ghost. So I went on, through the spring and summer. I made it as far as the North Domain just as autumn was closing in, through a small pass that the stonecaster who came to cast for the seamstresses had told me about. It was harder but faster than going all the way around to Golden Valley. I climbed steep goats’ trails that I would never have dared if I had not needed to get Snow safe to the Plantation before winter set in. I saw no one.

On the evening of the second day after I cleared the pass, I came down from the foothills into a small, wooded valley, no more than a dale full of upright birch trees, where the first autumn colors were late appearing so that the trees seemed like green pillars with a faint veil of yellow fire at their tips. It was a beautiful place. I was glad, because I could hear a stream trickling nearby. I had slung Snow across my chest in my shawl, and now he woke and began to cry for his feed. I drank from a cup made of birch bark, and I was so thirsty I forgot to ask the tree for permission to strip the bark. I drank and sat and fed my babe and was smiling at his tiny fingers kneading my breast when I realized someone was standing before me.

My heart thumped in surprise. I hadn’t heard any sound. I looked up but there was no one there. A trick of the light. I looked down to Snow and again, the figure stood in front of me.

I had known terror, when they came for Lidi, when they killed him, but this fear was different. A holy fear. I have never had the Sight, or heard the gods, but I knew that whatever I had seen was from the other world that they inhabit.

Snow finished and burped, loudly. I flinched and looked down at him without thinking, and again I saw the figure. This time I kept my head down. The edges of the figure were shimmering, moving yet anchored, as leaves move but the trunk stays still. It was not green, though, or any color I knew. More like a lack of color, like heat haze over rocks in the summer. I couldn’t see through it. It was solid, but—not there. Not wholly here, in this world.

“Greetings,” I whispered.

The figure bent and picked up the bark cup I had torn from the tree. It cradled the cup in its—were they hands, or something else? I couldn't see, couldn't quite make it out. It hissed, a strange sound like wind through leaves.

I was certain that this was the spirit of the birch tree, come to punish me for stealing the bark.

"I'm sorry, truly, truly," I stammered. "But the baby needed to be fed and I was so thirsty, I acted without thinking."

The figure reached a hand toward Snow and I jumped up and pulled him away. As soon as I stood it disappeared from my sight, but not from hearing. The hissing continued.

"It's not his fault!" I cried. "It's mine!"

I lowered my head to look at the ground and I could see it, faintly, before me, its hand stretched toward Snow, but stopped, considering. Its head turned up and I realized it was smaller than I was, but its arms were much longer and, perhaps, there were more of them. I couldn't see, and not being able to see frightened me more than I would have thought. To have the threat to my son disappear when I raised my head... It could be anywhere, go anywhere, spring out from anywhere... I kept my head down and watched it as close as I could.

It looked at me and the hissing increased, until it sounded like a forest in a gale, an ocean of trees tossing in the wind. The hissing came in waves and, although I cannot understand the gods, I understood this. This was not the spirit of one tree, but the guardian of many. And it wanted retribution.

"It was my fault," I said, "and I will pay the cost. But not now, I beg of you." My voice broke on the words and I bit back a sob. I didn't think this thing would understand tears.

"Let me get my son to safety, let me raise him, and then I will pay."

The spirit hissed more softly, but still not pleased.

"What are a few years to you? Just a few seasons, that's all. Then I will pay the forfeit."

I stared at the ground as if it were my beloved's face, praying to all the gods that were. The hissing dropped away to a faint shushing noise. It understood, I felt. It accepted. Then it reached one threatening hand to my son and poised its long fingers over his throat. The meaning was clear. If I did not pay, Snow would.

"I understand," I whispered. "When he is grown, I will come."

But it was not satisfied. It wanted something else. I thought frantically, and remembered the old stories, about bargains between humans and spirits. There were certain words that were always used. I had thought it was just a storyteller's trick, but perhaps it wasn't.

"I am Dila, daughter of Sarni. I swear by my blood that I will return to pay the forfeit."

The spirit fell silent, accepting the bargain. Then it disappeared into the earth, sank into it as one sinks into a bog, but the earth was firm where it had stood.

I went from that place as fast as I could, and I made it to the Valuer's Plantation the next day. They took us in, just as Lidi had said they would, in those winter nights when we'd planned this trip together. They gathered us in like lost lambs, and I felt a bit like a lost lamb, I was so shaken by my meeting with the tree spirit.

But then there was just life—working in the dairy was my main job, milking and cheese-making, although I helped with the sowing and the harvesting, like everyone else. And like everyone else I voted for the council members and said my say in the open meetings, which was one thing I would not have had in a free town, where only people who own property can vote. We had some fights in those meetings, I can tell you! Everyone helped me build a little cabin and I planted a circle of rowan trees around it to safeguard Snow while we slept, and underplanted them with larkspur, which protects from illusion. But nothing happened, except winter turning to summer and back again.

Until the evening of Snow's fifteenth birthday, when I had to pay the forfeit.

I had known it was coming. Every new moon I marked his height on the back of the cabin door, and it was three months since that mark had changed. He'd reached his full growth. I had promised to return when he was grown, and that was now. How I wished I'd said it some other way: when he was an adult, when he was settled in a home of his own—anything but this, which had come so soon.

For the last three days, every time I had walked outside the wind had risen, whipping my cheeks and tearing my hair out of its plait. Even the rowan trees seemed to hiss at me. When I walked out to empty the evening slop pail in the pig trough and the larkspurs were laid flat under the rowans by the wind, I knew in my gut it was time to go.

I'd never told Snow about the forfeit. No need to grow up knowing a thing like that. He was a happy soul, a lot like his father, and the Plantation was the safest place in the Domains—maybe in the world—so he'd grown free and wild like children should; grown up to look everyone in the eye and respect only those who'd earned it. He was best friends with a much bigger family—four boys and three girls—who lived a stone's throw from our cottage. He spent more time there than with me, and I knew they'd take him in, if he wanted it, and cherish him as I would. So early the next morning I went to talk to Cherry, the mother and a good friend of mine, and told her the story.

"I have to go tomorrow," I concluded. "Or the forfeit will fall on Snow."

Well, she was troubled and a bit disbelieving, but I'm not one for fancies or telling tall tales, so she took me at my word after the first surprise.

"Do you think you'll be coming back?" she asked, looking down and pleating her skirt with her fingers so she didn't have to meet my eyes.

"I doubt it."

"That's a high price to pay for a bark cup!" she said indignantly. "We could get the men and go and chop those trees down! That would sort it out."

I laughed. It was so like her, to fire up in defense of someone she thought was being hard done by. Cherry was the loudest voice for justice in our meetings, and I loved her for it. "More likely sort us out. No. I made a bargain, Cherry, and it was a good one. I got to raise my Snow, didn't I?" My voice broke a little on that, and she hugged me. I hugged back, glad of the comfort.

"I'll look after him," she said.

"I know." I collected my thoughts and smoothed my skirt. "I'm not going to tell him where I'm going," I said. "Just in case I do come back. No need to worry him. It's a hard thing to ask, but will you tell him, if I'm not back in a day or so?"

She made a face, but she nodded. “He can come and stay with us while you’re gone,” she said.

“You’re cramped for space here,” I said, looking around the small house as I stood up to leave. “After I . . . afterward, why not let the two eldest move in with Snow? They could still come back for meals, but they’d be out from under your feet.”

“Time enough to think of that later,” she said quietly. “Gods go with you, Apple.”

Apple was the new name they had given me, my Valuer name, taken to show my connection to all living things and my respect for the people of the old blood and their ways. It was a good name. Homely, ordinary, but useful and sweet on occasion. I had liked the idea of being Apple, and I liked it still.

I kissed her cheek, which was not a thing we did, normally, and went to find Snow.

It was hard to pretend that I was just going on a trading trip to Oakmere, when what I wanted to do was grab him and cry over him and make him promise to be a good man, a man like his father, and promise to look after himself and eat properly and clean up after himself and to choose a kind, sweet girl to marry—oh, and all the rest of the things a mother worries about. But I just hugged him and kissed his brow, as I had done other times, when I went trading, and he noticed nothing, because what fifteen-year-old boy notices anything about his mother?

Somehow that was comforting, that he was so—workaday. So unknowing that danger could lurk unseen in the wild. That he was safe here.

Then I went. I took just enough food and drink to get me there, because I didn’t expect to come back. I didn’t take Lidi’s backpack, just a potato sack. I wanted Snow to have the backpack.

I was surprised by how much I remembered about the way, considering how upset I had been fifteen years ago. I slept under the same holly bush I had sheltered under then, and next morning found the trail easily enough, but though I had worked hard and was still strong I wasn’t as young as I had been then, and the climb was hard. I was breathless when I reached the ridge that rimmed the little valley where I had seen the tree spirit, and I paused a moment. It was mid-morning, with the sun gilding the young leaves and the birch trunks shining brightly in the shade, almost glowing, it seemed, with the stream chuckling between ferns as though it laughed.

I thought then, and I still think, that it was a place worth protecting. That if I were a tree spirit, I would act, too, to save it from desecration.

I went down the slope and stood by the stream, where I had seen the spirit before, and put my sack on the ground.

"I have come to pay my forfeit," I said. Nothing happened. No figure, no change of sound, nothing. Then I remembered, and looked at the ground.

There it was, waiting. Silent. It raised its arms, the long fingers wavering as it shimmered in the sun, looking both real and unreal at the same time.

In the old stories, the words had to be said again, almost the same as when the bargain was made. So I took a breath and said, "I am —" and then I stopped, because I did not know what to say. I had made the bargain as Dila, but now I was Apple, and glad of it. I stared at the figure in confusion, and of course it vanished as soon as I lifted my head.

I looked back down at the ground. "I don't know what my name is," I said. I must have sounded daft, but it was the truth, and maybe it could hear the truth in my voice, because it hissed—to my surprise—in laughter, like a spring breeze playing in the branches. That gave me confidence.

"I was Dila when I made your bargain. But now I am Apple."

The spirit hissed again, and this time it was like the wind that rises before a storm.

"I don't know what to tell you," I said. "I'm here to pay whatever forfeit I have to, to keep my son safe. But I can't say to you, 'I am Dila,' because I'm not, anymore."

It tilted its head, considering, and I considered, too. Was there nothing of Dila in me? Just my love for Lidi, I thought.

Its hissing increased, and now it was a question.

"There's a little part of me that is still Dila," I confessed. Should I tell it what? It was growing impatient, I could tell. The wind was rising around us, the trees beginning to shake and the stream had small white waves. "My love for my husband. He's dead. He died while I was still Dila, so that part of me is her."

It was a poor explanation, and sounded sentimental to me, but the thing paused and the wind died. For a moment, the glade was silent, waiting. The back of my neck was getting sore from staring down for so long. Then the spirit reached out a hand and placed it on my chest. I thought, goodbye Snow, and I hoped—I remember hoping—that Lidi had waited for me so we could be reborn together.

Then I felt... Oh, I can't explain. A kind of tearing, in my heart, in my mind, all through my body. There was blood flowing, but not from any wound, just out of my skin, out of my eyes, out of my ears. It hurt. But not unbearably. The pain was not as bad as giving birth, not nearly as bad. The strangest thing was that the blood did not sink into my clothes. It flowed over my skin and down into the ground, disappearing as the spirit had disappeared the first time I had met it.

The spirit took its hand away.

There I stood, whole, unmarked, the blood leaving not a trace on my hands or anywhere that I could see, the pain fading, and me still alive.

The spirit hissed with satisfaction, and disappeared. That was it.

I stood there stupidly for a while, expecting something else to happen, but nothing did. The golden day went on around me and the stream chuckled its way along its bed, and I stood like a booby on the grass with tears running down my cheeks, because I had expected to die and now I was alive.

I climbed back out of the valley slowly, relishing every moment, and it wasn't until I had reached the ridge and was looking back at the valley that I thought of Snow, and how now I would be able to tell him the story, and I thought of Lidi, who would have to wait for me a bit longer. Then I realized what the spirit had taken. The last bit of Dila. The part that loved Lidi.

I could remember him. I could remember loving him. I could remember my grief when I lost him. But the feeling itself was gone. The part of my heart that had been full since the first day he kissed me was empty. He was just a memory, as though I'd heard about him in a story.

I felt the empty part of my heart every day, as I went about my milking and my sowing and my cooking. I felt both lighter and less solid, as though I had been hollowed out like a gourd. I had no grief, but nothing came to take its place, and I did not think anything ever would, because that was the nature of the forfeit, that that part of me should die.

It was a fair bargain. Blood and love and pain, for the life of my son. I would pay it again. But this was the thing: I knew that Dila badly wanted for Lidi to wait for her, so they could be reborn together. I knew that Dila, that *I*, thought that it was more likely he would wait for her because she continued to love him so much. So I wondered: I was Apple, wholly Apple, and Apple did not love him. So would he wait? Did I want him to?

I didn't care. It seemed to me that I would greet him after death merely as someone I once knew, with no more feeling than I have for the weaver in Oakmere who made my cheesecloths. But perhaps the part of me that had died already, the part that was Dila, will come back when it is time for me to go onto rebirth, and make me whole in death as I was not in life. Perhaps I will love him again, and greet him with joy.

I will have to wait to find out.

LEOF

THEGAN CAME WITH him to his horse the next morning, a great mark of favor. He handed Leof the stirrup cup himself, and said, "Keep me informed. You are doing well, but don't forget to keep the officers on their estates up to date. We will be calling the levies in soon enough, I suspect."

Leof nodded, feeling like a traitor because his heart was leaping at the thought of returning to Sorn. He was determined not to betray Thegan, but the image of her, waiting in her hall, that shaft of sunlight gilding her autumn hair, her green eyes wide and welcoming, made his heart turn over. And there was betrayal, right there, whether he did anything about it or not.

He had opened his mouth to say a formal goodbye when a shriek like a cold demon dying deafened them. Arrow and Bandy's horse, Clutch, reared and Thegan stood back, swearing. Leof fought with Arrow and got her under control, but Clutch bolted down the main street, straight for the harbor.

The shriek came again and this time Arrow stood, feet planted, head down, shaking uncontrollably. Leof looked up. Thegan was staring at the clear blue sky, his face pale. Leof followed his gaze and saw...something. A ripple in the sky, like a shadow on water; not quite a cloud, not quite anything.

"Wind wraiths," Thegan said, tight-mouthed.

They were hard to see, but now he knew what was there, Leof could make out vague figures, misty and curving through the sky, long arms out as though reaching for the ground. He expected them to pass over the town.

"Where is he?" one of them screamed. The sound scraped over Leof's nerves and Arrow trembled so hard he thought she would collapse. He dismounted and went to her head, soothing her. She turned her face into his chest like a child seeking comfort.

"Where is the enchanter who will feed us? Find him!" The voice was neither male nor female; it was high and low together, as a storm will have a deep voice and yet wuther high at the same time.

Thegan stared straight up at them, his face stern. "There is no enchanter here. Begone! You are forbidden in this realm."

"Hah!" The shriek rose high and passed the border of hearing, but Leof's ears still hurt as though the sound continued. "Soon!" it declared. "He will feed us spirit and body! Find him! Find him!"

The wraiths swirled out over the town, for all the world like hunting dogs looking for a scent. They shrieked and screamed and laughed so sharply that every dog started howling, or hid in terror, and every horse they passed panicked.

Thegan turned to Leof with sudden urgency. "Quick! Follow them. If they find this enchanter for us, so much the better!"

Leof mounted Arrow, who was still trembling. He bent low over her neck, patting her and murmuring reassurance. Bandy had regained control of Clutch and was trotting up the street from the harbor.

Thegan watched the wraiths intently. They were gathering around the town's southern gate. It was hard to see them, but it looked like there was a local mist there, or a low cloud. Then it disappeared and the shrieking died away.

"South," Thegan said. He slapped Arrow on the rump and she jumped forward and then began trotting up the slope to the gate. "After them, Leof! Find me this enchanter!"

Bandy clattered behind them, but Arrow was already picking up the pace. They swept through the gate at a canter and on the level ground of the cliff plateau Leof urged her on.

She responded to his hands and knees and began to gallop. Not her best pace, but one that she could sustain, if need be, for some time. He thanked the gods that he'd lost weight recently, having had so little time to sit down for meals and so little appetite when he did. Bandy was already far behind. Leof allowed himself a fleeting thought of Sorn, and then settled in the saddle.

He kept his eyes on the horizon, where a flowing mist, a ripple in the sky, showed where the wraiths were flying. As he watched, they began to veer inland, following a minor road toward the farmlands of Central Domain. This was his chance to catch up with them. They were following the way the enchanter had taken, and he had clearly kept to the roads. But Arrow and he weren't bound to marked routes. They could go cross country and perhaps even get ahead of the wind wraiths.

Leof headed Arrow at a low stone wall and she pricked her ears with pleasure. Like all chasers, she loved the sport and had missed it in Sendat. She took the jump flying and landed with precision on new hay. Leof couldn't bother, this time, about wrecking farming land or crops. Too much was at stake.

"We have to win this one, sweetheart," he said to Arrow. "This is the chase of chases."

ASH

After Ash had learned the truth about the demons of the Deep, he had been wild to discover his true shape, his animal nature. Now, with the truth promised to him, he had to wait, and wait, and wait . . .

"I am so hungry!" Flax complained for the sixth time.

"Well, you can always walk out of the Deep and take Cam and go back to Gabriston and eat," Ash said, annoyed. Flax looked sheepish.

"I don't know what you're complaining about," Ash added. "You only have to fast until after the ceremony. I've got two more days to go."

"Stop talking, you boys!" Vine ordered. "We're trying to sleep!"

Ash and Flax exchanged glances of mutual long-suffering. They were in a group with three other young men who had arrived with their fathers during the afternoon. Each of them was at a different stage of his journey to the Deep, but each had to fast the day through before he could go to the appropriate cave and learn what he had to learn. Ash had been through all this preparation in previous years, but he was about to skip over the last couple of steps and go straight to the final test, the climb to discover his true shape. For that, he had to fast for three days, taking only water, and staying silent for the last full day.

The first day went slowly. At sunset, the men disappeared into the caves and reappeared a little while later in their true shapes. Individually, the boys were chosen and led away. Flax was last. Rowan came for him, with Skink, whose true shape was a fox. Flax made a nervous face at Ash and stood, half-unwillingly, and began to strip off his clothes. He seemed both attracted to and uneasy with the Deep, which was not a bad thing, necessarily. Ash just hoped he was trustworthy. Tonight he would have the demon warnings, the threats about keeping silent, the solemn vows of secrecy. They made an impression, as they were meant to.

Once Flax was naked, the demons led him to join Ash at the mouth of the cave. Ash patted his shoulder reassuringly. Rowan the badger led them forward, around the leaping fire, to the first of the chasms, a split in the rock that blocked the exit from the cave. Black as pitch, it was a couple of paces wide. From below the sound of water thundered up. Rowan gestured to Ash. He nodded, remembering. This warning was usually given in daylight, when the men could talk. The youngest boys were shown this cave on their third day in the Deep, to prepare them for the night, which was hard.

"This is the beginning of the Deep," Ash said, echoing what he had been told precisely. "This is your first glimpse of the River. This is not the Hidden River, which flows from the Lake for all to see. This is the Dancing River, the Lake's little sister. She flows throughout the land, underground, never seen except by us, here, where she reveals herself to us that we might know who we truly are. She flows from cliff to cove, from sand to snow, binding the Domains as no man ever could, making this all one country. Our country, given to us by water and fire and never taken away, no matter what the fair-haired ones think. But beware! The River is not the Lake. She is wild, not tame; she is joyous and terrible; she is lover and she is Death herself. Beware. Do not betray her, or her punishment will be unthinkable. Do you swear allegiance to the River, to finding your truth?" Gently, he added, "You don't have to, but if you don't you can't go any further. You'll just have to wait in the clearing until morning."

Flax gulped and glanced back to where the demons waited in the shadows made by the leaping fire. "With them?" He shook his head and opened his mouth. "I —"

Ash cut in quickly. "Don't say it if you don't mean it. This is for life, Flax. There's no going back."

Flax met his eyes, uncertain. "Doesn't everyone want to know who they truly are?" he asked.

"No. Not everyone," Ash said. "Some are afraid. Some are so happy in themselves they don't need it. And some . . . some think they already know, and don't want it confirmed in front of others. Not everyone comes to the true Deep."

Around them, the men waited patiently. No one moved. Ash could feel the pull of the River, feel its power flowing up from the slit in the rock. It was a different power to the gods; wilder, happier, more grief-stricken. It *felt* more, as humans feel. The River desired them to go forward. He sensed that desire, the desire to know and be known, to accept and be accepted, which lay at the heart of the River mysteries. He had always found it irresistible, but Flax was not him.

Flax stared down into the dark, listening. "I swear," he said suddenly.

As one, the men took in a deep breath and howled triumph to the roof of the cave. It was the sound they had heard the first night, but this time it buoyed them up instead of chilling them. Ash felt himself grin, and Flax smiled widely, puffing his breath out in a long sigh.

"Now what?" he asked.

Ash flicked him a glance full of mischief, and backed away. "Now you jump," he said.

"Over *that*?"

Ash nodded. The howling grew louder and Rowan ran and leaped, high and long, over the black chasm, over the pounding waters, landing in a crouch and waiting there for Flax.

"You next," Ash said. "Come on."

Flax blew out his breath again and then backed up as far as he could go, until the fire was almost licking at his legs. Then he ran forward and leapt.

It wasn't a high leap, and for a moment Ash had a terrible fear that he would fall, and he would be left to explain his death to Zel. I promised to look after him, he thought in a quick panic, but then Flax was over safely and half-collapsed at Rowan's feet, panting much harder than he should have been from the jump. Yes, Ash thought, we learn about fear here. Rowan helped Flax to his feet and thumped him on the back in congratulations.

They went down the passageway and Ash returned to the clearing and settled down to wait. Tomorrow Flax would be taken to within touch of the River for the first time. The night after that, she would touch him. That was the night that Ash would climb.

All night he tended the fire and tried to ignore his rumbling stomach. The hunger would get worse, he knew. He had seen other young men go to the climb stumbling, light-headed with hunger. Fasting made the climb more dangerous, but cleansed the spirit and opened the heart to the River. It was necessary.

As he fed the fire, Ash realized that there was music building in his mind; a complex kind of music which he had no words for, no way of describing to anyone. He brooded over Skink's words after he had sung. He had been on pitch. His voice was true, even if it was horrible. If he could find someone willing to listen, he could share his music at last. But he doubted, as intertwined patterns of flute and drum and harp and voice ran through his mind, that simple singing could convey what he wanted. Perhaps this music simply wasn't meant to be heard by others. Perhaps it was only for the gods.

He resisted the temptation to take out the casting stones and ask. Casting for oneself was notoriously unreliable. But he decided to ask Martine, the first chance he got.

Because he was determined that there would be a future; that they would defeat this Saker; and he would not be a safeguarder in that future. Returning to the Deep had rekindled his love of music. He thought about Flax and the beauty of his voice. But it was the song that displayed that voice, and Flax was only a singer, not a maker of songs. Ash felt that, perhaps, he might be able to make songs that could rival the beauty of *The Distant Hills*. If he could find a way to teach the songs to others.

The young men came back just before dawn, exhausted, and ate cold meat and greengages and cheese. Ash sat away from them so he couldn't smell the food. Then the dawn lit the red rock walls as though drenching them with blood, the men came back from the caves in their true shape, ate breakfast, and all of them, Ash included, fell asleep in the early morning light.

He dreamt of water, running, endlessly running; of waves that took and carried him away; of Bramble smiling at someone out of sight; of fountains. Underneath the constant water sounds was music.

LEOF

OVER THE POST and rail fence, around the big willow tree and splashing across the stream, up the slope beyond, around the herd of dairy cows. The bull took objection to their appearance and put his head down to charge, bellowing defiance. Arrow scrambled out of the way and leaped over the dry-stone fence beyond. Leof leaned low over Arrow's neck and grinned. It was like the best of chases—he felt like he was out alone, leading the field, the way Bramble used to do on Thorn.

Ahead of him the Kill raced, but this was one Kill he didn't want to catch. He shivered at what might happen if the wind wraiths realized he was following them. Then he grinned again and urged Arrow on. She was tiring, but her heart was so big that whenever he asked her for more she gave it.

Leof thanked the gods that he had spent so much time at chases when he first arrived from Cliff Domain. He knew most of this countryside, had ridden over a great deal of it. It was a mixture of pasture and crops, intercut with many, many streams and small rivers. One of the most fertile areas of the country, this farmland was the reason Thegan had wanted Central Domain so badly. Leof thought ruefully of the crops he had trampled since he left Carlion, but it would have wasted too much time to avoid them. The mixture of animals and crops meant that the fences were frequent and sturdy, and that the ground beyond them was usually firm and reasonably level—perfect chasing country.

In the next field, Arrow soared over the post and rail fence, took long low jumps over three streams that divided the field, cantered for a moment to catch her breath, then gathered speed again across the pasture, scattering ewes and lambs as she went. Leof stood in the stirrups to ease her back for a while.

The wraiths were following a winding route among villages and small towns. They had stopped twice to investigate something, the second time for so long that Leof had a chance to spell Arrow. Without that respite, she would have foundered. He might have been able to catch them, but that wasn't his task. He had to let them lead him to the enchanter.

He would very much have liked to see what had interested them so. They had swooped close to the ground, over and over, and seemed to be *smelling* it. But they had taken off so fast afterward that he had no time to look. He had to take the straight line after them. He noted the locations and left them for another day. Right now, all he had to do was chase.

It was a glorious chase: over walls and streams, under shade trees and around coppices, over logs and through new hay that brushed his boots and smelt of summer. He felt vaguely guilty about enjoying it so much, when the safety of the Domains was at stake.

By the time the sun was overhead, out of his eyes, Arrow was tiring badly. He cast about for somewhere where he might get a change of horse, but the last village had been tiny and would have no messenger horses stabled there. He eased Arrow to a walk, watching the wraiths streak ahead of them, knowing he had probably failed, but clinging to the hope that they would keep going in that straight line and he would be able to find them again.

Then they stopped, in midair, hovering like hawks before a kill. And like hawks they stooped, shrieking. Leof wasn't close enough to see exactly what they had found. They were over a small grassy hill just outside the next village—Bonhill, that was it—and when they stooped they disappeared behind the hill.

He dismounted and walked Arrow slowly toward them, hoping that they would give her time to recover before speeding off again. Then he got close enough to hear a man's voice, speaking to them, and realized he had found the enchanter.

SAKER

ROWAN'S SONGS HAD been so precise. Saker gave thanks for the musician who had taught him all the old songs, the invasion songs which told how many of the old blood were killed in each place, and where they were buried. He wondered, briefly, where Rowan was now, and Swallow his wife, and Cedar their drummer. He had Traveled with them for months, learning the songs, and it had been the happiest time of his life.

Until now. Saker smiled as he turned over the ground and the spade revealed the graves. They had been shallow when made, but the centuries had covered them with layer after layer of dirt. He had had to dig deep. These bones were not in such good condition as others he had found. They were much browner, and soft, crumbling as he touched them. It was the damp. Water was a great destroyer of bones. The grave here was in a hollow which must have collected rainwater for untold years, making a lush patch in an otherwise scrubby field. Fed by the blood of his ancestors, Saker thought, and watered by the friendly rains of their home.

This was the fourth site he had excavated since Carlion, and it was almost routine. He sorted through the bones until he had taken fingerbones from each skeleton. Sometimes it was hard to decide which bone belonged to which body, and then he took extras just to be sure. After he had the fingerbones he laid them out on a piece of cloth and called to them, going over his litany of names. When he felt the twitch in his mind that told him the spirit had not gone on to rebirth, he placed that bone into the sack with the rest of his collection, and made a note of the name on his scroll. He had amassed quite a collection of names, now. He felt both triumphant and sad to read them over. So many, ready to fight. So many lost to Acton's greed.

He had sorted through almost two-thirds of the bones from this site and had gathered another dozen names when he heard the shrieking. He froze, immediately remembering the sound from terrible nights with Freite, the enchantress who had trained him. Wind wraiths. He began to shake with fear, as though he were still a child.

She had used the horrible spirits to cow him into obedience—had threatened to give him to them to be eaten, or worse. She never said what the worse was, but she didn't have to. The sight of them, their long, clawed fingers, their sharp teeth and, most frightening of all, their hungry eyes, filled him with terror. He had given up his strength to her, holding nothing back, rather than be delivered into their hands. She had lived so many extra years because of that, but he had been much older when he had discovered what she was doing with his power.

They came over the hill and swooped down into the pasture, crying out, crying triumph. He had never seen them in daylight before. They were barely visible, merely a suggestion of movement in the sky, like a ripple in water. But their harsh voices were as strong as ever, and he shook at the sound.

Then he set his mouth. No. He was not a child to be terrorized anymore. Never again. He was an adult, and more powerful than any sorcerer had ever been, even Freite. He had seen her tame them. He could do the same.

Except that Freite had tamed them with music, with whistling and fluting, and Saker was as deaf to music as he was indifferent to dancing. He could not use her spell, the five repeating notes. But if he could find the right words, the right sounds, that would work as well. He thought frantically, quicker than he had ever thought in his life, while they swooped and jeered above his head.

"Feed us, enchanter!" they screamed. "Feed us flesh and spirit!"

Saker paused. Feed them? That was what they had asked of Freite, and she had fed them, he knew, on vagrants and unwanted children. He had been excluded from those ceremonies as part of her obsessive desire to keep her secrets safe, but he could guess what had happened there. Perhaps he did not need to fear them after all.

She had told him, once, that they could not take what was not given. "At least, it's so in the settled lands," she had said. "A prohibition was put on them by an enchantress. My tradition says it was done by a woman named Tern, but where she lived and how long ago I don't know." She had smiled, the smile that she used to terrify him. "They cannot take, but they can be fed. Beware, child."

He shook off the unease of memory.

"Not yet," he answered the wraiths.

"When? Whennnn?" they screeched.

"Soon," he said, "soon."

He was disturbed, and unsure. Flesh he could give them in abundance. They could have all they could eat of Acton's people's flesh. But spirit? Now he realized what the "worse" was that Freite had threatened. To have the spirit eaten . . .

Should he set them loose on the warlord's men? Should even justice go so far? He did not know. He did not know how to decide.

But if he wanted to restrain them, he had better find a spell that would work. Or they would turn on him and his ghosts, too. The ghosts' bodies might be unassailable, but what of their spirits? It might be that they were even more vulnerable to the wind wraiths than the living. He could not risk it. The warlord's men would have to lose their chance at rebirth as well as their lives. Unless he could find the right spell.

MARTINE

THEY LEFT THE Valuer's Plantation early. Apple rousted them out of bed before dawn and they set off as soon as they had eaten breakfast.

Travel with a warlord was easy, Martine discovered. No one looked sideways at a dark-haired woman in the warlord's party. Food just appeared out of inns as they stopped to water the horses; carts pulled to the side of the road to let them go past. Even with Arvid, who was probably as good as warlords got, there was still the forelock-tugging and the curtseys and the obsequiousness that all sensible people show to anyone who travels with a party of armed guards. She got angrier as the day went on, and noticed Zel felt the same.

Martine maneuvered her horse next to Zel's chestnut, and they dropped back a little so they could talk. Trine came up next to them, still on a leading rein, but to Martine's surprise she didn't try to bite or kick. Perhaps she was beginning to accept Zel.

"It puts a bad taste in my mouth," Zel said, nodding to where a goose girl was bending double, she was curtseying so hard. Martine discovered a desire in herself to defend Arvid. Which was ridiculous. She had to change the course of this conversation. "The Valuers want to do away with warlords," Martine said. "Will you join them?"

That silenced her. Zel wasn't a joiner by nature, that was clear. She leaned over to pat Trine, perhaps taking as well as giving reassurance. Trine snorted at the touch, but didn't bite. It might do her good to be with Zel, someone else she could learn to trust. Martine thought they were all having a lesson in trust, herself included.

It was two long days' ride to Foreverfroze, so they stopped overnight at an inn which did nothing but service the traffic to the port. There was barely a village surrounding it, and the countryside around was pure forest. The road here was only a cart's width, although the ground on either side had been cleared for a bow-shot by Arvid's orders to prevent bandits ambushing trading parties.

They ate in the inn parlour. Martine sat as far from Arvid as she could, but the fire was still disturbing her, still churning at her every time she looked at him, every time she heard his voice. Her hand shook with desire as she poured cider into her cup, and she put the jug down abruptly to conceal it. This was worse than her infatuation with Cob, when she'd had the excuse of youth. The fire was taking a difficult revenge. She went to her room early, ignoring Arvid's attempt to catch her eye.

What was she doing here? Martine wondered. She stood in the inn chamber and stared at her empty bed, too restless to go to sleep.

When she and Ash had left Turvite, she had meant to go to the Hidden Valley, to visit Elva and Mabry. She had done that, and the winter she had spent with them and the new baby had been a golden time, despite the shadow of the ghosts hanging over them. But since leaving the valley—since the gods had told her to leave—she had just moved from one place to another without a plan, without any idea of what she was supposed to be doing. Finding Bramble, bringing her to the Well of Secrets, the journey into the Great Forest, sending Bramble on her mysterious journey, even taking horse for Foreverfroze, had seemed to make sense because she felt some responsibility for Ash, and then for Bramble.

But now, with Ash gone to the Deep and Bramble gone gods knew where, what was she doing here? Her gifts weren't needed—Safred could do all the future sensing anyone could ask, and more. Any part she might play in this gods'-driven attempt to stop Saker was probably over when she gave Acton's brooch to Bramble.

Martine was used to being in control of her own life. Now she felt adrift, and she didn't like it. She sat down on the side of the bed and took off her right boot, then noticed the sole. All around the edge it had been nibbled away, as though rats had got to it, and the bottom was pitted with holes that went almost all the way through the thick leather. She stared at it in puzzlement, then suddenly understood. She had walked in these boots out on Obsidian Lake, not once but six times, and the water of the lake had done this. Eaten tanned leather, hard leather, like vitriol did. She shivered, remembering the sting of the waters as she and Zel had cowered away from the fire. If the fire hadn't burnt off the water so quickly, she and Zel might look like this boot, or worse.

Martine felt a sudden desire to go home, back to Hidden Valley, and protect her daughter and grandson. But she had promised to meet Ash, and she would keep that promise.

They rode on the next day into increasing cold. Although it was summer, the Foreverfroze peninsula was swept by winds that blew across the never-melting northern ice. Yet the country teemed with life under the horses' hooves. As they turned north and began the journey up the peninsula, the trees grew sparser and more crooked, bent like old women toting loads of kindling home. Under the trees, though, there was lush grass and blazing wildflowers, and a constant scurrying of small animals making paths through the long stems. In the distance they saw elk and deer browsing. Birds were everywhere, and ignored them as if they had never seen humans. Terns, swallows, herons in the hundreds of low-lying pools, hawks high above in the vaulting pale blue sky, flocks of geese and ducks, waders and moorhens and cranes, even an albatross sailed above them and went on, riding the wind further out to sea.

The wind made Martine glad of the felt coat Drema had made for her in Hidden Valley. It seemed a long time ago, although it was less than a month since they had left. She spent a while wondering how little Ash was and how Elva was coping with motherhood. She realized with amusement that she *had* turned into a grandmother... at least in her thoughts.

With some determination, she forced herself to think about the present place and time. At least the wind kept the insects at bay. She was sure that in the lee the midges would attack furiously.

As though he had been waiting for her to finish her thoughts, Arvid brought his horse next to hers and smiled at her. The smile seemed to split her mind in two. One part was full of the suspicion of a lifetime: what would a warlord want with a Traveler woman? That had an easy answer! The other part came from deeper down, the part that had been brought back to singing life by the fire. The easy answer was the answer it wanted. The fire inside her urged her to simply drag him from his horse and take him there, on the ground, in front of everyone. No, the fire's voice seemed to whisper to her, it would be better in private, where he would not be distracted. She was increasingly sure that this was her punishment from the fire—to be tormented by desire that could never be fulfilled.

His smile was tentative and he looked like a boy of sixteen approaching his first Springtree dance partner. There was a sweetness in that smile that disarmed her. Sweetness wasn't a quality she associated with warlords.

But he was also an experienced negotiator, and he was too canny to begin with anything personal.

"Safred is still upset with your friend who has gone," he said, a trace of the smile lingering at the corner of his mouth.

She smiled involuntarily. "Bramble's hard to predict," she said.

"You know her well?"

Martine considered. "I've not known her long," she said. "But I have some understanding of her, I think."

"Safred has told me about your undertaking," Arvid said, his face completely serious.

Martine was shocked, and then wondered why she should be. They would need all the help they could get—this was a problem for the whole of the Domains. They were not spies, on a secret quest for their lord! Of course Safred had told him. No doubt all the warlords would know soon enough anyway. They kept each other informed of any threats to the Domains.

"Do you think Bramble is committed to her task?" Arvid asked.

That was the warlord talking, and Martine resented it. "Oh, no, I think she's gone off on a holiday," she said.

He winced. "She is young, and perhaps afraid," he suggested.

"Hah! That one's never been afraid of anything in her life," Martine retorted. "She says she's found a quicker way. She'll meet us in Sanctuary. Well then, we should go to Sanctuary."

"'We'?" Arvid asked delicately.

"Safred and Zel and Cael and I," Martine said. She didn't look at him. Would he offer to come with them? It was unheard of for a warlord to enter another warlord's territory without formal invitation: an act of war. He could come as far as Turvite, but after that . . .

"And Trine?" he asked with a smile, then paused. "I could come as far as Turvite, if you think it would be helpful."

She paused, struggling with herself. The two halves of her mind were in conflict. One wanted nothing to do with him. The other craved his company. Then her Sight reared up and swept all personal feelings aside. It was one of the strongest sensings she had ever had. Her hands shook with the power of it and the chestnut she was riding skittered a little. She clutched at the reins, still unsure on horseback.

"Yes," she said, eyes staring blindly at the stream they were passing. "Yes, we will have need of you in Turvite. Great need."

He nodded silently, but then let his horse fall back as though unsettled by her. She felt a flash of an old bitterness. She had lost her first love because he couldn't accept her gifts. Elva's father, Cob, had turned to Elva's mother instead, but fathered a babe far stranger than Martine. It was so long ago that most of the time she rarely thought of Elva as anything but her own child, but their relationship was the result of a man rejecting the uncanny twice over, in her and in his own flesh. With no excuse, because he was of the old blood. The oldest blood.

She shook her head free of the thoughts. Time she accepted that no man wanted to lie next to a seer, in case she could see into his soul and perceive the small, grimy secrets that lie in the center of all human hearts. Well, that rejection had given her a daughter, and now a grandson, so she should thank Cob instead of resenting him.

But when they stopped for lunch and to water the horses, she kept a distance from Arvid, all the same. There was no use inviting hurt. Or thwarted desire.

In mid-afternoon they passed a long train of ox-carts lumbering along the track, piled with high, canvas-covered loads. This was the merchandise the Last Domain was shipping to Mitchen, no doubt. A party of Arvid's guards protected them, although what bandits would attack them out here Martine couldn't imagine.

"Go on," Arvid said. "I'll just have a word."

They rode around the carts, raising their hands to the drivers who sat hunched against the wind and who occasionally lifted a whip to their oxen. The drivers nodded back, staring at Safred, whom they clearly recognized. Martine wondered how often Safred had visited Arvid at his fort, and why. Well, no doubt the gods had given her reasons, but consorting with warlords still seemed strange to her. It was disconcerting, after so many years spent avoiding warlords and their men, to be riding with them, part of their group, as safe as if she were among friends.

Arvid consulted briefly with the group's leader and then cantered up to rejoin them. "They'll be in Foreverfroze tomorrow, maybe the day after if the wagons get bogged down again. It happens a lot in this season. Easier on sledges in winter, really, but then the harbor is ice-locked."

He spoke absently, as though mentally computing the oxen's speed and endurance against a private timetable.

"Do all warlords concern themselves with trade?" Martine asked him, trying for a normal conversation with him.

He grimaced. "They don't have to. They have the free towns to organize trade for them."

"And you have no free towns?" Despite her intentions, the comment came out accusingly.

He glanced shrewdly at her, and smiled a little. "All our towns are free towns," he said. Martine shut her mouth firmly. Enough talk. No matter what she said, he would twist it. That was what warlords did. But Arvid went on. "Unfortunately, there are not enough people living in them to take all the goods that we produce. The things worth the most, the furs and the sapphires and the timber, those are worth more in the southern Domains, so it pays us to ship them down, but no one town is big enough to hire a ship for itself. So I do it."

"And take a cut!" Safred said.

Arvid laughed. "Of course! I have to support my people, after all, and that takes silver. Better a tax on exports than on grain, or cattle, or houses. This way, only the people that can afford it pay."

Safred sniffed. "You don't need so many guards."

"Tell that to the people on the borders of the Ice King's land. We have repelled two attacks this year already."

"Why aren't you there, then?" Martine asked. It struck her as odd that a warlord would leave a battlefield. It went against their whole code.

"*Because*," Arvid said, provoked at last and glaring at Safred, "*someone* told me the gods forbade it. So my men have to face the enemy alone and I am here, counting wagons like a merchant, instead of leading them as I should."

Ah, Martine thought. There's the warlord. He's been hiding, but he's there. The thought gave her some satisfaction, but also brought pain, as though a needle had slid into her heart.

Safred shrugged. "Complain to the gods," she said. "It's not my fault."

Involuntarily, Martine exchanged a glance with Arvid, both of them amused at Safred. It was hard not to smile back. She had never thought of blue eyes as being warm before.

To distract herself from the heat spearing through her, she said a prayer for Elva and Mabry and the baby. The gods don't pay much attention to humans, she thought, but sometimes they do; sometimes they take a liking, and they liked both Elva and Mabry. Loved them, even. So perhaps the prayer would work. She said none for Ash or Bramble. They were already in the hands of the gods, and no prayers of hers would change the outcome.

BRAMBLE

WALKING WITH THE hunter was like stalking deer. Bramble had to move stealthily but also quickly. The hunter was entirely silent; no footfall, no rustle of grass or branches. Bramble had roamed the woods all her life, but still, inevitably, she brushed aside grass stems which sighed, or occasionally placed her foot on a twig which groaned under her. Each time, the hunter flicked her a look that was impossible to decipher. Scorn? Disbelief? Astonishment?

They moved through the darkening Forest so fast they were almost running. Her skills came back to her, but she would never equal the hunter in stealth. It seemed to realize this and slowed its pace, just a little.

Bramble knew they were traveling further north, but she asked no questions. She had taken the leap and was in midair; she just hoped there was firm footing on the other side.

As the night grew darker, the hunter realized that Bramble was having more trouble following it. "Soon," it promised, and went more slowly. They came, after a while, to a space where a huge tree grew. Some kind of conifer, that was all she could tell in the darkness, but enormous, its trunk larger around than Gorham's house in Pless. Much larger. The tree looked almost as wide as the Pless Moot Hall, and its upper branches disappeared into the stars. As they ducked down to pass under its branches the faint light disappeared altogether. Bramble stood still, her head just below its lowest limbs, lost in a sighing black that moved around her as the wind soughed.

She wanted to ask where they were, but knew it was a foolish question. They were in the Forest, they were underneath an old tree. Any other answer was a human answer, one the hunter would not know.

"Come," it said. It took her by the arm and led her to the trunk of the tree, a journey that took some minutes.

They stood between huge writhing roots and the hunter said, "Do you remember where you want to go?"

"Um . . ." Bramble thought about it. She had to be very clear about this. "I remember it in the past."

"Soooo," the hunter said, and listened to the Forest. "Do you remember it clearly? Tell it to the Forest."

"It's a cave," Bramble said. "In the Western Mountains. A cave with drawings on the wall from long, long ago."

The hunter sniffed. "All times are long ago," it said. "But we cannot go to a cave. That is the domain of the stone-eaters. I cannot take you there."

"But —"

It ignored her interruption. "Do you remember outside the cave?"

The memory flooded back: being in Red's body, watching Acton ride up the slope toward the cave. Watching him disappear into the trees. Into what had been the Forest, in those days when the Forest had covered the whole country. The hunter hissed with satisfaction.

"So. You remember. The Forest remembers. It will take you there. The journey will take much time and no time."

"How?"

"The Forest remembers. We will go to your memory and then come back to your moment, this moment you are tied to so strongly."

Bramble half understood, but only half. I'm still in midair, she thought. She felt, immediately, the exhilaration of the chase. The hunter smiled, showing sharp teeth, as though it too felt the surge of excitement.

"Put your hand on the tree, prey," it said. "Its roots go back far. Very far."

Bramble reached out and placed her palm on the crinkled bark. Just as before starting a chase, all her senses seemed more alert. She felt the faint breeze on her cheek, heard owls and, high above, a flock of smaller birds. The small songbirds were migrating to their summer breeding grounds. They always flew at night, to avoid the hawks: black caps, warblers, swallows. Their wings flurried the night air, there were so many of them. Bramble could feel the tiny shiver along the tree as the owl launched itself from the upper branches in pursuit of the flock. Was it possible that she had really felt that? The night shifted and seethed around her, full of life. She could smell something: cedar? A strong, heady scent that dizzied her.

"Take a step forward," said the hunter. She did, and it was broad day.

She stared at the hunter. It leaned casually against the tree, its elegant bones jutting in the wrong places. She had been right, it was a kind of cedar tree, although a type she had never seen before. Her instinct told her never to show weakness to the hunter, so she disguised her disorientation.

"I thought cedars needed warm places to grow," she said.

The hunter shrugged. "Not this one."

They stepped away from the trunk. More than the light had changed. The tree seemed much smaller. It was, surely, only a young tree. Even allowing for the magnifying effects of night, Bramble was sure it had been huge before.

"We're in the past," she said.

"Not in *your* past yet," the hunter said reprovingly, as though she had been stupid. "There are more steps to that memory. Come."

It set off through the Forest at a slower pace than the night before. Almost strolling. "No hurry now," it said.

"Why not?" Bramble was concerned that the question might sound like a weakness, but she had to know. The whole *point* of this was that she didn't have any time to waste.

It listened to the Forest, and lost the disdainful look on its face, as though it had been chastised. "We travel in the past," it said as though explaining to a child. "So no time is lost in your *moment*. Then we return to your moment. I told you."

Bramble wondered how far back they had come. A hundred years? Five hundred? She felt light-hearted and light-headed. There was no task waiting for her here, and no grief. Maryrose was not yet dead. There was no one being slaughtered—at least, not more than there had always been, as the warlords extended their territory. The thought sobered her. She had seen too much death recently to be flippant about it, even five hundred years in the past.

The hunter slipped through the Forest and Bramble took off her boots and followed it, barefoot as it was barefoot, treading where it trod, trying to see with its eyes. There was no difference between this Forest and the one they had been in last night. It renewed itself eternally and time, to it, Bramble realized, was a matter of concentration, of where it put its attention. There was no *present*, no *past*, perhaps no *future*. Just the Forest.

The sense of timelessness was a gift from the Forest, she thought, as keeping the mosquitoes away had been a gift from the Lake. A gift to the Kill Reborn. Bramble wondered fleetingly if they would have done as much for Beck, if he had made the same journey. Then she thought, with a little satisfaction: the hunter would have killed Beck. She knew that she had been saved from fear because she had already been dead, had experienced the death-in-life for so long before becoming the Kill Reborn. Beck would not have had that toughening, and he would have feared, and died. It was all the roan's doing.

For the first time since his death, she could think of him with simple gratitude untouched by guilt. Perhaps seeing his death reflected in the eyes of the Well of Secrets was responsible, but she thought it more likely because of all the death she had seen, all the grief she had shared, while watching Acton's life. Everyone dies. What matters is the life shared beforehand.

But, just as she had learned acceptance through living other people's grief, she had also learned fear. Her body had learned what it felt like to be afraid; had learned how fine the line was between excitement and terror. So here she was, with a creature not human, who yearned to kill her, who *needed* in some way to kill her, in a landscape full of wolf and bear and sudden dangers, in a past she had no way of escaping. Her body wanted to be afraid, as Elric had been afraid, as Baluch had, waiting for Sebbi to die. But she refused. To understand fear was a good thing. The knowledge might make her kinder, she thought. But to let it fill her, let it take over, would lead to more than death at the hunter's knife. It would mean losing herself, the self that would survive death and go on to rebirth.

So she looked at the unfamiliar Forest, at the undergrowth which could conceal anything, and laughed, and the hunter laughed with her, a deep belly laugh.

The days went past as they walked the Forest, and Bramble let them go without counting them. They had not come back exactly in the year; it was full summer, and the best time to be wandering under the green shade.

They stopped occasionally to find food for Bramble. The hunter didn't seem to need food, only a sip of blood from each creature it killed, but it did need that, although not, perhaps, the way she needed to drink. It showed her how to stand so still that the deer would come up and surround her and she could reach out and plunge her knife into a throat.

"A moment," it said. "Just pause a moment for the fear to come before you thrust. Then you will be cleansed."

But she wasn't cleansed, just the opposite, so she left that to the hunter, after the first time, because it seemed calmer, happier, after a kill. Although it might be covered in blood afterward, the blood vanished immediately, with a little shiver in the light so that the hunter became momentarily hard to see. A ripple in time? Bramble wondered, but didn't comment on anything except the excellence of the hunt.

"It is my purpose," it said simply, gutting and butchering the carcase of a fallow deer for her with swift, beautiful strokes of its black rock knife.

She asked it no questions about its name, or its life, or anything not directly related to their path. The need to know would be seen as a weakness, she was sure. An indication of fear. She remembered too well the feeling of its knife at her throat. Then, she hadn't been afraid; now, she had a task to complete, which made it harder to face death without regret. She owed it to Acton to find his bones. Let him be a hero in death the way he had wanted to be in life but wasn't, quite.

Although she guarded always against showing any fear, Bramble was happier than she could remember being except for when she was racing the roan. This was where she belonged.

She found blueberries and raspberries as they walked, collected greens and wild carrots and onions, found tiny, sweet plums and small black cherries. The hunter could find anything Bramble wanted, but she was determined to feed herself. She had done it hundreds of times before, after all. As the days went past, the hunter seemed to acquire some respect for her knowledge of plants. They seemed irrelevant to it;

not needing to eat anything except death, plants were known but not important.

The hunter did not need to eat, but it did need sleep, as she did. At night they found soft grass to cradle them. Bramble offered to share her blanket, but the hunter refused. "Cold and hot are the same," it said, lying easily on its side.

Bramble watched it sleep and saw that it simply closed its eyes and was still, stiller than any human sleeper. Although that stillness was strange, it was real, and she was reassured by it. The hunter was not tricking her into vulnerability. She closed her own eyes and fell into slumber as easily as it had.

Four days after they left the tree—or was it five? Bramble couldn't remember, and was warmed by the thought that it didn't matter—they arrived at a ridge, and Bramble realized that they were looking down into what would become Golden Valley. The valley was wild, still, although the bottom was studded with the poplars that still grew there. But the rest of the valley was pure Forest.

She smiled at the sight. "I like this time," she said.

The hunter gave a small puff of laughter. "All time is the same," it said, shaking its head at her.

They traveled through the Valley for some days, then headed west from the bluff at its mouth, going southwest on a long diagonal that would bring them to the foot of the Western Mountains, near where Actonston would lie. On a cloudy day which threatened storm, in a sparser, drier section of the Forest that favored pines and larches, they found themselves at the edge of a cleared area of ground that led down to a farmhouse by the side of a river. It looked primitive. Not like the solid timber halls of Acton's time, nor the stonemasonry of her own. This farmhouse was slab construction, flung up in a hurry in summer to make sure there would be shelter by the time winter came. A short line of skinny cows was heading for a shed which no doubt doubled as the milking barn. In a pen near the barn, a scurry of calves bellowed for their mothers.

They stood looking down on the scene in silence. From a distance, the sound of axe blows cut through the late afternoon. The hunter and she both winced, then looked at each other in a kind of comradeship.

"Come," it said. "There are too many humans here."

It led her through the edges of the Forest toward the mountains, until they could no longer hear the axe or the lowing of the cows. The hunter went into a deep defile in the hillside, a narrow valley that raised its sides high above their heads in minutes. At the end of the valley, where it could gather all the water that run off the hillside, stood a lone chestnut tree, dominating the valley.

"Its roots do not go far enough, but it will take us some way," the hunter said. "This is a good place of remembrance, this. The tree remembers strongly."

This time, the step forward, hand on the bark of the tree, took her to early, early morning, a winter morning which lay ice still, frost covering the ground, tiny icicles edging each bare branch. Bramble looked up. The chestnut branches were dark against the pale, cloudless sky. As she watched, the sun crested the rim of the valley and lit the tree: each icicle flashed rainbows of colors, the whole tree flickered with brilliant light, with sparks and flames and ripples of cold fire.

This is what rebirth must feel like, Bramble thought. Shivering, she stood transfixed until, only a few moments later, the sun had warmed the icicles enough so that droplets hit her face and shocked her out of the reverie. She turned to the hunter, who was watching her with approval and a slight unease, as though her appreciation of the tree worried him somehow.

"Come," it said, "we must cross the river."

Unnervingly, although her breath was making steam, the hunter's did not, as though its breath was as cold as the air. She tried to remember the moment when its knife had been at her throat. She had been close enough to feel its breath, but she didn't remember feeling it at all.

Bramble fished her boots out of her saddlebags. Barefoot was all very well for the hunter, who seemed not to notice the cold, but frostbite was something she'd rather avoid. She wrapped her blanket around her shoulders as well, but even so she was very cold. She followed the hunter across snow dotted with the tracks of hare, followed by fox tracks.

The hunter chuckled. "The fox seeks its prey. Good luck, little brother."

She smiled, too, until she saw that the hunter left no tracks in the snow, although she saw its feet sink in. It saw her looking back at the single line of footprints in the powdery snow.

"I am here, in truth," it assured her. "I just allow the snow to remember what it was before I passed. I will show you."

It took a few steps and suddenly there were tracks behind it. Then it turned and waited, and the snow smoothed itself out. Bramble couldn't see any movement of snowflakes; it was just, suddenly, as though the tracks had never existed. It was a much smaller manipulation of time than the one which had brought her back to this moment, but it unsettled her more, because it was done so casually. As though time was infinitely malleable.

She needed to control her upset immediately, before the hunter sensed it and saw it as fear. She grabbed for the first thing she could think of: Acton. If time *was* so malleable, did that mean she could journey back again? Change things? Stop Red plunging that knife down, and up again? She shivered, and it was not just the chill air. What if he lived? What if he lived *while she was there*? Her heart beat faster at the thought. She could guide him; warn him. If she went back far enough, she could even prevent Hawk's massacre of Swef's steading, and the resettlement from over the mountains would have been peaceful. She longed for that; remembered the lightness and joy she had felt when she had thought that the invasion was not going to happen.

But like a shadow over the too-bright, snow-covered landscape, the memory of Dotta's warning came back. She had said that if Acton didn't invade, others would. Nothing could save the Domains . . .

"How far back can you take me?" she asked the hunter as they trudged down the slope to the frozen river.

"Far."

She left it at that, but she kept thinking about it; wondering which was the right moment to go back to. Where could she do the most good? It kept her mind off the cold.

In this time, the steading they had seen did not exist; the Forest reached all the way to the river. They crossed by sliding on the ice like children, laughing and falling and making faces at the water sprites who stared up, impotent and hungry, from beneath the ice. These moments of gaiety came on and off to the hunter, and its laughter was infectious.

It led her through several more seasons, finding places of remembrance every few days. One was a vast holly thicket, which seemed exactly the same in the earlier time. Another, a shaded clearing full of mushrooms.

"They go deep," the hunter said, smiling.

Although she left her boots off unless it was very cold, by the time they came to the mushroom glade the soles were almost worn through. They had traveled a very long way, and not by the shortest route. The hunter diverted them often; to hunt, to investigate the health of a herd of deer, sometimes simply to see something it considered significant, although there was no pattern to what was important: a single leaf, a spring, a small grouping of rocks. It never took her near a black rock altar, and she didn't ask why not, but she noticed that the gods left her alone. The whole journey was free of their presence; she felt liberated and forsaken at the same time.

MARTINE

THEY REACHED FOREVERFROZE at mid-afternoon. Martine had never been there, not in all her wanderings, and she stared as openly as Zel.

The town was sheltered by a ridge of light gray rock to the north which ran down to the sea, forming one headland of the huge harbor. The other was a flat tongue of land to the south, which curved like a fishhook. The long, long wharves for which Foreverfroze was famous ran out into the curve of the fishhook but were still in the lee of the ridge. The town looked exposed, compared to the high-cliffed ports of Turvite and Mitchen, but it offered the best harborage available in the north, and had prospered as the southern cities had grown—there was always a market for smoked whitefish.

There were no houses, as such—most of the buildings were underground, or at least dug in to roof level, so that the town looked like a collection of hats left lying on the ground by careless giants. Some were roofed with straw, some with turves. They were spaced in a series of circles, surrounded by gardens, so that no one was far from a neighbor's door, but each household had a green space around it. The gardens were full of vegetables but there were no flowers except the ones which bloomed casually along the side of the street.

Foreverfroze was a casual place overall. Green-eyed, fair-skinned children ran by their horses, calling up at them in a sweet, singing language, their black hair cut short, boys and girls alike. Martine realized that she was among people of her exact coloring: the pale skin, the green eyes, the black straight hair. A wave of excitement rose in her. There were still places, then, where the old blood lived together. Survived. Thrived. The last time she had been in a village of her own kind seemed a lifetime ago. Was it twenty-two, twenty-three years, since the twin villages of her birthplace had been destroyed by the Ice King's men? She had thought that the old blood was permanently scattered, flung in droplets across the Domains, harassed and driven and cheated and spat upon. She had thought there was no resting place for her people anymore. But here they were, just living. Tears rose in her eyes and her heart felt hot and tight. She was grateful that the town itself was different from her home. But the people were so similar, she almost expected to see Cob, or her mother, or one of her many aunties, come around the side of one of the roofs.

Instead, men sat in groups by the small doorways of their houses, weaving baskets; or tended the gardens; or nursed a baby. One lifted a hand as the party rode by. Occasionally an old woman mending a fishing net nodded to them as they went past. They saw only one younger woman. She was heavily pregnant. Otherwise, Martine knew, she too would have been out on the fishing ships.

On the horse, looking out across rooftops, it struck Martine forcefully that there was nothing in the town taller than an adult human. She felt like a giant, and was reminded of stepping back across Obsidian Lake with Bramble in tow, when she had felt immense, like one of the old gods.

The road curved through the circles of houses until it came to a half-circle set back from the wharfs, which were the only things that looked like their equivalent in the south. There were no large boats tied up, although there were quite a few small skiffs with blue sails out in the harbor. Martine noticed a few nets spread to dry. The largest building in the semi-circle was a big hall with an entrance held up by pillars of carved wood—precious in this landscape of sparse and stunted trees.

A few men and two older women ambled across to meet them at the doors. They dismounted and Holly took the reins, being careful to avoid Trine's teeth. One of the men beckoned her to bring them around the back of the hall. Arvid looked at Safred and then at Martine. He seemed to be debating whether or not to take the lead.

"Skua, Fox, greetings," he said to the older women. It was hard to tell them apart, they were both so wrinkled and bent and white-haired, although Fox had a more determined mouth and Skua's eyes were so creased with good humor that they almost disappeared when she smiled.

They nodded at him and then at the rest of the party, examining Martine with interest. She smiled at them, and Skua came forward and patted her cheek and said something, something she could almost understand. It was as though the language of her childhood had been taken and twisted back onto itself. The rhythm was right, some of the syllables were right, but the meaning eluded her.

"Skua says, you look like one of them," Arvid said, surprised as he took in the resemblance.

Fox said something seriously.

"Fox says the old blood will never be gone from the land while you are alive."

Martine shivered a little. That seemed too much like a prophecy for her taste.

"Let's hope I live forever, then," she said lightly. From their reaction it was clear they understood her, because both women firmed their mouths in a wry half-smile, and Skua patted her on the shoulder, as though she read her thoughts as well.

"Come to hall," Skua said, pronouncing the words with difficulty and some pride. She pushed Martine in the back to get her moving.

That simple touch, full of authority, made Martine feel young and vulnerable. *I am a grandmother*, she reminded herself, but with the two old women next to her, taking an arm each and shepherding her along the path, she felt like a child again, being taken by her aunties to see the village Voice because of some naughtiness. It had happened, once, when she had Seen the villages being attacked and raised a false alarm. She had been belted well and truly by Alder that day. He had a hard hand and her parents hadn't spoken to him or his family ever again. She had tried to forget the whole thing. Now, as she was being chivvied along, she realized it had not been a false alarm. She *had* Seen the attack which eventually destroyed the villages. She had just Seen it too early. Although, in her vision, the attackers had been warlord's men, not the Ice King. That memory pulled at her for the first time since the beating, and she wondered what her Sight had truly meant. When she had some time and solitude, she would try to remember it more clearly.

ASH

On the second night, when the men went into the caves to become their true selves, Rowan stayed behind with Ash. He didn't say anything until Skink came back and took Flax away, naked and scared but eager, too.

Rowan nodded toward the cave entrance after they were gone. "He's a fine singer, that one," he said.

Ah, Ash thought. That's why he's stayed with me. To have the "Flax will join us" conversation. He was a little light-headed with hunger and he found it vaguely funny.

"Yes," he said. "Mam'll be pleased as a bear cub with a honeyfall. You'll be able to perform all the duets, now." He waved expansively. "All the difficult stuff that needs more than one voice." He found he was avoiding the word "song" as he would avoid using a sore finger. That made him both sad and angry. "All the *songs* you couldn't do while I was with you."

Rowan looked down at his hands, fiddling with the flute he carried everywhere. "I won't say that hadn't occurred to me," he said. "But it's not what I wanted to talk about."

He paused, as though waiting for Ash to prompt him with a question. Ash kept silent. Rowan sighed. "We've missed you," he said.

"I've been gone two years," Ash said. "You know where Turvite is. You could have visited."

"We did," Rowan said. "We went back this winter past, but you were gone, and Doronit wouldn't answer any of our questions. If it wasn't for a man named Aelred, we wouldn't have known if you were dead or alive. He told us you'd left with a woman named Martine."

It was a question.

"Yes," Ash said. What could he say? Tell the whole story—Doronit's use of him, the attack on Martine's life, his decision to reject everything Doronit stood for? That was past, and no sense going over it. "She's Elva's mother. Little Ash's grandmother. That's how I met Elva and Mabry."

At the word "grandmother," Rowan had relaxed, no doubt imagining some white-haired old dodderer instead of the brazen seducer he had feared. Ash smiled, thinking of Martine's calm beauty and the times he had forced himself not to desire her.

"When you leave here," Rowan said quietly, "to sing the songs... do you want me to come with you?"

Astonishment kept Ash silent. This was one thing that had never occurred to him. He had imagined, when he first felt the power in his casting stones, joining his parents back on the Road. But he had never imagined his father joining *him*. He didn't know what to say.

"Will I need you, to sing them?" he asked finally.

Rowan went very still, and then shook his head. "I doubt it."

"Well, then," Ash went on, suddenly sure. "I'll be going into the middle of this fight. Better for you and Mam to be a long way off. Where I don't have to worry about you."

Rowan looked rueful. "Where you don't have to safeguard us?" he asked. "No, don't answer. You're right. You have more to concern you than us, now, and that's as it should be."

Ash wasn't sure if he'd offended his father or not. He never did anything right, it seemed.

"Your mother wanted you to go to Doronit. She said it would be the making of you. I wasn't so sure, but she was right." As usual, Ash thought. You always think she's right. "From what you're not saying, it may have been unpleasant," Rowan added, "but it's made you grow up."

That's a good thing, isn't it? Ash wanted to shout at him. Why look so sad?

Rowan stood up and clapped him on the shoulder, then started to undress, getting ready to join the others in the caves. He hesitated, his eyes unreadable in the firelight. "Did you find anyone to love, since you've been gone?" he asked.

Ash thought of Doronit, Martine, Elva, Bramble... "No," he said. "Other things have concerned me."

He hadn't intended it as a rebuke, but his father stiffened.

"It's a hard road, when the gods hold the reins," Rowan said. "Take care of yourself." Then he walked into the cave, disappearing behind the entrance fire like a spirit.

Ash sat for a while, staring into the narrow sky above the clearing, and wondering why he felt both loved and lonely at the same time.

BRAMBLE

GRADUALLY THEY APPROACHED the mountains and their path grew more difficult, over ridges and through steep valleys, down into chasms and up the other side, climbing with fingertips and toes. Halfway up a cliff face, barely hanging on over a sheer drop, they looked at each other and laughed, united in joy.

Then the hunter led her to an oak tree and said, "Take a step forward."

When she did so, it was winter. The air bit at her cheeks and hands.

"You are in your moment, now," the hunter said. "Your place is over there."

It pointed west of south. Bramble's mouth went dry. She had stopped thinking days ago; had relaxed into the rhythm of walking and climbing and hunting. Acton had retreated in her mind; now her need to make a decision surged forward. Her breathing quickened, and that was a mistake, because the hunter's hand went to its knife in anticipation.

"Are you afraid?" it said.

"Look," Bramble said, finally exasperated, "I'm not going to be afraid of you, all right? Just accept it."

It smiled, painfully. "Until I kill you, I am in your world," it said. "Bound to share your time. Your death will free me. Return me to what I was."

"Fine. Later. I'll try to be afraid of you later, after all this is over, and then you can kill me." It nodded, seriously, as though satisfied, and she thought wryly that she might regret that promise. "Can you take me further back?" she asked. "Can you take me back another five years?" If she warned them, then, of what was going to happen, surely she could divert history's path?

But the hunter shook its head. "The Forest told me to bring you here. Nowhere else. No other time." It looked at her suspiciously. "Why do you want more of the Forest's time?"

"So I can change things," she said. "Make them better."

The hunter took a step back in shock. "No, no, no. Do you not understand? These are places of *remembrance*. They are not to be changed. Never. Memory is sacred."

"But —"

It drew its knife. "I would kill you uncleansed first," it said, "and die."

"Why?"

It searched for words, its face troubled, like a child who had been asked too hard a question. "Time is knotted together with memory. With the places of remembrance. Make a change, and the knots come undone altogether. Not only the future unties. The past, too."

Its voice was earnest, and she knew it told the truth. Her shoulders sagged. She might have known it wouldn't be possible. Over and over the gods had put her in a place where *if only* she had changed things, the future would have been better, and over and over they had prevented her from acting. She supposed it was time to accept it. Her role was to watch, and to retrieve. To witness, and to remember. Just like the hunter.

It was watching her with concern, an expression she had never seen before on its face.

"You don't want to kill me," she said, wonderingly.

It flinched and looked away, then lifted its chin and stared her in the eyes. "You are too like one of us," it said. "Fearless and joyful. But you are still my prey, and one day you will fear, and I will be there and claim my kill, and then I will be a true hunter once again. One who has not let the prey escape."

She nodded. "That will be a good death," she said. "I forgive you for it, and release you from reparation."

The hunter paled. "What is it that you have done?"

Bramble smiled and touched its shoulder, just once, lightly. "It is how we cleanse each other of killing."

That troubled it again. It stared at her, golden eyes unblinking, like a hawk's. "I do not know if that is a good thing or a curse," it said.

She didn't know either, so she shrugged and grinned. "That's a risk you'll have to take, then," she said, and it caught her gaiety and chuckled, suddenly full of energy.

"Come," it said. "This way."

She followed it, expecting another long trek, but within a few minutes they were standing at the edge of the woodland, looking down on Wili's steading. It was very cold and her breath—but only hers—steamed in the air. The view she had of the steading was very much like the view Red had had. Startled by the thought, she looked around quickly and saw him, concealed from the steading by a large tree but clearly visible from their vantage.

She took a step forward into the shelter of a juniper tree so that he would not be able to see her. The hunter was already concealed there. She watched Red closely. He *was* a big man, shambling, looking uneasy and excited. He looked subtly different from seeing him with Baluch's eyes, although she wasn't exactly sure how. She saw him more clearly, saw the details of his clothes, the shape of his head. Perhaps it was just the difference between a woman's gaze and a man's, or perhaps Baluch's attention was so often on the music inside his head that he noticed little.

She had watched Red, wondering, for too long. With a shock she heard the puffing breath of a horse trudging through snow behind her. She wheeled around, and there he was.

Through her own eyes Acton seemed bigger than ever, particularly on the small horse. Tall, so broad across the shoulders that he reminded her of a blacksmith. His hair was uncovered and the new beard lit his chin with gold sparks in the winter sunshine. It was different, profoundly different, from seeing him through Baluch. Emotions roiled through her and she couldn't separate them. She had hated him for so long, and then learned not to hate him, and then to hate him again. He had killed so many people... But here she was, standing in the past, and seeing him in the flesh made it real to her that he came from this time, as she did from hers, and he carried its strengths and weaknesses as his own. He was a killer because he had been trained to be, encouraged to be by everyone he respected. What excuse did she have? At least he tempered his killing with generosity and kindness and a great, encompassing enjoyment of life.

Her heart thumped wildly. He was so *big*. She had seen him, most often, through the eyes of a man as tall as he was, almost as strong. In her own body she was sharply aware of how much larger he was, how male.

As he came abreast of her, some instinct made him glance over. She couldn't move. The gods would have to witness for her that she was frozen in shock. She was so used to being an unseen observer that it just hadn't occurred to her that he could see her now. Surely this was tampering with memory; with history? Would all the past and future come unraveling around them because she had made a stupid *mistake*?

Then he smiled at her, that crooked sideways smile he used for courting, and she realized that she had seen this happen before, through Red's eyes—that she was already a part of this time, this history. Relief hit her, but it wasn't relief that made her smile back. It was him. His glance seemed to invite her to share joy in the day, the trees, the crispness of the air. It was a look full of celebration and invitation, and she could not resist it. Any more than any other woman ever resisted it, she scolded herself, and schooled her face into composure. But he had seen that first, irrepressible reaction, and he winked at her.

She wanted to pull him down from the horse and shake some sense into him; to take him by those broad shoulders and drag him away from the path he was riding; to drag him to safety. He was so reckless! To go riding off to who knew where without even Baluch at his back. She was reckless herself, and she understood why he took risks; had gloried in them with him. But this time, just *this* time, she desperately wanted him to be careful... If only he had been careful!

He smiled wider at the frown on her face and raised a hand in farewell, then rode on. There was something in the gesture that implied, "I'll see you some other time." The movement cut to her heart and reminded her where he was riding to. She regretted frowning. The last woman's face he saw should have smiled at him.

"Are you done?" the hunter asked.

Bramble watched Acton ride into the apron of trees; watched Red leave his position and follow; and watched them both disappear behind evergreen. She thought of the burial ceremonies of her youth: the pine sprigs placed between the fingers, the Wooding Voice saying, "In your hands is evergreen; may our memories of you be evergreen." Her eyes filled with tears, and she blinked them away.

"Yes," she said. "I'm done."

"I must touch you," the hunter said. She realized that it wanted her to know that it wasn't attacking her and understood that it must rarely touch. She reached out a hand, and it took it, its palm dry and rough, like a dog's paw. They had been through the shift in time often enough for her to know what to do: she took a step.

Instantly the world shifted and tilted around her. The earth under her feet moved; instead of a slope, she was standing on level ground. Trees vanished. Buildings appeared. Men, turning, shouting, "Ghosts! The ghosts have come!" They raised weapons to their shoulders and one ran in and swung straight at Bramble.

"No!" the hunter cried. It leapt in front of her and the weapon—a pickaxe, the end wickedly sharp—pierced its body. It fell.

"Stop!" Bramble yelled, pushing and shoving the man away. She didn't even have time to find her knife. She was defenseless. But the attackers jumped back, as though she had stung them.

"They're talking! They're talking! Ghosts don't talk!" The men started to babble, the one with the pickaxe looking sick. He sank to his knees, the handle loose in his grasp.

"Gods of cave and dark," he whispered. "I've killed him."

The hunter was spouting blood from the big vein under the heart. Nothing could stop it, Bramble knew. Except perhaps enchantment, or the power of the Forest. She looked around wildly, but there were no trees here. They were in a place of gray stone and nothing else: stone buildings, flagstones, a great gash cut into the side of the hill. A mine. That's why the men had the pickaxes ready. They weren't an army, just men coming home from a shift in the pit.

Bramble gathered up the hunter, supporting its head. "I thought you lived forever," she whispered.

"In the Forest. As a true hunter. Me, neither, now," it gasped. It looked at the man who had killed it. "I fear," it said. "You must taste the fear and be cleansed." It dipped one finger in its own blood and held it out to the miner, who stared at it in confusion.

"That's not how we do it," Bramble said.

"No . . . I remember." The hunter's words were coming harder now, and weaker. It coughed; there was blood on its lips. "I remember . . . Forgive. I forgive . . ." Its head drooped but it turned its face to the miner. Its voice was hardly audible. "I forgive and . . . and release from reparation."

Bramble was crying. The tears she had held back all these weeks in case they had made her seem afraid were pouring down her cheeks and dropping onto its face, its hawk-feathered hair, its body.

"Why did you save me?" she said.

"You are *my* prey." Its voice became stronger for that one sentence, then faded away. "No one but me should kill you."

"In our next life," she said, trying not to laugh, because surely there was nothing to laugh at. "I promise. In our next life you can kill me."

"Too late," it said, smiling with an echo of its old joy. The slitted pupil in the hawk eyes narrowed and disappeared until the eye was entirely golden. Then its flesh grew insubstantial in her hold and vanished away like a water sprite pulled out of water. The wind blew away only a mist, a scent of pines, a whisper. Bramble bowed her head over her empty hands and wept.

LEOF

LEOF TURNED ARROW to the road and trotted sedately into Bonhill like any normal traveler. It wasn't a large village, but it had an inn. He called up the ostler and handed Arrow over to her with strict instructions about water, feed and grooming. Before he let her be led away he patted her and told her how marvelous she was. She knew it—tired as she was, she tossed her head and flirted with him.

Then he found the innkeeper and ordered a message be sent to . . . He hesitated for a moment. The enchanter had moved in a serpentine route. Although finding him had taken many hard riding hours, they were not that far from Carlion. Sendat was further, but he was sure that Thegan would not want to take the garrison out of Carlion. Two messages, then, one to Sendat and one to Thegan. While the best horses the inn had—sturdy little cobs which usually pulled the wagon—were being saddled, he wrote quick notes to Thegan and Sorn.

This was the first time he had written to her, and he reflected that he should take a lesson from the circumstances—the only communication between them should be like this, an officer's note to the warlord's wife. He signed it formally: "Thy willing servant, Leof son of Eric." He wrote with truth that he would be her servant, if nothing else.

Sendat was a day's march away, and they couldn't wait for the foot soldiers to catch up. He asked her to send the mounted troops, and to double each trooper with a pikeman. Hard on the horses, but it wouldn't be a long campaign and the roads were good.

Thegan had put a lot of silver into repairing roads when he first came to power in Central Domain, as he had done in Cliff Domain, and for the same reason. The people thought it was to improve trade and connection between towns, but Leof knew it was in preparation for moments like this, when he needed to move large numbers of men quickly.

Once he had sent the messages and checked on Arrow, he grabbed a piece of cold roast chicken from the flustered cook in the kitchen and went out the back way, taking a threaded, concealed path to where he had seen the wraiths hover.

Farmland wasn't ideal for stalking, but Leof had been well trained in scouting and by the time he had finished the chicken he had managed to worm his way to the side of the hill near the enchanter. He kept well back, away from the circle the wind wraiths were endlessly tracing above the rise.

He had been half-expecting Thegan to be right: to see the white-haired man from the pool. In any event, he was expecting such a powerful enchanter to be old. Perhaps very old. But the man who was digging and sorting out the bones he unearthed was around the same age as Leof: twenty-five, twenty-eight, no older than thirty.

Leof was tempted to simply kill him before he could raise more ghosts. He didn't look like a warrior—he was tall but had no muscle, and his mannerisms were nervous. Leof suspected that confronted unexpectedly with a sword, the enchanter would have no defense.

Two things stopped him. If he failed—if the enchanter had protective spells of some kind, or if the wind wraiths protected him—Thegan would have lost any chance of surprise. And the other thing: he just didn't know enough about the spell on the ghosts. Maybe the enchanter kept them under some kind of control, and if that control disappeared…Leof shuddered at the thought of the Carlion ghosts let loose on the rest of the Domains.

So he just watched. The enchanter was afraid of the wraiths. Leof had assumed that the wraiths were his servants. But judging by the looks he cast over his shoulder as he worked, he didn't trust them anymore than Leof did. They were circling and calling to each other in a language he had never heard; half wind noise and half speech. Occasionally, they darted at the enchanter and laughed when he flinched. But they seemed to respect his right to work, and they were interested in what he was doing.

He worked without pause, following a strict routine. He dug a new section, taking the turf off in squares with a sharp spade and laying it aside, then digging deeper until he found bones. Then he put the spade aside and took up a spoon, loosening each bone carefully and laying out skeletons. From each skeleton, he took a bone—a fingerbone, usually. He bent his head over this bone for a moment. Sometimes it was a long moment, sometimes short. After this, he either put the bone and its skeleton carefully back in the earth and buried it, or he put the bone even more carefully into a sack, and then buried the rest of the bones. The work was painstaking, and for a while he seemed to become unaware of the wind wraiths.

After a couple of hours, Leof realized that he urgently needed to piss. He eased back from his vantage point, losing sight of the enchanter, and retraced his path step by careful step until he was hidden in a dense coppice of willow trees and it was safe to relieve himself. He stood in the green shadow for a while, trying to decide what to do. The enchanter was so caught up in his work and, from the size of the hill, had a lot more digging to do. Leof decided he was better off going to meet Thegan and guide him to the spot.

So he left the willows and made for Bonhill, not sure whether he was deserting his post. The wind had risen as the sun began to lower; every gust or wuther made him look behind him, in case the wind wraiths were following.

BRAMBLE

There were far too many questions and too much exclaiming and explaining by the miners, particularly explanations to the mine boss, a middle-aged man named Sami whose brown eyes trusted no one. Sami insisted on knowing who she was and how she had got into the mine.

Bramble was sick of talking, and disconcerted by the appearance of a group of young boys who poked their way in to the center of the circle and listened, their eyes wide. She bit back a curse as she met the eyes of a pale child surely not more than nine or ten.

"Enchantment, all right?" she snarled at Sami.

He took a step back and then recovered his authority. "You've got no right here."

"You've heard about the ghosts?"

"One of our buyers told us," Sami confirmed. "The news is all over the Domains."

Bramble wondered how long it had been in this time since the attack on Carlion; since Maryrose's death. "How long ago did it happen?" she asked.

Sami shrugged. "Three, four days. We haven't heard anything else yet." His eyes narrowed. "What's it to you?"

She didn't have time for this. She didn't have the time *or* patience. "My sister was killed there."

There was silence. Bramble used the moment of shock to take charge. "I need to find the animal cave," she said, gesturing to the mine. "There's something in there that we need to defeat the enchanter who set the ghosts on Carlion."

"Are you an enchanter, too?" The miner who had killed the hunter stepped forward, his pickaxe still in his hand. She could see that he wanted to feel justified; to not be guilty of murder. He didn't look like a murderer: he was strong enough, but his face was gentle and his voice quiet. She felt sorry for him. If she had heard the stories about Carlion and then had seen two figures appear out of nowhere, what would she have done?

She shook her head. "No, it was the hunter who had the power, not me. I'm just ordinary."

They looked skeptical, and she supposed she didn't blame them. But she was wound up with tension and grief and purpose, and she couldn't baby them.

"I need the animal cave," she said again. "Then we might be able to stop the bastard who raised the ghosts."

"Why should we trust you?" Sami asked.

"Oh, shag it, I haven't got time for this." Bramble drew her belt knife, grabbed Sami by the collar and put the knife to his throat. She was faster than she had been, she thought. Hunting every day had made her more dangerous. She grinned at his frantic eyes, pretending to enjoy his fear. Her stomach roiled in disgust.

"Because I could kill you right now. But I won't." She let him go, and only then thought of the right thing to say. "Because the Well of Secrets sent me."

These were truly powerful words. Each man there relaxed, as though everything had been explained.

"What animal cave?" the miner asked.

"The cave with the animal drawings on the wall, from the very old times," Bramble explained. "The aurochs, and the elk and deer."

The miners exchanged glances and shook their heads.

"Never seen ought like that," one said. "What about you, Medric?"

The miner pushed out his lip and shook his head, too. "No," he said. "I don't know it."

Bramble felt her guts cramp. The cave *had* to be there. She had been sure the miners would have found it.

"There's another cave," she said. "I could find my way from there . . ." She looked up at the mountainside, trying fruitlessly to spot any familiar landmarks. She had seen this mountainside only a few moments ago, as Acton rode up. Surely she could remember? That big peak, yes, but that was miles away . . . a thousand years of mining had altered the side of the mountain beyond recognition. The area where

Dotta's cave had been—that was where the entrance to the mine was. Inside were not caves but tunnels, wide enough for carts to be pushed up and down.

Despair began to creep over her, but she pushed it down. "Who knows the caves best?" she asked.

There was silence, but everyone looked at Medric. He rested his pickaxe on the ground and stared at it, as if unwilling to meet their gaze.

Sami cleared his throat. "Think you'll be able to find him, Medric?"

Medric took a breath, and let it out again as if unsure what to say. He shrugged. "If I call him, he might come," he said eventually, in a voice that gave nothing away.

"Who?" Bramble asked.

"A friend. Fursey. He, uh . . . he lives in there." Medric indicated the mountain with a jerk of his head.

"Human?" Bramble asked.

A couple of the men looked at the ground as though unsure of the answer. One shorter man grinned and said, "Well, we've had our doubts," and then shut up as Medric glared at him.

"Human," Medric confirmed.

She was glad of that confirmation as she followed Medric and his lantern down the tunnel and felt the weight of the earth above her, encountered the absolute darkness of underground for the first time with her own body. The dark hadn't seemed as bad when she was looking through Gris's eyes.

He led her down a long way, through tunnels that sometimes required her to crawl, and sometimes took them through caverns where the roof echoed high above her head. They stopped, finally, in a small cave—no, a tunnel. She saw the marks of pickaxes and chisels on the rock walls. This was the bottom of the mine, but there were fissures in the rock, passages like the ones Dotta had shown her, leading further down. Medric put down the lantern and stood for a moment, as if gathering courage.

"Fursey," he called softly. "Fursey! I've come back!"

He waited a few moments, and then called again, and then again.

There was silence. The earth seemed to grow heavier above them.

Medric checked the candle in the lantern—it was more than half gone. He tightened his lips and sighed. "Fursey," he called again, but this time reluctantly. "I need your help."

Nothing.

He raised his voice in frustration. "There are people dying, Furse, and I need your help!" Echoes rang along the tunnel walls, so that the whole mine seemed to be whispering, "help, help, help . . ."

Medric turned to Bramble and shrugged. "If he doesn't want to help . . ."

Behind him, from the thinnest of the fissures, a slight figure appeared. A man. Yes, human, Bramble was sure, although there was something about the way he moved that reminded her of the hunter. He stood staring at Medric for a moment as someone might stare at a picture of devastation. Then Medric realized where Bramble's eyes were staring and whirled around.

"Fursey!" He took a step forward and clasped the man to him, but the slight figure slipped out of his grasp and stood looking at him, head to one side.

"I thought," he said in a soft voice, "that if you came back, you would come alone. Is this your *wife*?" There was venom in his voice.

Medric flinched. "Of course not. I only just met her. She needs help, and you're the only one . . ."

"So you came back for her, not for me? How was your family?"

The question threw Medric. "They were fine. Da's dead. Mam's remarried. My sisters're fine. So I came back to find you."

Somehow, the words took the tension out of the cave. "But you hate the mine," Fursey said.

"Yes," Medric confirmed. "I hate the mine."

"Then you should not have come back."

Medric bent his head, as he had after he had killed the hunter, and stared at the floor of the tunnel.

Bramble had had enough of all this melodrama. "I need to find the animal cave, the one with the paintings on the wall," she said directly to Fursey. "Will you help?"

"That's a sacred place," Fursey said.

"I know." This man might have been human, but he was strange.

Well, she had dealt with stranger things than him. “I need to find some bones,” she said.

“Are they calling you?” he asked.

Very strange. But in a way, they were.

“Yes,” she said. “They have called me for a thousand years.”

He nodded. “Then I will take you.”

MEDRIC'S STORY

THIS IS HOW it was.

It's cold and windy. Da's hand is the only warm thing in the world, and there won't be that much longer.

The man from the mine is not too impressed; this one's too skinny, his look says, too bloody hungry. My boys'll eat him for breakfast. But he clinks some coins in his pocket.

"Five silver pieces."

Da's hand tightens. Too much, or too little? It's hard to tell. What's five silver pieces worth, anyway?

"He's worth more than that," Da says. "He's a good boy, obedient. He's a hard worker, aren't you, Medric?"

Oh, yes. Da's strong enough to make sure of that. He's got a hard hand, has Da.

"Say something, why don't you?"

The man interrupts before Da does more than raise his voice. "Five and a half. That's it."

"It's robbery." But he takes it.

The man from the mine is called Sami. He's from the north, with fair hair but brown eyes. Traveler blood in there, somewhere. A middling-size man, running a little to fat. But a man with a hard hand. It's not difficult to pick them, once you've known one.

"Come on," he says. "I'll put you in with the pushers. They'll start you off right."

He leads the way to a long stone building with a slate roof. It'd be impressive in a town, but stone's cheap here, after all. All it costs is the labor of getting it out of the ground.

A chill strikes off the stone as he leads the way through the doorway. Inside, the floor is packed dirt. The little windows are so high up that at this time, late evening, there's almost no light at all. There are wide wooden bunks in rows on both sides of the room. In the closest bunks are boys, two or three to a bed: every age from ten up, and all of them asleep with the sleep of exhaustion. They sprawl uncaring, arms hanging out, legs uncovered by the one blanket. The mine whistle blew an hour ago, as Da hurried up the steep path to the mine, saying, "By all that's holy, hurry up."

An hour from leaving the mine to this oblivion.

Da said, "Forget your bloody big words and your bloody airs and graces, boy. You're here to work, and don't you forget it." Good advice. The only good advice Da ever spoke. Maybe not such a good farewell, though.

Sami gestures to a bunk in the far corner where there are only two boys. "Nav and Fursey. Bunk in with them tonight and they'll show you around tomorrow. You'll be pushing. Get some supper over at the kitchen."

He points northward, through the stone wall, then considers. "You'd better give me your duffel. This lot'll steal anything that's not nailed down. Don't worry, I'll look after it. You can get it back when you leave."

Right. In seven years, at nineteen. Those clothes are going to be really useful then.

Sami grins. A clip over the ear is clearly his normal way of saying goodbye. It could be worse.

The kitchen is bright with firelight but there's not much food left. The cook grumbles as he fills a bowl with lentils and scrounges around until he finds a crust to go with it. The food's not too hot, but it's good. Solid. Sustaining. After all, you have to feed boys if they're going to hew out a mountain for you the next day.

Nav and Fursey both grumble about having to train a newcomer, but only Nav means it. Nav's a city boy from Turvite, mean-eyed and suspicious, sold to pay his "uncle's" gambling debts. His mother let him go without a word, he says, scared that if she objected his "uncle" would leave her.

"She'm a twitty bitch," he says, "no shagging good on her own. I's well off without her."

Fursey's an orphan, with nowhere to go and no one to complain about. He's yellow-haired and blue-eyed, so his folks must have come from the south, but that's all he knows. He's been here since he was five; he doesn't remember before that.

"I was somewhere else," he says. "I don't care. Now I'm here." He smiles, sweetly.

Fursey's the smallest of the pushers, but the others let him alone.

"Go easy with him," Nav says quietly. "He looks like he's a soft one, but if he takes against you he'll kill you. He don't never forget nothing; and he don't never forgive."

Fursey looks people in the eye, even the hewers. He smiles like a much younger boy, but his stare is too strong for even Sami to bear for long. So Sami doesn't look at him.

"Get moving," Sami shouts at all of us. "You think it's a holiday?"

Fursey leads the way. Pushers don't really push—they pull the ore-laden carts out of the mine, up the steep, stony ramps. The traces go around the chest, and a long strip of leather rests against the forehead and is attached to the sides of the cart. A trained twelve-year-old boy who leans into the leather headband and puts his whole weight into it can haul a fully laden cart up a mile of mine ramps in twenty-two minutes. That's how fast Fursey is, but Sami doesn't know it. Fursey stops halfway up, every time, in the darkest part of the ramp, and just looks around.

The leather strap cuts. The ramp is stony and sharp on bare feet. The mine's not cold, exactly, not like up above, where the wind cuts through clothing like it was paper. But it's dark. By the gods, it's darker than anything. A darkness that settles down, heavy, like thick cloth over your mouth. The pale yellow of the candles at the turning points of the ramps can barely be seen. There is only the great bear of the dark. The roof feels like it's caving in.

"Look for the gold," Fursey says urgently. His hand is warm. The boy-smell of him is comforting.

"What?"

"Look for the gold. There's always sparks of it, even here. That's why I stop, to see the gold."

There are sparks. Tiny, flickering at the corner of your eyes. Barely there.

"There's a reef behind there," Fursey says, pointing at the wall. "But those fools up top don't know it. They've passed it by."

"How do you know?"

"I know," Fursey says, and settles the leather strap onto his brow. "Back to your cart, Medric. Follow me. I'll go slow."

With the strap around your forehead you have to look down and the dark doesn't seem so heavy. But it's a long, long way to the top of the ramp. To the sunlight. There are four more trips to make before mid-meal.

Well, you get used to anything, they say. Even to unending work, eat, sleep, work again. Not every day is pushing. The mine closes down at the dark of the moon for two days, and the free hewers go down-valley, to their families, those who have them.

"Dead unlucky to be underground at the dark o' t'moon," Nav explains to me. "That's when the delvers come out."

"Delvers?"

Nav looks quickly over his shoulder, and makes the sign against hexing. "The dark people, the little people, the eaters of rock, the owners of the blackness," he says, and it's clear those aren't his words, that he's learned them off by heart. But from whom, he won't say.

Even with the mine closed, the pushers don't stop working. There's always work: scything the grass around the barracks, cutting wood, weeding the kitchen garden. That's not so bad, with the sun warm on your back and the smell of fresh earth; living earth. Different from the dark, dead smell of underground rock.

These two days, Fursey is twitchy as a cat. Snapping at everyone. His wide-eyed stare has become a glare.

"He just hates being out o' t'mine," Nav says. "I told you, he'm crazy."

It's true. Back in the mine, Fursey sings as he pushes; and stops to look at the gold twice as long.

In bed that night, he talks about it, whispering. "I know none of the others understand, but you do, don't you, Medric? It's so beautiful down there, with the gold shining all around me. The gold calls to me,

I can hear it, I know where it is underneath the rock. It wants to be taken out, to be melted down and made into beautiful things. It wants to be admired and treasured. It yearns for the pain of the pick cutting through the reef."

His hand is warm. He is the only warm thing here.

"I don't really understand. But I suppose . . ."

"You'll see," he says with confidence. "You'll get to love it, too." He snuggles closer. His hair smells of dust and leather.

In time, pushers become hewers. Hewing is better. Striking hard at the rock face, choosing your spot so the whole slab falls away with just one blow. There is skill in hewing, and responsibility. It's easy to make a mistake, to bring down a section of wall on your fellows.

That's how Nav dies, when a new hewer takes out part of a supporting wall and the tunnel collapses. The mine closes for a day. The free hewers walk down the valley to the gods' altar stone to pray for him and for once the bonded hewers and pushers are allowed to go with them, under Sami's watchful eye.

"Why don't they have a proper funeral? Why don't they dig him out?"

"The delvers will have taken his body," Fursey says matter-of-factly.

He is right. Expecting the worst, it's hard to go down into the dark the next day. But Nav's body is gone and the tunnel floor partly cleared.

"No one knows where the bodies go, but nothing bad could happen. They only eat rock," Fursey says. "I think gold is like dessert for them." He pauses. "I'd like to meet them someday."

"Don't say that! You might meet them the way Nav has."

He smiles. In the pale light of his candle his eyes have no irises; they are wholly black, like the dark of the mine halfway up the shaft. The flickering of the candle puts gold into his eyes. Sometimes it is there even in daylight.

"There are worse places to die."

The bed is bigger and colder without Nav. At home, the night seemed dark. But after the heavy darkness of the mine, even the blackest night is full of light. Fursey's head shines in it. Now there is some privacy, but Fursey thinks it's best to wait until the others are asleep.

They know anyway. All the boys who share beds share pleasure as well. What else is there? Where else can warmth be had? But Fursey is like that; secretive, solitary.

"Except with you, Medric. I'd never keep a secret from you."

When Fursey finally becomes a hewer, months behind the other sixteen-year-olds, it's a relief to everyone, even Sami. Fursey was like a chained bear, sullen and dangerous, those last two months.

"If Medric can start hewing, I can too," he argued. "I've been here longer than anyone. You know I know the mine like no one else. I can pick a reef better than you can!"

But Sami was firm. No one becomes a hewer until they reach the height mark on the kitchen doorway. Not even Fursey, no matter how he argued and cursed.

His first day, Fursey fairly races down to the rock face, laughing and swinging his pick. He chooses a completely different part of the wall to work on. Ignores the foreman.

"Here, Medric," he calls. "This is where the reef is thickest." He talks to the rock. "I can hear you," he says. "I'm coming to get you out. Fall to my left," he says. He swings his pick as though he's been doing it all his life. The pick head hits the rock and a whole section falls off, to his left. The way only the best and most skilled hewers can do, after years of practice.

Underneath there is pure gold. The full seam, shining so bright in the weak candlelight it looks molten, glowing. The hewers gather around silently. Even the bonded ones, who have no choice about being here, even they sigh a little, looking at the gleam of it. Fursey reaches out and touches it, traces the broad river of it down the wall.

"Hello," he says.

That's the way it goes. Fursey chooses where we hew. Each time, he talks to the rock, tells it where to fall, how to split. And it does. The mine production triples. Fursey is Sami's pet. He gets new clothes, the best food. No one minds because, with Fursey telling them where to lay their picks, and talking to the rock face, no one dies. There are no more tunnels collapsing.

At night, he lies staring at the ceiling, smiling.

The other hewers in the barracks whisper to each other of the girls down in the valley, whisper and touch and groan. They talk about what they'll do when their bond time is up. Where they'll go. Sandalwood. Carlion. Foreverfroze. Who they'll shag, and how. Then they touch again.

Fursey talks about gold, and then touches.

"Gold and you, Medric. What else do I need?"

Only three months until the seven years are up. Fursey was sold in for fourteen years. He has another nine months to go.

"I'll work the nine months with you, Furse. Then we can leave together." It's a faint hope. There's no chance.

"Leave?" he says, not understanding.

"My bond is up in three months. Yours is up in nine. I'll work the extra six months with you, get a bit of pay in my pocket. Then we can both leave together."

He stares. "*Leave?*"

He's right, of course. It would be crazy for him to go. As soon as his bond is worked out, Sami will hire him back at three times a normal hewer's pay. He's worth twice as much again. He could have a house in the valley, live a good life doing what he loves. Why should he leave?

"I never chose to come here, Furse. I've got family, somewhere to go."

"Your own da sold you!"

"Not my da. I wouldn't spit on him. But I've got two sisters. I want to find them. Make sure they're all right."

He relaxed. "Well, you can do that and then come back. No need to go for good."

No need. Except the dark and the cold and the flickering of gold at the edges of vision like madness, waiting.

Except the hard slog of the walk up the mine ramp. Except the ugliness of the barracks and the dirt and the smell. Except having to watch the young pushers heave their hearts out and no way to help.

Except the girls in the valley. And the girls in the world beyond the valley. And the idea of children, someday. Children to be loved. To be cared for. Not hit, not terrorized. Loved. Never, ever, sold.

Nine months can seem longer than years put together. And shorter than a day.

Three days to go, Sami tries a recruiting talk. "You're a good hewer, Medric. You've got a real gift for it." That's true. "Why not think about staying? Fursey's going to have his own house up here, you know. The two of you could have a good life."

He's frightened that Fursey might desert the mine. He can't afford it.

"It's not such a bad life, when you're not a bondsman," he says confidentially, leaning close. "The valley girls like a free hewer." He winks, then thinks again as he sees Fursey's face. "Course, there's no need for you to go anywhere, really. Nice house of your own, good food, good company. There's many a man in the outside world would cut off his right arm for a life like that." He chuckles. "Course, he wouldn't be any use to us then!" His hand descends in what he means to be a friendly pat on the back. But he's a heavy-handed man, like my da, and it hurts.

"Don't go," Fursey says when Sami leaves. It's the first time he's said it straight out.

"I can't take the dark any longer than I have to, Furse. I'm not like you. I've never loved it. There's a whole world out there. Don't you want to see it?"

He shakes his head. "And the valley girls?" he asks bitterly.

"Oh, gods, Furse, I don't want them like I want you. But don't you want a family? A real home?"

He looks up with his eyes full of tears. "You're my family. You and the gold."

"Well, you'll still have the gold. I hope you enjoy it."

Maybe that wasn't kind. But he talks always like gold is human. Like it has feelings.

On the last day, he stays at the rock face until after the mine whistle, until the other hewers have gone up the ramp and there is no one else around. No one will come back. They let him make his goodbyes in private.

"Don't go, Medric," he says.

"I have to."

"No, you don't. You can change your mind and stay here, where you belong. With me."

His eyes are as black as always, down here, but they are shining gold, too. Strong flickers of gold. Nav's warning comes back to mind, from the first day. "He don't never forget nothing; and he don't never forgive."

Love is not a word that's ever used at the mine, and it's too late to try it now, anyway. But it's true. Even when he's acting like a madman.

"I only stayed in the world because of you," he says. "I never wanted to go up into the light. You know that. I went up there for you."

"I know, but —"

"I'm not going back again. Not without you. I'm staying down here." He pulls up the pickaxe, hoisting it casually, as hewers do, and I'm suddenly aware of the muscles in his shoulders and arms, the broad hewer's chest. The pickaxe can hew rock—it would go straight through blood and bone. Who knows what he's going to do, but he has to be stopped.

"You won't be able to help the gold anymore. What will it do without you?" It's a forlorn, stupid argument, but it makes him frown, considering.

He stands at the tunnel mouth and smiles, fair hair shining in the candlelight, just like gold. The only warm thing in the world.

"The mine will still go on," he says. "A little slower without me, that's all. But I'll be here forever." Then he walks right up to me and kisses me, the pickaxe held between us so that all I feel is soft lips and rough wood and cold steel against my neck. Then he walks past me, down into the darkest part of the mine.

As he walks, he whispers to the gold, "Show me where they are, the delvers, lead me to them, honeyfall, bright stream, sweet gold, you're my only love now, lead me to the people of stone . . ." And he disappears into the darkness.

The only warm thing. How could I help but go back?

MARTINE

THE PEOPLE OF Foreverfroze had gathered in the open space before the hall, examining the strangers with interest. Fathers hoisted their children onto shoulders so the little ones could see the warlord and his companions. Larger children wormed their way to the front. There was a holiday atmosphere, cheerful and expectant. Martine felt that she was as much a focus of interest as Arvid—the strange woman who looked like one of them.

Skua and Fox led her through the crowd, following the others. Safred, Arvid, Cael and Zel reached the hall steps first and turned to watch Martine come through. Men and children and old women touched her lightly as she passed: on the arm, the shoulder, the back, patting, saying "Welcome," a word that sounded exactly as it had in her own village. Tears rose in her eyes and a woman clucked gently at her, "Now, now." She felt overwhelmed by the sense of family. She wondered if she could come back here to live after . . . afterward. Perhaps, finally, she had found somewhere she could belong. Then she looked up and saw Arvid.

He was staring at her as though she were a miracle. She flushed, the lingering cold of the wind banished by pulses of heat, by a deep blush that swept through her, from head to foot, the fire spreading as though she stood before the altar in the middle of the ritual. She kept walking, trying to control her face, but she could see from his expression that he had seen her reaction. His breath was coming faster, his eyes darker than normal. As Martine reached the group, trying to focus on Safred and Zel instead of Arvid, Skua gave her a little push so that she stumbled and landed in his arms.

Skua said, "Hah!" and Fox slapped her hand, mock reproving. Martine was only just aware of them. One of Arvid's hands was under her elbow, the other on her back. Her own hands were spread across his chest, fingers splayed. Every point where they touched was alive, warm, intense. She didn't dare look at his face, although they were almost the same height and all she had to do was raise her eyes to his. She could feel his breath, warm on her cheek; fast breaths that comforted her because it was clear that whatever was happening, was happening to both of them.

"She's cold! Better warm her up, lad!" Skua said. The crowd cheered and laughed and Martine broke away from Arvid and turned, glaring at Skua.

"I'm too old for these games," she said sternly, and Fox, for the first time, laughed.

"Never too old," she cackled, digging Skua in the ribs. The two of them chuckled and made some clearly lewd comments to an old man standing behind Skua, speaking too fast in their own language for Martine to understand. He took it with a private smile buried under a long-suffering air, and exchanged a glance of sympathy with Martine. She had forgotten this part of having a family—the lack of privacy, the assumption that the aunties knew best, the interference. She *was* too old for this, too old to get accustomed to it again. Her vision of a future homecoming wavered.

Then they took pity on her and chivvied everyone into the blessed warmth of the hall, and fed them fried whitefish and salmon roe, mushrooms and greens, snowberries and smoked eel. Martine made sure she wasn't sitting next to Arvid, but she ate the whole meal with every sense tingling, aware of each move he made.

Toward the end of the meal, Arvid spoke directly to Skua. "The ship?" he asked.

"Tomorrow," she said.

He nodded, satisfied, then said, "There may not be room for the horses."

For a moment, Martine didn't realize what he meant, then she and Zel and Cael all spoke at the same time. "Trine's coming!"

Arvid was perplexed. "It's just a horse."

"Bramble's horse," Safred said quietly.

He shrugged. "Very well then. The wagons will arrive tomorrow, we can load and sail with the next tide," he said. He grinned at Martine and she had to bite her tongue to stop herself smiling foolishly back. "One thing about Foreverfroze, there's always lots of strong men around to help load ships!"

"Why is that?" Martine asked Safred.

"The shipmasters prefer women fishers," she said absently, picking over a platter for the last of the mushrooms.

"But why?"

Arvid turned toward her. "Because the shipmaster has to pay a levy to the family if a fisher is lost at sea, and when a ship is blown far off course and has to limp home, women take starvation better than men and are more likely to survive," he explained seriously.

Martine smiled grimly. "So it's a matter of silver," she said, leaning forward so she could hear him better above the hubbub in the hall.

"Silver and gold," Arvid agreed. "A ship that loses its crew will bankrupt the shipmaster and he will lose the ship."

"Shipmasters are men?"

He shook his head. "Not always. But to steer a ship in rough weather, you need a man's strength, so the shipmaster is either a man or has a steersman as a husband."

"You know a lot about it," Martine observed.

"They are my people," he said simply. "It is my job to know them."

She realized abruptly that she had been lured into private conversation with him, and sat back, trying to seem calm. The memory of the moment outside rushed back and to cover her embarrassment she spoke with severity. "And to make sure they know you," she said. "And your guards."

"Of course," he agreed gravely, but with a hint of a smile, "they must know their warlord and the people who protect them."

She sniffed with disbelief, and he laughed.

"Don't judge me so swiftly, stonecaster! Things are different up here in the north." Heads had turned as he laughed, and indulgent glances were cast at them.

Martine couldn't wait to get out of Foreverfroze, and preferably without Arvid. She pushed herself back from the table and stood up. "If you'll excuse me," she said.

He let her go, but called after her, "Go breathe the northern air," he said. "It clears the head."

She threw him a withering look, but he looked back without a smile, his guard down, eyes dark with emotion and desire. For her. The fire flared up inside her again.

Martine went out the door fast and into the bracingly cool air. She turned away from the houses and made for the ridge, where she might find solitude and time to reflect. The climb was a stiff one, but there was a path and she ploughed up it, glad of the movement after the day spent riding. At the top, she had used up enough energy to stop and appreciate the view. The sun was setting and the light had changed quality, losing its brilliance and becoming misty and golden. The moon was just rising, huge over the dark, moving sea. She stood on the ridge and reached out her hands, one east and one west, until the sun and the moon seemed to sit in her palms, and felt herself and the world come into perfect balance, poised on the ridge as if she were riding some great beast, one of the giant bulls of the Ice Giants, or a sea serpent, and she a hero out of the legends of her people: Mim, or the Prowman, or old Dotta herself, savior of the fire.

For the first time since the fire had roared and rejected her, she was herself again. Whole. Calm. Back where she ought to be. Her breathing eased and grew slow as the sun slipped out of her hand and disappeared, and the moon swam slowly aloft, turning silver as she swam, and laying down the gleaming hero's path on the shifting sea. Martine lowered her arms.

Arvid's footsteps below her came as no surprise. She half-smiled, expecting to find that this, too, had returned to normal. That now the fire was gone, she would be able to look at him as she looked at any other man.

Then he reached the top of the ridge and she met his eyes.

ASH

Boys were not allowed to take the risk of finding their true shape until they were fully grown. On the third night of his fast, the thought returned to Ash with some comfort, watching Flax strip uncertainly in the forecourt of the big cave, that he himself was now fully grown, and strong enough to risk it.

They jumped the chasm and proceeded to the inner cave, much smaller than the first, and lit only by the glowworms and the faint flicker of light from the first cave. Here, a small stream sprang from the wall and flowed across the floor of the cave, spreading itself into a shallow pool and then flowing out another crack in the rock to fall to the River below. The deer and squirrel took hold of Flax and made him lie down in the pool, his face just clear of the water. His teeth started chattering immediately. Ash remembered that sudden chill, the freezing water clinging to his skin.

"This is the third test," Ash said. "Lie still and trust the River. Listen to her voice. Learn her. Love her. If you trust in her, you will be safe."

That was all he could do for Flax. He had been told the same, the first time he came here, by an older boy who had not yet found his true shape. Now it was up to Flax. Ash walked toward the next passageway, where his father waited for him.

"Where are you going?" There was a note of panic in Flax's voice.

"Not far," Ash said. "But you must meet the River alone."

Flax stared at him. Ash could barely see him in the dimness, but he could hear his breathing, fast and shallow.

"Trust her," he said gently. "But don't drink any water from anywhere in the Deep unless you have been given leave."

He followed his father down the passageway, leaving most of the men behind with Flax. A wolf and a fox followed them: Vine and Skink. His excitement built further, and with it came apprehension.

Was this the night when he would find his true shape? Outside the Deep you did not think about the Deep, but you couldn't stop yourself from dreaming. After his first visits here, he had dreamed again and again about becoming truly himself, about finding his animal self. His dreams had ranged from the grandiose—wildcats, bears—to the ridiculous—moles, water-rats, shrews—to the disturbing. He didn't want to be a weasel. Truly, he didn't want that.

They took him ever deeper, through dark caves without a single green star, through passageways which were rough underfoot, down and further down until they came at last to a place with another small fire.

They were on a broad platform which ended in a cliff. Beyond was darkness. There was no way to tell how large the cavern was, but the river roared loudly and echoed through the darkness. There was a large pool to one side which reflected the light of the fire in a perfectly still surface.

A man came from behind the fire, and unlike every other man in this place, he wore a human face, and was clothed in leggings and tunic. Ash had never seen him before, and wondered why. He was very, very old, his skin hanging in wrinkles and folds, his hair so white that it was impossible to tell what color it might have been in his youth, although Ash felt sure it would have been jet black. He wore his hair in braids that reached past his shoulders, tied off with threads and feathers and beads. Immediately, Ash felt that his own short hair was out of place. He wondered how this old man managed in the world outside; only warlords' men were allowed to wear their hair long. Any Traveler who did so risked a beating or worse from warlords' men.

The man, surprisingly, had bright blue eyes, so his blood was not purely Traveler blood. This was a person with a complex past, a long and convoluted history that took in both Traveler and Acton's people. Ash found that reassuring, somehow, although he didn't know why. He put the thought away to examine later, and stared into the man's bright eyes.

"Will you meet your true shape?" he asked Ash. His voice was beautiful, the voice of a singer born and trained.

Ash felt a sharp stab of envy, but pushed it down. He nodded. The small movement made his head spin. Fasting cleansed you, but it left you weak. "I will," he said.

"Then climb, and drink, and know."

The man led him to the edge of the cliff which descended into blackness, the small light from the fire making it seem even darker. Rowan came forward and placed both hands on his shoulders. He hissed. Ash could tell it was a blessing. He tried to smile at his father, but managed only a tight grimace. The fear was climbing up his stomach to his heart.

The old man came forward and placed a hand on his head. "Take our love to the River," he said. "Climb, and drink, and know."

Ash turned and backed over the cliff in the place the man pointed to. At least he was strong, and fit, thanks to training all winter with Mabry. He felt cautiously for toeholds and handholds. He didn't like heights; had always felt a treacherous desire to throw himself off. The darkness made it a little better, but it was impossible to see where his hands and feet were. As his head went below the edge of the cliff, he closed his eyes. Better to trust to his sense of touch than strain his eyes uselessly.

He didn't know how deep the cliff was. The last two years he had come with his father to the Deep, he had been brought to watch, as youths a little older than he was had made the climb. Not everyone survived the climb itself. Not everyone survived the knowledge of who they were. Some went mad. Some, when they returned up the cliff and were shown their true self in the reflecting pool, jumped off the cliff. Ash had seen it happen to a boy who found himself in a field-mouse shape.

As a watcher, the climb had always seemed a long time. Now it seemed endless. Fumbling in the dark, knowing one misstep, one bad handhold, could send him plummeting, screaming perhaps, into the dark, thundering river...He controlled his breathing as Doronit had taught him to, concentrating on only the next movement, the next shift of weight. This was a test of patience and self-control as much as skill and strength. Not to hurry, that was the main thing. Take it slow and sure, think of nothing else...He tired faster than he expected to and realized that strength wouldn't get him through this, but determination might.

The wind from the water below dried the sweat on his bare skin and made him shiver. His fingers were bleeding and his feet were cut. Why did a stubbed toe *hurt* so much? He had never understood that. The thought worried him. He was becoming light-headed. When he next had a foothold which would bear his whole weight he stopped and breathed deeply for a few moments, calming down before starting again.

The noise of the river was getting louder. He began to feel splashes on his legs: small droplets of water hitting and tickling as they rolled down. Then larger splashes, small waves flung up from the surface over his feet. The rocks grew slippery and he moved more slowly. There was no bottom to the cliff, he realized. Nowhere to stand. He would have to cling precariously to the rock and lean down to drink.

He decided that the safest way was to keep climbing until his knees, at least, were under water. Although the current might tug at him, he wouldn't have to bend so far down. He wasn't sure if he was being brave or foolish, but perhaps the River favored fools, because as he carefully edged his feet down into the chilling water and waves slapped against his thighs, he found a ledge to stand on. The current was much faster and more turbulent than he had expected: he teetered and grabbed for a protruding knob of rock to steady himself. He could hold against it, just, but not for long.

He bent to the water, and then paused. It didn't seem polite to just drink, as though he had a right. He didn't know what to expect, but he felt he had to ask first.

"Lady," he said quietly, "may I drink?"

Immediately the water began to flow more quietly; the current stopped tugging at him, the waves grew still. The River seemed to pause in its course.

"Lady, I thank you," he said, and scooped a palmful of water to his mouth. It tasted of chalk and iron, sweet and harsh at once, strong. Dizziness swept over him and he clutched at the cliff face in a panic. Then he felt the power of the River reach up to him, steadying him.

Trust me, it said in a voice unlike any he'd ever heard; a woman's voice, for certain, but with harmonies no human voice could carry, as though many voices spoke in rhythm with each other; and behind the voice was music so intricate, so complex, that it was almost unrecognizable as melody. He was ravished by it. His heart swelled with it until he felt it would burst with emotion. But there were no echoes from the voice and that was when he understood that she spoke inside his head.

"I do trust you," he answered aloud, and it was true.

She laughed, bells and nightingales and waterfalls of laughter, and then was silent. He was left to climb the cliff again, his dizziness replaced by a wild curiosity. What had he become? He hadn't felt his face change, but perhaps that moment of dizziness had been the shift to his true shape. He knew not to touch his head, and that it was forbidden to guess the shape before he saw it in the reflecting pool.

The climb up was quicker but just as physically demanding. The cold of the River had leached strength from his muscles and he had to force himself upward by sheer will. Eventually, he became aware of the light growing brighter, the flames flickering. His eyes were almost blinded as his head crested the cliff edge and he pulled himself up onto the platform.

His father was there, helping him over the lip and then standing back to stare at him, open-mouthed. Oh gods, Ash thought. I'm a vole. Or a weasel.

The old man was staring, too, and the fox and the wolf, all staring as though they'd never seen anything like him. What if I'm a *snake?* he thought wildly. Or a tame animal like a sheep? Please, not a sheep.

He walked forward, stiff-legged, to the reflecting pool, and the others followed behind him. He bent over its still surface, its perfect reflection, and saw himself.

Just himself. His own face, his normal face, a little pale but just the same as always.

A great grief rose in him and he hid his face from his father, from the other men. The River had rejected him. Why? *Why?* When it took squirrels and voles, yes, and even field-mice men, why would it reject *him?* He was worthless, he had always known it, useless for anything... No wonder his father hadn't taught him all the songs. Not just because of tradition, they had said that to put him off. He was flawed deep inside. The River had probably told his father not to share the deep secrets with him. He fought back tears because he felt that if he started to cry he would never stop.

"Ah . . ." the old man let out a great sigh as he hid his face, and came forward. "My son, welcome. I have waited a long time for this." He laughed a little. "You don't know how long!"

He took hold of Ash's hands and pulled them away from his face. Ash wanted to look away, but a last remnant of pride made him meet the man's gaze, expecting scorn and derision. The blue eyes were full of joy and comradeship. The man put his arm around Ash's shoulders and turned him to face the others. Ash looked away, down at the ground, anywhere but at his father.

"Rejoice with me," the old man said. "The River has found another lover."

LEOF

THEGAN ARRIVED BEFORE sunset, with a small body of men—all sergeants, except for his personal groom. Leof smiled to himself. Any old campaigner knew that when you used oath men in battle, you'd better have some good sergeants keeping them in line and making sure they didn't break and run for it.

"My lord," Leof said as Thegan sprang down from his horse.

Thegan clapped him on the back and looked out over the landscape, which glowed golden and rose from the setting sun. It was a scene of perfect peace: dairy cattle wound their accustomed way to the milking sheds, birds settled to their nests, a sheepdog barked in warning at an errant ewe as it herded her into the fold for the night, and down the street mothers called their children in. Bonhill was full of the best possible reasons for resisting the enchanter.

"Where is he?" Thegan asked.

Leof pointed out the hill and described the work the enchanter was doing. "I'd say he'll be there several days, if he wants to make sure he gets all the buried bones. It's a big area for one man to cover."

"The bones . . ." Thegan brooded. "You think that's what he's using to raise the ghosts?"

"What else would he want them for?"

Thegan nodded, his face dark. "Is it the enchanter you met?"

"No. He's a young man, under thirty, I'd say. Not a warrior."

"Hmph. If he were a warrior he wouldn't have resorted to tricks and spells." Thegan nodded in decision. "Well done. When will the Sendat troops arrive, do you think?"

"Depends if they march through the night. If they do, we might be in place before sunrise. If not, then midday."

Thegan called his groom. "Sandy, take the road to Sendat and tell whatever officer you find leading my troops that I want them to take no more than two hours' rest tonight. Tell them we have to be in position before it gets light."

The groom nodded and ran for the stables.

"There's no guarantee that the wind wraiths won't smell us out anyway," Leof cautioned.

"We'll deal with that if it happens," Thegan said. "Come, let's eat and rest while we can."

It was good advice, and Leof took it. He and the sergeants ate and lay on the inn benches, jackets under their heads for pillows. Thegan lay more comfortably in the innkeeper's bedroom. They were all experienced men, so they slept, waking quickly as Thegan's groom barged in through the inn doors.

"They're almost here!" he called. "My lord! My lord! They're coming!"

Leof sprang up and pulled his jacket on, feeling the familiar sense of tension and excitement he always felt before battle. This time, there was no unease. These were no innocents, like the Lake People; this was a monster aided by monsters, and he would hew the enchanter's head off with great satisfaction, if Thegan didn't get to him first.

Thegan appeared from the bedroom looking, as always, pristine. Leof retied the combination of leather thong and brown velvet ribbon that kept his hair back and pulled his jacket into shape over his hips, then followed Thegan out into the dark. On the eastern horizon, the sky was just beginning to gray.

The road leading to Bonhill curved around a series of hills, so that they could make out glimpses of movement and shadow, and hear the sound of horses hooves and harnesses clinking. Wil and Gard were at the head of the column, with Alston behind leading the first group.

"Privy break!" Alston called as they came to a halt two lengths away from the first village house, near an orchard. It was a well-practiced routine. The men swung down from their horses and helped their pillion passengers, the pikemen, off. Then three out of four riders handed their reins to the fourth and disappeared into the coppice, followed by their passengers. When they emerged the fourth man went, too. Then they stood by their horses, waiting for orders. Leof could smell the piss from the inn door, and the nervous sweat. Thegan always ordered a privy break before a battle; the men knew they would be fighting soon.

While the men relieved themselves, Wil and Gard dismounted and came for orders.

"The enchanter is on the hill, over there," Thegan said. "There's no chance that we will completely surround him before he hears us, but I want to get a small force up close and hidden before the main charge starts, so that if he sets a spell loose we have a surprise up our sleeve." They nodded, nervous as the men. Neither of them liked the idea of fighting an enchanter.

Leof put an arm around Wil's shoulders, and shook him slightly. "I've seen him. He's a scrawny bastard, and he doesn't look too brave to me. He'll probably run when he sees us, and then we'll have him!"

Thegan nodded approval at him. "Twenty pikemen, Leof, under your command. Take them to your observation post and keep them there until you get my order. Use your own judgment if he sees us and starts to fight. I'll give you a count of three hundred to get into position before we move."

Leof nodded. He went to Alston and relayed the order. Alston gathered the twenty men and gave them a brief speech about keeping low and staying silent. He had chosen experienced men, not the oath men. Leof paused. He knew Alston liked to pray before he went into battle, but this time he just motioned the men to start moving.

"No prayers?" Leof asked curiously.

"No need to ask for forgiveness from the one we are about to kill," Alston said. "He has forfeited any rights to life or to rebirth." His voice was flat with a kind of hatred that Leof had never heard from him before. "This is a blasphemer of the worst kind," he added. "He will rot in the cold hell for eternity."

The words sounded so unlike his normal sensible self that Leof was troubled. Could anyone forfeit their right to life or to rebirth? That was one of those questions that had never worried him before he knew Sorn. Her belief had made an impression on him without him realizing it, just as she had herself. He felt a quick, aching yearning for her; to be sitting calmly with her, gazing quietly at her beauty. Although he knew that if he were there, there would be no quiet inside him, only raging desire and desperation. He shook off the thought and concentrated on leading his men quietly through the convoluted path that led to the willow coppice.

They only just made it within the count of three hundred. Once there, Leof led the men under the trailing curtain of willow boughs, to the hard task of waiting. They heard nothing from the hill of bones except the wuthering of the wind, which might have been wind wraiths or might have been merely air. From beneath the trailing willow branches they could judge the quiet onset of day. The light grew brighter until they could see each other's faces, then eyes. The men listened hard, pikes clutched in sweaty hands.

Leof alone peered out, trying to make out any movement from the hill. He fancied he could hear the soft noises of Thegan's approach, but he knew how easily imagination magnified every sound before a battle. Thegan would not have had time to get everyone into position yet.

Then, as the highest leaves of the willow trees were lit into bright yellow green, they heard the wind wraiths crying, "Ware! Ware! Master, beware of men with iron!"

Leof looked out to see Thegan still some way away, and the enchanter springing up from sleep. Frantically, he grabbed the bags of bones and poured them out in a circle around him. Leof realized it was the first step in making a spell, and he charged out of the screen of leaves, yelling, "For Thegan!"

"Thegan! Thegan!" his men shouted. The enchanter faltered as he saw them, then he grabbed his knife and gabbled some words, holding the knife over his palm.

Leof ran up the slope at full pelt, but he was too late. The enchanter drew the knife down as Leof grabbed for it, scattering blood over the bones around him. He spun around, showering as many bones as he could before Leof grabbed him and pressed his hand against his own jacket to stop the bleeding. But it was too late. Around them, a circle of ghosts was forming. The first one, a short man with hair in beaded plaits, was the leader. The ghost aimed a sword at Leof's head. Leof let go of the enchanter and brought up his own sword in defense. He was stunned by the strength of the blow. For the first time, he understood to his marrow how dangerous the ghosts were.

The enchanter was backing away, terrified, protected by a phalanx of ghosts. The ground shook as Thegan's men charged the hill, horns blowing the attack. Leof's men had reached the hill just as the ghosts appeared and were now engaging them as they had been taught.

"Aim for the arms!" he heard Alston shout, and the men shouted acknowledgment.

Leof was fighting bitterly. The ghost wasn't a warrior, that was clear, but it didn't have to be when it didn't have to guard against death. It attacked furiously but without trying to defend, so that for a moment Leof had to put all his energies into protecting himself. The strangest thing was that the ghost was not breathing. Leof had often fought at close quarters, and he knew the interplay of gasp and breath and grunt as each man gave or took blows. This time only he breathed and gasped; it was disconcerting; strangely impersonal. Yet the hatred in the ghost's eyes was very personal. After a flurry of blows he maneuvered the ghost around until he could take the blow he wanted. As he raised his sword for the cut, he was aware of Thegan's horse arriving, of the riders bringing axes down on ghost after ghost, targeting the shoulders and arms and legs, as they had been instructed.

He grinned and brought his sword down on the shoulder of the ghost's sword arm. He had done this before, to one of the Ice King's men. He knew how much effort was needed to actually cut someone's arm off. But he did it. The ghost's arm fell to the ground. Astonished, the ghost looked down at it and Leof used the moment to bring his sword around and up for a backstroke that cut off its head. The head tumbled to the ground.

The ghost itself did not fall. The body swayed and then, sickeningly, the head and arm disappeared from the ground, and reappeared on the ghost's body. Complete with sword in hand. Leof stood watching in shock, his mind racing, his hands trembling. He and his men were all going to die. The Domains were going to die. There was no way to fight this—none at all.

The ghost twisted its head slightly, as if testing the surety of its neck, then looked down at its sword hand. It looked slowly up at Leof and smiled mockingly, then raised its sword again and struck. Leof blocked it but it drove him to his knees.

"Regroup!" Thegan shouted. "Withdraw!" He spurred his horse closer to the hill and reached down to hoist Leof up behind him just in time to avoid the ghost's killing blow. Thegan wheeled the horse and hacked with his own sword at a group of ghosts, giving his men time to get away. Leof spun from side to side, guarding their backs.

All around them, men were screaming and running as they realized that the ghosts were not being harmed by even their worst strokes. The horns sounded the retreat, a pattern of notes Leof had only ever heard in training. Thegan had never retreated before.

"Abandon it!" Thegan yelled to the remaining men. "Barricade yourselves in the houses." He pulled his horse away.

A few of the men were down, lying dead or dying, and as the horns rang out the wind wraiths appeared as though summoned by them. They descended toward the battlefield with shrieks of joy, like enormous ravens. The ghosts stopped still to watch them, their faces distorted by fear.

"Feed us!" the wraiths shouted. Thegan checked his horse as the wraiths hovered over the enchanter, safe in his circle of ghosts.

"You may feed," the enchanter cried and the wraiths dived on the dying. The men screamed, long bubbling screams that made Leof's gorge rise. The ghosts backed away, except for those around the enchanter, and then turned and ran, streaming down the hill, heading for the village and beyond. Leof blanched at the likely outcome; he hoped the inn had stout doors and a good strong bar. If the past pattern stayed true, they had all day before them. Sunset seemed a very long way away.

The ghost Leof had fought stood beside the enchanter now, and it raised its sword and shook it threateningly, grinning with satisfied malice.

"Archers!" Thegan shouted. A rain of arrows left the trees, where archers had been concealed, all aimed at the enchanter, who was just within bowshot. But as the shafts hissed through the air they were overtaken by the wind wraiths, who snatched them up in mid-flight and cast them down to the ground, shrieking with glee.

Thegan tensed and leaned forward, staring at the enchanter, clearly considering whether he could reach him and drag him out, or perhaps rescue some of the men.

"Don't do it, my lord," Leof said. He put a hand on Thegan's rein, and dragged his horse's head around, heading him back to Sendat. "It's useless. No army alive could stand against them."

BRAMBLE

FURSEY LED THEM. He needed no lantern, finding his way with uncanny ease up and down and up again, past walls through which they could hear the rushing of water. The sound reminded Bramble too vividly of the many times water had seemed to sweep her out of Acton's life and back into it again. It was only an hour or so since she had seen him, vividly alive. She smiled despite herself as she remembered that sideways smile, the promise and admiration it had held, the energy of every movement he made. She was going to miss that energy.

In the darkness it was easier, somehow, to think about all the people she had come to know through Baluch's eyes, and Ragni's, and Piper's—all dead and gone. She remembered her mother telling her about a man whose whole family had been killed in a fire. "Never really got over being left alive," she had said. "Hung himself on the first anniversary." At the time, she hadn't understood how anyone could regret being alive. She didn't, she *didn't* regret it. Maryrose had told her to live, and she would live, as long as she had to. But she understood, for the first time, how lonely that man must have been, when everyone he loved was gone and he was left to carry on. She thought that, after all this was over, she would find her parents and maybe stay with them for a while.

After that she would find a song-maker, and tell him or her the truth about Acton and the past, and set the record straight. Damn Asgarn's name for eternity. The thought made her slightly more cheerful.

Then Fursey turned a corner and suddenly she was in a passage she recognized, one Dotta had led her down. Her heart beat faster. Not far now. She recited the turns in her head as Fursey took them—yes, he did know the way. Finally, they made the turn into the cave, and Medric raised his lantern high, looking at the walls in amazement. The painted animals seemed to leap and buck, as though they were still alive. Fursey stood for a moment with bowed head, as if praying.

The lantern candle was almost burnt out. Medric took another from his pocket and replaced it. The new candle burned with a whiter light, allowing Bramble to examine the corners of the cave. She searched thoroughly, but there were no bones, not even animal bones. In the furthest corner, however, was a shaft, and the smell from it was dry. No murmur of waters, no sense of damp. If the bones were in there, they might be retrievable.

"The bones must be down there," she said. "We'll have to bring tackle and try to fish them out."

"No." Fursey's voice was adamant. "That is a place sacred to the stone-eaters. We can't go there. We can't *fish* there."

"We need the bones," Bramble said, equally adamant. They stood, glaring at each other.

Medric cleared his throat. "Um . . . can we ask the delvers?"

"No one can summon them!" Fursey said indignantly.

He was wrong. Of course, Dotta had known. Bramble realized with shame that Dotta had warned her about this, and she had forgotten. She remembered another thing Dotta had told her: "The prey must be called with love, though, or it does not come. Remember that."

Were the delvers her prey, or was she theirs? It didn't matter. She was moving once again in a bizarre world where the impossible was necessary. She touched the images of the earth spirits which someone had painted thousands of years ago and sent out the call, as the hunter had taught her, as the hunter had done, with love. Come to me, she said silently, as she had been silent in the Forest when the deer came and nuzzled her before their deaths; as she had been silent when the hunter had his knife to her throat; as she had been silent when Red had brought the knife up. Prey or hunter, it was the same thing. Come to me, for I have need of you.

Medric's gasp alerted her. She turned to see Fursey kneeling, separated from her and Medric by a river of dark rocks. They were slow moving but inexorable, filling the cave not from the outer cave or through fissures but from out of the walls themselves, sliding through the rock as easily as she moved through snow, but leaving no trace of their passage behind. They were half her height, and glinted in the light from the lantern as polished granite glints, but they were rough, not smooth.

They were far more strange than water sprites or wind wraiths; dangerous and alien. Bramble grinned at them in the darkness, feeling the familiar lift of excitement, and moved forward, slowly, giving them time to get out of her way. They made an aisle for her and she reached the shaft at the edge of the cave easily—but now she was alone, in a little island surrounded by earth spirits.

"There were bones," she said clearly, "thrown here a thousand years ago. The bones of a man. I need them. I am sent by the gods to recover them."

She had no idea if they would understand her, and when they spoke to her in grating rock-sliding-on-rock voices she knew that they hadn't. She looked at Fursey.

He lifted his shoulders. "I don't understand them, either," he said.

The delvers edged forward, pushing Bramble closer to the shaft. Medric sprang forward too, shouting, "No!" but he was too late. They pushed suddenly, hard and impossible to resist, and she felt herself falling. The sensation was like the waters sweeping her away once again and she forced herself to relax, as she had then, to let the current take her where it willed.

She landed with a thump that knocked breath and thought from her body and lay for a while in darkness so complete that her eyes made light for her, peopling the cave with specks and fireballs, with colors and sparks.

There was something sharp under her. She moved with difficulty and edged it out. If Acton's bones had broken her fall—she laughed silently. That would be rich. She drifted off into semi-consciousness.

"Bramble! Bramble!" Medric's voice roused her.

"Mmm," she said. "I'm all right." That was a lie. She hurt all over.

"The delvers have gone," he shouted. "I'm sending down a candle. Do you have a tinderbox?"

No, of course she didn't have a tinderbox. What a stupid question.

"No," she managed to say.

She dragged herself up and sat with head hanging. A moment later a thin cord with tinderbox and candle came snaking down through the shaft and hit her on the head.

"Oh, dung and pissmire!" she said. The box had bounced off her head and fallen somewhere nearby. She felt for it cautiously. The rock beneath her was covered with bones. Whether they were Acton's or animals', she didn't know.

Then at the same moment, her left hand touched the tinderbox and the right one found a smooth surface... rounded, with holes. Oh, gods, it was a skull. She grabbed the tinderbox but her hands were shaking too much to undo the knot. She put it on the rock next to her foot and reached out again for the skull. His skull. The bone was silk covered in dust. She rubbed it on her trousers to clean it and held it in both hands, leaned her head down until her forehead was on his.

He was dead. He had been alive, smiling at her, only a few hours ago. But he was dead. He had been dead all this time, lying here, flesh withering away to dust, to nothing but bone. He was dead and she would never see him again.

The grief rose in her overwhelmingly; worse than for the roan, or the hunter, or even for Maryrose. The strength of it burned her as it rose, choking her, stopping her breath so that she thought she would die, racking her with so much pain that her eyes could not fill with tears, and at last she recognized it for what it was. She had felt this grief before, when she was Piper, looking at the ghost of Salmon. This was the grief of love.

Alone in the dark, she cradled his skull to her and rocked backward and forward and remembered him, because all she would ever have was memory, and she would love no human never, because he was no longer human, because they had never been human together except for that one moment on the hillside, where he had smiled at her with such promise, such delight. She remembered him vividly, gold hair shining in the sunshine, flecks of gold glinting on his jaw from the new beard, blue eyes bright and mischievous, mouth curved with desire. For her. Her, not Wili or Freide or the girl on the mountain. He had smiled at her, only two hours ago.

And now he was dead, and his bones were as dry as her eyes.

SAKER

INVINCIBLE. THEY WERE invincible. All day the warlord's men fell before them, or ran before them. They cowered behind locked doors, they pleaded for mercy before the killing stroke came. Nothing could save them.

Saker himself was invulnerable—guarded not only by undying men, but by the wind wraiths as well. Safe against archers, safe against blades, safe against blows. Invincible.

He was buoyed by victory, elated and exalted and set free from all fear, at last. He had thought that the wraiths were a terror, but they had saved his life. The gods were truly with him, supporting him. *They* had sent the wind wraiths.

He left the cart behind on the hill and took only the casket of bones and the scrolls with him. Now that he had been discovered, he must hide until the next time. They would keep a lookout, to stop anyone digging for bones. This army was all he had, and probably all he could get, for now. It was enough.

Enough for Sendat. Enough to raze the warlord's fort and kill everyone within. Enough to gather all the weapons they would need.

Then, Turvite. He would raise Alder, his father, to participate in that great fight.

As the day ended, he found an abandoned water mill whose course had run dry, and hid the bones and scroll under the decaying wheel before holing up himself in the mill loft. Owl went with him. They looked out the window slit across what seemed peaceful, prosperous country lying golden in the last light of the sun. Owl smiled ferociously and gestured wide, then began to fade, still smiling.

"Yes," Saker confirmed as he disappeared. "Yes, we will have it all."

He ignored his empty stomach and settled down, smiling, to plan for massacre and conquest.

Book Three
FULL CIRCLE

To Stephen and Robert

BRAMBLE

I'M SENDING a rope down!" Medric said. "There's nothing to hitch it to here, so don't pull on it until I'm braced and I give you the word."

"All right," said Bramble. She was lucky, she supposed, that she had come down into the caves with Medric, an experienced miner, but part of her wished he would let her stay down here at the bottom of this shaft, alone in the middle of a mountain with Acton's bones, until she too had died and her flesh had sifted into dust.

"Ready?" Medric called.

Bramble adjusted the rope under her armpits and clasped her arms around the fragile bundle of Acton's bones. She pushed down all feeling. She didn't have time for grief, or love, or anything but revenge. Saker the enchanter was going to come to grief himself, and she would be there to destroy him. For her sister Maryrose. For all the innocents killed by Saker's ghost army.

"Ready," she said.

"Now!"

She began to climb, bracing herself against the shaft wall with her feet as Medric hauled from above. The rope cut her, but she was making steady progress when Medric yelled something from above and the world came tumbling down.

Dirt and small rocks hit her face first, blinding her, and then Medric's heavy body slid down the shaft, slamming them both to the ground, with rubble and pebbles cascading after them, covering the candle stub and plunging them into darkness.

They lay gasping for a long moment before Bramble could move.

"Everlasting dark!" Medric swore, his voice shaky. "The edge just gave way."

Somehow, it made Bramble grin. Gods and powers, delvers and hunters from the Great Forest, all had conspired to get her here to find these bones, and now a simple accident could undo it all. She rather liked that, liked the feeling of being, for the moment, free from destiny and instruction. No one had foreseen this, as far as she knew. That meant she could react as she liked and do as she pleased in response.

So she laughed.

"Bramble!" Medric reproved, much as her mother used to.

"Well, it could have been worse," she said. "You're not really hurt, are you?"

She sat up and felt both the jacket full of bones and herself for injuries. Scrapes, bruises (gods, lots of bruises!), and a swelling above one ear—although it seemed very large for something that had just happened, so it may have been a legacy from her first fall down the shaft.

Medric searched around in the rubble until he found the tinderbox, then fished a spare candle out of his belt pouch and lit it. She *was* lucky that Medric had proved so steadfast. She wouldn't have blamed him if he had run away when the delvers came and pushed her down this shaft.

"Always carry a few," he said, although earlier he had intimated that they would run out of light if they didn't turn back soon. He really didn't like being underground, Bramble thought, with a flicker of worry. They weren't likely to get out of here anytime soon.

"Will your friend go for help?"

"Fursey?" Medric shook his head, sending dust flying out of his hair like gold in the candlelight. "He left after the delvers came. Doesn't even know we're down here." His voice was dark with abandonment; he'd hoped that Fursey would stay with him, Bramble thought.

She ignored his sigh; they didn't have time to worry about love affairs gone wrong, no matter how strange the beloved or how deep the hurt. "So we'll have to find another way out."

"I might be able to climb out," Medric said doubtfully, but when they examined the shaft they found it was clogged with rubble, and with her saddlebags, which had slid down the shaft with Medric. Bramble dislodged them, sending gravel spinning off, and emptied out everything in them: spare clothes, hairbrush, boot ties, rags, salt were all moved to one bag, leaving the other empty, ready. Almost empty.

At the bottom, where she had put it before leaving Gorham's farm, months ago, was the red scarf she had won when she became the Kill Reborn. It was the only colour in this dark world, and she let it stay where it was, not sure if she were being sentimental or prudent. It was tangled with the brooch Ash had given her. She had tucked it in there when they left Obsidian Lake.

She left the brooch and scarf and put Acton's bones in on top of them. The leg bones didn't fit, and she had to suppress a feeling of panic that she had to leave them behind. She placed them carefully on a low rock, feeling both solemn and silly; they looked ridiculous, like pickings from a giant's plate, but they were Acton's, and she couldn't just throw them away.

Medric tried pulling a few rocks out from the shaft, but more just shifted down into their place. "There's been a big rockfall," he said, in a far more confident tone, the voice of the miner. "No getting out that way, not without a gang of men working from above."

"So," Bramble said, turning and staring into the dark. "We go exploring."

They were standing under a low roof in a flat-bottomed area which sloped gently down to their left and rose more steeply to their right, where the roof became too low for them to walk. There was only one way to go.

"Just as well it's heading the right way," Bramble said.

"Everything gets turned around underground," Medric said warningly. "Don't depend on your sense of direction down here."

"But—" Bramble always knew where she was, and that sense seemed to be working fine. She pointed down the slope and slightly to the right. "The mine entrance is that way."

Medric looked sceptical. "No choice either way," he said. "We follow the river bed."

"What?"

"This would have been a river course, one time," he explained as he led the way down, candle held high. "That's why the walls are so smooth."

Bramble hitched Acton's bones over her shoulder more comfortably, and reached out to touch the wall with the other hand. It was smoother than she'd expected. "So if we follow it down, we find water?" she suggested.

"If we're lucky. If it doesn't narrow too much, or if there's been no rockfalls, or if the land hasn't shifted since the river flowed—which it probably has, which is why the course is dry now." He turned to look seriously at her, his hazel eyes reflecting the spark of candlelight. "We'll be lucky if we get out alive."

Bramble smiled. At least this was *real* —not god-given dreams or time shifting beneath her feet. And it distracted her from thoughts of Acton, which she wasn't ready to face. She thumped Medric on the shoulder and saw him wince as she hit a bruise. "I'm hard to kill," she said. "Let's go."

They went carefully but as fast as they dared, not knowing how long they'd be down here. The candles wouldn't last forever. They followed the old river, ignoring narrower side passages, even though some of them sloped upwards, because in the larger course there was a faint stream of air across their faces.

"Follow the air," Medric said, as though it was the one rule of life, Bramble thought, and maybe it was, in a mine.

Medric settled down into a plodding careful state. He looked at the floor, mostly, leaving it to Bramble to look ahead. She realized that this shutting off was how he had managed to survive the long years of mining.

The old river bed was leading them gradually astray, further down, further north. Bramble reckoned they had passed the mine entrance some time back, and they were now much deeper than when they had started, but she was encouraged by the fresh air which still blew gently in their faces. It had to come from somewhere.

They reached a section where the passage closed in, so they had to crouch, and then slither along. Medric started breathing more heavily. He was a big man, and it was a tight fit.

"I'll go up ahead," Bramble said, "and see if it widens out."

He nodded thankfully and backed out to where he could sit up, his hands shaking. Bramble left the candle with him and went backwards on her stomach, feeling with her toes. The passage narrowed until she could only just move, and she felt a sudden spurt of panic. The walls seemed to press down upon her, the dark she had found soothing only a few minutes before was now full of death, the earth itself a grave where she would be pinned, helpless, forever…

She set the fear aside, but it gave her more sympathy for Medric. If he felt like this all the time, he was being heroic just for not screaming. With an effort of will, she kept moving.

As if to reward her, the toe of her boot, sliding carefully backwards, fell into empty air. A ledge, dropping off. How far down? She bent her leg up and found that at the edge her toe couldn't reach the upper wall. The passage widened just before the drop—perhaps enough to let her sit up and turn around. She snaked sideways so that she wouldn't be hanging half-off and half-on the ledge and edged carefully down.

She could feel the air moving more freely around her head and shoulders as she came closer to the drop, and cautiously sat up, bumping her head just a little. She could sit crouched over easily enough, and she could sense a huge empty space in front of her, full of sound…whispering, plinking, rushing…

"It opens up," she called back to Medric, "but come carefully—there's a drop on the other side." She sat and listened hard as her voice echoed out and round. Other noises, too. Water and air, air and water…

Medric came face first, pushing the candle in front of him. That's not going to do much good in a place this size, Bramble thought, but she took it from him and raised it high as he shuffled closer and sat up, more hunched than she but a safer distance from the drop.

The tiny light from the candle was caught, reflected, from a million places, a million drops of water. They were at the top of what must have once been a short waterfall, at the edge of a cavern so large that every sound they made was taken and echoed and echoed again.

There was just enough light to see boulders and arches of rock, icicles and ant hills of rock reaching down and up from ceiling and floor, joining in places into pillars. The cave—the cavern—stretched up in places so high that no light reached. It seemed to reach up into the dark of the night sky, so Bramble felt surprised not to see any stars.

"There are no wonders like the wonders of the dark," Medric said quietly. Bramble suspected that was something Fursey had once said to him, but whoever said it was right. The echoes of Medric's voice climbed and soared and flew back to them in high cascades of sound.

"Wonders..." the echoes said, and, "Dark..."

The echoes were surrounded and supported by another sound. Everywhere, from the icicles of rock and from points on the cavern's roof, the tiny drops of water fell, onto rock or into shallow pools. Each small *plop* or splat was magnified and transmuted into a thin, ceaseless, mourning cry. The rocks were weeping, and this was the sound of their tears.

The falling water caught the candlelight and sent sparks of it back to them, so that they were caught in a small pool of dazzle, of rainbow glimpses and fleeting lines of light.

"You know where we are, don't you?" Medric said. "These are the Weeping Caverns. The home of Lady Death herself. We'll never get out."

ASH

Like harp music, the sound of the river rippled far below them. It sounded calm, now. Soothing, as though it had never leapt high, never threatened. The old man smiled, his long white hair casting a shining circle around his head in the firelight. Ash was aware of the other men, his father included, standing in the shadows of the cave, but he couldn't bring himself to look at them. Desperately, he stared into the old man's intense blue eyes.

"She calls you," the man said. "She calls your name. Close your eyes. Listen."

Bewildered, hoping that he was not beyond acceptance, that the human face which had reflected back at him from the pool did not mean that he was worthless, Ash closed his eyes. He had so hoped to find his true shape when he climbed down to meet the River. Every other Traveler man did so, after all. Why should he be different? Did he *have* no true shape? No animal spirit deep in his soul which the River could call out? What did that make him?

Ash shuddered with a combination of grief and horror at the thought and felt the old man pat his back in comfort.

"Listen," he said gently. "She will speak to you."

The river was growing louder. Ash concentrated. He had heard the River speak only minutes ago, when he stood in her waters and asked permission to drink. She had laughed, and granted it. Now there were no words, only sounds, like music, like the music he carried in his head, day after day.

The music built in his mind, speaking of emotion deeper than thought, deeper than words, stronger than time. Love was only a small part of it, on the edges. Desire ran through it, but was not the center. He strained, listening harder, and felt it slip away.

"Be still," the old man said.

The hand on Ash's back was warm and reassuring. He let out a long breath, forcing his muscles to loosen, and found the center of the music, the rhythm that controlled everything. *Welcome*, it said. *Belong*.

He began to cry. He had yearned towards homecoming when he lived with Doronit, hoping past sense that she could give it to him. He had seen belonging like this and envied it, watching Mabry and Elva hold their baby, his namesake. He had dreamt of returning to the Road with his parents as a stonecaster, earning a place with them as he had not been able to do as a musician. Each dream had withered, sending him back to the Road, and finally pushing him here. Perhaps he had been Traveling towards the River all his life.

Yes, said the music. *All your life*.

Ash raised his face to the old man, who was smiling.

"She has been waiting for you for a long, long time, child," he said, as he had said once before. "And so have I."

Ash found his voice with difficulty. "Who are you?" he whispered.

"I am the Prowman."

It was a term Ash knew from old river songs—the Prowman stood at the front of the boat and signalled to the steersman which direction to take, to avoid the rapids and treacherous currents. He found the name reassuring.

Ash's father, Rowan, came forward hesitantly. His head was a badger's; each of the men there wore his true nature in the form of an animal, revealed to them through the power of the River. The sweat on his naked skin reflected the torchlight in slabs of gold and red.

Rowan put a hand gently on Ash's shoulder. The dark badger eyes searched his. And then Rowan let Ash go, turned to the other men and lifted his arms high in a gesture of victory. He howled triumph and the other men joined in, dancing and shouting, the animal screams and yowls echoing off the cave walls until Ash was nearly deafened. It was a terrible sound: harsh, cacophonous, wonderful. It lifted him up into a kind of exaltation. He still didn't understand what had happened, or why he had not been given his true shape like the other men; but he did understand that they accepted him, honored him, just as he was. The moment was over too soon. Rowan and the other men ran off into the darkness which led to another cave. Some of them carried torches, the flames and smoke flickering behind them as they ran.

They left one torch behind, stuck in a crevice in the rock wall. The dark closed in around, making the cave seem even bigger, the echoes sharper. Ash was aware of his wet feet and calves, suddenly cold where the River had splashed him as he climbed.

The Prowman walked behind one of the boulders near the passage and came back with a blanket and pack. He threw the blanket to Ash, who hesitated. All the other men were naked, except for the Prowman, who wore leggings and a tunic.

"Am I... allowed?"

The old man shrugged, the beads at the end of his long braids clicking softly. "Animals go naked," he said. "We are not animals."

"What are we?"

The Prowman gestured to the floor and they sat, cross-legged, Ash pulling the blanket around himself. The pack held food: cooked chicken, bread, apples, dried pear. Ash fell on it thankfully. He hadn't eaten in three days.

"Slowly," the Prowman said. "Or you'll just throw it all up again."

It was good advice, but it was hard to follow. Ash forced himself to start with the bread and chewed it thoroughly instead of wolfing it down.

"What are we... Well, that's a little hard to say," the Prowman said, smiling. "We are... Hers. I can tell you some things about yourself, although I do not know you. You are a musician."

Ash shook his head vigorously, glad his mouth was full of bread so he didn't have to say the disappointing words out loud.

"No?" The Prowman paused, surprised. "You *don't* make up music?"

Ash stilled, his hand over the chicken. *Did* he make up music? The moment seemed to stretch for hours.

"In my head," he said finally. "Only in my head."

"Ah, well, that's where all music starts."

"But I can't sing!" Ash said. "Or play anything."

"The River doesn't care about that. She wants what's inside you, not what you do outside."

"What? What's inside me?"

"The thing that makes the music, that *thinks* the music. The center of you. It's why She chose me, why She chose you."

"Chose us to do what?"

For the first time, the Prowman seemed unsure. "Different things. Be Her voice, for one. Be Her eyes in the world, Her... life, Her..."

"Her lover, you said," Ash prompted. He wasn't sure how he felt about that, except intensely curious.

"Mmm... you'll find out about that in time, although it won't be what you expect."

"Nothing ever is!" Ash exclaimed, tired of being told only part of things, tired of always being at the beginning of understanding. Enough of this mysticism. He had a job to do. "I need to learn the secret songs."

The Prowman shook his head, and Ash jumped to his feet, infuriated. "Don't tell me there's *another* shagging test!"

"No, no, don't worry," the Prowman said, laughing sympathetically. "You don't need to learn the songs because when you need them, She will give them to you. How do you think the men learnt them in the first place? She gave them to me, and I gave them to the men. She will be your teacher, lad, when the time comes."

But Ash had a better idea.

"*You* can sing them!" It was a relief, to hand over the responsibility to someone he was sure could fulfil it. But the Prowman put up a hand in refusal.

"No. This is your job. Your time to be active in the world. I have had my time, and it was more than enough." There was a note of sorrow, of loss, of relinquishment, in his voice. "So there is nothing to keep you here," the Prowman went on. "Go where you need to go, and She will be there waiting for you."

"Sanctuary," Ash said without thinking. "I have to go to Sanctuary."

The Prowman's face became shadowed; tears stood in his eyes. With their bright blue clouded, he looked very old, the torchlight showing hundreds of wrinkles, his hands browned with age spots, his hair snow white.

"Sanctuary," he whispered. "That is a name I have not heard in a very long time." He looked up, tears disappearing. "Why do you go to Sanctuary?"

Ash hesitated, overwhelmed by how much he had to explain.

"To raise the ghost of Acton," he said simply. "So that Acton can lay this army of ghosts to rest."

The Prowman went very still.

"Acton," he said. "She did not tell me that. I wonder why." He sat for a long moment and then stood up, as supple as a young boy. "If you go to raise Acton's ghost, lad, I think you will need me with you."

Relief washed over Ash. "You'll come with us?"

"I will take you the River's way."

LEOF

AT NOON the enchanter had sent the wind wraiths away and the ghosts moved off to the south, and Leof, Alston, Hodge and Horst followed them on Thegan's orders. The other troops had returned with Thegan to Sendat after the ghosts had routed them at Bonhill, but there was just a chance that a small group of horsemen could pick off the enchanter from a distance.

"Take any chance you have," Thegan had said. "At any cost."

Leof nodded. "The other reports say that the ghosts faded at sunset or sunrise," he reminded Thegan. "We might get our chance then."

Thegan clapped him on the shoulder in a parody of his usual comradeship. It was a show for the men watching, and Leof was glad that Thegan could still make a show. He had never seen his lord angry like this, not even when Bramble had defied him and escaped.

Now the four warlord's men followed as the ghost army, frustrated by the solid doors and shuttered windows of Bonhill, headed out into the countryside, looking for easier prey. Horst strung his bow, the short bow he kept for using on horseback.

"My lord," he said to Leof, indicating the enchanter and the bow.

During the battle, the wind wraiths had plucked their arrows out of the air and they had lost their best chance to take the enchanter. If the wraiths stayed away now, Leof knew they might have a chance. "Yes," he replied. "Anytime you get a clear shot, take him."

But as they rode, slowly, always at a distance, they could see that the wraiths were hovering far overhead. The enchanter probably couldn't see them, but they were ready to protect him.

Leof turned to Alston. "If we can charge them suddenly, Horst might get a shot away. He only needs one."

He expected Horst to preen at the praise, but the man just nodded. Something was worrying Horst, more than the ghosts. He had arrived back from the Last Domain only just in time to come south with Thegan, but without Sully, who had been killed in an ambush in the Golden Valley. Another problem for Thegan to deal with, but not one Leof could think about now.

Perhaps Horst was missing his friend. He kept glancing at the sky and wiping his hands on his breeches. Well, wind wraiths were enough to make anyone nervous. Gods knew they made Leof jittery enough.

"Do you know this country, Alston?" Leof asked. He knew it well himself, from riding chases all over it.

Alston nodded. "Aye, my lord, a little."

"The road goes between a small hill and a stream, up ahead, about a mile away. Once they pass the hill, we can come after them fast and catch them up on the other side. If we come in fast enough, the wind wraiths may be taken by surprise. It might give us a chance."

Nodding, Alston considered it.

"We should close up the gap, maybe," he ventured, and Leof agreed.

"But slowly, and gently. Don't alarm the wraiths."

Hodge and Horst both shivered at the thought, then exchanged embarrassed glances. Horst set his face in a scowl, as though preparing himself for the worst.

They urged the horses to a faster walk and gradually, as the ghosts and the enchanter strode on, unheeding, they closed the gap little by little. The wraiths seemed unaware of them, but Leof didn't hold out much hope. As soon as they moved in, the wraiths would swoop to protect the enchanter. He wondered if he should give Horst his own horse Arrow to ride—she was by far the fastest, and would get him closest to the ghosts. But she wasn't used to her rider shooting as he rode, and Horst's bay was. He would just have to take care not to get in Horst's line of fire.

Ahead, the last of the ghosts disappeared as the road bent behind the hill. "Draw weapons. Horst, ready bow. Now!" Leof ordered.

They spurred their horses, Arrow getting away first, but the others catching up fast as Leof held her back a little. Horst took the lead, arrow nocked and bow held down, reins between his teeth. His horse knew what was expected of her, and she gave it: a steady pace, like a regular drum beat, so that Horst could loose the arrow at precisely the right moment in her gait.

As they rounded the hill, Horst was just in the lead.

"Spread out!" Leof commanded, and he and Alston took point either side of Horst while Hodge brought up the rear, his own bow out and ready.

The ghosts turned at the sound of their hoof beats, but they were too far from the horsemen to interfere. Horst was almost within bow shot. The enchanter turned.

"Wait, wait, not too soon," Leof called.

Horst took aim and the enchanter put up a futile hand to ward him away. As the arrow left the bow the ghosts moved in front of the enchanter, but too late.

Then, in the split second before the arrow reached him, the wraiths dived between, snatching the arrow from the air, screaming. They turned towards Horst, claws out, teeth bared, and lunged.

"Fire again!" Leof commanded, but Horst screamed, too, and turned the terrified horse, kicking her away. The other horses were also panicking, and the ghosts had closed in around the enchanter. They had lost their chance. Bitterness in his mouth, Leof shouted, "Back! Back!" and they turned their horses and took off after Horst, who was well down the road, his bay galloping faster than ever before.

The wraiths nipped and scratched at them as they went, scoring the horses' rumps and scratching long furrows in their scalps. It was terrifying. The wraiths' shrieking seemed to sap all the strength from Leof's muscles, but he was bolstered by fury, and he rounded on them and shouted, "We are in settled lands and there has been no betrayal. Begone!"

They were the words his father had taught him, to banish wind wraiths. The words had worked for a long, long time, part of the compact between the spirits and humans, which had been established so long ago that its beginning had passed out of memory. The spirits—water, wind, fire, forest, earth—were free to hunt in wilderness but forbidden to attack humans in settled lands. Unless a human betrayed one of their own to the wraiths, as humans sometimes did. But that did no harm to the compact itself. Without the compact, the wraiths could feast on body and soul right across the Domains, with nothing to stop them. They were even harder to fight than ghosts. Without the compact every stream would be full of water sprites, every wind a carrier of death, every step into a wood a step into peril...

Leof wasn't sure the compact still held, and the thought that it might have broken irrevocably was frightening. But the wraiths hovered behind him and screamed disappointment, their claws dripping blood. Arrow would not be held. She pulled her head around and made off after the other horses, the herd instinct taking over.

Leof let them run half a mile or so before he called them in. The horses' sides were lathered and their eyes still showed too much white. He had to let them rest and drink before following the enchanter again. For all the good that would do, he thought.

The stream was close to the road here, and Hodge walked the horses for a few minutes to cool them down, then watered them. He was shaking, still.

"Horst," Leof said. "Come."

He took Horst aside. The man wouldn't look him in the eyes. Like Hodge, he was still shaking, but Leof suspected it was with shame as much as with the aftermath of fear.

"You did not follow my order, Horst." Leof kept his voice deliberately calm.

"I'm sorry, my lord! Please—please don't tell my lord Thegan."

Leof considered that. Could he blame this man for panicking in the face of those deadly claws and teeth? A human enemy was one thing, but a foe who could eat your soul was something very different. Thegan, on the other hand, would blame him and punish him. And Horst was Thegan's man. He worshipped his lord. A hard word from Thegan was enough to cause anguish—real punishment, real shame, would be unbearable.

They needed every archer they could get, if they were to have any chance at this enchanter. There would be opportunities in the next battle. Horst was the best they had.

"There will be another time," Leof said slowly, "when we may confront the enchanter again, *with* his wraiths, and only an archer can save us."

"It won't happen again, my lord. I swear it. I swear it."

There was something else here, something Horst wasn't saying, something that accounted for the panic. Leof took a guess. "You've met wind wraiths before."

Horst looked astounded "Aye, my lord," he mumbled. "They almost killed me."

"And now you have faced them again. Tell me honestly, Horst, if I needed you to face them one more time, could you?"

Horst stared at the ground for a long moment, then looked up and deliberately met Leof's eyes, as a common soldier rarely did to an officer. "I could," he said firmly.

"Then I think Lord Thegan may not need to know any more than that the wind wraiths stopped our attack."

Horst's face was flooded with relief. "Thank you, my lord."

"Don't let us down, Horst."

"I'd die first," Horst promised.

Leof slapped him on the shoulder. "I'd prefer you didn't. We have need of you."

They remounted and took the road again, watching with beating hearts for the first sign of wind wraiths in the sky above them. Where there were wind wraiths, they would find the enchanter.

The horses were rested and their wounds staunched, but they didn't like being asked to go back down the road towards the spot where they had been so terrified. Hodge's black gelding dug in his hooves and refused to move.

"We might do better on foot," Leof said. "The horses won't face the wraiths without bolting."

Hodge cleared his throat the way sergeants do when officers are about to make a big mistake.

"Well, sergeant?" Leof asked.

"Without the horses, we'd've been dead back there. Sir." Hodge said it simply, and he was right, of course.

"Very well, then. Our aim is to keep them in sight until sunset, when the enchanter will be without his army, at least, and we may have a chance to waylay him without the wraiths seeing us."

They nodded together, Alston, Hodge and Horst. Good men. Experienced, level headed. Leof wondered if they would all make it back home, but shoved the thought away, down where it belonged, in the well of shadows that every soldier avoided thinking about.

"We'll go across country, then," Leof said. "Skirt the hill and find him on the other side."

The black gelding—Canker, a bad name for a horse, Leof thought—was happy enough to take to the fields and the other horses followed Arrow eagerly.

By mid-afternoon they had traced a big circle around the hill and made their way back to the road. But there was no sign of the enchanter.

"A hand canter until we have them in sight," Leof ordered. "Horst, you lead. Keep an eye out for signs they've left the road."

It was a strange journey. The sun was shining brightly, the breeze was warm, Leof could hear thrushes in the hedgerows and grasshoppers shrilling. A beautiful day, and a lovely ride. But behind them lay death and before them terror. It was as though they rode in a bubble of safety that might be popped at any moment. He shook his head to clear it. It had been a long night and longer morning, and he was much too tired. He should eat something, although he felt at the moment as though he'd never again be hungry. He dug some dried grapes out of his belt pouch and chewed on them stolidly, the sweetness making him thirsty, so he drank. The others were doing the same, he noted, except Horst, who had no attention to spare from the dust of the road.

They should have caught up with the enchanter quickly enough, despite their long detour, but the road stretched on and they came eventually to the next village, Feathers Dale, which lay so quiet and orderly under the sun that Leof knew immediately that the ghosts had not come this far.

"We've missed them," he said, turning Arrow. She moved reluctantly, smelling water and stables and hay in the town somewhere. "Come on, lass," he encouraged her, and they went back again to investigate more thoroughly.

It turned out the ghosts had left the road just after the hill where they had tried to ambush the enchanter. They'd wasted more than an hour and a half. Hodge swore, and Leof felt like joining him. "Let's go," he said instead, taking Arrow through a gate into a field. The ghosts had left the gate open, and he made sure Alston closed it again behind them. For some reason, that carelessness with the gate made him angry, angrier even than during the battle.

He was suddenly sure that this enchanter had never worked with his hands, never sweated in a field to get the hay in as he had, next to his father and brothers and all the inhabitants of their town, as just about every person in a warlord's domain had at one time or another. Bringing in the hay, harvesting the grain or the grapes or the fruit or the beans, these were a part of life, one of the patterns of life which brought people together in comradeship and common purpose.

Up until this moment, he had feared the enchanter's scheme, but he had not thought about the man himself. Now he was filled with hatred. Contempt. This man was a destroyer of lives and he deserved to be destroyed in return.

The trail was clear enough, and they followed as fast as the horses could bear. Arrow was tiring badly, after her great run from Carlion the day before, and the others, not as fit as she, were in much the same case. The wounds the wraiths had made weren't deep but the horses had bled enough to weaken them.

The country here was a series of dales and small hills, fields separated by coppices of beech and birch and ash, the trees for spears and chairs and trugs and charcoal. Settled country, with farms regularly spaced. Peaceful.

Cantering down a gentle hill towards a farmhouse, they heard screams. Dying screams, familiar to them all from many battles. They urged the horses forward, Leof feeling sick, because what could they do to protect these people? Nothing. Nothing except try to get them inside and barricaded.

"Hunda!" they heard someone scream. "Run!"

A young man came skittering out of the farmyard, a ghost close behind, two wind wraiths sailed down from the heights and swept across his path. Perhaps it was fear that made him stop in his tracks and watch them as they sailed up again into the sky and disappeared, but it gave the ghost behind him time to catch up and bring down his scythe. The youth fell, fair hair darkening with blood.

"There they are!" Alston shouted.

The ghosts were outside a barn, arguing with the enchanter, it seemed. There were three bodies already on the ground, but no wind wraiths, thank the gods. The ghosts looked up as the horsemen approached, and the leader, the short one with beaded hair, hefted Leof's own sword and grinned at them. But the enchanter pulled him away, speaking urgently, and the ghosts, reluctantly, followed him out of the farmyard, running.

"See to the wounded," Leof told Hodge, and he kicked Arrow forward to her best pace. He rode into the pack of ghosts, Arrow following her battle training, kicking out behind her to stop pursuers, allowing Leof precious seconds to swoop on the enchanter and drag him across the saddlebow.

He almost made it. Would have made it, despite the ghosts. But the wraiths descended from where they had been perched, unseen, on the far side of the barn roof, and flapped and clawed and spat and dragged the enchanter back into the air with them. He looked almost despairing as he vanished into the sky.

Leof pulled Arrow away as the ghost leader aimed a huge blow at her neck. He blocked it with his borrowed sword and slashed down at the man's head. The blow cut right through his neck. The head didn't fall, as a living man's would have, but he reeled and swayed and gave Leof enough time to back Arrow and turn her.

The other wraiths, he realized, were attacking his men. "Back!" Leof shouted. "He's gone. Get back!"

Then the ghosts had run after their enchanter and the wraiths flew away, and they were left, the four of them, looking at the bodies, the youth, an older woman and two young girls barely out of childhood, whose blood gleamed darkly in the sun.

HUNDA'S STORY

IN THE end, we are animals, and all we can touch is flesh.

Our spirits are imprisoned in clay, and every day, every night, we yearn to break free. I know you have—surely you've had the flying dream? The swimming dream? The one where you're soaring, weightless, swooping and gliding and shifting on a thought, on a prayer…

We've all had those dreams, which are the yearning of our spirits.

I think this world is punishment. My da says that if we are noble and good in this life, we will be reborn, but I think he's got it wrong. I think if we are good enough we are *not* reborn, at least, not as humans. Not as heavy flesh.

We are animals. That's why they eat us, because they know us for what we are.

The first time I saw one, I was three summers old. Maybe four. We were down at the stream, Hengi and Caela and me, where we weren't supposed to be on our own, because of them. Hengi was showing off, the way he always does, dipping his toe into the water, trying to prove that he was braver than anyone else.

"Come and get me!" he yelled. "I'm not afraid of you!"

It came. It snatched for his toe but he jerked back as it came up at him from the green depths, and it missed. I could hear it hiss with annoyance, even from under the water. Hengi and Caela scrambled away from the bank and ran screaming to the cottage, but I stayed, staring, and it stared back at me. She stared. It was a girl, no doubt.

The stonecasters say that there are moments when your life shifts its path, when what you do, what you decide, changes everything from then on. So. That was my moment. If I'd run, I wouldn't have seen her clearly.

I wouldn't have seen that she was beautiful. And young. Not a child, like me, but not old like my mam. More like Ethelin, Caela's big sister. Her eyes were green and long, and they were green all the way, with no whites to them. They gleamed like a cat's. She looked at me, and smiled. Beckoned.

I wasn't stupid, not even at four. I shook my head and kept my feet planted firmly on the ground. But I didn't run. And then...then she started to sing.

There are no words for it. If you haven't heard it, I can't recreate it. No human could. It went too high for a human voice, and too low as well. It was like a dozen voices singing, but it was only one. It was water and laughter and silver in the sun...It called to all the parts of me that were *not* animal. It filled my chest with hot tight longing because it spoke of everything I could never have—spirit, pure and simple, flying free of flesh, free of earth, free of death.

I didn't think those things then. Not at four. But I felt them. Cried for them. Sank down on my haunches and wept silently, until my mam and the other adults came running to beat the waters and shout until she went away.

They made sure we didn't go anywhere near the stream after that. I crept down, sometimes, but she was never there, even when I stuck my toe in the water and shouted, "Come and get me!"

I heard her singing in my dreams, but what good was that? It wasn't her I wanted, it was the freedom I heard in her song.

SAKER

THE DARKNESS covered Saker like a shield. His army was somewhere behind him and would have faded by now, with the sunlight. The wind wraiths had deposited him next to an old mill and sped back into the air on his order, so he was safe and concealed, where no one would look for a great enchanter.

And yet... He drank from the millrace, relieved himself against the cracked wall of the mill, went back to the loft and wondered why he felt so... alone. He had always been alone, since the day the warlord's men had killed his family, his whole village. Even when he lived with Freite, the enchanter who had trained him, he had been alone. It was no different now.

But today the ghosts had protected him, defended him, drawn around him. Without that defence, he felt vulnerable. Saker frowned. There had to be a way to enable the ghosts to stay after the sun shifted. It seemed that he could call them up for a day, or for a night, but no longer. Sunset or sunrise drew them back into death, into the darkness before rebirth, and he had to summon them all over again the next time he needed them.

At least the wind wraiths had gone.

"You may not stay near me," he had said to them when they let him down from that horrifying flight. "The Warlord's men will see you, and after dark I am vulnerable."

"Do not fear, human," one of the wraiths had replied. "We will protect you."

Saker shook his head. "You cannot protect me against an army of archers, and that is what they will bring against me if they find me. I will summon you when I next have need of you."

"And we will feast!" the wraiths shrieked.

"You will feast," Saker confirmed, close to vomiting at the thought of them eating the spirits as well as the bodies of their victims. "But now you must go."

"We will watch from a distance," the wraith said. "And be ready when you need us, master."

They had streamed up into the sky, laughing and screaming.

Lying in the dark of the mill, Saker felt very small and too young, somehow, for his task. Perhaps he should raise his father's ghost. Call him: Alder, son of Crane. Let his own blood flow to call his father back, give Alder strength so that Saker could lean into his embrace...

But he was too weak. He had lost a lot of blood already, raising the ghost army to defend himself against the warlord. And he knew, if he were honest, that his father would rather plan the next battle than fold him in his arms.

His father would be right, Saker knew. He had to plan.

Turvite was his goal. He wanted to take the city that Acton had despoiled. But that day's futile battering on the solid doors and walls of Bonhill had shown him that taking a city would be a long, long fight. And he could not allow himself to be unprotected each night. It would only take one assassin and the whole great scheme of reclamation and revenge would be over.

He had to find a way to keep the ghosts alive. Until their work was finished.

ASH

"You can't come the River's way," Ash said.

"How will I get to the meeting place?" Flax asked, caught between surprise and uncertainty.

"My father will take you there," Ash said. He had made the plan as soon as the Prowman had explained that the two of them would have to go alone. Rowan would take Flax to meet Ash's mother, Swallow, and then journey together to Sanctuary. It would mean that Ash wouldn't have to see that first meeting, his mother's delight at Flax's voice, their first song together... Ash wondered if he was grasping at the Prowman's offer so eagerly just to escape that.

But no. If there were a faster way to Sanctuary, he had to take it. He looked around the clearing where the other men, restored to their normal human selves, were dressing and eating, laughing as they did so. Not demons any more, but singers and musicians, discussing their craft. Ash caught snatches of melody as one man—Skink, the leader—pulled a pipe from his pocket and began to play. A dawn song, greeting the day, the same one Flax had sung to him in Golden Valley.

A bass voice picked up the words and a tenor joined in, not Flax, an older man, without Flax's purity of sound but with a richer timbre. Ash and Flax both paused to listen.

Up jumps the sun in the early, early morning
The early, early morning
The early dawn of day
Up wings the lark in the early light of dawning
The early light of dawning
When gold replaces gray

The voices supported each other and echoed richly from the cliffs. When they had finished they began discussing the song, the best instruments to use, the timing, all the daylight talk of the Deep. With the night gone, the Deep was almost ordinary. Not quite. The high red-streaked sandstone walls which enclosed them were always a reminder of the need for secrecy, the need for silence about what happened here. It had taken them days to reach it, and the way had been dangerous, but Rowan would guide Flax back.

"Take the horses," Ash said to Flax. "For all our sakes, get them back to Bramble safely!"

Flax grinned at that, but seemed uncertain still. "Are you sure I can't come with you?"

Ash was reminded of his promise to Zel, to look after Flax as if he were his own brer. It made him feel guilty, but he reasoned that if Flax *were* his own brother, he would do exactly the same thing—entrust him to his parents.

"My father wants you to meet my mother. She's a singer like you, you know—better than you!" He was deliberately provocative to get Flax bristling, but instead the youngster's face lit up.

"She'll teach me? Certain sure?"

"Certain sure," Ash confirmed, a sour taste in his mouth. Teach him and rejoice. He pushed the thought away, all thoughts away except the miraculous one that the River was waiting for, and wanting, *him*. Not Flax or his father or any other in these long, long years. Him. He was overtaken by a sense of his father's vulnerability, out there in the world which contained murderous ghosts and unknown terrors. "And—look after my father, too."

Flax nodded, as though he'd been given a task by the gods. He would have to do something about that hero worship, Ash thought as Skink handed him some fresh-cooked fish. He ate hungrily without tasting the food and walked over to Rowan.

"Sanctuary," Rowan said musingly as he approached. "I know it. A cursed place, they say it is. There's a song..."

"Yes," Ash said, surprising himself by finding a need to be gentle with his father, who was not accustomed to fighting or fearing or struggling with anything except a difficult melody. "I know the song. But it is just a meeting place. Get there as soon as you can."

Rowan nodded and embraced him, and it was only as Ash raced

into the cave to meet the Prowman that he realized it was the first time he had given his father a direct order. Yet it had seemed so natural. This was his craft, it seemed—action.

He said as much to the Prowman as they made their way back to the inner cave, where Ash had climbed down only the night before.

"Action and music," the old man agreed. "That is our craft, to meld the two." He grinned. "And, I'm afraid, to do as we are told. We are followers, boy, not leaders."

Ash digested that. It struck a sour note, but he knew it was true. He had always followed: his parents, Doronit, Martine, Safred. Even Bramble, half-conscious, had made the decisions. And now the River.

"If you are to survive Her," the Prowman said, "you must know yourself."

Filled with a sudden impatience, Ash snapped, "That's the sort of thing old men say."

The Prowman laughed. "Aye, that's so! That is so indeed. Well, lad, perhaps you know yourself too well already. Perhaps what you need is to lose yourself in Her instead."

Ash grinned, sure suddenly that he could speak his mind as freely as he liked. Somehow, he was at ease with the Prowman as he had never been at ease with anyone before. "Enigmatic," he teased. "Very like an old sage from the stories."

The old man smiled and flicked him on the shoulder with the back of his hand, as boys do to each other. "Race you to the water," he said.

Together they ran through to the caverns where the green stars on the walls never faded, following the winding, crooked path, laughing as they went, and as they came to the final cave, the final cliff, and Ash slowed, the Prowman called back over his shoulder, "Trust Her!" and leapt out high over the rushing water.

As he disappeared from sight, Ash took a deep breath, full of sudden joy and sudden fear, and leapt after him.

There was music.

He couldn't recognize the instrument, and that frightened him, but the River's voice soothed him with wordless harmonies. *Home*, She said, *Belonging*, and he was calm.

But not still. Ash was rushing, rushing past rock walls, rushing through openings surely too small for his body, spinning and splashing and sliding. As fear left him and he let the music fill him instead, he was equally full of joy and something he'd never known before... but the feeling, like the instrument, had no name, because it was outside human experience. It was not happiness, or joy, or satisfaction. It was all of those.

A sense of purpose—of *being* the purpose, rather than fulfilling one.

A sense of power.

Liberation.

Speed.

Deep, deep calm and stability, hidden in the middle of the rushing, as water, swung in a bucket quickly over one's head, stays firm in the center and cannot fall.

He was the water, the bucket, the swinging arm. The center which moved.

He was the River's way.

BRAMBLE

BRAMBLE DIDN'T believe they were in the Weeping Caverns. There were too many stories about them—the entrance was supposed to move, certainly, but it was always on the surface. This was just a large cave with water in it. She looked over at Medric, "So, if no one can get out, how did the stories get told?"

He had no answer for that, but his hands shook as they slowly climbed down the rock wall to the floor of the cavern.

As she moved down the solid rock face with her saddlebags over her shoulder, she could feel Acton's bones shift and slide with each step. The movement unsettled her as nothing in her life had ever done. She had tried to pack them tightly but they shook loose, as though Acton was determined in death, as he had been in life, not to be trammelled. As though at every step he tapped her on the back, saying, "Remember me?"

It was bad enough to bear her grief for him; to bear his bones as well, to be a packhorse for his remains, was too much. She wanted to be rid of them. Wanted fiercely to see him again, even as a ghost, and also wanted fiercely not to see him as a ghost, pale and insubstantial. She thought it was a good thing the gods were driving her, because if it had been up to her she was not sure whether she would have brought him back.

But she would complete her task and stop Saker. Kill him, too, if the gods were kind. And then, only then, could she stop and consider what Obsidian Lake had done to her, and who she might be afterwards.

So if Lady Death tried to stop her, too bad for the Lady.

They reached the cavern floor with legs and arms shaking, and collapsed on a damp rock. When they had recovered they drank water from one of the clear pools, water that tasted of nothing except, faintly, chalk.

"Follow the air," Medric said again, and the air seemed to be curving around the high wall to their left, so that was the way they walked, picking their steps between shallow pools and small spires of rock, past pillars and grotesque shapes that looked, again and again, as though a hunched human figure had been turned to stone by the endlessly dripping water. Yet it was beautiful. There were wings of rock, and towers and colors that glowed in the candlelight: cream and ochre and orange and green. And everywhere, the murmuring sigh of water and air.

"Who brings light into the darkness?" a voice boomed from above them. "Who disturbs this holy place?" The echoes took the words and grew them into an accusation, a promise of punishment, a death knell.

"Oh, Swith!" Medric whispered, but Bramble peered further ahead, holding the light high, although her heart was beating fast. This was one of those times, she thought, when other people feared, but she had never been on good terms with fear and she wasn't planning to start now.

"Who wants to know?" she demanded.

"Oh, hells, Bramble, you might at least squeal!" It was Ash's voice, coming from a platform of rock to their right.

Bramble laughed, as she felt the gods smile in her head and leave her to stream towards Ash. He was staring at her with a broad grin, looking fitter and happier than when she had last seen him.

"I don't squeal," she said. "How did you get here?"

He shrugged as he walked to the edge to help them climb up. "The same way you did," he said casually. "Enchantment."

She nodded and let it go. If he wanted to tell her more, he would. She handed the candle to Medric and surprised herself by embracing Ash. "This is Medric," she said, stepping back. "He was a miner—helped me find the place I had to go."

Medric stared at Ash. "Like scaring people, do you?" he asked.

"It was a fair question," Ash replied absently, "I couldn't see who you were." He turned and waved someone forward from the gloom.

Medric held the candle higher to reveal an old man walking towards them, making no sound.

Bramble felt a slight shock—he was dressed the way Acton's people had dressed a thousand years ago: leggings and tunic, long hair with beaded braids in the front, sheepskin boots with the fleece still inside. All that was missing was a beard.

He reached the circle of candlelight and smiled at them. "Greetings," he said. "We are well met, it seems."

A wave of cold went over her and she began to shake. She knew that voice. Surely she knew it, would know it to her grave.

"This is the Prowman," Ash said to her. "Prowman, this is Bramble."

The old man's eyes were puzzled as she stood there in silence. She swallowed the lump in her throat and forced herself to talk, although there were tears gathering in her eyes and her legs were still shaking. She had to force herself not to embrace him, not to throw herself at him as she would have at Maryrose, or her grandfather. He didn't know her, after all.

"He was a prowman once," she said. "But his shipmates called him Baluch."

Bramble stared into blue, blue eyes. Eyes that she remembered as clearly as she remembered Maryrose. Those eyes were bright with interest and she could almost, almost hear the music that was no doubt going on behind them. Some kind of pipe music, she'd be willing to bet, high and trilling. She was finding it hard to catch her breath.

Ash was standing very still, paler even than usual, as though he were looking at a puzzle that suddenly made sense but had an answer he didn't like. "You're *Baluch?*" he asked.

The old man nodded, slowly, his face carefully blank.

Baluch.

Here. A thousand years later. Still here. Bramble was overwhelmed by a cascade of memories: Baluch as a toddler, reproving Acton; Baluch as a young boy, a lad, a young man, a man full grown... Baluch whooping with laughter as Acton's boat went over the rapids. Baluch shouting with rage as his sword cut through his enemies. Baluch standing by the edge of the White River, saying, "There's something up north that calls me..."

"The Lake," Bramble said, clutching at the only possible explanation so her head would stop swimming. "The Lake transported you in time."

Baluch's eyes were alive with curiosity and a kind of pleasure, as though he enjoyed having someone know him.

"Often," he said. "I come by my wrinkles honestly, but I've earned them in a dozen different times, whenever She had need of me. I've skipped from time to time like a stone over water. But how did you know me?"

Trying to work out how to explain made her legs, finally, give out from under her. She sank down onto a rock, knees trembling.

"Thank the local gods," she said eventually. "They showed me your face." Which was true enough, even if it was woefully incomplete. But how could she explain Obsidian Lake and her own, very different, travels in time? Baluch smiled as though some of what she was thinking showed in her eyes and she smiled back, a rush of pleasure swamping her. Someone else who remembered... It was a kind of homecoming, to look into Baluch's blue eyes, as she had when she was Ragni, or even the girl on the mountain.

"Who is he?" Medric asked her softly, while Baluch went to talk quietly to Ash. Ash stood straight and disapproving, but listened.

Whatever Baluch said didn't convince him. He shook his head, and Baluch slapped his own thigh, his voice growing louder. "I've spent my whole life protecting the Lake People, from attack after attack!" he said. "Ask her!"

He paused for a moment, and waited. Finally, Ash nodded, but his face was still troubled. Bramble could understand that. Baluch was, after all, implicated in everything Acton had done. It wasn't easy to face your enemy and realize he wasn't a monster, after all.

Baluch clapped Ash on the shoulder, a gesture he and Acton had used often to each other. It made Bramble's heart clench.

"Baluch. You know—from the old stories, Acton's friend," she said to Medric.

"Donkey dung!" Medric exclaimed. "He's dead!"

"Apparently not."

It was a bit much to take, she supposed, for someone whose life had until yesterday been as solidly sensible as a life could be. But he was the man who had fallen in love with Fursey, so he *could* cope with oddity if he chose. He'd just have to. The trick was to keep him busy. And they should all be busy, because if Ash were here and she were here... "I have the bones," she called to Ash. A trembling began in her gut at the thought of what they were about to do, but she ignored it and got up, forcing her knees to stay firm. "Do you have the songs?"

Ash hesitated, looking to Baluch, any remnants of hostility vanishing into a need for guidance.

"There are songs," Ash said slowly. "But they don't seem to be enough... in themselves."

"When Tern the enchanter raised the ghosts of Turvite against Acton, she used her own blood," Bramble said. "She sang the song and then cut herself and scattered the blood on the corpses."

Ash raised his eyebrows. "That's not in the old story. It just says she raised the ghosts of Turvite to fight Acton, and failed, then jumped off the cliff."

"Her name was Tern?" Baluch said. "I remember her. But as Ash said, she failed."

"She failed to give them fighting strength," Bramble corrected him. "But she raised the ghosts well enough, which is what we want to do."

She knelt and took off her jacket, spreading it out on a flat piece of ground, and then slid her hand to the very bottom of one saddlebag and pulled out the red scarf. It was the symbol of rebirth, and perhaps it would help, now, to bring him back. She spread it on her jacket.

Her heart faltered. Stuck to the scarf, in the folds, were hairs. Horse hairs, from the roan. She had brushed them off her own clothes too often to mistake them. Gently, she brushed them together into a small pile. There were only a few, but it was as though the roan were with her, encouraging her.

Unpacking the bones was next. She slid her fingers gently over the curve of his skull, a secret caress, and the only one she'd ever have. Enough. She drew out the bones as though they were just anyone's, and laid them on the scarf, placing the skull over the roan's hair, to keep it safe. It was the first time she'd looked at the bones closely in the light, even in the poor candle glow. They seemed ridiculously small.

"I had to leaves the leg bones behind," she said, almost in apology to Acton. "I couldn't fit them."

Baluch crouched next to the scarf and put his hand out to touch the skull. His hand shook. "Acton," he whispered.

But of course there was no answer. Bramble turned aside. She knew too much of what Baluch was feeling, and it unsettled her. She wondered how much he had changed, living his life in snatches, moving from time to time for a thousand years at the whim of the Lake. His smile hadn't changed, or his eyes. Or that voice.

Ash was staring at the bones like a rabbit stares at a weasel, eyes wide and stuck.

"*Ash*," Bramble said sharply. He blinked and turned to her in relief. "Sing," she said.

"I'm not sure..." He looked at Baluch and lowered his voice. "She's given me a kind of pattern of song, but not the words and not the exact melody."

Baluch nodded. "There are some songs which must be sung new each time. You will have to find your own version of what she has given you."

Bramble wondered if "she" were the Lake, but the men clearly weren't going to say. Fair enough. She had secrets of her own.

Ash fished his belt knife out of its sheath and held it a little uncertainly, and began to sing.

The first notes, harsh as rock grating on stone, startled Bramble and made her deeply uneasy. She'd heard this sound before, when Safred tried to heal Cael. It was the sound of power, which should have been reassuring given what they were trying to do, yet it wasn't. It just felt wrong.

Ash seemed to feel that, too, because after a moment he fell silent, shaking his head. "It's not right," he said.

"That song felt old to me," Baluch said mildly. "I think you have to make it new." His head tilted to one side as though he were listening to something, someone, else. "You have to make it *yours*," he added.

Ash nodded, and knelt down beside the bones. He put his hand out, hesitating, over the skull, then slid it sideways and rested his palm on the curve of the collarbone. "Acton," he said quietly.

Bramble remembered something and dug quickly in the bottom of the other bag for Acton's brooch. She had always meant to give it back to Ash at some point. This seemed like a good time—it might help him as it had helped her.

She knelt beside him and put the brooch down next to Acton's skull. Baluch gasped. His grandfather had made it, Bramble remembered. Eric the Foreigner had made it for the chieftain Harald to give to his wife, who had given it in turn to her daughter Asa, Acton's mother. And Asa had given it to Acton. Acton's murderer, Asgarn, had ripped it from Acton's cloak as he lay dying and given it to his accomplice, Red, the traitor. And from there, who knew whose hands it had passed through before it came to Ash? A thousand years of ownership. This brooch had come to their time by the long road, as though it had walked slowly through the undergrowth of a forest, while Baluch had, as it were, jumped from tree to tree.

Bramble weighed the brooch in her hand as if it should have grown heavier with each year. She placed it on the scarf, next to Acton's skull.

"I give this back to you," she said, not sure if she were talking to Ash or to Acton.

Ash nodded gratefully and put his other hand on the brooch, shivering slightly as his fingers touched the cold metal. "Acton, I call you back from the darkness beyond death," he said, and began to sing in the voice of the healer.

His first notes faltered, but when Baluch came forward and placed a hand on his shoulder his voice gained strength, the notes and the words building, gathering power and authority.

It felt irresistible. The words were unfamiliar to her, although she caught echoes of the languages that Gris and Asa and Hawk had spoken. The notes were not really a melody—they seemed more like half a conversation, a chant rather than a song.

Ash began to shake, but he gripped the knife in his hand more surely and raised it, then brought his other hand off the brooch and held it ready over the bones. It trembled slightly, although Bramble couldn't tell if that was from fright or from the passage of power through him.

Ash brought the knife down on his palm, and blood flicked out over the bones.

Bramble held her breath, feeling shaky. Ash's voice climbed to a climax and stopped on a high note that brought the echoes ringing and ringing after it. She was staring at the bones so hard her eyes started to burn.

Nothing happened.

The blood trickled down over the skull and dripped into the empty eye sockets. A small, slightly mad, part of Bramble's mind was concerned about getting blood stains on the scarf; she was thinking about anything, bloodstains, washing, the cold of the stone floor through her thin boots, anything rather than face the possibility that everything they had done had been for nothing. That she would never see him again.

Ash sighed and sat back, his face carefully blank.

There was a long silence.

"So," Medric said, "is that it?"

"It was not complete," Baluch said gently.

Bramble was reminded of Tern on the cliffs of Turvite, and her own sense that what was missing from Tern's spell was feeling, some emotion apart from the desire for revenge. "You have to really want him back," she said, her voice trembling a little. She breathed in deeply, controlling it. "And you don't, do you?"

"Of course I do!" Ash said. "We need him."

"But you hate him," she said. Ash stared at her and Baluch stared at him, as though surprised at the idea.

"Of course I hate him," Ash said impatiently. "He invaded my country and massacred my people."

"No, no, that's not how it happened!" Baluch protested.

"Yes it was," Bramble said. She wasn't minded to let Baluch paint Acton in rosy colors, no matter how much she loved him.

"You weren't there —" Baluch started.

"Really?" Bramble said. "I have two words for you, Baluch son of Eric who never took part in massacres. River Bluff."

Baluch fell silent, staring at her as if she were the Well of Secrets herself. Bramble felt a quick flash of sympathy for Safred. That look made her feel not fully human.

"There *were* massacres," Bramble said quietly. "Whole towns, killed or dispossessed. He wanted T'vit, didn't he, and he did whatever it took to get it. So don't tell me Ash doesn't have reason to hate him. Anyone with Traveler blood has reason to hate him."

"Including you?" Baluch asked.

"I have reason," Bramble said. "And none of that matters. What matters is how to get him back."

"The problem is," Ash said, "I think it needs a memory in the middle of it, or a true longing, and I don't have either."

"I could help," Baluch said, "but it might upset the song to have two singers."

"I'll do it," Bramble said.

"You?" Baluch gazed at her in astonishment. "You remember Acton?"

It was too much, suddenly. "Better than you," she hissed. "You let him go off to that meeting with Asgarn while you went to your precious Lake, didn't you? You let him go off to be killed!"

"Asgarn..." Baluch breathed, his eyes hardening. "I knew. I *knew* it was him, but I could never prove it. Never even find the body."

"Enough!" Ash said firmly. "We can discuss the past later. Right now we have a job to do." He turned to Bramble. "Prepare your memory," he said gently. He had gained in authority, somehow, since she'd last seen him.

She knew it would need more than memory. It needed the longing he had spoken of. Gods knew she had that, but she would have to share it with Ash for the spell to work. She turned aside for a moment, her face burning. How much was she prepared to give to stop Saker? All her certainties were gone, all her defences were down. Now it seemed her privacy and dignity had to be sacrificed too.

Maryrose, she thought. This is for you.

She turned back, her face calm again, and joined hands with Ash, her other hand resting on the familiar curve of the brooch, Asa's brooch, Acton's brooch. Red's, after he had thrust the knife into Acton's back. That memory brought the rush of feeling that she needed, they all needed, to bring him back: longing, regret...love. Ash felt it sweep through her and he gulped in surprise, then started singing, a little faster, a little more urgently than before, the harsh notes rising and rising, words a bit different, rhythm altered so that it matched her breathing as she thought of him, remembered him, *needed* him as the heart needs blood, as the loom needs thread, to be whole.

And this time, it was her hand that Ash slashed, her blood that spilled over his pale, pale bones. She welcomed the pain because it was easier to bear than the loss of him, easier to think about than the emptiness which he had filled. Memories of his life flooded her, and it was as though she were him as well as Baluch, as well as Asa, seeing the world through his eyes briefly as she had seen it through theirs: climbing the mountain to find Friede, she was both Baluch and Acton; guiding the boat down the river to Turvite, she was both steersman and prowman, both exulting; fighting the people of River Bluff, she wielded two swords, and both killed... Standing on the mountain, watching him climb to his death, she was him, too, looking at a dark-haired wild-looking girl, feeling his heart leap...

Come back from beyond death, she willed into the darkness. We have need of you. Come back. *I* have need of you.

She could feel something happening, and hear something, too, a whisper without body, a bodiless chant without words, a high whine. It made her feel sick, and suddenly she thought, this is unnatural. Wrong. The gods had deserted her, as though they wanted nothing to do with it, although they had sent her here for just this moment.

She heard Medric gasp suddenly and Baluch's breath hissed out, but she could not look up from the bones where gently, hesitantly, a mist was gathering.

Her breath was hard to find. At the edge of her vision shapes twisted, pale shadows of writhing bodies. She willed herself not to look at them and concentrated on Acton, Acton. Come, I have need of you.

Ash pulled her back, still singing, but she kept hold of the brooch as he guided her to her feet so she could see more, back a few steps until their legs knocked against a rock pillar and they stood and stared at the ghost standing before them, white and clear as a sculpture in ice. There were no shapes in the darkness now, no twisting forms, no sense of wrongness. Just him.

MARTINE

Trine was housed in a small hold that opened up directly to the deck.

"Fish hold," the shipmaster had said, and it smelled like it. Trine hadn't settled easily, but it was much better than trying to get her below decks. Half of the hold was covered over to give her shelter from rain and sun, but she could get her nose up into the open air and move around on her tether a little.

"Look. That's my Aunty Rumer," Zel said blankly, staring up at the rigging where a dark-haired woman flipped open a sail and let it drop free. "Or maybe Rawnie." She blinked, as if trying to make her eyes see better. "They're twins."

Trine snorted and tried to shy as the sail bellowed, but Zel held her firmly and patted her, taking the excuse to look away from the rigging and attend to the horse.

"Don't give her too much freedom," the shipmaster told her. "If the swell gets up, we'll have to lash her down and she won't like that, so keep her close tied."

Zel had frowned but seen the sense to it, and they'd loaded Trine first and let her get used to her quarters well before they set sail. Martine and Zel had kept her company. She was beginning, Martine thought, to accept them as inadequate substitutes for Bramble. As the ship left the dock, Zel began rebinding Trine's forefoot with a padded bandage, designed to stop her being bruised in bad weather, and she was carefully not looking up.

"Nice for you, to meet family," Martine said lightly, but she wondered. Zel's face was bemused, as though she wasn't quite sure what she should be feeling. She certainly wasn't feeling anything uncomplicated like pleasure at meeting family.

Then, when was family ever uncomplicated? Martine mused on her own four aunties, all dead, who were as fine a mixture of love, interference, exasperation and pride as any niece could have had. She wondered how she'd feel if she'd encountered them unexpectedly, in those years she'd been on the Road before they'd all been killed by the Ice King's men. Somehow she thought there was more in Zel's eyes than the ambivalence an independent girl might feel about kin.

"Your mam's sisters?" Martine asked politely. "Or your da's?"

"Mam's," Zel said, her lips tucking back as soon as she said the word, as if she wanted to unsay it.

Yes, there it was. Something about Zel's mam. Martine's Sight nudged her, but she didn't need it to know that Zel and her mam had had a difficult time of it together. Perhaps seeing these aunties brought back bad memories. But later she saw Zel eating her supper with two women as alike as two hen's eggs, and the three of them were laughing.

They sailed into Mitchen in the early morning, on a grey day with a chill wind. Unlike Turvite, the Mitchenites had built right up to the edge of their headlands, so coming into harbor meant passing below houses and shops, aware of people out early in the streets pointing to them, calling out, running down to the docks, clutching their money pouches.

"No ships in port," Arvid said, looking worried.

By the time the sailors were tying up at the big dock, a crowd was pushing its way to the ship. Mostly men, but some women carrying babies or leading children by the hand. There were no dark heads among them, or none Martine could see. She wondered if all the Travelers of Mitchen had taken shelter somewhere. She hoped so—with news of the massacre at Carlion clearly spreading across the country, it wouldn't be long before someone decided all Travelers were somehow responsible.

The shipmaster called, "Don't put the gangplank out!"

Rumer and Rawnie, who were holding it, laid it down. The sailors on the mooring ropes let out a little slack, so that the people on the dock couldn't touch the ship.

"Captain! Captain! I can pay, all the way to the Wind Cities!"

"Take my children if you won't take me!"

They shouted and pleaded with her, becoming more agitated, until the shipmaster held up her hands for quiet. Gradually, they fell silent, their upturned faces a mixture of anxiety and hope.

"We are not going to the Wind Cities," she shouted. "We're going to Turvite."

They started shouting again: "You're mad! You're fools! The ghost'll go there, sure as fire burns! They love ghosts in Turvite!"

The shipmaster just stood there and gradually, one by one, the crowd dispersed, turning back home with heavy treads and slumped shoulders.

The only one who stayed was an old, grizzled sailor who said, "I'd rather be where they know how to deal with ghosts," and spat over the side of the dock to mark his words.

"Fair enough," the shipmaster said, and threw him a rope to climb up. "We might need an extra steersman," she added to Arvid. "The waters around Turvite are liable to be rough, this time of year, when the current changes."

The harbor master emerged from his house and organized the unloading of the cargo and the restocking of the boat's larders and water barrels.

Safred was first off the gangplank, sitting down thankfully on a crate. "When my stomach settles down, I might even be able to eat something," she said, half-laughing.

Apple and the other two merchants started heading for town. "Don't know what kind of bargain we're going to make," she called back to Arvid from the deck. "Frightened people hold on hard to their purses."

But she seemed cheerful enough, her blond hair swinging in its single long plait. She looked younger than she had at the Plantation, Martine thought. Probably comes of not having to look after anyone, or cook any meals. Or wear the big, heavy jackets you needed in the Last Domain. Martine herself felt much freer now they were far enough south that she could pack away her felt coat.

Arvid came up behind Martine and put his hands on her waist. A squirm of pleasure went right through her. She bit back a smile.

"Not going into town?" he asked.

"I'm thinking about it," she replied. "Times of trouble, a stonecaster can make good money. But by the same stone, a stonecaster can get into a lot of trouble if the answers aren't to everyone's liking."

"So stay with me," he breathed. "I have no duties here at all. It's Apple and her friends who do the bargaining. I just turn up for the celebration meal afterwards, so our customers can brag about having dinner with the warlord."

Martine sniffed. "Not much to brag about."

"Not from where I sit," he agreed, nuzzling her ear. The hot breath melted her.

"Oh, all right," she said, feigning reluctance. "I suppose I don't have anything else to do right now."

Laughing, he pulled her by the hand down the companionway and into his cabin. As they tumbled onto the bunk, she could hear Trine's hooves clunking down the gangplank, with Zel's footfalls in between. So they were all right, and she could concentrate on Arvid.

They didn't come out until it was night.

On deck, Safred and Cael were having a late supper: "Just something light," Safred said. "My stomach isn't quite settled yet." There were more sailors on board than she had expected—didn't sailors just disappear off to the inns and brothels when a ship was in port?

Rumer and Rawnie were having a cha with Zel in Trine's hold while she curried the mare down. Martine asked them.

"Everything's locked up," they said. "Brothel's open, but the inn's not letting strangers drink. Only place we could get an ale was a Traveler's hut, out on the edges, and that wasn't the best place to drink for two women. Lot of young'uns, full of beer and piss and thinking they're cock of the dunghill. And *they* wouldn't serve blondies, so most of the crew can't get a drink anywhere. Might as well be here."

Martine and Arvid moved to the side and looked at the town. Shuttered up tight; no one on the streets. Martine had been to Mitchen many times before, and it was a town, like Turvite, that enjoyed its summer nights. This quiet readiness disturbed her greatly.

"Have we heard from Apple and the others?" she asked the shipmaster.

"No, but I wouldn't worry. We've made this trip a dozen times before. The merchants always stay late."

"But they usually call for me to come to the dinner," Arvid said, looking worried. "Holly, Beetle, on duty, now!"

His guards had been playing dice aft. They threw down the cup and sprang up, running to Arvid's side.

"We're going to check on the merchants," Arvid said. "Stay close."

"I'd better come," Safred said, her eyes wide in the darkness, glinting in the light from the lantern hung on the mainmast. "You might have need of me."

The guards checked their weapons and settled their uniforms into place, then followed Arvid down the gangplank. "They'll be at the Moot Hall, most likely," he said.

Safred went after them, and Martine followed. Arvid glanced back and saw her, and opened his mouth to order her back on board. She could see the moment he realized he had no right to give her orders—particularly in a free town!—and closed his mouth with some chagrin.

She smiled grimly. So. He didn't like that. Serve him right for falling for an outsider.

His guards had moved into formation around them, hands on swords even though it was illegal in a free town for warlords' men to use weapons. Martine found herself glad of them, and reflected that it didn't take much for even a Traveler to range herself with the stronger party when danger threatened. If danger threatened.

Her Sight was showing her nothing. But many distressing things happened without Sight warning her. It was only when the gods thought that the event was important that Sight intervened.

Walking through the silent town was unnerving, like a dream that was about to turn into a nightmare.

It was a relief to hear some noises coming from the center, near the Moot Hall: voices, singing, shouting. They quickened their pace.

Men's voices, singing snatches of a drunken song: "Kill 'em all, kill 'em all!" they roared. It was the chorus of one of the best-known songs about Acton. She expected to find a mob of burly blonds and red-heads sitting on the steps of the hall, swinging their tankards.

They rounded the corner to the central square. There were no market stalls left here; they'd all been packed away, and the eating houses were closed, as was the Moot Hall.

There were no people, either. The only sign of life was that the lanterns on the walls next to the Moot Hall doors had been smashed and were dripping oil down the bricks.

The singing continued, from a road that led up and out of town.

Arvid hesitated. "We should ask at the hall," he said.

Then the singing stopped and became shouting, and the sounds of crashing and splintering wood.

They ran, Holly and the other guards taking the lead, but Arvid not far behind. Safred and Martine kept pace. Martine's heart was thudding hard.

The shouting was getting louder.

"That's right, you bastards, hide behind your bars and shutters! We're going to get you all!"

"Thass it, you tell 'em, Bass!"

"Scared of *us*, now, aren't you? Where's your bloody Acton now, eh? Our people are comin' back and you can't stop us!"

"Look, Bass, lookee 'ere."

"Show 'em how we can fight, Bass!"

"Take that, blondie!"

A woman screamed.

It was only a few more paces. They could see figures struggling, hear them gasping, panting.

Holly drew her sword as she ran and the others copied her, Arvid included.

Martine tried to sort it out in the meagre light leaking from between the shutters of the surrounding buildings. Four men, five, six...two women. One of them was screeching and trying to pull two fighting men apart. The other hit her attacker as he brought both hands down on her head. Was one of them Apple?

"Break them apart," Arvid ordered, and Holly leapt into the struggling group and pulled one back, throwing him towards another guard, who hit him and pushed him down to sit groggily, holding his head.

Arvid went in after Holly, ramming one tall figure with his shoulder, using the hilt of his sword under the man's chin. He crumpled on the spot. The other guards were equally efficient, pulling the combatants away one by one until there were six separate men instead of a fight, and two women, one of them still swearing and the other lying still, legs sprawled.

Martine went to her, making room for Safred by her side. It was Apple, her blue eyes half-open, her knife lying in one slack hand.

"Too late," Safred said sadly. She turned immediately to lay her hands on another man who had a wound from Apple's knife. He was the only other one seriously hurt. Safred began to sing, the harsh song, the healing song.

Martine shivered and her eyes filled with tears as she closed Apple's eyes and straightened her clothes. She thought of Snow, Apple's son, waiting for her to come home, and her heart clenched, her mind inevitably going to her own daughter, Elva, and how she would feel in the same situation.

Arvid crouched beside her. "Drunken thugs," he said bitterly. "Travelers, attacking anyone who came along."

"Because they could," Martine said. "For once, people were afraid of them."

She turned and confronted the man who had killed Apple. Safred had finished. Martine looked at him. She could see him clearly, now her eyes had adjusted to the light. No more than twenty, probably, and not too bright. A life spent looking at the ground instead of in people's eyes, in case they hit you or dragged you off to the warlord for insolence. A life spent being hated, or despised, or overlooked. She should be filled with compassion for someone like this, who had been so warped by the hatred of Acton's people.

She spat in his face.

"You have become just like them," she said. "You've let them win."

Then she turned and walked away, back to the ship, and didn't look to see if anyone followed.

BRAMBLE

ASH'S SONG ended and he cleared his throat, staring at Acton. Bramble had forgotten, again, that he was so big. Baluch and Ash were tall men, and Medric was solidly muscled, but he dwarfed all of them, or seemed to.

Baluch moved towards him, and Medric followed, his mouth open in wonder at a childhood hero standing right there in front of him. Ash stood next to her, glaring, bristling with hatred now that he confronted his people's enemy. All Acton had to do was stand there, Bramble thought, and he created followers and enemies just like that; his whole life had been the same. Even Baluch had put loyalty over friendship—he would have obeyed Acton's orders, she was sure, even if it had meant both their deaths. Had Acton ever known anyone who wasn't either follower or enemy?

As the ghosts of Turvite had been when Tern raised them, he seemed a little confused at first, and looked around, blinking. His gaze passed over Medric, Baluch, Ash, and came to her. And then he smiled. Her heart turned over, because it was the smile he had given her on the hillside, in the one moment where he and she had been alive in the same place at the same time, a smile of promise, of complicity, of mischief and delight. It broke her heart, but she couldn't help smiling back even while she lifted her chin and squared her shoulders. Curse him. She might not be his enemy any more, but she'd walk into the cold hell on her own two feet before she'd be his follower, before she'd let him cozen her the way he'd cozened the girl on the mountain. No matter how much she loved him.

Acton took a step towards her and she braced herself, unsure why. He was a ghost. He couldn't touch, or talk, or... She looked at Ash. "You can make them talk, can't you?"

Ash nodded and moved in front of Acton. "Speak," he said.

Acton's face was clear, even in the dim light, as though he had merely been dusted with flour and the real man, hearty and hale, was waiting underneath the pale covering. It made her want to weep.

"You can talk, now," she said, wondering what he'd say.

"Am I dead, then?" Acton asked in the language of the past. She understood the words, after so long hearing them, but he spoke in the healer's voice, the prophet's voice, rock on grating stone. Soul-destroying. Bramble trembled with revulsion and anger. This was not *fair*!

Acton was startled by the sound, too, and closed his mouth firmly. He raised his hands apologetically and smiled at her, inviting her to understand his silence. But she hadn't gone through all this to not be able to talk to him.

"Ash," she said. "Make him talk in his own voice."

Ash looked at her with pity in his eyes. "I can't. From the grave, all speak alike."

It was a great disappointment, but she would have to deal with it. Acton was looking at Baluch, puzzlement all over his face.

Baluch came forward, moving quietly, like a man in a sick room, and stood in front of him. "You've been dead a very long time," he said gently, in the language they shared.

"Bal?" Acton said. His incredulity showed only in his face; the voice stayed as it was, stone. Baluch winced at the sound, and then nodded. Acton grinned, looking him up and down in a mime of astonishment at how old he was, teasing.

Baluch smiled back, the boy he had been showing clearly through the wrinkles. "At least I got to be old," he said. "They all thought you'd been killed by a jealous husband somewhere. Why else would you ride out alone, but to some secret meeting with a lover?"

Acton shook his head. "Not a lover."

"Bramble says it was Asgarn."

Acton turned to her. She could see his lips make the motions of saying her name, but he didn't say it out loud, and she was thankful for that. She didn't want to hear her name in that terrible voice. But he spoke anyway, looking puzzled.

"By the way Baluch looks it's been, what—sixty years or so? But you're young."

"A thousand years," she said.

He blinked. "Swith the Strong! How —"

He looked at her with an assessing gaze, as he'd look at a stranger, as he'd looked at Tern the enchanter on the headland outside Turvite. He mistrusted her. She had appeared just before his death and here she was a thousand years later, unchanged. Of course he mistrusted her. But the look hurt.

She felt herself empty out, as though her ribs were a hollow ring around nothingness. If she let herself feel it, she would break apart, bones clattering onto the weeping rocks. She would not show him weakness. He shielded weakness from harm, he took responsibility for the weak, and she would rather he mistrusted her than have him feel paternal.

"There's a lot to explain," she said briskly. "But we can talk as we go. We have to get to Sanctuary." She began to pack his bones back into the saddlebags. The roan's hairs were stuck to Acton's skull with her blood. That seemed fitting, somehow, and she left them there, turning the skull inward so the hairs wouldn't rub off. She felt, irrationally, that the roan would keep Acton safe, somehow.

"Wait," he said, gazing at the bones in sudden understanding. "You raised my ghost?" He looked at Baluch, at Ash, at Medric. "Why?"

"We don't have time for this." Bramble said. "We'll explain on the way."

"Really?" Ash asked dryly. "And do you know how to get out?"

"You got in," she said. "Don't you know the way?"

"The way we came, you can't travel," Baluch said.

Bramble pulled shut the drawstring on the bag and closed the flap. The scarf had absorbed the blood and was dry, although the spots on her jacket were still wet. It was only her blood, not his; she put on her jacket and slung the bags over her shoulder.

"I suspect," she said, "that what guided you here knows the way."

Baluch and Ash exchanged an unreadable look, and then she saw Baluch's eyes go unfocused, the way the Well of Secrets looked when she communed with the gods.

"Aye," Baluch said slowly. "We will be guided."

He had carefully avoided saying who would be guiding them, but

Bramble would be willing to bet it was the Lake, somehow reaching out. "Glad she's on our side," she said. Ash and Baluch looked startled, and she laughed.

She knew the others didn't think it was funny, but she didn't care. Grief and loss were walking beside her wearing the face of a man a thousand years dead. The only way she could cope was to laugh. Then Acton grinned at her, his eyes lighting with shared amusement at Baluch's discomfiture, and the clench of muscles around her heart eased a little. She wasn't so foolish as to think he'd come to love her—*could* ghosts love? She knew that what she felt, she felt alone. But perhaps they could be comrades, at least.

Then she stumbled a little on the broken ground and Acton instinctively put out a hand to support her elbow.

She expected his hand to pass through her, but instead she came up with a jolt. He was solid. The cold of the burial caves washed over her, crept up her arm from where he touched her and chilled her heart, but he was solid, like the enchanter's ghosts. He had touched her.

Ash looked astonished.

Acton let go of her slowly, staring at his own hand. He hadn't expected this, either. "So..." he said, and his hand went to where his sword should have hung. But he hadn't taken it to that meeting with Asgarn a thousand years ago. He moved to draw his belt knife instead, but it had fallen to the floor of the cave when Red had knifed him. He looked at Baluch. "I'll need weapons."

Baluch smiled, slowly, and stepped forward to clasp forearms with Acton. They stared into each other's eyes for a moment, smiles growing. "We'll find you a sword. You can take my knife until then."

He handed over his belt knife.

Acton flipped it in the air and caught it again by the blade, a boy's trick, then tucked it into the sheath on his belt.

"We didn't bring you back to fight," Bramble said, as angry as she had ever been at any warlord. Why was fighting the first thing he always thought of? She knew the answer to that—had lived through battle after battle with him—but he had *died*. Hadn't that changed anything in him?

Acton looked at her, and his surprise turned into that intense gaze that he used when something important was happening. Bramble wondered what was in her face to make him look like that, but it didn't matter. She had to explain, and she had to do it well. She couldn't let Acton leave these caves thinking that another fight would solve things.

"We brought you back because we have need of you. A thousand years have passed, and the land you invaded is now known as the Eleven Domains." His language was easy for her, it had become part of her mind, part of her heart, as familiar as her mother's voice. "Asgarn set up the warlord system that he described to you, using your name to justify it. The original inhabitants of this land were massacred and dispossessed..."

He listened intently, the commander taking a briefing from an officer, assessing everything she said, looking occasionally to Baluch for a confirming nod. He was not looking at her as a young woman any more, which was a different kind of grief, and one she had not expected.

As they followed Baluch through dark and echoing caverns, across pools and over cracks that pierced the heart of the earth, while water dripped like a reminder of time passing, she painted a history of blood and division and oppression, painted it as vividly as she could, so that he would understand what he had done, what he had allowed to happen. So that he would want to help.

She knew exactly what to say, because she knew his weaknesses, knew his strengths, his dreams and his nightmares. It felt a little like betraying him, to use her knowledge of him this way. But it would have been a greater betrayal—of him, as well as Maryrose—not to.

"So we need your help," she said at last, stopping for a moment to stare him right in the eyes. Not a follower, not an enemy. An ally, perhaps.

"You will have it," he said. The echoes took his voice and amplified it, so that it became a god's voice, Swith's voice, booming from the walls and the roof, high above.

She couldn't avoid suspecting that he said it mostly to please Baluch; he had been fascinated by the story of the Domains but not shocked by her tales of endless battles. That had been his life, after all—death didn't change who he had been, who he was.

"Whatever I can do," he went on, "I will do." The echoes answered, "I will do, will do, will do..." and she knew he would stand by that oath.

"Then the next task," Bramble said, "is to find Saker."

FLAX

WATCHING ROWAN try to ride was even funnier than watching Ash. At least Ash was fit and strong—Rowan was wiry with the endurance built up by decades of walking the Road, but he had very little strength in his shoulders or arms. When Mud decided to go one way and Rowan wanted him to go differently, the man had no chance.

Flax grabbed the reins from him. "I'll lead you," he said, pushing down his amusement.

Rowan dropped his head, his face reddening. "Not so good at this, am I?"

"You'd not expect me to play the flute right first try, would you?" Flax said cheerfully. "Riding's just as complicated."

Rowan's eyebrows lifted and he settled back more comfortably in his saddle while he thought it through. That reassured Mud, and he followed Flax and Cam willingly enough as they made their way along the flat-bottomed valley that led back to Gabriston.

The other singers and musicians had left before them, one by one, slipping off into the darkness with a simple, "Wind at your back"—the Travelers' 'bye.

The horses needed light to pick their way out along the rocky defiles that surrounded the Deep, so he and Rowan had waited until dawn, Rowan sitting on a rock playing the flute while Flax had curried and groomed both horses and made sure they were fit to travel. Each to his own trade, he supposed, and all of a part with this strange time in the Deep, where he had been very much the apprentice. A youngling, just learning the first notes of a new song, that's what he had been.

He shivered as he saw the canyon opening up before them and the long slit of daylight widen to show the valley beyond. He had to put away all thoughts of the Deep, now, all the memories of the River, her water flowing over his skin like silk and blood, all thoughts of the fires in the caverns where the demons had taught him mysteries. A surge of excitement went through him and he felt tinglingly alive. He was truly becoming a man! He had been Zel's little brer for so long, following along after her, doing what he was told. But this was beyond her, forbidden to her, and no matter what she said, he was coming here again next year, to learn more. To become a man like Ash. A man who had no fear, not even of warlords and their men.

He turned in the saddle to smile at Ash's father, who had skills of a different sort to teach him. He was excited—to think that Ash's mother was the legendary Swallow! He had heard about her so often, from other musicians on the Road: her voice, her skill, her dedication. If anyone could teach him what he still needed to know about singing, it was her.

"When we get to Gabriston," he said to Rowan, "we'll have to earn some silver."

Rowan shook his head. "No, not so close. Never that close to the Deep, coming or going. Swallow's at Baluchston. We'll head straight there."

"The canyons change," he added. "Every year is different. I just follow the sun."

Following the sun, they found their way to a path up the cliff, which would skirt around Gabriston and take them on a secondary road to Baluchston.

"Now we are back to country I know," Rowan said, climbing down from Mud with difficulty. He would be sore the next day.

"Make sure you stretch your legs t'night," Flax said. "Or you won't be walking tomorrow."

Rowan grimaced and stared up the cliff, looking at Mud with doubt.

"I'll lead," Flax said, grinning. Cam was happy to be led, Mud was happy to follow Cam.

The climb was stiff but Flax found himself oddly happy. He had always wanted his life to be exciting, and since meeting Ash, it had been. Great things at stake—life and death, the future of the world. He began to sing without even thinking about it, as he often did, a wedding song from the South Domain.

A new day, a new day
Seed and fruit,
Fruit and seed
A new life, a new life
Tree and root
Root and tree.
Growing, growing, growing…

Rowan smiled. "Thinking of settling down?"

Flax laughed, too pleased with himself to even be embarrassed, and they climbed in companionable silence.

The road was deserted all afternoon. In the fields, the grapes were untended. They were not ripe, but there should have been workers out, checking for bugs and weeds. It was odd. Unchancy. As the day went on they both became increasingly nervous. The horses picked up on their anxiety and began to sidle and shy at blown leaves. Rowan had no hope of controlling Mud, so they dismounted and began walking along the empty track.

"Usually like this?" Flax asked.

Rowan shook his head. "No. No. There are usually Travelers, farmers, workers. There's a village up ahead. Let's go quietly, eh?"

"Let's mount up," Flax said. Rowan looked at him and Flax shrugged. "Just in case."

The village was busy, at least. This was where everyone had gone—they were barricading their houses and the inn, nailing shutters closed, dragging barrels of water indoors, carrying food from sheds and barns into the houses. They had clearly heard news of the enchanter and his ghosts.

No one paid them any attention at first, beyond a quick look to make sure it wasn't the warlord's men. Then one of the women, a skinny red-head with big hands, who was rolling a barrel towards one of the cottages, looked at them more closely.

"Traveler!" she shouted. All over the village heads swivelled, and the hands that were nailing and sawing hefted their tools.

"Go!" Flax said, kicking Cam into a trot and looking back to make sure Rowan had heard.

Rowan wasn't quick enough. A burly man in a butcher's leather apron had grabbed Mud's bridle and was trying to pull Rowan out of the saddle. Rowan kicked at his head, and the man fell back a moment, but came on again. Mud was spooked and lashing out with his back hooves. Flax reined Cam in, unsure of what to do.

The other villagers were gathering, staying away from Mud's hooves but preparing to rush in. Some of them ran towards Flax and for a moment he was gripped by the desire to run—to urge Cam into a gallop and race away, as he and Ash had raced from the warlord's man in Golden Valley. He could hear Zel's voice in his head, screaming, *Get out of there!*

But Rowan...

Ash would never leave Rowan behind, even if Rowan were a stranger. Look how he'd rushed to save Bramble. Ash would *act*, even if it meant risking his own life.

Flax pulled Cam's head around and kicked her back towards the struggling group. They almost had Rowan out of the saddle, and then there would be no chance for him if they did. Flax noticed a boy with a hoe watching, dancing from foot to foot with excitement. He leant down and grabbed it, then used it to beat aside two women who were screeching and grabbing at Mud's head.

Cam didn't like it. Her ears were flat on her head and the whites of her eyes were showing. She wanted to shy away, but he used every bit of skill he had to force her ahead, towards Rowan. "Come on, girl, come on, take the bastards down!" he called, and the sound of his voice steadied her.

He put a foot in the face of the butcher and poked the hoe into the stomach of another man, who wrenched it out of his hands. Just as well, he thought—time to clear a path out of here. He whistled the signal Gorham taught all his horses that meant "Run! Follow me!"—praying to all the gods that Bramble had taught her horses the same way.

He whirled Cam and set her straight at the woman who had called out. She didn't believe he would ride her down at first, standing there grinning and waving a knife—a carving knife, big enough to disembowel Cam if she got in the right blow. Flax yelled, screamed as he picked up pace, no words, just anger and hate making a sound to raise the dead. The woman's face changed as he came towards her. He knew he was moving fast, but to him everything seemed to move slowly. She'll be dead if she don't move, he thought, screaming, and the red-head jumped out of the way just in time.

Mud followed immediately. They left the village at a gallop, with a thrown axe whistling past Rowan's ear, clattering on the ground under Cam's heels. She kicked backwards and kept going, Flax urging her on. He had stopped screaming, his throat raw. He wouldn't be able to sing for a while.

"Dark-haired bastards!" the red-head yelled after them. "Don't bother running! We'll get the shagging lot of you!"

As though they understood her words, the horses increased their pace, Mud coming up level with Cam. They rode at a good pace for another half mile, until they were sure no one in the village had a horse to follow them on, then slowed.

"Walk them," Flax said. "Let them cool down and catch their breath. We may need them again later."

"Gods of field and stream!" Rowan gasped. "They would have killed us."

"Reckon they know the enchanter are a Traveler," Flax said grimly. "Have you got a hat?"

Rowan bit his lip; Flax could see he didn't like the idea of pretending to be one of Acton's people. But he wasn't a fool. He fished a knitted cap out of his backpack and slid it on, covering his hair and ears. Odd in full summer, but by the time someone started to wonder about that they would be gone.

Flax wished it were winter: the long summer twilight seemed to make them more conspicuous. So much for his cheerful mood of the morning.

"I know another way," Rowan said. "It's longer, but it avoids most of the towns between here and Baluchston."

"You've convinced me!" Flax said, trying to sound encouraging. Ash was depending on him to look after Rowan, but it was more of a responsibility than he had realized. The older man looked very tired, and he squirmed in the saddle, making Mud roll his eyes back and flatten his ears. Flax clucked reassuringly at him and he settled down.

"We should travel at night," Rowan said.

"Certain sure. And find a place to spell the horses."

It was a long time before they came to the small path that led off to the left, towards Baluchston. The track was rocky under the horses' hooves, and Cam picked up a stone. Flax noticed almost immediately and dug it out, but she still went lame for a while, slowing them to the point where Flax wanted to scream—in his highest register—in frustration.

They stopped to rest themselves and the horses at a tiny clearing where deer were drinking from a rill. The hinds startled away, bounding off into the shadows.

Flax realized with satisfaction that it was almost dark. "An hour," he said, loosening Cam's girth and motioning Rowan to do the same for Mud. "We'll give them an hour."

"I could use more than that," Rowan said, sitting on a flat rock at the water's edge. He looked up at Flax seriously. "Thank you, lad. I'd have been hacked to pieces if you hadn't come back for me."

Flax grinned at him, feeling buoyed up and as strong as an ox. All right, they were in the wilderness with everyone's hand raised against them, but it was still better than trailing around behind Zel from inn to inn, singing to clods who wouldn't know a true note from a pig's fart. And he had taken action when danger threatened. Like Ash.

"Have a drink," he said. "There's a long night ahead of us."

MARTINE

THE SHANTYMAN was singing as they brought up the anchor.

Lady Death will ring her knell
Heave away
Haul away
And call us all to the coldest hell
Raise the anchor, maties!

Martine stood at the stern and watched the huge anchor, wood bounded by iron, slide slowly up out of the dark green water, dripping weed.

The Last Domain cargo having been finally off-loaded and paid for, and Trine well exercised by Zel while that was done, they were catching an evening tide out of the small harbor, back onto the open sea. Without Apple. The men who had attacked her had been taken by the Moot staff, and would be tried and punished. The two merchants who had come with her were riding back north.

"Didn't have no Travelers there to start with," one had said. "May not be no ghosts there, either."

Martine was full of foreboding, but her Sight couldn't tell her about what. No matter what happened, the next few weeks were unlikely to go well. People would die; the dead would walk; not even the gods knew what the outcome would be. Perhaps her jitters were no more than that; or perhaps, since Safred didn't seem to share them, they were more personal. Perhaps this new-found joy with Arvid was doomed to end when they reached Turvite.

Perversely, that thought cheered her. If all she had to worry about was a love affair gone wrong, she was in good shape.

On the thought, Arvid appeared from below decks and joined her. "Safred's sick again. Cael's tending her."

"Never take a seer over water," Martine said lightly.

"*You* don't get sick."

She ignored the implication. "Cael's not well himself."

"No." Arvid's face darkened with worry and he pushed a hand through his light brown hair. "He's worse."

"If Safred can't heal him, and the ship's healer can't..."

"Cast the stones again for him," Arvid said.

It was worth a try. She sat cross legged on the bare warm deck and pulled out of her belt the square of blue linen she used to cast on, and spread it on the deck. She spat in her hand and held it out to Arvid. He spat in his and clasped hands. The familiar ritual calmed her, reminded her of who she was. Not Arvid's bed mate, but a stonecaster, Sighted and strong.

"Ask your question," she said.

"Why can't Cael be cured?" Arvid asked.

Her right hand went into the pouch and the stones leapt to her fingers, the ones she needed seeming almost to stick, as they always did. She brought them out and cast them across the linen, her head bent to watch their fall, her ears ready.

"Death," she said, a catch in her voice, because she liked Cael. "Destiny. Sacrifice." She reached out to turn the other two over. Although she recognized each of her stones no matter which way they lay, they spoke to her only when they were face up, and other stonecasters she knew had told her that it was the same for them. "Time, and Memory, both hidden."

"Dragon's fart!" Arvid said angrily. It was so unexpected she just gaped at him, and he was puzzled for a moment. "It's a northern saying," he said. "I just meant—well, it's clear, isn't it, even to me?"

Martine bent her head over the stones and listened. They spoke quietly but surely. Lady Death was coming for Cael, and coming soon, but there was a reason for it, not just blind malignant chance. She said so to Arvid.

"And that's comforting, is it?" he said, staring at the stones. "I'd hoped to give Safred better news."

Martine felt that pang that all stonecasters knew. They were only the heralds, the messengers, but somehow they felt responsible for the bad news they delivered—and certainly, customers tended to act as though they were. It irritated Martine when the questioners stared at her with anger and suspicion, but when they didn't she felt even more culpable. Like with Ranny of Highmark. She was still unsure if she'd made the right choice there. It had seemed right, to deny Ranny the knowledge the stones had given her of the time and date of her death. But had she the right to censor the stones? She didn't know.

She felt so young, all her old certainties dissipated. Who was she to withhold information from anyone? She sighed and packed the stones away in her pouch, folded her casting cloth. When they reached Turvite she'd find Ranny and tell her what she wanted to know.

Then Arvid touched her hand and smiled tentatively at her. He was unsure, too, even after a week of sharing a bed, and that gave her more confidence. She smiled back, touching his cheek lightly, and he lit up from within, glowing with desire and what she had to suspect was love. Oh, gods. How could she love a warlord?

Cael came up on deck not long after, while Arvid was aft talking to the captain. He was sweating and pale, a bad combination, and he sat next to her at the bow heavily, turning his face into the wind with relief. Zel followed him like a shadow and sat at his feet, her face serious.

"I'm dying," he said conversationally.

He wasn't asking for reassurance, so there was nothing to say except the truth. Zel sat perfectly still, waiting for Martine's response.

"Yes," she said. "I think you are."

A shiver ran through Zel and her face twisted, fighting tears, but Cael nodded and simply sat for a time.

"Why, do you think?" he asked. "Why won't it heal?"

She had puzzled over that many times, with few answers. "It may be because your wound was given... somewhere else, some other time. May be it can only be healed then, too."

He frowned, thinking back to the stream in the Great Forest which had seemingly taken him to somewhere else, to be attacked and wounded. "So I have to go back to the stream? But we each went to a different place."

"No," Martine said, sure of this at least. "A different time."

"So there's no guarantee that I'd go to the time I needed. And I'd have to take Saffie back too, back to where those...things are."

"I think so."

He shook his head with decision. "Not a chance."

"No."

It was a fine day and they sat for a while, enjoying the sunshine and the breeze. Zel pulled out some tiny balls and juggled for a while, keeping in practice.

Cael's eyes seemed to look at a different horizon, somewhere in the past. "I had a family, you know," he said. "We were Valuers, born and bred. Sage, my wife, she died of a fever when Safred was two. We had two girls, March and Nim. They married. There were three little ones: a girl and two boys. Linnet, Birch and Eagle. Nim was so excited when she saw an eagle from the birthing chamber—she thought it meant he would be something great in the world."

"What happened?" Martine asked, as gently as she could.

"Safred's father, the warlord, came looking for her. I took Saffie to safety, so he couldn't take her and use her as a warlord's weapon. He killed them, one by one, until someone in the village told him where we had gone."

Martine was plunged into deep empathy and old grief. Her village, too, had been killed off; everyone she loved, gone, except the young Elva, because Martine had taken her on the road. She sent a prayer to the gods for Elva's safety.

There were tears on Zel's cheeks. She turned her head away and scrubbed at them with the back of her hand, then went on juggling.

"They should have told straight away," he said with old anger. "When it came down to it, they didn't believe in Valuing after all—her life, my life, was no more important than theirs. But it's hard to believe that where she's concerned. And she'd helped so many of them. Healed so many...They loved her."

"And she escaped," Zel said, still not looking at him.

"Aye. The delvers rescued her." He paused, staring at his hands. "I'll be glad to see Sage and March and Nim again. If they've waited for me."

The lump in Martine's throat was so hard she couldn't talk.

"You're lucky that your dead love you," Zel said, then pushed herself up, hard, and tucked the balls in her pocket as she walked away, her eyes resolutely turned up, to find her aunties in the rigging.

"That one carries a lot of grief, still, even after Safred helped her," Cael said sadly.

"Everyone carries grief," Martine said, "if they live long enough."

Memories of her own dead came back to her: Elva's parents, Cob and Lark, her own parents, her aunties and uncles, cousins, grammers and granfers. Everyone in the two villages was related, one way or another.

The Ice King's men had come on them so unexpectedly, early, very early in the season...too early, you would have thought, for them to have made it over the snow-choked mountains.

Once again she remembered her girlhood vision of the villages being attacked. Not by the Ice King, but by the warlord and his men. That was crazy, though. Why would the warlord have attacked his own people? The thought came, inevitably: they weren't *his* people. Dark-haired villagers were never his people. But why would he have done it? She searched her memory more closely, trying to piece together the separate parts of the vision. It was so long ago, she'd only been fifteen...She had seen a young officer leading, not the warlord himself. Not even the warlord's heir, Masry. She hadn't known this officer, but he had definitely been in charge.

She rubbed at her side, where an old scar still sometimes ached. She owed that scar to Alder, the village voice at Cliffhaven, who had beaten her for telling about that vision, for raising a false alarm. Yet it had seemed so clear, so true to that young self. The danger had seemed...so real.

Oh, what was the point? False visions happened sometimes, particularly to the young. And sometimes the Sight couched itself in riddles, leading you astray, even though, looking back, the meaning was clear.

It didn't matter now, anyway. No matter who had attacked Cliffhaven, it was a long time ago and over and done with.

She touched Cael on the back of his hand. He was too warm to the touch. "I'll make you a tisane to bring down the fever," she said.

He nodded heavily. "Aye. But don't let Saffie know. She worries too much as it is."

Rumer and Rawnie dropped down out of the rigging and draped an arm each over Zel, laughing about something.

"Family," Cael said, and sighed.

RAWNIE'S STORY

I ALWAYS WANTED to be beautiful, like my little sister Osyth. She had that Traveler kind of beauty, dark and elegant and lithe. Well, we was lithe enough, my twin Rumer and me, but that was because we was tumblers and worked hard at it. She were—oh, I don't know. Her eyes was big and her nose were straight and there were just something about her that made men look.

Rumer and me, we was ordinary, as ordinary as Travelers can be in the Domains. Not ill-featured nor even so plain, but ordinary. Osyth stood out like a dark moon. After she married that Gorham (and he worshipped the ground she walked on, that were clear), me and Rumer took to the Road alone, and had a good time of it. Osyth said we'd be short of silver within a month, and she were near enough right, for neither of us had the knack of keeping money. Sweet in, sweet out, we thought, and if we had to shag for our shelter more often than we'd like, well, everything has a price. It was a bad summer, too, that year, the worst I remember, and there was no silver to be had for tumbling, not even tumbling in someone's bed.

So we decided to head north, where the weather is different and the year might not have been so bad. And since we was heading north, we thought we'd go see our mam, in Foreverfroze. She were a fisher, our mam, like one of the Seal Mother's people, and she loved the clean colors of the ice and the sea and the sky, white and blue and green and gray. Fishing was her passion, I reckon, and Da came a cold second to it.

She's a funny one, my mam. I mean, look at the names she gave us: Osyth and Rumer and Rawnie. Whoever heard of Traveler girls with names like those? But Mam never did think much of tradition, and Da thought that whatever Mam did was right. We talked about her and him, in the nights after a tumbling performance, but we could never seem to understand her right. Guess we never will.

I think we was a bit kin-hungry without Osyth, and maybe a bit mother-hungry too, cause Osyth used to boss us around just like Mam and it felt a bit rootless, somehow, not to have anyone telling us what to do.

We got up to Foreverfroze at the end of summer, which wasn't so smart, maybe, but it let us spend the winter with Mam and Da, helping to salt down the fish the women had brought back and helping Da weave the sweet-grass baskets the men traded down south. And Mam filled the long nights with stories about the fisherwomen and their freedom and prosperity. It sounded good enough, all right.

The next spring Mam said, "Come out and try it for yourselves," and she got us berths on her ship, the *Flying Spray* , as a hooking and gutting team. All the fishers are women on those ships, and they work in partnerships, one woman hooking the fish and flipping it back to deck, the other gutting it and rebaiting the hook.

Well, we tried it and we didn't like it, although Rumer and I could work like one body when we wanted to, and the rhythm of hooking and gutting the fish was easy enough for us to learn. But it was boring, boring as walking a long road between high walls, and before three days were out we was up on the rigging with the sailors, laughing as we raced each other to the topsails.

They marvelled at us, but it weren't hard for professional tumblers to keep balance, even on a swaying rope fathoms above the deck and the icy sea.

So that's how we found our passion, Rumer and me, the passion of high places and wide horizons, of swell and spray and sea and sail. Of always moving, even in port. Of always seeing new things, good things and bad. Of taking your home with you wherever you go, so that you are always where you belong.

Now there's lots of stories about the fishing women, about what they get up to on those ships, alone for months without men except for a few of the sailors. I notice those stories are always told by men.

Oh, there were a couple of teams shared more than their bed space, but mostly fishers are too tired to even think about shagging—sleep is precious and hard won when the fish are biting, and when they're not the fishers are more likely to snipe at each other than throw kisses. And put a lot of women together in one place, you get them all having their monthlies at the same time—that's a recipe for arguments and tears and friendships broken and made up again; oh, Rumer and me, we stayed way up in the rigging those days.

We've always liked sweet young men, Rumer and I, and on the *Flying Spray* we learnt to like sweet older men, too. There was always a few men sailors 'cause there are things that need pure strength on any ship and men are best for that, no question. Takes three women to hold the steerboard against a current, and one strong man does a better job. So we had some men to choose from.

Unlike most of the women, we didn't have men to go home to, so we were popular. No complications, see? We didn't have to give up any pleasures, except food. You can get good and tired of fish stew.

But for all that, it was a fine life and we loved it. Mam too. And Da seemed happy enough with his men friends, working and looking after the childer in the winter. He started making comments about needing grandchildren to look after, but we was in no hurry, Rumer and me. It would mean a full year on land, and we was still in the early stages of the passion, where even a day away seems too long.

And then... You can't trust the gods. Not for long.

We was on the *Cormorant* three days out from Foreverfroze, when the storm come up out of a clear sky.

The sea were on a nice even swell, we had a good following wind—but not so much to make her dig her nose in, which that ship was prone to do, like many two-masters that came out of Mitchen's yards. The sun were shining. The gulls that was following us didn't even notice anything, though usually they're more weather-wise than we humans.

Then, *whoomp*! A huge clap of wind, like a hand sweeping across the surface of the sea and hitting us broadside. The ship reeled and staggered, but thank the gods we hadn't caught much in those three days so she were still riding light. She righted herself with an effort we could all feel.

There was a pause. We was all shouting. The ship owner were also the steersman, and she went dead pale and called to bring down the sheets, but it were too late. The wind hit us before the riggers had cleared the first crossbar.

And the sky stayed clear. Clear as poverty soup, that sky, but wind screeching down on us and tearing the rigging apart, pushing every hand that wasn't lashed to her post right across the deck to the steer-board side. Me and my twin clung to a bollard and each other and the wind whipped tears up in our eyes like we was mourning each other already.

Wind wraiths, I thought. Can't be nothing else.

And I worked my mouth, trying to bring up spit, because the story goes that if you're of Traveler blood whistling will tame them, but you can't whistle with a mouth dust dry with fear, so most folks never get to test if it's true.

Then they came.

They're hard to describe, and I can't do it, but they was only half in the world, it seemed, and half somewhere else. And they laughed.

The wind dropped as they hovered, just above the poop deck, and the master came to meet them. She passed us as she went and avoided our eyes, and that was bad, I knew.

They hailed her in screeching voices. "Master!" they said. "We have found you."

She worked her mouth for enough spit to form an answer. She didn't want to say anything, it looked like, but she had to. "You have found us."

The spirits sent up a triumphant laugh, a howl more like, that sent cold down into my marrow bones.

"Present your sacrifice," one of the spirits said.

And the master turned her head and looked at us.

Pity in her eyes.

We looked around, wildly, but the others was turning away from us, ashamed, crying or stony-faced, and we knew we was dead as we stood.

We'd heard the stories. In the dead watch, by a crescent moon, sailors love to tell the wind wraith stories. About the compact, made no one knows how long ago, where the wind wraiths and the humans made a deal—if the spirits found a ship in the wide wastes of the ocean, they could take a single soul but the ship and the rest of the crew had to be left safe.

It was a good deal for the shipowner, for the sailors, for the fishers. For everyone except the one they threw to the spirits. The newest sailor on board.

"Last on, first off," the master said. I will say she was sorrowing as she said it, but she meant it, nonetheless. "Which of you was last on?"

"Me," Rumer said.

"Me," I said in the same moment.

The master were taken fair aback. Even the spirits looked confused. I didn't look at Rumer, and she didn't look at me. Nothing to say. But we gripped hands tight, like just before a performance, or afterwards, when we was taking our bows.

"Both…" the wind wraith said in a voice half venom and half hiss.

"No! I was last on." The voice had come from the hooking deck below us. We spun around and there was Mam, laying down her rod like it were made of ruby, nodding to her partner and the other fishers, climbing up the companionway from the hooking deck to stand beside us.

"Not true," Rumer and I said together, with one voice.

"True enough," Mam said. She didn't look at us, after one quick glance that were full of warning, like she used to look at us when we was half-grown, after she'd told us to do something we didn't want to. We knew that look, right enough. It meant, "Do as you're told or suffer the consequences."

My guts was churning and I were sweating like a smith. I didn't know what to want. What to hope for. Seemed to me it would be easier to die than see either Rumer or Mam taken, but maybe they felt the same.

The master looked helplessly from Mam to us, and we all looked stonily back at her.

"We have to give one," she said. "But only one."

"*Three* have volunteered," the spirit said, swooping closer, mouth agape.

That seemed to strengthen the master. "*One* was agreed to. Do you break the compact?"

It seemed disturbed by that idea, and slid away from her, higher up, and hung next to its companions. "No," it wailed. "One. One is enough."

"Well, then," Mam said. "Here I am."

"No!" we shouted, but the master and Mam locked gazes for a moment, and the master nodded.

The spirits stooped at Mam, and dragged her from the deck. I felt them swipe by me, their flesh like cold cloth dragging on my skin, and then they launched into the sky, dragging Mam with them, screeching and shrieking with triumph. We tried to pull her back, Rumer and me, grabbing onto her feet, but they was too strong, strong like the sea, unstoppable, and they ripped her away from us and left us sprawling on the deck.

She turned her head back to see us, but by then she were too far up for us to see into her eyes. But she didn't scream, our mam. She didn't give them any fear to play with. She didn't give them anything except herself.

And in a heartbeat, two, three, they were gone across the wide, level sea, and we was left fallen on the deck under a calm blue sky, with a steady following wind bringing us the sound of gulls.

We just sailed on and all we was left with was questions, and too much imagining about where they took her to, and what they did when they got there.

We had nightmares every night, after.

And yet, it's like she answered a question for us that we'd never of dared to ask, and that's left a sweetness as well as a pain behind.

For Rumer to offer to die instead of me, well, that's easy to understand. She's my twin. Of course we'd die for each other. And maybe others would say, well, she were your mother, of course she'd die for you. But I tell you, it came as a shock to both of us. It weren't something I'd have ever predicted. Tell the truth, I don't think even a stonecaster could've predicted it.

What I want to know is, what did the master see in Mam's eyes that made her nod? 'Cause I don't think we ever seen it, and when I wish, that's what I wish for: to see those eyes and see if it were love that made her a sacrifice. Or something else.

LEOF

THEY LEFT the farmyard and quartered as much ground as they could, but it was useless. The gods only knew where the wraiths had flown to with their enchanter. And at dusk, if things went as they had in Spritford and Carlion, the ghosts themselves would fade.

An hour before sunset, Leof ordered his men to turn around and head for Sendat. Wearily, they turned the horses' heads towards home. It was a measure of the quality of these three men, Leof thought, that even after all the unsettling events of the day, they unerringly turned towards the fort at Sendat. It was one of the first things his own father had taught him—always know where you are, always know where you can retreat to if necessary, so that in the heat of battle you are not disoriented, so that if you need to run you don't run the wrong way.

Although he'd always followed that advice, today was the first time he had really needed it. Today was the first time Thegan had ever retreated. Leof considered how livid his lord was going to be when they returned empty-handed. They made the trip in silence, and he suspected that the others were considering the same thing, and wondering how Thegan would greet them. Leof was heart-sick that he wasn't returning with the enchanter—Thegan had risked his own life to save his, back at Bonhill, and the only way he could repay that was to deal with the enchanter. He had failed, and it weighed on him as nothing ever had. His lord would be angry, and rightfully so.

But when he walked into the hall at Sendat just after the evening meal had ended, Thegan took one look at his face and, although his mouth tightened, he waved Leof into his workroom calmly. At Thegan's signal, Sorn rose and followed them. Leof felt his heart lift and clench at the same time. Seeing her was a blessing from the gods, but also a danger, with Thegan watching.

"No luck?" his lord asked.

"We found him, followed him. Tried to take him down by bow,

but the wraiths intervened. Then we found him and the ghosts in a farm—they'd killed the people there—and I rode in to grab him, almost had him, but the wraiths dragged him up into the sky and we don't know where they took him. We searched, but they could be anywhere. Out of the Domain, maybe." He shrugged, suddenly bone weary.

Thegan listened closely, and Leof knew that later, tomorrow maybe, his commander would take him through it all again, in detail, looking for any weakness they could exploit.

"Enough, now," he said. "Eat and rest. Tomorrow we take action."

It was comforting to realize that Thegan had already devised a strategy; but alarming, too. Any action they took was likely to be desperate.

"There is food," Sorn said, her voice soft. "Come and eat."

In a dream he followed her back into the noise and movement of the hall. He really was very tired. It seemed impossible that it was only two days ago that he had left her here to go to Carlion. With a shock, he remembered the white-haired man, the Lake's ambassador. His warnings had made the trip to Carlion necessary. The Lake seemed the least of their problems, now, and with a surge of relief Leof realized that it was, indeed, the least of their problems. Thegan was unlikely to move against Baluchston anytime soon. That was one thing he could stop worrying about. He wondered when he had started being someone who worried.

Sorn signalled to a maid and as if by enchantment food appeared in front of him. Good, solid food: soup, sausages, bread. Comforting food. He set to, relying on Sorn to make sure that Alston and the others would also be fed. He could always rely on her. For a moment his gaze rested on her as she spoke to one of the serving maids, her head bent to listen to the girl's answer. She was as calm as always, and watching her he could almost believe that the world outside was safe. Then he realized he was staring and looked down at his plate.

He slept like the dead. Better than he deserved. Better than the dead were sleeping, around here.

The next morning Thegan called him to his office.

"Take Alston and fortify the old barn," he said. "Use our own masons, not the Travelers. Make sure it's secure." He paused, weighing his words. "We are building a prison. I want it watertight."

Leof was speechless for a moment, looking at Thegan from across the warlord's desk. "You think the ghosts can be imprisoned?" It was an intriguing idea.

"No, no. How would we get them here? No." He seemed to come to some decision, and moved around his desk, resting his thigh against it so that he looked casual. Leof could tell that he was anything but relaxed.

"To save Sendat, we will need hostages," Thegan said. Leof had no idea what he meant.

Thegan nodded at the papers on his desk. "I compiled reports while I was in Carlion. The ghosts ignored some people and killed others. Not a single Traveler was killed. Not one. And when I questioned the survivors, it was the same story. A Traveler grandmother, a Traveler great-grandfather. Some of them had never heard of Travelers in the family, but that's not surprising. Families hush it up. But most knew it was somewhere in their bloodline. Far back at times, but there."

Leof slowly absorbed the information. He felt as though his head were full of horsehair, like a cushion. It had always been likely that the enchanter was a Traveler—like the first enchanter who tried to make ghosts solid, in Turvite. But this was proof. "He's making the ghosts kill—for Travelers, you think?"

"I think he wants to take back what Acton took and he is protecting his own people."

"The ghosts don't kill their own," Leof said slowly.

"Exactly. And more than that—they *will* not kill their own, or all his work is for nothing. Which is why we need hostages."

Leof nodded, understanding. It was purely logical; he ignored a feeling of dismay. Time to trust his lord. Thegan had proved, yesterday, that Leof could trust him, even to the risk of his own life.

"So—set Alston to fortify the barn, and then you and Gard will take a detail to collect every Traveler within a day's ride of Sendat. Explain to Alston so he can prepare here."

"My lord, what if they will not come?"

Thegan smiled sourly. "They'll come all right. Once people know that the ghosts spare the Travelers, this will be the only safe place in the Domain for them. And that's what you will offer them, Leof—safety. Safety from their neighbors behind the strong walls of the warlord's fort." He paused, weighing his words. "I will not let this enchanter destroy life in the Domains. I will crush him one way or the other. I swear it."

Leof left, wondering how he had come to a place where he questioned his lord's orders. But Thegan was right. The news about Travelers and ghosts would get around, no doubt, spurred by Thegan's own questions, if by nothing else, and then he shivered. No Traveler would be safe. He was doing them a favor by offering shelter. And if the ghosts really did respect the lives of their own, then the Travelers and Sendat would survive. It was the only way. The only choice they had.

But as he explained the plan to Alston and saw the ready acceptance in his eyes, he was troubled. If the ghosts did not respect Traveler lives, what then? Were they all to be slaughtered, their own people and the Travelers alike? If the ghosts overwhelmed their defences—well, then, he would die. The road was long only if you were lucky. The thought made him oddly cheerful and he whistled as he went to the stables to find Thistle.

BRAMBLE

THEY WALKED through the dark, following Baluch, with only Medric's small candle to light their way. They were using one candle at a time, not knowing how long it would take them to reach the surface.

Ash motioned Bramble away from the others and they walked together. "You must keep the bones with you at all times," he said. "We can find another singer, if we have to, but you are the key."

The ghosts Ash and Martine had seen at Spritford had faded at sunset. If Acton faded too… She pushed down her grief at the thought. They would have to raise him again, that was all.

"I'm rather glad I can't raise him on my own," she said. It would be both a temptation and a torment, to be able to call him to her.

"The way you feel about him, I thought you'd want to be able to." His voice was accusing.

She flushed. "He's not as bad as history paints him."

"He's the enemy of our people."

"I'm from both, remember?" she replied. "I've come to realize that I have no enemies but the warlords. And no matter what the stories say, he didn't start the warlord system."

That gave him pause. "So he's not a killer?"

Her step faltered a little. "Aye," she said. "He's a killer." The words sent a pain straight through her chest. "But so are we."

Ash flinched at that, and said nothing for a while. His hand went to his belt, as though to reassure himself, and Bramble noticed a pouch hanging there, the type stonecasters used.

"Are you a caster now as well?" she asked him.

Ash nodded. "I can cast." But his tone was doubtful.

She left it at that and they walked companionably until they were in a dry, smooth area of the caves, a round pocket in the middle of a long corridor of stone. The air was fresh, and they knew they were getting closer to the surface, because there was a narrow crack letting in a tiny lozenge of light. It glowed in the darkness and left afterimages on her eyes.

Medric blew out his candle. Their eyes were so adjusted to the dark that the cave seemed like bright daylight.

"Let's take a break," Ash suggested.

Bramble went over to the crack and looked up; the slender chimney seemed to go up forever. Her sense of time was unsettled in here, but still it seemed she could feel the sun setting. Would Acton fade at sunset? The thought made her shiver. She wouldn't look at him. Better to turn around and have him gone than watch him fade away. Then he came to stand beside her, making all the hairs on her arms stand up. She didn't know if that was because he was a ghost, or because he was... him.

"What would you see, if you stood on top of this hill?" Acton asked.

Bramble shrugged. "Farms, villages, towns—as far as the horizon and beyond."

"So much..." he said, wonderingly. "We've built a great country!"

"Out of the blood of my people," Ash reminded him.

Acton turned, and the last red light of sunset caught him, gilding him so that for a moment Bramble could see the man he had been, hale and rosy. She strangled something like a sob, and felt irritated with herself. She had to take control of these ridiculous surges of emotion.

"Aye," Acton said. "You are right. It was badly done. By me, by others." He paused, choosing his words, and Baluch paused too, a curious look on his face, as though he were remembering old and difficult times. "We tried for peace. But we were betrayed by your people."

"You murdering bastard!" Ash snarled. He somehow looked larger, as though rage had swollen him. Medric moved behind Acton, not understanding Acton's words but aware of conflict, and immediately taking his side. It enraged Ash further. "You can't excuse massacres with a lie about betrayal."

Bramble moved to Ash's side, sensing his approval, as though she were ranging herself on the side of right. "He's telling the truth, Ash," she said. Startled, he whirled to face her, a protest on his lips. She held up her hand. "Oh, yes, he's a killer, he's a murdering bastard all right, he invaded, all of that. But it's true he tried to do it peacefully and the original inhabitants massacred his kin."

Ash stood silent, his breath rasping.

Baluch came forward and laid a hand on his arm. "True," he said quietly. "Acton's mother, my sweetheart, all our friends... butchered by the dark haired ones. Our girls raped and degraded. Our home burnt."

"Hawk," Bramble said. "The leader's name was Hawk. It was his steading."

Fumbling with the shards of everything he had ever believed, Ash latched on to that. He knew that name. "Hawk? Hawksted? Like in 'The Distant Hills'?"

The words of the song, the tune, slid back into Bramble's mind, and the pieces fell into place. She realized that she had even heard the tune forming in Baluch's head, as he had looked down at the corpse of Friede's killer, but she hadn't recognized it then. "For Friede?" she asked Baluch. " 'The Distant Hills' was for Friede?"

"*You* wrote that?" Ash looked awe-struck, as though he had met a god.

Baluch's mouth firmed and he turned away. Bramble felt cold. Shaky. Baluch had written "The Distant Hills." She had known that song all her life; she had known it before it was written. The thought unsettled her. Time whirled in her head.

Ash was staring at the ground, his face confused and wondering.

"You know too much," Baluch said, staring at bare wall.

"Aye," Bramble said. "I do."

"You were right," Baluch said at last, in her own language. "I went to the Lake just before Acton's death. The calling was so strong... I intended to be back before the Moot, before Acton went to Hawksted, but I didn't understand, then, about how She takes time. It was thirty years, that first time. She brought me forwards to where the Lake People were being attacked for the first time. I... advised on their defense. Asgarn was an old man, then. I killed him without knowing who he was. She only told me afterwards. I felt... It was a bad moment, finding out I'd killed someone I'd fought with."

"So you avenged Acton without knowing it," Bramble said. Baluch laughed bitterly.

"Do you think She knew he had killed Acton?" she asked.

"The Lake? I doubt it."

Bramble looked at Acton, finally, needing to see his reaction, although it seemed like a weakness in her that she needed it. In the moments when Baluch had claimed her attention, the sun had set, but Acton was still there, still staring at them with concern, not understanding. She felt a surge of relief.

"He doesn't fade..." Bramble said. She didn't know if she were glad or not. Ash looked up, his face set, giving nothing more away, but she was sure there was turmoil in his mind. Gods knew, there was turmoil in hers. The past, the present, the future were too mixed for peace of mind.

"He should have faded," Ash said. "If it's the same spell."

"Who knows?" Baluch mused. "It may be different in some small way..."

"Who cares?" Bramble said, and Acton smiled at her tone, although he hadn't understood their words.

"We can stay the night here," Ash said, in the old language.

"I will guard you," Acton said immediately. Ash looked irritated, resenting the easy way Acton took over. A lifetime of giving other people orders—the habit lasted even beyond the grave, Bramble thought. But it was sensible to leave the watch to him. He didn't need to sleep.

Ash avoided Baluch's eyes as he lay down next to Bramble. "Even if they did kill Acton's people, did that excuse him going on to murder thousands of innocent people?" he muttered to her.

She paused, as though she didn't want to answer. "No," she said. "There was no excuse for killing the men of Turvite, or all the people of River Bluff. No excuse. But Hawksted—what would you have done if your parents and all your friends had been betrayed, massacred, by a stranger?" Ash didn't answer, just sat with his shoulders hunched. "Pray you'll never have to find out." She turned her back on him and settled down, her head on the bag that contained Acton's bones. It had taken living all of Acton's life for her to understand him even a little. Poor Ash—all his certainties were being challenged in a single day.

Baluch, instead of resting, had moved aside to talk to Acton.

"Teach him our language," she called to Baluch. "He's going to need it." She sighed, watching them. They had a lot of information to share. A lot of memories. She felt a pang of resentment—she knew so much, shared so many of those memories, but had no right to them...and no chance of making new ones with him, not in this life.

The shock of the dead voice woke her fully. "Well then, Bramble the beautiful, the resolute," Acton said. "Who are you, then? And how do you know so much about me and mine?" He was sitting beside her, Baluch was asleep next to Ash.

He was not charming her, not trying to seduce her into following him. He just wanted to know. So she told him about Obsidian Lake, and he listened, and although his brows knit a time or two, he didn't interrupt.

"Just how much did you see?" he asked cautiously.

"Wili, for example?" she mocked. He flinched, but a smile tugged the side of his mouth as though he laughed at himself. She smiled involuntarily. For the first time she thought about his reaction, were she to betray her love for him. Apart from risking her own dignity, it wouldn't be fair to him, to burden him in an instant with a love that had taken all his life to form, which he couldn't possibly return. "I didn't see enough to make you blush," she said. "Or me either." Which was stretching the truth.

His mouth twisted wryly. "Good," he said. "I wouldn't mind making you blush, but not that way."

He said it so easily, she was sure it was a habit left over from before the grave, like the habit of command. Always, wherever he'd gone, he'd charmed his way into beds and into hearts. It was nothing to do with her personally. Nothing to make her heart leap. But her heart beat faster anyway. At least she had the satisfaction of knowing he would have desired her, if they'd met for more than a moment. Would have acted on the desire.

She tore her thoughts off that path as he cocked an eyebrow at her, laughing at her so easily, with such an invitation to share his amusement, that she melted into laughter and then into something else entirely. He reached out towards her face, but she flinched back. She never wanted to feel that bone deep chill again.

He froze, chagrin on his face, and brought down his hand. "I forgot," he said. He seemed to brood for a moment, then looked up at her. "But on the mountainside? You were really there, weren't you? Not a vision?"

She told him about the hunter, and the journey to the place where she could find his bones.

"You looked so . . . wild, like a spirit from the forest," he said. She wasn't sure if it were reminiscence or mistrust.

"I'd been living like one for months," she said.

He grinned. "You smiled and then you frowned, and I thought—Oh, that one won't ever be tamed!"

It was a compliment. It seemed the strangest thing yet, to hear the words that had haunted her for so long transformed in his mouth into something good. "So a demon once told me," she said lightly, passing it off.

"Now that's a story I'd like to hear!"

She shook her head, remembering the rest of the demon's prophecy, which had been proven with such a twisting truth: *Born wild and died wild . . . No one will ever tame thee, woman, and thou wilt love no man never*. She never would, because the only one she'd ever loved was a ghost, not a man.

"I need sleep," she said brusquely. "Even if you don't."

His mouth twisted again, but not in amusement this time. "Aye," he said. "Sleep. I will guard you."

Because of the grating voice of the dead, she couldn't tell if his tone was protective or resentful. She thought his pale shadow beside her would keep her awake, but she dropped into sleep as a stone into a well, and did not dream.

FLAX

WE'LL BE safe in Baluchston," Rowan said.

Flax grimaced and stared forward, down the long, winding, overgrown track that led north and west, eventually.

"Are you sure? They're Acton's people, even if they do live with the Lake."

Rowan smiled. "The Lake is more than water, lad, remember? She will keep us safe. She always has kept her people safe."

"I thought that were only the Lake people themselves, the ones that set their roots down there."

"Old blood is known," Rowan sang, in a light, clear tenor.

Flax turned more towards him in excitement. "I don't know that song," he said. He hadn't thought about that—the chance to learn new songs. With luck, whole new cycles of songs... His heart lifted and he smiled. "Teach me," he said.

A shadow went over Rowan's face as though the words brought back a difficult memory, but he fished out a little pipe—the sort of thing shepherds whittled while they watched their flocks—and began to play a simple melody. It sounded old. Flax hummed along as Rowan repeated the refrain.

"One of the oldest we have," Rowan said. "From before the land-taken. I'll teach you the new words, the translation, first, and then the old words, so you'll know what you're singing."

"Does Ash know many of the old songs?" Flax asked.

"Aye," Rowan said. "He knows them all, now."

They camped for the night in a tiny, tight space under two big willows—one for them and one for the animals. Once they were settled and he had groomed the horses, Flax crept out and foraged in a nearby field of oats for horse feed, trying to take a little from each row so that the farmer wouldn't raise the alarm in the morning. He had been brought up to buy, not steal, but that didn't worry him. We's owed a little fodder, he thought, after all that stravaging.

He came back with his arms full, and Mud and Cam nosed at him eagerly, so that he almost dropped it all. He carefully divided his booty into two equal piles, and then stood between them so that Mud, who ate faster than Cam, wouldn't steal her portion too.

"They need more than grass, if we're going to keep riding each day," he explained when Rowan asked. "These are just ripe—they're early, but it's protected down here in the valley and that far slope's a sun trap."

Rowan was a good campfire cook, even with the meagre rations they had left. After they'd eaten, he pulled a fishing line from his pack and baited the hook with the last bit of cheese, then edged out over the stream on a willow root and tied the line off.

"Never know your luck," he said.

The River might have been looking after them, because there was a nice sized pike on the hook the next morning, and pike weren't known for liking cheese.

Rowan built a small, almost smokeless fire and cooked it quickly, dousing the embers straight afterwards. It was delicious, even without salt, which they'd run out of the day before. Flax could have eaten two more.

The day that followed was one of constant tension and boredom. Keeping a lookout became Flax's obsession. Sweat trickled down his back, and he had to remember to relax his hands so that Cam wouldn't get nervous. The memory of that axe whistling through the air past their ears, the memory of the hate in the red-head's face came rushing back, over and over again, every time he heard a noise or saw a distant figure across the fields.

Nothing happened when he did. There was no shout of "Traveler!". At this distance, they looked respectable, as people did on horseback. Flax raised his hand genially as they passed, and no one even looked twice at them.

By the time Baluchston rose up across the water he was exhausted.

He hoped that Rowan was right about the Lake protecting them, because he didn't think he could.

They caught the ferry across the narrow end of the Lake, and they were the only passengers. The ferry man looked sharply at them, but said nothing except to name the fare. Rowan handed over some coppers and they led the horses onto the flat-bottomed boat. There were ferries of many different sizes, depending on what had to be taken across; they had boarded the large one, which could take horses and wagons and dogs.

Flax expected Mud and Cam to be nervous, but although they snuffled at the side of the ferry, they stood calmly, as though they were used to boats. He wondered just where Bramble had been, and what she had done there.

There was a man waiting for the ferry on the other side; a man with a tight mouth, greying hair and a wonderfully decorated tan leather belt cinching in his spreading waist. Flax eyed it enviously.

Rowan noticed his glance, and smiled. "My friend likes your work, Reed. He's a singer, like Swallow," he said, looking over at Flax. "Reed's the leatherworker in these parts."

Flax blushed a little. He wasn't greedy, but the belt was truly beautiful, covered with intricate scrollwork, and it was nice to be distracted by something attractive after the last few days. He said so, a little defensively, and Reed laughed, the lines around his mouth loosening.

"My shop's in the main square," he said. "I'll give you a discount, same as I give Rowan, if you'll give me a song."

"One of Reed's belts'll last you a lifetime," the ferryman confirmed.

"I wish I could," Flax said honestly. The idea of doing something as simple as shopping appealed to him greatly.

As Reed climbed in the ferry they waved goodbye and walked towards the town square. Flax had been more reassured by the conversation than he would have believed.

Baluchston was a normal free town, it seemed. People in the streets, maybe more with dark hair than was usual, all of them busy about their daily tasks. A few glances came their way; each time, Flax tensed.

"Calm down, lad," Rowan said. "We're safe here."

Rowan led the way straight to a small cottage on the outskirts, near the road that wound south towards Sendat. It belonged to Swallow's cousin, the man Skink who had been with them in the Deep. Swallow always stayed there when Rowan was away.

And there was Swallow, laying clothes out to dry on the lavender bushes along one side of the cottage. Would she take him as a pupil?

He could feel his stomach trying to climb up his throat with nerves, and his mouth was dry. She looked him up and down, a question in her eyes, not moving to greet Rowan until the question had been answered.

"This is Flax, a singer for you to train," Rowan said, and he looked around as if to check whether anyone was listening.

She noticed, and then walked over to Rowan and kissed him. It were an act, put on for whoever were watching, Flax thought, and yet it weren't an act. She loved him. Had missed him. But she went through the motions of greeting her man with her eyes watchful and her mind alert.

As they passed through the door into the main room of the cottage—kitchen, eating and sitting room combined—Rowan whispered, "Ash sent him."

Swallow's steps halted for a moment, a tiny heartbeat while her hands tightened to white knuckles at her side, and then she loosened her fingers and kept going as if she hadn't heard.

"I'll take the horses round the back," he said, wanting to leave them to their hellos in private. "Best to get them out of sight."

"There's a shed," Swallow replied. Even in those few words, Flax could hear the flexibility and control of her voice. The muscles along her cheeks and jaw were strong, and she carried her shoulders well back, to keep her breath clear. She was aware of him assessing her and smiled, amused. "Get on with you," she said. "Do your tasks and come back here for food."

"Aye, my lady," he said, half mocking and half serious, and she took it as he intended, with a smile, so that he left the house with a jaunty step, feeling welcomed.

Over supper of cheese melted on toast with salted fish for flavor, Rowan told Swallow a carefully edited account of what had happened. It was hard to leave out the Deep and the River, but Flax realized that he—that all Traveler men—had lots of practice at it. Years. The story was disturbing enough, likewise that her son was about to raise the dead.

"Those songs are forbidden!" Swallow said, her voice sharp.

"For a reason," Rowan agreed mildly. "Time to set that reason aside when the need arises."

SAKER

SAKER RAN his hand through the stones in his pouch, feeling their familiar tingle and click.

He knew that casting the stones for himself was a fool's task, but he had nowhere else to turn for counsel. If only his father could talk! But although he could bring his father back, solid and real, he could not give him a voice.

Right now, he had several problems.

They knew what he looked like, and they would be searching for him.

His army needed weapons—and tools, particularly steel axes, to hack their way into the houses where the invaders cowered away from them.

The ghosts faded. That was his main problem.

He knew where to get the weapons he needed—Sendat, the warlord's fort. All reports said that Thegan had been stockpiling weapons and goods against a war with the Lake People. If the ghosts could take the fort, they would have all the weapons they needed.

But reports also said that Thegan had strengthened the town's defenses. It might take longer than a day or a night to storm the fort to defeat him. And if the ghosts faded in the middle of that—the siege could stretch on for days, months even, with his army attacking by day and the fortifications being rebuilt at night. He would win, eventually, but... each night he would be left defenseless, in the middle of the warlord's territory.

This whole great enterprise rested on his shoulders, and he must *not* let himself be killed. He told himself he wasn't afraid.

His first task was to make the ghosts perpetual. He did not need to cast the stones after all. The decision made him more cheerful. This was a matter of skill.

He tucked his pouch into his belt and sat with his back against the mill loft wall. He was tired of this hiding place. Tired of hiding. If he could just craft a spell to give the ghosts continuance...

Somehow the ghosts were tied to the sun's rhythms, but how? The only thing they were tied to was his blood.

The blood dried out... The ghosts faded exactly at sunset or sunrise. But blood... Was *that* tied to the sun; or to time?

He couldn't work out how.

As the day waned, he set himself to remember everything his teacher, Freite, had said about blood spells. To remember every time she had used one.

The memories were unpleasant, and made him shake. But he forced himself on, remembering day by day, night by night, every time Freite had raised that black stone knife and used his blood, or a cat's blood, or someone else's... those were the worst memories. One made him stagger outside to puke. He had puked back then, too, when he'd seen what she was doing to an old man she'd bought from a Wind Cities trader, a slave who couldn't work any more. The man wasn't even drugged, as they usually were, so his eyes were wide open, pleading with Saker to intervene. To save him. She put those eyes out with her bare hands, and when he vomited, she laughed at him, said he was weak.

"We are power itself, boy," she hissed. "Blood is breath, pain is strength, death is the wind in our sails."

"Other people's death," he muttered.

"Well, ours wouldn't be much use, would it!" She cuffed him on the back of the head so that his ears rang. "You remember, boy. Death is the wind in our sails."

Then she brought the knife down across the old man's throat, and he felt the surge of power go through her.

Was that what his ghosts needed? Other people's blood?

Saker was filled with excitement. Was it, could it be, that simple? There was always blood on the battlefield. If that was all, it would have worked already. There must be another ingredient...

He washed his mouth out and sat back down to sift through his memories once again. This time, he would control his gorge. And he would find the missing piece.

LEOF

THEY STARTED in Sendat, and that was easy. Leof simply sent messengers to the town to announce that Lord Thegan wanted all Travelers to report to the fort. He knew that the Travelers would assume that the warlord was putting restrictions on their movements, as had often happened in the past, that they would be forbidden to enter towns, for example, or forced to pay extra taxes. They would grumble among themselves, but they would come, and Alston would put them in the barn when they did, to wait for Thegan. The masons and carpenters who were working on the fortifications would join them. Minus their tools.

He had the harder job of collecting people from the outlying villages.

"Don't you worry, sir, it'll be just like requisitioning horses," Hodge said comfortably, as their squad rode down the hill from the fort. The first Travelers were walking up the road, and stood aside to let them pass, bowing and bobbing their heads in respect. Leof nodded his thanks to them and raised a hand in greeting to a family with a small boy who stared openly at the horses. The father, who had been moving to cuff the boy for disrespect, stared at Leof instead, doubt and gratitude warring on his face. It was curiously disturbing. What had he expected? Reprisal against the boy for staring? What treatment did these people get from warlords' men usually?

"People aren't horses, sergeants."

Hodge looked sceptical. "Some may as well be, sir."

Leof let it pass. They were facing a huge job. "I want scouts on messenger horses sent to the outlying villages to find our people," he said. "Then small squads—four men should be plenty—to go out and bring them in. They should bring their goods, too, and any food they have. No sense us feeding them if they can feed themselves."

Hodge nodded. "What if they won't come?"

"My lord Thegan is sure they will," Leof said, but he had private doubts. "I'll ride out with the first squad. There are reports of Travelers in Pigeonvale. We'll start there."

Pigeonvale was half an hour's ride away. The weather was threatening rain, and Leof wondered if they'd be able to get the hay in safely this year. There was never a good time to go to battle, but the weeks between spring sowing and the hay harvest were best—the oath men could concentrate on their duties instead of worrying about their families being left hungry over winter.

A mile out of the village, Hodge, who was riding at point, put up a hand to signal a stop where the road widened into a camping place near a stream. There was a small tent there next to the ashes of last night's fire, and a handcart, the kind Travelers often used.

"Gather them in, sergeant," Leof said.

Hodge nodded to one of the oath men and he dismounted and went over to the tent. He was a young one, green as grass, and only in this detail because he was good with horses. Scarf, they called him, because he always wore a brown scarf around his neck. The men joked that his mother had knitted it for him to keep her darling safe from fever, but he said it was a gift from his sweetheart. Leof smiled, remembering the look on his face as he'd said it—a mixture of pride and embarrassment.

Scarf called out, "Ho, Travelers!" in a voice meant to sound full and stern, but which came out squeaky with nerves. He flushed and bent down to the tent opening, shouting, "Out here now!" to cover his discomfiture.

Then he went still and turned, retching into the stream, vomit and tears mingling on his face. Leof jumped down from Thistle and strode to the tent. He didn't want to know what was in there, but had to.

Two bodies, a man and a woman, in their mid-years by the beginnings of gray in their hair. Stabbed, throats cut. A terrible smell from where their bowels had loosened as they died. The flies were all over their staring eyes. But nothing had been taken—all their meagre belongings were around them, cooking pots, tinderbox, food... This was murder, not banditry.

He felt a cold anger take him over, and motioned Hodge to come and look.

Turning away from the tent, the sergeant's face was unreadable, but he went over to Scarf and patted him on the shoulders. The man had stopped vomiting and was washing his face in the stream.

"Come," Leof said. "Let us talk to the people of Pigeonvale."

"We can't just leave them there." Scarf said, pointing to the tent.

Hodge looked at him pityingly. "Lad, they're dead. No harm's going to come to them now. We'll get a burial detail out here from the village."

Scarf climbed back on his horse with unsteady legs. The other men clustered around him, keen to find out what had been in the tent and telling them gave him back a little of his dignity.

"Ride on," Leof said.

Pigeonvale was shuttered and barricaded. They rode into the market square—an open space more dirt than grass, which barely deserved the name of square—and immediately people came flooding out of their houses, clamoring for help. There were only twenty or so—it was a small, poor village.

"My lord, my lord, are they coming, the ghosts?" a man called.

"We got rid of the Travelers, lord. The ghosts are a plot of those dark-haired bastards," a woman yelled.

Leof held up a hand for silence. "You got rid of the Travelers?"

"Aye, my lord," the woman said proudly. "When we heard from Lord Thegan's man that the ghosts were sparing Travelers, we killed them!"

"Stuck 'em like pigs," another man said. "They didn't even fight."

Leof felt ice travel through his veins. Thegan had seeded this. Deliberately. Knowing that murders would result. Used the information to get the rumors started so that Travelers would be under threat and come to the fort willingly. To save himself time, and trouble. And it would, the cold trained officer's part of his mind confirmed. It would make things much easier.

"My lord Thegan's man told you that?" he asked.

"Aye, my lord, one of his own officers."

"My lord Wil, it was," an older man said. "Him what comes from over Bonhill way."

"You did wrong," Leof said. "My lord does not wish Travelers killed." He was amazed that he could keep his voice steady. "Lord Thegan wishes all Travelers to come to the fort at Sendat, where they will be safe."

The older man grinned. "Ah, that's right. My lord Thegan wants to do the job himself, eh? Well, there's a few left. Cherry and her boys have shut themselves in and we couldn't get to them, and there's a farmhand over at Esher's place with a head as dark as night on him, though he swears he's one of us."

"Aye, and that woman down near Barleydale," a young woman said eagerly. "She's a red-head, but she's got dark eyes, and you know there's always Traveler blood with dark eyes. She's got two girls, too."

"Take a list down, sergeant," Leof said, and he rode away, no longer able to listen. He had studied old battles, old campaigns. Humans would sacrifice anyone, especially strangers, to save their own. Nothing more ruthless existed than a man—or woman—with children to protect and someone weak to kill.

And he knew, too, the fury that rose against the victim precisely because he was weak. Leof had felt it himself, in battle, when an enemy couldn't protect himself. When fighting turned to slaughter anger filled you, made you implacable, as though the enemy's weakness was an insult. He had never understood that, but he had felt it, and now he recognized it in the eyes of these people. They hated the Travelers even more than they had yesterday, because they had been easy to kill.

"Cherry and her boys" turned out to be the local candlemaker, living in a respectable house on the outskirts of the village. The house, like all the others, was shuttered and barred.

Hodge banged on the door and shouted, "Warlord's men, mistress! Here to take you and your boys to safety at the warlord's fort."

There was a scuffling behind the door and then a woman's voice: "Why would the warlord protect *us*?"

A good question, Leof thought bleakly.

"You pay your taxes, don't you?" Hodge asked. "Warlords don't like people who pay taxes being killed off."

Leof frowned at that, but the cynicism of the answer was reassuring to the woman, and she opened the door slowly, her three boys craning to see from behind her.

"Gather up whatever food you've got, and some blankets and clothes, too," Hodge said. "We won't wait long."

His impatience also reassured her. She nodded and vanished into the house, calling out instructions to the boys, and reappeared a few minutes later with bundles and bags, while the eldest boy, about twelve years, trundled a handcart around from the back yard where the candles were made. The handcart had a couple of dozen candles in the bottom, and the woman looked shyly up at Leof.

"It may be the lady would like some extra candles?" she asked.

He smiled warmly at her. "I'm sure she would, with so many people coming to the fort. That was well thought of."

Cherry bobbed her head and dumped the food and blankets on top of the candles, more cheerful now she felt that she wasn't going empty-handed. That she could prove her respectability.

Leof suspected that the respectable and the not-so-respectable would be lumped together in Thegan's mind. "Let's go, sergeant," he said, and they rode off to "near Barleyvale" where the red-headed woman lived with her family.

It went on like that all day.

They came across the remnants of other massacres: a family of four cut down on the road and left on the verge for the crows; an old man garotted in a parody of a warlord's execution, and hung up from a tree as the warlord hung criminals in the gibbet; a house that had been fired and still stank of burnt meat. Scarf puked each time, and Leof found himself feeling grateful to the boy for expressing simple human revulsion, as he could not, being the officer.

He had to remain in control of himself, although his anger rose higher as the day went on and they heard more reports about "my lord's officer" spreading the news about the ghosts sparing Traveler lives.

His own messengers did their job thoroughly. By the end of the day as soon as they rode into a town the inhabitants were ready, either with a group of stony-faced Travelers surrounded by guards with pitchforks and scythes, or with directions to where the "black-haired bastards" had barricaded themselves in. At least the messengers had stopped the slaughter. But across the Domain, Leof estimated, hundreds would have been killed.

They turned for home at noon with a band of about sixty Travelers, a mixture of small families and singles, most with handcarts or backpacks full of food and clothing.

"To Sendat, sergeant," Leof ordered, and he rode at the back of the group so the dust from Thistle's hooves wouldn't get in their eyes. It was a long boring ride, and it gave him far too much time to think about Thegan, and Wil, and what was going to happen to the Travelers when they reached the fort.

But what could he do? There was nowhere else to take them, and they were definitely not safe where they were. At least in the fort they had a chance. He lashed himself with blame. He should have killed the enchanter when he had the chance, before Thegan's troops arrived in Bonhill, when it was just him and the enchanter up on the hill. If he had borrowed a bow from the town, he could have shot him without even the wind wraiths being alerted. If he had been quicker in the farmyard he could have slit his throat before the wraiths rescued him.

Unbidden, the image of Sorn's face rose in his mind, smiling at him, and he felt comforted. She would not blame him, and she would tell him not to blame himself. But although he kept his face calm, as befitted an officer, he felt that he wanted to ride home crying like a baby.

They arrived back at Sendat late, in the dark, long after the evening meal. Leof left the settling of the Travelers in the barn to Alston and Hodge, and went straight to Thegan's workroom.

"Leof," Thegan greeted him. "Good. How many did you bring in?"

"Sixty-two," Leof said, walking into the warlord's workroom. He stood looking straight at Thegan, unsure what to say. "There were massacres," he managed finally. "Murders. All over the Domain."

Thegan nodded. "Yes."

That was all. But it wasn't enough.

"Wil spread the news about the ghosts protecting Travelers."

Thegan was looking at him strangely, a small smile curling the corners of his mouth. "On my orders," he confirmed, and he sat back in his chair, waiting for Leof's response.

"Why, my lord?"

"Difficult times call for difficult measures," he said. "Of course it would be better if we didn't have to take this action. On the other hand, the Travelers have always been a weakness in the Domain's defense. And in the future, they would have been a weakness in the defense of Actonsland."

Actonsland. The united country Thegan was trying to create. With him as its overlord. He was still planning for the long term—and wasn't that what you wanted in a warlord? Someone who thought ahead, who took pains to ensure the future of his people?

"You think they would join the enchanter?" Leof asked, feeling deflated. Thegan was as logical as always.

"Of course they will, as soon as they understand what he's trying to do. The young men, at the very least. The hot heads. The kind who end up in the gibbet."

He smiled, not the miraculous smile, nor the one that invited you to join his select group of friends, but a kind smile, the sort of smile Leof might have given Scarf.

Leof was so tired that he couldn't think properly.

"You did your duty," Thegan said, absently, as he looked back at the map spread out on his table. "Now go and eat, and rest. There will be more to do tomorrow."

Leof was almost persuaded that Thegan had done what he had to do—the right thing, the reasonable thing—and then he walked back into the hall, looking for food, as he had been ordered, and saw Sorn.

She was standing at the door to the kitchen, her little dog Fortune hiding in her skirts as he always did. She was discussing something with the cook. She looked up and he was shocked by how drawn her face looked, how pale. Her eyes were desperate.

He went towards her without thinking, but halfway across the room he realized how fast he was walking, and slowed so that the men and serving girls gathered around the tables wouldn't notice. He had been ordered to get food. He was following orders, he told himself. But his heart was beating uncomfortably fast and he was angry at whatever, whoever, had put that fear into her eyes.

"My lady," he said, and bowed, as etiquette demanded.

She bowed back, eyes down. "My lord Leof." She looked up to the cook. "My lord is hungry. Get him food."

"Yes, my lady," the man said, and he raced back to the kitchen, leaving them, for the moment, in a pocket of silence.

"Are you all right?" he asked. It was breaking their rule of never saying anything personal in public, but he had to know what had brought that look of grief, of anger, he wasn't sure what it was.

"Is it true?" she asked in a low voice. "Is it true that my lord sent Wil out to spread a rumor that the ghosts protect Travelers?"

"Not a rumor. The truth."

She looked up sharply and met his eyes. "And that makes it all right? To connive at the murder of innocents?"

It was as though she had turned a picture the right side up, so that he could see it all clearly, recognize his lord's scheme for what it was. "No," he replied. "That does not make it all right. But for now, the Travelers are safer here."

"We must make sure they stay safe," she said, low and insistent.

He nodded.

They stood, quietly, until the cook returned with a tray of food, pretending to the world, even to each other, that they had not just committed themselves to treachery—he against his sworn lord, she against her husband.

BRAMBLE

WHEN THEY woke, the world had changed around them. Instead of a small cave in a long passage, they were in one of the huge caverns, water dripping from the walls, pillars of rock forming on roof and floor, the friendly little lozenge of light nowhere to be seen. Next to them, a dark river flowed silently, its quiet ripples threatening in the flickering candlelight. It disappeared between a high, thin crack in the wall.

On the river's banks were strange shapes in rock: a huge bird, wings outspread, a winter tree, perfect but only as high as Bramble's chest, an old woman hunched over a fire. Others looked more monstrous, like water sprites or wild boars, tusks shining. The sound of water trickling, slapping gently at its banks, echoed constantly.

"The Weeping Caverns," Medric said, glancing from one rock form to the next with a hint of panic in his voice. "They never let you out."

"Fear weakens you, lad," Acton said. "Breathe deep."

Medric didn't understand the words, but the smile that went with them heartened him and he put his shoulders back and nodded. Acton nodded approval at him, and he swelled with pride.

Men! Bramble thought. They just lined up to worship him. "This isn't the one we were in before," she said firmly. "We haven't been brought back to where we were."

"How can you know?" Baluch asked, curiously. "We could be in a different part of the same cavern."

Bramble shook her head stubbornly. "No. That cavern ran north and south. This one runs east and west." She repeated it in the old language, for Acton.

Medric didn't believe her, but the others did.

"Can you tell where we are?" Ash asked.

"South of where we were, I think." She concentrated. "The mine entrance is far behind us. The White River may be close. It comes out of these caves." She paused. "I am getting tired of being thrown around in time and space at the whim of the gods." She turned in to the cavern, her hand on one of the cold, slippery rock pillars, and shouted, "Tell us what you want!" Acton came to stand beside her. Even as a ghost, he was a reassuring presence.

Just as when she had asked for help from the Lake, something came.

Along the river bank, shapes stirred. Not every one—not the water sprite, but the boar, not the tree, but the woman. They moved, but they moved silently. The figures straightened and turned towards them in unison, blind rock eyes seeming to focus.

Bramble stood still, but Medric and Ash and Baluch all moved towards her until they were standing in a tight group. Acton walked forward to meet the shapes. The old woman, the boar, a weasel, sinuous even in rock, a fox, brush held high, an ox.

The boar stopped in front of Acton, but the others moved around him with the same unstoppable force as delvers had. The woman stood a little way from Bramble, mouth in a smirk. The weasel faced Ash, the fox, Baluch, the ox lumbered around to the back of the group to confront Medric.

Bramble moved forward a little, until she was face to face with the figure of the old woman. She held up her candle so that she could see the woman's face. It was no one she had ever seen, in her life or in Acton's. The kind of face a doll maker would carve for an evil-old-woman puppet—nothing but wrinkles and spite lines.

Acton's head flicked around, and he grinned at her, and then at Baluch. She smiled back, feeling the familiar rush of pleasure and excitement that danger brought.

The old woman raised a finger, as if reproving her. Her face writhed, and Bramble couldn't tell if the stone really shifted and warped, or whether it was simply the flicker from the candle.

Behind her, Ash cleared his throat, the first sound any of them had made since the shapes moved.

"Wild!" the old woman hissed immediately. "Ungrateful, undutiful, unwomanly! Not fit for anyone. The unloved daughter. The unwanted one."

Bramble flinched. Her voice was like the voice of the dead, rock grating on rock, but lighter, with changing tones like water falling. Behind her, she could hear the other figures speaking, and in front, the boar was roaring at Acton in his own language: "Murderer! Despoiler!"

The ox lowed accusations at Medric: "Coward, unwanted son! Sold for garbage. Unmanly, weak!"

She was glad that the weasel spoke quietly, and she couldn't hear what Ash was hearing. But her anger was building, because she knew that Medric, in particular, would be vulnerable to this kind of attack.

"Be quiet!" Ash's voice cut through with the resonance of power, and they were silent immediately.

"Oh, let them speak!" Acton said. "Words can't hurt us."

The others stared at him. Bramble saw that Medric had tears on his cheeks and Ash and Baluch both looked shaken. Acton had his solemn face on, the one that so often preceded some explosive physical action. Like smashing the rocks to splinters.

Then the old woman put out a hand and placed it heavily on Bramble's shoulder. She tried to move away, but her feet were stuck. She looked down: the bottoms of her boots were encased in rock, and the rock was spreading. She glanced at the others. The figures in front were touching each of them now, and the stone was slowly growing up their legs. They were being trapped.

The boar put a foot on Acton's, who promptly kicked it hard, unbalancing it and sending it crashing onto its side.

Acton came to Bramble's side, but waited to see what she would do. She glared at the woman. "What do you want?" she asked.

"Speak," Ash said reluctantly.

"These are the Weeping Caverns. None but the worthy leave here. And you, girl, are empty inside," the woman said. "You are the less loved, less wanted, carrying death with her like a plague! You betray the ones who trust you. You allow your loved ones to die like beasts!"

Bramble's earlier exhilaration drained away, but she was not the young girl who had left her family knowing she would not be missed. She thought of the hunter, and of Acton, and of Maryrose, who was waiting for her on the other side of death. And of the roan, dead because she had been afraid, just once, and let fear rule her. She wasn't going to do that again. Acton was right. These were just words.

"Yes," she said. "That's right. That's me."

Shocked, the woman moved back. As soon as she lifted her hand away from Bramble's shoulder, she froze back into rock. The stone around Bramble's boots melted into a watery slurry. She kicked it off and turned to face the others. "It's all true," she said. "Everything they say to us is true. You might as well accept it."

Baluch immediately spoke to the fox, which held his tunic in its jaws. "True," he said. "All true." The fox moved away and froze in position, its paw raised, its brush low.

Medric's shoulders were hunched and he was swaying his head from side to side, like a horse with the weaves. She went to him, ignoring the ox, whose heavy hoof was pinning Medric's foot down. Acton followed her and shoved the ox aside, despite its great weight. But the stone continued growing over Medric's feet.

"The worst of us is not the best of us," she said gently. "You can be everything they say, and still be worthy, because of what else you are." He stared at the ox as if he hadn't heard her. "Would Fursey have loved you if you weren't worthy?" she asked. "Would I have trusted you? Would you have bothered to help me? So your father didn't want you! What does that matter now?"

The ox spoke at the same time, "Coward! Weak! Always fearful!"

She stared at Medric, rubbing his shoulder, urging him to understand. Acton smiled at him and Medric blinked, turning his head to stare at Bramble for the first time.

He seemed to take something from her—not strength, something more like love.

Slowly, he turned towards the ox. "Yes," he said heavily. "I am."

The ox fell silent.

Ash understood, but Bramble could see that he found it hard to say the words. He managed, eventually, to concede whatever the weasel had said to him, but the weasel snapped, "Liar!" back at him and he flinched.

"Remember," Acton said to him, "we are all guilty of something." Ash stared at them.

Bramble felt her store of compassion, usually reserved for poddy calves and sick rabbits, rise like yeast. She smiled at him, like the big sister she felt she was to him. "I've been many people now, Ash, and I can tell you—we all fear the same things."

He stared at her, uncomprehending. The weasel was whispering, too quiet for her to hear, but Ash bit his lip.

"All of us," she said. "We fear being unwanted, alone, unloved. We fear the death of those we love. We fear that no one will miss us when we're gone."

She thought of all the eyes she had looked through: Ragni, old and facing her own death stoically, but distraught at the death of Asa; Piper of Turvite, fearing for her children, mourning Salmon; Baluch, hating himself for killing children but following Acton anywhere; Wili, letting Edwa kill herself because she understood the fear of being discovered as they were, used and degraded, worthless... Warmth overtook her and she hugged Ash, ignoring the weasel as though it were not there. "Come on, Ash. We need you."

"Worthless..." the weasel hissed.

The word was the same in both languages, as words sometimes were, so Acton understood. "This one? Worthless? Hah!" he said, evading the boar again as he spoke.

Ash blinked and turned to Baluch. "I can't hear her," he said.

"No," Baluch said, smiling with reassurance. "She lets you fight your own battles." He clapped Ash on the shoulder and perhaps that was what he needed, a physical shock, or perhaps it was the right reassurance.

Ash stared at the weasel. "I have been unloved," he said. "I have been useless. But not now."

"Truth at last," the weasel sneered, but it moved away and stiffened into rock.

The boar was shouting at Acton and trying to catch his tunic with a tusk.

"Oh, just talk to it!" Bramble said. "Or we'll never get out of here."

He gave her the sideways smile, but he obediently spoke to the boar: "Yes, yes, I am a killer, I am an invader. Those aren't secrets."

The boar stopped and froze in place. Bramble wished she felt better about it—Acton's tone had been so off-hand, so casual, as though the accusations hadn't bothered him at all.

But something else was disturbing her. All these things...had been alive once. She faced the old woman. "You're dead. Why haven't you gone on to rebirth?"

"Speak," Ash said. His voice was stronger, as if he were regaining confidence. The blind rock face stirred but only the mouth moved. "None are reborn from the Weeping Caverns," she said, and the eyes came alive, too, to stare despairingly at her. "None."

"I don't believe that," Bramble said. "It can't be true. The gods wouldn't allow it."

"The gods are young and this is not their realm, girl." She took a step towards Bramble. "Stone is ruler here."

"Not just stone," Baluch said from behind her. "Water, too."

"We can't leave them here," Bramble said.

"We'd never get them out," Baluch replied, assessing the size and weight of the rocks.

"None shall leave," the old woman said.

"The turns are turned!" the fox echoed.

"There is no way." The weasel rose up on his hind legs and giggled. Ash reached out and pushed it off balance so that it fell with a crash to the floor and lay there, panting and glaring.

"Then we will make a way," Acton said.

"Acton," Baluch said, "what are you thinking?"

"I am thinking stone can be broken." He came to Bramble. "How close are we to the surface?"

She extended that part of her mind that told her where she was, and figured it.

"Not far, I think." She pointed east. "That's the way we were going before the cave changed around us."

"If we can find a way out, perhaps our miner here can show us how to widen it enough to let these poor creatures out."

"That might work," Bramble said, "but not if the spell that holds them won't let them walk. They're too heavy to carry."

"But we have an enchanter," Acton said, looking at Ash. "Can you not find a way to bring them to the light?"

Ash looked at the old woman, his face full of pity. "Stone is no match for water."

He looked up. "Let them go, and the Caverns will be safe." His voice echoed in the dark around them, full of warning.

"Wait," said Acton, and he turned to the woman. "Who tasked you?"

"Dotta, daughter of fire," she said in his own language. "None shall leave but the worthy."

"Dotta," he repeated, the grating voice slow and considering.

"She was protecting you, Acton," Bramble said. "She knew I'd come back for your bones, and I think she was making sure no one too arrogant to accept their shortcomings would steal them first. But Dotta wouldn't have stopped spirits going on to rebirth."

The old woman spread her hands and shrugged with one shoulder, like a fishwife bargaining in the marketplace. "That is the Caverns. It has always been so. We have no power over it."

"Then it is time to end the Caverns," Ash said. Baluch came to stand beside him, to link arms. Acton watched him go with a curious look on his face, as though realizing for the first time that Baluch had had a life—a long life—which had changed him in ways Acton didn't understand.

The old woman stared at Ash as though not understanding, and slowly the other figures stirred into life and ranked themselves behind her—not just the animals, but all the other figures, human and otherwise, which had lined the bank of the river.

They did not threaten. They did not speak. But Bramble saw a kind of hope in their blank eyes and slack muscles, as though they had been tasked for too long. Then Ash looked at Baluch and together they closed their eyes and sounded a single low note, their voices matching like one voice.

Bramble had no idea what was happening, but "water," Ash had said, so she moved away from the river, up to a promontory of rock that stood high. Medric and Acton followed her, but Ash and Baluch stayed still, standing in front of the stone figures, hands splayed, eyes closed, humming and singing without words.

The river began to sing in tune with them.

FLAX

THE WARLORD'S men came beating a gong that set every horse in Baluchston whinnying.

Flax ran out to calm the horses and went to the gate instead, to watch them going by on the main road—a party of messengers, just three of them.

Rowan and Swallow appeared at his shoulder.

"I'll start packing," Swallow said.

Rowan nodded. "Saddle up, boy," he said. A few moments was all it took and then they were ready, leaving the cottage tidy.

"When will my cousin be back?" Swallow asked.

"He was on foot," Rowan answered absently, head cocked, still listening to the now distant gong. "It will take him a few more days."

"Then we'll take all the bread," she said, darting back to collect it and stow it in her pack.

They led the horses by back paths, paths that Rowan knew well, it seemed; and they paused in a coppice of beech trees just outside town. There was no need to discuss why they were running. When warlords' men came beating gongs, Travelers made themselves scarce.

"Those were Thegan's men," Rowan said. "We should avoid Sendat."

Swallow nodded. "We could cut across the plains. It's a long way on foot . . ."

"Down river to Carlion and then to Turvite by boat?" Rowan mused.

In the end, they decided to cut across the Domain, avoiding towns, until they reached South Domain.

Swallow wasn't a rider and didn't intend to become one, so Flax tied their packs onto Mud and they all walked.

"It's a change, not carrying anything," Swallow said. "It makes me feel light. Now, Flax, tell me what you know about melody."

It was an inquisition. Swallow questioned him about every aspect of music, made him demonstrate breathing, projection, scales...He was woefully ignorant of the theory, but he could see that she liked his actual singing.

"Your breathing is shoddy," she said. "You could get much more power with proper control."

She waited to see his response, but he knew that look; his mam had used it on him often enough. He knew how to be humble when it counted.

"Will you teach me?" he asked, which was, after all, all he wanted to know.

She sniffed a little and settled back into walking. "We'll see," she said. But the look she exchanged with Rowan was amused and pleased, and he knew the answer was "yes."

This was plains country, a mixture of pasture and cropping, wheat, sheep and goats, some orchards. The dairies which leant against every barn were for ewes and nannies; cheesemaking was a major occupation. In this kind of country Travelers were regarded with great suspicion, and there were few officers' manors where musicians could find work.

"I've got silver," Swallow said. "We can buy what we need, if they'll sell it to us." They had stopped outside a small town to discuss food.

"Lucky at dice again?" Rowan said quizzically, and Swallow blushed a little.

"Aren't I always?"

"Better if I buy," Flax said. He got out a comb and slicked his hair back into a small ponytail. It was just long enough—Zel would have been at him this last week to get it cut, he thought. He groomed Cam until she shone and her tail was free of burrs and straw, then pulled out his good blue jacket and buffed his boots to a shine.

"That'll have to do," he said. "Do I look the part?"

He mounted and put on a haughty air, as an officer's son might, or the child of a wealthy merchant.

Swallow looked amused, but disapproving. "You could mimic an ape from the Wind Cities, I'm thinking," she said. He grinned and made ape noises at her, and she flapped her hands at him, then tossed him a purse. "Traveling food," she said. "But don't make it too obvious."

"I'll meet you on the other side of the village," he said.

The township was larger than a village. It had three shops: one for chandlery and farm goods, a butcher's and a store that sold everything else.

He tossed Cam's reins to a boy along with a copper. "Give her some water," he ordered, then walked in without looking to see if he'd been obeyed. Assume they'll obey and they will, he told himself, his heart thumping irregularly and his palms wet.

The shopkeeper hastened to serve him, and he bought all they needed without trouble. He even made a joke about young men with big appetites, and winked at the man's daughter, although she was squint-eyed and on the wrong side of thirty.

Cam was waiting at the horse trough, well-watered, and he tossed the boy another copper as he mounted and rode off south, feeling as though an arrow would hit him in the small of the back at any moment, or another axe would come singing out of thin air to take him down. But he made it away without incident and he went on down the hedge-lined track feeling very pleased with himself.

A half-mile went past before he began to get worried. There was no sign of Swallow or Rowan. There were hoof prints, and he recognized the worn shoe on Mud's off fore, where he pecked at the ground when he got bored; so they had come this way. But then he came to a widening of the road, a place where Mud's prints were scuffed over by other horses', several of them, it looked like, and riding horses, not the big half-moons that would have meant draught animals. There were droppings to the side as though the other horses had waited there for a while. But Cam wasn't reacting, which meant they were gone now, not hiding in the bushes and lying in wait, as his imagination feared.

Horses probably meant warlord's men.

Run, came Zel's voice in his head, but he couldn't do that. Ash wouldn't do that.

He sat down in the saddle carefully so that Cam stepped out gently, slowly, at a pace where Flax could listen for other horses up ahead. Then he thought that Cam would hear them long before he would, so he quickened her a little and watched her ears, ready for when they pricked forward, hoping he could stop her whinnying a greeting in the moment afterwards.

He puzzled out the tracks as he went. There were four horses, he thought, and perhaps a dozen people on foot. Some of the footprints looked like children's. They wouldn't be moving very fast, so he slowed down, then dismounted. They couldn't possibly be far ahead of him, not on foot. He hadn't been that long in the village.

As he neared a bend in the track, at a place where the road dipped into a hollow, he saw Cam's ears prick and her nostrils flare as she took in air to neigh. He lunged forward and pinched her nostrils closed, almost falling over her hooves.

"Shh, shh, sweetheart," he said, and although she rolled her eyes at him as though he'd gone mad, she snuffled out the air she'd taken in and let him lead her back the track a ways, until he could tether her between a hedge bright with unripe blackberries and a hayrick. She pulled contentedly at the loose strands of hay sticking out of the rick, as Flax ran back along the grass by the track, trying to be as silent as possible. He crept up to the bend and peered around, keeping low to the ground.

Warlord's men. Four, on horseback. Thegan's, again, like the ones in Baluchston. This was still Central Domain, and they held sway here. And with them—a group of Travelers, he thought, although one family had red-haired children and looked too prosperous, too fat, to be on the Road. They had stopped and were drinking from the stream which crossed the path in this hollow. He spotted Swallow and Rowan, who was still leading Mud. The warlord's men were lounging around, trading jokes with each other, and weren't threatening anyone. The sergeant was a big hairy man with red-gold stubble beginning to show on his face—the kind of man who had to shave twice a day to look smart. He was the only one who bothered to watch the Travelers, and even he did it lazily, as though he were sure they wouldn't run off.

Flax had no idea what was going on. He wished Zel were here—the burden of making decisions was heavier than he'd expected.

Rowan looked around at intervals, seeming casual, but Flax realized he was looking for him. He didn't want to make any movement so he stared directly at Rowan, concentrating on him. If you looked long enough, somehow people sensed you. Sure enough, after a moment Rowan looked in his direction, rubbing the back of his neck as though it prickled.

His gaze met Flax's and immediately he flicked a quick glance at the warlord's men. That told Flax what he wanted to know—this was not some nice picnic by the stream. They were prisoners, no matter what it looked like. Rowan tilted his head fractionally to signal, "Get away." Flax nodded, and wriggled backwards from his vantage point until he could stand up and run back to Cam.

Not that he was running away. His blood fizzed with excitement. Those warlord's men were sloppy, not expecting any trouble from mere Travelers. It wouldn't be hard to spirit Rowan and Swallow away from them. Mud would be harder. He considered that. He wondered how many of Thegan's horses his father had trained, and grinned. It only needed a few. Horses were herd animals. Where some of the herd went, the others would follow.

But he would have to wait until dark.

As the afternoon drew on, Flax became certain the warlord's men were taking Rowan and Swallow and the other Travelers to Sendat.

Why were they going with the warlord's men so willingly? Flax had grown up on stories of Travelers escaping from persecution by the skin of their teeth and their willingness to do anything to save their children: hide in cesspits, share caves with sleeping bears, even crouch in streams despite fear of water wraiths. But these people were just following along.

He had no idea why, and it disturbed him.

He trailed behind them just far enough so that Cam wouldn't try to join the other horses. He could follow their tracks, and when he came to a fork in the road it was easy to see which way they had gone. After that he relaxed a little.

By evening, they had turned on to the main road from Baluchston to Sendat. Flax blessed the lengthening shadows, and the fact that fear of the ghosts was keeping everyone close to home. There was no other traffic, which meant he was safe, as long as he kept well back from the warlord's party.

The sergeant called a halt at a broad meadow leading down to a small spring-fed mere. Flax tied Cam up on the other side of the coppice that edged the camp site, and made his way silently through the trees to spy. He watched the warlord's men organize the camp, giving a couple of the men shovels to dig privies in the coppice, getting the children to gather kindling for the fire, telling the women to get on with the shared task of cooking.

It was better not to make contact with anyone but Rowan or Swallow. That was his mother in him, he thought; she had never trusted anyone, and it had annoyed him. But this was the time for mistrust, and secrecy, and pretence, and all those other things she had practiced in order to be accepted in Pless. Shame she never lived to see his father a town councillor. She'd wanted it so badly. Part of him knew it was that desire which had pushed her to attack him, but the thing was, he didn't remember it. She had drugged his cha, Zel said, and tried to smother him, but he was asleep and so it all seemed more like a story than reality. He believed Zel—believed she had no choice, or thought she had none. But he couldn't really imagine his mother killing him, and so he struggled to think of her with any anger or resentment. He wondered if that made him weak. What would Ash think?

The image of Ash in his mind smiled at him, and he was reassured. Aye, Ash'd choose pity over anger any day, he reckoned. So. It may be that Ash wouldn't choose to kill the warlord's men, either. He wished Ash were here.

When it was full dark, he pissed against a tree to make sure he wouldn't need to go later, then slowly made his way towards the camp. One of the guards was on watch, of course, but he was lying back, looking at the stars instead of the road. With any luck he was actually asleep. Then Flax realized that the man was lying on his front, not his back, and he was crying, trying to keep quiet by muffling the sobs in his sleeve. Flax's heart contracted. It was the young one, the one with the brown scarf at his throat. He wondered what a soldier had to cry about.

He knew where Rowan and Swallow were sleeping—near the edge of the trees, well-positioned for slipping away. No fools, them. But the horses were on the other side of the camp, the Sendat side. Was it better to go quietly off on foot, and lose Mud? Again he was racked with indecision. If they were on foot, the warlord's men would hunt them down easily. It was the memory of dogs baying on his trail, back in Golden Valley, that decided him. He never wanted to hear that sound again.

So instead of waking Rowan, he slipped across the road and made his way behind the bordering hedge to where the horses were tethered, then crossed back over and slid silently among them. His heart pounded the whole way and he was sweating. The horses didn't mind. They whuffled and sniffed at him. He was counting on the warlord's horses being accustomed to having many different people look after them, and he was right. They didn't treat him as a stranger. Mud shouldered others out of the way to get to him, nickering gently.

Flax froze, but there was no sound from the soldiers. Horses do make noises at night. 'Course they do.

"Shh, shh, there," he murmured, patting Mud on his side and gathering all the leading reins up, pulling the tethers off their pegs until he had all five animals on a rein. He collected a couple of saddles and slid them onto Mud's back, looping up the girths so they didn't trail. Mud shook his head but didn't try to dislodge them. They were the small, flat saddles the good riders used, so they weren't a burden to him.

Gently, quietly, he whistled the "follow me" signal his father had taught all his animals. Mud and two others pricked up their ears at the sound, and gladly fell in behind him. The others came along, as he had thought they would.

He led them further down the track and tied them to a gatepost. The "wait" whistle was long and soothing, and even the two horses who didn't know it seemed to settle when he tried it on them. Then, trying to move like Ash did in the dark, like a shadow himself, he crept back to where he had tethered Cam.

This was the big problem.

He could move silently, but Cam was much too big and heavy footed to pass the camp in silence.

He saddled her up and took her in a wide circle, thankful for the crescent moon as it showed itself above the hills as he threaded his way through the first field, trying not to damage too much—or leave a trail that could be easily followed.

Cam seemed to enjoy the ramble, walking quite confidently across the shadowy fields. He brought her back to the road well down from the other horses, then tethered her and began to run back the way he had come. Time was passing too fast. The moon had climbed from the horizon already, seeming to shrink as she swam higher, becoming colder and less welcome.

Flax threaded through the trees again as quietly as he could, to where Rowan and Swallow were lying.

He reached out and touched Rowan's shoulder. Immediately, they got up, slid their packs on and followed him behind the hedge and down the road to the horses; only then did they make a noise.

Rowan gasped as the big shapes loomed up in the darkness, but Swallow hissed. "Are you mad?" she demanded. "Horse stealing's a killing offence!"

"We're not stealing theirs!" Flax said, shocked. "I'm not stupid. We're just leaving them here so they can't come after us easily. Although, if we took just one, we'd each have a mount..."

Swallow considered it. "They're telling us they're here to protect us from massacres but it doesn't mean they won't stage one of their own when it suits them. No warlord ever cared about Travelers and none ever will." Her voice was bitter.

Rowan touched her arm. "Come, we must go."

Fumbling in the dark, Flax saddled Mud and a steady black cob he'd marked out during the day as the most sensible of the others. Then he helped Swallow and Rowan to mount, and they headed off towards Sendat.

"The one way they won't expect us to go," Rowan said. "We can turn off to the right before Garvay, I'm pretty sure."

"It's a long time since we walked those roads," Swallow said, and Flax couldn't tell if she were doubtful or nostalgic.

Rowan smiled at his wife reassuringly, "The road is long..."

Flax clicked his tongue to Mud and they moved off, the other horses trying to come with them at first and then settling, complaining, when their tethers held.

Under the cold moon, the Road looked very long.

"If we're lucky," Flax said to himself.

LEOF

THE SQUADS went out the next day, but Thegan kept Leof back at the fort, organizing the Travelers into work groups.

"We might as well get some use out of them," he said over breakfast. "They'll be working for their own defense, after all."

When Leof went out to the big barn he was surprised at how much at home their guests had made themselves: cooking fires in a row outside, privies off behind the barn, each family's area marked off with rope. Alston had been very busy, it was clear.

The Travelers crowded towards Leof, and Alston motioned them back to give him room to speak. "As you know," he began, "we are fortifying against the enchanter's ghosts. You will be staying here until the menace is gone and there is no more reason for you to be afraid. That means that the fort's defenses are your defenses, and we would like your help in the work."

Some nodded, some looked sceptical; they probably thought Thegan had organized this to save himself the cost of a workforce. Well, let them. It would stop them from thinking darker thoughts.

Each of the masons and carpenters was assigned helpers from the mob in the barn.

"Keep them together with their own people, if you can," Leof told Alston. "The dry-stone waller, that big man from up north who is working on the rampart—give him a group of ten or so. Most of his time is being spent carrying the stones."

Alston nodded, but hesitated before he moved away. "My lord...I wanted to thank you. Faina and I, we wanted to thank you."

"For what?"

"The house..."

He had no idea what the man was talking about, and he didn't have time to find out now. A house in the town, married quarters? Probably something Sorn had organized. "I don't know anything about a house," he said. "Get to work."

As though the words had been a secret message, Alston grinned. "Of course, my lord. Of course!"

With an extra sixty people, the fort reminded Leof of home during a campaign against the Ice King's people. Cliffhold had been like this: always ringing with hammer blows from the smithy, horses whinnying to each other in the muster yards, the oath men drilling to their sergeants' shouts, children running, screaming, laughing. As he approached to inspect the fortification, he noticed there were lots of children today, most of them dark-haired, which was curiously disconcerting.

The waller—what was his name…? Oak, that was it—didn't look pleased when Alston spoke to him, but then he hadn't looked pleased for weeks. He looked exhausted, in fact. The work near the gate was almost finished but Leof felt he had been remiss in not giving the man help earlier.

On his way back he saw Sorn and her maid Faina gathering the children into the barn. Probably lesson time, he thought, and wondered how many of these children had any schooling. Well, he knew Sorn would sort it out. Some of these Travelers were perhaps even better off for staying at the fort for a time. Maybe.

It was a curious pleasure to watch her while she was unaware of him. She would be a lovely mother, he thought, seeing her cradle a toddler in her arms, smiling at him and tickling him under his arm. *If Thegan can't sire children, she'll never be a mother*. The thought slid treacherously under his guard, and he turned abruptly and headed for the smiths. They needed boar spears. Lots of them. Pin the bastard ghosts to the ground and see them fight then!

That evening Thegan and Leof spent an hour working out the details for the fortifications, provisioning, guard duties, night soil collection and the common meals. Sorn joined them for that part of the planning, and Leof marvelled again at her quiet competence. She seemed to have anticipated all of Thegan's questions, and found solutions to problems they had not imagined, like how to wash the babies' loincloths. She smiled a little at their blank faces.

"We're not accustomed to worrying about children on a battlefield," Leof said.

"Let us pray we never have to," Sorn replied, and it was a true prayer; he could hear it in her voice.

Thegan was oblivious to it, simply pleased with their combined efficiency. "Good. Good. Put all this in action."

A messenger knocked at the door and Thegan called him inside.

"Baluchston is refusing to give up its Travelers," he said. "Tomorrow go and get them. I've sent messengers warning them of your coming. If they will not surrender them, you will bring the town council back here to me."

That was all. Thegan turned immediately to Gard, who was waiting with a list of supplies commandeered from the various towns where they had collected Travelers. Thegan nodded dismissal to them both, and they rose together and walked back into the hall, which was silent and empty now that the meal was over and the cleaning done.

Leof could think of nothing to say that would be safe, so he bowed and left without a word, casting a quick glance at Sorn's face. But he could read nothing there except her normal serenity, which he knew now was a sham. She was so beautiful.

That beauty tightened his chest into an insistent pain, so that he had to stop outside the hall doors to breathe and compose himself before attending to the next task.

Baluchston was not—yet—part of Central Domain. Except in Thegan's eyes, apparently. Leof wanted Alston for this, not Hodge. Someone he could count on to do the gods' will.

He tried not to think about what that might be.

Leof checked the saddlebags his groom, Bandy, had packed for him. Never trust anyone with the necessities of life, his father had taught him, and it was just as well, because Bandy had forgotten parchment and inkstone for sending messages.

He came with many apologies and rechecked everything himself, worried that Leof would leave him behind.

"Come on then," Leof said. "Mount up."

They set out very early, Leof riding a horse from the common herd, a bay gelding with two white socks. There was no way he'd risk Arrow or Thistle near the Lake, and besides, they had both worked hard this last week and needed the rest. This was one of the horses Bramble and Gorham had trained and, though it had an odd trick of tossing its head whenever another horse came near, it didn't bite or kick, so he counted his blessings. He led his men out, twenty of them, to escort the Travelers or Town Council of Baluchston back to Sendat, and thereby proclaim to the world at large that Baluchston was part of Central Domain now, like it or not.

Leof didn't think the people of Baluchston would like either option, which was why there were twenty horsemen instead of four, as there had been with the other collecting parties.

It was a relief to be out of the fort.

The rain was holding off, just, although the clouds were thickening and the wind rising slowly. Everyone who could be spared was out in the fields, gathering in the hay before the storm struck and the crop was ruined. His instinct was to go and help, knowing what a difference twenty workers would make; but Thegan's orders didn't allow for delays.

He sent a prayer to the local gods, to hold off the rain, and thought that the farmers' families in the fields were surely doing the same.

SAKER

THE FARM was heavily shuttered, like every building in Central Domain now. Even though the farm dogs were barking madly from the end of their chains, lunging at his scent, the farmer and his brood stayed cautiously, safely behind solid wood. Saker smiled grimly. It was a kind of victory, to make them cower behind their doors. But it made finding food harder.

He wished he had learnt to fish, or forage, or learnt any other way of feeding himself from the land; but that had not been part of Freite's skills. She knew only enchantment, so that was all he knew.

He could eat the dogs, he supposed. He knew how to kill dogs. Knew how to kill just about anything that was tied up, thanks to her. But he preferred something else.

The dairy was the best place. He made for it boldly, certain that the more noise he made the less likely the farmer was to come out and confront him. The dairy was shuttered, too, but it couldn't be bolted from inside, so he had no trouble forcing the door latch.

He set the door ajar so that the moonlight streamed in. Inside, there wasn't as much as he'd hoped, but there was enough: curds and whey, but no hard cheese that he could take away with him, milk in settling pans, the cream like clouds. There were stirring spoons on the drying rack, so he sat down on a churning stool and helped himself. Fatty cream, sharp curds, bland whey...He hated the smell of curds on the turn. He couldn't bring himself to take the rennet, which was soaking in a bucket. Goat's stomach *could* be eaten, he knew, but even roasting it to cinders wouldn't take away that smell.

He'd kill for a loaf of bread.

For a moment, he paused, realizing that the idle thought was true. He would kill for a loaf of bread, or a handful of strawberries, or even a mouthful of hard cheese. Why not kill for that, when they had to die anyway?

He teetered for a moment between dismay and exhilaration at the thought but it was exhilaration that led him out to see what was growing in the kitchen garden. Strawberries *would* be nice. He kept his knife in his hand, just in case.

Action was what he needed now. He had sat, hour upon hour, racking his mind for memories, for theory, for any hint as to how he might amend the spell. Blood was the key to prevent the ghosts from fading, but how it was tied to the sun's rhythm he did not know.

He found, by touch, peas twining around cones of sticks, and snapped off the almost full pods to stuff in his scrip. The leaves were soft and pleasantly furry, but his fingers, questing, poked their way into a fat caterpillar, which squelched.

He jerked his hand back and left the peas alone to venture further along the rows.

Didn't carrots have these plumy tops? He knew that if he'd spent any time at all on a farm, he'd have a better idea. He pulled experimentally and when the noise came he thought it was the carrot screaming as it was wrenched from the ground. His guts clenched and he jumped back, dropping the carrot.

But it was just a carrot, and it lay there, seeming to mock his fear. The scream came again. A wind wraith, coiling and curling just above him. He felt a strong urge to void his bowels, but fought it back.

"Master!" it hissed in his ear. "What do you seek?"

He wasn't going to say he was foraging. Gods alone knew what food they'd offer him.

"I seek ingredients for a spell," he said. "A spell to allow the ghosts to stay in this world past the setting of the sun."

He could see the wraith now, almost invisible in the moonlight. The moon was only a sliver and it lit the creature from behind, so that it seemed he was looking at the crescent through a curtain of impossibly fine fabric. Finer than silk, and silver-gray. For a moment, he simply looked at it, without fear, and recognized its beauty. Freite had been beautiful too, in her own way. It seemed to him that evil often was.

"Ingredients?" the wraith said. "What more do you need, than blood?"

Freite had received many of her spells from the wraiths. There was no such thing as human spells, she'd told him once, on a day when he'd pleased her by giving her all the power from him she needed. He'd lain, exhausted, on a couch, while she strolled the room full of vitality, younger than the day before, lightly touching her collection of precious glass, piece by piece.

"All spells are stolen from or traded for with the spirits," she had said. "We have none of our own."

Hope stirred his guts into turmoil. "Blood alone is not enough," he said to the wraith.

"Blood and memory," it howled.

"Whose blood?" Saker demanded.

"The blood of thy heart, the blood of thy heart's enemy, what matter? Thy memory, thy army's memory, what matter? Feed us night and day, master. Day and night!" It shrieked with anticipated rapture and soared up in that fountain of movement he had seen so often and feared so greatly.

His heart thumped. Blood and memory. He ran through the spell in his mind. Yes. There were always memories that flooded over him at the start of the spell. He hadn't realized how important they were. He smiled.

Blood and memory. A way to renew the spell—to constantly renew it.

His ghosts were beings of memory. And they would find blood. Fountains of blood.

ASH

HE SAW with the River's eyes, which were not eyes at all. Every crack in the stone where water had once flowed was clear to Her; every opening, even a sliver, where she could reach was mapped. She knew the Caverns as his father knew his flute; it was instrument, where she sang, and home, and long familiarity.

"Smash it," Ash said to Her. "Crack it like an egg."

Was it asking too much, to demand that She destroy this long-held sanctuary? He and Baluch waited, breaths bated, hearts pounding, humming the notes that asked Her to help. The answer was not in words.

She laughed. It was wild, alive, unstoppable: the random, untameable force of flood let loose, delighting in destruction, wedded to change. She laughed, and the river rose.

It swirled around them as it came, sliding intimately between their clothes and their skin, tinglingly cold, pushing them but never so hard they were unbalanced. She curled past them, the current strengthening, the quiet flow of the river turning to rushing power, aimed like a spear at the crack where the river disappeared into the cavern wall. Like a spear, like a wedge for chopping hardwood, like the axe itself.

She did not let the river flow too widely as the rock resisted: it built up in a straight line, a long column of water banked only by air and Her will, far above the rocks. The water pounded in waves into the slit, against the far wall, over and over. Sound buffeted them, and Ash could faintly hear the stone figures screaming.

She laughed again as the rock resisted, and some power in the rock also, in the Cavern itself, whatever power kept the spirits from rebirth. He could sense it: this was the power of stone itself, as She was the power of water. The water sprites were hers and were like her, beautiful and dangerous. The delvers belonged to the earth, and were like it, unforgiving and irresistible. Except to water.

Ash could feel the battle building as tingling under his skin, across his hair, which stood on end.

"Give me your strength," She said, and although he thought She didn't really need it, not for this battle, it was his battle, and so it was right that She take strength from him. As he had helped Safred when she was healing Bramble, he sent support to her in a way he didn't understand. She relished it and grew stronger, wilder, the river rising higher and pounding more heavily until he felt, then heard, then saw the rocks at the end of the Cavern split apart like halves of a walnut and sunlight dive in, blinding them all, and rocks tumbled and danced and leapt and shattered, hurting his ears.

"Thank you," he said to Her.

The earth rumbled, a mixture of anger and defeat as the River sighed, "It's an old battle. I always win."

In the same moment, the stone figures cried out, throwing up hands and paws and tails in defense against the light.

As the sun hit the stone figures, they began to dissolve into the same slurry of water and rock that had come off Ash's boots when the weasel had let him go. Only bones were left as the stone melted away, some human, some animal. The weasel had really been a weasel, by the sinuous backbone, but one of normal size. The ox was a skeleton, but flesh still covered the old woman's bones. Bramble knelt beside her, supporting her head. It seemed that her body hadn't decayed before the Caverns had taken her.

Through the tears in his eyes from the harsh light, Ash could see she was younger than the stone had made her look, not much older than Bramble, with long blonde hair and fine clothes, the kind an officer's wife might wear. Around her waist, where simple women wore a belt, she had a sash embroidered with two names entwined: Brea and Calin. It was a marriage belt, sewn by an officer's daughter for her wedding.

"How did she end up here?" Ash marvelled.

"Unluckily," Bramble said. She bent and picked the body up easily and laid it out on a rock, smoothing the eyelids and crossing the hands over the chest. There was, surprisingly, no smell except that of chalk and water. She stepped back and bowed her head. "Brea, may you not linger on the roads, may you not linger in the fields. Time is, and time is gone."

"Time is, and time is gone," Ash and Medric said.

"May you find friends, may you find those you loved," Bramble said. "Time is, and time is gone."

"Time is, and time is gone," Baluch joined in.

"We have no rosemary, but remember us. We have no evergreen, but may our memories of you be evergreen. Time is, and time is gone."

"Time is, and time is gone," all of them said, except Acton. Perhaps, Ash thought, his people had had a different ceremony.

Ash began to gather rocks, to cover the girl over, but Bramble stopped him.

"No," she said. "Let her lie in sunlight."

So they left the body laid out on its rock, bathed in the white sunlight of early morning, and made their way out.

The river had sunk to its earlier level but it was still a hard, slippery climb over the rocks and out. They were huge, great slabs of limestone that shifted as they put weight on them, and settled into new positions with no more than a gentle push.

It took them until the sun was high above to reach the peak of the rock pile and all that time the River was silent in Ash's head. When he balanced on the topmost rock and looked out, he thought he understood why. She had carved out half a mountain to free them—the scar of the Cavern's collapse cut across acres of steep ground. The cavern river now cascaded down the mountain to join a larger river at the base. The White River? Bramble had said it was near.

The power involved...He shook a little. This had happened because he had asked for it.

"You'll pay for it, in time," Baluch said quietly, and it took Ash a moment to realize that he meant it literally, that he would pay with time, his own time, as Baluch had done. Ash shivered and wondered when he would have to start paying. He didn't want to leave everyone he knew just yet.

"No town here, thank the gods," Bramble said as she looked out beside him. She put her hand on his shoulder. "You have power, Ash."

"Not my power," he said.

BREA'S STORY

WE START out different, but we end at the same place.

So my mother would say to me after a funeral, after the stone had been rolled back over the burial cave. But it seems to me we come to the same place earlier than that, no matter what our life is like, no matter if we are rich or poor or loved or unloved.

We come to the place where we first meet Lady Death face to face and decide whether or not to take her as ally.

There were two of us; and on the surface we were alike, Linde my cousin, and I. Born the same year, within days of each other. Grown up the same—we could wear each other's clothes, and did, and from the back no one could tell us apart, for we both had the same wheat-coloured locks, and we dressed each other's hair in the knot of plaits they call the Maiden's Prayer. From the front—well, Linde was always prettier than I was, no doubt, but her figure wasn't as good, so I got the boys who looked at a girl's body and she got the ones who looked at her face. That did not trouble me. When a boy looked at my breasts and started breathing fast, I felt strong and alive, heady with power. It was the only power I could recognize in myself, then. One who has no right to make choices has no real power, and I had no such right about anything more serious than how to braid my hair.

Our fathers were twins, officers to the warlord, both of them, as their father and father's father had been. Their lands adjoined. They had built their houses on the edges of their lands so they could be close together, and so Linde and I and our brothers and sisters grew up in two houses, and both of them were home.

Officers' daughters don't choose their husbands. There's more to marriage than four legs in a bed, my grandmother told me. Your task is to make alliances for this family that will keep us safe and strong, that's your life's work, she said.

And my mother nodded, warmly, because she'd been sent off halfway across the Domains to marry my father, to cement an alliance between our family and Cliff Domain. "Love doesn't count when you measure it against family and children and safety and loyalty and strength," she said. She touched my plaits, gently. "And you must trust your father to choose you a good husband, as mine did."

I smiled. It was a byword around the Domain, how my parents loved each other. I realize now that that was a bad thing for me. It brought me up to expect better than I was ever likely to get, being portioned off for strategic purposes as all girls must be.

At least I was not ugly, I thought, and *would* get married, unlike my aunt Silv, who was hare-lipped and squint-eyed and kept mostly to the kitchen and the linen closet. No one had even tried to find her a husband.

Linde went first. My uncle found her a young one, an auburn-haired officer from Western Mountains Domain, one of the warlord's officers who lived at the fort. Cenred, the warlord, was old and this officer was one of his son's best friends, so it was a good marriage. The bridegroom's name was Aden, and he came, blushing, to collect her.

"How you're going to miss her!" the aunts all said, because Linde and I spent all our time together, though we fought like water sprites when their backs were turned. We lived a layered life, she and I. On top, we were the good girls, the obedient, friendly, happy girls. Underneath, there was more going on and always had been.

We'd decided to do it that way one afternoon when we'd both been sent to Linde's room for pulling each other's hair. We can't have been more than seven or eight.

Linde climbed up to the wall slit and looked out into the golden autumn afternoon. "It's not worth it," she said. "Fighting with you isn't worth missing nut-gathering for."

I agreed with her.

"We shouldn't do it," she said. "We shouldn't fight in front of them."

"I don't like you," I said.

"I don't like you either," she snapped back. "But they don't have to know that."

It was a new idea to me, the idea of deceit, but Linde had been lying a long time. That was one of the reasons we fought—she put the blame on me for things she'd done. I saw a way to stop that. I remember feeling very clever and crafty at that moment, satisfied with myself, as young children are sometimes.

"I'll stop fighting in front of them if you stop getting me into trouble," I said.

She considered it, then slid down off the chest she was standing on and came over to me. She spat in her hand and held it out to me. I spat in mine and we sealed the bargain. And from then, we were known as best friends, the best in the world, though we snarled and scratched at each other in private.

It was excellent practice for marriage.

Because we were always together—therefore always chaperoned—they let us have more time alone than the other girls. And we became experts at stealing extra hours, at sneaking off and exploring the places we should not have known about. It even bought us time truly alone, because after a while they stopped verifying our stories, and we could go off by ourselves, ready with an alibi.

Linde found the enchanter's house, off the road to town, back from the road up a narrow drive lined with yew trees.

Freite, her name was, and she was dark haired but not a Traveler, because Travelers have pale skin and she was brownish, like someone from the Wind Cities. So we were unsure of the etiquette when she invited us in. A Traveler we would have scorned. But an exotic like Freite . . .

We drank cha with her in a lavish room full of carpets and cushions, with glass winking from shelves. There was more glass than I had ever seen in one place, more than the warlord had in his hall.

Linde was fascinated. Here was a woman who owned her own house, a woman who, she told us, made her own decisions. A woman of power. It was hard to know how old she was but I thought, *old*, though her face was unlined.

Linde wanted all the kinds of power there were, but Freite just smiled when she asked questions. It was like she was fishing for something, like she was using Linde to get something she wanted, but it wasn't Linde. She wasn't interested in Linde, though my cousin couldn't see that truth. She wanted me.

Half a dozen times she made a move as if to touch me—not as a man would touch, for pleasure, but just a gesture. A pat on the arm to get my attention, say, or reaching to brush a hair away from my collar. I pulled back, each time, sure somehow that no good would come of a touch from her. Her eyes grew angrier and darker as the time went on and I became nervous.

"We must get back," I said to Linde, but she was headstrong as ever and concentrated on getting this woman to reveal something—anything—about how she had come to this marvelous position, of being on her own, with wealth of her own, with no man to control her.

I stood up and said firmly, "We must go now."

Linde glared at me, but she came. That was the bargain—we would not disagree, even in front of a stranger. Freite invited us to come again, "Anytime," she said, "I am always here."

Linde smiled and said she would be back soon, sweet as honey, but two minutes out the door and she was berating me for being rude, for being stupid, for not seeing that we should be learning all we could from Freite.

"I don't want to learn what she could teach," I said, and shivered. It was true. Out of the house I felt clean, and that made me realize that inside it had felt dirty, filthy, though the floors had been spotless and the glass gleaming. It was Freite who had felt filthy, a grime on her soul spreading over everything. I said so.

No doubt the fight that followed would have lasted until we got home, but as we walked down between the towering yews a boy stepped out in front of us. Auburn hair, hazel eyes, younger than us, but not bad looking and well dressed. Linde took all that in with a blink and smiled and bowed, but he was looking at me, and I was looking at his pale cheeks and tired eyes.

"Don't go back," he said to me. "She wants your power."

"What power?" Linde asked sharply. "Brea hasn't got any power."

"*You* know," he said, still looking at me. "Stay away from her."

I nodded and he stepped back into the trees. Linde surged forward to see where he had gone, but there was no sign of him.

"What was all that about?" she demanded. "Do you know him?"

I shook my head.

"What power?"

And there it was, the underlayer that I had never shared with anyone, not even Linde. The shameful secret sleeping inside me. The power that only Travelers had, only the people with tainted blood, whose family line was not pure. I looked my blonde cousin in the eye and lied.

"I don't know what he was talking about," I said. "All I know is that she's a creepy old woman who kept trying to touch me. And you know what grandmother told us about women like her."

It was enough to distract her: a girl-fancier, or a girler looking for a blonde to ship to the Wind Cities' brothels, either option fuelled her speculation. Her vanity told her that Freite would want *her*, not me, and that she was in most danger. That gave her a pleasant thrill, but she was no fool, my cousin. The danger was real, and it kept her away from Freite. Fear of being used by her, of being *tainted* by her, kept me away too.

Then Linde got married, and I did miss her. Not she herself, but the time and space her companionship had bought me. I was drafted into the everyday work of the households, and trained intensively in the duties of a wife, the duties of an officer's woman.

But it was as though Freite's eyes and the young man's words had woken the power in me, from where I had buried it as deep as I could. I began to know things before they were told to me, to read people's eyes and see their thoughts showing as clear as speech. That was when I blessed Linde. Our life of dissimulation was a perfect preparation for this. For not showing what I truly was.

If I wanted a husband, I had to conceal myself. No one would want a wife with Traveler blood in her; it would shame the entire family, spoil the marriage chances of my brothers and sisters, possibly even get my father's lands taken away from him. Warlords don't trust Travelers.

Nor should they, because I found in myself layers and layers of deceit. Everything about me was a lie. My looks, my speech, my smiles, everything but my desire for my father to find me a husband so I could have my own place and my own family.

He found me one, all right, and the irony was he thought he was doing me a favor when he betrothed me to Linde's husband's cousin. He was an even better match than Aden, my father said, with a bigger estate and more silver. Moreover, he lived at the warlord's fort just as Linde did, and had his land, up near the mountains, managed for him by a kinsman.

"You'll be glad to see her, no doubt," he said to me, beaming with satisfaction at having given me so great a boon. I thanked him properly, almost swooning with delight, it seemed, but my spirit darkened with fear. Linde knew me better than anyone. If she were to see the power which had awakened in me...

But then I reasoned with myself. She would not dare to speak out, because it would taint her family as well as mine. She would not dare take that risk. I was safer with her than with anyone. As I realized that, tears came to my eyes and my father hugged me, a thing he rarely did.

My husband Calin came to collect me soon after.

What is there to say? He is dead, after all. He was a boor and a bully but not an evil man. He was merely used to getting his own way, and Cenred's fort was a place of drunkenness and license. Calin had lived like that for years, since he was a very young man, and it had shaped him to fit.

Cenred's wife was an invalid who wanted only solitude, and his son had not married, so there was no one to keep a check on the officers' young wives. For Linde and me it was a continuation of our old life, except that we avoided the hall, where the officers drank and whored and gambled.

Linde was besotted with her husband, Aden. A nice enough boy and with eyes only for her. I dealt with mine as best I could, and cursed my parents for filling my head with romantic ideas. But it was Calin who taught me my true power, a power I learnt in pain and dread, night after night in our bed. Night after night I wished him dead.

And day by day he died.

A wasting disease, the healer called it. He looked furtive when he said it, so I stopped him as he went out the door, pretending to want to thank him, and I asked, "What is wrong?"

He looked down at his hands, as though weighing his words. "Does your husband have any enemies, lady?"

I stiffened. "He is an officer. There are many who hate all officers." I paused, but I had to ask. "Why?"

"There is a feel about this... It's come on very fast for such a young man. It may be... wished upon him."

The blood rushed from my head to my feet and I swayed. No doubt he thought he'd frightened me, because he took my arm to steady me, and began to babble, "No, no, no reason to be frighted, lady, it was just a shadow on my mind, but it does happen so quickly sometimes, out of the deep sea and nowhere as they say... "

I forced my voice to be calm. "If this got out, there would be reprisals on innocent people."

He nodded, and never spoke of it again.

Calin was too frail now to come to our bed with any thought but sleep, but that night I caressed his head and wished him well because, although I dreaded his touch, I had never meant to harm him. Never meant to kill. I wished with all my heart, and I wished night and day, but it made no difference. I had no power to heal, only to curse.

He died only four months after our wedding day, and I thanked the gods that I was not carrying his child.

I went through the patterns of grief. I laid him out in proper form, cried at the funeral, Swith knows I looked pale enough. And on the third day I shut myself up in our room, the room where he had died, saying I wanted no one but myself at his quickening, if quickening there was.

I even hired musicians, saying that music often helps the spirit find rest. A flautist, a drummer and a singer, it was—typical Travelers, but the woman had a voice that would charm the soul out of your body. I set them to play outside the door, hoping that if I had to acknowledge my guilt the music would cover my words.

I was ready. Ready with the knife, ready to take the blame and offer reparation. Ready for Calin to accuse me silently.

He had died, as men often do, just before dawn. I sat up the night waiting, for it isn't always three days to the minute. I sat and listened to the flute and drum, listened to the woman sing songs about peace and love and the winds of dawn. I could hear nothing else, and even now I cannot close my eyes without hearing her voice again. I waited while the candle guttered, and the gray dawn slid in through the shutters, while the smooth bed seemed to grow bigger and brighter moment by moment, so that I strained my eyes time and again, thinking the white sheet was his ghost forming, thinking the pillow was his head, the bolster his body. The knife grew slick and I had to change hands and wipe the sweat on my dress. I felt sick with shame, feverish with guilt. As the first yellow rays cut through the gap at the window, I tensed. Surely now, surely this was when he would come, accusing and angry.

I waited until noon, until dusk, but he did not come. The healer had prepared him well for death, and even in the grave, it seemed, he did not realize I had killed him.

As I unbolted the door and came out into the corridor, the woman singer rose to greet me. They had played unstinting the whole time, taking turns towards the end so that it would be flute, or drum, or singer, to eke out their energy until it was over.

I gave the woman the purse I had ready.

"I hope all went well," she said, which was an impertinence from a Traveler, but she was pale and weary-looking and I felt grateful to them.

"He did not come," I said.

"That is good," she said gently. "He is at rest."

My eyes filled with tears, and they were real, because I hoped against hope that she was right, that my curse had not poisoned his afterlife as well.

Then her eyes narrowed a little and her head tilted to one side.

"If you try to deny who you are," she said, very quietly, "the power will overwhelm you."

I stared at her in shock, not believing that she could have said it, half-believing that I had imagined the words out of my own guilt and confusion. She turned away to help her colleagues pack their instruments, as though she had said nothing. What had she seen? How had I betrayed myself?

I took her by the arm and she turned to look at me, and saw my fear. "You are not the only one with power," she said reassuringly. "Others will see nothing."

But how could I be sure ? Worse—how could I be sure that I would not curse someone again, unthinking?

So I came to my husband's lands, and to his house, which was mine now until I died, and I became, like Freite, a woman free of men, as widows mostly are. And I became, like her, a woman who lived alone, and saw no one unless they knocked at the door, and in the time honored way I made sure that no one knocked, by being rude and parsimonious and meagre. They thought me a mad miser, down in the village.

So I protected others from a stray thought, a moment's anger, by becoming solitary. I protected myself from the guilt of their deaths, as well, and closed my eyes each night to the memory of the singer, of her songs about love and the winds of dawn, though I found no peace there. The only peace I found was walking in the mountains, and how could I know that my lonely explorations would lead so deep and to so much pain?

For one thing I was sure, and still am. Loneliness is better than murder.

FLAX

"WE NEED to be out of sight by dawn," Swallow said. She didn't like the idea of hiding, it was clear, but she accepted it. They had stopped at a stream to let the horses have a breather.

"This is mostly flat country," Rowan said, pulling at his ear in a way that Flax had seen Ash do when he was thinking. "Farm land. Not much shelter."

"There are coppices," Flax suggested and they nodded.

"The next one we see, then," Swallow said. She cast a worried look at the sky, which was now filling with clouds as a cool north wind picked up.

The moon would soon be covered, Flax thought, and they would be in pitch black—no riding then, they'd have to lead the horses. He touched his heels to Cam's flanks and they set off again with him in the lead. But there were no coppices on this stretch of road. It was all fields, mostly vegetables, from what they could see in the moonlight: cabbages, beanpoles, some hay fields and pasture. The hay hadn't been mown here; there weren't even any hayricks to hide behind and the hedgerows weren't high enough to offer shelter.

Not much further on, they came to a junction with a much wider track, a real road marked by wagons and horse traffic.

"Baluchston or Sendat?" Rowan asked the world in general.

To their left, the main route to Baluchston ran straight. To the right, the road led to Sendat.

"We've missed the turn, then," Swallow said.

Rowan nodded. "We could turn around and try to find it—I think maybe it was that little track about three miles back."

Somehow, that seemed like a bad idea. Flax felt a real urgency to keep moving, to get as far away from Baluchston as they could.

The sky was growing lighter.

"There are coppices on this road," Swallow said. "All the way down to Sendat. And there's another road about ten miles on that would take us east, to the Hidden River and North Domain. We could get a boat down to Mitchen and then one to Turvite from there."

She had the ordering of the family group usually, that was clear, just like his mam.

"We'd better get under cover then, before dawn," Rowan said.

The lightening sky was like a threat, like a deep dark chord sounded on that Wind Cities instrument with the big belly. He desperately wanted to sing, something cheerful to keep his spirits up, but it was too dangerous. The farmhouses were close to the road here, and villages too frequent.

They came to a village before they found a coppice, but they had no time to go around it. "Straight through," Swallow said, and they went on at a gentle canter, hoping the inhabitants wouldn't wake, or would think it were warlord's messengers coming back to the fort.

Flax, in the lead, came up on the first house, his heart beating fast, ears straining to hear anything, anyone, any sign that they were noticed. The village was revealed in flickers of moonlight as the clouds raced across the sky. All the houses were shuttered and barred. There was none of the usual clutter around: no handcarts or barrels outside the inn, no washing left out, no toys forgotten when it had been time to go inside. The tidiness gave the village an unnatural air, as though the townsfolk were already dead. That wasn't a comfortable thought. The dead were as dangerous as the living, now. It took only a minute to ride through the small collection of houses, but by the time they were on the other side he was drenched in sweat, and he wondered how Ash managed to live this kind of life all the time.

When there was no sound of pursuit, they relaxed a little, but Flax was still searching for any sign of cover—even a copse would do.

They left the plain behind as the road began to wind between small hills. Flax felt more comforted as the slopes rose up around them; they couldn't see ahead very far, but at least no one would be able to spot them a long way off.

The sun was winning over the clouds. It was a late dawn, but it was coming, slowly. The horses were tired, and Flax kept them to a walk, despite the urgency he felt.

Cam's ears pricked forward and she raised her head. He was too slow; he wasn't expecting it. She whinnied loudly and was answered from around the bend just ahead of them. Flax looked around wildly. Nowhere to hide. They would have to brazen it out, no matter who was around the bend.

He straightened in his saddle, reminding himself that he was a young merchant, travelling with his servants to—to where? Sendat? Carlion? Yes, going to Carlion to find out about their family's steward there, to get solid information about what had happened, rather than rumors and scare stories.

He took a breath and got ready to smile as they came around the turn.

Warlord's men. Thegan's men. Camped, but packing up in the early light, getting ready to move on. Flax's face froze, but he kept Cam moving, raising a hand to the soldiers as if in casual greeting. But one of them, a solid good-looking man in his thirties, moved across their path and raised a hand to stop them. He had the arm ring that identified him as a sergeant.

Flax reined in amiably, and nodded. "Morning."

"You're out early," the man said.

"Heading for Carlion. Long way, so we got off early."

"Where are you from?"

"Baluchston," Flax said, hoping it was the right choice. But it was the only free town on this road, and they needed to be from a free town if they were going to get away with this.

"Really?" the sergeant said, and he looked back at Swallow and Rowan. That was bad. Flax forced himself to not look. "Just stay here a moment, lad."

The sergeant walked back to speak to another man, a tall pale-haired officer wearing the signature ponytail, who was about to mount a big bay gelding.

He looked just like a warrior out of the old stories, the kind of man that Flax had secretly wanted to be as a very young boy, before he'd found his voice. He'd been ashamed of it, but all the same he'd dreamt about riding tall and fair on a chaser stallion—though he knew, as a horse trainer's child, that few stallions made really good chasers. For the first time, he thought that maybe he could go back, someday, when he tired of the Road, and help his father…

If he didn't deal with this, there'd be no future, and no chance of ever seeing his father again. He swallowed down his fear, and prepared to lie until his face turned inside out, the way the old mothers said it would if you fibbed.

But he didn't have the chance.

The officer took one look at Rowan and Swallow, and a closer look at him, and simply said, "I'm sorry, but all Travelers from Baluchston must go to the fort at Sendat."

"I'm not a Traveler!" Flax tried to put as much indignation into his voice as he could.

"No?" The man seemed prepared to grant him exemption, but then one of the soldiers came and whispered to him. The officer firmed his mouth—gods, a gorgeous mouth!—as though he were disappointed, and turned to Flax. "Dern says he's seen you singing. A voice like a lark, he says. A Traveler."

That was bittersweet, to be skewered by his own talent. Flax shrugged and smiled as charmingly as he could. He didn't think it would make any difference with this one, but flirting worked with astonishing people sometimes.

"It was worth a try," he said.

The officer smiled, genuinely amused, but unfortunately not attracted at all. "You misunderstand. My lord Thegan is offering sanctuary to all Travelers—there have been killings right across the Domain and my lord is gathering Travelers for their own protection."

"So we've been told," Swallow said. "But we were in no danger in Baluchston."

"You were in great danger, whether you knew it or not," the officer said firmly. He turned to an archer. "Horst, take them to the fort." With a shock, Flax recognized the man who had pursued him and Ash in Golden Valley—the man Ash had saved from the wind wraiths.

The archer stared at him, and flushed as if remembering his fear of the wraiths, then turned away, pretending he didn't know Flax. Good. Flax was happy to go along with that. The officer looked at the ground for a moment, as though trying to decide what to say, then looked up and met their eyes, gazing at each of them separately, as though he wanted them to pay great attention. "My lord is generous, but he requires his orders to be followed. I would advise you to go with Horst."

It was clear he meant it. Just to add weight, Horst shifted his bow and fingered the arrows in his quiver. The officer hadn't ordered him to bring them down if they tried to escape, but it was clear that he would. They all knew it. Flax was suddenly, sharply glad that Zel was safe with Safred. No one would attack the Well of Secrets party.

"Our horses need rest," Flax said. "We've been riding all night."

"Take a break here, then, Horst, and have them back to the fort by tomorrow evening." Horst nodded. "Alston," the officer said to the sergeant, "let's be off."

The men mounted and rode on, the sergeant leading the squad.

The officer lingered a moment. "See my lady Sorn if you need anything," he said, then shook his reins and his horse began to trot after the others.

Flax looked warily at the archer.

"Down you come," Horst said. "Don't think I'm going to help you with your animals."

Well, that was clear enough. They dismounted and led the horses to the stream, where Flax, with some clumsy help from Swallow and Rowan, unsaddled, fed and watered the horses, then groomed them thoroughly before throwing himself on the grass and eating the food Swallow had ready for him. Flax was tired of resisting things. He was much, much better at just going with the current, like the little boats children made from leaves and twigs.

Of course, those boats always sank eventually, but once he'd made one that had floated right down a stream and launched itself off the cliff into the sea. It had flown, buoyed up by the air, for quite a way before it sailed down to the waves and was sucked from sight.

The archer kept them on the road all day and only found a camping place when the horses started to visibly labor. They were still some hours out of Sendat, but in such a settled, busy part of the Domain that Flax knew they had no chance of escape. As Horst had followed them along, they had been glared at, spat and shouted at, and threatened in every village, by every farmer, by every child with a handful of dung to throw, and only the soldier's presence had kept them from being dragged off their horses and kicked to death.

There would be no refuge in this country.

After they'd set up camp in a field with a stream that Horst simply commandeered from the farmer—"Warlord's business"—they ate their cold food in silence.

"What about a song, then?" Horst said finally, wiping the crumbs from his jacket.

Flax was astounded. Did this man really think they would entertain their gaoler? Then he looked more closely at the man. There was no scorn in his eyes, not even a demand. He'd asked as one person would ask another person for a favor, no more. Did he really believe all that nonsense about the warlord offering refuge? Did he think he was the hero in this story, saving Travelers from their deaths?

It worried Flax that the archer might be right. Maybe he was the hero.

Swallow cleared her throat, and looked meaningfully at him when he turned around. "Why not?" she said. "We have to practice anyway."

That was true, but it made Flax want to laugh. Practice, in the middle of all this!

Rowan found his flute in his pack and took out a small tambour as well. "Do you drum?" he asked Flax.

"Not as well as Ash," he said. They looked startled, as though they'd forgotten he and Ash had Traveled together, or as though they were surprised that Ash would drum for him.

"Try, anyway," Swallow said. He took the drum and sounded it—light but true. Good enough for a field and a warlord's man.

"Do you have a favorite song?" Rowan asked the archer.

The man seemed embarrassed. Probably liked some invasion song about killing Travelers, and wasn't sure whether he should ask for it.

"What about 'Homecoming'?"

Flax blinked, but he had his performing face on now, so he didn't show his surprise. "Homecoming" was a western mountains song, a miners' song, melancholic and somewhat sentimental. Not the sort of song a soldier often asked for.

Rowan set the beat by tapping on his thigh. Flax picked it up, holding a regular rhythm, then Rowan set the flute to his lips and played the simple melodic introduction.

Then Swallow began singing, and Flax's fingers faltered on the drum. He picked up the rhythm again, though, as she glared sideways at him, and he kept it up. Her voice was as pure as snowmelt—perfect, even after this long, long day, even without a chance to practice, to warm her throat and muscles.

The mountain is deep
And the mine is dark
And I have only one small light
Oh, pray keep me safe
In the pit-dark night
And bring me home
To the evening light

He came in on the chorus, softly, as he thought she would like, and saw her eyes flick sideways—in approval, this time.

Chains of gold, chains of gold
Bind me to you
Chains of gold, chains of gold
Bring me home

Afterwards, as the last notes of the flute died away, the warlord's man cleared his throat and said, "My mam was western mountains born." That was all, but it was enough. And they slept just as they would have if the archer had been another Traveler.

Sendat was a big town. They reached the outskirts in mid-morning and here, unlike every other place they'd passed, no one spat at them. The merchants in the market stared at them, and the townspeople too, but they nodded at Horst and a few shouted remarks—like, "More for my lord, eh? Fort's getting pretty full!"

Horst ignored their remarks with a shrug and an occasional glare, until one man yelled, "My lord must be crazy, feeding all those dark-haired bastards!" and then he was off his horse, his hand around the man's throat, his boot knife drawn and poised at the man's privates.

"Did you question my lord's orders?" he hissed.

The man shook and denied it and babbled about what a great lord Thegan was, and Horst dropped him, resheathed the knife and remounted without another word. The three travelers followed him up the hill to the fort, leaving complete silence behind them. Once they were out of earshot of the market, Horst cleared his throat and said, "No one questions my lord when I'm around."

"Loyalty is a valuable quality," Rowan said quietly, and Flax could tell that he meant it. The archer realized that, too, and his face cleared of its bad mood.

"Aye," he said. "The most valuable thing a man like me has to offer."

There were many people, men and women and even children, working on the fortifications around the top of the hill. Stakes, palisades, ditches—a whole ring of defenses—showed the sharp edges and colors of new work. Thegan was serious about defending his fort from the ghosts. But would it be enough? For the first time, Flax wondered whether the Travelers were to be used as some other form of defense. He shivered slightly and turned to Horst. "What about our horses?"

"My lord's commandeered all horses. Travelers are sleeping in the barn, over there." Horst pointed to a group of dark-haired women and children cooking over fires. It smelt good. Rabbit stew, perhaps. Flax hoped there'd be dumplings.

But his appetite fell away as they walked through the heavily guarded gate and he noticed that half the warlord's men on the wall faced inwards, watching the Travelers.

LEOF

LEOF ORDERED his men to set up camp outside Baluchston. Their twenty men seemed a very small party when he remembered the army Thegan had assembled here only a few weeks ago. It was twilight by the time they had pitched tents, and he decided to give Vi and her council the night to talk the problem over.

He took Alston with him, but no other guards. Alston didn't comment. Thank the gods for a sergeant who didn't chatter! Leof could do things Thegan's way, or he could do his best to avoid conflict. This time, he wouldn't let his pride or his temper get the better of him.

Outside Vi's shop, they dismounted and found a youth to take the horses to a nearby inn. "Tell them my lord will want dinner," Alston said to the lad.

Leof usually ate with the men when he was on campaign, but Alston deserved a good meal, so he didn't contradict the order.

He ducked his head as he went through the doorway to avoid a swathe of white cloth across the lintel. That was a sign of mourning in these parts. He hoped that it wasn't Vi who was dead.

But there she was, lumbering forward to greet him, her shrewd eyes bright in the light from several lamps. Her mouth opened to greet him, then she noticed Alston following him, and changed what she had been about to say.

"Welcome back, Lord Leof," she said.

"Mistress Vi," he acknowledged. "This is my sergeant, Alston."

"Pleased to meet you," Vi said. "Come on through to the kitchen. The others are there."

The kitchen was even brighter than the shop, with a big fire in the hearth and lamps set around. Four men and women looked up from a table in the center of the room as he came in, and his heart sank. Most of them had the closed-off look that meant they'd already made up their minds to deny him whatever he asked. Only truth would serve here, and he hoped Alston understood that.

There were two chairs vacant, at either end of the table. He took one and Vi took the other and there was a moment of silence. Alston came to stand behind him, in the second's position which, in an officer's court, meant that there was no trust in the host. Leof didn't know if Vi knew that custom, but she flicked her eyes over Alston and the corners of her mouth tucked back in a little.

"This is Reed, our leather worker," Vi said, indicating the older man to her left. "Minnow the chandler, Sar the weaver, Drago the ferryman, and Eel."

Leof nodded to them all in turn, and they nodded back, silently. The lack of any trade for Eel made Leof look closely at him. One of the Lake People, he thought, dark hair and dark eyes and skin that had spent a long time in the sun. And wise, humorous eyes. He nodded to Leof with a smile.

Vi ceremoniously poured them each a mug of water. "Lake water, for wisdom," she said as she passed one to Leof.

Eel dipped his finger in the water and drew a circle on the back of his hand, then drank. A sign that he belonged to the Lake? That he respected Her power? Leof pretended not to have seen, and drank at the same time as Vi and the others. The water tasted of nothing—or of everything: life and rock and moonlight. He shook his head to clear it of fancies. It was just water.

"What does Thegan want?" Vi asked.

"For now, he wants all the Travelers in the town," Leof replied. There was an intake of breath around the table. "Not the Lake People," he assured them. "Just any Travelers who are passing through." He had decided that it would be impossible to sort out the Settled Travelers from the Lake People, and this partial request might possibly be granted. "There have been massacres," he said seriously. "Many, many Travelers have been murdered. You must have heard."

They nodded, but kept silent, so he ploughed on. "My lord is offering sanctuary to all Travelers in his Domains. Messages have gone to Cliff Domain, as well, instructing his officers to protect Travelers, to gather them together in Cliffhold and keep them safe. He is doing the same in Central."

"But we are not part of Central Domain." It was the youngest of them, Minnow, a red-headed woman with startling blue eyes. She was someone Leof would have appreciated before he knew Sorn.

Leof chose his words carefully. "It's true you have not traditionally been part of Central Domain, but I think you must realize that you are now part of Lord Thegan's territory."

"So, Lord Leof, are you come to tell us our days as a free town are over?" Vi asked.

There was no way to soften the truth. "They were over some time ago, Voice. My lord has had no objections from other warlords to his intentions for Baluchston. Your independence is long gone."

They sat for a moment, taking that in.

"Others have tried to conquer the Lake in the past," Eel said softly.

Leof hesitated. He would not insult the Lake to these people. Not only would it make them antagonistic, Leof felt that it was profoundly dangerous to belittle the Lake so close to it. And whether Thegan would approve or not, he was going to honor that feeling.

"The Lake is the Lake," he said. "But my lord is able to bring armies on either side, this time. And he will have learnt from the last encounter. He won't try the same thing twice. And he will not give up." Leof spaced out the last words, because they had to understand Thegan; they had to believe he was implacable.

"Nor will She," Eel said.

Vi put her hand on his arm. "Eel, I think what my lord Leof thinks about the Lake and what his master thinks may be very different."

Leof forced himself not to look at Alston. Alston hadn't been part of the attack on the Lake, and he had no understanding of how powerful She could be.

"The Travelers are at risk as soon as they set foot on the road," he said. "We will take them to safety."

"They are safe already," the older man, Reed, said, "safer than they could ever be in a warlord's fort!"

"Are you sure?" Leof asked. "Are you sure the Lake can protect you against the dead?"

"It's not the dead we have to fear," Eel said softly. "It's what will follow them."

Leof decided that he had said enough. "Extend our invitation to the Travelers here. We will be in the town square tomorrow, two hours after dawn, to take them to safety." He stood up and bowed to them all, a gesture Thegan would not have approved of. And he could not tell them of the consequences of disobedience, or they would take to the Lake and be outside his reach. "I wish you a good night."

Leof left without looking back, but he could hear, and they said nothing until he was outside the shop. "Come on," he said to Alston. "Let's eat."

Alston paced silently by his side over to the inn. Just outside, he turned and said, "My lord, is the Lake so powerful?"

Leof paused, weighing his words. "I believe the Lake and the gods work together for our good. And that their power is Hers."

"Hers?"

Leof grinned. "Oh, yes, sergeant. She's definitely female. And that should be enough to tell us not to cross her!"

The town council was waiting in the square in the morning, the Lake behind them blindingly bright in the morning sun. Leof shaded his eyes and looked around the square, but of course there were no Travelers waiting compliantly to be herded off. Just the council, and behind them the people of Baluchston, standing in family groups, waiting. They didn't seem concerned. He noticed that some of them wore that smirk that meant they expected a good show. Leof's pride flicked at him. They seemed to think he was negligible, that Thegan could be flouted with impunity.

They would have to learn.

"Voice of Baluchston," he said formally, pitching his voice so it could be heard right across the square, "I am come to escort the Travelers of this place to safety."

"Sure enough," Vi said. "We're here and ready."

She swept a hand to indicate the people behind her. All of them.

He kept his face under tight control. "I informed you yesterday that we are inviting only those of Traveler blood to the fort."

Aye," Vi said. "So it is. All of us in Baluchston have the old blood, one way or another. There's been a lot of marrying with the Lake People over the years. If your lord wants to protect all of the old blood, he'll have to take us all. The whole town."

Leof fought down a smile. Swith, she was a cunning old fox! She knew Thegan couldn't possibly accommodate all of them. But they had, in a way, defied his lord, and he could not allow that, so it was time to fall back on the second part of Thegan's orders.

He had given his instructions back in camp, so when he raised his hand and dropped it the men went forward smartly, two to a councillor, riding them down and scooping them up without warning. It was a trick Thegan had used in battle before, to isolate the Ice King's officers from their men. They whooped as they split into pairs and targeted a councillor, bending down and grabbing one armpit each. Once the man was in the air, the right hand rider bent further to get an arm under the knees and flip him up over the opposite withers. It was a little harder with a woman, Leof noticed, and the men with Vi were having some problems, she was so stout. The red-headed woman fought tooth and nail and drew blood with both, but the men hardly noticed and dumped her face down with a slap on the rump for good measure.

Leof sat implacably, although something in him cheered when Eel wriggled out of the way like his namesake and ran for the Lake. The soldiers followed, but the townspeople were in the way; they shifted unwillingly aside, and boys ran under the horses' hooves, startling them into rearing.

Leof kicked his horse and chased him—he couldn't let Eel escape. His speed made even the boys jump out of the way, and he was gaining on Eel as they came to the end of the square, where the long piers stretched out into the water.

His gelding's hooves drummed onto the wooden boards of the pier and the horse spooked, planting his forefeet solidly, refusing to move, shaking all over. Leof almost fell. He jumped off instead and ran flat out after Eel, but there was a moment, just a moment, when his legs had to adjust to being on solid ground, and he was a pace or two behind when

Eel, still running, flew straight off the end of the pier, and leapt high in the air, arms flailing. He hit the water and disappeared and only then did Leof realize that the people of Baluchston had been cheering Eel on, as now they fell silent, waiting for him to come back up.

Leof scanned the surface methodically. The water stayed an unbroken silver plain, except where the current stirred up choppy waves. Everything other than the ferry boats was swept away in that current, to the waterfall that fell hundreds of feet to the Hidden River. Leof wondered if even the Lake could save a man from that. He waited until there was no possibility that Eel was still holding his breath, still swimming under water, and then turned and walked slowly back, leading the gelding gently onto the solid earth and mounting. The stories of old battles said the Lake could move a man through time, into the future or the past—he wondered if she had done so to Eel, to keep him safe, or if he were drifting down the Hidden River, food for the fish.

"Regroup," he ordered his men, and they came, four of them with struggling councillors across their saddlebows. Three, rather. Vi just lay there like a sack of meal. He couldn't stop to check on her now. He pushed his gelding to a trot and the others followed, the people in the square running after them, some pleading, some cursing, some threatening.

"The Lake will save them!" one old woman screamed, eyes blazing, and Leof believed her, which was why they were not stopping anywhere within wave's reach. He managed to maneuver his horse to Vi's side and found that she was stoically staring upwards, mouth compressed.

She glared at him. "Didn't warn us about this, did you?" she accused him.

"Would you rather I had razed your town?" he asked. "I follow my lord's orders." He moved away before she could elicit more guilt from him.

Three miles out, when he was sure the Lake could not reach them, he halted so that the councillors could climb on double with their captors. He looked at Vi, perched precariously on the rump of a piebald mare, and his lips twitched. "Give the Voice her own mount," he told the soldier in front of her. "You double with Bandy."

"Aye, my lord," the soldier said, half resigned and half relieved.

Leof looked severely at Vi. "If you try to ride off, you'll be shot," he said, but he didn't really mean it and she knew it. The problem was, the five archers with them heard too, and put their bows at the ready. Leof looked at them and back at Vi. "Don't try," he said.

She nodded. "Thegan's orders, eh?" she said. "So you're following a man who doesn't even believe in the gods?"

Alston took a shocked breath. Leof paused. It would be stupid to reply directly. "Criticizing the Lord Thegan is not permitted, Mistress Vi," he said firmly.

She sniffed, but stayed silent. She was a little pale; the ride couldn't have been easy for her. And it wouldn't get any better before Sendat. Leof sighed. When he had dreamt about being a warlord's officer, it had never been like this.

"Sendat," he said, and his men moved off immediately, in perfect formation, with perfect trust.

Too many people trusted him, Leof thought. He couldn't possibly satisfy them all.

It was slow riding, and instead of camping, they stayed at inns along the way. He had no orders to treat the council with anything but respect, and rumors would soon reach the other free towns. He didn't want to add fuel to an already dangerous fire. If Thegan wanted to keep both Baluchston and Carlion, he had to be seen to act as though he had no choice. And he could not treat the councillors of a free town like prisoners.

So he did not commandeer the rooms, he paid for them, as Thegan usually did, with a tax chit, and he allowed the councillors to sleep without guards; although some were posted at the outside doors. He didn't think they'd try to run.

Over dinner, he had asked Vi, "Did the Lake not give you instructions?"—not trying to be provocative, but wanting truly to know.

May be she sensed that, because she stared at him steadily for a moment, and then said, "Aye. She did. We're buying time, lad."

"Time for what?"

"Time for the enchanter to be defeated," Reed answered for her.

Leof had leant forward, as focused as he was during battle. "How?" he demanded.

Vi patted his hand, for all the world like she was his grammer. "Don't you worry, lad, the gods have it in hand."

"How many people will die before they settle it?" he said, remembering the bodies in the farmyard, his men at Bonhill, screaming as the wind wraiths feasted.

She paused, her face clouded. "Well, now, the gods don't worry much about deaths," she said. "Death and life, it's all the same thing to them. But coming back from death—that's a worry, and no mistake."

"There's things unseen in the world, lad," Reed broke in, his voice husky. "And things that aren't meant to be seen. The Lake says the enchanter could open the doors to the cold hell, and let the soul eaters in."

Leof could feel the blood leave his face. "They're *real?*" he said. He had always believed the soul eaters were a fireside story, a terror made up to scare children into being good: "If you don't do what you're told, when you die the soul eaters will get you and you'll never be reborn!" Horrible images filled his mind, ghouls that waited beyond death and ate the souls of the evil, the vain, the cowardly... There was no compact with the soul eaters as there was with the wraiths. If they entered the world of the living, it would not stay alive very long.

Vi gazed at him. "Aye, lad, they're real. And they're hungry. So it seems to me that your lord should concentrate on finding that enchanter."

"He's doing whatever can be done."

"So are we all," Vi replied.

"Pray it's enough," Reed said, and he shivered and looked up to the rafters of the inn, as though he expected to see something there, a demon, perhaps. He began to eat again, but his face was grave, as though he were preoccupied with more than the food.

No, Leof didn't think they would try to run. Whatever the Lake had in mind, she was buying time for the people of Baluchston, and the councillors were the price.

REED'S STORY

THERE'S NO saying what will happen next. That's what I learnt, that summer, that winter, watching her change. Losing her. They said at first that it was madness, wandering wits, but I knew better.

The gods talk to us but we don't see them. What if we could? What if *she* could, my Eaba? The first time, she looked up from the table where she was stringing beans for dinner, and her face lit up, as though she had seen a friend come in. I turned from punching a pattern into a belt length, but there was no one there. I raised my eyebrows at her, but she just smiled.

Well, Eaba and I have managed to share the same workspace for thirty years by keeping our noses out of each other's business. So I shrugged, although I puzzled over it later, in bed, her hand resting on my chest as it always did.

Then our children started noticing things. We've got eight, some grown and some half-grown and some still running about bare-legged. Two are married, though not the eldest boy, Wyst, and he was the one to say something.

"What are you looking at, Mam?" he asked one day, when she was smiling into the branches of the plum tree, though the blossom had long since disappeared and the fruit hadn't swelled yet.

"Why, that," Eaba answered, waving her hand to the sky as though it was obvious. But when we looked, we didn't see anything.

She picked her washing off the rosemary bushes and went inside, and Wyst and I stared at each other, then shrugged. Women! I think we both thought.

But it niggled at me and that night in bed I asked her, "What did you see in the plum tree, love?"

She laughed at me. "Don't try that on me, husband," she said, as though I were trying to trick her. "As if you didn't see it!"

"I didn't see anything except the tree," I said.

"No?" she replied, unconvinced, and settled down to sleep.

That shook me. What had she seen so clear that neither Wyst nor I could see? I wondered if it might be something to do with her being a woman, after all. *Could* they see things we couldn't? Nothing about women would surprise me, not after thirty years with Eaba.

The next time she got that look, she was combing the winter wool from her favorite nanny out in the goat shed, and I asked her straight out, "What are you looking at? And don't say 'that'! I can't see anything here except the shed and the goats."

Her face clouded over and she looked worried. She peered up again into the rafters—it was always up she looked, never down, when she had that expression.

"You don't see it?" she asked slowly.

I shook my head. Her eyes almost disappeared, she frowned so much. Then she looked up again.

"Why can't he see you?" she asked, and cocked her head as if listening to an answer. She wasn't pleased by it, whatever it was. Her lip stuck out in that stubborn way I knew so well, and she muttered, "That's no answer!"

She turned to me, still frowning, and asked, "I suppose you couldn't *hear* that, either?"

"No. I heard nothing."

She sighed. "It says that you don't have the right kind of eyes, but what sort of answer is that? It told me last week that I've only just got the right kind myself. Something to do with the veils."

Ah, I thought. Her eyes *had* been changing lately, growing the milky veils that had blinded her mother and her grandmother before her. She'd been resigned to it, starting to learn the house by touch as well as sight. Perhaps this—whatever it was—was just a missight, so to speak, because her eyes weren't working properly.

But she heard this thing as well.

"What's *it*?" I asked.

She opened her mouth as though to explain, and then shut it. She peered upwards, then shook her head.

"I don't know how to describe it," she said, tapping the wool comb on her knee in frustration. "The words aren't the right words..."

"Just give me an idea."

She paused, searching her mind, but shrugged helplessly.

"Is it alive?" I asked.

"Oh, yes!" she said.

"Is it human?"

"Oh, no!"

"A spirit?"

She shook her head. "Not like the water sprites, or the wind wraiths...I don't rightly know what it looks like."

"Well, what color is it?"

She went very still, as though realizing something for the first time.

"I don't know..." She looked up again, then slumped back on her stool. "Oh. It's gone. I don't think it likes being talked about."

"But —"

"It *is* beautiful," she said eagerly. "It's *very* beautiful. Like...like joy would be if it had a shape."

"But what shape?" I said, a bit loudly, frustrated myself. She looked hurt.

"I can't say. Can't, husband, not won't. I don't have the words."

After that, she didn't want to talk about it, but whatever the thing was, it came more and more often. The children all noticed, first, and then the villagers.

The little ones were convinced it was a wish sprite, like the ones in their stories. The older ones were worried, but no child likes to think their mother is going mad, so they didn't actually say it aloud.

We prayed, Wyst and I, at the black rock altar, but the gods have never spoken to anyone in our family, and they didn't now. When the villagers started muttering about wandering wits, I decided to go find a stonecaster.

Eaba was lighthearted. "It's like a holiday," she giggled, as she did when we were courting, and tucked her hand through my arm and snuggled close, and it was suddenly a good day, even if my worry for her was tugging at my mind.

She didn't look away from me the whole walk, and it was only then I saw that what I liked least about this *it* was how Eaba's face lit up when she saw it; the way she used to light up when she looked at me, or our babies. It was a kind of love she felt, not just delight, and I resented it hot and fierce once I realized it.

The stonecaster was a woman named Sylvie, a woman a few years younger than us, but not so young that I felt she wouldn't understand.

"You ask," Eaba said when we got there. "You're the one as wants to understand." And that was another annoyance. Eaba never seemed to care what the villagers were saying. Didn't even seem to be curious about this *it*—as though the presence of it answered all her questions, even when she couldn't tell anyone else what it was.

Well, I thought, I'm not going to beat around the bush. I spat in my palm and clasped hands with the stonecaster. "Is it real?" I asked.

She blinked in surprise and felt in her pouch for the stones. Brought them up, cast them.

They looked just like ordinary stones to me. Four landed face-up, with their marks showing. The other, a dark rock, face-down.

"New beginnings, Joy, Family, Spirit, face-up," she said, touching them lightly. Then she put her fingertip on the dark stone. "Chaos," she said quietly, and seemed to listen. Then she sat back and shook her hand as if her finger had been bitten. "Well," she said. "Whatever it is, it's real enough." She looked at the stones again, then sighed. "They're not saying much. There is some kind of spirit or sprite come to you, but what kind it is I cannot say. It brings joy."

"Yes!" Eaba said. "Only joy."

Sylvie looked her straight in her milky eyes. "For you. It brings joy for you. But for others it brings chaos, upheaval. A change in everything they have known or believed."

Eaba sat back on her haunches, brow puckered. "But why?" she asked. "What does it matter to them?"

"Because you love it more than you love us!" I burst out. "You'd rather stare up at it than do anything—*anything*—else."

She blinked and stared at me with more attention than she'd given me for a month. For a moment I could see through the veils in her eyes to the woman I loved. But her eyes filled with tears, and I lost her.

"I'm going blind, husband," she said softly. "I have loved you for thirty years, and I will love you until the day I die. But in all the world, it's the only thing that is bright to me. Would you take that light away from me?"

What could I say? I loved her. Love her.

I took her home and told the children and the neighbors what the stonecaster had said. I think some of the neighbors didn't believe me. I didn't care. I cared for her and I did her chores when she was too busy staring at the sky to notice what needed doing. She stared more and more, longer and longer, as though the sight was food and drink to her. I became father and mother, both, to our children and was relieved when they grew old enough to care for themselves and to help care for her.

I loved her. Love her. But when Vi told me the plan to stymie the warlord, and that like as not he'd take all of us councillors as hostage if we went to the square and defied him, I went anyway.

I'd like to think she noticed that I was gone.

BRAMBLE

HALFWAY DOWN the tumbled mountainside, they saw people gathering below, drawn by the thunder of the breaking rocks. Young men, the fastest runners, arrived first. Then children, then the adult villagers, more stolidly, but betraying in their bodies a mixture of fascination and fear. Not warlord's men, thank the gods. But dangerous for all that. There wasn't a dark head among them.

Acton waved cheerfully to them and Bramble suppressed a smile. Medric was excited and rather proud, Bramble thought, to be coming out of the mountain with Acton. She hoped he was right not to be afraid.

Ash looked worried, but with a touch of anticipation. "See if he can talk his way out of being a ghost," he muttered to Bramble.

"You talk for me, Baluch," Acton said, before they reached the waiting group.

"What do I say?" Baluch asked, a little out of breath. He was having more trouble climbing down than they were, Bramble thought, and she remembered the young Baluch, climbing a mountainside, springing from boat to shore, running.

"Tell the truth!" Acton said, his face surprised. "Tell them who I am and that I've come to defeat the enchanter."

The villagers were whispering to each other, pointing at Acton. Some carried scythes, sickles or hoes as weapons.

They halted a few feet above the crowd, and Baluch announced, in that clear, singer's voice: "People of the Domains, Acton has returned to you to lead you in victory against the enchanter!"

The suspicious faces cleared immediately, and they cheered. It astonished Bramble.

"It's the legend from the songs," Ash said. "The last thing he said as he rode away was, 'I'll be back before you need me.' In their hearts, they believed it, so they believe him, now."

Bramble laughed. "If they only knew!"

Acton sprang down from the rock and the villagers crowded around him. They wanted to touch him, despite the graveyard chill, and he let them, as if understanding the need to make sure he was real. He smiled, but it wasn't his mischievous smile, it was the smile of the commander, trustworthy and responsible and strong. She realized that it wasn't a false face. He just shifted as the need arose, because he could be whatever people needed. Maybe that's what he had always done—served other people's needs. The only thing he'd ever wanted, really wanted, for himself was to go to sea, and he'd never had the chance. That was what Tern, the enchanter of old Turvite, had done to him. She had cursed him: he would never have what he truly wanted.

The crowd grew more excited. "Acton! Acton!" they called.

Bramble was reminded of other scenes, battles, where Acton's warriors had done the same thing just before they killed. She hoped it wasn't a portent for the future. She drew Ash aside. "You gave him the perfect introduction. A mountain bursts apart, and Acton appears! The stuff of legend."

Ash scowled. "We're wasting time."

Acton put up a hand and the villagers drew back a little. He turned to Baluch and pointed to his own throat.

Baluch nodded. "Acton has returned from the grave for you, and he speaks with the voice of the dead. Be prepared. It is a harsh voice, but it is the voice of strength from the darkness beyond death."

The smith took a step forward. The village voice, may be.

Acton nodded gravely to him and said, "Where are your Travelers?"

It was the last thing Bramble had expected. Ash was as surprised as she was.

Baluch translated and the smith, a curly headed blond with hazel eyes, stared at them all, astonished. "Travelers?" he asked, looking around as if to find some. "Most escaped, my lord."

"Who from?" Acton said sharply. Again, Baluch translated.

"The warlord's men came," the smith replied. "And took a few of them. The others ran."

"Find them," Acton commanded. "They are your only defense."

Baluch translated again, but this time the smith and his people were mutinous. "Travelers? What good are they?" He stared with narrowed eyes at Bramble and Ash, and she looked impassively back at him. She had no idea what Acton was planning. Medric moved slightly in front of her.

"The enchanter seeks to kill all of my blood," Acton declared. "Only Travelers, standing shoulder to shoulder with you, can defy him."

"He's mad," Ash whispered, and Bramble could see the same thought in the smith's eyes.

"No," she said slowly. "He's right. The enchanter may think he's doing what Travelers want. If they challenge him —"

Acton spoke again. "Find your Travelers. Reassure them. Plan your defenses with them. And treat them well—because they are your shield and your sword."

"Stupid idea," a woman muttered. "Acton wouldn't say that. He just killed the bastards."

Acton turned slowly towards her and she backed away a little, reacting to the authority in his look. Bramble wasn't sure how he did it; his face was calm, not stern, but nonetheless he suddenly felt dangerous.

"For a thousand years this land has been divided, in part because I chose poorly at times. Division has led us to the dead taking revenge upon the living. Unity is our only defense. If we are not divided, if the people of the old blood stand with us, we cannot be defeated."

"Is that true, lord?" the smith asked. "We can't be defeated?"

Acton stared at him with compassion. "We will be defeated, my friend, if we are fighting each other. Work together, or die."

As soon as Baluch finished echoing him, he strode off. Northeast.

"Tell everyone what Acton wants," Baluch added. "Spread the word."

The smith nodded in obedience. It made Bramble's gut curl in a knot. Obedience, deference—Acton and Baluch expected them, just like any warlord's man.

But then she caught sight of the puzzlement and uncertainty of the other villagers, and almost laughed. It was so like him, to upset everything, to come back and take over, to do what everyone least expected.

"This wasn't quite what I imagined we'd be doing," she said. Ash was annoyed.

"He's heading the wrong way. We're supposed to go to Sanctuary."

But when they caught up with Acton, he refused to turn around.

"Sanctuary's too close to T'vit," he said. "We have to stop this enchanter before he gets there."

"Since when is that *your* decision?" Ash demanded.

Medric moved in front of Ash and glowered. "That's Acton you're talking to!"

For a moment, Ash looked at him with hatred. Medric hunched himself, preparing for a fight. Bramble began to move forward, ready to intervene. She knew how Ash could fight. If he exploded, Medric would die. But Ash turned away from him, towards Acton.

Acton considered him. It had been a long time, Bramble thought, since anyone had challenged his leadership. Even Asgarn had pretended, until the end, to follow him gladly.

"Enchanter," he said with courtesy, "your business is spells and power. Mine is fighting. It's bad strategy to let your enemy get to your most valued stronghold. You must stop him early, before he reaches it. Or people die."

Bramble wondered which battle he was thinking of—one where he was a defender, or an attacker? Either way, he was right.

"We agreed to meet the Well of Secrets in Sanctuary," Ash said.

"She is a great prophet and healer," Baluch explained to Acton.

"We don't need her," Acton said. "From what you say, I must confront these ghosts. Do we need this Well of Secrets for that?" They hesitated, and he kept speaking. "Does it matter *where* I do it?"

"Not so far as we know," Baluch said. "But we may not know everything."

"Nobody knows everything," Acton said, his cheerful face at shocking odds with the terrible grating voice. "Baluch tells me that there is a stream in Central Domain which ran red with the blood of dead soldiers."

Information from the Lake, Bramble thought.

"Draw me a map," Acton said to Baluch, who crouched and sketched a rough outline of the Domains in the dirt. Acton beckoned over one of the young men from the village who had followed them.

"Show us where we are," Baluch said to him. The boy dragged his eyes away from Acton and pointed. They were much further east than she had thought. The Caverns had transported them a long way. Good, she thought, that would save them time.

"Thanks, lad," Baluch said, and Acton clapped the boy on the shoulder. The dead-cold sent him on his way shivering, but he was walking tall.

"Central Domain is where?" Acton asked. Baluch pointed to the map and Acton nodded. "Then the enchanter will make his way down to Turvite this way." His finger traced a route and stopped at the Fallen River.

"There's only two places to cross that river," Bramble said. "Up near the source, and here"—she pointed—"at Wooding." Her voice had been steady, she thought, but Acton glanced up at her as though she'd betrayed her unease. Her parents and grandfather were in Wooding. If the enchanter crossed the River there…"That's where I'm from," she added. "I know that countryside."

Acton nodded and stood up, brushing the dirt from his hands. "We make for Wooding, then," he said.

Bramble reached in her mind for the local gods, as she had done so often. *Wooding?* she asked, but they didn't answer. All their attention was on Acton. Perhaps that meant they approved of his plan.

She had sworn not to become one of his followers. Giving in to her own desire to go to Wooding seemed like a betrayal of that, a betrayal of Maryrose. Then she remembered Ash's pouch. The gods could decide for them.

"Cast for us, Ash," she said.

Ash looked relieved to take some kind of action. He sat down on the grass and spread out the square of linen he kept tucked in the top of his pouch. Acton's face lit with interest, as it had in the cave when Dotta had cast the stones for him. He crouched next to Bramble as she sat opposite Ash, spat in her palm and clasped hands with him.

"Which way should we go?" she asked.

Ash cast five stones. They clinked as they fell. Four of the faces were up.

"Necessity, Danger, Travel, Uncertainty," Ash said, touching them one by one. As when he had sung Acton back, his voice was the voice of the dead, harsh and grating. As Baluch had said, it was a voice of power. The final stone was plain black, blank faced. She waited for Ash to turn it over, but instead he touched it lightly as it lay. The blank stone, then, the one that meant anything could happen.

But Ash said, "Evenness," his tone full of dread.

"Evenness?" Bramble said. "Never heard of that one."

"It's new," Ash said, his face carefully blank.

Bramble stayed very still for a long moment. The other two, who came from a culture without stonecasters, looked puzzled.

"Change the stones, change the world," Bramble quoted, and Ash nodded. "But what does it mean?"

Ash took a long breath and let it out. "I'm not sure." He sounded light and young and a little afraid. "Justice? Equality?" His face seemed strained, as though this was not a responsibility he relished.

"So what do these stones mean for us?" Acton asked.

Ash looked down at the casting. "They mean that neither choice is perfect," he said. "We will be taking a chance either way, and the chances are evenly balanced, good and bad."

"Wooding, then," Acton said immediately, standing up.

"Because it's your choice?" Ash said, standing to face him.

"It's *Acton*," Medric protested again.

Acton waved Medric silent and turned to look at Ash seriously. "You brought me back because you have need of me," he said. "I think you need more of my skills than you know. We are enemies—I understand that. But I have stood shoulder to shoulder with my enemies before, because we were both confronted with a greater threat. And I think that is what you and I must now do against this enchanter."

"Under your command," Ash said bitterly.

"Are you a commander? If you are, I will follow you," Acton replied.

It was the simplicity of it that disarmed Ash. If Ash was a commander, Acton *would* follow. That truth was clear in his face.

Ash turned away and crouched down to pick up his stones and put them back in the pouch. Bramble expected his face to be red, but instead he was pale, as though Acton had said more than she had heard.

Acton nodded as if Ash had answered and began walking north-east, Baluch following after a backward look at Ash.

Bramble waited for Ash to pack up then slung her saddlebags back over her shoulder, in their accustomed place. She'd walked the length and breadth of this country, and it looked like she was going to walk halfway back. Her boots would be worn through, she thought with a grin, and she'd be forced to go barefoot, as she preferred.

"My family are in Wooding," she said, not looking at Ash. He walked ahead without meeting her eyes and she turned to Medric. "If you want to go home now, Medric, no one will think less of you."

He was surprised. "Go *now?* Oh, no. I'm following Acton." His eyes were alight with a vision of glory, of being part of legend.

"It will be risky."

"Fine with me," he said. That was bad, Bramble thought. That was very bad.

"We're not going on some kind of adventure," she continued, "where you can get yourself killed so you don't have to feel guilty any more, or so you can die in glory." Her voice was deliberately harsh, to startle him. "I need to be able to trust you, or you get out of this right now."

"You can trust me!" he protested.

"Trust you not to take the easy way out if an opportunity presents?" she demanded. "Not to dive into death to get away from your own thoughts?"

He flushed and looked away, and she knew she'd been right. He had been courting Lady Death in his mind as a way out of dealing with his need for Fursey, and Fursey's need for the gold buried deep in the mine Medric hated to enter. Lady Death would help him forget what the ox had said to him, back in the Caverns. And the promise of fighting with Acton had just made it easier to court her. Deliverance and glory, all in one.

But to Bramble's surprise he looked back at her, chin up. "Aye," he said. "I'll back you best I can till you don't need me."

She nodded. "Good then." Her voice softened. "Maybe by then Lady Death won't look so fair to you."

Medric grinned, a sudden sweep of humor across his face that brought an answering smile from her. "It's the first time a female's had any attraction, so might could be you're right!"

Acton and Baluch walked together and Bramble could hear that Baluch was still giving language lessons—the names of things, the words he had used to the villagers, Domain and town names.

And they weren't traveling alone. Like Medric, some of the young men from the village chose to follow Acton at a respectful distance.

The first step, Bramble thought. He's raising an army.

LEOF

WHEN THEY arrived at the fort, Leof took Vi and the other councillors to the hall, moving through the muster yard slowly, to let them take a good look at the men training, the smiths hammering, the masons working on the defenses. He had no hope that the huge, complicated apparatus of war being created here would impress Vi, but he wasn't sure of the others; it was worth a try.

He left them in the empty hall with Alston and went in search of Thegan, but found Sorn first, supervising the cleaning of Thegan's office. His heart jolted and then lifted as he laid eyes on her. She was instructing a young maid, a new girl by the looks of her, about leaving Thegan's map table strictly alone. Her voice was like rain after drought. He took a deep breath and let it out, glad she hadn't seen that first, unmistakable reaction.

Then she turned and saw him and he saw her eyes light, her mouth open to say his name and then close again, firmly, as she took control of herself. It broke his heart, an actual pain inside his chest, to see her in difficulty, but he could do nothing that wouldn't make it worse.

"Lady Sorn," he said formally, bowing. "I seek my lord."

"With the smiths, Lord Leof, I believe," she said.

"There are . . . guests, in the hall."

Her eyes lifted sharply to his, but they betrayed nothing.

"The town council of Baluchston," he said.

"They will be treated with honor and offered comfort," she said, the formal oath of a warlord's lady. It was a serious thing to say, and he was both solaced and worried by it. Sorn would honor that oath, and it might cost her dearly.

He bowed again and walked slowly back to the hall so his breathing would be as calm as her voice by the time he reached it.

The older man, Reed, spoke as he entered the room. "Where are the Travelers being kept?"

"In the barn." Distaste crossed their faces, and he was nettled. "I assure you, we have done what we could to make them comfortable, but as you have seen, our accommodations are stretched to breaking point. Stay here. My lord is with the smiths. I will come back after I have seen him."

Irritation at them went with him across to the smiths' forge and hardened his voice when he found Thegan with Affo, the head smith, and a group of other men he didn't know.

"I've brought those bloody Baluchstoners back," he said. "The whole town turned out and said they had Traveler blood and we should take all of them. I brought the council back. I've stuck them in the hall."

Thegan nodded. "Let them wait. I've been talking to the smiths and the weavers from town about making heavy weighted nets, like the ones the northern fishers make to catch the fish that are too strong for their lines."

Leof gladly dived into the discussion, gloom lifting from his spirits. Defense, weaponry, the organization of their forces: these were what he had been trained for, and what he loved. Let Thegan deal with politics.

Sorn rose as Thegan entered, and bowed. "My lord," she said, and waited, hands by her sides.

Leof and Thegan had returned to the hall to find Sorn sitting with the town councillors at one of the lower tables, discussing, it had appeared, the music of the Lake People and how it differed from that of Acton's people. Leof hadn't realized she knew anything about music. There was so much he didn't know about her.

Vi lumbered to her feet and the others followed, a little reluctantly, and faced Thegan. Leof wondered what they saw: he himself was looking at Thegan a little differently nowadays, but he still saw a handsome, strong man in the full possession of his power. Vi's face gave nothing away, her heavy-lidded eyes blank.

"Our guests," Thegan said to Sorn, "have informed the Lord Leof that they have Traveler blood, so I think they are best housed in the barn with the others."

He ignored the council completely. Vi didn't react at all but Reed was furious, and the two younger ones showed a mixture of relief and indignation. Sorn nodded, and with her agreement Thegan simply turned and walked out.

Leof exchanged a quick glance with Sorn, and followed him, trying not to laugh. Punctured expectations were so often funny, even in people he quite liked.

Thegan turned and found him chuckling and smiled, the real smile. He couldn't help but return it. "They have no idea they have given us a weapon that we can use against this enchanter."

"My lord?"

"Not only Travelers as hostages, now, but Lake People." His tone was full of satisfaction. "After this is over, they will not be going home unless they tell me the secrets of the Lake."

There he was again, planning for the future. Leof found it both reassuring and irritating. He wanted to say, "How can you be so sure it will be over?" but knew it was possible that Thegan was *not* sure, and was just putting on a good face for his officers. Leof didn't want to find out that was true.

He left Thegan and went to check on the mason's gang strengthening the wall under Oak's direction. No time to rest just yet.

Sorn and her maid, Faina, crossed the yard, headed for the dairy. Oak's eyes followed them, and Leof stiffened. He would brook no indignity from a Traveler towards Sorn. But Sorn disappeared inside the dairy and left Faina outside, talking to Alston. Their bodies inclined towards one another. Oak's mouth tightened and he turned away suddenly, his trowel striking hard against the high stone block that was wrapped with ropes ready to be lifted, the note ringing out across the yard. Faina, not Sorn, then. Leof relaxed, filled with sympathy. No wonder the poor fellow looked unhappy.

"Keep up the good work, mason," he said. Oak looked surprised, as though Leof's words had contradicted something he had been thinking. Not feeling valued, maybe? Leof hadn't been an officer all his adult life without knowing how to deal with that. "Without you, mason, and your colleagues, we would be in a dangerous situation. Our lives are in your hands."

Leof looked around at the small gang preparing to use pulleys and rope to haul the heavy stones up into place, and clapped Oak on the shoulder. He expected the man to puff up a little with importance, or nod with understanding, but Oak stopped still, as though he had never thought of his role in this way. Finally, he nodded and turned away, trowel still in hand, to give an order to the lad he'd been assigned, a young man with light brown hair and soft hands, who'd clearly never done a hand's turn of work in his life. He looked familiar, and then Leof placed him—the one who had pretended not to be a Traveler, on the road to Baluchston.

"Flax!" Oak ordered. "We need to raise these blocks. Give us a work song to keep us in time."

The lad nodded. "Sea shanties are best for that," he said in a light voice, and waited until all hands had grasped the rope, then he gave out a note so strong and full that Leof almost jumped.

Lady Death will ring her bell
Heave away
Haul away
Call us all to the deep cold hell
Raise the mains'l maties

The men hauled on the ropes in time and the stone block slowly rose. Oak steadied it so it wouldn't swing.

There waves are taller than the sky
Heave away
Haul away
They'll crush your ribs and blind your eyes
Raise the mains'l maties

Oak called, "Hold it there," and then Leof heard the solid thunk of the stone settling into place.

Although he'd spent the day in the saddle, he felt the sudden need to get out of the fort, to prepare himself for dinner, the first meal he'd had in both Thegan and Sorn's company since he'd found himself loving her. He needed surcease. He checked that Thegan did not need him.

"Arrow will need exercising," he said. "If you'll excuse me, sir."

"You and your horses!" Thegan replied, waving Leof away.

Arrow did need exercising. She was spritely and affectionate and danced her way down the long road from the fort, shying at everything—wind blown leaves, a boy trundling a cart full of stone up to the walls, her own shadow. Leof found her innocent antics a great relief; and they kept his mind off everything else.

He rode down to the pool where he had seen the old man, half hoping to find him there again, but there was nothing except the cool, spreading water and moss-covered stones, which seemed to promise continuity, a sense of time far beyond a human lifespan. He dismounted and stayed there for a while, until Arrow grew bored and nudged him in the back. He reluctantly turned to go back, then paused and walked towards the water, Arrow's reins looped over his arm.

He stood with his toes just in the pool, feeling the cool wetness seep slowly into his boots. "Lady," he said, feeling absurd, "What should I do?" He didn't expect a reply. Part of him hoped fervently that there wouldn't be one.

But a voice sounded in his head, as though she were speaking from another room. "You are not one of mine," it said, which was curiously hurtful, because it was said in his mother's voice.

"I am in need of guidance," he said.

"No," the voice said. "You know what is right, which is all the guidance you need. If you will not go home to your mother, you must take the consequences." The voice was curiously soft and sorrowful, as his mother's voice had never been in his memory, and yet he knew that his mother could sound like this, as though she had crooned over him in this tone when he was too young to remember.

"But I will give you a gift," the voice said, "because you believe in me. Because you have tried your best to protect my people."

Something nudged his toe. He looked down and saw a little circle floating on the water. He picked it up. It was woven reeds, a simple ring as large as a woman's bracelet.

“For luck,” the Lake said, her voice warm with laughter. “Just a token, to help you think of me. Keep it with you.”

The water stilled, the ripples from where he had picked up the ring disappeared, smoothed away, and he knew she was gone.

He tucked the ring in his left pocket and felt a little flushed, as he had at sixteen when Dorsi’s daughter, Gret, had chosen him for the Springtree dance: embarrassed and happy, with an undercurrent of fear.

FLAX

As always when Travelers came together, the barn that night was full of music, a complex lively music of drum and flute and oud, bells and rhythmic clapping, horn and gong. Rowan, Swallow and Flax were at the center of it, of course, and Flax found it comforting.

"Give us a song, lad," Reed, one of the councillors from Baluchston, said to him, and he muttered to Rowan, "What will I sing?"

Rowan smiled at him and played the first notes of "The Distant Hills."

From the high hills of Hawksted, my lover calls to me
The breeze is her voice, the wind becomes her breath
From the high hills of Hawksted, above the settled plain
My lover sings so sweetly, sings the song of death

The last time Flax had sung this song was in the Deep, asking for acceptance from a group of demons. This audience was much easier.

By the time he finished, there were more than a few wet eyes. Even Oak looked teary, which he hadn't expected.

"Singing's all very well, my dearies," Vi said, "but that Lord Thegan's a cold-hearted boy and he'll sacrifice us all, sooner or later."

"Aye, that's so." It was Reed's voice, grave. "He'll not keep feeding us, not for long."

"We're not prisoners," Oak objected.

"I'd rather be here than back home," a woman said. "They slaughtered my cousins—and we've been Settled three generations!"

Disquiet circled the barn like a swarm of bees.

"It's bad out there," Vi agreed, "and we're better off here for the meanwhile. But let's not think he's doing it out of the goodness of his heart. We may not be prisoners, but we're hostages, sure as eggs is eggs."

"What would you know? You're not a Traveler." It was a man's voice, deep and authoritative. Flax looked around but didn't recognize the old man. There were people here from all over Central Domain.

"I've got the old blood in me, same as everyone in Baluchston," Vi replied. "I may not have been on the Road, but as far as Thegan is concerned, I'm tainted and he can do what he likes with me."

That silenced them.

Flax hesitated, but the memory of Ash confronting wind wraiths came back to him. Surely he could face a few questioning eyes? "We have to be ready," he said. "Sooner or later they'll turn on us, and we have to be ready. Have our escape routes planned, hide some weapons, figure out who stands with whom, and where."

Some in the crowd looked at each other, judging reactions, and Vi nodded.

"Aye," she said. "But quietly. Sing again now, in case they wonder why we've stopped."

Rowan's flute started and Swallow began to sing; it was beautiful and spare and delicate, in a language Flax didn't know. From the Wind Cities? No, something else. The melody sounded strange, too, with an unusual choice of notes. With a shock, Flax realized that she was singing in the old language, the tongue used by the people Acton had invaded. He'd had no idea that it survived. His parents had certainly never taught him any.

Then the words changed into his own tongue, as though Swallow were translating:

Water, fire, earth and air
Spirits live and spirits die
Flame upon the mountain
Wind across the sky
Water dark and dreamless
Earth in which we lie
Water, fire, earth and air
Blood is everlasting

"We're better off where we are," the old man said, when Swallow had sung the last note.

"But we have to be ready," Flax objected, "for when we're not better off."

"Young man's talk," the man said. Flax could see clearly now; he was a very old man, half bent over with rheumatism. "Young man's talk, young man's death."

A Traveler saying, and true enough. There were a few scattered chuckles.

"Old heads on young shoulders, sometimes," Reed said, and Flax laughed.

A child began to cry, and then another as the first cry woke the sleeping ones.

A woman groaned and got up to settle her child, and the assembly began to break into family groups. Some headed out to the privies.

Flax joined Oak and Vi and Reed in a corner of the room to plan.

OAK'S STORY

I CAN MAKE a wall will stand for a thousand years. I've seen 'em. Fences built in Acton's time, still there, snaking across the country like a stream. You can't build a straight wall that'll last, though. Have to follow the lay of the land, get the feel of the earth roundabout and put the wall where it lies lightest on the ground. Try to build a straight wall and it'll tumble over come spring, when the groundwater shifts with the snowmelt; it'll bulge when the tree roots feel their way through the cracks in the bedrock to get to the rivers beneath; it'll shake itself to death, slowly, with the heat and cold and heat of summer and winter and summer, over and over, making the rocks snap and crack apart, like as not—and then the wall has to bind those rocks together so that, even snapped apart, the wall still holds. Can't do that with a straight wall.

Build a straight wall, and you're having to repair it, year after year. That's most of my business, repairing straight walls. Guess I shouldn't complain about 'em then.

I know where I am with rock. Know my granite and my schist, sandstone and bluestone, basalt and limestone. Harder the better. Nothing beats a granite wall. Nothing.

But people... I have no idea about people. Never have had. Like my father, Mam said. Just like him. That's all right with me. My Da was a good worker. I've never seen a man make a wall with less wastage of stone. He could find the right chink even for a bit of rubbish—tufa, or even scoria, rocks that hardly deserve the name of stone. He taught me. Never said much. Didn't need to. Piece by piece is how you build a wall, and there's not much to say about it that you aren't better off showing.

He taught me masonry, too, working with mortar, even bricks. Some places just got no stone. I can build anything, near enough, thanks to Da.

So I never minded being no good with people. My da found himself my mam, and I guessed one day I'd meet myself a girl who didn't want a chatterer, and it'd be sweet.

And maybe I would have, and maybe I could have, if I hadn't met Faina first.

Course I always thought I'd meet a Traveler girl. Who else? I'm no fool, ready to get beaten up or worse for looking above myself. And when did I meet other girls anyway? Walling, you deal with the man of the farm, or the house, not the woman. But my mam liked to visit the local gods wherever we went, and I came with her, though I don't feel them the way she did. So there we were a few years ago near Sendat, in a little village, and we went to the black stone altar early for the dawn greeting, just like a hundred times before, in a hundred little villages all over the Domains. And there she was. Fair-headed, blue eyed. Praying like she meant it.

My mam says my da made up his mind about her the first time he laid eyes on her. Takes some men like that. Guess I'm like my da that way, too.

Like I said, I'm not a fool. Didn't even think about it. Didn't even imagine...

But I knew there wouldn't be anyone else for me.

I did my job for a local farmer and we went on our way. Nothing else I could do.

My mam died the next year, and after that I Traveled alone. I had my round, meaning I called in to regular customers once every three years. Never short of business. South in the winter, north in the summer. Then this last year the call went out for wallers and masons to come to Sendat. My lord Thegan was building better fortifications.

I went because it was good money and it's better not to say no to a warlord.

So. She was there. At the fort. Acting as maid to the Lady Sorn. That first day, I was working on the new storage sheds and I saw her walk through the mustering yard after the Lady, so the next morning I was there at the altar stone before dawn, and sure enough she came. A little older; just the same. It was just the same for me, too. I don't think she even saw me. She was with a sergeant. He had a good face, that one, and tall, blond. I found out later his name was Alston and they were hand-plighted. I could tell, the way she looked at him.

There never had been any chance for me, so I wished her well. But I didn't go back to the altar at dawn. Made my visits during the day, when she was busy in the hall with the Lady.

She's a real lady, that Sorn. The weather was getting hot, and she made sure that there was small beer for all the workers, and good food at mealtimes, and decent lodgings, even for the Travelers. Alston organized things so that the Travelers and the blondies weren't working together, which made life better, too. He was all right.

But I heard that they couldn't get married yet. Alston didn't have a house to take Faina to, and her father wouldn't let her live in the barracks with the other soldiers' women. Don't blame him. No place for a gentle girl.

I heard Alston talking about it to my lord Leof. "I've got land," he said, "down by the stream, that my lord ceded to me after I got my sergeant's badge. But no house." He sounded rueful.

"And no chance of getting one until all this work is done," Leof said, looking at us, laboring to shore up the walls around the fort.

Alston shrugged. "We can wait," he said. But he sounded wistful, and I thought she was probably wistful too. "Even one sound room would be enough for the present."

I found out where the land was, and went to have a look. It was a good place. Alston must have pleased Lord Thegan, to get that land.

I used some of the things the demons had taught me in the Deep, and I scried the land underneath, to learn its strengths and faults. It's not a thing I do often. It takes too much from you.

The bedrock beneath it was solid, there was a spring as well as the stream, the earth flowed gently into a naturally level place, which is where, no doubt, they meant to build. But that place was where the spring started, and it traveled underground a ways before it came up. Put a house there and it would sink to one side in a year.

But down the other side was an outcrop of granite, which had calved enough stone to build with, and if that was cleared away there was enough room for a house. I scried that place, too, and felt the layers speak back to me, clear as quartz in the sun. Granite bedrock, solid as the earth itself. That was where they should put their house.

Well, I was a waller, and there were walls to build. What else could I do for her? It was for living in, so I used mortar to give them straight walls (and maybe I thought I could come back and repair those walls in the future, and see her). I worked at night, after Lord Leof let us go from the fort.

I was tired, of course. Got tireder, working two jobs. Didn't matter. Walls went up, slow and then quicker once the foundations were done. I made her a good house. Strong. Facing south-east, with two windows, but none on the north side where the wind whistled.

Two rooms. Didn't let myself think about what might happen in that second room, between him and her. It didn't matter.

I made her a solid house, a house she could trust, with a chimney of river stones, all blue and grey, and a good white doorstep and a high-pitched roof to slide the snow off, because they told me it snowed mightily in Sendat. I traded some silver for slates in another village, told the man it was for my lord's work. Cut the trees for the rafters from their own land. I even put a floor in, flagstones, hard to cut. Didn't get much sleep that week. Alston got a bit short with me—told me to pick up the pace or get a whipping. Didn't hold it against him, much. He was right. I had been slacking.

Didn't matter. What mattered was, I couldn't figure a way to be there when she saw it.

I couldn't tell her. Alston was so much at the fort that he hadn't been to the land in weeks. I'd counted on that, but now the house was finished it was not so good.

I went to the altar at dawn and she was there, right enough, but —

I'm no good with people. Don't understand how they work. But I thought, if I tell someone else, and they told Alston, or her…

Couldn't think of who to tell.

So I went to the new stonecaster, Otter, down in the village. Didn't tell him what I wanted. You don't have to. He cast, but the stones were so mixed up, he said, that he couldn't make head nor tail of 'em. An empty house, he said, and a forlorn love. He looked curious, but trustworthy enough. So I told him. Not everything. Just that someone had built a house on Alston's land and I didn't know how to tell him. Didn't want to get involved, I said, but I think he could tell I was already involved, up to my armpits.

"I'll mention it to my lord Leof," he said gently. "Next time I go up to the fort."

He was there next day. I was working on the gate with Lord Leof inspecting the work when he arrived. I saw him talking to the Lord, and he was good to his word, because he didn't so much as look my way. He visited the Lady, too, while he was there.

So then I kept a watch and, sure enough, after dinner, Faina slipped out with Alston and they went down the hill together, taking the back way to the land.

I followed 'em. Heard 'em find the place. Alston had brought a lantern to light their way, though it wasn't full dark, and he took it inside. I saw them in the window, saying, "But *who?*" and concluding that it was my Lord Leof and the Lady Sorn, together, had organized it. She couldn't think of anyone else who would do something like this for her.

She was crying. That was all right. I'd seen my mam cry like that when my brother had his child. It meant I'd built her a good house, and she liked it. That was my satisfaction, right there. All I needed, I thought. Then he came up behind her and she turned her face to his shoulder and he put his arms around her.

I went away.

Nothing else I could do. For her. For me. Not while she loved him. Not even if she hadn't. Only time in my life, though, I've wondered what my life would have been if I'd had blond hair. If I could have gone up to her that first time, in her old village. Said, "Nice morning, isn't it?" as we walked away from the altar. Courted her. Won her. Built her a good house, a strong house that she could trust, for the both of us to live in.

Not in this life. Not nowhere in the Domains. Not now, and not never, probably. But I wondered. Wanted. Got angry for the first time, about how it wasn't fair and never had been. Thought, "It shouldn't be like this."

It shouldn't.

SAKER

SOLDIERS LINED the road ahead of him, checking everyone. Not that there were many people on the road to stop. Everyone who could be was hunkered down behind their shutters, shivering with fear.

Saker smiled, but his smile faded as he saw the merchant's party ahead of him sorted into two groups. One, blonds and red-heads, who were allowed to go on their way. The other, dark-hairs, kept in a group to one side, where the road widened into a water meadow.

His own hair was its customary reddish brown. He always carried some rosehips to make the dye, because they looked so innocuous if he was ever searched—"Oh, yes, sergeant, rose-hip tea is very good for you, you know." Whereas anyone found with henna traded up from the Wind Cities was assumed to be a Traveler in disguise and treated badly. He had dyed his hair very carefully before venturing out of the mill. But would it fool the soldiers?

The pouch of stones he tucked inside his jacket. Stonecasters were not always Travelers, but most were. He remembered the red-headed woman from Carlion who had had Traveler blood—perhaps, like her, the stonecasters who were not Travelers had old blood in them after all.

His throat tightened as he walked towards the soldiers, conscious that if they found the bones in his pack he was dead on the spot. A sergeant was in charge of them, a large gray-haired man in his fifties. "Ho, sir!" he said with professional geniality. "Where are you off to?"

"Sendat," Saker replied, smiling. "I have family there, and they say it's the safest place in all the Domains right now."

"Family, eh?" The sergeant looked at him closely. "Who would that be, then?"

Saker blessed his years of roaming from town to town as a stonecaster. "Old Lefric, the chairmaker," he said confidently. "He's my great-uncle." And Lefric would confirm that, too, because he had decided, hearing Saker's made-up ancestry over a drink in the inn, that he was his niece Sarnie's boy from Whitehaven. He'd invited Saker home with him that night and he'd stayed with the old man several times since, thinking there might come a time when being able to claim a family would come in handy. He was feeling rather satisfied with his forethought right now.

"Lefric?" the sergeant asked. "Bit of a drinker, that one."

It was a test.

"I think you may have him mixed up with someone else, sergeant," Saker said. "My uncle never drinks anything stronger than small ale."

The sergeant smiled. "All right, go along with you." He turned his attention to another party coming along the road, dismissing Saker without another glance.

Saker went on, deliberately ignoring the group of Travelers as he passed them.

He made it twenty paces down the road before his hands started to shake, his heart pound. Why would he be afraid now? It was over. He'd passed the test and he'd survived. It must be anger at the treatment the Travelers were receiving. But he had to tuck his hands well into his pockets and breathe deeply for more than a mile before he had himself under control.

Unlike the farms and villages he had passed on the way, Sendat was open for business. The market square was as full as always—perhaps fuller, although there was not as much produce on sale as there had been the last time he had visited two years ago. Saker thought that the farmers were not willing to risk the journey to town.

He noticed, too, that there were very few tools out in the open, and no axes at all. Had the warlord given orders to lock up the one type of weapon that would make these people vulnerable to his army?

He made straight for Lefric's house, in case the sergeant from the road, who had looked no fool, checked up on him. Lefric was in his yard, as usual, setting the legs into a stool.

He looked up as Saker came through the gate, and his face brightened. "Penda!" he called. He got up creakily and put the stool down on his workbench, then hobbled over to greet Saker. His knees and hands were even more swollen with arthritis than when Saker had last visited, but his eyes were still bright blue, unfaded. "It's good to see you, lad!"

He clasped his hands around Saker's arms and gave him a small shake of welcome.

Saker smiled. Although Lefric was one of Acton's people, he had always liked the old man. "Ho, uncle!" he said, smiling. "Thought I'd come and see how you were faring, these strange days."

"You're a good lad, Penda, a good lad, and it's good to see you. Come away in and have a bite. You look like you've been journeying a good while."

Saker glanced down at his clothes. They showed the wear and tear of sleeping rough and washing little. "Aye," he said, "I've come a fair step."

Over supper, he and Lefric exchanged news. He made up stories about his supposed mother, Sarnie, and his siblings; Lefric told him, in detail, all the goings-on of the warlord and the fort. Saker listened intently. Travelers being gathered together? Offered shelter and safety? He was shaken. Surely a warlord would never protect Travelers at the risk of his own people? Such an action would be beyond generous...He had always heard that this Lord Thegan was a hard man, although loved by his people. Could he be a just man, too? And if he were, what did that mean for Saker's plan?

The next day, he quartered the town, looking for the best place to cast his spell. With his army so large, now, Lefric's yard wasn't big enough. It wasn't easy to find a suitable place. He had to be sure of enough time to raise the ghosts, and the more he looked, it became clearer that there was nowhere within the town where he could ensure privacy.

He came back to the yard preoccupied, and was greeted by Lefric's request that he go to the coppice south of the town, to cut ash for chair backs. He had marked the tree with his colors, so Saker would have no trouble finding it.

"Save me the trip, lad," Lefric said, beaming as Saker nodded. "It's good to have family to help out." He paused. "Might could be it's time for you to settle down here, lad. Take on the business."

For a moment, Saker had a vision of what life might be like, living here, working at a solid, simple craft. Making friends. Marrying, even.

His vision faltered at that. His time with Freite had made him wary of touching any woman.

Just as well.

The guards on the road leading south refused to let him take an axe to the coppice. "Saws only," they said, and made him take the small hatchet that Lefric had given him back to the yard and lock it up.

"Aye, aye," Lefric grumbled. "I'd forgotten. Those are the new rules."

He couldn't set the ghosts to batter down door after door if the axes they needed were locked up in chests and cellars. They could get them, eventually, but the effort... Increasingly, he was looking to the fort for the weapons they needed.

It wasn't hard to find the tree Lefric wanted. The coppice was small enough, and useless for his needs during the day, being frequented by other crafters who shared Lefric's rights here: trug makers, wattlers, carvers. But at night... He looked around speculatively as he sawed at the ash tree.

Perhaps not right here, but behind the coppice looked promising. He put down his saw and wiped his brow as if tired, then walked towards the stream beyond the trees, in the little valley. At the stream's edge, he scooped water in his hand and drank, honestly relishing it. He poked at his hand, where a blister was already forming. No, he really wasn't suited to this kind of work.

By the stream was no good for his needs, either, at least not here. But a little way along there was a spreading pool under a large tree—a cedar? Its branches hung low, almost sweeping the ground in places. Under there he would be private, safe from interference. If he could get out here; if the guards were not too vigilant; if Lefric slept soundly enough.

He knew what his father would say to that—"Kill the old man. He's no kin of ours." But he was reluctant to repay Lefric's kindness with murder. "Weak!" He heard his father's voice again, and felt sweat break out on his brow. If he couldn't get out of the town, he'd need to stay at Lefric's until he could. He needed to keep him alive.

It was enough of a reason to still the accusing voice.

Tonight, Saker thought. I'll call them up tonight, and then tomorrow it won't matter what happens to Lefric.

The thought brought a mixture of excitement and terror.

ASH

THE STRAGGLE of youths behind them grew larger as they passed each farm. They were starting to resemble a parade, like harvest time in the northern towns, Ash thought sourly. And they were all so *young*. He knew, objectively, that some of the gawking youths were his own age, but somehow they seemed more like childer. They certainly acted like childer, larking about and making jokes. They didn't seem to realize the magnitude of the problem.

Acton, of course, just laughed at them.

"We need horses," Bramble said as they approached the next village.

Ash groaned inwardly at the thought of riding, but he knew she was right. It would take them weeks to get to Wooding at this pace.

"Will one carry me, d'you think, sweetheart?" Acton asked.

She shook her head. "Not a chance. But you're dead—there should be no limit to how fast you can run."

It had taken courage to say that out loud, Ash thought, remembering the searing longing that had flowed from Bramble when he and she had raised Acton.

Acton grinned at her. "I never was very fast on my own legs. Might be fun as long as I don't spook the horses."

In the village, Acton and Baluch went through their performance again. Ash had to resist the urge to give them a low, regular drumbeat as a background, because it *was* a performance. This time, there were a few wary Travelers hailed out of their houses—or hauled out, Ash suspected. They arrived in the town square with frightened or defiant or deliberately blank faces, and gazed at Acton as though he were Lady Death herself. Ash was glad to see that gave Acton pause.

"Without you," Acton said to them as gently as his death voice would let him, "these people are all lost."

One dark-haired woman at the back of the crowd, her arm around a young boy protectively, seemed to think that would be a good idea, and Ash wondered how badly she'd been treated in the past. He felt pushed to speak to her, so he slipped around the side of the crowd. She took in his dark hair and looked less suspicious.

"The ghosts slaughter," he said. "Children, women, old people, they don't care. They just kill."

She looked quickly at a group of very young children who, bored by the adult talk, had started a game of chasings around the village well. One of them had dark hair.

"That's what we're working for," Ash said quietly. "So they can play and work and live together without fear."

"A few hearts and minds'll have to change for that to happen," she said, and touched a scar on her arm. A warlord's brand, the punishment for insolence in these parts.

"Aye," Ash said. "They will."

She flicked her eyes at Acton. "That really him?"

"Yes."

"Shame he's dead already. I'd of killed him where he stood, otherwise."

"We need to stand together against this enchanter."

She sniffed. "And after that? When they don't need us any more?"

Ash touched the pouch at his side.

"There's a new stone in the bag—evenness. Who knows what that means?"

"A new stone?" she asked, her eyes alight. "Then the world *is* changing."

"Aye," he said. "And how it changes will depend on us."

Ash realised that this was his task—as Acton raised the countryside, he would spread the news about Evenness. Everyone knew the adage: change the stones, change the world. If hearts and minds had to shift, thinking about the new stone might be the first step. He felt better, having a task, instead of just trailing behind Acton.

The Voice found them horses. Not good ones, by Bramble's expression, but saddle horses nonetheless. Bramble claimed the best of them, a lumpy bay, Medric was given a piebald, which looked half-carthorse but could carry him and the feed bags, and Ash and Baluch got shaggy dappled geldings, clearly brothers. Baluch simply paid for them, and for food.

"Where did you get that much silver?" Bramble asked him.

He smiled, looking older than ever. "Singing," he said, and for some reason that made Bramble laugh.

The horses didn't like Acton at first, but Bramble took them, one by one, and whispered to them and made them smell him until they stopped skittering away with wild eyes at his approach.

"But don't touch them," she warned him, "and don't talk to them."

He made a face, but obeyed in silence. Baluch, standing next to Ash, chuckled, and Ash wondered if Acton had ever obeyed anyone before.

The horses let them leave their escort of youths behind, which was a great relief. The boys were planning to mass at the borders of their Domain, Travelers and blonds alike. Acton wished them well and waved goodbye.

"Run!" Bramble called, turning the head of her ungainly mare to the north-east. "Run, little rabbit!"

Acton laughed and they surged off together, Bramble pushing the mare to a canter, Acton seeming to will himself to go faster, and faster, until he was keeping pace easily. His feet weren't quite touching the ground, Ash noticed.

Ash and Baluch enticed their horses to keep pace, but their slow start meant that Bramble and Acton remained some way ahead of them. Medric lumbered along behind, but the carthorse was faster than it looked.

"She loves him," Baluch said, glancing across at Ash.

"He's dead," Ash replied.

"Aye, but —" Baluch watched the two flying figures jump a low wall, Bramble's hair escaping from its tie and streaming out on the wind. "He may have met his match in her."

"And what's *she* met in him?" Ash asked, and wished he hadn't because no matter what the answer was, it couldn't be good for Bramble.

MARTINE

THEY WERE rounding the cape between Mitchen and Carlion, and the captain was looking worried.

"Bad water around here," one of Zel's aunties said. Martine could never tell them apart they were so alike—sun-browned, wiry, greying. "Things happen," she explained grimly.

Zel cast her a cynical look as she filled Trine's hay net. Trine butted her on the shoulder, but not unkindly. They had come to a closer understanding in the last few days. "Sailors' stories, Rawnie," Zel said.

Rawnie shrugged. "Believe what you like. But we'll be saying our prayers till we're past Carlion, Rumer and me."

"And keep a lookout for sea serpents?" Martine asked. She was sitting on the side of Trine's enclosure. She wanted to swing her legs like a child, she was so happy whenever she thought about Arvid. He was doing his accounts nearby, sorting out how much each Last Domain farmer and crafter had to be paid from the cargo they had sold in Mitchen. He glanced up briefly and gave her a look that recalled the night before, when he had stared into her eyes and said her name as he made love to her.

Her mood over the past days had veered from happiness so great she had felt drunk, to pessimism and gloom. The weather matched her: the clouds flitted across the sun, sending them from glare to shadow moment by moment.

She turned back to Rawnie and Zel, who were staring at her knowingly. She flushed.

"Well, sea serpents?" she prodded, embarrassed.

"No," Rawnie said seriously. "They swim further south, past the Wind Cities. Stranger than them."

The captain whistled. Rawnie jumped out of the hold to run to the mast. She seemed to skip up it, moving from rope to cross-mast to belaying pin.

Zel watched her thoughtfully. "Useful on ship, being a tumbler," she said, as if she'd never realized her physical skills might have any other application than performing.

"Your aunties seem happy," Martine said. It would be good for both Zel and Flax, she thought, if Zel took some time on board a ship.

"But what would Flax do?" Zel muttered as she shovelled Trine's dung into a bucket. She washed down the deck before spreading a fresh layer of straw.

Martine enjoyed the sun on her back as she watched Zel complete her chores. But slowly, subtly, she became aware that something was wrong. The sun was on her back, all right, but she wasn't growing any warmer. It wasn't the breeze—she was in a protected corner here. The sun's rays were growing weaker instead of stronger, although it was approaching noon.

"Something's wrong," she said. "Call Safred."

They didn't have to. As they came out of the hold Safred emerged from below deck, followed by Cael. The captain was at the steering arm, conferring with the steersman, and they both looked unhappy. Arvid came from the stern to join them as Martine and the others approached.

"What's happening?" Arvid asked.

The captain pointed off the starboard bow. Between them and the coast was a long, low bank of fog, rolling silently over the water towards them. It was a pure, cold white, and it should have reflected the sun brilliantly, but instead it seemed to drink the light in.

Martine found it terrifying. "Can we outrun it?" she asked.

The captain shook her head. "Normal fog, maybe. Not it. That's peril fog, that is. No escaping. All we can do is batten down until it gets what it came for."

"What is it coming for?" Cael asked.

"Memories," the captain said, in the same way she might have said "murder." The fog was coming faster. "Keep hold!" she called, bracing herself against the steering board, the steersman on the other side equally braced.

Martine moved back to the mast and grabbed a stay. She saw Arvid vaulting over a crate to get to her and then the fog reached them.

It blanked out not only sight but also every other sense. Martine couldn't hear, or speak, or feel her hands or feet. As though she had been imprisoned in fleece, but she couldn't even struggle against it. She tried stamping her feet on the deck, but it made no noise.

Then she heard, finally, and wished she hadn't. Someone was weeping. The steersman, she thought. The voice was a man's, close by, but he was crying like a child. Martine moved, without thought, to go to him, but without any sense of her body she had no idea how or which way she was moving, and she froze in fear. She could walk straight off the side of the ship unwittingly.

Then another voice—Safred's—cried out, "No!"

Martine sensed power in that rejection: the fog seemed to thin in that direction. Having a direction at all was so great a relief that Martine wanted to sink down and collapse, but she moved towards Safred as fast as she could.

Safred was muttering, "I will not..." over and over, and Martine used the words as a home line, like the ones they strung between houses in the Last Domain in winter, so that someone caught out in a blizzard could grab on and follow it to safety. She followed the words and found the white nothingness dissipating, so much that she could finally see Safred, in a column of clear air.

Others were coming, too: Arvid was next to her, Cael sprawled on the deck at Safred's feet—had he been weeping? A small whirlwind of fog lingered above Safred's head, seeming to be drilling down. Martine's Sight struck her and she almost fainted. She could feel the hunger in the fog, a hunger that could not be satisified. The hunger of the dark for the light, the hunger of the dead for life, the hunger of emptiness.

"I will not. I will not..." Safred's face was set but she kept repeating the words.

The captain stumbled into the clear air. "Let them have it!" she pleaded. "It'll go if you let it have the memory. It only ever takes from one or two."

"No!" Safred cried out. "They want all of them. They're not mine to give!"

Martine understood. Safred had not only her own memories, but the memories of all the people she had helped over the years. All those secrets, the deepest part of herself, were not hers to give. She had a hunger for secrets equal to the fog's, which meant that to it she was a feast. The fog would not let her go.

"We'll be stuck here forever!" the captain said. "I beg you, Well of Secrets."

Cael dragged himself up and put his hand on her shoulder. "Niece, I think you must."

"They trusted me," she said, eyes fixed on nothing.

He pressed her shoulder. "They are only secrets. You are more than the secrets you hold."

The fog crept back slowly over them, so that Martine gradually lost feeling in her toes, her feet, her legs.

"*Now* , child," Cael said, in the voice of a father.

Safred closed her eyes, and the fog enveloped her. She screamed; it sounded like a toddler's tantrum, but then it changed and Martine could hear real pain in it, searing distress.

Tears ran down Cael's face. The fog around her head darkened, became more like smoke, formed curls and wisps. Complex patterns emerged, like watermarks in silk, and Martine realized that it was, in its own way, beautiful. And her Sight told her that it was satisfied after all.

The screaming softened to a whimper, and Safred slumped to the deck. Cael gathered her into his arms, wincing as his own wound pained him. They were now only vaguely shrouded by the swirling patterns of light and dark.

Then they were not—the fog was gone, speeding across the water towards the open sea. It looked darker, but still pale, still formless.

Martine crouched beside Safred and took her hand.

"All gone," Safred moaned, laying her head on Cael's shoulder. "All of them, gone."

The steersman stumbled forward, and it was clear from his face that he had indeed been the one weeping.

The captain embraced him. "What did it take?" she asked.

"My childhood, I think," he said. "I can't remember anything before I was twelve, when I came on board ship the first time."

The captain breathed out a sigh of thankfulness. "That's all right," she said, smiling and hugging him. "You had a bastard of a childhood anyway!"

She waved at the crew and they cheered.

"Saf? What can you remember, sweetheart?" Martine asked coaxingly.

"They took the secrets," Safred said, without opening her eyes. "Only that. So much." She was exhausted.

"Your own memories?" Cael asked.

"I don't think so. Some small ones, perhaps." She sat up. "I can't remember the first time I healed someone," she said.

"Your childhood?" Cael prompted.

"I remember you, and Sage, and Nim and March," she said slowly. "So I think they left me that."

"They?" Arvid said. "The captain said *it*."

Safred shook her head. "They," she said definitely. "Like a swarm, like a hive of wasps feeding off a beehive. Parasites."

She shivered then leant over and vomited. They helped her up and Martine and Zel supported her towards the companionway, passing the steersman. They stared at one another with pity and comradeship.

"It was a bastard of a childhood," he said. "But now all I have is—emptiness."

She nodded, shivering still. "A great emptiness," she said. "It will never be filled."

SAKER

ALL DAY Saker wondered when he should raise his army. What if his new spell didn't work? What if they attacked the fort and then the ghosts faded, leaving him helpless?

He decided to cast the spell just before dawn, and wait until sun-up. If they faded, no harm done. If they didn't—on to the fort.

After they had retrieved the axes they needed from the fort, they would turn back and go through the town. He smiled to himself. It was a good plan.

He ate dinner with Lefric and enjoyed it, the first meal he had really enjoyed for weeks. The old man made dumplings and treacle for dessert, something he'd had only rarely—inns hardly ever cooked them, and Freite had never cooked, unless it was for a spell.

He licked the sweetness from his fingers and smiled at Lefric. When they went through the town, he would make sure this one was saved. The decision made him feel powerful and magnanimous; life and death were in his hands, but he would use it wisely.

The sky was still black. He had mapped out his route that afternoon, but finding it again, now, just before dawn was proving difficult. He hadn't brought a lantern; it was too dangerous to show a light. So he fumbled his way along the street, grateful for the chinks of light that came from an inn door, from an upstairs chamber where someone was getting ready to go to work, or making love, or sitting up at a sickbed.

As he stumbled past the locked houses, each one with its own occupants, each its own world, Saker felt completely alone. He was always alone, but having to go past each house and know he had no place there, no family, no role to play, tonight it seemed more difficult. He felt like a ghost himself, forever excluded from human company, human love. He touched wall after wall to keep himself walking straight, and each touch was another place he didn't belong, each house another rejection. His breath came loud in his ears, ragged and sobbing.

He was almost running by the time he reached the last house, along a laneway that he had earlier calculated wouldn't be guarded. Just as well he'd been right—he hadn't thought to go slowly, carefully. He simply needed to get away from those houses, from all the things he would never have.

But after Acton's people were gone, surely then he could think about a place of his own, even a family...His steps slowed and his breathing returned to normal.

It was no lighter, but the clouds were lifting and soon there would be starlight to see by. The wind seemed to blow the loneliness away—being alone out here was different from being alone in a town. He walked briskly along the lane, which curled in a wide loop before it came back to the coppice.

When he reached the pool, with its overhanging branches, something made him hesitate. It wasn't a strong feeling, like Sight, but...He turned and walked towards the coppice instead.

There was a small clearing where the charcoal burners worked, but in early summer they were long gone, leaving only the smell of charred wood behind. Here he made his preparations, laying out the bones on a linen cloth, bringing his father's and Owl's skulls out last and placing them in the front row. His father would be impressed by their army, Saker was sure. He looked up. The sky was beginning to lighten to that clear gray that meant it would be a sunny day.

Saker waited for as long as he dared. He couldn't risk the ghosts being seen if they were going to fade at sun-up. But the remaining clouds were turning pink. It was time.

"I am Saker, son of Alder and Linnet of the village of Cliffhaven. I seek justice..."

The strength of the spell lay in memories, and finally he understood that, could draw on them and on the memories that had been buried with these bones: phrases of music, a particular scent, a scream. It was harder than he had expected, to draw on the memories in the bones as well as his own. It meant he had to experience their despair. And their anger. Yes. Their anger would feed his own righteous rage, giving him enough strength to call them again.

"Arise Alder and Owl and all your comrades, know my blood as your own, seek only the blood of strangers..."

He heard something, and paused—something high and disquieting, like bat calls, a sound so high he almost felt it rather than heard it. It ran along his veins like ice water. He looked around quickly, but there was nothing to be seen except the trees and the lightening sky. Perhaps it was the souls of his army, keening to be brought back from death. He raised his knife and brought it down, despite his unease.

When the blood spattered on the pale bones, his father and Owl rose up first, by a heartbeat, before the blood had stopped spouting from his palm, and were followed by the others. The sound at the edge of his hearing grew as they appeared until he could barely hear anything else.

Then he said the final words in the old tongue, the new part of the spell: "Blood and memory raised you. Blood and memory feed you. Blood and memory keep you."

The sound in Saker's ears vanished. At least his father would understand him easily. No need for the few words of the old tongue he had to use with Owl and the others.

"We are outside Sendat, a large town with a warlord's fort at the top of the hill. Inside the fort are weapons—axes, halberds, tools we can use to get *inside* the houses."

Alder nodded enthusiastically.

"This is our second big raid—we took Carlion." Saker was both proud and a bit worried that Alder would be angry he had been excluded. "I wanted to make sure we were ready for this," he added as Alder frowned. "This is the important one, the one that will allow us to take Turvite back."

Alder looked like he wanted to argue it, but Owl clapped him on the back and urged him out of the coppice.

"No!" Saker ordered. "Wait!" He held up a hand to them all to mime "Stop." "Wait until the sun is up." He pointed to where the sun was beginning to show above the hills.

"Blood and memory!" he said in the old tongue. "Remember your losses."

Each person there, man and woman, turned solemnly to face the sun, grief and anger on their faces. The light crept across the landscape and finally came to them, there in the hollow, last of all.

They did not fade.

Saker felt himself shaking inside. He had not really believed it would work... "Now!" he said to his father, buoyed by relief and triumph. "Let us take the fort!"

The ghosts understood. They raised a silent chant of triumph and shook their weapons in the air. When they stamped their feet, the ground shook.

His father stepped forward and embraced him, his face glowing with pride. Saker leant into him and laid his head on his father's icy shoulder. Just a moment, that was all, to fortify him for the task ahead. He stepped back and took a breath.

A shepherd out early saw their approach and raced ahead to raise the alarm. Saker let him go. Let the townsfolk shut themselves up in their houses. It cleared the way for the real fight.

By the time they reached the first houses, in full sunlight, there was nothing but silence and children crying behind closed doors. Signs of work just begun and hastily abandoned were everywhere—a spindle unravelling its new thread, a butter churn spilling cream onto a doorstep, a last with a shoe half-stitched overturned outside the cobbler's shop. Every door was barred, every window shuttered.

He and his men passed them without a glance. The road to the fort led clear and easy, right up to the first gate and palisade.

Over the main gate was an observation post, a roofed platform raised above the line of the wall. Saker could see officers gathered there, watching. The warlord's men lined the walls, weapons ready. The new sun glinted on their armor, their weapons.

The might of the warlords, ranged against them. Every other time, Acton's people had won. Every other time, this concentration of weaponry and trained men had smashed his people's defenses, and each defeat had ended in a massacre. There would surely be a defeat, today, but it would not be his people slaughtered. Not this time.

Saker stood outside the gate, out of bow range, and motioned Owl forward. He was expecting arrows, shouts, spears from the waiting men, but there was nothing. Then a handsome blond man standing at the observation post cupped his hands and shouted, "Enchanter! Do you hear?"

Saker exchanged glances with his father and Owl. What would he do if this warlord simply surrendered? His father's eyes were hard. Saker knew what he would say—exactly what Acton had said: *Kill them all.*

"I hear," he shouted back.

"Behind these walls I have one hundred and thirty-six Travelers," the warlord said. "Leave Sendat now, and they live. Attack, and they die."

Rage overwhelmed him. Treacherous, murderous bastards! Come and live in my fort, I will give you protection, he'd told them. And they'd come, because the rest of their people were being slaughtered in their beds. He knew his people would have come with trust, and faith, and hope. And now they were to be turned into cattle for the slaughter. Goods to be bargained with.

The warlord motioned behind him and a young woman was brought forward—black-haired. He put a knife to her throat, and seemed to spit words in response to another man, an officer, standing behind him. That man was dragged away by soldiers.

Saker looked around—his ghosts were staring at him. They hadn't understood the first exchange, but the girl was clearly one of them, and the threat was one they understood.

She was crying, sobbing, pleading for her life. Saker swallowed hard. He couldn't condemn her. Not one of his own people. His head lowered until he stared at the stones of the road.

Alder pushed him hard, to make him look up. Saker stared into his father's face, a face from childhood, the one that made even the strongest men of the two villages back down.

Owl, behind him, raised his scythe, and the ghosts around him followed his lead.

Saker looked at them, not understanding how they could demand to go on. Then he realized. This was the moment. If they backed down now, every warlord, every town, would hold their people hostage. Prisoners, forever. Instead of bringing people of the old blood freedom, he would have brought them slavery.

One hundred and thirty-six sacrifices to buy freedom forever.

He closed his ears to the girl's sobbing, and stared up at the warlord. "Each of their names will be remembered. They will be honored for the freedom their deaths have bought." Saker saw approval in his father's eyes.

"Did you think I would not do it?" the warlord shouted, and dragged his knife across the girl's throat, blood spurting out and falling in a shining red cascade over the wall.

Owl howled silent anguish, then leapt forward onto the gate. Alder boosted him up and over, where the warlord's men slashed and hacked at him in vain, then ran.

Saker stood, watching, as his men and women climbed and scrambled, hit and killed. He heard the screams of Acton's people as the old blood took their revenge.

But the girl on the hill was silent.

DAISY'S STORY

I WERE UGLY, ugly as an unkind word, my gran used to say. I'd had pox when I were just walking, and the scars'd stretched into ridges and holes. Bad to look on. She were kind, but she spoke as she saw, my gran, and so when my mam said, "Oh, don't listen to her, you're beautiful," I didn't believe it. Travelers don't have mirrors, much. Too expensive, too breakable. But I looked in still pools and I saw that my gran were right. My body were all right, but my face were ugly as an unkind word.

Even when I were little it itched at me. My sister were pretty, with hair so light brown she could've pretended to be one of Acton's folk, if we'd had the right clothes and boots. But we was Travelers, and poor, like most Travelers. My mam was a painter—she did those patterns, friezes, around the inside walls of houses. Clever as clever, my mam. She taught me: ships for Turvite, dolphins for Mitchen, wheat sheaves for the northern towns, flowers for Pless and leaves for Sendat, the standing wave for Whitehaven, fish for Baluchston, pots and scales for Carlion, the moon in all its phases for Cliffhold.

I don't think Mam were a woman of power, cause otherwise she'd'oa' warned me not to mix 'em.

I found out first in Baluchston, after she died of the wasting fever and my ser married a tinker and I took the Road alone. I were painting a main room for a ferryman. His wife were new to the place, from Sendat, and she wanted something as reminded her of home, but he were Lake through and through, and he wanted fish. So I mixed 'em up for them, autumn leaves and fish, and it felt funny as I painted, but I put that down to the lack of air in the room. The fish seemed to thrash around a bit in the corner of my eye, and the leaves floated gently down—but when I turned around to check, there they were, safe on the wall.

I were almost finished when the Voice come rushing in, all wheeze and pant, for she's a big woman, Baluchston's Voice, and older'n stone.

"Stop!" she said. I were just about to paint the last fish, and I were cross and a bit flummoxed. What was it to her what I painted? It weren't her house.

"Stop," she said again, but gentler, like. "Lass, you have danger in your hand."

I looked down at my brush and its load of gray paint. I'd never seen anything less dangerous in my life. "Mad," I said.

She laughed. "Aye, may be so. But mixing those two... They'll be pulling up nets of leaves and the fish will be jumping up in the trees by day's end if you keep going."

"Nah," I said, laughing too.

"Aye," she said, and she weren't joking.

The Lake had sent her, and that shook me up properly, 'cause my mam had told me oft and oft about that Lake, and how never to go against Her or Hers.

So I painted over each leaf and put fish instead—a different kind, trout instead of pike, so the design would stay balanced. Afterwards, Vi, the Voice, took me for a meal at the inn and talked it over with me serious, like.

"Painting's a kind of enchantment," she said. "You call what you paint, if you paint with love. And each frieze must be a circle."

"Aye, they must be unbroken." I nodded. "That's why they have to run over the top of doors and windows."

"Haven't you ever wondered why?"

I thought it through, then shrugged. "I always reckoned it was just... design."

She shook her head so hard the flesh on her arms wobbled. "Nay, lass, each circle's a spell to bring prosperity."

"Autumn leaves aren't prosperous."

"Harvest time," she said. "Don't mix them up, lass. Every place has its wellspring of prosperity, and it's bad luck to mix them."

Well, I kept to her advice, because I were no fool, and I still remembered the way the leaves had seemed to fall out of the corner of my eye. But I brooded over it, and brooded more when the lad I wanted, a tall, strapping cobbler I met in Gardea, wanted nothing to do with me. He mooned after a pretty little tumbler who tumbled him and then left him behind without a backward glance, I heard. But I was long gone by then, because I couldn't bear to watch him watching her perform outside the inn, her and her brer, a skinny boy who sang like a nightingale.

I thought about power a lot that summer, and calling, and how painting might be a path to power, and I wondered, wondered, wondered, until the wondering turned into planning and the planning, finally, became decision.

To work, I needed somewhere I could paint a frieze that would be unbroken and stay undisturbed forever—or at least until I were in the burial caves. And that thought gave me an idea. Most caves are taken for the dead, but in the Western Mountains there are still some, high up, where no one goes but bear and wolf. Seemed to me that were a good place to set a spell down in paint.

I Traveled that way so as I got there in the summer, when the bears were out of their caves, and I went up past Spritford to Hidden Valley, which I'd not been to but I'd heard it had caves in the valley walls.

So it did, right enough. Oh, that's a pretty place, Hidden Valley. I thought I'd like to go back there, someday. Maybe even Settle.

I found me a cave was just right, with a low entrance that hollowed out into a space about the size of a room. There was old bear scat there, but none recent, so it didn't trouble me. The bear wouldn't hurt the paintings—all its scratching points, which were rubbed smooth, were below where I'd paint.

I took my gear as well as my paints up there, 'cause I knew it would take me more than a day, and I set to work as the dawn light first channelled into the cave, gray and pale. I painted, and I painted, until the light was red with sunset, and I left the brush still wet so that the painting would know it was not done yet, and I started before dawn the next morning, as soon as I could see my hand in front of my face, and by dusk it was finished.

This frieze was me, and I painted it with love. Painted the way I *ought* to be, the way I *should* have looked: better than my sister, even, with two sides of my face the same, and big eyes and soft lips and the smooth, smooth curve of skin like that tumbler had, but *me*, and I painted it around the cave until the design met above the door. But the faces weren't all the same, and that was where the power lay.

No, they were different, each one: side face and full face, laughing and smiling, serious and mocking, all the expressions I could think of, except crying. Each one I finished, I could feel the power build, feel something shift inside me. And when I put the last stroke in, the final brush mark that tied the last image to the first, the power burst out.

Ah, gods, it hurt! I fell to the ground, screaming. My face were being ripped off, it felt like, ripped and torn and seared with vitriol. I would have scrubbed out the brushstrokes, but I couldn't stand up. I were curled around myself in pain, spasms rippling through me so I arched and jerked like someone with the falling sickness.

Pain like that seems eternal when you're in it, so I don't know how long it took. I fell asleep, or maybe unconscious, after, and next I knew it was day. I got up, carefully, not touching my face in case a touch made the pain come back. I ached in every bone. When I looked up at the frieze, I didn't know whether to laugh, or cry, or purge myself. Each of those images was ugly. Ugly as an unkind word.

I touched my face then. No pock scars—not one. And I felt different even down to the bone. Beautiful. Aye. I knew it in that moment, and I were full of triumph and...I don't know the words for that feeling, but it were good.

I walked out into the early morning and though it were a gray, wet day, it felt like sun and blue skies to me. I were weak as a kitten, and it took me long, long months to get strong enough to Travel. I had to work in the inn there, and the nightmares of pain came every night, but I didn't care, because the inn had a little mirror in the stairway and I could see myself as I went past with the chamber pots or the wood basket. I were beautiful.

When I got strong I went looking for my cobbler, thinking, hoping...and I found that Traveling on your own as a beautiful young woman has problems of its own. But I had what I wanted, and I knew I would find him again, and he would look at me the way he looked at that tumbler, and we would be happy. We would Settle in Hidden Valley, and I would paint our house with happiness.

I heard he was in Sendat, so there I went. My cobbler, he were there all right, gathered up with the rest of us Travelers, there with his new wife and his new baby and though I hated him, hate him, I hope he's all right, hope that baby's still alive, hope for them better than I got.

The lord picked me because of my face. That lord, that bastard, he looked at all the girls—just the girls—and he picked the most beautiful, to make a better show for the enchanter.

So I got my throat cut because I were good-looking, and that were such a joke, don't you think? A joke on me.

His new wife weren't even pretty.

LEOF

LEOF, ON duty at the gate, saw the messenger come up from the town just after dawn, sweating and gasping, "They're coming!" A mixed band of townsfolk followed him, the ones who had no homes, or who didn't trust the stoutness of their doors.

"In quick as you can!" Leof told them. They needed no urging, moving as though Lady Death herself was after them—and maybe she was.

He despatched a runner to ring the alarm bell and he made sure the gate was secured behind them.

As the bell tolled out, all of Thegan's people, men and women alike, well-drilled over the last week, went into action. The muster yard boiled briefly as soldiers, sergeants and civilians ran desperately to get to their posts. Sorn crossed the yard at a quick walk, even in this emergency a center of calm. Leof smiled involuntarily at the sight of her.

Only the Travelers stood still, until they were chivvied into the barn by a picked handful of soldiers, led by Horst. Leof, watching to make sure they weren't treated roughly, saw him talk briefly to a couple standing next to the boy who had flirted with him on the road. Flax, Oak had called him. The couple nodded at Horst and moved to the back of the barn, but the youngling shook his head and stayed put.

Leof continued watching as Horst corralled the Travelers behind the line of the open doors, and set his men on guard outside, back and front. The Travelers, impassive, watched the activity in the yard; and Vi, Reed and the other councillors from Baluchston took positions at the front, near the boy.

The yard was now clear again, and Leof knew that Sorn and her women would be in the big hall, ready with bandages and strong drink and, gods help them, saws and hot pitch in case they needed to cauterize a stump. He prayed for her safety, and touched the amulet in his pocket, then turned his attention back to the road.

They approached, rounding the bend below. Thegan had had all trees and bushes cut back from the roadside, so they had a clear view. The enchanter was leading his army, flanked on one side by the same ghost who had almost killed Leof at Bonhill, a short man with beaded plaits, and another stronger looking man.

And there was no sign of wind wraiths.

Leof prayed that they would stay away, but he didn't hold out much hope. A shudder went through him at the thought, but he kept his face calm, as an officer must.

"My lord!" Leof called, as Thegan appeared at his shoulder. Wil and Gard and some of the sergeants followed, Hodge and Alston among them. They crowded into the observation platform above the gate and stared down the road.

Thegan's mouth tightened as he saw the ghosts. "Get her," he said over his shoulder to Hodge.

Hodge started towards the barn and Leof didn't want to know who Thegan meant by "her," but he could guess. If he were a warlord showing a hostage to an invader, he'd pick the prettiest little thing he could find. It wasn't sensible—an older man's life was just as valuable as a young girl's—but it wasn't sense they were dealing with.

Leof forced himself to watch. Hodge disappeared into the barn and came out dragging exactly what Leof had pictured: young, pretty, frightened. Flax tried to block Hodge's way, but Horst and two men forced him aside and back into the barn.

Vi's face was unreadable, but the set of her shoulders told him what she was thinking. She spat something at Hodge, and his face flamed bright red, but he held the girl's arm firm.

Leof was sweating, the cold sweat of fear. He could smell it on himself. He couldn't let Thegan just murder this girl to make a point. He couldn't, even if it was his warlord's direct order. Could he?

He'd never prayed harder in his life than he prayed that the enchanter would respect the hostages' lives and retreat. It was their only hope.

Hodge brought the girl over to Thegan. Eighteen, maybe, and a bit like Bramble would have looked at that age. She was frightened, sobbing. Even if she didn't know what was happening, being dragged off by a warlord's man to a group of soldiers was a terrifying situation for any girl. Unlike Bramble, she wasn't even trying to be brave.

On the faces around him, Leof recognized that mixture of pity and irritation that a weak victim so often evoked in the strong. But Thegan's face was completely expressionless, as he waited for the enchanter to come within earshot. He didn't even glance at the girl. The rising sun glinted off his hair and made a nimbus around it, so that he looked like a vision sent by the gods.

"Enchanter! Do you hear?" Thegan shouted.

Behind him, in the yard, on the walls, in the barn, there was complete silence.

"I hear," the enchanter shouted back.

"Behind these walls I have one hundred and thirty-six Travelers," the warlord said. "Leave Sendat now, and they live. Attack, and they die."

The Travelers began to shout and protest from the barn, Flax the loudest.

Let it work, Leof prayed. Gods of field and stream, gods of sky and wind, gods of earth and stone, make it work.

Thegan motioned to Hodge and the sergeant brought the girl forward.

Yes, Leof thought. Show him the girl. Make the enchanter see her face. Move his heart.

Then Thegan brought out his knife and placed its tip at the girl's throat.

The world went very still for Leof. He was aware of a stir among the men there, but none moved. None protested. Was it fear of the ghosts, or loyalty, that kept them silent? Or did they just not care because she wasn't one of theirs?

The moment, the heartbeat, seemed to stretch forever, as though he were poised at the crest of a wave that would never break. Loyalty was the officer's creed, central to the warlord system, the heart of their beliefs, the core of their lives. Loyalty and obedience. He owed Thegan his life. Thegan had saved him at Bonhill at the risk of his own life. He had commanded him in so many battles, and Leof had followed blindly, sure that whatever his lord said would be right, and it had *proved* right, time and again. What if he was right now? From the corner of his eye, he spotted Sorn, hurrying towards the gate, followed by Faina, and that meant he had no more time to think, because Sorn would do anything, would throw herself under the knife, to save this innocent, and he couldn't let her.

"My lord!" he said, moving forward, putting his hand on Thegan's arm. "No, my lord!"

"Take him and chain him," Thegan said calmly to Hodge, as though Leof were merely another law-breaker brought before the warlord's justice. The blue eyes were as cold as hell. As though Leof's years of loyalty and comradeship meant nothing to Thegan—had never meant anything. He had been a tool, like all the others.

"He is no officer of mine," Thegan said. "Cut his hair off."

Leof grabbed at the knife at the girl's throat, trying to twist it from Thegan's grasp, but Wil and Gard and Hodge were on him and dragging him away, hands grabbing his arms, his legs, picking him up bodily, one limb each, in that lift that is the hardest to break free from. He had nothing to push against. He kicked, tried to wrench his way loose, but three to one was too much.

As they dragged him back he heard the girl pleading, and saw Alston, white-faced, take a step towards Thegan.

"Did you think I would not do it?" Thegan shouted at the enchanter. The girl screamed and the scream was cut off in the gurgle of a cut windpipe, a sound they all knew too well from the battlefield, and it was too late.

Leof stopped struggling. They lowered his legs to the ground and he stood, shaking, hung between Wil and Gard, who were shaking too. Wil, apology mixed with determination on his face, drew his belt knife and sawed off Leof's ponytail, and threw the bright hair on the ground, where the wind lifted a few strands of it into the air, whirling it around. Leof watched it, feeling oddly calm. There was his old life, he thought. Maybe some birds would use it to line their nests.

Sorn no longer hurried. She stood in the middle of the yard, Faina clutching her arm, tears on her cheeks and staining the front of her plain gray gown. She stared at Leof and took a deep breath, wiping emotion from her face.

"We have to chain you," Wil said. Leof nodded and they trudged towards the whipping post beside the barn, past the Travelers standing in the doorway, looking between Horst and his men, who stood with bows strung and arrows nocked.

Flax glared at them, fury flushing his cheeks, and Oak, the mason, stood at his side with shoulders hunched and heavy. The red-headed councillor wept silently, and Reed's face was turned away, covered by his hand. Vi simply stared at him.

"Don't blame him," Wil said, nodding at Leof. "He tried to stop it."

Leof wondered why he said it. It was an acknowledgement, of a kind, that what had happened to the girl was wrong, but it was worthless, because Wil had done nothing.

"What will happen to you?" Vi asked him.

Leof shrugged. "The noose or the pressing box." He didn't much care. He'd spent his life under Thegan's command, keeping their Domain safe from attack, and now it seemed that all he had done was help evil rule.

"Hope you make it that far," Vi replied. "That enchanter, he won't respect hostages. We'll all be dead, come sunset."

She was probably right.

They chained his hands and looped the chains through the high hook above the whipping post, dragging his arms up painfully. He could hear in the distance the unmistakable sounds of battle starting.

Sorn stared at him, her face expressionless but her hands clenched at her sides. He turned his head deliberately away from her towards the Travelers in the barn, and then back again. He had tried to save the girl, and failed. But there were still one hundred and thirty-five more souls to be saved.

Sorn nodded. Her hand on Faina's arm, she walked around the side of the barn. There was a back door, a back gate. If she could get the guard away... *Run*, he thought. *Save yourself as well as them*.

A scuffle at the barn door brought his attention back. Flax and Oak were trying to push out, shoving against the soldiers, who pushed them back.

Flax turned to the Travelers clustered close to the door, but hanging back. “Are you going to wait here to be slaughtered by the warlord?” he demanded. “If we wait, it will be too late.”

The boy was right. “Do it!” Leof called.

Horst whipped around, his face contorted with anger. “That’s treason!” he yelled, and he brought his bow up to aim at Leof. His arm drew back, and Leof braced. Better Horst’s arrow than the pressing box.

The soldiers at the door had turned at Horst’s shout. Flax slid past them, jumped Horst from behind, dragging him down. Oak acted at the same moment, thumping the next archer on the side of the head, and the barn erupted as Travelers came flooding out, barrelling towards the soldiers.

Reed snatched the knife from Horst’s boot and went for one of the archers, but he was too slow—an arrow took him in the chest and he fell soundlessly, still clutching the knife.

Horst twisted beneath Flax, bringing his arms up to break free, but the boy was stronger than he looked and held on grimly, bashing Horst’s head against the ground. Young Scarf lunged at Flax from behind and plunged a knife into the boy’s side. Flax arched backwards, astonishment on his face. Horst sprang to his feet and drew his sword, slicing towards the nearest Traveler.

Leof lost sight of them as the Travelers spilled out into the yard, the alarm bell ringing.

Thegan strode back from the gate, directing archers on the walls with hand signals.

“Kill them all!” he shouted and turned back to the wall defense.

Arrows rained down. Leof was protected by the whipping post at his back and the barn wall next to him, but the Travelers were too slow to take cover. They fell, one by one: the red-headed councillor went first, shouting defiance. She fell on top of Flax’s body. His head faced Leof, his eyes wide and blank. There was a trickle of blood drying at one nostril.

Vi and Oak had been pushed back towards the barn by the fighting. They both ducked in behind the door, marshalling the few who had escaped the arrows towards the back where, surely, Sorn was waiting.

Run, Leof thought towards her. *Run.*

But of course she came back for him. Striding through the barn, she carried the pole that could unhook his chains from the whipping post.

"Don't let them see you help me!" he yelled, but she ignored him, moving even faster towards him.

Then the wind wraiths came, shrieking hunger and delight, and the walls began to spill ghosts from three sides. Her steps faltered, then steadied, and she came on.

"Run! *Please*, Sorn!"

Ghosts streamed over the walls, but she didn't seem to care. She was braver than anyone. Braver than he was, for sure and certain. Brave to the core.

Then Thegan came from the gate, running hard, followed by Wil and Alston and Hodge, and swept her up in one arm, sword in the other. He dragged her to the back door of the barn, but she managed to throw the pole to Leof, for what good it would do, before she was gone.

Thegan didn't even look at him.

The archers were scrambling from the walls, soldiers with boar spears massing to form a line to cover their retreat. The ghosts simply walked up the spear, ignoring the shaft through their bodies, as a boar will run up it, until they reached the end. Thegan's men had thought of this, and had set the crossbar much further back than normal, allowing for their reach with a sword, so the line was holding.

Then, from behind, Oak came lumbering, swinging a halberd, chopping at the spearsmen and shouting.

Once the line was broken it was outright massacre. Affo was there, wielding an axe as tall as himself, buying time by hacking at the ghosts' arms and legs. It took a moment or two for each one to reform, the delay too short for them to gain any real advantage.

Oak was not the only Traveler fighting alongside the dead army. Living flesh was grabbing swords and bows and axes from the withdrawing soldiers and wielding them inexpertly.

"Retreat!" Leof shouted at the soldiers. "Get yourselves away!"

It brought the wind wraiths' attention.

They descended, screaming, from the wall heights, talons reaching out. Leof braced himself and stood tall, taking hold of the chains with both hands.

As the first wraith came at him, he took all his weight on the chains and swung his legs up high in the strongest kick he could manage. It took the wraith in the chest and it fell backwards with a squawk, although Leof could feel a sharp sting from where a talon had cut his leg.

They regrouped and began circling him, just above head-height.

"Master, master!" they called. "Come and feed us the pretty one!"

The enchanter appeared in the yard, flushed and triumphant. He carried no weapon, but the ghost with beaded hair followed him, hefting an axe. Leof recognized the weapon and turned away. Affo's. The wind wraiths made another darting sortie towards him, and he swung from side to side, kicking them off.

The enchanter nodded to the ghost. "Kill him, Owl. *Disgara*."

Owl raised the axe.

"No!" It was Oak, running heavily out of the fray. "He tried to stop Thegan."

They stared at him for a moment, Owl slightly lowering the axe but clearly not understanding anything but Oak's tone. He didn't look like he enjoyed being stopped. He looked enquiringly at Saker, hefting the axe again.

"He's one of them," the enchanter said. "An officer." He nodded to Owl to strike, and Owl raised the axe high with satisfaction.

At that moment the wraiths plunged towards Leof again, shrieking. He had to lift his legs above his waist to kick them off, the Lake's amulet falling from his pocket to the ground.

Owl let the axe drop. He knelt, cautiously, by the amulet, and looked closely at it. Then he stood up and looked at Leof, suspiciously. He mimed dipping his fingers into water and drawing a circle on the back of his hand, then with his eyes, put the question to Leof.

Leof remembered seeing Eel make the same sign with his cup of Lake water. A sign of respect for the Lake, he had thought at the time. Leof nodded to Owl. Oh yes, he respected the Lake.

Owl stood for a moment.

The enchanter laid a firm hand on Owl's arm. "*Disgara!*"

Owl shook his head, but Leof wasn't sure if it was in disagreement or in puzzlement. He stepped forward and tried to use the axe to unhook Leof's chains from the top of the whipping post, but he was too short. He looked at Oak and gestured for him to help, and Oak reached up with the halberd and let them loose.

The relief on Leof's shoulders was immense, though he hadn't been aware of any pain up until then. He shrugged movement back into his shoulders and bent down slowly to pick up the woven circle of reeds. The wind wraiths had moved on to easier prey; he could hear the screams. He looked up and shock kicked him in the gut—the wraiths carried Faina. She was bleeding from a hundred wounds and as he watched she stopped screaming and her head dropped back, eyes closed. Then, from below, an arrow took her in the chest; Leof knew from the fletching it was Horst's arrow. He had saved Faina's spirit, at least.

Leof looked around wildly—did they have Sorn? Faina never left Sorn. He would drag this enchanter's heart from his body if Sorn had been taken by those monsters.

But there was only Faina.

"Your lord has run away, with his lady and his men," the enchanter taunted him. Leof relaxed. Smiled. Sorn safe.

The enchanter stared at him and Leof stared back. Not a strong face, he thought, a nothing face, an ordinary face on an ordinary body. He wished he had killed this man when he'd had the chance, at Bonhill.

"Owl refuses to kill you," the enchanter said. "Why?"

Was it more dangerous to tell him or not to tell him? Leof's inclinations ran to the truth. "Because the amulet was given to me by the Lake," he explained. "To keep me safe."

The enchanter frowned. "The Lake? What does she have to do with this?"

So, Leof thought. Thegan was wrong. The wave that defeated them outside Baluchston was conjured by the Lake, not this murderer. He kept his face blank.

"Let him go, then, Owl. *Vara, vara.*" The enchanter pointed to the gate and Owl nodded.

Owl kept a tight hold of his arm until they breasted the gate, then he reached out and gently touched the amulet in Leof's hand. It was a gentle gesture.

Leof looked at him, surprised, and saw tears in his eyes. Then the dead man looked towards the town and his eyes grew fierce. He hefted the axe and gestured for Leof to go.

Leof ran down the hill, shouting, "Ware! Ware! Run! They have axes! They're coming!" expecting any moment to feel an arrow or a spear in his back.

BRAMBLE

THEY VISITED three villages on their way, stirring the young men into dreams of glory and ensuring that Travelers were included in any defense. They learnt to leave Medric on the outskirts with the horses, because the animals—all animals—went crazy at the sound of Acton's voice booming out across the village green.

Ash spread his own news more quietly, Bramble at his side. The Travelers of each village, reassured by the promise that the world was changing, cooperated with their neighbors and began to forge a new kind of alliance.

It was late afternoon when Bramble called a halt on behalf of the horses. They had reached a stopping place near a stream, which was clearly used by Travelers. There was a pile of kindling next to the fire circle, and the ground had been flattened by boots and bed rolls.

"We need to keep moving," Acton said. "There is sunlight left."

"You can't just ride horses like you ride a boat," Bramble replied, looking him right in the eye. "They need rest. And *we're* still alive, remember. We need rest too."

Acton nodded reluctantly but Bramble was irritated. She knew he had ridden horses—well, the sturdy ponies that passed for horses in his day. He should have more sense. But he'd been buoyed up by the reception he'd received in each village, by the excitement of a great enterprise, and he was impatient to continue.

When they dismounted, Bramble was piercingly reminded of her first riding days, learning on the roan, and how sore she had been. In months of walking through the Forest with the hunter she had lost her riding muscles. Ash was in a better state, but Baluch and Medric could barely walk.

They tethered the horses and Bramble recruited Medric to help groom and feed them while Ash and Baluch built the fire and prepared the meal: cold beef and cheese, fresh bread, onions, raisins. Baluch used the opportunity to give Acton another language lesson.

By the time they ate, it was growing dark and the fire was welcome.

"How about some music?" Bramble asked Baluch. He smiled at her and pulled a small pipe from his belt pouch.

"Play that one you made up for your father's wedding," Acton said.

Bramble sat up straight. "Eric got married again? Who to?"

"Ragni's daughter, Sei," Baluch replied. "She was a widow. Her husband was killed by the River Bluff People."

Her face must have changed.

"What?" Ash asked.

"These two and their men killed every last man, woman, child and baby in that village," she said bitterly.

"They chose to fight!" Baluch protested, but he looked pale, and he put down the pipe like an old, old man.

"I thought..." Acton said slowly, considering, "I thought they would go on to Swith's Hall, to feast forever. I believed that."

Ash stared at him with contempt. "You were wrong," he spat. "You just murdered them."

"They killed one of my men," Acton said.

"And that justified killing a whole village?" Ash said, his voice like a whip.

Acton flinched back from it. "No," he said. "No. But it seemed to, at the time."

Ash rounded on Baluch. "Why is there no song about River Bluff?"

Baluch looked at him, fighting for calm. "Because I was ashamed of it." He paused. "Perhaps we should make one now."

Acton looked down at his hands. "The beer was good. Put that in." Ash made a wordless exclamation of disgust, but Acton put up a hand in defense. "No, no, I meant that honestly. They were clever people. They built good houses, they made good beer, they fought like wolverines, even the women and children." His voice, even through its stone-on-stone harshness, was admiring. "They were fine enemies."

Ash stared at him with a kind of bewilderment, as you might stare at a slug that had perched on the top of your shoe in the night. It was a stare that asked, *What are you?* Medric, too, was troubled, staring at Acton as though he wanted the legend to explain everything away, to make it all right again.

"Times were different then," Baluch said, and Medric's face cleared a little. That was an excuse he could accept.

Bramble wasn't minded to let Baluch off so easily, remembering the mixture of exhilaration and horror he had felt in that battle. He had known they were doing wrong, even if Acton hadn't.

"People were the same," she said. "They grieved just as much when someone they loved was killed."

Baluch looked at her, a thousand years of memory in his eyes. "That's true," he said. "Love doesn't change."

In the morning, Bramble was as stiff as any old grandam and every sinew protested each movement. She swore quietly to herself and went off to piss away from the camp.

They breakfasted on the leftover bread and cheese and then caught and saddled the horses, which took longer than it should have because the dappled geldings had chewed through their tethers and were two fields away, happily gorging on a haystack.

"We should avoid villages if we can," Ash said, readying to mount. "We don't have time to stop everywhere."

To her surprise, Acton nodded. "Agreed. We stop only where we must," he said, the sound of his voice sending the horses into a panic. Bramble swore at him and he raised his hands placatingly at her, smiling.

Gods help her, that smile was enough to melt her clean through. He didn't have to know that, though.

They bypassed five villages, but now, mid-afternoon, they faced a broad stream that seemed to have only one crossing—the ford at a small town.

"We need food," Bramble said to Ash. "Acton might as well give his speech while I buy it."

Acton smiled at her and Ash nodded.

"I doubt they'll let us through without questions, anyway," he said.

"Medric," Bramble said, "take the horses across the ford and wait for us on the other side."

Medric looked long-suffering. He loved to stand next to Acton, proud as a boy with his first bow. Taking the horses across the ford wasn't his idea of glory. But they had taught him to obey orders at that mine of his, because he never complained.

This was clearly a village that had heard of the slaughter at Carlion. The windows were heavily shuttered, even though it was the middle of the day, and there were no tools in sight.

A party of strangers riding in to any town was usually all it took to bring villagers out from their midday meal.

But Acton's presence sent a couple of men running off, and women pulled their children behind closed doors and watched fearfully through gaps in the shutters, leaving brooms and spindles littering the street. Only two men grabbed axes and stood their ground.

They dismounted and Medric took the horses and began to lead them away. Acton raised his hands peacefully and nodded to Baluch to start.

"Good people," Baluch said sonorously. "Do not be afraid. This is no ghost come back from the dead to seek revenge. This is," he paused for effect, "Acton, returned to defeat the enchanter!"

There were exclamations from the villagers. Bramble could hear women talking to each other behind the shutters. She realized that this was the first village which was too far from the Weeping Caverns to have heard the mountain burst asunder; she wondered if they would find it as easy to convince the villagers that Acton was back. The legend of his return in times of danger had always been strong in the west, where he had died, but not so much in the central and eastern parts of the Domains.

Then the men who had run off walked back into the village, followed by five of the warlord's men, pushing Medric in front of them. Three of them had strung bows and quivers on their backs. One of them, a blond sergeant, seemed young to have gained that rank. A villager led their horses.

Dung and pissmire, Bramble thought. Trouble.

Baluch moved to address the sergeant. "Good day —"

"Enchanters! Shoot them!" the sergeant yelled, staring at Acton. He nocked an arrow as he spoke, and aimed straight at Ash.

Medric turned at the shout and saw him take aim. "Don't!" he cried and cannoned into the man, sending him sprawling. The other two archers hesitated, but aimed and fired at Acton.

The arrows stuck in him and stayed there, quivering. He looked down at them and Bramble saw that irrepressible sense of humor rise up and take over. He put one finger on the end of an arrow and flicked it, making it twang, and grinned. She couldn't help but grin, too. The archers turned pale, nocked and aimed again.

"Not the ghost, you fools!" the sergeant said, scrambling up. "The enchanter!" He pointed at Ash, the only dark-haired man in the group.

Ash grabbed a broom and held it like a singlestave, but Acton had already moved forward and had seized the man's arm as he reached for his bow. "Would the enchanter come with a single ghost?" he asked.

The dead-cold touch and terrible voice froze the sergeant in place and Acton took advantage of the moment to snatch the bows from the other two archers. One of them ran, the other stayed stock-still, brittle with fear. The two men with swords weren't sure who to attack, so they faced down the only one with a weapon. Ash.

"I am Acton, come back from beyond death to defeat the enchanter." Acton said the words in their own language and released the man's arm; he stood back, waiting.

"Oh, that's likely, that is," the sergeant said.

Bramble noticed his strong South Domain accent and knew they had to be near home. The warlord's men of South Domain were both badly trained and brutal. The sergeant stood firm, full of bravado and furious about being disarmed in front of his men. She had seen this kind of thing too many times before, whenever someone in Wooding had dared to question anything a warlord's man did.

She stepped forward and laid a warning hand on Acton's arm.

The sergeant drew his own sword and turned to Ash, ostentatiously ignoring Acton. "Enchanter!" he said. "Surrender to my lord's justice."

"I am *not* the enchanter," Ash said. "We are not a threat to you. Call off your men."

The sergeant swivelled and aimed a great blow at Acton's shoulder. With no sword, no shield, he shifted back with a fighter's instinct and the sword sliced down on his upper arm.

Bramble felt the shock as it hit him. The arm fell cleanly off, the bows in his hand clattering to the ground. Acton just stood, looking puzzled. Her heart stopped, and thudded, leapt and steadied as she realized that he was not really hurt.

The men with swords began to close in on Ash and the sergeant raised his sword again, this time to strike Bramble. She braced herself so she could kick him in the groin and then hestitated, remembering the last time she had kicked a warlord's man, and killed him.

"No!" Medric yelled, and he flung himself at the sergeant, who jumped back and swung his sword around. Acton spun and shouldered him aside, but although the blow went awry, it still landed, hitting Medric in the neck. Acton smashed his left hand down on the sergeant's arm and the sword went spinning. Bramble kicked him in the groin, then turned to Medric.

There was blood all over her. All over Acton, the sergeant, Medric himself. It spurted out as though glad to be free of his body. She knelt next to him as he fell and he gasped for breath, reaching for her. She took his hand and held on tight, knowing it would be only a matter of seconds. Acton would deal with the sergeant.

"Thank you," she said to Medric, though her throat was so tight she could barely make the words.

His eyes were already unfocused. "The only warm thing," Medric breathed, and then he stopped breathing.

She closed his eyes, laid his hand carefully down, and stood up with murder in her eyes, rage scorching her. All the times that warlord's men had ridden roughshod over the people of Wooding boiled up in her, all the times she'd bitten her tongue or held back her blow because it would cause danger to her family, all the times she had watched and fumed and hated. She would kill him, now, and die for it if she had to.

A lot had happened in those seconds.

Ash was standing over one swordsman, pressing the broom handle hard against his neck. Baluch had the other sword, but the soldier who had held it was running away. Acton, his arm whole again, yanked the arrows out of his chest and drove them up under the sergeant's chin until the points drew blood. The two soldiers stood very still, watching.

Bramble hoped he'd simply push them through, and make the sergeant's lifeblood spurt out as Medric's had. Baluch tossed a sword to Acton, who caught it one handed. He let the arrows fall to the ground and held the sword to the sergeant's throat.

"You killed one of my men," Acton said, low and furious. He looked up at the villagers, who were still watching, not sure which side they should support. Then Acton said accusingly to the villagers, "And you let him."

Neither the sergeant nor the villagers understood him, but the words were like ice down Bramble's spine, an unwelcome echo of the past. She took a step forward, the red rage draining out of her and leaving cold behind. "This is not River Bluff," she said, forcing the words out.

At the same moment, Ash said to Baluch, "This is not Hawksted."

Both men flinched. Baluch lowered his sword. Acton paused for a moment, long enough for Bramble to wonder what she would do—what she could do—if he chose to strike. Was she prepared to die to save the sergeant? To throw herself on Acton's blade? She didn't think she was, but she wished she were. She wished, for the first time, that she didn't hate warlord's men so much. Because then she could save Acton from another murder.

The sergeant was brave, she had to give him that. He stared ahead, unflinching, and his bladder hadn't loosened with fear.

"He was doing his duty for his lord," she said quietly. "Would you have believed it, if you were him? A ghost from a thousand years ago, come back to save everyone?" She smiled at him wryly.

Acton's sense of humor reared up, as she'd hoped, and his hand loosened on his hilt. He took a step back and let the sergeant move away. "Aye, it's hard to believe, right enough," he said. He flicked a glance at Baluch, who came obediently to stand next to him. "Tell this man that I am who I say I am, and he owes fealty to me before his fealty to any other lord, because I am the Lord of War."

Bramble watched it happen as Baluch spoke. The sergeant, who had been so hostile, so disbelieving, suddenly believed. Because Acton had spared his life? Or because he had had more time to observe the ghost, and he saw now that he truly looked and behaved like a Lord of War?

Men simply followed him. They felt greater in themselves when they did. Even poor Medric. She knelt by his body and wished she had known him better, wished she had asked him about how he and Fursey had met, about his family, his work. She'd had the chance, on the walk and the ride from the mountain, but she'd been too preoccupied with Acton.

Because when people followed him, they stopped seeing anything else.

Not her, she swore to Medric. Not her any longer.

Thornhill, the fort above Wooding, was visible in the late afternoon light even from across the river. It was on the only high ground, and its palisades picked up the late sunlight in a gray gleam. Far below it, they could just make out the roofs of the town, the herringbone pattern of reeds visible on each thatch. That was Udall the thatcher's pattern. Unmistakable. The only other thatcher who used it was that girl who'd been his apprentice, Merris, who married the butcher over in Connay.

Her whole life rushed back into her head: Widow Forli, the brewer Sigi and her children, old Swith with his arthritic hands. Her parents, and grandfather. Maryrose.

They were a few leagues above the narrow bridge which spanned the deep chasm that she and the roan had jumped, once, escaping from Beck and the other warlord's men. She had died, here. Right here. She dismounted and looked down. Below, the Fallen River resounded, its spray climbing in swirling clouds of mist. Swifts rode the air currents, constantly in motion.

Looking at the astonishing jump the roan had made, pride and love and grief for him rushed into her heart. No other horse could have done it. She dragged her eyes from the chasm and looked back at the town she had grown up in. She could just make out the roof of her own house.

In old songs and stories, when someone came back home they either felt right at home, and sentimental with it, or they felt like a complete stranger. Neither was true of her. Perhaps it was because she had never felt at home here to begin with.

Ash and Acton were arguing. Again.

"Who is in command there?" Acton said, gesturing at the town. "If we go to him, he can help us get information, better horses —"

"Go to the *warlord?* " Ash and Bramble exclaimed together.

Acton blinked at their vehemence. "Even Asgarn would have understood this situation," he said. But Bramble shook her head decidedly.

Baluch put up his hand in peacemaking.

"I don't think you understand about warlords and Travelers, yet," he said. "Just take my word for it, Acton, no warlord is going to believe two dark-haired people who show up with what they claim is your ghost."

Acton opened his mouth to argue, but Ash lost patience. "Silence," he said, and Acton could no longer speak.

Bramble had had enough of this sniping. "I'm going home," she said, and she strode off, then thought to look back and say, "You'll have to lead the horses; they won't cross the bridge otherwise. They panic."

The men were staring after her. Acton had that look—a mixture of admiration and laughter, and she thought of Medric saying "the only warm thing." She was pretty sure he'd been talking about Fursey. Men did think of the person they loved most, just before they died. She'd heard enough men in the pressing box calling for their mothers to know that. But although his look warmed her, it was the same admiration he'd shown to Wili, or the girl on the mountain. To any woman. She was just another in a long line whom he'd looked at like that.

Suddenly, she wanted fiercely to go home, to see the familiar look of exasperation and puzzlement in her mother's eyes, to see her father's slow smile, to feel her grandfather's hug. To feel *normal* again, as if she had not died twice, as if she had never loved a ghost or seen the battles and love affairs of a thousand years ago.

As she stepped off the bridge, leading her lumpy bay, the men following behind, she could feel familiarity rise up through her boot soles, and her spirits lifted. In her mind, she sent a greeting to the local gods, as she had done every day in her childhood.

They did not reply.

"We have to go to the altar," she said, and mounted.

She led their party the woods way to the altar, along narrow trails used mostly by deer. The black rock altar looked as it always did. Bramble slid to the ground and led the horses to a large chestnut and tethered them, then approached the altar.

Greetings, she thought to the gods. She laid her hand on the cold rock and felt relief wash through her. They were there, they were there after all. But their attention was elsewhere, far away.

Greetings, she thought again, and this time a small spark of their notice flickered towards her. When they recognized her, suddenly all their attention turned to her.

Child, they greeted her. *Why are you here? Go to Turvite.*

And that was all. Their attention immediately turned away from her. She had the sensation that they had returned to a battle, a fight of their own, and a sliver of the same coldness, the same dread, that she had felt as they raised Acton went through her.

She backed out of the clearing and rejoined the others. "We have to go to Turvite," she said. "Now."

Ash simply nodded, and Bramble thought that perhaps he had heard them too. But Acton set his mouth and frowned. Bramble turned to Ash.

"Let him speak," she said.

"Speak, then," Ash said.

"Why Turvite?" Acton asked immediately.

"Because the gods say so," Bramble said.

He considered that, shaking his head. "But —"

"It's the *gods*, you idiot," she said, furious. No one could stir her to greater annoyance than Acton. No one.

"They're not *my* gods," he said simply, the statement sounding doubly blasphemous in the dark grating voice. "Who knows how much they know? They could be wrong."

She could see them getting dragged down into an argument which would go on for too long. They didn't have time for this.

"*I* am going to Turvite," she said. "Ash is coming with me."

Acton glanced at Ash and saw his assenting nod.

"And without *Ash*, oh Lord of War," she continued, "*you* cannot speak."

"The gods are not the only powers in this land," Baluch said, as if unsure of his own words. "We all agreed to follow Acton's leadership—"

"No," Bramble interrupted. She faced Acton and stared right into his eyes. "I am not your follower. I never will be."

He smiled at her, the sideways smile that had melted hearts over and over again, but her heart kept a steady beat. The nuthatches that nested in this glade were calling to one another, an alarm call because of the noisy humans. She had seen them nest and raise their young every year. This was the place where she had always been strongest, the most at peace. Where she knew who she was, and who she was not.

Acton stared into her eyes and gradually she saw his face change. The warm expression shifted into a frown, then into something else. She was reminded of old Swith's face as she rubbed the swelling from his arthritic hands—a combination of pleasure and pain. But this was deeper than anything Swith had ever felt. It seemed to her that Acton's pale eyes flickered with the vivid blue she remembered, as though the living man had looked out, for a moment, from the ghost's eyes.

His face showed a mixture of exaltation and loss, the expressions flowing so fast that she wasn't sure she'd even seen them. Her heart beat faster, and she flushed.

He turned away from her for a long moment, as if regaining his composure, then faced her, and smiled. It was not the cozening smile. She had never seen him smile like this before—in his life or his death. It was a smile of regret at something lost. Something precious. Did he regret that she wouldn't follow him? Was the loss he felt the loss of his life? His vitality? She couldn't tell, but it seemed to her that he had grown older in those few minutes, and it sent a spear through her heart, robbing her of breath. His eyes were pale again. He was dead, and she had to remember that.

Acton turned to Ash and gestured to his mouth.

"Speak," Ash said, in almost a whisper, as if he, too, had seen something that moved him.

"We must raise the defenses of this place first," Acton said firmly.

She nodded, unable to speak. Yes, that was right, she thought. Even the gods would want that. She felt a flash of relief that her parents would be protected, at least as well as they could manage before they left.

"We'll start with my family," she said. "They're used to Traveler and blondies working together."

"Let's go, then," Ash said.

Although the houses were shuttered fast, the shops around the market square had their counters down as usual for evening business. Wooding had a big market square, being the warlord's town. They stopped on the edge of the open space, not sure if they should attract notice or not. In every other village Acton had just walked straight out into the open, but here... A warlord's town was different, and even Acton seemed aware of it. Bramble thought that after Medric's death, he didn't want to risk her or the others by being overconfident.

"Hey!" a voice called. They started, and Acton drew his sword. He had kept the sergeant's and had seemed happier with a weapon in his scabbard.

One of the warlord's men had taken a loaf of bread from a stall, it looked like, and the owner, a very young man, was objecting. "The warlord's son said you had to pay for what you took!" the man, a redhead, insisted.

Beck. The warlord's man was Beck, the man who had trained the roan with whips and spurs. The man who had chased her and the roan until she had jumped that chasm out of desperation, and died. Beck, the man the gods had intended to be the Kill Reborn. The roan had decided otherwise, and changed her life.

Beck was a veteran of too many encounters like this one. He simply walked over to the stall and spat on the biggest basket of loaves set out on the counter, then turned and hit the man across the ear with his fist. The man fell to the ground groaning, and Beck's companions helped themselves to the clean loaves from the other baskets.

They walked away without saying a word, leaving the man still moaning and clutching his head on the ground.

Acton started to surge forward, his face thunderous, but Bramble called him back. "What do you think you're going to do?" she said bitterly. "Even if you beat the piss out of all four of them —" he opened his mouth and she cut him off—"yes, I know you could beat all four, but what then? Those are warlord's men and there's a barracks full of them up at the fort. Are you going to fight them all?"

Acton stood still, angry and unhappy.

Ash was obviously enjoying Acton's discomfort. "Speak," he said.

"Something should be done," Acton said. "Warriors should protect their people, not exploit and beat them!"

"Yes," Bramble said seriously, "they should. But they don't. And they haven't, for a thousand years."

For a moment, there was such anguish in Acton's eyes that Ash looked away.

"We'll go around the back street," Bramble said. "And find my family. They'll know what's happening." She added, with a flicker of humor, "Or we could ask the Widow Forli. She always knows all the gossip."

Her parents' house was shuttered tight, but so was every other house. She led the others around the back and left Ash to tether the horses while she tried the door. It had been nailed shut with a board across it. No one around here could afford proper locks, so this was the way a house was left secure when the owners were away.

They weren't here.

A mixture of relief and regret swept over her. She wouldn't have to face her parents' grief for Maryrose—but there would be no homecoming.

"What are you doing, there, you?" A sharp voice, as familiar as the roses growing over the walls came from behind them. Widow Forli. Bramble turned to face her, smiling despite herself.

Widow Forli was plumper than she had been. She looked like she'd been eating properly at last. Then Bramble remembered. Maryrose had told her that her parents had come back to Wooding for the Widow Forli's wedding to . . . to whom? She couldn't remember.

"Bramble!" Forli exclaimed, and her hands went to her mouth in a genuine display of surprise.

Bramble glanced around. Acton was nowhere to be seen, nor Baluch. There was just Ash, with the horses.

Forli cast one look at him and jumped to the obvious conclusion, with avid interest. "Brought your young man to meet them, have you? They're not here. They're up to Carlion —" She faltered to a stop, face crumpling a little as she realized she'd have to tell Bramble why her parents had gone.

Bramble took pity on her. "To bury Maryrose?"

Forli nodded, solemn, pity in her eyes. She seemed kinder than she had been, Bramble thought, or maybe it was she who had changed.

"You know then? Aye, they went as soon as they heard the news, though I told them it was too dangerous."

"Nowhere is safe, these days," Bramble said.

Forli made the sign against the evil eye. "So I hear." Her old pleasure at knowing all the gossip took over, and she added, "The warlord's gone to Turvite, they say, for a warlords' council about this enchanter and his ghosts. And Eolbert, the warlord's son, too. That Beck is acting overlord!" She looked sideways at Ash. "They're taking everyone's horses. I'd be careful if I were you."

Bramble nodded. "Thank you, Forli," she said, and the woman looked surprised. Bramble remembered just how rude she'd been to her in the past. "We'll stay tonight, and be off in the morning. But if they're taking horses, I'd appreciate you didn't tell anyone that we're here."

Disappointment shone in Forli's eyes, but she nodded. "Aye, that's best. Sure and secret."

To reward her, Bramble said, "I hear you have some news? You're married again?"

"To the smith," she said proudly.

"Congratulations. He's a good man."

Astonishingly, Forli blushed. A love match? Amazing. Anything was possible, if Forli was in love.

Ash gave Forli some coppers and she went off to the market to buy them bread and milk and cheese. "And some pasties!" Bramble called after her. "Some of Sigi's ale would be good, too."

As soon as she'd left, Acton and Baluch came out from behind the shed and with his sword Acton prised off the board nailing the door shut.

Bramble stood for a moment in the doorway before going in. This house was full of memories of Maryrose, and hatred of Saker surged back, stronger than ever. He would pay for his murders. She set her mouth and walked in, dropping her saddlebags in the corner; she took the bucket and fetched water from their well.

She sat down, finally, on her stool. Her own stool, at their own table. Although her parents had gone to Carlion to live with Maryrose and Merrick, it was clear the house was well kept. Her grandfather must have stayed here, or come back for frequent visits. That made sense. He'd never liked towns anymore than she did. She blinked back tears. Time to get on with the job.

"How do you say 'new beginning' in their language?" Acton asked Baluch, catching her thought.

She left them repeating words like "peace" and "justice," and went into the room she and Maryrose had shared. Her mother had kept it as it was, except that there was a new cover on Maryrose's old bed. Her mother had woven it—she recognized the pattern as one her mother had been working on in the year Bramble left home.

That made her want to cry, suddenly, but she forced the tears back and fed her anger instead. Saker would suffer. She would turn the knife in the wound, herself, and make sure.

MARTINE

WITH A good following wind, they came to Turvite faster than Martine had dared to hope for, and found other ships heading the same way. Safred was still keeping to her bed; she shook every time she tried to stand up, and Cael spent most of his time sitting on a stool next to her, keeping watch. He seemed a little stronger after days on the water, and Martine hoped against hope that his wound would heal after all.

"That's Eni's colors," Arvid said, shielding his eyes from the afternoon sun so he could sight the two-master a league or two ahead of them. It was just about to make the tack into the narrow entrance to Turvite harbor. He turned to look astern, where a three-masted galley rowed. "And those are Coeuf's."

"You haven't displayed your colors," Martine said.

Arvid grinned. "I didn't bring them with me. Didn't think of it, to tell truth. I was just going on a trading trip to Mitchen, remember?" He ran a hand through his brown hair and frowned. "Someone must have sent out the muster for the warlords' council. It's always held in Turvite."

There was a note in his voice she hadn't heard before, a mixture of wariness and distaste. "You don't like the council?"

It was a daring thing for a commoner to ask a warlord, but he didn't seem to notice that. He seemed to view her as his equal. She found herself testing him like this all the time, trying to find out, once for all, if he really believed in Valuing or was just mouthing the words. He hadn't failed, even a little bit, not once. She should stop doing it.

He sidestepped the question. "I wasn't brought up to politics. It's different in the Last Domain. We're so isolated that we're all in it together. There are very few officers' families, and most of them have intermarried with merchants and farmers and even crafters. We don't stand on ceremony much."

Martine imagined what it was like, going from that to a warlords' council, with its rigid and exacting etiquette, its precise gradings of status and worth…And he was so young, much younger than the other warlords she knew of.

She slipped a hand through his arm and hugged it to her, the most spontaneous show of affection she'd given him in public. "You'd better not be seen with me," she said. "I'd destroy your standing completely."

He went still, avoiding her eyes, and she realized that this was something he'd thought about, had already made a decision on. Her mouth went dry. This was the moment when he would say, "I'm sorry, but you're right…" Because the truth was that warlord and Traveler just couldn't be together, and this time on the ship was stolen time, honeyed time, like childhood summer days that seemed to stretch on forever but had to end in darkness.

He picked up a short length of rope from a barrel in front of them, and started twisting it in his hands, as though he wanted a reason not to look at her.

That was when she realized that she *did* love him, because instead of being angry about it, she wanted to make it easier for him, even if her heart felt that it was splitting in two.

"It's all right," she said, letting go of his arm. "I understand. You have a job to do. The council is more important —"

He turned to face her, grabbing at her hand, his mouth set stubbornly.

"I will not deny you," he said furiously. "If what we are building in the north means anything, then I *must* not deny you. Let them say whatever they want—I am the warlord, I will do as I choose!"

She stared at him for a moment, astonished, and then laughed, helplessly laughed until she sank down on the deck, gasping. He stared at her in bewilderment.

"Meet arrogance with more arrogance?" she managed to say. "Protect equality by demanding respect for your rank?"

A smile tugged at the corners of his mouth and he raised his head in a parody of a proud officer. "Ex-actly," he said, exaggerating each sound. "Pre-cisely."

"Let's hope it works," she said.

He stared at her, as if suddenly uncertain, running the length of rope through his hands. "So... you will stand with me?"

It wasn't ex-actly, pre-cisely a marriage proposal, which was good because she wasn't ready for one yet. But it was a big thing, a large question. It would change her life forever. She should think it over sensibly before she gave him her answer.

"Of course I will," she said.

LEOF

LEOF RAISED the alarm well enough for some of the people of Sendat to run. But not all. Not even most.

The ghosts didn't chase the ones who ran. Perhaps they thought they'd have time later to track and slaughter them. Perhaps they were right. If no one could stand against them, nowhere was safe.

Leof stopped running, and stood in the middle of an open field of hay, hay that should be harvested, and let the sweat cool on his back and neck.

He had nothing. Was nothing.

He sank to the ground and sat cross legged, his head hanging. No longer an officer. Forsworn. A traitor. Without allegiance, or family, because his family was cut off from him now, for their own safety. Without home, or goods, or even a horse. He had a sword he was no longer permitted to use, a small pouch of silver, and a woven ring of reeds.

Should he go to the Lake? The Lake, alone, could keep her people safe from the ghosts, he was sure. He thought he would be welcomed there, but what would he do? Learn to fish?

With everything else taken away, there was only one place he wanted to be—within sight of Sorn.

Sorn was on her way to Turvite.

A free town, where traitors were protected.

He might catch a glimpse of her there, make sure she was safe. Make sure she was still alive.

He picked up a handful of dirt and let it run through his fingers. It was good soil, in Central Domain. Full of life. He didn't want to see it become a wasteland peopled only by ghosts. He could offer his services to the Turvite Council, to other warlords even. He could still fight.

Leof dusted off his hands and stood up, his head swimming a little. He hadn't eaten for a while, or drunk . . . There was a stream nearby.

He went to it and drank, then took the reed ring from around his neck and held it in his hand. "Lady?" he said, not expecting a reply.

He remembered her last answer: *If you will not go home to your mother, you must take the consequences.* Going home to his mother was no longer possible, not if he wanted to keep her safe.

"I can't go home to my mother now, Lady," he said. "I am a traitor. Should I go to Turvite?" But this time there was no answer. Perhaps he had exhausted her patience, or maybe the answer was so obvious she didn't need to give it.

It was a long way to Turvite, so he stole a horse, one of Thegan's breeding stock from a farm across the valley. It was a good mare, by Acton out of Dancing Shoes. Not as good as Arrow, but fresh. He took a spare mount, a chestnut gelding, so he would lose as little time as possible. He wished he could have taken Arrow, but he knew she would have been taken by Thegan's party.

He stole saddle and tack as well, from the empty stable block. The farm workers were holed up in the strongest part of the farmhouse, behind shutters and bars. He saddled the horse and rode up to the door. He could at least give them a warning.

"Take the horses and go to Turvite," he yelled. "My lord Thegan will meet you there."

An eye peered out from a crack in the shutters. "My lord Leof?"

"The ghosts have taken the fort," he said. "Make your escape while you can. Take the horses to Turvite and my lord will be pleased."

The eye stared at him, and he was suddenly conscious of his short hair, blowing across his face.

"The fort's gone?" The man's tone was incredulous, as though he couldn't imagine it.

"Aye," Leof said. "And the ghosts have tools, now, axes." The eye disappeared and he heard a flurry of activity start inside. "Be safe!" he yelled, and he kicked the mare into a canter, down the wide grassy ride to the back road which led south. The main road would be choked with those who were fleeing Sendat. He hoped enough people had got out for that to be true. Or else there was no good that had come from his betrayal of his lord.

SAKER

HIS NAME was Oak. He was a man about Saker's age, dark haired and thick-shouldered, with gray eyes that burned.

"I want to join you," he said. "It shouldn't be like this."

Saker nodded. Oak was talking about the bodies around them—bodies with dark hair like his, who had been slaughtered by Thegan's men, cut down by arrows, most of them. They were being collected and reverently prepared for burying by some of the ghosts. The rosemary bushes in the kitchen garden were almost stripped bare; and they'd had to send a party to the coppice to collect enough pine sprigs.

"We all want to fight. Take back what was ours."

A group stood behind Oak—about thirty people. All that they could save of the Travelers in the barn, although Oak had told him that some had escaped before the ghosts stormed the walls.

Saker was filled with elation. This was what he had hoped for, dreamt of: his people, joining him in the fight. Living comrades, fighting for justice.

Tears came to his eyes. "You are welcome," he said. He clasped arms with Oak and then turned to the others, a mixed group of men and women, all ages from fifteen to sixty. "We've taken over the warlord's hall. Go find yourselves food and drink. Tomorrow we bury our dead and then we march."

They stood together in the muster yard in the red, dying light of dusk and used one of the warlord's men, a young officer named Wil, to get the blood they needed. Oak had found him hiding in the barn loft.

"Blood and memory," Saker said as he wielded the knife, trying not to remember Freite with her knife, trying to convince himself that this was no different to killing in battle. It was the first time he had killed a human with his own hands. The man was his own age and some quirk had also given him hazel eyes. He was on his knees, not pleading, his head up. But his eyes showed white as Saker raised the knife.

"Gods of field and stream," he began, "gods of sky and wind, gods of earth and stone —"

His father, impatient, seized the knife from Saker's hand and slashed it across the boy's arm. The blood welled up, not pulsing, but streaming steadily. It would last long enough for each ghost to taste, or touch, or whatever they pleased.

Saker heard again, at the edge of his hearing, the thin, high keening he had heard as he had called up the ghosts in the coppice. No one else, not even his father, seemed to hear it. There were others, he thought, whose bones he'd not found, who watched them and wanted to join their fight. It was their grief he heard when the spell was loosed.

Alder dipped a finger in the man's blood and drew a line across his forehead. It stood out startlingly dark against his pale skin. Owl followed suit.

Saker swallowed. His father should have left the knife stroke to him. But he said nothing and turned to the ghosts, who were queuing for their share of blood.

"Blood *and* memory," he said to them as they walked past. Most chose to mark their faces, like Alder, but some bent and licked at the blood. The officer shuddered at each touch.

There were hundreds, and by the end, when the sun was almost gone, the last of them were hustling to claim their share, so that the man was pulled this way and that, his blood smeared uselessly on the ground. He fainted, moaning, his face as pale as theirs.

And then the sun disappeared.

For a moment, only a moment, Saker found part of himself hoping that it hadn't worked, that they wouldn't have to go on, day after day, finding blood, sacrificing.

Saker waited a heartbeat, two, three. The ghosts stopped moving, turned their faces to the west. But they did not fade.

His father slapped Saker on the back, smiling, and Owl nodded at both of them, his face intense with satisfaction.

Alder indicated the land below them, spreading his arm wide, and Saker grinned.

"Yes," he said, "we take back all of it. Starting with Turvite."

How wonderful it was to finally talk to someone freely—to be honest, truly himself. Saker tried to remember the last time he had been able to tell the truth. He thought it was when he'd warned that officer's daughter against Freite. A long, long time ago.

He discussed it with Oak, over a dinner of fine roast kid and carrots, strawberries from the garden, clotted cream and honey. It gave him great satisfaction to sit in the warlord's chair and drink mead out of an actual glass goblet.

And to discuss conquest with a friend of the old blood was a joy he had anticipated for a very long time.

"Turvite's the key," he said, leaning to fill Oak's glass again. "It always has been, which is why Acton wanted it."

Oak nodded, reflecting. "Lot of people in Turvite."

"It's the only way. Otherwise they will regroup and take it back from us. If we wipe them out, our people can live in peace and plenty."

"There's some good folk, though," Oak replied, "with Acton's blood."

Saker scoffed. "So tell me how to sort them out from the other kind, and I'll save them. I've thought this through, Oak. There's no other way."

Oak looked thoughtful and downed the last of his drink.

"Get some sleep," Saker said. "Early rise tomorrow."

He slept in the warlord's bed, which smelt still of the Lady—gardenias and roses. Saker dreamt of gardens torn apart by wind wraiths, and woke in the hour before dawn, that high, ominous shrilling in his ears, ready to provide more blood for his army. But by the time he got out to the muster yard in the gray light, Owl and his father had already bled two victims dry, a blonde dairymaid and a saddler.

Saker watched the ceremony with a sinking feeling in his gut. They hadn't bothered with a prayer to the gods, and no one was reminding the ghosts of blood and memory. It was far more businesslike than the day before, with two orderly lines that meant no one had to hustle for their share. All arranged without him.

As the saddler slumped back on the ground, dead, Saker saw something move out of the corner of his eye—a tall, sinuous shape. He spun, mouth open to call an alarm, but there was nothing there except an aspen, shivering in the dawn wind. He shivered too. An illusion. Nothing more.

His army was getting ready to march.

He wondered, for the first time, whether he had the power to break the spell and send the ghosts back to the grave.

ASH

THE WARLORD'S men slammed both doors open just after dawn. They came in two groups, yelling, "Out, the lot of you!", waking Ash from the deepest sleep he'd had since Oakmere. He roused instantly, rolled out of bed and jumped through the window; but they were outside, too, and grabbed him roughly, dragging him around to the front door where the officer stood.

He had just enough sense not to fight back. They threw him on the ground and he rolled to his knees, hands ready, just in case. But there were at least ten men, and he had no chance; they held boar spears and bows, as well as swords. He didn't even have his belt knife. He'd taken his belt off the night before, wanting for once to sleep comfortably, and feeling safe in Bramble's house. That had been stupid, although it had probably saved his life—he'd have used the knife, if he'd had it, and he'd be dead by now.

They threw Bramble down after him. She grimaced at him and wiped a smear of blood away from her mouth. She'd fought, then.

The River reached to him, sensing his fear. "*Beloved?*" She said.

"I am here," Ash replied, calmed by Her touch.

"*Stay alive*," She ordered, with a flicker of humor.

"Good idea," he answered in kind, and She laughed and retreated, as though She trusted him to deal with this current danger. It gave him confidence.

The officer was a man in his forties, maybe, with a small beard, and a hard voice. "Travelers," he said, "you are fortunate. The warlord has decided to give you shelter at the fort."

"Shelter from what?" Ash asked.

"From those who would take revenge against all dark-haired folk because of your enchanter's evil." He said it like he didn't believe it. Like he didn't care if it were true or not.

Bramble drew a breath and one of the warlord's men looked at her with some interest. That look was unmistakable. Where in the cold hell was Acton?

"Beck!" a voice called from inside. "There's another one!"

Bramble flashed a look at Ash and he wondered what she meant, then remembered. *Beck*. He'd heard that name. The Well of Secrets had named Beck as the man whom the gods had intended to be the Kill Reborn. A man of mixed blood, as Bramble was.

Baluch walked out the door, hands spread wide to show that he was weaponless, followed by a couple of men who were clearly not sure whether Baluch was a Traveler. He looked strange enough, it was true, in his leggings and tunic, his plaits hanging around his face. But he had blue eyes, the particular blue that you only got with no trace of the old blood, and that might save him.

"Beck, is it?" Baluch asked, his beautiful voice taking on a tone of authority, as an officer's would in these circumstances.

"Second in command at Thornhill fort, in temporary command in my lord's absence," Beck answered immediately, responding to the tone.

Baluch nodded. "I hope you have good reason for rousting us from our beds."

"My lord's orders. All Travelers come to the fort." There was no room for negotiation in that voice. "Everyone with Traveler blood in them, Settled or not," Beck added, to make it clear that Bramble living in a cottage didn't make her safe.

Ash could see the pattern, suddenly. There was a song from four centuries ago, "The Red-headed Lord," told the story of a warlord who took his enemy's children as hostages to prevent a massacre.

"Hostages," he said, the refrain of the song running through his head. "You want us as hostages."

"What my lord wants with you is no one's business but his," Beck said, and gestured to his men to haul Ash and Bramble to their feet.

"Your lord is wrong." Acton's voice had come from the corner of the house. Dark and grating and terrible, it was as though Ash heard the voice of the dead for the first time, inspiring the terror of death. Acton had spoken in the modern language—a fast learner, Ash thought, or Baluch had taught him the words he would most likely need.

The warlord's men whirled, then stopped, faltering, as they saw Acton.

"Stand fast!" Beck snapped. The men settled into formation, clutching their weapons.

Acton held his sword, the one he had taken from the sergeant who had killed Medric, and it looked menacing against his white hands and white chest.

"Your lord is wrong," Acton repeated. He took a step forward and the men started to back away slowly; he kept one eye on Beck, who had drawn his own sword.

"Where are the rest of you?" Beck asked, circling for a better approach.

"You don't recognize me," Acton said gently. "I have been gone a thousand years, but I'm back now."

Beck stared at the ghost before him. "Impossible," he said, finally.

Acton needed no translation—the tone was clear. He smiled.

"You're not Acton," Beck said loudly, for the benefit of his men. "You're an imposter trying to sow discord." He smiled back at them. "You—" he spaced the words for effect—"are a creature of the enchanter's."

The men firmed in their ranks, gripping their spears and swords more tightly.

"No matter who I am," Acton said, "I resist the enchanter, and I advise you to do the same."

"We are—"

"Hostages won't work," Bramble cut in. She stood up and took a step forward, facing Beck down. "The enchanter kills Travelers who get in his way."

Acton came forward, sword point on the ground, Baluch next to him, ready to translate.

"The enchanter will sacrifice these people if he has to, for all Travelers. Instead of holding them hostage, you should be begging these people to save you." Baluch translated so fast that it was as though he were Acton's echo.

Beck looked disbelieving, but a murmur came from the men. "And how can they save us?" he asked.

"Stand together with them in defense. Let them convince the enchanter that they don't need his help. That they are strong and respected and safe in this town."

"Hah!" Bramble scoffed, and Beck flicked her a glance of dislike.

"You must make them your shield and sword," Acton insisted, speaking the modern words himself.

"I will make them our shield," Beck said. "As my lord ordered." He gestured to Ash and Bramble. "Take them to the fort."

Acton smiled and stood next to Bramble. There was something in his face that made Ash shiver. Something primitive. For the first time, Ash felt in his gut that Acton was a thousand years dead, because the light in his eyes, his willingness to slaughter with a smile on his face, came from another time. And it was clear, from the way he stood, that he would protect Bramble at the cost of a hundred lives.

Ash was filled with a vast impatience. Beck's men didn't deserve to die because their officer was too hard-headed to submit to fate.

"Do you want to die?" Ash exclaimed. He pointed at Acton. "Don't you understand? That's *Acton*. Alive he could have crushed each one of you. But he's dead. He has a sword and he *cannot be killed*. Lay one hand on her and he'll slaughter the lot of you."

The men backed away but Beck grabbed Ash, pointing a knife at his gut. "Which is why we need hostages," he said.

For a long moment no one moved. Then Beck turned to Acton. Ash kicked Beck in the groin and as the man bent over in pain he brought up joined hands fast under his chin, snapping Beck's head back. The warlord's man fell, retching.

Ash stepped back, panting a little, Beck's knife in his hand. He knelt by Beck's side and held the knife in the same place Beck had used on him, under the ribs ready to strike up at the heart. His hand shook with the desire to push it in. But this wasn't a decision he could make on his own. He looked up at Bramble. Her eyes were hard with hatred, too, but she shook her head, flicking her eyes at the other men, poised now to attack. The River touched his mind again as if sensing his turmoil. *Stay alive.*

"I could kill him," Ash said slowly, for the benefit of the men. "But we are not here to kill." He stood up and tucked the knife into his belt.

Beck vomited again and rolled up onto his knees, then climbed to his feet, wiping his face.

He looked at Ash, a long measuring look that marked Ash down for later retribution.

"I could kill all of you," Acton said. "But we're not here to kill."

It gave Ash a jolt of satisfaction to hear Acton follow his lead. Acton had been telling the truth, earlier—he was prepared to follow if someone else led. But they had reached an impasse, and Ash didn't know how to break it.

Bramble walked over to Beck and spoke quietly to him. "You have the old blood in you, just like me," she said.

Beck's face went blank and he shook his head. No, not true: Ash could see the thoughts hitting him, making him shake a little. "You're lying," he said.

Bramble said, "The Well of Secrets told us."

He dragged a breath in and held it, then let it out slowly, fighting for calm, to not let his men see his reaction. It was as though Bramble had told him something he had always feared. Then his face hardened. "Acton or not, I take these Travelers to the fort."

"We'll go," Bramble said, and then to Acton and Ash, "there may be someone with more sense up there."

Beck waved his men back to let them walk freely. The men were visibly relieved.

As they walked up to the fort, through the busy market square, the center of all eyes, Acton grinned at Ash. "So," he said, "you're a warrior as well as an enchanter."

"No," Ash said quietly. "I've been a killer. And sometimes I'm a safeguarder. But I'm not a warrior, and I never will be."

The townsfolk followed them, drawn by the sight of Acton, not knowing if he were a messenger from the enchanter, or an advance scout for an army.

At the gate of the fort, with guards outside and inside, Ash felt his stomach churn. To be escorted into a fort by warlord's men was a verse from a song which ended on the gibbet. The soldiers unbarred the gate at Beck's order and it swung open slowly.

As Ash readied to walk forward, one of the soldiers looked up over Ash's shoulder to the sky, and horror twisted his face.

"Run!" he screamed and ran inside the fort, throwing his spear to the ground.

They all spun around.

Wind wraiths. Gods preserve them. Wind wraiths were arrowing their way across the sky, turning and dipping and dancing with joy. Ash was flooded with shame. Were these the wraiths he had sent south unintentionally, from the cliffs above Golden Valley? Had he saved himself then at the cost of other lives? He had saved Flax and Horst, too, he reminded himself, but the shame stayed, mixed with fear as the wraiths came closer to the fort.

They circled high above, shrieking down to them. "Our master has conquered the central fort and we have feasted! Soon, soon, we feast here, humans!"

They cackled and played in the air before disappearing north, towards Central Domain. The silence they left behind was broken by one of the men sobbing.

"He has broken the compact," Baluch said, his voice shaking.

"He commands spirits as well as ghosts in his army," Acton said, not seeming to understand what the compact meant. But the thought that a human being had deliberately invited wind wraiths to feast on other humans made Ash want to retch.

"Sendat has fallen," Bramble said slowly. She looked up at Beck, who was white around the eyes but who stood firmly, not showing fear to his men. "Did Thegan have hostages?"

Beck nodded.

"Much good it did him," said Bramble. "I hope the wind wraiths ate his heart out."

Ash shivered. There was a terrible intensity to Bramble's eyes. She hated Thegan—it was his men who had tried to kill her in Golden Valley, when she and Ash first met.

Acton came forward and stood in front of Beck.

"Hostages are useless, it seems. Work with your Travelers and you may survive."

"Why would they stand with us?" he asked. "If I were them —" He stopped, unable to frame the words.

Ash felt the weight of the pouch at his belt grow suddenly heavier, as if the stones wanted to remind him of their presence. "I can convince them," he said. "Let me talk to them."

The warlord's house had fine stone steps and Ash stood on them, Beck by his side, while the soldiers chivvied a small crowd of Travelers from one of the outbuildings to stand in front of them. Behind, the townsfolk clustered at the gate.

Acton and Baluch stood behind Ash, but Bramble slid away from them as they climbed the steps and joined the crowd.

Ash had never made a speech before, but he'd performed often enough, and seen his parents control a crowd.

He took the pouch from his belt and held it up. "I am a stonecaster," he said, realizing that it was the first time he had said those words. "And in this pouch is a new stone."

A shock ran through the crowd like a drum roll. He could feel the River listening, and he knew that the gods were leading him.

"Change the stones, change the world," he said as the murmurs quietened. He let his voice build, as his mother would at the climax of a song. "The stones have spoken. It is time for us to change the world."

LEOF

IN THE shadows of the enchanter's progress, Leof made mental notes about the ghost army's numbers, groups, skills. He was an officer, trained in scouting and assessing an enemy, and knew they would want that information in Turvite. So Leof curbed his desire to just ride until he reached the city where he was sure Thegan had taken Sorn.

But they were a rabble, not an army. Their only show of organization was at dusk and dawn, when a ceremony took place in which they queued for something. Leof couldn't get close enough to see exactly what.

More worrying was the number of Travelers who had already joined their ranks. Two hundred, maybe, men and women and children. Leof suspected that many didn't want to fight, but felt safer with the ghosts than they did with Acton's people; and who could blame them?

He rode across country to avoid the hordes of people fleeing along the roads, streaming in every direction, but mostly towards Turvite. Carlion was closer, but clearly no one trusted that it was safe. Turvite would need warning, he decided, that it was about to receive a domain's worth of visitors, hungry and probably without any silver to pay their way. And for how long?

Cross country on a decent horse was faster, anyway. They were in Three Rivers Domain now, and the warlord here did not spend money on roads the way Thegan did. They would be in South Domain soon, and the roads there were even worse. Should he stop at the fort at Wooding and let them know what was coming?

Over his evening campfire—the ghosts didn't travel at night, although he didn't understand why not—Leof considered his own position. His short hair meant he no longer looked like an officer. His sword—if he had any sense, he'd throw his sword away and figure out how else he could earn his living. It was the pressing box for anyone but a warlord's man to carry a sword. But he couldn't throw it away. He'd trained with the sword from the time he was old enough to walk—toy swords, wooden practice-swords, blunt half-size blades, and finally the real thing. He couldn't just discard it.

Besides, he might need it.

The decision settled him, made him feel less like a dandelion clock floating willy-nilly on the breeze. If they all made it through, there would be time enough to worry about the rest of his life.

The people running ahead of the ghosts had left a lot behind them. He'd had no trouble finding a ham and some cheese in the last farmhouse. He'd hesitated about whether to leave silver for them, but figured that if he did, the farmer would probably never get it. So he had ignored the guilt of theft and packed his spare horse with a light load of food that would last—plus a good supply of oats. If worse came to worst, the horses could make do with grass, and he could live on porridge. He'd done it once before, when he'd been snowed in to a cave for two weeks on a scouting trip.

That time Thegan had come to find him. When the blizzard had stopped, Thegan had led a rescue party and dug him out. So many qualities: loyalty, courage, intelligence, foresight. Tears pricked Leof's eyes; it felt like his commander, the commander he'd fought behind for so long, believed in for so long, was dead. But he had never existed.

Leof watched the ghost army as it approached the bridge over the chasm of the Fallen River. He was near Wooding, on a small rise, obscured from view. A scout from the town, an older man with gray hair, was cut down by one of the ghosts as he tried to make it back to the small force holding the bridge. Men with axes stood ready to hack through the bridge supports and send the bridge crashing into the chasm. The ghosts would then have to go the long way, down to the ford near Three Rivers Domain. If they didn't break the bridge Leof knew the people wouldn't live long.

Then someone moved forward, towards the ghosts, and stopped, the people behind pushing, trying to see what was happening.

Leof expected the ghosts to surge forward, killing as they went, but nothing happened. The enchanter came to the front, flanked by the two ghosts who had seemed to control the fighting in Sendat. They talked—talked!—to the man on the bridge and then, astonishingly, the entire ghost army turned and began to walk down the river towards the ford. It seemed impossible.

Leof found himself shaking. What had happened here? Had the South Domain warlord found a way of defeating the ghosts? He rode a little closer for a better look at the men still ranged across the bridge. They weren't warlord's men, most of them, although their leader seemed to be an officer. Were they…Travelers?

By the time the ghosts and their human allies had walked down river, the men on the bridge were relaxing, sitting down and pulling out flasks and bread, celebrating. Leof rode up and dismounted, tying the horses to a nearby tree.

The officer stood up, ready to be welcoming, and then hesitated as he saw Leof's short hair.

Brazen it out, Leof thought. "Greetings," he said with an officer's authority. "I'm Lord Leof, from Sendat. Congratulations. You're the first group to have been successful against the ghosts. How did you do it?"

The man smiled with thin pride. "Beck, second-in-command to Coeuf, Warlord of South. We heard about Sendat, so we knew the hostage plan wouldn't work." He hesitated. "Do you know about Acton, Lord Leof?"

That was a strange question, Leof thought. Beck read his expression and went on quickly. "He's back. His ghost, that is. And he can talk. He told us to make the Travelers our shield and our sword."

Leof stared at him. The man seemed to believe what he was saying. And why not? If all the other ghosts had risen, why not Acton? He felt a flicker of hope. If Acton were fighting with them…perhaps they had a chance at last.

"So our Travelers told the ghosts, 'This is our home. Go elsewhere'," Beck continued. "The old ghost, the big one, didn't like it, but the enchanter said we had the right to make the decision for ourselves. He said, 'They have weapons. They don't need us to fight for them.' I think he was pleased about that."

Leof raised his voice so they could all hear.

"You've done very well indeed. You are the only people to save their homes so far. We need to send messengers to other districts to let them know of your success." He spoke more quietly, to Beck, "Your warlord can organize it."

Beck shook his head. "Coeuf's gone to Turvite for the warlords' council. His son, too. I'll do it."

"I'll take the news to Turvite," Leof said. "They will be glad of it there."

Beck grinned. "If they can get their Travelers to do it. Without the stonecaster journeying with Acton I'd've had trouble convincing them."

MARTINE

THEY ENTERED Turvite Harbor on an evening tide, riding the swell through the narrow channel with the captain shouting instructions as fast as she could speak and the sailors up and down the rigging like wrens in a berry bush.

Their party met on deck, Safred and Cael both looking pale, but Safred more cheerful at the thought of land ahead.

"I must go to the Moot Hall," Arvid said, turning to Martine. "You will come with me?"

"Not immediately," Martine answered. "I have business here. I have to see Ranny of Highmark."

"She'll be at the Moot Hall. She's in the council. With so many warlords arriving, the council will be there."

Martine felt her back crawl, as it had when she had last walked through Turvite, expecting a knife between her shoulder blades from Ranny. She had no idea if the woman still wanted to kill her, but it seemed likely.

"All right, then, I'll go with you. But the others must go straight to Sanctuary."

Arvid looked at them with surprise. "It's too late for that," he said. "Too late for secrecy. If the warlords are out in force, whatever must be done should be done before them, with their support. We will send to Ash and Bramble, bring them to Turvite."

Cael looked at him kindly. "Lad, do you really think they'll believe us?"

"The Well of Secrets? Of course they'll believe her!"

Zel refused to go, and none of them pressed her. She wanted to take Trine off to the inn Arvid always used, The Red Dawn.

Trine had recovered all her old snappiness, seeming to object to everything about Turvite—the noise, the smell of fish, the lumbering handcarts, the hawkers.

"She'll look after me," Zel said, smiling, and they smiled back, but as she walked off down the road in front of them, leading Trine because the horse's legs were a little unsteady after the long voyage, she looked very small.

"Perhaps you should go to the inn too, and rest," Safred said to Cael. He looked pallid and shaky, but he shook his head.

"I'll see it through. If they've all come, you know —"

"Yes. My uncle will be there," Safred said. "Perhaps my father."

She was staring off at the sea, but her hands were clasped tight. Martine couldn't tell if she was frightened, or hopeful, or simply confused. Perhaps all three. It was the most she had spoken since the fog had been fed. That should be encouraged.

"Your uncle?" Martine asked briskly. "Which one's that?"

"Thegan," Safred said. "My father was Masry, his older brother, the heir to Cliff Domain, but after... When I ran away from him, he followed me into the caves and we met delvers. They say it warped his mind. Changed him. He became very religious, went into seclusion. So Thegan took over the Domain when my grandfather died. Then, of course, he married that poor little Sorn and now he has from cliff to cove, except for the Lake."

"Poor little Sorn?"

"Married off to cement alliances, like all the warlords' daughters. That's what my mother saved me from. What a prize I would have been!" Her voice was bitter. She had paid a high price for her freedom, and she hadn't been the only one who had made sacrifices.

Martine glanced at Cael, but he was concentrating on his balance. Holly, Arvid's guard, stepped forward and gave him her arm. The fact that he took it told Martine that he was very bad. But how he used the last of his energy was his choice.

"Do the gods tell you what we must do next?" Arvid asked her.

Safred shook her head. "I am hollowed out," she said. "I think they will not speak to me again."

There was nothing they could say to that without sounding falsely hearty.

They walked down the dock guarded by Arvid's soldiers, Holly still supporting Cael, and made their way through the streets to the Moot

Hall past some locals, staring and speculating at the new arrivals. Martine could hear them:

"That's the young warlord from up north!"

"No, no, it's Coeuf's son from South. Has to be—look at that nose. Just like Coeuf's. You could hide a horse up there!"

Martine felt happiness sliding over her, as it did so unexpectedly these days. She managed not to giggle, but she couldn't resist peeking at Arvid's nose. It was a definite nose, admittedly, but surely not so prominent as all that?

Immune to public attention in a way she would never become, Arvid ignored it all and chatted with Safred and his guard. Finally, as they approached the hall, he turned to Martine. "Do you have yourself under control now?" he asked, his own mouth twitching just a little.

It almost undid her. What was it about this man that brought out the giggling youngling in her? Then the fear at the heart of love overtook her and her eyes stung with tears. "Be careful," she said. "In there, all the rules are already overturned."

She could hear it as she said it, the Sight coming through without her intention. His gaze sharpened on her as he heard it too, and he nodded, once, the warlord's nod acknowledging information from an officer.

One of his guards called out to the safeguarders on the doors, two big men Martine recognized as working for Doronit: "My Lord Arvid of the Last Domain requires entrance."

The men swung back the big doors and they entered in strict precedence: Arvid, then Safred, Cael, then Martine, the soldiers flanking them all.

At the door to the great hall the Turvite councillors, Ranny among them, stood to greet the arrivals. Arvid went through the formalities, but when he looked around in preparation for introducing his party, Martine shook her head very slightly.

Ranny had seen Martine already, and didn't look pleased. There was no need to antagonize her by making her formally acknowledge someone she thought of as an enemy. Martine wished that she had never withheld the full casting she had done for Ranny. But then—perhaps she would never have left Turvite, never seen Elva or been sent to the Well of Secrets. Never met Arvid. Too many connections, tumbling like stones in a landslide.

"My adviser, the Well of Secrets," Arvid said.

A stir went through the people assembled, and Martine saw someone slip out the door to the hall to spread the news.

Ranny smiled, a genuine smile of relief. "We are glad indeed to see you here, my lady," she said.

"Lady?" Safred said, her freckles standing out against her pale face. "I think not."

Martine winced. The whole of the Domains knew that Safred, Well of Secrets, had refused her heritage as a warlord's daughter; refused to be part of the ruling elite.

Ranny realized she had misspoken, but she carried on with the aplomb of the seasoned diplomat. "Please, enter."

The others walked on, but Martine lingered, moving closer to Ranny. "Two weeks after mid-summer, twenty-three years from now, here in Turvite," Martine said softly, ensuring no one else could hear.

Ranny stared at her, instantly suspicious. "What?"

"I swear to you, that is what the stones told me," Martine said.

Safred had returned and overheard. "That was an old fate," she said gently, "cast before the enchanter arose with his army. All fates have been broken by that—it was outside the gods' control. No fate cast is certain, now."

Shocked, they both stared at her. Then Ranny smiled. "So you do *not* know. No one knows when I will die." Tension went out of her shoulders and her head lifted. "Good. That's as it should be."

"Are you ready?" Arvid asked reprovingly. He had come back to collect them.

Inside the hall the servants had taken the tables up and set one large, long table in the middle. The Turvite councillors were at one end, the titular head of the Council, Garham the wine merchant, in the center. Garham had been a customer of Martine's—a blustering but not stupid man, he rarely listened to anyone other than Ranny, who stood beside him.

Warlords and their men stood around, eyeing each other and the table, working out precedence and who would sit where.

Martine recognized a few of them: old Coeuf was there with his son, Eolbert. She smiled to herself when she saw that he had inherited his father's nose. Merroc from Far South was easily picked out, too, as he was famous for his bright red hair. He was in his fifties but still robust. He'd outlived three wives; two dead in childbirth and the other from a fever. They said he was cursed: even as a warlord, he'd had trouble finding a fourth wife.

Some others: Eni from Three Rivers, so stout he could hardly walk; Berden from Western Mountains, it must be, he was supposed to be very tall and despite the stoop of age he towered over them all still. Then a young man, younger even than Arvid, with reddish-blond hair. Would that be Gabra, who held Cliff Domain for his father, Thegan? But not all the eleven were represented. Some would still be traveling, she figured, and Henist from Northern Mountains might not come at all; he ran his domain as though it were separate from all the rest.

Garham called out, "My lords! Councillors! Please take a seat."

She moved towards the wall with Cael, certain she didn't belong at that table. "Let's find you somewhere to sit down," she said to him, taking his arm.

He nodded with effort and they walked slowly towards the door.

After some initial jostling, the warlords sat at the table, their officers standing behind. The councillors were grouped at the head of the table, Ranny on Garham's left hand. Safred sat at his right, her spine straight and her head high. But Martine could tell she was unhappy about being there.

Garham cleared his throat. "This council was called by the Lord Thegan —"

"And it was a warlords' council!" Merroc snarled. "What do you think *you're* doing here, merchants?"

Garham paused, trying to control his temper.

Martine and Cael had almost reached the door when it slammed back and a man strode into the room, followed by several officers and a woman. The leader was tall and blond and ridiculously good looking, and he moved like he owned the world. He wore Central Domain's colors, as did the officers. The woman was auburn haired and graceful, but looked tired and drawn. Thegan and Sorn? Martine wondered. It seemed likely.

Thegan walked to the foot of the table and suddenly, like a picture turned upside down, it became the head, simply because he stood there. Everyone there turned subtly to look at him.

He stared down the table challengingly—not at the warlords or the councillors, but at Safred. "Are you satisfied?" he asked her. "If you had done your duty by our family we would have had warning of this before it happened!" He slammed his fist down on the table. Safred winced, but recovered.

Cael was already halfway to the table. Martine followed helplessly, sure this was going to end badly.

"Well?"

"Don't blame her for your own incompetence," Cael said.

Thegan whirled on him, hand going to his sword. He was unshaven and tired, Martine saw, and deeply, vigorously angry.

He checked when he saw it wasn't an officer insulting him, and looked to his officers as though expecting them to drag Cael away. Then he realized that they were in Turvite, a free town, and Cael had the right to say anything he wanted. That no warlord had power within the city bounds. Martine could see it happen, because his face went very calm, and behind her the woman drew in a sharp breath, as though frightened.

"You look a bit like your brother," Cael went on casually. "I suppose we're some kind of relation, since my sister married your brother."

It took the wind out of Thegan's sails as nothing else could. Martine smiled.

"Your brother couldn't capture her, and you have no right to even try," Cael said, the amiable tone at odds with his sharp gaze.

Safred stood up. She still looked pale to Martine's eye, but she spoke firmly enough. "Thank you, uncle," she said formally. "But I am sure this council has more pressing things to discuss than our family disagreements."

"She's right!" Merroc snarled. "What can you tell us, Well of Secrets? Can we stand against this enchanter and his dead?"

Thegan and Cael still glared at each other, but Thegan turned away after a moment, preserving dignity by pretending to discount Cael. Martine saw him flick a glance at one of his officers, and saw the man nod in return. Cael's life wouldn't last long if that man got near him.

Martine forced herself to approach Cael. "Come," she said. "Leave her to explain."

Safred nodded, and Cael turned to go, all his energy deserting him so that he had to lean heavily on Martine's arm to make it out of the hall.

Behind them, as the door closed, they heard Safred's warning, "The gods have provided a way of defeating the ghost army, but it will not be easy, and we must not kill the enchanter before it is done. That would be the worst folly…"

The woman who had accompanied Thegan followed them out and sat on a bench in the corner, collapsing the last few inches onto the seat as though exhausted. Martine helped Cael onto the bench beside her.

"I am Sorn," the woman said, gathering herself.

"My lady," Martine acknowledged, and Cael echoed her.

"No lady now, I think," she said bitterly. "Sendat is taken by the enchanter."

"Then he'll come here soon," Martine said.

"They will have axes," Sorn said. "Many of them."

Martine considered the possibilities. "The stonecasters of Turvite bespell their doors against ghosts," she said slowly. "Is it possible, do you think, to bespell a whole city?"

SAKER

SAKER ADDRESSED each new group of allies the same way. "There's no need to steal. No need to loot. Everything will belong to us, by the time we have finished. Just take what you need now and decide which house you want later, after we have conquered. There will be enough for everyone."

They cheered him, each time, and joined him, more every day. Whenever they were sighted, Acton's people ran for their lives and the Travelers came out to meet them. The warlords further south hadn't been as efficient as Thegan at gathering up the Travelers. Or massacring them. But there were no more towns like Wooding; no Travelers asked them to just pass by.

"No safety being Settled, not any more," one old man said to him in a small, prosperous town. "Is there? We might as well fight."

Saker clapped him on the shoulder and smiled as his people gathered whatever they needed from the market square. They didn't linger and didn't loot, but finding enough food for their growing army always took some time.

His father and Owl were impatient with the needs of the living.

"These people are our future," Saker reminded them. "Once the invaders are destroyed, these are the ones who will build our new land."

Alder and Owl shared a glance that Saker could not read. Then, almost reluctantly, Alder nodded.

They took over that village for the night. All of Acton's people had vanished, except for the innkeeper, who pretended to be glad to see them. "Welcome, welcome, come in!" he babbled, clutching at his apron.

He had the same brownish hair as Saker himself, but Owl shook his head when Saker asked if the man had Traveler blood, and used him as one of the evening sacrifices. Oddly enough, his family had old blood in plenty, and the wife served them with tears running down her cheeks, two young childer hiding in her skirts.

"You're safe now," Saker told her, but he could see that only fear stopped her spitting in his face. Fear for her children. "Your children will grow up able to look anyone in the eye," he said earnestly. It was important that she understand why they fought. "No more warlords. No more Generation Laws. No more injustice."

"My husband was a good man. Where's the justice in his death?" she demanded, her voice breaking into sobs.

"We all have to make some sacrifices to bring the future into being," he said, but his words sounded hollow even to himself, and he wondered if they should have spared the man, for the sake of his children.

Each night and morning, Alder and Owl conducted the blood ceremony. Saker had nothing to do with it, but by this time he was glad. The shrilling sound grew stronger in his ears each time, until he could hardly bear it. On the third day, as he watched his father slit the arm of a young woman, a blonde-haired woman much the same age as the girl Thegan had killed at Sendat, he realized something. The sound was not the yearning of spirits beyond the grave who wished to join them. It was the keening of those they had killed and sent to the darkness beyond death, calling out for revenge. No one else seemed to hear it, and Saker accepted the sound, and the shapes he saw, writhing in the corner of his vision, as part of the price he had to pay to secure their victory. He was haunted by the dead—that was fitting. He would bear that alone, so that none of his people, alive or dead, would feel the burden. After each ceremony, exhausted by pretending to be unaffected by the deafening shrill, by controlling his reactions to the horrible, distorted shapes which clambered at the corner of his eyes, he sat down and found some consolation in that thought. He was protecting his people, as he should, from evil.

BRAMBLE

BRAMBLE RODE through the day half-expecting Swith himself to descend from the clouds. Anything might happen, she felt. Beck, hated for as long as she could remember, was an ally. Acton, despoiler and invader, was her—well, call it friend. Wind wraiths were abroad in settled land. Ash, whom she had thought of as a younger brother to be looked after, had stood on the warlord's steps and made a speech that had stirred an entire town to cooperation and action.

And here she was, riding to Turvite to confront an enchanter who was capable of the darkest betrayal in all human history. To confront him, and make him powerless, and then kill him. The peace she had felt in the forest with the hunter was so far away she could barely remember it.

Acton ran at her side like a young deer, tireless and oddly comforting. Occasionally he would grin up at her, and although she grinned back she felt there was something false about it, as though he were forcing himself.

Close to twilight, deep in South Domain, they entered a long stretch of woodland, to Bramble's relief. The summer green of the trees, the rustle of life, bird calls, everything was a blessing.

After an hour's riding, they found a clearing with a stream that crossed the road, and decided to camp there.

Bramble was grooming the bay when the hair on the back of her neck stood up. The bird calls were all wrong. She could hear woodpeckers' *ki-ki-ki-ki* alarm calls from some way ahead.

"Ware," she said. "Someone's coming."

They drew off behind an enormous holly bush and waited. A few moments later a band of Travelers came into view, but Travelers like she had never seen before. A big group—far larger than the Generation Laws allowed. Twenty, maybe, mostly men and a few young women, although there was one family with a small child and a babe in arms. They walked warily, carrying hatchets and knives like weapons.

Bramble stepped out and raised a hand in greeting. They stopped and scanned the trees for anyone else, then relaxed a little as they noticed her coloring.

"Fire and water," she greeted them, remembering her grandfather's lessons in Traveler ways.

"Fire and water and a roof in the rain," the man in front replied. "Are you alone?"

She shook her head and the others came out of hiding. The Travelers gripped their weapons more tightly at the sight of Baluch, smiled as they saw Ash, and seemed excited when Acton finally appeared.

"Are you with the enchanter?" a young man asked eagerly.

"No," Bramble said. "Why?"

"We're going to join him," the leader said. "We've had enough."

"Enough of what?" Baluch asked.

The leader glared at him. "Enough of being murdered in our beds! Do you know what's been happening?"

Bramble answered quickly, before the others could say anything. "Some of it. But joining the enchanter isn't the way to —"

"It might keep us alive!" the mother with the baby exclaimed. "They killed my sister and her two sons. For nothing! Nothing…" She began to weep. Her husband put an arm around her shoulders and glowered at them, as though her tears were their fault.

"The enchanter can't be stopped, they say. His ghosts will protect us." He looked at Acton, assessing his bulk and the sword at his side with some satisfaction.

Acton was listening thoughtfully, assessing each member of the group, but he stayed behind Baluch and said nothing.

"The enchanter wants to kill everyone in the Domain without Traveler blood," Ash said.

The Travelers looked at each other. It was news to them, and a shock. Some faces were troubled, some implacable, but others wore a touch of satisfaction.

"Might be the only way," the leader said finally. He looked up at the canopy of leaves. It was growing darker. "Camp here," he ordered.

These were people who lived on the Road. Bramble admired their competence as they set up camp, built fires, dug a privy. They kept their bags packed, so they could leave at any moment. She and the others helped and by the time they were all sitting down to eat, the Travelers made a place for them in the fire circle.

They shared what they had, and it was the best meal Bramble had eaten since the morning she'd woken up in Oakmere, unexpectedly alive and ravenous. Carrot soup, roasted rabbit and greens, griddle scones and a dark fruitcake that the woman with the baby said kept well on the Road.

After they'd cleaned up and repacked their gear, Ash took out his pouch and glanced at Bramble. She nodded. It was worth a try.

"There is a new stone in the bag," he began, more gently than he had at Wooding.

They listened, but unlike the Travelers at Wooding they had seen recent murder, and not by ghosts. They would not be convinced. Acton tapped Ash on the knee.

"Speak," Ash said readily.

"Greetings —" he began.

The dark, grating voice brought the Travelers to their feet. Parents lifted children into their arms and two of the littlest began to cry.

"There's no need to be afraid —" Ash said.

"I am Acton, come from the darkness beyond death —"

They stared at him white-faced. One man picked up his pack. The woman with the baby took a step backwards, covering her child's face to shield it.

"He won't hurt you," Bramble said.

"Ghosts don't speak," the youngest man said. "Ghosts don't speak!"

He began to back away, his eyes fixed on Acton. The others moved too, slowly backwards, gathering their packs as they went until they were at the edge of the clearing.

"We mean you no harm," Baluch said in his most soothing voice, but they weren't listening, Bramble saw. Their whole attention was given to Acton. Acton the invader.

"Are you really Acton?" the leader asked, his voice rough.

Acton spread his hands in a gesture of good faith and took a step forward.

"I am Acton," he confirmed. I am here to —"

The young man broke and ran and the others followed, disappearing into the trees.

"Come back!" Ash cried.

He might as well have been mute. In a few moments, they were alone in the leaping light of the fire.

Acton looked down at his hands. They were shaking. "Afraid. So afraid of me," he whispered.

Bramble wanted to reassure him, tell him that they feared a nightmare story, a figure out of legend, not him. But it was him they were afraid of—and if it had been a thousand years ago, they would have been right to run.

Ash said so. Bramble thought for a second that Acton would hit him, but he clenched his fists and walked a little way into the trees.

He came back some time later.

"Speak," Ash said.

"They will join the enchanter," he said.

"They're right," said Baluch, the first time he had spoken since the Travelers had gone. "They're safer with him."

Acton said nothing, but something had changed in his face; a new awareness, Bramble thought, of the consequences of his actions. He would not be so fast to declare himself the next time they met Travelers.

The next day they passed through fields and woodland and more fields.

They were ahead of the enchanter's march, which fretted Acton. When they stopped for the night where a stream formed a clear pool he paced around the fire circle.

"We should make our stand here," he said, indicating the broad sweep of pastureland they had ridden through that afternoon. "Before he gets to Turvite."

Bramble hesitated. What if he were right? She drew Ash aside.

"Why not cast?" she said.

Ash looked over at Acton. "See what the gods say? You're right, now is a good time."

Since the wind wraiths had appeared he had barely spoken, except to spread the word about Evenness and a new world waiting on the other side of this crisis. Bramble had believed him, too. The world was shifting. But somehow she couldn't see the new one. It seemed too far away, as though she only had the time she was living in, moment by moment. As the hunter had lived, moment by moment.

They stepped through the ritual and Ash examined the stones. "They say we must go faster."

"Well, we can't!" Bramble said, exasperated. "The horses won't stand it."

"There's another way." He hesitated, as though he were about to say something she shouldn't hear. Baluch, sitting beside him, put a hand on his arm.

"Bramble has met her," he said reassuringly.

Ash looked startled. "You've met the River?"

Bramble shook her head. "Not me. I met the Lake."

Baluch waved his hand dismissively. "The same being in a different mood."

"The River is the Lake's little sister," Ash said, as though he parroted something he'd heard many times.

"All rivers, all streams, all lakes in the Eleven Domains are part of her," Baluch said gently. "It's why we can hear her everywhere." He looked at Bramble. "She will take us the River's way to Sanctuary, if you wish."

The River's way, she thought. Faster than horses? The way Ash came into the Weeping Caverns? Acton moved closer, listening with interest, and Ash sat back, saying nothing more.

"Will She take Acton, too?" she asked.

Ash and Baluch both considered for a moment, as though listening to someone speak, then shook their heads. Acton moved away, his face expressionless for once.

"Sorry, Bramble," Ash said, as if he were not sorry at all. "We'll have to raise him again when we get there."

Bramble felt her gorge rise at the thought. She had been able to do it once, when she hadn't known what it would take, but to deliberately banish Acton back to the darkness beyond death and then go through that, that flaying alive. "No," she said.

"Bramble —" Ash said, exasperated.

"With you two gone, we can make a better pace," she said briskly. "I can ride each of the horses in turn, and go cross country. We'll be there much sooner. It's better this way." She forced herself to grin at him. "Neither of you are really riders, after all."

At least there was no argument about her not being safe on her own. She could have no better protection than Acton. His own people worshipped him and he terrified the Travelers.

"You won't be able to talk to him," Ash warned.

She shrugged. That might be a relief.

Ash looked at her with some compassion in his eyes. "If you have anything to say, say it now."

She did have something to say, and knew that she had better say it convincingly. She walked around the fire to where Acton was saying goodbye to Baluch.

"I want to make something clear," she said. "We are not going to confront the enchanter here. We are going to Turvite as quickly as possible. I will not wait for you. I will not turn aside. Whatever dreams you have of raising an army and marching on Turvite, forget them. That's not going to happen twice."

"I want to protect it, this time," he said, and paused. "A way of paying part of my debt."

"You're not here to fight," she said. "You're here to help others, not to lead."

He smiled at her. It had a hint of the cozening smile in it, but it was far warmer, and full of laughter. "Yes, Mother," he said.

"You've been spoilt from the day you were born," she said in mock reproof. "You've always had everything you wanted."

"Not now," he said, suddenly serious, looking younger, eyes open with that impossible flicker of blue. "I can't have what I truly want."

He meant her. It was clear. He wanted her. But was it real, or just that, for the first time, he couldn't reach out and take what he fancied?

She stared at him, but she didn't know what to say. She was not going to pour her heart out in front of Baluch and Ash.

"You will be together in your next lives," Baluch said.

She blushed, hard, feeling the red climb up from her heart to her face.

Acton looked startled and then laughed. "I promise," he said, serious again. "In our next life."

She couldn't speak. Not in front of the others. But she nodded, feeling exultation climbing through her, filling her with something wilder than joy. They both smiled. Whatever linked them was as tight as a bowstring.

"I think we can go now," Baluch said to Ash, and his voice was a mixture of amusement and a kind of regret. He looked older than before, as though their exchange had exhausted him.

"Aye," Ash said.

He hugged Bramble goodbye and the warm pressure of his arms was both comforting and a reminder of what Acton would never feel like to her. She let out a breath as Ash and Baluch walked to the pool and stood beside it.

They looked back and raised their hands, then took a step forward into the water, and were gone.

She walked down to look at where their footprints ended, then turned back to Acton.

He was gone too.

MARTINE

MARTINE DID not want to go back into the council chambers, but Sorn insisted. "Come with me," she said.

They left Cael sitting on the hall bench and opened the door.

The warlords were still arguing.

"Apologies won't stop them!" Thegan said forcefully. "He's prepared to sacrifice any number of his own people to take his revenge—do you think apologizing would make any difference to him?"

Sorn coughed politely and he whirled, impatience clear on his face.

"My lords, councillors," Sorn said. "This is Martine, a stonecaster who lived formerly in this city. She has a suggestion."

"Well?" Thegan said, pre-empting Ranny or Garham's right to speak first.

Garham's face closed in with anger, and somehow that bolstered Martine's courage. "In Turvite," she said calmly, "we bespell the doors of stonecasters' houses, to prevent ghosts from entering."

"Can you bespell the whole city?" Ranny asked.

"I don't know," Martine said. "I've never tried to do more than my own door. But I am not the only stonecaster who can use that spell. If we worked together..."

"Good!" Garham said. "At last, a sensible suggestion. Boc, send for the stonecasters of the city. I want them here now!"

Boc hurried out with a spring in his step, and faces lightened around the table.

"If it works for Turvite..." Merroc said.

"We can protect all our towns and villages," Arvid said, finishing Merroc's thought. He shot Martine a look of admiration and mischief. "If our stonecasters agree."

"I am sure they will," Martine replied. What was the man thinking, to even suggest otherwise? Did he *want* to see stonecasters imprisoned and forced to work?

"And we have the Well of Secrets," Merroc said, inclining his head politely to Safred.

Safred raised a hand in denial. "My lords, I am not a stonecaster, nor a caster of spells. I can relay messages from the gods, and I can heal, but that is all. If I can help, I will, but do not rely on me for spell casting."

Thegan scowled at her as though she had personally betrayed him. The others got to their feet and stretched.

"No sense waiting here while these casters are gathered," Coeuf said, leaning heavily on his son's arm. "I'll be at my inn."

He was followed out by the rest of the warlords and councillors, Ranny last. Thegan nodded to his men to take a break and they left too. Only Thegan, Sorn, Safred and Thegan's son, Gabra, remained.

Martine was struck by the resemblance between Safred and her cousin. They might have been mother and son, if she'd had him young. Safred was looking at him, too, and then at Thegan.

Martine's Sight stirred, and she moved forward to Safred's side. "Don't," she whispered. "Whatever it is, don't say it."

"I have to," Safred said. "It's part of this pattern, I can feel it." She turned to Gabra and nodded. "It's good to meet you, brother," she said slowly.

He frowned. Thegan stood very still, his face blank.

"Cousin," Gabra said.

Safred ignored him, looking at Thegan. "Did you really think I wouldn't know my father's son?" she asked.

Sorn was even stiller than Thegan. Then she took a deep breath in, her face pale, her green eyes cold, and faced him. "Time we had a child, you said. Were you going to pimp me, too?"

Impatience swept over him. "I didn't *pimp* her! She always wanted Masry, but he was obsessed with the green-eyed Valuer bitch. She only took me as second best, and when I gave her the chance to lie down with him, she jumped at it!"

Gabra stood with his mouth tightly closed, looking more like Thegan than he had done before.

"And me?" Sorn demanded. "Who did you have in mind for me?"

He looked at Gabra.

Sorn laughed, her voice hard. "Your *nephew?* Oh, perfect!"

"It's the bloodline that counts," Thegan snarled. "Masry was the true heir anyway—his son inherits, his son's son inherits. The way it should be."

"As if you cared!" Sorn shot back. "If you'd been a *man* and sired your own sons, you would never have allowed Masry's get to have any part of your lands."

He struck her across the face, a full back-handed blow that sent her sprawling on the floor. Gabra and Martine both moved between them as he took a step towards her.

Sorn did not cry out. She fell in silence, as though she'd done it many times before, and climbed back to her feet in silence, and faced him down. "I am my father's daughter, and the true heir to his Domain," she said softly. "I renounce you as husband."

Thegan smiled. "I own you, wife."

"I have had time to study my position, these last years," Sorn continued, "since I have not had children to occupy me." He flinched, and her voice gained strength. "There are ancient laws, little used but still valid. Since the Domain passes through my bloodline, if you are not able to give me heirs, I can renounce you for the sake of the Domain, and take another husband."

"I'll kill you first," he said. "You know I will."

"This is not Sendat. You are not ruler here. If you kill me without heirs, my cousin Coeuf's son inherits."

"He'd have to take it by blood."

"It's already been taken," Martine said, annoyed. "Have you forgotten?"

Thegan nodded, still looking at Sorn. "She's right. Truce, until the enchanter is defeated?" His voice was as soft as honey, as reasonable as rain after drought.

Sorn stared heavily at him, red from his blow spreading across her cheek, and then nodded. "But I will not sleep where you sleep," she said.

"Stay with us," Safred said immediately.

Thegan flicked a hand as if to say "Do what you like," then walked out of the room. Gabra hesitated, but followed him.

Martine and Sorn and Safred looked at each other.

"Don't trust him to keep this truce," Safred said.

Sorn gave a half-smile. "I know him too well to trust him with anything," she said. She sat, exhausted, on one of the chairs and raised a hand to her face.

"That wasn't the first time he'd done that," Martine said.

"No, no, he's never struck me before," Sorn said.

"It wasn't the first time you've been struck, though."

Sorn bit her lip and shrugged. Safred laid a hand over the red cheek and sang softly under her breath. When she took the hand away the skin was back to its normal pale glow.

Sorn looked up with awe. "A true prophet," she said. "The gods are good, to have sent you to us."

A flush swept up over Safred's freckled face. "The gods love *you*," she said. "They yearn for you."

But Sorn only laughed, as though that were impossible. She dug inside her belt pouch and brought out a small scroll of paper. "I don't know who to give this to," she said. "I made a list of the Travelers at Sendat. I've marked the ones who escaped before the ghosts came. Most of the others were killed, although some may have survived. I thought someone, somewhere, would want to know who they were..."

Safred took the list gravely, and looked over it. It was long. Halfway down, her expression lightened.

"Rowan and Swallow escaped," she said to Martine. Martine knew that they were Ash's parents. Ash had been going to find his father...

"What about Ash?" she asked, in sudden fear.

"There is no Ash on the list," Sorn replied.

Martine realized only then that her heart had stopped beating, when it resumed with a sudden thud. But there were tears on Safred's cheek.

"Who?" Martine asked. "Who is it?"

"Flax," Safred said numbly.

Martine drew in a sharp breath. No, she prayed. No.

"A young man," Sorn said. "A beautiful singer. I know he died, trying to lead the others to escape. I am sorry...you knew him?"

Martine turned away. Zel. Gods of field and stream, what would Zel do?

"I should have known this had happened," Safred said numbly. "*Why didn't they tell me?*"

"Because," Martine said bitterly, "human death doesn't matter to them, remember?"

"I have to tell Zel," Safred said.

Martine and Sorn went with her. Martine passed other stonecasters coming to the Moot Hall, but didn't stop. Let them sort out a strategy, she thought, and she would help. They knew as much about spell casting as she did. She had to be with Zel.

As soon as they came around the stable door, Zel realized something was wrong. "Are the ghosts here?" she asked, springing up from a straw bale, bridle and cleaning cloth in her hands.

Safred just stood there. Martine didn't know what to say, either.

"What's wrong?" Zel asked.

Sorn moved forward, her face full of compasssion. "I am sorry, but we have bad news. You have a brother named Flax? A singer?"

Zel nodded slowly.

"He is dead."

Her head moved from side to side in denial. Sorn took her hands, pressing them in sympathy.

"He was very brave," she said. "He was trying to free his people when he was cut down."

"Free them?" Zel whispered. "From the ghosts?"

"No." Sorn's voice was even gentler. "The warlord at Sendat held Travelers for hostage against the ghosts. But the enchanter attacked anyway, and the hostages...Some managed to escape, but your brother..."

"The warlord killed him," Zel said flatly. "What about Ash? Is he dead, too?"

Sorn looked at Martine for help.

"We don't know what's happened to Ash," Martine said. "Oh, Zel, I'm sorry."

"He promised he'd keep Flax safe," Zel explained to Sorn, as if it were very important that she understood. "He *promised*. He's a safeguarder, see, and he said he'd look after Flax like he were his little brer." Her voice cracked on the word and she drew in a long, sobbing breath.

"So he's still alive? Right? He's alive and my brer dead?" She turned to Safred. "That right?"

Safred nodded. "I think so. But we don't know why—"

"Don't matter *why!*" Zel said. "Don't matter. He's alive and my boy's dead and he promised." She threw the bridle and cloth on the floor. "Where's the enchanter now?"

"On his way to Turvite," Safred said. "Zel—"

"Warlords gatherin" to fight, eh? Kill more people? Seems to me this enchanter are the only one stayed honest." She walked out the door.

Sorn went to follow her, but Safred stopped her. "Let her go."

"Is this part of the pattern, too?" Martine asked with bitterness.

"I pray so," Safred said.

SAKER

SAKER LOOKED across the plain to the rising hills in the distance. Turvite, and beyond that, the sea.

It had been fifteen years since he had been here, the year that Freite had come to barter with the trader from the Wind Cities for some special herbs for a particular spell against plague.

The trader had refused to sell them to her, and she had been furious. Saker found himself thankful for that, now that he thought about it. Had she been planning to loose a plague on her enemies, and refrained only because she could not guarantee her own safety? It seemed likely, looking back.

He had been only a boy, then, cowed and obedient. He had gawked at the high hill with its golden houses, flinched at the noises that clamored in every street, slept lightly on a pallet at the end of Freite's bed, and slept heavily on the nights after she drew strength from him. She'd had customers: a woman with eyes the color of sapphire, a man with a raddled nose, an old man in rich clothes who ordered her about like a lackey. She hadn't liked that, but after he was gone she turned to Saker and said with satisfaction, "He's got a canker and he'll be dead in a year, no matter how high his mark is!"

There had been some significance to that, which he hadn't understood, some complex bit of politics or social interaction that she had never bothered to teach him. Now, he realized with a jolt of surprise, none of that mattered. The old ways were about to end: old families would die, old wealth would be shared among his people. Social standing would vanish; equality would stand. Evenness. All the things he had never quite understood would be unimportant.

They would work their way through Turvite street by street, and no one, this time, would escape.

ASH

ASH STEPPED onto the riverbank.

The smooth curve of bank was dotted with small jetties, and here and there clumps of willows and alders grew down to the water. He and Baluch used the branches of one to swing up the steep bank, the sky bright above them, mackerel clouds a coverlet of rose and gold. Ash's safeguarder instincts made him assess their position immediately. There was no one in sight.

A light wind seemed to blow them dry in the instant that they stepped ashore. That moment, leaving Her, was full of sorrow and loss.

He saw his pain reflected in Baluch's face.

"It's always so," Baluch said gently. "To leave Her is to break your heart. Every time."

Ash nodded. It was the same as human love, then, like the songs said. A mixture of joy and pain, desire and longing, delight and misery.

He accepted it with some relief. If his bond with the River had been unalloyed happiness, it would have felt false to him, like the happiness poppy juice bought. Temporary.

"The heart of love is the dagger, the soul of love is the lance," he quoted. It was a song from the north, a couple of hundred years old. His mother liked it.

Baluch smiled with quiet satisfaction. "That was one of my good ones," he said.

Ash stared for a moment, then burst out laughing in a kind of shock. Had Baluch written every song he liked from the last thousand years? He sobered, thinking about that song, "The Warrior's Love." A life of fighting and music, that was Baluch, and that song brought both of them together. He wondered if Acton were as complex, if that were the reason Bramble loved him.

There were voices, beyond the curtain of trees. Many voices, talking in a low contented buzz. They paused to listen. Occasionally a voice was raised in a shout or a laugh.

"Sounds like an inn," Baluch said.

Ash nodded, and now he brought his attention to it, he could smell beer, and piss, and sausages cooking. "I think it's the Dancing Bear, at Sanctuary," he said. "I've been here before." Several times, he remembered, on jobs for Doronit. The innkeeper was one of her customers. His stomach growled. It had been a long time since the last of the cheese. "I could do with some food."

"An inn is the best place to get news," Baluch said.

They moved to the edge of the green willow curtain and paused, listening still. It felt dangerous to Ash, to push aside that curtain and walk back out into the world. He had a deep conviction—almost Sight—that the world had changed since he entered the River. That he would walk into the inn in another time, another place, another country, even.

He put his hand out and pulled the trailing willow withies aside, and walked into the inn yard.

There were tables set out on the river bank, full of people drinking, and the inn behind them was busy. It *was* the Dancing Bear, the largest inn on the river outside Turvite, so large that he couldn't see beyond it to the town. As he stood there, assessing, someone inside lit candles and the night suddenly seemed darker.

He and Baluch took a couple of steps towards the drinkers, and the people at the nearest table turned around to look.

Dung and pissmire! Ash thought. It was Aylmer, Doronit's right-hand man. Aylmer, and Hildie, and tall blond Elfrida, and two of the Dung Brothers. The third Dung Brother walked out of the inn, carefully carrying three tankards. He stopped dead when he saw Ash.

There was a moment when everyone froze. Then the others looked at Aylmer—even Hildie.

"You've got a hide thick as an ox, coming back," Aylmer said. "She'll take you apart, and she'll do it slow."

For a moment Ash's memory played for him a recent song: the speech he had made about the world changing, there on the steps of the warlord's house, in the stronghold of the enemy. He had taken the crowd with him, lifted them up with the image of a better world, a greater world where justice was the same for everyone, officer or commoner, Traveler or Acton's folk. It had been a great and wonderful feeling, while it lasted, while they listened, and then afterwards as they worked together for the first time. He had felt like a different person, as though nothing was beyond him.

But the eyes that looked at him now saw just Ash, the Traveler boy whom Doronit had employed, trained, been betrayed by. A nothing. A cipher. Ash felt his confidence drain away with the memory of Wooding. This was Sanctuary, Turvite, the real world, and here he was just a safeguarder.

Baluch was still behind him. Ash motioned with his hands behind his back: go, stay hidden. Baluch melted back into the willow fronds.

This situation, he realized, wasn't about his task, it was simply about his own survival. Perhaps this meeting was why the stones had sent him here. He only had one chance to get Doronit's people on his side. What would do it? All he had was the truth.

"She wanted me to murder Martine, on Ranny's orders. I don't do murder for hire."

The two Dung Brothers scratched the backs of their necks as if in puzzlement. The third moved to do the same and spilt some beer, then put the tankards down on the table and stared at him. They weren't hostile, but they weren't important. It was Aylmer and Hildie who would decide. Ash kept his eyes on them. Hildie looked scornful and somehow satisfied, as if she'd always known he was weak and was glad to have it confirmed. Aylmer pressed his lips together, but he seemed—wistful? As though he wished he'd made the same choice.

"She'll take *us* apart if we doesn't turn him over to her," Hildie said.

"Aye," Aylmer said slowly. "That she will." He sounded regretful, but there was no hesitation in the way he got up and came to Ash's side.

Ash knew better than to fight them. Or to run. Hildie was faster, the Dung Brothers stronger, and Aylmer more cunning. Even Elfrida had put him through a window, one time. All of them together could have stopped Acton himself. He shivered at the thought, and remembered Baluch, hiding and listening.

"What are you doing in Sanctuary? Who needed so many safeguarders?" Ash asked.

"Big shipment of jewels and velvet, coming down the river from Whitehaven," Aylmer said. "Merchant's landing it here so his rivals won't get wind of it. Not till early tomorrow, though. We thought we'd make a night of it."

"And we're going to," one of the Dung Brothers said, settling more comfortably in his chair. "Don't need all of us to take him to Doronit."

Aylmer looked at him steadily. "Well, if you don't want to share the reward, that's fine by me. Come on, Hildie. I reckon you and I can keep him in line."

Hildie laughed. "Sure and certain," she said. "Off we go, cully." She came behind Ash and he felt the nudge of a knife in his back. They had been colleagues, he and Hildie, but he knew she wouldn't hesitate to use that knife. "It'd be more work to deliver you to her with your hamstrings cut, but we c'd do it," she said.

He laughed. "Aye, that's for sure." He felt almost free; he could make no decisions here except to go with them or die fighting, and that was no decision at all.

They walked him from the inn yard, Aylmer on one side and Hildie just behind. "So, cully, you've come full circle," she said.

"Not yet," Ash said.

Sanctuary was almost connected to Turvite. Houses and market gardens lined the road between the two, and at halfway there was another inn called the Last Chance. Last chance to get good beer before leaving the city, or last chance to buy beer at country prices? Both, maybe. His good mood continued, and he could just make out, at the edges of his hearing, Baluch whistling "The Warrior's Love." Following, then, but not trying to break him free. Just as well.

He pretended to have caught a stone in his shoe, and as he bent over to dislodge it, he saw Baluch watching from behind a house a hundred yards or so back. He shook his head and flicked his fingers discreetly to say, no, don't try. Baluch looked puzzled, but nodded and disappeared behind the corner of the house. Ash knew Baluch wouldn't do anything stupid. He had been a fighter once, but he was no match for Aylmer or Hildie now.

Walking back into Turvite proper, they strode up the long hill that he and Martine had struggled down in that storm, close to a year ago. Ash felt like a different person to the boy who had left, but he wasn't sure why. It wasn't just the passage of time. It wasn't even the sense of being involved in a task of huge importance. It was mainly the memories of young Ash and of the River. He had a home, now, and a stake in the future; a year ago he had been without any ties, without anywhere he would be welcome, without the sense he had a future. It was why he'd followed Martine so doggedly—she was all he'd had.

Turvite itself hadn't changed. It was still loud and busy and smelly, and full of people going about their many businesses, even though it was coming on to full dark. The ghosts lingered, too, pale and insubstantial compared to the warriors Saker the enchanter had summoned, but still clear in the fading light. They looked at Ash with concern, recognizing him from the Mid-Winter's Eve when he had commanded them, on Doronit's orders, to reveal their secrets. It was her source of power in this city, all those secrets stolen from the dead. It was a bad memory, but it was important to remember what he had done, what he was capable of.

A year ago, being a Traveler in Turvite had attracted no comment. This evening, he and Hildie were given black looks and mutterings. Men spat on the ground as they passed, women made the sign against evil.

"What's that about?" Ash asked Hildie, after a woman had cursed her for a black-haired slut. Hildie just shrugged.

"Don't say you haven't heard about this Traveler enchanter?" Aylmer cut in.

"I've heard," Ash said. "But I didn't know people were sure he was a Traveler."

"Lord Thegan announced it," Aylmer said. "Figured it out somehow from what had been done in Carlion."

Ash felt cold sweep over him. If people in Turvite, famed for tolerating anyone from anywhere, were spitting at Travelers in the street, what was happening in the rest of the Domains? Stories of massacres abounded in the old songs, and some not so old. The Generation Laws had been enacted originally to stop large Traveler groups being attacked on the Road—the warlords decided that their various services were too useful to lose. With a touch of panic, Ash wondered about his father and Flax.

He sent a prayer to the local gods, and heard them reply, saying his name over and over, as they had when he lived here. Then, it had filled him with panic and a kind of shame. Now, he welcomed the sensation. He reached out to the River in his mind and found her, very faint, far below the city. *Belonging*, he felt her say, and was comforted.

As they climbed the hill, coming into the richer quarters, lanterns were hung at gates, candles lit inside houses, curtains drawn, and the streets began to empty. By the time they reached the very top and walked past the huge, sprawling mass of Highmark, they were the only ones around.

Then there he was, back at Doronit's house, back to where he'd sweated and yearned and maybe even loved a little. He'd always heard that places seemed smaller when you went back to them, but Doronit's house loomed larger: she'd built another story on, half-timbering, painted sand-color to mimic the sandstone houses further up the hill.

He was glad it looked different.

The office was the same, though, and Doronit herself, when she finally walked in, looked just as she had the day he'd killed the girl in the alley: wide navy trousers tucked into yellow boots, skirt and blouse of a lighter blue, a shawl pinned by a sapphire brooch. And her face, he thought, meeting her eyes at last, looked as smooth, as beautiful, as…cold.

The thought reminded him of what he carried with him, and he reached out gently to the River, sensing Her to the north, and deep below. A phrase from "The Distant Hills" played in his mind; his love was far away.

Ash stared into Doronit's sapphire eyes and wondered how she was going to kill him.

BRAMBLE

HE WAS gone.

She looked around wildly, but there was nothing except the silent pool, and the fire burning low.

Acton was gone, as a ghost fades after quickening and never comes back.

She felt as if she were disintegrating, shredding apart on the wind, her heart flaking away, uncoiling like a ball of thread. She couldn't breathe.

Ash. It was because Ash had left. Ash had sung him up, and without Ash he had faded. He had not gone on to rebirth, as a ghost that fades after quickening. He could not have, because he had promised he would help her, and he never broke his word.

That thought steadied her. He had promised, and what he had promised he would do. That was a certainty, and she clung to it. They could bring him back. She would take his bones to Turvite and find Ash and they would sing him up again. It would be all right.

Bramble deliberately put her feet down in the cold water, trying to shock some sense into herself. She had lived without Acton until now. She would survive without him, as she had survived without the roan, without Maryrose. But as she walked over and picked up the pack full of his bones, part of her didn't believe it. They felt even lighter than before, as though some essence of him had gone, too.

It was a long, lonely night with only the horses for company.

In the very early morning, Bramble saddled the mare and took the other two on a leading rein. They weren't as fast, but at least she could spell the mare. As they cantered along the grass by the side of the road, she found anxiety growing in her chest. Not her anxiety—at Obsidian Lake she had become adept at sorting her own emotions from those of others. This was coming from somewhere else.

Then she saw the black rock altar among the trees and realized that the gods were calling her. Thankfully, she headed the mare towards the clearing and slipped off her back, tethering her to a sapling.

As she placed her hand on the altar, the anxiety rose to an almost panic.

Why are you here, child? they asked. *You should be in Turvite. Now! You should be in Turvite now!*

She cursed Acton. If she hadn't listened to him, they would have gone straight down the river and been in Turvite by now.

I will hurry, she said to them.

Too late, too late, they said with sorrow, and turned away from her towards whatever battle they were fighting.

She backed away and stood by the horses, fighting her own anxiety. She could ride—of course she could ride, but on these horses it would take too long. If only she had the roan.

She remounted and urged the horses to their best pace, but she knew they couldn't keep it up for long. They weren't chasers; they weren't even in top condition.

Rounding a bend screened by willow trees, she saw the barred fences, white-striped, that marked a horse farm. A stud, because in the fields beyond were chasers. Long legged, short backed, beautiful. Valuable.

Horses that could get her to Turvite much faster than the slugs she had.

Horse stealing was a killing offence, but that wasn't what made Bramble hesitate. She didn't want to take a horse who might be loved as she had loved the roan. But she had no choice. She'd bring them back, if she had the chance.

She wondered if any of these horses had come from Gorham's farm. There was an easy way to find out. Perched on the fence, she whistled them up: the come-to-me call all Gorham's horses learnt.

Across the field, three of them threw their heads up, whinnying, and whirled to canter over to her. Her heart lifted as they came—she was sure she remembered at least one of them. By Acton out of Silver Shoes—a great lineage, but the colt had been so wild that the owner had gelded him. He'd be fast. With him were two mares, a bay and a liver chestnut who lagged behind the others.

She took the tack off her other horses and turned them loose with reassuring pats. They were happy to graze and went off to meet the others in the field, who were now crowding towards them with that insatiable equine curiosity.

She saddled the gelding and put the bay on a leading rein, and then left, wondering why no one on the stud had come out when the horses had whinnied. Too afraid they'd meet ghosts?

The gelding's canter was smooth as they rode down the flat even road. Not bad, and the mare could keep pace. But could they jump? If they could ride cross country it would be much, much faster.

There were wooden fences all along this stretch of road—perfect. She set the gelding at one and he sailed over, the mare following willingly on a very long rein.

Chasing had always been her great passion, the one thing that could set her alight: the speed, the freedom, the thundering, shaking ground flicking past like a dream. On the roan, chasing, she had lost any sense of a separate self; they were one being, acting as one, and her exhilaration was his, and his was hers.

It wasn't like that with these horses, but it was still wonderful. In the broad light of morning, over field and stream, over wall and ditch, over hedge and fence, the three of them raced together, and Bramble laughed each time they jumped. They sped like an arrow towards Turvite, her sense of direction taking them in a straight line, no matter what the obstacle. There were no big rivers between here and there, and nothing smaller that they couldn't jump.

They galloped and jumped and trotted and walked, Bramble switching from horse to horse every couple of hours, until the sun set, and they had to rest.

With these horses, she would be in Turvite by the next night.

MARTINE

MARTINE WENT back to the gathering of stonecasters, because there was nothing else to do. She had left Sorn and Safred together eating an evening meal, but she wasn't hungry. Flax and Zel. She'd only known the boy a very short time, but he'd been as sweet as new butter. She wondered, again, where Ash was and why he'd let Flax go anywhere alone.

Zel had a right to her anger, but surely Ash had had good reason. Safred thought he wasn't dead, but she didn't know for sure. The gods were being coy, apparently. Martine felt a quick surge of anger. She should be grateful they were intervening at all, she supposed, but their lack of care for individual humans set her teeth on edge. At least the fire saw *you* —the individual woman, the actual person. He knew each of them by name, by more than name...but He was no help now.

The stonecasters were in the big hall, with Ranny trying to organize them from the mayor's podium. It was like herding snakes, as the saying went. They were talking to each other, sitting on the floor, some of them, casting stones; some argued over the right spell to use. There were only twenty or so, but the noise was immense. When Martine came in, they quietened and turned to face her, their backs to Ranny. Another thing for Ranny to get upset about, she thought. She found their deference surprising. She was a good stonecaster, yes, but she'd never claimed to be better at it than anyone else. Still, she did know most of them...She realized that they'd all come to her for readings at one time or another, which showed they trusted her skill, if nothing else.

"The ghost army is almost certainly on its way here," she said, pitching her voice as loud as she could. "We thought we could try to bespell the city the way we bespell our houses, to keep ghosts out."

"But that only works because they're *our* houses," a portly auburn-haired man objected. She'd forgotten his name, perhaps because she'd never liked him.

"And this is *our* city, isn't it?" Martine asked. "Do you want to find a new home in a countryside ruled by ghosts? I doubt they need castings very often!" She tried for a laugh, and got a few chuckles.

Wila, who cast mostly for the whores down by the harbor, cleared her throat. "My spell is for walls and door," she said. "I don't think it would work for streets. Or squares. Not empty space, see?"

Martine looked over their heads to Ranny. "Can we get barricades built across the outer streets? If we can make a ring of bespelled houses and barricades..."

Ranny nodded, shortly, and jumped down. "I'll get it organized. You assign them districts. Don't forget the harbor."

Fortunately, most stonecasters lived in the poorer parts of town—near the harbor and on the outskirts. The middle of the city, on its hill, was the preserve of the respectable. Martine found a clerk to fetch a map of Turvite and allocated an area for each stonecaster to cover, the area nearest to their own home whenever possible.

One of them was a stranger to her, after all—he had come with Thegan from Sendat, an odd-looking bald man without any eyebrows. Otter, his name was. He studied the map with intensity and spoke of the enchanter with real hatred.

"The others are afraid of the enchanter," Martine said to him. "But you hate him."

Otter's mouth thinned. "I'm from Carlion." He stared unseeing at the map of the city. "For twenty years I've been working towards equality for Travelers. Me and others, some Traveler, some not. We were getting close to having the laws repealed in Carlion. We had the ear of the town clerk, a few other councillors. We were so *close*! Twenty years...and that blood-hungry bastard destroyed it all in a night. We'll never recover from this."

He turned abruptly and walked out with the others, as though he were sorry he had said so much. He was strong, Martine thought, feeling regret for the future he had been working for, and slightly ashamed that it had never occurred to her to do so. She hoped he could cast a good spell—and the others. But she knew it would only buy them time.

Where was Ash? And Bramble, where was she?

Since Martine had no home in Turvite now, she took a part of the city that no stonecaster had a stake in—around the road to Sanctuary. It was the route into the city the ghosts were most likely to take; and she might see Ash. She stood at a barricade made of carts and barrels and boards, stretched across the road.

"Why don't stonecasters do more spells, if you can?" Sorn had asked her, back at the inn.

"There aren't many to cast," she had told her. "Only a handful, and most of those backfire on you—cast a love spell, someone ends up hating you; give the evil eye, your eye sees only ugliness afterwards."

"Balance," Sorn mused.

"Something like that. The spell to keep ghosts away is different, somehow. Maybe because it doesn't try to change anyone, just preserve what is—your privacy."

So here she was, trying to preserve a whole city's privacy.

The stonecasters had agreed that the spell might be stronger if they all cast it at the same time—at sunset. It wasn't a difficult spell, but to do it on this scale required all their strength, and sunset or sunrise were the easiest times to cast a spell. Martine didn't know why, but dusk and dawn seemed to enhance Sight and other gifts.

She waited, conscious of the Turviters who had built the barricade, and others who lived nearby, watching her critically, hopefully, nervously.

It had been three years since she'd cast this spell. It was usually done alone, inside your own home. She had never performed any public enchantments before. She took a deep breath, feeling like the butterflies in her stomach were as big as sparrows. She looked around to embed the area in her mind and saw Arvid, standing beside one of the houses, a few steps away. He smiled at her. She was flooded with warmth; she hadn't expected him to be there. The nerves retreated as though they had never existed, and she spread out her hands on top of the barricade, feeling the timber warm from the afternoon sun, slightly rough under her fingertips.

She had loved living in Turvite. This *was* her city; these were her people. She knew them inside and out—their fears, their hopes, their loves and hates, their greed and generosity. They had brought all of themselves to her and she had cast the future for them, for good or ill.

Take that feeling, she thought, and weave it into the spell.

"I am Martine, of Turvite," she said aloud, "and this is my home. Spirit without living body, come not within my home; spirit without living body, be barred from my home; spirit without living body, enter not my door."

The usual spell—"Spirit without body, enter not my door unless I set it ajar for you"—left two big holes for the ghost army. They would have needed only one sympathizer within the city to undo the protection; and who knew if the ghosts had an actual body rather than merely having bodily strength?

The rest of the spell wasn't in words, but in feeling—the desire to protect, the desire to make whole, the desire to be safe. Martine's Sight could sense the other spells reverberating on either side of her.

She could feel her energy flowing out with the spell, and she gave all she had; the others were doing the same. She had to push the spell from the barricades to the walls of the houses on either side, and then further. She thanked the gods that Turviters didn't like trees or shady yards; their houses abutted each other. But each house needed a spell in itself, and pushing the protection from one house to the next took more energy than she had expected. She pushed sideways and out to the limit of the barricades and houses, to the space that was neither city nor countryside. The edge of Turvite.

Her head was light and empty now, her legs shaking; but they weren't finished yet, they hadn't joined. She wished Ash were here, to give her strength in the way he had given it to Safred once, but she was alone. She swayed, fighting dizziness, and felt Arvid's hands come under her elbows, to support her. He wasn't Ash; he didn't have the ability to channel strength to her. But his presence, his warm body behind her, his concern, steadied her.

She reached out as best she could, ensuring that her protection reached the casters' on either side, closing the gaps. Her Sight took her around the spell, which now stretched all the way around the city. It was like a protective girdle shaped like a crescent, because it took a curve in at the harbor. But there, at the point where the crescent curved inwards, there was a weak spot. A lack of feeling, a lack of desire. She knew who it was. Otter, from Carlion. He didn't feel strongly enough about the city to protect it properly.

She sent her own love, her own strength, to that part of the spell, and felt it firm up, like a rope pulled taut. It was a maternal kind of love, she realized, as though the city and its people were her child. She could sense other weak spots being shored up by the stronger stonecasters.

The words of spells were taught when a stonecaster took an apprentice. But only the words—you couldn't teach the feeling. How could you teach the searching out, the recognizing, that Sight allowed?

The protection grew, and grew, and then stopped. The rope was taut, all around the city. It *felt* all right. But whether it would keep out solid ghosts, she had no idea.

She had just enough strength left to end the spell, tying it off as one tied embroidery thread when a design was done, and as it ended her legs gave way and she fell.

Arvid caught her.

"I'm all right," she whispered. She was not all right. She could barely feel her legs and hands. Every bone in her spine hurt. But she was breathing, and the spell was tight and full.

LEOF

IN EVERY town he passed through, Leof told of the success of the Wooding Travelers. To the Travelers left alive, to the village voices, to any warlord's man he found. Most Travelers were too scared, or too angry, to do anything; but a few began to band together to protect those of Acton's people who had been good to them.

There were at least some of these: people who had given Travelers shelter when scared mobs came for them, or those who had hidden Travelers in barns or haylofts or in their own bedchambers, and denied all knowledge of them. Sometimes there were family bonds to explain their actions—but sometimes, as far as Leof could tell, they had acted out of sympathy, and abhorrence of murder.

But there were fewer of those stories than of Travelers massacred, or imprisoned, or sent to the warlord.

When he told one voice about the Wooding group, the woman said, "Why would they protect us?" Leof couldn't fault her logic: why, indeed?

As he neared the outskirts of Turvite, his two horses tired but still sound, Leof remembered his last visit to the city, two years ago, to ride in a Spring Chase. It had been after he had met Bramble, but before he had recognized his love for Sorn. Before Thegan had actively planned war. Before the enchanter, before the Lake, before he had been anything but an enthusiastic officer who liked chasing and idolized his warlord.

He had been a child.

Coming up the hill to Turvite he saw the entrances to the city were barricaded. Flimsy constructions of boards and carts that wouldn't keep an army of children out, let alone the ghosts. Surely the Turviters weren't relying on these inadequate defenses?

When he reached the barricade he found some of the Moot staff, with what looked like hastily recruited deputies, allowing people in and out of a small gate.

One of the staff, an older man, was instructing a young deputy. "You *must* close the gate after each person," he said. "The stonecasters say the spell will only work if we keep a wall around the whole city, like the walls of a house, see? So people can go in and out of a house, but to keep the house safe you have to close the door."

The younger man, a tanner by the smell of his clothes, nodded earnestly. "Aye," he said. He looked up at Leof, clearly preparing to put his training into practice. "Are you blooded?" he demanded.

"What?"

"Show us your blood," the older man said.

Leof frowned. "How?"

"You may," said the young man, parroting, "pull down your eyelid and let us see the red; cut your hand and bleed; or punch yourself on the arm and show us the reddening."

"Isn't it obvious that I'm alive?" Leof demanded, both amused and affronted.

"It will be when you show us," the older man said stolidly.

Chuckling, Leof dismounted and pulled down an eyelid. The young man inspected him solemnly and then opened the gate, closing it again carefully once Leof had led the horses through.

"The stonecasters?" Leof queried.

"They're casting a spell to keep these ghosts out," the older man said happily. "We'll be safe in Turvite!"

"There are a lot of people hoping you're right, and they're all on the way here," Leof warned him.

He rode to the Moot Hall first. He had considered his options all the way to the city, and had decided that Turvite's council needed warning of the countryfolk fleeing to their city, and to learn of the success at Wooding, although he doubted *any* argument would convince the enchanter to turn away from Turvite. He would have to risk meeting Thegan.

At the door of the Moot Hall he was inspected again for blood, and then passed from clerk to clerk until he was in a small room with a thin, blonde woman.

He hesitated on the threshold, but she waved him to a seat. "I'm Ranny of Highmark," she said.

He'd heard of the Highmark family. They had a breeding farm which produced wonderful piebald chasers. "Leof, originally of Cliff Domain," he said. He'd thought quite a bit about how to present himself. "Former officer to Lord Thegan."

She raised an eyebrow at that, but let it go. "You have news?"

"Thegan is in the city?" he countered.

She paused, weighing whether it was valuable information, but he could have found out from anyone at the hall. "Aye," she said. "He came straight here."

"So he would not know, I suspect, that the whole countryside is following his example. Half of Central Domain is on its way here, hoping for shelter."

"We can't take them all in," she snapped.

"Best be prepared, then, to send them elsewhere. There may be alternatives." He explained the situation in Wooding, where the Travelers had protected their village. "I've been encouraging other towns to do the same," he said. "I'm hopeful at least some areas will remain untouched."

"Interesting," she mused. "We have quite a few Travelers here. Settled for generations, some of them. We might call a muster..." She stood up and bowed. "Thank you for your assistance, Lord Leof. Perhaps, since you are no longer on Thegan's staff, we can call on you for advice about our defenses?"

"I'll give you some advice right now—the enchanter has acquired human allies. Travelers who were attacked by our people and who see him as their saviour. Your barricades may stand against the ghosts, but the humans will demolish them in a single charge."

"What do you suggest?"

"Archers at high points and behind the barricades, pikemen in front, and a good solid group of soldiers set in ambush behind them. The humans will be at the back, I think, when they attack, and if you surprise them you could cut them down easily enough with a trained force, particularly if you have enough archers. They are not trained fighters, you understand."

Part of him sorrowed as he said it—there were women in that group, and children, too. Perhaps they would not fight, and might be saved.

"We would prefer not to call in assistance from warlords."

"Set the ambush on Merroc's soil—then you won't need to let his men into the city." Merroc was the warlord of Far South Domain, which surrounded Turvite.

Ranny nodded. "Will you command the city forces?"

"Not if you want to keep Thegan as a friend," he said. "In fact, I would count it as a favor if you did not mention me to him."

Ranny assessed that information. She nodded. "Agreed, for now, if you keep me informed of your whereabouts."

"As to that, can you recommend an inn? Something modest, I'm afraid." He smiled at her, the smile that so often helped him make a friend.

It worked on her, too. Her lips twitched, even if she didn't smile back. "The Red Dawn is not a bad place," she said. "And I think Lord Thegan is unlikely to go there."

The Red Dawn was stripped of staff. The innkeeper had to come out and take the horses himself, apologizing and promising that he'd be with his lord as soon as he'd put them in the stables and found the stable boy to groom them. He suggested that Leof wait in the inn chamber, he was sorry, but there would be no one there to serve his lord. Everyone was out working on the city defenses; he hoped his lord understood. Of course he understood.

The first person he saw when he walked into the inn chamber was Sorn.

She was sitting alone in a window seat, gazing up at the sky. He had never seen her in repose before, and for a moment he simply didn't believe it *was* her. Why would she be here, instead of at the Moot Hall, or a more expensive inn? Then he saw the curve of her cheek, the light coming through the window onto the warm glow of her hair, the long hands clasped around her knees, and knew without doubt that it was her. It was as though someone had punched the breath out of him; the moment of shock was followed by a surge of feeling so great he couldn't identify it. It brought tears to his eyes, set his hands shaking.

She was alive. She was here. He didn't care whether Thegan punished him—he had to speak to her.

She hadn't noticed him. He set his bags on the floor and walked slowly between the inn tables towards her.

He stumbled a little, pushing a chair across the floor with a sharp noise, and she looked over at him. He stood still, thinking of nothing. Just looking at her.

Sorn looked back for a moment, eyes wide, and he had just enough time to wonder what to say before she sprang from the seat and flung herself across the room to him. "You're alive, you're safe! You're alive!" she babbled—quiet, controlled Sorn! He caught her, held her close. Her hands were at his face then, cradling it, then at his chest, grasping his tunic, shaking him a little. "You're *here*!" she said breathlessly.

He was already a traitor. What did one more betrayal matter? But he couldn't do it—couldn't hold her and kiss her the way he ached to. It was the only shard of honor he had left.

She saw it in his face. "I've renounced him," she said, and pulled Leof down so she could kiss him. "I'm free."

He didn't understand how she could do that, but he had no resistance left. They kissed as though parched for each other, kissed and held—the urge to pull her tight to him, to make sure she was really there, was as strong as the urge to make love to her. He twined his hands in her long hair and held her head firmly as he kissed her. Desire overwhelmed his relief at seeing her alive, and she felt it.

"Come," she said, pulling him by the hand upstairs.

They didn't make it to the bed, falling to the floor instead. He had never felt this need before, not even with Bramble. It wasn't a need for pleasure, or release, but to be with, to be *one*. Joined together, joined forever... He fought against climax because it would be the beginning of separation; he slowed but she wouldn't let him, moaning his name. Her voice, his name; it started an avalanche in him, of pleasure and tears and joy and sharp, sharp pain at the center. He clutched at her and said her name in return, and felt her tears start, her body clutch his.

They lay in a welter of clothes, still half-dressed, feeling cold air and warm skin and sweat cooling. Shaking, both of them, still, and not from pleasure.

He'd always thought that shagging was shagging, no matter who the partner: always good, always fine. He tightened his arms around Sorn and she made a curious little snort of satisfaction, and he laughed.

She looked up at him, laughing too, and then fell silent. "Too much need for too long," she said.

He stroked hair back from her eyes. "I love you," he said.

She closed her eyes as if in pain, and he winced, wondering if he'd completely misunderstood. Then she turned her brow into the curve of his shoulder, and he realized she was weeping. He wiped the tears away for some time before she raised her head.

"No one, in all my life, has ever said those words to me," she said.

"Your parents, surely!"

"My mother died in childbirth. My father…was not a loving man."

"Your wetnurse?" he ventured. "Your maid?"

"They changed, depending on who owed tax bondage."

He was appalled at the vision of the lonely little girl, growing up without comfort or affection in all the isolation of the fort.

"Then how did you become so wonderful?" he exclaimed.

She laughed with more freedom than he had ever seen in her. Then she sobered. "Thank the gods," she said. "They were my refuge."

The words brought them back to the present, and to the dangers of the present.

"There's a good deal you don't know," she said.

As they dressed she shared all the information she had, including the plan to raise Acton's ghost.

"The Well of Secrets says that Bramble has gone after his bones." Sorn was pretending to fold a scarf, but looking sideways at him.

He caught her at it. "Wondering about her and me?" he asked. "One night, a long time ago, and never again."

She relaxed and continued her story, finishing with Thegan's intention to have Gabra sire a child on her. He stood rigid at that point, every instinct telling him to find Thegan and kill him.

She came and clasped her hands over his. "I have renounced him," she said. "Before witnesses, including the Well of Secrets. After—after this is over—I will choose me a new husband." She smiled coquettishly at him, a look he had never seen from her before. "I wonder who I might choose?"

He laughed, but sobered quickly. "We must not be seen together, or Thegan will claim you are only renouncing him to have me, and I am a traitor, condemned to death. I'll find another inn."

"No," she said, blinking slowly. "You will take a separate room, but you will stay here."

It was the warlord's daughter speaking, and his impulse was to obey, but he had to make her see that it was dangerous for her. "Sorn —"

"I am willing to take your oath of allegiance, Lord Leof."

Even with her hair tumbled around her shoulders and her lips red from his mouth, she looked older suddenly, and far stronger.

"You need to put your case to the other warlords before Thegan gets to them," he warned, then he picked up his sword from where his belt had fallen, and drew it, presenting it hilt first to her in the ancient ceremony, but she shook her head.

"I am not a commander," she said. "I value the oath more than the sword."

"Thou art my lady," he said, "and I shall be loyal unto thee until death." They were not the same words he had used to Thegan. To Thegan he had pledged his sword and his honor. Thegan had used his sword and trampled on his honor. So for Sorn, whose honor was brighter by far than his own, he could offer only loyalty. But it seemed to be what she wanted.

Formally, she placed her hands over his. "I am thy lady," she said. "In return for thy loyalty, I shall care for thee until death."

It was the promise warlords made to officers who did not serve directly in their command—the officers who husbanded their lands and paid tribute. They were both aware of the double meaning of the words; it sounded like a wedding pledge. He smiled at her and she turned her head away slightly, trying not to smile back, then punched him lightly in the arm as if to rebuke him for levity.

She plaited her hair swiftly and pinned it up until she was once again the poised warlord's daughter.

"So, now you're mine and I can do what I like with you," she teased him as they walked out of the room.

His breath caught in his throat at that thought, but he brought his attention back to the needs of the moment. "We need to find Bramble. Where's the stonecaster?"

The sun had lowered while they had been in the chamber, and the innkeeper had lit the lanterns below.

"I have reported to my lady," Leof said. "What room have you put me in?"

The innkeeper looked slyly at him. "I wasn't sure you'd be needing a separate room."

Leof crossed the room in two paces and pushed the man back against the counter. "You cannot possibly have meant to insult my lady."

The innkeeper didn't cower, but he lost the knowing expression. "Nay," he said. "No insult. I'll put you in the room at the end of the corridor."

Leof nodded and let him go. Another woman was coming down the stairs: stocky, sandy-haired, around forty.

"Safred!" Sorn said thankfully, going to meet her. "Leof, this is the Well of Secrets."

It was strange to meet a legend in the flesh. Leof bowed very low and straightened feeling curiously exposed. It was said that the Well of Secrets knew the past and the future and everything in between. The way she flicked a glance between him and Sorn, and then lifted her eyebrows just a fraction made him believe it.

She walked over to him, closer than was polite. He didn't know whether to move back. Then she put out her hand and touched the circle of woven reeds that hung around his neck. "Are you a man of power, Lord Leof?" she asked.

He shook his head. "It was given to me. As a great boon. It saved my life."

"You are blessed," Safred said. "Keep it close. If we survive this, you will have a son. Give it to him, when he is born."

A shiver went through him. Prophecy. True prophecy. It felt different from stonecasting, where the stones somehow seemed to have the power. The Well of Secrets was linked tight to the gods... A son. *If we survive this*, she had said.

"Will we win against this enchanter?" he asked.

She sighed. "You want a prophecy? Fine, here it is." Her eyes looked into space, and she spoke as if from a long way away. "The dead will be reborn, the quick and the quickened will both taste blood, the killers will be brought together to confront the killed. The voices of the dead will echo through the world, and the evil dead shall triumph over the evil living. If we're lucky."

Her gaze sharpened on him again and he was sure she could see the trembling in his body.

"Happy?" she asked.

"Don't take it out on him, Safred," Sorn said sharply.

Safred turned to look at her closely. "So, you've found your strength, have you? Don't let Thegan intimidate you again."

"I won't."

The three of them stood there as if waiting for something. Outside, the sun set.

A shiver went through Safred and she clutched at a chair back to steady herself. "They have set the spell," she said. "The city is protected from ghosts."

"As long as the barricades are intact," Leof said. "It will be a fight to remember, keeping them so."

ASH

"TELL ME everything you know," Doronit said. It was the part of her that he'd never fully understood, the merchant in information. But more than that, there was a need to know what was happening, as though knowing could protect her. He thought for a moment of Safred, to whom secrets were meat and drink, but this was different: more rational, more ruthless.

"And then you kill me?" he asked.

"That depends on what you tell me," she said, sitting down behind her desk. She didn't offer one of the chairs she kept for clients, but he took one anyway, staring at her, not sure how he felt.

Thanks to the River, his desire for Doronit had been washed clean away. But the other emotions—especially gratitude for her taking him in when no one else wanted him, not even his parents—stayed with him and made his mind whirl. He knew she'd had her own reasons for taking him, but she'd given him the first home he'd ever known and she had truly valued him, the first person to ever do so. The skills she had taught him had saved his life, and Bramble's.

So he told her the truth. Exactly, leaving nothing out but the River.

At the end, she looked at him closely. "What are you not telling?"

He brushed the question away. "Nothing important to you."

She assessed that, a look on her face he could not read, and for the first time he could take breath and simply look at her. Just a Traveler woman. Richer, cleverer, but important only because of the secrets she held. He would never share her desire for power, but having walked through the streets of this city and seen the contempt and hatred for Travelers that lay just under the surface, he understood what had driven her to compel the ghosts of Turvite to give up their secrets. Compassion for her twisted in his gut.

"This enchanter wants to take back the Domains for our people?" she asked, looking away at last, twisting the fringe of her shawl between her fingers, something he'd never seen her do before.

"Yes. By killing everyone."

She nodded slowly and raised her head to gaze at him. Her eyes were alight. "That would work," she said.

He pushed out of the chair, sending it spinning to the floor behind him. "Thousands of people!"

"*Their* people," she breathed.

He should have seen this coming—he'd known how much she hated Acton's people. He had to appeal to the merchant in her. "There'd be no trade," he said. "Life would just collapse! No customers, no merchants, no *farmers*. You'd starve in a month."

"You think our people couldn't learn to be farmers, if they had the best land available to them, tools, animals, barns and all just handed to them? Some of them already know how! I grew up on a farm, Ash. I could run one. With a little help."

He was as startled by the idea of Doronit on a farm as by the plea in her voice. "You would let thousands of people—children—be slaughtered, just for revenge?"

She smiled, hard as the sapphires in her brooch. "Not for revenge. For justice! This is *our* land, and always has been. Do the old powers come for the blondies? No! Does the River acknowledge them? You know she doesn't."

Shock hit him, a moment ahead of understanding. She had all the secrets that the ghosts could tell. Of course some Traveler man had told her about the River. She didn't know, couldn't know, about him and Her.

Outside, the sun set. A shiver went through both of them at the same moment, and Ash's head reeled. Something was happening, outside, at the edge of the city—at all the edges of the city. A spell... One that felt familiar.

Doronit was quicker than he was, as always. "The spell to keep out ghosts! They've set it all around the city."

They stood for a moment silently. Doronit smiled.

"They'll be resting secure now, in their feather beds. Thinking they're safe. But all we have to do is break the barricade, and they're all dead."

She saw the revulsion on his face and came closer.

"We could help him, Ash, you and I. There's no sign that he can make them talk. Think how much more effective he'd be if he could talk to them, discuss plans of attack, strategy. We would be his most valuable officers."

He knew that voice. It was the voice she'd used to try to convince him to kill Martine. Then he had been torn, but not this time. He moved closer to her, as though drawn despite himself. For a moment, he'd lost his compassion for her, but now it came back. She was like a child, not caring how she got what she wanted, just wanting it now. In that thought, at last, he found affection for her as well as compassion and gratitude; she could have been so much more. In another world, a different time, before the landtaken, she could have been anything she chose.

Her eyes warmed as she came closer, seeing the warmth in his. "We could tip the balance," she said softly. "You and I together. The way it was meant to be."

"Yes," he said. "We could tip the balance. *You* could tip the balance."

He could see it, too clearly. Turvite overrun. She would simply send out her people and tell them to break the barricades where it wouldn't be detected. The ghosts would storm through into an unprepared city. The enchanter, so far, had shown no great sense of strategy or cunning. His strikes had been clean, simple, brutal. With Doronit to advise him, with her capacity to communicate freely with the ghosts, with her huge network of spies and safeguarders—and worse, with her viciousness—Acton and Bramble had no chance of even reaching the ghost army. Doronit's agents would find and stop them before they came anywhere near. She would destroy any hope they had, and condemn thousands to death, right across the Domains. And one of those thousands would be young Ash, probably, and Mabry his father, certainly. Their precious home in Hidden Valley would be smashed apart with swords and screams and death, and the child he had sworn to protect would be the most vulnerable thing there.

He didn't reach to the River for guidance. She had no say in this. Just this once, he was not following. This time, he had to decide for himself.

Ash reached up, gently, delicately, and took Doronit's face between his hands. He felt very calm, as though time had slowed. She smiled, triumphant, blue eyes finally alight for him.

He broke her neck.

MARTINE

SORN WANTED to go back to the Moot Hall immediately. If she were to claim Central Domain, she needed to be part of any discussion, to set herself in the council as if it were natural. Turvite was the perfect opportunity—she had as much right to be there as the warlords did.

Martine would have preferred to rest, but she followed Sorn. Curiosity drove her as much as duty, she acknowledged to herself. And the desire to see Arvid.

When they walked into the hall, Ranny and Garham were poring over a map of Turvite spread out on a huge table. They were allocating areas. Each warlord was to defend a section of the city, using his own men to direct and train Turviters.

Martine kept back, but Sorn joined the group around the table, ignoring Thegan's glare and the questioning stares of the others. Ranny glanced at her and nodded; Garham scarcely seemed to notice her. Arvid looked up and saw Martine at the back of the hall and smiled involuntarily, as though his whole spirit had lightened because she was there. Her thoughts wandered: to his arm, supporting her during the spell; his gentleness as he had returned her to the Red Dawn, the way he had stroked her hair back and handed her over to Sorn and Safred reluctantly. She forced her attention back to the present, to the discussion around the table.

Ranny had given the harbor to Coeuf, Martine suspected on the grounds that his senility would be least dangerous there, and put Eolbert, his son, in actual control. Thegan was given the southern sector.

"I should take the north-west," he demanded. "I'm the only one who has experience against them!"

"Much good it did you," Sorn said mildly.

Each warlord snapped his head around to stare at her. Thegan couldn't hide his astonishment, which gave Martine some satisfaction. He'd never so much as spoken a word to her directly, but her dislike was already deep and burning.

Merroc smiled at Sorn in appreciation. "I will take the north-west," he said. "It leads to my domain."

Thegan stared at Merroc; then, with a slight nod, accepted this as reasonable. Or appeared to.

The others took their assignments more graciously, and were introduced to the Turvite Moot staff who would be their offsiders.

Before Merroc left, he bowed to the council and said, "Far South Domain is at the service of Turvite!" It was a display for the benefit of the assembled officers and councillors.

"South Domain is at the service of Turvite," Eolbert followed quickly, simultaneously, with Arvid: "The Last Domain is at the service of Turvite." The two men smiled at each other, a little embarrassed. The other warlords waited for each other to speak.

Sorn noticed Thegan open his mouth. "Central Domain is at the service of Turvite," she said.

There was a pause, as people registered who had spoken. The women councillors smiled slightly.

"Cliff Domain is at the service of Turvite," Thegan said smoothly, smiling at Sorn as though at an errant child. "And the men of Central and Cliff Domains will fight together, as always."

It was a good recovery, Martine thought. But Sorn had sown a seed, at least, in people's minds. Eolbert's, for example. He was her age, after all, and not married, although rumor said he had a mistress who lived at the fort and had borne him several children. That was no barrier to a formal alliance between warlord families. Sorn would have to encourage Eolbert to hope that, if she renounced Thegan, he would be in the running to marry her.

She clearly knew that, because she smiled at him gently, and walked out the door with him, and let Thegan hear her say, "You have several children, do you not, my lord, at Wooding?" It was a dangerous game, and Sorn was braver than Martine had thought to play it, but Thegan was too fully occupied with the enchanter to focus on her just yet. It would come. An attempt to kill her, probably, before she could announce her intention, so he could inherit from her. And then he could forget about siring a son on her.

"I would so love to have children myself," Sorn said.

Eolbert's eyes widened and the dissipated folds around his mouth deepened. So, he had understood, and was rapidly calculating her intentions. "A big family is every warlord's dream," he said. "One I certainly share." He glanced at Thegan. "But not in this current situation. We must deal with this enchanter before any of us can think of the future."

Say something, Martine urged Sorn silently. Reassure Thegan of your promise, or he will draw sword and slice you down right here.

As though she had caught the thought, Sorn nodded. "Indeed, my lord," she said gravely. "Nothing can be thought of until after this crisis."

Arvid came up behind Martine and, careless of who was watching, put his hands on her waist and drew her back to rest against him. She allowed herself to relax. Sorn was safe for now.

It made sense for the council to use the most experienced commanders, but the people of Turvite didn't like it, and showed they didn't like it by obeying orders slowly or sloppily or by simply ignoring them. Martine and Sorn and Safred watched as Merroc tried to organize the defense of the western road. He had made an inn his headquarters, despatching orders from there, but it wasn't going well.

Martine almost laughed. It was one of the things she'd always liked about Turviters, their independence. But it might get them killed. She yawned behind her hand. Every bone still ached slightly, as though the spell had hollowed them out. But how could she rest? She'd never sleep, not tonight.

"I can't be everywhere at once, man!" Merroc snapped when an aide asked him to talk to the tanners who were forming the guard at the gate.

"Perhaps an extra officer would be useful, my lord Merroc?" Sorn queried.

He frowned. "An *experienced* officer would be invaluable, my lady, but —"

"I have one in my train," she said smoothly. "He has . . . parted ways with my lord Thegan, but he is an excellent officer."

"Who is it?"

"Lord Leof."

"The chaser? Gods, yes, get him here as soon as you can."

"Thegan won't like it," Safred warned.

Merroc smiled. "Let me worry about Thegan. Time he learnt he's not the warlord of the whole eleven!"

They sent a messenger to fetch Leof from the Red Dawn. When he walked in, Sorn bit back a smile, and he flicked a quick, searching glance at her before bowing formally. Ah, Martine thought. Sits the wind in that quarter? That explained a great deal. He was certainly good looking enough to make a young woman's heart beat faster. Sorn was playing a much more dangerous game than she had realized. Thinking of Arvid, Martine was sympathetic. You couldn't choose who you loved, could you? Especially a warlord's daughter, married off when she was still half a child to a ruthless man twice her age. Poor Sorn, she thought. Yet when she looked at Sorn, who was following Merroc's plans intently, a small frown on her face, her body upright in her chair, *poor Sorn* seemed inappropriate. Sorn was no longer a child—and she had a strength that men might not easily see, hidden inside the calm poise of the warlord's wife.

Leof had no time to even speak to them. Merroc sent him out immediately to place the archers in the houses nearest the road.

More people were going to die, Martine thought. More and more.

ASH

HE WALKED out into the training yard, putting every ounce of energy he had into seeming confident.

Aylmer was waiting, sitting on a bench honing a knife in the light from a lantern. Hildie was lying full length on another bench. They both tensed as he walked out the door, and Hildie swung her legs to the ground, eyes on his.

"She's letting you live?" Aylmer asked, voice neutral.

"Better than that," Ash forced himself to grin. "I'm the heir again!"

Hildie swore, but Aylmer raised both brows and half-grinned back, caught between admiration and disbelief. He stood up and made for Doronit's office.

"Wouldn't go *just* yet if I was you," Ash said slowly, before Aylmer had reached the door. "She might need a few minutes to, er..."

Aylmer's grin was genuine this time. "Shagged your way back in, did you, lad?"

Hildie laughed and lay back down on the bench. "Old fool," she said, and it wasn't clear if she were talking about Doronit or Aylmer.

Neither thought for a moment that he might have been a threat to Doronit. A year ago they would have been right.

His hands felt heavy with the memory of her weight sagging down on them as he'd lowered her to the floor.

"I need a drink!" he said with feeling, and raised a hand casually to them as he simply walked out of the yard, and kept walking slowly until he reached the inn on the corner. Hildie watched him go. He didn't turn to confirm it, but he knew she would be watching. She was less trusting than Aylmer, and immune to men's charms.

So he walked into the inn and past the outside benches into the quiet of the parlor, ordered a mead and, after he'd had a few sips of its dizzying sweetness, headed out to the privy in the back lane.

He couldn't see anyone watching the lane, so again he kept walking. He had to find Baluch. Meet Bramble. Be ready for the enchanter's next strike.

But he didn't make it to the end of the laneway before the Dung Brothers caught up with him.

They stripped him of weapons, purse and pouch and hauled him in front of the council, where Doronit's limp body lay on a sheet on the floor as evidence. She looked like a stranger, some brown-haired woman he'd never met. Small, much smaller than she'd seemed to him alive. Ash drew a deep breath and looked away from her.

Turvite's Town Council was five members, including Ranny. They stared at him with identically suspicious blue eyes, and he had never been so aware of his black hair.

The Council were furious, especially Garham, who shouted and banged the table in front of him.

When he drew breath, Ash said, "Clear the room."

"What?" Garham yelled. "Don't you give me orders, you black-haired bastard!"

Ash looked at Ranny, who had sat composed through Garham's tirade. The last time he had seen her had been in her own office at Highmark, with Martine. He could tell she remembered him. He spoke directly to her. "Clear the room."

The other councillors began to object, but Ranny cut through them. "Why?"

"Because you don't want anyone else to hear why I killed her."

That silenced all of them.

"Clear the room," Ranny said.

Reluctantly, Hildie, Aylmer, the Dung Brothers, Boc and the other Moot staff trailed out and shut the double doors behind them.

"Well?" Garham demanded.

He told them almost everything. Acton's brooch, the gods in Hidden Valley sending him and Martine to the Well of Secrets, meeting Bramble, meeting Safred and Cael, the tasks the gods had given them. They listened impassively, although their eyes widened when he described raising Acton's ghost.

"You left him behind?" Garham said. "With some chit of a girl?"

"The gods sent me ahead—perhaps to get you ready for when he arrives, so we can meet this enchanter next time he comes, to lay the ghosts to rest and bring peace."

"His story matches that of the Well of Secrets," Garham said reluctantly, at the end.

"She's here?" Ash asked eagerly. "Let me see her."

"Later," Ranny said. "Perhaps."

"You say someone has to give Acton his voice, let him acknowledge his wrongdoing, like at a quickening." That was the thin one, a spice merchant Ash had once worked for, guarding a saffron shipment.

Ash nodded.

"What if he won't acknowledge it?"

"Why should he?" a thickset, red-faced man broke in. Wine merchant, that was it. Garham, his name was and he was as influential as the Highmarks, Doronit had told him. "He didn't do anything wrong! He's a hero!"

The others were silent.

"No matter what we think of him in the present day," Ash said carefully, "to the ghosts he is the man who invaded their homeland and organized their deaths. And he has promised that he will go through the ceremony."

"Why not just kill the enchanter?" Garham said, looking crafty.

"Someone else will raise the ghosts. And the ghosts will come, and it will all start over again. It is the ghosts who must be—dealt with."

"What do you want us to do about it, eh?" Garham asked.

"Let me go. The Well of Secrets and I will go to bring Acton here."

They stared at him.

"You need me to finish the task the gods have given me."

"Wait. There is still the matter of Doronit's death," Ranny said.

"Doronit was going to support the enchanter," Ash replied. "To break the barricade and, once the city was overrun, hand over her entire organization to support him. You know how much information she had..." They looked, shiftily, at each other, as though assessing how much each knew. "...but you don't know how she got it."

"How?" Ranny demanded.

"She was like me. She could make ghosts speak. She made the ghosts of Turvite tell their secrets. And she was going to join the enchanter, so he could talk to his army whenever he liked, discuss strategy, plan attacks . . . ”

They shivered in unison.

“So I killed her.” Ash kept his voice flat. “It was the only chance we had.”

“Why would Doronit . . . ?” the thin spice merchant asked.

“Because she wanted to be sitting where you are sitting, and she knew she never would.”

“She was ambitious, yes, but surely she never imagined that a *Traveler . . .* ” Garham spluttered.

“No,” Ash said. “She knew better than that.”

That was all he trusted himself to say. He ached all over. Head and legs and back and stomach, where the Dung Brothers had kicked him and Hildie had punched him. He'd fought, but to stop them he'd have had to kill them, and he'd had enough of killing.

Ash waited all night in a small room off the hall. They didn't bother to bring him a candle. He sat away from the window, staring at the green wall with its frieze of little ships, to represent the mercantile wealth of Turvite. The longer he stared, the more they seemed to dip and lift with the stylized waves they rode upon.

Safred had called him a killer, in her kitchen back in Oakmere. He'd known it was true, even then, but he'd hoped that he could leave that behind him. Become someone else. When the River had chosen him he had felt washed-clean, new, ready for a different life. To be a different person.

But here he was with blood on his hands, again. Doronit. He sat with his hands hanging between his knees, remembering her. He hoped, with all his heart, that he had killed her for the reason he had told the council. To save them all. Not because he had hated her. Not because he had loved her. Not because she was beautiful and untrustworthy and unrepentant.

He didn't think he had killed her for those reasons. Before the River, maybe he would have. Since She had accepted him, he had felt no desire for anyone else. So, surely, he had closed his hands around Doronit's neck for good reason. Surely.

Killer.

He did not reach for the River, and She did not try to contact him. He refused to wonder if she would ever touch his mind again. If not, he deserved it.

He didn't know what would happen, but he clung to two things: Acton walked; and Safred was here, nearby, and would no doubt find him eventually. But he might still hang for Doronit's murder, if the ghosts were defeated.

BRAMBLE

SHE RODE for a day and a night, stopping only for water and privy breaks. When the horses tired, she stole new ones from abandoned farms. By the end, she was lightheaded from lack of food and sleep, in a high exalted mood.

The Turvite headland hadn't changed much in a thousand years. She had seen it then through Piper's eyes, coming up from the harbor. Now she stood on its northern edge, where it started to rise from the surrounding fields, and saw that it formed a quarter circle, bounded by the cliffs on the sea and harbor sides, and by the stream to the north. It rose and became a plateau at its height, dotted by boulders and rocks, turfed by hardy grass and small shrubs in the lee of the boulders. There was a clear path up from the town which, protected a little from the rising wind, seemed as good a place as any to wait.

She drank from the stream and then leapt over it, her body feeling heavy after the fast ride. She had no food, but that didn't seem to matter. Perhaps she should sleep, though, before she went looking for Ash. It was very early, the sky only just beginning to lighten. A couple of hours, and then she would go searching. She trudged up the hill towards the ring of high rocks. As she approached, she realized that someone, a man, was waiting for her.

Baluch. Without Ash.

"Where is he?" Bramble called, unable to disguise her urgency.

"If Ash can get away, he will come here," Baluch said. "The River will tell him where I am. He is imprisoned in Turvite, but not harmed."

"We need to get him out," Bramble said. "We need him to sing Acton back."

"He is not with you?" Baluch said tentatively, then realized what must have happened. "Could you not sing him yourself?"

She shook her head. "Ash has the brooch. I don't think...I don't think I could do it alone." She didn't know why she was so sure, but she was. The thought of trying to sing Acton back by herself was nauseating. "Can you do it?"

"I can try," Baluch said, but he was troubled by the thought, too, she could tell.

They spread the scarf out and laid Acton's bones on it. "Best to wait for sunrise," Baluch said, and she nodded understanding—sunrise or sunset were the best times.

So they waited, and they talked over other things—memories in common, Ragni and Sebbi, Harald and Swef... Friede.

"I loved her," he said. "I've never said that to anyone else, because no one else knew her."

"So you wrote songs for her."

He dropped his head for a moment, then brought it up again. "Yes... a poor monument."

" 'The Distant Hills' will keep her alive forever," Bramble said, but he shook his head.

"I should have put her name into it. *Then* she would have lived forever." He paused. "Strange. I put all those memories aside, but talking with you has brought back all the pain."

"It's the same pain the ghosts are feeling. Just as fresh." He looked at her with surprise, but she was angry again, at the way people talked themselves out of guilt. "You're a good man, Baluch, but you killed a lot of people in your day. Acton has taken responsibility for that. Time you did, too."

She pushed herself to her feet and walked out of the circle of boulders, feeling the salt spray on her face and hands. The wind was building again, clouds scudding across the sky, waves smashing into the cliff. She walked to the edge and peered down. The rollers were crashing against the sheer rock, sending spray shooting up and over the cliff face. Bramble grinned, tilting her head back to the sky and letting the spray coat her face and neck, letting the wind whip her hair out of its tie. Her spirits rose. Too much talk. She wished she were back in the forest again with her hunter, but this rampant display would do. Wind, water, stone. The things that lasted. The same as they were a thousand years ago.

She took comfort from that; the land, at least, would remain no matter what the enchanter did.

After a while she turned and went back to Baluch, whom she found watching her, standing, leaning on one of the boulders as if he'd been there a long time.

She was wet from sea spray, but she didn't care.

"I can see why he looks at you the way he does," Baluch said. Her heart skipped a beat with sudden longing to see Acton again, even as a ghost. To see how he looked at her. To see that berserker grin he gave just before he did something outrageous. The hollow under her ribs was enormous. She felt like a shell around thin air, as light and empty as an egg whose hatchling has flown away.

As the sun showed its first edge, Baluch began to sing. His voice was much better than Ash's—more trained, more controlled—and the song rose like a bird song, like water flowing. Bramble hung her head and yearned for Acton, feeding all her longing into the music. It was harder than with Ash, which surprised her, because she wasn't revealing anything this time that Baluch didn't already know. But she and Ash had been attuned, and she and Baluch were not, exactly. Perhaps it was the missing brooch. Perhaps it was the place, so far from where he met his death.

She remembered being Baluch, being inside his head, inside his music, and felt the connection between them grow stronger.

Come back, she sent to Acton. *We need you. I need you.*

But she could tell, even before Baluch's voice faltered to a stop, before she lifted her head, that he had not come.

SAKER

SAKER WOKE and looked out the window to the east. A day's march to Turvite. Perhaps two. The road curved and looped between low hills, following the path of the river. There were well-built villages along the way, smaller streams with bridges over them, large inns next to docks on the river, all the marks of prosperity.

He ran his fingers over the rim of the wash basin. He had to make sure that, when the spoils of war were distributed, it was done fairly. His people had had everything taken from them: they should receive everything equally.

But that might be difficult, sometimes. There were not so many ceramic basins of this quality... Who should get this level of goods?

Better to smash the luxuries and start even than have disputes about mere things, Saker resolved. Or else inequality would be built into the foundation of their new world, and he would not let that happen.

The yard below was seething with ghosts. They had finished their morning blood ceremony. Saker had decided to let Owl and his father just do it. He tried not to admit to himself that he was relieved not to have to use the knife on another person—it was not because of that, not at all. It was because he was finding it increasingly harder to avoid reacting to the terrible whining of the spirits of those they had killed. With each sacrifice, the sound grew louder, though no one else could hear it. Each dawn and dusk, the distorted shapes crowded his vision more and more, writhing towards him against an invisible barrier. He had nightmares about what would happen if that barrier ever broke, and he shuddered.

In a corner of the yard, the wind wraiths devoured the remains of the sacrifice. Saker turned away from the sight. Better to avoid the whole ceremony, lest he break down in front of his army.

They had organized themselves into groups for the march: ghosts first, human allies behind them. It was time he went down.

As he came out of the house into the bright glare of the dawn sun, the lead wraith flew to him like a scrap of cloud and hovered.

"Master," it said. "Today you go to the city of the woman."

"The woman?"

The wraith shivered. "The enchanter who made the compact, long ago. The compact is strong, there. Too strong for us to follow you, unless you break the walls and invite us in. Can you?"

Saker felt his spirits rise. At last, a battle without the horrific shrieking of the wraiths. "I will try," he said graciously.

"Call us and we will come." The wraith shot up in the air and was joined by his companions, until they were no more than specks in the sky, and then were gone.

Saker looked down, his eyes blinded by the morning light, and he noticed a woman walk through the gate into the yard. She stood for a moment, staring at the ghosts, and then she shrugged and came in. A black-haired woman, young, with the grace of an acrobat. Saker realized he was staring, and flushed.

It had been longer than he could remember since he had looked at any woman that way.

She asked a question of one of the living, and made her way over to him. He could see that she had cried a lot, recently. His heart contracted a little with pity.

"My name's Zel," she said. "My brer was killed by Thegan at Sendat."

She has come to reproach me, Saker thought immediately. And she is right—I am responsible for those deaths.

"So. Can I join you?"

It was like a reprieve; she did not blame him. He nodded. "Welcome, Zel," he said. She bobbed her head, as though she didn't know what to say but felt she should say something. He reached out and put his hand on her shoulder. "Walk with me today," he said, "and I will explain our plans."

She half-smiled at him; it was the best she could do, he surmised. Her grief ran deep, very deep. Freite had taught him how to draw on the power of such emotions, but he didn't need to. The ghosts were all the power he needed. That realization made him feel light, free of the past. He walked with Zel to the head of the army and took the front wagon.

They found Owl, Oak and his father waiting for him to lead.

"This is Zel," he told them. "She has suffered greatly from the warlords, as we all have." They nodded to her with respect, and Oak smiled at her, stirring a flick of jealousy in Saker. He put a hand on her back, to guide her into place, and saw that Oak registered the touch.

"Come," he said, raising his voice so they could all hear. "Let us make Turvite our own."

They drove off to the sound of human cheering and the deathly percussion of the ghosts banging their weapons together. Even without the wind wraiths, they were invincible.

Saker and Zel talked, and he learnt that her brother had been a singer, and she a tumbler, as he had thought. She was so slight that she made him feel stalwart, and he was determined that she should go to the back when the fighting began.

"Why should I?" she demanded. "I want to fight the blond bastards."

"I understand. But it's better if the ghosts can swing their weapons without worrying about hitting a living ally." He dropped his voice and leant closer confidentially, her scent suddenly warm in his nostrils, making him dizzy. "They're not trained soldiers, you know, and half the time they hit each other!" She turned surprised eyes to him and he chuckled a little. "It doesn't matter, of course, with them. But with you..." He shook his head magisterially. "It would hinder our fight, and that cannot be allowed."

She stared at her feet resentfully. Her boots were scuffed and worn, from long Travel. He would find her a cobbler to make a new pair. All his people would have new boots, he amended hastily. Not just her.

On the outskirts of Turvite, they passed through a deserted village.

"This Sanctuary?" Zel asked, looking around intently.

"Aye," Saker said. "They've all hidden in the city, but it won't help them."

Zel frowned, and kept frowning on the long slope up the hill towards the city. He tried to engage her again in conversation, but she replied absently and he let it drop. She looked at him often, and he took comfort from that, although she never smiled, just looked around at the ghosts and the city ahead. It was natural that she should be afraid. He said so.

"Not fear, cully," she said.

"What, then?"

There were tears in her eyes as she looked up at him. "Just the past coming back to bite me," she said. "I'm going to die. I knew it when I found out about Flax. And I thought, if I'm going to die, I'd rather die fighting with my own kind."

"You're not going to die!" he protested. "I'll look after you."

"You'll have enough trouble looking after yourself. D'you think they'll just let you stroll in?"

"They can't stop me! Us!" he said. "We're invincible!"

She smiled at him then, but it was the smile of a mother to a young child who had said something foolish.

"No such thing in the world as invincible," she said. "Not in this world or the next. Sorry."

That was all she would say.

As they came through the houses and market gardens that surrounded the city, Saker could see that the road had been blocked off. But this was no proper fortification, as there had been at Sendat. This was just a motley collection of carts and barrels and boards. No one stood guard, although he noticed faces at windows nearby, watching. It was unnerving. Then, as they came closer, he felt the hum of enchantment running through the barricade.

It seemed familiar to him, somehow, but he couldn't place it. He called a halt a few hundred yards from the barricade and got down from the cart. Owl, his father and Oak came to him with questions in their eyes.

"There's a spell on the barricades," he said. "I don't know what it is, but I don't want our living allies anywhere near it. We'll have to storm it and see."

Owl nodded and hefted his battleaxe. He was hung with other weapons: knives, a short cudgel.

Oak stepped forward. "Are you sure you should send the ghosts against a spell?" he asked, and Alder nodded strongly, as though he shared Oak's doubts.

"It's not that type of a spell," Saker said. He was sure of that. "Believe me. It feels quite different from a destruction spell." He looked at his father, who was still frowning. That annoyed him and put a sharper note into his voice. "Spells are my business. This is *not* a destruction spell."

Reluctantly, Alder nodded and moved back with Owl to the head of their forces. They exchanged glances and grinned at each other. Saker, as he had before, felt suddenly excluded. Owl, he thought, was the kind of son Father really wanted. Warlike. Fearless. He set his shoulders straighter. Well, it wasn't Owl who had brought them to this moment of triumph. It was him.

"Attack!" he shouted.

The ghosts moved forward, men and women and youths armed with axes or swords, moving more quickly as they neared the flimsy barricade.

A few yards away from it, Owl recoiled, pushing back against the men behind him. Alder flung up a hand and skidded to a stop, putting out a hand for balance and pushing over the woman next to him. The line came to a standstill. Saker watched, puzzled. What had happened?

Owl tried again, walking forward as if through deep water, thrusting his leg ahead at each step with visible effort. Then, head down, pushing as hard as he could, he could go no further. Saker felt the spell's power surge against him. It was very strong.

Owl turned and walked back, and the power in the spell waned.

"I know what it is," Saker said, turning to Zel. "It's the spell stonecasters use in Turvite to keep ghosts out of their houses." He thought for a moment. "It will only work if the barriers go all the way around the city."

Oak planted the handle of his axe in the dirt and smiled a little.

"Time for us to do some work, I reckon," he said.

LEOF

OAK? SURELY that was Oak, the stonemason from Sendat. Leof felt sick to his stomach. He was angry with Oak as though the man had betrayed him personally, but he remembered that the last time he had seen Oak, Thegan's men had been trying to kill him. It wasn't surprising that he had joined the enchanter's army. Where else could he go? Who should he side with—the man who was trying to take his country back for him, or the ones who had tried to murder him?

Merroc had given orders that the barricade should appear deserted. They had waited, sweating—in attics and bed chambers, a rabble of safeguarders and huntsmen for archers—while the enemy sorted themselves into the dead and the living, and the dead had advanced upon them. Behind them, in the city, Leof had heard the news of the ghost army's approach spread. Shouts, screams, weeping, running feet loud against the cobbles. He had hoped that Eolbert, down by the harbor, would realize that he'd have to hold the barricade against the Turviters trying to get out, more than against the enemy. *Just let them through*, he thought, *let them run if they want, as long as the spell stays strong*.

And it stayed strong, but now the enchanter's human allies were massing together—too close for proper fighting—and walking up the road, led by Oak, axe in hand. There were women, too, but Leof was relieved to see the men kept them at the back out of harm's way. Except, of course, that would put them closer to his spearmen who were waiting for just this moment, when the living enemy was between them and the archers.

Merroc was in the house across the road, with a sightline to Leof. He nocked his bow and looked at Merroc, who had his hand raised, waiting for the Travelers to advance enough to be sure targets, but not so close that any could break through the barricade. The others in the room found places at the windows, bows ready but not pulled.

Leof watched. They were within bowshot now.

He took aim, but not at Oak. He couldn't bring himself to cut the man down. Two along from him were a pair of twins, tall men with shiny black hair like raven's wings.

Leof pulled back and aimed at the one on the left. He felt the familiar heart-stopping anticipation that built just before battle—a mixture of dread and excitement, nausea and exhilaration.

Merroc's hand dropped, and the archers let fly. The whir of arrows was loud, shouts and screams erupted from the enemy. Leof's man dropped. Oak reeled back with a shaft in the shoulder. He dropped his axe, picked it up again with his other hand and tried to rush forward.

Leof took another arrow. This was where practice paid off.

He was twice as fast as the others so it fell to him to stop Oak from reaching the barricade. There was no choice: a living city depended on it. He pulled back and let fly, then nocked another arrow and shot again as Oak's throat blossomed with blood. The third arrow hit him in the side as he spun away; he fell.

Around him, his companions were panicking. They had been prepared for hand-to-hand fighting, Leof thought, not for death falling from the sky. Just as his men at Bonhill had not been prepared for the wind wraiths. He hardened his heart and shot, and shot again.

The line broke and ran back towards the ghosts, who had started advancing. But the spearmen emerged from hiding and spears sliced through the air towards them. A few realized what was happening. Leof saw one young woman jump over a fence like an acrobat and run between houses, away from both the spearmen and the ghosts. He followed her flight to avoid looking at the slaughter; she ran, but she ran in a wide circle, coming up behind the ghosts and rejoining the enchanter, who stared, stricken, calling his people back.

The ghosts turned on the spearmen, but Merroc waved and a horn sounded in warning. The spearmen turned and ran back into the houses on either side; bespelled against ghosts, they were temporary havens.

The spearmen slammed the doors closed and the shutters were already nailed up. Outside, the ghosts couldn't even reach the walls; one strained to touch the door, but couldn't make contact. He snarled frustration—even at such a distance, the expression was clear.

In the street below him, people began to cheer. He should be happy, too, Leof thought, but he could see Oak's body, and the others he had killed, sprawled on the road. He could not quite feel the elation he had always felt before when a battle went well.

They were retreating, all of them: the few remnants of the living, the dead, the enchanter. Leof thanked the gods that the wind wraiths had not come; that had saved the spearmen.

He realized then, with a little shock, that they had not lost a single man; and at last a sense of achievement came to him.

BRAMBLE

SHE WOULD not let herself panic. She would not. "We need Ash," Bramble said. Briskly, she began packing Acton's bones back into the bag. She refused to dwell on the feel of bone beneath her fingertips, the curve of his skull. "We'll have to go into Turvite and find him."

She had to raise her voice. Baluch had walked away after their attempt to raise Acton had failed, and was looking down at the city from the landward side of the boulders.

"That might be harder than it sounds," he answered over his shoulder.

Bramble moved to stand beside him, gazing down at Turvite, which was spread out before them like a bowl, the tiers of houses leading down to a harbor full of white caps from the night's wind.

A thousand years ago a woman named Piper had looked down at what had been a simple fishing village. Bramble felt as though she saw both places at the same time, as one sees frost on the windowpane and the scene outside, overlaid on one another. She shook her head. *This* Turvite she could smell, a combination of old fish and spices, woodsmoke and cooking bacon. She was starving.

Then she saw, around the town, a continuous barrier blocking all the inward streets, with men behind it, guarding. "They're trying to keep the ghosts out," she said.

"Doesn't mean they'll let us in," Baluch said. "People from the countryside will be flooding in soon, when the ghosts advance. Their only hope of survival is to keep everyone out except their own people."

Bramble remembered when Baluch's folk had made the same choice—to accept the people running from the Ice King or fight them off. They had chosen to fight. It was the constant attacks from those pushed from their land that had led to Acton planning the settlement over the mountains.

Instead of going down the slope to the harbor, they walked along the ridge that connected with the hill at the back of the town. They found a well-worn track, and halfway along they understood why; they had to stand aside to let the milked cows return to their pasture. They passed in stately file, their udders swinging loose, and their solid warmth was reassuring to Bramble, their twice-daily trek seemed the only unchanging thing.

"I want to see what's happening on the other side," Baluch said. He was assessing the city with a warrior's eye, as he had once assessed River Bluff.

The barrier extended all the way around the city, but as they came closer it was clear that it was so flimsy it wouldn't keep anyone out.

"A spell," Bramble said with surety. "They're using enchantment to strengthen it."

"Let's hope they know what they're doing."

The headland grazing area ended on a high knoll. Beyond it on one side were market gardens stretching down to the river. Lilac, rosemary, lavender and dung from the gardens mixed in Bramble's nose. Down the hill, the road west cut through a mixture of houses and vegetable patches.

It was strange to see her enemy, finally, coming down the road towards Turvite. It had been months for her since that day in Oakmere when Safred had told her that a man named Saker had killed Maryrose, and offered her the chance to stop him.

They needed Acton, right now. "We have to try again," she said.

But Baluch shook his head. "It won't work. I could feel it—something is missing in the spell. I'm not sure if it's the brooch or Ash, but we can't do it as things stand."

"Then we have to find Ash."

"Battle is about to be joined," he said, flexing his right hand as though a sword might appear there. "And Ash is in the middle of the city, somewhere. I don't know where."

"But he's alive?"

Baluch nodded, and she felt a surge of relief. It wasn't hopeless, then. Risky, but not impossible.

She grinned and hoisted her bag of bones onto her shoulder. "If they're coming in the front way, let's you and I go in the back, round the harbor."

They retraced their steps to where the path began to lead down towards the water, but Baluch put out a hand and stopped her. "Look," he said.

There was a fight at the barricade leading to the harbor. People were panicking, trying to reach the few ships in port. The guards at the barricade were letting people through one by one, closing the gate after each one, but it wasn't fast enough to satisfy the crowd. Some leapt over the barriers, others climbed up inside the houses that formed part of the city's defence, and jumped from their windows. The ones who made it through rushed to the ships, all of which had pulled up their boarding planks and were making ready to sail.

It didn't stop the crowd. They pulled on the mooring ropes until the ships were crammed up against the dock, then swarmed up the sides. The sailors fought them off with belaying pins and knives. Bodies dropped back onto the dock—some sailors, but most Turviters.

"Don't go down," Baluch said. "Please, Bramble. I can't protect you down there."

She spared a flick of a smile for the idea that he had to protect her—that came from his old life, for sure—but the scene below was sobering enough. Going down into that mob was too foolhardy even for her. She had Acton's bones, and they could not be risked.

The desperate Turviters had almost overwhelmed the ships when a horn blasted out from the top of the hill.

"The ghost attack!" Baluch said.

They ran back to the knoll in time to see the ghosts retreat, confused, leaving a welter of dark-haired bodies in front of the barrier.

"More deaths," Bramble said.

"More will come, unless we do our job," Baluch said.

SAKER

HE CALLED his people back in horror, and they died as they came, bodies falling, pierced by spears or arrows; some screamed as they lay in the dust of the road, their blood coating themselves and their colleagues.

Blood.

He could smell blood, and the stench of guts cut open.

Blood and memory.

"Arise!" he cried, putting all his grief and terror into the call. "Arise, comrades-in-arms! Oak and Ber and Eldwin and Fox, arise! We seek justice for you, my friends. Arise!" He called, and kept on calling, as long as their blood flowed.

It was easier, this spell, than any other had been, fuelled by his pain, strengthened by his sorrow.

They rose as they died, one by one, the ghosts forming quickly, their weapons still in their hands. There was no confusion—they knew what had happened, they had died hearing him call. Their ghosts moved with purpose as soon as they formed, gathering with the others; they were the newest part of his army, the most valuable.

Zel had arrived, panting, at his elbow as he began the spell, and she supported him as it ended, when his legs gave way and his head spun. She was stalwart; he gave thanks to the gods that she was still alive.

Saker turned to his ghosts again, and whispered, "Try the barrier again."

Owl and his father looked sceptical, but they went, all the same. The bigger group overwhelmed the road and spilt off into the yards on either side. Saker could feel the spell again as they approached the barricade: just like last time, its strength rose as his army came nearer. But this time, this time, it was almost not enough. He closed his eyes so he could sense it better. The spell only just held, now that there were more ghosts trying to break it.

Saker opened his eyes. His father looked furious, storming back to him, brandishing his sword. Owl followed, just as angry, and the others came behind, disappointed, frustrated.

"We almost had it," Saker said to them. "With the new ghosts, we were almost enough to break it. I need to think. I need somewhere quiet to think."

"Up on the headland," Zel said, pointing. "It's quiet up there."

She was right. The headland was deserted.

The wagons were no good up there. He left them with the few living allies in the yard of an inn halfway down the slope. Zel organized guards, shifts, rosters—he had needed someone like her. Then they walked up to the headland together, near the river, the ghosts trailing behind. His father brushed past them, impatiently, and Owl followed him. They climbed to the highest point and stood, looking down at the city.

When Saker turned away and sat by the stream, Zel followed. He didn't think that his father saw Turvite as he did, as a jewel to present to their people, a symbol of everything they had lost. His father, he suspected, just wanted to destroy it and everyone in it.

They needed more ghosts. That was the key. Those just arisen had almost been enough. But to get more... Travelers had to die. Or else he had to find more bones.

He outlined the problem to Zel, relieved to have someone to talk to, someone to share with. "If only I didn't need the bones!" he said despairingly.

She patted his hand as it lay on the grass, and he flushed. He turned his hand over quickly, so that her hand came down on his palm, and he curled his fingers around hers. It was the first time he could remember welcoming a human touch. It was so different from all the times he had taken a hand wet with spit and stiff with excitement. Zel's hand was gentle, although rough with calluses from her tumbling.

He smiled at her, and she smiled back.

A hand came down on her shoulder and pulled her roughly away, sending her sprawling almost into the water. His father.

Alder grabbed him by the shirt and shook him like a terrier shakes a rat, pointing in rage at Zel, frothing that he couldn't shout, couldn't berate him. Saker knew why his father was angry—because he had taken a moment, just a moment, to be simply Saker, a Traveler man, sitting with a Traveler woman in peace, instead of being committed, heart and soul, every moment, to their cause.

Unforgivable.

His father threw him down and hit him across the face, the shoulders, the back, as he curled into a ball to protect himself.

There had been many beatings in his childhood. Alder was known for having a hard hand. One family had even cut off all contact with his because Alder had beaten their daughter for lying.

Saker was vaguely aware that Zel had scrambled up and pulled Alder away, shouting insults at him. Alder shrugged her off, but he stopped and moved back a pace.

Saker forced himself to hands and knees, panting with pain. So much pain, all his life, from his father, from Freite...

Anger bloomed in him. Wild anger, so huge it seemed about to split him in two. He seemed to swell larger than any human, as vast as the sea, as vast as the sky. His sight was red, as though his very eyes were bleeding pain. He could kill his father easily, just by removing the spell from him. He'd *never* have to see him again, never see the look of disdain on his face, never... No! No, that wasn't right. Couldn't be right. His anger was for the invaders. If his father had lived, seen him grow to be a man, surely they would have found mutual respect, understanding...

It was the invaders' fault, all of it. Acton's fault. All over the Domains, people lay in shallow graves and burial caves because of him. The invaders had to be crushed. His father was right. But the anger... the anger was still there, still building. He felt as though his eyes were going to break open; his heart was beating too fast, it would burst itself and there was no one to bring him back, no one to call *his* spirit back from the darkness beyond death... He felt like a wind was rushing through him, lifting him to his feet.

His father backed up a step as he rose, and Saker was glad to see it. Glad to see alarm on his face.

Blood and memory.

He remembered them all. All the songs that Rowan had taught him, all the names he had conned over the months of collecting bones, all the faces, the places, the pain, the death...He remembered them all.

Blood and memory and anger would bring them all back.

He took out his knife and slashed his palm wildly, and the anger swelled as he cut and cut, the blood swirling out as he began to spin, so that all the Domains would be touched by it, south and north and west and east—all corners blessed by his blood.

He called them: "Arise, brothers and sisters! Arise, all of you. All who have died who would not have died without Acton; all who have died untimely and unjustly; all who have been murdered, had the life ripped from them because of Acton's invasion; come to me, all of you, all my brothers and sisters, all the dead who rage; all whose lives were shorter because the invaders came through Death Pass. Arise and come! Come! Come now! Come and be given all my strength!"

And as the spell grew, as the power grew, the terrible singing in his head returned, louder than ever, but he ignored it. Let them rage, those he had killed! Let them shriek against the barrier of death for revenge. No one would call them back. He didn't care if the ululation split his head wide open, he would not stop. He would call them all, all his kin.

The anger and the pain and the loneliness spun out of him and spread out across the Eleven Domains. He could feel it go, feel it spread, feel it fly across the landscape like clouds before a gale. It spread like night, like shadow, like sunlight. As fast as dawn.

He felt it hit the nearest burial caves, felt the spirits stir within. Felt it go further, further, traveling as a dove flies, straight and quick. It was huge, growing no weaker as it spread, pushing all other enchantments before it. Something about that troubled him, but he did not know what it was.

The high whining in his head began to pulse and move, as though whoever made it was looking for a weak spot in him, a chink they could use to climb through, to come back like his kin was coming. But he was too strong, too fearless. He resisted, thrust it away from him.

Then he felt the first of the new ghosts moving up the hill, faster than anyone could walk, faster than a chaser; and the whining died away. They were invisible: flying, swimming through time and air to be with him. They only firmed to visible shapes when they came near enough, and they kept moving until they stood before Saker, dazed and wondering.

A young girl was in front, holding a knife with comfortable familiarity. She looked around and blinked, then tilted her head to the side as though assessing the situation. She looked Saker up and down, then Alder. Owl. Then she saw Zel, and relaxed a little, as though the presence of a young woman reassured her. The others were a mixture: old and young, men and women, clothes of different fashions and quality.

Saker saw that his father, at last, was looking at him with some respect. But somehow it mattered less, now. He could not turn aside for Alder. He had to stay here, until the spell was complete.

They were coming with the speed of dawn light. And when they were assembled, nothing would stand against them.

BRAMBLE

BRAMBLE COULD hear shouting from the other side of the headland, a rhythmic shouting. The bones in the bag on her shoulder seemed to move in time to it. A half-familiar noise rang in her head—the same noise she'd heard when they raised Acton's ghost. It was the sound of the dead being brought back. She dropped the bag and watched, in a mixture of relief and consternation, as Acton's ghost rapidly formed.

He seemed to be fighting against something that was pulling him towards the top of the headland. He was being dragged up towards the shouting. She reached out to help him, but her hand went through. He was a real ghost, then. She moved closer to him, desperate to help but helpless, barely able to think through the ear-splitting noise in her head. And then the shouting above stopped.

His hand clasped hers with the chill of the burial caves.

She almost let him slip from her grasp, but grabbed hold with her other hand as the whining howl subsided. The enchanter had called up more ghosts, she realized, and Acton had been in the ambit of his spell.

"Hold on to him!" she called breathlessly to Baluch. The pull up the hill was very strong. "We have to keep him here!" She dug in her heels and despite Acton fighting it, too, with all his massive strength, they were dragged up a yard or so before Baluch added his weight, coming around and leaning against Acton from higher up the slope.

From the harbor below, ghosts appeared and rushed past them: sailors, city people, all the recent dead.

Acton shook his head as if to clear it, set his jaw in that look she knew so well, and simply stopped. Immovable, like a mountain.

Bramble exchanged glances with Baluch, and they both smiled, very slightly. If this were a battle of wills, they had no doubt who would win it.

Acton seemed to send down roots into the ground, so that his feet were planted as solidly as an oak tree. Still, it was not only will, but power, being used against him, and even an oak tree may be pushed over by a strong enough wind.

It brought out the best and the worst in him. When strength of will faltered, stubbornness took over. She saw it happen, saw the mulish set to his mouth, the same expression he had worn when he set himself to explore the Ice King's realm.

Her hands, on his cold, cold arms, were going numb. She would reach a point where she couldn't grasp, and then what? "Gods of field and stream," she hissed, holding on. "Gods of sky and wind, gods of earth and stone, help us!"

Her shoulders and legs were alight, burning with effort. She looked at him and laughed to herself—this was not how she had imagined touching him, that moment back on the hillside when he and she had been alive. He grinned at her as if catching the thought, and mimed a kiss. They both laughed silently, Bramble gasping for air, hearing only her own heartbeat and Baluch's panting breath.

Bramble was suddenly aware of noise above them. It wasn't talking, but a *shush*, like the sound of people moving silently over grass.

And Acton seemed to be planted solidly now, as though the spell were running thin.

She released Acton's arms and waited a moment to make sure he was firmly set, then put a finger to her lips and climbed the hill half-crouched, hands steadying her against the high slope. She lay down before she reached the top, and slithered up to peer over the edge.

Ghosts. Hundreds.

They were many, many more than had attacked the city that morning. Thousands, maybe.

Silent. Roaming the headland in small bands. More arriving, dragged to the spot by the spell, just as Acton was being pulled. They flew, it seemed, or came through the ground itself, and formed on the hillside in front of a man, the enchanter. Saker.

It was her first close sight of him, and she was disappointed. He was just a man. Not old, not handsome, not ugly, not tall or short or anything unusual. Just a man that she might have passed in the street.

How could this... *nothing* be responsible for so much grief?

He looked exhausted, and when the arrival of ghosts slowed and then stopped, he slumped to the ground. Good. Acton should be free. But she didn't go back immediately, because something was happening.

The few humans and some of the ghosts which were already there were organizing the new ghosts into lines, as if they were assembling for inspection. Then Bramble saw that at the head of each line was a person, hogtied. Scared. Next to each prisoner was a ghost with a knife. Two ghosts, a big man and a small one with the beaded hair of Hawk's people, seemed to measure how far the sun had to go in the sky, then nodded to the ghosts at the heads of the lines. They bent as one and cut the arm of the person kneeling in front of them, and tasted the blood that welled up.

Bramble scanned the scene and her stomach clenched as she registered the ceremony unfolding before her. Blood was part of the spell. Blood to keep the ghosts there, blood to give them strength. Some of the new ghosts were hanging back, reluctant to taste the blood of a living sacrifice.

The enchanter came to address them, supported by one of the Travelers. A girl. Zel.

Bramble stared, uncomprehending. How could Zel? *Why* would she? Some plot of the Well of Secrets? It had to be. Zel was probably feeding information back to the city. That could be useful. And it meant that Safred and Martine were here, which had to be good.

"Take some blood before sunset," the enchanter called to the ghosts. "It will keep you from fading. But it is not only blood you need, but memory. Blood and memory will keep you here, to take your revenge." Some seemed confused, and his voice sharpened. "You will fade without it, back to the darkness beyond death."

Bramble didn't wait to see if they were convinced. Acton needed blood, right now.

She scrambled down the hill, fumbling for her belt knife. Acton was free, standing, moving his shoulders as if to get the kinks out of them.

Cutting her arm just above the wrist, she offered it to him. He stared at her, puzzled.

"Blood and memory will keep you from fading at sunset," she said.

"The enchanter is feeding all his ghosts blood, and you have to drink, too, like in a quickening ceremony."

His people hadn't had quickenings. They happened only in the Domains, like stonecasting. He didn't understand, and shook his head.

Baluch put a hand on his arm. "Take the blood, Acton. We need you."

It was a hard thing for him to do, she could see, and she was filled with a familiar impatience with him. Why couldn't he *see* what was happening? "Just drink the blood, idiot!" she snapped.

His eyes lit with laughter at that, and he bent obediently, his tongue flicking out to her skin. She shivered violently as the death-cold hit her, but at the same time was pierced with sudden desire; heat and cold striking through her with equal force, leaving her trembling. His eyes were no longer laughing; he swallowed her blood down and stared at her with matching need. Baluch turned away.

Acton put his hand out to stroke her cheek, but instead of touching her, he curved his palm so that his fingers followed the line of her jaw without contact. Slowly, sadly, he shook his head.

Her chest was tight with desire, but he was right. There would be no surcease for them, not in this life. Not in any, may be. She turned away, fighting tears.

"Acton can face the ghosts and acknowledge his guilt," Baluch said thoughtfully, looking at the cut on her wrist. "But the quickening ceremony needs blood, as well."

He and Acton exchanged glances. Bramble didn't trust that look; she knew it too well. "What?" she demanded.

"I think," Baluch said slowly, "I think if we are offering acknowledgment of the landtaken, I should be the one to offer blood."

Bramble badly wanted to argue against him. Let the warlords do it! They're the real criminals. But she had to accept that he was right. He had been there. He had killed, and more than once. He owed blood.

"There are a lot of ghosts," she said. "That much blood might kill you."

Baluch grinned at her, a familiar gleam in his eyes. The music in his head would be horns and drums, she thought.

"I have to die *some* time," he said.

MARTINE

Sorn walked into the hall without considering etiquette, Safred, Martine and Cael behind her. She was gaining in authority with every passing hour, Martine thought, as though the free air of Turvite was feeding some part of her that had been starved all her life.

The council was consulting with the warlords, Merroc included. Thegan looked up and anger flashed across his face so quickly that probably only they had seen it. Then he smiled. "My lady! Come to join our celebrations?"

"Celebration is premature," Sorn said, standing stiffly in front of the council table. "The enchanter has let loose another spell. The Well of Secrets tells me that he has begun calling for reinforcements; that there will be more ghosts arriving, from all over the Domains."

A buzz arose as the warlords turned back to their map, reassessing the defenses.

Martine spoke reluctantly. "With this number of ghosts against it, I don't think the protective spell will survive."

"It's time to negotiate," Ranny said.

"I'm not negotiating with that piece of filth!" Merroc snarled.

"I will negotiate with him, if none of you will," Arvid cut in.

Martine wanted to smile at him, to give him support, but she forced herself to look at Sorn instead. It would do him no good in the warlords' eyes to get encouragement from her.

Ranny dismissed one of her people to find a set of antlers, the sign of parley across the Domains. In Turvite, so far from the nearest forest, they weren't common.

"I will take your spell workers with me, my dear," Thegan said to Sorn. "We might have need of them."

"I will take them with me," Sorn said, staring him straight in the eyes as she had never done before. She saw fury flare up in him, and she nodded calmly before walking away to join Martine and Safred.

"It's a fine line you're walking," Martine murmured to her.

"It's necessary. There has to be someone in that parley who respects the gods."

"One thing more," Safred said to Ranny. "I believe you have a young man arrested. Ash. A safeguarder."

Martine's gut clenched. Safred hadn't mentioned this—how long had she known? And who had told her? Were the gods talking to her again?

"A murderer!" Garham said. Martine flinched. What had Ash done?

"Even so," Safred said. "We need him."

"If the Well of Secrets needs him, Garham, I think we have more to worry about than a single death," Ranny intervened smoothly. Seeing Garham's slow nodding agreement, Ranny turned to one of the Moot staff. "Get him."

As the parley group gathered and bickered over precedence, until it was established that Ranny was the least threatening person to hold the antlers, they brought Ash in.

His shoulders were hunched, hands in pockets. He looked profoundly unhappy. But his expression lightened as he saw Safred, and even more when he saw Martine.

She smiled as easily as she could. "In trouble again, are you?"

He tried to grin, but couldn't. "I killed Doronit," he said baldly, as if he wanted to get the worst over with immediately.

Martine paused, her breath stilled. Without willing it, her gaze flicked to Arvid, for support, but she looked back at Ash immediately. This was no business of Arvid's. Ash was watching her as if waiting for a sentence of death. Martine remembered the night he had refused to kill her on Doronit's orders—he had given up everything so that he would not have to murder. Only extreme need would have pushed him to killing Doronit.

"No doubt you had good reason," Martine said gently. Ash's shoulders relaxed.

Safred turned to him. "It's time to meet the enchanter."

SAKER

THE WIND wraiths were circling, over the sea, as though they were waiting for something. Saker watched them with unease. They had said they could not come close to Turvite. Why had they appeared now? He remembered, with a twist in his stomach, the feeling that some other spell had weakened when he called in the spirits.

But the wraiths were offshore, a league or so away, so he didn't have to think about it now. It was time to address the new ghosts. There were so many of them. And such a variety. He now knew that Traveler blood existed in the most unlikely people, but even so, some of these new arrivals seemed strange to him. A beautiful woman in modern dress, her shawl held by a brooch, looking around with calculating eyes. A scraggy old woman dressed in fur skins. She had laughed and refused the blood, but Owl had taken some and smeared it across her face. Saker wondered if they had known each other.

Owl had then soaked a rag in blood and unceremoniously dabbed blood on the cheek of each new ghost. It was much more efficient; the sacrifice hadn't even died.

So many. There was even one who seemed not quite human, who was hard to see, except out of the corner of Saker's eye. It moved like a cat instead of a person, with hawk's feathers in its hair.

He could feel that the spell was still subtly working—the last of the ghosts had not yet arrived.

He moved to higher ground and clapped his hands to draw their attention. What language should he use? The old or the new? He decided to start with the old and then repeat himself.

The ghosts gathered around. His heart was breaking, there were so many untimely dead. He found the words he needed in the old tongue and pieced them together in his mind before he spoke. He could wait no longer.

"Welcome!" he shouted. "I called you so we can take back the land that was stolen from us."

Some of the ghosts nodded and clapped their hands together, but others looked blank. The old woman in skins shook her head in dismay. He didn't understand, but he kept on.

"The invaders are in fear of us, because we can overcome them. We will attack the city—" he swept his arm towards Turvite—"take back what was ours."

When he repeated the words in his own language, he saw with astonishment that some ghosts shook their fists at him, or turned their backs. His father and Owl seemed as puzzled by the dissent as he was.

Zel came up behind him. "Not all of them are Travelers, Saker," she said. "Her, for example." She pointed to a young woman dressed in current fashion, not like an officer's daughter, but better than most. The woman had an arrow in her breast and was kneeling, praying. "She's one of Acton's people, sure and certain."

He recognized the woman. It was the maid, the warlord's wife's maid, from Sendat. He had never expected this. Brothers and sisters, he had called for, the ones cut down before their time by the invasion.

"Your spell were broad," Zel went on. "I reckon it called *everyone* who died because of the invasion. Including the ones you've killed."

Saker searched the crowd more carefully and recognized the tall red-headed woman from Carlion who had thrown herself in the way of Owl's blow. She had been of the old blood, but she was standing next to the husband she had tried to protect, and he had been one of Acton's people. He saw some others from Sendat. Not many, because the wind wraiths had feasted there. Those spirits were truly dead. But there were some soldiers, and there—the first sacrifice, the young officer they had bled to keep the ghosts alive. He was standing, arms folded, staring at Saker as though calculating the best way to kill him.

And there was a young man coming towards them, looking excited. Zel stared as though she couldn't believe it.

"Flax?" she whispered, and then ran to him, throwing herself into his arms. She pulled back, shaking him. "I told you to stay out of trouble! I told you to be careful!" Saker felt his heart skip a beat, but it wasn't a lover's voice she used as she scolded him. "You went and got yourself *killed*!" Her brother, maybe? She began to weep, hands covering her face, and the boy patted her on the back, a curious expression on his face, a mixture of pity and consternation at the tears.

Saker noticed an older woman, dark hair showing clearly despite her paleness, staring intently at Zel and Flax, but standing away from them as though she didn't have the right to come closer. She seemed to hesitate, then turned and walked to the back, losing herself in the crowd.

Saker forced himself to look away from Zel. The important thing was that they had more than enough ghosts to break Turvite's defenses. Perhaps not all of them would join in, but that didn't matter. They were invincible.

Alder began organizing the ghosts who had come to Turvite into groups, to march down the hill to the city. Owl gathered the new ones who had welcomed Saker's words, and directed them to Alder's groups, which were swelling rapidly.

They would take the groups down and the force of numbers would overwhelm the protective spell. The other ghosts could wait here.

Flax looked across and realized what was happening. His face, so soft before, firmed and he looked older. He moved away from Zel, searching for others in the crowd. He found an older man, a couple of young ones. His face lit up when he saw Oak, and he went towards him enthusiastically. Then he saw that Oak was one of a group preparing to fight—checking weapons, settling knives in belts. He shook Oak's arm, but Oak stared at him stonily and drew his belt knife. Flax backed away.

He moved into the crowd. Saker watched him closely; he didn't know why, but his Sight was telling him that Flax was important. Zel was watching, too, and her face was unreadable. Flax approached the young officer they had bled to death. They faced each other. Flax pointed at the city, and shook his head. The officer spread his hands—they were empty, of course, because he had not died fighting, with a weapon in his hand.

Flax made a motion dismissing that as an excuse, then turned and marched towards the path down to the city. He stood on it, feet planted, and stared challengingly at the officer, and at the other ghosts who were not joining the groups. Saker couldn't believe it. This boy had been killed by the warlord's men only days ago! He should have been hungry for revenge. Why was he siding with the Turviters?

Other ghosts were joining him. A tall beautiful blonde woman in ancient dress, who stood next to Flax and regarded everyone with a calm eye. The scraggy old woman, the tall red-head and her husband, the maid, a girl leaning on a crutch, and others, following them, seeming to realize that they had a choice of who to support. They stared at Saker with varying expressions, a mixture of disdain, hatred, and fear.

He wished, agonizingly, that he could talk to them properly, and have them talk back. That he could explain everything, so that they would understand, and respect him, and join him.

Owl and Alder, occupied with readying their troops, realized what was happening too late. The path was blocked by a solid phalanx of ghosts, of all sorts and sizes, Traveler and Acton's people alike, standing ready. More joined them, including the young officer. Although their numbers were not large, there were too many for the path, so they spread out along the ridge, forming a half-circle of resistance.

Flax looked at Zel, and motioned her to join him, but Saker reached out and took her hand tightly. She made a movement towards Flax, but stopped. Her hand tightened around Saker's, and he was filled with a warmth he'd never known before.

Alder snarled at Saker as he pushed past him to confront the newcomers. For once, Saker was glad the ghosts could not talk.

The sun was lowering. Saker was overcome with impatience. They had to act now! Or it would be too late. He didn't know why he was so sure—it wasn't Sight, not as it normally felt. It was something else, some animal sense that told him they had very little time left.

"Push them aside," he said to Owl. "Don't hurt them."

Owl laughed at him. Then he took a step forward and swung his battleaxe straight at Flax. Zel cried out and leapt forward, pushing Owl to the ground before the blow could connect.

Flax dragged her upright and pushed her back to Saker, making shooing motions with his hands as he might have shooed chickens back to roost. He was right, Saker thought. Zel was one of the few who could be hurt. One of the few still left alive.

Owl stood up, his face contorted with rage, and raised the axe again.

"Stop!" Saker said. This time he put power into it, and Owl, thank the gods, stilled with his axe high, then slowly put it down, resting the blade on the earth.

"Fighting each other will not help," Saker continued. But Alder turned to him and took him by the shoulders, shaking him. Shaking his teeth loose in his head, making his neck feel it was about to crack.

"Someone's coming from the city!" Zel shouted. Saker followed her to a vantage point. The ring of new ghosts parted to let them look down.

There was a party coming up the path: the leader, a small blonde woman, carried antlers, a symbol that warlords had used for centuries in the borderlands between domains, to show that they were a hunting party, not a party of war.

"Someone's coming up this way, too!" a man shouted from the back of Alder's group. "A man and a Traveler woman—they've got a ghost with them!"

Saker relaxed. More recruits. He looked down the hill again. There were warlords in that band—he recognized Thegan, from Sendat. How dare he show his face! And others—Merroc, from Far South; old Coeuf, from South. There were women, too, and a handful of officers.

They would want to negotiate. To save their city. But they had chosen badly, if they thought he would negotiate with Thegan—with any of them! Sendat had shown there could be no peace, no justice, no surrender.

He could feel that the ghost coming up the other side of the hill was the last one, that the spell was finally ending. He glanced over and saw the ghost, a big man, flanked by a Traveler couple, step onto the plateau.

The spell faded away. Then the world shook beneath him.

BRAMBLE

As they climbed the hill, Bramble was aware of a great hissing murmur. The ghost army couldn't talk, but the noise of their movement was like the noise of the sea on a calm day.

Acton looked out over the plateau. It was filled with ghosts, and they had spilt into the market gardens below as well. Thousands upon thousands.

"They are opposing him," Baluch said thoughtfully, pointing to a group blocking the path to the city. "They are refusing him access to the town."

Acton wasn't listening. He was still looking down, his face stricken. He gestured widely, to include all the ghosts, then tapped his own chest and looked at Bramble questioningly, pleading.

"All your fault?" Bramble asked. She paused. What should she say? What did she truly believe? It was hard to find the right words. She had tussled with this herself: how could she love a killer? Unless she accepted that she, too, would have fought and killed and invaded, if she had been him. But although she loved him, could finally allow herself to accept him as he was, that didn't mean he had been blameless.

"Some are not your fault. The ones Hawk killed. The ones that someone now has killed. But there are others. River Bluff. T'vit. More. You invaded, and you killed, and you took. I accept that Hawk had to die, if only to rescue Wili. But after that—after that you just took what you wanted, because you wanted it. Because you wanted a harbor. Because you wanted to go to sea. Because you thought a death in battle was a good death, but it's not. It's just death."

Tears were riding down his cheeks, and he bowed his head as though accepting her judgment. Bramble looked away from him, and once she had she couldn't look anywhere else but at Maryrose, who was staring down the enchanter's forces with disdain. Bramble's heart was flooded with warmth and she felt her hands loosen from fists.

"He's called them all," Bramble said, finding her voice, fighting tears. "He's said the wrong words, and called everyone who died because of the invasion."

Acton pointed and she looked and saw another group of ghosts forming—warlord's men, and by the way they were behaving, they knew each other. Men Saker's army had killed, perhaps. They'd died with weapons in their hands, so they had swords and pikes now. They began to make their way across the headland towards Saker, swords drawn, a wedge of order in the throng. They were going to attack.

Acton ran onto the plateau, straight for Saker, grabbing a sword from another ghost as he passed. Baluch ran after him.

Bramble took a few steps after them when something under her feet shifted, putting her off balance. Then the gods cried out to her: *Help us!* And she fell to the ground as it seemed to shake beneath her. The force of the cry was so great that she began to crawl back down the slope, to get to them. They needed her.

She scrambled back to her feet and looked down to the harbor below, the quickest way to the altar from here. The ships were bursting into flame, the harbor boiling with water spirits. The mob that had clamored to get onto the ships now scrambled to get off, pushing and shoving back along the docks to the city. The entrances were now held by warlord's men, and they were ruthless; they chopped down anyone who tried to break the barricade.

The only other way into the city was to cross the plateau through the army of ghosts.

She turned back to the headland. Below her, Acton was fighting off a group of warlord's men, standing in front of Saker like Lady Death herself. She ran down, pushing the cold bodies of the ghosts aside as she went, so that it felt like she was running into winter, her veins freezing moment by moment. It was hard to run away from the city—the call of the gods was still drawing her, pulling her hard.

As she ran, she shouted. "Don't kill him! We need him! Don't kill him!"

She heard Baluch's voice added to hers. "The Well of Secrets says not to kill him!"

Those were words of power. When she reached the enchanter, the two sides had stopped fighting and were facing off. Baluch stepped between them and Bramble wished hard that Ash were there, to let Acton speak for himself.

"The Well of Secrets," Baluch said slowly, looking at the ghosts of the warlord's men, "has told us to keep him alive until she gets here."

The leader was a young officer, very young, with only a small wound, a cut on his arm. He gazed at the enchanter and at the ghosts around him with absolute hatred. The officer sheathed his sword and motioned to his men to do the same. But he stood his ground, as though merely waiting for permission to attack.

The enchanter turned to Acton. "I thank you, sir," he said formally.

Bramble was impatient. She had to get back to the altar in the city. But the pressure to return to Turvite suddenly lifted, as though the gods no longer needed help. Or had found it elsewhere.

Ash, Bramble thought, taking a deep breath. Martine. Maybe Safred. She relaxed a little, but it didn't feel as though the crisis was over; the gods were not shouting in her ears but they were still distressed.

Maryrose smiled down at her. Touching Acton had been horrible, but she couldn't help it: she threw her arms around Maryrose, ignoring the burial cave scent and the cold, cold skin. Maryrose hugged her. Stroked her hair. And for a moment, just a moment, everything stopped. They were at the center of the world, the center of life itself. But her body rebelled against the chilly embrace, and she shivered, the movement bringing her to the here and now.

Bramble pulled back and blinked tears away. "We'll solve this," she told Maryrose. "And then you can just wait for me, so we can go on to rebirth together."

Maryrose nodded seriously, her eyes approving. Bramble felt a familiar warmth grow under her ribs; only Maryrose had ever really approved of her. Maryrose and Acton, maybe.

When she moved up the ridge to get a better view of the city, her gaze was drawn by an odd movement in the sky. She gasped. Wind wraiths were streaming towards the city from out at sea, a long arrowhead of wraiths heading straight for them. They had a long way to come, but they were so *fast*. Bramble had never seen them before, but she knew immediately.

Wind wraiths, fire spirits—Tern's compact was crumbling. That was why the gods had cried out.

Bramble grabbed the enchanter by the shoulder and spun him around. "Look what you've done!" she cried, pointing to the sky. "The compact is broken apart!"

He paled and took a step back, as if to run from the wraiths, then stood his ground. "I did nothing to the compact," he said.

"Your shagging spell broke it!" she hissed. "Fix it or we're all dead."

He stared at her and she realized he was no older than she was, certainly no more than thirty.

"I don't know how," he said. He frowned, his eyes unfocusing as she had seen Martine's do, and Safred's, when they used the Sight. She thought to the gods, urgently, *What should he do?* but they didn't reply.

ASH

ASH AND Martine kept in the back of the parley group as they walked out of the Moot Hall and up the hill, Ranny in the front with the antlers. Martine pushed Arvid forward, her hand in the small of his back so unconsciously intimate that Ash stared, and she flushed. What was it with women and warlords? First Bramble, now *Martine*? He felt like all certainty was crumbling. *Martine?*

"He's a good man," she said defensively. "A Valuer."

Of course he was a Valuer. A warlord Valuer. That made perfect sense. Ash snorted his disbelief.

They walked up the hill in silence, towards the waiting death, danger, stone and water.

Safred came back to join them. She gave a brief outline of the attack on the city and how the ghosts and their human allies had been repulsed. "There was panic, though, and people stormed the ships in port," she said. "I healed the ones I could, but many of the sailors died. Zel's aunty, for one."

Zel's aunty? He'd never even heard of Zel's aunty. He didn't know what to say.

"Ash... are you all right?"

He shrugged. What could he say? Yes? No? Both were lies.

"You killed Doronit?"

"Broke her neck," he said harshly, glad in a way to make her wince. It may be he *was* dangerous. "She would have broken the barricade and joined the enchanter, else."

Safred nodded sadly. It infuriated him, as though this was all her fault.

"Well, you wanted a killer, didn't you? You needed someone who could do whatever needed to be done. *Didn't you?*"

"Yes," she said. Her green eyes were bright with tears, but she didn't cry.

The fury drained out of him. At the same moment the gods cried out. He and Safred and Martine all jerked to a stop. *Help us!* the many-layered voices cried into their minds.

They all forgot the parley and turned to run downhill, towards the old part of the city where the black rock altar stood under its canopy of oak leaves. Martine called back: "Sorn, the gods need us!" Sorn ran after them.

As they came towards the open space where the great oak tree grew, Ash could hear the local gods shouting, *No! NO!*

A shudder went through them all and the ground shifted under their feet. Ash was thrown to the ground. He didn't know what was happening. Part of him felt a strong urge to run, run to the headland. Another part wanted to run as far from there as he could.

"His spell of calling is ending," Safred said, her voice shaking. "He has called all the ghosts. All the angry dispossessed of the Eleven Domains. All of them are here, now."

The pressure of the spell increased before it tapered off, but underneath it Ash could feel something else—something being pushed, stretched, bent past breaking point. Another spell, old, old, deep in the ground...it was cracking under Saker's power, as a weir will crack in a flood. The water doesn't care. Doesn't even notice the weir. But the cracks widen...

"The compact!" Safred gasped. She was white with terror. "The spell is breaking apart the compact. Breaking into pieces!"

Ash dragged himself up and they ran on. In quick flashes, Ash remembered: water spirits lying in wait in the Sharp River; wind wraiths above the cliffs of Turvite, long claws reaching for his throat; wraiths in the uplands of Golden Valley, slashing at Horst, harrying him for sport. Only the compact stopped that happening, all over the Domains.

They could hear screams coming from the harbor. He looked involuntarily down a side street, and saw the topmost masts above the nearby houses. As he watched, balls of yellow light descended on them and they burst into flame. He had never seen a fire wraith before, and his whole body went cold. The protective spell might keep them from the city, but for how long?

At last, they reached the open space where the altar was. The ground around the altar was churning, in a wide circle that matched the oak tree's shade.

"Delvers!" Safred gasped.

In the circle of broken earth there were boulders moving, seeming to wade through the ground, pushing cobblestones aside in waves. They advanced slowly, but inexorably, towards the altar. Their circle grew smaller.

Ash hesitated. Delvers: no one knew their weaknesses; they did not vanish in air, they could not be hurt by sword or spear or fire or water or any human strength. He gathered his courage and ran towards the altar, leaping over the circle of delvers and turning to face the nearest ones, his back to the altar.

Safred and Martine gathered their skirts up around their knees and leapt, too, crowding as close to the altar as they could. Safred spoke out in the voice of the dead, the healing language transmuted into a challenge. Ash had the impression that they had turned their backs as if uninterested, although the shapes didn't actually turn. They moved towards the altar with purpose, and all Ash and the others could do was stand and watch.

"We have to strengthen the compact!" he said to Safred.

"I don't know how!" she wailed.

"It's hurt." He shook her shoulders. "Heal it!"

"I'm empty! Ever since the ship . . . I am empty!"

He didn't know what she was talking about, but they had to act, or it would be too late. He put his hand on her shoulder and willed his strength to her, as he had done when Bramble was dying.

"I'm full," he said. "Use me. You've done it before."

She put her hands flat on the altar and closed her eyes, Ash's hands on her shoulders from behind. Ash closed his own eyes, and straight away he could sense the cracks in the old spell. Beyond them was chaos. Safred began to sing, her harsh voice cutting through the air.

Ash reached for the River, to see if She could lend her strength, but She was distant. He could feel a strange ambivalence from Her, and realized, with a shock, that the water sprites were Her creatures, after all, born of Her, living only within Her. He would think about that later.

Now he turned his attention to Safred and poured whatever strength he could find to her. There was a curious emptiness about her, a hollowness in the center of her presence, but it was surrounded by power and strength, and he guided her to that, drew on it himself and fed it back to her.

He might be a killer, but he could also help heal.

Safred's song wound itself down into the altar, into the spell itself, but it was as though it was as insubstantial as the air she used to make it. It did nothing, merely seeped between the cracks and dissipated.

She stopped singing and looked at Ash in despair. The delvers had slowed, but they were still advancing, and they were closer than before, inside the circle of oak tree shadow.

Martine joined hands with Safred. "Let's try again."

They closed their eyes and Safred started to sing again. This time, as the song went down, Martine's strength was there. She was speaking.

"It's like the other spell, to keep the ghosts out," she whispered. The words were like a shout in Ash's ear. "Safred, it goes like this: 'Spirits, come not within my home; spirits, be barred from my home; spirits, enter not my door.' "

Astonished, Ash realized that she was singing the same five notes that Doronit had taught him, to send away the wind wraiths.

Safred sang the same tune, but the cracks kept growing. Safred worked harder, her voice hoarse with effort. There were layers to the compact spell, Ash realized. It was like a cloth with four layers, and the bottom layer was unravelling. That was why the delvers could come right inside the city while the fire and wind spirits were still kept outside. But to get to that layer, to repair it, Safred had to go through the top layers, and it was only where the cracks were deepest that she could do it without causing more damage.

"The spell's not right!" Ash said. "There are four layers. There has to be four—something."

They paused for a moment; Safred's song stopped. They could feel the old spell breaking further apart every moment, and the noise of the delvers grinding through the earth was louder each moment.

What would happen when they reached the altar? Ash wondered.

Would they simply grind it into pieces, the compact destroyed, the gods made homeless?

"Wind, water, stone... " Martine hesitated. "Fire, too, I suppose. Try this, Safred: 'Spirits of wind, come not within my home, spirits of water, come not within my home, spirits of fire, come not within my home, spirits of air, come not within my home.' "

"No," Safred said. "Didn't you see what was happening? Ash's strength went to the third layer, yours went to the second, and mine to the top. We can repair one layer each, I think, but I don't know why."

Ash knew. Of course, now he thought about it.

"The third layer is water," he said.

Martine looked down at her hands, as if admitting something embarrassing. "The second is fire," she said. "I think the top one must be air."

"We sing to our strengths?" Safred said doubtfully, but they had no time to debate it. "We have no one for earth, then."

"Use me," Cael said. He had limped into the square after them without Ash noticing and was being supported by Lady Sorn.

"Cael is earth," Martine said. "Anyone can see that."

Cael looked at Safred, and smiled slightly.

"No choice, niece," he said.

Safred bit her lip and held out her hand.

He gauged the height of the delvers—barely past his knees, but he shook his head. Sorn lent him her arm for balance and he simply walked over the top of one, putting his boot down on it firmly and thrusting off. The delver made a crashing noise that almost split Ash's head in two but Cael was unaffected, although the effort of stepping down opened his wound again—Ash could see lines of blood and pus seeping through his shirt.

Cael leant thankfully on the altar. They joined hands again and all began to sing the words Martine had suggested, each taking one element.

"Spirit of water, come not within my home," Ash sang, in the voice of the dead, feeling like a traitor to the River, knowing there would be a reckoning with Her, one day, for this, but also feeling that it was one way to make up for sending the wind wraiths south.

"Spirit of fire, come not within my home," Martine sang, and the words felt sad, as if she were relinquishing something valuable.

"Spirit of air, come not within my home," Safred sang, in the voice of the dead.

"Spirit of earth, come not within my home," Cael sang, his voice gravelly and low.

This time the cracks started joining, supporting, reforming.

Cael had no power of Sight or healing, yet his voice resonated somehow with the lowest layer and at first they were hopeful, as they saw the cracks slow in their progress. Ash marvelled at the size and complexity of the compact spell. Whoever had done it had been a great enchanter, with a mind as complicated as—Ash didn't know what to compare it to.

But the lowest one was the hardest to reach, and the one that had cracked most, and it resisted every effort he made. After the three top layers were mostly healed, they tried to help him, all singing "Spirits of stone, come not . . . ", until they were all exhausted, propped up on the altar stone like drunks against an inn table, but it did no good. Cael was not strong enough. His song was barely reaching the top part of the lowest layer. Caught in the middle of the spell, Ash could sense how weak he was. How near death.

They paused, just for a moment. The three top layers stayed firm and steady, but the lower one began to fragment further immediately.

"Don't try to heal me, niece," Cael said, and took a deep breath.

"No, don't!" Safred cried, but it was too late. Cael let out the breath in a last, long, passionate song.

"Spirits of stone, come not within my home," he sang, and poured out all the strength he had down into the lowest layer of the spell. All his love. All his devotion to Safred. All his decent, kind, cheerful life. The life of someone without gifts, without power, without anything except circumstance to make him special. The life of someone who had wanted to be an ordinary husband and father, until those things were ripped away from him. Ash felt it go; honored him; envied him. It wouldn't have been enough. Ash could See that it wouldn't have been enough; but as his life poured out, something else went, too—the remnant power of the Forest, which had been keeping his wound fresh, which had been killing him slowly. That power went down deep, deeper even than the River, and as Cael died that power left him, spearing into the earth, returning home by a route deeper even than the fourth layer. That spear of power took Cael's strength with it, down deep enough, strongly enough, to reach the cracks.

Then Cael was dead, and his body fell against Ash's shoulder. But the cracks in the lowest layer had stopped growing.

And the delvers had disappeared. Ash sighed with relief. He took a deep breath and stepped back, well away from the altar. Martine rolled her shoulders and shook her head like a dog coming out of water.

Safred rubbed at her eyes, her face white. "It's not fully healed," she said with difficulty. Trying to stay intent on their task. Ash wanted to pat her on the shoulder, but guessed that would take away the last of her self-control. "That lower layer is beginning to fray again."

The ground burst open beneath their feet.

Ash staggered, tripping and falling on his back, rolling as he had been taught and coming to his feet with his knife in his hand—but of course there was no human enemy to face. Safred had fallen on her side. He hauled her up and away from the altar. Martine backed away on the other side of the altar.

"They're coming!" Safred cried.

The ground was roiling around the black rock, heaving and splitting, cobblestones spinning away, mounds rising and falling. Then some of the mounds shook themselves and became the dark shapes of delvers, hard to see in the bright sunlight. They had moved slowly before, but now they were much faster, as though they were running out of time.

The gods were silent. The delvers crowded around the altar and it began to sink into the ground, as a foundering ship sinks into the sea.

"No!" the lady Sorn cried out, as though her heart was being ripped away.

It was so quick, Ash didn't have time to move. The altar, Cael's body still on it, was sucked into the dirt and disappeared in a few heartbeats, and the delvers followed it, leaving the ground beneath the oak tree looking like it had been dug over for planting.

The tree itself seemed unharmed. Everything was exactly the same; but the altar was gone.

Sorn sank to her knees and wept.

Ash, Safred and Martine went to the spot where it had been, and stared helplessly at the ground. Where had they taken him? Then Martine knelt and brushed away some dirt. The toe of Cael's boot. Safred's face sagged with relief, and she looked a decade older than she was.

"They have buried him," Martine said. "As a mark of respect, I think. But the altar . . . "

"This is what the gods feared," Safred whispered to herself. "The enchanter has broken the compact—the lower layer kept the delvers out." She turned and looked at Ash, green eyes wide in a white face. "We must defeat him and rebuild the compact. Or the world crumbles for everyone, including Travelers."

BRAMBLE

"DO SOMETHING!" she screamed at the enchanter.

He shook his head, his mouth open, watching the wind wraiths with clear terror. Useless. The wind wraiths were closing in, and someone by the stream yelled out, "Water sprites! There's water sprites in the creek!"

On the edge of the plateau, the ground shifted slightly, as though something moved underneath. Bramble knew what it was. Delvers. She was glad there was nothing to burn on the headland to tempt fire wraiths. They would head for the city. Then she was ashamed of the thought.

Suddenly the wind wraiths paused in their arrow flight. She could hear their harsh shrieking even from here. They were protesting something.

The gods had found help, Bramble thought. Safred? Ash? Where in the cold hells were they?

The fine trembling beneath her feet died out of the ground, and the world felt solid again. Almost. Something was still not right. But the wind wraiths cawed frustration and wheeled again out to sea, and the water spirits let the cascade of the stream take them over the cliff into the wild sea. Bramble took a breath, and looked at the enchanter. He smiled at her in relief and she wanted to hit him more than she had ever wanted anything. But she couldn't kill him yet. The compact had to be fixed, first, and the ghosts laid to rest. *Then.*

Acton moved behind the enchanter, and Saker turned his head and nodded, as though Acton was one of his men. Of course he would believe that of someone who had just saved his life, but Bramble wondered why Acton was letting him believe it.

"Where is Ash?" she asked Baluch.

He swallowed as though he found it difficult to talk. "He was helping the gods," he said. "She isn't happy about that."

Too bad for Her, Bramble thought. She turned and noticed a parley group being led up the hill by a woman carrying antlers as a sign of peaceful intent. Warlords, most likely. Yes, there was Thegan. It was a measure of how perilous their world had become that Thegan seemed barely a threat to her now. She recognized Coeuf from Wooding, puffing and wheezing after the climb, and Leof. It was odd to see him again, as if she'd met him in another life. He looked older, tired.

Flax motioned his ghostly allies back, to let the parley group through, and Bramble looked around for Acton. She found him staring at the crowd with intent eyes. Assessing, as a commander sums up the situation before attacking. A female ghost moved to his side and touched his arm. Asa! His mother. She hadn't gone on to rebirth, had waited all this time…and Friede was with her, greeting Baluch with mock astonishment at his advanced age. Baluch's eyes were bright with tears and she touched his cheek comfortingly.

Other people were greeting their dead—Thegan's sergeant, even Thegan. He went to the band of warlord's men and greeted them; they stood straighter, and whatever he said made them feel proud. Then he motioned them back. That isn't over, Bramble thought. He's the only warlord here with armed men at his back, now. He'll use them, sooner or later. She looked at Acton to warn him, but he was already watching Thegan, eyes narrowed.

Saker stepped forward, looked around at each member of the parley group, and said, "My name is Saker, son of Alder." He indicated the scowling ghost standing behind him.

"What do you want?" Thegan asked in a reasonable tone, as if he were in command of the parley. But Saker had Thegan's measure, she could see.

"Justice," Saker said. "Justice for murder and dispossession that has lasted a thousand years."

"There's no justice this side of the grave," Thegan said.

"Then we shall send you to the other side to seek it," Saker said through gritted teeth. "My ghosts —"

Flax shook his head and raised his hand outwards against Saker, and so did the others with him. Saker stopped speaking, as though waiting for them to move back.

The ghosts who had stood with Flax moved closer together to show their support. The parley now stood in a circle of ghosts. As more ghosts came from lower down the slope to see what was happening, the circle widened to let them see, until it took up almost all of the plateau.

Bramble watched Acton. He seemed to just stand there, but the ghosts on either side of him had moved back, without realizing it, she suspected, to leave him a little ahead. Baluch stood, as always, at his shoulder. The ghosts who had noticed Acton looked at him as often as they looked at the enchanter and the parley group. None seemed to recognize him.

The parley leader laid the antlers at Saker's feet, as though the warlord hadn't spoken. "I am Ranny of Highmark, of the council of Turvite," she said. "I come to parley with the enchanter Saker, son of Alder."

"I greet you, Ranny of Highmark," Saker said.

"Saker, enchanter, we in Turvite seek to do no harm to you or yours. We ask for truce, so that a peaceful settlement can be reached which is satisfactory to us both."

"Our land was taken from us. We want it back. That would satisfy us."

"All of it?" she said disbelievingly.

"All." Saker looked disdainfully at her. He glanced behind him to his father, who was nodding approval.

"You would have to kill thousands of people," Ranny said.

"Yes," Saker said.

Bramble grew hot with rage, and then cold. She would gut this madman from stem to stern, and be doing the world a favor. He spoke as though lives were nothing, as though he were Lady Death herself, with the right to pick and choose who would die.

The ghosts moved on the grass, some in excitement, but some in unease. Not all of Saker's army wanted to kill. But that solved nothing. At the worst—or the best—it meant an unending battle between Saker's ghosts and the others, with neither side vulnerable, neither side bearing any losses.

Saker sensed his army's unease and turned to them, his face reassuring. "The world will become safe again, for us and our blood," he said. The Turviters who had been summoned during the last spell shouted silently at him, shaking their fists. They shouldered their way through the crowd and came to stand behind Flax, their arms linked to block the path. Bramble realized that Cael was one of them, and felt her stomach clench. He winked at her and she smiled a little back.

"Not all your army is of your blood," Ranny said. "Not all obey you."

Saker whirled. "Do you think I cannot winnow them out? Do you think I cannot send them back to the darkness beyond death?"

"Wouldn't surprise me if you couldn't," Bramble spoke up. "As long as they feed themselves blood before sunset. Blood and memory."

He turned to her, his face white, and she fought down the urge to take out her boot knife and gut him. It wouldn't solve anything. She drew breath and let it out again.

Zel came up to Saker and laid a hand on his arm.

"Don't matter," she said. "Don't worry about that. What matters is this: we've got the upper hand first time in a thousand years, and we gotta use it right."

The enchanter's father nodded urgently, staring at Zel approvingly. Saker shook himself and stood upright, opening his mouth to make some kind of proclamation.

There was a disturbance on the path leading down to the city. The solid ghosts of Turvite were moving aside, shoving each other out of the way, as four people clambered up hastily.

Thanks the gods! Ash, Martine, Safred. And Sorn.

Sorn walked straight to Saker, still panting from the climb. She was more beautiful than when Bramble had last seen her, and seemed stronger, somehow.

Sorn caught her breath. "Saker, son of Alder, do you respect the gods?" she asked in a gentle voice.

He drew himself up as though she had insulted him. "Of course I do!"

"But your actions have harmed them. Your spell—your last spell—damaged the compact."

The enchanter paled and cast a look over his shoulder at the wind wraiths. They had pulled back, but they were still there. He cleared his throat. "The compact was repaired. I felt it."

Sorn shook her head. "Not fully. It will fragment again, soon." She turned and motioned Safred forward. "Saker, enchanter, greet Safred, the Well of Secrets."

Safred paused, weighing her words. "If you continue, there will be nothing for anyone—for the Travelers you want to help, the other inhabitants of this land, even the gods themselves. Is that what you want?"

Alder gestured vigorously, mouthing angry words. It was time to act, because apparently Acton wasn't going to do anything. Yet. Bramble nodded at Ash.

"Speak," he said to Alder.

"If we can't have the land as we should, no one will!" Alder shouted, in the deep voice of the grave. It made the words harsher, and everyone recoiled, ghosts and humans alike. Except the smaller ghost at his side, who shook his axe. Saker looked stunned, Acton thoughtful. The language lessons had worked well enough for him to understand Alder—their two languages were separated mostly by changes in pronunciation.

"You can make them speak!" Saker exclaimed.

"Kill them all," the small ghost said in the old tongue. Bramble bit her lip—that phrase brought back too many memories.

"When our land is regained, I will repair the compact," Saker said. Martine and Ash and Safred all shook their heads immediately. Saker turned to Ash. "You are lying."

"No," Ash said. "The compact is made of four spells, and needs four—four with power—to repair it. I can weave back the water strand, Safred the air, Martine the fire. We need you to stop the earth spirits. But you need *us*. You'll never do it alone."

Ash looked up at someone over Saker's shoulder, and Bramble saw his face freeze, then he nodded slightly at one of the ghosts, an attractive woman in modern dress. She bowed slightly, mockingly.

He turned back to the enchanter, ignoring her. "We must work together."

SAKER

SAKER STARED at the dark-haired enchanter. A man of his own blood, but working with the enemy. He had spoken with authority and conviction. Saker was sure he told the truth. He glanced up—the wind wraiths were closer. He shuddered at the thought of the compact broken, but to work with the enemy, to delay their revenge... His father glowered at him, but above his father's head were wind wraiths, high in the sky, and they were closer, just a little, than before. From the harbor below, smoke rose. He shuddered again, to think of fire spirits loosed upon his Travelers.

The ground beneath his feet seemed to tremble slightly, and the Well of Secrets caught her breath. "Now, Saker, enchanter," she said. "Or it all ends here."

The shrieking of the wind wraiths grew louder and the water in the stream—were shapes there again?

The tall dark-haired woman stepped forward. "You need to know us," she said. "I am Martine. This is Ash. Safred you have met."

She reminded him of his childhood, when everyone in his village had had that dark hair and pale skin. He bowed a little, trying to look formal, but feeling panic rise. If they were going to do it, let them do it now, before the wind wraiths broke through. They were advancing, inexorably, no longer in a single arrowhead but in several lines, as though they were approaching along rips in the spell. Attacking the weak points. His heart pounded hard in his chest. If they broke through, no agreement with him would stand. They would spare no one, including him. Including Zel. He glanced at her and she nodded encouragingly. She seemed to trust these people.

That gave him the courage to draw breath. "The compact spell ends just before the cliffs."

"So we repair it from here, back into the land," Ash said. He held out his hand and Saker hesitatingly took it.

He was used to grasping hands when he cast stones, but this was different. This was a kind of fellowship. Something he had never known. He had never cast a spell with someone before as an equal. Only as Freite's slave.

Martine took Ash's other hand and Safred completed the circle. She began to sing: "Spirit of air, come not within my land..."

Saker twitched and almost lost Ash's grip on his hand. It was an unbearable sound, like the voice his father had spoken in. A voice of power.

"Spirit of fire, come not within my land," Martine sang. Her voice, thankfully, was human.

"Spirit of water, come not within my land," Ash sang, also in the voice of the dead.

Saker felt weak in comparison to this young man. Not only an enchanter, but one who could make the dead speak, and spoke with their voice.

Ash squeezed his hand and Saker cleared his throat. The five notes were awkward, as they didn't quite fit the spell, so he had to concentrate to put words and notes together. "Spirit of earth, come not within my land," he sang, and knew his voice sounded thready beside theirs.

They closed their eyes, and there it was, the compact spell resting deep in the earth, woven out of the earth itself, it almost seemed, its layers distinct but closely adhering.

Ash squeezed Saker's hand again, and Saker gathered his strength and directed the song to the deep cracks in the lowest layer. He felt Ash follow him down to the third layer and sent his song into the fissures, which were growing. He sensed Martine and Safred doing the same to their levels. It was difficult, much more difficult than raising the dead, but there were no hissing spirits from beyond the grave to distract him. And to work a spell with others...to be in company with people like him, to use power to build and strengthen, that was a new thing, and it filled him with a kind of joy.

Saker had no sense of the passage of time, just of his growing weariness. The layer they had given him was the most damaged. Part of him resented it, but the part Freite had trained recognized that they were not suited—not strong in the right way—to knit the fabric of earth together into the spell. Each of the others, he could sense, was connected to something else, something greater than themselves. When he Saw Martine, she was surrounded by a nimbus of fire; Ash had a melody of running water twined around his spell song; Safred, a strangely empty presence, was a vessel, a pathway, for the power of the gods. They were here, through her, and Saker realized that they had inspired the compact in the beginning, had given their strength to the first compact spell, as they were giving Safred strength now. But the gods were not sending all their strength this time. Their attention was elsewhere.

The four of them sent their song out across the compact to the very edges of the Domains. They sang until their throats were raw, until none could draw more power from anywhere; and the fissures closed, slowly, until the world was whole again.

Finally, finally, Ash let his hand go and Saker opened his eyes.

MARTINE

THE WIND wraiths were disappearing, fleeing out to sea like tatters of mist before a gale. The waters of the stream were clear again. The fire wraiths had risen from the harbor in a ball like a second sun and now were gone. The ground no longer trembled beneath her feet.

They were safe.

Martine dropped Ash's hand and stood for a moment with him, coming back to the here and now. Saker stood dazed, hands at his sides. He seemed younger than he had, and much weaker, swaying with exhaustion. Safred merely looked pale.

"Horst," Thegan said softly. Martine turned to catch the warlord whispering to his archer. Thegan nodded towards Saker.

"My lord," Horst said urgently, "we need him alive! The Well of Secrets said —"

"Do what you are told," Thegan replied quietly.

Horst looked down at the bow in his hand, then up where the wind wraiths were scudding away across the sky, and his brows twitched. His eyes met Ash's, and Ash shook his head, pleadingly. Horst's hand opened, slowly, and the bow fell to the ground.

"You will obey me!" Thegan drew back his hand and felled Horst with one blow. Sorn's Leof tried to catch him but had been too far away; Horst came down against one of the many small boulders that dotted the headland.

Something woke in Martine's mind. Not Sight but the memory of Sight. The vision she had had when she was a girl, which Alder had beaten her for. The destruction of Cliffhaven by a warlord's man. By *this* man. He was much older, two decades older, but surely it was him.

She burned inside. This man had killed everyone she had ever loved. Her parents, Elva's parents, her brother, aunties, uncles, cousins...Everyone was gone when she had returned, and strangers lived in her dearest places. She was dizzy with rage and a grief that felt new-minted.

Leof knelt next to Horst and held his shoulders up. He was bleeding heavily from the nose and ears. Ash came and knelt next to them.

"You were right," Horst whispered to them both. "Shouldn't have trusted him." Then his head fell back and blood bubbled out of his ears.

Leof eased him back down to the ground. Another one of Thegan's sergeants arranged his sprawled limbs neatly, smoothing his hair down with a shaking hand.

"He won't obey you again, Thegan," Ash said bitterly. "Not ever."

Saker stepped forward. He held his hand above Horst's body and concentrated.

"This man was of our blood, too, although his blood was thin," he said. "Arise, sergeant."

Horst's ghost rose, hands empty. He stared at Thegan and moved to stand near Leof and Sorn. Saker turned slowly towards the parley group.

Now, Martine thought. If he can be swayed, it's now. She pushed Ash in the back and he took a step forward, put a hand out to Saker.

"There is something you don't know," he said. He held out his pouch of stones. "There is a new stone in the bag."

"What?" Saker said, thrown off his course. "New?"

"Evenness." Ash fished in the bag and brought out a small black stone. It was singing, a high simple song that Martine had never heard from any other stone. A single note, but with overtones and harmonies wreathed around it. It looked so innocent, lying there in his hand, she thought. How could it change anything?

"Change the stones, change the world," Saker whispered, staring at it.

Martine was aware that they were all staring at the new stone, ghosts and warlords and soldiers and councillors. The whole world seemed to be staring at Ash's hand, where the future lay.

"You're a stonecaster," Ash said, indicating the pouch at Saker's waist. "Can't you hear it sing?"

It was singing more loudly, and the other stones in his pouch sang, too. Saker nodded slowly, eyes fixed on the stone. "Evenness," he said. "It sings of fairness. Balance. Justice."

"Yes," Ash said. "Balance." He hesitated. "You were right—it is time for the world to change. But Balance needs *two* sides, not one. Acton's people as well as Travelers."

"Equal," Saker said. He raised burning eyes to Ash, as though the stone had sung him a vision of the future. "Balance means both sides equal."

They looked at each other carefully, and Martine was struck by their similarities: same age, height, powers. What could have pushed Saker to the extremes he had taken? She was filled with pride for Ash—he had said exactly the right things, exactly the right way, and now the world was about to change.

Saker turned slowly and faced the parley group.

"What do you want?" Ranny asked.

"Justice," Saker said. "Equality." He paused, as if thinking through something new to him. "All the laws that push my people into the dirt. The Generation Laws. The laws against owning property. The laws against Travelers being on town councils, or being village voices. The laws must be repealed!"

Saker's army started banging their weapons against each other in support. Flax's group joined in. Only Thegan and his soldiers stayed still.

Even Bramble was stamping now. Martine and Ash joined in, too. Saker was right about this, at least. The laws should change. She watched the warlords. They didn't look happy. Except Arvid. She smiled involuntarily. He had nothing to be ashamed of.

"We have no such laws," Arvid said to Saker.

"The laws will be repealed in Central Domain," Sorn said, in her soft voice. Thegan stepped forward but she stared up at him reprovingly. "They are not just, those laws, and should never have been made."

He stared back at her for a long moment, then turned aside, his fists clenched.

"I'll repeal the laws," Merroc said. "We all will." He looked around, and each warlord nodded, some more readily than others.

"Our land," Saker said, but his voice no longer had the flat tone of obsession, as it had before.

Martine's gaze shifted to a ghost dressed in the ancient style, who moved from behind Saker to Ash's side.

"Speak," Ash said readily, with a flick of a glance at Bramble. Martine realized that this was Acton. *Acton.* They had done it, then. She felt dazed, staring at him. Acton, the invader.

"*Enough* land," he said in the grating voice of the dead. "This country was not fully settled when we came, but there were villages and towns. Give enough back to settle all who wish to be settled."

He hadn't identified himself. Why? The warlords looked at him closely. Thegan's eyes narrowed, as if assessing his identity, but Martine could see they never suspected who he truly was.

"I suppose," Merroc said grudgingly, "we could give you land—enough land to support you."

"Two or three villages in each Domain," Coeuf said, nodding. "Safe havens for you and your kind."

"Good land," Acton put in. "Productive. From the warlords' own estates. Mixed in with everyone else, not fenced off, and separate."

He was enjoying this, Martine saw. Enjoying the game, enjoying hiding who he was, enjoying challenging the warlords. She saw him exchange a smile with Bramble and felt a sudden shock. Sympathy for Bramble overwhelmed her. It was hard enough to love a living warlord, but to love the dead... Martine shivered, imagining Arvid dead. She looked up to find him staring at her, his hazel eyes intent on her face, as though he saw something new there. She could feel her expression soften as she met his gaze, despite herself, and his whole face responded. It was only a moment, and then he turned back, but Martine knew that they had crossed some boundary and were in new territory. Love.

"Two villages in Central Domain," Thegan said, in the tone of one who had no choice, "and two in Cliff Domain. In good farming country. Your people will be safe there. You have my word."

Rage erupted through her. How dare he promise safety and deal only in treachery.

Saker had been looking at the ground, but at Thegan's words he looked up, a rage burning in him, too. "'You have my word'?" he spat. "There were two villages of the old blood in Cliff Domain twenty-three years ago. Warlord's men destroyed them!"

Martine stepped forward, heart pounding, and pointed at Thegan, her whole arm extended so that even those at the back could see. "*You* destroyed them!"

Thegan simply nodded. "It was necessary," he said. He turned to the warlords. "The Ice King was gathering his troops, but I couldn't convince my father that we had to do the same. I *knew* he was going to attack. We had to prepare. So I sacrificed a couple of Traveler villages. I let my father believe the Ice King had attacked them, and he threw everything we had into preparation. And the next year, the king tried to invade. If we hadn't been prepared, the entire Eleven Domains might have been destroyed!"

The other warlords listened with suspicious eyes but nodded slightly, as if to say that they understood.

Martine was full of rage and grief, and Saker's face showed the same mix of emotions. The big ghost next to him was incandescent with fury. He was shouting, shouting and screaming silently with anger. She recognized him, finally. Alder. Of course. The Voice.

"There was a Saker, a young boy, the son of the Voice in Cliffhaven..." she whispered. "I was from Cliffhaven." Saker looked at her, startled. She stared into his eyes. "Saker, son of Alder —" she flicked a glance at his father—"I am Martine, daughter of Swift and Stickleback. I was away from Cliffhaven when..."

Saker swallowed visibly, his face a mixture of joy at finding her and anger at Thegan. He turned back to Thegan. "I was from Cliffhaven. Your men missed me!"

Martine's heart was skipping beats. Saker was Elva's cousin—Alder had been Elva's grandmother's brother.

"All this," Saker said, arms spread wide to encompass the whole ghost army, "is *your* doing."

As though that had been a signal, Alder charged forward, sword raised like a club.

Martine heard a sudden high buzzing, a terrible scraping like fingernails down glass, like an animal in unbearable pain. It split through her skull and she dropped to her knees with the force of it. Ash was holding his head, too, and Bramble was swaying as if dizzy. Saker staggered a few steps, his face chalk white.

Everyone else was stunned into immobility. Except Leof. He ran forward followed by one of Thegan's sergeants, but Alder simply shouldered them aside and brought down his sword.

The blow was blocked, not by Thegan, but by Acton. Alder snarled and swung again, intent on getting to Thegan. What happened next was too fast for Martine to follow, but in a moment Alder was on the ground, his face in the dirt, and Acton's boot was on his back, his hands holding both swords.

The whining stopped. Martine climbed back to her feet slowly, head still ringing. Safred had fainted, and Sorn was ministering to her.

Alder bucked and threshed on the ground under Acton's foot, with Acton staring down at him with pity. Bramble, her face pale, squatted next to his head.

"You can't win, Alder," she said. "That's Acton."

SAKER

ALDER LAY still.

Saker looked at the ghost who had so easily vanquished his father. Knowledge of his identity wiped out any thought of the screaming from beyond the grave which had erupted when his father lifted his sword.

Acton. Evil incarnate. Invader. He moved only to defend his own, the warlord Thegan. He was dead, Saker reminded himself; Acton could not be killed again. His own tongue swelled in his mouth with rage, gagging him.

Acton moved back, slowly, and Alder got up and faced him, his shoulders hunched and wary. He was frightened.

Frightened. Saker had never seen his father frightened before. Come to that, he'd never seen anyone burlier than his father. Or better able to fight—although, now that he thought of it, Alder never had fought, except as a ghost, when he could not be hurt. His size meant that he only needed to threaten; and he was good at threats.

As though he saw him for the first time, Saker looked at his father. At the fear in his eyes, the servile tilt to the shoulders. He remembered Martine, now. She was the young woman his father had beaten so badly that her whole family had refused to ever speak to Alder again. His father, a beater of women. A coward in front of a stronger man. A bully.

His heart began to beat in long, slow strokes, and he cast around for Zel. Her clear eyes would help him understand all this. She was standing next to her brother, but her gaze was stony on Thegan. Something else they shared, Saker thought. Thegan had killed both their families.

Thegan bowed to Acton, his eyes wide. "My thanks, my lord," he said. Saker thought, now is the proof. The invader will clasp the murderer in his arms and praise him. Acton looked him up and down.

Every warlord there, every warlord's officer, every attendant and council member, waited for his response.

Acton mimed spitting in the dust at Thegan's feet, and moved away.

Thegan paled.

"Speak," Ash said to Acton, with some satisfaction.

But Acton ignored Thegan and turned to Alder and Saker. "The dead should not kill the living," he said.

"Who heard them?" Safred asked, leaning on Sorn for support. "Who heard the crying from beyond death?"

Martine raised her hand. Then Ash, Bramble. Saker, finally, raised his own, and then others in the crowd of ghosts followed him. There weren't many—perhaps one in a hundred. Saker remembered the other times he had heard that sound: when he had raised the ghosts. It had started after the first battle at Spritford, he realized. After the dead had first killed the living.

He had thought it was the spirits of those he had killed shrieking for revenge. But... they were here. He had raised them all, and they stood before him. Who was it, then? Who was calling from beyond the burial caves?

The last sunlight disappeared, and they were left in the gray light of dusk.

Safred broke the silence, speaking to Martine and Ash. "We will deal with that later, I think," she said.

Safred turned back to him from the crowd. "Acton is here," she said, "to make reparation. Just as at a quickening. To acknowledge the wrongs that have been done in his name, and to offer sorrow for those wrongs."

A susurration went around the ghosts. Then one began to gently stamp her feet in approval. It was taken up immediately by the other ghosts, of both sides, so that they were surrounded by a circle of noise, so many ghosts stepping together that the rhythmic tread made the ground shake.

"Wait!" Saker cried. He flung up his hands, palms out, to quieten them. Gradually, the stamping died away. "Yes!" he said. "The warlord should acknowledge what was done. But I have acted to safeguard the future of your descendants. It's still undecided where they are to go."

"They're welcome in the Last Domain," Arvid offered.

Saker nodded to him, then addressed the ghosts: "Do you wish your descendants to live in the Last Domain, safe?"

Many of the ghosts began to stamp again, but Zel came forward, hotly. "No! That means they've finally won. They've got rid of us altogether!" She turned to Saker. "Can't you make another spell? Let them—" she pointed at the warlords, "let them change the laws and give us land, and you put a spell on them so that if they break their word and hurt us, the ghosts will rise again?"

Saker was uncertain. That was a very complex spell, and would he be left in peace to make it? He doubted that. He hesitated. "We cannot trust any warlord after what *he* did," he said, pointing at Thegan.

"But Thegan is no longer lord of Central Domain," Sorn said clearly. "I have renounced him, since he cannot give me heirs."

Thegan started towards her but Acton intercepted him and two of the other warlords moved to flank her, staring Thegan down. One of them, the younger one, smiled, and Saker saw a sudden resemblance to Thegan. Was this Gabra, his son, who held Cliff Domain for him?

"And I," Gabra said, "have discovered my true father is Masry, past warlord of Cliff Domain, and I will hold that Domain as his only son." He paused, as Thegan stared at him, face showing nothing. "Travelers will be safe in my Domain. The villages of Cliffhaven will be given back to them, complete, as they were taken, and the laws will be repealed."

Saker smiled at his father. Their villages regained! But his father only scowled at him and Saker realized, as if for the first time, that nothing would satisfy Alder but death, and more death. That he was so angry about his own death that he would kill the entire world. He thought, Father has never looked for others from Cliffhaven. Never tried to find out what happened to the others. Only him.

Thegan stood very still, and smiled at both Sorn and Gabra, as if at children, then turned to the other warlords. "These things," he said, "are not to be decided here. Do you want this man to hold you ransom? To threaten that if you do not treat his people well enough, he will raise another army? How well is 'well enough'? If one of them gets a stubbed toe because your roads are not smooth enough for them, will he blame you?"

They were frowning. Oh, he was so persuasive. So *reasonable*. Saker could see them listening to him, but didn't know what to say to make them realize that they were listening to one of the soul eaters in human flesh.

Then Ash stepped forward. "Right here, right now, we have seen this man strike down an innocent man," he said loudly. "Is this someone who should be *listened* to?"

The ghosts stamped their approval.

"Who are you to ask?" Thegan hissed.

Ash looked him straight in the eye. "I am the one who raised Acton's ghost. I am the one who allows him to speak. Don't you think it's time we heard from the real Lord of War?" The ghosts pounded their feet; the ground trembled. "Speak, Acton," Ash said. He looked around the waiting circle. "And remember, the dead cannot lie."

Acton turned, slowly, giving each ghost in the circle a chance to look at him. The moon was coming up, and it painted him silver, quicksilver.

"I am Acton, Lord of War," he announced in the ancient language, but in the same voice his father and Safred and Ash had used. The voice of the dead. The voice of power. A rustle went through the crowd. "But I am *not* a warlord!" Then he repeated himself in the common tongue. This time, there were exclamations from the parley group.

They gave way to a silence so intense that Saker felt the rocks themselves were listening.

"I opposed the warlord system," Acton proclaimed, first in one language, and then in the other. "I wanted everything to be run by councils, as it was in Turvite. And that is why they killed me, and hid my bones."

Saker was dumbstruck. That couldn't be true. But Ash said the dead couldn't lie. The ghosts stared, openmouthed; the warlords listened, their cheeks blanched, seeing their world crumbling. Ranny and the other Turvite councillors smiled.

But Owl came forward and shook his sword in Acton's face, and spat on the ground at his feet.

Acton's face changed, from challenge to compassion. "Yes," he said gently, in the old language. "I led the invasion. And I killed." He turned to the ghosts. "I am your killer. Lo, I proclaim it: it was I who took your lives from you. I am here to offer reparation—blood for blood." He repeated it so everyone would understand.

"You have no blood to offer," Thegan said.

Acton turned slowly to look at him. Thegan backed a pace.

"If *you* had not destroyed Saker's village, Thegan," Safred said, "none of this would have happened. It seems to me that it is up to you to offer blood for blood."

Saker couldn't take in what Acton had said. Not responsible for the warlords? Did it make any difference? He'd said he *was* responsible for the invasion. Who was to blame? Who was *really* to blame? Saker spoke as if he were in a dream: "The blood must be offered freely."

"I offer nothing," Thegan said. "Anything you get from me you must take."

I will take it willingly, Saker thought. This was one sacrifice he was happy to cut himself. Only the past knew who was responsible for the warlord system. But Thegan, he knew for certain, was the killer of all he had held dear. He took a step forward and Thegan bent, whipped a knife from his boot and struck out at him. Lightning fast, lightning sharp. One of the officers lunged, Ash took a quick step and drew his own knife, but they were too late. As Thegan moved on him, Zel threw herself between them with a tumbler's litheness and the blade meant for Saker's heart sliced into Zel's neck. The two men each grabbed one of Thegan's arms, but he did not fight them. He simply turned his head to the blond officer and said, "You fool. You could have killed him more easily than I, and this would be over."

Saker made a wordless sound, feeling as if the knife had cut his heart open. He caught Zel as she fell, her blood pumping out in spurts from the wound. Safred came to stand next to them then, as if compelled, she sank down to her knees and placed her hand on Zel's chest. Saker looked up in sudden hope, but Safred shook her head. Zel's brother had dropped to the ground and buried his face in his hands.

Zel's blood slowed, and stopped. It was fast, Saker thought, fast and painless, and he clung to the thought to stop the tears, which were hard in his throat, from bursting out.

Saker lowered Zel gently to the ground and stood up, his eyes blank. His hands were stained red and he stared at them, then raised both so that he could smear his forehead and cheeks with streaks of her blood, willing her to rise and join him, willing it as he had never willed anything before.

She rose instantly and stood beside him, smiling at Thegan.

"This crime was committed on Turvite soil," Ranny said, hurrying her words to forestall him. "He will be punished. Hanged."

Saker turned his gaze towards her, not able to think, barely able to feel. He took Zel's cold hand and looked at Acton. "Blood is not enough," he said. He could hear that his voice was the voice of madness: flat, emotionless, empty. "You do not know how much pain you have caused. You offer blood, but you do not offer sorrow." He swung his hand in a wide arc and his heart seemed to swell in his chest. He felt as if he were going to die, and he welcomed the feeling. He wanted to die. Wanted to join her. Every ghost here had felt like that, had suffered as he was suffering. "Look at them!" he whispered. The silence was so intense that the words reached the whole plateau. "Look at them. Each of them was hurt. Each of them died. Each of them grieved." His voice gradually took on feeling, each sentence louder and darker. Anger was building in him, as thunder builds before a storm. He let it loose: "You cannot ask forgiveness when you do not know the evil you have done!"

He whirled on Ash, clutching him by the shoulders. "Make them speak!" he pleaded. "Make them all speak! Let them tell the true story of what has been done. Let it all be remembered."

The ghosts were listening hard. Saker let Ash go and went into the middle of the circle, turning so that he could see them all.

"You must be heard!" he shouted. "You must be listened to! Your deaths were an evil which should never have happened, but your stories can be told. Your stories can be *remembered*."

The ghosts, hesitantly, stamped their approval.

"Come," Saker said to Acton. "Come and hear."

Acton walked to stand beside him, and Ash took a step forward. Ash, his first ever real ally.

"Speak," Ash said quietly, fervently, turning on the spot so he could see every one of them. "Speak."

As one, they opened their mouths and spoke, in the terrible voices of the dead.

ASH

THE NOISE was so great, so huge, it sent Ash staggering to the ground. Saker, likewise, lost his footing. Acton held his arm to steady him. The voices were stabbing into his head. This wasn't what he had wanted; no one could hear anything in this.

"Quiet," Ash called out.

The silence then was like the ringing after your ears have been boxed. Ash needed advice, and there was only one person who could give it. Ash levered himself up and scanned the crowd for Doronit.

She saw him and came forward, smiling at him with malicious pleasure that he needed her.

"Doronit," he said. "Do you know a way to give them back their voices?"

She indicated her own mouth, and Ash flushed. "Speak," he said, expecting her to refuse to help him. But she was serious.

"All I know is what a wind wraith once told me," she said. "To give them back their voices, you must find yours."

"My voice *is* theirs," Ash said, feeling stupid, as if he should see an answer in her words. But the thought had flung open a door in his mind: Ash knew what to do, and it was something he could never have done before he met the River. He began to hum, the note he and Baluch had used to summon the water in the cavern—*Her* note—and then to sing the single word "speak."

He saw the others wince at the sound, and closed his eyes. This had nothing to do with them; and, in a way, nothing to do with the River. The ghosts spoke with the voice of the dead because they had left behind all human contact, all links. They were cold.

The way to his voice, to their voices, was through the simple warmth he could feel from Martine; the trust in Bramble's eyes; the memory of baby Ash sucking his finger on the day they had left Hidden Valley; Drema's gift of the felt coat; Baluch's comradeship. Even the fellowship of drumming for his parents, the three of them united in music. And the River's welcome, the River's acceptance.

He sang, thinking of these things, and felt a change in the sound, but it wasn't enough. The words themselves had to be new, he thought, as well as the voice. So instead of "speak" he began to craft a new song, a song about the most valuable thing he knew in this world, the baby Ash. A song about new life. It wasn't a song in the way his father's songs were. It didn't tell a story. It didn't have sentences. But into it he put all the words about life and love that he knew, from the three languages the ghosts held between them: the language of the old blood, of the landtaken, and of his own time. He repeated, mixed and merged the words over the notes and the music tied them together into something never heard before, never dreamt of before, building in strength and sweetness and joy and the fear in the heart of love.

His voice changed.

It wasn't trained, like his mother's or Flax's. It had cracks in it, and his breath control was terrible. But the notes rose purely, a full tenor that carried to the furthest edge of the plateau. He began to include all the words for "speak" and "story" he knew from the three languages, and he settled into a rhythm of calling, as the goatherds of the Sharp River call the goats home at evening, their voices rising and falling on the evening air.

"Speak your story; tell your truths; show your selves; speak and be satisfied; speak and be at rest," he sang, his voice fully human.

The ghosts were pressing in closer, the song drawing them, their lips working as they tried to talk, but the spell was incomplete.

Finally, Ash flung up his arms and cried "*Speak!*" on a long high note.

They spoke. It was still loud, but each voice was its own again. Acton moved from group to group, trying hard to listen, to hear, to understand.

Each of those alive was trying to listen, understanding somehow that Saker was right: in order to repair the wrong done, the wrong must first be understood, the pain given voice, the injustice exposed. But they could not possibly hear them all.

Safred was kneeling, her face upturned, transfigured by a kind of ecstasy as the words, the stories, the secrets, poured over her.

A pretty girl, with the mark of a cut throat, said to Sorn: *I were ugly, ugly as an unkind word, my gran used to say...* The small beaded ghost spoke to Acton: *I couldn't stop them. I didn't even realize the village was being attacked, until they burst the latch like it wasn't there...* A gray-haired man had found Bramble, whom he seemed to know, and told her: *It began on Sylvie's roof. My hands were cold...* Maryrose, Bramble's sister, spoke to Ranny, a half-smile on her face. *Before you were born and after the sun first shone, there was a girl.*

Zel and Flax, where were they? He found them finally, at the back of the crowd, listening to an older woman who strongly resembled Zel. Their mother? Zel spoke to both her and Flax: *Murder's an ugly word, don't never doubt that. But it's a solid one, like a stone in your hand.* Saker stood next to her, attentively.

He found Doronit. She'd been waiting for him: *It's true my parents were Travelers by blood, but they were as settled as can be by nature.* He listened to her story with horror and pity, and held her hand as her throat constricted with grief and she found it hard to go on. Understanding her, at last, he found a way to love her with a father's love, with sorrow. So much grief, all around him. So much anger, so many lives cut short.

Da came round the back of the milking shed in the middle of the morning, a girl said to Thegan's sergeant.

There were fishers on the bank, Cael said to Gabra, and Gabra's eyes were intent.

Ash found Acton listening to an older woman who smiled at him as though he were the center of the world. She was dressed in ancient style. Was she his mother? *The women stay in the women's quarters. Yes, of course*, she said, ironically.

An old woman in animal skins grabbed his arm, the cold sliding through his muscles. *Listen to this one*, the River said sharply, so he focused on her bright eyes and listened hard. *My Aunty Lig was one of three sisters, as her mother had been, and her mother before her*, she started, and he took it all in, open-mouthed. The wrath of the Fire god! he realized, astonished, and wondered what the River would do if he rejected her. *I do not kill my lovers*, She said, amused. *They never leave me.*

Ash turned and noticed Baluch standing with a woman who carried a crutch; they both listened to a small man with a weak chin who faced them half-defiantly, half-ashamed: *I'd do it again. Even having to kill her, I'd do it again .*

What good was it? Where was the use? I had served, worked, been loyal—for what? Merroc knelt by a fair woman in her forties and, astonishingly, cried.

They were all listening, with Safred in the center. So many stories.

In the end, we are animals, and all we can touch is flesh.

I always wanted to be beautiful, like my little sister, Osyth. She had that Traveler kind of beauty, dark and elegant and lithe.

There's no saying what will happen next. That's what I learnt, that summer, that winter, watching her change.

A stonecaster walked up to Ash, pouch hanging at his belt, a man with no hair at all and no eyebrows, with terrible burn marks down one side of him. He noted the pouch at Ash's belt and weighed his own pouch in his hand.

The desire to know the future gnaws at our bones, he said, and Ash listened.

BRAMBLE

THE STORIES flowed out of them like honey, like vinegar, like wine and water and vitriol.

So much grief. So much joy. So many questions unanswered. Safred knelt still through it all, drinking it in. Around the circle, the living humans also sank to their knees under the weight of the emotions pouring out around them. Most cried, or clutched their chests in shared pain, or sighed yearningly for those lost, long ago.

Some stories were longer than others, so that the voices fell out one by one until the last drifted to a close: *I wished the tanner was still alive so I could try his spell one more time…*" It was Osyth. Zel and Flax were next to her, listening hard, tears on their cheeks, and as she finished she reached out to them and they went to her as babies go to their mothers, with trust and love.

Acton touched Bramble gently on the shoulder, the cold sliding through her and settling her. Then he stepped forward to Safred and helped her up. She stumbled, white and unsteady, but her face was full of a kind of joy, of completion.

"I have them all," she said in wonder. "I was empty and now I'm full."

Baluch moved next to Acton, took the knife from his own belt, and poised it over his hand. Acton hesitated. He shot a look at Ash, as if to ask for guidance, and then squared his shoulders. She had seen him do that once before, when he spoke to the Moot as a young man. He had convinced his audience then; would he be able to now?

Saker waited; he looked exhausted. Bramble prayed that Acton would find the right words.

"I am Acton, Lord of War," Acton said, and in his own voice his words were strong, and her throat tightened. "I have heard you. I acknowledge the truth of your lives. And I say: What was done to you was wrong. What you have suffered should not have happened. What you have witnessed should never have occurred. What you have lost —" His voice faltered, as if he were remembering the many stories he had heard. "Those you have lost should have remained with you. And I say to you: Whatever I have done to make these things happen, I regret from the depth of my heart. From the center of my soul, I am sorry."

Some wept softly, some looked to the ground, others away, as if his words had unlocked a part of themselves that had been separated for a long time.

Then Acton glanced at Baluch and he moved forward. "I am Baluch, second to the Lord of War," he said, his singer's voice reaching out like sunlight. A buzz of amazement went through the crowd.

"I was part of the landtaken and I regret my actions. I acknowledge my guilt and offer blood for blood in reparation." He hesitated. "I have killed others, of my own people, in defense of the Lake, and to those, too, I offer reparation. I offer myself as symbol of repentance."

He brought down the knife and cut the back of his hand, then held it out. Acton stood behind him, unmoving, his hand on Baluch's shoulder, so that they were offering tribute together.

One by one, they came and took blood. A few drank, but most simply touched.

One of the ghosts, the one Ash had called Doronit, hesitated for a while, until Ash went over to her.

"There's a new stone in this bag, remember," he said, showing her his stone pouch. "It says Evenness. Fairness. Say what you think."

She made a face at needing his help, but she spoke, "You think it means what?"

"I think the world is changing."

"The world is always changing, and rarely for the better," she said, with a shadow of charm. But she moved forward, and touched her hand to Baluch's, and smeared her face with his blood.

There were so many.

The whine started almost too low to hear. It crept into Bramble's head, slightly, very slightly, louder with each ghost that took blood. She shook her head to try to clear it, but the sound kept on, a high unpleasant vibration, like very loud screaming, very far away. She saw that Safred, Martine and Ash heard it too.

Baluch began to grow pale, and Ash and Martine rolled a rock over for him to sit on.

Bramble wasn't sure what she had expected—perhaps that as each ghost took the blood, it would fade, as ghosts did after a quickening. That didn't happen. They merely took their places back in the circle, and waited with inhuman patience.

The noise, now, was loud enough to give her a headache. Then, at the corner of her eye, she seemed to see movement, but when she turned her head there was nothing there. She walked over to Safred and Martine. Ash joined them, his hands at his ears.

"Can you hear that?" Bramble asked.

"It's the soul eaters…" Safred said, her eyes white-rimmed.

Bramble went cold. This—*this*—was what the gods had feared. This was the battle they had been fighting, against a myth, a story to frighten children: be good or the soul eaters will get you after death. If the soul eaters were here, in the land of the living, what would that mean?

"They came when we were at Obsidian Lake," Martine said, "but they faded once you were back."

Bramble looked over at Baluch. The noise had started, when? When Alder had tried to kill Thegan, when the soldiers' ghosts had tried to kill Saker, when the ghosts had bled a captive so they would not fade.

"The dead should not kill the living," she whispered. In the corner of her vision, shapes writhed. She let her eyes go out of focus, and saw them more clearly: distorted human shapes, elongated or swollen almost past recognition. Repulsive, hungry for life, for spirit, for everything that they were not.

Safred was nodding. "I think when the dead walk the land in solid bodies, and especially when the dead kill the living, the barrier between life and death grows thinner. If it grows thin enough, they will break through."

"What do they want?" Ash seemed paler than before, but he spoke forcefully.

"Life," Safred said.

Martine reeled, as if she had Seen something terrible. "They want to eat," she said. "Everything. All life. Not just humans. Everything."

"Once the ghosts are gone..." Bramble said. "The barrier will be strong again."

"Baluch will die, though," Martine whispered. She was ashen, and clung to Arvid's hand. "That one death might be enough to breach the wall."

"The ceremony's started," Arvid said. "Can we replace him before he dies? Can I give blood?"

As one, they shook their heads. Bramble wasn't sure why she was so certain, but she was. If this was going to work, it had to be Acton and Baluch, the ones who had begun it all.

"We just have to hope that the barrier can take one more death," Safred said.

When Baluch finally fainted, Acton sat on the rock, his friend's body lying across him. He supported Baluch's neck and laid the bleeding hand over his own, ready for the ghosts.

The whine had grown and the shapes filled half of Bramble's vision now, the writhing forms strangely overlaid on the real world, as though they were a thin curtain she could see through.

The ghosts came, and kept coming, in their thousands.

The leader of Saker's army, a ghost with beaded hair, approached last, when Baluch's blood had almost stopped flowing.

He came reluctantly, staring at Acton, and stood over Baluch but did not reach for him. His face was impossible to read, emotions changing on it rapidly.

Ash took pity on him. "Speak," he said gently.

"I swore revenge for the death of my wife," he said. "I thought she'd wait for me...but she hasn't. She's gone on."

"Perhaps she is waiting in the darkness beyond death," Ash said.

"I swore revenge," he repeated, as though it were the only truth he knew.

Acton smiled mirthlessly. "One more will finish him off. Take your blood and you'll kill the friend I held dearest in the world. Will that satisfy you?"

The man looked into his eyes and his face calmed. "I thought revenge would be sweet."

"So did I," Acton replied. "But it's like poisoned mead—sweet at first and then a spear in your vitals."

The ghost nodded and reached out to touch Baluch's hand; he smeared the blood across his face. "I am Owl. I release you from your debt," he said.

A sigh went up from the ghosts and Acton laid Baluch down, tears ice white against the paleness of his face. He knelt for a moment beside the body, his hand on Baluch's chest. Bramble thought of their two baby heads crowding together over a bowl of soup, a thousand years and a lifetime away, and her throat was too tight to speak. She put a hand on Acton's cold shoulder.

Ash came forward to Baluch and hesitated, looking at Saker.

"No," Acton said. "Leave him be. No need to bring him back."

Ash nodded and touched Baluch's face, as if saying goodbye. The ghosts watched. Some even wept.

Now, Bramble thought. Now they'll fade. But they did not, and the shrieking of the soul eaters rose higher and higher in a triumphant scream.

SAKER

"NO FORGIVENESS," Alder said flatly, staring at Owl in disgust. "Never."

Saker was huddled on a rock to one side. He raised his head, slowly, exhausted, the sound in his head driving him to madness. Of course his father would refuse. The chance to exercise power? He couldn't resist it. Hadn't he heard those stories? Hadn't he understood what they meant?

He went to his father. "We have a chance to find peace. For everyone. Justice for the future. Fairness."

Alder sneered at him. "They've cozened you, boy. They'll back out of it as soon as we're gone and you'll have done it all for nothing."

Saker felt emptied, calmer than he had ever felt in his whole life. Listening to the stories had changed him, shown him how much he shared with others. He was not a freak, an outcast. The stories had changed everyone there—he had seen it in their faces. Everyone except Lord Thegan. And his father. They were the same, Saker thought, men who saw others only as servants or enemies. He couldn't be angry with his father; but he could pity him. And he could control him.

"I raised you, Alder, son of Snipe, and I can cast you back into the darkness beyond death," he said.

"Hah!" Alder said. "Try it."

Saker cast a quick look at the sky, which was already lightening, the short summer night almost over.

"Alder, son of Snipe!" he called. "I seek justice. I seek balance. And in their name, I banish you to the darkness you came from."

His father turned, livid, his bull shoulders pulled up and his fists clenched, ready to strike Saker down as he had many time before.

Saker held out his own hand, palm up. "I strike you still!" he cried, a spell he had seen Freite use but never tried himself before.

Alder slowed and stopped like a man caught in treacle, then gathered his strength and tried to forge on against the spell.

His will against his father's. For a moment, Saker faltered. Then Zel came to his side, and Martine to his other like a mother, like his own mother whom she looked so much like.

He firmed his voice. "Alder, I cast you out—I cast you out of this company, into the arms of Lady Death!"

His father's ghost faded and was gone.

Now, Saker thought, the others can go on to rebirth. He took a long breath and looked around, waiting for the circle of ghosts to fade with the morning light.

But they did not.

The shapes at the corners of his eyes grew wilder and stronger.

BRAMBLE

THE SOUL eaters' constant whine was now an agonizing shriek. Around them, others were beginning to hear it. Merroc and Ranny looked around as if searching for its origin. The ghosts moved uneasily and formed small groups again, instead of the united mass they had been.

"Something's wrong," Bramble said, barely able to see anything beyond the twisting shapes that blurred her vision. "The ghosts have to fade, and soon, or the barrier will breach. Safred, can you ask the gods?"

Safred's eyes glazed, as they had seen her do so many times before. This time, she shook her head. "They are not there. There is no space in me for them any more. I am filled." She paused, as if trying to decide whether she was glad or hurt, and then seemed to choose. "I will never hear them again," she said contentedly.

Bramble reached for the gods in her head, but they were so very far away, too far to hear clearly. "Can you cast, Martine?" she asked.

Saker came up and reluctantly she moved back to let him join their circle. She had hated him for so long... she could kill him now, and the ghosts would fade. This was her chance to take revenge, in a righteous cause. She drew her knife and looked across at Acton. He was staring at Saker with a deep compassion, and somehow that allowed her to let go of anger. Pity for Saker flowed through her, and a bemused understanding. She slid her belt knife back into its sheath, and the movement was like a sigh.

"I think," he said hesitantly, looking at the ground instead of meeting their eyes, "that they have lost their way. They are ready to go, but they don't know how. The spell has cut them off from the darkness beyond death, and they need to find a way back."

"Perhaps the soul eaters are concealing the way," she said slowly.

Saker blanched and looked wildly around at the twisting shapes. "Soul eaters?" His hands shook. "What have I done?"

"If you could banish me the way you did your father, could they follow me?" Acton asked.

"I don't think so. I sent him back to where he had been—which was not on the path to rebirth." The words came haltingly.

Then Maryrose came towards them, and they moved back to give her room. She looked at Ash.

"Say what you wish to say," he said.

"The door to rebirth opens at death," she said. "I have seen it, and did not go through. But if someone were to die and go through, we could follow, I think."

"Is that my job?" Saker asked. "To die? I could do that, I think."

That felt almost right to Bramble, but not quite. It was too easy, somehow.

"Ash," Martine said, "remember that song you sang us, in Hidden Valley, about the prey?"

Ash said the words aloud:

The gods' own prey is galloping, is riding up the hill
Her hands are wet with blood and tears and dread
She is rearing on the summit and her banner floats out still
Now the killer's hands must gather in the dead.

"The gods' own prey," Bramble said, thinking of Sebbi, speared upon the Ice King a thousand years ago. It was hard to think clearly, the noise was growing so loud. "That's me. The prey is the Kill, and I'm the Kill."

"The Kill Reborn," Martine said. "Are you ready to die?"

"I've died twice already—third time counts for all."

She wanted to laugh aloud. If she had any Sight—and she still wasn't sure about that—it was telling her loud and certain sure that this was the right thing to do. Acton looked at her sadly, but she smiled back with relief. No need to kill anyone. No need for anyone else to die.

The shapes grew stronger and across the plateau exclamations came thick and fast.

Swords were drawn and swiped at thin air, people tried to bat the shapes away from them, Friede picked up her crutch, swung it wildly and then stood stone still, realizing she was hitting out at nothing solid. But the shapes grew stronger, fuller, as though they were drawing strength from the reactions. From the fear.

Bramble looked with blurred eyes at the shapes twisting just beyond death. "Now you won't have to wait at all for me," she said to Acton. "We can be reborn together, right now. And after all this, the gods owe us a good life!"

He laughed.

"I had a good life," he said. "But one with you will be better!"

Everyone else was solemn, but Bramble was filled with elation. She knelt and fished out the red scarf from her saddlebags, then hunted in the crowd of ghosts until she found a woman with a lance. She borrowed it and tied the scarf to the tip as it was in the Spring Chase.

It was almost sunrise. The gray light before dawn showed them all clearly: the warlords and their men, the Turviters, the wide circle of ghosts bedabbed with Baluch's blood. Bramble met the eyes of those she had known and nodded.

She stood holding the lance, ready—but something was missing.

"Wait," Martine said, her eyes blank with Sight. "Someone is coming."

Someone on horseback, galloping. Bramble could hear the hoofbeats, growing louder. They seemed, impossibly, to come from across the river. Closer now, but no horse in sight. Her heart started to beat in rhythm. She dropped the lance. As the sound seemed to pass through the circle of ghosts, a figure condensed out of the air, a figure that she knew, of course, who else? A gift from the gods—or may be he'd just decided to come back himself.

He came straight to her, trotting, his roan hide gleaming, his wise eyes welcoming her. She ran to him and threw her arms around his cold neck, until he butted her side and whinnied. Then she pulled back and looked him in the eye.

"I'm sorry," she said.

He butted her again, but this time impatiently, as if she were wasting time, so she swung up onto his back. He had only the old blanket she had used in Wooding. No saddle, no bridle, no bit. Her heart was singing. Acton came over to them and handed her the lance, the red scarf beginning to stir in the wind before dawn.

Then she touched the roan's neck and brought him over to Maryrose.

"Come up?" she asked, reaching a hand down. Maryrose eyed the horse dubiously, but grasped her hand. Acton helped her to mount behind Bramble, then stood with one hand on the roan's shoulder. Merrick came forward to stand at his other shoulder.

"What are you going to do?" Ash asked.

She looked up to where the cliff ended abruptly, far above the waves. "He's a jumper," she said. "We're going to jump."

Their faces were so solemn, she wanted to laugh, but she could feel tears prick her eyelids, too. Each of them, in turn, touched her leg in farewell: Ash, Martine, Safred, Leof, Sorn.

Even Saker. "Thank you," he said.

The twisting shapes were moving faster, the gestures clearer, more violent, the shrieking louder; those who could hear it clearly dropped to the ground clutching their heads, and others clapped hands uselessly to their ears.

They were trying to frighten her, she realized. Her death would only mend the Domains if she were not frightened. If she feared as she died, it would open the door to them, and they would burst into this world to destroy, a greater plague than ever the wind wraiths could be, because all of life was their enemy.

Then she let herself smile, the familiar pleasure she always felt before a chase rushing through her. She had never been on good terms with fear, and she wasn't going to start now, not with her love running beside her, not with the jump of her life before her.

She raised the lance above her head and the ghosts fell in behind her, Cael and Owl at their head.

She clicked her tongue to the roan.

He moved forward, gathering speed, cantering up the hill into the morning sun. Maryrose held on tightly. In the last yards he sped into a gallop and launched himself as he had from the edge of the chasm in Wooding, that vast, impossible leap that felt so much like flying. They went up into a fractured world of light and air, the red scarf streaming out behind her, and they were poised for a moment in space, waves beneath them, white water and cliffs beckoning, and she laughed as they fell.

ASH

ASH'S BREATH caught in his throat when he saw them outlined like shadows against the rising sun, and then saw the shadows fade in mid-air, dissipating as a water sprite shreds itself on the wind.

The rest of the ghost army followed, Cael leading the way, Flax and Zel next, more and more, faster and faster, as those behind realized what was happening and became urgent to move, to jump, to be released.

None of them looked back.

As each one jumped and faded, the shrill threat from the soul eaters grew a little less, the shapes moving across his vision retreating.

They were gone by the time the sun was fully up, ghosts and soul eaters alike, and Ash slowly became aware of the normal sounds of the headland. Cows lowed somewhere, waiting to be milked. The sea washed the rocks below. The dawn breeze wuthered gently through the rocks.

Ash looked around the headland, at the weapons discarded by the ghosts lying like a tribute pile around Baluch, at the humans left there. As he turned, he saw that they were surrounded by people: not just the parley group, but many more Turviters, and others, people who'd been on the Road by the look of them. The folk from the countryside who had run to Turvite for protection had finally arrived, including his parents. Rowan and Swallow walked towards him, smiling. He walked towards them stiffly, knowing that if he tried to run he'd fall down. His mother said his name, and there was a sob in the word, as if she'd been afraid for him. He fell into their embrace, exhausted but happy.

He turned to beckon Martine over, and saw that she was facing down a squad of the Moot staff from Turvite who wanted to arrest Saker. Saker wasn't resisting, but Martine held up a hand.

"Wait," she said. She took Saker and led him towards the cliff. Was she going to give him the option of jumping off? That didn't seem like her.

The crowd started shouting curses and threats at Saker.

Arvid walked towards them, looking troubled. Ash agreed with him. Saker had to be arrested. Of course. It was a waste, in a way, but . . . the River spoke sharply to him, more reprovingly than he had ever heard her.

We do not approve of waste, She said.

The ground around Saker's feet began to churn, just as the ground around the altar had churned.

"Martine!" Ash called, and raced towards her. She jumped back and took a few steps down the slope, but Saker stood still, staring at the earth without understanding. He looked so tired it was a miracle he was standing at all.

Then the delvers burst from the earth and surrounded him.

The crowd was silent. Some were running away, others were praying. Ranny, to Ash's admiration, walked forward. She stood next to Ash and Martine. Safred joined them, looking helpless.

"I can't stop them," she called to Saker apologetically.

He will be taken for healing, the River said to Ash. *And punishment.*

Then the ground flew up around Saker and he and the delvers disappeared, just as the altar had disappeared, as Cael had, leaving only ploughed earth behind.

Ash cleared his throat and turned to the crowd.

"He has been taken for punishment," he said. After a moment's silence, the crowd started cheering. It made Ash feel sick, which was stupid. These people had lost everything because of Saker, he told himself. Of course they want him punished. But he remembered the inhuman power that had destroyed the Weeping Caverns, and the cold, beautiful eyes of the water spirits, and shivered.

Sorn stepped forward and held up a hand and the crowd quieted, curious.

"Before witnesses on this last night, the spirit of Acton proclaimed that he had intended this land to be ruled by councils, not by warlords." She let the stir in the crowd die down before she went on, eyeing Thegan. "It is my purpose, as Lady of the Central Domain, to honor his wishes. The warlords' council is met here already. I suggest that it be made permanent, so that the Eleven Domains can become truly united, and that each Domain establish an advisory council such as exists already in the Last Domain, similar to the councils in the free towns. What say you?"

The crowd roared its approval and Sorn turned to the warlords with a smile. Thegan stepped forward to object, and Merroc waved him away.

"You have no voice in this council, Thegan. Your *nephew* is Lord of Cliff Domain, Sorn is Lady of Central. You have nothing, and you will not be listened to."

Ranny cleared her throat. "More than that, Lord Merroc. The officer Thegan is under charge of murder, of Horst the archer and Zel the Traveler. As we all witnessed."

Thegan smiled contemptuously at her. "Horst was my own man. You have no rights in his death."

He's going to get away with it, Ash thought. Again. Just like it's always been since the warlords took over. But this was not the same group of people who had climbed up the headland the day before.

"You will hang for Zel's death," Ranny said. "I promised that you would face justice, and I will not be forsworn."

Garham looked at the Moot staff and pointed to Thegan. "Arrest the officer and take him to the Moot Hall cells."

They surrounded Thegan and Boc held out his hand for Thegan's sword, which he surrendered reluctantly.

Ash moved over to Merroc and said, "If you don't support Turvite in his death, he'll have the Domains at war within a year." Merroc stiffened and nodded, once.

"I heard the stories," Merroc said. "If he has not been changed by them, he has the heart of a soul eater, and deserves to die."

"He carries three knives as well as his sword," Sorn said. Thegan shot her a glance of pure hatred; but he handed over the knives and went with Boc and his men, down the hill, head still high.

Eolbert offered his arm to Sorn, who took it after a brief look and smile to Leof. "Come, my lady. Let us go back to the Moot Hall out of this sun and discuss the best way to run this council of ours."

"Here is someone who can advise us," Sorn said, stopping next to a fat old lady in dusty clothes. "Vi, the Voice of Baluchston, is deep in the confidence of the Lake and wise in the ways of managing a free people."

Vi smiled at her approvingly. "As to that, lass, I don't know, but I wouldn't mind a chance to put my feet up."

Sorn laughed and offered Vi her other arm. They led the parley group and most of the Turviters down the hill towards the city. Arvid glanced back to Martine before he left, and she waved him away with a reassuring smile.

Ash stared out over a landscape which was coming back to life. Farmers were harvesting, wagons were back on the roads, boats on the river. Everywhere seemed alive but here; the plateau was enormous without the crowd. The trampled grass was already turning yellow under the sun.

Safred was standing in a daze of fatigue. Ash hoped that was all it was. He put a hand under her elbow and guided her towards the path, Martine taking her other arm. She moved slowly, as though she were wading through high water. His parents went ahead of them down the hill.

"What about you?" Martine asked him. "What are you going to do now?"

Ash paused, then took a deep breath and sang, in Flax's memory: "Up jumps the sun in the early, early morning..." His parents whirled around, his mother's face alight with a kind of joy he'd never seen there before. For a moment, he was full of regret for the life that he'd thought he'd wanted. He could have it now, if he chose. But the River and the music twined together in his mind, and he knew that Road was closed to him.

"I'm going to make music," he said. He looked his father in the eyes. "New music. Make it up and write it down. Bramble's story first."

His father seemed to understand but said nothing. His mother put a hand on his father's arm, and they turned and walked on.

Ash and Martine paused, looking back at the place where Bramble had seemed, for a moment, to fly.

"That will be a good song," Martine said.

Ash hoped so. He could hear it in his head, and feel the River listening with approval. They walked down to the city together as the music played for him, flute and drum and oud, twining together around the sweet notes of a horn, crying out her beauty and her courage. And her bloody-mindedness, too. He knew the refrain, already:

The road is long and the end is death
If we're lucky .

meet the author

Alison Casey

PAMELA FREEMAN is an award-winning writer for young people. She has a doctorate of creative arts from the University of Technology, Sydney, Australia, where she has also lectured in creative writing. She lives in Sydney with her husband and young son. To find out more about the author, visit pamelafreemanbooks.com.